PRAISE FOR WILBUR SMITH

22.11.22

'Wilbur Smith rarel[...]
Sunday T[...]

'The world's leading adventure writer'
Daily Express

'Action is the name of Wilbur Smith's game and
he is a master'
Washington Post

'The pace would do credit to a Porsche, and the invention
is as bright and explosive as a fireworks display'
Sunday Telegraph

'A violent saga . . . told with vigour and enthusiam
. . . Wilbur Smith spins a fine tale'
Evening Standard

'A bonanza of excitement'
New York Times

'. . . a natural storyteller who moves confidently and
often splendidly in his period and sustains a flow of
convincing incident'
Scotsman

'Raw experience, grim realism, history and romance welded
with mystery and the bewilderment of life itself'
Library Journal

'A thundering good read'
Irish Times

'Extrovert and vigorous . . . constantly changing incidents
and memorable portraits'
Liverpool Daily Post

'An immensely powerful book, disturbing and compulsive,
harsh yet compassionate'
She

'An epic novel . . . it would be hard to think of a theme that
was more appropriate today . . . Smith writes with a great
passion for the soul of Africa'
Today

'I read on to the last page, hooked by its frenzied
inventiveness piling up incident upon incident . . . mighty
entertainment'
Yorkshire Post

'There is a streak of genuine poetry, all the more attractive
for being unfeigned'
Sunday Telegraph

'. . . action follows action . . . mystery is piled
on mystery . . . tales to delight the millions of addicts of the
gutsy adventure story'
Sunday Express

'Action-crammed'
Sunday Times

'Rattling good adventure'
Evening Standard

THE TRIUMPH OF THE SUN
and
WILD JUSTICE

WILBUR SMITH was born in Central Africa in 1933. He was educated at Michaelhouse and Rhodes University. He became a full-time writer in 1964 after the successful publication of *When the Lion Feeds*, and has since written over thirty novels, meticulously researched on his numerous expeditions worldwide. His books are now translated into twenty-six languages.

THE NOVELS OF WILBUR SMITH

THE COURTNEYS

When the Lion Feeds   The Sound of Thunder
A Sparrow Falls   Birds of Prey   Monsoon
Blue Horizon   The Triumph of the Sun

THE COURTNEYS OF AFRICA

The Burning Shore   Power of the Sword   Rage
A Time to Die   Golden Fox

THE BALLANTYNE NOVELS

A Falcon Flies   Men of Men   The Angels Weep
The Leopard Hunts in Darkness

THE EGYPTIAN NOVELS

River God   The Seventh Scroll
Warlock   The Quest

Also

The Dark of the Sun   Shout at the Devil
Gold Mine   The Diamond Hunters
The Sunbird   Eagle in the Sky
The Eye of the Tiger   Cry Wolf
Hungry as the Sea   Wild Justice
Elephant Song

WILBUR SMITH

THE TRIUMPH OF THE SUN
OF THE SUN
and
WILD JUSTICE

PAN BOOKS

The Triumph of the Sun first published 2005 by Macmillan
First published in paperback 2006 by Pan Books
Wild Justice first published 1979 by William Heinemann
First published in paperback 1968 by Pan Books

This omnibus first published 2008 by Pan Books
an imprint of Pan Macmillan Ltd
Pan Macmillan, 20 New Wharf Road, London N1 9RR
Basingstoke and Oxford
Associated companies throughout the world
www.panmacmillan.com

ISBN 978-0-330-50801-8

A CIP catalogue record for this book is available from
the British Library.

Typeset by SetSystems Ltd, Saffron Walden, Essex
Printed in the UK by CPI Mackays, Chatham ME5 8TD

THE TRIUMPH
OF THE SUN

This book is for

my helpmate, playmate, soulmate, wife and best friend

Mokhniso Rakhimova Smith

The earth burns with the quenchless thirst of ages, and in the steel blue sky scarcely a cloud obstructs the relentless triumph of the sun.

The River War, Winston S. Churchill, 1905

OMDURMAN

1. The Mosque
2. Mihrab
3. Kubbet el Mahdi (Mahdi's tomb)
4. The tin Mosque
5. Khalifa's enclosure
6. Khalifa's special court
7. Khalifa's Palace
8. Khalifa's Harem
9. Khalifa's kuran school
10. Houses of Khalifa's Mulazemin (body guard)
11. House of Mahdi's son
12. Khalifa's stables
13. Khalifa's stores
14. Mahdi's Harem
15. House of Mahdi's family
16. Khalifa Ali Wad Helu's house
17. Houses of Khalifa Ali Wad Helu's Mulazemin & relations
18. House of Khalifa's son (Osman)
19. Great stone wall of Omdurman
20. Mud wall of Omdurman
21. House of the Khalifa's relations
22. Slatin's new house
23. } Houses of Kadis
24. }
25. Yac ub's old house
26. Quarters of Osman Atalan and his Beja Arabs
27. Houses of Yacub's katebs
28. Slatin's old house
29. Beit el Amana
29a. Flags & drums stores
30. Other houses of Khalifa's relations
31. Prison
32. Arms factory
33. Quarters of the Western people
34. Quarters of Borgo & Takarna people
35. Mashra (Ferry)
36. Khalifa's house on the Nile
37. Old fort of Omdurman
38. House of the commandant of Jehadia
39. Quarters of the Black Jahadia
40. Khalifa's house in Dem Yunes
41. Hillet (village) of the Fetihab Arabs
42. Quarters of Bornu, Fellata & Gowama people
43. House of Nur Angara
44. Quarters of Homr Arabs
45. Quarters of Kababish and other camel-owning Arabs
46. Quarters of Hamar Arabs
47. Quarters of Habbania Arabs
48. Quarters of Rizighat Arabs
49. Quarters of Kanana Arabs
50. House of Abdulla Wad Ahmed
51. Quarters of Degheim Arabs
52. Quarters of White Nile tribes
53. Quarters of Jaalin Arabs
54. Carpenters' shops
55. Market courts of justice
56. Scaffolds
57. Salt Market
58. Linen & cloth market
59. Barbers' shops
60. Tailors' shops
61. Vegetable market
62. Butchers' shops
63. Forage market
64. Grain & date market
65. Grain & date stores
66. Wood market
67. Women's market
68. European cook shops
69. The Muslimania quarter
70. Old house of Father Ohrwalder
71. Cemetery
72. Houses of Ahmed Sharfi & family of Khalifa Sherif
73. Quarters of Kunuz Barabra
74. Quarters of the Danagla
75. Quarters of the Beni Jarrar Arabs
76. Tombs of the Martyrs
77. Quarters of different tribes
78. Tombs of the Mahdi's family & relations
79. Powder factory
80. Beit el Mal
81. Slave market
82. Commissariat stores of the Mulazemin & Katebs
83. Quarters of the Fur tribes
84. Quarters of the Egyptians (Ibrahim Pasha Fauzi, Said Bey Guma, Yusef Effendi Mansur & others)
85. Khalifa's Hejra house
86. Khalifa Ali Wad Hulu's Hejra house
87. The Hejra Mosque
88. Quarters of the Wad el Besir & Hellawin Arabs

TUTI ISLAND

89. Powder Magazine
90. Tuti village

KHARTUM

91. Mukran fort
92. British Consular Palace
93. Church
94. Sanitary Department
95. Post and Finance offices
96. Austrian Consulate
97. Government House (Hekemdaria)
98. Governor's palace (Saraya)
99. Grain stores
100. Arsenal
101. Barracks
102. Hospital
103. Fort Burri
104. Small arms, ammunition stores
105. Artillery ammunition stores
106. Cartridge factory
107. A place of worship
108. French Consulate
109. Italian Consulate
110. Houses of the natives
111. Bab el Messallamia
112. Fort Kalakia
113. The Eastern palace (Saraya)
114. North Fort

115. Khojali
116. Burri
117. Kalakla
118. Shagaret Muhhi Bey
119. Halfaya

KHARTUM AND OMDURMAN

YARDS

0   1000   2000   3000

MILES

0   ½   1   2

RIVER NILE

O M D U R M A N

TUTI

BAHR EL AZRAK OR BLUE NILE

K H A R T U M

Ryder
Courtney's
compound
and
menagerie

THE CANAL

BAHR EL ABIAD OR WHITE NILE

Stone & Mud Walls
The light blue indicates
portions inundated during
high Nile.

Rebecca leant her elbows on the sill of the wide, unglazed window, and the heat of the desert blew into her face like the exhalation of a blast furnace. Even the river below her seemed to steam like a cauldron. Here it was almost a mile wide, for this was the season of High Nile. The flow was so strong that it created whirlpools and glossy eddies across the surface. The White Nile was green and fetid with the taint of the swamps through which it had so recently flowed, swamps that extended over an area the size of Belgium. The Arabs called this vast slough the Bahr el Ghazal, and the British named it the Sud.

In the cool months of the previous year Rebecca had voyaged upstream with her father to where the flow of the river emerged from the swamps. Beyond that point the channels and lagoons of the Sud were tractless and uncharted, carpeted densely with floating weed that was perpetually shifting, obscuring them from the eyes of all but the most skilled and experienced navigator. This watery, fever-ridden world was the haunt of crocodile and hippopotamus; of myriad strange birds, some beautiful and others grotesque; and of sitatunga, the weird amphibious antelope with corkscrew horns, shaggy coats and elongated hoofs, adapted for life in the water.

Rebecca turned her head and a thick blonde tress of hair fell across one eye. She brushed it aside and looked downstream to where the two great rivers met. It was a sight that always intrigued her, though she had looked upon it every day for two long years. A huge raft of water weed was sailing down the centre of the channel. It had broken free of the swamps and would be carried on by the current until it dispersed far to the north in the turbulence of the cataracts, those rapids that, from time to time, broke the smooth flow of the Nile. She followed its ponderous progress until it reached the confluence of the two Niles.

The other Nile came down from the east. It was fresh and sweet as the mountain stream that was its source. At this season of High Nile its waters were tinted a pale blue grey by the silt it had scoured from the mountainous ranges of Abyssinia. It was named for this colour. The Blue Nile was slightly narrower than its twin, but was still a massive serpent of water. The rivers came together at the apex of the triangle of land on which the City of the Elephant's Trunk stood. That was the meaning of its name, Khartoum. The two Niles did not mingle at once. As far downstream as Rebecca could see they ran side by side in the same bed, each maintaining its own distinct colour and character until they dashed together on to the rocks at the entrance to the Shabluka Gorge twenty miles on and were churned into a tumultuous union.

'You are not listening to me, my darling,' said her father sharply.

Rebecca smiled as she turned to face him. 'Forgive me, Father, I was distracted.'

'I know. I know. These are trying times,' he agreed. 'But you must face up to them. You are no longer a child, Becky.'

'Indeed I am not,' she agreed vehemently. She had not intended to whine – she never whined. 'I was seventeen last week. Mother married you when she was the same age.'

'And now you stand in her place as mistress of my household.' His expression was forlorn as he remembered his beloved wife and the terrible nature of her death.

'Father dear, you have just jumped off the cliff of your own argument.' She laughed. 'If I am what you say I am, then how can you prevail on me to abandon you?'

David Benbrook looked confused, then thrust aside his sorrow and laughed with her. She was so quick and pretty that he could seldom resist her. 'You are so like your mother.' This statement was usually his white flag of defeat, but now he struggled on with his arguments. Rebecca turned back to the window, not ignoring him but listening with only half her attention. Now that her father had reminded her of the terrible peril in which they stood she felt the cold

2

claws of dread in the pit of her stomach as she looked across the river.

The sprawling buildings of the native city of Omdurman pressed up to the far riverbank, earth-coloured like the desert around them, tiny as dolls' houses at this distance, and wavering in the mirage. Yet menace emanated from them as fiercely as the heat from the sun. Night and day, the drums never stopped, a constant reminder of the mortal threat that hung over them. She could hear them booming across the waters, like the heartbeat of the monster. She could imagine him sitting at the centre of his web, gazing hungrily across the river at them, a fanatic with a quenchless thirst for human blood. Soon he and his minions would come for them. She shuddered, and concentrated again on her father's voice.

'Of course, I grant that you have your mother's raw courage and obstinacy, but think of the twins, Becky. Think of the babies. They are your babies now.'

'I am aware of my duty to them every waking moment of my day,' she flared, then as swiftly veiled her anger and smiled again – the smile that always softened his heart. 'But I think of you also.' She crossed to stand beside his chair, and placed her hand on his shoulder. 'If you come with us, Father, the girls and I will go.'

'I cannot, Becky. My duty is here. I am Her Majesty's consul general. I have a sacred trust. My place is here in Khartoum.'

'Then so is mine,' she said simply, and stroked his head. His hair was still thick and springing under her fingers, but shot through with more silver than sable. He was a handsome man, and she often brushed his hair and trimmed and curled his moustache for him, proudly as her mother had once done.

He sighed and gathered himself to protest further, but at that moment a shrill chorus of childish shrieks rang through the open window. They stiffened. They knew those voices, and they struck at both their hearts. Rebecca started across the room, and David sprang up from his desk. Then they relaxed as the cries came again and they recognized the tone as excitement, not terror.

3

'They are in the watch tower,' said Rebecca.

'They are not allowed up there,' exclaimed David.

'There are many places where they are not allowed,' Rebecca agreed, 'and those are where you can usually find them.' She led the way to the door and out into the stone-flagged passage. At the far end a circular staircase wound up the interior of the turret. Rebecca lifted her petticoats and ran up the steps, nimble and sure-footed, her father following more sedately. She came out into the blazing sunlight on the upper balcony of the turret.

The twins were dancing perilously close to the low parapet. Rebecca seized one in each hand and drew them back. She looked down from the height of the consular palace. The minarets and rooftops of Khartoum were spread below. Both branches of the Nile were in full view for miles in each direction.

Saffron tried to pull her arm out of Rebecca's grip. 'The *Ibis!*' she yelled. 'Look! The *Ibis* is coming.' She was the taller, darker twin. Wild and headstrong as a boy.

'The *Intrepid Ibis*,' Amber piped up. She was dainty and fair, with a melodious timbre to her voice even when she was excited. 'It's Ryder in the *Intrepid Ibis*.'

'Mr Ryder Courtney, to you,' Rebecca corrected her. 'You must never call grown-ups by their Christian names. I don't want to have to tell you that again.' But neither child took the reprimand to heart. All three stared eagerly up the White Nile at the pretty white steamboat coming down on the current.

'It looks like it's made of icing sugar,' said Amber, the beauty of the family, with angelic features, a pert little nose and huge blue eyes.

'You say that every time she comes,' Saffron remarked, without rancour. She was Amber's foil: eyes the colour of smoked honey, tiny freckles highlighting her high cheekbones and a wide, laughing mouth. Saffron looked up at Rebecca with a wicked glint in those honey eyes. 'Ryder is your beau, isn't he?' 'Beau' was the latest addition to her vocabulary, and

4

as she applied it solely to Ryder Courtney, Rebecca found it pretentious and oddly infuriating.

'He is not!' Rebecca responded loftily, to hide her annoyance. 'And don't be saucy, Miss Smarty Breeches.'

'He's bringing tons of food!' Saffron pointed at the string of four capacious flat-bottomed barges that the *Ibis* was towing.

Rebecca released the twins' arms and shaded her eyes with both hands against the glare. She saw that Saffron was right. At least two of the barges were piled high with sacks of dhurra, the staple grain of the Sudan. The other two were filled with an assorted cargo, for Ryder was one of the most prosperous traders on the two rivers. His trading stations were strung out at intervals of a hundred miles or so along the banks of both Niles, from the confluence of the Atbara river in the north to Gondokoro and far Equatoria in the south, then eastwards from Khartoum along the Blue Nile into the highlands of Abyssinia.

Just then David stepped out on to the balcony. 'Thank the good Lord he has come,' he said softly. 'This is the last chance for you to escape. Courtney will be able to take you and hundreds of our refugees downriver, out of the Mahdi's evil clutches.'

As he spoke they heard a single cannon shot from across the White Nile. They all turned quickly and saw gunsmoke spurting from one of the Dervish Krupps guns on the far bank. A moment later a geyser of spray rose from the surface of the river a hundred yards ahead of the approaching steamer. The foam was tinged yellow with the lyddite of the bursting shell.

Rebecca clapped her hand over her mouth to stifle a cry of alarm, and David remarked drily, 'Let's pray their aim is up to the usual standard.'

One after another the other guns of the Dervish batteries burst into a long, rolling volley, and the waters around the little boat leapt and boiled with bursting shells. Shrapnel whipped the river surface like tropical rain.

Then all the great drums of the Mahdi's army thundered

out in full-throated challenge and the ombeya trumpets blared. From among the mud buildings, horsemen and camel riders swarmed out and galloped along the bank, keeping pace with the *Ibis*.

Rebecca ran to her father's long brass telescope, which always stood on its tripod at the far end of the parapet, pointing across the river at the enemy citadel. She stood on tiptoe to reach the eyepiece and quickly focused the lens. She swept it over the swarming Dervish cavalry, who were half obscured in the red clouds of dust thrown up by their racing mounts. They appeared so close that she could see the expressions on their fierce dark faces, could almost read the oaths and threats they mouthed, and hear their terrible war cry: 'Allah Akbar! There is no God but God, and Muhammad is his prophet.'

These riders were the Ansar, the Helpers, the Mahdi's élite bodyguard. They all wore the *jibba*, the patched robes which symbolized the rags that had been the only garb available to them at the beginning of this *jihad* against the godless, the unbelievers, the infidels. Armed only with spears and rocks the Ansar had, in the past six months, destroyed three armies of the infidels and slaughtered their soldiers to the man. Now they held Khartoum in siege and gloried in their patched robes, the badge of their indomitable courage and their faith in Allah and His Mahdi, the Expected One. As they rode they brandished their double-handed swords and fired the Martini-Henry carbines they had captured from their defeated enemies.

During the months of the siege Rebecca had seen this warlike display many times, so she swung the lens off them and turned it out across the river, traversing the forest of shell splashes and leaping foam until the open bridge of the steamboat sprang into sharp focus. The familiar figure of Ryder Courtney leant on the rail of his bridge, regarding the antics of the men who were trying to kill him with faint amusement. As she watched him, he straightened and removed the long black cheroot from between his lips. He said something to his helmsman, who obediently spun the wheel and the long wake

6

of the *Ibis* began to curl in towards the Khartoum bank of the river.

Despite Saffron's teasing Rebecca felt no love pang at the sight of him. Then she smiled inwardly: I doubt I would recognize it anyway. She considered herself immune to such mundane emotions. Nevertheless she experienced a twinge of admiration for Ryder's composure in the midst of such danger, followed almost immediately by the warming glow of friendship. 'Well, there is no harm in admitting that we are friends,' she reassured herself, and felt quick concern for his safety. 'Please, God, keep Ryder safe in the eye of the storm,' she whispered, and God seemed to be listening.

As she watched, a steel shard of shrapnel punched a jagged hole in the funnel just above Ryder's head, and black boiler smoke spurted out of it. He did not glance round but returned the cheroot to his lips and exhaled a long stream of grey tobacco smoke that was whipped away on the wind. He wore a rather grubby white shirt, open at the throat, sleeves rolled high. With one thumb he tipped his wide-brimmed hat of plaited palm fronds to the back of his head. At a cursory glance, he gave the impression of being stockily built, but this was an illusion fostered by the breadth and set of his shoulders and the girth of his upper arms, muscled by heavy work. His narrow waist and the manner in which he towered over the Arab helmsman at his side gave it the lie.

David had taken the hands of his younger daughters to restrain them, and leant over the parapet to engage in a shouted conversation with someone in the courtyard of the consular palace below.

'My dear General, do you think you might prevail on your gunners to return fire and take their attention off Mr Courtney's boat?' His tone was deferential.

Rebecca glanced down and saw that her father was speaking to the commanding officer of the Egyptian garrison defending the city. General 'Chinese' Gordon was a hero of the Empire, the victor of wars in every part of the world. In China his legendary 'Ever Victorious Army' had earned him the sobriquet. He had come out of his headquarters in

7

the south wing of the palace with his red flowerpot fez on his head.

'The order has already been sent to the gunners, sir.' Gordon's reply was crisp and assertive, edged with annoyance. He did not need to be reminded of his duty.

His voice carried clearly to where Rebecca stood. It was said that he could make himself heard without effort across a raging battlefield.

A few minutes later the Egyptian artillery, in their emplacements along the city waterfront, opened up a desultory fire. Their pieces were of small calibre and obsolete pattern, six-pounder Krupps mountain guns; their ammunition was ancient and in short supply, much given to misfiring. However, to one accustomed to the ineptitudes of the Egyptian garrison, their accuracy was surprising. A few clouds of black shrapnel smoke appeared in the clear sky directly over the Dervish batteries, for the gunners on both sides had been ranging each other's positions during all the months since the beginning of the siege. The Dervish fire slackened noticeably. Still unscathed, the white steamer reached the confluence of the two rivers and the line of barges followed her as she turned sharply to starboard into the mouth of the Blue Nile and was almost immediately shielded by the buildings of the city from the guns on the west bank. Deprived of their prey the Dervish batteries fell silent.

'Please may we go down to the wharf to welcome him?' Saffron was dragging her father to the head of the staircase. 'Come on, Becky, let's go and meet your beau.'

As the family hurried through the neglected, sun-bleached gardens of the palace, they saw that General Gordon was also heading for the harbour, with a group of his Egyptian officers scampering behind him. Just beyond the gates a dead horse half blocked the alley. It had been lying there for ten days, killed by a stray Dervish shell. Its belly was swollen and its gaping wounds heaved with masses of white maggots. Flies hovered and buzzed over it in a dense blue cloud. Mingled with all the other smells of the besieged city the stench of rotting horseflesh was sulphurous. Each breath Rebecca drew seemed to catch in her throat and her stomach heaved. She fought back the nausea so that she did not disgrace herself and the dignity of her father's office.

The twins vied with each other in a pantomime of disgust. 'Poof!' and 'Stinky-woo!' they cried, then doubled over to make realistic vomiting sounds, howling with delight at each other's histrionics.

'Be off with you, you little savages!' David scowled at them and brandished his silver-mounted cane. They shrieked in mock alarm, then raced away in the direction of the harbour, leaping over piles of debris from shelled and burnt-out houses. Rebecca and David followed at their best pace, but before they had passed the customs house they encountered the city crowds moving in the same direction.

It was a solid river of humanity, of beggars and cripples, slaves and soldiers, rich women attended by their slaves and scantily clad Galla whores, mothers with infants strapped to their backs, dragging wailing brats by each hand, government officials and fat slave traders with diamond and gold rings on their fingers. All had one purpose: to discover what cargo the steamer carried, and whether she offered a faint promise of escape from the little hell that was Khartoum.

The twins were rapidly engulfed in the throng so David lifted Saffron on to his shoulders while Rebecca grasped Amber's hand and they pushed their way forward. The crowds recognized the tall, imposing figure of the British consul and gave way to him. They reached the waterfront only a few minutes after General Gordon, who called to them to join him.

The *Intrepid Ibis* was cutting in across the stream and when she reached the quieter protected water half a cable's length offshore she shed her tow lines and the four barges anchored in line astern, their bows facing into the strong current of the Blue Nile. Ryder Courtney placed armed guards on each barge to protect the cargoes against looting. Then he took the helm of the steamer and manoeuvred her towards the wharf.

As soon as he was within earshot the twins screeched a welcome: 'Ryder! It's us! Did you bring a present?' He heard them above the hubbub of the crowd, and had soon spotted Saffron perched on her father's shoulders. He removed the cheroot from his mouth, flicked it overboard into the river, then reached for the cord of the boat's whistle, sent a singing blast of steam high into the air and blew Saffron a kiss.

She dissolved into giggles and wriggled like a puppy. 'Isn't he the most dashing beau in the world?' She glanced at her elder sister.

Rebecca ignored her, but Ryder's eyes turned to her next and he lifted the hat off his dense dark curls, sleeked with his sweat. His face and arms were tanned to the colour of polished teak by the desert sun, except for the band of creamy skin just below his hairline where his hat had protected it. Rebecca smiled back and bobbed a curtsy. Saffron was right: he really was rather handsome, especially when he smiled, she thought, but there were crinkles at the corners of his eyes. He's so old, she thought. He must be every day of thirty.

'I think he's sweet on you.' Amber gave her serious opinion.

'Don't you dare start that infernal nonsense, Mademoiselle,' Rebecca warned her.

'Infernal nonsense, Mademoiselle,' Amber repeated softly – and rehearsed the words to use against Saffron at the first opportunity.

Out on the river Ryder Courtney was giving his full attention to the steamer as he brought her into her mooring. He swung her nose into the current and held her there with a deft touch on the throttle, then eased the wheel over and let her drift sideways across the stream until her steel side kissed the matting fenders that hung down the side of the wharf. His crew tossed the mooring lines to the men on the jetty, who seized the ends and made her fast. Ryder rang the telegraph to the boiler room, and Jock McCrump stuck his head through the engine-room hatch. His face was streaked with black grease. 'Aye, skipper?'

'Keep a head of steam in the boiler, Jock. Never know when we might need to run for it.'

'Aye, skipper. I want none of them stinking savages as shipmates.' Jock wiped the grease from his huge calloused hands on a wad of cotton waste.

'You have the con,' Ryder told him, and vaulted over the ship's rail to the jetty. He strode towards where General Gordon waited for him with his staff, but he had not gone a dozen paces before the crowd closed round him and he was trapped like a fish in a net.

A struggling knot of Egyptians and other Arabs surrounded him, grabbing at his clothing. 'Effendi, please, Effendi, I have ten children and four wives. Give us safe passage on your fine ship,' they pleaded, in Arabic and broken English. They thrust wads of banknotes into his face. 'A hundred Egyptian pounds. It is all I have. Take it, Effendi, and my prayers for your long life will go up to Allah.'

'Gold sovereigns of your queen!' another bid, and clinked the canvas bag he held like a tambourine.

Women pulled off their jewellery – heavy gold bracelets, rings and necklaces with sparkling stones. 'Me and my baby. Take us with you, great lord.' They thrust their infants at him, tiny squealing wretches, hollow-cheeked with starvation, some covered with the lesions and open sores of scurvy, their loincloths stained tobacco-yellow with the liquid faeces of cholera. They shoved and wrestled with each other to reach him. One woman was knocked to her knees and dropped her infant under the feet of the surging crowd. Its howls became weaker as they trampled it. Finally a nail-shod sandal crushed the eggshell skull and the child was abruptly silent and lay still, an abandoned doll, in the dust.

Ryder Courtney gave a bellow of rage and laid about him with clenched fists. He knocked down a fat Turkish merchant with a single blow to the jaw, then dropped his shoulder and charged into the ruck of struggling humanity. They scattered to let him pass, but some doubled back towards the *Intrepid Ibis*, and tried to scramble across to her deck.

Jock McCrump was at the rail to meet them with a monkey

wrench in his fist and five of his crew at his back, armed with boat-hooks and fire axes. Jock cracked the skull of the first man who tried to board and he fell into the narrow strip of water between the ship and the stone wharf, then disappeared beneath the surface. He did not rise again.

Ryder realized the danger and tried to get back to his ship, but even he could not cleave his way through the close pack of bodies.

'Jock, take her off and anchor with the barges!' he shouted.

Jock heard him above the uproar and waved the wrench in acknowledgement. He jumped to the bridge and gave a terse order to his crew. They did not waste time unmooring, but severed the lines to the shore with a few accurate strokes of the axes. The *Intrepid Ibis* swung her bows into the current, but before she had steerage way more of the refugees attempted to jump across the gap. Four fell short and were whipped away downstream by the racing current. One grabbed hold of the ship's rail and dangled down her side, trying to lift himself aboard, imploring the crew above him for mercy.

Bacheet, the Arab boatswain, stepped to the rail above him and, with a single swing of his axe, neatly lopped off the four fingers of the man's right hand. They fell to the steel deck like brown pork sausages. His victim shrieked and dropped into the river. Bacheet kicked the fingers over the side, wiped his blade on the skirt of his robe, then went to break out the bow anchor from its locker forward. Jock turned the steamboat out across the current, and ran out to anchor at the head of the line of barges.

A wail of despair went up from the crowd, but Ryder glowered at them, fists clenched. They had learnt exactly what that gesture presaged, and backed away from him. In the meantime General Gordon had ordered a squad of his soldiers to break up the riot. They advanced in a line with their bayonets fixed and used their rifle butts to club down any who stood in their way. The crowd broke before them, and disappeared into the narrow alleys of the city. They left the dead baby, with its bleeding mother wailing over it, and half a dozen moaning rioters sitting, stunned, in puddles of their own blood. The Turk who Ryder had floored lay quiescent on his back, snoring loudly.

Ryder looked about for David and his daughters, but the consul had shown the good sense to get his family away to the safety of the palace at the first sign of rioting. He felt a lift of relief. Then he saw General Gordon coming towards him, stepping through the litter and bodies. 'Good afternoon, General.'

'How do you do, Mr Courtney? I am pleased to welcome you. I hope you had a pleasant voyage.'

'Very enjoyable, sir. We made good passage through the Sud. The channel is well scoured out at this season. No necessity to kedge our way through.' Neither deigned to remark on the gauntlet that the steamboat had run through the Dervish batteries, or the riot that had welcomed it to the city.

'You are heavily laden, sir?' Gordon, who was fully six inches shorter, looked up at Ryder with those remarkable eyes. They were the steely blue of the noonday sky above the desert. Few men who looked into them could forget them. They were hypnotic, compelling, the outward sign of Gordon's iron faith in himself and his God.

Ryder understood the import of the question instantly. 'I have fifteen hundred sacks of dhurra sorghum in my barges, each bag of ten cantars weight.' A cantar was an Arabic measure, approximating a hundredweight.

Gordon's eyes sparkled like cut sapphires, and he slapped his cane against his thigh. 'Well done indeed, sir. The garrison and the entire population are already on extremely short commons. Your cargo might well see us through until the relief column from Cairo can reach us.'

Ryder Courtney blinked with surprise at such an optimistic estimate. There were close to thirty thousand souls trapped in the city. Even on starvation rations that multitude would devour a hundred sacks a day. The latest news they had received before the Dervish cut the telegraph line to the north was that the relief column was still assembling in the delta and would not be ready to begin the journey southwards for

13

several weeks more. Even then they had more than a thousand miles to travel to Khartoum. On the way they must navigate the cataracts and traverse the Mother of Stones, that terrible wilderness. Then they must fight their way through the Dervish hordes who guarded the long marches along the banks of the Nile before they could reach the city and raise the siege. Fifteen hundred sacks of dhurra was not nearly enough to sustain the inhabitants of Khartoum indefinitely. Then he realized that Gordon's optimism was his best armour. A man such as he could never allow himself to face the hopelessness of their plight and give in to despair.

He nodded his agreement. 'Do I have your permission to begin sales of the grain, General?' The city was under martial law. No distribution of food was allowed without Gordon's personal sanction.

'Sir, I cannot allow you to distribute the provisions. The population of my city is starving.' Ryder noted Gordon's use of the possessive. 'If you were to sell them they would be hoarded by wealthy merchants to the detriment of the poor. There will be equal rations for all. I will oversee the distribution. I have no choice but to commandeer your entire cargo of grain. I will, of course, pay you a fair price for it.'

For a moment Ryder stared at him, speechless. Then he found his voice. 'A fair price, General?'

'At the end of the last harvest the price of dhurra in the souks of this city was six shillings a sack. It was a fair price, and still is, sir.'

'At the end of the last harvest there was no war and no siege,' Ryder retorted. 'General, six shillings does not take into account the extortionate price I was forced to pay. Nor does it compensate me for the difficulties I experienced in transporting the sorghum and the fair profit to which I am entitled.'

'I am certain, Mr Courtney, that six shillings will return you a handsome profit.' Gordon stared at him hard. 'This city is under martial law, sir, and profiteering and hoarding are both capital crimes.'

Ryder knew that the threat was not an idle one. He had

seen many men flogged or summarily executed for any dereliction of their duty, or defiance of this little man's decrees. Gordon unbuttoned the breast pocket of his uniform jacket and brought out his notebook. He scribbled in it swiftly, tore out the sheet and passed it to Ryder. 'That is my personal promissory note for the sum of four hundred and fifty Egyptian pounds. It is payable at the treasury of the Khedive in Cairo,' he said briskly. The Khedive was the ruler of Egypt. 'What is the rest of your cargo, Mr Courtney?'

'Ivory, live wild birds and animals,' Ryder replied bitterly.

'Those you may offload into your godown. At this stage I have no interest in them, although later it may be necessary to slaughter the animals to provide meat for the populace. How soon can you have your steamer and the barges ready to depart, sir?'

'Depart, General?' Ryder turned pale under his tan: he had sensed what was about to happen.

'I am commandeering your vessels for the transport of refugees downriver,' Gordon explained. 'You may requisition what cordwood you need to fuel your boilers. I will reimburse you for the voyage at the rate of two pounds per passenger. I estimate you might take five hundred women, children and heads of families. I will personally review the needs of each and decide who is to have priority.'

'You will pay me with another note, General?' Ryder asked, with veiled irony.

'Precisely, Mr Courtney. You will wait at Metemma until the relief force reaches you. My own steamers are already there. Your famed skill as a river pilot will be much in demand in the passage of the Shabluka Gorge, Mr Courtney.'

Chinese Gordon despised what he looked upon as greed and the worship of Mammon. When the Khedive of Egypt had offered him a salary of ten thousand pounds to undertake this most perilous assignment of evacuating the Sudan, Gordon had insisted that this be reduced to two thousand. He had his own perception of duty to his fellow men and his God. 'Please bring your barges alongside the jetty and my troops will guard them while they are offloaded, and the dhurra is taken to the customs warehouse. Major al-Faroque, of my staff, will be in command of the operation.' Gordon nodded to the Egyptian officer at his side, who saluted Ryder perfunctorily. Al-Faroque had soulful dark eyes, and smelt powerfully of hair pomade. 'And now you must excuse me, sir. I have much to attend to.'

As the official hostess to Her Britannic Majesty's consul general to the Sudan, Rebecca was responsible for the running of the palace household. This evening, under her supervision, the servants had laid the dinner table on the terrace that overlooked the Blue Nile so that David's guests might enjoy the breeze off the river. At sunset the servants would light braziers of eucalyptus branches and leaves. The smoke would keep the mosquitoes at bay. The entertainment would be provided with the compliments of General Gordon. Every evening the military band played and there was a fireworks display: General Gordon intended the show to take the minds of Khartoum's population off the rigours and hardships of the siege.

Rebecca had planned a splendid table. The consular silver and glassware had been polished to dazzling brilliance and the linen bleached white as an angel's wing. Unfortunately the meal would not be of comparable quality. They would start with a soup of blackjack weeds and rose hips from the ruins of the palace garden. This would be followed by a pâté of boiled palm-tree pith and stoneground dhurra, but the *pièce de résistance* was supreme of pelican.

Most evenings David took his station on the terrace above the river with one of his Purdey shotguns at the ready, and waited for the flights of waterfowl to pass overhead as they flew in to their roosts. Behind him the twins waited with the other guns. Such a matching trio of firearms was known as a garnish of guns. David believed that any woman who lived in Africa, that continent of wild animals and wilder men, should be competent in the use of firearms. Under his tutelage

Rebecca was already an expert pistol shot. At ten paces she was usually capable with six shots from the heavy Webley revolver of knocking at least five empty bully-beef cans off the stone wall at the bottom of the terrace to send them spinning out across the waters of the Nile.

The twins were still too small to withstand the recoil of a Webley or Purdey, so he had trained them to serve the spare shotguns until they had become as quick and dexterous as a professional loader on a Yorkshire grouse moor. The moment her father had fired both barrels, Amber snatched the empty gun from him and, at almost the same instant, Saffron thrust the second into his hands. While he picked his birds and fired again, the girls reloaded the empty weapon and were ready to serve him with it as soon as he reached for it. Between them they could keep up an impressive rate of fire.

David was a celebrated shot and seldom wasted a cartridge. While the girls squealed encouragement he might on occasion bring down five or six birds in quick succession from a flight of teal speeding high overhead. In the first weeks of the siege wild duck had regularly come within range of the terrace, teal, shovellers and more exotic species, such as Egyptian geese and garganey, all of which had provided important additions to the palace larder. But the surviving duck learnt quickly, and now the flocks habitually gave the terrace a wide berth. It was only the more stupid and less palatable birds that could still be brought to table by David's marksmanship. A brace of heavily billed pelicans were his most recent victims.

The accompanying dish Rebecca planned to serve was the boiled leaves and stems of the sacred Egyptian water-lily. When he had recommended this plant to her Ryder Courtney had told her that its botanical name was *Nymphaea alba*. He had a vast fund of knowledge of all the natural world. She used the lovely blue blossoms as a salad – their peppery flavour helped to disguise the pervading fishy taste of pelican flesh. These plants grew in the narrow canal that cut off the city from the mainland. At this season the water in the canal was waist deep, but in the Low Nile period it dried out. General Gordon had set his troops to widening and deepening the

17

canal into a moat to bolster the city's fortifications and, much to Rebecca's annoyance, they were destroying the source of this nutritious delicacy in the process.

The consular cellars were almost bare, except for a single case of Krug champagne that David was saving to celebrate the arrival of the relief force from the south. However, when Ryder Courtney sent Bacheet up to the consulate to accept the dinner invitation, he also sent three calabash gourds of Tej, the powerful native honey beer, which tasted like poor-quality cider. Rebecca intended serving it in crystal claret decanters to give it an importance it did not normally warrant.

Now she was putting the finishing touches to the dinner arrangements, and the table's floral decoration of oleander from the neglected gardens. The guests would start arriving in an hour and her father had not yet returned from his daily meeting with General Gordon. She was a little worried that David might be late and spoil her evening. However, she was secretly relieved that General Gordon had refused the invitation: he was a great and saintly man, a hero of the Empire, but scornful of the social graces. His conversation was pious and arcane, and his sense of humour, to be charitable, was impaired if not totally lacking.

At that moment she heard her father's familiar tread reverberating down the cloisters and his voice raised as he summoned one of the servants. She ran to greet him as he stepped out on to the terrace. He returned her embrace in a distracted, perfunctory manner. She stepped back and studied his face. 'Father, what is it?'

'We are to leave the city tomorrow night. General Gordon has ordered all British, French and Austrian citizens to be evacuated at once.'

'Does that mean you will come with us, Daddy?' These days she seldom used the childish term of endearment.

'It does indeed.'

'How are we to travel?'

'Gordon has commandeered Ryder Courtney's steamer and barges. He has ordered him downriver with all of us on board. I tried to argue with him, but to no avail. The man is intractable and cannot be moved from his chosen path.' Then David grinned, seized her round the waist and spun her into a waltz. 'To tell the truth, I am vastly relieved that the decision has been taken out of my hands, and that you and the twins will be conveyed to safety.'

An hour later David and Rebecca stood under the candelabrum in the reception lobby to greet their guests, who were almost entirely male. Months before, nearly all the white women had been evacuated north to the delta, aboard General Gordon's tin-pot steamers. Now those vessels were stranded far south at Metemma, awaiting the arrival of a relief force. Rebecca and the twins were among the few European females who remained in the city.

The twins stood demurely behind their father. They had prevailed on their elder sister to allow them to be there when Ryder arrived and to watch the fireworks with him before Nazeera, their nurse, took them to the nursery. Nazeera had been Rebecca's nurse too and was a beloved member of the Benbrook household. She stood close behind the twins now, ready to spring into action at the first stroke of nine. Much to the twins' disappointment, Ryder Courtney was last to arrive, but when he did they giggled and whispered together.

'He's so handsome,' said Saffron, and did her swooning act.

Nazeera pinched her and whispered in Arabic, 'Even if you are never to be a lady, you must learn to behave like one, Saffy.'

'I have never seen him in full fig before.' Amber agreed with her twin: Ryder wore one of the new dinner jackets that the Prince of Wales had recently made fashionable. It had watered satin lapels and was nipped in at the waist. He had had it copied from an picture in the *London Illustrated News* by an Armenian tailor in Cairo, and carried it off with a casual elegance far from his rumpled workaday moleskins. He was freshly shaven and his hair shone in the candlelight.

'And, look, he has brought us presents!' Amber had seen the telltale bulge in his breast pocket. She had a woman's eye for such details.

Ryder shook hands with David and bowed to Rebecca. He

refrained from kissing her hand in the Frenchified gesture that many members of the diplomatic corps, who had arrived before him, had affected. Then he winked at the twins, who covered their mouths to suppress giggles as they dropped him a curtsy in return.

'May I have the honour of escorting you two beautiful ladies to the terrace?' He bowed.

'Wee wee, Moonseer,' said Saffron, grandly, which was almost too much for Amber's self-control.

Ryder took one on each arm, stooping a little so that they could reach, and led them out through the french windows. One of the servants in a white robe and blue turban brought them glasses of lemonade, made from the few remaining fruits on the trees in the orchard, and Ryder presented the twins with their gifts, necklaces of ivory beads carved in the shape of tiny animals: lions, monkeys and giraffes. He fastened the clasps at the backs of their necks. They were enchanted.

Almost on cue the military band down on the maidan beside the old slave market began to play. The distance muted the sound to a pleasing volume, and the musicians succeeded in embellishing the familiar repertoire of polkas, waltzes and marching tunes of the British Army with beguiling Oriental cadences.

'Sing for us, Ryder, oh, please do!' Amber begged, and when he laughed and shook his head, she appealed to her father, 'Please make him sing, Daddy.'

'My daughter is right, Mr Courtney. A voice would add immeasurably to the pleasure of the occasion.'

Ryder sang unselfconsciously, and soon had them all tapping their feet or clapping in time to the music. Those who fancied their own vocal prowess joined in with the chorus of 'Over the Sea to Skye'.

Then the firework display began, General Gordon's nightly treat. The sky cascaded with sheets of blue, green and red sparks from the ship's signal rockets, and the watchers oohed and aahed in wonder. Over on the far bank of the Nile the Dervish gunner whom David had dubbed the Bedlam Bedouin fired a few shrapnel shells at the point from where he guessed the rockets were being set off. As usual, his aim was awry and nobody sought shelter. Instead, everyone booed his efforts with gusto.

Then the twins were led away, protesting vainly, to the nursery, and the company was summoned to the table by one of the robed Arab footmen tapping on a finger drum. Everyone was in fine appetite: if not yet starving, they were at least half-way there. The portions were minuscule, barely a mouthful each, but Herr Schiffer, the Austrian consul, declared the blackjack weed soup to be excellent, the palm-pith pâté nourishing and the roast pelican 'quite extraordinary'. Rebecca convinced herself that this was meant as a compliment.

As the meal drew to a close, Ryder Courtney did something to confirm his status as the hero of the evening. He clapped his hands and Bacheet, his boatswain, came out on to the terrace grinning like a gargoyle and carrying a silver tray on which reposed a cut-glass bottle of VSOP Hine Cognac and a cedarwood box of Cuban cigars. With their glasses charged and the cigars drawing until the tips glowed, the men were transported into an expansive mood. The conversation was diverting, until Monsieur le Blanc joined in.

'I wonder that Chinese Gordon refused such fine entertainment.' He giggled in a girlish, irritating manner. 'Surely it is not possible to save the mighty British Empire twenty-four hours of every day. Even Hercules had to rest from his labours.' Le Blanc was head of the Belgian delegation sent by King Leopold to initiate diplomatic contact with the Mahdi. So far his efforts had not been crowned by success and he had ended up a captive in the city like the rest of them. The Englishmen at the table looked upon him pityingly. However, as he was a foreigner and knew no better, he was excused the solecism.

'The General refused to attend a banquet while the populace was starving.' Rebecca rose to Gordon's defence. 'I think that was very noble-minded of him.' Then she hurried on modestly, 'Not that I claim my humble offering as. a great banquet.'

Following her example David initiated a eulogy to the General's inflexible character and his marvellous achievements.

Ryder Courtney was still smarting from Gordon's last demonstration of his adamantine character and did not join in the chorus of praise.

'He wields an almost messianic power over his men,' David told them earnestly. 'They will follow him anywhere, and if they don't he will drag them by their pigtails, as he did with his Ever Victorious Army in China, or kick their backsides black and blue as he does to the Egyptian riff-raff with which he is forced to defend the city at the moment.'

'Your language, Daddy,' Rebecca chided him primly.

'I am sorry, my darling, but it is true. He is completely fearless. Alone, mounted on a camel and in full dress uniform, he rode into that murderous rogue Suleiman's encamped army of rebels and harangued them. Instead of murdering him out of hand Suleiman abandoned the rebellion and went home.'

'He did the same with the Zulus in South Africa. When he walked alone among their warlike *impis*, and turned his extraordinary eyes upon them, they worshipped him as a god. At that, he thrashed their *induna* for blasphemy.'

Another spoke up: 'Kings and potentates of many nations have competed to secure his services – the Emperor of China, King Leopold of the Belgians, the Khedive of Egypt and the premier of the Cape Colony.'

'He is a man of God before he is a warrior. He scorns the clamour of men, and before he makes any fateful decision he enquires in solitary prayer what his God requires of him.'

I wonder that God required him to steal my dhurra, Ryder thought bitterly. He did not voice the sentiment but changed the direction of the conversation dramatically: 'Is it not remarkable that in many ways the man who faces him now across the Nile shares many characteristics with our gallant general?' A silence followed this remark, which was almost as bad as Le Blanc's gaucherie, not at all worthy of a man of the calibre of Ryder Courtney.

Even Rebecca was aghast at the idea of comparing the

saint with   ister. Yet she noticed that when Ryder spoke other men listened. Even though he was the youngest man at the table, the others deferred to him for his fortune and reputation were formidable. He had travelled indefatigably where few men before him had ventured. He had reached the Mountains of the Moon and sailed on all of the great lakes of the African interior. He was a friend and confidant of John, the Emperor of Abyssinia. The Mutesa of Buganda and the Kamrasi of Bunyoro were his familiars and had granted him exclusive trading rights in their kingdoms.

His Arabic was so fluent that he could debate the Koran with the mullahs in the mosque. He spoke a dozen other more primitive tongues and could bargain with the naked Dinka and the Shilluk. He had hunted and captured every known species of the wild beasts and birds of Equatoria, and sold them to the menageries of the kings, emperors and zoological gardens of Europe.

'That is an extraordinary notion, Ryder,' David ventured cautiously. 'It strikes me that the Mad Mahdi and General Charles Gordon stand at opposite poles. But perhaps you can point out some characteristics they have in common.'

'First, David, they are both ascetics who practise self-denial and abstain from worldly comforts,' Ryder replied easily. 'And both are men of God.'

'Different Gods,' David challenged.

'No, sir! One and the same God: the God of the Jews, Muslims, Christians and all other monotheists is the same God. It is simply that they worship Him in different ways.'

David smiled. 'Perhaps we can debate that later. But for now tell us what else they have in common.'

'They both believe that God speaks directly to them and that therefore they are infallible. Once their minds are set they are unwavering and deaf to argument. Then again, like many great men and beautiful women, they are both betrayed by their belief in the cult of personality. They believe that they are able to carry all before them by the blue of their eyes or by the gap between their front teeth and their eloquence,' Ryder said.

'We know who possesses the blue aı.   pelling eye,' David chuckled, 'but to whom belongs the gap-toothed grin?'

'To Muhammad Ahmed, the Mahdi, the Divinely Guided One,' said Ryder. 'The wedge shaped gap is called the *falja* and his Ansar consider it a mark of the divine.'

'You speak as though you are familiar with him,' said Le Blanc. 'Have you met the man?'

'I have,' Ryder confirmed, and they all stared at him as though he had admitted to supping with Satan himself.

Rebecca was the first to rouse herself. 'Do tell us, Mr Courtney, where and when? What is he truly like?'

'I knew him first when he lived in a hole in the bank of Abbas Island, forty miles up the Blue Nile from where we now sit. Often when I passed the island I would go ashore to sit with him and speak of God and the affairs of men. I could not claim that we were friends, nor would I ever wish to do so. But there was something about him that I found fascinating. I sensed that he was different, and I was always impressed by his piety, his quiet strength and unruffled smile. He is a true patriot, as is General Gordon – another trait they have in common.'

'Enough of General Gordon. We all know of his virtues,' Rebecca interjected. 'Tell us rather of this terrible Mahdi. How can you say he has in him a grain of the same nobility?'

'We all know that the domination of the Sudan by the Khedive in Egypt has been iniquitous and brutal. Behind the magnificent façade of imperial dominion has flourished unspeakable corruption and cruelty. The native population has been subject to greedy and heartless pashas, and an army of occupation forty thousand strong, which was used to collect the extortionate taxes the pashas imposed. Only half went to the Khedive in Cairo and the rest into the personal coffers of the pashas. The land was ruled by bayonet and kurbash, the vicious hippo-hide whip. The effete pashas sitting here in Khartoum delighted in devising the most savage tortures and executions. Villages were razed and their inhabitants slaughtered. Arab and black man alike cowered under the shadow of the hated 'Turk', but no man dared protest.

24

'The Egyptians, while aspiring to civilization, fostered and encouraged the trade in slaves, for that was how the taxes were paid. I have seen such horrors with my own eyes, and I was amazed by the forbearance of the population. I discussed all this with the hermit in his hole in the riverbank. We were both young men, although I was by some years the younger. We attempted between us to discover why this situation persisted, for the Arab is a proud man and has not lacked provocation. We decided that two essential elements of revolution were missing, and the first of these was the knowledge of better things. General Charles Gordon, as the governor of the Sudan, provided this. The other missing element was a uniting catalyst among the oppressed. In the fullness of time Muhammad Ahmed provided this. It was how the new Mahdist nation was born.'

They were silent, until Rebecca spoke again, and hers was a woman's question. The political, religious and military facets of the Mahdi's history interested her very little. 'But what is he really like, Mr Courtney? What of his appearance and his demeanour? How does his voice sound? And tell us more of this strange gap between his teeth.'

'He possesses the same vast charisma as Charles Gordon, another trait they have in common. He is of medium height and slim in stature. He has always dressed in robes of spotless white, even when he lived in the hole in the ground. On his right cheek is a birthmark in the shape of a bird or an angel. This is seen by his disciples and adherents as a touch of the divine. The gap between his teeth rivets your attention when he speaks. He is a compelling orator. His voice is soft and sibilant, until his ire is aroused. Then he speaks with the thunder of one of the biblical prophets, but even in anger he smiles.' Ryder drew out his gold pocket-watch. 'It lacks only an hour of midnight. I have kept you late. We should all get a good night's rest, for as you have been told it is my duty, allotted to me by General Gordon, to make certain that none of you here tonight will ever be forced to listen to the voice of Muhammad Ahmed. Remember, please, that you are to be aboard my steamer at the Old City wharf before midnight tomorrow. It is my intention to sail while it is still too dark for the Dervish gunners to pick us out clearly. Please restrict your luggage to the minimum. With good fortune we may run clean away from them before they get off a single shot.'

David smiled. 'That will require a certain amount of luck, Mr Courtney, for the city is crawling with Dervish spies. The Mahdi knows exactly what we are up to almost before we know it ourselves.'

'Perhaps this time we will be able to outwit him.' Ryder half rose and bowed to Rebecca. 'I apologize if I have overstayed my welcome, Miss Benbrook.'

'It is still far too early for you to leave. None of us will sleep yet. Please sit down, Mr Courtney. You cannot leave us high and dry. Finish the story, for you have intrigued us all.'

Ryder made a gesture of resignation and sank down again on his chair. 'How can I resist your command? But I fear you all know the rest of the story, for it has been often told and I do not wish to bore you.'

There were murmurs of protest down the length of the table.

'Go on, sir. Miss Benbrook is right. We must hear out your version. It seems that it differs greatly from what we have come to believe.'

Ryder Courtney nodded acquiescence, and went on: 'In our western societies we pride ourselves in glorious traditions and high moral standards. Yet in savage and uneducated peoples ignorance provides its own source of great strength. It engenders in them the overpowering stimulus of fanaticism. Here in the Sudan there were three giant steps on the road to rebellion. The first was the misery of all the native peoples of the country. The second was when they looked about them and recognized that the source of all their ills was the hated Turk, the minions of the Khedive in Cairo. It needed but a single step more before the mighty wave of fanaticism crashed over the land. That was the moment when there arose the man who would become the Mahdi.'

'Of course!' interjected David. 'The seed had been sown long ago. The Shukri belief that one day, in the time of shame and strife, a second great prophet would be sent by Allah, who would lead the faithful back to God and sustain Islam.'

Rebecca looked sternly at her father. 'It's Mr Courtney's story, Father. Please let him tell it.'

The men smiled at her fire, and David looked guilty. 'I did not mean to usurp your tale. Pray go on, sir.'

'But you are right, David. For a hundred years the people of the Sudan have always looked in hope to any ascetic who rises to prominence. As this one's fame spread, pilgrims began flocking to Abbas Island. They brought valuable gifts, which Muhammad Ahmed distributed to the poor. They listened to his sermons, and when they left to return to their homes they took with them the writings of this holy man. His fame spread throughout the Sudan until it reached the ears of one who had waited eagerly all his life for the coming of the second prophet. Abdullahi, the son of an obscure cleric and the youngest of his four brothers, journeyed to Abbas Island in wild expectation. He arrived at last on a saddle-galled donkey, and he recognized instantly the devout young hermit as the true messenger of God.'

David could not restrain himself longer: 'Or did he recognize the vehicle that would convey him to power and wealth undreamed?'

'Perhaps that is more accurate.' Ryder laughed in accord. 'But, be that as it may, the two men formed a powerful alliance. Soon news reached the ears of Raouf Pasha, the Egyptian governor of Khartoum, that this mad priest was preaching defiance to the Khedive in Cairo. He sent a messenger to Abbas to summon Muhammad Ahmed here to the city to justify himself. The priest listened to the messenger, then stood up and spoke in the voice of a true prophet: "By the grace of God and his prophet, I am the master of this land. In God's name I declare *jihad*, holy war, on the Turk."

'The messenger fled back to his master and Abdullahi gathered around him a tiny band of ragged wretches, then armed them with sticks and stones. Raouf Pasha sent two companies of his best soldiers by steamer upriver to capture the troublesome priest. He believed in the incentive method

27

of conducting warfare. He promised promotion and a large reward to whichever of his two captains made the arrest. At nightfall the steamboat captain landed the soldiers on the island, and the two companies, now in competition with each other, marched by separate routes to surround the village in which the priest was reported to be sheltering. In the confusion of the moonless night the soldiers attacked each other furiously, then fled back to the landing. The terrified steamboat captain refused to let them embark unless they swam out to his boat. Few accepted this offer for most could not swim, and those who could feared the crocodiles. So the captain abandoned them and sailed back to Khartoum. Muhammad Ahmed and Abdullahi, with their tatterdemalion army, fell upon the demoralized Egyptians and slaughtered them.

'The news of this extraordinary victory spread throughout the land, that men with sticks had routed the hated Turk. Surely it must have been the Mahdi who led them. Knowing that more Egyptian troops would be sent to kill him, the newly self-proclaimed Mahdi began a *hegira*, very much like the exodus of the One True Prophet from Mecca a thousand years before. However, before the retreat began, he appointed the faithful Abdullahi as his *khalifa*, his deputy under God. This was in accordance with precedent and prophecy. Soon the retreat became a triumphal progress. The Mahdi was preceded by tales of miracles and prodigious omens. One night a dark shadow obliterated the crescent moon, the symbol of Egypt and the Turk. This message from God high in the midnight sky was plain for every man in the Sudan to see. When the Mahdi reached a mountain fastness far to the south of Khartoum, which he renamed Jebel Masa in accordance with the prophecy, he deemed himself safe from Raouf Pasha. However, he was still within striking distance of Fashoda: Rashid Bey, the governor of the town, was braver and more enterprising than most Egyptian governors. He marched on Jebel Masa with fourteen hundred heavily armed troops. But, scornful of this rabble of peasants, he took few precautions. The intrepid Khalifa Abdullahi laid an ambush for him. Rashid Bey marched straight into it, and neither he nor any single one of his men survived the day. They were slaughtered by the ragged ill-armed *Ansar*.'

Ryder's cigar had gone out. He stood up, took a glowing twig from the brazier of eucalyptus branches and relit it. When it was drawing brightly again he returned to his chair. 'Now that Abdullahi had captured rifles and vast military stores, not to mention the treasury of Fashoda in which was deposited almost half a million pounds, he had become a formidable force. The Khedive in Cairo ordered that a new army be raised here at Khartoum and gave the command of it to a retired British officer, General Hicks. It was one of the most abysmally inept armies ever to take the field, and Hicks's authority was diluted and countermanded by the bumbling Raouf Pasha, who was already the author of two military disasters.'

Ryder paused and as he poured the last of the Hine into his glass he shook his head sadly. 'It is almost two years to the day that General Hicks marched out of this city with seven thousand infantry and five hundred cavalry. He was supported by mounted artillery, Krupps guns and Nordenfelt machine-guns. His men were mostly Muslims and they had heard the legend of the Mahdi. They began to desert before he had covered five miles. He clapped fifty men of the Krupps battery in chains to encourage them to greater valour, but they still deserted and took their manacles with them.' Ryder threw back his head and laughed, and although the tale had been terrifying the sound was so infectious that Rebecca found herself laughing with him.

'What Hicks did not know and what he did not believe even when Lieutenant Penrod Ballantyne, his intelligence officer, warned him, was that by now forty thousand men had flocked to the Mahdi's green flag. One of the emirs who had brought his tribe to join the array was none other than Osman Atalan of the Beja.'

The men around the table stirred at the mention of that name. It was one to conjure with, for the Beja were the fiercest and most feared of all the fighting Arabs, and Osman Atalan was their most dreaded warlord.

'On the third of November 1883, Hicks's motley force ran headlong into the army of the Mahdi, and they were cut to pieces by the charges of the Ansar. Hicks himself was mortally wounded as he stood at the head of the last formed square of his troops. When he fell the square broke and the Ansar swarmed over it. Penrod Ballantyne, who had warned Hicks of the danger, saw the General empty his revolver into the charging Arabs before his head was sliced off by a swinging broadsword. Ballantyne's own superior officer, Major Adams, was lying shot through both legs, and the Arabs were massacring and mutilating the wounded. Ballantyne sprang to horse and managed to lift Major Adams up behind his saddle. Then he hacked his way out through the attackers, and broke clear. He caught up with the Egyptian rearguard, which was by this time in full flight for Khartoum. He was the only surviving European officer so he took command. He rallied them and led a fighting retreat back into Khartoum. Ballantyne brought back two hundred men, including the wounded Major Adams. Two hundred men – of the seven and a half thousand who had marched out with General Hicks. His conduct was the one single ray of light in an otherwise dark day. Thus the Mahdi and his *khalifa* became masters of all the Sudan, and they closed in with their victorious forty thousand on this city, bringing with them the captured guns that torment us to this day. And so the populace languishes and starves, or perishes from pestilence and cholera, while awaiting the fate that the Mahdi has in store for Khartoum.'

There were tears in Rebecca's eyes as Ryder stopped speaking. 'He sounds a fine and brave young man, this Penrod Ballantyne. Have you ever met him, Mr Courtney?'

'Ballantyne?' Ryder looked surprised by this abrupt change in the focus of his tale. 'Yes, I was here when he rode back from the battlefield.'

'Tell us more about him, please, sir.'

Ryder shrugged. 'Most of the ladies I have spoken to assure me that they find him dashing and gallant. They are particularly enamoured of his moustache, which is formidable. Perhaps Captain Ballantyne might agree rather too readily with the general feminine opinion of himself.'

'I thought you spoke of him as a lieutenant?'

'In an attempt to garner some tiny grain of glory from that terrible day the commander of the British troops in Cairo made a great fuss of Ballantyne's role in the battle. It just so happens that Ballantyne is a subaltern in the 10th Hussars, which is Lord Wolseley's old regiment. Wolseley is always ready to give a fellow Hussar a leg up, so Ballantyne was uplifted to the rank of a full captain, and if that was not sufficient he was given the Victoria Cross to boot.'

'You do not approve of Captain Ballantyne, sir?' Rebecca asked.

For the first time David detected in his daughter's attitude towards Ryder Courtney a definite coolness. He wondered at the rather excessive interest she was evincing towards Ballantyne, who presumably was a stranger to her, when suddenly, with a small shock, he recalled that young Ballantyne had visited the consulate some weeks before Hicks's army had marched away to annihilation at El Obeid. The lad had come to deliver a despatch from Evelyn Baring, the British consul in Cairo, which had been too sensitive to be sent over the telegraph, even in cipher. Although nothing had been said at the time he had guessed that Ballantyne was an officer in the intelligence section of Baring's staff, and that his seconding to Hicks's motley army was merely a cover.

Damme, yes! It's all coming back, David thought. Rebecca had come into his office while he was engaged with Ballantyne. The two young people had exchanged a few polite words when he introduced them, and Rebecca had left them alone. But later, when he was showing Ballantyne to the door, David had noticed her arranging flowers in the hall. On glancing out of his office window a short time later, he had seen his daughter walking with Ballantyne to the palace gates. Ballantyne had seemed attentive. Now it all fell into place. Perhaps it was not pure chance that Rebecca had been lingering in the hall when Ballantyne emerged from his office. He smiled inwardly at the way his daughter had pretended never to have met Ballantyne when she asked Ryder Courtney his opinion of the man.

So young, but already so much like her mother, David reflected. As devious as a palace full of pashas.

Ryder Courtney was still responding to Rebecca's challenge: 'I am sure that Ballantyne is an authentic hero, and I am indeed impressed by his facial hair. However, I have never detected in him any excess of humility. But then again I am ambivalent about all military men. When they have finished thrashing the heathen, storming cities and seizing kingdoms, they simply ride away, their sabres and medals clinking. It is left to administrators like your father to try to make some order out of the chaos they have created, and to businessmen like myself to restore prosperity to a shattered population. No, Miss Benbrook, I have no quarrel with Captain Ballantyne, but I am not entirely enamoured of that branch of the state apparatus to which he belongs.'

Rebecca's eye was cold and her expression severe as Ryder Courtney stood up again to leave, but this time with greater determination. Rebecca did not attempt to delay his departure any longer.

It was after midnight before Ryder rode back to his godown. He slept only a few hours before Bacheet woke him again. He ate his breakfast of cold, hard dhurra cakes and pickled salt beef while seated at his desk, working over his journal and cash book by the light of the oil lamps. He felt a sinking sense of dread as he realized how finely drawn were his business affairs.

Apart from six hundred pounds deposited in the Cairo branch of Barings Bank, almost all his wealth was concentrated in the besieged city. In his warehouse he had over eighteen tons of ivory, worth five shillings a pound, but only when it reached Cairo. In beleaguered Khartoum it was not worth a sack of dhurra. The same could be said of the ton and a half of gum arabic, the sap of the acacia tree, which had been dried into sticky black bricks. It was a valuable commodity used in the arts, cosmetics and printing industries. In Cairo his stock would sell for several thousand pounds. Then he had four large storerooms stacked to the ceiling with dried cattle hides bartered from the pastoral Dinka and Shilluk tribes to the south. Another large room was filled with trade goods: rolls of copper wire, Venetian glass beads, steel axe and hoe heads, hand mirrors, old Tower muskets and kegs of cheap black gunpowder, rolls of calico and Birmingham cotton goods, with all the other trinkets and gewgaws that delighted the rulers of the southern kingdoms and their subjects.

In the cages and stockades at the far end of his compound he kept the wild animals and birds that formed an important part of his trading stock. They had been captured in the savannahs and forests of Equatoria and brought downriver in his barges and steamer. In the stockades they were rested, tamed and made familiar with their human keepers. At the same time the keepers learnt what food and treatment would ensure their survival until they were transported north up the Nile to be auctioned to the dealers and their agents in Cairo and Damascus, and even to Naples and Rome where prices were considerably higher. In those markets some of the rarer African species might fetch as much as a hundred pounds each.

His most valuable possessions were concealed behind the steel door of the strongroom, which was hidden by a large Persian wall-hanging: more than a hundred bags of silver Maria Theresa dollars, that ubiquitous coin of the Middle East, minted with a portrait of the buxom queen of Hungary and Bohemia. This was the only coinage acceptable to the Abyssinians in their mountainous kingdom and his other more sophisticated trading partners, such as the Mutesa in Buganda, the Hadendowa and the Saar of the eastern deserts. At the moment there would be little trading with the emirs of these desert Arab tribes. Almost all had gone over *en masse* to join the Mahdi's *jihad*.

He smiled sardonically in the lamplight. I wonder if the

33

Mahdi might be open to an offer of Maria Theresa dollars, he thought. But I expect not. I hear he has already accumulated over a million pounds in plunder.

In the strongroom alongside the canvas bags of dollars were even greater treasures. Fifty sacks of dhurra corn, a couple of dozen boxes of Cuban cheroots, half a dozen cases of Hine Cognac and fifty pounds of Abyssinian coffee.

Chinese Gordon is shooting hoarders. I hope he offers me a last cheroot and a blindfold, he mused. Then he became deadly serious again. Before Gordon had commandeered the *Intrepid Ibis* Ryder had made plans to move as much as possible of his stock and stores downriver to Cairo. Then he would run the blockade of the river.

He had also planned that, while he was occupied with this voyage, Bacheet would take the bulkier and less valuable stocks by camel caravan to Abyssinia and perhaps even to one of the trading ports on the coast of the Red Sea. Although the Mahdi had deployed his armies along the western bank of the Blue Nile, and the northern bank of the Blue Nile, and was blockading the river, there were still many gaps in his besieging cordon. Principal of these was the broad wedge of open desert between the two rivers, at whose apex stood the city. Only the narrow canal protected this part of the city perimeter, and although General Gordon's men were deepening and widening it there was nothing beyond: no Dervish army, only sand, scrub and a few stands of acacia thorn for hundreds of miles.

Said Mahtoum, one of the few emirs who had not yet gone over to the Dervish, had agreed a price with Ryder to bring his camels close in to the city, just out of sight of it behind a low, rocky ridge. There, under Bacheet's supervision, he would load the cargo and smuggle it over the Sudanese border to one of Ryder's trading stations in the foothills of the Abyssinian mountains. All of those plans must now go by the board. He would be forced to leave all his possessions in the beleaguered city, taking only a boatload of refugees with him.

'Damn General bloody Chinese bloody Gordon!' he said, stood up abruptly and moved around the room. Apart from the cabin of the *Intrepid Ibis* this was his only permanent home. His father and his grandfather had been wanderers. From them he had learnt the itinerant lifestyle of the hunter and the African trader. But this godown was home. It needed only a good woman to make it complete.

A sudden image of Rebecca Benbrook opened in his mind. He smiled ruefully. He had a feeling that, for no good reason he could fathom, he had burned his bridges in that quarter. He crossed to a pair of massive elephant tusks that were fastened by bronze rings to the stonework of the wall and stroked one of the stained yellow shafts absently. The feeling of the smooth ivory under his fingers was as comforting as a string of worry-beads. With a single bullet through the brain, Ryder had killed the mighty bull who had carried these tusks at Karamojo, a thousand miles south of Khartoum on the Victoria Nile.

Still fondling the ivory, he studied the faded photograph in its ebony frame on the near wall. It depicted a family standing in front of an ox-wagon in a bleak but unmistakably African landscape. A team of sixteen oxen was inspanned and the black driver stood beside them, ready to crack his long whip and begin the trek towards some nameless destination out there in the blue yonder. In the centre of the picture Ryder's father sat in the saddle of his favourite mount, a grey gelding he had named Fox. He was a big, powerfully built man, with a full dark beard. He had died so long ago that Ryder could not remember if it was a reasonable likeness. He was holding the six-year-old Ryder on the pommel of his saddle with his long skinny legs dangling. Ryder's mother stood at the horse's head gazing serenely at the camera. He remembered every detail of her lovely features and, as always when he looked on them, he felt his heart squeezed by the memory. She was holding his sister's hand. Alice was a few years older than Ryder. On the other side of her stood Ryder's elder brother, with one arm protectively round their mother's waist. That day had been Waite Courtney's sixteenth birthday. He was ten years older than Ryder, and had been more a father to him than a brother after their own father had been killed by a wounded buffalo during the course of the journey on which the five in the photograph had been about to embark.

The last time Ryder Courtney had wept was when he received the telegraph from his sister Alice in London with the terrible news that Waite had been killed by the Zulus on some God-forsaken battlefield in South Africa under a hill called Isandlwana, the Place of the Little Hand. He had left his widow Ada with two sons, Sean and Garrick; fortunately they were almost grown men and could take care of her.

Ryder sighed and drove those sad thoughts from his mind. He shouted for Bacheet. Although it was still dark, there was much they must do today if they were to be ready to sail before midnight.

The two men walked past the ivory warehouse to the gate of the animal stockade. Old Ali met them coughing and grumbling.

'O beloved of Allah,' Ryder greeted him. 'May the wombs of all your beautiful young wives be fruitful. And may their ardour fire your heart and weaken your knees.'

Ali tried not to grin at this levity, for all three of his wives were ancient crones. When a chuckle almost escaped him he turned it into a cough, then spat a glob of yellow phlegm into the dust. Ali was the keeper of the menagerie, and although he seemed to hate all mankind he had a magical way with wild creatures. He led Ryder on a tour of the monkey cages. They were all clean, and the water and feed in the dishes was fresh. Ryder reached into the cage of Colobus and his favourite jumped on to his shoulder, bared his teeth and exposed his fangs. Ryder found the remains of the dhurra cake from his breakfast in his pocket and fed it to him. He stroked the handsome black and white coat as they went on down the row of cages. There were five different species of ape, including dog-faced baboons, and two young chimpanzees, which were hugely in demand in Europe and Asia, and would find eager buyers in Cairo. They clambered up and hugged Ali round the neck; the youngest sucked his ear as though it were its mother's teat. Ali grumbled at them in soft, loving tones.

Beyond the monkeys there were cages full of birds, from starlings of vivid metallic hues to eagles, huge owls, long-legged storks and hornbills, with beaks like great yellow trumpets. 'Are you still able to find food for them?' Ryder indicated the carnivorous birds tethered by one leg to their posts. Ali grunted noncommittally, but Bacheet answered for him.

'The rats are the only animals that still thrive in the city. The urchins bring them in for two copper coins each.' Ali looked at him venomously for having divulged information that was none of his business.

At the far end of the stockade the antelopes were penned together, except for the Cape buffalo who were too aggressive to share with other animals. They were still calves, barely weaned, for young animals were more resilient and travelled better than mature beasts. Ryder had left for last the two rare and lovely antelope he had captured on his last expedition. They had lustrous ginger coats with stark white stripes, huge swimming eyes and trumpet-shaped ears, and were also still calves; when fully mature they would be the size of a pony. Buds bulged out between their ears, which would soon sprout into heavy corkscrew horns. Although the cured hides of the bongo had been described before, no live specimen had ever been offered for sale in Europe, as far as Ryder knew. A breeding pair like this would command a prince's ransom. He fed them dhurra cakes and they slobbered greedily into his palm.

As they walked on Ryder and Ali discussed how best to maintain a constant supply of fodder to keep their charges nourished and healthy. The bongos were browsing animals, and Ali had discovered that they accepted the foliage of the acacia tree. Al-Mahtoum's men regularly brought in camel loads of freshly cut branches from the desert in exchange for handfuls of silver Maria Theresa dollars.

'Soon we will have to capture another floating reed island because if we do not the other animals will starve,' Ali warned lugubriously. He relished being the bearer of worrisome tidings. When rafts of swamp weed and papyrus broke free from the dense masses in the lagoons and channels of the Sud they were carried downstream on the Nile. Some of the rafts were so extensive and buoyant that often they brought large animals with them from the swamps. Despite the best efforts of the Dervish, Ryder and his crew were able to secure these living rafts with long cables and heave them on to the bank. There, gangs of labourers hacked the matted vegetation into manageable blocks and moored them in the moat of the channel. The grasses and reeds remained green until they could be used as fodder.

There was scarcely enough daylight for Ryder to finish his preparations to leave Khartoum, and the sun was setting by the time he and Bacheeet left the compound with a string of baggage camels for the old harbour. Jock McCrump had steam up in the boilers of the *Intrepid Ibis* when they went aboard.

Ryder was painfully aware of the spying eyes of the city upon them as they loaded the last bundles of cordwood for the boilers into one of the barges. The sun had been down for two hours before they had finished but the heat of the day still held the city in a sweaty embrace as the moon began to show its upper limb above the eastern horizon and transform the ugly buildings of the city with its pale romantic rays.

Unremarked among the other sparse river traffic, a tiny felucca used the last of the evening breeze to leave the Omdurman bank and slip downriver. Under cover of darkness it passed not much more than its own length beyond the entrance to the old harbour. The captain stood on one of the thwarts and stared into the entrance. He saw that torches were burning, and with the rays of the moon he was able to make out all the unusual activity around the *ferenghi* steamer moored in the inner harbour. He heard the clamour and shouting of many voices. It was as he had been informed. The *ferenghi* ship was making ready to leave the city. He dropped back on to his seat at the tiller and whistled softly to his three-man crew to harden the big lateen sail so that he could bring her closer to the night breeze, then put the tiller hard up. The small boat shot away at an angle across the current and headed back for Omdurman on the western side of the river. As they came under the loom of the land the captain whistled again, but more piercingly, and was challenged almost immediately from the darkness: 'In the name of the Prophet and the Divine Mahdi, speak!'

The captain stood up again and called to the watchers on the bank. 'There is no God but God, and Muhammad is his prophet. I bear tidings for the Khalifa Abdullahi.'

The *Intrepid Ibis* still lay at the Old City wharf. Jock McCrump and Ryder Courtney were checking the row of Martini-Henry rifles in the gun rack at the back of the open bridge, making certain they were loaded, and that spare packets of the big Boxer-Henry .45 calibre cartridges were to hand, should they run into the Dervish blockade when they left the harbour.

No sooner had they completed their final preparations than the first of the most important passengers came up the gangplank, Bacheet leading them to their quarters. The *Ibis* had only four cabins. One belonged to Ryder Courtney, but over Bacheet's protests he was going to relinquish it to the Benbrook family. There were only two bunks in the tiny cabin. They would be crowded, but at least it had its own bathroom. The girls would be afforded some privacy in the crowded steamer. Presumably one of the twins could sleep with her father, while the other would be with Rebecca. The foreign consuls had been allocated the remaining cabins, while the rest of the almost four hundred passengers must take their chances on the open decks, or crowded into the three empty barges. The fourth barge was laden with the cordwood so that they would not be forced to go ashore to cut supplies of this precious commodity.

Ryder looked towards the eastern horizon. The moon was only a few days from full, and would give him just enough light to descry the channel down towards the Shabluka Gorge. Unfortunately it would also light up the target for the Dervish gunners. Their aim was improving each day as they had more practice and experience with the laying of the Krupps guns that they had captured at El Obeid. They seemed to possess an endless supply of ammunition.

Ryder looked back at the wharf and felt a prickle of irritation. Major al-Faroque of General Gordon's staff had lined up a company of his troops to guard the perimeter of the harbour. With fixed bayonets they were prepared to prevent a mob of refugees without General Gordon's pass trying to storm the little steamer and force themselves aboard. The desperate populace would go to any lengths and take any chance to escape the city. What annoyed Ryder was that al-Faroque had allowed his men to light torches so that they could examine the faces and papers of those would-be passengers who were lining up at the entrance. The torchlight now illuminated the entire expanse of the wharf to the scrutiny of the Dervish sentries across the river.

'In God's name, Major, get your men to douse those lights!' Ryder bellowed.

'I have General Gordon's strict orders to allow no one to pass until I have checked their papers.'

'You are calling the Mahdi's attention to our preparations to sail,' Ryder shouted back.

'I have my orders, Captain.'

While they argued, the crowd of passengers and hopefuls was swelling rapidly. Most were carrying infants or bundles of their possessions. However, they were becoming anxious and panicky at being forbidden entry. Many were shouting and waving passes over their heads. Those who had no pass stood stubborn and grim-faced, watching for their opportunity.

'Let those passengers through,' Ryder shouted.

'Not until I have examined their passes,' the Major retorted and turned his back, leaving Ryder fuming helplessly at his bridge rail. Al-Faroque was stubborn and the altercation was having no effect except to delay the embarkation interminably. Then Ryder noticed David's tall figure pushing through the throng with his daughters pressing close behind him. With relief he saw that al-Faroque had recognized them and was waving them through the cordon of his troops. They hurried to the gangplank, burdened with their most valued possessions. Saffron was lugging her paintbox and Amber a canvas bag stuffed with her favourite books. Nazeera pushed the girls up the gangplank for David had used all his influence and the dignity of his office to obtain a pass for her.

'Good evening, David. You and your family will have my cabin,' Ryder greeted him, as he stepped aboard.

'No! No! My dear fellow, we cannot evict you from your home.'

'I will be fully occupied on the bridge during the voyage,' Ryder assured him. 'Good evening, Miss Benbrook. There are only two narrow bunks. You will be a little crowded, I am afraid, but it's the best available. Your maid must take her place in one of the barges.'

'Good evening, Mr Courtney. Nazeera is one of us. She can share a bunk with Amber. Saffron can share with my father. I will sleep on the cabin floor. I am sure we will all be very comfortable,' Rebecca announced with finality. Before Ryder could protest an ominous chanting and shouting came from the large crowd held back by the guards at the head of the wharf, like floodwaters by a frail dam wall. It provided him with a welcome excuse to avoid another confrontation with Rebecca. There was an ominous glitter in her dark eyes, and a mutinous lift to her chin.

'Excuse me, David. I will have to leave you to install yourselves. I am needed elsewhere.' Ryder left them and ran down the gangplank. When he reached Major al-Faroque's side he saw that the crowd beyond the line of soldiers was growing larger and more unruly with every minute that passed, and they were pressing right up to the points of the bayonets. Monsieur Le Blanc was the last of the diplomatic corps to arrive. Incongruously he was decked out in a flowing opera cloak and a Tyrolean hat with a bunch of feathers in the band. He was followed by a procession of his servants, each heavily laden with his luggage. Born aloft on the shoulders of his porters was a pair of brassbound cabin trunks, each the size of a pharaoh's sarcophagus.

'You cannot bring all that rubbish on board, Monsieur,' Ryder told him, as the guards allowed him to pass.

Le Blanc reached him with sweat dripping off his chin, fanning himself with a pair of yellow gloves. 'That "rubbish", Monsieur, as you call it, is my entire wardrobe of clothing and is irreplaceable. I cannot leave without it.'

Ryder saw at once the futility of arguing with him. He stepped past Le Blanc and confronted the first party of trunk-bearers as they staggered through the cordon with their load.

'Put those down!' he ordered, in Arabic. They stopped and stared at him.

'Do not listen to him,' squealed Le Blanc, and rushed back to slap at their faces with his glove. 'Bring it along, *mes braves*.' The porters started forward again, but Ryder measured the huge Arab who was clearly the head porter, then stepped up to him and slammed a punch into the point of his jaw. The porter dropped as though shot through the head. The trunk slipped from his fellows and crashed to the stone flags. The lid flew open and a small avalanche of clothing and toiletries poured out on to the wharf. The rest of the porters waited for no more but dropped their load and fled from the wrath of the mad *ferenghi* captain.

'Now see what you have done,' cried Le Blanc, and fell to his knees. He began gathering up armfuls of his scattered possessions and trying to stuff them back into the trunk. Behind him the crowd sensed an opportunity. They pressed forward more eagerly, and the guards were forced back a few paces.

Ryder grabbed Le Blanc's arm and hauled him to his feet. 'Come along, you Belgian imbecile.' He tried to drag him towards the gangplank.

'If I am an imbecile, then you are an English barbarian,' howled Le Blanc. He reached back and grabbed a trunk's heavy brass handle. Ryder could not break his grip, although he hauled with all his strength.

From the back of the crowd a large rock was hurled at the head of Major al-Faroque. It missed its target and struck Le Blanc's cheek. He shrieked with pain, released the trunk handle and clutched his face with both hands. 'I am wounded! I am gravely injured.'

More stones flew out of the crowd to fall among the soldiers and bounce off the pavement. One struck an Egyptian sergeant, who dropped his rifle and went down on one knee clutching his head. His men fell back, glancing over their shoulders for a line of retreat. The crowd yammered like a pack of hounds and pressed them harder. Someone picked up the sergeant's fallen rifle and aimed it at Major al-Faroque. The man fired and a bullet grazed the major's temple. Al-Faroque dropped, stunned. His men broke and ran back, trampling his prostrate form. They had been transformed in an instant from guards to refugees. Ryder picked up Le Blanc and ran with him kicking, screaming and struggling in his arms like a child in a tantrum.

Ryder dumped the Belgian on the deck, then raced on to his bridge. 'Cast off!' he shouted to his crew, just as the first wave of rioters and half the Egyptian *askaris* scrambled on board. The decks were already so overcrowded that the crew were shoved from their positions and were unable to reach the mooring lines. More and more rioters raced down the wharf, and leapt on board the steamer or scrambled into the barges. Those already on board tried to beat them back and the decks were buried under a mêlée of struggling bodies.

Saffron popped her head out of the main cabin to watch the excitement. Ryder picked her up and thrust her bodily into her elder sister's arms, then pushed them both into the cabin. 'Stay out of the way,' he shouted, and slammed the door. Then he snatched the fire axe from its bracket at the head of the companionway. More rioters were coming out of the darkness, unending hordes.

Ryder felt the deck of the *Ibis* heel over under the uneven distribution of weight. 'Jock!' he shouted desperately. 'The bastards are going to capsize us. We have to get her off the

43

jetty.' He and Jock fought their way through the throng. They managed to cut the mooring lines free, but by this time the *Ibis* was listing dangerously.

When Ryder reached his bridge again and opened the throttle, he could feel the enormous drag of the overloaded barges. He glanced back and saw that the nearest had less than two feet of freeboard. He spun the wheel towards the harbour entrance.

The *Ibis* was driven by a Cowper engine, a powerful unit with three cylinders. This modern design incorporated an intermediate steam reservoir for compound expansion that allowed much higher boiler pressure than previous models. The *Ibis* needed all this power to enable her to drag the string of heavily loaded barges up through the fast-flowing waters of the cataracts. Now, under the thrust of the Cowper, she built up speed and a white wave blossomed under the bows of each barge, faster still and the water curled over their bows. A chorus of despairing cries rose from the passengers in the barges as they began to flood and settle even lower in the water. Ryder cut back the power, and managed to con the *Ibis* and her tows out through the harbour entrance into the open river where he would have more space in which to manoeuvre – but the increased turbulence of the surface exacerbated the build-up of the bow waves.

Ryder was forced to throttle right back until he barely had steerageway. The ship was picked up by the current and slewed across the channel with her tow lines becoming fouled. The barges ran down on the *Ibis*. The first of the heavy vessels crashed into her stern, and she shuddered with the shock.

'Cut them loose!' Le Blanc screamed, his voice so shrill with terror that it cut through the din. 'Cut them loose! Leave them behind! This is all their fault!'

The tangle of vessels, still bound together by their tow lines, drifted past the last buildings of the city, then into the broad reach of the combined Niles. Ryder realized he would have to anchor to give himself time to adjust the trim of the barges so that they would tow obediently. He considered turning back to put the stowaway passengers ashore. As they were now, they might flounder in the Shabluka Gorge. Even if they won through, his legitimate passengers would not be able to endure this overcrowding during the heat of the passage through the Desert of the Mother of Stones. Ryder gave the orders to break out the heaviest anchor before they were carried beyond the protection of General Gordon's artillery. Suddenly there was a warning cry from Bacheet.

'Boats coming fast! Dervish boats from the other bank!' Ryder ran to him and saw a flotilla of dozens of small rivercraft appearing swiftly and silently out of the darkness from the direction of Omdurman, feluccas, nuggars and small dhows. He ran back to the bridge. The ten-thousand-candle-power lamp was mounted on the bridge coaming. He turned its brilliant white beam on the approaching craft. He saw that they were crammed with armed Ansar. The Dervish must have been fully aware of their escape plans and had been lying in ambush for the *Intrepid Ibis*. As they closed with the steamer and her tangled string of barges the Ansar shrieked their terrible praise of God, and brandished their broadswords. The long blades glimmered in the light, and the passengers in the barges wailed with terror.

'Man the rail!' Ryder shouted to his crew. 'Stand by to repel boarders!'

His crew understood this drill well. They had practised it regularly for the Upper Nile was a dangerous place and the tribes who lived upon its banks and in its marshes were savage and wild. They struggled to reach their places at the ship's side to meet the enemy, but the passengers were packed shoulder to shoulder and they found it almost impossible to force their way through. The ruck of human bodies surged forward as they were shoved from behind, and some of those nearest the side were thrown overboard. They screamed and splashed on the surface until they were borne away on the current or sank beneath it. A young wife with her newborn infant strapped to her back went over and although she paddled desperately to keep her baby's head above the surface, they were sucked back into the *Intrepid Ibis*'s propeller.

It was fruitless to attempt to rescue any of those in the

water. Nor was there time to anchor, for the Dervish boats closed in swiftly: as they reached the barges they hooked on to the sides and the Ansar warriors tried to clamber aboard, but they were unable to obtain a foothold on the packed decks. They hacked and stabbed at the screaming passengers with their swords, trying to clear a space. The barges rolled wildly. More bodies splashed overboard.

The next wave of Dervish boats came at the *Ibis* from her starboard side. Ryder dared not open the throttle of his engines for fear of swamping the leading barge. If that happened the drag on the tow line would be so powerful the barge might drag *Ibis* under with her. He could not run from them so he must fight them off.

By this time Jock McCrump and Bacheet had passed out the Martini-Henry rifles from the gun rack. Some of the Egyptian *askaris* had brought their Remington carbines on board with them and stood shoulder to shoulder with the crew at the rail. Ryder played the spotlight on the approaching boats. In its stark beam the faces of the Ansar were murderous with battle lust and religious ardour. They seemed as inhuman as a legion from the gates of hell.

'Aim!' shouted Ryder, and they levelled their rifles. 'One round volley. Fire!'

The hail of heavy lead slugs ripped into the closely packed Arabs in the feluccas, and Ryder saw one Dervish flung backwards into the river, the sword spinning from his hands and half of his skull blown away in a bright cloud of brains and blood, sparkling crimson in the spotlight beam. Many more were struck down or hurled overboard by the impact of the 450-grain bullets at such close range.

'Load!' Ryder yelled. The breech-blocks snickered metallically, and the spent cases pinged away. The riflemen thrust fresh cartridges into the open breeches, and snapped the loading handles closed. 'One round volley. Fire!'

Before the men in the small boats had recovered from the first volley, a second smashed into them, and they sheered away from it.

At that moment Ryder heard David's voice carry above

the wails and shrieks of the other passengers. 'Behind you, Mr Courtney!' David had climbed up on to the roof of the cabin. He was balanced there with one of his shotguns held at high port across his chest. Ryder saw Rebecca at his side. She held one of her father's Webley revolvers in each hand, and handled them in a businesslike manner. Behind them stood the twins, each with a loaded shotgun ready to pass forward to their father. Their faces were moon pale but determined. The Benbrook family made a heroic little group above the struggling turmoil on the deck. Ryder felt a quick upthrust of admiration for them.

David pointed over the opposite rail with the barrel of his shotgun, and Ryder saw that another wave of Dervish boats was closing in from that side. He knew he could not get his men back across the crowded deck before the attackers came aboard. If he did he would leave the starboard side undefended. Before he could make the decision and give the order, David took matters into his own hands. He raised the Purdey shotgun and let fly right and left into the crew of the nearest boat. The spreading cloud of goose shot was, at this range, more potent than the single Boxer-Henry bullet. The instant carnage in the felucca stunned the Dervish attackers. Four or five had gone down and were struggling on the deck in puddles of their own blood. Others had been knocked over the side and, flotsam, washed away on the stream.

Saffron slipped the second Purdey into her father's hands while Amber reloaded the empty gun. Rebecca fired the Webley revolvers into the nearest felucca. The recoil from each shot threw the heavy weapons high above her head, but their effect was deadly. David fired again in such quick succession that the shots seemed to blend together in a single jarring concussion. As this havoc of lead pellets and revolver bullets sprayed over the boats, and they saw the tall white man on the cabin roof raise a third gun and aim at them, two of the felucca captains put their helms over, and turned away, unwilling to accept such punishment.

'Good man!' Ryder laughed. 'And well done, you lovely ladies!'

The Dervish feluccas gave up on such dangerous, vicious prey and turned on the overladen and defenceless barges. Now that all the attackers were concentrating on them, their fate seemed sealed. Dervish Ansar hacked their way on board and the passengers were driven like sardines before a barracuda to the far rail of the ungainly craft. The bulwark was driven under by their combined weight and the river rushed in and flooded her. The barge foundered and rolled over. Her weed-carpeted bottom pointed for a moment towards the moon. Then she plunged under and was gone.

Immediately the sunken barge acted like a great drogue on the tow line, and the *Intrepid Ibis* was cruelly curbed, like a horse pulled on to its haunches. The tow line had been made by twisting together three ordinary hawsers. It was immensely powerful, far too strong to part and release the barge. The *Ibis*'s stern was dragged down irresistibly and the water flooded the afterdeck in a rush.

Ryder tossed his rifle to one of the *Ibis*'s stokers and seized the heavy fire axe from him. He sprang down on to the flooding deck and shouldered his way to the stern. He was already knee deep in water, which cascaded in over the transom. Soon it would flood the engine room and quench the boiler fire. Ryder gathered himself and balanced over the tow line, which was now stretched tight as an iron bar through its fairlead in the stern plating. It was as thick as a fat man's calf, and there was no give or elasticity in the water-laid strands.

Ryder swung the axe from full reach above his head with all his strength and, with a crack, a dozen strands parted at the stroke. He swung the axe high once more and put every ounce of muscle behind his next stroke. Another dozen strands gave way. He kept swinging the axe, grunting with the power behind each stroke. The remaining strands of the cable unravelled and snapped under the fierce drag of the submerged barge and the *Ibis*'s driving propeller. Ryder jumped back just before the rope parted and slashed at him like some monstrous serpent. Had the parting cable end caught him squarely it might have broken both his legs, but it missed him by a few inches.

He felt the *Ibis* lurch under him as she was freed of the drag, then spring back on to an even keel. She seemed to shake the water off her decks as a spaniel shakes when it comes ashore with a dead duck in its jaws. Then the propeller bit in hard and *Ibis* surged forward. Saffron was shaken from her perch on the cabin roof. Her arms windmilled and Rebecca tried to catch her, but she slipped through her fingers and fell backwards with a shriek. If she had struck the steel deck she might have caved in the back of her skull, but Ryder threw aside the axe, dived under her and snatched her out of the air. For a moment he held her to his chest.

'A bird you certainly ain't, Saffy.' He grinned at her, and ran with her towards his bridge. Although she tried to cling to him, he dumped her unceremoniously in Nazeera's arms. Without a backward glance, he jumped behind the *Ibis*'s wheel, and pushed the twin throttles wide open. With a rush of steam from her piston exhausts, she tore away, rejoicing to be free of her towing cable, building up swiftly to her top speed of twelve knots. Ryder brought her round to port in a narrow arc of 180 degrees until he was rushing straight back towards the tangled mass of barges and feluccas.

'What are you going to do?' David asked, as he appeared at Ryder's side with his shotgun over a shoulder. 'Pick up swimmers?'

'No,' Ryder replied grimly. 'I am going to add to, not subtract from, the number of swimmers.' The bows of the *Ibis* were reinforced with a double thickness of half-inch steel plate to withstand contact with the rocks of the cataracts. 'I am going to ram,' he warned David. 'Tell the girls that we will hit with an almighty thump and they must hang on tight.'

The Dervish boats were thick as vultures round an elephant carcass. Ryder saw that some of the Ansar were freeing the tow lines that held the barges together and passing the cables down to the dhows. Obviously they intended dragging them one at a time into the shallows of the west bank where they could complete the slaughter and plundering at their leisure. The rest were still hacking at the cowering bodies on the crowded decks or leaning over the sides to stab at those who were struggling in the water and screaming for mercy. In the beam of the *Ibis*'s spotlight the waters of the Nile were stained the colour of mulberry juice by the blood of the dead and dying, and rivulets of blood trickled down the sides of the barges.

'The murderous swine,' Rebecca whispered. Then, to Nazeera, 'Take the twins to the cabin. They should not witness this.' She knew it was a forlorn command. It would require more bodily strength than Nazeera possessed to remove them from the bridge. In the reflection of the spotlight's beam their eyes were huge with dreadful fascination.

The capsized barge was floating bottom up, but sinking swiftly. Suddenly its stern rose, pointed at the moon, then slid below the surface and was gone. Ryder steered for a cluster of three big feluccas, which had tied on to the side of the nearest surviving barge. The Ansar were so busy with their bloody work on the deck that they did not seem to notice the *Ibis* bearing down on them. At the last moment one of the dhow captains looked up and realized the danger. He shouted a warning, and some of his comrades were scrambling back into the feluccas as the *Ibis* struck.

Ryder brought her in so skilfully that her steel bows tore through the wooden hulls in quick succession, the timbers shrieking and exploding with the sound of cannon fire as the boats capsized or were driven under the bloody waters. Although the *Ibis* touched the side of the barge as she tore past, it was a glancing blow and the vessel spun away.

Ryder looked down into the terrified faces of the surviving refugees and heard their piteous entreaties for rescue. He had to harden his heart: the choice before him was to sacrifice all or rescue some. He left them and brought the *Ibis* around, still under full throttle, then aimed at the next group of Dervish attack boats as they wallowed helplessly without steerageway alongside another drifting barge.

Now the Ansar were fully aware of the danger. The *Ibis*

bore down on them and the blazing Cyclops eye of the spotlight dazzled them. Some threw themselves overboard. Few could swim and their shields and broadswords drew them under swiftly. The *Ibis* crashed at full throttle into the first felucca, shattered it, and ran on with scarcely a check. Beyond was one of the largest Dervish dhows, almost the length of the *Ibis* herself. The steamer's steel bows sliced deeply into her, but could not sever her hull. The impact threw her back on her heels and some of those on her deck were hurled overboard with the crew of the dhow.

Ryder threw the *Ibis* into reverse, and as he backed off from the mortally stricken dhow he played the spotlight beam around her. Most of the Dervish boats had recovered their boarding parties from the barges, abandoning their prey in the face of the *Ibis*'s ferocious onslaught. They hoisted sail and steered back towards the west bank. The three surviving barges were no longer linked together, for the Ansar had succeeded in freeing the lines. Independently of each other they were spreading out and drifting in towards the west bank, thrust across the wide bend of the river by the current. In the powerful beam Ryder could just make out the Dervish hordes waiting to welcome them and complete the massacre. He swung the *Ibis* around in the hope that he could reach at least one and pick up the tow line again in time to drag it off the hostile shore.

As he tore towards the barges he saw that the one that contained the cordwood, heavier than the others, was being carried more slowly on the current. The remaining two were still in its teeth, their decks piled with the dead and wounded, blood painting their sides, glistening red in the spotlight beam. They would soon be into the shallows where the *Ibis* could not follow them.

Ryder knew every shoal and bend of the river as intimately as a lover knows the body of his beloved. He narrowed his eyes and calculated the angles and relative speeds. With a sinking feeling in the pit of his stomach, he realized he could not reach them in time to rescue them all. He kept the *Ibis* tearing downstream under full steam, but he knew it was hopeless. He saw first one barge, then the other check sharply and come to a halt, stranded on the shoals. From the shore the waiting Dervish warriors plunged into the river and waded out waist-deep to finish the slaughter. Ryder was forced to throttle back and watch helplessly in horror and pity as the Ansar scrambled aboard and their bloody work began again. In vain he directed the rifle fire of his crew at the hordes of Dervish still wading out to the stranded vessels, but the range was long and the bullets had little effect.

Then he saw that the cordwood barge was still floating free. If he acted swiftly he might still be able to salvage it before it, too, went aground. He opened the throttle and raced down to intercept it. It was of crucial importance to recover this stock of fuel for his boilers. With it, they might reach the first cataract without being forced ashore to cut more timber. Ryder shouted to Jock McCrump to prepare a new tow line, then brought the *Ibis* alongside the barge and held her in position while Jock and his boarding party jumped across to fix the fresh line.

'Quick as you like, Jock,' Ryder shouted. 'We're going to touch bottom at any moment.'

He looked anxiously at the enemy shore. They had now drifted within pistol shot, and even as he thought it he saw muzzle flashes as the Dervish riflemen opened fire on them from the bank. A bullet struck the bridge rail and ricocheted so close past David's ear that he ducked instinctively, then straightened, looking embarrassed. He turned sternly to Rebecca: 'Get the twins below immediately, and make sure they stay there until I tell you.'

Rebecca knew better than to argue with him when he used that tone. She gathered the twins and drove them off the deck with her fiercest tone and expression. Nazeera needed no urging and scuttled down to the cabin ahead of them.

Ryder played the spotlight along the bank, hoping to intimidate the Ansar marksmen or, at least, to illuminate them so that his own crew could return fire more accurately. Although Jock worked fast to rig the new tow line, it seemed like an eternity as they drifted swiftly towards the shallows and the waiting enemy. At last he bellowed across, 'All secure, Captain.'

Ryder reversed the *Ibis* slowly until the gap between the two vessels was narrow enough for Jock and his team to leap back on board the steamer. As soon as his feet hit the *Ibis*'s steel deck he yelled, 'Haul away!'

With a rush of relief Ryder eased the throttles ahead and gently drew the barge after him until she was following like an obedient dog on a leash. He began to haul her off into the main stream of the river, when a rushing sound filled the air and something passed so close above him that his hat spun off his head. Then, immediately afterwards, there followed the unmistakable boom of a six-pounder cannon, the sound following the shell from the west bank.

'Ah! They've brought up one of their artillery pieces,' David remarked, in a conversational tone. 'Only wonder is that it has taken them so long.'

Quickly Ryder doused the spotlight beam. 'They could not fire before for fear of hitting their own ships,' he said. And his last words were drowned by the next shell howling overhead. 'That was not so close.' He kept his right hand pressing down on the throttle handles to milk the last turn of speed out of his vessel. The weight and drag of the barge cut at least three knots off their speed.

'They are close enough to be using open sights,' David said. 'They should be able to do better than that.'

'They will – oh, I am sure they will.' Ryder looked up at the moon, hoping to see the shadow of a cloud fall across it. But the sky was brilliant with stars and the moon lit the surface of the Nile as if it were a stage. For the gunners the *Ibis* would stand out against the silver waters like a granite hillock.

The next shell fell so close alongside that a shower of river water fell over the bridge and soaked those on it so that their shirts clung to their backs. Then there were more cannon flashes along the shore behind them as the Dervish gunners dragged up gun after gun and unlimbered to bring the *Ibis* under fire.

'Jock, we will have to give them the best of it and cut the barge loose,' Ryder called to the engineer.

'Aye, skipper. I had a notion ye would say just that.' Jock picked up the axe and started towards the stern.

Another Dervish gun-carriage galloped along the bank until it was slightly ahead of the straining *Ibis* and her burden. Though neither Ryder nor David was aware of it, the master gunner commanding the mounted battery was the Ansar whom David had dubbed the Bedlam Bedouin.

From astride the lead horse of the team, he gave a sharp command and they wheeled the gun carriage into line with the gun's muzzle pointing out across the river, and unlimbered. The number two and three loaders stamped the heavy steel base plate into the soft earth of the riverbank. They set the point of the trail into its slot in the plate. While they worked the master gunner was shrieking orders, wild with excitement: he had never in all his brief career been offered such a fine target as the *ferenghi* ship now presented. It was almost broadside on. Its silhouette stood out crisply against the shimmering waters. It was so close that he could hear the terrified voices of the passengers raised in prayer and supplication, and the peremptory commands of the captain speaking in the infidel language the gunner could not understand.

He used a hand-spike to traverse the gun round the last few degrees until the long barrel was aiming directly at the ship. Then he wound down the elevation handle until he was gazing over the open iron sights at his target.

'In the Name of Allah, bring the bomboms!' he screamed at his loaders. They staggered up with the first ammunition box and knocked off the clips that held the lid in place. Inside, four shells lay in their wooden cradles, sleek and glistening ominously. The gunner, self-taught in the art of gunnery, had not yet fathomed the arcane principle of fuse delays. In fumbling haste, he used the Allen key he wore round his neck to screw the fuses to the maximum setting in the belief that this imparted to each missile the greatest amount of destructive power. The *Ibis* was a mere three hundred yards off the bank. He set his fuses at two thousand yards.

'In God's Name let us begin!' he ordered.

'In God's Name.' His number two flung open the breech of the Krupps with a flourish.

'In God's Name,' intoned the number three, and slid one of the long shells deep into the chamber until it was snug against the lands. The number two slammed the breech-block shut.

'God is great,' said the Bedlam Bedouin, as he squinted over his sights to make certain of his aim. He traversed the mount four degrees left until he was aiming at the base of the *Ibis*'s funnel. Then he jumped back and seized the lanyard. 'Allah is mighty,' he said.

'There is no other God but God,' chorused his team.

'And Muhammad and the Mahdi are his prophets.' The gunner jerked the lanyard, and the Krupps slammed back against its base plate. The discharge deafened the crew with its report and blinded them with the muzzle flash and the flying dust.

On an almost flat trajectory the shell howled over the river and struck the *Intrepid Ibis* two feet above the waterline and just astern of midships. It passed obliquely through her hull as readily as a stiletto through human flesh, but by virtue of the maximum fuse setting it did not explode.

Had it been three inches higher or lower it would have done minimal damage, nothing that Jock McCrump with his gas welding equipment could not have repaired within a few hours. But that was not to be. In passing it slashed through the main steam line from the boiler. Steam heated to twice the temperature of boiling water and under pressure of almost three hundred pounds to the square inch erupted in a shrieking jet from the ruptured pipe. It swept over the nearest stoker as he bent to thrust a faggot of timber into the open firebox of the boiler. He was naked in the heat, except for a turban and loincloth. Instantly the steam peeled the skin and the flesh off his body in great slabs to expose the bones beneath.

The agony was so terrible that the man could not utter a sound. Mouth gaping in a silent scream, he fell writhing to the deck and froze into a sculpture of the utmost agony.

Steam filled the engine room and boiled in dense white clouds from the ventilation ports to pour over the decks, shrouding the *Ibis* in a dense white cloud. Rapidly the ship lost power and swung idly broadside to the current. The Bedlam Bedouin and his gun-crew howled with excitement and triumph as they reloaded. But their quarry was now obscured by her own steam cloud. Although shells from many Krupps batteries along the bank plunged into the water alongside, or ripped the air overhead as though a giant was tearing a canvas mainsail in two, no more struck the little *Ibis*.

Jock McCrump had been on the bridge with Ryder when the shell struck. He grabbed a heavy pair of working gloves from the locker beside the forward steam winch, and pulled them on as he ran back to the engine-room hatchway. The steam that billowed through the opening stung his face and the bare skin of his arms, but the pressure in the boiler had dropped as the steam bled off through the ruptured pipe. He ripped the heavy canvas curtain that covered the hatch from its rail, and snapped at Ryder, 'Wrap me, skipper!'

Ryder understood instantly what he was going to do. He shook out the thick curtain, then wound Jock in it, cloaking his head and every part of his body but for his arms.

'The grease pot!' Jock's voice was muffled by the folds of canvas. Ryder seized it from its hook beside the winch, scooped out handfuls of the thick black grease and spread it over the exposed skin of Jock's muscular arms.

'That will do,' Jock grunted, and opened a slit in his canvas head cover to draw one last deep breath. Then he covered his face and plunged blindly down the steel companion ladder. He held his breath and closed his eyes tightly. But the steam scalded the exposed skin, melting away the coating of black grease from his bare arms.

Jock knew every inch of his engine room so intimately that

he did not need to see it. Guiding himself with a light touch of gloved fingers over the familiar machinery, he moved swiftly towards the main pressure line. The shrieking of high-pressure steam escaping from the rupture threatened to burst his eardrums. He felt his arms cooking like lobsters in the pot and fought the impulse to scream, lest he use the last air in his aching lungs. He stumbled over the stoker's corpse, but recovered his balance and found the main steam line. It was wrapped with asbestos rope to prevent heat loss so he was able to run his gloved hands along it until he found the wheel of the stopcock that controlled the flow of steam into the line. Swiftly he spun the wheel and the rushing sound of escaping steam rose sharply, then was snuffed out as the valve closed.

It took ineffable pain to make a man like Jock McCrump sob, but he was crying like an infant as he staggered back to the foot of the companion ladder, then clambered painfully up to the deck. He stumbled out into the night air, which felt cold after the hellish atmosphere of the engine room, and Ryder caught him before he fell. He stared in horror at the huge blisters hanging from Jock's forearms. Then he roused himself and scooped more grease from the pot to cover them, but Rebecca had appeared suddenly and pushed him aside.

'This is woman's work, Mr Courtney. You see to your boat and leave this to me.' She was carrying a hurricane lamp and, by its feeble light, examined Jock's arms, pursing her lips grimly. She set the lamp on the deck, crouched beside Jock and began to work on his injuries. Her touch was deft and gentle.

'God love you, Jock McCrump, for what you've done to save my ship.' Ryder lingered beside Jock. 'But the Dervish are still shooting at us.' As if to underline the fact another Krupps shell plunged into the river, so close alongside that the spray rained down on them like a tropical cloudburst. 'How bad is the damage? Can we get power on at least one of the engines to get us out of range of the guns on the bank?'

'I couldnae see much at all down there, but at the best odds the main boiler will not have as much pressure in her as a virgin's fart.' Jock glanced at Rebecca. 'Begging your pardon, lassie.' He stifled a groan as Rebecca touched one of the pendulous blisters, which burst open.

'I'm sorry, Mr McCrump.'

'It's naught at all. Dinna fash yourself, woman.' Jock looked up at Ryder. 'Maybe, just maybe, I can knock together some kind of jury-rig and get steam to the cylinders. It just depends on the damage she's suffered down there. But at the best I doubt we'll get more than a few pounds of pressure into the line.'

Ryder straightened up and looked around. He saw the dark shape of Tutti Island no more than a cable's length downstream from where they wallowed, powerless, under the Dervish guns. What the Dervish cannon fire lacked in accuracy, it made up for in rapidity. From the sheer weight of shells being hurled at them, it could not be long before they received another direct hit.

He watched the changing bearing of the island for a moment longer. 'The current is carrying us past the island. If we anchor in its lee it will screen us from the guns.' He left them and shoved his way through the passengers, shouting for Bacheet and his mate Abou Sinn. 'Clear this rabble out of the way, and prepare to anchor at my command.'

They jumped to their stations, shoving and kicking aside the bewildered *askari* and stowaways to give themselves room to work. Bacheet freed the retaining tackle from the ring of the heavy fisherman's anchor that hung at the bows. Abou Sinn stood over the chain where it emerged through the fairlead of the chain locker with the four-pound hammer ready.

Ryder peered back at the land, watching the muzzle flashes of the Dervish guns and judging his moment. For a few minutes he held his breath while it seemed that they would be driven ashore on the island, then an eddy in the current pushed them clear and they drifted so close to the eastern side of the island that they were sheltered from the Dervish batteries.

'Let go!' Ryder shouted to Abou Sinn, and with a blow of

the sledge-hammer he knocked the pin out of the anchor shackle. The anchor splashed into the river, the chain roaring out after it, and found the bottom. The chain stopped running and Bacheet secured it. The *Ibis* came up hard and short, and spun round in the current to face upstream, with the timber barge behind her on her tow line. The Dervish cannon fire tapered off as the gunners found themselves deprived of their target. A few more shells screeched high overhead or burst ineffectually into the sandbanks of the screening island, then the gunners gave up and silence descended.

Ryder found Jock sitting on the bunk in the cabin, being attended to by all the Benbrook ladies. 'How are you feeling?' he asked solicitously.

'Not so bad, skipper.' He indicated his arms: 'These bonny little lasses have done a fine job on them.' Rebecca had bandaged both arms with strips that the twins had torn from one of the threadbare cotton bedsheets, then fashioned a double sling from the same material. Now she was brewing a mug of tea for him on the stove in the tiny galley next door. Jock grinned. 'Home was never so good. That's why I ran away.'

'Sorry to interrupt your retirement, but can I trouble you to take a peek at your engine?'

'Just when I was really enjoying meself,' Jock grumbled, but rose to his feet.

'I'll bring your mug down to the engine room for you, Mr McCrump,' Amber promised.

'And I'll bring one for you, Ryder,' Saffron called.

Jock McCrump followed Ryder down to the engine room. Bacheet and Abou Sinn carried away the stoker's corpse, and by the light of a pair of hurricane lamps they assessed the damage. Now that Jock was able to examine his beloved engine more closely, he grumbled bitterly to disguise his relief. 'Bloody heathens! Can't trust them further than you can throw one of them. No sense of common decency, doing this to my bonny Cowper.' However, only the main steam line shot was through; the engine itself was untouched.

'Well, there's naught I can do for the steam line this side

of my workshop in Khartoum. In the meantime, though, perhaps I can cobble something together to get a mite of steam through to the engine, but I reckon we'll not be breaking any speed records with the old girl.' Then he held up his bandaged arms. 'You'll have to do the donkey work, skipper.'

Ryder nodded. 'While we're at it, I'm going to send Bacheet to move all our uninvited passengers across to the barge. That will correct my trim and give me a little more manoeuvrability and control. It will also give the crew more room to work the ship properly.'

While the passengers were transhipped, Ryder and his engineer began the repairs. Working quickly but carefully, they bled off the remaining steam from the boilers and drew the fires from the grate. Then they used the in-line valve cocks to isolate the damaged section of the main steam line. Once this was done, they could begin rigging a bypass line to carry steam through to the power plant. They had to measure the lengths they needed and cut the new pipe sections to length by hacksaw, then clamp them into the heavy vice on Jock's workbench and cut threads into the ends of the pipes with the hand dies. They packed the joints with asbestos thread and tightened the elbows and connectors with their combined weight on the long-handled pipe wrench. They ended up with a mare's nest of convoluted improvised piping.

The work took the rest of the night, and by the time they were ready to test its integrity dawn was showing through the engine-room portholes. It took another hour to set the fires in the grates and work up a head of steam in the boiler. When the needle of the pressure gauge touched the green line Jock gingerly eased open the cock of the steam valve. Ryder stood beside him and watched anxiously, hands black with grease, knuckles bruised and bleeding from rough contact with steel pipes. They held their breath as the needle on the secondary pressure gauge rose, and watched the new pipe joints for the first sign of a leak.

'All holding,' Jock grunted, and reached across to the port-engine throttle. With a suck and a hiss of live steam the big triple pistons began to pump up and down in their cylinders, the rods moved like the legs of marching men, and the propeller shaft rotated smoothly in its bearings.

'Power up and holding.' Jock grinned with the pride of accomplishment. 'But I cannae take the chance and open her full. You'll have to take what you get, skipper, and thank the Lord and Jock McCrump for that much.'

'You're a living, breathing miracle, Jock. I hope your mother was proud of you.' Ryder chuckled. When he wiped the sweat off his forehead, the back of his fist left a black smear. 'Now, stand by to give me everything you can just as soon as I can get the anchor weighed and catted.' He charged up the ladder to the bridge. Abou Sinn followed him and ran to the controls of the steam winch.

As the *Ibis* pushed slowly forward against the river current, the anchor chain came clanking in through the hawserhole. The flukes broke free from the riverbed and Ryder eased open the throttle. The *Ibis* responded so sluggishly that she made little headway against the four-knot current. Ryder felt a cold slide of disappointment. He glanced over the stern at the barge. Drawing deeply under its cargo of cordwood and uninvited passengers, it was behaving with mulish recalcitrance. Dozens of pathetic faces stared across at him.

By God, I've half a mind to cut you free and leave you to the mercy of the Mahdi, he thought venomously, but with an effort set the temptation aside. He turned instead to David, who had joined him silently. 'She'll never be able to hold her own in the Shabluka Gorge. When the entire flow of the combined Niles is forced through the narrows the current reaches almost ten knots. With only half her power the *Ibis* will be helpless in its grip. The risk of piling up on the rocky cliffs is too great to accept.'

'What other choice do you have?'

'Nothing for it but to battle our way back to Khartoum.'

David looked worried. 'My girls! I hate to take them back to that death-trap. How long will Gordon be able to hold out in the city before the Dervishes break in?'

'Let's hope it's long enough for Jock to finish his repairs so that we can make another run for it. But now our only hope is to get back into the harbour.' Ryder turned the *Ibis* across the current and headed her for the east bank. He tried to keep the bulk of Tutti Island between the ship and the Dervish batteries, but before they were half-way across the first shells were howling above the river. However, with the current giving him some assistance Ryder opened the range swiftly, and the skill of the Bedlam Bedouin and his comrades was not up to the task of hitting a target as small as the *Intrepid Ibis* at a range of over a mile, except by the direct intervention of Allah. This day, however, their prayers went unanswered, and although there were a few encouraging near misses the *Ibis* and her barge made good their crossing of the main-stream, then turned south for the city, hugging the furthest edge of the channel at extreme range for the Krupps.

The Dervish feluccas sallied out from the west bank and made another attempt to intercept the steamer, but by now the sun was high. General Gordon's artillery on the riverfront of Khartoum was able to direct furious and remarkably accurate fire upon the enemy flotilla as it came within easy range. Ryder saw four small boats blown into splinters by direct hits with high explosive and correctly fused shells. The severed limbs and heads of the crews were hurled high in the yellow clouds of lyddite fumes. This discouraged all but a few of the bravest, most foolhardy captains, and most of the small boats turned back for the shore.

Three of the attack boats pressed on across the river, but the wind blew strongly from the south and the current was at five knots from the same direction. Two of the feluccas were swept downstream and were unable to make good a course to intercept the *Ibis*. Only one of them stood in her way. But Ryder had been given plenty of time to prepare a reception for it. He ordered all the deck passengers to lie flat, so as to offer no target to the attackers. As the enemy vessel raced towards them, heeled over by the wind and pushed along by the current, Bacheet and Abou Sinn were crouched below the starboard bulwark.

'Let them get close,' Ryder called down from the bridge, as

he judged the moment. Then he raised his voice to full pitch: 'Now!' he bellowed.

Bacheet and Abou Sinn sprang up from hiding and aimed the brass nozzles of the steam hoses down into the undecked hull of the felucca. They opened the valves and solid white jets of live steam from the *Ibis*'s boiler engulfed the warriors crowded into the open boat. Their bloodthirsty war cries and angry challenges turned to screams of anguish as the dense clouds of steam flayed the skin and flesh from their faces and bodies. The hull of the felucca crashed heavily against the steel of the *Ibis*'s hull, and the impact snapped off the mast at deck level. The felucca scraped down the steel side of the steamer, then spun out of control in her wake. She now wallowed directly in the path of the heavily laden barge. The Ansar were so blinded by the steam that they did not see her coming. The barge smashed into the frail craft and trod her under the surface. None of her crew surfaced again.

'That takes care of that,' Ryder murmured, with satisfaction, then forced a smile at Rebecca. 'Forgive me for depriving you of the comfort of the cabin floor, but tonight you will have to make do with your own bed in the palace.'

'That is a hardship I am determined to endure with the utmost stoicism, Mr Courtney.' Her smile was almost as unconvincing as his, but he was amazed at how pretty she looked in the midst of so much mayhem and ugliness.

General Charles Gordon stood on the steps above the harbour entrance and watched the *Ibis* limp in. When Ryder looked up at him from the bridge, his regard was cold and cutting as blue ice, with no trace of a smile nor any hint of sympathy. When the steamer was tied up at the stone jetty Gordon turned away and disappeared.

Major al-Faroque remained to welcome the bedraggled passengers as they staggered ashore from the barge. His head was swathed in a white bandage, but his expression was ferocious as he picked out those of his men who had deserted their posts and attempted to escape. As he recognized them he lashed each offender across the face with the kurbash whip he carried, and nodded to the squad of *askari* who were lined up behind him. They seized the marked men and locked manacles on their wrists.

Later that afternoon, when Ryder was summoned to the general's office in the consular palace to make his report, Gordon was distant and dismissive. He listened without comment to all that Ryder had to say, condemning him with his silence. Then he nodded. 'I am to blame as much as anybody. I placed too much responsibility on your shoulders. After all, you are not a soldier, merely a mercenary trader.' He spoke scornfully.

Ryder was about to make an angry retort when a volley of rifle fire rang out from the courtyard of the palace below. He turned quickly to the window and looked down.

'Al-Faroque is dealing with the deserters.' Gordon had not risen from his chair. Ryder saw that the ten men of the firing squad were leaning nonchalantly on their weapons. Against the wall of the courtyard facing them sprawled an untidy row of corpses. The dead men were all blindfolded with their wrists tied behind their backs, their shirts bloodsoaked. Major al-Faroque was walking down the line, his service revolver in his right hand. He paused over a body that was twitching spasmodically and fired a single shot into the blindfolded head. When he reached the end of the line he nodded to a second squad of men, who ran forward and piled the corpses into a waiting cart. Then another group of condemned men were led up from the cells into the courtyard and lined up along the wall. While a sergeant tied their blindfolds, the firing squad came to attention.

'I hope, General, that the consul's daughters have been warned of these executions,' Ryder said grimly. 'It is not something that young gentlewomen should witness.'

'I sent word to him that they should keep to their quarters. Your concern for the young ladies does you credit, Mr Courtney. However, you might have been of greater service to them by affording them safe passage downriver to a place of security.'

'It is my intention to do so, General, as soon as I am able to effect repairs to my steamer,' Ryder assured him.

'It might already be too late for that, sir. Within the last few hours I have received the most reliable intelligence that the Emir Osman Atalan of the Beja tribe is in full march with his array to join the Mahdi's besieging force out there.' General Gordon pointed out of the window across the White Nile at the Omdurman bank of the river.

Ryder was unable to conceal his alarm. With the notorious Osman Atalan opposing them, the nature of the siege would change. Any escape from Khartoum would become incalculably more difficult.

As if to endorse these grim thoughts, the next volley from the execution squad crashed out, and immediately afterwards Ryder heard the soft sounds of human bodies flopping lifelessly to the ground.

The Emir Osman Atalan, beloved of the Divine Mahdi, was riding at large. In response to the Mahdi's summons to Khartoum, he had been for many weeks on the march up from the Red Sea Hills with his army. His warrior spirit chafed at the monotony and drudgery of the pace set by the great agglomeration of animals and people. The baggage train of camels and donkeys, the columns of slaves and servants, women and children was strung out over twenty leagues, and when they camped at night it was like a city of tents and animal lines. Each of Osman's wives rode in a curtained litter on the back of her own camel, and slept at night in her own commodious tent, attended by her slaves. In the van and in the rearguard rode the legions of the forty thousand fighting men he commanded.

All the subservient tribes had massed to his scarlet and black banner: the Hamran, the Roofar of the hills and the

65

Hadendowa of the Red Sea littoral. These were the same warriors who, within the last few years, had annihilated two Egyptian armies. They had slaughtered Baker Pasha's superior numbers at Tokar and El Teb and left a wide road of bleached bones across the desert. When the wind came from the west the inhabitants of Suakin on the coast twenty miles away could still smell the unburied dead.

Many of the tribes under Osman Atalan had played a major role at the battle of El Obeid where General Hicks and his seven thousand had perished. They were the flower of the Dervish army, but in their multitudes they moved too slowly for a man such as Osman Atalan.

He felt the call of the open desert and the silence of wild lands. He left the teeming legions to continue the march towards the City of Infidels while he and a small band of his most trusted aggagiers ranged out on their horses to indulge in the most dangerous sport known to the bravest of the tribes.

As he reined in his steed on the crest of a long wooded ridge that overlooked the valley of the Atbara river, Osman Atalan cut a romantic, heroic figure. He wore no turban, and his thick black hair was parted down the middle and drawn into a long plait that hung to the level of the blue silk sash that girt the waist of his ornately patched *jibba*. He held the scabbard of his broadsword clamped under his right knee against the saddle. The hilt was exquisitely fashioned from rhinoceros horn with a patina like amber, and the blade was inlaid with gold and silver. Under the fine loose cloth of his *jibba* his body was lean and wiry, the muscles of his legs and arms like the woven sinews of a bowstring. When he swung down from the saddle he stood tall beside his horse's head and stared out across the wide land below, searching for the first glimpse of the chase. His eyes were large and dark with the thick, curling lashes of a beautiful woman, but his features seemed carved in old ivory, hard flesh and harder bone. He was a creature of the desert and the wild places, and there was no soft flesh on him. The inexorable sun had gilded but not blackened his skin.

His aggagiers rode up behind him and dismounted. The title of honour was reserved for those warriors who hunted the most dangerous game on horseback, armed only with the broadsword. They were men carved from the same stone as their lord. They loosened the girths of their horses' saddles, then tethered the animals in the shade. They watered them, pouring from the waterskins into leather buckets, then spread mats of plaited palm fronds before them and put down a small heap of dhurra meal for them to feed. They themselves did not drink or eat, for abstinence was part of their warrior tradition.

'If a man drinks copiously and often, he never learns to resist the sway of the sun and the sand,' the old men said.

While the horses rested the aggagiers took down their swords and shields from where they were tied to the saddles. They sat in a small, companionable group in the sunlight, and began to strop their blades on the cured giraffe hide of their shields. The hide of the giraffe was the toughest of all wild game, yet not so heavy as that of the buffalo or hippopotamus. The shields were round targes, unadorned with image or emblem, marked only by the blade of the enemy, or the claw and fang of the chase. Blade-honing was a pastime with which they filled their leisure, as much part of their life as breathing, more so than eating or drinking.

'We will sight the quarry before noon,' said Hassan Ben Nader, who was the emir's lance-bearer, 'praised be the Name of God.'

'In Allah's Name,' the others chorused softly.

'I have never seen a spoor such as this lead bull leaves upon the earth,' Hassan went on, speaking softly so that he did not offend his master or the djinns of the wilderness.

'He is the bull of all bulls,' they agreed. 'There will be sport for a man before the sun sets.'

They glanced sideways at Osman Atalan, showing respect by not staring at him directly. He was deep in contemplation, squatting with his elbows on his knees and his smooth-shaven chin in the cup of his hands.

There was silence except for the susurration of steel on

leather. They paused in this endless activity only to test an edge with a thumb. Each blade was about three and a half feet in length, and double-edged. It was a replica of the broadswords of the crusaders that, centuries before, had so impressed the Saracens before the walls of Acre and Jerusalem. The most treasured blades had been forged from the steel of Solingen, and handed down from father to son. The marvellous temper of this metal imparted immense power to the blade, and it was capable of taking an edge like that of a surgeon's scalpel – the lightest stroke would split hide and hair, flesh and sinew to the deepest bone. A full stroke could divide an enemy at the waist, cutting him in two as effortlessly as though he were a ripe pomegranate. The scabbards were fashioned from two flat pieces of soft mimosa wood, held together and covered by the skin of an elephant's ear, dried hard and strong as iron. On the flat of the scabbard were two raised leather projections about twelve inches apart, which held the weapon securely under the horseman's thigh. Even at full gallop it would not flap and bounce in the ungainly manner of the swords of European cavalry.

The aggagiers rested while the high sun moved through an arc of three fingers across the sky. Then Osman Atalan rose to his feet, in a single flowing, graceful movement. Without a word the others rose also, went to their mounts and tightened the girths. They rode on down the slope of the valley, through open savannah in which the stately flat-topped acacia trees stood along the banks of the Atbara river. They dismounted beside one of the deep green pools. The elephant had been there before them. They had filled their bellies with water, then bathed riotously, hosing powerful jets from their trunks over themselves and the surrounding sandbanks. They had scooped up cartloads of thick black mud and plastered it on their heads and backs as protection against the sun and the swarms of biting insects. Then the three mighty grey beasts had wandered away along the bank, but the sand and mud they had left on the edges of the pool were so fresh that they were still damp.

The aggagiers whispered excitedly together, pointing out

the huge round tracks of the largest bull. Osman Atalan laid his war shield upon one of the pad marks. The circumference exceeded the giraffe-skin targe by the breadth of his finger.

'In God's Name,' they murmured. 'This is a mighty animal, and worthy of our steel.'

'I have never seen a greater bull than this,' said Hassan Ben Nader. 'He is the father of every elephant that has ever lived.' They filled the waterskins and let the horses drink again, then mounted up and followed the trail through the open acacia forest. The three bulls were moving head on to the faint breeze so that they would detect any danger ahead. The aggagiers moved up quietly and intently behind them.

The lead bull had dropped a pile of bright yellow dung in a clearing. It was stringy with chewed bark that he had stripped from the acacias, and lumpy with the stones of the Doum palm tree. A swarm of bright butterflies hovered over it. The scent was so strong that one horse snorted nervously. His rider calmed him with a reassuring touch on his neck.

They rode on, with Osman Atalan a length ahead. The trail was plain to see even from the distance of a hundred paces or more, for the bulls had ripped long slabs of bark from the boles of the acacias. The pale wounds were so raw and recent that they glistened with the running sap, which would dry into sticky black lumps of the precious gum arabic.

Emir Osman rose high in the stirrups and shaded his eyes to gaze forward. Almost half a mile ahead, the shaggy head of a tall Doum palm rose above the lesser trees of the savannah. Although the breeze was so faint as to be barely palpable the distant palm top was whipping from side to side as though it were being battered by a hurricane.

He looked back at his companions and nodded. They smiled, because they understood what they were witnessing. One of the bulls had placed his forehead against the bottle-shaped trunk of the palm and was shaking it with all his massive strength as though it were a sapling. This brought the ripe Doum nuts showering down on his head.

They reined in their steeds to a walk. The horses had scented the chase and were sweating and trembling with fear and excitement, for they knew what would happen next. Abruptly Osman laid his hand on his mount's withers. She was a creamy honey-coloured mare. She lifted her lovely Arabian head and flared the wide nostrils that were the mark of her breed, but stopped obediently. Her name was Hulu Mayya, Sweet Water, the most precious substance in this thirsty land. She was six years old and in her prime, swift as an oryx and as gentle as a kitten, but with the heart of a lioness. In the clamour of battle and the fury of the chase she never faltered.

Like her rider she stared ahead for the first glimpse of their quarry. Suddenly there he was, one of the lesser bulls standing separated from his companions, dozing under the spreading branches of a mimosa tree. The dappled shadows blurred his outline.

Osman gestured with his right hand, and they went forward, the horses stepping warily as though they expected a cobra to rear up under their hoofs. Almost imperceptibly the shapes of the other two beasts emerged from among the trees. One, tormented by the stinging flies, shook his head violently so that his ears clapped thunderously against his shoulders. His tusks gleamed dully in the shade, darkened by sap and vegetable juices to the colour of a meerschaum pipe stained by tobacco smoke. The curved and tapered pillars of ivory were so vast that the aggagiers grunted with satisfaction, and touched the hilts of their broadswords. The third bull was almost hidden by a patch of kittar thornbush. From this angle it was impossible to judge how his tusks compared with those of his companions.

Now that Osman Atalan had placed the position of each bull, he could plan his attack on them. First they must deal with the nearest, for if they passed across his wind their scent would be carried to him. The smell of man and horse would send him away at a rush, trumpeting the alarm to the others, and only hard riding would bring them up to the herd again. In a whisper that was barely a movement of his lips, but with expressive gestures of the hands Osman Atalan gave his commands to the aggagiers. From long experience each man knew what was expected of him.

The bull under the mimosa tree was angled half away from them, so when Osman led them forward again he circled out to the right, then came in more directly from behind. The eyesight of the elephant is poor, when compared with that of other creatures of the wild, such as the baboon and the vulture. But if it has difficulty distinguishing shape it picks up movement readily enough.

Osman dared not approach closer while he was mounted. He slipped from the saddle and girded up the hem of his *jibba* with the blue sash, leaving his legs covered only with baggy breeches. He tightened the straps of his sandals, then drew his broadsword. Instinctively he tried the edge and sucked the drop of blood that welled from the ball of his thumb. He tossed Sweet Water's reins to Hassan, and started towards the massive grey shape in the shade of the mimosa tree. The bull seemed as majestic as a three-decked man-o'-war. It seemed impossible that such a mighty beast could fall to the puny blade.

Osman stepped lithely and lightly with the grace of a dancer, carrying the sword in his right hand. However, he had bound the first hand's breadth of the blade above the cruci-form crosspiece of the hilt with a strip of skin from the ear of a freshly killed elephant: now that this had dried and cured it formed a double grip for his left hand.

As he approached the bull he heard the soft rumbling of its belly – the animal was sharing its contentment and pleas-ure with the rest of the herd, who were also dozing in the somnolent midday heat nearby. The bull was swaying gently, and swishing lazily at the flies with his stubby tail; the wiry bunch of hair at the end was almost worn away with age. The gigantic stained tusks were so long and thick that the bull was resting the blunt tips on the hard-baked earth. His weathered, corrugated trunk hung slackly between the ivory shafts. He was fondling the sun-dried, bleached femur bone of a long-dead buffalo with the tip, rolling it against his front foot, then lifting it to his lips as if to taste it, rubbing it between the fleshy finger-like projections on each side of the nostril openings, much as an ancient Coptic priest might play with his beads as he sat dreaming in the sun.

Osman changed his grip, two-handed now for the fatal stroke, and moved down the bull's flank close enough to touch him with the point of the sword. The riven grey hide hung down in bunches around the bull's knees, and in loose flaps under his sagging belly, like the clothing of an old man, too baggy for his wizened body.

His aggagiers watched him with awe and admiration. A lesser warrior would have chosen to hamstring his quarry, approaching the unsuspecting beast from behind and, with swift double strokes, severing the main tendons and arteries in the back of the legs above the huge, splayed feet. That injury would allow the hunter to escape, but cripple and anchor the bull until the severed arteries had drained the life from him, a slow death that might take up to an hour. However, to attempt the head-on approach as their emir was doing, increased the danger a hundredfold. Osman was now well within the arc of the trunk, which was capable of delivering a blow that would shatter every bone in his body. Those huge ears picked up the smallest sound, even a carefully controlled breath, and at such close quarters the rheumy little eyes would detect the slightest movement.

Osman Atalan stood in the bull's shadow, and looked up at one of those eyes. It seemed much too small for the huge grey head, and was almost completely screened by the thick fringe of colourless lashes as the bull blinked sleepily. The dangling trunk was also shielded by the thick yellow tusks. Osman had to entice the bull into extending it towards him. Any untoward movement, any incongruous sound would trigger a devastating response. He would be clubbed down by a blow from the trunk, or trampled under the pads of those great feet, or transfixed by an ivory tusk, then knelt upon and ground to bloody paste under the bulging bone of the bull's forehead.

Osman twisted the blade gently between his fists and, with

the polished metal, picked up one of the stray sunbeams that pierced the leafy canopy above his head. He played the reflected sunbeam on to the bull's gently flapping ear, then directed it forward gradually until it shot a tiny diamond wedge of light into the bull's half-closed eye. The elephant opened his eye fully and it glittered as it sought out the source of this mild annoyance. He detected no movement other than the trembling spot of sunlight, and reached out his trunk towards it, not alarmed but mildly curious.

There was no need for Osman to adjust his double grip on the hilt. The blade described a glittering sweep in the air, fast as the stoop of the hunting peregrine. There was no bone in the trunk to turn the blow so the silver blade sliced cleanly through it and half dropped to the ground.

The elephant reeled back from the shock and agony. Osman jumped back at the same instant and the bull spotted the movement and tried to lash out at it. But his trunk lay on the earth, and as the stump swung in an arc towards Osman, the blood hosed from the open arteries and sprayed in a crimson jet that soaked his *jibba*.

Then the bull lifted the stump of his amputated trunk and trumpeted in mortal anguish, his blood spraying back over his head and into his eyes. He charged into the forest, shattering the trees and thornbushes that blocked his path. Startled from the brink of sleep by his trumpeting screams, the other bulls fled with him.

Hassan Ben Nader spurred forward with Sweet Water on the rein. Osman snatched a lock of her long silky mane and leapt into the saddle without losing his grip on the hilt of his broadsword.

'Let the first bull run,' he cried. The pumping of the massive heart would drive the blood more swiftly out of the open arteries. The bull would weaken and go down within a mile. They would return for him later. Without checking his horse, Osman passed the spot where the dying animal had turned sharply aside. He rose in the stirrups more clearly to descry the trails of the two unwounded bulls. He followed them until they reached the first hills of the river valley where they parted company. One bull turned southwards and stormed away through the forest, while the other clambered straight up the rocky slope. There was no time to study the spoor and decide which was the larger animal, so Osman made an arbitrary choice.

He signalled with his raised sword and the aggagiers separated smoothly into two bands. The first party rode on up the escarpment after one animal, and Osman led the rest after the other. The dust of its flight hung in the still hot air, so there was no need to slow down to read the spoor. Sweet Water flew on for another mile until, four hundred paces ahead, Osman made out the dark hump of the bull's back crashing through the grey kittar thorn scrub, like a whale breaching in a turbulent sea. Now that he had the chase in sight Osman slowed Sweet Water to an easy canter, to save her strength for the final desperate encounter. Even at this pace they gained steadily on the bull.

Soon the gravel and small pebbles thrown up by the bull's great pads rattled against his shield and stung his cheeks. He slitted his eyes and rode in still closer, until the bull sensed his presence, and turned upon them with speed and nimbleness astonishing in such a massive beast. The horsemen scattered before his charge, but one of the aggagiers was not quick enough. The bull reached out with his trunk and, at full gallop, plucked him from the saddle. The broadsword with which he might have defended himself spun from his grip, throwing bright reflections of sunlight before it pegged into the hard earth and oscillated like a metronome. The bull turned aside and, with his trunk coiled round the aggagier's neck, swung the man against the trunk of a Doum palm with such force that his head was torn from his body, then knelt over the corpse and gored it with his tusks, driving the points through and through again.

Osman turned Sweet Water back and, although she tossed her long mane with terror, she responded to the pressure of his knees and his touch upon the reins. He rode her in directly across the bull's line of sight, and shouted a challenge to attract the animal's full attention, 'Ha! Ha!' he cried. 'Come, thou spawn of Satan! Follow me, O beast of the infernal world!'

The bull leapt up with the corpse dangling from one of his tusks. He shook his head and the dead man was hurled aside. Then he charged after Osman, squealing with rage, shaking his great head so that the ears flapped and volleyed like the mainsail of a ship-of-the-line taken all aback.

Sweet Water ran like a startled hare, carrying Osman swiftly away before the charge, but Osman slowed her with a lover's touch on the bit. Though he lay forward over her neck he was looking back under his arm. 'Gently, my sweetest heart.' He moderated her speed. 'We must tease the brute now.'

The bull realized he was gaining and thundered after them like a squadron of heavy cavalry. He thrust his head forward and reached out with his trunk. But the mare ran like a swallow skimming the surface of a lake to drink in flight. Osman kept her streaming tail an arm's length ahead of the tip of the waving trunk. The bull forced himself to even greater speed, but as he was about to snatch down the horse and her rider Osman pushed her gently so that she ran tantalizingly ahead, just beyond the bull's reach. Osman spoke softly into her ear and she turned it back to listen to his voice.

'Yes, my lovely. They are coming on.' Through the dust of the bull's run he could make out the shapes of his aggagiers closing in. Osman was offering himself and his mount like the cape to the bull, giving his men the opportunity to ride in and deliver the lethal strokes. The elephant was so absorbed with the horseman in front of him that he was unaware of the men who rode up under his out-thrust tail. Osman watched Hassan Ben Nader leap lightly from the saddle to the ground right at the bull's pounding heels. His outrider seized the loose reins and held the head for the instant that Hassan needed.

As he touched the earth he used the impetus of his horse's gallop to hurl himself forward. As the bull placed his full weight on the nearest leg, the rope of the tendon bulged tightly under the thick grey hide. Hassan slashed his blade across the back of the fetlock, a hand's span above the point where the straining tendon was attached to the joint. The gleaming steel edge cut down to the bone, and the main tendon parted with a rubbery snap that, even in the uproar of the chase, carried clearly to Osman's ear. In the same instant Hassan Ben Nader snatched back the reins from his outrider and leapt into the saddle. His horse plunged into full gallop once more. It was a marvellous feat of horsemanship. With three lunges his horse had carried him clear of the bull's tusks and trunk.

The bull lifted his wounded leg from the earth and swung it forward to take the next pace, but as his full weight came down on to the pad, the leg buckled and the fetlock joint gave way. An elephant is unable to run on three legs, as other four-legged creatures can, so he was instantly crippled and anchored to the spot. Squealing with agony and rage he groped for his tormentor. Osman spun Sweet Water about and, with his heels, drove her back almost under the outstretched trunk, shouting at the bull to keep his attention riveted, turning just out of reach. The bull tried to chase him, but stumbled heavily and almost went down as the crippled leg gave way under his weight.

In the meantime Hassan had circled back and, again undetected by the struggling animal, rode in now under his tail. He jumped down once more, and then, to demonstrate his courage, let his steed run on as he stood alone at the bull's heel. He waited an instant for the bull's full weight to come down on its uninjured leg, and when the tendon stood out proud beneath the skin he severed it with the skill of a surgeon. Both of the bull's back legs gave way under him and he sank helplessly on to his haunches, screaming his anguish to the pitiless sky and the triumphant African sun.

Hassan Ben Nader turned his back on the struggling animal and walked away unhurriedly. Osman jumped down from Sweet Water and embraced him. 'Ridden like a man, and killed like a prince.' He laughed. 'This very day you and I shall take the oath and eat the salt of brotherhood together.'

'You do me too much honour,' Hassan whispered, and fell

to his knees in homage, 'for I am your slave and your child, and you are my master and my father.'

They rested the horses in the shade and watered them from the skins while they watched the last struggles of their quarry. The blood spurted from the gaping arteries in the back of the bull's legs, in rhythm with the pulse of his heart. The earth beneath his pads dissolved into a bath of mud and blood, until his crippled legs slipped and slid as he shifted his weight. It did not take long. The bright crimson flow shrivelled, and the lassitude of approaching death settled over him. At last the air rushed out of his lungs in a long, hollow groan and he toppled on to his side, striking the earth with a sound that echoed off the hills.

'Five days from now I will send you back here with fifty men, Hassan Ben Nader, to bring in these tusks.' Osman stroked one of the huge ivory shafts that thrust up into the air higher than his head. It would take that long for the cartilage that held them in the bony sockets of the skull to soften with decay so that the great shafts could be drawn out undamaged by careless axe strokes. They mounted and rode easily back along their own spoor to find the first beast that Osman had attacked. By this time he, too, would have bled to death from the terrible wound. It would be easy to track him down to the spot where he had fallen, for he must have left a river of blood for them to follow.

They had not gone half a league before Osman held up a hand to halt them and cocked his head, listening. The sound that had alerted him came again from across the rocky ridge over which the other band of aggagiers had pursued the third bull. The intervening hills must have damped down the echoes so that they had not heard them before. The sound was unmistakable to these experienced hunters: it was the sound of an angry elephant, one that was neither crippled nor weakened by its wounds.

'Al-Noor has failed to kill cleanly,' said Osman. 'We must go to his aid.'

He led them up the slope at a gallop, and as they crossed

the ridge the sounds of conflict were loud and close. Osman rode towards them, and found a dead horse lying where it had been struck down, its spine shattered by a blow from the bull's trunk. The aggagier had died upon its back. They rode past them without drawing rein, and found two more dead men. At a glance Osman read the signs: one had been unhorsed in the face of the charging animal. The hooked, red-tipped thorns of the kittar had plucked him from the saddle as he had tried to escape the bull's charge. The other dead man was his blood-brother, and he had turned back to save him. As they had lived so they died, their blood mingled and their broken bodies entwined. Their horses had run free.

The elephant trumpeted again. The sound was closer now, and sharper. It rang out from a forest of kittar not far ahead. They slammed their heels into the flanks of their mounts and galloped towards the kittar. As they approached, a rider broke at full gallop from out of the thorn barrier into the open. It was al-Noor on his grey, which was in the extremes of terror and exhaustion. Al-Noor was almost naked: his *jibba* had been ripped from his body by the thorns and his skin was lacerated as though it had been clawed by a wild beast. The grey was staggering, throwing out its hoofs sloppily at each stride, and was too far gone to see and avoid the antbear burrow in its path. It stumbled and almost went down, throwing al-Noor over its head, then ran on, leaving its rider stunned, in the track of the great bull elephant that burst out of the thorn forest behind him. This was the patriarch bull, whose tracks had first astounded them. There was blood on one back leg but too high and too far forward to have struck the tendon. Al-Noor had inflicted a flesh wound that did not slow or impede the animal. As he came on, he held his head high to keep his long tusks clear of the thorn scrub and stony earth. They extended from his lip twice as far as a tall man could reach with both arms spread wide. They were as thick as a woman's thigh with almost no taper from lip to tip.

'Ten cantars a side!' Hassan shouted, amazed. This was a legendary animal, with almost two hundred pounds of ivory curving out on each side of his great grey head. Still dazed al-

Noor rose shakily to his feet and stood, swaying drunkenly, with blood and dust coating his face. His back was turned to the charging bull, and he had lost his sword. The bull saw him, squealed again, and rolled his trunk back against his chest. Al-Noor turned. When he saw death descending upon him he raised his right hand, index finger extended as a sign that he died in Islam, and cried, 'God is great!' It was his moment of acceptance. He stood without fear to meet it.

'For me and for Allah!' Osman called to his mare, and Sweet Water responded with her last reserves of strength and speed. She dashed in under the vaulted arch of tusks, Osman flat on her neck. The bull's trunk was rolled. There was no target for his blade. He could only hope to draw the charge off the man. The bull's gaze was so focused on al-Noor that he was unaware of the horse and rider coming in from the flank until they flashed past, so close that Osman's shoulder glanced off one of the tusks. Then they were gone, like the darting flight of a sunbird. The bull wheeled aside, forsaking the standing man and following the more compelling focus of his rage. He charged after the horse.

'O beloved of Allah,' al-Noor shouted his gratitude after the emir who had saved him, 'may God forgive all your sins.'

Osman smiled grimly as the words floated to him above the murderous trumpeting, the clash of hoofs and bursting thorn scrub. 'God grant me a few more sins before I die,' he shouted back, and led the bull away.

Hassan and the other aggagiers rode in his wake, shouting and whistling to attract the bull's attention, but he held on after Sweet Water. The mare had run hard but she was not yet spent. Osman looked back under his arm and saw that the bull was coming on apace, so swiftly that neither Hassan nor any other could get into position to attack his vulnerable back legs. He looked ahead and saw that he was being driven into a trap. Sweet Water was running into a narrow open lead between dense stands of the kittar thorn, but her path was blocked by a solid wall of thorn. Osman felt her check under him. Then she turned her head, gazed back at her beloved rider, as if seeking guidance, and rolled her eyes until the red linings showed. White froth splattered from the corners of her mouth.

Then horse and rider ran into the kittar, which closed round them in a green wave. The thorns hooked into hide and cloth like eagle's talons, and almost at once Sweet Water's graceful run was transformed into the struggles of a creature caught in quicksand. The bull thundered down upon them, its mighty progress unchecked by the kittar.

'Come, then, and let us make an end.' Osman called the challenge, dropped the reins and kicked his feet out of the stirrups. He stood up, tall, upon the saddle, facing back over Sweet Water's rump, his eyes on the level of the bull's. Man and beast confronted each other over a rapidly dwindling gap.

'Take us if you are able,' Osman called to the bull, knowing how the sound of his voice would infuriate the animal. The bull flattened his ears against the sides of his skull, and rolled the tips in rage and aggression. Then he did what Osman had been waiting for: he unrolled his trunk and reached out to seize the man and lift him high off the back of his horse.

Balancing to Sweet Water's violent lunges and struggles, Osman held the long blade poised, and as the serrated grey trunk was about to close round his body, he struck. The steel whickered in flight, and dissolved into a silver blur of light. The stroke was full, and seemed to meet no resistance: the steel sliced through hide, flesh and sinews, as though they were mist. It severed the trunk close to the lip as smoothly as the guillotine blade takes off a condemned man's head.

For an instant there was no blood, just the sheen of freshly exposed flesh and the gleam of nerve ends and white tendons. Then the blood burst forth, engulfing the great grey head in a crimson cloud as the arteries erupted. The bull screamed again, but now in agony and dismay. Then he lurched to one side as he lost his balance and sense of direction.

Osman dropped back into the saddle and guided Sweet Water with his knees, steering her out of the arc of the bull's blood-dimmed eyesight. The animal blundered in a wide uncertain circle as Hassan rode in behind him to make the cut in the back of his left leg. Then he jumped back into the saddle, leaving the bull anchored by his crippled leg. Osman slipped down from Sweet Water's back and, with another stroke of his blade, cut through the other hamstring.

The heart blood pumped from the terrible wounds in his back legs and trunk, but the bull remained upright for as long as a mullah might take to recite a single *sura* of the Koran. Osman Atalan and his aggagiers dismounted and stood at their horses' heads to watch his death throes and pray for him, praising his might and courage. When at last he fell with a crash to the stony earth, Osman cried, 'Allah is almighty. Infinite is the glory of God.'

The word flashed through the alleys and souks, and was shouted from the rooftops and minarets. As it spread, a sombre, funereal mood descended on the city of Khartoum. Whispering dolefully as they came together, the inhabitants hurried to find a vantage-point from which they could gaze across the river and behold their fate.

Ryder Courtney was in the workshop in his compound behind the hospital and the red mud walls of Fort Burri when a servant brought him a note from David Benbrook, scribbled on a torn sheet of consular paper. Since first light that morning Ryder had been working with Jock McCrump on the repairs to the *Intrepid Ibis*. When they had disconnected the punctured steam piping they discovered more damage than they had first suspected. Some of the metal fragments had been carried into the cylinders and had scored the liners. It was surprising that they had been able to make the return trip to the harbour.

'Damn good job I didnae let you go tearing away at full throttle,' Jock muttered morosely. 'We would have had a right ballocks if I had.'

They had been obliged to sway the heavy engine out of the *Ibis*'s hull on to the stone jetty. Then they transported it to the compound by ox-wagon, taking a circuitous route to avoid the narrow alleyways. They had been working on it for the last ten days, and the repairs were almost completed. Ryder wiped his hands on a ball of cotton waste, then glanced through the note. He handed it to Jock. 'Do you want to come and watch the Lord Mayor's show?'

Jock grunted. With long tongs he lifted a glowing sheet of metal from the forge and carried it to the anvil. 'Like as not we'll be having a gutful of that worthy Oriental gentleman Osman bloody Atalan without running out to stare at him now.' He hefted the heavy blacksmith's hammer and began to pound the metal to shape. He ignored Ryder as he plunged it into a trough of water. It cooled in a hissing cloud of steam and Jock measured it critically. He was shaping a patch for one of the shell holes in *Ibis*'s hull. He was not satisfied with the result, and whistled tunelessly as he returned it to the forge. Ryder grinned and went out to the stables for his horse.

He crossed the canal on the earthen causeway, and rode through the scurrying crowds to the gates of the consular palace. He hoped to avoid running into General Gordon, and was pleased to see his unmistakable khaki-uniformed silhouette on the upper parapet of Mukran Fort with half a dozen members of his Egyptian staff gathered around him. Each man had either a telescope or a pair of field-glasses focused on the north bank of the Blue Nile, so Ryder was able to ride past the fort and reach the consulate without drawing their attention. He handed his horse over to one of the syces at the gate of the stableyard and strode through the barren gardens to the legation entrance of the palace. The sentries recognized him at once and saluted him as he entered the main foyer.

An Egyptian secretary came hurrying to meet him. Like everyone else he wore a nervous, worried expression. 'The consul is on top of the watch-tower, Mr Courtney,' the man told him. 'He asked you to be good enough to join him there.'

When Ryder stepped out on to the balcony the Benbrook family did not notice him immediately. They were grouped around the big telescope on its tripod. Amber was taking her turn, standing on a cane-backed chair to reach the eyepiece. Then Saffron looked round and let out a squeak of delight.

'Ryder!' She ran to seize his arm. 'You must come and see. It's so exciting.'

Ryder glanced at Rebecca, and felt a tightening in the pit of his stomach. She showed no ill effects from their recent curtailed voyage downstream. On the contrary, she looked cool, even under the layers of green georgette petticoats that ballooned out over her crinoline. There was a bright yellow ribbon around the crown of her straw hat, and her hair was arranged in ringlets over her shoulders. It caught the sunlight.

'Don't let that child pester you, Mr Courtney.' She gave him a demure smile. 'She has been in an overbearing mood since breakfast.'

'Overbearing means regal and queenly,' said Saffron, smugly.

'It does not.' Amber looked back at her from the telescope. 'It means bumptious and insufferable.'

'Peace be unto both of you.' Ryder chuckled. 'Sisterly love is a beautiful thing.'

'Glad you could come,' David called to him. 'Sorry to tear you away from your work, but this is worth a look. You have had enough of the telescope, Amber. Let Mr Courtney have a turn.'

Ryder stepped up to the parapet, but before he stooped to the eyepiece he stared out across the river. It was an extraordinary spectacle: as far as he could see the land seemed to be on fire. It took a moment to realize that this was not smoke that gave the sky a dun, fuming aspect, but the dustcloud thrown up by a vast moving mass of living things, human and animal, that stretched away to the eastern horizon.

Even at such a distance there was a low reverberation in the air, like the muted hum of the beehive, or the murmur of the sea on a windless day. It was the sound of braying donkeys, lowing herds, fat-tailed sheep and thousands of hoofs, marching feet, the creaking of camel burdens and the squeal of axles. It was the clatter of giraffe-hide war shields, of spears and blades rattling in their scabbards, the rumble of the gun-carriages and the ammunition train.

Then, more clearly, he heard the trumpeting of the

ombeyas, the Sudanese battle trumpets carved from a single ivory tusk. The warlike call of these instruments carried an immense distance in the desert airs. Underlying it was the throbbing bass beat of hundreds of huge copper drums. Each emir rode at the head of his tribe with his drummers, trumpeters and banner-bearers preceding him. He was closely surrounded by his *mulazemin*, his bodyguards, his brothers and blood-brothers, and his aggagiers. Though they rode united now by the holy *jihad* of the Divine Mahdi most of these tribes carried their centuries-old blood feuds, and none trusted another.

The banners were of rainbow hues, embroidered with texts from the Koran, and exaltations to Allah. Some were so large that it took three or four men to hold them aloft, rippling and snapping in the hot desert breeze. The banners and the harlequin-patched *jibbas* of the warriors made a gorgeous show against the drab landscape.

'How many do you estimate there are?' David asked, as though he was speaking about the race-day crowd on Epsom Down.

'The devil alone knows.' Ryder shook his head doubtfully. 'From here, we can't see the end of them.'

'Fifty thousand, would you hazard?'

'More,' said Ryder. 'Maybe many more.'

'Can you make out the entourage of Osman Atalan?'

'He will be in the van, naturally.' Ryder placed his eye to the telescope and trained it forward. He picked out the scarlet and black banners. 'There is the devil himself. Right at the forefront!'

'I thought you said you had never before laid eyes upon him,' David said.

'No introduction necessary. That's him, I tell you.'

In all that hubbub and bustle the slim figure on the cream-coloured horse was unmistakable for its dignity and presence.

At that moment there was a sudden commotion among the vast congregation on the far bank. Through the telescope Ryder saw Osman rise in the stirrups and brandish his broadsword. The front ranks of his *mulazemin* broke into a furious charge, and he led them straight at a small group of horsemen that rode to meet them from the direction of Omdurman. As the masses of cavalry and camels dashed forward they discharged volleys of joyous gunfire into the air. The blue smoke mingled with the dustcloud, and the spearheads and sword blades twinkled like stars in the murk.

'Who is that they are riding to meet?' David asked sharply.

Through the lens Ryder concentrated on the small group of horsemen, and exclaimed as he recognized the green turbans of the two leading horsemen. 'Damme, if it's not the Divine Mahdi himself and his *khalifa*, the mighty Abdullahi.' Ryder tried to make his tone sardonic and pejorative, but no one was deceived.

'With that merry band of cut-throats sitting across it, the road to the north is firmly closed.' Although David said it breezily, there was a shadow in his eyes as he looked to his three daughters. 'There is no longer any escape from this wretched place.' Any retort that Ryder could make would have been fatuous, and they watched in silence the meeting of the men who held the fate of the city and all its inhabitants in their bloody hands.

With bared sword and his long plait thumping against his back, Osman Atalan charged straight at the mounted figure of the Mahdi. The prophet of Allah saw him coming in a whirlwind of dust, to the deafening bray of the war horns and the pounding of drums. He reined in his white stallion. Khalifa Abdullahi stopped his horse a few paces behind his master, and they waited for the emir to come on.

Osman brought Sweet Water to a plunging, skidding halt and shook his broadsword in the Mahdi's face. 'For God and his Prophet!' he screamed. The blade that had slain men and elephants in their hundreds was now only a finger's breadth from the Mahdi's eyes.

The Mahdi sat unmoved with that serene smile on his lips and the *falja* showing between them.

Osman spun Sweet Water round and galloped away. His bodyguard and banner-bearers followed him at the same wild gallop, firing their Martini-Henry rifles into the air. At a distance of three hundred paces Osman rallied his men and they regrouped at his back. He lifted his sword high, and again they charged in a serried phalanx, straight at the two lone figures. At the last instant Osman pulled up the mare so violently that she came down on her haunches.

'*La ilaha illallah!* There is but one God!' he yelled. 'Muhammad Rasul Allah! Muhammad is the prophet of God!'

Five times the horsemen retreated and five times they charged back. At the fifth charge Muhammad Ahmed, the Divine Mahdi, raised his right hand and said softly, '*Allah karim!* God is generous.'

Immediately Osman threw himself from Sweet Water's back and kissed the Mahdi's sandalled foot in the stirrup. This was an act of the utmost humility, a rendering up of one man's soul to another. The Mahdi smiled down at him tenderly. He emanated a peculiar perfume, a mixture of sandalwood and attar of roses, known as the Breath of the Mahdi. 'I am pleased that you have come to join my array and the *jihad* against the Turk and the infidel. Rise up, Osman Atalan. You are assured of my favour. You may enter with me into the city of Allah, Omdurman.'

On the flat roof of his house, the Mahdi sat cross-legged on a low *angareb*, a couch covered with a silk prayer rug and strewn with cushions. There was a screen of reed matting over the terrace to shield them from the sun, but the sides were open to the cooling breeze off the river and to provide a view across the wide expanse of the Victoria Nile to the city of Khartoum. The ugly square blockhouse of Mukran Fort dominated the defences of the besieged city. Emir Osman Atalan sat facing him, and a slave maid knelt before him with a dish of water on which floated a few oleander petals. Osman dipped water from it and made the ritual ablutions, then dismissed the woman with a wave. Another lovely Galla slave girl placed between them a silver tray that bore three jewelled long-stemmed silver cups: chalices looted from the Roman Catholic cathedral in El Obeid.

'Refresh yourself, Osman Atalan. You have travelled far,' the Mahdi invited him.

Osman made an elegant gesture of refusal. 'I thank you for your hospitality, but I have eaten and drunk with the dawn and I will not eat again until the setting of the sun.'

The Mahdi nodded. He knew of the emir's frugality. He was well aware of the peculiar religious enlightenment and the sense of dedicated purpose brought on by fasting and denial of the appetite. The memories of his sojourn on Abbas Island were as fresh as if it had taken place the previous day, and not three years before. He lifted a silver cup to his lips, displaying for an instant the gap between his front teeth, sign of his divinity. Of course, he never drank alcohol but he was partial to a drink made from date syrup and ground ginger.

Once he had been lean and hard as this fierce desert warrior, but he was no longer a solitary hermit. He was the spiritual leader of a nation, chosen by God. Once he had been a barefoot ascetic who had denied himself all sensual pleasures. Not long ago it had been boasted through all the Sudan that Muhammad Ahmed had never known a woman's body. He was virgin no longer and his harem contained the first fruits of all his mighty victories. His was first choice of the captured women. Every sheikh and emir brought him gifts of the most lovely young girls in their territory, and it was a political imperative that he accept their largesse. The numbers of his wives and concubines already exceeded a thousand, and increased each day. His women fascinated him. He spent half his days among them.

They were dazzled by his appearance, his height and grace, his fine features, the winged birthmark and the angelic smile that disguised all his emotions. They loved his perfume and the gap between his teeth. They were intoxicated by his wealth and power: his treasury, the Beit el Mal, held gold, jewels and millions in specie, the spoils of his conquests and the sack of the principal cities of the Nile. The women sang, 'The Mahdi is the sun of our sky, and the water of our Nile.'

Now he set aside the silver cup and held out his hand. One of the waiting girls knelt to offer him a scented silk cloth with which to dab the sticky syrup from his lips.

Behind the Mahdi, on another cushioned *angareb*, sat the Khalifa Abdullahi. He was a handsome man with chiselled features and a nose like the beak of an eagle, but his skin was dappled, like a leopard's, with the scars of smallpox. His nature was also that of the leopard, predatory and cruel. Emir Osman Atalan feared no man or beast, except these two men who sat before him now. These he feared with all his heart.

The Mahdi lifted one gracefully shaped hand and pointed across the river. Even with the naked eye they were able to make out the solitary figure on the parapets of the Mukran Fort.

'There is Gordon Pasha, the son incarnate of Satan,' said the Mahdi.

'I will bring his head to you before the beginning of Ramadan,' said his *khalifa*.

'Unless the infidel reaches him before you do,' suggested the Mahdi, and his voice was soft and pleasant to hear. He turned to Osman. 'Our scouts report to us that the infidel army is at last on the move. They are sailing southwards in a flotilla of steamers along the river to rescue our enemy from my vengeance.'

'At the beginning they will move at the pace of the chameleon.' The *khalifa* endorsed his master's report. 'However, once they pass through the cataracts and reach the bend of the river at Abu Hamed, they will have the north wind behind their boats and the current will abate. The speed of their advance will increase six-fold. They will reach Khartoum before Low Nile, and we cannot assault the city before the river falls and exposes Gordon Pasha's defences.'

'You must send half of your army northwards under your most trustworthy sheikhs and stop the infidels on the river before they reach Abu Klea. Then you must annihilate them, just as you destroyed the armies of Baker Pasha and Hicks Pasha.' The Mahdi stared into Osman's face, and Osman's spirits stirred. 'Will you deliver to me my enemy, Osman Atalan?'

'Holy One, I will give him into your hands,' Osman replied. 'In God's Name and with the blessing of Allah, I will deliver to you that city and all those within.' The three warriors of God gazed across the Nile like hunting cheetahs surveying herds of grazing gazelle upon the plains.

Captain Penrod Ballantyne had been waiting in the ante-chamber of Her Britannic Majesty's consulate in Cairo for forty-eight minutes. He checked the time on the clock above the door to the inner office of the consul general. On the left-hand side of the massive carved door hung a life-sized portrait of Queen Victoria as she had been on her wedding day, pure and pretty with the bloom of youth still on her and the crown of Empire on her head, On the opposite side of the door there was a matching portrait of her consort, Albert of Saxe-Coburg and Gotha, handsome and marvel-lously bewhiskered.

Penrod Ballantyne shot a glance at himself in the gilt-framed ceiling-high mirror that adorned the side wall of the antechamber and, with satisfaction, noted his own likeness to the young Prince Consort, now long dead while Penrod was young and vital. The captain's epaulettes on his shoulders and the frogging of his uniform jacket were bright new gold. His riding boots were polished to a glassy sheen, and the fine glove leather creased around his ankles like the bellows of an accordion. His cavalry sabre hung down along the scarlet side stripe of his riding breeches. He wore his dolman slung over one shoulder and clasped at his throat with a gold chain, and carried his Hussar's bearskin busby under his right arm. On his left breast he wore the purple watered silk with the bronze cross inscribed 'For Valour', which had been cast from the

Russian guns captured at Sebastopol. There was no higher military decoration in the Empire.

Sir Evelyn Baring's secretary came in. 'The consul general will see you now.'

Penrod had been standing to preserve the pristine appearance of his uniform – creases at the elbows, down the back of his tunic and at the knees of his breeches were unsightly. He replaced the tall busby on his head, glancing in the mirror to make certain it was centred low on his eyebrows with the chain across the chin, then marched through the carved doors into the inner office.

Sir Evelyn Baring was seated at his desk, reading from a sheaf of despatches in front of him. Penrod came to attention and saluted. Baring beckoned him in without glancing at him. The secretary closed the door.

Sir Evelyn Baring was officially the agent of Her Britannic Majesty's Government in Egypt, and her consul general in Cairo with plenipotentiary powers. In truth he was the viceroy, who ruled the ruler of Egypt. Since the Khedive had been saved from the mobs of rebellion by the British Army and the fleet of the Royal Navy in Alexandria harbour, Egypt had become, in all but name, a British protectorate.

The Khedive Tawfig Pasha was a weak youth and no match for a man like Baring and the mighty Empire he represented. He had been forced to abdicate all his powers, and in return the British had given him and his people the peace and prosperity they had not known since the age of Pharaoh Ptolemy. Sir Evelyn Baring possessed one of the most brilliant minds in the colonial service. The Prime Minister, William Gladstone, and his cabinet were aware of and highly appreciative of his qualities. However, towards his underlings, his manner was patronizing and condescending. Behind his back they called him 'Sir Over Bearing'.

Now he ignored Penrod as he went on with his reading, making notes in the margins with a gold pen. At last he stood up from his desk, and left Penrod standing while he went to the windows that overlooked the river to Giza and the stark silhouettes of the three mighty pyramids on the far bank.

That damned idiot, Baring mused to himself. He has got us into this pretty pickle of rotten fish. From the outset he had opposed the appointment of Chinese Gordon. He had wanted to send Sam Baker, but Gladstone and Lord Hartington, the Secretary of War, had overruled him. It is in Gordon's nature to provoke conflict. The Sudan was to be abandoned. His job was to bring our people out of that doomed land, not to confront the Mad Mahdi and his Dervishes. I warned Gladstone of precisely this, Gordon is trying to dictate terms and force the Prime Minister and the cabinet to send an army to reoccupy the Sudan. If it were not for the unfortunate citizens that he has incarcerated with him, and for the honour of the Empire, we should let Chinese Gordon stew in his own juice.

As Baring turned away from the window and the contemplation of those immemorial monuments across the Nile, his eye fell on a copy of *The Times* of London that lay on the table beside his favourite armchair. He frowned more deeply. And then we have also to take into account the uninformed and sentimental opinions of the sweating masses, so readily manipulated by those petty potentates of the press.

He could almost recite the leading article from memory: 'We know that General Gordon is surrounded by hostile tribes and cut off from communication with Cairo and London. Under these circumstances the House has the right to ask Her Majesty's Government whether they are going to do anything to relieve him. Are they going to remain indifferent to the fate of the one man on whom they have counted to extricate them from their dilemmas, to leave him to shift for himself, and make not a single effort on his behalf?' was what Lord Randolph Churchill had said to the Commons, as reported on 16 March 1885. Damned demagogue! Baring thought now, and looked up at the Hussar captain. 'Ballantyne, I want you to go back to Khartoum.' He spoke directly to Penrod for the first time since he had entered the room.

'Of course, sir. I can leave within the hour,' Penrod responded. He knew that the one word the master of Egypt liked to hear above all others was 'yes'.

Baring allowed himself a wintry smile, an extraordinary mark of his approval. His intelligence system was wide-reaching and pervasive. Its roots burrowed into every level of Egyptian society, from the highest levels of the government and the military to the forbidden councils of the mullahs in their mosques and the bishops in their cathedrals and Coptic monasteries. He had his agents in the palaces of the Khedive and the harems of the pashas, in the souks, bazaars and brothels of the greatest cities and the meanest villages.

Penrod was nothing but a tiny tadpole in the festering swamp of intrigue in whose waters Sir Evelyn Baring set his lines and into which he cast his net. However, recently he had become quite fond of the lad. Behind the good looks and dandified appearance, Baring had detected a bright, quick mind and an attention to duty that reminded him of himself at the same age. Penrod Ballantyne's family connections were solid. His elder brother was a baronet and had large estates on the Scottish Borders. He himself had a significant income from a family trust, and the purple ribbon on his chest bore ample witness to his courage. Moreover, the young dog had shown a natural aptitude for intelligence work. Indeed, he was gradually and subtly making himself valuable – not indispensable, for nobody was that, but valuable. The only possible weakness that Baring had so far detected in him he carried in his trousers.

'I will give you no written message, for the usual reasons,' he said.

'Naturally, sir.'

'There is one message for General Gordon, and another for David Benbrook, the British consul. The messages are not to be confused. It may seem to you that they are contradictory, but pray do not let that trouble you.'

'Yes, sir.' Penrod divined that Baring trusted Benbrook well enough because he lacked brilliance. Just as he trusted Chinese Gordon not at all because of his brilliance.

'This is what you are to convey to them.' Baring spoke for half an hour without consulting any slip of paper, barely pausing to draw breath. 'Have you got that, Ballantyne?'

'I have, sir.'

One of the fellow's assets is his appearance, Baring thought. No one can readily believe that behind those whiskers and those wonderfully pleasing features is a mind that can assimilate such a lengthy, complicated message at the first recital, then deliver it accurately a month later. 'Very well,' he said flatly. 'But you must impress on General Gordon that Her Majesty's Government has no intention whatsoever of reconquering the Sudan. The British Army now making its way up the Nile is in no way an expeditionary force. It is not an army of reoccupation. It is a rescue column of minimal strength. The objective of the desert column is to insert a small body of regular first-line troops into Khartoum to bolster the defences of the city long enough for us to evacuate all our people. Once this has been achieved we intend to abandon the city to the Dervish and come away.'

'I understand, sir.'

'As soon as you have delivered your messages to Benbrook and Gordon you are to return northwards and join Stewart's relief column. You will act as guide, lead him across the bight of the Nile to where Gordon's own steamers are waiting at Metemma to take them upriver. You will attempt to keep in contact with me. The usual codes, mind.'

'Of course, Sir Evelyn.'

'Very well, then. Major Adams of General Wolseley's staff is waiting for you on the second floor. I understand that you are acquainted with him.'

'I am, sir.' Of course Baring knew that Penrod had won his VC by rescuing Samuel Adams from the bloody battlefield of El Obeid.

'Adams will give you a more detailed briefing, and provide you with the passes and requisitions you will need. You can catch the Cook's steamer this evening and be in Assouan by Tuesday noon. From there you are on your own. How long to Khartoum, Ballantyne? You have made the journey many times before.'

'It depends on conditions in the Desert of the Mother of Stones. If the wells are holding I can cut the great S-bend of the river and reach Khartoum in twenty-one days, sir,' Penrod answered crisply. 'Twenty-six at the outside.'

Baring nodded. 'Make it twenty rather than twenty-six. Let yourself out.' Baring dismissed him, without offering to shake hands. He was lost in his despatches again before Penrod reached the door. It was not important to Baring that people liked him. Only that they did their job.

Colonel Sam Adams was delighted to see Penrod again. He was walking with only a single stick now. 'The sawbones tells me I'll be playing polo again by Christmas.' Neither mentioned the long ride back from the battlefield of El Obeid. All that needed to be said on that subject had been said long ago, but Adams glanced admiringly at the bronze cross on Penrod's chest.

Penrod composed a cipher telegraph to the intelligence officer with the vanguard of the Desert Column that was assembling at Wadi Halfa eight hundred miles up the Nile. Adams's adjutant took it to the telegraphist on the ground floor and returned with the confirmation that it had been sent and received. Then Colonel Adams invited Penrod to lunch at Shepheard's Hotel, but Penrod begged a prior engagement. As soon as he had his travel papers he left. A groom had his charger at the gate and it was less than half an hour's ride along the riverbank to the Gheziera Club.

Lady Agatha was waiting for him on the Ladies' Veranda. She was just twenty and the youngest daughter of a duke. Viscount Wolseley, the commander-in-chief of the British Army in Egypt, was her godfather. She had an income of twenty thousand a year. Added to this, she was blonde, petite and exquisite, but an enormous handful for any man.

'I would rather have the French clap than Lady Agatha,' Penrod had recently overheard a wag remark at the Shepheard's bar, and had been undecided whether to laugh or call the fellow outside. In the end he had bought him a drink.

'You are late, Penrod.' She was reclining in a cane chair and pouted as he came up the steps from the garden. He kissed her hand, then glanced at the clock over the garden entrance to the dining room. She saw the gesture. 'Ten minutes can be an eternity.'

'Duty, I am afraid, my lovely. Queen and country.'

'How utterly boring. Get me a glass of champagne.' Penrod looked up, and a waiter in a long white *galabiyya* and tasselled fez appeared as miraculously as a genie from the lamp.

When the wine came, Agatha sipped it. 'Grace Everington is getting married on Saturday,' she said.

'A mite sudden?'

'No, actually, just in time. Before it begins to show.'

'I hope she enjoyed the chase.'

'She tells me no, not at all, but her father is being beastly and says she must go through with it. Family honour. It is to be quiet and discreet, of course, but I have an invitation for you. You may escort me. It might be fun to watch her making an ass of herself, and of him.'

'I am sorry to say it, but by then I shall be far away.'

Agatha sat up straight. 'Oh, God! No! Not again. Not so soon.'

Penrod shrugged. 'I was given no choice.'

'When are you leaving?'

'In three hours' time.'

'Where are they sending you?'

'You know better than to ask.'

'You can't go, Pen. The reception at the Austrian embassy is tomorrow evening. I have a new dress.' He shrugged again. 'When will you come back?'

'That is blowing in the wind.'

'Three hours,' she said, and stood up. The movement attracted the gaze of every man on the veranda. 'Come!' she commanded.

'Lunch?' he asked.

'I think not.' Her family kept a permanent suite at Shepheard's, and Penrod rode beside her open gharry. As the door to the suite closed she pounced on him, like a kitten on a ball of wool, lithe, playful and earnest all at once. He picked her up easily and carried her through to the bedroom.

'Be quick!' she ordered. 'But not too quick.'

'I am an officer of the Queen, and an order is an order.'

Later, she watched him as he dressed again while she lay stretched full length, languid and replete, inviting his appraisal. 'You won't find better than this, Penrod Ballantyne.' She cupped her hands under her breasts. They were pale and large in comparison to her girlish waist. She squeezed out her nipples, and he paused to watch her. 'You see? You do like it. When will you marry me?'

'Ah! May we apply ourselves to that question at some later date?'

'You are an utter beast.' She combed her fingers through the mist of strawberry curls at the base of her belly. 'Should I pluck myself here? The Arab girls do.'

'Your information on that subject is probably more accurate than mine.'

'I heard that you like Arab girls.'

'Sometimes you are amusing, Lady Agatha. At other times you are not. Sometimes you behave like a lady, and at others not at all.' He slung his dolman over his shoulder and adjusted the chain as he turned to the door.

She flew off the bed like a wounded leopard, and he only just had time to turn and defend himself. She went for his eyes with her sharp, pearly talons. But he seized her wrists. She tried to bite his face, small white teeth clicking together an inch from his nose. He bent her backwards so she could not reach. She kneed at his groin, but he caught the blow on his thigh and turned her round. She was helpless in the circle of his arms with her back to his chest. She pressed her firm round buttocks into him, felt him swelling and hardening, and gave a breathless but triumphant little laugh. She stopped struggling, sank to her knees and lifted high the twin half-moons of her buttocks. She wriggled her thighs apart so that the nest of pink curls peeked out between them. 'I hate you!' she said.

He dropped down behind her, still booted and spurred, his sabre belted at his side. He ripped open the front of his breeches, and she screamed involuntarily as he transfixed her. When he stood up again she collapsed and lay panting at his feet. 'How do you always know what I want you to do? How do you always know what to say, and when to say it? That terrible name you called me a moment ago was like chilli powder on a sweet mango – it took my breath away. How do you know these things?'

'Some might call it genius, but I am too modest to agree.'

She looked up at him. Her hair was tangled and her cheeks were flushed rosily. 'Call me that again.'

'No matter how richly you deserve it, once is enough for now.' He went to the door.

'When will you come back?'

'Perhaps soon, perhaps never.'

'You beast. I hate you. I truly hate you.' But he was gone.

Three days later Penrod stepped off the fast steamer at the Assouan jetty. He was wearing tropical khaki uniform without decorations or regimentals. He had exchanged the busby for a pith helmet with a wide brim. There were at least another fifty soldiers and officers within sight who were dressed almost identically, so he excited no attention. A ragged porter in a filthy turban seized his kit-bag and ran ahead of him into the maze of streets of the old town. Striding out on long legs Penrod kept him in sight.

When they reached the gate in a nondescript mud wall at the end of the narrow, twisted alley, Penrod tossed the porter a piastre and retrieved his bag. He tugged the bell cord and listened to the familiar chimes. After a while there were footsteps beyond the gate, soft and faltering, and a voice quavered, 'Who is it that calls? There is nothing here for we are poor widows and deserted by God.'

'Open this gate, you houri of Paradise,' Penrod replied, 'and swiftly, before I kick it down.'

There was a moment's stunned silence, broken at last by a wild cackle of laughter and a fumbling at the bolts. Then they were shot back and the gate creaked open. An ancient head, like a turtle's but partly covered with a widow's veil peered round the jamb. The gaping grin exposed two crooked teeth widely separated by an expanse of pink gum. 'Effendi!' The old woman squealed, and her entire face puckered with wrinkles. 'Lord of a thousand virtues.'

Penrod embraced her.

'You are shameless,' she protested with delight. 'You threaten my virtue.'

'I am fifty years too late to pluck that fruit.' He let her go. 'Where is your mistress?'

Old Liala glanced significantly across the courtyard. In the centre of the garden a fountain splashed into a pool in which Nile perch circled tranquilly. Around its border stood statues of the pharaohs: Seti, Thutmose and great Rameses, lifted from their tombs by grave-robbers back in the mists of time. It never failed to amaze him that such treasures were displayed in so humble a setting.

Penrod strode across the courtyard. His heart beat faster. He had not realized until that moment how much he had been looking forward to seeing her again. When he reached the beaded curtain that covered the doorway he paused to regain his composure, then jerked it aside and stepped through. At first she was merely a dim, ethereal presence, but then his eyes adjusted and her shape emerged from the cool gloom. She was slim as a lily stem, but her robe was shot with gold thread, and there was gold at her wrists and ankles. As she came towards him, her bare henna-painted feet made no sound on the tiles. She stopped in front of him and made obeisance, touching her fingertips to her lips and her heart.

'Master!' she whispered. 'Master of my heart.' Then she hung her head and waited in silence.

He lifted the veil and studied her face. 'You are beautiful, Bakhita,' he told her, and the smile that blossomed over her features enhanced that beauty a hundredfold. She lifted her chin and looked at him, and her eyes glowed so that they seemed to light the dimmest recesses of the room.

'It has been only twenty-six days, but it seems like all my life,' she said, and her voice quivered like the strings of a lute plucked by skilled fingers.

'You have counted the days?' he asked.

'And the hours also.' She nodded. Roses coloured the waxen perfection of her cheeks, and the long lashes meshed over her eyes as she glanced away shyly. Then her eyes crept back to his face.

'You knew I was coming?' he accused her. 'How could you when I did not know it myself?'

'My heart knew, as the night knows the coming of dawn.' She touched his face as though she were blind and trying to remember something with her fingertips. 'Are you hungry, my lord?'

'I am famished for you,' he replied.

'Are you thirsty, my lord?'

'I thirst for you as a traveller thirsts for the waterhole when he has been hunting seven days in the desert under the relentless sun.'

'Come,' she whispered, and took his hand. She led him into the inner room. Their *angareb* stood in the centre of the floor and he saw that the linen upon it had been washed, bleached and smoothed with a hot iron, until it shone like the saltpan of Shokra. She knelt before him and removed his uniform. When he stood naked she rose and stepped back to admire him. 'You bring me vast treasure, lord.' She reached out and touched him. 'An ivory sceptre, tipped with the ruby of your manhood.'

'If this is treasure, then show me what you bring in exchange.'

Naked, her body was moon pale, and her breasts bulged weightily, the nipples as large as ripe grapes, wine dark and swollen. She wore only a slim gold chain round her waist, and her belly was rounded and smooth as polished granite from the quarries above the first cataract. Her hands and feet were decorated with fine acanthus-wreath patterns of henna.

99

She shook out the dark tresses of her hair, and came to lie beside him on their mattress. He gloated over her with his eyes and fingertips, and she moved softly as his hands dictated, raising her hips and twisting her shoulders so that her bosom changed shape and no secret part of her body was hidden from him.

'Your quimmy is so beautiful, so precious, that Allah should have set it in the forehead of a ravening lion. Then only the valiant and the worthy might dare to possess it.' There was wonder in his voice. 'It is like a ripe fig, warmed in the sun, splitting open and running with sweet juices.'

'Feast to your heart's content upon the fig of my love, dear lord,' she whispered huskily.

Afterwards they slept entwined and their own sweat cooled them. At last old Liala brought them a bowl of dates and pomegranates, and a jug of lemon sherbet. They sat cross-legged on the *angareb* facing each other and Bakhita made her report to him. There was much for her to relate, great and dire news from the south, from Nubia and beyond. The Arab tribes were all in a state of flux and change, new alliances forged and century-old ties broken. At the centre of all this turmoil sat the Mahdi and his *khalifa*, two venomous spiders at the centre of their web.

Bakhita was older than Penrod by three years. She had been the first wife of a prosperous grain merchant, but she was unable to bear him a child. Her husband had taken a younger woman to wife, a dull-witted creature with broad, childbearing hips. Within ten months she had given birth to a son. From this position of marital power she had importuned her husband. He had tried to resist her, for Bakhita was clever and loyal and with her business acumen he had doubled his fortune in five short years. However, in the end the mother of his son had prevailed. Sorrowfully he had spoken the dread words: '*Talaq! Talaq! Talaq!* I divorce thee!' Thus Bakhita had been cast into that terrible limbo of the Islamic world inhabited only by widows and divorced women.

The only paths that seemed open to her were to find an old husband with many wives who needed a slave without having to pay the headprice, or to sell herself as a plaything to passing men. But she had honed the wiles of a merchant while serving her husband. With the few coins she had saved she bought shards of ceramics and chipped, damaged images of the ancient gods from the Bedouin and from the orphans who scratched in the ruins, the dry riverbeds and nullahs of the desert, then sold them to the white tourists who came up the river on the steamers from the delta.

She paid a fair price, took a modest profit and kept her word, so soon the diggers and grave-robbers brought her porcelain and ceramics, religious statuettes, amulets and scarabs that, after four thousand years, were miraculously perfect. She learnt to decipher the hieroglyphics of the ancient priests on these relics, and the writings of the Greeks and Romans who came long after them; Alexander and the Ptolemy dynasty, Julius Caesar and Octavian who was also Augustus. In time her reputation spread wide. Men came to her little garden to trade and to talk. Some had travelled down the great river from as far afield as Equatoria and Suakin. With them they brought news and tidings that were almost as precious as the trade goods and the relics. Often the men talked more than they should have for she was very beautiful and they wanted her. But they could not have her: she trusted no man after what the man she had once trusted had done to her.

Bakhita learnt what was happening in every village along the course of the great river, and in the deserts that surrounded it. She knew when the sheikh of the Jaalin Arabs raided the Bishareen, and how many camels he stole. She knew how many slaves Zubeir Pasha sent down to Khartoum in his dhows, and the taxes and bribes he paid to the Egyptian governor in the city. She followed intimately the intrigues of the court of Emperor John in high Abyssinia, and the trade manifests in the ports of Suakin and Aden.

Then one day a small ragged urchin came to her with a coin wrapped in a filthy rag that was like no coin she had seen before or since. It filled the palm of her hand with the weight of fine gold. On the obverse was the portrait of a

101

crowned woman, and on the reverse a charioteer wearing a laurel wreath. The surfaces were so pristine that they seemed to have been struck the previous day. She was able to read the legend below each portrait readily. The couple on the coin were Cleopatra Thea Philopator and Marcus Antonius. She kept the coin and showed it to no one, until one day a man came into her shop. He was a Frank and for a while she was speechless, for in profile he was the image of the Antony on her coin. When he recovered her tongue, they talked for a while with Bakhita veiled and old Liala sitting in close attendance as chaperone. The stranger spoke beautiful poetic Arabic, and soon he did not seem to be a stranger. Without knowing it she began to trust him a little.

'I have heard that you are wise and virtuous, and that you may have items to sell that are beautiful and rare,' he asked at last.

She sent Liala away on some pretext, and when she poured another thimble of thick black coffee for her guest she contrived to let her veil slip so that he could glimpse her face. He started, and stared at her until she readjusted it. They went on speaking but something hung in the air, like the promise of thunder before the first winds of the *khamsin*.

Bakhita was gradually overtaken by an overpowering urge to show him the coin. When she placed it in his hand he studied the portraits gravely, then said, 'This is our coin. Yours and mine.' She bowed her head in silence and he said, 'Forgive me, I have offended you.'

She looked up at him and removed the veil so he could look into her eyes. 'You do not offend me, Effendi,' she whispered.

'Then why do your eyes fill with tears?'

'I weep because what you said is true. And I weep with joy.'

'You wish me to leave now?'

'No, I wish you to stay as long as your heart desires.'

'That may be a long time.'

'If it is God's will,' she agreed.

In the years that followed that first meeting she had given

him everything that was in her power to give, but in exchange had asked from him nothing that he would not give freely. She knew that one day he would leave her, for he was young and came from a world where she could never follow him. He had made her no promise. At their first meeting he had said, 'That may be a long time,' but he had never said, 'always'. So she did not try to exact a pact from him. The certainty of the ending added a poignancy to her love that was sweet as honey and bitter as the wild melon of the desert.

This day she sat with him and told him all she had learnt since they had last spoken twenty-six days before. He listened and asked questions, then wrote it all out on five pages from his despatch notebook. He did not need to consult a cipher for he had learnt by heart the code that Sir Evelyn Baring had given him.

Old Liala covered her head with her widow's cloak and slipped out into the alley carrying the despatch tucked into her intimate undergarments. The sergeant of the guard at the British military base knew her as a regular visitor. He was under strict orders from the base intelligence officer, so he personally escorted her to the headquarters building. Within the hour the message was buzzing down the telegraph line to Cairo. The following morning it had been deciphered by the signals clerk at the consulate and the *en clair* text was on the consul general's silver tray when he came in from breakfast.

Once she had sent Liala to the base with the report, Bakhita came back to Penrod. She knelt beside his stool and began to trim his sideburns and moustache. She worked quickly and, with the expertise of long practice, had soon reduced his fashionable whiskers to the ragged shape of a poor Arab *fellah*. Then she turned to his dense wavy curls and the tears slid down her cheeks as she hacked them away.

'They will soon grow again, my dove.' Penrod tried to console her as he ran his hand over the stubble.

'It is like murdering my own child,' she whispered. 'You were so beautiful.'

'And I will be beautiful again,' he assured her.

She gathered up his uniform from where it lay in the

corner of the room. 'I will not let even Liala touch it. I will wash it with my own hands,' she promised him. 'It will await your return, but never as eagerly as I.'

Then she brought the cloth bag in which she had kept his stained and ragged clothing from his last journey to the south. She wound the filthy turban round his cropped head. He strapped the leather purse round his waist and tucked the service revolver into the light canvas holster, then slipped the curved blade of the dagger into its sheath beside the Webley. They would not show under his dirty *galabiyya*. Then he strapped on a pair of rough camel-hide sandals and was ready to leave.

'Stay with God, honoured lady.' He bowed obsequiously and she was amazed at how easily he had made the transformation from swaggering Hussar to humble peasant, from *effendi* to *fellah*.

'Return to me soon,' she murmured, 'for if you perish, I shall perish with you.'

'I shall not perish,' he promised.

The harbour master took only a glance at the military travel pass before he assigned Penrod to the gang of stevedores on the next ammunition ship to leave for the south. Penrod wondered again if the elaborate precautions he was taking to avoid recognition were truly necessary. Then he reminded himself that the owner of almost every black or brown face in the swarming docks was a sympathizer of the Dervish. He knew also that he was a marked man. His heroics at El Obeid had been widely discussed, for they were the one blemish on a perfect victory for the Mahdi and his *khalifa*. Bakhita had warned him that when his name was uttered in the souks along the riverfront it was with a frown and a curse.

The steamer's cargo was made up entirely of military stores for the army, which was assembling at Wadi Halfa in preparation for the drive upriver. The loading continued all that night and most of the next day. It had been a long time since

Penrod had indulged in such hard and debilitating labour. A pause to straighten an aching back or even the slightest hesitation invited the flick and snap of the kurbash whip from one of the overseers. It required all his self-restraint to grovel to the blows and not retaliate with a clenched fist. The ship settled lower into the water as the heavy ammunition cases were heaped on her decks. At sunrise as she left the wharf, pulled into the channel of the river and thrust her ugly round bows into the current she had less than two feet of free board.

Penrod found a space between the tall piles of crates and stretched out in it. He clasped his skinned knuckles and raw fingers under his armpits. He ached in every joint and muscle. It was almost twenty hours' steaming against the stream to the port of Wadi Halfa. He slept for most of the voyage, and was fully recovered by the time they arrived early the next morning. Fourteen larger steamers were anchored in the main stream of the river. On the south bank was a vast encampment, lines of white canvas tents and mountainous piles of military stores. Boatloads of helmeted troops were being ferried out to the steamers by nuggars and small dhows.

Sir Evelyn Baring had explained the rescue-expedition plan in detail. This was the River Division of the double-pronged advance southwards. The flotilla was preparing to set out on the detour around the great western bend of the river. They would be forced to negotiate three dangerous cataracts along the way. The men going on board would have to tow the steamers on long lines from the bank through those boiling rock-strewn narrows.

Ahead of them, the Desert Column would travel swiftly across the bend of the Nile to Metemma, where Chinese Gordon's four little steamers were waiting to carry a small detachment of hand-picked men to Khartoum, to reinforce the city until the arrival of the main relief column.

The ammunition ship moored against the riverbank and the porters were immediately roused to begin offloading. Penrod was one of the first ashore and again his travel pass, when displayed to the subaltern in charge of the detail, worked its small miracle. He was allowed through. He picked his way through the encampment and was challenged often before he reached the guardpost at the entrance to the zareba that contained the Desert Column.

Its four regiments, commanded by General Sir Herbert Stewart, were drilling and exercising on the parade ground in preparation for the long trek across the loop. But it might be weeks or even months before they received the final marching orders from London.

The sergeant of the guard must have been forewarned of Penrod's arrival for he did not quibble when the dirty Arab labourer addressed him in the idiom of the officers' mess, and demanded to be taken to the adjutant's tent.

'Ah, Ballantyne! I received the telegraph from Colonel Adams in Cairo, but I didn't expect you for three or four days yet. You have made good time.' Major Kenwick shook hands, but refrained from mentioning Penrod's unusual garb. Like most of the senior officers he was rather fond of this young scamp, but a little envious of his escapades. He seemed to have a knack of popping up whenever the bullets were flying and promotion was in the air.

'Thank you, Major. Do you know, by any chance, if my men are here?'

'Yes, damn it! And that sergeant of yours has helped himself to five of my best camels. If I had not been firm he would have made off with a whole troop.'

'I'll be on my way, then, if you'll excuse me, sir.'

'So soon? I rather hoped that we might have the pleasure of your company in the mess for dinner this evening.'

Penrod saw that he was eaten up with curiosity about this mysterious visitation. 'I'm in rather a hurry, sir.'

'Perhaps we might see you in Khartoum, then?' The adjutant kept fishing resolutely.

'Oh, I doubt it, sir. Shall we agree to meet at the Long Bar of the Gheziera Club when this little business has been settled?'

Sergeant al-Saada was waiting for him at the camel lines. Many eyes were watching so his greeting was cold and dismissive, a measure of the wide social chasm between a sergeant in a regiment of the Queen, and a common *fellah*. They rode into the dunes, Penrod trailing behind him on the grey she-camel. His spirits surged as she moved under him: he knew at once that al-Saada had chosen a wind-eater for him. As soon as they were out of sight of the camp al-Saada reined in. As Penrod came up alongside him his forbidding expression split in a flashing grin, and he snapped his clenched fist across his chest in the riding salute. 'I saw you on the deck of the steamer when she came round Ras Indera. You have travelled fast, Abadan Riji.' The name meant the One Who Never Turns Back. 'I told Yakub you would be here in less than five days.'

'Fast I came,' Penrod agreed, 'but even faster must we go.'

Yakub was waiting for them a mile further on. He had the other camels couched behind an outcrop of black rock. Their shapes were rendered grotesque by the waterskins they carried, like huge black cancerous growths on their backs. Each camel was capable of carrying five hundred pounds, but in the Mother of Stones desert each man needed two gallons of water every day to stay alive. As they dismounted Yakub hurried to greet Penrod. He went down on one knee and touched his lips and his heart. 'Faithful Yakub has waited for you since Kurban Bairam.'

'I see you, Beloved of Allah.' Penrod smiled back at him. 'But did you forget my pack?'

Yakub looked pained. He ran back, untied it from one of the camels and brought it to him. Penrod unrolled it on the baked earth. He saw that his *galabiyya* had been freshly laundered. Swiftly he changed his rags for the fine wool robe that would protect him from the sun. He covered his face with the black cotton headdress in the fashion of the Bedouin, and tied the black sash round his waist. He tucked the curved dagger and the Webley revolver into the sash over his right hip, and his cavalry sabre on the opposite hip to balance them. Then he drew the sabre from its plain leather scabbard and tested the edge. It stung like a cut-throat razor and he nodded approval at Yakub. Then he made a few practice strokes with the steel, cutting to both sides, lunging high and low, recovering instantly. The sabre felt good in his hand and seemed to take on a life of its own. In this age of breech-loading rifles and heavy ordnance Penrod still revelled in the *arme blanche*.

Almost every Arab carried the long broadsword, and Penrod had observed their use of the blade in contrast to his own. The heavy weapon did not suit the Arab physique. Unlike the mailed crusaders from whom the heavy blade had been copied they were not big, powerful men: they were terriers rather than mastiffs. They were devils to cut and lunge, and the broadsword could inflict a terrible wound. But they were slow to recover their blade. They did not understand the parry, and they used their round leather shield almost exclusively to defend themselves. Against a skilled swordsman they were vulnerable to a feint high in the natural line. Their instinctive response was to lift the shield and to lose sight of the opponent's point, and they would not see the thrust that followed the feint like a thunderbolt. At El Obeid when the square had broken and the Dervish had swarmed in, Penrod had killed five in as many minutes with that ploy. He ran the blade back into its scabbard and asked Yakub, 'Is the Mother of Stones open?'

'There is water at Marbad Tegga.' In the Taka dialect, the well's name meant Camel Killer. 'Little and bitter, but just sufficient for the camels,' Yakub replied.

Yakub was a Jaalin Arab who had been driven from the tents of his people by a blood feud that started in a quarrel over dishonour to Yakub's sister. Yakub was quick and expert with the blade and the man had died. However, he had been the son of a powerful sheikh. Yakub had been forced to flee for his life.

One of Yakub's eyes gazed in a different direction from the other. The ringlets that dangled from under his turban were greasy and his teeth, when he smiled at Penrod, were yellow and crooked. He knew and understood the desert and the mountains with the instinct of a wild ass. Before he had been driven out of the tribe he had taken a knife wound that had left him with a limp. Because of this affliction he had been refused service in the armies of the Queen and the Khedive. Thus, with no tribe and no other master, Penrod was all he had. Yakub loved him like a father and a god.

'So we can still cut the snake?'

When Penrod posed a question of such weight, Yakub gave it all his respect and attention. He tucked the skirts of his *galabiyya* between his legs and squatted. With his camel goad he scratched a large figure S in the dirt, but the upper loop was smaller by half than the lower. It was a rough charting of the course of the Nile from where they stood to the mouth of the Shabluka Gorge. To follow the riverbank through this serpentine meandering would add many weeks to the journey. This, of course, was the route that the flotilla of the River Division would be forced to take. The Desert Division, on their camels, would cut across the great loop and regain the river at Metemma. This shortcut was well marked by the caravans of the ages and by the bleached bones they had left behind them. There were two wells along the way that gave the traveller just sufficient water to make the crossing. Once they reached Metemma they could follow the upper limb of the Nile, keeping always in sight of the river as it swung back west again, until eventually it settled once more on its southerly course and headed for Khartoum. It was a hard road, but there was a harder one yet. The caravan masters called it 'cutting the snake'.

Yakub made a bold slash with the goad, drawing a straight line from their present position directly to the city of Khartoum. The line cut the S bend of the river neatly in half. It saved hundreds of miles of bitter, gruelling travel. But the trail was unmarked and to take a wrong turning meant missing the single well of Marbad Tegga, and finding instead a certain, terrible death. The well lay deep in the furnace-hot belly of the Mother of Stones, and it was well hidden. It would be easy to pass it by a hundred paces and never know it was there. The camels could drink the water, but its caustic salts would drive a man mad. Once they had watered the camels at Marbad Tegga it was still another hundred miles to the bank of the Nile at Korti below the fourth cataract. Long before they reached the river all the water in the skins would be finished. They might be twenty-four hours without a drop before they saw the Nile again, longer than that if the *djinni* of the desert were unkind to them.

Once they reached the riverbank, they must cross the river. At this point the current was swift, the stream was a mile wide and the camels were reluctant swimmers. But there was a ford known to few. Once they had crossed, drunk their fill and recharged the waterskins, they would be forced to leave the Nile again and face the Monassir desert on the other bank, another two hundred waterless miles. Yakub reiterated all this, drawing it all on the earth with his goad. Penrod listened without interruption: although he had cut the snake three times before and won through to the river crossing at Korti, there was always something fresh to learn from Yakub.

When he had explained it all Yakub announced, 'With the fearless and cunning Yakub to guide you, and angels to watch over you, perchance we may indeed cut the snake.' Then he rocked back on his haunches and waited for Penrod to make the decision.

Penrod had been considering the gamble while he was talking. He would never have attempted it without Yakub. With him to lead, the gains in time and distance to reach Khartoum were worth the gamble, but there was another even more telling consideration.

Bakhita had told him that the Mahdi and his *khalifa* were well aware of the British preparations to rescue Gordon. Their spies had kept them fully informed of the concentration of British regiments and the flotilla at Wadi Halfa. She said that the Mahdi had ordered a dozen of the most important emirs to leave the siege of Khartoum and take their tribes north-wards along the river, to contest the way, to meet the enemy at Metemma, Abu Klea and Abu Hamed. She said that already both banks of the river from Khartoum down to the first great bend were swarming with Arab horsemen and camel troops.

'The Mahdi knows that he must stop the Franks before they reach the city.' She used the word that described all Europeans. 'He knows that their army is small and poorly equipped with horses and camels. They say he has sent twenty thousand men northwards to meet the British and to hold the river line until Low Nile, when he can complete the destruction of Khartoum and send General Gordon's head to his queen.' She had added, 'Be careful, my dear lord. They have cut the telegraph lines to the north and they know that the generals in Cairo must send messengers to Khartoum to keep in contact with the general. The Mahdi will be expecting you to try to win through to the city. His men will be waiting to intercept you.'

'Yes, they will be looking for us to cross the loop, but will they guard the road to Marbad Tegga, I wonder?' Penrod mused aloud. Yakub shook his head for he had no English. Penrod switched back into Arabic: 'In God's name, brave Yakub, take us to the bitter well of the Camel Killer.'

They mounted up on the high wooden saddles. Penrod checked the rifle in its scabbard under his leg, and the bandolier of ammunition tied to the crosspiece of the saddle, then prodded the grey camel. Groaning and spitting, she lurched to her feet.

'In God's Name let us begin,' sang al-Saada.

'May He open our eyes to make the way clear,' Yakub cried. 'And may He make the Camel Killer plain for us to behold.'

'God is great.' Penrod said. 'There is no other God but God.'

Each led a pack camel and the water sloshed softly in the skins. At first, loose equipment squeaked or clattered to the rocking gait of the camels, but quickly they readjusted the straps and bindings that held the burdens. Once they stopped briefly and bled the air from the waterskins so that they no longer gurgled. When they went onwards it was in silence, a weird and unnatural silence in the void of heat and unfathomable horizons. The spongy pads of the camels' feet fell soundlessly on the sands. The men wrapped their heads so

111

that only the slits of their eyes showed and they did not speak. They slumped low on the tall wooden saddles and gave themselves over to the rhythm of the camels' gait.

They followed the ancient caravan road across a level expanse of orange-coloured sand that glowed in the sunlight until their eyes ached with the glare. The way was only faintly marked by the pale bones and desiccated carcasses of long-dead camels, preserved by sun so that some might have lain there for centuries. The air they breathed scalded and abraded the lining of the throat. The horizon wavered and dissolved in the silver lake of the mirage. The camels and their riders seemed to hang in space and though they rode forward as soundlessly as wraiths, they seemed never to move against the shimmering background. The only point of reference was the tenuous outline of the caravan trail, but even that seemed not to be attached to the earth but to rise up before them like a drifting tendril of smoke.

Penrod let himself lapse into the mesmeric trance of the desert voyager. Time was suspended and lost all significance. His mind ranged free and he thought how easy it would be to believe, as the Bedouin did, in the supernatural powers that inhabited this otherworldly landscape. He dreamed of the jinn, and of the ghosts of lost armies that had perished in these sands. Though Yakub was only half a pistol shot ahead of him he seemed at times to be as distant as the mirage, fluttering like a sparrow on the wings of his robe. At other times he loomed gigantically on the back of his elephantine beast, swollen and elongated by the treacherous play of light. On they went, and silently on.

Slowly something began to appear before them, a mighty pyramid that dwarfed the man-made constructions of the delta. It quivered in the silver mirage, detached from earth, hanging inverted above the horizon, balancing on its point with the flat base filling the southern sky. Penrod stared at it in awe, and again his credibility was taxed as it shrank swiftly, disappearing to a dark spot, then began to grow again, this time with its pointed summit uppermost and its base anchored to the earth.

They rode on and now it assumed its true form, a cone-shaped hill with two smaller ones standing close behind it. In a clairvoyant flash Penrod perceived that natural features such as these must have been the model for those other man-made pyramids that had astonished mankind over the ages. The caravan trail ran straight towards them, but before they reached the first Yakub turned aside, leaving the trail on the left hand. He led them forward into a wilderness that was no longer marked by the faintest trace of man or of his passing. This was the hidden way to Marbad Tegga.

Penrod was lulled back into the hypnotic suspension of time and feeling, and the hours passed as the sun made its noon and began its fiery descent to earth. At last he was roused by the altered gait of his she-camel. He looked around quickly and saw how the landscape had changed. The sand was no longer orange but ashen grey and seared. On the horizon all around were heaps of volcanic ash and lava several hundred feet high, as though all the worlds of the universe had been cremated and their remains dumped in this infernal cemetery and covered by these forbidding tumuli. The breath of ancient volcanoes had charred the very desert. There was no vestige of vegetation or of any living thing, except the three men and their pacing beasts.

Penrod saw why his mount's gait had changed. The earth was thickly littered with boulders and stones. Some were as large and perfect as round shot for heavy cannon, and others as small as musket balls. It was like the detritus of some long-forgotten battlefield. But Penrod knew that these were not the munitions of war. These rocks were the efflorescence left over from the eruption of the volcanoes. The liquid lava had been expelled into the sky in a deadly rain. As it fell back to earth it had cooled and solidified into these shapes. The camels were forced to pick their way across this dangerous footing, and their speed was much reduced.

The sun sank, and as it touched the earth it seemed to erupt in an explosion of green and crimson light, then fall away to give the world over to sudden night.

'Sweet night!' Penrod whispered, and felt his lip crack.

113

'Blessed cool night!' They couched the camels and fed them a small ration of crushed dhurra meal, then checked their harness and saddles for any sign of galling or chafing. While the men laid out their prayer mats and prostrated themselves towards Mecca, Penrod walked out into the desolation to loosen his cramped muscles and stiff joints. He listened to the night, but the only sound was the evening breeze along the dunes, whispering with the voices of the jinn.

When he returned Yakub was brewing coffee on the tiny brazier. They drank three cups each, and ate dates with thin rounds of dhurra biscuit. They anointed their lips and exposed skin with mutton fat to prevent them flaking and cracking. Then they lay down beside the camels and slept. Yakub roused them after two hours' rest. They mounted and went on southwards in the night.

The heavens were brilliant with stars, such a profusion that it was difficult to find the major navigational bodies in the silver dazzle. The air was cool and tasted sweet, but it was so dry that it baked the mucus in Penrod's nasal passages into pellets hard as buckshot.

Hour after hour the camels paced on. At intervals Penrod swung down from the saddle and strode along beside his mount, to rest her and stretch his legs. They stopped again before dawn, drank hot, unsweetened coffee, slept for an hour, then remounted and went on with the sun coming up on their left hand. The first rays struck and they quailed beneath the tyranny, covering their heads.

The desert was never the same. It changed its character and aspect as subtly as a beautiful courtesan, but always it was dangerous and deceptive. At times the dunes were soft and fleshy, pale ivory as the breasts and belly of a dancing girl, then turned the colour of ripe apricots. They flowed like the rollers of the ocean, or writhed together as sinuously as mating serpents. Then they collapsed over jagged escarpments of rock.

The hours and the miles fell behind them. When they paused to rest in the shade of the waterskins, it was often too hot to sleep. They lay and panted like dogs, then went on. The camels groaned and bellowed softly when they were couched and again when they were forced to their feet to resume the march. Their humps shrivelled. On the fifth day they refused to eat the small ration of dhurra meal that Yakub offered on the straw feeding mats.

'That is the first sign that they are nearing the limit of their strength,' Yakub warned Penrod. 'We must reach the well before dusk tomorrow evening. If we do not they will begin to die.'

It was not necessary to speak of the consequences for the men if the camels failed. The following morning, as they paused on the rim of a deep saucer of ground, Penrod pointed ahead. Along the opposite rim a frieze of gazelle stood in silhouette. They were as tiny and dainty as creatures in a dream, the colours of cream and milk chocolate, with lyre-shaped horns and white masked faces. After a moment they disappeared down the far side of the ridge as silently as if they had never existed.

'They drink at Marbad Tegga. We are close now.' It was the first time Yakub had spoken in many hours. 'We will be there before sunset.' He squinted with satisfaction.

At noon the camels refused to couch. They grumbled and moaned and shook their heads. 'They have smelt the water. They are eager to go to it,' said Yakub happily. 'They will lead us to the well like hunting dogs to the quarry.' As soon as the men had prayed and drunk their coffee, all three mounted again and rode on.

The camels quickened their pace and moaned with excitement as the scent of the water grew stronger in their nostrils. When they stopped again in the late afternoon Penrod recognized the terrain ahead from the last time he had passed that way. It was a fantastic array of shale hillocks, sculpted by wind and the ages into a gallery of weird shapes and fanciful carvings. Some resembled marching armies of stone warriors, others were crouching lions, and there were winged dragons, gnomes and jinn. But above them all stood a tall, striking column of stone that resembled a woman in a long robe and a widow's veil in an attitude of mourning.

'There is the Widow of Ahab,' said Yakub, 'and she faces

towards the well where her husband died.' He prodded his mount with the long goad and they started forward again, the camels even more eager than their riders.

'Wait!' Penrod shouted urgently, and when Yakub and al-Saada looked back he stopped them with a peremptory gesture. He turned his own camel into a shallow wadi that hid them completely. They followed him unhesitatingly. They had to wrestle with the camels to force them to couch, goading and twisting their testicles before they sank down, bellowing in protest. Then they hobbled them with rawhide ropes so they were unable to rise again. Al-Saada stayed to guard them, and make certain they did not try to break away to reach the water. Then Penrod led Yakub to the top of the ridge and they found a vantage-point among the shale hills. Penrod lay stretched on his belly and panned his field-glasses over the rugged ground beyond the Widow of Ahab. Yakub lay beside him, squinting hideously into the sunset. After a long wait he muttered, 'There is nothing but the sand and the rocks. You saw a shadow, Abadan Riji. Not even a jinn would inhabit this place,' and he began to stand up.

'Get down, imbecile,' Penrod snapped. They were silent and unmoving for another half an hour. Then Penrod handed Yakub the field-glasses. 'There is your jinnee.'

Yakub stared through the lens, then started and exclaimed when he picked out the distant shape of the man. Sitting in the shade at the base of one of the shale monoliths, he had been invisible. Only the pinprick of reflected light on the blade of the sword he was honing had alerted Penrod to his presence. Now he came to his feet and walked out into the slanting sunlight, an alien shape in the brooding landscape.

'I see him, Abadan Riji,' Yakub conceded. 'Your eyes are bright. He wears the patched *jibba* of the Mahdists. Is there more than one?'

'You can be certain of it,' Penrod murmured. 'Men do not travel alone in this place.'

'A scouting party?' Yakub hazarded. 'Spies sent to wait for the soldiers to come?'

'They know that the well of the Camel Killer is too small

and the waters too bitter to supply a regiment. They are waiting to intercept messengers carrying despatches to Gordon Pasha in Khartoum. They know there is no other road. They know that we have to come this way.'

'They are guarding the water. We cannot go on without water for the camels.'

'No,' Penrod agreed. 'We must kill them. None must escape to warn those men of our passing.' He stood up and, using the cover of the hillock, went back to where al-Saada waited with the camels. They dared not brew coffee while they waited for night to fall, for the smell of the smoke might carry to the enemy and betray their presence. Instead they drank water sparingly from the skins, and sharpened their blades as they ate the evening meal of dates. Then the Arabs spread their mats and prayed.

Darkness fell hot and heavy as a woollen cloak over the hills, but Penrod waited until Orion the Hunter was at his zenith in the southern sky before they left the camels and went forward on foot, Penrod leading with the Webley in the sash at his waist and the bared sabre in his right hand. They had done this many times before and they moved well separated but always in contact. Penrod circled downwind of the spot at which they had last seen the Dervish sentinel, and was grateful for the evening breeze, which covered any small sounds they might make as they closed in. He smelt them first, the smoke of their brazier, the sharp odour of burning camel dung. He snapped his fingers softly to alert Yakub and al-Saada, and saw them crouch obediently, dark blobs in the starlight behind him.

He crept forward again, into the wind, keeping the smoke directly ahead. He stopped when he heard a camel belch and grumble softly. He lay flat against the earth and peered ahead, waiting with the patience of the hunter. His eyes scanned slowly over the broken ground in front of him, picking out every rock and irregularity. Then something changed shape and his eyes flicked back to it. It was small, dark and round, not twenty paces ahead. It moved again and he recognized it as a human head. A sentry was sitting just over the lip of a

117

shallow nullah. Although it was after midnight the man was still awake and alert. Penrod smelt Yakub beside him, the odour of sweat, snuff and camels, and felt his breath warm in his ear. 'I have seen him, and it is past time for him to die.'

Penrod squeezed his arm in assent, and Yakub slithered forward silently as a desert adder. He was an artist with the dagger. His shape merged with the rocks and star shadows. Penrod watched the sentry's head, and suddenly another appeared behind it. For a moment they became a single dark patch. Then there was a soft exhalation of breath and both heads sank from view. Penrod waited but there was no outcry or alarm. Then Yakub came out of the nullah with his peculiar crablike limp. He sank down beside his master.

'There are five more. They are sleeping with their camels in the bottom of the nullah.'

'Are the camels in harness?' He needed not have asked. The men were warriors and would be ready to jump into the saddle and ride the moment they were roused.

'The camels are saddled. The men sleep with their weapons beside them.'

'Is there another sentry?'

'I did not see one.'

'Where is the well?'

'They have not been foolish enough to camp beside the water. It is three or four hundred paces in that direction.' Yakub pointed to the right end of the hidden nullah.

'So, if there is another man he will be there, watching the water.' Penrod thought for a few moments, then snapped his fingers again. Al-Saada came to crouch beside them.

'I will wait between the camp and the well to watch for another sentry. The two of you will go in and make a place in Paradise for these sons of the Mahdi.' Penrod tapped each of them on the shoulder, an affirmation and a blessing. They were better at this kind of close work than he was. He was never able to suppress his squeamishness when he had to kill a sleeping man. 'Wait until I am in position.'

Penrod moved out swiftly to the right. He reached the rim of the nullah and looked down into it. He saw the body of the man Yakub had killed lying under the lip. The man's knees were drawn up to his chest and Yakub had covered his head with his turban to make it appear that he had fallen asleep at his post. Further on, the men and animals on the floor of the nullah were a dark huddle, and he could not tell one from another. Yakub must have crawled in close to count them. He moved into the shadow of a boulder from where he could keep an eye on the nullah and cover any approach from the direction of the well.

He felt his nerves tingle as, first, Yakub and then al-Saada slipped over into the nullah below him. They blended with the mass of men and animals, and he could imagine the bloody knifework as they moved swiftly from one sleeping man to the next. Then, suddenly, there was a ringing scream and his nerves jumped tight. One had missed his stroke, and he knew it was not Yakub. There was instant confusion as the quiescent mass of bodies exploded into violent movement and sound. Camels lurched, bellowing, to their feet, men shouted and steel clashed on steel. He saw a man spring on to the back of one of the animals and burst out of the camp, riding up over the far wall of the nullah. Another Dervish escaped from the mêlée and bounded to the bottom of the nullah; he had gone only a short way when a figure raced after him in the unmistakable crablike style that covered the ground with deceptive speed. The two disappeared almost at once.

Penrod was poised to run down into the nullah and join in the fighting, when he heard footsteps behind him and stayed low. In the starlight he saw another figure running towards him from the direction of the Widow of Ahab. This must be the second Dervish sentry. He was carrying his sword in his right hand and his shield on the other shoulder. When he was too close to escape, Penrod jumped into his path. The Dervish did not hesitate but charged at him, swinging with the long blade. Penrod parried easily, steel resounding on steel, and feinted at his head. The Dervish lifted his shield to counter the blow, and instantly Penrod sent his blade home, a classic straight thrust into the centre of his chest so that the blade went clean through, and shot out two hands' span from the

119

back of his ribs. With almost the same movement he cleared and recovered his blade, and the Dervish dropped without a cry.

Penrod left him and raced down the bank into the nullah. He saw al-Saada stooped over a fallen body, slashing with his dagger across his victim's throat; black blood sprayed from the severed artery. Al-Saada straightened and looked about him, but his movements were sluggish. Three corpses were lying where they had slept.

'Botched! Two have got away,' Penrod snapped angrily. 'Yakub has chased one, but the other is mounted. We must go after him.'

Al-Saada took a pace towards Penrod and the blood-smeared dagger fell from his hand. He sagged slowly to his knees. The starlight was bright enough for Penrod to make out his expression of surprise.

'He was too quick,' al-Saada said, his speech slurred. He took his other hand away from his chest and looked down at himself. The blood from the wound under his ribs darkened his robe to the knees. 'Chase him, Abadan Riji. I will follow you in a little while,' he said, and toppled on to his face. Penrod hesitated only a moment as he fought his instinct to aid al-Saada. But he could tell by the loose-limbed way in which he had fallen that he was already beyond any help that he could give, and if he allowed the Dervish to escape his own chances of getting through to the besieged city would be seriously threatened.

'Go with God, Saada,' he said softly, as he turned away. He ran to the nearest Dervish camel and mounted it. With his sabre he cut free the knee halter. The camel reared on to its feet and plunged into a gallop that carried them up over the rim of the nullah. He could just make out the shadowy shape of the other camel flitting ahead, like a moth in the starlight. Within a few hundred paces he had adjusted to the pace of the animal beneath him. It seemed strong and willing, and it must have been well watered and fed during the vigil at the Marbad Tegga. He used his body to urge it forward, like a jockey pushing for the post. A quick glance at the stars confirmed what he already knew: that the fugitive was heading directly south towards the nearest point on the Nile.

They covered another mile, then Penrod realized that the Dervish had slowed his camel to a trot. Either he had been wounded in the skirmish, he was unaware that he was being followed or he was saving his mount for the long and terrible journey that lay ahead if he hoped to reach the river. Penrod urged his own camel to its top speed, and closed the gap swiftly.

He was beginning to think that he might still come up with the Dervish before he realized his danger, but suddenly he saw the pale flash of the man's face turned back over his shoulder. The moment he spotted Penrod he lashed out with his goad and urged on his mount with sharp cries. The two camels ran as though linked together, down through a dry wadi and up the stony ridge beyond. Then, gradually, Penrod's mount began to exert its superior speed and stamina and closed in remorselessly. Penrod angled slightly across the enemy's rear, planning to come in on his left, gambling on the chance that he was right-handed and would be least able to defend himself on this side.

Suddenly, unexpectedly, the Dervish swung his camel at a right angle from its track, and brought it plunging to a halt only a hundred paces ahead. As he swivelled on the high wooden saddle Penrod saw that he had a rifle in his hands, and was lifting it to level it at him. He had thought the Arab was carrying only his sword, and had not considered the possibility that there might be a weapon in the gun-scabbard behind the saddle.

'Come on, then, you eater of pork!' Penrod shouted, and reached for the Webley tucked into his sash. The range was too long for the weapon, and the back of a running camel was not a steady platform from which to fire, but he must try to spoil his opponent's aim so he could get close enough for the blade.

The Arab fired from the back of the standing camel. Penrod knew from the muzzle flash of black powder and the distinctive booming report that he faced a Martini-Henry carbine, probably one of those captured at El Obeid or Suakin. A fraction of a second later the heavy lead bullet tore into flesh and the camel stumbled beneath him. The Dervish whirled away, bowed over the carbine as he tried to feed another cartridge into the breech. Riding hard Penrod came up on his left-hand side with the sabre at cavalry point. The Arab realized he could not reload in time and let the carbine drop. He reached over his shoulder and drew the broadsword from the scabbard strapped across his back. He stared across at Penrod, and started back in the saddle with the shock of recognition.

'I know thee, infidel!' he shouted, 'I saw thee on the field of El Obeid. Thou art Abadan Riji. I curse thee and thy foul, three-headed God.' He aimed a heavy cross-bladed cut at the head of Penrod's camel. At the last moment Penrod checked his beast and the stroke went high. The blade lopped off one of the animal's ears close to the skull and the camel shied to one side. Penrod steadied it, but felt it stumble as the bullet wound in its chest began to weaken it. The Dervish was just beyond the reach of his sabre and although he thrust at him he could not touch him. His camel groaned. Suddenly its front legs collapsed, and it went down in a tangle. Penrod kicked his legs clear and landed on his feet, managing to stay upright.

By the time he had recovered his balance the Dervish on his camel was a hundred paces ahead and drawing away swiftly. Penrod snatched the Webley revolver from his sash and emptied the magazine after the dwindling shapes of rider and camel. There was no thumping sound of a bullet strike to encourage him. Within seconds they had dissolved into the darkness. Penrod cocked his head to listen, but there was only the sound of the wind.

His camel was struggling weakly to regain its feet, but suddenly it emitted a hollow roar and rolled over on to its back kicking its huge padded feet convulsively in the air. Then it collapsed and stretched out flat against the earth, its head thrust forward. It was breathing heavily and Penrod saw twin streams of blood spurt from its nostrils each time it exhaled. He reloaded the Webley, stooped over the dying animal, he pressed the muzzle to the back of its skull and fired a single shot into its brain. He took another few minutes to search the saddle-bags for anything of importance, but there were no maps or documents, except for a dog-eared copy of the Koran, which he kept. He found only a bag of dried meat and dhurra cakes, which would supplement their frugal rations.

He turned away from the carcass and set off along his own tracks back towards Marbad Tegga. He had covered barely half a mile when he saw another camel and rider coming towards him. He knelt in ambush behind a patch of jagged black rock, but as the rider came up he recognized Yakub and called to him.

'Praise the Name of Allah!' Yakub rejoiced. 'I heard a shooting.'

Penrod scrambled up behind his saddle and they turned back towards Marbad Tegga. 'My man escaped,' he admitted. 'He had a rifle and he killed my mount.'

'My man did not escape, but he died well. He was a warrior and I honour his memory.' Yakub said flatly. 'But al-Saada is dead also. He deserved to die for his clumsiness.'

Penrod did not answer. He knew there had been little love lost between them, for although they were both Muslims, al-Saada was an Egyptian and Yakub a Jaalin Arab.

In the bank of the nullah beyond the enemy camp Penrod found a deep cleft in the rocks and laid al-Saada in it. He wrapped his head in his cloak and laid the captured Koran on his chest. Then they piled loose shale over him. It was a simple burial but in accord with his religion. It did not take long, and neither spoke as they worked.

When they were done, they hurried back to the Dervish camp, and set about making preparations to continue the journey. 'If we go swiftly we might still pass through the enemy lines before the alarm is spread by the one who got away.'

The captured camels were all fat, well watered and rested. They transferred their saddles to them, and turned loose their own exhausted animals to find the water in Marbad Tegga, then make their way to the distant river. In the Dervish waterskins they had more sweet Nile water than two men needed. Among the provisions they found more bags of dhurra meal, dates and dried meat.

'Now we have supplies enough to win through to Khartoum,' Penrod said, with satisfaction.

'They will expect us to head for the ford of the river at Korti, but I know of another crossing further to the west, below the cataract,' Yakub told him.

They mounted two of the fresh animals and, leading three others loaded with bulging waterskins, rode on southwards.

They rested through the middle of each day, lying in the meagre strip of shade cast by the animals. The camels were couched in direct sunlight, which would have brought the blood of any other man or beast to the boil but they showed no discomfort. As soon as the tyranny of the sun abated, they rode on through the evening and the night. In the dawn of the third day, while the eternal lamp of the morning star still burned above the horizon, Penrod left Yakub with the camels and climbed to the top of a conical hill, the only feature in this burnt-out, desolate world.

By the time he reached the summit, day had broken, and an extraordinary sight awaited him. Two miles ahead, something white as salt and graceful as the wing of a gull glided across this ocean of sterile sand and rock. He knew what it was before he lifted the field-glasses to his eyes. He stared at the single bulging lateen sail, which seemed so out of place in such a setting. He wasted a little more time revelling in the sense of relief and accomplishment that settled over him: the white wing of the dhow sailed upon the waters of the Nile.

They approached the river with the utmost caution. While the terrors of the Mother of Stones were behind them, a new menace lay ahead: men. The dhow had passed out of sight downstream. When they reached the riverbank it was deserted, revealing no sign of human habitation. Only a flock of white egrets flew eastwards in an arrowhead formation, low across the steely waters. There was a narrow fringe of vegetation along each bank, a few clumps of reed, scraggy palms and a single magnificent sycamore tree with its roots almost planted in the mud at the edge. An ancient mud-brick tomb had been built in its shade. The plaster was cracked and lumps had fallen out of the walls. Faded coloured ribbons fluttered from the spreading branches above it.

'That is the tree of St al-Maula, a holy hermit who lived at this place a hundred years ago,' said Yakub. 'Pilgrims have placed those ribbons in his honour so that the saint might remember them and grant any boon they seek. We are two leagues west of the ford, and the village of Korti lies about the same distance to the east.'

They turned away from the riverbank so that they would not be seen by the crews of any passing dhows and made their way westward through wadis and tumbled hillocks until they reached a tall stone bluff that overlooked a long stretch of the Nile. For the rest of that day, they kept their vigil from the summit of the cliff.

Although the Nile was the main artery of trade and travel for an area larger than the whole of western Europe, not another vessel passed, and there was no sign of any human presence along this section of the banks. This alone made Penrod uneasy. Something must have disrupted all commerce along the river. He was almost certain that this was what Bakhita had warned him of, and that somewhere close by a massive movement of the Dervish armies was under way. He wanted to get across into the wastes of the Monassir desert as soon as possible, and to keep well away from the banks until he was opposite the city of Khartoum and could make a final dash into Gordon's beleaguered stronghold.

When the angle of the sun altered, it penetrated the water, and the darker outline of the shallows was just visible. A submerged spur of rock pushed half-way across the stream, and from the opposite side an extensive mudbank spread out to meet it. The channel between the two shallows was deep green but narrow, less than a hundred and fifty paces across. Penrod memorized its position carefully. If they used the empty waterskins as life-buoys, they could swim the camels across the deeper section. Of course, they must cross in darkness. They would be terribly vulnerable if they were caught in midstream in broad daylight, should a Dervish dhow appear unexpectedly. Once they had reached the far bank they could refill the skins and press on into the Monassir.

In the last hour of daylight Penrod left Yakub with the animals on the heights of the bluff and went down alone to examine the bank for tracks. After casting well up- and downstream he was satisfied that no large contingents of enemy troops had passed recently.

As darkness fell Yakub brought down the string of camels. He had emptied the last of the water from the skins, blown them up and stoppered them again. Each camel had a pair of these huge black balloons strapped to its flanks. They were roped together in two strings so that they would not become separated in the water.

The camels jibbed at entering the water but Penrod and Yakub goaded them down the bank and out on to the spur. As they headed into the middle of the Nile the water rose until it reached the men's chins, and they had to cling to the camel harness. The long legs and necks of the beasts allowed them to cross almost to the far side before they lost their footing and were forced to swim awkwardly. But the water-skins buoyed them up, and Penrod and Yakub swam beside them, urging them on and pointing their heads in the right direction, taking care to keep clear of their driving front legs below the surface. They swam them to the mudbank on the far side, and when they had regained their footing led them out on to dry ground. Quickly they refilled the waterskins and gave the camels their last drink for many days.

The crossing had taken longer than Penrod had bargained on, and the eastern sky was already paling before they were ready to leave the Nile, the skins filled tight and the camels' bellies swollen with water. Before they set out they tried to obliterate their tracks from the riverbank, but with that number of heavily laden animals and working in darkness it was impossible. They had to take a chance that the wind and the river waters would wipe away their tracks before they were discovered by Dervish scouts.

However, a dark premonition of evil rode on Penrod's shoulders as they headed out into the Monassir desert. After a few hours' travel the feeling grew so pervasive that he knew he must sweep the back trail to reassure himself that their crossing had not been discovered. He picked out the fleetest, most willing animal from their string – by now they knew each beast well by temperament and capability. He sent Yakub ahead with the others while he returned along their back trail. When he was still some miles from the river, he left the trail and headed for a line of low hills he had noticed earlier that overlooked the river. He couched and tethered his mount below the skyline, then crept forward. As he neared the crest of the hill he dropped to his belly, slithered up behind an outcrop of rocks and peered down into the valley of the Nile. His heart jumped against his ribs, and his nerves whipped tight at what he saw below him.

A small party of Dervish scouts was dismounted on the near bank of the Nile, and it was obvious that they had discovered the spoor as it emerged from the water. Through the field-glasses he studied the enemy intently. There were six of them. He thought that one might be the man he had chased from Marbad Tegga, but he could not be certain. They were all lean, hard desert Arabs, probably of the Beja tribe. They wore the gaily patched *jibbas* of the Mahdists, and carried the distinctive round targes and long-sheathed swords. They were leaning on the shafts of their spears and animatedly discussing the tracks on the bank. One turned and pointed south along the run of the spoor, and they all looked in the direction he had indicated. They seemed to be gazing directly towards the spot where Penrod lay.

He ducked behind the rocks while he assessed his situation. It seemed obvious that the man he had chased from Marbad Tegga, even if that was not him down there, had reached the river ahead of them. He must have spread the warning to

127

the forward elements of the main Dervish army coming down from the north. Perhaps one of the commanding emirs had sent this scouting party ahead to reconnoitre the river crossings and intercept them. Penrod could tell at a glance that these were aggagiers, the finest Dervish warriors. He and Yakub were outnumbered by three to one, and the Dervish were on the alert. He put out of his mind any notion of a fight. Their only salvation lay in flight.

Now he switched his attention from the men to their mounts. Each rode a handsome horse. They had only one pack camel to carry the leather bags of small gear, food and ammunition, but there were no waterskins. Obviously they were a swift scouting party, but because they carried no water they were confined to the narrow strip of ground a few miles each side of the river. They were not equipped for a deep foray into the Monassir. To intercept Penrod's caravan they would have to ride hard round the great loop of the river and try to get ahead of them on the riverbank opposite Khartoum. That journey was almost two hundred miles longer than the one that faced him and Yakub. He felt a great wave of relief as he realized that even the swiftest horses would not be able to cut them off before they reached their goal.

'I leave you to the mercy of Allah,' he murmured, in sardonic blessing, then wriggled back from the skyline to return to his mount and catch up with Yakub. Then an unexpected stir among the men below made him pause. Quickly he refocused the field-glasses. Two of the aggagiers had run back to the single pack camel and forced it to kneel. They unstrapped some equipment from the animal's back. One of the Arabs squatted cross-legged with what appeared to be a writing tablet on his lap. He wrote with great concentration and care.

The other man took down a small crate from the camel's load and removed the cotton cover that protected it. He opened a trapdoor in the lid and reached inside with both hands. Penrod quailed as he saw a small birdlike head bobbing and weaving between the man's fingers. The writer laid aside his pen, carefully folded his message and stood up. The other man proffered the creature he held, and they were busy for a moment longer.

Then the scribe stood back and nodded. With both hands the other tossed the sleek grey pigeon high into the air. The bird exploded into flight, its wings clattering softly as it rose higher and higher above the river. All the Arabs watched it, heads thrown back. Their faint cries of encouragement reached Penrod even at that distance.

'Fly, little one, on the wings of God's angels!'

'Swiftly to the bosom of the Holy Mahdi!'

Up and up the pigeon climbed, and then it described a series of wide circles in the sky, a speck against the blue, until at last it found its bearings and shot away in a straight, swift line, headed into the south across the loop towards the Dervish city of Omdurman.

Penrod watched it out of sight, longing to see the knife-winged silhouette of one of the desert Saker falcons towering above it, then beginning the deadly stoop, but no predator appeared and the pigeon vanished.

Penrod ran down the back slope of the hill and sprang into his camel's saddle. He turned its head in the same southerly direction as the pigeon had taken and urged it into the pacing gait that it could maintain for fifty miles without rest. But the pigeon would reach Omdurman before nightfall, while he and Yakub still had at least two hundred and fifty miles to ride. He knew now what a terrible gauntlet they had yet to run before he could reach Khartoum and deliver his despatch to Chinese Gordon.

Osman Atalan marched in the horde of worshippers towards the great mosque of Omdurman. Over his head floated his personal banner, which had been awarded to him by the Mahdi. It was worked with texts from the Koran, and it was carried by two of his aggagiers. All around him throbbed the massive copper war drums. The *ombeyas* bleated and brayed, and the crowds shouted praises to God, to the Mahdi and his *khalifa*. The heat clamped down upon the moving mass of humanity and the dust rose in a cloud from the trampling feet and hung over their heads. As they approached the outer wall of the mosque the excitement built up steadily for they knew that today the Mahdi, the light of Islam, would preach the word of God and his Prophet. The Ansar began to dance. Once they had been called Dervish, but the Mahdi had forbidden the use of that name as demeaning.

'The Holy Prophet has spoken to me several times and he has said that whosoever calls my followers Dervish should be beaten seven times with thorns and receive a plague of stripes. For did I not give a proud name and a promise of Paradise to my own true warriors who triumphed on the battlefield of El Obeid? Did I not decree that they be known as my Ansar, my helpers and partisans? Let them be known only as Ansar, and let them glory in that name.'

The Ansar danced in the sunlight, whirling like dust devils, faster and faster, spinning so that their feet seemed barely to touch the earth, and the ranks of worshippers that pressed around them ululated and shouted the ninety-nine beautiful names of Allah: 'Al-Hakim, the Wise. Al-Majid, the Glorious. Al-Haqq, the Truth . . .' One by one the dancers were overtaken by holy ecstasy and fell to the ground, frothing at the mouth and twitching until their eyes rolled back in the sockets and only the whites showed.

Osman entered the gates of the mosque. It was a vast enclosure open to the sky, and surrounded by a twenty-foot-high wall of mud bricks. It was eight hundred paces square and the whole expanse was packed with the kneeling ranks of *jibba*-uniformed faithful. At the far end of the mosque an opening was screened off by a rank of black-robed Ansar, the Mahdi's executioners.

Osman made his way slowly through the crowds towards this space. The ranks of kneeling figures gave way to him and called his praises as he passed, for he was the foremost of all the great emirs. In the first row of worshippers his aggagiers spread out his prayer mat of fine dyed wool. Beside it they piled the six great tusks that they had taken in the hunt in the Valley of the Atbara. Osman knelt on the mat and faced the narrow gate in the wall, which led to the private compound of the Mahdi.

Gradually the wild hubbub of the worshippers descended to a hum, and then to a charged, expectant silence. This was shattered by a ringing blast on an *ombeya* and through the gateway appeared a small procession. At the head were the three *khalifas*. In appointing these men as his successors the Mahdi had simply followed the precedent set by the first Prophet Muhammad.

There should have been a fourth *khalifa*, Al Senussi, the ruler of Cyrenaica. He had sent an emissary to the Sudan to report to him on this person who claimed to be the Mahdi. The man had arrived while the sack of the city of El Obeid was in full swing. He had watched in horror the massacre, the pillage, the torture, the children being chopped into pieces by the Ansar. He did not tarry to meet the Mahdi and fled from the carnage to report back to his master the inhumanities he had witnessed.

'This monster cannot be the true Mahdi,' Al Senussi decided. 'I want no truck with him.'

Thus there were only three *khalifas*, of whom Abdullahi was the first. Compared to him the other two were of no significance. Abdullahi led them to the prayer mats that had been laid out for them on the raised dais. When they had taken their places there was another expectant pause.

The *ombeya* shrieked once more and the Mahdi's sword-bearer entered through the gateway. He carried before him the symbol of the Mahdi's temporal powers: a sword with an extraordinarily long, bright blade. Its gold hilt and guard were worked with jewelled stars and crescents, and the steel was inlaid in gold with the double-headed eagle of the Holy Roman Empire, beneath which was the legend 'Vivat Carolus'. It was not an Islamic relic but must once have belonged to a Christian crusader. It was an heirloom that had been passed down over the centuries until it had become the sword of the Mahdi. Behind his sword-bearer came the prophet of God himself.

131

The Mahdi was dressed in a spotlessly clean and beautifully quilted *jibba*. On his head he wore a gold casque with chain mesh cheekpieces that might once have belonged to one of Saladin's Saracens. He began a slow, dignified progress through the congregation of kneeling worshippers. Their ranks opened before him, and sheikhs, warriors, priests and emirs crawled forward to kiss his feet and proffer gifts.

They held up handfuls of pearls and gold jewellery, of precious stones and beautifully wrought objects of silver. They laid bolts of silk and pure gold embroidery at his feet. The Mahdi smiled his angelic smile and touched their heads in acceptance of each gift. While his Ansar followed behind him and gathered up the offerings, the Mahdi preached to them.

'Allah has spoken to me many times, and he has told me that you should be forbidden to wear fine clothes and jewellery, for this is conceit and pride. You should wear only the *jibba*, which marks you as a lover of the Prophet and the Mahdi. Therefore it is right and wise that you should deliver these trinkets and fripperies into my keeping.'

Those close enough to hear the words shouted them aloud so that all might hear and know the wisdom of the Mahdi, and others further on repeated them so by the end they had been shouted to the furthest reaches of the vast enclosure. The worshippers praised God that they should be allowed to hear such wisdom.

They lifted up leather bags of gold and silver coins and poured them at his feet, glittering piles of Maria Theresa dollars, gold mohurs and English sovereigns, the currency of the Orient and the Occident. Osman Atalan crawled forward under the weight of the largest of the six tusks and his aggagiers followed him with similar offerings. The Mahdi smiled down on Osman and stooped to embrace him.

The watchers hummed with amazement at such favour bestowed.

'You know that these riches cannot buy you a place in Paradise. If any man hold back treasures and does not bring them to me freely and of his own accord, Allah will burn him with fire and the earth will swallow him. Repent and obey my words. Return to me all that you have taken for yourselves. The Prophet, grace be upon him, has told me many times that any man who still keeps the spoils of looting in his possession shall be destroyed. Believe the revealed word of the Prophet.'

They shouted again with joy to hear the word of God and his Prophet and the Divine Mahdi, and shoved their way to the front to deliver up their treasure.

Once the Mahdi had completed his progress round the mosque he returned to the dais and took his seat on his silk prayer mat. One at a time, his three *khalifas* knelt before him and offered their gifts. One clapped his hands and his grooms led in a black stallion that shone like washed obsidian in the sunlight. Its saddle was carved from ebony, while its bridle and reins were of gold lace, tasselled with the feathers of marabou and eagles.

The second *khalifa* offered him a royal *angareb* bed, whose frame was cunningly carved of ivory and inlaid with gold.

Abdullahi was the *khalifa* who knew his master best. He offered the Divine Mahdi a woman, but no ordinary woman. He led her into the enclosure himself. She was cloaked from head to ankles, but her outline beneath the silk was as graceful as that of a gazelle, and her bare feet were elegantly shaped. The *khalifa* opened the front of her cloak, but held it so that she was screened from all eyes other than those of the Mahdi. She was naked under the cloth.

The Mahdi leant forward on one elbow and stared at her. She was a lovely child of the Galla who, at fourteen years, had eyes as dark as pools of oil, and skin as smooth as butter. She moved like a newly woken fawn. Her breasts were small and girlish, but shaped like ripe figs. Every hair had been meticulously plucked from her sex, so that the pink tips of her inner lips peeked out at him shyly from the plump little cleft. This emphasized her tender age. The Mahdi smiled at her. She hung her head, covered her mouth with a tiny hand and giggled coyly. The Khalifa Abdullahi covered her again and the Mahdi nodded at him. 'Take her to my quarters.'

Then he rose, spread his arms and began to speak again.

'The Prophet has told me many times that my Ansar are a

133

chosen and blessed people. Thus He has forbidden you to smoke or chew tobacco. You shall not drink alcohol. You shall not play a musical instrument except the drum and the *ombeya*. You shall not dance, except in praise of God and his Prophet. You shall not fornicate, nor shall you commit adultery. You shall not steal. Behold the fate of those who disobey my laws.'

He clapped his hands, and from the side gate his executioners led in an elderly man. He was barefoot and dressed only in a loincloth. His turban had been stripped off and his unwashed hair was a dirty white. He looked confused and hopeless. He had a rope round his neck. When he stood in front of the dais one of the executioners jerked it and threw him to the ground. Then four surrounded him with their whips poised.

'This man has been seen smoking tobacco. He must suffer a hundred blows with the kurbash.'

'In the Name of God and his victorious Mahdi!' the congregation assented, with a single voice, and the executioners laid on together.

The first stroke raised a red welt across the man's back, and the second drew blood. The victim writhed and shrieked as others followed in quick succession. At the end he moved no more and they dragged him out of the gate through which he had entered. Behind him the dust was damp with his blood.

The next offender was brought in at the rope's end, and the Mahdi gazed down on him with a mild and benign smile. 'This man stole the oars from his neighbour's dhow. The Prophet has decreed that he shall have one hand and one foot cut off.'

The executioner standing behind him swung his broadsword low and hard, and lopped off the right foot at the ankle. The man collapsed in the dust and as he put out a hand to save himself, the executioner stood on it to pin it to the ground, then hacked down and cut through the wrist bone. Quickly and expertly they cauterized the stumps by dipping them into a small pot of boiling pitch from the brazier. Then

134

they tied the severed hand and foot around the man's neck and dragged him out through the side gate.

'Praise the justice and mercy of the Mahdi,' howled the worshippers. 'God is Great and there is no other God but God.'

Osman Atalan watched from his seat in the front rank of the mosque. He was amazed by the wisdom and perception of the Mahdi. He knew instinctively that new religious orders are not forged by granting luxurious indulgences but by enforcing moral austerity and devotion to the word of God. No man who witnessed the rule of this prophet could doubt that he wielded the authority of God.

The Mahdi spoke again: 'My heart is as heavy as a stone with sorrow, for there is a couple in our midst, a man and a woman, who have been taken in adultery.'

The congregation roared with anger and waved their hands above their heads, crying, 'They must die! They must die!'

They brought in the woman first. She was little more than a child, a waiflike figure with stick-thin arms and legs. Her hair had come down in a tangle over her face and shoulders, and she wailed piteously as they tied her arms and legs to the stake below the dais.

Then they led in the man. He also was young, but tall and proud, and he called to the woman, 'Be brave, my love. We will be together in a better place than this.'

Despite the rope round his neck he strode forward towards the edge of the dais as if he wished to address the Divine Mahdi, but the executioner pulled him up short. 'No closer, thou foul beast, lest your blood soil the raiment of the Victorious One.'

'The penalty for adultery is that the man suffer beheading,' said the Mahdi, and his words were repeated and shouted across the wide enclosure. The executioner stepped up behind his victim and touched the back of his neck with the blade of the sword, marking his aim. Then he drew back and struck, and the blade fluted through the air. The girl at the stake screamed in despair as her lover's head seemed to spring from his shoulders. He stood a moment longer as a bright stream fountained into the air, then cascaded over his torso. The Mahdi stepped back fastidiously but a single drop splashed the skirt of his white *jibba*. The dead man fell in an untidy tangle of limbs and his head rolled to the foot of the dais. The girl wailed and struggled with her bonds to reach him.

'The penalty for the woman taken in adultery is that she be stoned,' said the Mahdi.

The Khalifa Abdullahi rose from his cushion and went to the girl at the stake. With a strangely tender gesture he swept the hair back from her face and tied it behind her head, so that the believers could see her expression as she died. Then he paced back to the pile of stones that had been placed ready to hand. He selected one that fitted neatly into his hand and turned back to face the girl-child. 'In the Name of Allah and the Divine Mahdi, may they have mercy on your soul.'

He hurled the stone with the strength and speed of a spearman, and it caught the girl in the eye. From where he sat Osman Atalan heard the rim of the socket crack. The eye popped out and hung by the vine of its nerve on her cheek, like some obscene fruit.

One after the other the *khalifas*, the emirs and the sheikhs came forward, took up a stone from the pile and threw it. By the time Osman Atalan took his turn the front of the girl's skull had been crushed and she was hanging lifelessly against her bonds. Osman's stone struck her shoulder but she did not move. They left her hanging there while the Mahdi finished delivering his sermon.

'The Prophet, grace and eternal life be upon him, has said to me on many occasions that he who doubts that I am the true Mahdi is an apostate. He who opposes me is a renegade and an infidel. He who wages war against me shall perish from this life and be destroyed and obliterated in the next world. His property and his children shall become the property of Islam. My war against the Turks and the infidel is by the order of the Prophet. He has made me privy to many terrible secrets. The greatest of these is that all the countries of the Turks, the Franks and the infidels who defy me and who defy the word of Allah and his Prophet shall be subdued by the holy religion and law. They shall become as dust and fleas and small things who crawl in the darkness of night.'

When Osman Atalan returned to his tent in the palm grove beside the waters of the Nile and looked across at the fortress of the infidel, he felt exhausted in the flesh as though he had fought a mighty battle, but he was as triumphant in the spirit as though the victory had been granted to him by Allah and the Divine Mahdi. He sat on the precious carpet of silk from Samarkand and his wives brought him a gourd of sour milk. After he had drunk, his principal wife whispered to him, 'There is one who awaits you, my lord.'

'Let him come to me,' Osman told her. When he came he was an old man but straight of limb with bright young eyes. 'I see you, Master of the Pigeons,' Osman greeted him, 'and may the grace of Allah be with you.'

'I see you, mighty emir, and I pray the Prophet to hold you to his heart.' He proffered the grey pigeon he held gently against his breast.

Osman took the bird from him and stroked its head. It cooed softly, and he untied the silk thread that held a tiny roll of rice paper to its scaly red leg. He smoothed it against his thigh and as he read it he began to smile and the weariness slipped from his shoulders. Carefully he reread the last line of the tiny script on the note.

'I have seen his face in the starlight. Verily, it is the Frank who escaped your wrath on the battlefield of El Obeid. The one who is known as Abadan Riji.'

'Summon my aggagiers and place the saddle on Sweet Water. We ride for the north. Mine enemy has come.' They scurried to do his bidding.

'By God's grace we do not need to search the length and breadth of the Monassir Desert,' he told Hassan Ben Nader and al-Noor, who stood outside the tent with him while they waited for the grooms to bring their horses. 'We know when

137

and where he crossed the loop, and there is only one place to which he can be headed.'

'It is two hundred and fifty miles from where he crossed to where he aims to reach the river here opposite Khartoum,' said al-Noor.

'We know he is a tough warrior for we all saw him at El Obeid. He will travel fast,' said Hassan Ben Nader. 'He will murder his camels.'

Osman nodded in agreement. He knew the type of man he was hunting. Hassan was right: this one would have no qualms about riding his camels to death. 'Three days, four at most, and like a little fish he will swim into our net.' The groom brought Sweet Water to him and she whinnied when she recognized Osman. He fondled her head and gave her a dhurra cake to crunch while he checked her bridle and girth. 'He will keep well away from the bank of the river until he is ready to cross.' Osman was thinking aloud with the mind of the chase. 'Will he cross south of Omdurman or to the north?' he mused, as he came back to the mare's head, and before any of his companions could speak he answered himself: 'He would not cross to the north, for as soon as he entered the water the current would push him back and away from the city. He must cross to the south so that the flow of the Bahr El Abiad,' he used the Arabic name for the White Nile, 'will carry him down to Khartoum.'

A man coughed and shuffled his feet in the dust. Osman glanced at him. Only one of his aggagiers would dare question his words. He turned to the most trusted of his men. 'Speak, Noor. Let your wisdom delight us like the singing of the heavenly cherubim.'

'It comes to me that this Frank is as wily as a desert jackal. He may reason as you have just done and, knowing your mind, decide to do the opposite. He may choose to cross far to the north, then swing wide towards the mountains and cross the Bahr El Abiad rather than the Bahr El Azrak.'

Osman shook his head. 'As you have said, he is no fool and he knows the lie of the land. He also knows that the danger for him will not be in the empty desert but on the rivers where our tribes are concentrated. You think he will choose to cross two rivers rather than one? No, he will cross the Bahr El Abiad to the south of the city. That is where we will wait for him.'

He swung up easily into the saddle, and his aggagiers followed his example. 'We move south.'

They rode into the cool of the evening, and a long veil of red dust spread behind them. Osman Atalan was in the van, with Sweet Water striding out in a flowing canter. They had covered only a few miles when he reined in the mare, and stood in the stirrups to survey the terrain ahead. The tops of the palm trees that marked the course of the river were just visible on the left, but on the right stretched the great void of the Monassir, which after two thousand miles would give way to the infinite wastes of the Sahara.

Osman swung down from the mare's back and squatted at her head. Immediately his aggagiers did the same. 'Abadan Riji will circle out wide to the west to keep well clear of the river until he is ready to make the crossing. Then he will come out of the wilderness, and in the night try to slip through our lines. We will lay our net thus and thus.' He sketched out the lines of his pickets in the dust and they nodded their agreement and understanding as they watched. 'Noor, you will take your men and ride thus and thus. You, Hassan Ben Nader, will ride thus. I shall be here in the centre.'

Penrod drove the camels at a pace that not even the hardiest men and beasts could keep up for long. They covered the ground at eight miles an hour, and kept it up for eighteen hours without rest, but it taxed even their endurance to the limit. Both men were also exhausted when he called the first halt. They rested for four hours by his pocket watch, but when they tried to rouse the camels to go on the oldest and weakest refused to come to his feet. Penrod shot him where he lay. They distributed the water that the dead beast was carrying among the other camels, then mounted up and went on at the same pace.

When they reached the end of the next eighteen-hour stage of the march Penrod calculated that they had roughly another ninety to one hundred miles to go to reach the Nile ten miles south of Khartoum. Yakub agreed with this estimate, although his calculations were based on different criteria. They had broken the back of the journey, but it had cost them dear. Thirty-six hours' hard going, and only four hours of rest. When they tried to feed them, the camels refused to eat their meagre ration of dhurra.

Once the six camels were couched Penrod went to each waterskin and lifted it to judge the remaining contents. Then he pondered over the equation of weights and distances and the condition of each beast. He decided on a deliberate gamble. He explained it to Yakub, who sighed, picked his nose and lifted the skirts of his *galabiyya* to scratch his crotch, all symptoms of doubt. But in the end he nodded lugubriously, not trusting himself to voice approval.

They selected the two strongest camels and took them out of sight of the other four weaker animals. They watered them from the skins they carried, pouring the sweet water into leather buckets. The animals' thirst seemed unquenchable, and they sucked down bucketful after bucketful. They drank almost thirty gallons each. The change in their condition was startlingly swift. They rested them another hour, then fed them all the rations of dhurra that their companions had refused. The two chosen beasts devoured it gluttonously. Now they were strong and alert again. The resilience of these extraordinary creatures never failed to amaze Penrod.

When the four hours of rest ended they led the two camels back to where the other four lay listlessly. They forced the used-up animals to their feet. Now when they began the next stage of the journey the two pampered animals carried nothing but their saddles. Between them the exhausted camels carried all the remaining water and equipment as well as the two riders. One collapsed after three more gruelling hours. Penrod shot it. He and Yakub drank as much of the water from its skins as their bellies would hold. Then they shared the rest between their two strong beasts.

They pushed on at the same pace, but within another ten miles the remaining two weaker beasts went down in quick succession. Half-way up the slip-face of a low dune one fell as though shot through the brain, and half an hour later the other groaned and its back legs gave way. It knelt to die and closed the thick double rows of lashes over its swimming eyes. Penrod stood over it with the Webley in his hand. 'Thank you, old girl. I hope your next journey is less arduous.' And he put her out of her misery.

They allowed the surviving camels to drink what they could of the water, then drank themselves. What remained they loaded up. The two camels were strong and willing. Yakub stood beside them, and studied the terrain that lay ahead, the outline of the dunes and the shape of the distant hills. 'Eight hours to the river,' he estimated.

'If my backside lasts that long,' Penrod lamented, as he climbed into the saddle. He ached in every nerve and muscle, and his eyeballs felt raw and abraded by the sand and the glare of sunlight. He abandoned himself to the pacing gait of the beast under him, the legs on each side swinging in unison, so that he pitched and rolled in the saddle. The desolate landscape fell away behind them, and the dunes and bare hills were so monotonously similar that at times he had the illusion they were making no progress but repeating the same journey endlessly.

Still clinging to the saddle, he slipped into a dark, leaden sleep. He slid sideways and almost fell off, but Yakub rode up alongside him and shook him awake. He lifted his head guiltily, and looked at the height of the sun. They had been riding for only two hours.

'Six more to go.' He felt lightheaded, and knew that at any moment sleep would overtake him again. He slipped to the ground and ran beside his camels' head until the sweat stung his eyes. Then he mounted up again and followed Yakub through the shimmering wasteland. Twice more he had to dismount and run to keep himself awake. Then he felt the

141

camel under him change its pace. At the same time Yakub shouted, 'They have smelt the river.'

Penrod pushed up alongside his camel. 'How far?'

'An hour, perhaps a little longer, before it will be safe for us to turn eastwards and head straight towards the river.'

The hour passed slowly, but the camels paced on steadily until they saw another low ridge of blue shale appear out of the heat haze ahead. To Penrod it seemed identical to hundreds of others they had passed since they had crossed the loop, but Yakub laughed and pointed at it: 'This place I know!' He turned his camel's head and the beast quickened its pace. The sun was half-way towards the western horizon, and their shadows flitted ahead over the barren earth.

They came up over the ridge, and Penrod stared ahead eagerly for a glimpse of greenery. The wasteland was unrelieved and unrelenting. Yakub was undismayed, and shook his lank curls in the hot wind, as the camels ran on across the plain.

Ahead another low shale bank seemed to rise no more than head high above the level ground. Yakub brandished his goad and leered across at Penrod with a satanic squint. 'Place your trust in Yakub, the master of the sands. Brave Yakub sees the land as a vulture from on high. Wise Yakub knows the secret places and the hidden pathways.'

'If he is wrong brave Yakub will have need of a new neck, for I will break the one on which he balances his thick skull,' Penrod called back.

Yakub cackled and pushed his mount into a cumbersome gallop. He reached the top of the bank fifty paces ahead of Penrod, stopped and pointed ahead dramatically.

On the horizon they saw a line of palm trees stretched across the landscape, but it was difficult to judge the distance in the flat, uncertain light. The bunches of palm fronds on each long bole reminded Penrod of the ornate hairstyles of the Hadendowa warriors. He estimated that it was under two miles to the nearest grove.

'Get the camels down,' he ordered, and jumped to the ground. Surprisingly he felt strong and alert. At first sight of

142

the Nile the weariness of the journey seemed to have left him. They took the camels behind the ridge and couched them out of sight from the river plain.

'In which direction lies Khartoum?' Penrod asked.

Without hesitation Yakub pointed to the left. 'You can see the smoke from the cooking fires of Omdurman.'

It was so faint on the horizon that Penrod had taken it for dust or river haze, but now he saw that Yakub was right. 'So we are at least five miles upstream of Khartoum,' he observed. They had reached the precise position he had aimed for.

He went forward cautiously and squatted on the high ground with the field-glasses. He saw at once that he had overestimated the distance to the riverbank. It was probably closer to one mile than two. There was no cover on the river plain, which was flat and featureless. It seemed that there was some cultivation under the palm trees, for he made out a line of darker green below the untidy fronds. 'Probably dhurra fields,' he muttered, 'but no sign of a village.' Again he checked the height of the sun. Two hours until dark. Should we make a run for the river before sunset, or wait for darkness? He felt impatience building in him, but he held it in check. While he considered the choice he kept the binoculars to his eyes. The riverbank could be far beyond the first trees of the grove, or it might be right there at the edge.

Movement caught his eye and he concentrated on it. A faint shading of pale dust was rising from among the palms. It was moving from left to right, in the opposite direction of Omdurman. Perhaps it was a caravan, he thought, following the road along the riverbank. But then he realized it was moving too fast. Riders, he decided, camels or horsemen. Suddenly the dustcloud stopped moving, hung for a few minutes at the same point, then gradually settled. They have halted in the grove, right between us and the riverbank. Whoever they were they had made the decision for him. Now he had no alternative but to wait for darkness. He went back to where Yakub sat with the camels. 'Mounted men on the riverbank. We'll have to wait for darkness when we can sneak past them.'

'How many?'

'I'm not certain. A large band. Judging by the dust there are maybe twenty or so.' There was little water left in the skins, no more than a few gallons. With the river in sight they could afford to be profligate so they drank their fill. By this time it was slimy with green algae and had taken on the taste of the crudely tanned leather, but Penrod drank it with relish. What they could not consume they gave to the camels.

Then they inflated the empty skins. This was a laborious job: they held each skin between their knees and blew into the nozzle, holding it closed between breaths by clamping a hand over the opening. When each skin was full and tight they stoppered it. Then they strapped them to the backs of the kneeling camels. All was ready for the river crossing, and Yakub looked at Penrod. 'Yakub the tireless will keep watch while you rest. I will wake you at the setting of the sun.'

Penrod opened his mouth to refuse the offer, then recognized the sense of it. The elation was wearing off, and he realized that, without sleep, he was nearly at the end of his tether. He knew, too, that Yakub was almost indefatigable. He handed him the field-glasses without protest, stretched out on the shady side of his camel, wrapped his scarf round his head and was almost instantly asleep.

'Effendi.' Yakub shook him awake. His voice was a hoarse whisper. With a single glance at his face Penrod knew that there was trouble. Yakub's squint was hideous, one eye fixed on Penrod's face but the other roved and rolled.

As Penrod sat up his right hand closed on the butt of the Webley. 'What is it?'

'Riders! Behind us.' Yakub pointed back along the way they had come. Far out on the sun-seared plain a tight bunch of horsemen was coming on fast. 'They are on our tracks.'

Penrod snatched the field-glasses from him and stared back at them. They wore the *jibba*. He counted nine. They were covering the ground at a canter. The leaders were leaning forward in their saddles to watch the ground ahead.

'They were waiting for us,' said Yakub. 'It was the pigeon that warned them.'

'Yes! The pigeon.' Penrod leapt to his feet. He took a last glance at the height of the sun. It was squatting wearily on the horizon and little daylight remained. The camels were ready to run, eager for water, and lunged to their feet at the first touch of the goad.

Penrod leapt into the saddle and pointed his mount's head at the distant line of palm trees. He used the goad and it lumbered into a gallop. From behind he heard the distant thud of a rifle shot and a bullet ricocheted off the stony ground in a puff of dust and chips, but it was fifty yards out on the left. Even at such long range it was poor shooting, but the Dervish favoured the sword and the spear above the gun. They considered any expertise in the use of firearms to be effete and unmanly. The true warrior killed with the blade, man to man.

Within seconds the camels had crossed the ridge and were screened by the shale bank from further enemy fire. Penrod knew that they were no match for a good horse over the short run, but he pushed his on with cries of 'Ha! Ha!', the sting of the goad and urgent movements of his body. Yakub was lighter, though, and his mount drew gradually ahead.

As they raced for the edge of the palm groves Penrod searched for any sign of the horsemen he had spotted earlier. He hoped they might have ridden on towards Omdurman, and left their path open to the river. Even the best of us needs a little luck, he thought, then heard faint but excited cries from far behind. He looked back under his arm, and saw the nine horsemen sweeping over the shale bank they had just crossed. They were strung out but riding hard. There were more shots, but they flew wide. The palm groves drew closer, and he felt his confidence burgeoning. They had a clear run to the bank of the Nile.

'Come, Effendi, watch Yakub and you will learn how to ride a camel.' The little Jaalin tribesman laughed with delight at his own sense of humour. Both their animals were extended in full gallop, and Penrod ducked as loose pebbles flew back from the pads of the camel in front of him and flicked past his ears.

Suddenly there was a different sound of gunfire, much sharper and clearer. The band of riders he had seen earlier raced out of the grove. They must have been halted and resting among the trees, but now they had been alerted by the shots of the pursuers. All of them wore the *jibba* of the Dervish and were armed with spear, sword, targe and rifle. They were on a converging course, racing in from the right along the edge of the grove to cut them off from the river. Penrod narrowed his eyes as he judged their speed and the distance to where their paths would cross.

We will make it, but with little to spare, he decided. At that moment a heavy Boxer-Henry .45 calibre bullet struck Yakub's camel in the head and killed it instantly. It dropped onto its nose and the long legs flew over its head as it tumbled. Yakub was thrown high, then struck the hard ground heavily.

Penrod knew that he must be either killed or knocked senseless. He dared not stop to help him. Baring's messages were more important than the life of one man. None the less he was filled with dismay at the thought of leaving Yakub to the mercy of the Dervish. He knew they would give him to their women to play with. The Hadendowa woman could castrate a man, then flay every inch of skin from his body without allowing him to lose consciousness, forcing him to endure every exquisite cut of the blade. 'Yakub!' he bellowed, with little hope of any response, but to his astonishment Yakub clambered shakily to his feet and looked about groggily.

'Yakub! Make ready.' Penrod leant out sideways from the saddle. Yakub turned and ran in the same direction, to lessen the shock as they came together. They had often practised this trick in preparation for just such a moment on the battlefield or the hunting ground. Yakub was looking back over his shoulder to judge his moment. As the camel swept by him he reached up and linked arms with Penrod. He was jerked clean off his feet, but Penrod used the momentum to swing him back over the camel's croup.

Yakub grabbed him round the waist and stuck to him like a tick to a dog. The camel ran on without check. The moment

Penrod was sure that Yakub was secure he twisted in the saddle and saw that the closest Dervish was only two hundred yards out on their right flank. He rode a magnificent cream mare with a flowing golden mane. Although he wore the green turban of an emir, he was not a greybeard but a warrior in his prime, and he rode with the menace of a couched lance, slim, supple and deadly.

'Abadan Riji!' To Penrod's astonishment the emir challenged him by name. 'Since El Obeid I have waited for you to return to Sudan.'

Then Penrod remembered him. His face and figure were not easily forgotten. This was Osman Atalan, emir of the Beja.

'I thought I had killed you there,' Penrod shouted back. The emir had chased him as he carried the wounded Adams out of the broken square, just as the Dervish charge overwhelmed it. Osman had been riding another mount, not that lovely mare. Penrod had been up on a big strong gelding. Even burdened with Adams it had taken Osman a good half-mile to catch him. Then they rode stirrup to stirrup and shoulder to shoulder, as though riding each other off the ball in a game of polo, Osman slashing and hacking with that great silver blade, and Penrod meeting it with parries and stop hits, until his moment came. Then he feigned a straight thrust at Osman's eyes. The Dervish threw up his targe to catch the point, and Penrod dropped his aim and hit him, driving hard under the bottom rim of the targe. He had felt his steel go well in. Osman reeled back in the saddle and his mount had swerved aside, breaking out of the trial of strength.

Looking back under his arm as he carried Adams away, Penrod had seen that Osman's mount had slowed to a walk, and that his rider was hunched over and swaying. He had thought he was probably mortally wounded.

But that was clearly not the case, for now Osman shouted, 'I swear on my love of the Prophet that today I will give you another chance to kill me.'

Osman's men rode close behind him and Penrod saw that they were as dangerous as a pack of wolves. One of the aggagiers aimed his carbine and fired. The black powder smoke erupted from the muzzle and the bullet parted the air so close to Penrod's cheek that he felt its kiss. He ducked instinctively, and heard Osman shout behind him, 'No guns! Blades only. I want this one for my sword, for he has tainted my honour.'

Penrod faced ahead, giving all his concentration to wringing the utmost from the camel under him. They rushed towards the palm grove, but behind him he could hear the thunder of hoofs riding to a crescendo. As they rode past the first trees of the grove, he saw that he had been mistaken; this was not a field of dhurra but a dense stand of second-growth palmetto. The long needle spines could stab through the hide of a horse, but not that of a camel. He turned his mount's head and it charged straight at the thicket.

He heard the hoofs closer behind him and the hoarse breathing of a horse at full gallop, then saw the mare's golden head appear in the periphery of his vision.

'Now is your chance, Abadan Riji!' Osman called, and pushed the mare alongside the camel. Penrod leant across the narrow gap and thrust at his turbaned head, but Osman swayed back and kept his targe low, sneering at Penrod over the rim. 'The fox never comes twice to the snare,' he said.

'You learn swiftly,' Penrod conceded, and caught the great crusader sword on his own slim blade, turning it in the air so that it flew past his head. He steered the camel with his toes against its neck into the thicket of spiny palmetto. The camel crashed through, but Osman turned aside, breaking off his attack rather than lame or cripple the mare.

He galloped furiously round the edge of the thicket while the camel ran straight through. He had lost at least a hundred paces as he came back into the camel's tracks and rode hard to catch up with it again.

Penrod saw the wide expanse of the Nile directly ahead, a shimmering luminescence in the fading light. The camel bounded forward under him as it, too, saw the river. Penrod carried the sabre in his right hand, with the goad and the reins in the left. 'Yakub, take my pistol!' he said softly. 'And for the love and mercy of Allah, try this time to aim fair and shoot straight.'

Yakub reached round his body and pulled the Webley from his sash. 'The remarkable Yakub will slay this false emir with a single shot,' he cried, took deliberate aim and closed both eyes before he fired.

Osman Atalan did not flinch at the crack of the shot: he came on swiftly, but he had seen how close they were to the riverbank. He swung the mare in across the camel's rump, and stood in the stirrups with the long sword poised.

Penrod saw that he had changed his attack, and that he meant to cripple the camel with a deep cut through the hamstrings. With a stab of the goad and a hard tug on the reins he swung the beast's shoulder into the mare. Standing off balance in his stirrups Osman could not respond swiftly enough to counter the turn, and the two animals came together with the impetus of their combined weights. The camel was almost twice the height of the mare at the shoulder, and half again as heavy. She reeled and went down on her front knees. Osman was thrown on to her neck.

With the skill and balance of an acrobat he retained his seat, and kept a grip on his sword. However, by the time the mare had found her feet again, the camel had pulled too far ahead for her to catch up before it reached the riverbank.

As he raced towards it Penrod had only a moment to survey the river before him. He saw that the bank was a sheer drop of ten feet and that the water below it was green and deep. It was at least a mile across to the opposite bank and three large islands of reeds and papyrus were floating down in stately procession towards Khartoum in the north. That was all he had time to observe. With Osman and his aggagiers racing up behind them he urged the camel straight to the top of the bank.

'In God's Name!' shrieked Yakub. 'I cannot swim.'

'If you stay here the Dervish women will have your balls,' Penrod reminded him.

'I can swim!' Yakub changed his mind.

'Sensible Yakub!' Penrod grunted, and as the camel hesitated he stabbed hard into its neck with the goad. It leapt outwards so violently that Yakub lost his grip on the Webley as he snatched at a handhold. With a gut-wrenching sensation they dropped to hit the water with a splash as high as the bank above their heads. The aggagiers reined in their horses and milled about on top of the bank, firing down at the two men floundering on the surface.

'Stop!' Osman shouted angrily, and knocked up the barrel of al-Noor's carbine. His intervention came too late, for a bullet fired by one of the others hit the camel and damaged its spine. The terrified beast swam desperately with its front feet, but its paralysed back legs anchored it so that it turned in small circles, bellowing and hissing with terror. Despite the crippling injury it rode high in the water, buoyed by the inflated waterskins.

'You think you have cheated me yet again,' Osman shouted across the water, 'but I am Osman Atalan, and your life belongs to me.'

Penrod guessed immediately from the emir's tone of false bravado that, like most desert Arabs, he could not swim. For all his wild courage on land, he would never expose himself and his beautiful mare to the attack of the jinn and the monstrous Nile crocodiles that infested these waters. He would not follow his enemy over the bank into the swift green river.

For a minute longer Osman wrestled with his chivalrous instincts, his passionate desire for single combat, to avenge himself on his enemy with the sword. Then he gave way to expediency, and made an abrupt, eloquent chopping gesture with his right hand.

'Kill them!' he ordered. At once his aggagiers jumped to the ground and lined the top of the bank. They aimed volley after volley at the group of bobbing heads. Penrod seized Yakub by one arm and dragged him behind the struggling camel, using it as a shield. The current carried them swiftly downstream and the aggagiers followed, running along the bank, and keeping up a hail of carbine fire. All the time the current was carrying them away from the bank and the range was opening. At last a lucky shot struck the camel in the head, and it rolled over like a log in the water.

Penrod drew the dagger from his sash, and cut loose one of the inflated skins from its saddle. 'Hold here, brave Yakub,' he gasped, and the terrified Arab seized the tag of rawhide rope. They abandoned the camel's carcass, and Penrod swam them slowly out across the current towards the middle of the river.

As darkness dropped over them, with the suddenness of the African night, the shape of the Dervish on the bank faded away and only the muzzle flashes of their rifles still showed. Penrod swam with a gentle sidestroke, kicking with both legs, paddling with one hand and towing Yakub with the other by the scruff of his neck. Yakub was clinging to the skin bladder, and shivering like a half-drowned puppy. 'There are crocodiles in this cursed river so large they could swallow a buffalo, horns and all.' His teeth chattered and he choked on a mouthful of water.

'Then they would not trouble themselves with a skinny little Jaalin,' Penrod comforted him. A huge dark shape loomed out of the gloom and bore down on them. It was one of the floating islands of papyrus and reeds. He caught a handful of reeds as it drifted by, and dragged himself and Yakub up on to it. The vegetation was so densely matted and intertwined it could have supported a herd of elephants. It undulated softly under their feet as they crawled across it to the side nearest Khartoum. They squatted there, regaining their strength and gazing across at the eastern bank.

Penrod was worried that, on such a moonless night, he might not see the city when they reached it and stared into the darkness until his eyes ached. Suddenly he thought he could make out the ugly square shape of Mukran Fort, but his eyes were playing tricks and, when he stared at it, it dissolved. 'After such a journey, it would be the height of stupidity to sail past Khartoum in the night,' he muttered, and then his doubts were dispelled.

From downstream there came the crash of artillery fire. He leapt to his feet and peered through the papyrus stems. He saw the brilliant orange muzzle flashes of cannon demarcating the Omdurman side of the river. Seconds later the shells burst on the east bank and illuminated Khartoum's waterfront. This time there was no mistaking the stark outline of Mukran Fort and, beyond it, the consular palace. He smiled grimly as he remembered the nightly artillery bombardment by the Dervish gunner, whom David Benbrook had dubbed the Bedlam Bedouin. 'At least he has not run out of ammunition yet,' he said, and explained to Yakub what they had to do.

'We are safe here,' Yakub demurred. 'If we stay here the river will push us in time to the bank and we can walk ashore like men, not swim like iguanas.'

'That will not happen until you reach the Shabluka Gorge, where this raft will surely be destroyed. You know well that the gorge is the lair of all the most evil river djinni.'

Yakub thought about that for a few minutes, then announced, 'Brave Yakub fears no jinnee, but he will swim with you to the city to watch over you.'

The skin bladder had leaked half its air, and they blew it tight again while they waited for the raft to reach the most advantageous point. By then the moon had risen, and although the Dervish bombardment had petered out, they could make out the city skyline clearly, and even see a few small cooking fires. They slipped into the water. Yakub was becoming more courageous by the minute and Penrod showed him how to kick with his legs and help to drive the bladder across the current.

After a laborious swim Penrod felt the bottom under his feet. He let the bladder go and dragged Yakub ashore. 'Fearless Yakub defies all the crocodiles and jinn of this little stream.' Yakub posed boldly on the bank and made an obscene gesture towards the Nile.

'Yakub should close his fearless mouth,' Penrod advised, 'before one of the Egyptian sentries puts a bullet in his defiant backside.' He wanted to get into the city secretly. Apart from the danger of being shot by the guards, any contact with the troops would result in him being taken immediately to General Gordon. His orders from Sir Evelyn Baring were to deliver his message to Benbrook first, and only then to report to Gordon.

Penrod had spent months in Khartoum before and after the disaster of El Obeid, so he was intimately aware of the layout of the defences and fortifications, which were concentrated along the riverfront. Keeping well outside the walls and the canal, he worked his way swiftly around the southern outskirts. When he was almost opposite the domed roof of the French consulate, he approached the canal bank. Once he was certain that it was clear, they waded across, the water only chin deep.

When they reached the other side they lay up in the palm grove to wait for the patrol to pass. Penrod whiffed the smoke of Turkish tobacco before he saw them. They sauntered past along the footpath, rifles trailing, the sergeant smoking. It was behaviour typical of the slovenly Egyptian troops.

As soon as they were gone he dropped into the drainage ditch that led to the outer city wall. The ooze stank of raw sewage, but they crawled through the tunnel, past the back wall of the French consulate and into the old town. Penrod was perturbed at how easily they had got through. Gordon's defences must be stretched to breaking point. At the beginning of the siege he had commanded seven thousand Egyptians, but that number must have been much reduced by the attrition of disease and desertion.

They hurried through the deserted alleys, stepping round the bloated carcasses of men and animals. Even the appetite of the crows and vultures was inadequate to the task of devouring such an abundance. The stench of a city under siege assailed his nostrils, death and putrefaction. He had heard it called the cholera bouquet.

Penrod paused to pull his pocket watch from its pouch and held it to his ear. It had not survived the dousing in the river. He looked at the moon, judged that it was well after midnight, and hurried on unchallenged through the deserted streets. When they reached the gates of the consular palace there was still lamplight in a few windows. The sentry at the front gate was asleep, curled like a dog in his box. His rifle was propped

153

against the wall, and Penrod took charge of it before he kicked him awake. It took some time and a great deal of argument with the sergeant of the guard, but despite his appearance and the smell of sewage that wafted from his robes Penrod was able at last to convince him that he was a British officer.

When he was led to David Benbrook's office, the consul was reading by lamplight. He looked annoyed by the intrusion, as he removed the reading glasses from his nose and stood up. He was dressed in a velvet smoking jacket and had been poring over a sheaf of documents. 'What is it?' he snapped.

'Good evening, Consul.' Penrod saluted him. 'I'm sorry to trouble you at this time of night, but I've just arrived from Cairo with messages from Sir Evelyn Baring.'

'God bless my soul!' David stared at Penrod in amazement. 'You're English!'

'I am, sir. I have had the pleasure of your previous acquaintance. I am Captain Ballantyne of the 10th Hussars.'

'Ballantyne! I remember you well. As a matter of fact we were speaking about you just the other day. How do you do, my dear fellow?' After they had shaken hands David held his handkerchief to his nose. 'First thing is to get you a bath and some fresh clothes.' He rang for the servants. 'I am not sure that there will be hot water at this time of night,' he apologized, 'but it should not take long to get the boiler going.'

Not only was the bathwater scalding, David Benbrook even produced half a cake of perfumed soap from Paris and lent Penrod a razor. While he shaved David sat on the lid of the commode across the tiled bathroom. He seemed oblivious to Penrod's nudity, and scribbled notes in a little red leather-bound book, as Penrod repeated Baring's long and involved message. Then he questioned Penrod avidly about General Stewart's preparations for the rescue expedition. 'Hasn't even left Wadi Halfa yet?' he exclaimed, with alarm. 'By Gad, I hope we'll be able to hold out until he gets here.'

David was of almost the same build as Penrod. Even a pair of his boots fitted as though they were made for the younger man. Penrod had considerably less girth, but he belted in the trousers and tucked in a freshly ironed white shirt. When he was dressed David led him back to his study. 'I cannot even offer you brandy to wash it down,' he said, as a servant placed a beautiful Sèvres plate before Penrod. On it sat a small portion of dhurra cake and a lump of goat's milk cheese no larger than the first joint of his thumb. 'Hard commons, I'm afraid.'

'Very nourishing, sir.' Penrod nibbled the dhurra.

'Damned pleased to have your despatches, Ballantyne. We've been completely in the dark here for months. How long did it take you from Cairo?'

'I left there on the nineteenth of last month, sir.'

'Damn me, but that was good going.' David nodded. 'Now, tell me what the London newspapers are saying.' He was eager for every scrap of news that Penrod could tell him.

'They are quite openly reporting the bad blood between General Gordon and Mr Gladstone, sir, and public opinion is strongly on General Gordon's side. They want Khartoum relieved, the General rescued, and the savages taught to mind their manners.'

'What is your opinion, Captain?'

'As a serving officer I do not allow myself an opinion on such matters, sir.'

'Very wise.' David smiled. 'But as a member of the public, do you think that the Prime Minister has shown lack of resolve?'

Penrod hesitated. 'May I speak frankly, sir?'

'That is what I am inviting you to do. Whatever you say will remain between us. You have my word on it.'

'I think that Mr Gladstone has shown neither cowardice nor indecision in refusing to send an army upriver to save the life of General Gordon, as most of the British public believes. The general had only to embark on one of his steamers and come home. I believe that the Prime Minister did not feel justified in involving the nation in costly and risky operations here in the heart of Sudan merely to vindicate the personal honour of one man.'

David drew a deep breath. 'My goodness me! I asked for

155

your frank opinion and I got it. But tell me, Ballantyne, don't you think that there is not some personal resentment in Whitehall for an officer whose rash and intractable actions have brought so much odium upon them?'

'It would be remarkable if that was not the case. It is clearly demonstrated in the despatches from Sir Evelyn that I delivered to you.'

David considered Penrod seriously. He was not just a pretty fellow, he thought, he had a thinking head on his shoulders. 'So you would oppose the despatch of Wolseley's force to our relief?'

'Oh, never!' Penrod laughed. 'I'm a soldier, and soldiers thrive on war. I hope to be in the thick of it, even if it doesn't make good sense, which is apparent, and if matters turn nasty, which is highly likely.'

David laughed with him. 'War seldom makes good sense,' he agreed. 'It is refreshing to hear a military man say it. But why has Gladstone changed his mind, and agreed to send an army?'

'The expressed desire of the nation is a force to which Mr Gladstone has always acceded. I understand from Sir Evelyn Baring that the Prime Minister was advised that only a single brigade would be needed for the expedition. Only after he had reluctantly taken the decision, and announced it to the nation, did the war ministry ask for a much larger force. It was too late then to reverse the decision so the relieving army has become not a single brigade but ten thousand men.'

The hours sped away as they talked until the grandfather clock in the corner chimed again. David stared at it in astonishment. 'Two o'clock, upon my soul! We'll have to give you a few hours' sleep before you meet Gordon. I imagine you're in for a torrid time with him.'

The servants were waiting up for him but David dismissed them and personally showed Penrod to one of the guest suites. The night was so sultry and he was so tired that he could not bother himself to don the thick flannel nightshirt that David provided. Instead he stripped naked and before he crawled beneath the single sheet he placed his dagger under the pillow. Then he went out like a candle in a high wind.

He awoke without a change in his breathing, and was immediately aware that someone was in the bedroom with him. While he feigned sleep, he tried to remember where he was. Through his eyelashes he saw that the curtains were drawn and the light in the room was muted. It was still early in the morning. He moved his hand infinitesimally slowly under the pillow until his fingers curled around the hilt of his dagger. He waited like a coiled adder for the strike.

There was a light footstep beside his bed, and someone coughed softly, nervously. The small sound gave him direction and he launched himself off the bed. He bore the intruder to the floor, held him by the throat with one hand, and with the other touched him with the point of the dagger. 'If you move I will kill you,' he whispered ferociously in Arabic. 'Who are you?'

Then he became aware that his captive smelt of rosebuds and the throat he held was silken smooth and warm. The body under him was clad in taffeta bodice and skirts and there were marvellous protuberances and hollows under the fine cloth. He released his hold and sprang to his feet. He stared down in astonishment and consternation as his captive sat up. It took him some seconds to grasp that he had assaulted and threatened a young woman with shining blonde hair. And that sitting on the floor, with her skirts in disarray around her, her eyes were at the same level as his naked groin, her gaze was fixed upon an object that happened to be a part of his anatomy seldom exposed to public scrutiny.

Still gripping the dagger, he spun round to grab the sheet from the bed. Before he could wrap it round himself he realized that he was offering the reverse view to the young woman. Haste made him clumsy, and he fumbled until at last, modestly covered, he faced her again.

'I am mortified, Miss Benbrook. I had no idea it was you. You startled me.'

Her pale cheeks were slowly suffused with a rosy blush, but

157

she was still panting for breath, as though she had run a distance. The effect this had on what lay beneath her bodice was riveting. 'If I startled you, sir, then you have no idea how you have alarmed me. Who are you and what are you doing—' Her hand flew to her mouth as she recognized him, despite his unflattering new haircut. 'Captain Ballantyne!'

'Your servant, madam.' His bow was spoilt by the need to retain a grip on both the dagger and his sheet. She scrambled to her feet, stared at him a moment longer with wide eyes, then fled from the room. He stared after her. He had forgotten how pleasing she was to the eye, a condition not at all spoilt by her confusion and dismay. Then he grinned. 'That alone was worth the journey,' he said to himself.

He whistled as he shaved and dressed, then winked at himself in the mirror and said aloud, 'Perhaps next time she will recognize me more readily, now that she has more to remember me by.' Then he went down the stairs.

David was already seated at the breakfast table, but apart from the white-robed servants he was alone. 'Have some of this.' He placed a spoonful of an amorphous pale green substance on Penrod's plate. 'The taste is execrable, but I have it on excellent authority that it is highly nutritious.'

Penrod peered at it suspiciously. It looked like green cheese. 'What is it?'

'I understand that it is the curds of papyrus and reed weeds, made by my daughters. We eat a lot of it. In fact, since the official rations were reduced to one cup of dhurra corn a day, we eat little else.'

Penrod put a morsel cautiously into his mouth. 'My compliments to your daughters. It is very palatable.' He tried to sound convincing.

'It's not bad really. Try it with Worcestershire sauce or Gentleman's Relish. You will soon grow accustomed to it. Now, shall we go and call upon General Gordon?'

General Gordon turned from the window through which he had been staring across the river at the enemy emplacements. He stared at Penrod with that disconcerting blue gaze as he saluted. 'At ease, Captain. I believe you made the journey from Cairo in record time,' he said.

How did he know that? Penrod wondered, and then it was obvious. We have the boasting of the fearless Yakub to thank.

In silence General Gordon listened to his report and the messages he had brought from Sir Evelyn. When he had finished speaking, Gordon did not reply immediately. He paced up and down the long room, finally stopping to stare at the large-scale map of the Sudan that was spread on the table under the windows. The view from them was unrestricted: the glass panes had been blown out by shrapnel from the Dervish artillery across the river, but Gordon had taken no steps to fortify his headquarters or to protect his person. He seemed to be concerned only for the safety of the city and the well-being of its people.

'I suppose that we must be grateful to the Prime Minister for coming to the rescue of the populace, even though he is several months too late,' he remarked at last. Then he looked up at Penrod. 'The only consolation for me is that now I have at least one British officer on my staff.'

At those words, Penrod felt the first chill breeze of unease blow down his spine. 'My orders from General Stewart, sir, are to return to Wadi Halfa as soon as I have delivered my despatches to you. I am seconded to the new Camel Corps with orders to assist in guiding them across the loop of the Nile to the assault upon Metemma.'

Gordon thought about that for a moment, then shook his head. 'If General Stewart has not yet left Wadi Halfa it will be months before he reaches Metemma. You will be more useful here than sitting at Wadi Halfa. Besides, there must be hundreds of other guides qualified to bring the Camel Corps across the loop. When the rescue column reaches Abu

Hamed, I shall reconsider. But in the meantime I need you here.'

He said it with such finality that Penrod knew argument was futile. His dreams of action and glory were shattered. Instead of riding into the city at the head of his corps after fighting his way up from Metemma, he was now sentenced to the dreary monotony of the siege.

I must bide my time, and choose my moment, he decided, and did not let his expression betray his true feelings. 'It will be an honour to serve under you, General, but I would appreciate having those orders in writing.'

'You shall have them,' Gordon promised, 'but now I must bring you up to date with the situation here, and our immediate and most pressing problems. Take a seat, Ballantyne.'

Gordon spoke quickly, almost with agitation, flitting from subject to subject, chain-smoking cigarettes from a silver case. Slowly Penrod began to understand the enormous strain under which he had been working, and to gain an inkling of the terrible loneliness of this command. He sensed that before his arrival, there had been nobody Gordon could trust to share with him some of the burden. If Penrod was not an equal in rank, at least he was an officer of a first-line British regiment, and as such was worth a dhow full of Egyptian staff officers.

'You see, Ballantyne, I have here the responsibility and duty without full control. I am daily afflicted not only by the incompetence of the Egyptian officers but by their unconscionable behaviour and total lack of morality or sense of duty. They wilfully disobey orders, if they think they can escape the consequences, they neglect their duties and spend most of their time with their concubines. Unless I chivvy them they seldom bother to visit the front-line defences. I am aware that they conspire and intrigue with the Dervish in the hope that they may win advantage when the city falls, which they are convinced it will. They steal from their own men. The troops fall asleep at their posts, and in their turn steal from the populace. I suspect that large quantities of dhurra have been stolen from the granary. The women and children of the city spit at me and revile me in the streets when I am forced to reduce the rations yet again. We are down to a cupful of grain per person per day.' He lit another cigarette and the flame of the match fluttered in his cupped hands. He puffed rapidly, then smiled coldly at Penrod. 'So you can imagine that your assistance will be welcome. That is especially true since you are so well acquainted with the layout of the city.'

'Of course you may rely on me, General.' Despite his cold, almost messianic gaze, Penrod wondered how close Gordon was to breaking point.

'I am going to delegate to you the following responsibilities at the outset. Until now Major al-Faroque has been in charge of the storage and distribution of food. His efforts have been at best pathetically inadequate. I suspect, though I cannot prove it, that he knows something of the missing grain. You will take over from him immediately. I want you to let me have an inventory of all the available supplies as soon as possible. Under the rule of martial law, you have the power of seizure. You may commandeer any stores you need. Any transgressions are to be treated with the utmost severity. You may flog or shoot looters and black-marketeers without reference to me. The troops and the populace must be forced to accept the unpleasant laws – you will make them fully aware that the alternatives are even worse. Do you understand that?'

'Of course, General.'

'Do you know a Ryder Courtney?'

'Only in passing, sir.'

'He is a trader and merchant of this city. I was obliged to requisition a shipment of his dhurra. As a mercenary without an altruistic bone in his body, he resents it. He has his own compound within the city, and behaves as though he is independent of all authority. I want you to make the true position clear to him.'

'I understand, sir,' said Penrod, and thought sourly, So now I am no longer a Hussar but a policeman and quartermaster.

Gordon was watching his expression, and saw the reaction, but he went on unruffled: 'Among other enterprises, he owns and operates a large river steamer. At present it is undergoing repairs in his workshop. Once it is serviceable again, it will be useful in future military operations and possible evacuation of our populace, should Stewart's column fail to arrive in time. Courtney also has horses and camels, and much else that will be vital to us as the Dervish noose tightens around us.' Gordon stood up as a signal that the meeting was at an end. 'Find out what he is up to, and what he knows of the missing dhurra, Ballantyne. Then report back to me.'

Penrod knew of Ryder Courtney's reputation: David Ben-brook had spoken of him and even Sir Evelyn Baring had taken note of him. It seemed that he was a resourceful and formidable character. If Penrod was to carry out Gordon's orders he would gain nothing by marching up to the front gate of Courtney's compound and announcing himself and his intentions. First, he thought, a little scouting expedition is called for.

He left the palace gardens by the river gate. It was unguarded, and he made a note of that. He moved swiftly along the waterfront, to prevent warning of his arrival being telegraphed ahead. At the first redoubt of the defences the sentries were recumbent, resting weary limbs and eyes. Penrod had heard of Gordon's swift justice, and he had no wish to precipitate a massacre and decimation of the Egyptian garrison, so he used cane and boot to remind them of their duty.

He went on along the line of fortifications and gun emplacements that had been erected since his last visit to the city. It was evident that these had been planned by General Gordon, for they had been laid out with a soldier's eye and understanding of terrain. He inspected the field guns, and though he was no artilleryman, he picked out the deficiencies in care and handling of the weapons. The shortage of ammunition was painfully apparent. When he questioned them, the gunners told him they were not allowed independent fire but had to wait for orders from their officers before they were allowed to send a single shell across the river. The Dervish on the opposite bank were under no such limitation, and morning and evening they indulged in uninhibited barrages, which made up in enthusiasm for any lack of accuracy. Usually the middle of the day was calm and peaceful while both sides rested from the heat of the sun.

Penrod moved quickly past the harbour, where he noticed a white river steamer with most of her machinery stripped out and spread on the stone wharf for repair. Her hull and superstructure were peppered with shrapnel hits. A gang of Arab workers was busy patching and painting over the damage. A white engineer supervised them, encouraging his crew with a chorus of oaths and imprecations that carried clearly across the water in the accents of the Glasgow docks. It was obvious that it would be weeks, if not months, before the steamer was ready to sail. Penrod moved on along the river frontage of the Blue Nile towards Fort Burri and the arsenal.

As he picked his way through the alleyways, which were almost clogged with shell debris and filth, brown faces looked down at him from the windows and rickety balconies that almost met overhead. Women held up their naked infants so that he could see the swellings and bruising of scurvy, the skeletal limbs. 'We are starving, Effendi. Give us food,' they pleaded. Their cries alerted the beggars, who hobbled out of the gloomy depths of the alleyways to pluck at his clothing. He scattered them with a few shrewd cuts of his cane.

The guns on the parapets of Fort Burri covered the north bank of the Blue Nile, and the Dervish fortifications facing them. Penrod paused to study them, and saw that the enemy were taking few precautions. Even with the naked eye he could see figures across the river moving about in the open. Some Dervish women were washing their laundry on the riverbank and spreading it out to dry in full view of Fort Burri. They must have realized how perilously depleted was Gordon's stock of shot and shell.

Behind Fort Burri stood the squat and ugly blockhouses of the arsenal and the munitions store. General Gordon was using them as the city granary. There were sentries at the entrance and at each revetment that supported the crumbling walls. From what Gordon had told him, even those guards and the repairs to the walls had been no match for the ingenuity of Ryder Courtney or the Egyptian officers, or whoever was to blame for the depredations in the granary. However, this was not the time to visit the arsenal or to conduct an audit of the stores. That would come later. Penrod was headed towards the sprawling complex of Ryder Courtney's compound, which lay a short way beyond, almost on the canal that defended the city from an assault out of the southern desert.

As he approached he saw that there was unusual activity in progress on the canal banks behind the walls of the compound. This puzzled him, so he left the road and followed the towpath that ran along the embankment. At first he thought that the many men working in the canal were constructing some form of fortification. Then he realized that women were carrying bundles on their heads from the embankment into the rear gate of Courtney's compound.

As he came closer he saw that a huge raft of river weed almost blocked the canal. It was similar to the mass of vegetation on which he and Yakub had escaped from Osman Atalan the previous day. Dozens of Arabs swarmed over the raft, clad only in loincloths and armed with scythes and sickles. They were cutting the papyrus and river weed and tying it into bundles for the women to carry away.

What the devil are they up to? He was intrigued. And how did that raft of weed get into the canal so conveniently placed for Courtney to harvest? Then the answer occurred to him. Of course! He must have captured and roped it in the main river, then used muscle power to drag it up the canal. They warned me that he is crafty.

The workers hailed Penrod respectfully, invoking Allah's blessing on him. They looked impressed when he returned the greeting in fluent, colloquial Arabic. Although he wore no uniform, they knew his name was Abadan Riji, and that he had ridden off Osman Atalan and all his most famous aggagiers to reach Khartoum. Yakub had seen to it that all the city knew of their heroics.

When Penrod followed the line of Sudanese women through the rear gate of the compound, no one challenged him. He found himself in a large walled enclosure, which swarmed with activity. The women piled their bundles in the centre and returned to the canal for the next load. Another team was seated in groups, chattering as they picked over the cut stems and sorted them into piles. They discarded all the dead and dried-out material, and chose only that which was still green and succulent. This they sorted into the various types of vegetation. The largest heap comprised the common papyrus, but there was also water-hyacinth, and three other types of grass and reed. The *nymphaea* was obviously the most prized plant for it was not piled on the dusty ground like the papyrus and hyacinth but carefully packed into sacks and carried away for pulping by another team of women. They were working over a long line of stamp mortars that usually crushed dhurra into flour. The women worked in unison, thumping the heavy wooden pole they used as a pestle into the bowl-shaped mortar, pounding the water-lilies with a little water into pulp. They sang as they swayed and rocked to the rhythm of the swinging poles.

Once the contents of the mortars were reduced to a thick green paste, another party of women collected it in large black clay pots, and carried it through the gate of a second enclosure. Penrod was interested and followed them. No sooner had he stepped through the gate when, for the first time, he was challenged in a peremptory treble. 'Who are you and what are you doing here?'

Penrod found himself confronted by two young females, neither of whom stood much taller than his belt buckle. One was dark brunette and the other was golden blonde. One had eyes the colour of molten toffee, while the smaller girl's were the bright blue of petunia petals. Both gazed up at him with a severe expression and pursed lips. The taller child had her fists on her hips in a pugnacious attitude. 'You're not allowed in here. This is a secret place.'

Penrod recovered from his surprise, gallantly lifted his hat and bowed deeply. 'I beg your pardon, ladies, I did not mean to trespass. Please accept my apologies and allow me to introduce myself. I am Captain Penrod Ballantyne of Her Majesty's 10th Royal Hussars. At present I am on the staff of General Gordon.'

Both girls' expressions softened as they continued to stare at him. They were unaccustomed to being addressed in such polite terms. Furthermore, like most other women, they were not impervious to Penrod's charms.

'I am Saffron Benbrook, sir,' said the taller girl, and curtsied. 'But you may call me Saffy.'

'Your servant, Miss Saffy.'

'And I am Amber Benbrook, but some people call me Midget,' said the blonde. 'I don't really like the name, but I suppose I am a little shorter than my sister.'

'I agree entirely. It is not a fitting name for such a lovely young lady. If you will permit me, I shall address you as Miss Amber.'

'How do you do?' Amber returned his bow with a curtsy, and when she straightened up she found herself in love for the first time. It was a sensation of warmth and pressure in her chest, disturbing but not altogether unpleasant.

'I know who you are,' she said, just a trifle breathlessly.

'Do you, indeed? And, pray, how is that?'

'I heard Ryder speaking to Daddy about you.'

'Daddy, I presume, is David Benbrook. But who is Ryder?'

'Ryder Courtney. He said you had the finest pair of whiskers in Christendom. What happened to them?'

'Ah!' replied Penrod, his face suddenly touched with frost. 'He must be a noted comedian.'

'He is a great hunter and very, very clever.' Saffron rushed to his defence. 'He knows the name of every animal and bird in the world – the Latin names,' she added portentously.

Amber was determined to wrest back Penrod's attention from her twin. 'Ryder says that the ladies find you dashing and gallant.' Penrod looked slightly better pleased, until Amber went on innocently, 'And that you agree wholeheartedly with their opinion.'

Penrod changed the topic. 'Who is in charge here?'

'We are,' the twins chorused.

'What are you doing? It looks very interesting.'

'We are making plant curds to feed our people.'

'I would be most grateful if you could explain the process to me.' The twins seized upon the invitation and competed vigorously for his attention, interrupting and contradicting each other at every opportunity. Each grabbed one of Penrod's hands and dragged him into the inner courtyard.

'When the most succulent leaves are crushed, then they have to be filtered.'

'To get rid of the pith and rubbish.' There was no longer any thought of safeguarding secrets.

'We strain it through trade cloth from Ryder's stores.'

'We have to squeeze it to get out all the goodness.'

Pairs of Sudanese women were pouring the green pulp into lengths of printed cloth, then twisting it between them. The juices dribbled into the huge black cast-iron pots, which stood on three legs over the smouldering cooking fires.

'We measure the temperature – ' Saffron brandished a large thermometer importantly.

' – and when it reaches seventy degrees,' Amber cut in, 'the protein coagulates—'

'I am telling it,' said Saffron, furiously. 'I am the oldest.'

'Only by one hour,' Amber retorted, and gabbled out the rest of the explanation. 'Then we sieve off the curds and make them into bricks and dry them in the sun.' She pointed triumphantly at the long trestle tables laden with square blocks set out upon them in neat rows. This was what Penrod had eaten for breakfast, and he remembered David's warning that there was precious little else.

'We call it green-cake. You can taste some if you like.' Amber broke off a morsel and stood on tiptoe to place it between his lips.

'Scrumptious!' Penrod exclaimed, and swallowed manfully.

'Have some more.'

'Excellent, but enough for now. Your father says it is even tastier with Worcestershire Sauce,' he said hurriedly, forestalling delivery of the next mouthful, which was already on its way in Amber's grubby little hand. 'How much green-cake can you make in a day?'

'Not enough to feed everybody. Just enough for ourselves and our own people.'

The efficacy of the green-cakes was apparent. Unlike the rest of the malnourished populace, none of the inhabitants of the compound was showing signs of starvation. In fact, the twins were blooming. Then he remembered his brief meeting with their elder sister that morning. Nothing wrong with her either. He smiled at the memory, and the two children took it as a sign of his approval and smiled with him.

Penrod realized that he now had staunch allies in the Courtney stronghold. 'You really are two very clever young ladies,' he said. 'I would be most obliged if you were to show me around the rest of the compound. I hear that there are all sorts of fascinating things here.'

'Would you like to see the animals?' cried Amber.

'The monkeys?' said Saffron.

'The bongos?'

'Everything,' agreed Penrod. 'I would like to see everything.'

It was soon apparent that the twins were the favourites of everyone and that they had the run of the Courtney compound. They were particular friends and intimates of Ali the animal-keeper. It was only with the greatest difficulty that the old man prevented himself grinning with delight as soon as he laid eyes on them. They led Penrod from cage to cage, calling to the animals by name and feeding them by hand when they responded.

'They didn't like the green-cake at all when we first tried to feed them with it, but now they all love it. Just look how they gobble it up.' Amber pointed.

'What about dhurra? They must like that too?' Penrod set a bait for her.

'Oh, I suppose they do,' Saffron cut in, 'but there isn't enough for the people, let alone the animals.'

'We only get a cupful a day,' Amber confirmed.

'I thought your friend Ryder had plenty of dhurra and that he was selling it.'

'Oh, yes! He had a whole boatload. But General Gordon took it all from him. Ryder was furious.'

Penrod was grateful that the girls' innocent disclosures virtually guaranteed that, despite the general's suspicions, Courtney was not guilty of the theft of grain from the arsenal. He had no reason to feel any warmth for the man, especially after his remarks about Penrod's whiskers and his good opinion of himself, but he was an Englishman and it would have been distasteful for Penrod to have to confirm Gordon's suspicions.

'I would very much like to meet your friend Ryder,' he suggested tentatively. 'Would you introduce me?'

'Oh, yes! Come with us.'

They dragged him from the menagerie, and across an inner courtyard until they reached a small door at the far end. The twins let go of his hands and raced each other to the door. They threw it open and burst into the room beyond. Penrod stepped up close behind them and, from the doorway, surveyed the room swiftly.

It was obviously both an office and the private living quarters of the owner of the compound. A massive pair of elephant tusks were mounted on the far wall, the largest Penrod had ever seen. The other walls were covered with magnificently woven Persian carpets, and dozens of murky yellowing photographs in dark wooden frames. More carpets covered the floors, and in a curtained recess, a large *angareb* bed was spread with golden leopardskins, dappled with black rosettes. The chairs and the massive desk were hewn from polished native teak. The bookcases held rows of leatherbound journals, and scientific books on flora and fauna. A row of rifles and muzzle-loading guns stood in a rack between the curves of the thick yellow tusks. Penrod's gaze slid over this untidy masculine display, then riveted on the couple who stood in the middle of the room. Even the tumultuous twins were frozen with shock at the sight.

Man and woman were locked in a passionate embrace,

oblivious to everything and everyone around them. Saffron broke the silence with a wail of accusation: 'She's kissing him! Becky is kissing Ryder on his mouth!'

Ryder Courtney and Rebecca Benbrook sprang apart guiltily, then stood, frozen, staring at the group in the doorway. Rebecca turned ice pale and her eyes seemed to fill her face as she looked at Penrod. He cut her a mockingly appreciative salute. 'We meet again so soon, Miss Benbrook.'

Rebecca dropped her gaze to the floor and now her cheeks turned the bright crimson of live coals. Her mortification was so intense that she felt dizzy and swayed on her feet. Then, with an enormous effort, she rallied. Without looking at either man she rushed forward and seized her little sisters by the wrists. 'You horrible children! How many times have you been told to knock before you enter a room?'

She dragged them out of the open door, and Saffron's voice receded in the distance: 'You were kissing him. I hate you. I'll never speak to you again. You were kissing Ryder.'

The two men faced each other as though neither had heard the sisterly accusations of betrayal. 'Mr Courtney, I presume. I hope my visit has not come at an inconvenient time.'

'Captain Ballantyne, sir. I heard that you arrived in our lovely city late last night. Your fame precedes you.'

'So it appears,' Penrod conceded. 'Though for the life of me I know not how.'

'Simple enough, I assure you.' Ryder was relieved that there was to be no heavy-handed banter regarding the romantic episode that Ballantyne had witnessed – it might have led to an outbreak of hostilities. 'Your outrider, Yakub of the Jaalin, is the intimate friend of the nursemaid of the Benbrook twins and a stalwart of their household, a good lady by the name of Nazeera. Her busy tongue is one of her most apparent failings.'

'Aha! Now I understand. Perhaps you were even expecting my visit.'

'It comes as no great surprise,' Ryder admitted. 'I understand that General Gordon, may all his enterprises flourish, has some questions for me regarding the dhurra missing from the arsenal.'

Penrod inclined his head in acknowledgement. 'I see you keep yourself well informed.' He was appraising Ryder Courtney with a penetrating gaze, cloaked by a disarming smile as they sparred.

'I try to keep abreast of affairs.' Ryder was not at all disarmed by the smile, and his own gaze was just as shrewd. 'But please do come in, my dear fellow. It is perhaps a little early, but may I offer you a cigar and a glass of first-rate Cognac?'

'I was convinced those two marvellous commodities no longer existed in this naughty world.' Penrod moved across to the chair Ryder indicated.

When their cigars were drawing evenly they regarded each other over their charged glasses. Ryder gave the toast: 'I congratulate you on your speedy journey from Cairo.'

'I wish I were already on my way back.'

'Khartoum is hardly a spa,' Ryder agreed. They sipped the brandy and talked guardedly, still sounding each other out. Ryder knew Penrod by sight and reputation so there were no real surprises for him.

Penrod learnt swiftly that he had not been misinformed, and that Ryder was a formidable character, tough, quick and resilient. He was also good-looking in a rugged, forthright style. No wonder the lovely Miss Benbrook had shown herself susceptible to his advances. *I wonder just how susceptible. It might be amusing to test her commitment to this fellow, man to man and hand to hand, so to speak.* Penrod smiled urbanely, masking the glint of steel in his eyes. He dearly loved a contest, pitting his skills and wits against another, especially if a handsome prize were at stake. There was more to it than that. The nubile Miss Benbrook's involvement with Ryder Courtney added a new dimension to the sharp attraction he had previously felt towards her. It seemed that, despite appearances, she was not made of ice, that there were depths beneath the surface, which might be fascinating to plumb. He was amused by his own choice of metaphor.

'You mentioned the missing dhurra,' Penrod broached the subject again.

Ryder nodded. 'I have a proprietary interest in that shipment,' he said. 'It once belonged to me. It was transported at great expense and no little hardship several hundred miles down the river, then commandeered, some might even say stolen, by the redoubtable Chinese Gordon the minute I landed it safely in Khartoum.' He fell silent and brooded on the injustice.

'Naturally you have not the faintest notion what happened to it once it passed out of your hands?' Penrod suggested delicately.

'I have made some enquiries,' Ryder admitted. Under his instructions Bacheet had spent several weeks pursuing them. Even the rabbit warren of ancient buildings and alleyways of Khartoum could not hide five thousand ardebs of grain indefinitely.

'I would be fascinated to know the results of those investigations.'

Ryder regarded the tip of his cigar with a frown of annoyance. The lack of humidity in the desert air desiccated the tobacco leaf and caused it to burn like a grass fire. 'Did you hear if, by any chance, the good general has offered a reward for the return of the missing dhurra?' he asked. 'Lord knows, he paid little enough for it on the first purchase. Six shillings a sack!'

'General Gordon has not spoken to me of a reward,' Penrod shook his head, 'but I will suggest it to him. I would think that a reward of six shillings a sack might bring forth information, don't you?'

'Perhaps not,' Ryder replied. 'However, I believe that an offer of twelve shillings would be almost certain to produce results.'

'I shall speak to him at the first opportunity.' Penrod nodded. 'Although that does seem a trifle steep.'

'None of his promissory notes, either,' Ryder warned. 'It is common knowledge that the Khedive has given him drawing rights of two hundred thousand pounds on the Cairo treasury. A few gold sovereigns would sing sweeter than all the paper canaries ever to come out of the forest.'

'A sentiment most poetically expressed, sir,' Penrod commended him.

Rebecca sat in her secret place in a hidden corner of the battlements in the consular palace. She was hidden by an ancient hundred-pounder cannon, a monstrous rusting relic that had probably never been fired in this nineteenth century, and would certainly never be fired again. She had covered her head and nightgown with a dark woollen cloak, and she knew that not even the twins would find her there.

She looked up at the night sky and could tell by the height of the Southern Cross above the desert horizon that it was well after midnight, but she felt as though she would never be able to sleep again. In a single day her whole existence had been thrown into uproar and confusion. She felt like a captive wild bird, battering its wings against the bars, bleeding and terrified, falling to the floor of the cage with heart racing and body trembling, only to launch itself at the bars again in another futile attempt to escape.

She did not understand what was happening to her. Why did she feel this way? Nothing made sense. Her mind darted back to that morning when, as soon as she had seen the twins bathed and dressed, she had begun her weekly housekeeping inspection. As soon as she entered the blue guest suite she had seen the strange figure occupying the four-poster bed. She had not been informed by the staff of the arrival of any guests and Khartoum under siege was the last place to attract casual visitors. Knowing this, she should have left the bedroom immediately and raised the alarm. What had made her approach the bed she would never know. As she stooped over the sheet-covered figure, it had launched itself at her with the suddenness of a leopard dropping out of a tree on its prey. She found herself borne to the floor by a stark naked man with a dagger in his hand.

Remembering that terrible moment, she bowed her head and covered her face with her hands. It was not the first time that she had seen the male body. When Rebecca turned sixteen her parents had taken her on a tour of the capital cities of Europe. She and her mother had gone to see Michelangelo's *David*. She had been struck by the statue's unearthly beauty but the cold white marble had invoked in her no troublesome emotions. She had even been able, unblushingly, to discuss it with her mother.

Her mother often described herself as emancipated. At the time Rebecca thought that this merely meant she smoked Turkish cigarettes in her boudoir and spoke frankly of the human anatomy and its functions. After her suicide Rebecca realized that the word had deeper significance. At the funeral in Cairo she had overheard some of the older women whispering together, and one had remarked tartly that Sarah Benbrook had made David a cuckold more often than she cooked him breakfast. Rebecca knew her mother never cooked breakfast. Nevertheless, she looked up the word 'cuckold' in her father's dictionary. It took her a while to work out the true meaning, but when she did she had decided that she did not want to be emancipated like her mother. She would be true to one man for life.

Rebecca had next seen the male body only last year. David had taken her and the twins with him on an official visit to the upper reaches of the Victoria Nile. The Shilluk and Dinka tribesmen who inhabited the banks of the river wore no clothing of any description. The girls recovered from the first surprise when their father remarked that it was merely custom and tradition for them to adopt the state of nature, and they should think nothing of it. From then onwards Rebecca looked upon the enormous dark appendages as a rather ugly form of adornment, rather like the pierced lips and nostrils on the tribes of New Guinea that she had seen illustrated.

However, when Penrod Ballantyne had leapt upon her that morning the effect had been devastating. Far from leaving her uninterested and rather pitying, she found emotions and feelings of whose existence she had never dreamed until that moment erupting into her consciousness. Even now in the darkness, with the cloak over her head and her face covered with both hands, she was blushing until her face felt as though it was on fire.

I won't think about it ever again, she promised herself. 'It' was as fully as she allowed herself to describe what she had seen. Never. Never again. She even eschewed that description on the second attempt. Then immediately she found herself thinking about it with all her attention.

After that long-ago visit to Europe, Rebecca had overheard her mother discussing the subject with one of her friends. They agreed that a woman in a state of nature was beautiful, while a man was not, except Michelangelo's *David*, of course.

'It wasn't ugly or obscene,' Rebecca contradicted her mother's shade. 'It was . . . it was . . .' But she wasn't sure what it had been, except very disturbing, fascinating and troubling. What had happened later between her and Ryder Courtney was connected with the first episode in some strange way that she could not fully understand.

Over the previous months she and Ryder had gradually become friends. She had realized that he was strong, clever and amusing. He had an inexhaustible fund of marvellous stories and, as Saffron had often remarked, he smelt and looked good. She came to find his company reassuring and comforting in the days of the siege, when death, disease and starvation gripped the city. As her father had observed, Ryder Courtney was a man of accomplishment. He had built up a thriving business enterprise and sustained it even though the world seemed to be falling apart. He took good care of his own people and his friends. He had shown them how to make the green-cake, and he could make her laugh and forget her fears for a few hours. She felt safe when she was with him. Of course, once or twice he had made physical contact with her – a light touch on the arm when they were talking, or his hand brushing hers as they walked together. But always she had pulled away. Her mother had warned her often about men: they just wanted to ravish you, then leave you sullied for ever so that you could never find a husband. That was bad enough but, worse, ravishment was painful and, in her mother's experience, only childbirth more so.

Then that very morning after her horrible experience in the Blue Bedroom when her emotions had been in turmoil, she had gone alone to Ryder's quarters. She had never done that before. She had always taken at least one of the twins with her as a chaperone. But this morning she had been confused. She felt guilty about her strange and ambivalent thoughts of Captain Penrod Ballantyne. She was terrified that she had inherited the bad seed from her mother. She needed to be comforted.

As always, Ryder had been pleased to see her, and ordered Bacheet to brew a pot of the precious coffee. They had chatted for a while, at first discussing the twins and their lessons, which, since the beginning of the siege, had fallen sadly into default. Suddenly and unexpectedly, even to herself, Rebecca had begun to sob as though her heart would break. Ryder had stared at her in astonishment: he knew she was neither a whiner nor a weeper. Then he had put his arms round her and held her tight. 'What has happened to you? I have never seen you like this. You have always been the bravest girl I know.'

Rebecca was surprised by how good it felt to be held by him. 'I'm sorry,' she whispered, but made no effort to pull away. 'I'm being very silly.'

'You're not silly. I understand,' he told her, in the deep, gentle tone he used when he was comforting a frightened animal or a hurt child. 'It is getting too much for all of us. But it will soon be over. The relief column will be here before Christmas, mark my words.'

She shook her head. She wanted to tell him that it was not the war, the siege, the Dervish or the Mad Mahdi, but he stroked her hair and she quietened, pressing her face to his chest, his warmth and strength, and his rich man-smell. 'Ryder,' she whispered and lifted her face to explain how she felt to him. 'Dear, dear Ryder.' But before she could say more he kissed her full on the lips. The surprise was so complete that she could not move. When she had recovered her wits sufficiently to pull away, she found that she did not want to.

176

This was something so new and different that she decided to indulge herself a few moments longer.

The few moments became a few minutes and when at last she opened her mouth to protest, an incredible thing happened: his tongue slipped between her lips and stifled her protest. The sensation this produced was so overwhelming that her knees threatened to give way and she had to cling to him to hold herself up. The full muscular length of his body was pressed hard against her, and her protest came out as mewing sounds, like the cries of a newborn kitten seeking the teat. Then, to her consternation, she felt a monstrous hardness growing up between their lower bodies, something that seemed to have a life of its own. It terrified her, but she was powerless. Her will to escape evaporated.

A shrill high voice sundered the bonds that held her and set her free: 'She's kissing him! Becky is kissing Ryder on his mouth!'

Thinking about that moment now, she spoke aloud in the darkness under the great cannon: 'Now even Saffy hates me, and I hate myself. It is all such a terrible mess, and I wish I could die.'

She did not realize how far the words had carried until a voice answered her from the darkness: 'So there you are, Jamal.' The name meant the Beautiful One.

'Nazeera, you know me too well,' Rebecca murmured, as the plump, familiar shape appeared.

'Yes, I know you well and I love you more than I know you.' Nazeera sat beside her on the carriage of the cannon, and placed her arms round her. 'When I found that you were missing from your bed, I knew I would find you here.' Rebecca rested her head on Nazeera's shoulder and sighed. Nazeera was as soft and warm as a feather mattress and smelt of attar of roses. She rocked Rebecca gently. After a while she asked, 'Now, do you still wish to die?'

'I did not mean you to overhear me,' Rebecca answered ruefully. 'No, I do not want to die. Not for a while yet. But life is difficult sometimes, isn't it, Nazeera?'

'Life is good. It is men who are difficult most of the time,' said Nazeera.

'Bacheet and Yakub?' Rebecca teased her. Nazeera's admirers were no secret within the family. 'Why don't you choose one of them, Nazeera?'

'Why don't you make a choice, Jamal?'

'I don't understand what you mean.' Rebecca lifted her cloak off her head and stared at Nazeera, her eyes large and dark in the starlight.

'I think you do. Why is it that the day the beautiful captain returns to Khartoum you rush for safety to al-Sakhawi, and when you find out that he does not think of himself as just your old friend, you decide you want to die?'

Rebecca covered her face again. Nazeera knew nearly everything, and had guessed the rest. In a few words she had helped Rebecca understand her turmoil. Nazeera went on rocking her. She started to croon a lullaby, an old tune with new words: 'Which one will it be? How will you choose, and who will it be?'

'You make it seem like a child's game, Nazeera.' Rebecca tried to sound stern.

'Oh, it is. Life is just a child's game, but often the games of children, like those of grown-ups, end in bitter tears.'

'Like poor little Saffy,' Rebecca suggested. 'She says she hates me, and she won't speak to me.'

'She thinks you have stolen her love from her. She is jealous.'

'She is so young.'

'No. She will soon be a woman and at least she knows what she wants.' Nazeera smiled tenderly. 'Unlike some older women I know.'

'Twelve shillings?' Ryder Courtney insisted. 'There can be no misunderstanding?'

'Twelve shillings. The word of an officer and a gentleman.'

'That description might be debated,' Ryder grunted.

'Will you not carry a weapon?'

'Yes.' Ryder hefted the heavy ironwood club.

'I meant a sidearm or an edged weapon.' Penrod touched the sabre in its scabbard on his belt.

'In the dark it will not be easy to tell friend from foe. I prefer denting heads with a fist or a club. Not so irrevocable.'

They were stepping out, shoulder to shoulder, along one of the sordid alleys of the native quarter of the city. They both wore dark clothing. The sun had set little more than an hour ago, but it was already dark. Just enough daylight lingered for them to pick their way along. Bacheet was waiting for them near the Ivory Tower, one of the more notorious brothels of the most dangerous section of the city. He whistled softly to attract their attention, then beckoned them into the ruins of a building that had been destroyed by Dervish cannon fire from across the river. The three found seats on the piles of masonry and shattered roof beams. The intermittent glow of Penrod's cigar shed just enough light for them to make out each other's features.

'Has Aswat arrived yet?' Ryder asked in Arabic.

'Yes,' replied Bacheet. 'He came an hour ago, at sunset.'

'Who is he?' asked Penrod. 'Who is responsible for this business?'

'I can't be certain yet. Bacheet has heard his men call him Aswat but he wears a mask, to keep his face well hidden. Nevertheless, I have my suspicions. We will know for sure before the night is out.' Ryder turned back to Bacheet. 'How many men with him?'

'I counted twenty-six. That includes six armed guards. They will work late tonight. They always do. There is a lot of dhurra, and the sacks are heavy to move about. Aswat divides them into two gangs of about twelve men each. When the curfew falls, and the streets are deserted, they carry the sacks to the customers in other parts of the city. Two of Aswat's armed men who know the password of the night go ahead of each gang to make sure the road is clear of patrols. Two others bring up the rear to make sure they are not followed. Aswat waits at the tannery. It seems he won't take a chance on the street.'

'How many sacks does Aswat distribute every evening?' Ryder asked.

'About a hundred and twenty.'

'So by now he has sold a few thousand,' Ryder calculated. 'Probably less than three thousand left in his store. Do you know what he is charging for a sack?'

'At first it was five, but he has raised it to ten Egyptian pounds. He takes only gold, no notes,' Bacheet told him.

Ryder shook his head. 'Chinese Gordon is getting another bargain. The going rate is ten pounds. He is offering me but twelve shillings reward.'

'I'll cry for you tomorrow,' Penrod promised. 'Where is Aswat storing the stolen grain?'

'At the end of this street,' Bacheet explained. 'He is using an abandoned tannery.'

'Who have you left to watch the building?' Penrod asked Bacheet.

'Your man, Yakub. He is a Jaalin. The most treacherous of all tribes. Even that slithering of snakes have driven him out from their nest. I do not trust Yakub at all. He has no sense of honour, especially with women,' said Bacheet, bitterly. It was well known that he and Yakub were rivals for the favours of the widow Nazeera.

'But he is a good man in a fight, is he not?' Penrod defended Yakub.

Bacheet shrugged. 'Yes, if you do not turn your back on him. He is waiting behind the tannery, on the canal bank. My men are hidden in the courtyard of the Ivory Tower. The mistress of the house is a good friend.'

'She should be,' Ryder murmured drily. 'You are one of her best customers.'

Bacheet ignored such a fatuous remark. 'I chose this place to wait because from these windows we will be able to keep watch on the alley.' He nodded at the empty window openings. The glazing had been blown out by the shell blast, and the frames had been stolen for firewood. 'It is the only way to reach the tannery.'

'Good,' Ryder said. 'Two of your best men must follow the gangs. I want the names of all the merchants dealing with him. As soon as we have them we shall drop in on Effendi Aswat at the tannery.'

At that moment they heard the muffled tramp of feet. Bacheet slipped out through a shell hole in the rear wall to carry out Ryder's orders. Penrod stubbed out his cigar and wrapped the butt in his handkerchief, then joined Ryder at the empty window. They stayed well back in the shadows so that they were not spotted from the alley. A group of dark, furtive figures moved past the window. The two guards were first: they wore khaki Egyptian uniform with a flower-pot fez. They carried their rifles, bayonets fixed, slung over the shoulder. The porters followed them, bowed under the heavy dhurra sacks. The two armed men of the rearguard followed a short distance behind.

When they had disappeared Penrod remarked, 'Now I understand why you would not allow me to bring any of the garrison troops, and why you insisted that we use only your Arabs. Gordon's Egyptians are in this up to their necks.'

'Deeper than their necks,' Ryder corrected him. Within a short time the unburdened porters and their escorts came hurrying back down the alley towards the tannery. Bacheet appeared again, with the suddenness of the genie from the lamp. 'Ali Muhammad Acrani, who has a house behind the hospital, has bought all twenty-four sacks of the first delivery,' he reported. They waited for the next delivery to pass the windows. It was after midnight before the heavily laden porters left the tannery for the sixth time and staggered down the alley.

'That will be the last delivery,' Bacheet told Ryder. 'In God's Name, it is time at last to catch the jackal while he is still gobbling up the chickens.'

'In God's Name,' Ryder agreed.

When they slipped out of the rear of the shelled building, Bacheet's band was waiting for them in the shadows of the rear wall, armed with broadswords and spears. None carried firearms. Ryder led them quietly down the alley, keeping close to the dark buildings on each side. The silhouette of the tannery rose against the starbright desert sky. It was a three-storeyed building, dark and derelict, that blocked the end of the alleyway.

'Very well, Captain Ballantyne. I think it's time for you to go and find your man, Yakub.'

While they waited in the ruined building they had discussed the last details of the raid, so now there was no hesitation or misunderstanding. They had agreed that, as this was Ryder's affair, he would make the decisions and give the orders. However, Yakub was Penrod's man and would take orders only from him.

Penrod touched Ryder's shoulder in acknowledgement and moved quickly to the enclosing wall of the tannery's yard. The gate was closed and locked, but Penrod sheathed his sabre and jumped up to grab a handhold in a crack in the masonry. He pulled himself up with a single lithe movement, swung his legs over the top of the wall and dropped out of sight.

Ryder gave him a few minutes to get clear, then led Bacheet and the rest of the party to the high gate. He knew the layout of the building. Before the siege he had sent almost all of the hides he brought up from Equatoria to be processed by the old German who had owned the factory. The tanner had fled Khartoum with the first exodus of refugees. Ryder knew that the gate led into the loading yard. He tried it, but found it locked from the inside. It was unpainted, dry and cracked. He drew out his knife, whose point sank into the wood as though it were cheese.

'Dry rot,' he grunted. He ran the blade through the narrow gap between the edge of the door and the jamb, and located the staple of the lock on the far side. He backed off a few paces, lined up, then stepped forward and slammed the flat of his right boot into the door. The screws that held the lock on the far side were ripped from the rotten wood and the gate swung open.

'Quickly now! Follow me.' Across the yard there was a raised loading platform with the main doors of the warehouse leading off it. This was where he had unloaded his bundles of raw hides for curing, and where he had collected the finished product. A broken-down wagon still stood against the platform. The entire place stank of half-cured leather. The glimmer of lamplight showed through slits in the boarded-over ground-floor windows, and beneath the main doors to the warehouse.

Ryder ran up the steps of the loading platform. Rats scurried into their holes as he crossed to the main door. He paused to listen and heard muffled voices through the woodwork. Gently he put his weight on the door, which eased open an inch, and peered through the gap. A man was leaning against the door frame with his back turned to Ryder. He wore the long dark cassock of a Coptic Christian priest and the hood covered his head. Now he turned quickly and stared at Ryder with astonishment in his eyes.

'Ah, Effendi Aswat,' Ryder greeted him, as he lifted the ironwood club. 'Do you have any dhurra for sale?' He swung the club with the power of his wide shoulders behind it, aiming at the cloaked head. It should have cracked on the priest's skull, but the down stroke crashed into the top frame of the door above Ryder's head with a force that numbed his wrist. The club flew from his grip and struck the cloaked figure a glancing blow on the shoulder that sent him reeling backwards with a howl of pain.

'To arms! Stand to arms! The enemy is on us!' the priest shouted, as he raced away across the open floor of the warehouse.

Ryder wasted a few moments retrieving his club from where it had rolled against the wall. As he straightened he glanced around the cavernous warehouse. It was lit by a dozen or more oil lamps hanging from the railing of the catwalk that ran round the high walls, just below the roof beams. In the dim light he saw that Bacheet had underestimated the strength of the opposition: at least twenty other men were scattered around the warehouse. Some were slaves, naked except for turbans and loincloths, but others wore the khaki uniforms and red fez of the Egyptian garrison troops. All had frozen in the attitude in which the priest's cry had caught them.

The slaves were stacking mountainous heaps of sacks in the centre of the warehouse and the floury smell of ripe dhurra blended with the ancient reek of raw hide and tannin. An Egyptian lieutenant and three or four non-commissioned officers were overseeing their efforts. It took them all some moments to gather their wits. They stared, aghast, at Ryder as he advanced on them brandishing his club. Then, with warlike shouts, Bacheet and his Arabs burst in through the main doors.

The Egyptian non-commissioned officers came to life and rushed to where their rifles were stacked against the far wall. Their lieutenant pulled his revolver from its holster and loosed off a shot before Bacheet and his gang were upon them, swinging swords and thrusting spears. The shouting, hacking, cursing mêlée surged back and forth across the warehouse floor. One of the slaves threw himself at Ryder's feet and clung to his knees, screaming for mercy. Impatiently Ryder tried to kick him away, but he clung like a monkey to a fruit tree.

At the far end of the long building Aswat was getting away. With the robes of his cassock billowing behind him, he jumped over a pile of loose dhurra sacks and darted to the foot of one of the vertical steel ladders that led up to the overhead catwalk. As he started to climb, his skirts flapped around his legs, hampering his movements. Despite this handicap, he climbed with agility. All the while he kept up cries of encouragement and exhortation to his men: 'Kill them! Let none escape! Kill them all!'

Ryder tapped the clinging slave across the temple with the club, and he released his grip and crumpled to the floor. Ryder jumped over his inert body and ran to the foot of the ladder. He stuffed the club under his belt and leapt on to the first rungs, following the priest and gaining on him rapidly. He saw that beneath the skirts of his cassock the fugitive wore polished riding boots and spurs, and that his legs were clad in khaki riding breeches.

The priest reached the catwalk, and clung to the handrail, heaving for breath. He peered back down the ladder. His voice shrilled with panic when he saw Ryder coming up fast behind him. 'Stop him! Shoot him down like a dog!' But his men were too occupied with their own problems to take any notice. He struggled with the skirts of his cassock, trying to hoist them high enough to reach the sidearm that bulged on his hip, but he could not free it. Now Ryder was almost on him and Aswat abandoned the effort. Instead he snatched one of the oil lamps that hung from the handrail. He lifted it high over his head. 'Stop! In God's Name, I warn you! I will burn you alive.'

The hood of the cassock fell off to reveal the khaki tunic of the Egyptian Army, with the epaulettes and scarlet tabs of a major on the shoulders. His curls were dark and wavy, lustrous with pomade. Ryder caught a whiff of a pungent eau-de-Cologne. 'Major Faroque. What a pleasant surprise,' Ryder said cheerfully.

Al-Faroque's expression was frantic. 'I warned you!' he screamed. With both hands he hurled the lamp at Ryder, who flattened himself against the rungs of the ladder. As the lamp flew past his shoulder, it spun a meteor's tail of burning oil through the air behind it. It struck the steel ladder near the bottom and exploded, spraying a sheet of fire over the closest stack of dhurra sacks. Rivulets of flickering blue flames poured over the tinder dry sacks, which caught swiftly and burned as brightly as candles.

'Don't come near me!' al-Faroque yelled down at Ryder. 'I warn you. Don't—' He grabbed the second lamp off its hook, but Ryder was ready for it and pulled the club from his belt. The major threw with all his strength, sobbing with the effort as the lamp left his hand.

It flew straight towards Ryder's face. He watched it coming and, at the last moment, swatted it aside. It spun down into the body of the warehouse, and burst over another stack of dhurra. The grain went up in a leaping conflagration.

Al-Faroque turned to run, but Ryder threw himself up the last few feet and seized him by the ankle. He squealed and tried to kick himself free, but Ryder held him easily and hauled him towards the edge of the catwalk. Al-Faroque grabbed on to the handrail, and clung to it, squealing like a pig being dragged to slaughter.

At that moment a pistol bullet, fired from below, grazed Ryder's shoulder and struck the steel ladder six inches in front of his eyes. It left a bright smear of lead on the steel. The sting of the passing shot was so intense and unexpected that he slackened his grip on al-Faroque's ankle. Al-Faroque felt him give, and kicked backwards. The rowel of the spur on his other riding boot ripped across Ryder's temple, and knocked him off balance. Ryder let go of the man's leg, and grabbed at the ladder rung before his eyes. Al-Faroque pounded away along the catwalk.

Another shot from the tannery floor hissed past Ryder's head and kicked a slab of plaster and cement dust from higher up the wall. He glanced down in time to see the Egyptian guards who had escorted the last delivery of grain run back into the warehouse. He realized they must have seen the flames and heard the gunfire. They were blazing away wildly, stabbing with bayonet and sword at Bacheet's men. The one who had fired at Ryder reloaded his carbine, then swung up the stubby barrel and took deliberate aim at him. Helpless, Ryder watched the flash of the muzzle blast, and the swirling bouquet of black powder smoke. Another bullet clanged on the steel footplate inches above his head. It galvanized him and he hauled himself up the last few feet on to the catwalk. He jumped to his feet and raced after al-Faroque.

The Egyptian had disappeared through the low door at the far end of the catwalk. Ryder reached the opening, expecting another bullet from the marksman below, but when he glanced down he saw the trooper flopping about on the concrete floor like a fresh-caught catfish in the bottom of the boat. Bacheet was standing over him with one foot on his throat, trying to pull the buried spearhead out of his chest. Just then one of the enemy charged at him. Bacheet gave one last heave, the spear came free and he levelled it at his new assailant.

Ryder saw that his own men on the floor below were heavily outnumbered, and although they were fighting like gladiators they were gradually being overwhelmed. He was on the point of letting al-Faroque escape and turning back to join them when another two men ran into the warehouse through a rear door.

'More power to the glorious 10th!' Ryder roared, as he recognized Penrod Ballantyne and Yakub with him, dagger in hand. Penrod parried the bayonet thrust that the Egyptian lieutenant levelled at his face, then caught him with the riposte, sabring him cleanly through the throat; the silver blade parted the lieutenant's vertebrae, and was blurred with pink blood as it came out through the back of his neck. Penrod recovered his blade smoothly, and the Egyptian fell to the ground. His heels drummed spasmodically on the concrete as he went into his death throes. Penrod had a moment to wave casually at Ryder, who pointed through the door at the end of the catwalk.

'It's al-Faroque!' he yelled at Penrod. 'He went that way. Try to cut him off.' That was all he had time for, and he did not know if Penrod had heard, let alone understood. The flames were roaring like a mighty waterfall, and the entire contents of the warehouse were burning furiously, flames racing up the dry timber beams that supported the walls and roof.

So much for my reward, Ryder thought bitterly. Coughing in the smoke, he ran on after al-Faroque. He reached the low door at the end of the catwalk through which the man had disappeared, and stuck his head through it. He sucked in a deep breath of sweet night air and, through streaming eyes, saw that beneath him another ladder ran down the rear wall of the tannery, to the towpath of the canal.

Al-Faroque was still struggling with the folds of his cassock on the bottom rungs of the ladder, but when he saw Ryder's head he let go and dropped the last six feet to land on his hands and knees. He scrambled up, unhurt, and looked up at

Ryder. 'Get back!' he shouted. 'Don't try to stop me.' He tried again to hoist the tangled skirts of his cassock, and succeeded in reaching the holster on his belt. He drew the revolver and aimed it at Ryder. The light of the flames through the rear windows of the tannery lit the towpath brightly. Ryder saw that the major's hand was shaking. Oily drops of sweat ran down his cheeks and dripped from his double chins. He fired two quick shots, which struck the wall on each side of the door. Ryder ducked back inside and heard al-Faroque's footsteps running away along the towpath.

If he reaches the alley, he might get away, Ryder thought, as he clambered out of the door and swung on to the top rungs of the escape ladder. He went down it swiftly, dropped the last ten feet and landed with such force that he bit his tongue. He spat out the blood, and saw that al-Faroque had a lead on him of at least a hundred yards. He had almost reached the corner of the building.

Still carrying his club Ryder raced after him, but al-Faroque dodged round the corner and was gone. Seconds later Ryder reached it, and saw he was half-way down the alley, moving with amazing speed for such a portly figure. Ryder launched himself after him. Once al-Faroque reached the end of the alley he would disappear into the tangled maze of streets beyond. He'll not wait for us to catch him. He'll clear out of Khartoum tonight, Ryder thought grimly. By dawn he will be across the river and converted into the Mahdi's most faithful disciple. What mischief he can do us over there! He was starting to gain on him. But not fast enough, he thought.

As al-Faroque reached the end of the alley, an elegant figure stepped out of a dark doorway and kicked his back foot across the other. Al-Faroque crashed to earth with a force that drove the air from his lungs. However, he wriggled forward on his plump belly and tried to reach the revolver that had flown from his hand as he went down, but as his fingers closed over the butt Penrod stamped hard on his wrist, pinning his hand.

Ryder came up, stooped over him, and cracked him across

the back of his skull with the club. Al-Faroque's face dropped and he snored into the filth of the alley floor.

'A perfect flying trip,' Ryder said to Penrod, with admiration. 'Doubtless perfected on the rugger fields of Eton.'

'Not Eton but Harrow, my dear fellow. And don't confuse the two,' Penrod corrected him. Then, as Yakub appeared at his side, he changed easily into Arabic: 'Tie him up tidy and tight. Gordon Pasha will be interested to talk to him.'

'Perhaps he will allow me to watch the execution?' Yakub asked hopefully, as he unbuckled al-Faroque's belt and used it to strap his arms behind his back.

'Gentle Yakub,' said Penrod, 'I have no doubt that he will prepare a place for you in the very front row of the entertainment.'

By now the sky and the rooftops of the city were brightly lit by the blazing tannery. They left al-Faroque to Yakub, and ran back to the main gate. The heat of the flames was so intense that the combatants were being driven out of the building into the open. As they emerged from the doors or jumped from the windows, Bacheet and his Arabs were waiting for them. There were pugnacious shouts and bellows, the clash of blades and a few shots, but gradually most of the renegade Egyptian garrison troops were rounded up. A few managed to escape into the alleys, but Yakub went after them.

Dawn was breaking as the survivors were marched in clanking chains up to the gates of Mukran Fort. General Gordon watched their arrival from the battlements, and sent for Penrod. His benign expression turned to cold fury when he learnt of the destruction of three thousand sacks of his precious dhurra. 'You let a civilian take command of the raid?' he demanded of Penrod, and his blue eyes blazed. 'Courtney? The trader and black-marketeer? A shabby fellow without a patriotic scruple or a shred of social conscience?'

'I beg your pardon, General, but Courtney was every bit as committed to the recovery of the missing grain as we were. In fact, his agents discovered where it was hidden,' Penrod pointed out mildly.

189

'His commitment went as far as twelve shillings a sack, and not a penny further. If you had taken command this fiasco might well have been avoided.' Gordon stood on tiptoe to glare at him. Penrod stood rigidly to attention and, with an effort, kept his mouth grimly shut.

With an obvious effort Gordon regained his equanimity. 'Well, at least you were able to apprehend the ring leader. I am not at all surprised to find that it was Major al-Faroque. I am going to make an example of him to stiffen the remainder of the garrison. I am going to have him and his accomplices shot from the mouth of a cannon.'

Penrod blinked. This was a particularly savage military punishment reserved for the most outrageous crimes. As far as he knew, it had last been performed on the captured sepoys after the suppression of the mutiny in India almost thirty years ago.

'I would shed no tears if that scoundrel Courtney were to share the same fate.' The little general stamped to the window of his headquarters and scowled across the river at the enemy lines. 'However, I don't suppose I can do that to an Englishman,' he growled, 'more's the pity. But I will decide on something that will leave him in no doubt of my true estimate of his conduct and his moral worth. It will have to be something that affects the contents of his purse. That is where he keeps his conscience.'

Penrod knew that by far his best policy was silence. The good Lord knows I cherish no great affection for Ryder Courtney, he thought. No doubt we will soon be at daggers drawn over the favours of a young lady of our mutual acquaintance. Yet it is difficult to suppress a sneaking admiration for the fellow's brains and courage.

Gordon turned back from the window and pulled his gold hunter from his pocket by its chain. 'Eight o'clock. I want this rogue al-Faroque and his minions tried, sentenced and ready for execution by five this afternoon. I want it done in public on the maidan to make the deepest impression on the populace. I cannot abide black-marketeering in this city where

190

most of the populace is starving. You are in charge, Ballantyne, and I want it done properly.'

I t had all gone off very well, Penrod decided, as he wandered
down the terrace of the consular palace before he retired
for the night. He came to a stately tamarind tree whose
branches overshadowed half the terrace and leant against the
trunk. He was smoking the Cuban cigar that Ryder Courtney
had pressed upon him when they parted. Courtney had
declined the invitation to attend the executions. 'I don't
blame him. I myself would rather have been employed elsewhere,' he murmured.

He felt slightly queasy as he thought about it now, and he
took a long, deep draw on the cigar. At five o'clock that
afternoon almost the entire garrison of Khartoum had paraded
on the maidan to witness punishment. Only the minimum
strength was left to man the defences of the city. Although
they had not been ordered to do so, it seemed that the entire
civilian populace, too, lined the perimeter of the parade
ground three and four deep. The eight Krupps guns were lined
up wheel to wheel and aimed at maximum elevation toward
the besieging Dervish hordes in Omdurman. The ammunition
shortage was too severe to waste even these eight rounds: after
they had completed the primary destruction they would fly on
across the river to burst among the legions of besiegers and,
with luck, kill a few more of the enemy.

The first to be marched out were the black-marketeers and
merchants of the city who had been caught red-handed with
stocks of al-Faroque's grain. Ali Muhammad Acrani was at
the head of the file. When Penrod had searched his premises
behind the hospital he had found six hundred sacks hidden in
the slave cells under the barracoons.

The prisoners were lined up close behind the guns.
Gordon Pasha had sentenced them to watch the executions.
In addition all their possessions, including the contraband

dhurra, were confiscated. Finally they were to be expelled from the city to take their chances on the clemency of the Mahdi and his Ansar across the river. Penrod considered their fate. Given the same choice, I think I would have preferred the kiss of the gunner's daughter, he decided.

His mind went back to that afternoon's programme of entertainment on the maidan. When all the spectators were assembled, Penrod had given the order and Major al-Faroque and the seven other condemned men were marched out from the cells of Mukran Fort. They wore full dress uniform. Each man stood to attention in front of the artillery piece to which he was allocated. The regimental sergeant major read out the charges and sentences in a stentorian voice that carried to every one of the spectators. They craned forward to catch the words '. . . that they shall be shot from guns.' A hum of anticipation went up from the packed ranks. This was something none of them had ever witnessed. They held up their babies and young children for a better view.

They watched the sergeant major roll up the charge sheet and hand it to a runner, who carried it to where Gordon Pasha and Captain Ballantyne stood. The man saluted and handed the roll to the general. 'Very well.' Gordon returned the salute. 'Carry out the sentences.'

The sergeant marched smartly down the rank of condemned men, halting before each in turn and ceremoniously ripping the insignias of rank and merit from their shoulders and the breasts of their tunics. He threw the golden crowns, chevrons and medals into the dust.

When the eight men stood in their torn clothing, forlorn and dishonoured, he gave another order. One at a time the condemned were led to the waiting guns and spreadeagled over them. The gaping muzzles were aimed into the centre of their chests and their arms strapped along each side of the shining black barrels. From this grotesque embrace they would receive the kiss of the gunner's daughter. Al-Faroque threw himself down in the dust of the parade ground. He howled, wept and drummed his heels. Finally he had to be carried to his gun by the soldiers.

'Prepared to carry out the sentence,' the sergeant major bellowed.

'Carry on, Sergeant Major!' Penrod snapped back, his face and voice expressionless.

The sergeant major drew his sword and raised the bare blade. The drummer-boy at his side raised his sticks to his lips, then dropped them to the drumhead in a long roll. The sergeant major dropped his sword blade, and the drummer stopped abruptly. There was a momentary silence and even Penrod drew a sharp breath. The first gun bellowed.

The victim disappeared for an instant in a cloud of dense grey powder smoke. Then the separate parts of his torso were spinning high in the air. There was a stunned silence after the explosion, then a spontaneous burst of cheering from the spectators as the head fell back to earth and rolled across the sun-baked clay.

The sergeant major raised his sword again. The drum rolled, and was again abruptly cut short. Another thunderous discharge. This time the spectators were anticipating the result and the wild applause was mixed with hoots of laughter. Al-Faroque was last in the line and as his turn came closer he screamed for mercy. The crowd yelled in imitation, and al-Faroque's bowels voided noisily. Liquid faeces stained the back of his breeches. The hilarity of the watchers swelled to a bellow as the drum rolled for the eighth and last time. Al-Faroque's head leapt higher in the air than that of any man who had preceded him.

Penrod examined the stub of his cigar and decided regretfully that he could not take another draw without scorching his fingertips. He dropped it on to the flags of the terrace and ground it out under his heel. Although it was late and he had already made his nightly rounds of the city's defences, he still had a pile of paperwork to complete before he could think of bed. Gordon would want all his lists and reports first thing in the morning. The little martinet made no allowances for the contingencies of the siege and the heavy load he had already placed on Penrod's shoulders: 'We have to keep up to scratch, Ballantyne, and set an example.'

At least he spares himself even less than he does me, Penrod thought.

He straightened up from the tree, preparing to make his way up to the quarters that David Benbrook had allocated to him, when a small movement on one of the second-floor balconies caught his eye. The door to the balcony had opened and he was able to see into the room beyond it. The interior was lit by an oil lamp that stood on a ladies' dressing-table, and he could just make out the upright posts and canopy of the bed. The wallpaper was patterned with red roses and sprigs of greenery.

A slim feminine figure appeared in the doorway, back-lit by the lamp, which spun a golden nimbus about her head, like a medieval painting of the Madonna. Even though he could not see her face, he recognized Rebecca immediately. She wore a robe of some lustrous material with a pale blue sheen, probably crêpe-de-Chine. It fitted her closely, emphasizing the curve of her waist and hip, and leaving her arms bare below the elbows. She came to the front of the balcony where the moonlight added subtle silver tones to the golden lamplight behind her.

She gazed down on to the garden and terrace below her but did not see him, half concealed by the wide branches of the tamarind. She gathered her skirts and, with a graceful movement, swung her lower body up until she was sitting on the balcony wall. Her feet were bare, and her legs exposed to the knees. Her calves were shapely, her feet small and girlish. Penrod was enthralled by their elegance. Now the lamplight struck her in profile and left the other half of her face in mysterious moon shadow. She held an ivory-backed brush in one hand, and her long blonde hair was loose. She stroked the brush through it, beginning at the pale parting that ran down the centre of her scalp and ending at her waist, where the tresses danced and rippled. Her expression was serene and lovely.

Penrod wanted to move close enough to study every plane and angle of her face and perhaps even to catch a trace of her perfume. Despite the gloves, the long sleeves and the wide-brimmed straw hat that she wore habitually during the day, the skin of Rebecca's bare arms and legs was not fashionably milky but a light gold. Her neck was long and graceful, her head tilted at a beguiling angle. She began to hum softly. He did not recognize the tune, but it was a siren song he could not resist. He moved closer to the balcony with the caution of a hunter, waiting for her to close her eyes briefly at the completion of each brush stroke before he took another small step towards her. Now he could hear the intake of her breath at the end of each bar of the tune and almost feel the warmth and texture of her lips under his own. He imagined the tremulous way in which they would part to allow him to taste the apple-sweet juices of her mouth.

At last she set aside the brush, twisted her hair into a thick rope and coiled it on top of her head. She drew a long hairpin with a jewelled head from the lapel of her gown and reached up to secure her hair. As she did so she turned her head away and Penrod took advantage of this to step forward again.

She froze like a gazelle sensing the stalk of the leopard. He stood still and held his breath. Then she turned to face him and her eyes flew wide. She stared down at him for a moment, then swung her legs back into the balcony and sprang to her feet. Her lips framed a silent accusation: 'You were spying!'

Then she whirled away through the open door and closed it behind her, with just a faint click of the latch, as though she did not want anyone else to hear. As though the fact that he had been spying on her was a secret between them. Penrod's heart was drumming and his breath came faster. He regretted that he had frightened her away. He wished he had been able to watch her a little longer, as though he might have learnt some secret by studying her unsuspecting face.

He left the terrace and, as he mounted the main spiral staircase to his own quarters, his predatory instinct, which, for a brief interlude, had been replaced by an almost reverential awe, reasserted itself. He smiled. At least we now know where to find Mademoiselle's boudoir, should the need arise, he thought.

Unlike her twin, Amber was unperturbed by what they had witnessed when they burst in upon their elder sister and Ryder. She was the only one of the Benbrook sisters who returned to his compound the following day. She arrived at the usual hour with Nazeera in tow and immediately took charge of the team of three dozen Sudanese women who were manufacturing the precious green-cake. She relished not having to share the authority with Saffron.

Bacheet found his master in the workshop at the harbour and whispered his report.

Ryder looked up from the *Ibis*'s main steam line, which he and Jock McCrump were welding. 'Her sisters?' Ryder demanded. 'Miss Saffron and Miss Rebecca?'

Bacheet shook his head. 'Only Miss Amber.' This was not a conversation that Ryder wanted to share with Jock McCrump and the *Ibis*'s stokers and oilers. He jerked his head towards the door and Bacheet followed him out.

They were half-way back to the compound before Ryder broke the silence. 'What happened, Bacheet?' Bacheet looked innocently uncomprehending, but Ryder was certain that he had shared Nazeera's mattress last night and knew every detail of what had transpired during the past twenty-four hours in the ladies' quarters of Her Britannic Majesty's consular palace.

'Tell me what you know,' he insisted.

'I am a simple man,' said Bacheet. 'I know horses and camels, the cataracts and currents of the Nile. But what do I know of a woman's heart?' He shook his head. 'Perhaps you should enquire of these mysteries from one much wiser than I.'

'Send Nazeera to me.' Ryder stifled a smile. 'I shall wait for her at the monkey cages.'

Nazeera approved of Ryder Courtney. Of course, he had

the par-boiled look of most *ferenghi*, and his eyes were a disconcerting and unnatural shade of green, but a man's looks and age counted for little if he was a good provider. This one's wives would never starve: he was a man strong in body and resolve, and he would protect his own. Yet there was a gentleness in him. He would never beat his women, unless their behaviour truly invited it. Yes, she approved of him. It was to be regretted that, so far, al-Jamal had not displayed equal good sense.

She came to the animal compound, and whispered to old Ali that he should stay within call but out of earshot. She might be a widow and almost forty years of age, but she was a devout, respectable woman. She had convinced herself that she was the only one who knew of her discreet friendships with Yakub and Bacheet.

She greeted Ryder, asked the blessings of the Prophet for him, touched her heart and lips, then squatted at a polite distance from him. She drew her shawl over the lower part of her face and waited for him to speak.

Ryder asked after her health, and she assured him that she was well. Then he asked after the health of her charges.

'Al-Jamal is well.'

'I am happy to hear that. I was worried about her. She has not come to help the women today.'

Nazeera inclined her head slightly but made no comment.

'Nazeera, is she angry with me?' he asked.

She drew a sharp breath of disapproval. The question lacked even a semblance of subtlety. She should not dignify it with a reply. However, this time she would make allowances for him: after all, he was an infidel.

'Al-Jamal feels that you took advantage of her trust. She was in need of comfort and counsel so she came to you as a friend, but you behaved like a lecher.'

Bacheet saw Ryder's face crumple with dismay.

'Lecher?' he asked. 'She is wrong. I bear her great respect and affection. I am not a lecher.'

Nazeera was balanced on a knife edge of loyalty. She could not tell him that the real offence was that they had been

197

discovered not only by the twins but also by the pretty captain. But she liked him enough to give him a light word of comfort. 'I love her like my own daughter, but she is a young girl and understands nothing, not even her own heart. She will change with the moon and the wind and the current, like a dhow without a captain. When she says she wishes never to see someone again, she means at least until midnight, but probably not until noon tomorrow.'

Ryder pondered this as he offered a morsel of green-cake through the bars of the cage to Lucy, the vervet monkey. She was due to give birth at any moment. She seized his wrist and licked the last crumbs from his fingers.

'What should I do, Nazeera?' He asked.

She shook her head. Men were such children. 'Anything you do now will only make matters worse. Do nothing. I will tell her how much you are suffering. Most young girls like to hear that. When it is time to do so we will speak again.'

Ryder was much cheered, by this offer of assistance. 'But what of Saffron? Why has she not come to help Amber?'

'Filfil feels as strongly about your behaviour as her eldest sister.' Filfil was the Arabic word for pepper, and also Saffron's nickname. 'She also has expressed an intention never to speak to you again. She says that she wishes to die.'

Ryder looked alarmed again. 'A single kiss, and a fairly chaste one at that. Now she wants to die?'

'Long ago she chose you as her future husband. She has even discussed the details with me. I should warn you now that she will never allow you to have more than one wife.'

Ryder burst out in incredulous laughter. 'What a sweet and funny child she is, but a child nevertheless.'

'In a few short years she will be of marriageable age,' Nazeera did not smile, 'and she has made her plans.'

Ryder laughed again, but this time with a note of trepidation. 'Nazeera, I do not wish to encourage her to believe in the impossible, but nor do I wish to hurt her. Will you give her my message? Will you tell her that there is important work for her to do? I need her here.'

'I will tell her, Effendi,' Nazeera rose to her feet and bowed, 'but she will need more encouragement than that to forgive your infidelity. But now I must go to help al-Zahra.' Amber's Arabic name meant 'the Flower'. 'We can never make enough of the green-cake to feed so many hungry mouths.'

After she had gone Ryder lingered a few minutes longer at the monkey cage, pondering his predicaments. Lucy perched at the bars, belly bulging between her knees, and offered her head to his caress. She loved to be scratched behind the ears, and to have her fur searched for vermin. At last Ryder sighed and made to leave the cage. Lucy seized his hand as he tried to pull it out through the bars, and sank her sharp white fangs into his thumb.

'You creature, you!' He cuffed her lightly. She shrieked, as though in mortal anguish, and shot to the top of the cage where she gibbered at him furiously.

'A plague on you, and all female wiles!' he scolded, and sucked his thumb as he left the enclosure to go down to the harbour. Today Jock McCrump hoped to complete the repairs to the hull and engine, and he was planning to take the *Ibis* out on her trials.

Penrod stood on the parapet of the forward redoubt on the riverbank opposite Tutti Island. He stamped on the sandbags to test their solidity. As the stores of dhurra were used up he had the empty sacks filled and worked into weak points in the fortifications. 'That will do!' he told the Egyptian sergeant in charge of the work detail. 'Now we need a few more timber baulks in the embrasures of the gun pits.' Under General Gordon's orders, he was stripping the abandoned buildings, and using their timbers to strengthen the fortifications.

He strode along the top of the sandbagged wall, pausing every fifty or hundred paces to survey the riverbank below. He had placed marker pegs in the strip of muddy earth between the foot of the wall and the edge of the water. A month ago the Nile had lapped the wall three feet from the top. Two weeks ago a few inches of mud had appeared at the foot of the wall. Now the strip of bank was six feet wide. Each day the river was falling. Within the next few months it would enter the stage of Low Nile. This was what the Dervish were waiting for. The wide banks would dry out to give a safe mooring for the dhows ferrying their legions across the river, and a firm footing from which to launch a final assault on the city.

Penrod jumped down on to the mudflat and moved his pegs out to the edge of the receding river. In places there were now fifteen or twenty feet of exposed bank. They will need a lot more ground from which to launch a full-scale attack, he decided, but the river is falling rapidly. The Mahdi had shrewd and experienced warlords commanding his army, men like Osman Atalan. Soon they would start probing the defences with midnight raids and sorties. Where will they strike us first? he wondered. He walked on along the perimeter, looking for the weak spots. By the time he reached Mukran Fort he had picked out at least two points where he could expect the first raids to strike.

He found General Gordon at one of his favourite lookouts on the parapet of the fort. He was seated under a thatched sunshade at a camp table on which were laid out his binoculars, notebooks and maps. 'Sit down, Ballantyne,' he said. 'You must be thirsty.' He indicated the earthenware water jug on the table.

'Thank you, sir.' Penrod filled a glass.

'You may rest assured that it has been boiled the full half-hour.' It was a barbed jest. Under threat of flogging, Gordon had ordered all the garrison water to be boiled to those specifications. He had learnt the necessity of this during his campaigns in China. The results were remarkable. Although at first Penrod had believed this was another whim of Gordon's he had since become a fervent believer. Cholera was raging among the civilian populace of the city, who openly flouted Gordon's decrees and filled their waterskins from the river and the canal, into which discharged the city sewers. By contrast the garrison troops had suffered only three cases, and all of those had been traced to disobedience and the use of unboiled water. All three victims had died. 'Damned lucky for them,' Penrod had remarked to David Benbrook. 'If they had lived Gordon would have had them shot.'

'The death of the dog, they call it. Reeking torrents of your own hot excrement and vomit, every muscle and sinew of your body knotted in agonizing cramps, a desiccated skeleton for a body and a head like a skull!' David shuddered. 'Not for me, thank you very much. I'll take my water boiled.'

Penrod felt his skin crawl as he recalled that description: it was so accurate. Yet thirst could kill as swiftly as the cholera. The heat and the desert air sucked the moisture from his body so his throat was parched. He raised the mug, savoured the smell of woodsmoke, which proved it was safe, then drained it in four long swallows.

'Well, now, Ballantyne, what about the north bank?' Gordon never wasted time in pleasantries.

'I have marked a number of weak spots in the line.' Penrod spread his field map on the table and pinned down a corner with the water jug. They pored over it together. 'Here and here are the worst. The river level is dropping sharply – it's down another three inches since noon yesterday. Each day exposes us more. We will have to strengthen those places.'

'Heaven knows, we are hard pressed for men and material to keep pace with the work.' Gordon looked up shrewdly at Penrod. 'Yes? You have something to suggest?'

'Well, sir, as you say, we cannot hope to maintain the entire line impregnable . . .' Gordon frowned. He could not abide those he referred to as 'dismal Johnnies'. Penrod hurried on before he could level the accusation. '. . . so it occurred to me that we should deliberately leave some gaps in our outer defences to entice the Dervish to attack them.'

'Ah!' Gordon's frown lifted. 'Poisoned gifts!'

'Exactly, sir. We leave an opening, then behind it we set a trap. We run them into one of the blind alleys, and cover it with enfilading fire from the Gatlings.'

Thoughtfully, Gordon rubbed the silver stubble on his chin. They had only two Gatling guns, the rejects of Hicks's expedition. He had declined to take them with him on the march to El Obeid as he had considered them too cumbersome. Each weapon was mounted on its own heavy guncarriage, a sturdy axle and two iron-shod wheels. It needed a span of at least four oxen to drag it into action. The mechanisms were fragile and prone to stoppages. Hicks had believed in traditional volley fire from squares of infantry, rather than sustained fire from a single exposed position. He conceded that the Gatlings might be useful in a static defensive position, but he was convinced that there was no place for them in a flying offensive column. He had left the two guns and a hundred thousand rounds of the special .58 bore ammunition in the arsenal at Khartoum when he marched away to annihilation at El Obeid.

Penrod had found them stored in a dark recess of the arsenal, where he had collected a pistol to replace the one Yakub had lost, under dusty tarpaulins. He was familiar with the Gatling. He had selected two teams of the most likely Egyptian troopers under his command, and within a week had taught them to serve the weapons. Even though it was a complicated firing mechanism, they had learnt swiftly. The copper-cased rimfire .58 bore cartridges were fed by gravity from a hopper on top of the weapon. The gunner turned a hand crank, and the six heavy brass barrels rotated around a central shaft. As each bullet dropped from the hopper it was seized by one of the six cam-operated bolts, locked into the breech, fired and ejected by gravity. The rate of fire depended on the vigour with which the gunner turned the crank handle. It required strength and stamina to keep up a sustained fire for longer than a few minutes, but in practice Penrod timed one gun at nearly three hundred rounds in a half a minute. Of course, as soon as it heated it jammed. There was no machine-gun he knew of that did not.

In one respect Hicks had been correct, the Gatling guns were not very mobile. Penrod had realized that, in the event of a surprise night attack, it would not be possible to move them swiftly from one position to another on the tenkilometre perimeter of the city's defence works.

Penrod summarized his plan: 'Suck them through the pretended weak spots on to the Gatlings and cut them up, sir.'

'First rate!' Gordon beamed. 'Show me again where you propose to set your traps.'

'Well, sir, I thought that here below the harbour would be the most obvious point.' Gordon nodded approval. 'The other spot would be here, opposite the hospital.' Penrod prodded the map with his forefinger. 'Behind both those positions there is a maze of narrow streets. I will block them with piles of rubble and timber baulks, then site the Gatlings behind strong brickworks . . .' They discussed the plan over the next hour.

'Very well, Ballantyne. Carry on.' At last Gordon dismissed him.

Penrod saluted and headed for the ramp that led away from the parapet of the fort. Half-way down he paused to peer into the north. Only eyes as sharp as his could have picked out the tiny dark speck in the cloudless steel blue sky. At first he thought it was one of the Saker falcons coming in over the wastes of the Monassir desert from the north. He had noticed that a pair of the splendid birds were nesting under the eaves of the arsenal roof. He watched the tiny shape approaching, then shook his head. 'Not the typical falcon wingbeat.' The distant shape grew in size and he exclaimed, 'Pigeon!'

He was reminded sharply of his last ride down from the north when he and Yakub had cut the loop of the river. He watched the pigeon's approach with keen interest. As it approached the river, it began a wide circle high in the steely sky with the city of Omdurman as its centre.

'Pigeon returning to loft.' He recognized the manoeuvre. A pigeon nearly always began a long flight with a number of circles to orient itself, and ended in the same way before it descended to its home. This bird swung wide over the river, then passed almost directly overhead where Penrod stood.

'It's another bloody Dervish carrier!' He had seen the tiny roll of rice paper tied to its leg. He pulled his watch from his hip pocket and checked the time. 'Seventeen minutes past four.' He had bought the watch from Consul Le Blanc at an exorbitant price to replace the one that had been doused on his last crossing of the river.

He watched the pigeon come round in another sweeping circle that carried it over the grounds of the consular palace, then begin a long, slanting descent across the broad waters of the Nile. The last glimpse he had of it was as it dropped in steeply towards the whitewashed dome of the small mosque on the southern outskirts of Omdurman.

As he slipped the watch back into his pocket he had the feeling he was being watched and looked round. General Gordon's head showed above the parapet. 'What is it, Ballantyne?' he called down.

'I can't be certain, General, but I would wager a gold sovereign to a pinch of dry pigeon droppings that the Mahdi is running a regular bird mail with his army in the north.'

'If you are right, I would give more than a gold sovereign to get my hands on one of his messages.' Gordon stared grimly across the river at the mosque where the pigeon had landed. It was almost a month since Penrod had arrived in the city. Since then they had received no news from Cairo. There was no way of guessing what had happened to General Stewart and his relief column. Had they begun the march? Had they been beaten back? On the other hand perhaps they were only days away.

'Ballantyne, how can you get me one of those pigeons?' Gordon asked quietly.

A little before four the following afternoon Penrod was waiting on the terrace of the consular palace with his head thrown back to watch the northern sky.

'Right on time!' he exclaimed, as the speck appeared in the north sky, slightly to the east of where he had expected it. As it passed over his head he estimated the bird's speed and height with narrowed eyes. 'Two hundred feet if it's an inch, and going like its tail's on fire. A long call!' he murmured. 'But there is no wind, and I have taken pheasant higher than that.' He stroked his moustache, which was approaching its former glory.

The consular dinner that evening was formal. There were a dozen guests, all that remained of the diplomatic corps and the civil administrators of the Khedive in Cairo. As usual, Rebecca was her father's hostess. David had sent an invitation to Ryder Courtney, without consulting either Rebecca or Saffron, either of whom would surely have exercised a veto if they had had the chance.

Ryder had been cherishing a young buffalo heifer in the expectations of selling it for an enormous profit when the city was relieved. The prospect of salvation was becoming daily more remote, and the buffalo had a voracious appetite that was increasingly difficult to satisfy. When he received David's invitation he slaughtered the animal and sent a haunch with two bottles of Cognac to the consular kitchens.

Rebecca recognized the gift as a peace-offering, and it placed her in a terrible quandary. Could she refuse it, when it would make the evening a triumphant success? It would mean acknowledging Ryder's existence, which she was not yet prepared to do. She solved the dilemma by sending him a note, delivered by Amber, accepting the gift on behalf of her father. She knew this was weakness on her part, but she salved her conscience by determining not to address a single word to him if he attended the dinner.

Ryder, as was his wont, was the last guest to arrive. He was looking so elegant in his dinner jacket, and seemed so at ease with himself and the world that Rebecca's anger was exacerbated.

Nazeera lied, she thought, as she watched from the corner of her eye as he chatted affably with her father and Consul Le Blanc. He isn't suffering in the least.

At that moment she became aware that she, in her turn, was being watched. She glanced round sharply to see Captain Ballantyne studying her from across the room with the knowing smile that had begun to infuriate her. He is always spying, she thought. Before she recovered her poise and looked away, she noticed that his hair and his whiskers had grown out in a rather fetching fashion. She felt her cheeks burn and that disconcerting sensation in her lower belly. She turned to Imran Pasha, the former governor of Khartoum who was now subservient to General Gordon.

Ten minutes later she glanced around surreptitiously to see whether Captain Ballantyne was still spying on her, and felt a twinge of annoyance when she saw that he was engrossed with the twins – or they were with him. Both Amber and Saffron were shrieking with laughter in a most unladylike fashion. She regretted that she had given in to their blandishments and allowed them to join the company instead of making them eat their dinner with Nazeera in the kitchen. She had scored a small point by seating Saffron beside Ryder Courtney: the child would have difficulty holding firm to her vow never to speak to him again. She had placed Captain Ballantyne as far away from herself as possible, at her father's end of the table.

The buffalo haunch was a glorious pink in the centre, and running with juices. The company fell upon it in ravenous silence. No sooner were the plates removed than Captain Ballantyne whispered a few words to her father, stood up, bowed to her and strode from the room. She knew better than to expect an explanation for his departure. After all, they were at war, and he was responsible for the city's defences. However, she regretted that she was to be deprived of the opportunity to snub him more profoundly.

She glanced down the table at the second object of her disapproval, and saw that Saffron had obviously forgiven Ryder. At the beginning of the meal he had ignored her haughtiness and had concentrated all his attention on Amber at his right hand. This had brought Saffron close to tears of jealousy. Then he had switched tactics and turned all his charm on her. She had been unprepared for this. 'Saffron, did you know that Lucy has had her babies?' Before she realized the trap, she was listening avidly as he told her Lucy had given birth to twins, what the babies looked like, how proud Lucy was of them. He had named them Billy and Lily.

'Oh, can I come and see them tomorrow? Oh, please, Ryder,' Saffron cried.

'But Saffy, Nazeera told me you were not feeling well,' Ryder said.

'That was yesterday. I *was* feeling rather peaky.' Ryder gathered that 'peaky' was one of her new words. 'But I am very well now. Amber and I will be with you at seven o'clock tomorrow morning.' The trial of wills had ended with a complete capitulation on her part.

Rebecca made a small *moue* at the silliness of the child, and turned her attention back to Consul Le Blanc. She had overheard her father remark to Ryder that he was as queer as a duck with four legs. It was a pity that she was unable to ask Ryder what that meant. It sounded intriguing, and Ryder knew everything. I suppose I will have to forgive him in time, she thought, but not just yet.

The dessert was pâté of green-cake with warm honey sauce: at David Benbrook's instigation Bacheet had robbed the nest that wild bees had built in the palace roof. He had been sternly restricted to the removal of a single honeycomb – David had a sweet tooth and was hoarding the bees' output. This dish was also warmly received, and the Limoges porcelain dessert bowls were scraped clean.

'I have not enjoyed a meal as much since my last visit to Le Grand Véfour in eighty-one,' Le Blanc assured Rebecca.

Despite his four legs, he is rather a dear old ass, she thought. In this new mood of benevolence she glanced back at Ryder, caught his eye, then nodded and smiled. His obvious relief was really quite gratifying. Am I becoming fast? she questioned herself. She was not certain what being fast entailed, but her father disapproved of fast women, or said he did.

After their guests had departed and they had climbed the spiral staircase to the bedroom floor her father placed his arm round her shoulders, hugged her and told her how proud he was of her, and what a lovely woman she was growing into.

So he does not think I am becoming fast, Rebecca thought, but nevertheless she felt strangely discontented. As she prepared for bed she whispered, 'There is something missing. Why should I feel so unhappy? Life is so short. Perhaps the Mahdi will storm the city tomorrow and it will all be over, and I won't even have lived.'

As if the monster had heard her and stirred in his lair, there came the crash of artillery fire from across the Nile. She heard a shell shriek overhead, then burst somewhere in the native quarter near the canal. With her hair in a golden cloud upon her shoulders she threw on her silk dressing-gown, turned the lamp down low and opened the door to the balcony. She hesitated, feeling guilty and uncertain. 'There won't be anybody there,' she told herself firmly. 'It's after midnight. If he's still awake, he'll be at the waterfront with those Gatlings.'

She stepped out on to the balcony and before she could stop herself she glanced down and searched beneath the outspread branches of the tamarind tree. She felt a nasty twinge of disappointment when she realized she had guessed right. Nobody was there. She sighed, leant her elbows on the wall and stared out across the river.

The Bedlam Bedouin is having an early night, she thought. Since sunset there had been only that single cannon shot, and now all was silent. In the moonlight she watched the bats diving and circling as they hunted insects in the top branches of the ficus tree at the bottom of the terrace. After a few minutes she sighed again and straightened up. I'm not sleepy, but it's late. I should go to bed, she thought.

A vesta flared in the shadows beneath the tamarind tree, and her heart tripped. The flame settled to a yellow glow, and she saw his face lit like the portrait in a cameo, while the rest of him remained shrouded in darkness. He had a long black cigar between his teeth. He placed the tip of it to the match and drew deeply. The flame burned up brightly. 'Oh, sweet Jesus, he is so beautiful.' The blasphemy was out before she could quell it. Still holding the burning match in front of his face he looked up at her. She stared back. He was fifty yards away but she was mesmerized, like a bird by a cobra.

He blew out the vesta, and the image of his face was gone.

Only the glow of his cigar remained, brighter then fading as he drew on it. The pain came over her again, pervasive and debilitating, until she no longer had control of her emotions. Like a woman in a trance she turned slowly, went back through her bedroom and out into the corridor beyond. She passed the door to her father's suite, and her bare feet danced faster over the silken carpet that led her to the head of the staircase. She ran down, and was suddenly stricken with the fear that he would be gone by the time she reached the terrace. She fumbled with the latch of the front doors – it seemed an eternity before they opened. She ran across the lawn, then stopped dead when she saw his dark shape exactly where it had been.

He took the cigar from his mouth, dropped it on to the stone flags and waited. Her feet moved again, of their own accord, slowly at first then faster. 'I don't – I won't—' she stammered.

'Don't talk,' he commanded. And she was overwhelmed by deep gratitude although she did not understand why. She went into his arms, which closed round her. She lost all contact with reality. His mouth tasted of cigar smoke mingled with precious musk, a distillation of masculine ambergris, a rare elixir of desire. She felt terrified and helpless, yet as safe and secure as though she had been spirited into the keep of a fairy fortress.

Her silk robe and the light cotton nightgown offered no obstacle to him. Her skin beneath them was burning hot, but his cunning fingers ignited deeper and more intense fires within her. She closed her eyes, threw back her head and surrendered to his touch. Suddenly she gasped and her eyes flew open at a sensation almost too exquisite to be borne. The painful knot in the pit of her stomach burst, and a new, wonderful sensation replaced it and diffused through her whole being. She looked down and realized that the front of her gown was open to her navel and his mouth was pressed to her breast. She could feel his teeth upon her nipple, and thought he might bite through to her very heart.

He picked her up and she felt weightless. He laid her on

the lawn, and the grass felt cool and soft under her back. He lifted the skirts of her robe and the night air caressed her thighs and belly. She felt his weight come over the top of her. He was touching her where she had never been touched before. Her thighs fell apart.

The cannon across the river roared. She heard the shriek of the approaching shell, and her legs snapped together like the blades of a pair of scissors. The shell flew so close overhead that it took her breath away so that she could not scream. It crashed into the east wing of the palace, and burst in a cloud of flame, dust, flying plaster and bricks.

With all her strength she thrust him away and rolled out from under him. She jumped up and, long pale legs flashing, ran like a fawn startled from its forest bed, back across the terrace and up the stairs. Frantically she raced to the twins' room, beside her father's suite. The door was never locked. She ran in to them, gathered them up and held them tight. She was sobbing with relief to find them safe, and for her own escape. 'Are you all right, my darlings? Oh, dear Jesus, thank you for keeping us all safe.' She hugged them closer, but the twins were sleepy and grumpy.

'Why did you wake us up?' demanded Saffron.

'What's wrong with you, Becky? Why are you crying?' Amber yawned and rubbed her eyes. 'Why are you being so silly?'

Before she could reply her father came in through the door, carrying a lantern. 'Are you girls all right?'

'What happened? What is all the fuss about?' Saffron clamoured.

'Didn't even wake you up, what?' David laughed. 'The Bedlam Bedouin will be mortified. He's been shooting at the palace for months. The first time he manages to hit it, you go on sleeping as though nothing had happened. Shows a lack of respect, I'd say.'

'Oh, was it a shell?' Amber said. 'I thought it was a dream.'

'Where, Daddy? Where did it hit?'

'The east wing, but it's deserted. Nobody hurt. No fires. Everything safe.'

The twins were asleep before Rebecca left them, but after she got back to her own bed she could not drop off. She tried a prayer. 'Gentle Jesus, meek and mild, thank you for looking after Papa and the twins. Thank you saving me from . . .' She did not think it necessary to elaborate: He knew everything. '. . . for saving me from a fate worse than death.' She had read that expression somewhere, and now seemed an appropriate time to use it. 'Please keep me from temptation.' But the prayer did not seem to help. She did not truly feel as though she had been saved; on the contrary, she felt as though she had been cruelly deprived of something of great value, something as dear as life itself.

She thought about how he had touched her and began to ache again, where his fingers had been. Timidly she ran her own hand down to make sure he had not hurt her. She started with panic as she felt that she was bleeding, all hot and running wet. She pulled away her hand and held it up to the moonlight streaming in through the window. Her fingers were indeed damp but not with blood. She replaced her hand, and felt the pain swelling up inside her. She was panting, and wicked images flashed before her tightly shut eyelids. Penrod Ballantyne standing over her, naked, with the knife in his hand. She imagined his fingers where hers were now.

The huge ball inside her exploded, and the pain was gone. She felt a wonderful sense of elation and freedom. She felt herself falling backwards through the mattress, sinking down into a warm dark nest of sleep. When Nazeera woke her, sunlight was streaming in through the open balcony door.

'What happened to you, Becky? You are glowing like a ripe peach on the bough with the morning sun upon it.'

Arabic is such a romantic language, Rebecca thought. It suits my mood perfectly. 'Darling Nazeera, I feel as though this is the very first morning of my life,' she replied, in the same language, and wondered why Nazeera suddenly looked so worried.

Penrod understood David's reluctance to part for even a few hours with his precious double-barrelled twelve-bore London best guns by James Purdey & Sons. They were extraordinary weapons and had probably cost him as much as fifty pounds each, he guessed. 'One hundred and fifty,' David corrected him. 'Tsar Alexander of all the Russias and Kaiser William of Germany both have guns almost identical to mine.'

'I assure you that they are needed in the furtherance of an excellent cause, sir. I give you my solemn word of honour that I will look after them as though they were my firstborn,' Penrod wheedled.

'I hope you treat them better than that. It is always possible to beget brats. Purdeys like mine are another matter entirely.'

'Perhaps I should explain why I need to borrow them,' Penrod suggested.

David listened attentively. He became more intrigued as Penrod continued. In the end he sighed with resignation. 'Very well, but there is a condition. The twins go with them.' As he saw Penrod's nonplussed expression he went on, 'They are my loaders and I have taught them to pay proper respect to my guns.'

Both girls were delighted to be chosen for the commission, Amber even more so than Saffron. This was an opportunity for her to have her hero to herself for a while. They were ready and waiting on the palace terrace an hour ahead of the appointed time.

When Penrod arrived they insisted on coaching him in the skills of passing and handing the guns. He soon saw how seriously they took their duties: to humour them he pretended ignorance and asked a few asinine questions. 'Where do you put the bullets in?'

'They are not bullets, silly. They are cartridges,' Amber explained importantly. She was chief instructress. She and Saffron had debated this issue the previous night, when the

212

lights were out and they were supposed to be asleep. Finally Amber had settled the matter: 'Saffy, you can have Ryder as your special friend, but Captain Ballantyne is mine. Remember that!'

When it came to handling the guns, Penrod was deliberately clumsy and slow so that he did not deprive Amber of the pleasure of correcting him.

'When I pass it to you, you must try to remember to hold out your left hand with the palm up, Captain Ballantyne, so I can place the fore-end into your hand.'

'Like this, Miss Amber?' He managed to keep a straight face, as he reflected that he had been about the same age that Amber was now when he had first been allowed to attend his family's grand shoot at Clercastle on the Borders, and to take his place in the line like a man.

'Don't hold your hand so high, Captain Ballantyne, otherwise I can't reach.' She hated to draw attention to the discrepancy in their heights. At last she was satisfied. She even commended him on his progress: 'I must say, you do learn quickly, Captain Ballantyne.'

'I think that you and I make an excellent team, Miss Amber,' he replied seriously, and Amber felt quite giddy with gratification.

'Yes, but have you actually ever shot before?' Saffron was feeling left out, a sensation to which she was unaccustomed.

'Once or twice,' Penrod reassured her.

'My papa is one of the best shots in England,' Saffron informed him grandly.

'I am sure Captain Ballantyne will do very well.' Amber pulled a disapproving face at her twin. Could not Saffy keep quiet for once?

'Well, we shall see about that,' said Saffron haughtily.

All three waited impatiently on the terrace, the twins vying with each other to be the first to spot the pigeon. They saw it in the same instant, and squealed with excitement. The bird's wing tips were bone white. They flashed in the sunlight. It was high as it came in across the river, much too high as it passed overhead. The Purdeys were choked full and full, giving them an effective pattern of pellets at a range out to sixty yards, but this pigeon was at least three hundred feet high.

'Why didn't you shoot?' Saffron demanded, as it flew on.

'It was well out of range,' Penrod told her. 'If I prick the bird and send it wounded to its loft, the Dervish might tumble to what we are up to. They will stop using the birds. We must have a clean kill.'

'Daddy would have killed it easily.'

'Look, it's coming round again.' Amber tried to prevent her sister baiting the captain.

The pigeon turned wide beyond the scattered buildings of Omdurman, then came back across the river, angling in towards the waterfront, losing height gradually.

'That should do well enough,' Penrod murmured, and brought up the gun. The movement was unhurried, almost casual. His left arm was extended almost straight in line with the barrels, his right cheek pressed to the comb of the butt-stock. He picked up the bird from behind its tail, and swung smoothly through its line of flight. At the final instant, as his forefinger tightened on the trigger, he gave the gun an extra forward flick. It fired and the muzzle kicked up at the recoil. Smoothly he remounted the gun, his hands, shoulder and head dropping into the same position as before. The gun thudded again and jumped with a spurt of black powder smoke from the right-hand muzzle.

'Miss!' cried Saffron.

The bird was so high that there was a perceptible delay after the sound of the shots before the pellets reached it. Then the pigeon lurched and tottered in the air. Its legs dropped and dangled down.

'Hit!' howled Amber.

Then the pattern of the second shot caught the wounded bird and they heard the pellets rattle on its plumage. One pellet struck it under the chin and it threw back its head as the lead cut through to its brain.

'Dead!' Amber shrieked. 'Stone dead in the air! Even Papa couldn't have done better.' The pigeon's wings folded and it plummeted to earth, but it still had the momentum of its flight and curled out towards the water.

'It's going to fall into the river,' Penrod shouted with alarm, and tossed the shotgun back to Amber. It took her by surprise but she caught it before it hit the earth. Penrod bounded away down the lawn towards the riverbank, and she ran after him, hampered by the heavy gun.

For a while it looked as though the dead bird might fall on firm ground, but then the breeze caught it. Penrod came up short on the muddy strip of ground above the water's edge and watched in dismay as the pigeon splashed in thirty yards offshore. The carcass floated in the centre of a spreading circle of ripples and loose blue breast feathers.

'Crocodile!' Amber screamed behind him. A hundred yards beyond the fallen pigeon Penrod saw the monstrous head push through the surface. The skin was gnarled and lumpy as the bark of an ancient olive tree. 'Big one!' Amber shouted.

'It's after the pigeon,' Saffron cried.

Penrod did not hesitate. He pulled off his boots and flung them aside, then ran to the water's edge ripping off his shirt so that the buttons flew away like sown wheat. His breeches went next and he was left with only his underpants, in a dashing crimson silk. He ran into the green water until it reached his waist, then linked his hands over his head and dived forward. The moment his head broke water again, he struck out in a powerful overarm stroke. The crocodile was drawn on by the commotion, and its great tail thrashed from side to side, driving it to meet Penrod.

'Come back!' wailed Amber. 'Leave the silly old bird!'

Penrod swam furiously, kicking hard with both legs, cleaving through the water. The crocodile moved much faster. This was its element, but it had three times further than Penrod to travel. He reached the carcass and thrust the pigeon's head into his mouth, then turned and started back towards the shore. 'Faster!' Amber shouted wildly. 'It's gaining on you! Faster, please! Please!'

The great saurian had fixed all its attention on the man. Instead of diving, it swam on the surface and the long tail drove from side to side, sending out a boiling wake behind it. It was so close that its eyes glittered like opaque yellow marbles. Long fangs protruded over its scaly lips, the rows interlocking with each other. It bore in on Penrod's naked legs.

'It's going to catch you!' Amber was wild with fear. She had not reloaded the shotgun, but now she pushed the slide across and broke open the breech. She fumbled a pair of cartridges out of the leather bag on her hip, thrust one into the breech, and dropped the other into the mud. There was no time to retrieve it or find another so she snapped the breech closed. As she ran into the water it rose to her knees, her hips, then her lower ribs.

Penrod was directly in front of her, crashing through the water like a maniac, kicking up a froth behind him. With cold horror Amber watched the monster close the gap between them. Suddenly it reared high out of the water, and its jaws gaped open. The lining of its mouth and throat was a lovely buttercup yellow. It was so close that she could clearly see the flap of skin at the back of its throat sealing off the opening of its gullet to keep the water from flooding into its lungs. The fangs were sharp and ragged. She could smell the obscene reek of its open maw. It lunged towards Penrod's legs.

Amber threw up the gun and thumbed back the ornate hammer. At any other time she would have needed both hands to work against the heavy spring of the sidelock, but she was possessed. The butt was too long to fit into her shoulder so she held it under her right armpit. She aimed, and kept her eyes open, as her father had taught her, as she pulled the back trigger. If she had pulled the front one the hammer would have fallen on an empty chamber. David had taught her well.

The gun bucked and bellowed and a blast of shot swept inches over Penrod's head. The muzzle blast deafened him. Amber and the gun were sent flying backwards by the recoil and she disappeared under the swirling river waters.

The full charge of shot flew down the crocodile's gullet. The great jaws shut with a clash like the slamming of steel

216

gates, and its body arched into a drawn bow of agony. The glistening black snout almost touched its tail. Half out of the water it performed a backwards somersault, then dived below the surface and was gone in a mighty swirl of green waters.

Penrod found the bottom and staggered to where Amber had gone under. His ears were ringing painfully with the concussion of the shot, and as he shook his head to try to clear them the sodden pigeon carcass he was still holding in his teeth flopped against his cheeks. Golden tendrils of Amber's hair floated on the surface like some lovely water plant. Penrod seized a handful and dragged her head to the surface. She spluttered and choked, but she still had a firm grasp on her father's Purdey. Penrod changed his grip, swung her under his arm and he waded with her, an undignified tangle of sodden skirts, hair and kicking limbs, to the bank.

'Put me down!' she gasped. 'Please put me down.'

He set her on her feet. 'Cough it all up,' he ordered. 'Don't swallow any.' He pounded her between the shoulder-blades. The city sewers spilled into the river upstream. He did not want to lose this little one to the blast of the cholera horn.

David and most of the palace staff had been watching from the terrace and were running down to the riverbank. Before they arrived Penrod knelt in front of her. 'Are you all right now?'

'Yes, I am,' she gasped, 'but Papa's gun is wet.'

'What a brave and wonderful girl you are.' Penrod hugged her hard. 'I'd choose you in a scrap every time.' As her father came running up, Penrod rose to his feet but he kept one arm round Amber's shoulders. 'Forgive the impropriety, sir, but I owe this young lady my life.'

'Quite right and proper, Captain. I'm going to give her a kiss myself.'

Before that could happen Nazeera and Rebecca arrived.

'That filthy river!' Rebecca avoided Penrod's eyes, and pulled Amber away from him. 'Nazeera, we're going to get her into a Lysol bath.' The two swept Amber away.

In the bathroom, as Rebecca and Nazeera stripped off Amber's bedraggled, mud-plastered clothing and Saffron poured another bucket of heated water into the porcelain hip-bath, Amber was in raptures, 'Did you hear what he said, Becky? He said he'd choose me in a scrap every time.'

Rebecca studiously avoided a reply, but went to the bath and poured a liberal measure of Lysol into the steaming water.

Saffron was not so reticent. 'So now I suppose you think that makes him your beau,' she mocked.

'He jolly well will be one day. You wait and see.' Amber placed her hands on her bare hips and glared at her twin.

'Don't be so silly, Midget,' Rebecca rebuked her. 'Captain Ballantyne is old enough to be your father. Now, come and get into this bath at once.'

Nazeera felt a pang as she watched Amber clamber into the bath. Changes seemed to have taken place in the child's body. Soon there would be womanly hollows and swells where before all had been flat and featureless.

I am losing all my babies, she lamented inwardly.

Once he had buckled on his breeches, Penrod could examine the pigeon. It was a large bird with body plumage of bronze and wing tips of white, probably a female for they made the best homers. The message it carried had been folded and rolled tightly into a spill no larger than the first joint of his little finger and secured to the bird's leg with a fine silk thread. With his pocket-knife he cut the thread, and kept the carcass to take to the kitchens. He wrapped the roll of paper in his handkerchief to mop up as much moisture as possible, then pulled on his boots and, leaving David to mourn his waterlogged shotgun, set out for General Gordon's headquarters in the west wing of the palace.

'I understand that you have had some success with your shooting. There was a great deal of excitement on the riverbank,' Gordon greeted him.

'I managed to bring down a pigeon, sir, and it was a carrier.'

'You retrieved the message?' demanded Gordon eagerly.

'I have it, but it took a soaking in the river. I have not dared to unfold it, because the rice paper might disintegrate.'

'Let's take a look at it. Put it here.' Obediently Penrod placed his bundled handkerchief on the general's desk, and carefully unfolded it. They studied the tiny roll of paper.

'Seems it's still in one piece,' Gordon murmured. 'It's your prize. You unfold it.'

Careful Penrod nipped the silk thread with the point of his penknife blade. The rice paper was so fine that it tore along the folds as he tried to open it, but the inner part of the message had been kept almost dry by the tightness of the roll. The ink had run, and in spots the words were indecipherable.

'We need a book,' Penrod said, 'to press it while it dries completely.'

Gordon handed him his leatherbound copy of the Bible.

'Are you certain, sir?'

'The good book for good works,' Gordon told him.

Penrod opened the Bible and gingerly spread the damp sheet between the pages. He closed it and pressed the heel of his hand on the outer cover. Gordon was visibly impatient. He paced up and down the room puffing at one of his Turkish cigarettes until he could contain himself no longer. 'Damned thing must be dry enough by now.'

Penrod open the Bible carefully. The sheet of rice paper was still intact, flattened by the pressure, and it seemed that the ink had not run further. Gordon handed him a large magnifying glass. 'Your eyes, and your understanding of Arabic, are probably better than mine.'

Penrod carried the Bible across to the table below the

219

window where the light was better. He pored over it, and after a moment began to read aloud the tiny flowing script: '"I, Abdullah Sayid, son of Fahl, Emir of the Baggara, greet the Victorious Mahdi who is the light of my eyes, and call down upon him the blessing of Allah and his other Prophet, who is also named Muhammad."'

'Standard salutation,' Gordon grunted.

Penrod went on: '"True to the orders of the Victorious Mahdi, I stand guard upon the Nile at Abu Hamed, and my scouts watch all the roads from the north. The infidel Frank and the despicable Turk approach on two separate routes. The Frankish steamers have this day passed through the cataract at Korti."'

Gordon slammed the flat of his hand on the desk. 'Praise God! This is the first hard intelligence I have had in six weeks. If Wolseley's steamers have arrived at Korti they should reach Abu Hamed before the end of Ramadan.'

'Sir!' Penrod agreed, though he was not so sure.

'Go on, man. Go on!'

'A trifle difficult here. The ink has run badly. I think it says, "The camel regiments of the Franks are still encamped at the Wells of Gakdul, where they have been now for twenty-eight days."'

'Twenty-eight days? What on earth does Stewart think he is playing at?' Gordon demanded. 'If only he had some gumption, he would make a bold dash for it. He could reach us within ten days.'

That is Chinese Gordon's own style – the bold dash and the grand gesture, Penrod thought, but he kept his expression neutral. 'Stewart is also a death-or-glory lad, but he has to bring up his supplies before he can make the final charge to the city.'

Gordon jumped up again, and flicked the butt of his cigarette through the open window. 'With two thousand of Stewart's first-line British troops I could hold the city until the desert freezes over, but still he shilly-shallies at Gakdul.' He spun on his heel and faced Penrod again. 'Go on, Ballantyne, what else is there?'

'Not much, sir.' He stooped over the tattered scrap of paper. '"In the name of the Victorious Mahdi, and with the blessing of Allah, we will meet the infidel at Abu Hamed and destroy him."' Penrod looked up. 'That's all. It seems that Sayid ran out of space.'

'Very little for our comfort,' Gordon observed, 'and the Nile is falling.'

'With a brace of Ryder Courtney's fast camels Yakub and I could be at the Wells of Gakdul in three days,' Penrod said. 'I could take Stewart your message.'

'You do not escape me so easily, Ballantyne.' Gordon laughed ironically, a short bark of sound. 'Not yet awhile. We will continue to follow the progress of the relief columns by intercepting the pigeons.'

'The Dervish might accept one or two missing birds as prey of the falcons,' Penrod demurred, 'but we must not frighten them off by killing every one as it arrives.'

'Of course, you have a point. But I must have news. I want you to shoot every fourth pigeon that comes in.'

Muhammad Ahmed, the Victorious Mahdi, walked in the cool of the evening along the bank of the great river. He was attended by his *khalifa* and his five most trusted emirs. As he walked he recited the nine-and-ninety beautiful names of Allah and his entourage murmured the response after each was enunciated.

'Al-Ghafur, the concealer of faults.'

'God is great!'

'Al-Wali, the friend of the righteous.'

'Praise be to God!'

'Al-Qawi, the strong.'

'May his word triumph.'

They reached the tomb of the saint al-Rabb, and the Mahdi took his seat in the shade of the tree that spread its branches over it. When his warlords were assembled, he called upon each to report his order of battle, and give an account of the troops that he commanded. One after another they knelt before him and described their array. Then the Mahdi knew he had seventy thousand men gathered before the walls of Khartoum; another twenty-five thousand had gone two hundred miles north to Abu Hamed on the bend of the river to await the approach of the two British forces. These Ansar were of the finest, their religious ardour and their devotion to the *jihad* against the infidel at its fiercest. The Mahdi knew that no infidel army could prevail against them.

The Mahdi smiled at Osman Atalan. 'Tell me what we know of the enemy,' he ordered.

'O Mighty and Victorious Lord, beloved of God and the other Prophet, know you that each day Abdullah Sayid, Emir of the Baggara, sends a pigeon from his camp at Abu Klea on the bend of the Nile. Some of the birds do not reach my lofts, for there are birds of prey and other hazards along their flight path, but most come to my hand.'

The Mahdi nodded. 'Speak to me, Osman Atalan. Tell us what news of the enemy movements these birds bring us.'

'Sayid reports that the infidel steamers, seven in number, have passed through the last cataract below Korti, and now that the worst of their voyage is behind them, they come on apace. They are travelling almost five times faster than they did below the cataract. They carry many men and great guns.'

'God shall deliver them to my hand, and they shall be destroyed,' said the Mahdi.

'God is great!' Osman Atalan agreed. 'The second infidel column has reached the Wells at Gakdul. There they have stopped. We do not know why this is. I believe that there is not sufficient good fodder to feed the camels for the heavy work they must do. They wait at Gakdul for more supplies to be brought up from Wadi Halfa.'

'How many infidel troops are at Gakdul?'

'Divine One, Sayid has counted more than one thousand Franks, and about the same number of camel drivers, guides and servants.'

'Are these Franks mad?' the Mahdi demanded. 'How can

they dream to prevail against my one hundred thousand Ansar?'

'It may be that they are waiting at Gakdul for reinforcements to join them,' Osman suggested delicately.

'These infidels shall be destroyed also. No mortal man can prevail against the will of God. All these things God has told me.'

'Allah is all seeing and all knowing.'

'Know you that on many nights Allah has come to me as an eagle of flame. He has told me many grave secrets that are too powerful for the common man to hear,' he said, in his soft mellifluous voice, and they bowed before him.

'Blessed is the Mahdi, for he alone hears and understands the word of Allah,' chanted Khalifa Abdullahi.

'Allah has told me that before the infidel and the Frank and the Turk can be driven for ever from the Sudan and the earthly kingdom of Allah and Islam, my enemy Gordon Pasha must be destroyed. Allah has told me that Gordon Pasha is the black angel, Satan, in the guise of a man.'

'May he be ever accursed, and never look upon the face of God,' they cried.

'Allah, the All Wise, has told me that the noble warrior of Islam who cuts the head of Gordon Pasha from his trunk, like some bitter and evil fruit, and brings it to me, and lays it at my feet, shall ever be blessed and that there shall be prepared for him a place in Paradise at God's right hand. He will also be given power and riches in this world of the flesh.'

'God is merciful! God is great!' they chanted.

'Allah has spoken to me, and he has told me the name of my servant who shall bring the head of the infidel to me,' quoth the Mahdi solemnly, and they prostrated themselves before him.

'Let the man be me!'

'If it be me, I shall want no other honour in this life or hereafter.'

The Mahdi held up his hands and they fell silent. 'Osman Atalan of the Beja, draw closer to me,' he said. On his hands

223

and knees Osman crawled to his feet. 'Allah has told me that you are that man.'

Tears of joy streamed down the emir's cheeks. He bowed his head over the Mahdi's feet and washed the dust from them with his tears. Then he unwrapped his turban and, with the locks of his long dark hair, he dried the feet of the Chosen Prophet of God.

'The Nile is falling,' said Osman Atalan, 'and God and the Mahdi have prepared a task for us.' His aggagiers drew closer to the campfire and watched his face by the light of the flames. 'They have chosen us above all the warriors of Allah. We are blessed beyond all other men, for we have been given the wondrous chance to die for the glory of Allah and his Mahdi.'

'Let us seize Allah's bounteous gift. Command us, Great Lord,' his aggagiers pleaded.

He studied their fierce expressions with pride. These were not men, but man-eating lions. 'Our sacred task is to bring to the Divine Mahdi the head of Gordon Pasha, for omnipotent and mighty Allah has decreed that when we achieve this the infidel will be driven from this land for ever, and that Islam will prevail throughout all the world.'

Al-Noor asked: 'Shall we wait for the time of Low Nile, so that we may find a firm foothold on the city shore and a passage through the walls?'

'Every day we delay, the forces of Satan march down upon us from the north. Already their steamers laden with men and guns sweep up the river. Yes, the river is still high, but God has made clear a road for us.' Osman clapped his hands. An old man limped into the firelight and knelt before him. 'Have no fear, Beloved of God. No harm shall come to you. Tell these men what you know.'

'I was born and I have lived all my life in the City of the Elephant's Trunk, Khartoum. But since the Victorious Mahdi has invested the city and laid siege, the curse of Allah has been laid upon the city. Those infidels and Turks who have thought to resist his wisdom and his truth have been made to suffer as no men before them. Their empty bellies cling to their backbones, their children are eaten up by the cholera, the vultures gorge on their rotting corpses, the fathers club the birds and eat them half cooked while their crops bulge with the flesh of their own children.' The aggagiers moved restlessly as they listened to this recital. What an abomination to eat the flesh of the bird that had devoured your children. 'Those who are not too weak of starvation flee the doomed city, and the defences are every day denuded and weakened. I am one of those who has flown. But, like you, I wish to see the infidel banished for ever from the Sudan, and the son of all evil, Gordon Pasha, destroyed. Only then may I return in the peace of the Mahdi to my home.'

'Let Allah accomplish this,' they murmured. The man was old and frail but they admired his spirit.

'The Turks who fight for Gordon Pasha are so reduced in number by disease, starvation and desertion that the infidel can no longer guard the city walls. In their place Gordon Pasha has placed men of straw, mere scarecrows, to frighten off the timid among you.'

'What is this talk of straw men?' Hassan Ben Nader demanded. 'Is it true?'

'It is true,' Osman confirmed. 'I have sailed close to the harbour mouth in this brave old man's dhow. There is a place in the defences where a creek runs into the river through a stone gateway. This is the main outflow from the city sewers. Gordon Pasha has manned the gateway and the walls on either side with dummy soldiers to replace those who have died or run away. Only their heads show above the parapets. At intervals a few old women move them so that from this bank they seemed to live. There is none to resist our onslaught. With one rush we can be through the gap. Then the city and all those within will be ours.'

'There will be great stores of gold and jewels,' al-Noor mused.

'There are women in the city, hundreds of women. As his

225

wives, concubines and slaves, the Turk has chosen the most beautiful women of the Sudan and all the surrounding lands. For each of us there will be a dozen women at least.' Hassan Ben Nader's eyes gleamed in the firelight. 'The women of the Franks have hair like yellow silk and their skin is like rich cream.'

'Speak not of gold and slaves. We fight for the glory of Allah and the Mahdi.' Osman reprimanded them for their greed. 'After that we fight for our own honour and a place in Paradise.'

'When will we attack these straw men?' Al-Noor laughed with excitement. 'I have sat too long with my harem, and I am growing fat. It is time to fight again.'

'Three nights from now it will be the dark of the moon, and in the night we will cross the river. At first we will land two hundred men on the beach – there is no space for more. When we have forced the breach a thousand more will follow us, and after them a thousand more. By dawn I will stand on the parapets of Mukran Fort with the head of Gordon Pasha in my hands, and the prophecy will be fulfilled.' Osman stood up and made a sign of blessing over them. 'Make certain that your swords are sharp and all your wives are with child before we cross the river.'

'The old fisherman, the uncle of Yakub, has given the signal. A handful of sulphur in the flames of his cooking fire, and the puff of yellow smoke that Yakub was watching for,' Penrod reported to the Chinese Gordon.

'Can we trust this fellow, Yakub? To me he seems an evil rogue.'

'I have trusted him often in the most dire circumstances and I am still alive, General.' Penrod kept his anger under control, but with difficulty.

'Has he been able to warn us when the Dervish will attack – if they do?'

'No, sir, we don't know that,' Penrod admitted, 'but I expect they will use the new moon.'

While Gordon consulted his almanac for the moon phases, David Benbrook, the third man in the room, gave his appraisal of the chances of success. 'He is a brave man, this uncle of Yakub. I know him well. He has been in my service ever since I arrived in Khartoum. His information has always been reliable.' David was sitting in a chair by the window. These days, he and the general spent much time together. They were unlikely companions, but as Gordon's tribulations increased he seemed to find solace with his own kind.

Without seeming to do so Penrod studied Gordon's face while he spoke to David. Even in repose, a nerve fluttered in his right eyelid. This was only a visible sign of how finely stretched Gordon was. One of the other deeper and more significant indications was in his behaviour: the brutal excesses of inhumanity. It seemed to Penrod that these were becoming more savage each day, as though by the kurbash, the firing squad and the noose he could delay the fall of the city. Even he must now see that our struggle is drawing towards the end, and the populace is beyond hope or caring. Does he believe that he can compel them to their duty by convincing them that the consequences of their disobedience will be far worse than anything that the Mahdi can do to them? Penrod studied Gordon's face as the general spoke to David Benbrook. At least Benbrook is a man of humanity, he thought. His influence on Gordon can only be for the good.

He put aside such considerations when Gordon stood up and addressed him abruptly. 'Let us go down to the harbour and inspect your preparations to meet this imminent attack, Ballantyne.'

Penrod knew it was unwise for Gordon Pasha to show himself on the walls where the attack was expected: too many spies were watching his every move, and the Dervish were too shrewd not to suspect that he was preparing something for their discomfort. However, he knew it was even more unwise to gainsay the little man.

But Penrod need not have concerned himself: Gordon was too sly an old fox to lead the hounds to the entrance of his earth. Before they left the palace, Gordon removed his distinctive fez and replaced it with a grubby turban, the tail of which concealed half of his face, then covered his uniform with a stained, nondescript *galabiyya*. From a distance he looked like any humble citizen of Khartoum.

Even when they reached the harbour Gordon did not show himself on the parapets. However, he was meticulous and painstaking in his inspection of Penrod's preparations. He peered through every embrasure that pierced the walls of the derelict buildings that overlooked the noisome sewage-clogged creek. He stood behind a Gatling and traversed the gleaming multiple barrels from side to side. He was dissatisfied with the dead area directly under the muzzles. He climbed out of the Gatling's nest into the ooze of the creek and placed himself in the line of fire, then moved closer to the redoubt.

'Keep the gun trained on me,' he ordered.

The gunner kept depressing his aim until he shook his head with exasperation. 'You are too close, General. It can no longer bear.'

'Captain Ballantyne, if they reach this point the Dervish will be under the gun.' Gordon looked pleased that he had caught Penrod out.

Penrod realized it was no excuse that Gordon overloaded him with responsibilities: he had been negligent, and he rebuked himself silently. Such an elementary oversight is almost as bad as starving the gun for ammunition, he thought bitterly. He ordered the engineers to tear down the wall of sandbags and rebuild it with a lower sill.

'Where have you placed the second Gatling?' Gordon demanded. He had Penrod on the defensive now, and was pushing his advantage.

'It is still in the redoubt in front of the hospital. That is the other obvious weak point in our perimeter. I dare not leave that gap undefended, and place all our bets on the attack striking us here. The Dervish may even mount two simultaneous strikes at both positions.'

'They will strike here,' Gordon said, with finality.

'I agree that is the highest probability. So I have built another machine-gun nest over there, where it can cover the beach and enfilade both banks of the creek. As soon as the attack develops and the enemy is committed, I can rush the second gun across from the hospital to this side. Equally, if we are mistaken and they strike at the hospital I can move this gun over to cover that position.'

'How long will it take to move the guns?' Gordon demanded.

'I estimate about ten minutes.'

'No estimates, Ballantyne. Run an exercise and time it.'

On the first attempt the gun-crew encountered a pile of fallen masonry in the alley behind the harbour. They had to clear it before they could bring the heavy carriage through. The second attempt was more successful: it took twelve minutes to run it through the streets and resite it in the prepared nest to cover the beach and the banks of the creek.

'It will be in darkness,' Gordon pointed out. 'The crew must be able to do it with their eyes closed.'

Penrod kept them practising the manoeuvre late into the night. They cleared all obstacles and shell damage from the streets and alleys, and filled in the potholes and gutters. Penrod designed new gun tackles so that twenty men at a time could pull it.

By the morning of the second day they had cut the transit time down to seven and a half minutes. All this had to be done in darkness after curfew. If the Dervish learnt that they were practising moving the Gatlings from one point to another on the perimeter they would suspect a trap. Penrod was not sure that they knew of the existence of the two guns: while in the arsenal they had been stored away from prying eyes, and had probably been forgotten. In any event the Dervish had a deep scorn for firearms. It was unlikely they had ever seen the Gatlings in action so they could not guess at their destructive potential. Until now he had been careful to exercise the gun-crew where they were not under observation from the enemy bank of the Nile. They only fired the weapons into the empty desert on the southern perimeter of the city. When they were not in use he kept them covered with tarpaulins.

'With your permission, General, I intend to take up permanent quarters here at the harbour. I want to be on the spot when the enemy launch their attack. As things stand at present, it might all be over during the time it would take me to get here from the palace.'

'Good,' Gordon agreed. 'But if the Dervish spies discover that you have set up permanent headquarters here at the harbour our plan will be compromised.'

'I have thought about that, General, and I believe I will be able to conceal my whereabouts without causing suspicion.'

They enlisted the co-operation of David Benbrook in concealing from everybody, including the Benbrook sisters and consular staff, that he had moved only as far as the harbour. The story was put about that Penrod had secretly left the city, sent on a mission by General Gordon to carry a message to the British relief column at the Wells of Gakdul.

Penrod found his new quarters a far call from the luxury of his suite in the palace. He set up his *angareb* in a tiny dugout in the back wall of the Gatling emplacement. He had no mosquito net, and spent most of the night swatting the insects: at dusk they rose in clouds from the creek. Previously the palace's paltry food supplies had been augmented by the ingenuity of the Benbrook sisters, Nazeera, the kitchen staff and, of course, by David Benbrook's marksmanship. In his new headquarters Penrod shared the same rations as his men. Gordon had been forced to reduce the issue of dhurra to below starvation level, and hunger was now a constant spectral companion. Yakub was able to scrounge a few dried fish heads and skeletons from his uncle's house and these went into the stew pot that Penrod shared with his gunners. Some of the Egyptians were eating the pith of the palm trees and boiling the leather thongs of their *angarebs*. Much as he had once disparaged the taste of it, Penrod now sorely missed the rations of green-cake that the Benbrook sisters had regularly brought home from the compound of Ryder Courtney.

Penrod could not afford to be seen in the city, so he had to confine himself strictly to the harbour. This self-imposed incarceration was even more irksome than his cramped quarters and the disgusting food. It was a relief to direct all his energy and imagination into preparations for the coming conflict.

His plan was in two parts. First he had to lure the Dervish through the drainage ditch in the outer wall, and into the narrow creek. Then he had to ensure there was no way for them to get out, at least not alive. Gordon restricted his inspection tours to the hours of curfew. Penrod never expected praise from Chinese Gordon, but made certain that he gave the general no further cause for criticism.

Once all the preparations were completed, Yakub was more forthcoming in his praise than Gordon had been. 'With the help of clever Yakub you have built an abattoir.' He chuckled. 'A slaughter house for the pigs of Ansar.' Instinctively he fiddled with the hilt of his dagger as he looked around the stockade they had built. The men were stacking dry timber from the derelict buildings of the city on the bonfires that Penrod had ordered to be constructed on both banks of the creek. He had taken great care that once they were lit the flames would illuminate the enemy, but would not dazzle his gunners and riflemen. Each evening at nightfall his men soaked the bonfires with lamp oil so that their combustion would be almost instantaneous.

Penrod's sudden mysterious disappearance caused varying levels of consternation and concern among the Benbrook sisters. The one who suffered least was Saffron. She merely found herself deprived of a whip to torment her twin. It was no longer satisfactory to tease Amber about her beau, when he had absconded. Besides, Amber's distress whenever she raised the subject detracted from Saffron's enjoyment. Teasing was fun; inflicting pain was not.

On the other hand Rebecca was adept at concealing her

231

true feelings so Saffron had no inkling as to how profoundly Penrod's disappearance had affected her. Had she guessed, she would have had richer fields to plough.

When Amber had almost convinced herself that she would never again set eyes upon Captain Ballantyne, and that suicide was the only solution to her tragic existence, Yakub saved her life. This was not a deliberate act of charity: it was in gratification of Yakub's baser instincts.

His strict confinement, by his master, to the harbour defences above the mosquito-ridden creek suited Yakub not at all. In the last months he had become accustomed to finer living. Each evening Nazeera had provided him with a bowl of the same food as the consul general and his family enjoyed. This was not a great feast, but it far surpassed the watery communal stew, which smelt and tasted of rotten fish and dried animal hides.

However, by far the most troubling element in this new existence was that each night he lay awake at the foot of his master's *angareb*, waiting for the Dervish attack and wondering if Nazeera was being faithful to him. If her previous behaviour was anything to go upon, this seemed highly unlikely. He brooded on the fact that the perfidious Bacheet, that illegitimate son of a Beja father and a Galla pleasure dancer, was under no restrictions as to his nocturnal movements. The thought of Bacheet creeping into his beloved's *angareb* each night kept Yakub from sleep more effectively than all the mosquitoes from the creek. He rose quietly, as if he was going to use the latrine bucket. One of the sentries challenged him at the harbour gate, but Yakub knew the password.

Amber was sitting sleepless at her bedroom window. It was three days since Captain Ballantyne had disappeared. She tortured herself with the thought that he might have been caught by the Dervish before he reached the British lines. She imagined him as a prisoner of the Mahdi. She had heard of the fate of those who fell into that monster's bloodstained hands, and knew she would not sleep that night.

Below her window someone moved in the shadows of the courtyard. She drew back quickly. It might be an assassin sent by the evil Mahdi, but at that moment the man glanced up towards her window and she recognized his squint. 'Yakub!' she breathed. 'But he should be with Penrod on the way to the Wells of Gakdul.' Yakub was Penrod's shadow: wherever he went Yakub followed.

The breathtaking truth dawned upon her. If Yakub is here, then Penrod is somewhere close by. He did not go to Gakdul after all. It was only recently that she had allowed herself to think of him as Penrod, and not as Captain Ballantyne.

Amber's melancholy and foreboding dropped away. She knew exactly where Yakub was going. She sprang up from the window-seat, ran lightly to her wardrobe and threw a dark cloak over her nightdress. She paused only long enough to make certain that Saffron was still asleep, then slipped out of the bedroom and crept downstairs, making certain to avoid the twelfth step, which always creaked and woke her father. She let herself out of the kitchen side door and crossed the stableyard to the servants' compound.

Nazeera's window was lamp-lit. She found a lookout position in one of the empty stables and settled in to wait. She passed the next few hours by trying to imagine what Yakub and Nazeera found to keep themselves busy for such a long time. Rebecca had said that the two of them made love. Amber was not sure what this procedure entailed: her most diligent enquiries had not greatly increased her understanding of the subject. She suspected that Rebecca herself, despite her knowing airs, was just as ignorant as she was.

'It's when people kiss each other,' Rebecca had explained loftily, 'but it's not polite to talk about it.' Amber found this unsatisfactory. Most of the kisses she had observed were fleeting and usually planted on the cheek or the back of a hand, which could only be considered fairly dull entertainment. The one glaring exception was the exchange she and Saffron had witnessed between Ryder and Rebecca, which had caused such a brouhaha. That had been much more interesting. Both participants had obviously enjoyed the process, but even that had lasted less than a minute. In comparison, Yakub and Nazeera had been at it half the night.

I will ask Nazeera, she decided, then had a better idea. As soon as I find out where he is, I will ask Penrod. He's a man, so he must know how they do it.

Shortly before dawn the lamplight in Nazeera's room was extinguished, and moments later Yakub crept out of the door and set off through the dark, silent streets in guilty haste. Amber kept him in sight until he reached the harbour, and she heard one of the sentries challenge him. Then she had to get back to the palace before they found out she was missing.

'Cat been at the cream?' Saffron demanded. Amber's ebullient mood was such a marked change from the days of gloom that had preceded it that she had to tackle her sister later that day as they worked side by side over the green-cake cauldrons in Ryder Courtney's compound.

Amber gave her a sweet but enigmatic smile, and would not be drawn.

That evening, an hour after curfew, Penrod Ballantyne was amazed to recognize Amber's voice arguing with the sentries at the entrance to his headquarters in the Gatling emplacement. He rushed out immediately, buckling on his sword belt. 'You silly child,' he scolded her severely. 'You know very well there is a curfew. You might have been shot.'

Amber had hoped for a warmer reception. 'I brought you some green-cake. I knew you must be starving.' She unwrapped the small bundle she was carrying. 'And one of Papa's clean shirts. I can smell your old one from here.'

Penrod was about to demand how she had learnt of his whereabouts when, in the light of the bullseye lantern, he saw tears of humiliation in her eyes. But she blinked them back and faced him with her chin up. 'Furthermore, Captain Ballantyne, I will have you know that I am not a silly child.'

'Of course you are not, Miss Amber.' He relented instantly. 'You took me by surprise. I just did not expect you. I apologize.'

She perked up. 'If you give me your old shirt I will take it back to wash it for you.'

Penrod found himself in a dilemma. With the threat of an imminent Dervish attack on the harbour, he should not allow her to stay here another minute. For the same reason he dared not leave the emplacement to escort her back to the palace, and he could not let her wander through the city alone after curfew. He could send Yakub with her, but he needed him at his side. There was no one else he could trust. He chose the lesser of all evils.

'I expect that you will have to spend the night here. I cannot allow you to break curfew and go home alone,' he muttered.

Her face lit up with pleasure. This stroke of fortune far exceeded her remotest expectations. 'I can cook your dinner,' she said.

'There isn't much to cook, so why don't you and I share your very generous gift of green-cake?'

They sat on his *angareb* in the dugout. There were no curtains to this alcove so the gunners were involuntary chaperones as they nibbled the green-cake and talked in low tones. It was the first time he had spent any time with her, and Penrod soon discovered that Amber was entertaining company. She had an impish sense of humour that appealed to him, and a quaint manner of expressing herself. She described her various travels with her father, which ranged from Cape Town to Cairo, and finally Khartoum. Then, abruptly, she fell silent, placed her chin in her hand and considered him thoughtfully. 'Captain Ballantyne, now that we have become friends, would you be civil enough to answer a question that has been troubling me lately? Nobody seems to know the answer.'

'I am honoured that you consider us friends.' Penrod was touched. She was such a funny little thing. 'I would be delighted to render you any assistance I can.'

'How do people make love?' she asked.

Penrod found himself deprived of words and the breath to

235

speak them. 'Ah!' he said, and smoothed his moustache to win time. 'I think that it is done in various ways. There do not seem to be any fixed rules of engagement.'

Amber was disappointed. She had expected more of him. Obviously he knew as little as Rebecca. 'I suppose they kiss each other like you and I saw my sister kissing Ryder. Is that how they do it?'

'Indubitably.' He grabbed thankfully at the opening. 'I think that is exactly how they do it.'

'I should think that would become rather boring after a while.'

'It seems to grow on some people,' Penrod said. 'There is no accounting for taste.'

Amber changed the subject again, with disconcerting suddenness. 'Did you know that Lucy, Ryder's monkey, has had babies?'

'I had no idea. Boys or girls? What are they like.' He followed her thankfully on to firm ground.

Minutes later Amber's eyes closed, she subsided against his shoulder and, like a puppy, dropped into instant sleep. She did not stir even when he laid her on the *angareb* and covered her with the threadbare blanket. He was in a good mood, smiling to himself as he left her and went on his midnight inspection of the harbour defences. For once every one of the Egyptian sentries was wide awake. Either they were stimulated by the proximity of the enemy and their own exposure in this forward position, or their hunger drove away sleep.

He found a comfortable place to sit on the forward firing platform and listened to the drums across the river. Their monotonous tempo became soporific and he found himself nodding. He stirred guiltily: If Chinese Gordon finds me I'll be up before the firing squad myself. He took a turn along the parapet, and came back to his seat. He let himself relax and drift to the edge of sleep, but every few minutes he opened his eyes. He had trained himself to tread this tightrope without falling off it. Across the river the drums fell silent.

He opened his eyes again and looked up. Red Mars, the god of war, was hunting across the southern quadrant of the moonless sky with Sirius, the Dog, in leash. It was the darkest and loneliest hour of the night. He was close to the edge of sleep, but he kept his eyes open.

'Penrod.'

Cool fingers brushed his cheek. 'Are you asleep?' He turned his head to her. He was touched that she had used his baptismal name. She must truly think of him as her friend. 'No, I am not, but you should be.'

'I heard voices,' Amber whispered.

'A dream, perhaps,' he replied. 'There are no voices.'

'Listen!' said Amber.

Faintly he heard a dog bark on the west bank and another answered it from Tutti Island, further downriver. No dogs remained in the city. The last had been killed and eaten months before. 'Nothing.' He shook his head doubtfully, but she seized his arm and her sharp little fingernails dug in painfully.

'Listen, Pen. Listen!'

He felt his nerve ends jump tight, like the strike of a heavy fish on the deep-run fly. It was a whisper so faint, so insubstantial on the night breeze that only sharp young ears could have picked it up. It came from far out on the river. Sound carries over water, he thought, and stood up swiftly and silently. Faint as the breeze in the palm fronds, he had heard the traditional word of command to lower and furl the lateen sail of a dhow as it came in to its moorings. Now that he was straining his hearing to its limit, he heard the soft slap of bare feet on a wooden deck, and the slatting of canvas. Seconds later came the creak of a muffled rudder in its yoke as the dhow put up its helm. 'They have come,' he whispered, and moved swiftly along the firing platform to alert each of his men. 'Stand to! Stand to your guns. The Dervish are here. Hold your fire until my command.'

The sergeant gunner stripped the tarpaulin off the Gatling. The stiff material crackled softly and Penrod hissed him to silence. He looked into the ammunition hopper that sat on top of the glistening weapon. It was filled to the brim: six hundred rounds. He lifted the lids of the spare ammunition cases. They were all unlocked. At the Hill of Isandlwana when the Zulu *impis* had broken the British square the spare ammunition cases had been locked and the officer who had the Allen key had ridden out on patrol. Every white soldier in the camp had died that day under the Zulu blades. Ryder Courtney had told him that his elder brother had been among them. Tonight the ammunition cases were unlocked and the four Egyptian loaders were standing by to keep the hopper filled.

He ran to the rear of the firing platform. The corporal of signallers with a detail of four men had their crates of rockets open, and a line of ten flares ready for firing in their launching brackets, nose cones pointed skywards. 'Send up a flare at the first shot. Keep one burning in the sky until the last shot is fired. I want the whole area lit up like daylight,' Penrod ordered.

There was no time for anything else. Penrod started back towards the forward firing platform to take command there. He could not trust the jittery Egyptians to resist blazing away at their first glimpse of the enemy boats before the Dervish were disembarked upon the beach and well inside the trap.

He tripped over Amber, who was at his heels. 'Sweet Mary! I had forgotten about you.' He caught her by the arm and dragged her to the rear entrance of the redoubt. 'Run!' he ordered. 'You have to get out of here right away. This is no place for you now. Even the streets are safer. Run, Amber, and don't stop until you get home.' He gave her a firm shove through the doorway to send her on her way, and did not wait to see if she had obeyed before he turned back towards the forward firing platform.

Amber ran a few paces down the alley, then turned and crept back to the entrance of the redoubt. She watched Penrod disappear into the darkness. 'I am sick and tired of being treated like a baby,' she whispered. She hesitated only a moment before she followed him.

She moved quietly and self-effacingly along the back of the parapet so as not to attract the attention of the troopers who were manning the firing embrasures. They are all too

238

busy to worry about me, she thought. Her confidence swelled, and she hurried forward to look for Penrod. What if he needs me? I will be no use sitting in my bedroom at the palace. She saw his tall figure just ahead.

Penrod was already standing at the parapet that overlooked the beach. The straw-filled decoys had been dragged away and now live riflemen leant on the firing sills, peering down upon the dark beach. He had his drawn sword in his right hand. Amber felt a prickle of pride. He is so brave and noble, she thought. She found a place to hide in a corner of the rear wall and sank down behind it. From here she could watch over him. A tight, brittle silence held all the men at the firing wall.

Suddenly Amber realized how few of them were spread out thinly along the wall, twenty paces between them. These men did not seem enough to stop the hordes of the Dervish.

Then a man close to where Amber knelt whispered so softly that she could barely catch the words. 'Here they come.' His voice quavered with fear. The breech-block of his Martini-Henry snicked as he chambered a round. He lifted the weapon to his shoulder, but before he could press the trigger an open hand slapped across his face.

As he reeled sideways Penrod seized him by his collar and spoke close to his ear: 'Fire before my command, and I will have you blown from the cannon's mouth,' he promised. Al-Faroque's execution had left a deep impression on all the Egyptians who had witnessed it. Penrod pushed the man back to his position and they waited.

Then Penrod drew breath sharply. The first Dervish boat glided in towards the beach below. As it touched the sand a dark horde of Ansar clambered out into the waist-deep water and waded on to the narrow strip of mud below the walls. They carried their swords at shoulder height and moved with barely a sound. From the dark waters behind them appeared a flotilla of small dhows and feluccas, each packed with a mass of men.

'Hold your fire!' Penrod strode back and forth along the parapet, keeping his puny force under control with his savage whisper. The feluccas and dhows kept coming in until the beach was packed with hundreds of Ansar. There was not room for all of them on firm ground and the ones in the rear were still waist deep in the river. Those in front began to rip down the barricade that blocked the entrance to the drainage creek.

'Steady now! Steady!' Penrod exhorted them.

Part of the barricade crashed down and the Dervish swarmed through. Their war cry went up: 'There is no God but God!'

'Volley fire!' Penrod shouted and the rifles crashed out. The Dervish rushed on through the hail of bullets. Then the first rockets soared into the night sky, and the masses of Dervish swarmed like columns of ants in the weird greenish light. The riflemen fired down into them but there were so many that the bullets had little effect. When the front ranks reached the harbour wall they clambered up it, the rear ranks shoving from below. As they came over the top the defenders thrust with the bayonets.

Penrod strode along the wall, firing his new Webley pistol point blank into their bearded faces. In his right hand he carried his sabre and when the revolver was empty he slashed and hacked with the blade. The dead and wounded Ansar toppled back on to their comrades who were climbing up behind them. The Egyptian line was too flimsy to hold them in check much longer: all along the top of the wall knots of Dervish were gaining footholds. Their two-handed crusader blades hissed through the air with the sound of bats' wings. One of the Egyptians reeled back from the parapet with his right arm sliced off cleanly above the elbow. His blood was inky black in the light of the rockets.

'Back!' shouted Penrod. 'Fall back to the second line!' Even in her own terror, Amber was startled by how clearly his voice carried above the uproar. His men formed quickly into a skirmishing line, bayonets facing outwards, and they retreated backwards along the top of the wall. For a terrible moment Amber thought she would be left behind, but she sprang up and ran like a startled hare. Instinctively she knew that the Gatling emplacement was the strongest point of the defence, and headed for it.

She reached it well ahead of Penrod and his men, and scrambled to the top of the wall of sandbags. As she hung there, someone grabbed her arm from the far side and dragged her over. She fell on top of her rescuer. He smelt of rotten fish heads, and glared at her with a horrific squint, his face green in the light of the flares. 'Nazeera will kill you with her bare hands if she finds out you are here.' He pushed her roughly into the dugout in the back wall, just as Penrod led his men back in a rush.

'Gatling gunner! Open fire!' Penrod had selected the man on the crank handle of the gun for his strength and stamina. Sergeant Khaled was a colossal black man from one of the Nubian tribes of upper Egypt. Men like him made the finest soldiers in all the army of the Khedive. He bobbed up and down like a marionette as he worked. The brightly burnished barrels spun, like the revolving spokes of a chariot wheel. The flickering glare of muzzle flashes lit the parapet as brightly as a stage.

With a sound like a giant ripping up a roll of heavy canvas, a continuous stream of bullets tore into the ranks of Ansar as they swarmed forward. The heavy lead bullets slogged into living flesh, and the ricochets screamed off the stone parapets, almost drowning the clamour of the Dervish force. Traversing back and forth the Gatling scythed them down, piling heaps of corpses along the front of the wall. Those who followed scrambled over them and grabbed at the barrels of the rifles that aimed at them through the embrasures, trying to tear the smoking weapons from the hands of the defenders on the far side of the wall. The soldiers thrust at them with their bayonets, screaming with battle rage, and the Dervish screamed back at the agony of the steel slicing deeply into their bodies. Then the barrels of the Gatling swung back and blew them away, like the *khamsin* wind. The last of the Dervish tumbled off the revetment, and lay in huddles or dragged themselves through the black slick of the creek bed.

Sergeant Khaled straightened up and the gun fell silent.

His black face was split with a white and ferocious grin, and his barrel chest ran with rivers of sweat that gleamed in the green light of the flares.

'Reload!' Penrod shouted, as he filled the chambers of his own revolver from the loops on his belt. 'Get ready for the next wave.'

The loaders came running up with the ammunition buckets, and the shiny copper-cased cartridges cascaded into the Gatling hopper. Other ammunition boys ran along the parapet, doling out paper packets of Boxer-Henry ammunition to the riflemen. The water-carriers followed them, squirting water from the nozzles of the skins directly into the parched mouths of the soldiers.

'Be ready for them. They are not beaten. They will come back through the creek again.' Penrod moved down the parapet, talking to the men. The trooper whose arm had been hacked off had died from loss of blood. They laid his body against the rear wall and covered him with a blanket. Penrod started back towards the Gatling to bolster the courage of Sergeant Khaled and his gunners, but as he passed the doorway to his dugout he saw a small white face staring out at him. 'Amber! I thought you had gone.'

Now that she was discovered she decided to brazen it out. 'I knew you didn't mean to send me away. Anyway, it's too late now. I have to stay.'

He was about to debate this point with her, but from the depths of the creek bed rose the dread chorus of Dervish war cries. The hordes poured back in a flood that filled the creek from side to side.

Penrod drew the Webley from the holster on his belt and broke it open to check that it was fully reloaded. He snapped the breech closed. 'I know you can use this. I have seen you practising with your father.' He thrust the weapon, butt first, into her hands. 'Get back into the dugout. Climb under the bed. Stay there until this is over. Shoot anybody who touches you. This time do as you're told. Go!' He ran back to the parapet.

Two hundred Egyptian riflemen did not wait for his command to reopen fire. The volleys crashed down into the creek bed, and the Gatling ripped and rattled, a stream of spent cartridge cases spilling into a glistening mound on the floor of the redoubt beneath its carriage. A succession of coloured flares burst high above the arena, illuminating with garish light the Dervish struggling upwards through the reeking mud. Their ranks were so closely packed that every bullet must strike. Surely mortal men must break under such punishment, yet they came on, clambering over the torn and twitching corpses of their comrades, their multi-coloured *jibbas* plastered with reeking black mud, never wavering, each man trying to fight his way to the front rank of the attack, scornful of death, eager to seek it out in the smoking muzzles of the guns.

But there was a line at the foot of the wall across which even their courage could not carry them. The Gatling stopped them there, as though they had reached a wall of glass, building up taller piles of dead men. Wave after wave of warriors came on to add their own corpses to the growing heaps. Swiftly the creek was transformed into a ghastly charnel house. Then, as the attack wavered, the Gatling fire ceased.

'Captain! Stoppage!' Sergeant Khaled yelled. 'The gun is jammed.' As the import of those words struck the Egyptian troopers, horror dawned on their faces in the light of the flares. As the full extent of this disaster struck them their fire dwindled, stammered, and fell silent. Even the Ansar in the creek were caught up in the spell. A weird and unnatural quiet fell over the battlefield, broken only by the groans and cries of the wounded. It lasted but a few seconds.

Then a single voice spoke. *'La ilaha illallah!* There is but one God!' It was a voice Penrod recognized. He looked down into the grisly creek bed and saw Osman Atalan in the first rank of the Dervish horde. Their eyes locked. Then the battle cry went up from hundreds of throats and the attack swept forward again. As though the wall of glass that had contained them was shattered, they clawed their way up the steep, treacherous bank of the creek towards the redoubt.

The heads of the Egyptian riflemen turned as they looked back to find a line of retreat. Penrod knew that gesture well.

He had seen it before, on the terrible day when the square broke at El Obeid. It was the prelude to flight and rout. 'I will kill the first man who breaks,' he shouted, but one ignored him.

As he turned to run, Penrod stepped forward and thrust for his belly. The long blade of his sabre slipped in as though it had been greased, and the point sliced out through the back of the man's khaki tunic. He dropped to his knees, and clasped the blade of the sabre with his bare hands. Penrod pulled out the razor-sharp steel between his victim's fingers, severing skin and flesh and sinew. The man screamed and toppled backwards.

'Stand your ground, and keep firing.' Penrod held high his blood-wet blade. 'Or sing the same song as this cowardly creature.' They turned back to the firing embrasures and poured their volleys down into the mass of Dervish clambering up towards them.

Sergeant Khaled was hammering on the breech mechanism of the silent Gatling with his bare fists, leaving the skin of his knuckles on the sharp metal edges. Penrod grabbed his shoulder and pulled him aside. By the light of the flares he saw the crushed cartridge case jammed in the jaws of one of the six cam-operated bolts. It was a number-three stoppage, the most difficult to clear. There was a trick to it that Penrod had learnt from hard experience. He snatched the bayonet from the sheath on Sergeant Khaled's belt and, with the point of the blade, worked to prise open the jaws of the bolt.

The Dervish came up the walls, climbing like squirrels up the trunk of an oak. The Martini-Henry rifles fell silent as the attackers wriggled through the embrasures and grappled hand to hand with those Egyptians who had stood their ground. The Gatling's bolt was still jammed solidly. Penrod glanced up: at that moment the fate of the city and all its inhabitants hung on him.

One of the many myths that had built up around the image of General Chinese Gordon was that his voice could carry above the din of any battlefield. Penrod heard it now in the uproar of this inevitable disaster. 'Number-two gun, open fire.'

Penrod had never expected to welcome those harsh and hectoring tones. They carried clearly across from the secondary emplacement that Penrod had built in anticipation of just such a moment as this. His knees went weak with relief. Then he braced himself, and turned his mind back to the jammed gun.

Waiting, sleepless, on the glacis of the hospital fortifications, Gordon had heard the opening volleys of the battle, and seen the rocket flares sailing up from the harbour into the night sky. He had roused his gunners. They limbered up the second Gatling and ran it through the alleyways and byways of the city. It took them eight and a half minutes to reach the harbour and unlimber the Gatling in the empty emplacement that had been prepared for it. True to his nature, Gordon had timed them. He nodded approval and thrust the hunter back into his pocket.

'Number-two gun, open fire,' he grated, and the monstrous thunder of the six rotating barrels smothered the frenzied war cries of the Dervish. A moving sheet of fire swept relentlessly across the revetment of the creek. From this angle he caught them in left flank and rear. His fire tumbled them off the walls like ripe apples from a wind-shaken tree. Most lost their weapons in the fall. Those who rose to their feet again were hurled forward by the press of bodies still surging up the creek, and were trapped against the footwall of the fortifications.

'Back! Go back! It is over,' shouted those in the forefront.

'Forward!' screamed those coming up from the beach, 'For God and His Ever Victorious Mahdi!' The creek became a massive log-jam of bodies packed so tightly that even the dead were held upright by their comrades.

Penrod could not witness all this taking place while he struggled with the jammed bolt. At last he forced the point of the bayonet behind the lug of the cam and hammered on the hilt with his palm. He ignored the pain, and shouted at Sergeant Khaled, 'Back up the crank!' Khaled heaved anti-clockwise on the handle, taking the pressure off the cam and suddenly the lug flew back, with a clanging force that would have taken off Penrod's thumb, had he not jerked it away. The crushed and deformed cartridge case flew clear. As Khaled released the handle, the next round dropped from the hopper and was fed smoothly into the breech. The bolt cocked with a sweet, almost musical clank.

'Number-one gun cocked and ready, Sergeant.' Penrod slapped Khaled on the shoulder. 'Commence firing!' Khaled stooped to the crank, and Penrod himself took hold of the twin traverse handles and depressed the barrels so they were aimed down into the struggling confusion of mud-smeared Ansar. The gun jumped, hammered and shook in Penrod's hands.

Not even the bravest could withstand the combined fire of the two Gatlings. It rolled them back until they jammed in the portal of the drain tunnel, then decimated their ranks, piling their bodies like faggots of firewood on that narrow strip of beach. As the survivors staggered through the shallows towards the boats, the bullets kicked foam from the surface around them. When at last they clambered aboard, the heavy bullets splintered the deck timbers and struck down the crew cowering within the hulls. Their blood dribbled out of the bullet-holes and trickled down the outside of the hulls, like claret spilt from the goblet of a drunkard.

With their cargoes of broken bodies on the decks, the dhows steered back across the river in the first flush of day. As the last pulled out of the bight of the harbour the Gatlings ceased their dreadful clangour. The timid silence of the dawn was marred only by the lamentations of the new widows across the river on the Omdurman bank.

Penrod stepped back from the Gatling, whose barrels glowed as though they had been heated in a blacksmith's forge. He looked around him like someone awakening from nightmare. He was not surprised to find Yakub at his side. 'I saw Osman Atalan in the front rank of the enemy host,' he told him.

'I saw him also, lord.'

'If he is still on this bank of the river, we must find him,' Penrod ordered. 'If he is alive, I want him. If he is dead, his head shall be sent to the Ever Victorious Mahdi. It may discourage him and his Ansar from another attack on the city.'

Before he left the redoubt Penrod called to Sergeant Khaled, 'See to our wounded. Get them to the hospital.' He knew how futile that would be. Both the Egyptian doctors had deserted from Gordon's regiment months ago, but not before they had stolen and sold all the medical supplies. At the hospital building a few old Arab midwives still treated the wounded with herbs and traditional potions. He had heard that Rebecca Benbrook had tried to teach some of the Sudanese women how to take care of the wounded in a more orthodox fashion, but he knew that she had no medical training. She could do little more than attempt to staunch bleeding, and make sure the wounded had clean boiled water to drink, and extra rations of dhurra and green-cake.

Before the words were out of his mouth he heard a scream. He glanced in the direction it had come from and saw a woman dressed in black robes bending over a wounded Dervish. The Arab and Nubian women of the city had an instinct for death and loot. The first were arriving even before the crows and the vultures.

The wounded Dervish wriggled and writhed as the woman prodded him into position with the point of her little dagger. Then, with an expert stroke that started in his throat under the ear and raked forward, she opened both his carotid and jugular arteries and hopped back so the blood would not soak her skirts. Long ago Penrod had learnt not to interfere in this type of business. Arab women were worse than the men, and this one had made no attempt to conceal what she was about. He turned away. 'Sergeant, I need prisoners for questioning. Save as many as you can.' Then he jerked his head to Yakub. 'Come, All-seeing Yakub. Let us seek the Emir Osman Atalan. The last I saw of him, he was on the beach trying to rally his men as they ran for the boats.'

'Wait for me, Pen. I am coming with you.' Amber had crept out of the dugout.

Once again he had forgotten her presence. Her hair was in tangled disarray, her blue eyes were underscored with plum-coloured bruises, and her yellow frock was filthy with smoke and dust. The revolver was too big for the hand that held it. 'Will I never get rid of you? You must go home, Amber,' he said. 'This is no place for you, and it never was.'

'The streets are not safe,' Amber argued. 'Not all the Dervish got away in the boats. I saw hundreds of them escaping that way.' She waved the Webley in an indeterminate gesture over her shoulder. 'They will be waiting to ravish me or cut my throat.' 'Ravish' was one of her new words, although she was uncertain of its meaning.

'Amber, there are corpses and dying men down there. It's no place for a young lady.'

'I have seen dead men before,' she said sweetly, 'and I am not a lady yet, just a little girl. I only feel safe with you.'

Penrod laughed a little too harshly. He always felt light-headed and detached from reality when fighting was over.

'Little girl? In stature, perhaps. But you have all the wiles of a fully fledged member of your sex. I am no match for you. Come along, then.'

They slipped and slid down the bank into the creek. The first rays of the sun were gilding the minarets of the city, and the light improved every minute. Penrod and Yakub moved cautiously among the bullet-torn bodies of the fallen Ansar. Some were still alive, and Yakub leant over one with his dagger poised.

'No!' Penrod said sharply.

Yakub looked aggrieved. 'It would be merciful to help his poor soul through the gates of Paradise.' But Penrod indicated Amber, and shook his head again even more definitely. Yakub shrugged and moved on.

Penrod was looking for Osman Atalan's green turban. As he ducked out under the stone arch of the tunnel on to the muddy beach, he picked it out: it was on the head of a corpse floating face down in the lap and wash of the wavelets at the edge of the bank. Through the clinging folds of the *jibba* he saw that the corpse was lean and athletic. There were two bullet-holes in its back. The Gatling had inflicted massive damage – he could have thrust his fist into the holes. A few fingerling Nile perch worried the ragged tatters of raw meat that hung from the wounds. The end of the turban floated free, waving like a tendril of seaweed in the wash of the current. Osman Atalan's long dark hair was entwined with the cloth.

Penrod felt his spirits plunge when only moments before he had been intoxicated. He felt cheated and angry. There should have been more to it than this. He had sensed that he and Atalan were caught up together in the ring of destiny. This was no way for it to end. There was no satisfaction in finding his enemy floating like the carcass of a pariah dog in a drainage creek with fish nibbling his flesh.

Penrod sheathed his sabre and went down on one knee beside the floating body. With a strangely respectful gesture he took the dead man's arm and rolled the body face up in the shallows. He stared at it in astonishment. This was an older, less noble face, with brutish brows, thick lips and broken teeth stained by the smoke of the hashish pipe.

'Osman Atalan has escaped.' He spoke aloud in his relief. He was overtaken by a sense of prescience. It was not over yet. Fate had linked him and Atalan, as a serpentine liana binds two great forest trees to each other. There was more to follow, much more. He knew it in his heart.

There was a soft sound behind him, but it did not alarm him. He thought it was either Yakub or Amber. He went on studying the features of the dead emir, until Amber screamed, 'Pen! Behind you! Look out!' She was some way to his right. Even as he turned he knew it was not her he had heard so close behind him. And he knew he was too late. Perhaps, after all, this *was* where it ended, on this strip of mud beside the great river.

He completed the turn with his right hand on the hilt of his sabre, rising from his knees, but he knew he could not regain his feet and draw his sword in time. He had only a fleeting glimpse of his assassin. The Dervish had been feigning death: it was one of their tricks. Coiled like a poisonous adder he had waited his moment. Penrod had fallen into the trap: he had turned his back and sheathed his sabre. The Dervish had come to his feet with his broadsword drawn back like a forester about to make the first cut on the trunk of a tree. Now he swung all his wiry frame behind the stroke. He was aiming a few inches above the point of Penrod's left hip bone.

Penrod watched the massive silver blade looping towards him, but it seemed that time had slowed. He was like an insect trapped in a bowl of honey, and his movements were sluggish. He realized that the blade would slice through the soft tissue of his midriff, until it struck his spinal column just above the pelvic girdle. That would not stop it. The entire circumference of his body would offer as little resistance as if it were the spongy stem of a banana tree. This single stroke of the blade would bisect him neatly.

The shot came from his right, a flat blurt of sound, the characteristic report of the Webley .44. Although he was not looking directly at her, Penrod was aware of Amber's small shape at the periphery of his vision. She was holding the weapon double-handed at the full reach of both her arms, but the heavy recoil threw it high above her head.

The assassin was a young man with a thin, unkempt beard, his pockmarked skin the colour of toffee. Penrod was staring at his face as the heavy Webley bullet struck him in the left temple and blasted through his skull just behind the eyes. It distorted his features as though they were an india-rubber mask. His lips twisted and elongated, and his eyelids fluttered like the wings of butterflies. His eyes bulged from their sockets, and the bullet erupted from his right temple in a cloud of bone chips and wet tissue.

Half-way through the sword stroke his fingers opened nervelessly and the weapon flew from his grip. It spun past Penrod's hip, missing it by a hand-span, and cartwheeled away to peg point first into the muddy bank. The assassin took a step back before his legs folded and he collapsed.

With his right hand on the hilt of his half-drawn sabre Penrod turned to stare in amazement at Amber. She dropped the revolver and burst into sobs. He went to her and picked up the Webley, thrust it into the holster on his belt and buckled the flap. Amber was sobbing as though her heart was breaking. She was shivering and her lips were quivering wildly as she tried to tell him something. He placed one arm round her shoulders and the other behind her knees and lifted her as though she were an infant. She clung to him with both thin arms round his neck.

'That is absolutely enough for one day,' he said gently. 'This time I shall take you home myself.'

Gordon was waiting for him in the Gatling redoubt as he came up the bank. 'A fair night's work, Ballantyne. The Mahdi will think once or twice before he comes again, and the populace will be much heartened.' He lit a cigarette and his hand was steady. 'We will throw the Dervish dead into the river, a floating warning to their comrades. Perhaps some may even be carried down through the gorge to our troops coming upriver. They will know that we are holding out. It may encourage them to a little more haste.' Now he glanced at Amber, who was still weeping silently. Her whole body shook with sobs, but the only sounds were small gulps of breath. 'I will take command here. You may escort the young lady back to her family.'

Penrod carried Amber into the street. She was still weeping. 'Cry if it makes you feel better,' he whispered to her, 'but, by God, you are as brave a little thing as any man I have known.' She stopped weeping but her grip tightened round his neck.

By the time he handed her over to Rebecca and Nazeera Amber had cried herself to sleep. They had to prise her arms from round Penrod's neck.

General Gordon used their little victory to counter the numbing despair of the civilian inhabitants of the city. He gathered up the corpses of the enemy, two hundred and sixteen, laid them out in rows on the harbour quay and invited the populace to view them. The women spat upon them, and the men kicked them and shouted abuse, calling down the curse of Allah and condemning them to the fires and torments of hell. They shouted with glee as the corpses were thrown into the river, where the crocodiles snapped at them and dragged them below the surface.

Gordon posted official bulletins in every square and souk of the city, announcing that the British relief columns were now in full march for the city and would almost certainly arrive within days. He also gave them the joyous tidings that the Dervish were so disheartened by their devastating defeat and the approach of the British columns that vast numbers were deserting the black flag of the Mahdi and marching into the desert to return to their tribal homelands. It was true that there was a large movement of Dervish troops on the enemy bank, but Gordon knew that they were being sent northwards in battle array to oppose the British relief columns.

More welcome bulletins announced that General Gordon had declared a double ration of dhurra from the stock he was holding in the arsenal. The same bulletin informed the people that the remaining stocks of grain were more than sufficient to feed the city until the arrival of the relief column. It assured them that when the steamers docked in the harbour they would offload thousands of sacks of grain.

That night Gordon lit bonfires on the maidan. The band played until midnight, and the night sky was lit up again by rockets and coloured flares.

Early the following morning he called a more sombre meeting in his headquarters. There were only two other participants: David Benbrook and Penrod Ballantyne.

Gordon looked at Penrod first. 'You have drawn up the latest inventory of the grain stocks?'

'It did not take long, sir. At ten o'clock last night there were four thousand nine hundred and sixty sacks remaining. Yesterday's issue of double rations expended five hundred and sixty-two. At the present rate of consumption, we have sufficient dhurra for another fifteen days.'

'In three days I will be forced to halve the ration again,' Gordon said, 'but this is not the time to tell the people.'

David looked shocked. 'But, General, surely the relief column will be here in two weeks. Your own bulletins gave that assurance.'

'I have to protect the people from the truth,' Gordon replied.

'What, then, is the truth?' David demanded.

Gordon contemplated the ash on his cigarette before he replied. 'The truth, sir? The truth is not a monolith cast in iron. It is like a cloud in the sky, constantly changing shape. From every direction that one views it, it offers a different aspect.'

'That description has great literary value, I have no doubt, but in this situation it is of little help.' David smiled bleakly. 'When can we expect the relief column to reach us?'

'The information I am about to disclose to you must not go beyond the four walls of this room.'

'I understand.'

'Six Dervish were taken prisoner at the harbour.'

'I thought there would have been more.' David frowned.

'There were.' Gordon shrugged. David knew better than to pursue the subject. This was the Orient where different standards prevailed. Interrogation under torture fell within those standards. 'The six prisoners were questioned by my Sergeant Khaled. We obtained much useful intelligence, none of it reassuring. The steamers of the River Division seem to have been delayed at Korti.'

'Good Lord! They should have been at Abu Hamed by now,' David exclaimed. 'What on earth is holding them back?'

'We do not know, and speculation is vain.'

'What of the Desert Division under Stewart?'

'Here it is the same sad story. Stewart is still encamped at the Wells of Gakdul,' Gordon told him.

'It does not seem possible that either of those divisions can reach us before the end of the month,' David mused, then looked at the others hopefully for a denial. Neither man responded.

Gordon broke the silence. 'What is the state of the river, Ballantyne?'

'Yesterday it fell five inches,' Penrod replied. 'Each day the pace of the ebb is accelerating.'

'Can one apply the word "ebb" to falling river waters?' David asked, as if to make light of the serious implications.

Gordon ignored the frivolous question. 'The prisoners had other information to give us. The Mahdi has ordered another twenty-five thousand of his élite fighting men northwards to reinforce his army. There are now fifty thousand Dervish gathered at Abu Hamed.' He paused, as though reluctant to continue. 'Stewart has two thousand. That means he is out-numbered twenty-five to one. The Dervish know exactly what route he must follow to reach the river. They will choose their ground with care before they attack.'

'Stewart is a fine officer.' David tried to sound confident.

'One of the best,' Gordon agreed. 'But twenty-five to one is long odds.'

'In God's Name we must warn Stewart of the danger.'

'Yes, that is what I intend.' Gordon looked across at Penrod. 'I am sending Captain Ballantyne to the Wells of Gakdul to warn him and guide him through.'

'How do you intend that he make the journey, General? As far as I am aware, there are no camels in the city. They have all been eaten. There is only one steamer, Ryder Court-ney's *Intrepid Ibis*, but the engine is still out of commission. It is highly unlikely that a dhow will get through the Dervish lines.'

Gordon gave a chilly smile. 'I have discovered that Mr Courtney is the owner of a fine herd of at least twenty racing camels. He has been prudent enough not to keep them in the city where I might have found them, but has sent them out into the desert, to a tiny oasis two days' travel to the south. They are grazing there under the care of some of his people.'

David chuckled. 'Ryder Courtney has more arrows to his bow than a monkey has fleas.'

'For somebody who recently queried my use of the language, that is as magnificently garbled an image as you are like to come across in a year of searching.' Penrod smiled with him.

'When taxed with the question of the camels, he at first denied ownership.' Gordon was not smiling. 'Then he denied that he had any intention of concealing them from me, and said that it was simply a matter of the availability of grazing for the beasts. I immediately commandeered them. If he had been honest with me from the beginning I might have considered compensation.'

'He may not comply with your orders,' David said. 'Ryder Courtney is a man of independent spirit.'

'And of avaricious instinct,' Gordon agreed. 'But in this case he would be unwise in the extreme to gainsay me. Even under martial law one would hesitate to shoot a subject of the Queen, but he has several warehouses full of ivory and a large menagerie of exotic but edible animals.' Gordon looked smug. 'My persuasive logic has prevailed. Courtney has sent word to his herdsmen at the oasis to bring the camels in, and I expect them to be at our disposal by the day after tomorrow.'

'I had no idea of the gravity of the situation,' David murmured. 'Had I done so I would have prevented my daughter arranging a celebration of your victory at the harbour. She has planned a soirée for tomorrow evening. Unfortunately our kitchens can no longer provide elaborate dinners. However, there will be piano recitals and singing. If you think this inappropriate, General, I shall ask Rebecca to cancel the evening.'

'Not at all.' Gordon shook his head. 'Although I shall not attend, Miss Benbrook's festivities will keep up pretences and spirits. She must go ahead, by all means.'

Amber and Saffron opened the musical programme with a piano duet of 'Greensleeves'. It mattered little that the consular palace's grand piano was in sorry need of tuning: the twins made up in enthusiasm for what they lacked in other areas.

This evening Rebecca was a gay and vivacious hostess, and her father could not help remarking her change of mood. Last week she had been sad and moping but now she sang 'Spanish Ladies' with Ryder Courtney, then prevailed on him to render a solo of 'My Bonnie Lies Over the Ocean'. This was well received by the company. Saffron, in particular, applauded him rapturously.

Then Amber dragged Penrod on to the floor. 'You have to sing also. Everybody has to sing or do something.'

Penrod gave in graciously. 'Can you play "Heart of Oak"?' he asked, and Amber ran to the piano. Penrod's voice startled and thrilled them all: it was easy, lyrical and true.

> 'Come, cheer up, my lads!
> 'Tis to glory we steer,
> To add something more
> To this wonderful year . . .'

When the song ended Rebecca tried to blink tears from her eyes, as she called gaily, 'Refreshments will be served before the next act.'

She served strong Abyssinian coffee in delicate Limoges porcelain demitasses. There was no milk or sugar. While she was serving Captain Ballantyne, she fumbled and spilt hot coffee on to his gleaming boots.

Her father watched her from across the room as she blushed bright scarlet, and thought her confusion was almost as uncharacteristic as her clumsiness. Suddenly he realized what it meant. *The pretty soldier has her deeply entangled in his web. She is all fluster and flutter whenever he is within fifty paces. When he disappeared she almost pined away, and now* he is back she is dizzy with delight. He frowned, and thrust his hands into his pockets. She does not realize that in two days he will disappear again. I would hate to see her badly hurt. It is my paternal duty to warn her. He thought about that for a moment. And perhaps I shall. After all, the identity of the father of my grandchildren is very much my business.

Rebecca recovered herself, and clapped her hands for attention. 'Ladies and gentlemen, I have a special treat for you this evening. All the way from Madrid, where she has danced before the King and Queen of Spain and other crowned heads of Europe, Señora Esmeralda Lopez Conchita Montes de Tête de Singe, the celebrated flamenco dancer.' There was a brief but mystified spattering of applause as from behind the curtains a plump Spanish lady in lace mantilla, clattering bangles and earrings swept into the room on the arm of Ryder Courtney. In the centre of the floor she sank into a deep curtsy, then rose to her feet with unusual grace for such a portly female. She clicked castanets above her head, and as Rebecca struck up the opening bars of the 'March of the Toreadors' Señora Tête de Singe launched a drumfire salvo of heel stamps.

David let out a snort of laughter. He had been the first to recognize Consul Le Blanc beneath the tall wig and hectic makeup. Then a howl of laughter went up from the entire room, and did not subside until Le Blanc sank to the floor in another theatrical curtsy, his makeup running.

In the ensuing pandemonium David crossed to Rebecca and took her arm. 'What an inspired entertainment, my darling. Le Blanc was superb. I do so love a good impersonation.'

Rebecca was in such high spirits that when he led her towards the french windows she went without protest. 'Ah!' he said. 'My kingdom for a breath of fresh air.' He led her along the terrace. 'Of course, Ryder Courtney has a fine voice. A man of many talents. He will make some lucky lady a wonderful husband.'

'Papa, you are always so subtle.' She tapped his shoulder with her fan.

257

'I have no idea what you are talking about. But I must say I was surprised by Captain Ballantyne. He also has an extraordinary singing voice.' She went still, and looked away.

'What a pity he is leaving, this time for good, and we shall probably never have the pleasure of listening to him again.'

'What are you saying, Daddy?' Her voice was small.

'Dear me, I should not have let that slip. Gordon is sending him north with despatches to Cairo. You know these military men. Ships in the night, all of them, I'm afraid. One can not rely on them.'

'Daddy, I think we should go in to entertain our guests.'

Rebecca looked at herself in the mirror of her dressing-table. Her face was so thin that the cheekbones cast shadows beneath them. There are no fat people in Khartoum, these days. Even Consul Le Blanc is skin and bones. She smiled at the exaggeration, and noted with pleasure the improvement the smile made. I must try not to frown. She dipped her powder puff in the crystal bowl and lightly dusted the hollows under her eyes. 'Better and better,' she whispered. She was thin but she still had the bloom of youth upon her skin. 'At least Daddy thinks I am beautiful. I wonder if he would agree.' Thinking of him brought a glow to her cheeks. 'I wonder if he is out there again.' She glanced towards the balcony doors. 'I am not going to look. If he is there, he will think I am encouraging him. He will think that I am a fast woman, which I am definitely not.'

She let her dress fall round her ankles, and reached for the crêpe-de-Chine gown. Before she slipped it on she looked at her reflection in the mirror. Then, on an impulse, she crossed the bedroom and locked the door. She had sent Nazeera away, but she did not want her to return unexpectedly. As she went back to the mirror she pushed the straps of her shift off her shoulders, and let it fall to the floor beside her dress. She looked at her naked body in the mirror. Her ribs showed beneath her white skin, and her pelvic bones stood proud.

Her belly was concave as that of a greyhound. She touched her breasts. Nazeera said that men did not like small breasts. 'Are they too small?'

Then she remembered the feel of his lips upon them, the brush of his moustache and the sharpness of his teeth. As she stared, the tips swelled and darkened with heat. Suddenly she was aware of that wetness again, hot as blood, spreading slowly down the inside of her thighs. From her breasts her fingertips traced downwards, but as they brushed the gossamer cloud of golden hair at the base of her hollow belly, she jerked her hand away. 'I shall never do that again,' she told herself.

She reached for the gown, and belted it round her waist. She looked at the balcony door. 'I should not go out there. I should blow out the lamp and go to bed.' She moved slowly across the floor and hesitated at the door. 'This is silly and dangerous. Heaven knows where it will lead. I only pray that he is not there.'

She placed her hand on the door handle and drew a deep breath as though she was about to plunge into an icy pool. She turned the handle and stepped out on to the balcony. Her eyes turned instantly to the base of the tamarind.

He was there, leaning against the trunk. He straightened and looked up at her. His face was in shadow and she stepped to the edge of the balcony to see him more clearly. They stood very quietly, staring at each other. Rebecca felt as though she might suffocate. Every breath was an effort. Her skin was hot and sensitive. Her whole body was on the rack, every nerve stretched to breaking point. The long sinews down the inside of her thighs were drawn tight as whipcord. She turned her head and gazed at a branch of the tamarind. It curled out from the trunk like a python, thick as her waist, and hung over the edge of the balcony beside where she stood. The twins used it as a ladder and a swing. The bark was lightly polished where they had slid along it. Now she laid one hand on it and looked down again at Penrod.

'I am not enticing him,' she told herself firmly. 'This is not an invitation. He must not think that it is.'

He went to the base of the tree, and began to climb

upwards. No! she thought. He must not do that! I did not mean that!

She was alarmed by the rapidity with which he came up towards her. He reached the bough, and instead of sliding along it in an ungainly manner, with his legs dangling on either side, he stood up and ran lightly along it as though it were a gangplank. He was twenty feet above the ground, and she was terrified that he might slip. She was even more frightened that he would reach the balcony safely – and what then?

She ran back into her bedroom, and closed the door behind her. She reached for the latch to lock it but her fingers disobeyed her. She backed away from the door into the centre of the floor. She heard his footstep on the balcony and her breathing came faster. The door handle turned and her fists clenched at her sides. She wanted to call to him to go away and leave her alone. But no sound passed her lips.

He pushed open the door very slowly, and she wanted to scream. But her father was in the room across the landing and the twins' room was even closer. She did not want to wake them.

Penrod stepped into the room and shut the door quietly behind him. She stared at him, huge startled eyes in a thin pale face. He came to her slowly, with one hand outstretched as though to calm an unbroken filly. She began to tremble.

He touched her cheek. 'You are very lovely,' he whispered, and she thought she might burst into tears. He placed both hands on her shoulders, and she stood rigid. He leant gently towards her. She could not tear her eyes from his: they were green in the lamplight, with golden flecks and stars round the iris. Lightly his mouth touched hers. His lips were hot and smooth. His hands slid down from her shoulders and settled on her waist. Her arms hung at her sides like those of a rag doll. He drew her towards him, and she was unresisting. His lips opened on hers, and the taste and smell of him overwhelmed her. His tongue forced her lips apart, and she lifted her arms from her sides and wound them round his neck. He pulled her harder, almost roughly, against his body. She felt that massive hardness growing up again between their lower bodies. Her own wetness welled up like a spring from deep inside her, and she clenched her thighs and buttocks to stop it overflowing, but it flooded creamily down her thighs.

He swayed back, and she felt deprived as the contact between them was broken. She tried to follow his body with her own. He untied her belt and opened her gown. She tried half-heartedly to cover herself but he held her wrists, and studied her pale body with a rapt expression. 'You are lovely beyond the telling of it,' he murmured, and his tone was husky.

Her shyness evaporated in the warmth of his praise, and instinctively she pulled back her shoulders. Her breasts were pert and pointed. She saw by his eyes that he did not consider them too small. Her nipples felt pebble hard. She wanted desperately to feel his mouth on them again. She was possessed by utter wantonness. She reached up and took a double handful of the dense springing hair at the back of his head, twisted her fingers in his curls and drew his face down.

She gasped as his mouth closed on hers. She would never have believed the plethora of sensations that followed from such a simple act. His breath on her skin was alternately cool and warm as he inhaled and exhaled, his lips at first firm and dry, then soft and moist. His tongue squirmed like an eel, then lapped like a cat at a saucer of cream. He suckled on her, tugging and biting, and she felt the sensation repeated like an echo deep inside her.

When she reached the threshold of pain, he broke off suddenly, lifted her and carried her to her bed. He laid her on it as though she were something fragile and precious, then stepped back. He unbuttoned the front of his shirt, turned to the lamp on her dressing-table, cupped his hand behind the glass chimney and drew a breath to blow out the flame.

She sat up quickly. 'No!' she said sharply. 'Don't blow it out. You have seen me, and now I must see you.' She could not believe that she had spoken so brazenly. He came back and stood over her. Without haste he stripped off his shirt. His skin was ivory smooth and unblemished where it had been protected from the sun. The muscles of his chest were hard and flat, forged by swordplay and hard riding. He stood on one leg to pull off his boot, and his balance was rock steady. He laid the boot aside, careful not to drop it, and she was grateful for his consideration. He did the same with the second boot. Then he unbuckled his belt and stepped out of his breeches. She had seen him naked once before, and she had believed that the image would remain with her for ever. But she had not seen him like this. She bit her lip to prevent herself crying out with shock. He came on to her bed and knelt over her. 'Please don't hurt me,' she begged.

'I would die first,' he said. She whimpered as she felt him at the threshold of her being. She thought that something must tear or give way and she braced herself for the agony. She felt a wall of resistance within her.

This cannot be happening, she thought, but she was suddenly reckless of any consequences. She pushed up hard with her hips to meet him, and she felt him break through. The pain was sharp but transitory. He glided on and on into her, until he had filled her to her very depths. The pain fell away, and she was carried out over the void, terrified at first, then soaring upwards as though she scaled a mighty mountain range. When she reached the peak, the need to scream out her triumph was so powerful that she pressed her open mouth into the hollow of his neck to gag herself.

'Stay with me,' she pleaded, as, later, he rose to dress. 'Don't leave me so soon.'

'You know I cannot stay. It is late. Dawn is close, and the household will begin to stir.'

'When are you going away?'

He paused in the act of buttoning his shirt. 'Who told you that I am going away?' he demanded sharply. She shook her head. 'That is dangerous knowledge, Becky. If the enemy find out it could cost my life, and worse besides.'

'I will not tell another soul,' she said miserably. 'But I shall miss you.' She wanted his reassurance that he would return. Papa had said, 'Ships in the night, all of them, I'm afraid. One can not rely on them.' She did not want it to be like that.

262

He did not reply, but shrugged on his khaki tunic.

'Promise me you will come back,' she pleaded. He stooped over her bed and kissed her lips. 'Promise me,' she insisted.

'I never make promises I may not be able to keep,' he said, and then he was gone.

She felt tears close to the surface, but she forced them back. 'I will never be a whiner or a weeper,' she promised herself. Despite her bursting heart, sleep came down on her like a dark avalanche.

She woke to the sound of guns, but the shells were bursting near the harbour, where the attack had been beaten off. The Dervish were venting their spite. Her bedroom curtains were wide open, and sunlight streamed in.

Nazeera was fussing ostentatiously around the room. 'It is after eight, Jamal. The twins have been gone two hours,' she said, as Rebecca raised her head sleepily from the pillow. 'I have filled two buckets of hot water, and laid out your blue skirt.'

Rebecca was still half asleep as she slipped out from under the sheet. Nazeera stared at her in astonishment, and she tried to brazen it out: 'Oh, Nazeera, you look as though you were frightened by a jinnee. How many times have you seen me naked?' She ran to the bathroom and poured one of the steaming buckets of water into the galvanized hip bath.

Nazeera gazed after her, then pursed her lips. She pulled back the bedclothes and started with alarm. There was a patch of dried blood on the undersheet. Nazeera knew at once that this was not menstrual issue: al-Jamal had seen her moon only twelve days before and it was too soon for it to rise again. This blood was bright and pure and virginal.

Oh, my baby, my little girl, you have made the crossing, and now you stand on a strange and dangerous new shore. She bent closer to the bed to scry the omen. The stain was no larger than her spread hand, but it was shaped like a bird in flight.

A vulture? That was an evil omen, the bird of death and suffering. No. She thrust away the thought. A gentle dove? A falcon, cruel and beautiful? A wise old owl? Only the future will tell us, she decided, and gathered up the sheet. She would wash it with her own hands, in secret. No other must be allowed to see this marking. Then she stopped, for she sensed that al-Jamal was watching her through the open bathroom door.

She dropped the bundled sheet on the floor and went through to her. She knelt beside the bath and picked up the loofah. There was no soap – they had finished the last bar a week ago. Rebecca held her hair on top of her neck, and leant forward. Nazeera began the familiar ritual of scrubbing her back.

After a while she whispered her question: 'Which one was it, Jamal?'

'I don't understand what you are asking.' Rebecca would not look at her face.

'Who climbed the tamarind tree last night?' But Rebecca pretended she had water in her eyes, and covered them with both hands.

'It could not have been Abadan Riji, the pretty soldier. He has another woman,' Nazeera said.

Rebecca lowered her hands and stared at her. 'You are a liar,' she said softly, but with deadly ferocity. 'That is a cruel and hurtful lie.'

'So it was the soldier. I wish it had been the other, who might bring you happiness. The soldier never will.'

'I love him, Nazeera. Please understand that.'

'So does she. Her name is Bakhita.'

'No!' Rebecca covered her ears. 'I don't want to hear this.'

Nazeera was silent. She took Rebecca's arm and ran the loofah over it. When she came to her fingers she separated them and washed them one at a time.

'Bakhita is an Arabic name,' Rebecca blurted at last, but Nazeera remained silent. 'Answer me!' Rebecca insisted.

'You did not want to hear.'

'You are torturing me. Is she an Arab? Is she very beautiful? Does he love her?'

'She is of my people and my God,' Nazeera answered. 'I have never seen her, but men say she is very beautiful, and

264

rich and clever. As to whether he loves her or not, that I do not know. Can a man like Abadan Riji ever love a woman in the same way that she loves him?'

'He is an Englishman and she is Arab,' Rebecca whispered. 'How can she love him?'

'He is a man and she is a woman before all else. That is how she can love him.'

'Nazeera, an hour ago I was happy. Now happiness has flown away.'

'Perhaps it is best that you are unhappy for today rather than unhappy for the rest of your life,' Nazeera said sadly. 'That is why I have told you these things.'

Two hours after the beginning of curfew the four men left the city. Penrod and Yakub wore turbans and Ansar *jibbas* for they would be riding north through the Dervish lines. Ryder and Bacheet wore simple *galabiyyas*, like common tribesmen, for they would return to the city.

Despite their outfits they were unchallenged as they crossed the canal behind Ryder Courtney's compound. The guard had been warned to let them pass. They were all heavily laden with weapons and woven sisal bags as they struck out into the desert. None spoke and they moved warily, keeping well separated but in sight of each other.

Bacheet led the way. He never slackened his pace even when the sand was ankle deep. They walked for two hours before they climbed a bank of shale that was frosty pale in the glimmer of the moon. One of the wadis that was carved out of the far side was filled with a dark amorphous mass of thorny scrub. There Bacheet paused and lowered his burden to the ground. He spoke a few quiet words to Ryder Courtney. Ryder handed him a leather bag of Maria Theresa dollars, and Bacheet went forward alone. The other three squatted to wait. In the distance they heard Bacheet utter the lonely haunted cry of a courser, the nocturnal plover of the desert. The call was answered from the wadi.

'So al-Mahtoum is here. He is a good man. I can rely on him,' Ryder said, with satisfaction.

'Let us go to join them.' Penrod Ballantyne stood up impatiently.

'Sit down,' Ryder ordered. 'Bacheet will come to fetch us. Al-Mahtoum will not allow a stranger to see his face. He lives a dangerous existence. When he has handed over the camels to Bacheet he will disappear back into the desert like a fox.'

An hour later the courser cried again, and Ryder stood up. 'Now,' he said, and led Penrod and Yakub forward. There were four camels couched among the scrub. Bacheet squatted beside them but al-Mahtoum was gone. Penrod and Yakub went to each of them to check their tack and their loads. There were dhurra loaves and dried dates in the food bags and one of the animals was loaded with camel fodder. The water-skins were less than a quarter filled.

Penrod remarked on this.

'Al-Mahtoum expects you to fill them at the river crossing. No sense in carrying more than you need. You should reach the Nile at Gutrahn before midnight tomorrow. Don't try to cross sooner. The Dervish are thick as tsetse flies this side of Gutrahn.'

Penrod replied tartly: 'Yakub and I have travelled this road before, but thank you for your excellent advice.' He went from one beast to the next, slapping their humps. They were plumped up with fat. Next he checked their limbs, running his hands down shoulder and haunch to the fetlock. 'Sound,' he said. 'They are in good condition.'

'They don't come any sounder,' Ryder said bitterly. 'These are *gimal*, the finest racing camels. They are worth fifty pounds each – stolen from me by your warlord Chinese Gordon.'

'I will treat them like my own children,' Penrod promised.

'I am sure you will,' Ryder said, 'although those who call you the Camel Killer, and they are legion, might have difficulty believing you.'

Penrod and Yakub mounted up, and Penrod gave Ryder an ironic salute with the goad. 'I shall give your respects to the ladies at the Long Bar in the Gheziera Club.' He knew that Ryder was not a member. It was another little burr in the rough texture of their relationship.

Yet Ryder was not particularly pleased to see him go. Penrod Ballantyne was never dull. He and Bacheet watched the little caravan meld with the night.

Bacheet grunted and spat. It was apparent that he did not share his master's feelings. 'The two of them ride together because they are both rogues and lechers, almost as quick with knife and gun as they are with their meat prods.'

Ryder laughed. 'You should rejoice that Yakub has gone. Perhaps you will now be able to enjoy a little more of Nazeera's company.' He swung the sling of his rifle over his shoulder.

'You should be equally grateful to see their backs,' Bacheet's tone was astringent, 'although the leopard has already been in the goat kraal, or so I have heard.'

Ryder stopped in his tracks and tried to fathom Bacheet's expression in the starlight. 'What leopard, and whose goats?'

'Yesterday morning Nazeera changed the linen in the palace bedrooms. She had to wash one set in cold water.' It was an oblique reference, but Ryder understood it. Hot water removes most stains, but not blood. For that, one used cold water.

They did not speak again until they had crossed the canal into the city. Ryder was still filled with disbelief and betrayal as he entered his compound and went to his private quarters. Of course he knew of Penrod Ballantyne's reputation as a lady-killer, but Rebecca Benbrook? Surely not. She was a young girl of excellent family and strict upbringing. His respect and affection for her had led him to expect certain standards of her, those a man might look for in his future wife.

Bacheet and Nazeera are notorious gossips – I do not believe it. Then, suddenly, he remembered an observation his elder brother, Waite, had once made: 'The colonel's lady and Katie O'Grady are both women under the skin. In certain circumstances both think with their organs of generation, instead of their brains.' Ryder had laughed at the time, but now it sickened him.

He did not feel better until he had shaved and drunk two large mugs of black coffee, almost the last of his hoarded supply. Even then when he sat down at his desk, he found it difficult to concentrate on his ledgers. The most lurid and disquieting images kept forming in his mind. It was with relief that he made the final entry in his journal, closed the heavy leatherbound book and went out to begin his morning rounds of the compound.

As he stepped into the animal enclosure, Saffron ran to meet him. She had Lucy the monkey on her shoulder. Unperturbed the remaining infant was clinging to Lucy's belly fluff with all four paws and suckling busily. Lucy had lost the other to a disease that not even Ali had been able to cure. Saffron skipped along beside him, blissfully relating every shred of information and gem of wisdom that Ali had shared with her that morning.

'Victoria is scouring,' she informed him.

'Are we discussing the female bongo, or the Queen of England and Empress of India?' Ryder asked.

'Oh, don't be silly! You know exactly who I mean.' Saffron laughed. 'Ali says that the acacia leaves do not agree with her. He and I are going to dose her as soon as he has brewed his medicine. It's what he uses for the horses.'

Ryder felt his dark mood lift a little. Saffron's company was always healing and distracting. 'Why aren't you helping Amber in the green-cake kitchens?' he asked, as they came to the last cages.

'My sister is a bore, so bossy and overbearing. She hasn't been here for weeks and today she appears and gives orders as though she was a duchess.'

They walked between the ranks of Sudanese women who were crushing the bundles of fresh greenery in the wooden stamp pots. Ryder greeted most by name and asked a question, which demonstrated his interest and concern for them. They giggled in gratification. Some of the younger girls were openly saucy and flirtatious for Ryder was a great favourite among them. He knew that the way to get the best out of his people was to make certain they liked him. Saffron took part in the banter with the women, for she shared their sense of fun and they enjoyed her sparkle. High spirits were rare in the city, where terror and starvation had turned the populace into wild animals. We have the green-cake to thank for that. It keeps all of us healthy and human, thought Ryder.

He tried not to show it but he was eager to get to the inner enclosure where the smoke was rising from the line of three-legged cauldrons. When they reached it they found Rebecca, Amber and five Arab girls weighing and packing the loaves of green-cake into woven baskets for distribution to those who needed it most. This was not easy to decide, for there was not nearly enough to go round. Rebecca was reading the scale and Amber was writing down the results as her elder sister called them out.

'This is our best day ever, Ryder. One hundred and thirty-eight pounds,' Amber announced with pride, as he came up.

'Excellent. You ladies have done wonderfully well.' Ryder turned to Rebecca. She wore long skirts and a wide-brimmed straw hat, for the sun was already high and hot.

'Miss Benbrook, I hope I find you well?' He could see that she had lost more weight. He was sure he would be able to encircle her waist with his hands. But the thought of touching her made him uneasy, and he shifted from one foot to the other.

She gave him the first direct smile since their indiscreet behaviour had been discovered, but it lacked her usual sparkle and verve. She seemed depressed and subdued. 'Thank you, Mr Courtney. For a while I was unwell but I am now fully recovered.' They exchanged a few more stilted pleasantries, while Saffron pouted because she had lost Ryder's attention.

'If you will excuse us we should get back to work.' Rebecca ended the conversation. 'Amber, we have finished with the scale and you may take it back to the shed. Saffron, you are killing Lucy and her baby with love. Go and put them back into their cage. We need your help here.'

Saffron pulled a face but went to do as she was told leaving Ryder and Rebecca alone.

'You are wearing Arab dress,' Rebecca remarked. 'That is unusual, is it not?'

'Not at all,' Ryder replied. 'I always wear it when I travel in the desert. It is cooler and more practical for riding and walking. Also, my people prefer me to do so. It makes me seem one of them, and less a stranger.'

'Oh? I thought it was because you and Bacheet went out to find camels for Captain Ballantyne and Yakub.'

'Who told you that?'

'For me to know and you to find out.'

'Nazeera's a chatterbox. You should not pay attention to everything she tells you.'

'You are jumping to conclusions, Mr Courtney. However, I have always found Nazeera's information highly reliable,' she replied.

If only you knew Nazeera's latest bulletin, he thought, but she went on, 'Tell me, sir, did Captain Ballantyne get away safely?'

It was a direct question to which she obviously knew the answer. Ryder considered it carefully. It occurred to him that Penrod's departure had left the field clear for him. On the other hand did he really want the pretty soldier-boy's discarded toy?

'Well, did he?' Rebecca insisted on a reply. 'It is of no interest to me, but Nazeera will want to know about Yakub. He is her particular friend.'

Ryder grimaced at her delicate description of their relationship. Did Rebecca think of the soldier-boy as *her* particular friend, he wondered. 'I don't think that we should discuss military matters that relate to the safety of the city,' he said at last.

'Oh, la, Mr Courtney! I am not a spy for the Mahdi. If you don't tell me I shall simply ask my father. However, I thought you might save me the trouble.'

'Very well. I cannot see any pressing reason why you should not know. Captain Ballantyne left a little after midnight. He and Yakub are heading north, and in all probability will cross the Blue Nile tonight. They plan to join up with the Mahdist army that is moving north along the river towards Abu Hamed.'

Rebecca paled. 'They plan to travel in company with the Dervish? That is madness.'

'It is known as hiding in full view. They will conceal themselves among the host,' he assured her. 'You need not worry, Captain Ballantyne is adept at disguise. He can change like a veritable chameleon.' And he thought, She can take that as a warning, if she wishes.

'Oh, I am not worried, I assure you, Captain.' The lie was transparent: she looked as though she might burst into tears.

There is no doubt now that Nazeera was telling the truth, and that Ballantyne has made her his doxy, but what of it? Ryder reflected. She was never mine, and I don't love her – at least, not now that she is spoilt fruit. Even in his own ears that did not ring true. He tried to be more honest with himself. Do I love her? But he did not want to face that question four square.

'I will leave you to your labours, Miss Benbrook,' he murmured, and turned towards the door of the shed. 'Amber!' he exclaimed. He and Rebecca had been so caught up in their own conversation that neither had noticed she had returned.

'How long have you been listening?' Rebecca demanded.

Instead of answering Amber asked, 'Are the Dervish going to catch Penrod?'

'Of course not. Don't be silly!' Rebecca turned on her. Both sisters were close to tears. 'Anyway you should not eavesdrop on other people, and you should not refer to Captain Ballantyne as Penrod. Now, come and help me to get the cauldrons filled again.'

Amber pushed past her and fled through the gates of the compound and back through the streets towards the consular palace.

Poor little thing, thought Ryder, but there are difficult days ahead for all of us.

Early each morning, the minute the bells of the old Catholic mission had tolled the end of curfew, the women of the city streamed from the ruins, huts and hovels and scurried to the arsenal for the daily distribution of grain. By the time the gates opened several thousand were waiting in a line that stretched almost as far as the harbour. It was an agglomeration of misery. Starvation and disease, those dread horsemen, rode so rampantly through every quarter of the city that all cowered beneath their lash. Each of these poor ruined creatures, gaunt and ragged, some barely able to totter along, infants strapped to their backs or sucking vainly on their empty, withered dugs, clutched a battered dish and the tattered ration booklets issued by General Gordon's secretariat.

At the arsenal gates an Egyptian captain was in charge, with twenty men under his command. The dhurra sacks were dragged out one at a time from the granary. None of the citizens were allowed to enter the gates. Gordon did not want the populace to see for themselves how perilously low the stocks had fallen.

As each woman reached the head of the line, a sergeant examined her booklet to make sure it had not been forged. When he was satisfied he scribbled the date and his signature. The day's ration for her family was doled out into her dish with a wooden scoop. Two masters-at-arms, with clubs, stood ready on each side of the gates to discourage any argument or disturbance. This morning an additional twenty armed troopers were drawn up in a double rank on each side of the gates. Their bayonets were fixed, their expressions grim and businesslike. The women knew from bitter experience what this show of force presaged. They became restless and rowdy, bickering spitefully, jostling each other. The children sensed the tension and were fretful.

When General Gordon came striding down the street from the fort towards the gates, the women held up their children to show him their bruised, distorted features, the skeletal semi-paralysed limbs, and how their hair had turned to a sparse reddish fuzz, all sure signs of starvation, scurvy and beri-beri.

Gordon ignored these marks of affliction, the curses and supplications of the mothers, and took his place at the head of the squad. He nodded to the captain to proceed. The young officer unrolled the proclamation, which had been run off on the consulate printing press, and began to read it: 'I, General Charles George Gordon, by the authority vested in me by the Khedive of Egypt as Governor of the province of Kordofan and the city of Khartoum, do hereby proclaim that, with immediate effect, the daily ration of grain issued to each citizen of the city of Khartoum shall be reduced to the volume of thirty decilitres *per diem*—' The officer could get no further: his voice was drowned by jeers and screams of protest. The crowd pulsed and seethed like a black jellyfish, the women shaking their fists and waving their arms over their heads.

Gordon gave a sharp order. The troopers lowered their bayonets to present a bristling steel hedge to the advancing mob. The women spat, shrieked and hammered on the metal dishes they carried as though they were drums. The captain drew his sword: 'Back! Get back, all of you!'

This infuriated them further.

'You want us to starve! We will open the city gates! If the Khedive and Gordon Pasha cannot feed our children, we will throw ourselves on the mercy of the Mahdi.'

The women in the front rank seized the blades of the bayonets, and held them in bloody hands, forcing the troopers back.

Gordon gave a quiet command to the young captain. There was a clash of breech-blocks as the troopers loaded their rifles. 'Company present arms, aim!' The troopers looked over the iron sights into the contorted faces of the mob. 'Fire!'

The rifles crashed out, aimed carefully over the women's heads. Black powder smoke enveloped them in a dense cloud and, stunned, they reeled back a few paces.

'Reload.' The crowd wavered before the menace of the

273

levelled rifles, but then a new sound erupted. The women had begun the high-pitched ululation that goaded and inflamed the passions of the mob.

'Throw open the granary! Give us full ration!'

'Feed us!' they screamed, but the soldiers stood firm.

One woman picked up half a brick from a shell-damaged wall and hurled it at the front rank of riflemen. It did no damage, but provoked the rest to rush to the wall and grab bricks, stones and shards of pottery. The mob was transformed. It was no longer a gathering of human beings but a single monstrous organism, mindless amoeba of violence and destruction.

The stones and bricks flew into the thin ranks of troops. The young captain was struck full in the face. The red fez flew from his head, he dropped his sword and sank to his knees. He spat out a tooth and his mouth ran with blood. The women rushed forward, trying to reach the open grain sack, trampling the captain.

Gordon stepped into his place. The women saw his blazing blue eyes. 'Devil eyes!' shrieked those in front. 'Shaitan! Kill him!'

'Give us bread for the children! Give us food!'

The bricks clattered among the soldiers. Another man fell.

'Aim!' Gordon's voice carried, clear as a trumpet call. 'One round. Fire!'

The volley smashed into the mob at point-blank range, they went down before it and lay squealing like pigs in the abattoir. Those still on their feet wavered, and the ringleaders tried to rally them.

'Bayonets!' Gordon called. 'Forward!' They stepped out briskly, the bright blades levelled and the mob shrank back, then turned on itself and broke. They dropped their stones and bricks, threw aside their dishes and ran back into the alleys.

Gordon halted his men and marched them back into the arsenal. As the gates closed behind them, the survivors crept out from their hiding-places in the warren of slums. They came to find their dead, their wounded and their lost children.

At first they were timid and terrified, but then one woman picked up a fist-sized stone and flung it against the barred gates of the arsenal. 'The soldiers are fat, their bellies stuffed full. When we beg for food they shoot us down like dogs.' She was a tall bony harridan, dressed all in black. She stood before the gates and raised both skinny arms towards the sky. 'I call on Allah to smite them with the pestilence and the cholera. Let them eat the flesh of toads and vultures, as we are forced to do!' Her voice was a high-pitched shriek.

The other women thronged to her. They began to ululate again, rolling their tongues so that their spittle flew as they emitted that terrible keening sound.

'The Franks also have food,' screeched the woman in black. 'They gorge like pashas in their palaces.'

'The compound of al-Sakhawi, the infidel, is filled with fat beasts. His storerooms are piled high with sacks of grain.'

'Give us food for our babies!'

'Shaitan is the ally of al-Sakhawi. He has taught him witchcraft. From grass and thorn he has taught him to make the Devil's manna. His people feast upon it.'

'Destroy the nest of Shaitan!'

'We are the children of Allah. Why should the infidel feast while our babies starve and die?'

The crowd wavered uncertainly, and the black-clad woman took charge. She ran to the head of the street that led to the hospital and beyond it to the compound of Ryder Courtney. 'Follow me! I will show you where to find food.' She broke into a shuffling dance, bobbing and ululating, and the crowd streamed after her, filling the narrow street from side to side with a dancing, keening flood of humanity.

The men heard the uproar and came out of their hiding-places among the ruins. The ululating of the women maddened them. Those who carried weapons brandished them. They joined the turbulent dancing procession, and burst into the war songs of the fighting tribes.

Ryder and Jock McCrump were in the main workshop. They had suffered many setbacks. This was the third time in as many months that they had been forced to remove the *Ibis*'s engine from the hull and painstakingly reweld the steam lines. Then they had discovered that the main drive-shaft bearings had also been damaged, and were knocking noisily at even moderate revolutions. Jock had made replacements: from a solid block of metal he had forged and filed the half-shells by hand. It was a monumental exhibition of skill and patience. At long last, after all these months of meticulous labour, the repairs were complete. Now they were putting it all together for a final check before they transported it to the harbour for installation in the steamer's engine room.

'Well, now, skipper, I think this time we've got it right.' Jock stood back with black grease to the elbows and his few remaining hairs plastered to his scalp with sweat. 'This time I think the old *Ibis* will be able to carry us out of this God-forsaken hell-hole. There is a shebeen in Aswan run by a lass from Glasgow, a lady of my acquaintance. She sells genuine malt from the Isle of Islay. I would fain have the taste of it on my tongue again. It is the true nectar of the Almighty, and that's no blasphemy, mind.'

'I will buy the first round,' Ryder promised.

'And the rest,' Jock told him. 'You havenae paid me this year past.'

Ryder was about to protest the injustice of this accusation but he heard racing footsteps coming across the compound and Saffron's breathless squeaks: 'Ryder! Come quickly.'

Ryder stepped to the doorway. 'What is it, Saffron?'

She was holding her skirts high and her hat was hanging down her back on its ribbon. Her face was flushed scarlet. 'Something terrible is happening. Rebecca has sent me to call you. Hurry!' She grabbed his hand and pulled him with her. They ran towards the cauldron yard.

'Can you hear it?' Saffron stopped and held up her hand.

'Now, can you hear?' It was faint babble and murmur, like wind in trees or a distant waterfall.

'Yes, but what is it?'

'Our women say it's a huge crowd of the people. They are coming from the arsenal. Our women say that the grain rations have been cut again, and there is going to be terrible trouble. They are terrified, and they are running away.'

'Saffron, go and fetch Rebecca and Amber.'

'Amber is not here. She is sulking in the palace. She has not come back since she heard that Captain Ballantyne had gone away.'

'Good. She will be safe there. Let the women go if they want to. Bring Rebecca, Nazeera and any others who want to stay to the blockhouse. You know how to shutter the windows and bar the doors. You also know where the rifles are kept. You and Rebecca arm yourselves. Wait for me there.'

'Where are you going?'

'To call the men. That's enough questions. Now, run!'

It was for just this sort of trouble that Ryder had fortified the compound. The walls were high and solid and the tops were lined with shards of broken glass. He had designed the interior of the compound as a series of courtyards, each of which could be defended, but when one was overrun they could fall back into the next. In the centre, the blockhouse comprised his private quarters, treasury and arsenal. All the windows and doors could be covered with heavy shuttering. The walls were pierced with loopholes for rifle fire and the reed roof was heavily plastered with river clay to render it fireproof.

The first line of defence was the outer wall with its heavy gates at front and rear. He sent Jock with three men to barricade the rear gates, and stand guard there. Then Ryder took Bacheet and five of his most reliable men to the front gates, which opened on to the narrow street. They were all armed with long wooden staves. Ryder made certain the gates were bolted and the heavy timber bars were in their slots. It would take a battering-ram to break them down. There was a low wicket gate in the wall to one side, wide enough to admit one man at a time. Ryder stepped through it. The city street was empty, except for a few of the women from the green-cake kitchens. They were scurrying away like frightened chickens, and within seconds the last had disappeared.

Ryder waited. He was deliberately carrying nothing more provocative than the wooden staff. A rifle was worse than useless against a mob. A single shot might drop one person, but would merely infuriate the rest, and they would be on him before he could reload. A certain way to get yourself torn to pieces, he thought, and leant casually on the staff, assuming a calm, relaxed pose. The noise of the crowd was nearer now, becoming louder as he listened. He knew what that keening chorus of women's voices meant. They were whipping themselves and their menfolk into a frenzy.

He stood alone in front of the gates, and the sound built up into a muted roar, coming down on him like the wild waters of a river in flash flood. Suddenly the front rank of the mob burst into view two hundred paces down the narrow street from where he stood. They saw him and faltered. The hubbub subsided gradually, and a strange hush fell over them. They knew him well and his reputation was formidable.

Damn me, if I don't do a Gordon on them. Ryder smiled inwardly. Chinese Gordon was famous for the hypnotic power he could wield over a tribe of hostile savages. It was said he could calm and control them by the sheer power of his personality and the gaze of his steely blue eyes.

Ryder straightened until he stood tall, and glowered at them with all the ferocity he could command. He knew that they looked upon green or blue eyes as those of the Devil. The hush became silence. For the moment it was a standoff. It needed but a small push to topple it one way or the other.

He started to walk towards them. Now he held the stave threateningly, and paced with calculated menace. They backed off slowly before his approach. One looked back over his shoulder. They were on the point of breaking.

Suddenly a tall, gangling female figure bounded into the alley. Her features were withered with starvation. Her lips had shrunk back to expose bone-white teeth, too large for her pale pink gums, which were studded with open ulcers. She was the harpy of mythology, swathed in black cloth. As she danced towards him, her shanks beneath the black skirts were thin as the legs of a heron, and her enormous feet flapped like the carcasses of stranded black catfish. She threw back her head and emitted the cry of a banshee. The mob behind her roared and poured after her, filling the alley.

Ryder held up his right hand in a placatory gesture. 'I will give you whatever you want,' he shouted. 'Stop.'

His voice was drowned by the wild shrieks of the harpy: 'We have come to take what we want, and we will kill all who stand in our way!'

Slowly Ryder lifted his left hand and made the sign of the evil eye. He pointed at the woman's face, and saw her eyelids flutter as she recognized the sign. She stumbled and checked, but then she gathered herself and leapt forward again. He saw the madness in her gaze and knew she was too far gone to respond even to the most dire witchcraft.

Still he stood his ground until she was almost upon him. Then he stepped forward to meet her and drove the point of his staff into her midriff just below the ribcage. The spleens of most river-dwellers were swollen with malaria. A blow like that could burst the organ and kill or maim. The harpy dropped like a bundle of black rags, but the leading ranks of the mob leapt over her body. The man in the forefront swung a broadsword at Ryder's head. He ducked and darted back through the wicket gate. Bacheet slammed and bolted it behind him. They heard and felt the impact as the mob crashed into it on the far side.

'We will let them through the gate one at a time, and we can crack their skulls as they come through,' Bacheet suggested.

'Too many.' Ryder shook his head. 'I will climb to the top of the gate and try to reason with them.'

'You cannot reason with a pack of rabid dogs.'

Somebody was tugging insistently at his coattails and Ryder tried to pull away. Then he looked back. 'I thought I told you to stay in the blockhouse,' he exclaimed angrily.

'I brought you this.' Saffron held up his gunbelt with the holstered revolver dangling from it and the rows of brass cartridges in their loops.

'Good girl!' He strapped it on. 'But now get back to the blockhouse and stay there.' He did not watch her to make sure she had gone but turned back to Bacheet. 'Fetch the long ladder from the workshop.'

They placed it against the wall. Hand over hand Ryder shot to the top and looked down into the street. The length and breadth of it was filled with humanity. He picked out the harpy he had felled: she was on her feet again, doubled over and hobbling with pain, but her voice was as shrill and strident as before. She was directing the crowd to gather anything that would burn from the buildings that lined the street. They were dragging out baulks of timber, dried palm fronds, old furniture, rubbish, and piling it against the outside of the compound gates.

'Hear me, citizens of Khartoum,' Ryder shouted in Arabic. 'Let the peace and wisdom of God guide you. There is nothing within these walls that I will not give you gladly.'

They looked up him uncertainly as he balanced at the top of the ladder.

'There is the disciple of Shaitan!' the harpy screamed. 'The infidel! Look at him, the pork-eater! The brewer of the green manna from hell!' She shuffled into a painful dance, and behind her the crowd growled. They threw stones and sticks at him, but the wall was high and the range was long. The missiles hit the wall and bounced back, clattering in the dusty street.

'What you call the Devil's manna, is cooked grass and reeds. If you will feed them with it, your children will thrive and regain their health.'

'He lies! These are the falsehoods that the Devil has placed in his mouth. We know you are eating bread and meat, not grass. Within these walls you have dhurra and meat. Give it to us. Give us your animals. Give us the dhurra you have in your warehouse.'

'I have no dhurra.'

'He lies!' screeched the harpy. 'Bring fire! We will burn him out of this nest of evil and sacrilege.'

'Wait!' Ryder shouted. 'Hear me!'

But the roar of the crowd drowned his voice. One of the women ran up the crowded street. She was carrying a lighted torch, a bundle of rags soaked in pitch tied to a broomstick. A thick black tarry smoke billowed from the flames. She handed the torch to one of the men, who ran with it to the gate. Ryder glanced down in alarm as he realized how high the rubbish had been piled against the main gates. The man threw the smoking torch on top of the bonfire. It rolled half-way down, then stuck. In the dry desert air the flames caught at once and licked upwards. The gates had stood in the sun for many years. Even though Ryder had his people paint them regularly, the wood dried out and cracked faster than they could repair it, and now the dried paint flared, and the flames shot high. They were almost colourless in the bright sunlight. Ryder considered ordering Bacheet and his men to form a bucket chain to douse the flames before they could burn through the gates, then realized that there were neither enough men nor buckets, that the river and the well were too far, and the flames were already leaping higher than the top of the wall. The heat was intense and drove him off the ladder.

'Bacheet, we could fight them here, but I don't want any shooting. I don't want to kill anybody.'

'It is me that I am worried about, Effendi. I don't want to be killed either,' Bacheet replied. 'These are animals, mad animals.'

'They are starving and they have been driven to this.'

'Should I send one of the men with a message to Gordon to bring the soldiers to drive them away?' Bacheet asked hopefully.

Ryder smiled grimly. 'Gordon Pasha is not our friend. He values us only for our dhurra and our camels. If you send one of our men out there the mob will tear him to pieces. I think we will be forced to save ourselves without the help of Gordon Pasha.'

'How will we do that?' Bacheet asked simply.

'We must fall back to the main compound. They will not be able to burn that gate. The fire hose will reach it.' He had to raise his voice above the howls and shouts of the crowd in the street outside and the crackle of the flames. 'Come! Follow me!' The paint on the inside of the gate was already charring.

He ran back to the inner gate, and gave orders to have the water pump and fire hose rigged. There was a firing platform along the top of the inner wall, and reluctantly Ryder issued Martini-Henry rifles to those who could handle them. Apart from Rebecca and Jock, he had trained only five of his men, including Bacheet. The Arabs took little interest in musketry and showed even less aptitude for it. Rebecca could outshoot most of them. He left the women and Jock in the blockhouse, guarding the loopholes.

From the firing parapet he watched the main gates sag slowly inwards, then crash to the dusty earth in a final burst of sparks and burning fragments. The mob poured through, leaping and pushing each other over the still flaming remnants of the gates. One of the older women lost her footing and fell into the flames. They caught at once in her voluminous robe. The rest of the crowd ignored her agonized shriek, and within seconds she lay still. The smell of her roasting flesh floated sickeningly to where Ryder stood on the parapet of the inner wall.

Once the leaders were inside, they came up short. They were in unfamiliar territory and they looked about curiously. Then they caught sight of the row of heads above the parapet of the inner wall, and the hunting chorus went up again. They charged straight at the inner gate like a pack of savage hounds. Ryder let them get half-way across, then fired into the hard-packed clay in front of the leaders. The bullet kicked up a spray of dust and gravel, then ricocheted away over their heads. It stopped them short, and they milled indecisively.

'Don't come closer!' he shouted. 'I will kill the next one who comes.' Some turned, and started to creep away. Then the harpy hobbled through to the front. She broke once more into her grotesque dance. From somewhere she had armed herself with a cowtail fly switch. She brandished this as she screeched her threats and curses at the men on the parapet.

'You foul and stupid old woman,' Ryder muttered, in frustration and despair, 'don't force me to kill you.' He fired at her feet, and when the bullet kicked up dirt under her, she leapt into the air, flapping the black wings of her robe like an ancient crow taking flight. The crowd howled again. She hit the ground and came straight on towards the inner wall. Ryder levered another round into the breech and fired. Again she jumped high, and the men behind her imitated her, laughing. The sound had a deranged, obscene quality that was as menacing as the shouts of rage had been.

'Stop!' Ryder muttered. 'Please stop, you old bitch.' He shot again, but now the mob had realized he would not shoot to kill and lost all fear. They came on after the prancing figure in a swarm. They reached the gate and beat against it with the weapons they carried and their bare hands.

'Wood!' shouted the harpy. 'Bring more wood!' They ran to fetch it, and came back to pile it against the gate as they had before.

'Get the pump started!' Ryder shouted, and two men seized the handles and swung them up and down. The empty canvas hose, laid out across the yard, swelled and hardened as the pressure built up and a powerful stream of river water spurted from the nozzle. Two men on the parapet pointed it down on to the kindling below. It struck with such force that the pile tumbled over.

'Aim at her.' Ryder pointed out the harpy. The stream hit her full in the chest and knocked her backwards. She struck the ground on her shoulder-blades and rolled. The hose stream followed her. Every time she regained her feet, it knocked her down again. At last she crawled out of range on hands and knees. Ryder turned the hose on the men in the front of the crowd and they scattered. Then they spread out to search the other buildings of the compound, which lay outside the inner fortifications. Within minutes Ryder heard hammering and banging coming from the direction of his warehouses.

'They are smashing down the doors of the ivory storeroom,' Bacheet shouted. 'We must stop them.'

'A thousand of them, and ten of us?' Ryder did not have to say more.

'But the ivory and skins?' Bacheet was entitled to a small share of Ryder's profits, and now at the thought of his losses his face was a pattern of dismay.

'They can have the elephant teeth and the animal skins, rather than my own teeth and skin,' Ryder said. 'Anyway, they cannot eat ivory. Perhaps when they find no dhurra in the stores they will lose interest.'

It was a vain hope, and he knew it. It was not long before the men were streaming back, egged on by the wild ululations of the women. They were carrying some of the largest elephant tusks and bundles of sun-dried animal hides. They piled these at the foot of the wall. Their intention was clear. They were building a ramp to scale the wall. Immediately Ryder ordered the men on the hose to direct the stream on to the pile. The tusks and the heavy bales were much more solid than the rubbish they had used in their first attempt and the hose stream made no impression upon them. Then they tried to drive off the men, but although the hose beat down on them most stayed on their feet and placed more tusks on the growing ramp. When one was knocked down, three others rushed forward to take his place. They kept piling up the heavy material until it reached just below the top of the wall. Then they reassembled in the outer courtyard out of range of the fire hose. The black harpy pranced among them.

'You should have hit her harder,' Bacheet muttered darkly, 'or, better still, you should have put a bullet through that ugly head. It's still not too late.' He lifted the Martini-Henry and aimed it over the top of the parapet.

'She is in no danger, with you doing the shooting,' Ryder remarked. Despite the hours of instruction he had lavished on Bacheet he was a long way from mastering the art of musketry. Bacheet looked pained at the insult, but he lowered the rifle. 'See? The old witch is picking out the best men to climb the walls.'

Bacheet was right. Somehow she had kept hold of the switch even when the hose had hit her squarely. It was secured round her wrist by a loop of rawhide. She was moving among the crowd and marking the ones she chose by slapping them in the face with it. Quickly she picked out thirty or forty of the youngest and strongest. Many were armed with broadswords or axes.

Encouraged by the harpy the women started that dreadful cacophony again. The assault troop brandished their weapons and rushed at the wall. The jet of water from the hose struck the leaders but they linked arms to support each other.

'Let us shoot, Effendi,' Bacheet pleaded. 'They are so close even I cannot miss.'

'I would not give odds on that,' Ryder grunted, 'But hold your fire. If we kill just one they will go berserk and start a massacre.' He was thinking of the women in the blockhouse. Little else mattered.

Even with the hose playing over them the attackers climbed swiftly to the parapet. Ryder and his men checked them there, swinging at their heads with clubs and staves. They had the advantage of height. At a range of only a few feet the fire hose was almost irresistible, and the long staves kept the attackers from getting close enough to use their swords. But when some lost heart and retreated down the ramp of bales and tusks the harpy was at the bottom to meet them, lashing their faces with the switch and screaming abuse. Three times they fell back and each time she sent them up again.

'They are giving up,' Bacheet panted. 'They are losing heart.'

'I hope Allah is listening to you,' Ryder said, and plied his staff, cracking it across the temple of the man in front of him. He rolled down the ramp and lay still at the bottom. Even the harpy's stinging blows with the switch could not rouse him.

Then a man pushed through the throngs of ululating women. He walked with the rolling long-armed gait of a silver-backed gorilla bull. His head was round, shaven and

285

shiny as a cannonball. His skin was the colour of anthracite and his features were Nubian, with thick lips and a wide, flattened nose. He had stripped to his loincloth and the muscles of his chest bulged under the oiled skin, and writhed like a black silk bag of pythons. 'I know this one,' Bacheet croaked huskily. 'He is a famous wrestler from Dongola. They call him the Bone Cruncher. He is dangerous.'

The Nubian climbed the ramp with astonishing agility. Ryder ran down the platform to confront him, but he was already at the parapet. He raised himself to his full height, balanced like an ebony colossus.

Ryder placed the butt of the long stave under his arm, like a lance, and ran at him. The sharpened point caught the Nubian in the centre of his chest and snagged in his flesh. Ryder threw his weight behind it, and the Nubian hovered at the point of balance, his arms windmilling, body arched backwards.

Bacheet sprang to Ryder's side and the two threw their combined weight on the staff. The Nubian went over like an avalanche of black rock. He tumbled into five men behind him, and they tumbled down the steep incline of the ramp in a confused jumble of arms and legs.

The Nubian hit the sun-baked earth on the back of his shaven head and the impact reverberated like the fall of a lightning-blasted mahogany tree. He lay quiescent, mouth agape and thunderous snores echoing up his throat. The harpy jumped on to his chest and lashed at his face.

The Nubian opened his eyes and sat up. He swatted her away with the back of one hand and shook his head groggily. Then he saw Ryder and Bacheet grinning down at him. He threw back his head, bellowed like a bull buffalo in a pitfall, then groped for his sword, lurched to his feet and charged straight back up the ramp.

'Sweet Mother of God,' said Ryder. 'Just look at him come.' He raised the staff again, and as the Nubian reached the top he thrust at him viciously. With a flick of the blade the Nubian lopped two feet off the end. Ryder stabbed at him again with the butt. The Nubian cut again back-handed and left Ryder with a stump no longer than his arm. Ryder hurled it at him. It struck the Nubian in the centre of his sloping forehead. He blinked and roared again, then came over the top of the parapet, hacking wildly.

'Back to the blockhouse!' Ryder yelled, as he ducked under the blade.

Suddenly he realized he was alone on the parapet. The others had anticipated his order and taken themselves off at top speed. He dived down the rickety ladder into the yard and raced for the door. He could hear the Nubian close behind him, and the swish of his sword fanned the short sweaty hairs on the back of his neck.

'Run, Ryder! He's right behind you,' Saffron shrilled from one of the loopholes. 'Shoot him – I gave you your gun! Why don't you shoot?' In theory it was good advice, but if he lost even a second in loosening the flap of his holster the Nubian would take his head off at the shoulders. He found an extra turn of speed and began to catch up with Bacheet and the other Arabs.

'Faster, Ryder, faster!' Saffron yelped. Close behind him he could hear the hoarse breathing. Ahead, the others burst through the blockhouse door.

Rebecca was holding it open for him. Now she levelled the rifle and seemed to aim straight at his head. 'I can't shoot without hitting you,' she cried, and lowered the barrel. 'Come on, Ryder, please, come on.' Even in the desperate circumstances, her use of his first name gave him a sweet thrill and added wings to his feet. He flew through the doorway and Rebecca and Saffron slammed it behind him. On the far side the Nubian crashed into it with a force that shivered the frame.

'He's going to smash it off its hinges.' Rebecca gasped. They heard the Nubian hacking and kicking at it.

'Steel door, steel frame,' Ryder reassured her, and grabbed the rifle Saffron handed him. He opened the breech and checked the load. 'We'll be safe in here.'

He stepped up to the loophole and Rebecca stood close beside him. Through the narrow opening they had a view across the yard to the door of the workshop and in the other direction to the inner gate of the menagerie. The broad sweat-gleaming back of the Nubian appeared in their field of vision. He had abandoned his assault on the blockhouse door. Now he was striding across the yard to the barred inner gates. When he reached them Ryder watched him lift the heavy teak locking bars and toss them aside. Then he stood back and kicked the brass lock off its hinges. As the gates swung open the harpy was first into the yard. The horde poured in behind her.

She headed straight for the blockhouse, and the rest followed her closely. It was a horrific spectacle, as though the gates of hell had burst open and spewed out the legions of the damned and long-dead. Their faces were ravaged by disease and hunger, their eyes too large for their wizened, emaciated heads, their lips and eyelids swollen and inflamed with running ulcers and carbuncles. Starvation and disease emit their own odour as the body devours itself and the skin releases the fluids of decay and dissolution: as they crowded to the loop-holes the stench oozed through into the hot, airless interior and filled it with the reek of open sepulchres. It was a miasma that was difficult to breathe. The ruined faces leered and grimaced through the openings. 'Food! Where is the food?' They thrust their arms through. Their limbs were thin and gnarled as dead branches. The palms of their hands were as pale as the bellies of dead fish.

'Oh, Jesus, have mercy on us,' Rebecca gasped, and shrank against Ryder, instinctively seeking his protection. He placed one arm round her shoulders. This time she made no effort to pull away from him. 'What will happen to us now?'

'Whatever happens, I will stay with you,' he said, and she pressed closer to him.

The harpy was shrieking orders to the mob. 'Search all the buildings! We must find where they have hidden the dhurra! Then we will smash the pots in which they have brewed the Devil's manna. It is evil and an offence in the sight of God. It is this that has brought misfortune upon the city, and visited us with pestilence and disaster. Find where they have hidden the animals. You shall feast on sweet meat this day.' Her shrill voice reached to the depths of their starved bodies. They responded to her with a kind of blind, hypnotic obedience and rushed away from the rifle slits so that Ryder could see out again. He and Rebecca pressed their faces to the same opening, breathing the cleaner air and watching the hordes streaming towards the gates of the menagerie, led by the colossal Nubian and the harpy.

'Well, them bongos of yours ain't going to be shitting on the decks of my ship again, skipper,' said Jock McCrump lugubriously. Suddenly he remembered his manners and touched the brim of his cap to Rebecca. 'If you'll forgive my French, ladies.'

'What are they going to do with them, Jock?' Saffron's voice was fearful.

'It's the cooking pot for all of them beasties, d'ye ken, Miss Saffy?'

Saffron flew at the door and tried to tear open the locking bars. 'Lucy! I have to save Lucy and her baby!'

Ryder took her arm gently but firmly, and drew her to his side. 'Saffron,' he whispered huskily, 'there is nothing we can do for Lucy now.'

'Can't you stop them? Please! Won't you stop them, Ryder?'

There was no reply he could give her. He held the two girls tightly, Saffron on one side and Rebecca on the other. They clung to him and watched some of the mob crowd the gate that led to the menagerie and try to break in, but it was stout and resisted their efforts. Then the Nubian shouldered them aside. He braced himself against the gate and shook it until it rattled in its frame, but it did not give way. He stepped back, charged and crashed into it with one massive shoulder. The hinges were torn from the frame and the door flew open.

Ali, the old keeper, stood in the open doorway with a rusty sword in his hands.

'Ali, you old fool,' Ryder groaned and tried to turn the

girls away so that they would not see what was about to happen. But they resisted and stared ashen-faced through the loophole.

Ali raised the sword above his head. 'Begone, all of you! You will not enter here.' His voice was high-pitched and quavering. 'I will not allow you to touch my darlings.' He hobbled towards the giant, threatening him with the dented weapon. The Bone Cruncher shot out one thick arm and seized the old man's sword wrist. He shook it as a terrier shakes a rat, and they heard the bone of the old man's forearm crack. The rusty sword dropped into the dust at his feet. Using the broken arm as a handle the Bone Cruncher lifted Ali's wriggling body above his head and slammed him into the jamb of the gate with such force that his ribs snapped like dry kindling. He dropped the broken body, and stepped over it. The crowd rushed after him into the menagerie, but as they passed they hacked at Ali's head with club or sword.

A great roar of greed and hunger went up from within the menagerie as the mob saw the rows of cages and the terrified animals they contained.

'Food! Meat!' screamed the harpy. 'I promised you a feast of fresh red meat. It is here for you.' She rushed at the nearest cage and tore open the door. It was filled with scarlet and grey parrots, a swirling screeching cloud of wings. She leapt in and slashed at them with the whisk, knocking them to the floor of the cage and stamping on them with both horny feet.

The crowd followed her example, breaking open the monkey cages and clubbing the terrified occupants as they bounded around. Then they attacked the stockades and pens of the antelope.

In the blockhouse they could hear what was happening. Above the crash of breaking cages and the uproar of the mob, Saffron was able to identify the terrified voices of her favourite creatures: the shrieks of the parrots and the howls of the monkeys.

'That's Lucy, my poor darling Lucy,' she sobbed. 'They can't eat her. Tell me they won't eat Lucy.' Ryder hugged her but could find no words of comfort.

Then there came wild bleating and bellows of pain from the larger animals.

'That's Victoria, my bongo!' Saffron struggled again. 'Let me go! Please, I have to save her.'

The female bongo bounded out through the gates of the menagerie where old Ali's corpse still lay in the bloody dust. She must have escaped from her pen as the mob tore it down and seemed unhurt.

'Run, Victoria!' Saffron screamed. 'Run, my baby.'

A dozen men and women ran after her with spears and swords. The large, strikingly coloured animal saw the open gate ahead of her and swerved towards it, her sleek hide glistening dark chestnut with creamy white stripes, ears pricked forward, eyes filled with terror, huge and dark in her lovely head. She had almost reached the open gate when one of the spearmen checked and swivelled his shoulders, his left hand pointing straight at her, the right cocked back and holding the spear. He swung his weight forward and the spear flew in a high arc, then dropped towards the animal. It struck her just forward of the croup and the spearhead buried itself. The point must have struck the spine, for her paralysed hindquarters dropped, and she stood still on her front legs.

A triumphant howl went up from the hunters and they crowded round the maimed animal. They made no effort to put her out of her misery, but hacked off lumps of her living flesh. The Nubian rushed up and, with a sweep of his sword, opened her belly as if it were a purse. The pale bag of her stomach and the entwined ropes of entrails bulged out through the gash. These were delicacies, and the mob dragged them out of her, and devoured them voraciously. The yellow contents of the uncleaned guts mingled with the blood, and dribbled from their lips and jowls as they chewed.

Rebecca gagged at the sight and turned away her face, but Saffron watched until at last the bongo collapsed and the crowd swarmed over her carcass like a flock of vultures hiding it from view. From the gates of the menagerie others ran out carrying bleeding lumps of meat and the battered carcasses of the birds and monkeys. They tried to escape before the latecomers from the city streets joined in. They were too late, and all across the compound vicious squabbles and fighting broke out. Saffron saw one of the children pounce upon a scrap. He stuffed it into his mouth and tried to swallow it. But the woman who had dropped it set upon him, beating him and pummelled him until he was forced to spit it out. Before she could pick it out of the dust, someone else snatched it and ran out of the gates with the woman chasing after her.

Another group broke down the door of the shed that contained the day's cooking of green-cake. They gathered up slabs in their shirts, but before they could make off with it the harpy fell upon them. She seemed to have risen above the simple need to find food and ran among them, striking at random with her whisk, screaming, 'That is the poison of Shaitan! Throw it on the fire. Throw it into the latrines where it belongs.' Although a few ran off with their booty, the harpy forced most to fling their share into the cooking fires or down the latrine pits.

'She has destroyed it all. What a shameful waste,' Rebecca cried in anguish. 'And she is making them smash our cauldrons. Now we shall all starve.'

Ryder watched the harpy helplessly. He saw how dangerous this raving demagogue was, that at any moment she might trigger another explosion of murderous passion and insanity. However, most of the mob had disappeared, and it seemed that the riot must soon die of its own accord.

Even though the damage they had wreaked was punishing, Ryder sought some small comfort in the fact that they were making no effort to take the ivory. It was clearly too heavy to carry far. Most of his other valuable possessions were locked in the strongroom in the blockhouse. Just as soon as the *Intrepid Ibis* was seaworthy again, he would load what was left of them and be ready for instant flight.

But the harpy was still prowling round the yard, stopping every few minutes to shake her whisk at the blockhouse and scream curses and insults at the white faces she could see watching her from the loopholes. When she paused at the door of the workshop, Ryder was not seriously alarmed. Some of the other looters had gone in there but had soon come out again. There was nothing in there for them to eat, nothing of obvious value for them to carry away. However, the harpy was in the workshop for only a minute, before she rushed out and screamed across the yard for the Nubian wrestler. Like a tame gorilla responding to its trainer, he crossed the yard with his massive rolling gait. She led him into the workshop. When the Nubian came out again he was carrying such a heavy burden that his legs were bowed under its weight.

'Look!' shouted Jock, in consternation. It was a burden that would have taken the strength of five ordinary men, but the Nubian was carrying the main steam pipe from the *Intrepid Ibis*. Jock had laboured over this piece of machinery for months and now it was ready to reinstall in the steamer.

The harpy screeched towards the blockhouse, 'You think to escape the wrath of the Mahdi? You think to run away in your little steamer? We are going to throw this thing into the Nile. When the Mahdi comes, your white and leprous corpses will rot in the streets of Khartoum. Even vultures will not eat them.' She drove the giant Nubian like an ox towards the gates.

'Even he can never carry it to the river!' Ryder exclaimed. But the harpy was now shouting for others to help him. A number were hurrying to his aid.

'I give you my solemn oath that he is taking my steam pipe nowhere,' Jock growled. He swung up the Martini-Henry, and the crash of the shot in the narrow confines of the room numbed their ears. The rifle kicked back, and the sweet stink of black powder smoke stung their nostrils.

The Nubian had reached the gates. He was less than sixty yards from the rifle slit. The heavy lead bullet caught him just behind the ear and angled forward through his brain. In a pink cloud of wet tissue, it burst out through his right eye socket. He collapsed, with the weight of the steam-pipe chest pinning his corpse to the sunbaked clay.

'You killed him,' Ryder exclaimed in disbelief.

'I aimed at him, didn't I?' Jock said brusquely. 'Of course I damn well killed him.' With his callused thumb he pushed another cartridge into the breech of the rifle. 'And I'm going to kill anybody else who touches my engine.'

In the yard there was an abrupt and breathless silence. The rioters had almost forgotten the presence of the white prisoners in the blockhouse. They stared at the huge half-naked corpse in awe.

The harpy was the only one not bereft of the power of movement. She snatched an axe out of the hands of the man nearest to her and rushed at the length of pipe. One of the many duties of a Sudanese woman is to cut the firewood for her household. As the first stroke of the axe clanged against his steam pipe, Jock knew she was an expert. She swung the axe again, and hit exactly the same spot. Jock could see that she was aiming at one of his welds. The metal there would be annealed by the heat of his torch. Already it was buckling. Two or three blows like that and she would puncture and distort it. It might take days to repair the damage she had already done. If he didn't do something to stop her she might inflict damage beyond repair.

'We will have no more of that nonsense,' he muttered.

Ryder saw him lift the rifle again. 'Don't shoot!' he shouted. 'Jock, *don't shoot her.*'

'Too late!' said Jock, without the least note of contrition in his voice, and again the Martini-Henry bucked and bellowed in his hands.

The bullet caught the harpy full in the chest. It picked her off her feet and threw her against the wall. She hung there, her mouth wide open, but the scream was trapped for ever in her throat. Then she slid down the wall, leaving a long bright smear on the whitewash.

The remaining rioters stared in consternation at the bodies of the two ringleaders. Retribution had come swiftly and unexpectedly. When would the next shot crash out, and who would fall? A wail of alarm went up, and they rushed for the gates.

'Keep them on the run!' Ryder had resigned himself to making the most of Jock's precipitate action. He snatched up his own rifle and fired over the heads of the rioters. Within minutes the yard was empty, except for the harpy and her Nubian.

Ryder opened the blockhouse door cautiously and called to Rebecca, 'Keep Saffron in here with you until we know it's safe for you to come out.' With rifles loaded and held at high port, ready to get off a quick shot, the men swept the compound to make certain no danger still lurked. Jock hurried directly to his steam pipe and knelt beside it. He peered anxiously at the axe marks on the metal, removed the greasy and battered cap from his head and polished the marred surface tenderly, then he replaced his cap and studied the marks again. He sighed with relief. 'Ain't too much damage done.' He picked up the whole pipe as easily as the Nubian had, and carried it lovingly back into his workshop.

Ryder walked over to the two corpses. The harpy was sitting with her back against the wall. Her eyes and her mouth were open and her expression was faintly quizzical. He prodded her with the toe of his boot. She flopped on to her face and lay still. He could have fitted his clenched fist into the deep dark bullet-hole between her shoulder-blades. He did not need to examine the Nubian. His head lay in a puddle of his own brains.

'I don't approve, but that was not bad shooting, Jock,' he muttered, then called to Bacheet, 'Dump them in the river. The crocodiles will take care of them. No need to report this. Gordon Pasha is a busy man. We don't want to give him more to worry about than he already has.' He waited until Bacheet and his Arabs had dragged the bodies out of the yard and through the gates that led to the canal. Then he went back to the blockhouse and opened the door. 'All is safe. You may come out.'

Saffron rushed past him and darted to the menagerie gates. Old Ali lay curled beside the gatepost. He had been her friend. He had loved the animals as much as she did, and he had taught her how to care for them. She knelt beside his body. In the months since the beginning of the siege she had been exposed to death in many of its most hideous forms, but now she gagged as she looked at her friend's body. The rioters had battered his head until it was shapeless, no longer recognizable as human.

'Poor Ali,' she whispered. 'You died for your animals. God will love you for that.' She found his bloodsoaked turban and covered his face. 'Go in peace,' she said in Arabic.

She left him and went on into the menagerie. There she stopped again. She gazed around at the devastation and her knees went weak under her. Every cage had been smashed open and every one of the animals was gone. Clouds of blue flies hummed over puddles of their blood that were drying and caking in the desert sun. With an effort, Saffron steeled herself and went on down the rows of empty cages.

'Lucy!' She called as she went, and she imitated the chittering sound that was the monkey's special recognition call. 'Billy! Billy, baby, where are you?' She reached Lucy's cage. The door had been torn off, and the cage was deserted. She stood before it, grieving. She had been so young when her mother died that she could barely remember it but she knew she had not felt as bereaved as she did now.

'They couldn't have done this. It's so cruel.' She knew that if she stood there longer she would start to blubber and her father would be ashamed of her. There was only one other place in the menagerie to search. She went to the feed shed at the far end of the enclosure.

'Lucy!' she called. 'Billy, where are you, my baby?' She peered into the gloom.

'Billy!' She made the chittering monkey sound, and a tiny dark shape shot out from behind a pile of straw. With a single bound it landed on her hip, climbed on to her shoulder and chittered softly in reply to her call.

'Billy!' whispered Saffron. 'You're safe!' She sank to the floor and hugged the small furry body to her chest. Despite everything her father had told her, she began to cry and could not stop.

Before sunrise the next morning, just after the mission bells had sounded the end of curfew, Ryder heard feminine voices in the yard, followed by the slamming of the door to the green-cake shed. He wiped the lather from the blade of his razor on to his wash-rag, and made one last pass from the bulge of his Adam's apple to the point of his jaw. He examined his cleanshaven image in the hand mirror, and grunted with resignation. Despite the kiss of the razor, his jaw was still blue. Not everybody can have whiskers like the pretty soldier-boy. He folded his razor, laid it carefully in the velvet slot in its fitted leather case and closed the lid. Then he left his private quarters in the blockhouse, and went out into the yard.

He glanced at the gate to the menagerie, and felt the surge of fresh anger and grief for the wanton slaughter of his animals. He could not yet bring himself to go into the enclosure. At least Bacheet had removed old Ali's body and buried it before yesterday's sunset, in accordance with the law of Islam.

Now Bacheet and his men were collecting tusks from where they were piled against the inner wall, and carrying them back to the warehouse. Ryder called Bacheet to him, and they went to inspect the main gates. There was nothing left of them but a few charred planks. 'We will have to abandon everything in the outer stockade,' Ryder decided. 'We will move into the inner fortifications. The gates are solid and strong. We can defend them.' He left Bacheet to carry out those orders.

For the last half an hour he had heard the hammering of metal on the anvil coming from Jock's workshop, but now there was silence. He crossed to the workshop and looked in at the door. Jock McCrump had just lit the blue acetylene flame of his welding torch and was lowering the smoked-glass goggles over his eyes. He looked up at Ryder. 'Old vixen could swing an axe like a lumberjack, and she packed a punch like

John L. Sullivan hisself. It's going to take couple or three days to fix this. Now make yourself scarce.' He bent over the damaged pipe and played the flame on to the gash in the metal.

'In one of our bloody moods today, are we?'

'Ain't nothing to laugh and dance about. You should have let me shoot her before she did this.'

Ryder chuckled. They had been together a long time and knew each other's foibles. He left Jock to get on with it and went to the green-cake shed. Nazeera and all three Benbrook sisters were there. They were wearing the working aprons and gloves they had made for themselves, and they were trying to restore order to the devastated kitchen.

'Good morning, Ryder.' Rebecca smiled at him. Ryder was taken aback by the warmth of her greeting and because she was still using his first name.

'Good morning, Miss Benbrook.'

'I would be obliged if in future you would address me by my Christian name. After the way you protected my sister and me yesterday, we need no longer stand on ceremony.'

'What little I could do for you was only my duty.'

'I was particularly pleased that you were so restrained in your use of force. A lesser man might have turned the riot into a massacre. You have the humanity to realize that those poor people had been driven to excess by the terrible dilemma in which they are caught up. However, I would like to express my sympathy for the grievous losses you have suffered.'

Saffron had been listening to her elder sister impatiently. She was not pleased by this new warmth between Rebecca and Ryder. She told me she despised him, but now she's cooing at him like a dove, she thought. 'You should have shot all of them, not just two,' she said sourly. 'Then we might have saved Lucy.'

'At least Billy seems none the worse.' Saffron's severe expression softened and Ryder took immediate advantage. 'How are you going to feed him? He isn't weaned yet,' he enquired solicitously.

'Nazeera has found a woman who lost her new baby from cholera. We're paying her to feed Billy and he guzzles her milk like a little pig,' Saffron replied.

Rebecca blushed. 'I am sure Ryder does not want to hear all the gruesome details,' she told her little sister primly.

'Then he should not have asked,' Saffron replied reasonably. 'Anyway, everybody knows how babies are fed, so why are you turning red, Becky?'

Ryder looked around for an avenue of escape, and found one. 'Good morning, Amber. You missed all the excitement yesterday.'

But Saffron did not want to relinquish Ryder's attention to yet another sister. 'Don't mind her,' she said. 'She has been grumpy since Captain Ballantyne went away.' Before Amber could protest she went on blithely, 'All the Sudanese women have run away. They won't come back to work here. They have been threatened by bad men in the town who say that we are doing the Devil's work by making green-cake.'

Ryder looked at Rebecca with concern. 'Is this true?'

'I am afraid it is. They were too terrified to come to tell us themselves. But one went to Nazeera. Even then she was taking a grave risk. She says that the Dervish sympathizers in the city have discovered how valuable the green-cake is to our survival, and they are trying to stop us making it. That female creature and the Nubian wrestler who led the riot against you were Mahdists.'

'That explains a great deal.' Ryder nodded. 'But what do you plan to do?'

'We will go on alone,' Rebecca replied simply.

'Just the three of you?'

'Four, with Nazeera. She is not afraid. We Benbrooks don't give up that easily. We have found two cauldrons that were not smashed and our first batch of green-cake will be ready by this evening.'

'Pulping the vegetation is hard work,' he protested.

'In which case you should let us get on with it, Ryder,' Rebecca told him. 'Why don't you go and help Mr McCrump?'

'A man knows when he is not wanted in the kitchen.' Ryder tipped the brim of his hat and hurried back to the workshop.

A little after noon Jock pushed the welding goggles to the top of his head and smiled for the first time that day. 'Well, skipper, that's about the best I can do. Maybe she'll hold up without blowing out under pressure and giving us another steam bath. We can only pray to the Almighty.'

They loaded the drive shaft and steam pipe into a Scotch cart and covered them with a tarpaulin to hide them from the eyes of Dervish agents while they moved them through the streets. No draught animals remained in the city. They had all died of starvation or been eaten. Ryder joined Jock, Bacheet and the Arabs in the shafts of the cart and they trundled it down to where the *Intrepid Ibis* lay at the wharf. By lantern light they worked on in the engine room long after dark. When even Jock was overtaken by exhaustion they stretched out on the *Ibis*'s steel deck plates and snatched a few hours' sleep.

They woke again at dawn. The food bag was almost empty, but Ryder ordered Bacheet to dole out a few dates and scraps of smoked fish for breakfast. Then they went back to work in the engine room. In the middle of the morning Saffron and Amber came down to the harbour. They had two small loaves of freshly made green-cake hidden in Saffron's paintbox.

'We put them there because we did not want anyone to know what we were doing. This is our first batch,' Saffron announced, with pride. She held up her hands, 'Look!' Amber followed her example.

Ryder saw the blisters in their palms. 'My two heroines.'

There were only a few mouthfuls for each of the men, but it was enough to boost their flagging energy. Saffron and Amber sat with Ryder on the edge of the deck, their legs hanging over the side, and watched him eat. He was touched by the womanly satisfaction that they showed, even at their age, to be feeding a man. They watched each piece go into his mouth just as his mother had so many years ago.

'I am sorry, but that's all,' Saffron said, as he finished. 'We'll make some more tomorrow.'

'It was delicious,' he replied. 'The best batch yet.'

Saffron looked pleased. She pulled her knees up to her chin, and sat hugging her long skinny legs. 'It makes me sick to think of all those horrible Dervish eating their heads off over there.' She stood up reluctantly and brushed down her skirts. 'Come on, Amber. We must get back or Becky will give us the sharp edge of her tongue.'

Long after the twins had gone, and the men were struggling to manoeuvre the long drive shaft into its chocks in the confines of the engine room, Ryder pondered Saffron's casual remark.

It was mid-afternoon when Jock announced at last that he was cautiously optimistic that this time the engine might perform as God and its makers had intended. He and his crew fired up the boiler, and while they were waiting for a head of steam to build up, Ryder shared one of his last remaining cigars with the Scotsman. They leant together on the bridge rail, both tired and subdued.

Ryder took a long deep draw on the cigar and passed it to Jock. 'The Mahdi has a hundred thousand men camped on the other side of the river. Tell me, Jock, how do you suppose he is feeding them?' he asked.

Jock held the smoke in his lungs until his face turned puce. At last he exhaled explosively. 'Well, first off they have thousands of head of stock that they've plundered,' he said. 'But I reckon he must be bringing dhurra downriver from Abyssinia.'

'In dhows?'

'Of course. How else?'

'At night?' Ryder persisted.

'Of course. On a moonlit night you can see the sails. Lot of traffic on the river at night.'

'Jock McCrump, I want you to get this old tub of ours working under a full head of steam by tomorrow evening at the latest. Earlier than that, if you like.'

Jock stared at him suspiciously, and then he grinned. His teeth were as ragged and uneven as those of an ancient tiger shark. 'If I didn't know you better, skipper, I'd think you were up to something.'

There were no clouds in the desert sky to provide a canvas on which the setting sun could paint its setting. The great red orb dropped like a stone below the horizon and almost immediately the night came down upon the heat-drugged land. Ryder waited until he could no longer make out the opposite bank of the river, then gave orders to Bacheet to cast off.

With his engine telegraph at 'dead slow ahead', he eased the *Intrepid Ibis* out through the harbour entrance and into the main stream of the river. As soon as he felt the tug of the current he turned the bows into it and rang down to Jock for 'half ahead'. They pushed up against the flow of the river and Ryder listened anxiously to the beat of the engine. He could feel the hull quivering under his feet, but there were no rough vibrations. He held her at that speed until they had rounded the first bend of the Blue Nile and a long deep glide of the river lay ahead.

He took a deep breath and rang down for 'three-quarters ahead'. The *Ibis* responded with the panache of a toreador parading into the bullring. Ryder let out a long sigh of relief. 'Take the wheel, Bacheet. I am going below.'

He slid down the engine-room companionway. Jock was shining the beam of his bullseye lantern on to the shaft, and Ryder went to stand beside him. They watched it turning in its new bearings. Jock lowered the lantern and in its golden light they studied the outline of the silver column minutely, looking for the tiniest flutter or tremble of distortion. Like a gyroscope, it was spinning so evenly that it seemed to be standing still.

Jock cocked his head. 'Listen to her sing, skipper.' He

raised his voice above the hiss and slide of the cylinders. 'Sweeter than Lily McTavish!'

'Who in creation is Lily McTavish?'

'Barmaid at the Bull and Bush.'

Ryder let out a roar of laughter. 'I never realized what a connoisseur of opera you are, Jock.'

'Can't really say I know much about it, skipper, but I do know a fine pair of tits when I see 'em.'

'Can I push the *Ibis* up to full revolutions?'

'Just like Lily McTavish, I reckon she's game for anything.'

'I'd like to meet this Lily.'

'Get in the queue behind me, skipper.'

Still laughing Ryder went back to his bridge and took the wheel from Bacheet. When he pushed the telegraph to 'full ahead', the *Ibis* surged forward against the current.

'Twelve knots!' Ryder shouted gleefully. He felt a great weight slip from his shoulders. He was no longer a prisoner in the fever city of Khartoum. Once more all three thousand miles of the Nile belonged to him, his high road to freedom and fortune.

He pulled back the lever of the engine telegraph to 'half ahead' and kept on up the river; before he reached the next wide bend he had counted five head of sail, all heavily laden trading dhows coming down from the Abyssinian highlands to Omdurman. He turned across the flow, and ran swiftly back downstream. Then he shouted down the voice tube to the engine room: 'Jock, come up here where we can talk.'

They leant on the bridge rail together. 'After what happened at the compound yesterday, I am not taking any more chances. The mood of the people is ugly and dangerous. The city is crawling with agents and sympathizers of the Mahdi. They will know by morning that the *Ibis* is seaworthy again. We must expect an attempt at sabotage. From here on, we must keep an armed guard on board twenty-four hours a day.'

'I was going to do that anyhow.' Jock nodded. 'I've already moved my bed and duffel back on board, and I'll be sleeping with a pistol under me mattress. My stokers will be taking turns at guard duties.'

'Excellent, Jock. But apart from that, as soon as it's light enough I want you to move her from the harbour into the canal and tie her up at the jetty at the back gate of the compound. She'll be much safer there, and easier to load.'

'You thinking about your ivory?' Jock asked.

'What else?' Ryder smiled. 'But also I want to be able to make a run for it if things go wrong again. I'll be waiting for you to bring the *Ibis* up the canal at first light.'

'What's all that din?' Ryder had been woken by Bacheet hammering on the blockhouse door.

'One of the Egyptian officers is here with a message from Gordon Pasha,' Bacheet shouted back.

Ryder's heart sank. No news from Chinese Gordon was ever good. He reached for his trousers and boots and pulled them on.

The Egyptian had two black eyes and a scabbed, swollen lower lip.

'What happened to you, Captain?' Ryder asked.

'There was a food riot at the arsenal when the general reduced the ration. I was hit in the face by a stone.'

'I'd heard that your troops shot twenty of the rioters.'

'That is not correct,' the officer said hotly. 'To restore order, the general was forced to shoot only twelve.'

'How abstemious of him,' Ryder murmured.

'You also had trouble with the rioters, and were forced to shoot,' the captain added.

'Only two, but they killed one of my men first.' Ryder was relieved to have confirmation of the shooting at the arsenal: Gordon was no longer in a position to point the finger at him. 'I understand that you have a message for me from Gordon Pasha.'

'The general wishes to see you at Mukran Fort as soon as

possible. I am to escort you there. Will you please make ready to leave at once?'

Schoolboy being called to the headmaster's study, Ryder thought wryly. He took his hat down from the peg on the wall. 'Very well. I am ready.'

Gordon was at his usual station on the battlements of the fort. He was standing behind his telescope, peering down-river towards the Shabluka Gorge. Two brilliant coloured flags flew from the flagstaff of the watchtower. The red, white and black of Egypt was surmounted by the red, white and blue of the Union Flag of Great Britain.

Gordon straightened up and saw Ryder's upturned face. 'Those flags will be the first thing that the relief force sees when they come up the river. Then they will know that the city is still in our hands, and that we have withstood all the forces of evil and darkness.'

'And all the world will learn, General, what one English-man alone and almost unaided has been able to achieve. It is a story that will be written large in the annals of Empire.' Ryder had meant it to be ironic, but somehow it did not come out that way. He was forced to admit, however reluctantly, that he admired this terrible little man. He could never feel the slightest affection for him, but he stood in awe of him.

Gordon raised a silver-grey eyebrow beneath which a cold blue eye glinted, acknowledging the barbed compliment from an adversary. 'I am informed that you took your steamer out on trial last night, and that it was successful,' he stated crisply.

Ryder nodded cautiously. The old devil misses nothing, he thought. Now he found himself hating the man as strongly as ever.

'I hope that does not mean you are planning to sail away in her before the relief arrives?' Gordon asked.

'The thought had crossed my mind.'

'Mr Courtney, despite your mercenary instincts you have

305

made, perhaps unwittingly, a significant contribution to the defence of my city. Your production of the foul-tasting but nutritious green-cake in itself has been of great assistance. You have other resources at your disposal that might save lives.' Gordon stared at him.

Ryder stared back into the sapphire eyes and replied, 'Indeed, General, and I feel I have done as much as I can. However, I have a premonition that you will try to convince me otherwise.'

'I need you to remain in the city. I do not want to be forced to impound your vessel, but I shall not hesitate to do so if you defy me.'

'Ah!' Ryder nodded. 'That is a compelling argument. May I suggest a compromise, General?'

'I am a reasonable man,' Gordon inclined his head, 'and I am always ready to listen to good sense.'

That is not a widely held opinion, Ryder thought, but he replied evenly, 'If I am able to deliver equal value, will you allow me to sail from Khartoum whenever I wish, with the cargo and passengers of my own choice without restriction?'

'Ah, yes. I believe you have become friendly with David Benbrook's daughters,' Gordon smiled bleakly, 'and that you have several tons of ivory in your warehouse. Those would be your passengers and cargo, would they not?'

'David Benbrook and the three young ladies will be among those I shall invite to sail with me. I am certain that this would not be in conflict with your sense of chivalry.'

'What do you offer, sir, as your part of the bargain?'

'A minimum of ten tons of dhurra grain – enough to feed the populace until the arrival of the relief force and forestall any further rioting. You will pay me twelve shillings a sack, in cash.'

Gordon's face darkened. 'I have always suspected that you had a hidden hoard of grain.'

'I have no secret hoard, but I will risk my ship and my life to obtain it for you. In return I want your word of honour as a gentleman and an officer of the Queen that on delivery to you of ten tons of dhurra you will pay me the agreed price and

306

allow me to sail from Khartoum. I suggest that this is fair, and that you have nothing to lose by agreeing to it.'

Ryder had spread a black tarpaulin over the *Ibis*'s white superstructure, and coated her hull above the waterline with black river mud. Using long bamboo poles they punted her quietly down the shallow canal to the open river. Under her camouflage she blended so well into the darkness, that even in the brilliant starlight she was almost invisible from any distance over a hundred yards. As she slid into the main current of the river and the long poles could no longer find the bottom, Ryder rang down to Jock in the engine room for 'half ahead'. He turned upriver and cruised eastwards along the Blue Nile. He was deliberately avoiding the main branch of the White Nile, because the Dervish artillery batteries were all concentrated on the northern approaches. It was plain that by this time they were expecting the arrival of the British gunboats from that direction. However, in making these dispositions they had left the other branches of the river to the east and south unguarded. Until the Dervish realized this mistake the *Intrepid Ibis* had the run of thousands of miles of river.

All the dhows coming down the Blue Nile would be Abyssinians. Like Ryder, they were just honest, hard-working traders, selling their grain to the highest bidders. Of course, it was to be regretted that their main customer was the Mahdi.

Ryder angled the darkened *Ibis* across the river. For all the obvious reasons, the captains of the grain dhows were keeping closely to the bank furthest from Khartoum. Ryder and Bacheet stared ahead, watching for the first flash of canvas or the shine of starlight on one of the reed-matting lateen sails. Ryder's lungs ached with the craving for a good cigar, but his stock was dwindling. Abstinence makes the heart grow fonder, he thought sadly. I might end up smoking black Turkish tobacco in a hookah. How have the mighty descended in the world.

Bacheet touched his arm. 'The first little fish swims into our net,' he murmured.

Ryder watched the other vessel materializing on the dark waters, and muttered regretfully, 'Small fishing-boat. Riding high in the water. No cargo on board. We will let her go.' He spun the wheel and sheered away from her.

There was a faint hail from the smaller vessel: 'In God's name, what ship are you?'

Bacheet called back: 'Go in peace, with blessings of Allah upon you.'

They cruised on. As they rounded the first wide bend of the river, two miles above the city, another hull seemed to spring miraculously out of the night. They were closing so rapidly that Ryder had only seconds to make his decision. It was a large dhow, broad-beamed and low in the water. She had only a foot of freeboard. Her bow wave creamed back in the starlight, almost slopping over her bulwarks.

'Heavy with cargo,' Ryder said, with quiet satisfaction. 'This one is for us.' He swung in sharply towards the prize, and as they closed there was a cry of alarm from the man at her helm. As the steel hull made heavy contact with the dhow's timber side, the three heavy grappling hooks shot from the *Ibis* and clattered on to her deck. They bit and held in the dhow's bulwarks, locking the two vessels together. With a burst of power and hard left rudder Ryder forced the dhow's bows to slew across the current, spilling the wind out of her sail so that she wallowed helplessly. Then his men swarmed over the rail.

Before they realized what was happening the crew of the dhow were trussed up securely. Ryder jumped down on to the deck, just as the captain came up from his stern cabin. Ryder recognized him immediately. 'Ras Hailu!' he exclaimed, then greeted him in Amharic: 'I see you are in good health.'

The Abyssinian started with shock, then recognized Ryder. 'Al-Sakhawi! So you have turned pirate.'

'I am no pirate, but you have been dealing with one such. I hear the Mahdi is gouging you on the price of your dhurra.'

He took Ras Hailu's arm. 'Come aboard my steamer. Let us drink a little coffee and talk business.'

Jock held the two vessels in mid-stream while they settled down in the *Ibis* cabin. After a decent exchange of pleasantries Ryder broached the matter in hand. 'How is it that you, a devout Christian and a prince of the house of Menelik, can deal with a fanatic who is conducting a *jihad* against your Church and your countrymen?'

'I am covered with shame,' Ras Hailu confessed, 'but, Christian or Muslim, money is still money and a profit is still a profit.'

'What price is the wicked Mahdi paying you?'

Ras Hailu looked pained, but his eyes were shrewd in the lamplight. 'Eight shillings a sack, delivered at Omdurman.'

'Christian to Christian, and friend to old friend, what would you charge me if I paid in silver Maria Theresas?'

They both enjoyed the trading for it was in their blood, but time was too short to savour it. Dawn was only hours away. They struck a bargain at nine shillings, which left both men pleased. Jock towed the dhow into a quiet bay off the main river, known as the Lagoon of the Little Fish. Screened by the papyrus reeds, all hands turned out to tranship the cargo of dhurra to the steamer. It took all day, for the dhow was fully laden.

As darkness fell Ryder and Ras Hailu embraced warmly and took leave of each other. The dhow caught the evening breeze and ran up the Blue Nile towards the Abyssinian border. Ryder took the *Ibis* downriver to Khartoum. She was so deeply laden that they had to tow her from the bank of the canal to her mooring at the rear of the compound.

As soon as curfew ended, Ryder sent Bacheet with a message to General Gordon. Within the hour the general had arrived on the canal bank. He was accompanied by a hundred Egyptian troops, and quickly set up a chain of men to unload the sacks of dhurra. The work went swiftly, and Ryder stood by, counting each one and making notations in his little red book. 'By my calculations, General, this is considerably more than the contracted amount.' He cast an eye over the column of figures with the rapidity of a book-keeper. 'Even allowing for ten per cent underweight in the sacks, it's more in the region of twelve tons than ten.'

Gordon laughed – a rare sound, for Chinese Gordon was not given to frivolity, 'Surely, Mr Courtney, you are not suggesting that I should return the excess to the Mahdi, are you?'

'No, sir. I am suggesting that I am entitled to recompense for the overflow,' Ryder replied.

Gordon stopped laughing. 'There must be some limit to your avarice, sir.'

'I have rendered unto Caesar.' Gordon frowned at the biblical reference, but Ryder went on unperturbed, 'And now I would like to keep a ton of the dhurra for my own use. My compound was pillaged by the rioters. My own people are as close to starvation as any in the city. I have a duty to provide for them, as if they were my family. That does not add up to avarice in my book.'

They bargained shrewdly. At last Gordon threw up his hands. 'Very well, then. Keep two hundred sacks for yourself and be thankful for my generosity. You can come up to the fort to collect your Judas shekels.' He stamped away towards the arsenal. He wanted to see his precious grain safely behind the walls. But there was another consideration behind his abrupt departure: he did not want Ryder Courtney to see the softening of his expression or the shadow of a smile in his eyes. What a pity to lose a young rascal like that. We should have had him in the army. I could have made him into a first-rate officer, but it's too late now. He is spoilt by the lure of Mammon.

The train of his thoughts led him on, and he thought of another likely lad. As he reached the gates of the arsenal he paused and looked towards the north.

Ballantyne has been gone fifteen days already. Surely by this time he must have reached Stewart's encampment at the Wells of Gakdul and given him my message. I know in my heart that God will not allow all my efforts to come to naught.

Dear Lord, grant me the strength to hold out just a little longer.

But he was tired to the marrow of his bones.

They had ridden five days in the vast assembly of men and animals. It rolled ponderously northwards across the desert. Penrod Ballantyne swivelled on the saddle of his camel to look back. The dust of their progress reached the horizon and rose to the sky.

Fifty thousand fighting men? he wondered. But we will never know for sure – nobody can count them. All the emirs of the southern tribes and all their warriors. What power does this man Muhammad Ahmed wield that he can bring together such a multitude, made up of tribes that for five hundred years have been riven by feud and blood feud?

Then he turned back in the saddle and looked to the north, the direction in which this vast host was riding. Stewart has only two thousand men to oppose them. In all the wars of all the ages did odds such as these ever prevail?

He put aside the thought, and tried to work out how far back Yakub and he were from the vanguard of this mighty cavalcade. Without drawing attention to themselves they had to work their way gradually to the front. It was only from that position that they could break away and make a final dash for the Wells of Gakdul. The Dervish were pacing their camels, not driving them so hard that they would be unfit to take part in the battle ahead. That they were moving so quietly and not rushing into battle reassured Penrod that Stewart must still be encamped there.

They passed slowly through another loose formation of Dervish. These were hard desert tribesmen with swords and shields slung across their backs. Most were mounted on camels, and each led a string of pack camels carrying tents and ammunition cases, cooking pots, food bags and waterskins. Trailing along behind them were the traders and petty merchants of Omdurman, their camels also heavily laden with

311

trade goods and merchandise. After the battle, when the Ansar were rolling in loot, there would be rich profits.

At the head of this formation rode a small group of Ansar on fine Arab steeds, which had been lovingly curried until their hides shone in the sunlight like polished metal. Their long silky manes had been combed out and plaited with coloured ribbons. Their trappings and tack were of painted and beautifully decorated leather. The horsemen sat upon their backs with the panache and studied arrogance of warriors.

'Aggagiers!' Yakub muttered, as they drew closer. 'The killers of elephant.'

Penrod drew the tail of his turban closer over his mouth and nose so that only his eyes showed, and edged aside his camel to pass the group at a safe distance. As they drew level with them they saw the horsemen staring across at them. They were animatedly discussing the two strangers.

'Damn Ryder Courtney for his taste in camel flesh.' For the first time since leaving Khartoum, Penrod bemoaned the quality of their mounts. They were magnificent creatures, more befitting a *khalifa* or a powerful emir than a lowly tribesman. Even in this vast assembly they stood out as thoroughbreds. Yakub urged his camel forward at a faster clip, and Penrod cautioned him sharply: 'Gently, fearless Yakub. Their eyes are upon you. When the mice run the cat pounces.'

Yakub reined in, and they continued at more leisurely pace, but this did not deter the aggagiers. Two broke away from the group and rode across to them.

'They are of the Beja,' Yakub said hoarsely. 'They mean us no good.'

'Steady, glib and cunning Yakub. You must deceive them with your ready tongue.'

The leading aggagier came up and reined his bay mare down to a walk. 'The blessings of Allah and His Victorious Mahdi upon you, strangers. What is your tribe and who is your emir?'

'May Allah and the Mahdi, grace upon him, always smile

312

upon you,' Yakub responded, in a clear untroubled voice. 'I am Hogal al-Kadir of the Jaalin, and we ride under the banner of the Emir Salida.'

'I am al-Noor, of the Beja tribe. My master is the famed Emir Osman Atalan, upon whom be all the blessings of Allah.'

'He is a mighty man, beloved of Allah and the Ever Victorious Mahdi, may he live long and prosper.' Penrod touched his heart and his forehead. 'I am Suleimani Iffara, a Persian of Jeddah.' Some Persians had fair hair and pale eyes, and Penrod had adopted that nationality to explain his features. It would also account for the slight nuances and inflections in his speech.

'You are a long way from Jeddah, Suleimani Iffara.' Al-Noor rode closer and stared at him thoughtfully.

'The Divine Mahdi has declared *jihad* against the Turk and the Frank,' Penrod replied. 'All true believers must hearken to his summons and make haste to join up with him, no matter how hard and long the journey.'

'You are welcome to our array, but if you travel under the banner of Emir Salida, you must ride harder to catch up with him.'

'We are solicitous of the camels,' Yakub explained, 'but on your advice we will move faster.'

'They are indeed magnificent beasts,' al-Noor agreed, but he was staring at Penrod and not at his mount. He could see only his eyes, but they were the eyes of a jinnee and disconcertingly familiar. Yet it would be a deadly offence to order him to unveil his features. 'My master Osman Atalan has sent me to enquire if you wish to sell any. He would pay you a good price in gold coin.'

'I have the utmost respect for your mighty master,' Penrod replied, 'but rather would I sell my firstborn son.'

'I have said before and I say again that they are magnificent creatures. My master will be saddened by your reply.' Al-Noor lifted his reins to turn away, then paused, 'There is aught about you, Suleimani Iffara, your eyes or your voice, that is familiar. Have we met before?'

313

Penrod shrugged. 'Perhaps in the mosque of Omdurman.'

'Perhaps,' al-Noor said dubiously, 'but if I have seen you before I will remember. My memory is good.'

'We go on ahead to find our commander,' Yakub intervened. 'May the sons of Islam triumph in the battle that looms ahead.'

Al-Noor turned to him. 'I pray that your words may carry to the ear of God. Victory is sweet, but death is the ultimate purpose of life. It is the key to Paradise. If the victory is denied to us, may Allah grant us glorious martyrdom.' He touched his heart in farewell salute. 'Go with the blessings of Allah.' He galloped away to rejoin his squadron.

'The Emir Atalan,' Yakub whispered in awe. 'We ride in the same company as your most deadly enemy. This is the same as carrying a cobra in your bosom.'

'Al-Noor has granted us permission to leave his banner,' Penrod reminded him. 'Let us make all haste to obey.'

They stirred up the camels with the goad, and pushed them into a trot. As they pulled away Penrod looked across at the distant group of aggagiers. Now that he knew what to look for he recognized the elegant figure of Osman Atalan in a bone-white *jibba* with gaily coloured patches that caught the eye like jewels. On his lovely pale mare he was riding a few lengths ahead of the rest of his band. He was staring at Penrod, and even at that distance his gaze was disturbing.

Behind his master, al-Noor drew his rifle from its boot under his knee and pointed it to the sky. Penrod saw the spurt of blue powder smoke a few seconds before the report reached his ears. He lifted his own rifle and returned this *feu du joie*. Then they rode on.

They were challenged several times during the rest of the day. The quality of their camels and their obvious haste marked them out even among this huge gathering of animals and men. Each time they asked for the red banner of Emir Salida of the Jaalin, they were told, 'He leads the vanguard,' and they were pointed ahead. Penrod pushed on rapidly: ever since the meeting with al-Noor he had felt uneasy.

They paused in their journey only once more. One of the petty traders who followed the armies called to them as they passed. They turned aside to inspect his wares. He had rounds of dhurra bread, roasted in camel's milk butter and sesame seeds. He showed them also dried dates and apricots, and goat's milk cheese, whose high aroma started their saliva. They filled their food bags, and Penrod paid the exorbitant prices with Maria Theresa dollars.

When they rode on the merchant watched them until they were well out of earshot, then called his son who handled the pack donkeys. 'I know that man well. He marched with Hicks Pasha to El Obeid, at the start of the war of *jihad*. I sold him a gold inlaid dagger, and he bargained shrewdly. I would never mistake him for another. He is an infidel and a Frankish *effendi*. His name is Abadan Riji. Go, my son, to the mighty Emir Osman Atalan, and tell him all these things. Tell him that an enemy marches in the ranks of the warriors of Allah.'

The sun was sinking towards the western horizon and the elongated shadows cast by their camels flitted across the orange yellow dunes when at last Penrod made out the streaming red banner of Emir Salida through the dustclouds ahead.

'This is the front rank of the army,' Yakub agreed. He rode close to Penrod's right hand so that he did not have to raise his voice: other riders were within earshot. 'Many of these men are Jaalin. I have recognized two who carry a blood feud against me. They are of the family who drove me out of my tribe, and made me an outcast. If they confront me I will be honour-bound to kill them.'

'Then let us part company with them.'

The Nile was only a mile distant on their left hand. The whole army had been following the course of the river since they had joined it at Berber. At this late hour of the day many other travellers were turning aside to water their animals on the riverbank. They were too intent on their own affairs to remark the presence of the two strangers among them. Nevertheless Penrod contrived to keep well clear of them.

The grazing closer to the riverbank was dense and luscious. The grass reached as high as the knees of their camels. Suddenly there was an explosion of wings from under the front pads of Yakub's mount, and a covey of quail rocketed into the air. These were the Syrian Blue variety of their breed, larger than the common quail and highly prized for the pot. Yakub swivelled in his saddle and, with a whipping motion of his right hand, threw the heavy camel goad he carried. It cartwheeled through the air and smacked into one of the birds. In a burst of blue, gold and chestnut feathers the quail tumbled to earth.

'Behold! Yakub, the mighty hunter,' he exulted.

The rest of the covey swung across the nose of Penrod's camel and he made his throw. The goad clipped the head off the leading cock bird, and spun on with almost no deflection. It thumped into a plump young hen and snapped her near wing. She came down heavily and scuttled away through the tall grass.

Penrod jumped from the camel's back and chased her. She jinked and fluttered up, but he snatched her out of the air. Holding her by the head he flicked his wrist and broke her neck. He retrieved his goad and the cock's carcass, then ran back to his mount and swung up into the saddle. 'Behold! Suleimani Iffara, the humble traveller from Jeddah, who would never boast of his prowess.'

'Then I will not embarrass him by speaking of it,' Yakub agreed ruefully.

So they came down to the river. Hundreds of horses and camels were spread out along the bank, drinking. Others were grazing on the green growth that bordered it. Men were filling their waterskins, and some were bathing in the shallows.

Penrod picked out a spot on the bank that was well away from any of these people. They hobbled the camels and let them drink while they filled the waterskins and cut bundles of fresh grass. They turned the hobbled camels loose to graze, and built a small cooking fire. They roasted the trio of quail, golden brown and oozing fragrant juices. Then Yakub went to the cow camel and milked her into a bowl. He warmed the milk and they washed down with it a round of dhurra bread topped with a slice of the cheese, which reeked more powerfully than the goat that had produced it. They ended the meal with a handful of dates and apricots. It was tastier fare than Penrod had ever enjoyed in the dining room of the Gheziera Club.

Afterwards they lay under the stars with their heads close together. 'How far are we from the town of Abu Hamed?' Penrod asked.

With his spread fingers Yakub indicated a segment of the sky.

'Two hours.' Penrod translated the angle to time. 'Abu Hamed is where we must leave the river and cut across the bight to the Wells of Gakdul.'

'Two days' travel from Abu Hamed.'

'Once we pass the vanguard of the Dervish, we will be able to travel at better speed.'

'It will be a great pity to kill the camels.' Yakub rose up on one elbow and watched them grazing nearby. He whistled softly and the cream-coloured cow wandered over to him, stepping short against her hobble. He fed her one of the rounds of dhurra cake and stroked her ear as she crunched it up.

'O compassionate Yakub, you will cut a man's throat as happily as you break wind, but you grieve for a beast who was born to die?' Penrod rolled on to his back and spread his arms like a crucifix. 'You stand the first watch. I will take the second. We will rest until the moon is at its zenith. Then we will go on.' He closed his eyes and began almost at once to snore softly.

When Yakub woke him, the midnight chill had already soaked through his woollen cloak and he looked to the sky. It was time. Yakub was ready. They stood up and, without a word, went to the camels, loosened the hobbles and mounted up.

The watchfires of the sleeping army guided them. The smoke lay in a dense fog along the wadis, and concealed their movements. The pads of the camels made no sound, and they had secured their baggage with great care so that it neither creaked nor clattered. None of the sentries challenged them as they passed each encampment.

Within the two hours that Yakub had predicted they passed the village of Abu Hamed. They kept well clear, but their scent roused the village dogs, whose petulant yapping faded as they left the river and struck out along the ancient caravan route that crossed the great bight of the Nile. By the time dawn broke they had left the Dervish army far behind.

In the middle of the next afternoon they couched the camels in the lengthening shadow of a small volcanic hillock and fed them on the fodder they had cut on the riverbank. Despite the severity of the march the camels ate hungrily. The two men examined them at rest but found no ominous swellings on their limbs or shale cuts on their pads.

'They have travelled well, but the hard marches lie ahead.'

Penrod took the first watch and climbed to the top of the hillock so that he could overlook their back trail. He panned his telescope over the south horizon in the direction of Abu Hamed, but could pick out no dustcloud or any other sign of pursuit. He built a knee-high wall of loose volcanic rocks to screen himself in this exposed position, and settled comfortably behind it. For the first time since they had left the Nile he felt easier. He waited for the cool of the evening, and before the sun reached the horizon he sat up and once more glassed the southern horizon.

It was only a yellow feather of dust, small and ephemeral, showing almost coyly for a few minutes, then dissipating and fading away as though it were merely an illusion, a trick of the heated air. Then it materialized again, and hovered in the heat, like a tiny yellow bird. 'On the caravan road, fairly on our tracks, the dust rises over soft ground and subsides again when the trail crosses shale or lava beds.' He explained to himself the intermittent appearance of the dustcloud. 'It seems that al-Noor's memory has returned at last. Yet these cannot be horsemen. There is no water. Camels are the only animals that can survive out here. There are no camels in the Dervish army that can run us down. Our mounts are the swiftest and finest.'

He stared through the lens of his telescope but could make out nothing under the dust. Still too far off, he thought. They must be all of seven or eight miles away. He ran down the hill. Yakub saw him coming and could tell from his haste that trouble was afoot. He had the camels saddled and loaded before Penrod reached them. Penrod jumped into his saddle and his mount lurched up, groaning and spitting. He turned her head northwards, and urged her into trot.

Yakub rode up alongside him. 'What have you seen?'

'Dust on our backtrail. Camels.'

'How can you tell that?'

'What horse can survive so far from water?'

'When the aggagiers are in hot pursuit of either elephant or men, they use both their camels and their horses. At the beginning of the hunt they ride the camels, and also use them to carry the water. That is how they save the horses until they have their quarry in sight. Then they change to them for the final chase. You have seen the quality of their horses. No camel can run against them.' He looked back over his shoulder. 'If those are the aggagiers of Osman Atalan, they will have us in sight by dawn tomorrow.'

They rode on through the night. Penrod gave no thought to conserving the water in the skins. A little before midnight they stopped just long enough to give each animal two bucketfuls of water. Penrod stretched out on the ground and used an inverted milk bowl as a sounding board to pick up the reverberation of distant hoofs. When he placed his ear against it, he could hear nothing. He did not allow this to lull him into complacency. Only when they sighted the pursuers at dawn would they know how far they were trailing behind them. They wasted no time and padded on through the desolation and the hissing silence of the desert.

As the first soft light of dawn gave definition to the landscape Penrod halted again. Once again he was prodigal with the remaining water, and ordered Yakub to give each of the camels two more buckets and the remainder of the fodder.

'At this rate, we will have emptied the skins by this evening,' Yakub grumbled.

'By this evening we will either have reached the Wells of Gakdul, or we will be dead. Let them drink and eat. It will lighten their load, and give strength to their legs.'

He walked back a hundred yards and once again used the milk bowl as a sounding cup. For a few minutes he heard nothing, and grunted with relief. But some deep instinct made him linger. Then he heard it, a tremble of air within his eardrum, so faint it might been a trick of the dawn breeze sweeping over the rocks. He wetted his forefinger and held it up. There was no wind.

He lowered his head to the bowl, cupped his hands round his ear and closed his eyes. Silence at first. He took a deep breath and held it. At the outer reaches of his hearing there was a susurration, like fine sand agitated gently in a dried gourd, or the breathing of a beloved woman sleeping at his side in the watches of the night. Even in this fraught situation an image of Rebecca flared in his memory, so young and lovely in the bed beside him, her hair spread over them both like cloth of gold. He thrust away the picture, stood up and went back to the camels. 'They are behind us,' he said quietly.

'How far?' Yakub asked.

'We will be able to see them clearly in the first rays of the sun.' They both glanced into the east. The sun cast a nimbus around a distant hilltop, as though it were the rugged head of an ancient saint.

'And they will see us just as clearly.' Yakub's voice was husky and he cleared his throat.

'How far to the Wells of Gakdul?' Penrod asked.

'More than half a day's ride,' Yakub answered. 'Too far. On those horses they will catch us long before we reach the wells.'

'What terrain lies ahead? Is there a place for us to take cover where we might evade them?'

'We approach the Tirbi Kebir.' Yakub pointed ahead. 'There is good reason why it is called the Great Graveyard.'

This was one of the most formidable obstacles along the entire crossing of the bight. It was a salt pan twenty miles across. The surface was level as a sheet of frosted glass, unmarred by a single ripple or undulation, other than the broad indentation of the caravan road. Both its verges were outlined by the skeletons of the men and camels who, over the centuries, had perished along the way. The noon sunlight reflecting off the diamond white salt crystals lit the noonday sky with a glare that could be seen from many leagues in every direction. A camel standing in the centre of this great white place could be clearly recognized from the perimeter. The unrelenting sunlight, reflected and magnified by the shining surface, could roast man and beast like a slow fire.

'There is no other way forward. We must go on.' They put the camels to the crossing. Refreshed by the copious draughts of water and the fodder they had eaten they paced out strongly. As the daylight strengthened, the sky ahead became incandescent, like a metal shield raised to white heat in the forge of Vulcan. Abruptly they left the area of dunes and undulated gravel hills, and rode out on to the pan. With theatrical timing the sun soared out above the eastern hills and struck into their faces with its stinging lash. Penrod could feel it sucking the moisture from his skin and frying the contents of his skull. He groped in his saddlebag and brought out a piece of curved ivory into which he had carved horizontal eye slits so narrow that they blocked out most of the reflected glare. He had copied this from an illustration in the book of Arctic travel by Clavering and Sabine that depicted a native Eskimo of Greenland wearing such a contrivance, carved from whalebone, to ward off snow blindness.

Under the goads, the camels broke into the gait that the Arabs called 'drinking the wind', a long striding trot that sent the miles swiftly behind them. With every few strides either Penrod or Yakub swivelled round and stared back into the shimmering glare.

When the enemy came it was with shocking suddenness. At one moment the pan behind them was bare and white with not the least sign upon it of man or beast. At the next the Dervish column poured out from among the gravel hills and rode on to the white expanse. The weird play of sunlight created an illusion of perspective and foreshortened distances. Although they were still several miles away, they seemed so close that Penrod fancied he could make out the features of each individual.

As Yakub had predicted they were riding camels, pack camels: the aggagiers sat up in front of the huge balloon-like waterskins. Each rider led his horse behind him on a long rein. Osman Atalan was on the leading camel. The folds of his green turban covered his lower face, but his seat in the saddle was unmistakable, head held high and shoulders proud. Beside him rode al-Noor. Bunched up behind the leading pair Penrod counted six more aggagiers. Both sides spotted each other in the same instant. If the pursuers shouted it was too far for the sound to reach him.

Without undue haste the aggagiers dismounted from their camels. Two men were acting as camel-handlers and they gathered up the reins. Osman and each of his men led out a horse and watered it. Then the aggagiers tightened the girths and swung up into the saddle. This changeover took only the time that a Red Sea diver might hold his breath when he goes down to fill his net with pearl oysters from the deep coral reef. Then the horsemen bunched up and came across the shimmering salt surface at an alarming pace.

Penrod and Yakub leant forward in their saddles and, with thrusting movements of their hips, urged their mounts to the top of their speed. The camels reached out in a long-legged gallop. For a mile and then another the two bands raced on, neither gaining nor faltering. Then Hulu Mayya, Osman's cream-coloured mare, broke from the pack. She came on with her mane and long golden tail floating in the wind, a pale wraith against the dazzling plain of salt.

Penrod saw almost at once that no camel could hold off this horse over any distance, and he knew the tactics Osman would adopt: he would ride up behind them and hamstring their camels on the run. Penrod tried to conjure up a plan to counter this. He could not rely on a lucky bullet to bring down the mare. Perhaps instead he should let her come close, then turn back unexpectedly, taking Osman by surprise, and use his camel's height and weight to rush down on the mare. He might be able to force a collision that would inflict such injury on her that she would be out of the race. In truth, he knew that such a plan was futile: the mare was not only fleet but nimble; Osman was probably the most skilled horseman in all the Dervish ranks. Between them they would make a mockery of any clumsy charge he could mount. If by some remote chance he succeeded in crippling the mare, the rest of the Beja aggagiers would be upon them in the next instant, their long blades bared.

The tail of the green turban had blown clear of Osman's face and now he was so close that Penrod could make out his features clearly. The crisp curls of his beard were smoothed back by the wind of the mare's run. His gaze was locked on Penrod's face.

'Abadan Riji!' Osman called. 'This is our moment. It is written.'

Penrod drew the Martini-Henry carbine from its boot under his knee, and half turned in the saddle. He could not make the full turn and face his enemy to mount the rifle to his shoulder, without throwing his camel off balance. He swung up the rifle with his right hand, as though it was a pistol and tried to settle his aim. The camel lurched and jerked under him, and the rifle barrel made wild and unpredictable circles. At the full reach of his right arm the muscles strained and tired swiftly. He could hold his aim no longer, and fired. The recoil jarred his wrist and the trigger guard smashed back into his fingers. His aim was so wild that he did not mark the flight or strike of the bullet. Osman's replying laughter was natural and easy. He was so close now that his voice carried over the sound of hoofs and the rush of the wind.

'Put up your gun. We are warriors of the blade, you and I.' His mare came on apace, now so close that Penrod could see the white froth flying from the snaffle between her jaws. The scabbard of Osman's broadsword was trapped under his left knee. He reached down and drew out the blade, then held up its shining length for Penrod to see. 'This is a man's weapon.'

Penrod felt the strong temptation to respond to his challenge and take him on with the sword. But he knew that more was at stake than pride and honour. The fate of an army of his countrymen, the city of Khartoum and all within the walls – Rebecca Benbrook too – hung on the outcome of this race. Duty dictated that he must eschew any heroics. He ejected the empty case from the breech of his rifle, and took another round from his bandolier to replace it. He locked the breech-block but before he could turn back to fire again at Osman Yakub called to him in urgent tones. He glanced at him, and saw that he was pointing ahead, standing high in the saddle, waving his arms above his head, screaming in wild excitement.

Penrod followed the direction of his finger and his heart bounded. Out of the white glare of the salt pan ahead a squadron of mounted men appeared, their camels racing towards him on a converging track. There was no mistaking that their intentions were warlike. How many? he wondered. In the clouds of white dust it was impossible to guess but they came on, rank upon rank. A hundred, if not more, he realized, but who were they? Not Arabs! That's certain. Hope stirred. None of them wore the *jibba*, and their faces were unbearded.

They rushed towards each other, and Penrod saw the khaki of their tunics and the distinctive shape of their pith helmets. 'British!' he exulted. 'Scouts from Stewart's Camel Corps.'

Penrod swivelled in the saddle and looked back. Osman was standing tall in his stirrups, peering at the approaching ranks. Behind him his aggagiers had reined down from the charge and were milling in confusion. Penrod looked ahead again and saw that the commander of the Camel Corps had ordered a halt. His men were dismounting and couching their camels to form the classic square. It was done with precision. The camels knelt in an unbroken wall, and behind each crouched the rider, with rifle and bayonet presented across his animal's back. The white faces, although tinted by the sun, were cleanshaven and calm. Penrod felt a breathtaking surge of pride. These men were his comrades, the flowering of the finest army on earth.

He ripped the turban from his head to show them his face, then waved the cloth over his head. 'Hold your fire!' he yelled. 'British! I am British!' He saw the officer standing behind the first rank of troopers, with drawn sword, step forward and give him long, hard scrutiny. Now he was only a hundred and fifty paces from the square. 'I am a British officer!'

The other man made an unmistakable gesture with his sword, and Penrod heard his order repeated by the sergeants and non-commissioned officers: 'Hold your fire! Steady, the guards! Hold your fire.'

Penrod looked back again, and saw that Osman was close behind him. Although his aggagiers were still in confusion, he was charging alone into the face of a British square.

Again Penrod raised the carbine and aimed at Osman's mare. He knew that this was the one thing that might turn him aside. Now they were no more than three lengths apart, and even from the unstable back of a galloping camel Penrod's carbine was a deadly menace. Nevertheless, if he had aimed at the man, Osman would not have been daunted by it. But by this time Penrod had learnt enough about him to know that he would not push the mare into the muzzle of the rifle.

Osman reined back, his face furrowed with rage. 'I was wrong about you, coward,' he shouted.

Penrod felt his own rage flare. 'There will be another time,' he promised.

'I pray God that it is so.' Within sixty yards of the British square Osman turned. He brought the mare down to a trot and rode away to rejoin his aggagiers.

The square opened to let in Penrod, Yakub following. He rode up to the officer and slid to the ground.

'Good morning, Major.' He saluted, and Kenwick stared at him in astonishment.

'Ballantyne, you do turn up in odd places. You might have got yourself shot.'

'Your arrival was at a most appropriate moment.'

'I noticed you were having a spot of bother. What in the name of the Devil are you doing out here in the middle of the blue?'

'I have despatches from General Gordon for General Stewart.'

'Then you are in luck. We are the advance guard. General Stewart is with the main body of the relief column, not more than an hour behind us.' He looked out over the camels and the kneeling men at the front of his square. 'But first things first. Who was the Dervish bounder chasing after you?'

'One of their emirs. Fellow called Osman Atalan, head of the Beja tribe.'

'My solemn oath! I've heard of him. He's a nasty piece of work, by all accounts. We had better deal with him.' He strode away towards the front of the square. 'Sergeant Major! Shoot that fellow.'

'Sir!' The sergeant major was a burly figure with a magnificent pair of moustaches. He picked out two of the his best marksmen. 'Webb and Rogers, shoot that Dervish.'

The two troopers leant across the backs of their couched camels and took aim. 'In your own time!' the sergeant major told them.

Penrod found he was holding his breath. He had told Kenwick of Osman's position and rank to discourage just such an order. He had vaguely hoped that some chivalrous instinct might have dissuaded Kenwick from shooting down an emir. At Waterloo, Wellington would never have ordered his sharpshooters to make Bonaparte their target.

One of the troopers fired but Osman was riding steadily away and the range was already over five hundred yards. The bullet must have passed close for the mare swished her tail as though to drive off a tsetse fly. But Osman Atalan did not deign even to look back. Instead he deliberately slowed his horse to a walk. The second trooper fired and this time they saw dust fly. Again the bullet had missed by very little. Osman continued to walk the mare away. Each marksman fired two more shots at him. By then he was out of range.

'Cease firing, Sergeant Major,' Kenwick snapped. Then, in

an aside to Penrod, 'Damned fellow has the luck of the fox.'
He was smiling thinly. 'But you have to admire his cool
performance.'

'We will almost certainly be treated to other virtuoso
performances in the near future,' Penrod agreed.

Kenwick glanced at him, sensing the note of censure in
his tone. 'A sporting sentiment, Ballantyne. However, I do
believe that one should not accord too much respect to the
enemy. We must bear in mind that we are here to kill them.'

And vice versa. But Penrod did not say it aloud.

In the distance they watched Osman Atalan join up with
his aggagiers and ride away southwards towards Abu Hamed.

'Now,' said Kenwick, 'General Stewart will probably be
pleased to see you.'

'And vice versa, sir.' This time Penrod voiced the thought.

Kenwick scribbled a note in his despatch book, tore out
the page and handed it to him. 'If you wander around the
countryside dressed like that, it's likely you'll be shot as a spy.
I shall send young Stapleton back with you. Please inform
General Stewart that we're making good progress and, apart
from this Atalan fellow, we have made no other contact with
the enemy.'

'Major, please do not be lulled into believing that happy
state of affairs will persist much longer. For the last several
days I have been riding in company with a vast concourse of
the Dervish. All of them are coming this way.'

'How large a force?' Kenwick asked.

'Difficult to say for certain, sir. Too many to count.
However, I would estimate somewhere between thirty and
fifty thousand.'

Kenwick rubbed his hands with glee. 'So, all in all, you
might say that we are in for an interesting few days.'

'You might indeed, sir.'

Kenwick called over a young ensign, the lowest rank of
commissioned officer. 'Stapleton, go back with Captain Ballantyne, and see him through the lines. Don't get him or
yourself shot.'

Percival Stapleton gazed at Penrod with awe. He was not

much more than seventeen, fresh-faced and eager as a puppy. The two rode back, with Yakub, along the ancient caravan road. For the first few miles Percy was struck dumb with hero-worship. Captain Ballantyne was a holder of the Victoria Cross, and to have the honour of riding with him was the pinnacle of his sixteen months of military experience. Over the next mile he summoned up his courage and addressed a few respectful remarks and questions to him. He was highly gratified when Penrod responded in a friendly fashion, and Percy became relaxed and chatty. Penrod recognized him as a prime source of information, encouraged him to speak freely, and quickly picked up most of the regimental gossip from him. This was highly coloured by Percy's pride in the regiment, and his almost delirious anticipation of going into action for the first time.

'Everybody knows that General Stewart is a fine soldier, one of the best in the entire army,' the youngster informed him importantly. 'All the men under his command have been drawn from the first-line regiments of guards and fusiliers. I am with the Second Grenadiers.' He sounded as though he could hardly believe his good fortune.

'Is that why General Gordon has been waiting so long in Khartoum for your arrival?' Penrod needled the boy with surgical skill.

Percy bridled. 'The delay is not the general's fault. Every man in the column is as keen as mustard, and spoiling for a fight.' Penrod lifted an eyebrow, and the boy rushed on hotly: 'Because of the haste with which the politicians in London forced us to leave Wadi Halfa, we were obliged to wait at Gakdul for the reinforcements to reach us. We were less than a thousand strong and the camels were sick and weak from paucity of fodder. We were in no fit state to meet the enemy.'

'What is the position now?'

'The reinforcements arrived only two days ago from Wadi Halfa. They brought up fodder, fresh camels and the provisions we were lacking. The general ordered the advance at once. Now we have men enough to do the job,' he said, with the sublime confidence of the very young.

'How many is enough?' Penrod asked.

'Almost two thousand.'

'Do you know how many Dervish there are?' Penrod asked, with interest.

'Oh, quite a few, I shouldn't wonder. But we are British, don't you see?'

'Of course we are!' Penrod smiled. 'There is nothing else to say, is there?'

They topped the next rise and on the stony plain ahead appeared the main body. It was advancing in a compact square formation, with the pack camels in the centre. There appeared to be many more than two thousand. They came on at a good steady rate, and it was clear that they were under firm command.

With young Percy in uniform to smooth the way, the pickets let them into the marching square. A party of mounted staff officers was coming up behind the front rank. Penrod recognized General Stewart. He had seen him at Wadi Halfa, but had not been presented to him. He was a handsome man, stiff-backed and tall in the saddle, exuding an air of confidence and command. Penrod knew the man at his side rather better: he was Major Hardinge, the Camel Corps senior intelligence officer. He pointed at Penrod and spoke a few words to the general. Stewart glanced in Penrod's direction and nodded.

Hardinge rode over. 'Ah, Ballantyne, the traditional bad penny.'

'Penny now worth at least a shilling, sir. I have despatches from General Gordon in Khartoum.'

'Have you, my goodness? That's a guinea's worth. Come along. General Stewart will be pleased to see you.' They rode back to join the staff.

General Stewart motioned to Penrod to fall in alongside his own camel. Penrod saluted. 'Captain Penrod Ballantyne, 10th Hussars, with despatches from General Gordon in Khartoum.'

'Gordon is still alive?'

'Very much so, sir.'

Stewart was studying him keenly. 'Good to have your confirmation. You can hand over the despatches to Hardinge.'

'Sir, General Gordon would not commit anything to paper in case it fell into the hands of the Mahdi. I have only a verbal report.'

'Then you had best give that to me directly. Hardinge can take notes. Go ahead.'

'My first duty, sir, is to inform you of the enemy order of battle, as we are aware of it.'

Stewart listened intently, leaning forward in the saddle. His features were lean and suntanned, his gaze steady and intelligent. He did not interrupt Penrod while he reported the condition of the defenders in Khartoum. Penrod ended the first part of his report succinctly: 'General Gordon estimates that he can hold out for another thirty days. However, the food supplies have been reduced to well below survival level. The level of the Nile is falling rapidly, exposing the defences. He asked me to emphasize to you, sir, that every day that passes renders his position more precarious.'

Stewart made no effort to explain the delays he had encountered. He was a man of direct action, not one who made excuses. 'I understand,' he said simply. 'Go on, please.'

'General Gordon will fly the flags of Egypt and Great Britain from the tower of Mukran Fort, day and night, while the city is still being defended. With a telescope the flags can be seen from as far downstream as the heights of the Shabluka Gorge.'

'I hope shortly to verify that for myself.' Stewart nodded. Although he listened to Penrod with attention, his eyes were constantly busy, watching over the orderly formation of his square as it moved steadily southwards.

'My journey from the city brought me through the midst of the enemy formations. I can give you my own estimate of their dispositions, if you consider that might be of use, General.'

'I am listening.'

'The commander of the Dervish vanguard is the Emir

Salida, of the Jaalin tribe. He has probably fifteen thousand warriors under his red banner. The Jaalin are the northernmost tribe of the Sudan. Salida is a man in his late sixties, but he has a formidable reputation. The commander of the centre is the Emir Osman Atalan of the Beja.' Stewart narrowed his eyes at the name. Obviously he had heard it before. 'Osman has brought approximately twenty thousand of his own men from the siege of Khartoum. They have Martini-Henry rifles, captured from the Egyptians, and a great store of ammunition. As I am sure you are well aware, sir, the Dervish prefer to get to close quarters and use the sword.'

'Guns?'

'Although they have Nordenfelts, Krupps and plentiful supplies of ammunition in Omdurman, I have seen none being brought north with this wing of their army.'

'I know you're an old hand at Arab fighting, Ballantyne, where will they meet us, do you suppose?'

'I believe that they will want to deny you the water, sir,' Penrod replied. In the desert everything came down sooner or later to that. 'The next water is at the Wells of Abu Klea. It is sparse and brackish, but they will try to prevent you using it. The approach to the wells is through a rocky defile. I would guess that they will offer battle there, probably as you debouch from the narrow way.'

Hardinge had the map ready. Stewart took it and spread it on the front of his saddle. Penrod pressed close enough to read it with him.

'Point out to me the spot where you think they may attack,' Stewart ordered.

When Penrod did so Stewart studied it for a short while. 'I had planned to bivouac tonight on the north side of Tirbi Kebir.' He placed his finger on the spot. 'However, in the light of this new information it may be better to force march today, and reach the head of the defile before dark. This will place us in a flexible position in the morning.'

Penrod made no comment. His opinion had not been asked. Stewart rolled the map. 'Thank you, Captain. I think you will be most useful with the vanguard under Major Kenwick. Will you ride forward again and place yourself under his command?'

Penrod saluted, and as he rode off Stewart called after him, 'Before you join Kenwick, go back and see the quartermaster. Get yourself a decent uniform. From here you look like a bloody Dervish yourself. Somebody is going to take a pot at you.'

In the early-morning light, Osman Atalan and Salida sat at the top of the burnt-out hills of Abu Klea. From this vantage-point they overlooked a deep defile. They were seated on a fine woollen carpet, laid on the edge of the dragon's back ridge of black basalt rock. An almost identical ridge of the same dark rock faced them across the pass. At its narrowest point it was some four hundred paces across.

The Emir Salida of the Jaalin had known Osman since he was a stripling of seventeen. At that age Osman had ridden into Jaalin territory from the east with his father's raiding party. They had killed six of Salida's warriors and driven off sixty-five of his finest camels. Osman had killed his first man on that long-ago raid. The Beja had also abducted twelve Jaalin girls and young women, but these in Salida's eyes were insignificant against the loss of his camels. In the twelve years since then their blood feud had run red and rank across the desert.

Only since the Divine Mahdi, may he ever triumph over his foes, had called all the tribes of the Sudan to unite in the holy *jihad* against the infidel had Osman and Salida sat at the same campfire and shared the same pipe. In *jihad* all personal feuds were suspended. They were united by a common enemy.

A slave girl set the hookah between them. With silver tongs she lifted a live coal from the clay fire pot and placed it carefully on top of the black tobacco packed into the bowl of the pipe. She sucked on the ivory mouthpiece until the smoke was flowing freely. She coughed prettily on the powerful fumes, and passed the mouthpiece to Salida, a mark of respect for his years. The water in the tall glass jar bubbled blue as he drew the smoke through it, held it in his lungs and passed the mouthpiece to Osman. The Mahdi had forbidden the use of tobacco but he was in Omdurman, and Omdurman was far away. They smoked contentedly, discussing their battle plans. When there remained only ash in the pipe bowl, they knelt and prostrated themselves in the ritual of morning prayers.

Then the girl lit another pipe, and at frequent intervals one of their sheikhs came up the ridge to report to them on the enemy movements and the disposition of their own regiments.

'In God's Name, the squadron of Sheikh Harun is in position,' reported one.

Salida looked at Osman from under hooded, sun-freckled eyelids. 'Harun is a fine fighting man. He has two thousand under him. I have placed him in the wadi where the buzzard perched yesterday evening. From there he will be able to rake the enemy rear when they come out on to the plain.'

A short while later another junior sheikh came up the steep slope. 'In the Name of God and the Victorious Mahdi, the infidels have sent forward their scouts. A patrol of six soldiers rode through the pass as far as the mouth. They gazed through their long glasses at the palm grove of the wells, then rode back. As you ordered, mighty Emir, we let them go unhindered.'

An hour after sunrise the final report came in, and all the Dervish forces were in the positions allotted to them.

'What of the infidel?' Salida asked, in his rusty high-pitched voice.

'They have not yet broken camp.' The messenger pointed to the head of the long defile. Salida offered his elbow to Osman, and his erstwhile enemy helped the old man to his feet. His joints were lumpy with arthritis, but once in the saddle he could ride and ply the sword like a young warrior. Careful not to show a silhouette against the early-morning sky, Osman led him solicitously to the edge of the cliff and they looked down.

The infidel camp was in full view less than two miles away. The previous evening the soldiers had thrown up a zareba of stones and thornbush around the perimeter. As always the camp was in the shape of a square. They had placed a Nordenfelt gun at each of the four corners, so it could throw down enfilading fire on the outer walls of the stockade.

'What machines are those?' Salida had never fought the Franks. The Turks he knew well for he had slaughtered them in their hundreds with his own hands. But these big, red-faced men were a different breed. He knew nothing of their ways.

'Those are rifles, which fire very fast. They can lay down fields of dead men, like grass under the scythe, until they grow hot and jam. It is necessary to feed them corpses to stop up their mouths.'

Salida cackled with laughter. 'We will feed them well today.' He made a wide gesture. 'The feast is ready. We await the honoured guests.'

The hills, valleys and narrow gullies appeared barren and deserted, but in truth they were alive with tens of thousands of men and horses, sitting on their shields, waiting with the patience of the hunter.

'What are the infidels doing now?' Salida asked curiously as his attention went back to the enemy camp.

'They are preparing for our attack.'

'They know that we are here, waiting for them?' al-Salida enquired. 'How do they know that?'

'We had a spy in our ranks. A *ferenghi* officer. A clever, crafty infidel. He speaks our sweet mother tongue, and passes readily as a son of the Prophet. From Berber he rode northwards with our array. Doubtless, he has counted our heads, divined our intentions and gone into the infidel camp.'

'What is his name? How do you know so much about him?'

'His name is Abadan Riji. He gave me the wound at El Obeid that almost carried me to my grave. He is my blood enemy.'

'Then why have you not killed him?' Salida asked, in a reasonable tone.

'He is slippery as a river eel. Twice he has wriggled through my fingers,' Osman said, 'but that was yesterday. Today is today, and we shall count the dead at the setting of this sun.'

'The infidel may not offer us battle this day,' Salida demurred.

'Look!' He passed Salida his telescope. The old man held it the wrong way round and peered through the large lens. Though he could see nothing but a vacant blue sky, he looked wise. Osman knew that he understood little of these infidel toys, so to spare him embarrassment he described the scene in the British camp for him.

'See how the quartermasters are passing down the ranks handing out extra ammunition.'

'By God, you are right,' Salida said, and the telescope wavered several degrees in the wrong direction.

'See how they are bringing in the Nordenfelts.'

'In the saintly name of the Mahdi, you are right.' Salida bumped his eyebrow on the brass frame of the telescope, and lowered it to rub the spot.

'See how the infidel mounts up, and you can hear the bugles sound the advance.'

Salida looked up and, without the hindrance of the lens, saw the enemy clearly for the first time. 'By the holy name of the Mahdi, you are right!' said he. 'Here he comes in full array.'

They watched the British break camp and ride out. Their orderly ranks immediately assumed the dreaded square formation. They moved deliberately into the mouth of the defile, and no gaps appeared in their lines. Their discipline and precision were chilling, even to men of Osman's and Salida's temperament.

'For them there is no turning back. They must win through to the water or perish as other armies have done, swallowed by the desert.'

'I will not leave them for the desert,' declared Salida. 'We will destroy them with the sword.' He turned to Osman. 'Embrace me, my beloved enemy,' he said softly, 'for I am old and tired. Today seems a good day to die.'

Osman hugged him and kissed his withered cheeks. 'When

you die, may it be with your sword in your hand.' They parted and moved down the back slope of the ridge to where the lance-bearers held their horses.

Penrod looked up at the stark black cliffs that rose on each side of them. They were barren as ash heaps from the pit of hell. As they moved into the gut of the defile the cliffs compressed and deformed their formations. But no gaps appeared in the sides of the square. Carefully Penrod scanned the cliffs. There was no sign of life, but he knew this was an illusion. He glanced across at Yakub. 'Osman Atalan is here,' he said.

'Yes, Abadan Riji.' Yakub smiled and his right eye rolled out of kilter. 'He is here. There is the sweet perfume of death in the air.' He drew a deep breath. 'I love it even more than the smell of fresh quimmy.'

'Only you, lascivious and bloodthirsty Yakub, could combine love and battle in the same thought.'

'But, Effendi, they are one and the same.'

They moved on down the narrow defile. Fear and excitement coursed like intoxicating wine through Penrod's veins. He looked around at the bluff, honest faces that surrounded him and was proud to ride in their company. The quiet orders and responses were given in the familiar accents of home, so diverse that they might have been different languages: the sounds of the Scottish Highlands and the West Country, of Wales and the Emerald Isle, of York and Kent, of the Geordies, the Cockney, and the elegant drawl of Eton and Harrow.

'They will be waiting for us on the far side of this pass,' Yakub said. 'Osman and Salida will want to work their cavalry in the open ground.'

'Salida is the emir of your tribe so you understand his mind well,' said Penrod.

'He was my emir, and I rode in his raiding parties with him and ate at his fire. Until the day his eldest son ravished my little sister and I took the dagger to them both, for it was she who enticed him. Now there is blood between me and Salida. If he does not kill me first, one day I will kill him.'

'Ah, patient and vengeful Yakub, this may be that day.'

They rode on through the narrow neck of the pass and the sides opened like the jaws of a monster on each side of them. Still there was no sign of life on the dead, seared hills, not a bird or a gazelle. The bugle sounded the halt, and the distorted square came to a jerky stop.

The sergeants rode down the ranks to redress them. 'Close up on the right!'

'Keep your spacing in the ranks.'

'Wheel into line on the left.'

Within minutes the integrity of the square was restored. The corners were at meticulous right angles and the spacings were precise. The lines of bayonets glittered in the relentless sunlight, and the faces of the waiting men were ruddy with sweat, but not one unhooked a water-bottle from his webbing. In this thirsty wilderness, to drink without orders was a court-martial offence. From the back of his camel Penrod surveyed the ground ahead. Beyond the funnel of hills it opened into a broad, level plain. The earth was carpeted with white quartz pebbles and studded with low, sun-blackened salt scrub. At the far end of this bleak expanse stood a tiny clump of palm trees that seemed to have fossilized with age.

Good cavalry country, Penrod thought, and turned his full attention back to the trap of hills on either hand. Still they were devoid of all life, yet seemed charged with menace. They quivered in the heat mirage like hunting hounds brought up short by the scent of the quarry, waiting only the slip to send them away in full tongue.

The cliffs were riven by gullies and wadi mouths, by rocky salients and deep re-entrants. Some were choked with rock and scree, others coated with sand like the floor of a bullring. Yakub giggled softly and indicated the nearest of these with the point of his camel goad. There was no need for him to speak. The tracks of a thousand horses dimpled the surface of the sand. They were so fresh that the edge of each hoofprint was crisply defined and the low angle of the sun defined it with bold blue shadow.

Penrod raised his eyes to the serrated tops of the hills. They were sharp as the fangs of an ancient crocodile against the eggshell blue sky. Then something moved among the rocks and Penrod's eye pounced upon it. It was a tiny speck and the movement was no more striking than that of a flea crawling in the belly fur of a black cat.

He brought his small telescope out of the leather saddlebag and focused on it, then saw the head of a single man peering down on them. He wore a black turban and his beard was black, blending well with the rock around him. It was too far to recognize his features but the man turned his head, perhaps to give an order to those behind him. Another head appeared beside his, and then another, until the skyline was lined with human heads like beads on a string.

Penrod lowered the glass and opened his mouth to shout a warning, but at that moment the air throbbed with the gut-jarring beat of the Dervish war drums. The echoes rebounded off the facing cliffs, and now the host of the Mahdi appeared, with miraculous suddenness, upon all the ledges, galleries and crests of the pass. The central figure stood clear upon the utmost pinnacle. His *jibba* sparkled white in the sun, and his turban was dark emerald green. He lifted his rifle with one hand and pointed it at the sky. The grey gunsmoke spurted high into the air like the breath of a breaching sperm whale, and the sound of the gunshot followed seconds later. A mighty shout went up from the serried Dervish ranks: '*La ilaha illallah!* There is but one God!'

The echoes shouted back: 'God! God! God!'

The bugle in the centre of the British square sang on a wild, urgent note, and the troops reacted with smooth, prac-tised precision. Down went the camels, kneeling in orderly lines, forming at once the outer ramparts of this living fortress. The baggage animals and their handlers moved back and couched in a dense mass in the centre. They were the inner keep. Swiftly the gunners unloaded the Nordenfelt machine-guns from the pack-camels and staggered with them to the four corners, from where they could lay down enfilading fire along the front of each wall of the square. General Stewart and his staff stood in a group just within the front wall. The runners knelt close at hand, ready to race to any corner of the square with the general's orders.

A deadly silence fell upon this assembly of warriors. The Dervish ranks stared down upon them, and time seemed frozen. Then a single Dervish horseman rode out from the stony mouth of the main wadi. At extreme rifle range, he stopped, facing the square. He raised the curved ivory war clarion, the *ombeya*, and its clear, deep voice resounded along the cliff.

From the mouth of every wadi and combe poured the Dervish host, rank upon rank, thousand upon thousand, camels and horses. They kept coming, wheeling into loose squadrons, facing the little square. Few man were dressed or armed in the same way: lance and spear, axe and round leather targe, rifle, jezail and the dreadful broadsword were poised. The drums started again, a slow rhythmic beat and the Dervish ranks started forward.

'Wait for 'em, lads.' The sergeants strolled down behind the front wall of the square.

'Hold your fire, boys.'

'No hurry. There's enough for everybody.' The voices were calm, almost jocular.

The drums beat faster and the Dervish lines broke into a trot, the Ansar in the front beginning to jostle each other to be first into the square. Faster still, and the dense, savage masses seemed to fill the valley floor. Drums crescendoed and hoofs thundered. The dust rose in a choking miasma. The war cries were shrill.

'Steady, boys, steady!' Calm English voices, responding to the pagan shrieks.

'Hold your fire, chaps!' Penrod recognized Percy Stapleton's clear, boyish voice as he called to his platoon. He was having great difficulty restraining his eagerness. 'Steady, the Blues!'

The scamp thinks it's the boat race. Penrod smiled to himself. The drums pounded feverishly, and the *ombeyas* squealed and sobbed. Like the flood from a burst dam, the Dervish cavalry came straight at the British square.

'Get ready! Rolling volleys, lads,' called the sergeants.

'By the book now, my boys. Remember your drills.'

'Rolling volleys! Make each shot tell.'

Penrod was watching a sheikh on a rangy ginger camel. He had forced his way well ahead of the front rank of the charge. His mouth was wide open as he screamed, and there was a black gap in the line of his front teeth. He was a hundred yards from the face of the square, then seventy, then fifty, and coming on at a wild gallop.

The bugle rang out sweet and high.

'Rolling volleys. Front rank, fire!'

There was that brief pause, characteristic of highly trained troops, as each man steadied his aim. Penrod picked out the gap-toothed sheikh. The volley crashed out, astonishing the ear. The front rank of the charge shuddered to the shock. Penrod's man took the heavy bullet squarely in the chest, and flipped backwards from his high saddle. His camel slewed round and crashed into the two horses coming up behind it, bringing one down heavily.

'Second rank, rolling volleys. Fire.' Again the rifles crashed out. The bullets struck flesh with the sound of wet clay slung against a brick wall. The Dervish charge wavered, and lost impetus.

'Third rank, rolling volleys,' sang out the sergeants. 'Fire!' The bullets churned the Dervish into confusion. Riderless animals milled and shied. Bearded warriors swore and struggled to break clear. Corpses and wounded men were trampled and kicked beneath the hoofs. At that moment the Nordenfelts added their spiteful chatter to the uproar. Their fire hosed down the line. Like a barracuda driving through a shoal of pilchards, it split them into small, isolated groups.

'Front rank, rolling volleys. Fire!' The orders were repeated. The troopers reloaded, aimed and fired, with the oiled precision of rows of bobbins on a carding machine. The charge stalled, broke, and the survivors streamed towards the cliffs. But before they reached them the drums called to them and the *ombeyas* sang: 'Go back! For Allah and the Mahdi, go back into the battle!'

Fresh squadrons streamed out from the rocks to swell their depleted ranks. They massed, shouted to God, and came again, tearing across the trampled field where so many of their comrades already lay. Charging in to break the British square.

But a British square does not break. The sergeants called the timing of those regular rolling volleys. The barrels or the Nordenfelt machine-guns began to glow like horseshoes in the blacksmith's forge.

Osman Atalan had told Salida, 'It is necessary to feed them corpses to stop up their mouths.'

The Nordenfelts gorged on human flesh, choked on it and one after another jammed. As their staccato chatter ceased so the Dervish cavalry pressed closer, right on to the thicket of bright bayonets. Still the volleys crashed into them. They struggled forward and were chopped down, until even their courage and resolve were exhausted. At last they shrank away and rode back to the cliffs.

Salida looked down on the unbroken square from the heights. 'These are not men,' he said, 'they are jinn. How does a man kill a devil?'

'With courage and the sword,' replied Rufaar, his eldest surviving son. Two other sons older than him had been killed in raids and tribal warfare, and one had died in a feud over a woman. That death was still to be avenged.

Rufaar was thirty-three, a child of the warrior blood. With his own sword he had killed fifty men and more. He was as his father had been at the same age: his ferocity was unquenchable. Three of his younger brothers stood behind him. They were of the same brood, and in their veins also Salida's blood ran true.

'Let me lead the next charge, revered father,' Rufaar pleaded. 'Let me shatter these pig-eaters. Let me cauterize this festering sore in the heart of Islam.'

Salida looked upon him, and he was pleasing to a father's eye. 'Nay!' He shook his head. The single word of denial cut deeper than any enemy blade ever had. Rufaar winced with the pain of it. He went down on one knee and kissed his father's dusty foot. 'I ask no other boon but this. Let me lead the charge.'

'Nay!' Salida denied him a second time, and Rufaar's expression darkened. 'I will not let you lead, but you may ride at my right hand.' Rufaar's face cleared. He jumped to his feet and embraced his sire.

'What of us?' His other three sons joined the chorus. 'What of us, beloved father?'

'You puppies may ride behind us.' Salida glowered at them to hide his affection. 'Perchance Rufaar and I may throw you some scraps from the feast. Now fetch my camel.'

'Stretcher-bearer!' The call came from a half-dozen points around the outer wall of the square, where troopers had been hit by random Dervish fire. Quickly the wounded were carried into the centre and the gaps were closed. The doctors operated amid the dust and flies, sleeves rolled to the elbow, blood clotting swiftly in the heat. The wounded who could still stand came back in their bandages to take their places in the square once more.

'Water-boys!' The shout went around the little square. The boys scurried about with the skins and spilled water into the empty felt-covered bottles.

'Ammunition here!' The quartermasters moved along the sides of the square, doling out the cardboard packets.

The gunners struggled to clear the blockages of the machine-guns. They splashed precious water over the barrels to cool them. It boiled off in clouds of hissing steam, and the metal crackled and pinged. But the actions were locked solidly, and though they hammered and heaved they would not budge.

Suddenly in the midst of all this frantic activity the bugle rang out again. 'Stand to!' shouted the sergeants.

'They are coming back.' The Dervish cavalry rode out from the fastness of the hills. Like a great wave building up beyond the surf, they lined up again along the foot of the hills, facing the square.

'There is your enemy,' Penrod murmured to Yakub. The red banner waved in the centre of the line, carried by two Dervish striplings.

'Yes.' Yakub nodded. 'That is Salida in the blue turban. The mangy jackal beside him is his son, Rufaar. I must kill him also. Those are some of his other brats carrying his flag. There will be no honour in killing them, no more than popping fleas between the fingernails, but it must be done.'

'Then we still have much work to do.' Penrod smiled as he broke open another paper box of cartridges and filled the loops of his bandolier.

'Salida is a clever old jackal,' Yakub murmured. 'By the sweet breath of the Prophet, he learns quickly. He saw how we broke their first charges. Look! He has hardened his centre.'

Penrod saw what he meant. Salida had changed his formation. His line was not evenly distributed. The flanks were only two ranks deep, but in his centre Salida had formed a hammer, a solid knot of six closely packed ranks.

On the other side of the square General Sir Herbert Stewart studied the emir through the lens. 'He appears very old and frail.'

'He is old, but not frail, sir,' Hardinge assured him. 'With only fifty men, he led the charge that broke up Valentine Baker's Egyptians at Suakin. That was less than two years ago. The old dog still has teeth.'

'Then we shall have to draw them for him,' Stewart murmured.

'Here he comes, sir.'

'Here he comes indeed,' Stewart agreed.

The Dervish ranks rolled forward, the horses trotting and the camels pacing steadily, the men upon their backs brandishing their weapons and chanting their war cries. The dust storm trailed behind them. They crossed the half-way line, and broke into a canter. The lines bunched up like a clenching fist. Ahead the ground was littered with their own dead. They lay thickly as cherry blossom beneath the wind-blown trees of an orchard. Their harlequin *jibbas* bore fresher, darker stains than the decorative patches, and the blue flies rose in a cloud as the thunder of the charge shook the earth. The hoofs of the front rank trampled the corpses, scattering the bloody heaps into fresh confusion, and they came on without check.

In the centre Salida leant forward in the saddle of his grey camel. His rifle was still in its boot beneath his knee, but he handled the heavy broadsword as lightly as if it were a toy. He shouted no war cry, reserving his scant breath for the main business. His expression was ecstatic; the rheum from his bloodshot eyes ran down his cheeks into his silver-grey beard. He was an obvious target for the rifles that lay ahead. The first volley crashed into them, and men and animals were shot down. But Salida and his sons rode on untouched. Men pushed forward from the rear ranks to fill the gaps, and they were just in time to receive the next volley, and the next. But Salida rode on.

On the left flank a Nordenfelt machine-gun opened up, slicing through the front of the Dervish charge with bullets. Then, almost immediately, it jammed again and fell silent. But the Martini-Henrys crashed out in unison, keeping their terrible unhurried beat. Camels bellowed as they were hit and went down. Horses plunged, reared and fell backwards, crushing their riders. But in Salida's centre new men rode forward, keeping up the impetus of the charge. Salida reached the point twenty feet in front of the wall of the square where each of the previous charges had failed and floundered. Rufaar's knee touched his own, his other sons backed him almost as closely. Although three ranks of the Dervish centre had been shot away, brave men still poured forward to give the hammer weight as it swung towards the frail wall of the square.

'This time we will break these dogs.' Rufaar laughed.

But the British line never breaks. Now it gave a little, as a blade of Damascus steel will bend, but it did not shatter. A wave striking the solid coral reef, they washed over the front rank. Khaki-clad figures fell under the swinging blades, and the Dervish fired down into them from the backs of the camels. But gradually Salida's hammer lost its momentum. It slowed and stalled and at last spent its weight and fury against the second rank of the little square. The big men in sweat-soaked khaki tunics held them, then hurled them back.

The Dervish cavalry turned and streamed away towards the cliffs.

Salida was reeling on the saddle. A bayonet thrust had gone in deep above his hip bone. He might have fallen, but Rufaar reached across and, with one arm around his shoulders, steadied him and led him back to the shelter of the wadi. 'You are sore wounded, Father.' He tried to lift him to earth.

'The battle has only just begun.' Salida struck away his son's hands. 'Help me bind up this little cut, then we will ride back and finish the task that God and the Mahdi have set us.'

With his own long blue turban they bound up the old man's wound, so tightly that the flow of blood was stopped; and the bandages stiffened his back so that he could sit tall in the saddle once again.

'Start the drums,' said Salida. 'Sound the *ombeya*. We are going back.'

Osman Atalan rode up on Sweet Water, Hulu Mayya. His Beja division had been waiting in reserve, ready to ride in and exploit when Salida and his Jaalin forced the breach. 'Revered and warlike Emir, you have done more than any man before you. Now let me take in my Beja to finish the work you have begun so well.'

'I will force the opening,' Salida told him firmly. 'You can follow after me, as we agreed.'

Osman looked into that haughty face, and saw that there was no merit in argument. If they delayed here another minute the day was lost. The British wall had almost broken. If they struck again in the same place before it could recover, perhaps they could carry it away.

'Ride then, noble Emir. I will follow close behind you.'

The entire Dervish army, two full divisions, poured out from the hills and advanced upon the little cluster of men on the open plain. In the van rode the emaciated figure in a bloody *jibba*, bareheaded, his grey hair covering his shoulders. His eyes glittered feverishly, like those of a saint or a madman.

'Gentlemen,' Stewart addressed his staff, 'we will move our station across to meet these fine fellows. I had not expected them to pound away at our rear wall like this. However, it seems that they are coming back for more of the same.'

They moved off in a group, just as Hardinge rode up to report. 'The Dervish did some damage with that last charge, sir. We suffered fifty-five casualties all told. Three officers killed – Elliot, Cartwright and Johnson. Another two were wounded.'

'Ammunition?'

'Still in good supply, but all four of the Nordenfelts are out of action.'

'Damned rubbish. I asked for Gatlings. What about the water?'

'Running low, sir. We must reach the wells before nightfall.'

'That is my intention.' Stewart pointed at the massed Dervish cavalry drawn up along the foot of the hills. 'It looks as though they are about to attack with everything they have. A last desperate throw of the dice. I want you to pass the order to the three other walls to have the quarter columns standing in reserve. Just in case these fellows get inside.'

'Oh, they'll never get in, sir.'

'Of course they won't, but see to the quarter columns nevertheless.'

During the battle the Dervish had hammered away at the northern wall of the square. The men in the other three walls had received only the very first charge. Since then they had taken little part. They were restless and frustrated. Now, in the face of this new threat, the sergeants strode down the ranks detailing the quarter columns. If the enemy broke one wall, the square must not be allowed to collapse in upon itself. The other three walls must stand firm, while every fourth man, the quarter columns, rushed to stop the gap and shore up the broken wall. Before they were ready the war drums began their frenetic rhythm, and the *ombeyas* brayed and blared. The Dervish cavalry rolled forward yet again.

With no troops under his direct command Penrod had time enough to squint up at the height of the sun through slitted lids. It's after noon, he thought, amazed. We have been in play for three hours and more.

Beside him Yakub was fretting: 'If Salida does not come to me, someone else will kill him first.'

'That will never do, gentle Yakub.' Penrod lifted his helmet, swabbed his brow with his kerchief and settled the helmet again at a rakish angle. Then he looked ahead as the rumble of hoofs and the babble of Arab voices swelled into the deafening overture of battle. They swept up to the threshold of the square.

'First rank, rolling volleys. Fire.' The sergeants began their chant and at regular intervals the massed gunfire thundered out. The ranks of cavalry shuddered and shook as the volleys raked them, and their advance slowed under the dreadful punishment, but they came on and on, struggling over the last few yards until they struck the wall for the second time. Like raging bulls the two sides locked horns, swayed and pushed, thrust and hacked.

The British gave a little, then heaved themselves back. The white soldiers were adept with the bayonet. These weapons were longer reaching and quicker to recover than the swinging broadswords. For the second time that day Salida's division began to crumple. The soldiers plied the bayonets at close quarters, and some went down under the heavy crusader blades, but the rest tightened their grip and the Dervish gave ground more rapidly.

Then Osman Atalan rode in at the head of his fresh reserves. He came up behind Salida, and threw his full weight into the balance. His Beja were an avalanche and nothing could stand before them.

'They are in!' Along the British ranks a terrible shout went up. The unthinkable had happened. A British square had broken. The Dervish poured in exultantly. They drove back the khaki line and chaos descended on the dense maul and ruck of struggling men. Isolated British soldiers dropped and died under the Dervish blades, and were trampled beneath the hoofs.

'There is but one God!' the aggagiers shouted, as they killed and killed again.

The troopers of the shattered north wall were swiftly broken up into tiny groups of three and four men under the weight of Osman Atalan's aggagiers. As they were pushed back, Penrod ran forward to meet them, and gathered some of the strays to his own command. 'Form on me, lads. Back to back, shoulder to shoulder,' he shouted.

They recognized his authority and presence, and fought their way to him. As they came together they hardened into a cohesive whole, a prickly hedgehog of bayonets in the fluid fury of the fight.

Other officers were rallying the scattered troopers. Hardinge had gathered up a dozen, and the two bands melded. They were no longer a pair of tiny hedgehogs, but a fierce porcupine rattling steel quills.

An Arab on a tall black camel smashed into them, and before they could cut him down, he had lanced Hardinge through the belly. Hardinge dropped his sword and seized the lance shaft in both hands. The Arab still had hold of the butt. With a single heave Hardinge plucked him off his saddle. They fell in a tangle together. Penrod snatched up the sword Hardinge had dropped and rammed the point between the Dervish's shoulder-blades. Hardinge tried to rise, but the lance tip was deep in his guts. He tried to pull it out, but the barb held. He sank down again, bowed his head and closed his eyes, clutching the shaft with both hands.

Penrod stood over him to protect him and his troopers closed the gaps on either hand. It was good to have a fine sabre in his hand again. The blade had wonderful balance and temper: it came to life in Penrod's hand. Another Dervish rushed at him, swinging overhand with the broadsword. Penrod caught the heavy blade high in the natural line, and deflected it past his shoulder. It sliced open Penrod's sleeve but did not break the skin beneath. Before the Dervish could recover Penrod killed him with a thrust through the throat. He had a moment to glance round: his little group was standing firm. Their bayonet blades were dulled, and their arms black with clotted Arab blood. 'Forward, lads,' Penrod called to them. 'Close the breach!'

'Come on, boys. Let's see these fellows off!' a familiar voice piped at Penrod's elbow. Percy Stapleton was beside him. He had lost his helmet and his curly hair was dark with dust and sweat, but he was grinning like a demented ape as he cut and thrust at another Dervish then hit him cleanly in the chest. Penrod saw at once that Percy was a practised natural swords-man. When a Dervish swung low at his knees, Percy jumped lightly over the blade and cut the Arab across the side of the neck, half severing it. The man dropped his broadsword and tried to grab at his throat with both hands. Percy killed him with a quick thrust.

'Well done, sir.' Penrod was mildly impressed.

'You are too kind, sir.' Percy flicked his hair out of his eyes, and they both looked round for another opponent.

But, quite suddenly, the Dervish charge ran out of momentum. It slowed and hesitated, heaved forward again, then ran up against the mass of couched camels of the British baggage train, and stopped dead. The two opposing sides clinched and leant against each other like exhausted boxers in the tenth round, too weary to throw another punch.

'Quarter columns, forward!' General Stewart took command of his reserves at this crucial moment when all hung in such fine balance. They wheeled in behind him. Sword in hand, he stalked ahead on long legs like a marabou stork. He led them round the bulwark of kneeling baggage camels and they took the stranded Dervish in their left flank. The scattered and exhausted bands of British troopers saw them coming, took new heart and hurled themselves back into the fray. The ruptured square began to contract, and repair the tear in its outer fabric.

Osman Atalan, with the sure instinct of the warrior, recognized the moment when the battle was lost. He turned his mare back, then he and his aggagiers fought themselves clear before the jaws of the trap could close on them. They galloped away to the safety of the hills and left Salida and his sons enmeshed in the British square.

Salida was still sitting high on his camel. But the wound above his hip had burst open again and blood was streaming down his legs. His face was yellow as the mud of a sulphur spring and the sword had fallen from his trembling hand. Rufaar sat up behind him and, with an arm round his waist, held him upright, despite the camel's terrified plunges. Salida was dazed by the lethargy of his wounds, and the shock of watching his younger sons die under the British bayonets. He looked for them in childlike bewilderment, but their broken bodies were lost under the trampling hoofs.

Yakub saw an opening in the Dervish ranks as they turned to meet Stewart's reserves. 'I have private affairs to attend to, Effendi,' he called to Penrod, but Penrod and Percy Stapleton had found three more maddened Dervish to deal with and did not notice as he slipped away.

As Yakub ran up behind Salida's camel he scooped up a broadsword from the hand of a dead Arab. The animal was kicking and plunging, but Yakub dodged the flying hoofs, which might have delivered a killing blow. With a powerful double-handed swipe he cut through the tendons in one of the beast's hind legs. It bellowed and lurched forward on three legs, but he ran after it and hacked through the other hamstring. The camel collapsed on to its hindquarters. Salida and Rufaar were hurled violently from its back. Rufaar kept hold of his father and tried to break his fall as they struck the ground at Yakub's feet.

Rufaar looked up and recognized him. 'Yakub bin Affar!' he said, and the bitter hatred of the blood feud roughened his voice. But he was holding his father with both hands and unable to defend himself.

'Mine enemy!' Yakub acknowledged, and killed him. He left the broadsword buried to the hilt in his chest, and drew his dagger. He caught a handful of Salida's silver beard and pulled his head back, exposing his throat. He did not hack at the windpipe, but drew the razor edge of the dagger across the side of the wattled throat. It sliced through the carotid artery under Salida's ear, and Yakub made no effort to avoid the jet of bright blood that spurted over his hands and arms.

'She is avenged,' he whispered as he daubed the blood on his forehead. He would not utter his sister's name for she had been a whore, and many good men had died because of her. He let go of Salida's beard and let his face flop into the dust. He left him lying beside his son and ran back to Penrod's side.

The breach in the British square closed on the Dervish like the mouth of a sea anemone on a small fish that had swum into its tentacles. The Dervish asked no quarter. Martyrdom was the way to eternal life, and they welcomed it. Stewart's men knew that they would not surrender. Like a poisonous serpent with a broken back, they would strike at any hand extended to them, no matter how compassionately.

Relentlessly the soldiers plied the bayonet and the sword, but it was dangerous, bloody work, for each Dervish had to be surrounded and cut down. While there was life in them they fought on. The slaughter went on through the afternoon, raging at first, then gradually subsiding.

Even when it seemed to be over, it was not. Among the mounds of corpses individual Ansar were feigning death, poised to leap on any unwary victim. They lost a half-dozen more men to these furtive assassins before General Stewart ordered the advance. They gathered up their own casualties, and there were many. They took with them ninety-four wounded and seventy-four British corpses, wrapped in their own blankets, as they marched away towards the palm grove at the limit of the plain that marked the Wells of Abu Klea.

Among the palms they threw up a zareba, and buried their dead, laying them gently in rows in the shallow communal grave dug hastily in the sandy earth. It was evening before Penrod could go to find Hardinge in the hospital bivouac. 'I have come to return your sword, sir.' He proffered the beautiful weapon.

'Thank you, Ballantyne,' Hardinge whispered weakly. 'It was a gift from my wife.' His face was as pale as candlewax. They had moved his stretcher close to the fire, because he had complained of the cold. He reached out painfully and touched the blade, as if in farewell. 'However, I doubt I shall have much further use for it. Keep it for me, and use it as you did today.'

'I will not accept that, sir. You will march with us into Khartoum,' Penrod assured him, but Hardinge sagged back on to the stretcher.

'I think not,' he murmured. He was right: he was dead before daybreak.

The rest of the men were too exhausted to move on. Although he was haunted by thoughts of the great and lonely man waiting for them in Khartoum, Stewart could not drive them on in their present state. He gave them that night and most of the next morning to recover. They rested until noon in the scanty shade of the palm grove around the wells. The water was filthy, almost as salty as seawater. They boiled it with black tea and the last of the sugar.

In the enervating heat of midday Stewart dared delay no longer. He gave the order to continue the march. They loaded the seriously wounded on to the camels, and when the bugler sounded the advance they toiled away across the burning land.

They marched on through the rest of that day, then on again through the night. They had covered twenty-three miles before sunrise, and then they stopped. They could go no further. They were utterly exhausted. There remained only a few cupfuls of water for each man. The camels were all played out: even though they could smell the river ahead, they could not go on. The wounded were in desperate straits. Stewart knew he would lose most of them unless he could bring them to the water. He sent a runner to summon Penrod. 'Ballantyne, I have need of your local knowledge again. How far is it to the river?'

'We are very close, sir, about four miles. You will be able to see it from the next ridge.'

'Four miles,' Stewart mused. He looked back over the exhausted British formation. Four miles might as well have been a hundred for all the hope he had of getting them there. He was about to speak again, but Penrod interrupted him.

'Look ahead, sir.'

Upon the ridge of higher ground that lay between them and the river a small band of fifty or so Dervish had appeared. All the officers reached for their telescopes. Through the lens Penrod at once recognized the banner of Osman Atalan. Then in the centre of the band he picked out his tall lean figure on the back of the cream-coloured mare.

'Not too many of them,' said Sir Charles Wilson, Stewart's second-in-command, but his tone was dubious. 'We should be able to brush them aside without too much trouble. I don't think they will have the temerity to come at us again, not after the lesson we gave them at the wells.'

Penrod was about to contradict him. He wanted to point out that Atalan was a clever tactician: he had pulled his men out of the lost battle at Abu Klea before they were utterly destroyed. During the previous day and night, his scouts must have shadowed the battered British square, waiting for this moment when they had used up all their strength and endurance and their camels were finished. With an effort Penrod bit back the words.

'You wanted to say something, Ballantyne?' Stewart had not lowered his telescope but he had been aware of Penrod's reaction.

'That is Osman Atalan himself on the cream horse. I think there are more than just that one troop. He got off comparatively lightly at Abu Klea. His divisions are almost intact.'

'You are probably right,' Stewart agreed.

'There is dust on the right,' Penrod pointed out. All the telescopes turned in that direction, and another group of several hundred more Dervish cavalry appeared upon the ridge. Then there was more dust further to the left. Swiftly the numbers of the enemy swelled from fifty to thousands. Their sullen squadrons stood squarely across the road to the Nile.

Stewart lowered his telescope and snapped it shut. He looked directly at Sir Charles Wilson. 'I propose to laager the baggage and the wounded here in a zareba, and leave five hundred able-bodied men to protect them. Then with a flying column of eight or nine hundred of the fittest men we shall make a run for the river.'

'The camels are done in, sir,' Wilson cut in quickly. 'They will never make it.'

'I am aware of that,' said Stewart, crisply. Privately he had come to think of his second-in-command as a man who could smell the dung in a bed of roses. 'We will leave the camels here with the wounded and proceed on foot.' He ignored the shocked expressions of his staff and looked at Penrod. 'How long would it take you lead us to the river, Ballantyne?'

'Without the wounded and the baggage I can have you there in two hours, sir,' Penrod answered, with all the confidence he did not feel.

'Very well. The company commanders will select their strongest and fittest men. We will march in forty minutes' time, at fifteen hundred hours precisely.'

'What kind of men are these?' al-Noor asked with wonder, as they sat on their horses and watched the depleted British square form up and march out of the zareba. 'They have no animals and no water and still they come on. In God's Holy Name, what kind of men are they?'

'They are descendants of the men who fought our ancestor Saladin, Righteous of the Faith, eight hundred years ago before Jerusalem,' Osman Atalan replied, 'They are men of the Red Cross, like the crusaders of old. But they are only men. Look upon them now and remember the battle of Hattin.'

'We must always remember Hattin,' agreed his aggagiers.

'At Hattin Saladin trapped an exhausted, thirst-crazed army of these men and destroyed it at a single blow. So great were the losses he inflicted upon the infidel that he tore from their bloody hands the entire kingdom of Jerusalem, which they had stolen from the faithful and held for eighty-eight years.' Osman Atalan rose in his stirrups and pointed the blade of his broadsword at the band of marching men, so tiny and insignificant on the stony grey plain. 'This is our field of Hattin. Before the setting of the sun we will destroy this army. Not one will reach the river alive. For the glory of Allah and his Mahdi!'

His aggagiers drew their swords. 'The victory belongs to God and his Mahdi,' they cried.

As the slow-moving British square climbed the gentle slope towards them the Dervish disappeared behind the ridge. The British toiled on. Every few hundred yards they halted to preserve the order of the wavering ranks and bring in their stragglers. They could not leave them for the Dervish and the castrating knife. Then they started again. In one of the pauses Stewart sent for Penrod. 'What lies beyond the ridge? Describe the ground ahead,' he ordered.

'From the ridge we should overlook the town of Metemma on the near bank,' Penrod assured him. 'There is an intervening strip of heavy scrub and dunes about half a mile wide, then the steep bank of the Nile.'

'Please, God, from the ridge let us also see Gordon's steamers moored against the bank and waiting to take us up to Khartoum.' As Stewart said it the ridge ahead was transformed. The entire length was sown with bright white puffs of powder gun-smoke, like a cotton field with ripe pods bursting open in the hot sunlight. The Boxer-Henry bullets began to whip around them, ploughing up the red earth and whining off the white quartz rocks.

'Should we not return their fire, sir?' Wilson asked. 'Clear that ridge before we move on?'

'No time for that. We must keep stepping out,' Stewart snapped. 'Pass the word for my piper.'

General Sir Herbert Stewart's personal piper, like his master, was a Highlander. His tartan was the hunting Stewart and he wore his glengarry at a jaunty angle, the ribbons dangling down his back.

'Give us a good marching tune,' Stewart ordered.

'"The Road to the Isles", sir?'

'You know my favourites, don't you, young Patrick Duffy?'

The piper marched twenty paces ahead of the front wall of the square, his kilt swinging and his pipes skirling the wild, outlandish music that inflames the warlike passions of all men who hear it. The bullets still whipped around them. Every few minutes a man was hit and went down. His comrades lifted him and carried him forward. The Dervish snipers retreated before the resolute advance until at last the ridge was silent and deserted. The square marched on towards it.

Suddenly the drums hidden behind the ridge began a deep bass beat that made the air tremble. Then the ground seemed to tremble in sympathy. To the rumbling thunder of hoofs, the Beja cavalry swept over the skyline ahead.

The square halted and tightened its formation, and the horde of horsemen rode into the first blast of gunfire and reeled back. The second and third volleys decimated them and they turned and galloped away.

The soldiers picked up their wounded comrades and started

forward again. The next Beja charge thundered over the skyline. The drums thudded and *ombeyas* shrieked. The British laid down their wounded and dead, and formed up in the impenetrable walls. The charge broke against them and, like a retreating wave, fell back. The weary march resumed. They passed over the fallen Dervish, and to forestall the treacherous suicidal attack of the warriors feigning death, they bayoneted the living and dead bodies as they stepped over them.

At last, the front rank came out on the skyline. A hoarse cheer issued from their parched throats and they grinned with cracked, bleeding lips. Before them lay the broad sweep of the Nile. The surface of the river splintered the sunlight into myriad bright reflections like spinning silver coins. There, against the far bank, lay the pretty little steamers of Gordon's flotilla, waiting to take them upriver to Khartoum.

Some of the men sank to their knees, but their comrades hauled them to their feet and held them erect. Penrod heard a youngster croak, 'Water! Sweet God, water!' But his voice was gagged by his swollen purple tongue.

The corporal who supported him answered, 'The bottles are dry, but there is all the water you can drink down there. Brace up, lad! We're going down to fetch it. Ain't no blackamoor going to stop us either.'

'No stopping, lads,' the sergeant major called to them. 'Not until you wash off the stink of your sweat in yon wee stream.'

Those who were still able to laughed, and with a new lift in their weary stride they started down towards the Nile. Ahead stood an undulating series of low dunes, the last barrier before the river. The sands were multi-hued: cinnamon and chestnut, puce and chocolate. The hollows between them were thick with thorn scrub and saltbush.

Beyond the dunes, along the riverbank, lay the labyrinthine native town of Metemma. The narrow winding alleys, huts and hovels pressed right up to the water's edge. It was silent and deserted as a necropolis.

'The town is a trap, sir.' Penrod offered his opinion diffidently. 'You can be certain that it is teeming with Dervish. If the men get into those alleys they will be cut to shreds.'

'Quite right, Ballantyne,' Stewart grunted. 'Make for the open stretch on the bank below the town.' The Dervish harassing fire still spurted and smoked from the tops of the dunes and from among the thick scrub in the hollows below them. Stewart took one step forward, then spun round as a heavy bullet thudded into him. He went down in a broken heap. Penrod knelt beside him and saw that the bullet had struck him in the groin, shattering the large joint of the femur. Shards of bone stuck out of the churned flesh, and blood bubbled over them. It was a wound that no man could survive.

Stewart sat up and thrust his clenched fist into the gaping hole in his flesh. 'I am hit,' he called urgently to Sir Charles Wilson. 'Take command, and keep the regiment pushing hard for the river. Let nothing stand in your way. Drive for the river with everything you have got.'

Penrod tried to lift him and carry him forward. 'Damn you, Ballantyne. Do your job, man. Let me lie. Take them on. You must help Wilson to get them to the river.'

Penrod stood up and two burly troopers rushed to the general.

'Good luck, sir!' Penrod said, and left him. He hurried to catch up with the front rank and lead them down into the dunes.

It did not seem that a squadron of cavalry could conceal itself in that low scrub, but as they came off the ridge, the bush ahead came alive with horses and figures in speckled *jibbas*. Within seconds the two sides were once more locked in savage, bloody conflict. Every time the soldiers drove them back with those flailing volleys, they reassembled and charged again. Now some of the white men in the front rank of the mangled British square were dropping, not from their wounds but from heat exhaustion and that terrible thirst. The men on each side hoisted them up again and pushed them forward.

The sweat dried in salt-ringed patches on their tunics; their bodies could no longer sweat. They reeled like drunks and dragged their rifles with the last of their strength. Penrod's vision wavered and darkened with cloudy shapes. He blinked eyes to clear his eyes, and each step was a monumental labour.

Just when it seemed that mortal man could endure no longer, the dense scrub ahead rustled and shook and out came the horsemen yet again. Riding at the head of the charge was the familiar figure in the green turban. The coat of the cream-coloured mare under him was dulled with sweat, her long mane matted and tangled. Osman Atalan recognized Penrod in the front rank of the square, turned the mare with his knees and rode straight at him.

Penrod tried to steady himself for his legs were rubbery under him. His light cavalry carbine seemed to have been transmuted to lead. It needed a painful effort to lift it to his shoulder. Even though they were still separated by fifty paces the image of his enemy, Osman Atalan, seemed to fill the field of his distorted vision. He fired. The sound seemed muted, and everything around him moved with dreamlike slowness. He watched his bullet strike the mare high in the forehead above the level of her magnificent dark eyes. She flung her head back and went down, struck the earth and rolled in a cloud of sand with her legs kicking spasmodically. She came to rest with her neck twisted back under her body.

With feline grace, Osman kicked his feet from the stirrups as she fell and sprang from her back to land lightly in balance. He stood and glared at Penrod with an expression of deadly hatred. Penrod tried to reload the rifle, but his fingers were numb and slow, and Osman held his eyes with a mesmeric spell. Osman stooped and picked up his broadsword from where he had dropped it. He ran towards Penrod. At last Penrod managed to guide the cartridge into the open breech and closed the block. He lifted the weapon and his aim wavered. He tried desperately to steady it, and when, for an instant, the bead of the foresight lay on Osman's chest he fired. He saw the bullet graze the emir's sword arm, and leave a bloody line across the muscle of his biceps, but Osman neither flinched nor lost his grip on the hilt of the broadsword. He came on steadily. Other troopers on either side of Penrod turned their rifles on him. Bullets kicked up sand or snapped through the scrub around him. But Osman's life seemed charmed.

'Kill that man!' shouted Wilson, his tone strident and nervous.

The rest of the Arab horsemen had seen their emir go down and their ranks broke up. One of his aggagiers swerved towards Osman's isolated figure. 'I am coming, master.'

'Let me be, Noor. It is not yet finished,' Osman shouted back.

'It is enough for this day. We will fight again.' Without slowing his mount al-Noor leant out of the saddle, linked arms with him and swung him up behind his saddle.

As he was carried away into the dense scrub, Osman glared back at Penrod. 'It is not finished. In God's Name, this is not the end.' Then he was gone. The rest of the Dervish cavalry disappeared as swiftly, and an eerie silence fell over the field. Some of the exhausted men in the British line sank to the earth again, their legs no longer able to support them, but the cries of the sergeants roused them: 'On your feet, boys. There is the river in front of you!'

Stewart's piper puffed up his bag and 'Scotland the Brave' shrilled on the desert air. The men shouldered their weapons, picked up their dead and the square moved forward yet again. Staggering along in the front rank, Penrod licked the salt and dried blood from his cracked lips, and the last few drops of his sweat burned his bloodshot eyes as he searched the scrub ahead for the next wave of savage horsemen.

But the Dervish had gone, blown away like smoke. The British came out on to the high bank of the Nile, and waved and shouted to the steamers across the river. They were pretty as model boats floating on the Serpentine on a bright Sunday morning in London Town.

They had won through. They had reached the river, and a hundred and fifty miles to the south in Khartoum, General Charles Gordon still endured.

Osman Atalan waited in the village of Metemma for shattered divisions of his Jaalin allies to reassemble, for their sheikhs to come to him and place themselves under his command. But their own emir, Salida, and all his sons were dead. So brave when he led them, they were now like children without a father. Allah had deserted them. The cause was lost. They disappeared back into their desert fastnesses. Osman waited in vain.

At first light the next morning he called for the master of the pigeons. 'Bring me three of your fastest and swiftest birds,' he ordered. With his own hand he wrote out his message for the Mahdi in triplicate, one copy to be carried by each bird. If falcons or other misfortune struck one or even two, the vital message would still reach the holy man in Omdurman.

'To the Mahdi Muhammad Ahmed, may Allah protect and cherish him. You are the light of our eyes, and the breath of our bodies. My shame and sadness is a great rock in my belly, for know you that the infidel has prevailed in battle against us. Emir Salida is dead, and his division destroyed. The infidel has reached the Nile at Metemma. I am returning in all haste with my division to Omdurman. Pray for us, Holy and Mighty Mahdi.'

The pigeon-master tied the folded messages to the legs of the birds, replaced them in their basket and carried them to the riverbank. Osman went ahead of him. The pigeon-master handed the birds to him one at a time. Before he launched them, Osman held each in his cupped hands and blessed it. 'Fly swiftly and straight, little friend. May Allah protect you.' He tossed the bird into the air, and it rose on the clatter of wings, circled the little village of Metemma, then picked up its bearings and shot away on rapid wingbeats into the south. He let each pigeon get well clear before he sent away the next, lest they should form a flock that would attract the attention of the predators.

When they were gone he walked back to the village and

climbed the mud dome of the mosque. From the top balcony of the prayer tower, whence the muezzin called the faithful to their devotions, he had a full view of both banks of the river. The cluster of small white steamers was still anchored downstream in the Pool of the Crocodiles. They were beyond his reach, for he had no artillery with which to attack them. Instead he turned his attention to the British camp. With the naked eye he could make out the men within the walls of their hastily constructed zareba. They had not yet made any effort to begin loading the steamers with either men or equipment. He wondered at their curious lethargy. It was much at variance with the energy and urgency they had displayed until now. If their goal was still to reach and relieve Khartoum as swiftly as possible they should have left their wounded on the riverbank, embarked their fighting men and sailed southwards without an hour's delay.

'Perhaps Allah has not yet forsaken us. Perhaps He will help me to reach the city ahead of these unpredictable men,' he murmured.

He went down from the tower to where the remnants of his division were waiting for him on the outskirts of the village. The horses and camels were already saddled and loaded, and al-Noor held his new steed. It was a big black stallion, the strongest animal in his string. Osman stroked the white blaze on his forehead. His name was al-Buq, the War Trumpet.

'You are without vice, Buq,' he whispered, 'but you could never match Hulu Mayya.' He looked back up the dunes to where she had fallen. The vultures and the crows still circled over the ridge. Will there ever be another animal as noble as she? he wondered, and the black tide of his anger flooded the depths of his being. Abadan Riji, you have much to atone for.

He swung up into the saddle and raised his clenched right fist. 'In the Name of Allah, we ride for Omdurman!' he cried, and his aggagiers thundered after him.

Khartoum lay in a torpor of despair, weak with plague and deprivation. The girls' voices were in penetrating contrast to the brooding silence around them.

'There's one coming,' Saffron sang out.

'I know. I saw it long ago,' Amber chanted.

'That's a lie. You never did!'

'I *did*!'

'Stop that squabbling, you two little harridans,' David Benbrook ordered sternly, 'and point it out to me.' Their young eyes were sharper than his.

'Over there, Daddy. Straight above Tutti Island.'

'Just to the left of that little cloud.'

'Ah, Yes. Of course,' David said, slipped the butt of the shotgun under his right armpit and turned to line up with the approaching bird. 'I was just testing you.'

'You were not!'

'Tut, tut. A little more respect, please, my angel.'

Nazeera heard their voices. She was on her way back to the kitchen carrying a pitcher of water that she had drawn from the well in the stableyard. She had been going to boil and filter it, but the voices distracted her. She set the pitcher on the table beside the front door next to the cluster of glasses on the silver tray, crossed to the window of the dining room and looked out over the terrace. The consul stood in the middle of the brown, burnt-out lawn. He was staring up into the sky. There was nothing unusual in this behaviour. For many weeks now he had spent each afternoon on the terrace watching for any bird to come within range of his shotgun. She turned back to the kitchen, but absentmindedly left the pitcher of unboiled water on the table with the glasses. Behind her she heard the thud of the gun and more excited squeals from the twins. She smiled fondly and closed the kitchen door behind her.

'You got him, Daddy!'

'Oh, clever paterfamilias!' This was Saffron's latest addition to her vocabulary.

The pigeon tumbled in the air as the pellets plucked a burst of feathers from its chest. It fluttered down and crashed into the top branches of the tamarind tree above the palace bedrooms. It stuck there, thirty feet above the ground. The twins raced each other to the base of the tree and clambered up it, arguing and pushing each other.

'Be careful, you little demons!' David called anxiously. 'You're going to hurt yourselves.'

Saffron reached the bird first. She was the tomboy. She balanced on the branch and stuffed the warm body into the front of her bodice and started down again.

'You are always so overbearing,' Amber accused her.

Saffron accepted the compliment without protest and jumped the last few feet to the ground. She ran to her father. 'It's got a note!' she shrilled. 'It's got a note just like the others.'

'Goodness gracious me, so it has,' David agreed. 'Aren't we lucky? Let's see what the gentlemen across the river have to say for themselves.' The twins danced after him as he carried the dead pigeon into the hall. He propped the shotgun against the wall and fumbled in his coat pocket for his *pince-nez* and clipped it on to the end of his nose. Then with his penknife he cut the thread that held the tiny roll of paper, and spread it carefully on the table beside the pitcher and the glasses. His lips moved silently as he deciphered the Arabic script, and slowly his benign expression changed. It became alert and businesslike.

'This is the most wonderful news. The relief column has smashed up the Dervish army in the north. Now they will be here within days. I must take this note across to the general right away,' he told the twins. 'Go in and ask Nazeera to pour your bath now. I will be a while, but I will come to your room to say goodnight.' He clapped his hat on to his head and set out down the terrace towards Gordon's headquarters.

Saffron snatched up the shotgun before Amber could reach it. She held it tantalizingly, like another trophy under her sister's nose.

'That's not fair, Saffy. You always do everything.'

'Don't be a baby.'

'I'm not a baby.'

'You are a baby, and you're sulking again.'

Saffron carried the shotgun across the lobby and into her father's gunroom. Amber watched her go with her clenched fists on her hips. Her face was flushed and her hair was sticking to her forehead with perspiration. She saw the pitcher on the side table where Nazeera had left it. With an angry flourish she poured herself a glass of water, drank it and pulled a face. 'It tastes funny,' she complained. 'And I'm not a baby and I'm not sulking. I'm just a bit cross, that's all.'

Ryder Courtney knew that his stay in Khartoum was drawing to an end. Even if the relief column arrived before the city fell, and was able to evacuate them all safely, the city would belong to the Dervish. He was clearing out the compound, ready to pull out at the first opportunity. Rebecca had volunteered to help him draw up an inventory and bills of lading for everything that was being loaded on board the *Intrepid Ibis*.

Ryder had become increasingly aware of the emotional turmoil she was going through. The uncertainty was wearing away at everyone's nerves, as conditions in the city deteriorated. The menace of the great army of the Dervish besiegers seemed to grow as the will of the trapped population declined and the relief column did not arrive. It had been ten months since the city had been invested by the Mahdi. A long time to live under the threat of horrible death.

Ryder knew how the responsibility of caring for her little sisters weighed upon Rebecca. Her father was little help in this regard: he was amiable and affectionate but, like the twins, he relied on her with almost childlike faith. None of the Sudanese women had returned to work since the mob attack on the compound. The running of the little green-cake kitchen had devolved almost entirely upon Rebecca. The twins were willing helpers, but the grinding labour was beyond their strength and endurance. Ryder's admiration and affection for her were enhanced as he watched her struggle to take care of her family. He considered once again the fact that at barely eighteen she had been saddled with this heavy load of responsibility. He understood how alone and isolated she felt, and tried to give her the help she needed. However, he was aware that his ill-considered unrestrained behaviour had damaged her trust in him. He had to be careful not to frighten her again, yet he longed to take her in his arms, comfort and shield her. He felt that since Penrod Ballantyne had left Khartoum he had made good progress in repairing their damaged relationship: she seemed so much easier in his company. Their conversations were more relaxed and she did not avoid him so obviously as before.

They were in the blockhouse, sitting at his desk across from each other. They were counting the piles of silver dollars into heaps of fifty, then wrapping them into rolls of parchment and packing them into wooden coffee chests, preparatory to taking them on board the *Ibis*. From the corner of his eye Ryder watched her brush back a strand of that beautiful silken hair. His heart ached as he noticed the calluses on her hands, and the little lines of worry and hardship at the corners of her eyes. A complexion like hers was more suited to the pleasant climes of England than to scorching sunlight and burning desert airs. When this is over, I could sell up here, and take her back to England, he thought.

She looked up suddenly and caught his eyes upon her. 'What would we do without you, Ryder?' she said.

He was astonished by the words and the tone in which they were spoken. 'My dear Rebecca, you would do well in any circumstances. I claim no credit for your strength and resolve.'

'I have been unkind to you.' She ignored his denial. 'I behaved like a little girl. You of all people I should have treated more kindly. Without you we might long ago have perished.'

'You are being kind to me now. That makes up for everything,' he said.

'The green-cake is just one of your valuable gifts to my family. I do not think it an exaggeration to say that with it you have saved our lives. We are healthy and strong in the midst of starvation and death. I can never repay you for that.'

'Your friendship is all the payment I could ask for.'

She smiled at him and the worry lines were smoothed away. He wanted to tell her how beautiful she was, but he bit back the words. She reached across the desk, spilling a stack of silver coins, and took his hand. 'You are a good friend and a good man, Ryder Courtney.'

For the first time she studied his face quite openly. He is not as beautiful as Penrod is, she thought, but he has a strong, honest face. It's a face one could see every day and not grow tired of. He would never leave me, as Penrod has. There would be no native girls hiding in a back room. He is a man of substance, not ostentation or pretence. There would always be bread on his table. He is a rock of a man and he would shelter his woman. The hand holding hers was powerful and competent, hardened with work. His bare arm reaching towards her was like the pillar of a house. His shoulders under the cloth of his shirt were broad and square. He was a man, not a boy.

Then, suddenly, she remembered where they were. Her smile crumpled. The precariousness of their lives rushed back upon her. What would happen if Ryder sailed away in the *Ibis* and left her and the twins here? What would happen to them when the Mahdi and his murderous army stormed into the city? She knew what they did to the women they captured. Tears swamped her eyes and clung to her lashes. 'Oh, Ryder, what will become of us all? Are we all going to die in this awful place? Dead before we have lived?' She knew in her woman's heart that there was only one certain way that she could bind a man like him to herself for ever. Was she ready to take that step?

'No, Rebecca, you have been so brave and strong for so long. Don't give up now.' He stood up and moved quickly round the desk.

She looked up at him as he stood over her, and the tears ran down her cheeks. 'Hold me, Ryder. Hold me!' she pleaded.

'I do not want to give you offence again.' He hesitated.

'I was a child then, a mindless girl. Now I am a woman. Hold me like a woman.'

He lifted her to her feet and took her gently in his arms. 'Be strong!' he said.

'Help me,' she answered and pressed close to him. She buried her face against his chest and inhaled his scent. Her terrors and doubt seemed to recede into insignificance. She felt safe. She felt his strength flowing into her, and clung to him with quiet desperation. Then, slowly, she was aware of a new, pleasant sensation that seemed to emanate from the centre of her being. It was not the divine and consuming madness that Penrod Ballantyne had evoked. It was, rather, a warming glow. This man she could trust. She was safe in his arms. It would be easy to do what she had contemplated.

This is something I must do not only for myself but for my family. Silently she made the decision, then said aloud, 'Kiss me, Ryder.' She lifted her face to him 'Kiss me as you did before.'

'Rebecca, my darling Becky, are you sure what you are about?'

'If you can speak only to ask daft questions,' she smiled at him, 'then speak not at all. Just kiss me.'

His mouth was hot and his breath mingled with hers. Her lips were soft and she felt his tongue slip between them. Once that had frightened and confused her, but now she revelled in the taste of him. I will take him as my man, she thought. I reject the other. I take Ryder Courtney. With that level-headed decision she let her emotions take control. She slipped the leash on all restraint as she felt something clench deep in her belly. It was a sensation so powerful that it reached the edge of pain. She felt it throbbing inside her.

It is my womb, she realized, with amazement. He has roused the centre of my womanhood. She pushed her hips hard against his, trying to ease the pain or aggravate it, she was not certain which. The last time Ryder had embraced her she had not understood what she had felt swelling and hardening. Now she knew. This time she was not afraid. She even had a secret name for that man's thing. She called it a tammy, after the tamarind tree outside her bedroom, which Penrod had climbed that first night.

His tammy is singing to my quimmy, she thought, and my quimmy likes the tune. Her mother, the emancipated Sarah Isabel Benbrook, had taught her the quaint word. 'This might be the last day of our lives. Do not waste it,' she breathed. 'Let us take this moment, hold it and never let go.' But he was diffident. She had to take his hands and place them on her breasts. Her nipples seemed to swell and burn with his touch.

She twisted the fingers of one hand into the hair at the back of his head to pull it down, and with the other hand she opened the hooks down the front of her bodice. She freed one of her breasts and as it popped out she pressed it into his mouth. She cried out with the sweet pain of his teeth on her tender flesh. Her essence welled inside her and overflowed.

She was overcome with a desperate sense of urgency. 'Quickly – please, Ryder. I am dying. Do not let me die. Save me.' She knew she was babbling nonsense, but she did not care. She clasped both her arms round his neck and tried to climb up his body. He reached behind her, took a double handful of the hem of her skirt and lifted it up round her waist. She wore nothing beneath it, and her buttocks were pale and round as a pair of ostrich eggs in the gloom of the shuttered room. He cupped them in his hands and lifted her.

She locked her thighs round his hips, and felt him burrowing into the silken nest of curls at the fork of her legs. 'Quickly! I cannot live another moment without you inside me.' She pressed down hard, screwing up her eyes with the effort, and felt all her resistance to him give way. She dug her fingernails into his back and pushed down again. Then nothing else in the world mattered: all her worries and fears dissolved as he glided in, impaling her deeply. She felt her womb open to welcome him. She thrust against him with a kind of barely controlled desperation. She felt his legs begin to tremble, and stared into his face as it contorted in ecstatic agony. She felt his legs juddering beneath them, and she thrust harder and faster. He opened his mouth and when he cried out, her voice echoed his. They locked each other in a fierce paroxysm that seemed as if it would bind them together through eternity, but at last their voices sank into silence, and the rigid muscles of his legs relaxed. He sank to the floor on his knees, but she clung to him desperately, clenching herself round him so that he could not slip out and leave her empty.

He seemed to return at last from a faraway place, and stared at her with an expression of awe and wonder. 'Now you are my woman?' It was half-way between a question and a declaration.

She smiled at him tenderly. He was still deep inside her. She felt marvellously powerful, deliciously lascivious and wanton. She tightened her loins, and gripped hard. She had not realized she was capable of such a trick. He gasped and his eyes flew wide. 'Yes,' she agreed, 'and you are my man. I will hold you like this for ever, and never let you go.'

'I am your willing captive,' he said. She kissed his lips.

When she broke off to draw breath he went on, 'Will you do me the great honour of becoming my wife? We do not want to shock the world, do we?'

Suddenly it was all happening very swiftly. Although this had been her intention, she could not think of a response both demure and yet binding upon him. While she considered it there was a loud knock on the blockhouse door. She pushed him away and hurriedly stuffed her breasts back into her bodice, looking anxiously towards the door. 'It is locked,' he reminded her in a whisper. With hundreds of pounds in coin lying on his desk, he had taken no chances. Now he raised his voice: 'Who is it?'

'It is I, Bacheet. I have brought a news bulletin from Gordon Pasha.'

'That is not important enough to worry me when I am busy,' Ryder retorted. Gordon issued his bulletins almost daily. They were designed to comfort the populace of the city and to bolster their will to resist. Thus his compositions were subject to wide literary licence, and were often separated from the truth by a considerable distance.

'This one is important, Effendi.' Bacheet's tone was excited. 'Good news. Very good news.'

'Push it under the door,' Ryder ordered.

He stood up and lifted Rebecca to her feet. They both adjusted their clothing: he buttoned the front of his breeches and she straightened her skirts. Then Ryder went to the door and picked up the crudely printed bulletin. He scanned it, then brought it to her.

DERVISH ARMY ROUTED.

THE ROAD TO KHARTOUM IS OPEN.

BRITISH RELIEF COLUMN WILL ARRIVE WITHIN DAYS.

She read it twice, the first time swiftly, the second deliberately. At last she looked up at him. 'Do you think it is the truth this time?'

'It will be a cruel hoax if it is not. But Chinese Gordon is not renowned for his restraint or his consideration for the delicate feelings of others.'

Rebecca pretended to reread the bulletin, but her mind was racing. If the relief column was truly on its way, was the need for a permanent relationship with Ryder Courtney really so pressing? As his wife she would be doomed to spend the rest of her days in this wild, savage land. Would she ever again see the green fields of England and have the society of civilized people? Was there any desperate urgency to marry a man who was pleasant and would care for her, but whom she did not love?

'True or not,' Ryder went on, 'we shall find out very soon. One way or the other you will still be my fiancée. There is a full head of steam in the *Ibis*'s boiler and her hold is loaded with every stick of cargo it can carry—' He broke off and studied her face quizzically. 'What is it, my darling? Is something worrying you?'

'I have not yet replied to your question,' she said softly.

'Oh, if that is all, then I shall repeat it and hope for your formal response,' he said. 'Will you, Rebecca Helen

Benbrook, take me, Ryder Courtney, to be your lawful wedded husband?'

'In all truth, I do not know,' she said, and he stared at her, appalled. 'Please give me a little time to think about it. It is a momentous decision and not one I can rush into.'

In this pivotal moment on which so much depended, a thought suddenly occurred to her: If the relief column arrives the day after tomorrow, will Penrod Ballantyne be with them? Then she thought, It is of no account, one way or the other, for he no longer means anything to me. I made a mistake in trusting him, but now he can go back to his Arab girls and his philandering ways for all I care. But she found herself unconvinced by this, and the image of Penrod persisted in her mind long after she had left Ryder's compound and was on her way back to the consular palace.

It took Sir Charles Wilson several days to bring in all his wounded, the baggage and the camel string. In the meantime he fortified the camp on the riverbank below Metemma, siting the Nordenfelt machine-guns to cover all the approaches, and he raised the walls of the zareba to a height of six feet.

On the third day after the battle the chief regimental surgeon reported to him that General Stewart's wound had developed gangrene. Wilson hurried down to the hospital tent. The rotten sweet smell of necrotic flesh was nauseating in the heat. He found Stewart lying in a bath of his own sweat under a mosquito net over which the huge hairy blue flies crawled, searching for some point of entry to reach the irresistible odour of the wound. It was covered with a field dressing, heavily stained with a custard-yellow discharge.

'I have managed to remove the bullet,' the surgeon assured Wilson, then lowered his voice to a whisper that the stricken man could not hear: 'The gangrene has a firm hold, sir. There is little or no hope, I am afraid.'

Stewart was delirious and mistook Wilson for General

Gordon as he stooped over the camp bed. 'Thank God we were in time, Gordon. There were times when I feared we would be too late. I offer you my congratulations for your courage and fortitude, which saved Khartoum. Yours is an achievement of which Her Majesty and every citizen of the British Empire will be justly proud.'

'I am Charles Wilson, not Charles Gordon, sir,' Wilson corrected him.

Stewart stared at him in astonishment, then reached through the mosquito net and seized his hand. 'Oh, well done, Charles! I knew I could trust you to do your duty. Where is Gordon? Ask him to come to me at once. I want to congratulate him myself.'

Wilson freed his hand and stood back from the bed. He turned to the surgeon. 'Are you sedating him sufficiently? It will do him no good to become so agitated.'

'I am administering ten grains of laudanum every two hours. But there is little pain in the site of a wound once the gangrene takes hold.'

'I will place him on the first steamer that departs downriver for Aswan. That will probably be in two or three days' time.'

'Two or three days?' Stewart had only picked up the last few sentences. 'Why are you sending Gordon down to Aswan, and why two or three days? Answer me that.'

'The steamers will set off for Khartoum imminently, General. We have run into unforeseen but unavoidable obstacles.'

'Gordon? But where is Gordon?'

'We must hope he is still holding out in Khartoum, sir, but we have had no news of him.'

Stewart looked around the tent with a wild, bewildered expression. 'Is this not Khartoum? Where are we? How long have we been here?'

'This is Metemma, sir,' the surgeon intervened gently. 'You have been here four days.'

'Four days!' Stewart's voice rose to a shout. 'Four days! You have thrown away the sacrifice made by my poor lads. Why did you not push on with all speed to Khartoum, instead of sitting here?

'He is delirious,' Wilson snapped at the surgeon. 'Give him another dose of laudanum.'

'I am not delirious!' Stewart shouted. 'If you don't set out for Khartoum immediately, I will see you court-martialled and shot for dereliction of your duty and cowardice in the face of the enemy, sir.' He choked and fell back, spent and muttering, on his pillows. He closed his eyes and was quiet.

'Poor fellow.' Wilson shook his head with deep regret. 'Completely out of his head and hallucinating. No appreciation of the situation. Look after him and make him comfortable.'

He acknowledged the doctor's salute, and ducked out through the fly of the tent. He blinked in the bright sunlight, then scowled as he realized that a small group of officers was standing rigidly to attention nearby. They had certainly heard every word that had been spoken. Their expressions left no doubt of that.

'Have you gentlemen nothing better to do than laze about here?' Wilson demanded. They avoided his eyes as they saluted and walked away.

Only one stood his ground. Penrod Ballantyne was the junior officer in the group. His behaviour was impudent. He was walking the tightrope across the lethal chasm of insubordination. Wilson glowered at him. 'What are you about, Captain?' he demanded.

'I wondered if I might speak to you, sir.'

'What is it, then?'

'The camels are fully recovered. Plenty of water and good feed. With your permission I could be in Khartoum within twenty-four hours.'

'To what purpose, Captain? Are you proposing a one-man liberation of the city?' Wilson allowed his scowl to change to an amused smirk – an expression that was no great improvement, Penrod thought.

'My purpose would be to take your despatches to General Gordon, and inform him of your intentions, sir. The city is sore pressed and at the limit of its endurance. There are English women and children within the walls. It can be only days before they fall into the clutches of the Mahdi. I was hoping I might be allowed to assure General Gordon that you have his plight and that of the populace in mind.'

'You disapprove of my conduct of the campaign, do you? By the way, what is your name, sir?' Of course Wilson knew his name: this was a calculated insult.

'Penrod Ballantyne, 10th Hussars, sir. And no, sir, I would not presume to remark on your conduct of the campaign. I was merely offering, for your consideration, my local knowledge of the situation.'

'I shall be sure to call upon you if I feel in need of your vast wisdom. I will mention your subordinate conduct in the despatches I shall write at the conclusion of the campaign. You are to remain in this camp. I shall not detach you on any independent mission. I shall not include you in the force that I shall lead to the relief of Khartoum. At the first opportunity you will be sent back to Cairo. You will take no further part in this campaign. Do I make myself clear, Captain?'

'Abundantly clear, sir.' Penrod saluted.

Wilson did not return his salute as he stamped away.

Over the days that followed, Wilson spent most of his time in his headquarters tent, busying himself with his despatches. He ordered an inventory of the remaining stores and ammunition. He inspected the fortifications of the zareba. He drilled the men. He visited the wounded daily, but General Stewart was no longer conscious. The steamers waited at their moorings with full heads of steam in their boilers. A mood of indecision and uncertainty descended on the regiment. Nobody knew what the next step would be, or when it would be taken. Sir Charles Wilson issued no orders of consequence.

On the evening of the third day Penrod went down to the camel lines and found Yakub. While he made a pretence of inspecting the animals, he whispered, 'Have the camels ready and the waterskins filled. The password for the sentries when you leave the zareba will be Waterloo. I will meet you at midnight by the little mosque on the far side of Metemma village.' Yakub looked at him askance. 'We have been ordered to take messages to Gordon Pasha.'

Yakub was at the rendezvous, and they set out southwards at a rate that would take them beyond pursuit by dawn.

Two days to Khartoum, Penrod thought grimly, and my career in ruins. Wilson will throw me to the lions. I hope Rebecca Benbrook appreciates my efforts on her behalf.

Osman Atalan, riding hard with a small group of his aggagiers, left the main body of his cavalry many leagues behind. He climbed up through the gut of the Shabluka Gorge. On the heights, he reined in al-Buq and leapt on to the saddle. Balancing easily on the restless horse, he trained his telescope on the City of the Elephant's Trunk, Khartoum, which lay on the horizon.

'What do you see, master?' al-Noor asked anxiously.

'The flags of the infidel and the Turk are flying on the tower of Fort Mukran. The enemy of God, Gordon Pasha, still prevails in Khartoum,' said Osman, and the words were bitter as the juice of the aloe on his tongue. He dropped back onto the saddle and his sandalled feet found the stirrups. He gave the stallion a cut across the rump with the kurbash, and al-Buq jumped forward. They rode on southwards.

When they reached the Kerreri Hills they met the first exodus of women and old men from Omdurman. The refugees did not recognize Osman with his black headcloth and unfamiliar mount, and an old man called to him as he cantered by, 'Turn back, stranger! The city is lost. The infidel has triumphed in a mighty battle at Abu Klea. Salida, Osman Atalan and all their armies have been slain.'

'Reverend old father, tell us what has become of the Divine and Victorious Muhammad, the Mahdi, the successor of Allah's Prophet.'

'He is the light of our eyes, but he has given the order for all his followers to leave Omdurman before the Turks and the infidels arrive. The Mahdi, may Allah continue to love and cherish him, will move into the desert with all his array. They say he purposes to march back to El Obeid.'

Osman threw back the headcloth that covered his face. 'See me, old man! Do you know who I am?'

The man stared at him, then let out a wail and fell to his knees. 'Forgive me, mighty Emir, that I pronounced you dead.'

'My army follows close behind me. We ride for Omdurman. The *jihad* continues! We will fight the infidel wherever we meet him. Tell this to all you meet upon the road.' Osman thumped his heels into al-Buq's flanks and galloped on.

He found the streets of Omdurman in turmoil. Heavily armed Ansar galloped down the narrow streets; wailing women were loading all their possessions on to donkey carts and camels; crowds hurried to the mosques to hear the imams preach the comforting word of Allah at this terrible time of defeat and despair. Osman scattered all before his horse, and rode on towards the mud-walled palace of the Mahdi

He found the Mahdi and Khalifa Abdullahi on the rooftop, under the reed sunscreen, attended by a dozen young women of the harem. He prostrated himself before the *angareb* on which the Mahdi sat cross-legged. He had agonized over his decision to ride for Omdurman and face the successor to the Prophet of Allah, rather than taking his aggagiers and disappearing into the eastern deserts of the Sudan. He knew that if he had taken that course the Mahdi would certainly have sent an army after him, but in his own territory he would prevail against even the largest and most skilfully led host. But to wage war on the Mahdi, the direct emissary of Allah on earth, would have meant the end of him as a Muslim. The risk of death he ran now was preferable to being declared by the Mahdi an unbeliever, and having the gates of Paradise closed to him through all eternity.

'There is only one God, and no other God but Allah,' he said softly, 'and Muhammad, the Mahdi, is the successor to his Prophet here on earth.'

'Look in my face, Osman Atalan,' said the Mahdi. Osman looked up at him. He was smiling, the sweet smile that showed the small, wedge-shaped gap between his front teeth. Osman knew, with the cold hand of death laid upon his heart, that this did not mean he was forgiven. The Mahdi was certainly infuriated by his failure to stop the relief column. It was necessary only for him to raise his hand and Osman would suffer death or mutilation. Often the Mahdi would offer the condemned man his choice. On the long ride up from Metemma Osman had decided that if the choice were offered him he would choose beheading, rather than the amputation of his hands and feet.

'Will you pray with me, Osman Atalan?' the Mahdi asked.

Osman's spirit quailed. This invitation was ominous, and often preceded the sentence of death. 'With all my heart and the last breath of my body,' Osman responded.

'We will recite together the *al-fatihah*, the first *sura* of the Noble Koran.'

Osman adopted the appropriate first prostration position, and they recited in unison: 'In the name of Allah, the Most Gracious, the Most Merciful,' then went on through the remaining four verses, ending, 'You alone we worship, and you alone we ask for help, for each and everything.' When they had finished, the Mahdi sat back and said, 'Osman Atalan, I placed great faith in you, and set a task for you.'

'You are the beat of my heart, and the breath in my lungs.' Osman thanked him.

'But you have failed me. You have allowed the infidel to triumph against you. You have delivered me up to mine enemy, and it is all finished.'

'Nay, my master. All is not finished. I have failed in this one thing, but not in all.'

'Explain your meaning.'

'Allah has told you that it will not be finished until a man brings you the head of Gordon Pasha. Allah told you that I, Osman Atalan, am that man.'

'You have not fulfilled that prophecy. Therefore you have failed your God as well as his prophet,' the Mahdi replied.

'The prophecy of God and Muhammad, the Mahdi, can never be brought to naught,' Osman replied quietly, feeling the breath of the dark angel upon his neck where the executioner's blow would fall. 'Your prophecy is a mighty rock in the river of time that cannot be washed away. I have returned to Omdurman to bring the prophecy to fruition.' He pointed across the river to the stark outline of Fort Mukran. 'Gordon Pasha still awaits his fate within those walls, and the time of Low Nile is upon us. I beseech you, give me your blessing, Holy One.'

The Mahdi sat silent and unmoving for a hundred of his rapid heartbeats while he thought swiftly. The Emir Osman was a clever man and an adroit tactician. To refuse his plea was to admit that he, Muhammad, the Mahdi, was fallible. At last he smiled and reached out to lay his hand on Osman's head. 'Go and do what is written. When you have fulfilled my prophecy, return to me here.'

An hour before midnight a small felucca lay in the eastern channel of the Victoria Nile. It was hove to against the night breeze and the current, with sail skilfully backed. Al-Noor sat beside Osman Atalan on the thwart. Both men watched the Khartoum bank. Tonight the rocket display was extravagant. Since the onset of darkness a continual succession of fireworks had soared into the sky and burst in cascades of multi-coloured sparks. The band was playing with renewed alacrity and verve, and at intervals they heard singing and laughter, carried faintly across the dark waters.

'Gordon Pasha has heard the news of Abu Klea,' al-Noor whispered. 'He and his minions rejoice in their heathen hearts. Hourly they expect the steamers to appear from the south.'

It was long after midnight before the sounds of celebration slowly subsided, and Osman gave a quiet order to the boatman. He let the lateen sail fill, and they felt their way in closer to the shore below the walls of Khartoum. When they reached a point opposite the maidan, al-Noor touched his master's arm and pointed at the tiny beach, now exposed by the retreating waters. The wet mud glittered like ice in the starlight. Osman spoke a quiet word to the boatman, who tacked and sailed in closer still. Osman moved up to the bows and used one of the punt poles to take soundings of the sloping bottom as they crept along the beach. Then they sat quietly, listening for the sentries doing their rounds, or other hostile movements. They heard nothing except the hoot of an owl in the bell tower of the Catholic mission. There was lamplight within the upper floor of the British consular palace which faced on to the river, and once they saw shadowy movement beyond the window casement, but then all was still.

'After their victory, the infidel is lulled. Gordon Pasha is not as vigilant as he was before,' al-Noor whispered.

'We have discovered the beach on which we can land. We can return to Omdurman now to make our preparations,' Osman agreed. He gave a quiet command to the boatman, and they headed back across the river.

When Osman and al-Noor reached his double storeyed house in the south quarter, which lay between the Beit el Mal, the treasury, and the slave market, dawn was breaking and a dozen of his aggagiers were sitting in the courtyard being fed by the house slaves a breakfast of honey-roasted lamb and dhurra cakes with steaming pots of syrupy black Abyssinian coffee. 'Noble lord, we arrived at dusk last night,' they told him.

'What kept you so long on the road?' he asked.

'We do not ride horses like al-Buq, who is the prince of all horses.'

'You are welcome.' Osman embraced them. 'I have more work for your blades. We must retrieve the honour that was stripped from us by the infidel on the plains of Abu Klea.'

David Benbrook insisted that he should host a victory party to celebrate the battle of Abu Klea, and the imminent arrival of the relief column in the city. Because of the paucity of food and drink, Rebecca decided on an al fresco dinner, rather than a formal display of silver and crystal in the dining room. They sat on folding canvas campaign chairs on the terrace overlooking the maidan, and listened to the military band, joining in with the better-known choruses. In the intervals, while the band regained their breath, they toasted the Queen, General Wolseley and, for the benefit of Consul Le Blanc, King Leopold.

After much inner communication with his conscience, David decided to bring up from the cellars the single case of Krug champagne that he had been hoarding all these months. 'A little premature perhaps, but once they arrive we will probably be too busy to think about it.'

This was the first time that General Gordon had accepted one of Rebecca's invitations to dinner and entertainment. He wore an immaculate dress uniform with a red fez. His boots were polished to a high gloss and the Egyptian Star of Ishmael glinted on his breast. He was in a relaxed, expansive mood, although Rebecca noticed the nervous tic below his eye. He nibbled a minute portion of the food on offer: green-cake, dhurra bread and cold roast bird of indeterminate species, which had been gunned down by the host. He chain-smoked his Turkish cigarettes, even when he stood to make a short speech. He assured the company that the steamers crammed with British troops were racing even at that hour up against the rapids of the Shabluka Gorge and that he confidently expected them to reach the city by the following evening. He commended the other guests and the entire populace, of every colour and nationality, for their heroic resistance and sacrifice, and gave thanks to Almighty God that their efforts had not been in vain. Then he thanked the consul and his daughters for their hospitality and took his leave. The mood of the remaining guests was at once much lighter.

The twins were given special dispensation to delay their bedtime until midnight, and were allowed a sherry glass of the precious champagne. Saffron quaffed hers like a sailor on shore leave, but Amber took a minute sip and made a face. When Rebecca was looking the other way, she poured the rest into her twin's glass, much to Saffron's glee.

Amber was becoming increasingly quiet and wan as the evening progressed. She took no part in the singing, which

Rebecca thought odd. Amber had a sweet, true voice and loved to sing. She refused when David asked her to dance the polka with him. 'You are so quiet and subdued. Are you feeling unwell, my darling?'

'A little, Daddy, but I do love you so much.'

'Would you like to go up to bed? I will give you a dose of salts. That will fix it.'

'Oh, no. Goodness me, no! It is not that bad.' Amber forced a smile, and David looked worried but did not pursue the matter. He went off to dance with Saffron instead.

Consul Le Blanc also noticed Amber's unusual behaviour. He came to sit beside her, held her hand in an avuncular manner and launched into a long, complicated joke about a German, an Englishman and an Irishman. When he reached the climax he doubled over with laughter and tears ran down his pink cheeks. Although she saw nothing funny in the story Amber laughed dutifully, but then stood up and went to Rebecca, who was dancing with Ryder Courtney. Amber whispered in her elder sister's ear, and Rebecca left Ryder, took the younger girl's hand and hurried indoors with her. David saw them leave and he and Saffron followed. When they reached the foot of the staircase, Rebecca and Amber were on the first landing above them.

'Where are you going?' David called after them. 'Is anything the matter?'

Still holding hands Rebecca and Amber turned to face him. Suddenly Amber groaned and doubled over. With an explosive rush of gas and liquid, her bowels started to empty. It poured out of her like a yellow waterfall, and went on and on, forming a deep, spreading puddle at her feet.

David was the first to recover his wits. 'Cholera!' he said.

At that dread word Saffron thrust the fingers of both hands into her mouth and screamed.

'Stop that!' Rebecca ordered, but her own voice was almost a scream. She tried to lift Amber, but the yellow discharge was still spurting out of her and splattered down the front of Rebecca's long satin evening dress.

Ryder had heard Saffron scream and ran in from the

terrace. He took in the scene almost instantly. He dashed back to where they had dined and swept the heavy damask cloth off the long table, sending silver candlesticks and table ornaments crashing to the floor. He raced up the stairs.

Amber was still voiding copiously. It seemed impossible that such a small body could contain so much liquid. It was running down the staircase in a rivulet. Ryder shook out the damask like a cape, and enfolded her in it, lifted her as though she were a doll and ran with her up the stairs.

'Please put me down, Ryder,' Amber begged. 'I will dirty your lovely new suit. I cannot stop myself. I am so ashamed.'

'You are a brave girl. There is nothing to be ashamed of,' Ryder told her. Rebecca was at his side. 'Where is the bathroom?' he asked her.

'This way.' She ran ahead and threw open the door.

Ryder carried Amber in and laid her in the galvanized bath. 'Get her soiled clothes off her and sponge her down with cool water,' he ordered. 'She is burning up. Then force her to drink. Weak warm tea. Gallons of it. She must keep drinking. She has to replace every drop of the fluid she has lost.' He looked at David and Saffron in the doorway. 'Call Nazeera to help you. She knows about this disease. I must go back to the *Ibis* to fetch my medical chest. While I am gone, you must keep her drinking.'

Ryder raced through the streets. He was fortunate that for this one night General Gordon had relaxed the curfew so that all the populace might celebrate the relief of the city.

Bacheet had stowed the medical chest in its usual place under his bunk in the main cabin of the *Ibis*. He rummaged through it swiftly, searching for what he needed to staunch Amber's diarrhoea and replace the mineral salts that she had lost. He knew he had little time. Cholera is a swift killer. 'The Death of the Dog,' they called it. It could kill a robust adult in hours, and Amber was a child. Already her body had been stripped of fluid. Soon every muscle and sinew would scream for liquid, terrible cramps would twist her, and she would die a desiccated husk.

For a dreadful moment he thought that the vital packets

of dirty white powder were missing, then remembered that he had moved them to the lockers in the galley for safety. In the cholera-torn city they were worth more than diamonds. The powder was packed in a woven sisal bag. There was enough to treat five or six cases. He had bought it at a usurious price from the abbot of a Coptic monastery deep in the gorge of the Blue Nile. The abbot had told him that the chalky powder was mined by his monks from a secret deposit tucked away in the mountains. Not only did it have a powerful binding effect on the bowels, it was also close in character and composition to those minerals purged from the human body by the disease. Ryder had been sceptical until Bacheet had been struck down with cholera, and Ryder had pulled him through with liberal doses of the powder.

He stuffed everything he needed into an empty dhurra sack and ran back to the consulate. When he climbed the stairs to the bathroom he found that Amber was still in the bath. She was naked, and Rebecca and Nazeera were sponging her from the basin of warm soapy water that Saffron held. David hovered ineffectually in the background holding a tin mug of warm black tea. The stench of vomit and faeces still hung heavily in the room, but Ryder was careful not to show disgust.

'Has she vomited?'

'Yes,' replied David, 'but only some of this tea. I don't think she has anything else inside her.'

'How much has she drunk?' Ryder demanded, as he snatched the mug from the other man's hand and poured a handful of the powder into it.

'Two mugs and a bit,' said David, proudly.

'Not enough,' Ryder snapped. 'Not nearly enough.'

'She won't take any more.'

'She will,' said Ryder. 'If she can't drink it, I will give it to her with an enema tube.' He carried the mug to the bath. 'Amber, did you hear what I said?' She nodded. 'You don't like enemas, do you?' She shook her head vehemently, and her sodden curls dangled in her eyes. 'Then drink!' He placed one hand behind her head and held the cup to her lips. She gulped it down painfully, then lay back gasping. Already wasted by prolonged starvation, her body was now dehydrated and skeletal. The change that had taken place in the hour he had been away was dramatic. Her legs were as thin as those of a bird, her ribs as distinct as the fingers of a hand. The skin on her sunken moon-pale belly seemed translucent so that he could see the network of blue veins under it.

Ryder poured another handful of powder into the mug, and filled it with warm tea from the kettle that stood close at hand. 'Drink!' he ordered, and she choked it down.

She was panting weakly, and her eyes had sunk into plum-coloured sockets. 'I have no clothes on. Please don't look at me, Ryder.'

He stripped off his moleskin jacket and covered her. 'I promise not to look at you if you promise to drink.' He refilled the mug and poured the powder into it. As she drank it, her belly bulged out like a balloon. The gases in it rumbled, but she did not void again. Ryder refilled the mug.

'I can't drink any more. Please don't make me,' she begged.

'Yes, you can. You made me a promise.'

She forced down that mug and another. Then there was a strong ammoniac odour and a yellow trickle of urine ran down the bottom of the bath to the plug-hole. 'You've made me wet myself like a baby.' She was weeping softly with shame.

'Good girl,' he said. 'That means you are making more water than you are losing. I am so proud of you.' He understood the trespasses he had already made on her modesty, so he stood up. 'But I am going to let Rebecca and Saffy look after you now. Don't forget your promise. You must keep drinking. I will wait outside.'

Before he left the bathroom he whispered to Rebecca, 'I think we may have beaten it. She is out of immediate danger. But the cramps will begin soon. Call me at the first sign. We will have to massage her limbs or the pain will become unbearable.' From his sack he handed her the bottle of coconut oil he had brought from the *Ibis*. 'Tell Nazeera to take this down to the kitchen and warm it to blood heat, no more than that. I will stay close.'

The other dinner guests had left hours ago, and everything was quiet. Ryder and David settled down to wait on the top step at the head of the staircase. They chatted in a desultory fashion. They discussed the news of the relief column, and argued about when the steamers would arrive. David agreed with Chinese Gordon's estimate, but Ryder did not: 'Gordon is always conservative with the truth. He says whatever suits his purpose best. I will believe in the steamers when they tie up in the harbour. In the meantime I will keep up steam in the *Ibis*.'

Out in the night an owl hooted mournfully, then again, and a third time. Restlessly David stood up and went to the window. He leant on the sill and looked down on the river

> 'When the midnight owl hoot thrice,
> To-wit-too-woo, with one breath,
> Then in a trice
> It heralds death.'

'That's superstitious nonsense,' said Ryder, 'and, what's more, it does not scan.'

'You are probably right,' David admitted. 'My nursemaid repeated it to me when I was five, but she was the wicked witch in person and loved to frighten us children.' Then he straightened up and peered down towards the riverbank. 'There's a boat out there, close in to the beach.'

Ryder went across to join him at the window. 'Where?'

'There! No, it's gone now. I swear it was a boat, a small felucca.'

'Probably a fisherman laying his nets.'

From the bathroom they heard Amber cry out in anguish. They rushed back to her. She was curled into a ball. The wasted muscles in her limbs were like whipcords as the spasms tightened them almost to snapping point. They lifted her out of the bath and laid her on the clean towels that Rebecca and Nazeera spread on the tiled floor.

Ryder rolled up his sleeves and knelt over her. Nazeera poured warm coconut oil into the cup of his hands and he began to massage Amber's twisted legs. He could feel the ropes and knots under the skin. 'Rebecca, take the other leg. Nazeera and Saffy, her arms,' he ordered. 'Do it this way.' While they worked, David dribbled more of the tea mixture into their patient's mouth. Rebecca watched Ryder's hands as he worked. They were broad and powerful, but gentle. Under them Amber's muscles gradually relaxed.

'It's not over yet,' Ryder warned them. 'There will be more. We must be ready to start again as the next spasms seize her.'

What depths there are to this man, Rebecca thought. What fascinating contradictions. Sometimes he is ruthlessly resourceful, at others he is filled with compassion and generosity of spirit. Would I not be foolish to let him go?

Before the hour was up the next cramps had locked Amber's limbs so they fell to work on her again, and were forced to keep it up through the rest of the night. Just before daybreak, when all were reaching their own limits of exhaustion, Amber's limbs gradually straightened and the knots softened and relaxed. Her head rolled to one side and she fell asleep.

'She has turned the corner,' Ryder whispered, 'but we must still take care of her. You must make her drink the powder mixture again as soon as she wakes. She must eat also. Perhaps you might feed her a porridge of dhurra and green-cake. I wish we had something more substantial, like chicken broth, but that is the best we can do. She will be weak as a newborn infant for days, perhaps weeks. But she has not scoured since midnight, so I hope and believe that the germs, as Joseph Lister is pleased to call the wee beasties that cause the trouble, have been purged from her.' He picked up his damp, soiled jacket from the floor. 'You know where to find me, Rebecca. If you send a message I will come at once.'

'I will see you to the door.' Rebecca stood up. As they went out into the passage, she took his arm. 'You are a warlock, Ryder. You've worked magic for us. I don't know how the Benbrook family can ever thank you.'

'Don't thank me, just say a prayer for old Abbot Michael who robbed me of fifty Maria Theresa dollars for a bag of chalk.'

At the door she reached up and kissed him, but when she felt his loins stir, she pulled away. 'You are a satyr as well as a warlock.' She managed a faint smile. 'But not now. We shall attend to that business at the first opportunity. Perhaps tomorrow after the relief force arrives, when we are all safe from the evil Dervish.'

'I will hold myself on a short rein,' he promised, 'but tell me, dearest Rebecca, have you given any further thought to my proposal?'

'I am sure you will agree, Ryder, that at this dire time in our lives, my first thoughts must be for Amber and the rest of my family, but each day my affection for you increases. When this dreadful business is over, I feel sure that we will have something of value to share, perhaps for the remainder of our days.'

'Then I shall live in hope.'

Osman Atalan picked out two thousand of his most trusted warriors for the final assault on Khartoum. He marched them out of Omdurman, making no effort to conceal his movements. From his roost on the parapets of Fort Mukran, Gordon Pasha would observe this exodus, and take it as another indication that the Mahdi was abandoning the city and fleeing with all his forces to El Obeid. Once his men were behind the Kerreri Hills, where they were concealed from the prying telescopes on the towers and minarets in Khartoum, Osman divided them into five battalions of roughly four hundred men.

A large assembly of boats on the Omdurman bank would warn Gordon Pasha that something was afoot. If he attempted to take such a large force across the river in a single wave, it would overcrowd the tiny landing beach below the maidan, and in the darkness create chaos and confusion. He decided to use only twenty boats for the crossing of the river, each vessel could carry twenty men safely. Once they had landed the first wave of four hundred men, the boats would return to the Omdurman bank to take on board the following battalions. The first wave of attackers would get off the beaches as soon as they could, and leave the way clear for the next. Osman estimated that he would be able to transport his entire force across the Nile in little more than an hour.

He knew his men so well that he gave simple orders to the sheikhs he placed in charge of each battalion, orders that they would not forget in the passion of battle and the heady excitement of looting the city.

Dervish spies within the city had drawn detailed maps of the exact layout of Gordon Pasha's defences. The Gatling guns were Osman's prime targets. The memory of his last encounter with those weapons was etched deeply on his mind. He wanted no recurrence of that slaughter. The first battalion ashore would go straight for them, and put them out of action.

Once the guns had been captured or destroyed, they could roll up the fortifications along the waterfront, then wipe out the Egyptian troops in the barracks and the arsenal. Only then would it be safe to turn his men loose on the populace.

The previous night Muhammad, the first Prophet of Allah, had visited Muhammad, the Mahdi, his successor. He had brought a message directly from Allah. It was decreed that the faith and devotion of the Ansar should be rewarded. Once they had delivered to the Mahdi the head of Gordon Pasha, they must be allowed to sack the city of Khartoum. For ten days the sack would be allowed to run unchecked. After that the city would be burned and all the principal buildings, particularly the churches, missions and consulates, would be demolished. All traces of the infidel must be eradicated from the land of Sudan.

At nightfall Osman marched his two thousand back from the Kerreri Hills to Omdurman. Across the river in the city of Khartoum, Gordon's nightly firework display and the recital of the military band were more subdued than they had been the previous evening. There was widespread disillusionment that the steamers had not yet arrived. When the rocket display fizzled out, and silence settled on the city, Osman led his first battalion down to the riverbank, where the twenty boats were moored. This small flotilla was an eclectic collection of feluccas and trading dhows. The crossing of the Nile through banks of river mist was conducted in an eerie silence. Osman was the first man to wade ashore. With al-Noor and a dozen of his trusty aggagiers close on his heels, he raced up the beach.

The surprise was total. The Egyptian sentries were sleeping complacently, in the certainty that dawn would show the steamers of the relief force anchored before the walls. There was no challenge, no shot or shouted warning, before Osman's aggagiers were into the first line of trenches. Their broadswords rose and fell in a dreadfully familiar rhythm. Within minutes the trenches were clear. The dead and wounded Egyptian troops lay in heaps. Osman and his aggagiers left them and raced for the arsenal. They had not reached it before the second battalion landed on the beach behind them.

Suddenly a rifle shot clapped on the silence, then another. There were shouts, and a bugle sounded the call to arms. Erratic and isolated gunfire built into a thunderous fusillade, and the ripples and echoes spread across the city as the startled Egyptians blazed away at shadows or cravenly fired into the air. Down near the little beach an *ombeya* howled and a war drum boomed as another battalion landed and rushed through the breach into the city.

'There is only one God and Muhammad, the Mahdi, is his prophet.' The war chant was carried through the city, and suddenly the streets and alleys were alive with running, struggling figures. Their screams and entreaties rose in a babble of terror and anguish like voices from the pit of hell.

'Mercy in the Name of Allah!'

'Quarter! Give us quarter!'

'The Dervish are within! Run! Run or die!'

All Gordon's famous forts and redoubts were sited to cover the river approaches. Taken in the rear they were swiftly overwhelmed. Osman's aggagiers massacred the stunned defenders in their trenches or hounded them through the streets and alleyways, rabbits before the wolf pack.

David was at his desk, working on his journal. He had kept it up to date faithfully throughout the ten long months that the city had been under siege. He knew that it was an invaluable document. With the promise of relief so near, it could only be a matter of weeks before he and his girls were aboard a P&O steamship on their way back to England. One of the first goals he had set himself on arrival was to work up his journal into a full-length manuscript. The public appetite for books of adventure and exploration in the Dark Continent seemed insatiable. Baker, Burton and Stanley had each made several thousands of pounds from their publications. Sam Baker had even received a knighthood from the Queen for his literary efforts. Surely David's own first-hand memoirs of the valiant defence of the city would please many, and his account of the bravery and suffering of his three girls would tear at the heartstrings of every lady reader. He hoped he might have the book ready for the publishers within a month of reaching England. He dipped the nib of his pen in to the silver inkwell, and wiped off the excess carefully. Then he stared dreamily into the flame of the lamp on the corner of his desk.

It might bring in fifty thousand. The thought warmed him. Dare I hope for a hundred thousand? He shook his head. Too much by far, I would settle happily for ten thousand. That would help immeasurably with re-establishing ourselves. Oh! It will be so good to be home again!

His musings were interrupted by the sound of a rifle shot. It was not far off, somewhere down by the maidan. He tossed down his pen, splattering the page with a blob of ink, and strode across his office to the window. Before he reached it there were more shots, a volley, a crackling storm of gunfire.

'My God! What is happening out there?' He threw open the window and stuck out his head. Close at hand a bugler played the shrill, urgent notes of 'stand to arms'. Almost immediately there came a faint but triumphant chorus of Arab voices: '*La ilaha illallah!* There is but one God!' For a brief moment he was rooted to the spot, too shocked to draw breath, then he gasped. 'They are in! The Dervish have broken into the city!'

He ran back to the desk and swept up his journal. It was too heavy to carry so he crammed it into the safe that was concealed behind the panelling of the back wall. He slammed the steel door and tumbled the combination of the lock, then closed the panelling that concealed it. His ceremonial sword was hanging on the wall behind his desk. It was not a fighting weapon and he was no swordsman, but he buckled it round his waist. Then he took the Webley revolver from his desk drawer and thrust it into his pocket. There was nothing else of value in the room. He ran out into the lobby and up the stairs to the bedrooms.

Rebecca had moved Amber into her own room so that she could care for her during the night. Nazeera was sleeping on an *angareb* in the far corner. Both women were awake, standing indecisively in the middle of the room.

'Get your clothes on at once!' he ordered. 'Dress Amber too. Don't waste a moment.'

'What is happening, Daddy?' Rebecca was confused.

'I think the Dervish have broken in. We must run to Gordon's headquarters. We should be safe there.'

'Amber cannot be moved. She is so weak it might kill her.'

'If the Dervish find her she will fare far worse,' he told her grimly. 'Get her up. I will carry her.' He turned to Nazeera. 'Run to Saffron's room, quick as you can. Get her dressed. Bring her here. We must leave immediately.'

Within minutes they were ready. David carried Amber, and the other women followed at his heels as he went down the stairs. Before they reached the bottom, there came the crash of breaking glass and splintering wooden panels from the main doors, and savage shouts of Arab voices.

'Find the women!'

'Kill the infidel!'

'This way,' David snapped, and they ran into the back rooms. Behind them came another thunderous clap of sound as the front door was torn from its hinges and fell inwards.

'Keep close to me!' David led them to the door into the courtyard. Gordon's headquarters were on the far side. He lifted the locking bar and pushed it open a crack. He peered out cautiously. 'The coast is clear, for the moment at least.'

'How is Amber bearing up?' Rebecca whispered anxiously.

'She is quiet,' David answered. Her body was as light as that of a captured bird. She did not move. She might already have been dead, but he could feel her heart beating under his hand, and once she whimpered softly.

Gordon's headquarters were only a hundred paces or so across the courtyard. The main gate at the opposite end was bolted. There were open staircases on the side walls leading up to the second store, where General Gordon had his private rooms. There was no sign of any Egyptian troops.

'Where is Gordon?' David asked, in consternation. It did not seem there was any shelter for them even in the general's stronghold. At that moment the main gates shook, and heavy blows resounded on the outside. A terrible chorus of Dervish war cries swelled the uproar. While David tried to make up his mind as to what he should do next, three Egyptian troopers emerged from the headquarters building and ran across the courtyard to the main gates. They were the first David had seen.

'Thank God! They are waking up at last!' he exclaimed, and was about to lead the women out through the door when, to his amazement, he saw the soldiers lifting the heavy locking bars. 'The craven bastards are surrendering, and letting in the Dervish without a fight,' he barked.

Now the soldiers shouted, 'We are faithful to the Divine Mahdi.'

'There is one God, and Muhammad, the Mahdi, is his prophet.'

'Enter, O ye faithful, and spare us, for we are your brothers in Allah.'

They swung open the gates and a horde of *jibba*-clad figures swarmed in. The first of the Dervish warriors chopped down the Egyptian traitors ruthlessly, and their bodies were trampled by the rush of hundreds of feet as the courtyard filled with the attackers. Many were carrying burning torches and the flick-ering yellow light of the flames lit up the horrific scene. David was about to shut and bolt the door before they were dis-covered, but at that moment a solitary figure appeared at the head of the stone staircase that overlooked the courtyard. Fascinated, David continued to peer through the chink.

General Charles Gordon was in full dress uniform. He prided himself on his ability to impress the savage and the barbarian. He had taken time to dress even when he heard the pandemonium in the streets. He wore his decorations but carried no weapon other than a light cane: he was fully aware of the danger of antagonizing the men he was trying to placate.

Calmly, the hypnotic gaze of those sapphire eyes glinting in the torchlight, he held up his hands to quell the uproar. To David this seemed futile but, astonishingly, an unnatural quiet descended on the courtyard. Gordon kept both arms raised, like a conductor controlling an unschooled orchestra. His voice was strong and unruffled, as he spoke good but heavily accented Arabic: 'I wish to speak to your master, the Mahdi,' he announced.

The listeners stirred like a field of dhurra when a breeze sweeps through it, but nobody answered him. His voice was sharper and more masterful when he spoke next – he had sensed he was taking control. 'Who among you is your leader? Let him step forward.'

A tall, strikingly handsome figure stepped from the mob. He wore the green turban of an emir, and mounted the first step of the staircase. 'I am the Emir Osman Atalan of the Beja, and these are my aggagiers.'

'I have heard of you,' Gordon said. 'Come up to me.'

'Gordon Pasha, you will give no more orders to any son of Islam, for this is the last day of your life.'

'Utter no threats, Emir Atalan. The thought of death troubles me not at all.'

'Then come down these stairs and meet it like a man, and not a cringing infidel dog.'

For another few seconds Chinese Gordon stared down at

him haughtily. Watching from the darkness of the doorway, David wondered what was going on in that cold, precise mind. Was there not, even now, a shadow of doubt or a flutter of fear? Gordon showed neither emotion as he started down the staircase. He stepped as precisely and confidently as if he were on a parade ground. He reached the step above Osman Atalan and stopped, facing him.

Osman studied his face, then said quietly, 'Yes, Gordon Pasha. I see you are indeed a brave man.' And he thrust the full length of his blade through Gordon's belly. In almost the same movement he drew it out again, and changed to a double-handed grip. The pale blue light in Gordon's eyes flickered like a candle flame in the wind, his cold granite features seemed to fall in upon themselves like melting beeswax. He struggled to remain upright, but the flame of his turbulent life was flickering out. Slowly his legs gave way under him. Osman waited for him with the sword poised. Gordon sagged forward from the waist and Osman swung his sword two-handed, aiming unerringly at the base of his neck. The blade made a sharp snick as it parted the vertebrae and Gordon's head fell away like the heavy fruit of the durian tree. It struck the stone stair with a solid thump, and rolled down to the courtyard. Osman stooped, took a handful of the thick curls and, ignoring the blood that splashed down the front of his *jibba*, held the head aloft to show it to his aggagiers. 'This head is our gift to the Divine Mahdi. The prophecy is fulfilled. The will and the word of Allah govern all of creation.'

A single abrupt roar went up to the night sky: 'God is great!' Then, in the silence that followed, Osman spoke again: 'You have made a gift to Muhammad, the Mahdi. Now he returns a gift to you. For ten days this city, all its treasures and the people in it are yours to deal with as you wish.'

David waited to hear no more, and while the full attention of the Dervish was on their emir, he closed and bolted the door. He gathered the women about him, settled Amber's head more comfortably against his shoulder and led them back through the scullery, past the pantries and the entrance to the wine cellars to the small door that led to the servants' quarters. As they hurried along they could hear behind them the crash of breaking furniture. The women looked up fearfully at the sound of running footsteps from the floor above as the Dervish rampaged through the palace. David struggled briefly with the servants' door before he could open it and lead them out into the night air.

They reached the entrance to the reeking sanitary lane that ran along the back wall of the palace. Along it stood stacks of the night-soil buckets. They had not been collected for months and the odour of excrement was overpowering. This was a place so unclean that any devout Muslim would avoid it assiduously so they could afford to pause for a few moments. While they regained their breath, they heard gunfire and shouting in the streets beyond the boundary wall, and in the palace they had just left.

'What shall we do now, Daddy?' Rebecca asked.

'I do not know,' David admitted. Amber groaned and he stroked her head. 'They are all around us. There does not seem to be any avenue of escape.'

'Ryder Courtney has his steamer ready in the canal. But we must go quickly, or he will set sail without us.'

'Which road to reach him is safest?' David's breathing was laboured.

'We must keep clear of the waterfront. The Dervish will certainly be looting the big houses along the corniche.'

'Yes – of course. You are right.'

'We must go through the native quarter.'

'Lead the way!' he said.

Rebecca grabbed Saffron's hand. 'Nazeera take the other.'

The women ran down the narrow alley between the buckets. David ploughed along heavily behind them. When they reached the far end of the lane Rebecca paused to make certain that the street ahead was empty. Then they ran to the next corner. Once more she checked the ground ahead. They went on like this, a stage at a time. Twice, Rebecca spotted groups of rampaging Dervish coming towards them, and was just quick enough to lead them down a side alley. Eventually they came out behind the rear of the Belgian consulate. Here they were forced to a halt to avoid another gang of Dervish, who were breaking into the building. They were using a pew from the Catholic cathedral as a battering ram. The tall carved doors gave way and the Dervish burst in.

Rebecca looked around for another escape route. Before she could find one the aggagiers dragged the portly figure of Consul Le Blanc through the shattered doors into the street. He was squealing like a piglet on its way to the abattoir. Although he fought and struggled, he was no match for the lean and sinewy warriors. They pinned him down on his back in the middle of the road, and ripped off his clothing. When he was naked one knelt beside him with a drawn dagger. He took a handful of Le Blanc's hairy scrotum, and stretched it out as though it was india-rubber. With one stroke of the dagger he sliced it away, leaving a gaping hole in the base of the pale, pendulous belly. Roaring with laughter the men who held him forced Le Blanc's jaws open with the handles of their daggers and stuffed his testicles into his mouth, gagging his shrieks. Then they completed the ritual mutilation by lopping off his hands and feet at wrists and ankles. When they were finished with him, they left him writhing on the ground, and rushed back into the consulate building to join the pillage. Le Blanc struggled up and sat like some grotesque statue of Buddha, clumsily trying to remove the flaccid sack of his scrotum from his mouth with his bleeding stumps.

'Sweet Jesus, how horrible!' Rebecca's voice was husky with pity. 'Poor Monsieur!' She started to go to his aid.

'Don't! They will have you also.' David's voice was choked not so much with pity, as with the brutal effort of running so far with Amber in his arms. 'There is nothing we can do for him. We can try only to save ourselves. Becky darling, we must keep going. Don't look back.'

They ducked down another alley, forced ever deeper into the warren of huts and hovels of the native quarter and further off the direct route to Ryder Courtney's compound.

After another few hundred yards David came up short, like an old stag run to a standstill by the hounds. His face was twisted with pain and sweat dripped from his chin.

'Daddy, are you all right?' Rebecca had turned back to him.

'Just a little winded,' he gasped. 'Not as young as I once was. Just give me a moment to get my breath back.'

'Let me take Amber from you.'

'No! Little mite that she is, she is still too heavy for you. I will be all right in a few seconds.' He sank to the ground, still holding Amber tenderly to his chest. The other three women waited with him, but every time there was another outburst of gunfire or shouting they gazed around fearfully and huddled closer together. From the direction of the Belgian consulate, flames towered into the sky, and illuminated the surroundings with a yellow, flickering light. David heaved himself back to his feet, and stood swaying. 'We can go on now,' he said.

'Please, let me take Amber.'

'Don't be silly, Becky. I am perfectly all right. Go on!'

She peered closely at his face. It was pale and shining with sweat, but she knew that to argue with him would be a dangerous waste of time. She took his arm to steady him and they went on, but their pace was slower now.

After another short distance David had to stop again. 'How far to where the *Ibis* is moored now?'

'Not far,' she lied. 'Just beyond that little mosque at the end of the road. You can do it.'

'Of course I can.' He staggered forward again. Then, from behind, they heard a shout and the baying of Arab voices. They looked back. There was another pack of Dervish down the road behind them, at least two dozen, brandishing their weapons and hooting with wild excitement as they saw the women.

Rebecca dragged David to the corner of the nearest building. For a moment they were out of sight of their pursuers. David leant heavily against the wall. 'I can't go any further.' He handed Amber to Rebecca. 'Take her!' he ordered. 'Take the others with you and run. I will hold them here while you get away.'

'I cannot leave you,' said Rebecca, staunchly. Her father tried to argue but she ignored him and turned to Nazeera. 'Take Saffron and run. Don't look back! Run for the boat.'

'I'll stay with you, Becky,' Saffron cried.

'If you love me, you will do as I say,' Rebecca told her.

'I love you, but—'

'Go!' Rebecca insisted.

'Please, Saffy, do as she says.' David's voice was rough with pain. 'For my sake.'

Saffron hesitated only a moment longer. 'I will always love you, Daddy, and Becky and Amber,' she said, and grabbed Nazeera's hand. The two dived down the alley. David and Rebecca turned back to face the Dervish as they poured round the corner. Their *jibbas* and the blades of their swords were wet with blood, their faces were mad with blood lust. David drew his sword. He pushed Rebecca and Amber behind him to protect them.

The Dervish formed a half-circle facing him, just out of reach of his sword. One darted forward and feinted at his head. When David slashed back at him he shouted with laughter and jumped away. David tottered unsteadily after him. The others joined in the sport. They baited him, just out of reach of his blade, forcing him to turn from one side to the other.

While the others kept him in play, one circled and came up behind Rebecca. He seized her round the waist with one arm, and with the other hand pulled up her skirts. She was naked below the waist and the other Arabs roared with approval, as their comrade butted his hips against her buttocks in a copulatory display. Rebecca shrieked with outrage and tried to break away but she was hampered with Amber in her arms. David staggered back to try to protect them.

The Dervish released Rebecca. 'We will all mount her like that and she will bear us twenty fine Muslim sons.' He laughed and leered.

David was maddened by the pain in his chest and the taunts they shouted at him. He charged again and again, but they were swift and nimble. Blinded by his own sweat, and crippled by the pain that was building swiftly in his chest, the sword slipped from his hand at last and he sank to his knees in the dirt. His face was swollen and contorted, his mouth was open and he gulped like a stranded fish. One of the aggagiers stepped up behind him and, with a surgeon's skill, sliced off one of his ears. Blood poured down his shirt but David did not seem to feel the pain.

Rebecca was still holding Amber, but she rushed to her father and knelt beside him. She placed an arm round his shoulders. 'Please!' she said in Arabic. 'He is my father. Please spare him.' The blood from David's wound sprinkled them both.

The Dervish laughed. 'Please spare him!' they mimicked her. One grabbed a handful of her hair, and dragged her away. He threw her full length in the dust.

She sat up, holding Amber in her lap. She was weeping wildly. 'Leave him alone!' she sobbed.

With a shaking hand David reached into the pocket of his jacket and drew out the Webley. He waved it in vague circles. 'Stand back or I shall fire.'

The aggagier who had cut off his ear stepped in again, and with another quick, controlled cut lopped off David's outstretched hand at the wrist. 'Spare us, O mighty infidel, for we are in great terror of you,' he jeered. David stared at his severed wrist from which spurted a jet of arterial blood.

Rebecca cried out, 'Oh, what have they done to you?'

David clutched the stump to his chest with the other hand, then bowed his head over it, in an attitude of devout prayer. The Arab swordsman stepped up to him again and lightly touched the back of his neck with the blade, measuring the distance for a clean blow. Rebecca shrieked with despair as he lifted the sword, then swung back into the stroke. It cut through David's neck without sound or check, and his head dropped free of his shoulders. His headless body collapsed and his legs kicked in a brief convulsive jig.

The Arab picked up the head, holding it by a handful of its grey hair. He came to where Rebecca crouched and thrust her father's head into her face. 'If he is your father, then kiss him farewell before he goes down to boil in the waters of hell through all eternity.'

Although Rebecca was sobbing hysterically she tried to cover Amber's eyes with one hand and keep her face averted. But Amber twisted back, and screamed as she looked into her father's face. The tip of David's tongue protruded between slack lips, and his eyes were open, but blank and sightless.

At last the Dervish lost interest in such mild sport. He threw aside the head, and wiped his bloody hands on Rebecca's bodice. Then, through the cloth, he pinched and twisted her nipples, laughing when she cried out at the pain. 'Take them!' he ordered. 'Take these two filthy infidel whores to the pen. They will be taught to serve the needs and pleasures of their new masters.'

They pulled Rebecca to her feet, still with Amber in her arms, and dragged her away towards the waterfront.

Saffron crouched in the angle of one of the ruined shacks. Nazeera was beside her as they stared back down the alley and watched the Dervish tormenting her father and Rebecca. Saffron was too shocked to speak or weep. When the executioner stepped up to David and held the sword over him she covered her mouth with both hands to prevent herself uttering a sound that might betray them but she could not tear her gaze away from the harrowing sight. When the Dervish made the fatal stroke and her father's corpse fell forward, Saffron was at last released from the spell. She began to sob silently.

She watched them tormenting Amber with their father's head, and could not control her tears. When at last they dragged Rebecca and Amber towards the waterfront, Saffron jumped to her feet and took Nazeera's hand. The two ran on towards Ryder Courtney's compound.

Dawn was breaking when they reached it, and the light was growing stronger. The gates of the outer compound stood wide and the buildings were deserted. The Dervish had not yet spread out from the centre of the town as far as this.

They ran on across the inner courtyard. Saffron paused long enough to peer through the open door of the blockhouse. It was empty, stripped of every item of value. 'We are too late! Ryder has gone!' she cried to Nazeera. With a despairing heart she ran on towards the canal gates. They were closed but unbarred. It required their combined efforts to push them open. Saffron was the first through. Then she stopped abruptly. The *Intrepid Ibis*'s mooring was empty, and the steamer was gone.

'Where are you, Ryder? Where have you gone? Why have you left me?' She gasped for breath and fought back the dark waves of panic. Once she had gathered herself, she turned and raced along the canal towpath towards its juncture with the Blue Nile. She had not covered more than half the way to the first bend in the canal before she smelt the woodsmoke from the *Ibis*'s funnel. 'He can't be too far ahead,' she told herself, and her spirits soared. She pulled quickly ahead of Nazeera, who was struggling to keep pace with her. When she reached the first bend in the canal and came round it she screamed at the top of her voice, 'Wait for me! I am coming. Wait for me, Ryder!' The *Ibis* was two hundred yards ahead. She was puffing away down the channel towards the open river. Saffron summoned every last ounce of strength, and raced after it. The little steamer was not yet under full power, but was easing her way carefully down the shallow, winding canal. With this last burst of speed Saffron began to overhaul it.

'Wait! Ryder, wait!' In the glowing sparks from the smoke stack she could just make out Ryder's dark figure in the angle of his bridge, but he was looking ahead. The pumping steam cylinders drowned her voice.

'Ryder!' she screamed. 'Oh, please, look round.' Then she saved her breath and ran with all her heart. Ahead of her the *Ibis* reached the entrance to the river, and increased her speed, pulling out into the stream of the Nile current. Saffron came up short on the edge of the bank. She cried out again, danced up and down and waved both hands over her head. The *Ibis* drew away rapidly into the softly swirling banks of silver mist that hung low on the water. Saffron dropped her arms and stood still. Nazeera came up beside her and the two hugged each other in despair. Suddenly a rifle shot rang out on the towpath behind them. They spun round and saw four Dervish running towards them. One halted and levelled his rifle. He fired another shot. The bullet kicked dust from the towpath at their feet and ricocheted across the river. Saffron turned back towards the rapidly departing shape of the *Ibis*.

The rifle shot had alerted Ryder and he was staring back at them. Saffron was lifted on a new wave of hope: she shrieked again and waved her arms. Then Ryder was bringing the little steamer round in a tight circle, and heading towards them. She looked back at the Dervish. All four were running towards her in a bunch. She saw at once that they would be upon her before the *Ibis* could reach the entrance to the canal.

'Come!' she called to Nazeera. 'We must swim.'

'No!' Nazeera shook her head. 'Al-Sakhawi will take care of you. I must go back to look after my other girls.' Saffron would have argued, even though the pursuers were closing in swiftly, but Nazeera forestalled her protests and ducked off the towpath. She disappeared into the swamp reeds that grew along the verge.

'Nazeera!' Saffron shouted after her, but the yells of the Dervish were louder still. She pulled off her shoes, tucked up her skirts and ran to the edge of the canal. She drew a deep breath and dived in. When her head broke the surface she launched out towards the approaching steamer in a determined dog-paddle.

'Good girl!' She heard Ryder's voice and kicked wildly with both legs, pulling at the water with her cupped hands. Behind her she heard another shot and a bullet kicked up a fountain that showered her head and ran into her eyes.

'Come on, Saffy.' Ryder was leaning over the side of the steamer, ready to grab her. 'Keep swimming.' At last she felt the current catch her and push her faster. Then she saw his face above her and reached up to him.

'Got you!' Ryder said. With a single heave he plucked her out of the river, as though she was a drowning kitten, and swung her up on to the deck. Then he shouted to Bacheet, 'Take her out again.'

Bacheet spun the wheel and the deck canted over into the turn. Once more they headed out into mid-stream. The Dervish was still firing at them from the towpath, but swiftly the river mist closed around them, and although the bullets still splashed about them or pinged off the steel superstructure the man had lost sight of them. At last the gunfire petered out.

'What happened to you, Saffy?' Ryder carried her down the deck to the cabin. 'Where are the others? Where are Rebecca and Amber, and your father?'

She tried to stop herself blubbering at his questions and put her arms round his neck, 'It's just too horrid to say, Ryder. Terrible things have happened. The very worst things ever.'

He sat her on his bunk in the cabin. Her distress touched him and he wanted to give her a few moments to recover. He handed her a dry but grubby towel. 'Very well. We'll get you tidied up first. Then you can tell me about it.' He pulled a faded blue shirt off the clothes-line above the bunk. 'Hang your dress up there. Put this shirt on when you're dry, and come to the bridge. We can talk up there.'

The tails of his shirt reached below her knees. It served well enough as a loose shift. She found one of Ryder's neckties in the drawer under the bunk, and tied it round her waist as a belt. She used his tortoiseshell comb to tidy her damp hair, then twisted it into a single pig-tail. A few minutes later, she went up to the bridge. Her eyes were pink and swollen with grief. 'They have killed my father,' she said hopelessly, and ran to Ryder.

He caught her up and hugged her hard. 'It can't be true. Are you sure, Saffy?'

'I saw it. They cut off his head, just like they did to General Gordon. Then they took Rebecca and Amber away.'

She fought back another sob. 'Oh, I hate them. Why are they so cruel?'

Ryder lifted her up and sat her on the coaming of the engine-room hatch. He kept one arm round her. 'Tell me everything, Saffy, every detail.'

Jock McCrump heard her voice and came up from the boiler room. He and Ryder listened in silence to her account. By the time she had finished, the top rim of the sun was showing above the horizon, and the river mist was burning off. The city was slowly revealed in all its stark detail. Ryder counted eight burning buildings, including the Belgian consulate. Thick smoke drifted across the river.

Then he turned his telescope on the square silhouette of Mukran Fort. The flags had been pulled down and the flagstaff was as bare as a gallows. Slowly he panned his lens across the rest of the city. Crowds of the faithful were dancing through the streets, and crowding the corniche in their brightly patched *jibbas*. There were outbursts of gunfire, black powder smoke spurting into the air, salvoes of *feu de joie* from the victors. Many were carrying bundles of loot. Others were rounding up the survivors of the attack. Ryder picked out small groups of women prisoners being herded towards the Customs House.

'What colour dress was Rebecca wearing?' he asked Saffron, without lowering the glass. He did not wish to look upon her anguish.

'Blue bodice, with yellow skirts.' Although he stared until his eye ached, he could not pick out a blue and yellow dress, or a head of golden hair among the captive women. But they were far off, and the smoke from the burning buildings and the dust from all the wild activity ashore confused the scene.

'Where will they take the women, Bacheet?' he demanded.

'They will pen them up like heifers in the cattle market until first the Mahdi, then the *khalifa* and the emirs have time to look them over and take their pick.'

'Rebecca and Amber?' he asked. 'What will happen to them?'

'With their yellow hair and white skin they are a great prize,' Bacheet answered. 'They will certainly be selected by the Mahdi. They will go to him as prime concubines.'

Ryder lowered the telescope. He felt sick. He thought of Rebecca, whom he loved and had hoped to make his wife, reduced to a plaything for that murderous fanatic. The thought was too painful to bear, and he forced it to the back of his mind. Instead he thought of sweet little Amber, whom he had nursed and saved from cholera. He had a vivid image of her pale childish body, the same body he had massaged back to life, being mounted and violated, sweet flesh torn and alien seed flooding her immature loins. He felt vomit rising to the back of his throat.

'Take us in closer to the shore,' he ordered Bacheet. 'I must see where they are so I can plan a rescue.'

'Only Allah can save them now,' said Bacheet softly. Saffron overheard, and fresh tears oozed down her cheeks.

'Damn you, Bacheet, do as I say,' Ryder snarled.

Bacheet turned across the current and they eased in towards the city waterfront. At first they attracted little attention from the shore. The Dervish were too preoccupied with the sack of the city. An occasional shot was fired in their direction, but that was all. They steamed downstream as far as the confluence of the two great rivers, then turned back, cruising in close to the Khartoum waterfront. Suddenly there was the boom of a cannon shot, and a Krupps shell burst the surface ahead of the bows. The spray flew back across the deck. Ryder saw the gun smoke on the harbour wall. The Dervish had turned the captured guns on them. Another Krupps in the redoubt below the maidan came into action and the shell screeched over the bridge and burst in the middle of the river.

'We are not doing much good here, except giving them artillery practice.' Ryder glanced at Bacheet. 'Turn back into mid-stream and head on upriver. We'll find a quiet place to anchor until we can gather more news and find out what they have done with Rebecca and Amber. Then I can plan more sensibly for their rescue.'

For miles up the Blue Nile both banks were deserted. Ryder headed for the Lagoon of the Little Fish in which he had transhipped the cargo of dhurra from Ras Hailu's dhow, When he reached it he anchored in a stand of papyrus, which hid the *Ibis* from curious eyes on the shore.

As soon as they had made everything onboard shipshape, he called Bacheet to the engine room where they could talk without being overheard by the rest of the crew. He wasted no time but put it to Bacheet straight and unadorned.

'Do you think you would be able to go back among the Dervish and discover what has become of al-Jamal and al-Zahra without arousing the suspicions of the Ansar?'

Bacheet pursed his lips and puffed out his cheeks, which made him look like a ground squirrel. 'I am as they are. Why should they suspect me?'

'Are you willing to do it?'

'I am not a coward, but neither am I a rash man. Why would I be willing to do something as stupid as that? No, al-Sakhawi. I would not be willing. I would be extremely reluctant.' He tugged unhappily at his beard. 'I will leave at once.'

'Good,' Ryder said. 'I will wait for you here, unless I am discovered, in which case I will wait for you at the confluence of the Sarwad river. You will go into the city and, if necessary, cross to Omdurman. When you have news for me, you will return to give it to me here.'

Bacheet sighed theatrically and went to his own tiny berth in the forecastle. When he emerged he was dressed in a Dervish *jibba*. Ryder refrained from asking where he had obtained it. Bacheet dropped over the side of the *Ibis* and waded to dry ground. He set off along the bank towards Khartoum.

On the waterfront Nazeera mingled unobtrusively with the milling crowds. There were as many Dervish women as men in the throng, and she was no different from them in her black ankle-length robes and the headcloth covering half of her face. The other women had come across from Omdurman as soon as they had heard that the city had been taken. They had come for the excitement of the triumphal celebrations, the loot, and for the thrill of the executions and torture that must surely follow the victory. The wealthy citizens of Khartoum would be forced to reveal the hiding-places of their valuables, their gold, jewellery and coin. Obtaining information was a skill that the Dervish women had learnt from their own mothers and honed to a high art.

Nazeera was part of the jostling, cavorting, ululating river of humanity that flowed along the corniche above the river. Ahead the crowd parted to allow a line of chained Egyptian soldiers through. They had been stripped of their tunics, then beaten until their bare backs looked as though they had been savaged by angry lions. The blood from the whip weals soaked their breeches and dripped down their legs. As they shuffled past on their way to the beach, the women rushed forward to beat them again with any weapon that came to hand. The Dervish guards chuckled indulgently at the women's antics, and when a prisoner fell under the blows they prodded him to his feet again with a sword point.

Although Nazeera was desperate to find where her charges had been taken, she was trapped in the mass of women. She could see down on to the beach where lines of rickety gallows of roughly trimmed poles were being hastily erected. Those that had been completed were already buckling under the weight of the bodies that dangled from them, and more captives were being dragged forward with nooses round their necks. In groups they were prodded by the executioners on to the *angarebs* placed as steps beneath the gallows. When the nooses had been fastened to the crosspiece the *angareb* was pulled away and the victims were left swinging and kicking in the air.

This was slow work, and further along the beach another gang of executioners was hastening the business with the sword. They forced their victims to kneel in long lines with their hands tied behind their backs, their necks stretched forward. Then two headsmen started at opposite ends of the line and moved slowly towards each other, lopping off heads as they went. The watchers shouted as each head fell into the mud. When one of the executioners, his sword-arm tiring from the work, missed his stroke and only partially severed his victim's neck they clapped and hooted derisively.

At last Nazeera extricated herself from the press of bodies and made her way towards the British consular palace. The gates were open and unguarded. She slipped through them into the grounds. The palace was extensively damaged, window-panes smashed and doors torn off. Most of the furniture had been thrown out of the upper-floor windows. She went stealth-ily to the front terrace, and found more devastation. Terrified that she might run into a looter she crept in through the french windows and made her way through the wreckage to David Benbrook's study. Papers and documents were strewn across the room.

However, the oak panelling on the walls was intact. She went quickly to one panel and pressed the hidden spring built into the carving of the architrave. With a soft click it jumped back to reveal the door of the large safe. Her father had allowed Rebecca to keep her jewellery there, and Rebecca had taught Nazeera how to tumble the combination so that she could fetch and return the pieces she needed. The com-bination numbers were Rebecca's birthdate. Now Nazeera fed them into the lock, turned the handle and swung open the door.

On the top shelf lay David's leatherbound journal. The lower shelves were filled with family valuables, including the jewellery that Rebecca had inherited from her mother. It was all packed into matching red-leather wallets. There were also a number of canvas money-bags, which held over a hundred pounds in gold and silver coins. It was too dangerous to carry all of this with her. Nazeera returned all of the jewellery and most of the cash to the safe, then relocked the door and closed the secret panel. This would be her secret bank when she needed money. She placed a few small coins in her sleeve pocket for immediate use, then lifted her robe and strapped a canvas bag with more round her waist, then smoothed her shapeless skirts over it.

She left the study and climbed the stairs to the second floor. She went to Rebecca's bedroom, and stopped involuntarily in the doorway as she saw the extent of the damage. The looters had smashed every stick of furniture, and scattered books and clothing across the floor. She went in and searched through the mess.

She was almost in despair when at last she spotted the sisal bag lying under the overturned bed. The drawstring had burst open and much of the cholera remedy had spilled out. Nazeera squatted, scooped it up and poured it back into the bag. When she had salvaged as much as she could, she knotted the drawstring securely and tied it round her neck so that it hung down inside her robe. She gathered up a few other feminine trifles that might be useful and hid them about her person.

She went back downstairs, and stole out of the palace. She left the gardens through the small gate at the end of the terrace and lost herself in the Dervish victory celebrations. It did not take her long to discover where the women prisoners had been taken: the news was being shouted in the streets and people were flocking to the Customs House. Many had climbed up the walls and were clustered at the windows to peer in at the captives. Nazeera tucked up her skirts and scrambled up one of the buttresses until she reached the highest row of barred windows. She elbowed two small urchins out of her way. When they protested she unleashed a torrent of abuse that sent them scampering off. Then she gripped the bars and pressed her face to the square opening.

It took a minute for her eyes to adjust to the dim light inside. The Egyptian women prisoners were the wives and daughters of Gordon Pasha's officers, who were probably now lying headless on the river beach or dangling from the gallows. The women were squatting in miserable groups, with their children huddled around them. Many were spattered with the dried blood of their murdered menfolk. Among them were a few white women, the nuns from the Catholic mission, an Austrian lady doctor, the wives of the few Occidental traders and travellers who had been trapped in the city.

Then Nazeera's heart bounded: she had spotted Rebecca sitting on the stone floor with her back against the wall and Amber on her lap. She was bedraggled and filthy with dust and soot. Her hair was lank and matted with sweat. Her father's blood had dried in black stains down the front of her yellow skirt. Her feet were bare and dusty, scratched and bruised. She sat aloof from the others, trying to fight off the waves of despair that threatened to overwhelm her. Nazeera recognized the stoic expression that concealed her courageous spirit, and was proud of her.

'Jamal!' Nazeera called to her, but her voice did not carry. The other women and their brats were making a fearful racket. They were weeping and wailing for their murdered menfolk, praying aloud for succour, entreating their captors for mercy. Above all else they were calling for water.

'Water! In the Name of Allah, give us water. Our children are dying. Give us water!'

'Jamal, my beautiful one!' Nazeera screamed to her, but Rebecca did not look up. She went on rocking Amber in her arms.

Nazeera broke a chip of plaster from the rotten windowsill, and threw it down through the bars. It struck the ground just short of where Rebecca was sitting, but skidded across the stone flags and hit her ankle. She lifted her head and looked around.

'Jamal, my little girl!'

Rebecca raised her eyes. She stared at the head in the window high above her, and her eyes flew wide in recognition. She looked around her quickly, to make certain that the Dervish guards at the doors had noticed nothing. Then she stood up and crossed the floor slowly, carrying Amber, until she stood directly under the high window. She looked up again, and mouthed a single word: '*Mayya!* Water!' She lifted Amber's face and touched her chapped, swollen lips. 'Water!' she said again.

Nazeera nodded and climbed down the wall. She pushed her way through the crowds, searching frantically until she found the old woman with the donkey she had noticed earlier. The animal was so heavily laden with waterskins and bags of dhurra bread that its legs splayed outwards. The old woman was doing a thriving business with the hungry and thirsty crowds along the waterfront.

'I wish to buy food and one of your skins, old mother.'

'I still have a little bread and dried meat to sell, and for three *pice* you may drink your fill, but I will never sell one of my waterskins,' said the woman firmly. She changed her mind when Nazeera showed her a silver dollar.

With the small waterskin slung over her shoulder, Nazeera hurried back to the front entrance of the Customs House. There were five guards at the main door. They stood with drawn swords, holding the curious throng at a respectful distance. Nazeera saw at a glance that they were all men of her tribe, the Beja. Then, with a twinge of excitement, she recognized one. He was of the same clan and had been circumcised at the same time as her dead husband. They had ridden beneath the banner of the Emir Osman Atalan, before the rise of the Mahdi when their world had been sane and sensible, not yet maddened by the new fanaticism.

She sidled closer to the doors, but the man she knew made a threatening gesture with his sword, warning her to come no closer.

'Ali Wad!' Nazeera called in a low tone. 'My husband rode with you on the famous raid to Gondar when you slew fifty-five Christian Abyssinians and captured two hundred and fifty fine camels.'

He lowered the sword and stared at her in astonishment. 'What is your husband's name, woman!' he demanded.

'His name was Taher Sherif, and he was killed by the Jaalin at Tushkit Wells. You were with him the day he died.'

412

'Then you are the Nazeera who was once reckoned beautiful.' His stern expression relaxed.

Her old feelings of affection for him stirred. 'When we were all young together,' she agreed, and lowered the head-cloth so he could see her face. 'It seems to me, Ali Wad, that you have become a man of great power. One who could still light the flame in any woman's belly.'

He laughed. 'Nazeera of the silvery tongue. The years have changed you little. What is it you seek from me now?' She told him and his smile faded. The scowl reappeared. 'You ask me to risk my life.'

'As my husband gave his life for you . . . and as, once, his young widow risked more than her life for your pleasure. Have you forgotten?'

'I have not. Ali Wad does not forget his friends. Come with me.'

He led her in through the main door, and the guards within deferred to him respectfully. She followed him, and Rebecca ran to her. They embraced ecstatically and tearfully. Even in her extremity Amber recognized her and whispered to her, 'I love you, Nazeera. Do you still love me?'

'With all my heart, Zahra. I have brought water and food.' She led them to a corner of the hall and they huddled close together. Nazeera mixed some of the powder with water in the mug she had brought from the palace. She held it to Amber's lips. She drank greedily.

While this was going on Ali Wad glowered at the other prisoners. 'These three women,' he indicated Nazeera and her charges, 'are under my protection. Interfere with them at your peril, for I am a man of ugly moods. It gives me great pleasure to beat women with this kurbash.' He showed them the wicked hippo-hide whip. 'I love to hear them squeal.'

They cringed away from him fearfully. Then he stooped and whispered in Nazeera's ear. She cast down her eyes and giggled coquettishly. Ali Wad stalked back to his post at the door, grinning and stroking his beard.

The water revived Amber miraculously. 'What has happened to my sister?' she whispered, 'Where is Saffy?'

'She is safe with al-Sakhawi,' Nazeera assured her. 'I saw her go on board his steamer before I returned to you.' At this wonderful news Rebecca was too overcome with relief to speak. Instead she threw her arms round Nazeera and hugged her.

'You must stop weeping now, Jamal,' Nazeera told her sternly. 'We must all be clever, strong and careful, if we are to survive the difficult days that lie ahead.'

'Now that you are back with us, and I know Saffy is safe, I can face whatever comes. What will the Dervish do with us?'

Nazeera did not answer at once but glanced significantly at Amber. 'First you must eat and drink to remain strong. Then we shall talk.'

She gave them a little of the dhurra bread. Amber managed a few mouthfuls, and kept them down. Nazeera nodded with satisfaction, and took her on to her own lap to allow Rebecca a chance to eat and rest. She stroked Amber's hair and crooned softly to her. The child fell asleep almost at once. 'She will be well again within days. Young ones have the most resilience.'

'What will happen to us?' Rebecca repeated her question.

Nazeera pursed her lips as she considered how much she should say. As much of the truth as is good for her, she decided. 'You and all these women are part of the spoils of war, as much as horses and camels.' Rebecca glanced at the sorry creatures around her, and felt momentary pity for them, until she remembered that she and Amber were in the same predicament. 'The Dervish will use them as they wish. The old and ugly will become house and kitchen slaves. The young and nubile will be used as concubines. You are young and surpassingly beautiful. Your hair and pale skin will intrigue all men.'

Rebecca shuddered. She had never imagined what it might be like to fall under the power of a man of different race. Now the thought sickened her. 'Will they draw lots for us?' She had read in Gibbon's *Decline and Fall of the Roman Empire* that that was what soldiers did.

'No. The Dervish leaders will select those they want. The

Mahdi will choose first, then the others in order of their rank and power. The Mahdi will choose you, there is no doubt of that. And it is good. He is the best for us, far better than any of the others.'

'Tell me why. Explain this to me. How can you know what he is like in his *zenana*?'

'He already has over three hundred wives and concubines, and his women talk. It is widely known where his tastes lie, what he likes to do with his women.'

Rebecca looked puzzled, 'Don't all men do the same thing, like—'

She broke off, but Nazeera finished the question for her: 'You mean the same as Abadan Riji and al-Sakhawi have done to you?'

Rebecca blushed scarlet. 'I forbid you to speak to me like that ever again.'

'I shall try to remember,' Nazeera replied, with a twinkle in her eye, 'but the answer to your question is that some men want different things from their women.'

Rebecca thought about that, then lowered her eyes shyly. 'Different things. What is the different thing that the Mahdi wants? What will he do to me?'

Nazeera glanced down at Amber to make sure she was asleep, then leant closer to Rebecca, cupped her hand to her ear and whispered. Rebecca jerked back. 'My mouth!' she gasped. 'That is the most disgusting thing I have ever heard.'

'Nay, silly girl. Think a moment. With a man you do not love, or one you hate, it is quicker, easier and less uncomfortable. You do not lose your precious maidenhead, or if you have already done so, nobody is any the wiser. Even more important, there are no undesired consequences.'

'I can see that with certain men this might be preferable.' Then another thought struck her, and her expression changed again. She looked intrigued. 'What is it like . . . to do that to a man or let him do it to you?'

'First, remember this. With the Mahdi you obey him in all things with every semblance of pleasure and joy. Only one thing is vitally important. With the Mahdi you must never

415

display repugnance. He is divine, but in these matters he is as vain as all other men. Unlike other men, however, he has in his hands the power of life and death, and he does not hesitate to employ it on all who displease him. Thus the next thing to bear closely in mind is not to gag or spit. To reject and expel his essence would be a mortal insult to him.'

'But, Nazeera, what if I do not like the taste? What if I cannot help myself?'

'Swallow quickly and have done. In all events you will grow accustomed to it. We women learn and adjust very quickly.'

Rebecca nodded. Already the idea was not so shocking. 'What else must I remember?'

'There is no doubt in my mind that the Mahdi will choose you. You must greet him as the Chosen of God and the successor to His Prophet. You must tell him what a deep joy and honour it is to meet him at last. You can add whatever else you wish – that he is the light of your eyes and the breath of your lungs. He will believe this. Then you must tell him that al-Zahra is your orphan sister. The holy law places a duty on him to protect and care for the orphan, so she will not be parted from you. There are quotations from the holy writings about orphans that you must learn by rote so that you are able to repeat them to him. I will teach them to you.' Rebecca nodded, and Nazeera went on, 'There is one other thing more important than all else. You must do or say nothing that might cause the Mahdi to pass you by. Show no anger, or resentment or disrespect. If he should reject you, the next choice will fall to his Khalifa Abdullahi.'

'Would that be worse?'

'Abdullahi is the cruellest, most wicked man in Islam. Better we should all perish than he take you or al-Zahra as his concubine.'

Rebecca shivered. 'Teach me the quotations.'

She was a quick learner and, before Amber woke, Nazeera was satisfied that she would acquit herself properly in the presence of the prophet of God.

Osman Atalan returned across the Nile from the city he had conquered. He came in glory at the head of the flotilla of boats that had carried his army to Khartoum. Every man, woman and child who could walk, toddle or totter came down to the riverbank to greet him. The war drums boomed and thumped and *ombeyas* blared. One groom held his weapons, his lance, spears and broadsword. Another groom held his warhorse al-Buq for him, fully caparisoned, with his rifle in the scabbard behind the saddle.

When Osman stepped ashore from the dhow he was preceded by al-Noor who carried over one shoulder a leather dhurra bag, whose bottom was stained a dark wine colour. The crowds shouted when they saw it, for they guessed the contents. They shouted again at the sight of Osman, so tall and noble in his gleaming white *jibba* decorated with the brightly coloured patches.

Osman mounted al-Buq and processed through the town. The crowds lined both sides of the narrow, winding streets, and the road was strewn with palm fronds. The children ran ahead of his horse and the women lifted their infants high so that they could look upon the hero of Islam and tell their own children that they had seen him. Brave men and mighty warriors tried to touch his foot as he swept past, and the women ululated and called his name.

At the Mahdi's palace, Osman dismounted and took the stained dhurra bag from al-Noor. He climbed the outside staircase to the flat-roof terrace where the prophet of Allah sat cross-legged on his *angareb*. He made a sign to the young women who attended him, and they prostrated themselves quickly before him, then moved gracefully backwards, leaving the terrace to the two men.

Osman went to the Mahdi and placed the sack before him. He knelt to kiss his hands and feet. 'You are the light and the joy of our world. May Allah always smile upon you, who are his chosen one.'

417

The Mahdi touched his forehead. 'May you always please God, as you have pleased His humble prophet.' Then he took Osman's hand and raised him up. 'How went the battle?'

'With your presence watching over us and your face before us, it went well.'

'What of my enemy and the enemy of Allah, the crusader, Gordon Pasha?'

'Your enemy is dead and his soul boils eternally in the waters of hell. The day you had foreseen has arrived, and those things you had prophesied have come to pass.'

'All that you tell me, Osman Atalan, pleases God. Your words are as honey on your lips and sweet music in my ears. But have you brought me proof that what you say is true?'

'I have brought you proof that no man may doubt, proof that will resound in the heart of every son of the Prophet throughout all Islam.' Osman stooped, gripped the corner seams of the dhurra bag and lifted it. The contents rolled out on to the mud floor. 'Behold the head of Gordon Pasha.'

The Mahdi leant forward with his elbows on his thighs and stared at the head. He was no longer smiling. His expression was cold and impassive, but there was such a glow in his eyes that struck fear even into Osman Atalan's valiant heart. The silence went on, and the Mahdi did not move for a long time. Then at last he looked up again at Osman. 'You have pleased Allah and his prophet. You shall have great reward. See that this head is placed on a spike at the gates of the great mosque that all the faithful may look upon it and fear the power of Allah and his righteous servant, Muhammad, the Mahdi.'

'It shall be done, master.' For the first time Osman used the title 'Rabb', which was more than 'master'. It meant 'Lord of all things'. 'Rabb' was also one of the ninety-nine beautiful names of Allah. Had his praise exceeded the limits of flattery? Was this not blasphemy? Osman was immediately stricken by his own presumption. He bowed his head and waited for the Mahdi to rebuke him.

He need not have feared. His instinct had been flawless. The serene smile blossomed once more on the Mahdi's beloved face. He held out his hand to Osman. 'Take me to the city you have won for the glory of Allah. Show me the spoils of this great victory that brings the *jihad* to its full flowering. Take me across the river Nile and show to me all that you have achieved in my name.'

Osman took his hand and brought him to his feet. They went down to the riverbank and embarked in the dhow that was waiting for them. They crossed the flow and went ashore in the harbour of Khartoum. When he walked along the corniche to the governor's palace the crowds spread before him bolts of looted silk, fine linen and wool so that the Mahdi need not soil his feet in the dust and filth of the captured city. The chorus of prayer and praise that went up from the prostrating crowds was deafening.

In the governor's audience hall the Mahdi took his place beside Khalifa Abdullahi, who was working with four black-robed *kadi*, the Islamic judges. They were questioning the wealthy citizens of Khartoum who had been brought before them in chains. They were asked to reveal where they had hidden their treasures. This was a protracted process, for it was not enough simply to reveal all one's wealth at the outset. The Khalifa Abdullahi and his *kadi* had to ensure that the victims were holding back nothing. The full answers were extracted with fire and water. The branding irons were heated in charcoal braziers and when the tips glowed red they were used to burn the texts of appropriate *sura* from the Koran into the naked bellies and backs of the victims. Their agonized shrieks echoed from the high ceilings.

'Let your cries be heard as praise and prayers to Allah,' the Mahdi told them. 'Let your riches be offerings that you render to His glory.'

When there was no space left on their blistered skin for further religious texts to be inscribed, the red-hot irons were applied to their genitals. At last they were carried to the water fountain in the middle of the atrium of the palace. There they were strapped to a stool and tipped backwards over the wall of the fountain until their heads were below the surface of the water. When they lost consciousness, they were tipped forward, mucus streaming from their mouths and noses. They revived, and were immersed again. Before they expired the judges were well satisfied that they had revealed all their secrets.

Abdullahi led his master to the governor's robing room, which they were using as a temporary treasury, and showed him all that they had collected so far. There were bags and chests of coin, piles of plate and chalices of silver and gold; some were even carved from pure rock crystal or amethyst and encrusted with precious and semi-precious stones. There were heaps of silk and fine wool in bolts, satins embroidered with gold thread, more chests of jewellery, fantastic creations from Asia, India and Africa, earrings, necklaces, collars and brooches set with fiery diamonds, emeralds and sapphires. There were even statuettes in images of the old gods, fashioned thousands of years previously and plundered from the tombs of the ancients. The Mahdi frowned angrily when he saw these. 'They are an abomination in the sight of God, and every true Muslim.' His usually mild tones thundered through the halls so that even the *khalifa* trembled. 'Take them hence, smash them into a hundred pieces and throw the fragments into the river.'

While many men scrambled to obey his order, the Mahdi turned to Osman and smiled again. 'I think only what Allah wishes me to think. My words are not my own words. They are the very word of God.'

'Would the blessed Mahdi care to see the women prisoners? If any please him, he might take them into his *zenana*.' The *khalifa* sought to placate him.

'May Allah be pleased with you, Abdullahi,' said the Mahdi, 'but first I wish some refreshment. Then we shall pray, and only thereafter will we go to view the new women.'

Abdullahi had prepared a pavilion in the governor's garden at a spot that overlooked the river and the beach beside the harbour on which the gallows had been erected. Under a tent of plaited reed matting, which was suspended on bamboo poles and open on all sides to allow a cooling breeze to blow through, they reclined on splendid rugs of the finest wool and pillows of silk. From clay pitchers that allowed the liquid to permeate through and cool the rest of the contents, they sipped the Mahdi's favourite beverage of date syrup and ground ginger. In the meantime they watched, with mild interest, the execution of Gordon's men. Some of the victims were cut down from the scaffold while they still writhed in the noose and thrown into the river, hands bound behind their backs.

'It is a pity that so many are of Islam,' said Osman, 'but they are also Turks, and they opposed your *jihad*.'

'For that they have paid the price, but in as much as they were of the true faith let them find peace,' said the Mahdi, and extended the forefinger of his right hand in blessing. Then he stood up and led them towards the Customs House.

When they entered the main hall the captured women had been lined up against the far wall. They prostrated themselves as the Mahdi entered and sang his praises.

The guards had erected a dais at the opposite side of the hall to where the women knelt. This was covered with Persian carpets. The Mahdi took his seat upon them, then motioned for his *khalifa* to sit at his right hand and the Emir Osman Atalan to sit on his left. 'Let them bring the captives forward, one at a time.'

Ali Wad, who was in charge of the women, presented them in inverse order of their appeal to masculine taste. The old and ugly to start with, and the younger and prettier to follow. The Mahdi dismissed the first twenty or so, who interested him not at all, with a curt gesture of his left hand. Then Ali Wad led forward a young Galla girl. The Mahdi made a sign with his right hand. Ali Wad lifted her robe over her head and she was naked. The three great men leant forward to examine her. The Mahdi made a circular movement with his right hand, and the girl revolved before them to display all her charms, which were considerable.

'She is, of course, too thin,' the Mahdi said at last. 'She will have eaten little in the last ten months, but she will plump up prettily. She is pleasing, but she has a bold eye and will be difficult. She is of the kind that causes trouble in the *zenana.*' He made the left-hand sign of rejection, then smiled at his *khalifa*. 'If you decide she is worth the trouble, you may take her, and I wish you joy of her.'

'If she makes trouble in my harem, she will have stripes on her lustrous buttocks to show for it.' The Khalifa Abdullahi flicked her with his fly whisk on the threatened area of her anatomy. At the sting she squeaked and stotted in the air like a gazelle ewe. Abdullahi made the right-hand sign of acceptance and the girl was led away. The selection went on at a leisurely pace, the men discussing the females in explicit detail.

The daughter of a Persian trader caught their particular attention. They all agreed that her features were unattractively bony and angular, but the hair of her head was red. There was some discussion about its authenticity, which the Mahdi settled by having Ali Wad remove her garments. The gorgeous ruddy tone of her dense, curling nether bush dispelled their doubts.

'There is every hope that she will bear red-headed sons,' said the Mahdi. The first Prophet Muhammad, of whom he was the successor, had possessed red hair. Thus she was highly valuable as a breeder. He would give her to one of his emirs as a mark of his divine favour. It would reinforce the emir's loyalty and strengthen the bonds between them. He made the right-hand sign.

Then Ali Wad led forward Rebecca Benbrook. Nazeera had covered her head with a light shawl. Amber had just enough strength to totter at her elder sister's side, clinging to her hand for comfort and support.

'Who is the child?' demanded Khalifa Abdullahi. 'Is she the woman's daughter?'

'Nay, mighty *khalifa*,' Ali Wad replied, as Nazeera had coached him. 'It is her little sister. Both girls are virgins and orphans.'

The men looked interested. A maidenhead was of great value, and bestowed a magical and beneficial influence on the man who ruptured it. Then, as Nazeera had told him, Ali Wad drew off the shawl that covered Rebecca's head. The

Mahdi drew a sharp breath, and both the *khalifa* and Osman Atalan sat straighter as they stared in astonishment at her hair, which Nazeera had combed out carefully. A beam of sunlight through one of the high windows transformed it into a crown of gold. The Mahdi beckoned Rebecca to come closer. She knelt before him. He leant towards her and fingered a lock. 'It is soft as the wing of a sunbird,' he murmured in awe.

Rebecca had been careful not to look directly into his face, which would have been a gesture of disrespect. With her eyes still lowered, she whispered huskily, 'I have heard all men speak of your grace and of your holy state. I have longed for sight of your beautiful face, as a traveller in the great desert longs for his first glimpse of Mother Nile.'

His eyes opened a little wider. He placed one finger beneath her chin and lifted her face. She saw at once that what she had said had pleased him. 'You speak good Arabic,' he said.

'The holy tongue,' she agreed. 'The language of the faithful.'

'How old are you, child? Are you virgin, as Ali Wad has told us? Have you ever known a man?'

'I pray that you might be my first and my last,' she lied, without a tremor, knowing just how much depended on his choice. She had been watching the *khalifa* during the selection of the other women and sensed that all Nazeera had told her was true: he was as slippery as a slime-eel and as venomous as a scorpion. She thought that it would be better to be dead than to belong to him.

When he whispered to the Mahdi his voice was oily and unctuous. 'Exalted One, let us have sight of this one's body,' he suggested. 'Is the bush of her loins of the same colour and texture as the hair on her head? Are her breasts white as camels' milk? Are the lips of her quimmy pink as the petals of a desert rose? Let us discover all these sweet secrets.'

'Those sights are for my eyes alone to gaze upon. This one pleases me. I will keep her for myself.' With his right hand he made the sign of acceptance over Rebecca's head.

'I am overcome with joy and gratitude that you have found me pleasing, Great and Holy One.' Rebecca bowed her head. 'But what of my little sister? I pray that you will take her under your protection as well.'

The Mahdi glanced down at Amber, who shrank from him and clung to Rebecca's dusty, bloodstained skirt. She stared back at him in trepidation and he saw how young she was, how weak and sickly she appeared. Her eyes were sunk into bruised-looking cavities, and she had barely the strength to stand upright. The Mahdi knew that a child in her condition would be a nuisance and the cause of disruption in his household. He was not lubriciously attracted to children, either male or female, as he knew his *khalifa* was. Let him have this wretched creature. He was about to make the left-hand gesture of rejection, when Rebecca forestalled him. Nazeera had coached her in what she must say. She spoke up again, clearly this time.

'The saint Abu Shuraih has reported the direct words of the Prophet Muhammad, the messenger of Allah, may Allah love him eternally, who said, "I declare inviolate the rights of the weak ones, the orphans and the women." He said also, "Allah provides for you only in as much as you protect the orphans among you."'

The Mahdi lowered his left hand, and looked at her thoughtfully. Then he smiled again, but there was something unfathomable in his eyes. He made the right-hand sign of acceptance over Amber and said to Ali Wad, 'I place these women in your charge. See that no harm befalls them. Convey them to my harem.'

Ali Wad and ten of his men escorted Rebecca, Amber and the other women chosen by the Mahdi to the harbour. Without drawing attention to herself, Nazeera followed them. When they were placed on board a large trading dhow to be carried across the Nile to Omdurman, she went on board with them, and when one of the crew questioned her presence Ali Wad snarled at him so belligerently that he scurried away to attend to the hoisting of the lateen sail. From then on Nazeera was accepted as the servant to al-Jamal and al-Zahra, the concubines of the Mahdi. The three squatted together in the bows of the dhow.

While Nazeera made Amber drink again from the water-skin, Rebecca asked fretfully, 'What am I going to do, Nazeera? I can never allow myself to become the chattel of a brown man, a native who is not a Christian.' The full extent of her predicament began to dawn on her. 'I think I would rather die than have that happen to me.'

'Your sense of propriety is noble, Jamal, but I am brown and a native also,' Nazeera replied. 'Also, I am not a Christian. If you have become so fastidious, then perhaps it would be better if you sent me away.'

'Oh, Nazeera, we love you.' Rebecca was immediately contrite.

'Listen to me, Jamal.' Nazeera took Rebecca's arm and forced her to look into her eyes. 'The branch breaks that will not bend with the wind. You are a limber young branch. You must learn to bend.'

Rebecca felt as though she were being crushed beneath a great weight. Wherever her mind turned it encountered only sorrow, regret and fear. She thought of her father, and touched the black stains of his blood on her bodice. She knew that the terrible moments of his beheading were engraved on her memory for the rest of her life. The sorrow was almost unsupportable. She thought of Saffron and knew she would never see her again. She held Amber close to her heart, but wondered if she would survive the disease that had already damaged her fragile body. She thought of the future that awaited them all, and gaped before her, like the black, insatiable maw of a monster.

There is no escape for any of us. As she thought it, there was an urgent shout from one of the crew. She looked about her as though she had been rudely awakened from a nightmare. The dhow had reached the middle of the river, and was sailing along on the light breeze. Now the entire crew was agitated. They crowded the weather rail, and gabbled at each other, pointing downstream.

A cannon boomed out across the water, then another.

Soon every one of the Dervish guns were blazing away from both banks. Rebecca handed Amber to Nazeera and jumped to her feet. She gazed in the direction in which everybody was staring and her spirits lifted. All her dark fears and uncertainties fell away. Close at hand she saw the Union Flag of Great Britain flying bravely in the bright sunlight.

Quickly Rebecca pulled Amber to her feet, held her close and pointed downriver. Less than half a mile away a squadron of ships was steaming towards them down the middle of the channel. Their decks were crowded with British soldiers.

'They are coming to rescue us, Amber. Oh, look.' She turned Amber's head. 'Is it not the finest sight you have ever seen? The relief column has arrived.' Now, for the first time, she allowed herself to succumb to her tears. 'We are safe, darling Amber. We are going to be safe.'

Penrod Ballantyne kept at a safe distance from the river as they rode the last few miles along the eastern bank of the Nile towards the smoke-hazed city of Khartoum on the horizon. Every mile they covered confirmed what was already a certainty in his mind. The flags on the tower of Mukran Fort were gone. Chinese Gordon had been overwhelmed. The city had fallen. The relief column was too late to save them.

He tried to arrive at some decision as to what he should do now. Every one of his calculations up to this point had depended on the survival of the city. Now there seemed to be no reason or logic in going on. He had seen a city captured and sacked by the Dervish. By the time he arrived the only living things inside the walls of Khartoum would be the crows and vultures.

But something drew him onwards. He tried to convince himself that this course of action was dictated by the fact that the doors behind him were shut. He had compounded the charge of insubordination that hung over him by disobeying Sir Charles Wilson's direct orders to stay in the camp at Metemma. There seemed little merit in turning back now to face the court-martial with which Sir Charles Wilson would welcome his return.

'On the other hand, what merit is there in going forward?' he asked himself. There were others who might still be alive and in need of his assistance: General Gordon and David Benbrook, the twins and Rebecca. At last he was honest with himself. Rebecca Benbrook had loomed large in his consciousness ever since he had ridden away from Khartoum. She was probably the true reason he was there. He knew he must find out what had become of her, or for the rest of his life her memory would haunt him.

Suddenly he reined in his camel and cocked his head towards the river. The sound of gunfire was close and clear. It mounted swiftly from a few random shots to a full artillery barrage. 'What is it?' he called to Yakub, who rode close behind him. 'What are they shooting at now?'

There was a scattered grove of thorn acacia and palms growing along the bank, obscuring their view of the river. Penrod turned his camel and urged it into a gallop. They rode through the intervening belt of trees and came out abruptly on the bank of the Nile. A forlorn and desperate sight lay before him. The steamers of Wilson's division were struggling upstream towards the city of Khartoum, whose skyline was clearly visible before them. From their mastheads they flew the red, white and blue Union Flag. Their decks were crammed with troops, but Penrod knew that between them they could not carry more than two or three hundred men. Most of the faces he could see through the lens of his telescope were those of Nubian infantrymen. There was a cluster of white officers on the bridge of the leading steamer. They all had their telescopes raised and were peering upstream. Even at this distance Penrod could pick out the tall, awkward figure of Wilson, his craggy features hidden by his large pith helmet.

'Too late, Charles the Timid,' Penrod whispered bitterly. 'If you had done the right thing, as General Stewart and your officers urged, you might have been in time to tip the scales of Fate and save the lives of those unfortunates who waited ten months for you to come.'

The Dervish shot began falling more heavily around the little vessels, and hordes of Arab cavalry came galloping down the banks from the direction of Omdurman and Khartoum to intercept the flotilla. The Dervish riders fired from the saddle as they kept pace with Wilson's steamers.

'We must join them!' Penrod shouted to Yakub, and they raced forward to mingle with the Dervish. It was the perfect cover for them. They were soon lost in the dust and confusion of the Arab squadrons. Penrod and Yakub fired as enthusiastically as all the riders around them, but they aimed low so that their bullets whacked harmlessly into the river.

The surface of the water all around the two steamers was lashed by musketry, and the leaping fountains of spray kicked up by the Krupps guns. The white hulls were quickly pockmarked by the bullets that hammered against the steel plate. The thinner steel of the funnels was riddled with holes. Suddenly there was a louder explosion and a cloud of silver steam flew high into the sky above the second vessel. The Dervish riding around Penrod howled triumphantly, and brandished their weapons.

'One of the Krupps has hit her cleanly in the boiler,' Penrod lamented. 'By all the gods of war, this day belongs to the Mahdi.'

With steam still erupting from her, the stricken vessel swung helplessly across the stream and began to drop back downriver. Almost immediately Wilson's leading vessel slowed and turned back to render assistance, and the rest of the squadron followed him round.

The Arab riders with Penrod shouted threats and derision at the two vessels: 'You cannot prevail against the forces of Allah!'

'Allah is One! The Mahdi is his chosen prophet. He is omnipotent against the infidel.'

'Return to Satan who is your father! Return to hell, which is your home!'

Penrod shouted with them, and exhibited the same jubilation, firing his rifle into the air, but inwardly his anger and contempt for Wilson seethed. What a fine excuse to break off your determined attack and betake your craven buttocks back to a comfortable chair on the veranda of the Gheziera Club in Cairo. I doubt, Sir Charles, that we shall be seeing much more of you in these latitudes.

In the hope that the crippled vessel would be carried on to the bank, hundreds of Dervish riders followed the squadron downstream, keeping up a rattling fusillade. The crews struggled to pass a towline between them. As the steamers drifted in towards the opposite bank, and out of rifle range, many riders gave up the chase and turned back towards Omdurman. Penrod moved along with them and his presence was unremarked in the effusive mood of victory and triumph. It took almost an hour to reach Omdurman. This gave him plenty of opportunity to listen in on many shouted conversations, all of which were discussions of the devastatingly successful night attack on Khartoum, led by the Emir Osman Atalan, and the subsequent sack and looting. At one point he overheard some discussing the captured white women whom they had taken to the Customs House in Khartoum.

They must be talking about Rebecca and the twins. His hopes were resuscitated. Apart from them there were hardly any white women remaining in Khartoum, except the nuns and the Austrian doctor from the leper colony. 'Please, God, let it be Rebecca they are speaking about. Even if that means she is a prisoner at least she has survived.'

Among the long, haphazard ranks of riders Penrod and Yakub rode into Omdurman. Yakub knew of a small caravanserai on the edge of the desert, which was run by an old man of the Jaalin tribe, a distant relative to whom he referred as Uncle. This man had often given him shelter and shielded him from the blood feud with the other powerful members of their tribe. Although he looked curiously at Penrod he asked no questions and placed at their disposal a filthy cell with one tiny high window. The only furniture was a rickety *angareb* covered with coarse sacking in which numerous blood-sucking insects had already set up home. They seemed to resent any human intrusion into their territory.

'To reward you for your service to me over the years, Yakub

the Faithful, I shall allow you to sleep upon the bed while I make do with the floor. But tell me how much we can trust our host, this man Wad Hagma.'

'I think my uncle suspects who you are, for I told him once, long ago, that you were my lord. However, Wad Hagma is of my clan and blood. Although he has sworn the oath of Beia to the Mahdi, I believe he did so with his mouth only, not his heart. He would not betray us.'

'He has an evil cast in his eye, Yakub, but that seems to run in the family.'

By the time they had watered and fed the camels and penned them in to the kraal at the back of Wad Hagma's caravanserai, darkness had fallen and they wandered into the sprawling warren of the holy city, seemingly without purpose but in reality to find some news of the Benbrook family. After dark Omdurman was still a holy city and under the Mahdi's strict moral code. Nevertheless, they found a small number of dimly lit coffee shops. Some offered in the back rooms a hookah pipe and the company of a young, beautiful woman or, should their tastes lean in that direction, an even more beautiful boy.

'It has been my experience that in any foreign town the most reliable sources of information are always the women of pleasure.' Yakub volunteered his services.

'I know that your motives are praiseworthy, Yakub the virtuous. I am grateful for your self-sacrifice.'

'I lack only the few paltry coins required to perform this onerous task for you.'

Penrod pressed the room price into his hand, and ensconced himself in a dimly lit corner of the coffee shop from where he was able to eavesdrop on several conversations between the other clientele.

'I have heard that when Osman Atalan laid the head of Gordon Pasha at the feet of the Divine Mahdi the angel Gabriel appeared at his side and made the sign of sanctification over the head of the Mahdi,' said one.

'I heard it was two angels,' countered another.

'I heard it was two angels and the Messenger of Allah, the first Muhammad,' said a third.

'May he live at Allah's right hand for ever,' said all three in unison.

So, Gordon is no more. Penrod sipped the viscous bitter coffee from the brass thimble, to cover his emotions. A brave man. He will be more at peace now than he ever was during his lifetime. A short while later, Yakub emerged from the back room looking pleased with himself. 'She was not beautiful,' he confided in Penrod, 'but she was friendly and industrious. She asked me to commend her efforts to her owner or he would beat her.'

'Yakub, saviour of ugly maidens, you did what was expected of you, did you not?' Penrod asked, and Yakub rolled one eye knowingly while the other remained focused on his master.

'Apart from that, what else did she tell you that might be of value to us?' Penrod could not refrain from smiling.

'She told me that early this afternoon, just after the infidel steamers were driven in confusion and ignominy back down-river by the ever-victorious Ansar of the Mahdi, may Allah love him for ever, a dhow brought five women captives across the river from Khartoum. They were in the charge of Ali Wad, an aggagier of the Jaalin who is well known hereabouts for his ferocity and his foul temper. Immediately on landing Ali Wad conveyed the captives to the *zenana* of Muhammad, the Mahdi, may Allah love him through eternity. The women have not been seen again, nor are they likely to be. The Mahdi keeps firm control of his property.'

'Did your obliging young friend notice if one of those captives had yellow hair?' Penrod asked.

'My friend, who is not particularly young, was less certain of that. The heads and faces of all the women were covered.'

'Then we must keep a watch on the palace of the Mahdi until we are certain that these women are who we hope they are,' Penrod told him.

'The women of the *zenana* are never permitted to leave

431

their quarters,' Yakub pointed out. 'Al-Jamal will never again be allowed to show herself beyond the gates.'

'Nevertheless you might learn something by watching patiently.'

Early next morning Yakub joined the large group of worshippers and petitioners who were always gathered at the gates of the Mahdi's palace, ready to prostrate themselves before him when the Chosen One went to the mosque to lead the ritual prayers and deliver his sermons, which were not his words but the very words of Allah. This day, as was his custom, the Mahdi emerged punctually for the first prayers of the day, but so great was the press of humanity around him that Yakub caught only a glimpse of his embroidered *kufi* skullcap as he passed. Yakub followed him to the mosque, and after the prayers returned in his train to the palace. He followed this routine five times a day for the next three days, without receiving any confirmation of the existence or whereabouts of the women. On the third afternoon, as had become his habit, he settled down to wait again in the sparse shade of an oleander bush from where he could keep one eye on the palace gates. He was beginning to nod off in the somnolent heat when there was a light touch on his sleeve and a woman's voice entreated him, 'Noble and beloved warrior of God, I have clean sweet water to quench your thirst, and freshly roasted *asida* flavoured with chilli sauce as fiery as the flames of hell, all for the very reasonable price of five copper *pice*.'

'May you please God, sister, for your offer pleases me.' The woman poured from the waterskin into an enamelled tin mug, and spread sauce on a round of dhurra bread. As she handed these to him she said, in a low voice muffled by the headcloth that covered her face, 'O faithless one, you swore a mighty oath that you would remember me for ever but you have forgotten me already.'

'Nazeera!' He was amazed.

'Dimwitted one! For three days I have watched you flaunt yourself before the eyes of your enemies and now you compound your idiocy by shouting my name aloud for all to hear.'

432

'You are the light of my life,' he told her. 'I shall give thanks every day that you are well. What of your charges? Al-Jamal and her two little sisters, are they with you in the palace? My lord seeks to know these things.'

'They are alive, but their father is dead. We cannot talk here. After the afternoon prayers I shall be at the camel market. Look for me there.' Nazeera drifted away to offer her water and bread to others who waited at the gates.

As she had promised, he found her at the well in the centre of the camel market. She was drawing water in a large earthenware pitcher. Two other women lifted it and placed it on her head, Nazeera balanced it with one hand and set off across the marketplace. Yakub followed her closely enough to hear what she was saying, but not so close as to make it obvious that they were together.

'Tell your master that al-Jamal and al-Zahra are in the palace. They have been taken by the Mahdi as his concubines. Saffron escaped on the steamer of al-Sakhawi. I watched her go on board. Their father was beheaded by the Ansar. I saw it done.' Under the weight of the pitcher Nazeera moved with a straight back and rolling hips. Yakub watched the lively play of her buttocks with interest. 'What are your master's intentions?' she wanted to know.

'I think that his purpose is to rescue al-Jamal and carry her off as his woman.'

'If he thinks to accomplish this alone, he is touched by the sun. They will be discovered and both of them will die. Come here again tomorrow at the same time. There is someone else you must meet,' she told him. 'Now, walk away and do not show yourself at the palace gates again.'

He turned aside to examine a string of camels that was being offered for sale, but from the corner of his eye he watched her go. She is a clever woman and skilled in the art of pleasing a man. 'Tis a pity she does not confine her affections to just one of us, he mused.

The following day Yakub was at the camel market again at the same hour. It took him some time to find Nazeera. She had changed her costume to that of a Bedouin woman, and she was cooking at a charcoal brazier. He might not have recognized her had she not called to him: 'Roasted locusts, lord, fresh from the desert. Sweet and juicy.' He took a seat on the stump of acacia wood that had been placed by the fire as a stool. Nazeera brought him a handful of locusts she had crisped on the brazier. 'The one I spoke of is here,' she said softly.

He had taken little notice of the man who sat on the opposite side of the fire. Although he was dressed in a *jibba* and carried a sword he was too plump and well fed to be an aggagier. In place of a man's beard his chin was adorned with only a few wisps of curly hair. Now Yakub looked at him with more attention, and then, with a thrill of jealous anger, he recognized him. 'Bacheet, why are you not cheating honest men with your shoddy goods, or prodding their wives with your inconsequential member?' he said coldly.

'Ah, Yakub of the quick knife! How many throats have you slit recently?' Bacheet's tone was every bit as chilled.

'From where I sit yours looks soft enough to tempt me.'

'Stop this childish squabbling,' said Nazeera sternly, although she found it more than a little flattering that she could still be at the centre of such rivalry for her waning charms. 'We have important things to discuss. Bacheet, tell him what you have already told me.'

'My master, al-Sakhawi, and I escaped from Khartoum on his steamer, the night that the Dervish attacked and captured the city. We found the girl-child, Filfil, and took her with us. Once we were clear of the city, we moored the steamer in the Lagoon of the Little Fish. My master sent me back here to seek out al-Jamal. However, he can tarry no longer at the lagoon. The Dervish are diligently searching both banks of the river for him, and within a short while they will surely find him. He is forced to flee further up the Blue Nile into the kingdom of the Emperor John of Abyssinia where he is known and respected as a trader. When he is secure there he will be able to make careful plans for the rescue of al-Jamal and al-Zahra. My master is not yet aware that you and your master are here in Omdurman, but when I bring him this news I know that he will wish to join his efforts with your master's to achieve the rescue of the two white women.'

'Your master is called al-Sakhawi for his generosity and liberality. It is rumoured that his courage surpasses that of a buffalo bull, although no man has ever seen him fight. Now you tell me that this renowned warrior intends to run away and leave two helpless women to their fate. On the other hand, I know that Abadan Riji will remain here in Omdurman until he has procured their escape from the blood-drenched clutches of the Mahdi,' Yakub said scornfully.

'Ha, Yakub, how edifying to hear you talk of blood-drenched clutches,' said Bacheet smoothly. He stood up to his full height and sucked in his belly. 'The yapping of a puppy must not be mistaken for the baying of the hound,' he said mysteriously. 'If Abadan Riji wishes the assistance of al-Sakhawi in arranging the rescue of al-Jamal, he may desire to send a message to my master. He can do so through Ras Hailu, an Abyssinian grain trader from Gondar whose dhows trade regularly downriver to Omdurman. Ras Hailu is a trusted friend and partner of my master. I will not waste more breath and time in arguing with you. Stay with God.'

Bacheet turned his back on Yakub and stalked away.

'You are like a small boy, Yakub. Why do I allow you to waste my time and breath?' Nazeera asked the sky. 'Bacheet was speaking good sense. It will need more than reckless courage to lift my girls from the zenana of the Mahdi, and to carry them thousands of leagues across the desert to safety. You will need money to place as bribes within the palace, more money to buy camels and provisions, still more money to arrange relays along your escape road. Does your master have that much money? I think not. Al-Sakhawi does, and he also has the patience and brains that your master lacks. Yet in your arrogance and conceit you turn away the offer of assistance that will certainly make the difference between success and failure in your master's enterprise.'

'If al-Sakhawi is a man of such merit and virtue, why do you not marry your beloved al-Jamal to him, rather than to my master, Abadan Riji?' Yakub demanded angrily.

'That is the first sensible thing you have said all day,' Nazeera agreed.

'Are you against us? Will you not help us to free these women? Knowing how much I love you, Nazeera, will you turn me away in favour of that beardless creature, Bacheet?' Yakub assumed a piteous expression.

'I am newly arrived in Omdurman. I know very few people in this city. I have no way to enter upon the pathways of power and influence. There is little in which I can help you. One thing only is certain. I will not risk the lives of the two girls I love to some wild and reckless scheme. If you want me to give you what help I can, you must work out a plan that has more chance of success than of failure. It must be a plan that above all, takes into account their safety.' Nazeera began to pack up her pots and dishes. 'It must be a plan in which I can place my trust. When you have made such a plan, you can find me here every sacred Friday morning.'

'Nazeera, will you tell al-Jamal that my master is here in Omdurman, and that soon he will rescue her?'

'Why would I kindle false hope in her heart, which has already been broken by her captivity, the death of her father, the loss of her little sister Filfil, and the sickness of her other sister al-Zahra?'

'But my master loves her and will lay down his own life for her, Nazeera.'

'As he also loves the woman Bakhita and fifty others like her. I do not care if he lays down his life for her, but I will not let her lay down her life for him. Have you never seen a woman stoned to death for adultery, Yakub? That is what will happen to al-Jamal if your plans fail. The Mahdi is a man without mercy.' She tied a cloth round her dishes and lifted it on to her head. 'Come to me again only when you have something sensible to discuss with me.' Nazeera walked away, balancing the parcel gracefully on her head.

'How much money do you have?' asked Yakub's putative uncle, Wad Hagma.

Penrod looked into his guileless eyes and replied with a question. 'How much will you need?'

Wad Hagma pursed his lips while he considered. 'I will have to bribe my friends in the Mahdi's palace to clear the way and they are important men whom I cannot insult with a paltry sum. Then I will have to find and pay for the extra camels to carry so many people. I must provide fodder and provisions along the road, pay the guards at the border. All this will cost a great deal, but of course I will take nothing for my own trouble. Yakub is like a son to me, and his friends are my friends also.'

'Of course, he does this willingly and without thought of his own rewards.' Yakub endorsed his uncle's altruistic intentions. They were sitting together by the small fire in the soot-blackened lean-to kitchen of the caravanserai, and eating the stew of mutton, wild onions and chilli. Considering the insalubrious surroundings in which it had been cooked and the venerable age of the flyblown ingredients, the dish was tastier than Penrod had expected.

'I am grateful to Wad Hagma for his assistance, but my question was, how much does he need?' It was only as a last resort that Penrod had agreed to enlist the assistance of the uncle in his plans. Yakub had convinced him that Wad Hagma knew many of the Mahdi's entourage and members of his palace household. With his uncle to help them, Yakub had considered it unnecessary to bring to his master's attention the offer of assistance conveyed by Bacheet on behalf of his own master, al-Sakhawi. In any case, his animosity towards Bacheet was so deep that he could not bring himself to do anything that might redound to his rival's credit or profit. He had refrained from mentioning to Penrod his meeting with Bacheet.

'It will not be less than fifty English sovereigns,' Wad Hagma said, in a tone of deep regret, watching Penrod's reaction.

'That is a small fortune!' Penrod protested.

Wad Hagma was encouraged to be dealing with a man who considered fifty sovereigns only a small fortune, rather than an extremely large one, so he immediately raised the bidding. 'Alas, it could be a great deal more,' he said lugubriously. 'However, the fate of these poor females has touched my heart and Yakub is dearer to me than any son. You are a mighty man and famous. I will do my best for you. In God's Name I swear this!'

'In God's Name!' Yakub agreed automatically.

'I will give you ten pounds now,' said Penrod, 'and more when you show your intent in deeds rather than in fine words.'

'You will see that the promises of Wad Hagma are like the mountain of Great Ararat, on which the ark of Noah came to rest.'

'Yakub will bring the money to you tomorrow.' Penrod did not want to reveal where he kept his purse. They finished the meal and wiped the last drops of gravy from the bottom of the dishes with scraps of dhurra bread. Penrod thanked the uncle and wished him goodnight, then he signed to Yakub to follow him. They walked out into the desert.

'There are already too many people in Omdurman who know who we are. It will be unsafe to stay any longer in your uncle's house. From now onwards we will sleep every night at a different place. Nobody must be able to follow our movements. We must see but never be seen.'

It was some months after she had been confined in the *zenana* before the Mahdi took any further notice of Rebecca. Then he sent her and Amber new wardrobes of clothing. Amber received three simple cotton dresses and light sandals. Rebecca was sent apparel of a more elaborate but modest design, as befitted a concubine of Allah's prophet.

The clothes were a welcome distraction from the boredom of the harem. By this time Amber had recovered sufficiently from her illness to take an active interest, and they tried on the dresses and showed them off to Nazeera and to each other.

The *zenana* was an enclosure the size of a small village. There was only one gate in the ten-foot-high wall of mud-brick that surrounded the hundreds of thatched huts that housed all the Mahdi's wives and concubines, the slaves and servants who attended them. The women were fed from the communal kitchen, but it was a monotonous diet of dhurra and river fish fried in ghee, clarified butter, and blindingly hot chilli. With so many mouths to feed, the Mahdi obviously believed that some economies were called for.

Those women who had a little money of their own could buy additional provisions and delicacies from the female vendors who were allowed within the walls of the *zenana* for a few hours each morning. From her hoard of coins Nazeera bought legs of mutton, thick cuts of beef, calabashes of soured milk, and onions, pumpkins, dates and cabbage. They cooked these in the small fenced yard behind the thatched hut that Ali Wad had had his men build for them. On this nourishing diet their bony bodies, the legacy of the long siege, filled out, the colour returned to their cheeks and the sparkle to their eyes. Twice during this time Nazeera had returned secretly at night to the ruins of the British consular palace across the river in the abandoned city of Khartoum. On the first visit she had brought back not only money but David Benbrook's journal.

Rebecca had spent days reading it. It was almost as though she was listening to his voice again, except that on these pages he was expressing ideas and feelings she had not heard before. Between the sheets she discovered her father's last will and testament, signed ten days before his death and witnessed by General Charles Gordon. His estate was to be divided in equal shares between his three daughters, but kept in trust by his lawyer in Lincolns Inn, a gentleman named Sebastian

Hardy, until they reached the age of twenty-one. Newbury was as remote as the moon, and the chance of any of them returning there was so slim that she paid scant heed to the document and placed it back between the pages of the journal.

She read on through her father's closely written but elegant script, often smiling and nodding, sometimes laughing or weeping. When she reached the end she found that several hundred pages remained empty in the thick book. She determined to continue with his account of family joys and tragedies. When next Nazeera crossed the river Rebecca asked her to find her father's writing materials.

Nazeera returned with pens, spare nibs and five bottles of best-quality Indian ink. She brought also more money and some small luxuries that had been overlooked by the looters. Among these items was a large looking-glass in a tortoiseshell frame.

'See how beautiful you are, Becky.' Amber held up the mirror so they could both admire the long dress of silk and silver thread that the Mahdi had sent her. 'Will I ever look like you?'

'You are already far more beautiful than I am, and you will grow more so every day.'

Amber reversed the mirror and studied her own face. 'My ears are too big, and my nose too flat. My chest looks like a boy's.'

'That will change, believe me.' Rebecca hugged her. 'Oh, it's so good to have you well again.' With the resilience of the young, Amber had put most of the recent horrors behind her. Rebecca had allowed her to read their father's journal. This had helped her recovery, and alleviated the terrible mourning she had undergone for him and Saffron. Now she was able to reminisce about the happy times they had all spent together. She was also taking a more active interest in their alien surroundings and the circumstances in which they now found themselves. Using her natural charm and attractive personality she struck up acquaintances with some of the other women and children of the *zenana*. With the money that Nazeera brought home, there was enough for her to take small gifts to the most needy of the other women. She was soon a favourite in the *zenana* with many new friends and playmates.

Even Ali Wad softened under her warm, sunny influence. This forbidding warrior had renewed the intimate friendship with Nazeera that they had once enjoyed. On many occasions recently Nazeera had left their hut immediately after they had eaten the evening meal, and only returned at dawn. Amber explained her nocturnal absences to Rebecca. 'You see, poor Ali Wad has a bad back. He was unhorsed in battle. Now Nazeera has to straighten his back for him to stop the pain. She is the only one who knows how to do it.'

Rebecca alleviated her boredom by attempting to bring some order into the social and domestic chaos she found all around them. First, she concerned herself with the lack of hygiene that prevailed in the *zenana*. Most of the women were from the desert and had never been forced to live in such crowded conditions before. All rubbish was simply tossed outside the doors of the huts, to be scavenged by crows, rats, ants and stray dogs. There were no latrines and everybody answered the call of nature wherever they happened to be when they received it. To navigate the labyrinth of path-ways between the huts required nimble footwork to dodge the odoriferous brown mounds that dotted open ground. For Rebecca the final provocation was coming upon two small naked boys competing to see which could urinate across the opening of the single well that supplied water to the entire *zenana*. Neither competitor was able to reach the far side and their puny streams tinkled into the depths of the well.

Rebecca, with the backing of Nazeera, prevailed on Ali Wad to set his men to dig communal earth latrines and deep pits in which the rubbish could be burned and buried, and to make sure that the women used them. Then she and Nazeera visited the mothers whose offspring were wasting away with dysentery and the occasional bout of cholera. Rebecca had remembered the name of the monastery from which Ryder had obtained the cholera powder, and Nazeera persuaded Ali Wad to send three of his men to Abyssinia to fetch fresh supplies of the medicine. Until they returned, the women used what remained of Ryder Courtney's gift sparingly and judiciously to save the lives of some infants. This earned them the reputation of infallibility as physicians. The women obeyed when they ordered them to boil the well water before they gave it to the children or drank it themselves. Their efforts were soon rewarded, and the epidemic of dysentery abated.

All of this kept Rebecca's mind from the threat that hung over them. They lived close to death. The smell of bloating human bodies wafted over the enclosure and their nostrils soon accepted this as commonplace. In the *zenana* Rebecca and Nazeera prevailed upon Ali Wad to enforce the Islamic custom: the bodies of the cholera victims and those who died of other illness were removed by his men and buried the same day. However, they had no control over the execution ground, which was separated from the *zenana* by only the boundary wall.

A line of eucalyptus trees grew along the back wall of the *zenana*. The children and even some of the women climbed into the branches whenever the braying of the *ombeya* horns announced another execution. From this viewpoint they overlooked the gallows and the beheading ground. One morning Rebecca even caught Amber in the branches, watching in white-faced and wide-eyed fascination as a young woman was stoned to death not more than fifty paces from where she was perched. She dragged Amber back to their hut, and threatened to thrash her if she ever found her climbing the trees again.

Yet her first thought when Rebecca awoke each morning was the dread that this day the summons from the Mahdi to attend him in his private quarters of the palace would be delivered. The arrival of the gift of clothing made the threat more poignant.

She did not have long to wait. Four days later Ali Wad came to inform her of her first private audience with the Chosen One. Nazeera delayed the inevitable by pleading that her charge was stricken by her moon sickness. This excuse could work only once, however, and Ali Wad returned a week later. He warned them that he would come back later to fetch Rebecca.

In the small screened yard at the back of their hut Nazeera undressed Rebecca, stood her naked on a reed mat and poured pitchers of heated water over her head. It was perfumed with myrrh and sandalwood that she had bought in the market. It was well known that the Mahdi detested unclean odours. Then she dried her and anointed her with attar of lotus flowers and dressed her in one of her new robes. At last Ali Wad came to escort her to the presence of the Chosen One.

Nothing was as Rebecca had expected. There was no grand furnishing or tapestries, no marble tiles upon the floor, no tinkling water fountains. Instead she found herself on an open roof terrace furnished only with a few quite ordinary *angarebs* and a scattering of Persian rugs and cushions. Instead of the mighty Mahdi alone, three men were reclining on the *angarebs*. She was taken aback and uncertain of what was expected of her, but the Mahdi beckoned to her. 'Come, al-Jamal. Sit here.' He indicated the pile of cushions at the foot of his bed. Then he went on talking to the other men. They were discussing the activities of the Dervish slavers along the upper reaches of the Nile, and how this trade could be increased tenfold now that Gordon Pasha and his strange Frankish aversion to the trade was no more.

Although she hung her head demurely, as Nazeera had cautioned her to do, Rebecca was able to study the other two men through her half closed lashes. The Khalifa Abdullahi frightened her, though she could barely admit it to herself. He had the cold and implacable presence of a venomous snake; an image of the sleek, glittering mamba came to her mind. She shivered and looked to the third man.

This was the first opportunity she had had to study the Emir Osman Atalan closely. During their first meeting she had been too immersed in the game of survival for herself and Amber that she had played out with the Mahdi. Of course, since she had been in the *zenana* she had heard the other women discussing his reputation as a warrior. Since his final victory over Gordon Pasha, Osman was now the senior commander of the Dervish army. In power and influence with the Mahdi he ranked only below the Khalifa Abdullahi.

Now she was able to watch him from the corner of her eye and found him interesting. She had not realized that an Arab man could be so handsome. His skin did not have the usual dingy umber tone and his beard was lustrous and wavy. His eyes were dark, but sharp and alert with stars of light in their depths, like jewels of polished black coral. In contrast his teeth were very white and even. It seemed to Rebecca that he was in a jubilant mood, waiting for the first opportunity to deliver some important tidings to the others.

The Mahdi must also have sensed his eagerness, for at last he turned his smile upon him. 'We have spoken of the south, but tell me now what news you have from the north of my domains. What do you hear of the infidels who have invaded my borders?'

'Mighty Mahdi, the news is good. Within the last hour a carrier-pigeon has arrived from Metemma. The last infidel crusaders who dared to march on your cities and attempt to rescue Gordon Pasha have fled from your sacred lands like a pack of mangy hyenas before the wrath of a great black-maned lion. They have abandoned the steamers that brought them to Khartoum, and which you and your ever-victorious army damaged and drove away. They have fled back past Wadi Halfa into Egypt. They have been vanquished, and will never again set foot upon your territories. All of Sudan is indisputably yours and, at your command, your ever-victorious army stands ready to bring more vast territory under your sway, and to spread your divine words and teachings to all the world. May Allah always love and cherish you.'

'All thanks is due to Allah, who promised me these things,' said the Mahdi. 'He has told me many times that Islam will flourish in Sudan for a thousand years, and all the monarchs and rulers of the world will relinquish their infidel ways and become my vassals, trusting in my benevolence and placing their faith in the one true God and his Prophet.'

'Praise be to God in his infinite power and wisdom,' said the others fervently.

The news of the withdrawal of the British army from the Sudan was devastating to Rebecca. Despite the fall of Khartoum and the repulse of the British river steamers, she had cherished a tiny flame of hope that one day soon British soldiers would march into Omdurman and they would be freed. That flame was cruelly snuffed out. She and Amber would never escape this smiling monster who now owned them, body and soul. She tried to fight back the dark despair that threatened to overwhelm her.

I must endure, she told herself, not only for my own sake but for Amber's. No matter the price I am forced to pay, no matter the obscene and unnatural practices forced upon me, I must survive.

With a start she realized that the Mahdi was speaking to her. Although she felt dizzy with grief she gathered her courage and gave him her full attention.

'I wish to send a letter to your ruler,' he told her. 'You will write it for me. What material do you need?' Rebecca was startled by this demand. She had expected to be roughly handled and treated as a harlot, not as a secretary. But she gathered her wits and told him her requirements. The Mahdi struck the brass gong beside the bed. A vizier scurried up the stairs and prostrated himself before his master. He listened to the orders he was given and backed away down the stairs, chanting the Mahdi's praises. In a short while he returned with three house slaves carrying a writing cabinet that had been looted from the Belgian consulate. They placed it in front of Rebecca, and because the sun was setting and the daylight fading, they placed four oil lamps around her to light her work.

'Write in your own language the words I will tell you. What is your queen's name? I have heard that your country is ruled by a woman.'

'She is Queen Victoria.'

The Mahdi paused to compose his thoughts and then he dictated: '"Victoria of England, know you that it is I, Muhammad, the Mahdi, the messenger of God who speaks to you. Foolishly you have sent your crusader armies against my might, for you did not know that I am under the divine protection of Allah, and therefore must always triumph in battle. Your armies have been vanquished and scattered like chaff on the winds. Your powers in this world have been destroyed. Therefore I declare you to be my slave and my vassal."' He paused again, and told Rebecca, 'Be certain that you write only what I tell you. If you add anything else I will have you thrashed.'

'I understand your words. I am your creature, and I would never presume to disobey your lightest wish.'

'Then write this to your queen. "You have acted in ignorance. You did not know that my words and thoughts are the words of God Himself. You know nothing of the True Faith. You do not understand that Allah is one God alone, and that Muhammad, the Mahdi, is his true Prophet. Unless you make full recompense for your sins you will boil for ever in the waters of hell. Give thanks that Allah is compassionate, for he has told me that if you come immediately to Omdurman and prostrate yourself before me, if you place yourself and all your armies and all your peoples under my thrall, if you lay all your wealth and substance at my feet, if you renounce your false gods and bear witness that Allah is one and that I am his prophet, then you shall be forgiven. I will take you to wife, and you will give me many fine sons. I will spread my wings of protection over you. Allah will set aside a place for you in Paradise. If you defy this summons your nation will be cast down, and you will burn for all of eternity in the fires of hell. It is I, Muhammad, the Mahdi, who orders these things. They are not my words, but the words that God has placed in my mouth."'

The Mahdi sat back, pleased with his composition, and made the chopping sign with his right hand to show that he had finished.

'This is a masterpiece that you have created,' said Khalifa Abdullahi. 'It gives voice to the power and majesty of God. Your words should be embroidered on your banner for all the world to read, and to believe.'

'It is plain that these are the very words of Allah delivered through your mouth,' agreed Osman Atalan, gravely. 'I give

446

thanks eternally that I have been privileged to hear them spoken aloud.'

If it ever becomes known that I wrote this traitorous nonsense, Rebecca thought, I will be locked in the Tower of London for the rest of my days. She did not look up from the page but, trusting that no other person in Omdurman could read English, she added a final sentence of her own: 'Written under extreme duress by Rebecca Benbrook, the daughter of the British Consul David Benbrook who was murdered along with General Gordon by the Dervish. God save the Queen.' It was worth the risk, not only to excuse herself but to send a message to the civilized world of her predicament.

She sanded the page and handed it to the Mahdi, with lowered eyes. 'Holy One, is this as you wished?' she whispered humbly. He took it from her and she watched his eyes move up the page from the lower right-hand corner to the top left, in the inverse direction. With a rush of relief she realized he was trying to read the Roman letters as though they were Arabic script. He would never be able to decipher what she had written. She was certain he would not admit this and show it to another person for translation.

'It is as I wished.' He nodded, and she had to stifle an instinctive sigh of relief. He handed the sheet of paper to Kalifa Abdullahi. 'Seal this missive and make sure that it is delivered with all despatch to the Khedive in Cairo. He will send it onwards to this queen, whom I will take as my wife.' He made a gesture of dismissal. 'Now you may leave me, as I wish to disport myself with this woman.'

They rose, made obeisance and backed away to the staircase.

With a sharp surge of fear Rebecca found herself alone with God's prophet. She knew that her hands were trembling and she clenched them into fists to keep them still.

'Come closer!' he ordered, and she rose from her seat at the writing cabinet and went to kneel before him. He stroked her hair and his touch was surprisingly gentle. 'Are you an albino?' he asked. 'Or are there many women in your country with hair this colour, and eyes as blue as the cloudless sky?'

'In my country I am one of many,' she assured him. 'I am truly sorry if it does not please you.'

'It pleases me well.' In front of him as he sat on the *angareb* her eyes were at the same level as his waist. Beneath the brilliant white cloth of his *jibba* she saw his body stir: the extraordinary masculine tumescence that she still found incomprehensible – a distinct creature with a life of its own.

His tammy is waking up, she thought, and almost giggled at the absurdity of the prophet of God with a tammy between his legs, just like other men less divine. She realized how close she was to succumbing to hysteria and, with an effort, she controlled herself.

'I can see the lamplight through your flesh.' The Mahdi took her earlobe between his fingers and turned it to catch the beam of the lamp, admiring the pink luminosity of light that shone through. She blushed with embarrassment and he remarked the change immediately. 'You are like a little chameleon. Your skin changes colour in tune with your moods. That is remarkable, but enticing.' He took her earlobe between his teeth and bit it, hard enough to make her gasp but not enough to break the skin or draw blood. Then he sucked on the lobe, like an infant at the breast. She was unprepared for her body's reaction. Despite herself she felt the heightened sensitivity of her nipples rubbing against the silk of her bodice.

'Ah!' He noticed her inadvertent response, and smiled. 'All women are different, but also the same.' He cupped one of her breasts in his hand and pinched the engorging nipple. She gasped again. He sat back on his haunches and unfastened the front of her bodice. He seemed in no hurry. Like a skilled groom with a nervous filly, he moved with gentle deliberation so as not to startle her.

She realized he was highly skilled in the amorous arts. Well, he has had much practice, hundreds of concubines. She set herself to remain aloof and unmoved by his expertise. But when he lifted out one of her breasts from the opening of her bodice, and bit her nipple as he had her earlobe, with a tender

448

sharpness that forced another gasp from her lips, she found her good resolution wavering. She tried to ignore the ripples of pleasure that radiated from her nipple through her body. When she started to pull away he held her with a light pressure of his teeth. The pleasant sensation was piqued by guilt and the conviction that what was happening was sinful. Not for the first time in her short life she realized that sin, as much as sanctity, held its own peculiar attraction. I do not want this to happen, she thought, but I am helpless to prevent it.

His mouth wandered over her breast, his lips kneading and plucking at her flesh, his tongue slithering and probing. She felt her sex melting, and the shame receded. She began to itch with a strange impatience. She needed something more to happen but she was not sure what.

'Stand up!' he said, and for a moment she did not understand the words. 'Stand up!' he ordered, more sharply. She rose slowly to her feet. Her bodice was still open and one breast bulged free. He smiled up at her as she stood over him, his smile sweet and almost saintly.

'Disrobe!' he ordered. She hesitated, and his smile faded. 'At once!' he said. 'Do as I tell you.'

She slipped the robe off her shoulders, and let it drop as far as her waist. He looked at her, and his eyes seemed to caress her skin. A light rash of goose pimples rose round her nipples. He reached out and drew the fingernail of his right forefinger over it, scratching the skin lightly. Her knees felt as though they might give way under her. Although she had known all along that this must happen, she felt her shame return powerfully. She was an English woman and a Christian. He was an Arab and a Muslim. It flew in the face of all her training and beliefs.

'Disrobe!' he repeated. Her dilemma was insoluble, until her father's words, which she had so recently read in his journal, returned to her: 'One must always bear in mind that this is a savage and pagan country. We should not seek to judge these peoples by the standards that apply at home.

449

Behaviour that would be considered outlandish and even criminal in England is commonplace and normal here. We should never forget this, and make allowance for it.'

Daddy wrote that for me! she thought. She hung her head demurely. 'No man has ever laid eyes on what lies beneath this silk.' Shyly she touched the swelling of her own pudenda beneath the cloth. 'But if you will remove my covering I will know that it is the Hand of Allah and not of a common man that does so. Then will I rejoice.'

Unwittingly she had hit upon the perfect response. She had abrogated the responsibility to him. She had placed herself in his power, and she could see that in doing so she had pleased him inordinately.

He reached out again and slipped the dress down over the bulge of her hips. As it fell round her ankles, Rebecca cupped her hands over her Mount of Venus. He did not protest at this last demonstration of modesty. It was what he expected of a true virgin, but he said softly, 'Turn.' She revolved slowly and felt one of his fingers trace the curve of her buttock where it met the back of her thigh.

'So soft, so white, but touched with pink, like a cloud at dawn with the first ray of sunrise upon it.' With the touch and pressure of his finger he guided her, inducing her to lean over with straight legs until her forehead almost touched her knees. She felt his warm breath on the back of her legs as he brought his face closer to examine her. Again his finger insisted and she moved her feet wider apart. She could feel his gaze, directed deeply into her most secret places. He was seeing things that no other person, nurse, parent, lover or herself, had ever laid eyes upon. In this respect she was truly a virgin. She knew she should resent this minute examination of her body, but she was too far gone, too deeply under his influence. He was possessing her with his dark, hypnotic gaze.

'Three things in this world are insatiable,' the Mahdi murmured. 'The desert, the grave and the quimmy of a beautiful woman.' He turned her back to face him again, and gently removed her hands, which still covered her mount. He touched her pubes. 'Surely this is not hair but spun thread of gold. It is silk and gossamer and soft morning sunlight.'

His admiration was so manifest and poetically expressed that she welcomed rather than resented his touch as he gently parted the outer lips of her sex. Of her own accord and without his further guidance she moved her feet apart.

'You must never pluck yourself here,' he said. 'I grant you special dispensation not to do so. This silk is too beautiful and precious to be discarded.'

The Mahdi took her hands, drew her down beside him on the *angareb* and laid her on her back. He lifted her knees and knelt between them. He lowered his face, and she was amazed as she realized what he was about to do to her. Nazeera had not warned her of this. She had believed that it would be the other way about.

What happened next exceeded her furthest imaginings. His skill was sure, his instinct faultless. She felt as though she were being devoured. As though she were dying and being reborn. In the end she cried out as if in mortal anguish and fell back on the *angareb*. She was bathed in perspiration and trembling. She was deprived of the powers of thought or movement. She seemed to have become merely a receptacle of overpowering bodily sensations. It seemed to last for an age, before at last the spasms and contractions deep within her stilled and she heard his whisper. Although his lips were at her ear, it seemed to come from far away. 'Like the desert and the grave.' He laughed softly. She lay for a long time, rousing herself only when she felt him begin to caress her again. When she opened her eyes she discovered to her mild surprise, that, like her, he was naked. She sat up and leant on one elbow looking down on him. He was lying on his back. After what he had done to her, all sense of modesty and shame had been expunged. She found herself examining him with almost as much attention as he had lavished on her. The first thing that struck her was that he was almost devoid of hair. His body was soft and almost feminine, not hard and muscled like Penrod's or Ryder's. Her eyes went down to his tammy.

451

Although it stuck up stiffly, it was small, smooth and unmarred by ropes of blue veins. The circumcised head was bare and glossy. It looked childlike and innocent. It evoked an almost maternal feeling in her.

'It's so pretty!' she exclaimed, and was immediately frightened that he would find the description effeminate and derogatory, that he might take it as an insult to his masculinity. She need not have worried. Once again her instinct had been correct. He smiled at her. Then she remembered Nazeera's advice: 'Master and Lord, would it give you offence if I presumed to do to you as you were gracious enough to do to me? For me it would be an undreamed-of honour.' He smiled until the gap between his front teeth was fully exposed.

At first she was clumsy and uncertain. He seemed to regard this as more evidence of her virginity. He started to direct her. When she was doing what pleased him, he encouraged her with murmurs and whispers and stroked her head. When she became over-enthusiastic, he restrained her with a light touch. She became absorbed in the task, and her reward was a gratifying sense of power and control over him, however fleeting it might be. Gradually he urged her to increase the tempo of her movements, until suddenly he gave her complete and undeniable proof that she had pleased him. For a moment she was at a loss as to what to do next. Then she remembered that Nazeera had advised her to swallow quickly and have done.

Like a barbellate catfish in the muddy waters of the Nile, Penrod Ballantyne allowed himself to be absorbed into the teeming byways, alleys and hovels of Omdurman. He became invisible. He changed his costume and appearance almost daily, becoming a camel herdsman, a humble beggar or a nodding, drooling idiot almost at will. Yet he knew that he could not remain in the town indefinitely without drawing attention to himself. So, for weeks on end he left the sprawling city. Once he found employment as a drover with a camel dealer taking his beasts downriver to trade them in the small villages along the banks. On another he joined the crew of a trading dhow, plying up the Blue Nile to the Abyssinian border.

When he returned to Omdurman he made it a rule never to sleep twice in the same place. On the warning of Yakub he did not attempt to make direct contact with Nazeera or anyone else who knew his true identity. He communicated with Wad Hagma only through Yakub.

The preparations for Rebecca's rescue were long drawn-out, seemingly interminable. Wad Hagma encountered many obstacles, all of which could only be surmounted with money and patience. Every time Yakub brought a message to Penrod it was for more cash to buy camels, hire guides or bribe guards and petty officials. Gradually the contents of Penrod's once-heavy money belt were whittled down. Weeks became months, and he fretted and fumed. Many times he considered making his own arrangements for a lightning raid to snatch the captives and run with them for the Egyptian border. But by now he knew just how futile that would be. The zenana of the Mahdi was impenetrable without inside help, and daily the Dervish were exerting more control and restrictions on strangers entering or leaving Omdurman. Alone Penrod was able to move around with relative freedom, but with a party of women it would be almost impossible unless the way had been carefully prepared.

At last he discovered a small cave in a limestone outcrop in the desert a few miles beyond the town. This had once been the haunt of a religious hermit. The old man had been dead for some years, but the spot had such an unhealthy reputation among the local people that Penrod felt reasonably secure in taking it over. There was a tiny water seep at the back of the cave, just sufficient for the needs of one or two persons, and for the small herd of goats he purchased from a shepherd he met on the road. Penrod used the animals to support his disguise as a desert herder. From the cave back to Omdurman was a journey on foot of a mere two or three hours. Thus he was always in contact with Yakub, who rode out at night to bring him a little food and the latest news from his uncle.

Often Yakub stayed in the cave for a few days, and Penrod was glad of his company. He was unable to carry openly the European sword that Ryder Hardinge had given him at Metemma. It would attract too much attention. He buried it in the desert from where he would be able to retrieve it, and perhaps one day return it to Major Hardinge's wife. He instructed Yakub to find him a Sudanese broadsword, then practised and exercised each day with it.

Whenever Yakub visited him they sparred in the wadi at the front of the cave where they were hidden from the eyes of a casual traveller or a wandering shepherd. Such was his skill that after half the day at practice Yakub disengaged their blades with the sweat dripping from his chin. 'Enough, Aba-dan Riji!' he cried. 'I swear, in the Name of God, that no man in this land can prevail against your blade. You have become a paragon of the long steel.'

They rested in the low mouth of the cave, and Penrod asked, 'What word from your uncle?' He knew the news could not be good: if it had been Yakub would have given it to him immediately on his arrival.

'There was a vizier of the Mahdi with whom my uncle had come to an understanding and everything was at last in readiness. Three days ago the vizier fell foul of his master on another matter. He had stolen money from the treasury. On the Mahdi's orders he was arrested and beheaded.' Yakub made a gesture of helplessness, then saw his master's face darken with rage. 'But do not despair. There is another man more reliable who is in direct charge of the *zenana*. He is willing.'

'Let me guess,' said Penrod. 'Your uncle needs only fifty pounds more.'

'Nay, my lord.' Yakub was hurt by the suggestion. 'He needs a mere thirty to seal the matter.'

'I will give him fifteen, and if all is not in readiness by this new moon at the latest, I will come to Omdurman to have further speech with him. When I arrive I will be carrying the long steel in my right hand.'

Yakub thought about this seriously for a while then replied, just as seriously, 'It comes to me that my uncle will probably agree to your offer.'

Yakub's instincts proved correct. Four days later he returned to the hermit's cave. When he was still some way off he waved cheerfully and as soon as he was within hail he shouted, 'Effendi, all is in readiness.'

As he came to where Penrod was waiting he slid down from the saddle of his camel, and embraced his master. 'My uncle, so honest and trustworthy, has arranged everything as he promised. Al-Jamal, her little sister, and Nazeera will be waiting behind the old mosque at the river end of the execution ground three midnights hence. You should return to Omdurman earlier that day. It is best if you come alone and on foot, driving the goats before you in all innocence. I will meet you and the three women at the trysting place. I will bring six strong fresh camels all provisioned with water-skins, fodder and food. Then I, Yakub the intrepid, will guide you to the first meeting place with the next relay of camels. There will be five changes of animals along the road to the Egyptian border, so we will be able to ride like the wind. We will be gone before the Mahdi knows that his concubines are missing from the harem.'

They sat in the shade of the cave and went over every detail of the plans that Wad Hagma had laid out for Yakub. 'Thus you will see, Abadan Riji, that all your money has been spent wisely, and that there was no reason to distrust my beloved uncle, who is a saint and a prince among men.'

Three days later, Penrod gathered up his few meagre possessions, slipped the sword in its scabbard down the back of his robe, wrapped the turban round his head and face, whistled up his goats and ambled off towards the river and the city. Yakub had given him a flute carved from a bamboo shoot, and over the months Penrod had taught himself to play it. The goats had become accustomed to him and they followed him obediently, bleating appreciatively whenever he struck up a tune.

He wanted to arrive on the outskirts of Omdurman an hour or so before sunset, but he was a little premature. Half a mile short of the first buildings he turned the goats loose to graze on the dried-out thorn scrub and settled down to wait beside the track. Although he wrapped himself in his robe and pretended to doze, he was wide awake. An old man leading a string of six donkeys loaded with firewood passed him. Penrod continued to feign sleep, and after calling an uncertain greeting the old man walked on.

A short while later Penrod heard singing accompanied by the tapping of finger drums. He recognized the traditional country wedding songs, and then a large party of guests came along the road from the nearest village only a short distance to the south of the city. In their midst walked the bride. She was covered from head to foot with veils and the tinkling jewellery of gold and silver coins that formed part of her dowry. The guests and her male relatives were singing and clapping, and despite the Mahdi's restrictions on these ceremonies, they were dancing, laughing and shouting ribald advice to her. When they saw Penrod squatting on the roadside they called to him, 'Come on, old man. Leave your flea-bitten animals and join the fun.'

'There will be more food than you can eat, and perhaps even a sip of *arak*. Something you have not tasted for many years.' The man displayed a small waterskin with a conspiratorial smirk.

Penrod answered them in a quavering unsteady voice: 'I was married once myself, and I do not wish to see another innocent fellow take that same hard road.'

They roared with laughter.

'What a waggish old rascal you are.'

'You can give wise counsel to our doomed cousin in how best to appease a demanding woman.'

Then Penrod noticed that all the guests had the broad, over-developed shoulders of swordsmen, and despite their humble attire their swagger and strutting self-confidence was

456

more that of aggagiers than cringing country oafs. He glanced down at the bare feet of the bride, all that was visible of her, and saw that they were broad and flat, not painted with henna, and that the toenails were ragged and broken.

Not the feet of a young virgin, Penrod thought. He reached over his shoulder and took a grip on the hilt of the sword concealed down the back of his robe. As his blade rasped from the scabbard he sprang to his feet, but the wedding guests had surrounded him. Penrod saw that they, too, had drawn weapons as they rushed at him from every direction. With surprise he realized that they were not edged blades but heavy clubs. He had little time to think about it before they were on him in a pack.

He killed the first with a straight thrust at the throat, but before he could disengage and recover, a blow from behind smashed into his shoulder and he felt the bone break. Still, he parried one-handed the next blow at his head. Then another hit him in the small of the back, aimed at his kidneys, and his legs started to give way. He stayed upright just long enough to send a deep thrust into the chest of the man who had broken his shoulder. Then a great iron door slammed shut in the centre of his skull and darkness descended upon him like an ocean wave driven by the storm.

When Penrod regained consciousness he was uncertain where he was and what had happened to him. Close by where he lay, he heard a woman moaning and groaning in labour.

Why does not the stupid bitch hold her mouth, and have her brat elsewhere? he wondered. She should show some respect for my aching head. It must have been cheap liquor I drank last night. Then, suddenly, the pain ripped through the roof of his skull and he realized that the groans were issuing from his own dried-out mouth. He forced his eyes open against the pain and saw that he was lying on a mud floor in an evil-smelling room. He tried to raise his hand to touch his damaged head, but his arm would not respond. Instead a new shaft of agony tore through his shoulder. He tried to use the other hand for the job, but there was a clink, and he found that his wrists were fastened together with chains. He rolled over painfully and cautiously on to his good side.

Good is a relative term, he thought groggily. Every muscle and sinew of his body throbbed with agony. Somehow he pushed himself into a sitting position. He had to wait a moment for the blinding agony in his head, caused by the movement, to clear. Then he was able to assess his situation.

The chains on his wrists and ankles were slaving irons, the ubiquitous utensils of the trade across the country. His leg shackles were anchored to an iron stake driven into the middle of the dirt floor. The chain was short enough to prevent him reaching either the door or the single high window. The cell reeked of excrement and vomit, of which traces were scattered around him in a circle at the limit of the chain.

He heard a soft rustle nearby and looked down. A large grey rat was feeding on the few rounds of dhurra bread that had been left on the filthy floor at his side. He flicked the chain at it, and it fled, squeaking. Next to the bread was an earthenware pitcher, which made him realize how thirsty he was. He tried to swallow but there was no saliva in his mouth and his throat was parched. He reached for the pitcher, which was gratifyingly heavy. Before he drank he sniffed the contents suspiciously. He decided it was filled with river water and he could smell the woodsmoke from the fire over which it had boiled. He drank and then drank again.

I think I might yet survive, he decided wryly, and blinked back the pain in his head. He heard more movement and glanced up at the window. Someone was watching him through the bars, but the head disappeared immediately. He drank again, and felt a little better.

The door to the cell opened behind him and two men stepped in. They wore *jibbas* and turbans, and their swords were unsheathed.

'Who are you?' Penrod demanded. 'Who is your master?'

'You will ask no questions,' said one. 'You will say nothing until ordered to do so.'

Another man followed them. He was older and grey-bearded, and he carried all the accoutrements of a traditional eastern doctor.

'Peace be upon you. May you please Allah,' Penrod greeted him. The doctor shook his head curtly, and made no reply. He set aside his bag, and came to stand over him. He palpated the large swelling on Penrod's head, obviously feeling for any fracture. He seemed satisfied and moved on. Almost at once he noticed that Penrod was favouring his left side. He took hold of the elbow and tried to lift the arm. The pain was excruciating. Penrod managed to prevent himself crying out. He did not want to give the two interested guards that satisfaction, but his features contorted and sweat broke out across his forehead. The Arab doctor lowered the arm, and ran a hand over his biceps. When he pressed hard fingers into the site of the broken bone, Penrod gasped despite his resolution. The doctor nodded. He cut away the sleeve of Penrod's *galabiyya* and strapped the shoulder with linen bandages. Then he folded and tied a sling to support the arm. The relief from pain was immediate.

'The blessing of Allah and his Prophet be upon you,' Penrod said, and the doctor smiled briefly.

From a small alabaster flask he poured a dark, treacly liquid into a horn cup, and gave it to Penrod. He drank it, and the taste was gall-bitter. Without having spoken a word the doctor repacked his bag and left. He returned the next day, and the four days that followed. On each visit the guards refilled the water pitcher and left a bowl of food: scraps of bread and sun-dried fish. During these visits neither the guards nor the doctor spoke; they did not acknowledge Penrod's greetings and blessings.

The bitter potions that the doctor gave him sedated Penrod, and reduced the pain and swelling in his head and shoulder. After he had completed his examination on the fifth day the doctor looked pleased with himself. He readjusted the sling, but when Penrod asked for another dose of the medicine, he shook his head emphatically. When he left the cell, Penrod heard him speaking in a low voice to the guards. He could not catch the words.

By the following morning the effects of the drug had worn off, and his mind was clear and sharp. The arm was tender only when he tried to lift it. He tested himself for any concussion he might have suffered from the head blow, closing first one eye and then the other while he focused on the bars of the window. There was no distortion or any double vision. Then he began to exercise the injured arm, starting first by simply clenching his fist and bending the elbow. Gradually he was able to raise the elbow to the horizontal.

The visits from the taciturn doctor ceased. He took this as a favourable sign. Only his guards made brief visits to leave water and a little food. This left him much time to consider his predicament. He examined the locks on his shackles. They were crude but functional. The mechanism had been developed and refined over the centuries. Without a key or a pick he wasted no more time upon them. Next he turned his mind to deducing where he was. Through the lop-sided window he could see only a tiny section of open sky. He was forced to draw his conclusions from sounds and smells. He knew he was still in Omdurman: not only could he smell the stink of the uncollected rubbish and the dungheaps but in the evenings he caught a softer sweeter whiff of the waters of the river, and could even hear the faint calls of the dhow captains as they tacked and altered sail. Five times a day he heard the wailing cries of the muezzin calling the faithful to prayer from the half-built tower of the new mosque, 'Hasten to your own good! Hasten to prayer! Allah is great! There is no God but Allah.'

From these clues he pinpointed his position with a certain precision. He was about three hundred yards from the mosque, and half that distance from the riverbank. He was due east of the execution ground and therefore approximately the same distance from the Mahdi's palace and harem. He could judge the direction of the prevailing wind from the occasional small high cloud that sailed past the window. When it was blowing the stench of rotting corpses from the execution ground was strong. This gave him a rough sense of triangulation. With a sinking sensation in his gut, he decided that he must be in the compound of the Beja tribesmen beside the Beit el Mal, the stronghold of his old enemy Osman Atalan. Next he had to consider how this had happened.

His first thought was that Yakub had betrayed him. He wrestled with this theory for days, but could not persuade himself to accept it. I have trusted my life too many times to that squint-eyed rascal to doubt him now, he thought. If Yakub has sold me to the Dervish, there is no God.

He used the shackle of his chain to scratch a crude calendar in the mud floor. With it he was able to keep track of the days. He had counted fifty-two days before they came to fetch him.

The two guards unlocked the chains from the iron stake. They left his legs and arms shackled. There was sufficient slack in this chain to enable him to shuffle along, but not to run.

They led him out into a small courtyard and through another door into a larger enclosure, around whose walls were seated a hundred or more Beja warriors. Their spears and lances rested against the wall behind them, and their sheathed swords were laid across their laps. They studied Penrod with avid interest. He recognized some of their faces from previous encounters. Then his eyes jumped to the familiar figure seated alone on a raised platform against the far wall. Even among this assembly of fighting men, Osman Atalan was the focus of attention.

The guards urged him forward and, with the chains hampering him, he shambled across the courtyard. When he stood before Osman a guard snarled in his ear, 'Down on your knees, infidel! Show respect to the emir of the Beja.'

Penrod drew himself to attention. 'Osman Atalan knows better than to order me to my knees,' he said softly, and held the emir's eyes coolly.

'Down!' repeated the guard, and drove the hilt of his spear into Penrod's kidney with such force that his legs collapsed under him and he fell in a heap of limbs and chains. With a supreme effort he kept his head up and his eyes locked on Osman's.

'Head down!' said the guard, and lifted the shaft of the spear to club him again.

'Enough!' said Osman, and the guard stepped back. 'Welcome to my home, Abadan Riji.' He touched his lips and then his heart. 'From our first encounter on the field of El Obeid I knew there was a bond between us that could not easily be sundered.'

'Only the death of one of us can do that,' Penrod agreed.

'Should I settle that immediately?' Osman mused aloud, and nodded at the man who sat immediately below his dais. 'What think you, al-Noor?'

Al-Noor gave full consideration to the question before he replied. 'Mighty lord, it would be prudent to scotch the cobra before he stings you again.'

'Will you do this favour for me?' Osman asked, and with one movement al-Noor rose to his feet and stood over the kneeling prisoner with the blade of his sword poised over Penrod's neck.

'It needs but the movement of your little finger, great Atalan, and I shall prune his godless head like a rotten fruit.'

Osman watched Penrod's face for any sign of fear, but his gaze never wavered. 'How say you, Abadan Riji? Shall we end it here?' Penrod tried to shrug, but his injured shoulder curtailed the gesture. 'I care not, Emir of the Beja. All men owe God a life. If it is not now, then it will be later.' He smiled easily. 'But have done with this childish game. We both know well that an emir of the Beja could never let his blood enemy die in chains without a sword in his hand.'

Osman laughed with genuine delight. 'We were minted from the same metal, you and I.' He motioned to al-Noor to go back to his seat. 'First we must find a more suitable name for you than Abadan Riji. I shall call you Abd, for slave you now are.'

'Perhaps not for much longer,' Penrod suggested.

'Perhaps,' Osman agreed. 'We shall see. But until that time

you are Abd, my foot slave. You will sit at my feet, and you will run beside my horse when I ride abroad. Do you not wish to know who brought you to this low station? Shall I give you the name of your betrayer?' For a moment Penrod was too startled to think of a reply, and could only nod stiffly. Osman called to the men guarding the gate to the courtyard, 'Bring in the informer to collect the reward he was promised.'

They stood aside and a familiar figure sidled through the gate to stand gazing about him nervously. Then Wad Hagma recognized Osman Atalan. He threw himself upon the ground and crawled towards him, chanting his praises and protesting his allegiance, devotion and loyalty. It took him a while to traverse the yard for he stopped every few yards to beat his forehead painfully on the earth. The aggagiers guffawed and called encouragement to him.

'Let not your great belly drag in the dust.'

'Have faith! Your long pilgrimage is almost ended.'

At last Wad Hagma reached the foot of the dais, and prostrated himself full length with arms and legs splayed out flat against the dusty ground like a starfish.

'You have rendered me great service,' said Osman.

'My heart overflows with joy at these words, mighty Emir. I rejoice that I have been able to deliver your enemy to you.'

'How much was the fee on which we agreed?'

'Exalted lord, you were liberal enough to mention a price of five hundred Maria Theresa dollars.'

'You have earned it.' Osman tossed down a purse so heavy it raised a small cloud of dust as it struck the ground.

Wad Hagma hugged it to his chest, and grinned like an idiot. 'All praise to you, invincible Emir. May Allah always smile upon you!' He stood up, head bowed in deep respect. 'May I be dismissed from your presence? Like the sun, your glory dazzles my eyes.'

'Nay, you must not leave us so soon.' Osman's tone changed. 'I wish to know what emotions you felt when you placed slavers' chains upon a brave warrior. Tell me, my fat little hosteller, how does the sly and treacherous baboon feel when it leads the great elephant bull into the pitfall?'

An expression of alarm crossed Wad Hagma's face. 'This is no elephant, mighty Emir.' He gestured at Penrod. 'This is a rabid dog. This is a cowardly infidel. This is a vessel of such ungodly shape that it deserves to be shattered.'

'In God's Name, Wad Hagma, I see that you are an orator and a poet. I ask only one more service of you. Kill this rabid dog for me! Shatter this misshapen pot so that the world of Islam will be a better place!' Wad Hagma stared at him with utter consternation. 'Al-Noor, give the courageous tavern-keeper your sword.'

Al-Noor placed the broadsword in Wad Hagma's hand and he looked hesitantly at Penrod. Carefully he placed the bag of Maria Theresa dollars on the ground, and straightened. He took a step forward, and Penrod came to his feet. Wad Hagma jumped back.

'Come now! He is chained and the bone in his arm is broken,' said Osman. 'The rabid dog has no teeth. He is harmless. Kill him.' Wad Hagma looked around the courtyard, as if for release, and the aggagiers called to him, 'Do you hear the emir's words, or are you deaf?'

'Do you understand his orders, or are you dull-witted?'

'Come, brave talker, let us see brave deeds to match your words.'

'Kill the infidel dog.'

Wad Hagma lowered the sword, and looked at the ground. Then, suddenly and unexpectedly, in the hope that he had lulled his victim, he let out a blood-chilling shriek and rushed straight at Penrod with the sword held high in both hands. Penrod stood unmoving as Wad Hagma slashed double-handed at his head. At the last moment he lifted his hands and caught the descending blade on his chain. Such was the shock as it hit the steel links that Wad Hagma's untrained hands and arms were numbed to the elbows. His grip opened involuntarily and the sword spun from his hands. He backed away, rubbing his wrists.

'In God's Holy Name!' Osman applauded him. 'What a fierce stroke! We have misjudged you. You are at heart a warrior. Now, pick up the sword and try again.'

'Mighty Emir! Great and noble Atalan! Have mercy on me. I shall return the reward.' He picked up the bag of coins and ran to place it at Osman's feet. 'There! It is yours. Please let me go! O mighty and compassionate lord, have mercy on me.'

'Pick up the sword and carry out my orders,' said Osman, and there was more menace in his tone than if he had shouted.

'Obey the Emir Atalan!' chanted the aggagiers. Wad Hagma whirled round and raced back to where the sword lay. He stooped to pick it up, but as his hand closed on the hilt Penrod stepped on the blade.

Wad Hagma tugged at it ineffectually. 'Get off!' he whined. 'Let me go! I meant nobody any harm.' Then he dropped his shoulder and lunged at Penrod with all his weight, trying to push him backwards off the sword. Penrod swung the loop of chain. It whipped across the side of Wad Hagma's jaw. He howled and sprang backwards, clutching the injury. With a loop of chain swinging threateningly Penrod followed him. He turned and scuttled across the yard towards the doorway, but when he reached it a pair of aggagiers blocked his way with crossed swords. Wad Hagma gave up, and turned back to face Penrod as he stalked after him, swinging the loop of chain.

'No!' Wad Hagma's voice was blurred, and the side of his face distorted. The chain had broken his jaw. 'I meant you no harm. I needed the money. I have wives and many children . . .' He tried to avoid Penrod by circling along the wall, but the seated aggagiers pricked him forward with the points of their swords and roared with laughter when he hopped like a rabbit at the sting. Suddenly he darted away again, back to where the sword lay. As he reached it and stooped to seize the hilt, Penrod stepped up behind him and dropped the loop of chain over his head. With a quick twist of his wrists he settled the links snugly under Wad Hagma's chin and round his throat. As Wad Hagma's fingertips touched the sword hilt Penrod applied pressure on the chain and pulled him up until he was dancing on tiptoe, pawing at the chain with both hands, mewing like a kitten.

465

'Pray!' Penrod whispered to him. 'Pray to Allah for forgiveness. This is your last chance before you stand before him.' He twisted the chain slowly and closed off Wad Hagma's windpipe, so that he could neither whimper nor whine.

'Farewell, Wad Hagma. Take comfort from the knowledge that for you nothing matters any longer. You are no longer of this world.'

The watching aggagiers drummed their sword blades on their leather shields in a mounting crescendo. Wad Hagma's dance became more agitated. His toes no longer touched the ground. He kicked at the air. His damaged face swelled and turned dark puce. Then there was a sharp crack, like the breaking of a dry twig. All the aggagiers shouted together as Wad Hagma's limbs stiffened, his entire body sagged and he hung from the chain round his throat. Penrod lowered him to the ground and walked back towards Osman Atalan. The aggagiers were in uproar, shouting and laughing, some mimicking Wad Hagma's death throes. Even Osman was smiling with amusement.

Penrod reached the spot where the sword lay, swept it up in a single movement and rushed straight at Osman, the long blade pointed at the emir's heart. Another shout went up, from every man in the yard, this time of wild surmise and alarm. Penrod had twenty paces to cover to reach the dais and the courtyard exploded into movement. A dozen of the aggagiers nearest to the dais leapt forward. Their swords were already unsheathed, and they had only to come on guard to present a glittering palisade of steel to prevent Penrod carrying his charge home. Al-Noor darted forward, not to oppose Penrod head on but cutting in behind him. He seized the dragging leg chain and hauled back on it, whipping Penrod's feet from under him. As he hit the ground the waiting aggagiers rushed forward.

'No!' shouted Osman. 'Do not kill him! Hold him fast, but do not kill him!' Al-Noor released his grip on the leg shackles and grabbed the loop of chain that held Penrod's wrists. He jerked this viciously against the half-healed shoulder. Penrod gritted his teeth to prevent himself crying out but the sword fell from his hands. Al-Noor snatched it away.

'In God's glorious Name!' Osman Atalan laughed. 'You give me great entertainment, Abd! I know now that you can fight, but tomorrow I shall see how well you run. By evening I doubt you will have the stomach for more of your games. Within a week you will be pleading for me to kill you.'

Then Osman Atalan looked down from the dais at al-Noor. 'You I can always trust. You are always ready to serve. You are my right hand. Take my Abd to his cell, but have him ready at dawn. We are going out to hunt the gazelle.'

News travelled swiftly in the *zenana*. Within hours it was known by all, including Ali Wad and the guards, that the Mahdi had expressed himself pleased with the infidel woman, al-Jamal. Rebecca's status was enhanced immeasurably. The guards treated her as though she was already a senior wife, not a low-ranking concubine. She was given three female house slaves to attend her. The other women of the Mahdi, both wives and concubines, called greetings and blessings to her as she passed, and they carried petitions and supplications to her hut, begging her to bring them to the notice of the Mahdi. The rations that were sent to her from the kitchens changed in character and quantity: large fresh fish straight from the river, calabashes of soured milk, bowls of wild desert honey still in the comb, the tenderest cuts of mutton, legs of venison, live chickens and eggs, all in such amounts that Rebecca was able to feed some of the sick children of the lowest-ranking concubines who were in real need of nourishment.

This new status was passed on to the others in her household. Nazeera was now greeted with the title Ammi, or Auntie. The guards saluted her when she passed through the gates. Because it was known that Amber was the sister of one of the Mahdi's favourites, she, too, was granted special privileges. She was a child and had not seen her first moon, so none of the guards raised any objection when she accompanied Nazeera on her forays beyond the gates of the *zenana*.

That particular morning, Nazeera and Amber left the *zenana* early to go down to the market on the riverbank to meet the farmers as they brought in their fresh crops from the country. Figs and pomegranates were in season, and Nazeera was determined to have the first selection of the day's offerings. As they passed the large edifice of the Beit el Mal there was a disturbance down the street ahead of them. A crowd had gathered, the war drums boomed and the ivory horns sounded.

'What is it, Nazeera?'

'I don't know everything,' Nazeera replied testily. 'Why do you always ask me?'

'Because you do know everything.' Amber jumped up to see over the heads of the crowd. 'Oh! Look! It is the banner of the Emir Atalan. Let's hurry or we shall miss him.' She ran ahead and Nazeera broke into a trot to keep up with her. Amber ducked between the legs of the crowd until she had reached the front rank. Nazeera forged her way in behind her, ignoring the protests of those she shoved aside.

'Here he comes,' the crowd chanted. 'Hail, mighty Emir of the Beja! Hail, victor of Khartoum and slayer of Gordon Pasha!' With his banner-bearer riding ahead and four of his most trusted aggagiers flanking him, Osman Atalan was up on the great black stallion, al-Buq. As this entourage swept past Nazeera and Amber they saw that a man ran at the emir's stirrup. He wore a short sleeveless shift and a loincloth. On his head was a plain turban, but his legs and feet were bare.

'That's a white man!' exclaimed Nazeera, and around her the crowd laughed and applauded.

'He is the infidel spy, the henchman of Gordon Pasha.'

'He is the one they once called Abadan Riji, the One Who Never Turns Back.'

'He is the prisoner of the emir.'

'Osman Atalan will teach him new tricks. Not only will he

468

learn to turn back, but he will be taught to turn in small circles.'

Amber shrieked with excitement, 'Nazeera! It is Captain Ballantyne!'

Even over the noise of the crowd Penrod heard Amber call his name. He turned his head and looked directly at her. She waved frantically at him but the cavalcade carried him away. Before he was gone Amber saw that there was a rope round his neck, the other end of which was tied to one of the emir's stirrups.

'Where are they taking him?' Amber wailed. 'Are they going to kill him?'

'No!' Nazeera placed an arm round her to calm her. 'He is far too valuable to them. But now we must go back and tell your sister what we have seen.' They hurried to the *zenana*, but when they reached the hut they found that Rebecca was gone.

Nazeera immediately taxed the house slaves. 'Where is your mistress?'

'Ali Wad came to fetch her. He has taken her to the quarters of the Mahdi.'

'It is too early in the day for the Mahdi to begin taking his manly pleasures,' Nazeera protested.

'He is sick. Wad Ali says he is sick unto death. He is struck down by the cholera. They know that al-Jamal saved her little sister al-Zahra and many others from the disease. He wishes her to do the same for the Holy One.'

As the news of the Mahdi's illness swept through the *zenana* a high tide of wailing, lamentation and prayer followed it.

As they reached the edge of the desert Osman reined in al-Buq lightly and at the same time urged him forward with his knees. It was the signal for the stallion to break into a triple gait, the smooth, flowing action so easy on both horse and rider. It is not a natural pace, and a horse has to be schooled to learn it. The emir's outriders followed his example and tripled away at a pace faster than a trot but not as fast as a canter.

At the end of the rope Penrod had to stretch out to keep up with them. They swung southwards, parallel to the river, and the heat of the day started to build up. They rode on as far as the village of Al Malaka, where the headman and the village elders all hastened out to greet the emir. They implored him to grant them the honour of providing him with refreshment. If Osman had been truly on the chase he would never have wasted time on such indulgences, but he knew that if the captive did not rest and drink he would die. His clothing was drenched with sweat and his feet were bloody from the prick of thorns and flint cuts.

While he sat under the tree in the centre of the village and discussed the possibility of finding game in the vicinity, Osman noted with satisfaction that al-Noor had understood his true purpose and was allowing Penrod to sit and drink from the waterskins. When Osman stood at last and ordered his party to mount up, Penrod seemed to have regained much of his strength. He had pulled his left arm out of the sling, although it was not yet completely healed: it unbalanced him, and hampered the swing of his shoulders as he ran.

They rode on and paused an hour later while Osman glassed the desert ahead for any sign of gazelle. In the meantime al-Noor let Penrod drink again, then allowed him to squat on his haunches, his head between his knees as he gasped for breath. Too soon Osman ordered the advance. For the rest of that day they described a wide circle through sand dunes, over gravelly plains and across ridges of limestone, pausing occasionally to drink from the waterskins.

An hour before sunset they returned to Omdurman. The horses had slowed to a walk and Penrod staggered along behind them at the end of his rope. More than once he was jerked off his feet and dragged in the dirt. When this happened al-Noor backed his horse until he was able to struggle up. When they rode through the gates and dismounted in the courtyard Penrod was swaying on his torn, bloody feet. He was dazed with exhaustion, and it required all his remaining strength merely to remain upright.

Osman called to him: 'You disappoint me, Abd. I looked for you to find the gazelle herds for us but you were more happy rolling in the dust and looking for dung beetles.'

The other hunters shouted with delight at the jest, and al-Noor suggested, 'Dung beetle is a better name for him than Abd.'

'So be it, then,' Osman agreed. 'From henceforth he shall be known as Jiz, the slave who became a dung beetle.'

As Osman turned towards his own quarters a slave prostrated himself in front of him. 'Mighty Emir, and beloved of Allah and his true Prophet, the Divine Mahdi has been taken gravely ill. He has sent word for you to go to him at once.'

Osman leapt back into al-Buq's saddle and galloped out through the gates of the compound.

The jailers came for Penrod and dragged him to his cell. As previously, they chained him to the iron stake. But before they locked the door and left him, one of the jailers grinned at him. 'Do you still have the strength to attack the great emir?'

'Nay,' Penrod whispered. 'But perhaps I could still twist off the head of one of his chickens.' He showed the jailer his hands. The man slammed the door hurriedly and locked it.

Standing within his reach were three large pitchers of water in place of the usual one, and a meal that in comparison to those he had previously been offered was a banquet. Rather than having been thrown on to the bare floor, the food had been placed in a dish. Penrod was so exhausted that he could hardly chew, but he knew that if he were to survive he must eat. There was half a shoulder of roasted lamb, a lump of hard cheese and a few figs and dates. As he munched he wondered who had provided this fare, and if Osman Atalan had ordered it. If that was the case, what game was he playing? They let him rest on the following day, but on the next his jailers woke him before sunrise.

'Up, Abd Jiz! The emir presents his apologies. He cannot

471

join you in the gazelle hunt this day. He has urgent business at the palace of the Mahdi. However, al-Noor, the famous aggagier, invites you to hunt with him.' They placed the rope round his neck before they removed his chains.

Penrod's feet were so swollen and torn that standing on them was agony, but after the first few miles the pain receded and he ran on. They found not a single gazelle, although they scoured the desert for many leagues. By the time they returned the nails on three of Penrod's toes had turned blue.

They hunted again, day after day. Osman Atalan did not accompany them and they killed no gazelle, but al-Noor ran him hard. The nails fell off his injured toes. Many times over the next few weeks Penrod thought that the infected wounds and scratches on both feet might turn gangrenous and he would lose his legs.

By the onset of the new moon that signalled the beginning of Ramadan, both his feet had healed and the soles were toughened and calloused as though he wore sandals. Only the sharpest thorns could pierce them. He was as lean as a whippet. The fat had been stripped from his frame, replaced with rubbery muscle, and he could keep pace with al-Noor's horse.

Penrod had not seen Osman Atalan since the first unsuccessful gazelle hunt, but when he returned to Omdurman from the field on the third day of Ramadan, he was running strongly beside al-Noor's stirrup. He looked like a desert Arab now: he was lean and bearded, sun-darkened and hard.

As they reached the outskirts of the holy city, al-Noor reined in. 'There is something amiss,' he said. 'Listen!' They could hear the drums beating and the *ombeyas* blaring. The music was not a battle hymn or the sound of rejoicing. It was a dirge. Then they heard salvoes of rifle fire, and al-Noor said, 'It is bad news.'

A horseman galloped towards them, and they recognized another of Osman Atalan's aggagiers. 'Woe upon us!' he shouted. 'Our father has left us. He is dead. Oh, woe upon us all.'

472

'Is it the emir?' al-Noor yelled back. 'Is Osman Atalan dead?'

'Nay! It is the Holy One, the Beloved of God, the light of our existence. Muhammad, the Mahdi, has been taken from us! We are children without a father.'

For weeks they waited at the bedside of the Mahdi. Chief among them was Khalifa Abdullahi. Then there were the Ashraf, the Mahdi's brothers, uncles and cousins, and the emirs of the tribes: the Jaalin, the Hadendowa, the Beja and others. The Mahdi had no sons, so if he should die the succession was uncertain. There were only two women in his sickroom, both heavily veiled and sitting unobtrusively in a far corner. The first was his principal wife, Aisha. The second was the concubine al-Jamal. Not only was she his current favourite, but it was well known that she possessed great medical skills. Together these two women waited out the long and uncertain course of his disease.

Rebecca's Abyssinian cure seemed highly effective during the first stages of the illness. She mixed the powder with boiled water, and she and Aisha prevailed upon the Mahdi to drink copious draughts of it. As with Amber, his body was drained of fluids by the scouring of his bowels and the prolonged vomiting, but between them the two women were able to replace the liquid and mineral salts he had lost. It was fourteen days before the patient had started along the road to full recovery, and prayers of thanksgiving were held at every hour in the new mosque below his window.

When he could sit up and eat solid food, the city resounded to the beat of drums and volleys of rapturous rifle fire. The following day the Mahdi complained of insect bites. Like most of the other buildings in the city the palace was infested by fleas and lice, and his legs and arms were speckled with red swellings. They fumigated the room by burning branches of the turpentine bush in a brazier. However, the Mahdi

473

scratched the flea bites, and soon a number were infected with the faeces of the vermin that had inflicted them. The temperature of his body soared, and he suffered alternating bouts of fever and chill. He would not eat. He was prostrated by nausea. The doctors thought that these symptoms were a complication of the cholera.

Then, on the sixteenth day, the characteristic rash of typhus fever covered most of his body. By this time he was in such a weakened condition that he sank rapidly. Near the end he asked the two women to help him sit up and, in a faint, unsteady voice, he addressed all the important men crowded around his *angareb*. 'The Prophet Muhammad, who sits on the right hand of Allah, has come to me and he has told me that the Khalifa Abdullahi must be my successor on earth. Abdullahi is of me, and I am of him. As you have obeyed me and treated me, so must you obey and treat him. Allah is great and there is no other God but Allah.' He sagged back on the bed and never spoke again.

The men around the bed waited, but the tension in the crowded room was even more oppressive than the heat and the odour of fever and disease. The Ashraf whispered among themselves, and watched the Khalifa Abdullahi surreptitiously. They believed that their blood-tie to the Mahdi superseded all else: surely the right to take possession of the vacant seat of power belonged to one of their number. However, they knew that their claim was weakened by the last decree of the Mahdi, and by the sermon he had preached in the new mosque only weeks before he fell ill. Then he had reprimanded his relatives for their luxurious living, their open pursuit of wealth and pleasure.

'I have not created the Mahdiya for your benefit. You must give up your weak and wicked ways. Return to the principles of virtue I have taught you which are pleasing to Allah,' he had ranted, and the people remembered his words.

Even though the claim of the Ashraf to the Mahdiya was flawed, if one or two powerful emirs of the fighting tribes declared for them, Abdullahi would be sent to the execution grounds behind the mosque to meet his God and follow his Mahdi into the fields of Paradise.

Sitting quietly beside Aisha at the end of the room Rebecca had learnt enough of Dervish politics to be aware of the nuances and undercurrents that agitated the men. She drew aside the folds of her veil to ask Aisha if she might take a dish of water to bathe the fevered face of the dying Mahdi.

'Leave him be,' Aisha replied softly. 'He is on his way to the arms of Allah who, even better than we can, will love and cherish him through all eternity.'

It was so hot and muggy in the room that Rebecca kept her veil open a little longer, making the most of a sluggish movement of air through the tiny windows across the room. She felt an alien gaze upon her, and flicked her eyes in its direction. The Emir Osman Atalan of the Beja was contemplating her bare face steadily, and though his dark eyes were implacable she knew he was looking at her as a woman, a young and beautiful woman who would soon be without a man. She could not look away: her eyes were held by a force beyond her control, as the compass needle is held by the lodestone.

Though it seemed an age, it was only a few moments before Abdullahi leant towards Osman Atalan and spoke to him so softly that his lips hardly moved. Osman turned his head to listen, and broke the spell that had existed between him and the young woman.

'How do you stand, noble Emir Atalan?' Abdullahi whispered, and his voice was so low that nobody else in the room could overhear.

'The east is mine,' Osman said.

'The east is yours,' Abdullahi agreed.

'The Hadendowa, the Jaalin and the Beja are my vassals.'

'They are your vassals,' Abdullahi acknowledged. 'And you are mine?'

'There is one other small matter.' Osman procrastinated a moment longer, but Abdullahi was ahead of him.

'The woman with yellow hair?'

So he had seen the exchange of glances between Osman and al-Jamal. Osman nodded. Like the rest of them, Abdullahi lusted after this exotic creature with her pale golden hair, blue eyes and ivory skin, but to him she was not worth the price of an empire.

'She is yours,' Abdullahi promised.

'Then I am the vassal of Abdullahi, the successor of the Mahdi, and I will be as the targe on his shoulder and the blade in his right hand.'

Suddenly the Mahdi opened his eyes and stared at the ceiling. He uttered a cry: 'Oh! Allah!' Then the air rushed from his lungs. They covered his face with a white sheet, and the opposing factions faced each other across the cooling body.

The Ashraf stated their case, which was based on their holy blood. Against this the Khalifa Abdullahi's case was manifest: he did not have the blood but he had the word and blessing of the Mahdi. Still it hung in the balance. The newborn empire teetered on the verge of civil war.

'Who declares for me?' asked the Khalifa Abdullahi.

Osman Atalan rose to his feet and looked steadily into the faces of the emirs of the tribes that traditionally owed him allegiance. One after the other they nodded. 'I declare for the word and wish of the holy Mahdi, may Allah love him for ever!' said Osman. 'I declare for the Khalifat Abdullahi.'

Every man in the room shouted in homage to the new ruler, the Khalifat, of the Sudan, although the voices of the Ashraf were muted and lacked enthusiasm.

When Rebecca returned to the hut in the *zenana*, Amber greeted her ecstatically. They had been parted for all the long weeks of the Mahdi's last illness. They had never been separated for so long before. They lay together on one *angareb*, hugging each other and talking. There was so much to tell.

Rebecca described the death of the Mahdi and the ascendancy of Abdullahi. 'This is very dangerous for us, my darling. The Mahdi was hard and cruel, but we managed to inveigle ourselves into his favour.' Rebecca did not elaborate on how this had been achieved, but went on, 'Now he is gone, we are at the mercy of this wicked man.'

'He will want you,' Amber said. She had grown up far ahead of her years while they had been in the clutches of the Dervish. She understood so much – Rebecca was amazed by it. 'You are so beautiful. He will want you just as the Mahdi did,' Amber repeated firmly. 'We can be sure he will send for you within the next few days.'

'Hush, my sweet sister. Let us not go ahead to search for trouble. If trouble is coming it will find us soon enough.'

'Perhaps Captain Ballantyne will rescue us,' Amber said.

'Captain Ballantyne is far away by now.' Rebecca laughed. 'He is probably at home in England, and has been these many months past.'

'No, he is not. He is here in Omdurman. Nazeera and I have seen him. All the town is talking about him. He was captured by that wicked man Osman Atalan. They keep him on a rope and make him run beside the emir's horse like a dog.'

In the lamplight Amber's eyes glistened with tears. 'Oh, it is so cruel. He is such a fine gentleman.'

Rebecca was astonished and dismayed. Her brief interlude with Penrod seemed like a dream. So much had happened since he had deserted her that her memory of him had faded and her feelings towards him had been soured by resentment. Now it all came flooding back.

'Oh, I wish he had not come to Omdurman,' she blurted. 'I wish he had stayed away, and that I never had to lay eyes on him again. If he is a prisoner of the Dervish, as we are, there is nothing he can do to help us. I don't even want to think about him.'

Rebecca spent most of the following day bringing up to date the journal she had inherited from her father, describing in small, closely written script all that she had witnessed at the death bed of the Mahdi, then her own feelings at the news that Penrod Ballantyne had come back into her life.

From time to time her writing was disturbed by the shouts from the vast crowds in the mosque, which carried over the *zenana* wall. It seemed that the entire population of the country had gathered. Rebecca sent out Nazeera to investigate. Amber wanted to accompany her, but Rebecca forbade it. She would not let Amber out of her sight in these dangerous, uncertain times.

Nazeera returned in the middle of the afternoon. 'All is well. The Mahdi has been buried, and the Khalifat has declared that he has become a saint and that his tomb is a sacred site. A great new mosque will be built over it.'

'But what is all the noise in the mosque? It has been going on all day.' Rebecca demanded.

'The new Khalifat has demanded that the entire population take the Beia, the oath of allegiance to him. The emirs, sheikhs and important men were first to do so. Even the Ashraf have made the oath. There are so many of the common people clamouring to swear that the mosque is overflowing. They are administering the oath to five hundred men at a time. They say that the Khalifat weeps like a widow in mourning for his Mahdi, but still the populace crowds around him. Everywhere I walked in the streets I heard the crowds shouting the praises of the Khalifat and declaring their promises to obey him as the Mahdi decreed. They say the oath-taking will go on for many more days and even weeks before all can be satisfied.'

And when it is done, the Khalifat will send for me, Rebecca thought, and her heart raced with panic and dread.

She was wrong. It did not take that long. Two days later Ali Wad came to their hut. With him were six other men, all strangers to her. 'You are to pack everything you own, and go with these men,' Ali Wad told her. 'This is ordered by the Khalifat Abdullahi, who is the light of the world, may he always please Allah.'

'Who are these men?' Rebecca eyed the strangers anxiously. 'I do not know them.'

'They are aggagiers of the mighty Emir Osman Atalan. Nazeera and al-Zahra are to go with you.'

'But where are they taking us?'

'Into the harem. Now that the holy Mahdi is departed from us, he has become your new master.'

There was much work to be done. The Khalifat Abdullahi was a clever man. He understood that he had inherited a powerful, united empire, and that this had been built upon the religious and spiritual mysticism of the Mahdi and the political imperative of ridding the land of the Turk and the infidel. Now that the Mahdi was gone, the cement that held it together was dangerously weakened. The infidel would soon gather on his borders and the enemies within would emerge and gnaw away, like termites, the central pillars of his power. Not only was Abdullahi clever, he was also ruthless.

He called all the powerful men to him in a great conclave. Their numbers almost filled the new mosque. First he reminded them of the oath they had sworn only days before. Then he read to them the proclamation that the Mahdi had issued the previous year in which he had made abundantly clear the trust that he placed in Khalifa Abdullahi: 'He is of me, and I am of him,' the Mahdi had written in his own hand. 'Behave with all reverence to him, as you do to me. Submit to him as you submit to me. Believe in him as you believe in me. Rely on all he says, and never question his proceedings. All that he does is by the order or the permission of the Prophet Muhammad. If any man thinks evil or speaks evil of him, he will be destroyed. He has been given wisdom in all things. If he sentences a man to death, it is for the good of all of you.'

When they had listened earnestly to this proclamation he ordered the emirs and the Ashraf to write letters that were sent out with fast horsemen and camel-riders to the most remote corners of the empire to reassure and calm the population. He announced the creation of six new *khalifs*. In effect they would become his governors. His brothers were elevated to this rank, and so was Osman Atalan. The Khalif Osman was awarded a new green war-banner to go with the scarlet and black, and granted the honour of planting this at the gates of Abdallahi's palace whenever he was in Omdurman. All the eastern tribes were placed under his banner. Thus Osman now commanded almost thirty thousand élite fighting men.

It took several months for all this to be accomplished, and when it was achieved Abdullahi invited Osman Atalan to hunt with him. They rode out into the desert. There are no eavesdroppers in those great empty spaces, and the two mighty men rode a mile ahead of their entourage. When they were alone Abdullahi disclosed his vision of the future.

'The Mahdiya was conceived in war and the flames of the *jihad*. In peace and complacency it will rust and disintegrate like a disused sword. Like spoilt children, the tribes will return to their old blood feuds, and the sheikhs will bicker among themselves like jealous women,' he told Osman. 'In the Name of God, we lack not real enemies. The pagan and the infidel surround us. They gather like locust swarms at our borders. These enemies will ensure the unity and strength of our empire, for their threat gives reason for the *jihad* to continue. My empire must continue to expand or it will collapse upon itself.'

'You wisdom astounds me, mighty Abdullahi. I am like an innocent child beside you. You are my father and the father of the nation.' Osman knew the man well: he fed on flattery and adulation. Yet the scope of his vision impressed Osman. He realized that Abdullahi dreamed of creating an empire to rival that of the Sublime Porte of the Ottoman Empire in Constantinople.

'Osman Atalan, if you are a child, and Allah knows that you are not, you are a warlike child.' Abdullahi smiled. 'I am sending Abdel Kerim with his *jihadia* northwards to attack the

Egyptians on the border. If he is victorious, the entire country of Egypt from the first cataract to the delta will rise up behind our *jihad*.'

Osman was silent as he considered this extraordinary proposal. He thought that Abdullahi had wildly overestimated the appeal of the Mahdiya to the Egyptian population. It was true that the majority were Islamic, but of a much milder persuasion than the Dervish. There was also a large Coptic Christian population in Egypt, which would oppose the Sudanese Mahdiya fanatically. Above all, there were the British. They had only recently taken over supreme power in that country, and would never relinquish it without a bitter fight. Osman knew the quality of these white men: he had fought them at Abu Klea where there had been a mere handful of them. He had heard that they were building up their armies in the north. Their battleships were anchored in Alexandria harbour. No army of the Khalifat could ever fight its way over those thousands of miles to reach the delta. Even if by some remote chance it did, then certain destruction awaited it there at the hands of the British. He was trying to find the diplomatic words to say this without incurring Abdullahi's ire, when he saw the sly glint in his eye.

Then he realized that the proposal was not what it seemed. At last he saw through it: Abdullahi was not intent on the conquest and occupation of Egypt; rather, he was setting a snare to catch his enemies. The Ashraf were the main threat to his sovereignty: Abdel Kerim was the cousin of the Mahdi and one of the leaders of the Ashraf. He had under his control a large army, including a regiment of Nubians who were superb soldiers. If Abdel Kerim failed against the Egyptians, Abdullahi could accuse him of treachery and have him executed, or at least strip him of his rank and take the Ashraf army under his own command.

'What an inspired battle plan, great Khalifat!' Osman was sincerely impressed. He realized now that Abdullahi, by virtue of his cunning and ruthlessness, was indeed fitted to become the one ruler of the Sudan.

'As for you, Osman Atalan, I have a task also.'

'Lord, you know that I am your hunting dog,' Osman replied. 'You have only to command me.'

'Then, my warlike child, my faithful hunting dog, you must win back for me the Disputed Lands.' This was the territory around Gondar, a huge tract of well-watered and fertile land that lay along the headwaters of the Atbara river, and stretched from Gallabat as far as the slopes of Mount Horrea. The Sudanese and the Abyssinian emperors had fought over this rich prize for a hundred years.

Osman considered the task. He looked for the pitfalls and snares that Abdullahi was setting for him, as he had done for Abdel Kerim, but found none. It would be a hard and difficult campaign, but not an impossible one. He had sufficient forces to carry it out. The risks were acceptable. He knew he was a better general than the Abyssinian Emperor John. He would not be forced to campaign in the highlands where the advantage would pass to Emperor John. The prize was enormous, and the recaptured lands would become part of his own domain. The thought of moving his personal seat of government to Gondar, once he had captured the city, was attractive. Gondar had been the ancient capital of Abyssinia. There, he would be so far removed from Omdurman that he could establish virtual autonomy while paying lip service to Abdullahi.

'You do me great honour, exalted lord!' He accepted the command. 'Before the rise of the new moon I shall leave Omdurman and travel up the Atbara river to reconnoitre the border and lay my battle plans.' He thought for a moment, then went on, 'I shall need some pretence to travel along the border, and perhaps even visit Gondar. If great Abdullahi should write a letter of greetings and good wishes to the Emperor that he orders me to deliver to the Abyssinian governor at Gondar, I could secretly inspect the defences of the city and the deployment of the enemy troops along the border.'

'May Allah go with you,' said Abdullahi gently. 'You and I are as twin brothers, Osman Atalan. We think with one mind and strike with the same sword.'

In a flotilla of dhows, Osman Atalan and his entourage sailed up the Bahr El Azrek, the Blue Nile, as far as the small river town of Aligail. Here, one of the major tributaries joined the Nile. This was the Rahad river, but it was not navigable for more than a few leagues upstream. Osman offloaded his aggagiers, his women and slaves, almost three hundred souls. The horses had come up in the dhows from Omdurman. At Aligail he sent his aggagiers fifty miles in all directions to hire camels and camel-drivers from the local sheikhs. Once the caravan was assembled they moved eastward along the course of the Rahad. The caravan was strung out over several miles. Osman and a select band of his aggagiers rode well in advance of the main column. Penrod ran beside his horse with the rope round his neck.

The country became more wooded and pleasant as they moved slowly towards the mountains. There were a few small villages along the river, but these were well separated and the land between was populated with wild game and birds. They came upon rhinoceros and giraffe, buffalo, zebra and antelope of all descriptions. Osman hunted as they travelled. Some days were passed entirely in the pursuit of a particular species of antelope that had caught his attention. Spurning firearms, he and his aggagiers used the lance from horseback to bring down the quarry. There were wild rides and Penrod was able to keep up only by grabbing hold of Osman's stirrup leather and letting himself be pulled along by al-Buq at full gallop, his feet touching the earth lightly every dozen paces or so. By this time he was in such superb physical condition that he delighted in the sport as much as any of the aggagiers. It was all that made his captivity bearable, for during the chase he felt free and vital once again.

Most nights Osman's party slept in the open under the starry sky wherever the day's hunting had taken them. They were usually far ahead of the main column. However, when they had killed some large animal, such as a giraffe or rhinoceros, they camped beside the carcass until the main body caught up with them. When the baggage train arrived, Osman's enormous leather tent was erected in the centre of a *zareba* of thorn bush. It was the size of a large house, furnished with Persian carpets and cushions. The smaller but no less luxurious tents of his wives and concubines were placed around it.

Unlike the Mahdi and the Khalifat Abdullahi, Osman had limited himself to four wives, as decreed in the Koran. The number of his concubines was also modest, and although it fluctuated, it did not exceed twenty or thirty. On this expedition he had brought with him only his latest wife: she had not yet borne him a child and he needed to impregnate her. He had also restricted himself to seven of his most attractive concubines. Among this small group was the recently acquired white girl, al-Jamal. Until now Osman had been so occupied with affairs of state and politics that he had not yet gathered and tasted her fruits. He was in no hurry to do so: the anticipation of this consummation added greatly to his pleasure.

Penrod knew that Rebecca was with the expedition. He had seen her going aboard one of the dhows when they embarked at Omdurman. He had also seen her from a distance on four different occasions since the land journey had begun. Each time she had avoided looking in his direction, but Amber, who was with her, had waved and given him a saucy grin. Of course, there was never an opportunity to exchange a word: Atalan's women were strictly guarded, while Penrod was kept on a leash during the day and locked in leg shackles each evening. At night he was confined to a guarded hut in the *zareba* of al-Noor and the other aggagiers.

Even though he was usually exhausted when he settled down on the sheepskin that served him as a mattress, he still had opportunity to think about Rebecca during the long nights. Once he had convinced himself that he loved her, that she was the main reason why he had defied Sir Charles Wilson's strict orders and returned to Khartoum after the battle of Abu Klea. Since then his feelings towards her had become ambivalent. Of course, she was still his fellow country-woman. Added to that she had surrendered her virginity to him, and for those reasons he had a duty and responsibility towards her. However, her virtue, which had initially made her so attractive to him, was now indelibly tarnished. Although she had not done so of her own free will, she had become the whore of not one but at least two other men. His strict code of honour would never permit him to marry another man's whore, especially if that man was his blood enemy and of a dark, alien race.

Even if he were able to subdue these feelings and take her as his wife, what good could come of it? When they returned to England the full story of her defilement and degradation at the hands of the Dervish would not remain secret. English society was unforgiving. She would be branded for life as a scarlet woman. He could not present her to his friends and family. As a couple they would be ostracized. The regiment would never condone his choice of wife. He would be denied advancement, and forced to resign his commission. His reputation and standing would be destroyed. He knew that in time he would come to resent and, later, even hate her.

As an ambitious man with a well-developed instinct for self-preservation and survival, he knew what his course of action must be. First, he would do his duty and rescue her. Then, painful as it might be, they must part company and he would return to the world from which she would be for ever excluded.

If he were to carry through this determination, and rescue Rebecca and her little sister, his first concern must be to find freedom himself. To achieve this he must gain the trust of Osman Atalan and his aggagiers, and lull any suspicions they harboured that the sole purpose of his miserable life was either to assassinate the Khalif or to escape from his clutches. Once he induced them to relax the conditions of his imprisonment he knew he would find his opportunity.

The closer they came to the Abyssinian border, the more
wild and grand the land became. Magnificent savannahs
gave way to forests of stately trees, interrupted by open glades
of green grass. Twenty-five days after they had left the Nile
they came upon the first herd of elephant. Closer to the towns
and villages, these great animals had been ruthlessly pursued
by ivory hunters and had been forced to withdraw deeper into
the wilderness.

This herd was drinking and bathing at a pool in the Rahad
river. The water was deep and broad, surrounded by fever
trees with canary yellow trunks. They heard the squealing and
splashing from a great distance, and manoeuvred downwind
to climb the low kopje that overlooked the pool. From the
summit they had a splendid view of the unsuspecting herd.
It was made up of fifty or so cows with their offspring. There
were three immature bulls with them, but they carried nondescript tusks.

One of Osman Atalan's young warriors had not yet killed
an elephant in the classical manner, on foot and armed only
with the sword. Osman described the technique to him. It was
a masterly dissertation.

Penrod listened with fascination. He had heard of this
dangerous pastime in which the aggagiers earned their title,
but had never seen its execution. Towards the end of his
lecture, when Osman was pointing out the exact point on the
back of the elephant's hind leg where the sword stroke must
be aimed to sever the tendon, it occurred to Penrod that
Osman was addressing him as much as the Arab novice. He
dismissed this as an idle thought. The herd finished drinking
and wandered away through the grove of fever trees. Osman
let them go unmolested. They were not worthy of his steel.
He ordered the aggagiers to mount up and they rode back to
the encampment.

Three days later they came across more elephant tracks.

The aggagiers dismounted to study them, and saw that they had been made by a pair of bulls. The pad marks were fresh and one set was enormous. With animation they speculated among themselves as to the size and weight of ivory that the larger bull carried. Osman ordered them to remount and led them forward at a smart walk, so that the sound of galloping hoofs would not alarm and stampede the quarry.

'They drank at the river early this morning and now they are returning to the hills to take cover in the thickets of kittar thorns where they feel secure,' Osman said. As they approached the hills they saw that the lower slopes were covered with the reptilian and venomous green thornbush, which contrasted with the brighter, fresher colour of the deciduous forest higher up the slope. They found the big bull standing alone on the edge of the thicket.

'The two bulls have parted company and gone their separate ways. This will make the hunt easier for us,' Osman said softly, and led them forward. The elephant was drowsing quietly, fanning his huge ears, rocking gently from one foot to the other. He was angled away from them and his head was lowered so that the thorn scrub reached to his lower lip and hid his tusks from view. The aggagiers reined in the horses to rest them before beginning the hunt. The breeze was steady and favourable and there was no reason to hurry. Penrod rested with the horses. He squatted on his haunches and drank from the waterskin that al-Noor unstrapped from the pommel of his saddle and dropped to the ground beside him.

Suddenly the bull shook his head so that his ears clapped loudly, then reached out with his trunk to pluck a bunch of kittar blossom. When he lifted his head to stuff the yellow flowers into the back of his throat, he revealed his tusks. They were perfectly matched, long and thick.

The hunters stirred and murmured in appreciation.

'This is a fine animal.'

'This is an honourable bull.'

They all looked to Osman Atalan to see whom he would choose for the honour, each hoping it would be himself.

'Al-Noor,' said Osman, and al-Noor pushed his mount forward eagerly, only to slump again in the saddle when his master went on, 'slip the leash off Abd Jiz.'

Penrod came to his feet with surprise and al-Noor removed the rope from round his neck.

'It is too great an honour for an infidel slave,' al-Noor whispered enviously.

Osman ignored his protest. He drew his sword and reversed it before he handed it to Penrod. 'Kill this bull for me,' he ordered.

Penrod tested the balance and weight of the blade, cutting with it forehanded, then backhanded. He spun it in the air and caught it with his left hand, then cut and thrust again. He turned back to Osman, on al-Buq. Penrod was balanced on the balls of his bare feet; he held the sword in the guard position. His expression was grim. The blade was steady as if fixed in the jaws of a steel vice, pointed at the Khalif's chest. Osman Atalan was unarmed and within the sweep of Penrod's sword arm. Their eyes locked. The aggagiers urged their mounts forward and their hands rested on their sword hilts.

Penrod brought the sword slowly to his lips and kissed the flat of the blade. 'It is a fine weapon,' he said.

'Use it wisely,' Osman advised him quietly.

Penrod turned away up the slope towards where the bull elephant stood. His bare feet made no sound on the stony earth and he stepped lightly. He felt the breeze chill the sweat on the back of his neck. He used its direction to guide him as he angled in behind the bull. It was an enormous creature: at the shoulder it stood over twice his own height.

Penrod had in mind every word of Osman's advice as he studied the hind legs. He could clearly make out the tendons beneath the grey and riven hide. They were thicker than his thumb, and as the beast rocked gently they tightened and relaxed. He fastened his gaze on them and moved in quickly. Unexpectedly the bull humped his back and braced both back legs. From the pouch of loose skin between his back legs his penis dropped out and dangled until the tip almost touched the ground. It was longer than the span of Penrod's outstretched arms and as thick as his forearm. The bull began to urinate, a powerful yellow stream that hosed out a shallow trench in the hard earth. The smell was rank and strong in the noonday heat.

Penrod closed in to within three yards of the bull's haunches, and stood poised, the sword lifted. Then he ran forward and swung the blade, aiming two hand spans above the bull's right heel. It sliced down to the bone, and with a rubbery snap the tendon parted. In the same movement Penrod stepped across to the other leg, reversed his blade and cut again. He saw the recoil of the severed tendon under the thick hide, and jumped back. The crippled bull squealed and dropped heavily to his hindquarters in a sitting position with both back legs paralysed.

Behind him Penrod heard the aggagiers shout in acclamation. He watched the jets of blood squirting from the twin wounds. The bull's struggles to regain his feet aggravated the flow. It would not be long. The bull saw him and swung his head to face Penrod. He tried to drag himself forward, but his movements were awkward and ineffectual. Penrod retreated before him, watching until he was certain that the bull was mortally wounded, then turned and walked unhurriedly back towards the group of watching horsemen.

He had covered half the distance when another elephant squealed on his right flank. The sound was so unexpected that he wheeled to face it. All this time the second, younger bull had been standing nearby, also asleep on its feet. The kittar bush had concealed it, but at the cries and struggles of its companion it burst out of the dense thornbush at full charge, pugnaciously seeking a focus for its alarm and anger. It saw Penrod immediately and swung towards him, rolling back the tips of its huge ears and coiling its trunk against its chest in a threatening attitude. It trumpeted wildly. As it began its charge the ground trembled under its weight.

Penrod glanced around swiftly for some avenue of retreat. There was no point in running towards the group of horsemen. They could offer him no help and would gallop away before he reached them. Even to climb into one of the tall trees that grew nearby would be of no avail. Standing on its back legs the bull could reach even to the top branches to pull him down, or it could knock over the whole tree almost effortlessly. He thought of the ravine they had crossed a short distance back. It was so narrow and deep that he might crawl down into it beyond the bull's reach. He whirled and ran. Faintly he heard the ribald shouts of the aggagiers.

'Run, Dung Beetle! Spread your wings and fly.'

'Pray to your Christian God, infidel!'

'Behold, the fields of Paradise lie before you.'

He heard the elephant crashing through the scrub behind him. Then he saw the opening of the ravine a hundred paces ahead. He was at the top of his own speed, his tempered, hardened legs driving so hard that the elephant was overhauling him only gradually. But he knew in his heart that it would catch him.

Then he heard pounding hoofs close behind him. He could not help glancing back. The bull was towering over him like a dark cliff, already uncoiling its trunk to swipe him down. The blow would smash bone. Once he was on the ground the bull would kneel on him, crushing him against the hard earth until every bone in his body was smashed, then stabbing those long ivory shafts repeatedly through what remained of his body.

He tore away his gaze and looked ahead. Still the sound of hoofs crescendoed. Without slackening his run Penrod braced himself for the shattering blow that must surely come. Then the hoofs were alongside him, and he saw movement from the corner of his eye. The black bulk of al-Buq was overtaking him. Osman was leaning forward over his withers and pumping the reins. He had kicked his foot out of the nearside stirrup, and the empty iron bumped against al-Buq's flank.

'Come up, Abd Jiz!' Osman invited him. 'I have not finished with you yet.'

With his right hand Penrod snatched the stirrup leather and twisted it round his wrist. Instantly he was jerked off his feet, and he allowed himself to be carried away by the racing stallion. As he swung on the end of the leather he looked back. The bull was still at full charge behind them, but losing ground to the stallion. At last he abandoned the chase and, still squealing with rage, turned aside into the kittar thorn. As he ran off he ripped down branches from the trees in his path in frustration and hurled them high into the air. He vanished over the crest of the hill.

Osman reined in al-Buq, and Penrod released the stirrup leather. He still held the hilt of the sword in his left hand. Osman threw his leg over the stallion's neck and dropped to the ground, landing like a cat in front of him. The other aggagiers were widely scattered and for the moment the two were alone. Osman held out his right hand. 'You have no further need of that steel,' he said quietly.

Penrod glanced down at the sword. 'It grieves me to give it up.' He reversed the weapon and slapped the hilt into Osman's right hand.

'In God's Name, you are a brave man, and an even wiser one,' Osman said, and brought out his left hand from behind his back. In it he held a fully cocked pistol. He thumbed the hammer and let it drop to half-cock, just as al-Noor rode up.

Al-Noor also jumped down and spontaneously embraced Penrod. 'Two true strokes,' he applauded him. 'No man could have done it cleaner.'

They did not have time to wait for the tusks to rot free so they chopped them out. It took until noon the next day to remove the long cone-shaped nerve from the cavity in the base of each. It was painstaking work: a slip of the blade would mar the ivory and reduce drastically its monetary and aesthetic value.

They loaded them on to the packhorses, and when they rode into the main encampment the drummers beat loud and the horns blared. The women, even the Khalif's wife and his concubines, came out to watch. The men fired their rifles in the air, then crowded around the packhorse to marvel at the size of the tusks.

'This must have been the father and grandfather of many

great bulls,' they told each other. Then they asked Osman Atalan, 'Tell us, we beg you, exalted Khalif, which hunter brought down this mighty beast?'

'The one who was once known as Abd Jiz, but who has now become the aggagier Abadan Riji.'

From then on no man ever called Penrod Abd Jiz again. That derogatory name was lost and forgotten.

'Command us, Supreme One. What must we do with these tusks?'

'I shall keep one in my tent to remind me of this day's sport. The other belongs to the aggagier who slew it.'

Early the following morning when Osman Atalan emerged from his tent he greeted his waiting aggagiers and discussed with them the usual business of the day, the route he intended to follow and the purpose and object of the day's ride. Penrod squatted nearby with the horses, taking no part until Osman called to him, 'Your style of dress brings your companions into disrepute.'

Penrod stood up in surprise and looked down at his shift. Although he had washed it whenever an opportunity presented itself, it was stained and worn. He had no needle or thread with which to mend it, and the cloth was ripped by thorn and branch, worn threadbare with hard use. 'I have become accustomed to this uniform. It suits me well enough, great Atalan.'

'It suits me not at all,' said Osman, and clapped his hands. One of the house slaves came scurrying forward. He carried a folded garment. 'Give it to Abadan Riji,' Osman ordered him, and he knelt before Penrod and proffered the bundle.

Penrod took it from him and shook it out. He saw that it was a clean, unworn *jibba* and with it were a pair of sandals of tanned camel hide.

'Put them on,' said Osman.

Penrod saw at once that the *jibba* was plain, not decorated with the ritual multi-coloured patches that had such powerful political and religious significance and constituted a Dervish uniform. He would not have donned the *jibba* if it had. He stripped off his rags and slipped it over his head. It fitted him

492

remarkably well, as did the sandals. Somebody had observed his size shrewdly.

'That pleases me better,' said Osman, and swung up easily into al-Buq's saddle. Penrod moved up to his usual position at the stirrup, but Osman shook his head. 'An aggagier is a horseman.' He clapped again, and a groom led a saddled horse from behind the tent. It was a sturdy roan gelding that Penrod had noticed in the herd of spare horses.

'Mount up!' Osman ordered him, and he went into the saddle, then followed the group of riders into the forest. Penrod was conscious of his inferior rank in the band, so he kept well back.

Over the first few miles he assessed the roan under him. The horse had a comfortable gait and showed no vices. He would not be particularly fast. He could never outrun any of the other aggagiers. If Penrod ever tried to escape, they would run him down quickly enough.

No great beauty, but a hard pounder with good temperament, he decided. It felt good to have a horse between his knees again. They rode on towards the blue mountains and the Abyssinian border. They were heading now directly for Gallabat, the last Dervish stronghold before the border. Though the mountains seemed close, they were still ten days' ride ahead. Gradually they left the wilderness behind. There were no more signs of elephant or of the other great game animals. Soon they were passing through fields of dhurra and other cultivation and many small Sudanese villages. Then they started to climb through the foothills of the central massif.

When they off-saddled to recite the midday prayers, Osman Atalan always left the others and spread his carpet in a shaded place that overlooked the next green valley. After he had prayed he would usually eat alone, but that day he called Penrod, and indicated that he should sit facing him on the Persian carpet. 'Break bread with me,' he invited. Al-Noor set out between them a dish of unleavened dhurra cakes and *asida*, and another dish of cold smoked antelope meat. He had hastily cut the throats of the animals before they died from

493

the lance wounds that had brought them down so the flesh was *halal*. There was a smaller dish filled with coarse salt. Osman gave thanks to Allah and asked for His blessing on the food. Then he selected a morsel of smoked meat and, with his right hand, dipped it in to the salt. He leant forward and held it to Penrod's lips.

Penrod hesitated. He was faced with a crucial decision. If he accepted food and salt from Osman's hand it would constitute a pact between them. In the tradition of the tribes it would be equivalent to a parole. If thereafter he tried to escape, or if he committed any warlike or aggressive act against Osman, he would break his word of honour.

Swiftly he made his decision. I am a Christian, not a Muslim. Also, I am not a Beja. For me this is not a binding oath. He accepted the offering, chewed and swallowed, then picked out a scrap of venison, salted it and offered it to Osman. The Khalif ate it and nodded his thanks.

They ate slowly, savouring the meal, and their easy conversation concerned the affairs that absorbed them both: war, hunting and the pursuit of arms. At first it was wide-ranging, then became more specific as Osman asked how the British trained their troops and what qualities their commanders looked for in their officers.

'Like you we are a warlike people. Most of our kings were warriors,' Penrod explained.

'This I have heard.' Osman nodded. 'I have also seen with my own eyes how your people fight. Where do they learn these skills?'

'There are a people called the French, a neighbouring tribe. We have sport with them on occasion. There is always trouble in some part of the Empire that must be controlled. During periods of peace we have colleges, which have been established for many generations, to train our line and staff officers. Two are famous: the Royal Military Academy at Woolwich, and the Royal Military College at Camberley.'

'We also have a school for our warriors.' Osman nodded. 'We call it the desert.'

Penrod laughed, then agreed. 'The battlefield is the best

494

training school, but we have found the academic study of the art of war invaluable too. You see, most of the great generals of all the ages from Alexander to Wellington have written of their campaigns. There is much in which they are able to instruct us.'

When they rode on eastwards, Osman summoned Penrod to ride at his side and they continued their discussion animatedly. At times they became heated. Penrod was describing how Bonaparte had been unable to break the British square at Waterloo, and Osman had mocked him lightly. 'We Arabs have not studied at any college, and yet unlike this Frenchman we broke your square at Abu Klea.'

Penrod rose to the bait, as Osman had intended he should. 'You never broke us. You penetrated locally, but the square held and healed itself, then became a trap for your emir al-Salida, his sons and a thousand of his men.' They argued with the freedom of blood-brothers, but when their voices rose the aggagiers looked at each other uneasily and pressed close to be ready to intervene if their *khalif* was threatened. Osman waved them back. He reined in on the skyline of another ridge in the series that climbed like a giant staircase towards the mountains.

'Before us lies the land of the Abyssinians, our enemies for many centuries past. If you were my general and I asked you to seize the territory as far as Gondar, then hold it against the rage of Emperor John, tell me how you, with your schoolroom studies, would accomplish this task.'

It was the kind of problem that Penrod had studied at the staff officer's college. He took up the challenge with enthusiasm. 'How many men will you give me?'

'Twenty-five thousand,' Osman replied.

'How many does the Emperor have to bring against me?'

'Maybe ten thousand at Gondar, but another three hundred thousand beyond the mountains at Aksum in the highlands.'

'They will have to descend through the high passes to bring me to battle, will they not? Then I must invest Gondar swiftly, and once the city is contained I will not pause to

495

reduce it, but I will drive on hard to seal the mouths of the passes before the reinforcements can debouch into the open ground.'

They discussed this problem in detail, considering every possible response to the attack. Their discussion continued unflaggingly over the rest of the march to Gallabat. It was only when they came in sight of the town that it occurred to Penrod that it had not been an academic discussion, and that this journey was a prelude to the Dervish invasion of the kingdom of Abyssinia. Osman was calling on his training as a military adviser.

So the Mahdi's *jihad* did not end at Khartoum, Penrod realized. Abdullahi knows that he must fight or he will languish and perish. Then he considered how much damage he had unwittingly done by giving encouragement and expert advice to Osman.

Even if the Dervish triumphs here at Gondar, Abdullahi will not be satisfied. He will turn his eyes on Eritrea, and he won't stop there. He cannot stop. He will never stop until he is forcibly stopped. That will not happen until Abdullahi has aroused the wrath of the civilized world, he decided. In my own humble way I may have done something to help bring that about. He smiled coldly. There are exciting days ahead.

The Dervish governor of Gallabat was almost overcome by the honour of receiving the mighty Khalif Osman Atalan as a guest in his city. Immediately he vacated his own mud-brick palace and placed it at the disposal of the visitors. He moved into a much smaller, humbler building on the outskirts of the town.

Osman decided to rest in Gallabat until the cessation of the monsoon period, which would make travelling in the hilly country around Gondar almost impossible. This would entail a delay of several months, but there was much to keep him occupied. He wanted to gather every scrap of information that might be of importance during the coming campaign. He sent out word that the local guides who had taken caravans up to Gondar through the high passes, and those warlike sheikhs who had raided the Ethiopian territories for cattle and slaves must come to him in Gallabat. They hastened to his bidding. He questioned them at great length, and recorded all they had to tell him. This information would comprise the bulk of his report to the Khalifat Abdullahi when he returned to Omdurman.

Osman recalled that the Mahdi had used the white concubine, al-Jamal, as a scribe and letter-writer. She was skilled in many languages. He ordered her to be present at these interrogations to write down the facts as they were revealed by the witnesses. He had seen little of al-Jamal since the beginning of the expedition for he had had marital obligations elsewhere. But Osman had barely settled into the governor's palace before the older women slaves of the harem came to him with the news that his youngest wife had at last responded to his repeated attentions by missing her moon. They informed him that she had not flown her red banner for two months past.

Osman was pleased. His fourth wife was a niece of the Khalifat Abdullahi and therefore her pregnancy was of great political importance. Her name was Zamatta. Although she had a pretty face, she enjoyed her food and had thick thighs, a pudding-shaped belly and a pair of soft, cow-like udders. At this time in his life Osman Atalan demanded more from his favourites than a musical giggle and a willingness to lie back and open their legs. He had done what had to be done, and now he felt no inclination to spend more time in the company of the dull-witted Zamatta.

During the first few days of the interrogations al-Jamal had taken up an unobtrusive position behind the governor's dais in the audience hall. On the third day Osman ordered her to move to a seat below the front of the dais. Here she sat cross-legged with her writing tablet on her lap, directly in his line of vision. He liked the quick movements of her slim, pale hands, and the texture of the cheek that was turned towards him as she wrote. As was fitting, she never raised her eyes from the parchment or looked at him directly. Once or twice while he was watching her a mysterious smile touched her lips, and this intrigued him. Seldom before in his life had he been concerned with what his women were thinking, but this one seemed different.

'Read back to me what you have written,' he ordered.

She lifted those strangely pale blue eyes to look at him, and his breath caught. She recited the evidence, without having to read it. When she finished she leant towards him and dropped her voice so that he alone could hear. 'Trust him not, Great Lord,' she said. 'He will give you little for your comfort.' They were the first words she had ever addressed to him.

Osman's expression remained impassive, but he was thinking quickly. He had let it be known that he was conducting these enquiries to facilitate trade with the Abyssinians and plan his state visit to Gondar. Had this woman guessed his true intentions, or had she been informed? What grounds did she have for the warning she had just given him? He went on with his enquiries, but now he studied the man before him more intently.

He was an elderly caravan master, prosperous from the cloth of his robes, intelligent judging by the depth of his knowledge. In all other respects he was unremarkable. He had stated that he was of the tribe of Hadendowa. Yet he did not affect the patched *jibba*, and there was something alien in his accent and the manner of his speech. Osman considered challenging his identity, but discarded the idea. He looked for the other signs that al-Jamal must have noticed. The man leant forward to take the small brass cup of coffee from the tray that had been placed before him, and the neck opening of his robe gaped to show a flash of silver. It was a fleeting glimpse, but Osman recognized the ornately engraved Coptic Christian cross that hung on a chain round his neck.

He is Abyssinian, Osman realized. Why would he dissemble? Are they spying on us as we are on them? He smiled at the man. 'What you have told me has been of great value. For this I thank you. When do you begin your next journey?'

'Great Khalif, three days hence I leave with two hundred camels laden with rock salt from the pans at al-Glosh.'

'What is your destination?'

'I travel to the new city of Addis Ababa in the hills, where I purpose to barter my salt for ingots of copper.'

'Go with God, good merchant.'

'Stay with God, mighty Atalan, and may angels guard your sleep.'

When the caravan owner left the audience hall, Osman gestured al-Noor to his side. When the aggagier knelt beside him he whispered, 'The merchant is a spy. Kill him. Do it secretly and with cunning. None must learn who delivered the blow.'

'As you order, so shall it be done.'

The staff left the hall, each making an obeisance to the Khalif as he passed, but when al-Jamal rose to follow them Osman said curtly, 'Sit by me. We shall talk a while.'

By this time Rebecca could act the part of a concubine. The Mahdi had taught her how to please an Arab master. Flattery was the one sure way to achieve it. She was always astonished at how they would accept the most extravagant hyperbole as nothing more than their due. While she spouted this nonsense she could efface herself and keep her true feelings hidden. She sat as he had ordered and, with her face veiled, waited for him to speak.

'Remove your veil,' he said. 'I wish to see your face while we discourse.' She obeyed. He studied her features in silence for a while, then asked, 'Why do you smile?'

'Because, my lord, I am happy to be in your presence. It gives me great pleasure to serve you.'

'Are all the women in your country like you?'

'We speak the same language, but none of us is like the others. Great Khalif, I am sure your women are no different.'

'Our women are all the same. The reason for their existence is to please their husbands.'

'Then they are fortunate, great Atalan, especially those who have the honour to belong to you.'

'How did you learn to read and write?'

'My lord, I was taught to do so from an early age.'

'Your father did not forbid this?'

'Nay, sweet master, he encouraged it.'

Osman shook his head with disapproval. 'What of his wives? Did he allow them to indulge in such dangerous practice?'

'My father had one wife, and she was my mother. When she died he never remarried.'

'How many concubines?'

'None, exalted Khalif.'

'Then he must have been very poor, and of little standing in this world.'

'My father was the representative of our queen, and well beloved by her. I have a letter from Her Majesty that says so.'

'If the Queen truly loved him, she should have sent him a dozen wives to replace the old one.' Osman was fascinated by her replies, each of which led him immediately to another question. He found it difficult to imagine a land where it rained almost every day and was so cold that the raindrops turned to white salt before they hit the ground.

'What do the people drink? Why do they not die of thirst if the water turns to *salt?*'

'My master, before very long the snow turns back to water.'

Osman looked up to the spade-shaped windows. 'The sun has set. You must follow me to my quarters. I wish to hear more of these wonders.'

Rebecca's spirits quailed. Since she had been taken into his *zenana*, she had been able to avoid this confrontation. She smiled prettily, and covered her mouth with one hand as she had seen the other women do when overcome with shyness. 'Again you fill my heart with joy, noble lord. To be with you is all in this life that gives me pleasure.'

The cooks brought up the evening meal to his quarters while Osman prayed alone on the terrace, which commanded a grand vista of distant mountains. As soon as he had completed the complicated ritual he dismissed the cooks, and ordered Rebecca to serve his food, but showed little interest in it. He took a few mouthfuls, then made her sit at his feet and eat from his leavings.

He continued to ply her with questions, and listened intently to her replies, hardly allowing her a chance to swallow before he asked the next question. Some time in the early hours of the morning she slumped over and fell into a deep sleep on the cushions from sheer exhaustion. When she awoke it was dawn and she was stretched out still fully dressed on his *angareb*. She wondered how she had got there, then remembered her dream of being a small girl again and her father carrying her up the stairs to bed. Had the Khalif carried her to bed? she wondered. If he had, that was some small miracle of condescension.

She heard excited shouts and galloping hoofs from below the terrace and rose from the bed, went to the window and looked down. In the courtyard Osman Atalan and some of his aggagiers were trying out a string of unbroken three-year-old horses that had been the gift of the governor of Gallabat. Penrod Ballantyne, almost indistinguishable from the Arabs, was up on a frisky bay colt that was bucking furiously around the yard with arched back and stiff legs. Osman and his other aggagiers shouted with laughter and offered ribald advice.

These days, whenever Rebecca laid eyes on Penrod her emotions were thrown into uproar. He was a heartbreaking reminder of that long-ago existence from which she had been snatched so untimely. Did she still love him, as she had once thought she did? She was not sure. Nothing was certain any longer. Except that the man who stood at the opposite end of the yard now ruled her destiny. She stared at Osman Atalan, and the despair she thought she had subdued returned in full force to overwhelm her like a dark wave.

She turned from the window and stared at the Webley revolver that lay on a side table across the room. She had seen the Khalif place it there before he went to his prayers the previous night. It had probably been taken from a dead British officer at Abu Klea or perhaps even looted at the sack of Khartoum.

She crossed the room and picked it up. She opened the action and saw that every chamber was fully loaded. She snapped it shut and turned to the mirror on the facing wall. She stared at her image as she cocked and lifted the pistol to point at her own temple. She stood like that trying to summon that last grain of determination to press the trigger.

Then she noticed in the mirror the initials engraved discreetly in the butt plate of the weapon. She lowered it and examined the inscription. 'D. W. B. From S. I. B. With love,' she read. 'David Wellington Benbrook from Sarah Isabel Benbrook.'

This had been her mother's gift to her father. She hurled it from her and ran from the room, back to the *zenana* to find Nazeera, the only person in the world to whom she could turn.

Penrod sat the colt easily and let him work himself into a lather as he whipped from side to side with long elastic jumps, then stood on his hind legs and pawed at the sky. When the colt lost his balance and toppled backwards, the watching aggagiers shouted and al-Noor beat on his leather shield with his scabbard. But Penrod jumped clear, still holding the long rein. With a convulsive heave the colt came up again on all four legs, and before he could break away, Penrod sprang lightly on to his bare back. The colt stood on planted hoofs and shivered with outrage and frustration at being unable to rid himself of the unfamiliar weight.

'Open the gates!' Penrod shouted, to the captain of the city guard, then lashed the colt across the shoulder with the end of the reins. He sprang into startled flight, and Penrod turned him towards the open gates. They flew through and out into the lane, scattering chickens, dogs and children, skirted the souk, then ran out into the open country, still at full gallop. Almost an hour later horse and rider returned. Penrod walked the colt round the courtyard, turning him left and right, halting him, making him back up and stand at last. He threw one leg over his neck and dropped to the ground, stood at the colt's head and stroked his sweat-drenched neck.

'What think you, Abadan Riji?' Osman Atalan called down from the terrace. 'Is this a horse fit for an aggagier?'

'He is strong and swift, and he learns quickly,' Penrod responded.

'Then he is my gift to you,' said the Khalif.

Penrod was astonished at this mark of approval. It enhanced his status yet again. He lacked only a sword to be counted a full warrior of the Beja. He clenched his right fist and held it to his heart in a gesture of respect and gratitude. 'I am not worthy of such liberality. I shall name him Ata min Khalif, the Gift of the Khalif.'

The following day Penrod loaded his ivory tusk on to one of the packhorses and carried it down to the souk. For an hour he sat drinking coffee and haggling with a trader from Suakin. In the end he sold the tusk for two hundred and fifty Maria Theresa dollars.

When he had entered the souk he had passed the stall of a fat Persian. In pride of place among the merchant's wares a sword was laid out on a sheepskin fleece. Now Penrod came back to him. He examined all his other stock, showing particular interest in a matched necklace and earrings of polished amber, and avoided glancing at the sword. He haggled the price of the amber jewellery, and drank so many more cups of coffee that his bladder ached. In the end he struck a bargain at three Maria Theresas for the necklace. He bid the Persian farewell, and was leaving his stall when his eye fell at last upon the sword. The Persian smiled: he had known all along where Penrod's true interest lay.

The slim curved blade was of the finest Damascus steel, unembellished by gold engravings and inscriptions for the graceful wavy patterns in the metal, caused by the strip forgings, were sufficient ornamentation. This was not a pretty bauble but a true killing blade. With the bright edge Penrod shaved a patch of hair off his forearm, then flicked his wrist.

The steel sang like a crystal glass. It cost him seventy-five Maria Theresas, the equivalent price of two pretty Galla slave girls.

Three days later Osman Atalan held an audience in the great tent that had been set up at the edge of the city. Penrod waited his turn among the supplicants, then knelt before the Khalif. 'What more do you require of me, Abadan Riji?' Osman asked, and his tone was sharp and brittle as flint.

'I beg the mighty and noble Atalan to accept the gift of one he has honoured with his benevolence.' He placed the roll of sheepskin at Osman's feet.

Osman unwrapped it and smiled when he saw the lovely weapon. 'This is a fine gift and one that I accept with pleasure.' He handed the sword back to Penrod. 'Carry it for me. If you must use it, use it wisely.'

Between them they had reached a compromise. The slave was still a slave, but accoutred like a warrior.

Rebecca sat at the Khalif's feet each day, recording the proceeds in the audience hall. Every evening she was sent back to the *zenana* in the governor's palace. At first his indifference was a relief to her, but after three days it irked her. Had she given him offence by falling asleep in his presence, or bored and annoyed him with garrulousness, she wondered. Or am I just unattractive to him? It really does not matter what he feels. Only what happens to Amber and Nazeera, and of course to me also. Endlessly she and Nazeera discussed this predicament, which involved them all so intricately and intimately. Their well-being and even their lives were in the Khalif's hands. From hating the thought of allowing Osman Atalan to touch her, Rebecca began to fear that he would not do so.

Nazeera held up to her the example of his fourth wife Zamatta. 'She was unable to hold his interest. And so, even though she is a relative of the Khalifat Abdullahi, he sent her back to Omdurman as soon as she had a babe in her belly.

She may never see him again, and will probably pass the entire remainder of her life locked in the *zenana*. Beware, al-Jamal. If he rejects you, you may not be so fortunate as Zamatta. He might sell you, or give you to some old emir or sheikh who smells like a goat. And Amber – what will he do with her? The Khalifat likes children, young children. He would welcome her into his own harem, if Osman Atalan offered her to him. You must strive to please him. I shall teach you how, for I have some small experience in these matters.'

With these threats as an incentive Rebecca determined to pay full attention to Nazeera's advice and instruction.

The following afternoon Nazeera returned from a visit to the souk, and displayed her purchase: the tusk from the lower jaw of a hippopotamus. 'We shall use this as a tool of instruction,' she informed Rebecca. 'There is much demand for toys such as this among the women of the harem and *zenana* who do not see their husbands from one feast of Ramadan to the next. They call them the jinn of the *angareb*. The Khalif Atalan has different tastes from those of the Divine Mahdi. Your mouth and sweet lips alone will not suffice. He will require more of you than the Mahdi ever did.' She held up the tusk. 'The Khalif will be this shape, but if he is so large you will be blessed indeed.' Nazeera went on to demonstrate her artistry.

Rebecca would never have dreamt that some of the behaviour Nazeera described between man and woman was possible, and she found herself becoming more interested in the subject than the cold contemplation of survival required. She thought about it a great deal at night before she slept, and if Amber had not been lying beside her on the same *angareb* she might have indulged in some preliminary experimentation with the ivory toy.

However, it seemed that Osman Atalan had lost interest in her even before he had pursued their relationship to its full potential. Eventually he finished questioning the last of the witnesses. He was about to leave the audience hall without having acknowledged her, when unexpectedly he turned to one of his viziers. 'This evening the concubine al-Jamal will serve my evening meal. See to it.'

Although she kept her eyes downcast Rebecca felt a lift of intense relief, tempered by a stirring of trepidation. I must play the game that Nazeera has taught me to arouse his carnal passions, and make our lives secure, she thought, then tried to suppress the flutter of excitement in the pit of her stomach. It seemed, however, that this particular evening the Khalif's passions were more conversational than concupiscent. He gave her little opportunity to try out her freshly acquired knowledge.

'I know that in your country the ruler is a woman,' he said, before he had finished eating.

'Yes. Victoria is our queen.'

'Does she rule firmly and are her laws strong?'

'She does not make the laws. The laws are made by Parliament.'

'Ah!' said the Khalif knowingly. 'So Parliament is her husband, and he makes the laws. That is clever of him. He must be cunning and wise. I knew that a man must be behind it all. I should like to write a letter to Lord Parliament.'

'Parliament is not a single man. It is an assembly of the people.'

'The common people make the laws? Do you mean the cooks and grooms, the carpenters and masons, the beggars, *fellahin* and gravediggers? Anyone of this riff-raff can make a law? Surely this is not possible.'

Rebecca struggled for half of the rest of the night to explain an electoral system of government and the democratic process. When finally she succeeded Osman was appalled. 'How can warriors like those Englishmen I have fought allow this obscenity to exist?' He was silent for a while as he paced the floor. Then he stopped in front of her, and his tone was diffident, as though he feared her answer. 'Women also have this thing you call a vote?'

'Women do not have a voice. No woman may cast a vote,' she replied.

Osman placed his fists on his hips and laughed triumphantly. 'Ha! Now at least I can still respect my enemies. At least your men keep control of their wives. But tell me, please. You say your ruler is a woman. Does she not have a voice, a vote?'

'I – I don't know. I don't think so.'

'You Franks!' He clutched his head theatrically. 'Are you mad? Or is it me alone?'

Rebecca found that she was beginning to enjoy herself. Like a pack of hunting dogs, their discussion ranged over wide territory and started some extraordinary game. This was like the unrestricted and open-ended discussions in which her father had indulged her. Beyond the open windows the cocks crowed at dawn while she was still trying to explain to him that the Atlantic Ocean was wider than the Nile or even, in God's Name, Lake Tana. When he sent her back to the harem unmolested, her relief was tempered by a strange feeling of inadequacy.

Before she joined Amber on the mattress she held up the oil lamp and studied herself in the small mirror. Most men find me appealing, she reminded herself, and thought of Ryder Courtney and Penrod Ballantyne. So why does this savage treat me like another man? she wondered.

The next morning she watched with Amber and the rest of the women from the terrace of the harem as Osman Atalan rode out at the head of a band of his aggagiers on a hawking expedition along the eastern border.

'Look!' cried Amber. 'There is Captain Ballantyne. They say that the Khalif gave him that horse. On him the *jibba* looks as dashing as a cavalry dolman. He is so handsome, would you not agree, Becky?'

Rebecca had barely noticed Penrod but she made a non-committal sound while she followed with her eyes the elegant, exotic figure at the head of the cavalcade of horsemen. He is as fierce and dangerous as the falcon on his wrist, she thought.

Osman Atalan was gone from the city for almost ten days. When he returned he sent for Rebecca. He stood behind her shoulder as he directed her to draw a detailed map of the ground he had covered in his foray across the Abyssinian border. When she had completed it to his satisfaction, he dismissed her. Then he called her back from the door, 'You will attend me after evening prayers. I want to discuss with you certain matters that interest me.'

When she found Nazeera in the harem, she whispered the news to her. 'He wants me to go to him again this evening, Nazeera. What shall I do?'

Nazeera saw the colour in her cheeks. 'I am sure you will think of something,' she said. 'Now I will prepare your bath.' She poured a liberal measure of attar of roses and sandalwood essence into the pitchers of hot water, then rummaged through the chests to choose a robe fitting to the occasion from the wardrobe that the Mahdi had provided for Rebecca.

'You can see through it,' Amber protested, when Rebecca put it on. 'With the lamp behind you it makes you seem *naked*!' She placed a powerful pejorative emphasis on the last word. 'You will look like a belly-dancer!'

'I shall wear my woollen shawl over it, and keep myself covered throughout the dinner,' Rebecca reassured her.

As soon as they were alone in his quarters, the Khalif picked up the subject of their conversation of ten days previously, as though it had not been interrupted. 'So this large water you call the ocean is alive. It moves backwards and forwards, and leaps up and down. Is that not what you told me?'

'Indeed, mighty Atalan, at times it is like a ravening beast with the strength of a thousand elephants. It can overwhelm ships fifty times larger than any that voyage on the Nile as though they were dried leaves.'

He looked into her eyes to discover if there was any truth at all in these improbable statements. All he found were points of light, like those in the depths of a sapphire. This diverted his train of thought and he took her chin and lifted it to gaze deeply into her eyes. His hands were strong and his fingers hard as bone from sword-play and from handling his hawks and horses.

He made her feel helpless and vulnerable. I must remember everything Nazeera has taught me. She felt her loins melt lubriciously. This might be the only opportunity he will ever give me.

'I shall send an expedition of a thousand of my most intrepid men to find this wild water and bring it back in large skins,' Osman announced. 'I will pour it into the Nile to overwhelm the British steamers when next they sail upriver to attack us.'

She was touched by his naïvety. Sometimes it was like talking to a small child. Not for the first time she felt an extraordinary tenderness towards him, which she had forcibly to suppress. This is no child. This is a shrewd, ruthless, arrogant tyrant. I am completely at his mercy. Why did that thought excite her, she wondered. But before she could decide the answer he made another disconcerting change of subject.

'But I have heard that their steamers are able to voyage on the land further and faster than the bravest horse. Is this true?'

'It is true, mighty Khalif. These carriages are different from the river steamers and are called steam locomotives.' It took her a few moments to rally her thoughts, and she described how she had journeyed from London to Portsmouth in a single day, including a stop for refreshment. 'That is a distance greater than from Metemma to Khartoum.' Her voice was husky and disturbed. He still held her chin, but now he stroked her cheek and touched a lock of her hair. She was surprised at the gentleness of his hard fingers, this savage warrior from the primal deserts.

'What unguent do you use to keep your skin and hair so soft?' he asked.

'This is how I was born.'

'It grows dark. Light the lamps so that I may see you more clearly.'

She remembered how Amber had disapproved of the transparency of the silk she wore. She slipped the light woollen shawl off her shoulder as she stood up, and tossed it over the table as she went to take a taper from the fire pot. She cupped the flame in her hands and carried it across to the lamp. It caught, then burnt brightly; the warm yellow light chased the shadows along the walls. She lingered there a little longer, trimming the wick until the flame was burning evenly. Her back was turned to him, but she was aware of the picture she made. I am acting like a harlot, she thought, then seemed to hear her father's voice: 'It's an honourable profession. The oldest in the world.' She smiled in confusion as the ghost voice went on, delivering his often repeated advice to her: 'Whatever you do, do it to the very best of your ability.' It was a blessing.

'I shall try, Daddy,' she replied inwardly, and at that she felt a touch. She had not heard Osman Atalan cross the room behind her. His hands on her shoulders were strong and steady. She smelt him. It was a good smell like a well-groomed horse or a cat. Muslim men of his rank bathed as many times in a day as an Englishman did in a month.

She stood submissively as his hands ran down from her shoulders, under her armpits, then reached in front of her to take her breasts. They filled each of his hands. He took her nipples and rolled them between his fingers, then pinched them until she gasped. The pressure was skilfully applied, just sufficient to startle and arouse her without inflicting pain. Then he pulled her back against him. It was some moments before she realized that he had shed his *jibba* and was now naked. Through the silk of her robe she could feel the hard muscular length of his body pressing against her back. Tentatively she pushed back with her buttocks, and found conclusive proof that he did not find her repellent. With Nazeera's advice and instruction still sharp in her mind, Rebecca stood without moving as she appraised that which the Khalif was pressing against her. It seemed to be of similar shape to Nazeera's hippo tusk, and it was certainly every bit as hard.

She turned slowly in his arms and looked down. It seems that I am to be blessed indeed, she thought. Like the ivory tusk, he was smooth and slightly curved. She touched him, then encompassed him with her hand. Her fingers were barely able to meet round his girth. She made the movements of her hand that Nazeera had demonstrated and felt him throb and leap in her grip.

'Great Khalif, in your manly attributes you are peerless and imperial.'

He took the word 'imperial' as a comparison to the Light of the World, Muhammad el Mahdi, who now sat at the right hand of Allah, and he was well pleased. 'I am your stallion,' he said.

'And I am your filly, in awe of your strength and majesty. Treat me gently, I beg you, sweet lord.'

She continued to hold him. She expected him to pounce upon her as Ryder Courtney had done, but his restraint surprised, then titillated her. She kept her grip on him as he undressed her, and was still holding him as she fell back on his mattress. She attempted to direct him to her source, using both hands and coming up on her elbows so she could watch him disappear inside her. But he resisted her urging, and began to examine her as though she were indeed a thoroughbred filly, turning her this way and that, lifting each limb in turn, admiring and caressing them. It was at first flattering to be at the centre of his attention, but he was so unhurried and deliberate that she became impatient. She longed for the delicious sensation of being deeply invaded that she had last known with Ryder Courtney.

Still he lingered over her, taking his time so deliberately that she felt she must scream in her desperation. She had once owned a tabby cat named Butter. In her season Butter would yowl and sob to attract feline admirers. Rebecca understood that imperative now. How many thousand women has he known? she wondered. For him there is no urgency. He cares not at all that he is causing me such distress.

She tugged at him again with both hands. 'I beg of you, great Atalan, lack of you is torture beyond my ability to endure. Please be merciful and end it now.'

'You asked me to treat you gently,' he reminded her, with a smile.

'I am a silly creature who does not know her own mind or nature. Forget what I have said, my lord. You know much better than I ever will what must be done. Make haste, I entreat you. I can wait no longer.' He did as she asked, and this time she could not forbear from screaming, louder and longer than Butter ever had. None of Osman Atalan's other women had ever acknowledged his mastery in such a comprehensive vocal fashion. He was flattered and amused.

He did not dismiss her on rising, as was his habit, but kept her beside him as he ate his breakfast. Soon none of the other concubines he had brought with him from Omdurman were honoured by a summons to his private quarters. Rebecca took up almost permanent abode in them. She did not bore him, as the others were wont to do.

Once Osman Atalan had assembled all the expert first-hand information of the local guides and hunters and traders, he employed Rebecca's artistic skills and penmanship to incorporate it into a large-scale map of the border and the disputed country immediately beyond, where he expected one day soon to do battle with the Ethiopians. He gave a tracing of this map to Penrod and sent him out on a scouting mission to check it against the terrain. He could not entrust this task to any of his aggagiers: for all their loyalty and dedication to him, none was more than barely literate and none possessed more than a vestige of map-reading skills. However, to exclude any from such an important expedition would be to afford them deep insult.

On the other hand he was still not certain how far out of his sight he could trust the slave Abadan Riji. He solved this delicate problem by selecting al-Noor and six other aggagiers to accompany him, ostensibly as his jailers but in reality as his bodyguard. Osman left them in no doubt that they should accede to the reasonable orders and directions of Abadan Riji in the accomplishment of the objects of the expedition. On the other hand if they returned to Gallabat without their charge, he would decapitate them.

After his scouts had left, Osman Atalan remained at Gallabat to review with the Dervish governor the state of his province, also to receive the Abyssinian emissaries from Aksum. Emperor John was anxious to discern the true reason for the presence of such an important Dervish on his borders. His ambassadors brought valuable gifts, and assurances of mutual peace and goodwill. Osman sent back a message that as soon as the season of the big rains ended he would travel to Gondar to meet the emperor.

Meanwhile the thunderstorms raged daily over the mountains, affording him ample opportunity for prolonged discourse with his new favourite.

Penrod's expedition left Gallabat in the middle of the morning, just as soon as the rain of the previous night had blown over and the sun broken out between the high cumulo-nimbus cloud mountains. They were as lightly equipped as a tribal raiding party. Each man carried his own weapons and bedroll on the pommel of his saddle, while three pack mules brought up the rear with leather bags of provisions and cooking pots bouncing on their backs. Half a mile beyond the last buildings of the town they came upon a group of five women sitting beside the track. They were engaged in the endless feminine pastime of hairdressing. This was the equivalent of the aggagiers' sword-honing, and filled their idle hours, of which there were many.

It was not possible for an Arab woman to arrange her hair alone: it was a social enterprise that involved all her close companions. The styling was elaborate and might take two or three days of patient, skilled creation. In the year that Amber had lived in the harem she had learnt the art so well that, with her nimble fingers and eye for detail, her skills were much in demand among the other women of Osman Atalan's *zenana*; so much so that she was able to charge a fee of two or three Maria Theresas, depending on the labour required.

First, the hair had to be combed out. It was usually wiry, matted with congealed cosmetics and twisted into tight curls from its previous dressing. Amber used a long skewer to separate the strands. After that she employed a coarse wooden comb to bring about some order to the dense tresses. All these preliminaries might occupy a full day, which was enlivened by laughter and the exchange of juicy morsels of scandal and gossip.

Once it was possible to burrow down as far as the scalp, a hunt for trespassers was conducted in which everyone participated. The sport was accompanied by cries of triumph and shrieks of delight as the scurrying vermin were hunted down and crushed between the fingernails. Once the field had been cleared, Amber dressed the locks with a concoction of oil of roses, myrrh, dust of sandalwood, and powder of cloves and cassia mixed with mutton fat. Then the most delicate part of the operation took place. The hair was twisted into hundreds of tiny tight plaits and set with a liberal application of sticky gum arabic and dhurra paste. This was allowed to dry until it was stiff as toffee. On the final day each tiny plait was carefully unpicked with the long tortoiseshell skewer, and allowed to stand on its own, free and proud, so the woman's head appeared twice its normal size. The finished work was usually greeted with squeals of admiration and approbation. After ten days the entire process was repeated, affording Amber a steady income.

This morning Amber was so intent on her work that she was not aware of the approaching band of aggagiers until they were less than a hundred paces off. All present were now placed in an invidious situation. Here were five of the Khalif Osman Atalan's women, unveiled and unchaperoned, except by each other, about to be confronted by a war party of the same Khalif's trusted warriors. The correct and diplomatic behaviour would have been for both sides to ignore the presence of the other, and for the aggagiers to pass by as though they were as invisible as the breeze.

'Captain Ballantyne!' screamed Amber, and jumped to her feet, leaving the skewer sticking from her customer's bushy curls. She flew down the road to meet him. None of the women knew quite what to do. So they giggled and did nothing. Al-Noor, at the head of the band of horsemen, was in a similar predicament. He scowled ferociously and glanced at Penrod. Penrod ignored both him and Amber and rode on expressionlessly. Al-Noor could think of no rules to cover this situation. Al-Zahra was still a child, not a woman. She was in sight of four other women, and six warriors. By no stretch of the imagination could she be in any danger of violation. In the event of any repercussions all the others present were in equal guilt. In the last resort, he could plead with the Khalif that Abadan Riji was the leader of the band and therefore responsible for any breach of etiquette or custom. He stared straight ahead and pretended that this was not happening.

'Penrod Ballantyne, this is the first opportunity I have had to speak to you since Khartoum.' Amber danced along beside Ata.

'And you know very well why.' Penrod spoke from the corner of his mouth. 'You must go back to the other women or we shall both be in serious trouble.'

'The women think you very dashing. They would never tell on us.' They were speaking English, and Penrod was sure that none of the aggagiers understood a word of it.

'Then take a message to your sister. Tell Rebecca that I will seize the first opportunity to arrange your escape, and bring both of you to safety.'

'We know that you will never let us down.'

His expression softened: she was so pretty and winsome. 'How are you, Amber? Are you bearing up?'

'I was very sick, but Rebecca and Nazeera saved me. I am well now.'

'I can see that. How is your sister?'

'She is also well.' Amber wished he would not keep harking back to Rebecca.

'I have a little gift for you,' said Penrod. Surreptitiously he slipped his hand into the saddlebag and found the amber necklace and earrings he had bought in the souk. He had wrapped them in a scrap of tanned sheepskin. He did not hand them to her directly but dropped them into the road, using his horse to conceal the move from the other aggagiers.

'Wait until we have gone before you pick it up,' he

instructed her, 'and don't let the other women see you do it.'
He pressed his heels into Ata's flanks and rode on. Amber
watched him out of sight. The eyes of the other women also
followed the band of horsemen. Amber scooped up the small
roll of sheepskin. She could barely contain herself until she
was alone in the *zenana* before she opened it. When she did
she was almost overcome with delight.

'It is the most beautiful gift I have ever had.' She showed
it to Rebecca and Nazeera. 'Do you think he really likes me,
Becky?'

'It is a very handsome gift, darling,' Rebecca agreed, 'and
I am sure he likes you very much.' She chose her words carefully. 'As does everyone who knows you.'

'I wish I could grow up soon. Then he would no longer
treat me as a child,' said Amber wistfully.

Rebecca hugged her hard and felt her tears just below the
surface. At times like this the peril of their situation and her
sense of responsibility towards Amber was a burden almost
too heavy for her to bear. If you do to this beautiful child
what you did to me, Penrod Ballantyne, she vowed silently, I
shall kill you with my bare hands and dance on your grave.

The principal object of the expedition into Abyssinian
territory was to scout the three main mountain passes
through which any army coming down from the highlands to
the relief of Gondar would have to march.

The major combe in the mountain chain was the gorge of
the Atbara river. Although the ground on the north bank
of this river was precipitous and guarded by sheer rock cliffs,
the slope of the south bank was less demanding. The ancient
trade route ran along this side of the river. It took Penrod's
party almost three weeks to reach the mouth of the pass.
It rained heavily almost every night, and during the day
the rivers and streams were swollen, the ground sodden and
swampy. The going was so heavy that on some days they

covered less than ten miles. The aggagiers suffered cruelly from the wet and cold, to which they were unaccustomed.

Once they reached the Atbara gorge they climbed the slope of the south bank and about three hundred feet above the level of the river they came upon a saucer of ground that was hidden from any traveller on the caravan road below. A tiny stream ran down the middle of this hollow. Fresh green grass grew along both banks of the stream. They had driven the horses and mules hard, and Penrod decided to rest them for a few days while he observed any traffic coming down through the pass.

Each morning Penrod and al-Noor climbed to the lip of the saucer and took up a position in a patch of dense scrub just below the skyline. On the first two days they saw no sign of any human activity. The only living creatures were a pair of black eagles who had their eyrie in the cliffs above the north bank of the river: they were curious about the two men and came sailing along the hills on their immense wings to pass close over their heads as they crouched in the scrub. During the rest of the day they were often in sight, carrying hare and small antelope in their talons to their young in the shaggy pile of their nest.

Apart from these birds, the mountains seemed barren and deserted, the silence so complete that the mournful cry of the eagles carried clearly to them, although the birds were mere specks in the blue vault of cloud and sky.

Towards evening on the third day Penrod was roused from a drowsy reverie by another alien sound. At first he thought it might be a fall of rock rattling down the hillside. Then he was startled to hear the faint sound of human voices. He reached for his telescope and scanned the caravan road as far as the first bend of the pass. He saw nothing, but over the next half-hour the sounds grew louder, and when the echoes picked them up and accentuated them he was no longer in any doubt that a large caravan was threading its way down the pass. He lay on his belly and focused the spyglass on the head of the pass. Suddenly a pair of mules appeared in the field of his lens.

They were heavily laden, followed immediately by another pair, then a third, until finally he counted a hundred and twenty beasts of burden and their drovers descending along the riverbank towards the vale of Gondar.

'A rich prize.' The sight had woken the bandit instincts in al-Noor and he watched the caravan hungrily. 'Who can say what is in those sacks? Silver Maria Theresas? Gold sovereigns? Enough for each of us to afford a hundred camels and a dozen beautiful slave girls. Paradise enow!'

'Paradise indeed! Who could ask for more?' Penrod agreed, grim-faced. 'If we lifted a finger to these good merchants, Abyssinia would be thrown into uproar. The plans of the exalted Khalif Atalan would be frustrated, and you and I would be sent to Paradise without our testicles with which to enjoy its pleasures. All things in their season, al-Noor.'

Slowly the leading mules of the column came closer until they were passing directly below Penrod's lookout. Three men were bringing up the rear. Penrod studied them. One was a young lad, the second was short and pudgy and the third was a powerfully built rascal, who looked as if he could give good account of himself in a fracas. As they rode closer still, their features became more distinct, and Penrod almost let out an exclamation of surprise. He checked the outburst before it passed his lips. He did not want to arouse curiosity in al-Noor. He looked again more carefully and this time there could be no doubt. Ryder Courtney! His mind had difficulty accepting what his eyes had seen.

He moved the lens to the plump figure who rode at Ryder's left side. Bacheet, the fat rogue!

Then he turned his lens to the third person, a stripling dressed in baggy crimson trousers, a bright green coat with long skirts and a wide-brimmed yellow hat that seemed to have been designed in anger or in a state of mental confusion. The boy was laughing at something Courtney had said. But the laughter had a decidedly feminine lilt, and Penrod started, then controlled himself. Saffron! Saffron Benbrook! It seemed impossible. He had believed she must have perished with her father in Khartoum. The thought had been too painful to contemplate squarely, and he had pushed it to the back of his mind. Now here she was, as lively as a grasshopper and pretty as a butterfly despite her outlandish garb.

'They are on their way down to Gondar from either Aksum or Addis Ababa.' Al-Noor gave his opinion morosely, still mourning the fortune in camels and nubile wenches that he was being forced to pass by.

'They are going into camp,' said Penrod, as the head of the long column turned aside from the route and drew up on a clear, level stretch of ground above the bank of the Atbara. He looked at the height of the sun. There would be at least another two hours of light by which to travel, but Ryder was setting up his camp. While the herders cut fodder from the riverbank and carried it back in bundles to feed the mules, the servants erected a large dining and sitting tent and two smaller sleeping tents. They set out a pair of folding chairs in front of the fire. Ryder Courtney travelled in comfort and style.

Just as the sun set and the light began to fade Penrod saw Ryder, accompanied by Saffron, who had divested herself of the yellow hat, making his rounds of the camp and posting his sentries. Penrod made a careful note of the position of each guard. He had seen that they were armed with muzzle-loaders, and he could be certain these were filled with a mixture of pot-legs, rusted nails and assorted musket balls, all of which would be unpleasant missiles to receive in the belly at close range.

Penrod and al-Noor kept watch on Ryder's camp until darkness obscured it, except for the area in front of the main tent, which was dimly lit by an oil lamp. Penrod observed that Saffron retired early to her small tent. Ryder remained by the fire smoking a cheroot, for which Penrod envied him. At last he threw the stub in to the embers, and went to his own bed. Penrod waited until the lamplight had been extinguished in both tents, then led al-Noor back to their own camp beside the stream. They built no fire and ate cold *asida* and roast mutton. Firelight and the smell of smoke might warn unfriendly strangers of their presence.

Al-Noor had been quiet since they left the ridge, but now he spoke through a mouthful of cold food. 'I have devised a plan,' he announced. 'A plan that will make all of us rich.'

'Your wisdom will be received as cool rain by the desert. I wait in awe for you to impart it to me,' Penrod replied, with elaborate courtesy.

'There are twenty-two Abyssinians with the caravan. I have counted them, but they are fat traders and merchants. We are six, but we are the fiercest warriors in all of Sudan. We will go down in the night and kill them all. We will allow none to escape. Then we will bury their bodies and drive their mules back to Gallabat, and the Abyssinians will believe that they were devoured by the djinni of the mountains. We will hand all the treasure to our exalted lord Atalan, and from him we will win great preferment and riches.' Penrod was silent, until al-Noor insisted, 'What think you of my plan?'

'I can see no vice in it. I think that you are a great and noble *shufta*,' Penrod replied.

Al-Noor was surprised but pleased to be called a bandit. To an aggagier of the Beja, the epithet was a compliment. 'Then this very night in the time when all of them are asleep, we will go down to the camp and do this business. Are we agreed, Abadan Riji?'

'Once we have been given permission by the Emir Osman Atalan, may Allah love him for ever, we will murder these fat merchants and steal their wares.' Penrod nodded, and another long silence ensued.

Then al-Noor spoke again: 'The mighty Emir Atalan, may Allah look upon him with the utmost favour, is in Gallabat two hundred leagues to the north. How will it be possible to solicit his permission?'

'That is indeed a difficulty.' Penrod agreed. 'When you have found an answer to that question, we shall discuss your plan further. In the meantime, Mooman Digna will take the first watch. I shall take the midnight shift. You, Noor, will take the dawn watch. Perhaps then you will have time to consider a solution to our dilemma.' Al-Noor moved away in dignified silence, rolled himself in his sheepskin and, within a short while, emitted his first snore.

Penrod slept fitfully and was fully awake at Mooman Digna's first touch on his shoulder, and his whisper, 'It is time.'

Penrod allowed almost an hour for the aggagiers to settle again. He knew from experience that once they were cocooned in their sheepskins, they could not be easily roused to face the bitter mountain cold. He rose from his seat on the rock that overlooked the camp and, barefooted, moved silently up over the lip of the ridge. He approached Ryder's camp with great caution. By this time there was a slice of crescent moon above the horizon, and the stars were bright enough for him to pick out the sentries. He avoided them without difficulty. As al-Noor had pointed out, they were not warriors. He crept up behind the rear wall of Ryder's tent, and squatted beside it. He could hear Ryder breathing heavily on the other side of the canvas, only inches from his ear. He scratched on the canvas with his fingernails, and the sound of breathing was cut off immediately.

'Ryder,' Penrod whispered, 'Ryder Courtney!'

He heard him stir, and ask in a sleepy whisper, 'Who is that?'

'Ballantyne – Penrod Ballantyne.'

'Good God, man! What on earth are you doing here?' A wax vesta flared, then lamplight glowed and cast a shadow on the canvas. 'Come inside!' Ryder urged him.

When Penrod stooped through the doorway, he was astounded. 'Is it really you, Ballantyne?' You look like a wild tribesman. How did you get here?'

'I don't have long to talk to you. I am a prisoner of the Dervish and under restraint. I would appreciate it if you waste no more time on fatuous questions.'

'I stand corrected.' Ryder's friendly smile faded. 'I shall listen to what you have to tell me.'

'I was captured after the fall of Khartoum. I had returned there in an attempt to discover the fate of those who had

521

been unable to escape, especially David Benbrook and his family.'

'I can reassure you that Saffron is with me. We managed to get out of Khartoum on my steamer at the last minute. I have been trying to contact her family in England, to send her back to them, but these things take a great deal of time.'

'I know she is with you. I have been keeping watch on your camp. I saw her this evening.'

'I have been waiting to receive a message from you,' Ryder said. 'Bacheet met your man, Yakub, in Omdurman. He told Yakub that Ras Hailu could carry messages between us.'

'I have not seen Yakub since the day I was captured in Omdurman. He did not tell me anything about a meeting with Bacheet, or about this man Ras Hailu,' Penrod said grimly. 'Yakub has disappeared. I think that he and his uncle, a rogue named Wad Hagma, betrayed me to the Dervish. I was able to deal with his uncle, and Yakub is next on my list of unfinished business.'

'You cannot trust any of these people,' Ryder agreed, 'no matter how long you have known them and how well you have treated them.'

'So you know, then, that David Benbrook was killed in the sack of Khartoum, and that Rebecca and Amber were captured by the Dervish and handed over to the Mahdi?'

'Yes. Bacheet heard all this terrible news from Nazeera when he was looking for you in Omdurman. It is hard to imagine those two lovely young Englishwomen in the clutches of that dissipated maniac. I hope and pray that Amber is young enough to have been spared the worst, but Rebecca! The good Lord alone knows what she has suffered.'

'The Mahdi is dead. He died of cholera or some other disease. Nobody can be certain what carried him off.'

'I had not heard. I don't suppose that will change anything. But what has become of Rebecca now?' Ryder's concern was apparent. He made little effort to hide his feelings for Rebecca.

So Courtney has also had the benefit of Rebecca Benbrook's liberal nature, Penrod thought cynically. She has had so much experience now that when she returns to London she can turn professional and ply her trade in Charing Cross Road. Although his pride was stung, it did not detract from the responsibility he felt for her safety, or for that of her little sister. Aloud he said, 'When the Mahdi died the two sisters, Rebecca and Amber, were taken into the harem of the new Khalif Osman Atalan.' As he said it, there was a gasp behind him, and he turned quickly with his hand on the hilt of his dagger.

Saffron stood in the tent doorway. She was dressed in a man's shirt, which was many times too large for her and hung well below her knees. She must been awakened by their voices, and had come from her own tent just in time to overhear his last words. The thin cloth of the shirt was artlessly revealing, so that Penrod could not help but notice her figure under it. She had changed a great deal from when he had last seen her. Her hips and bosom were swelling and her face had lost its childish roundness. She was already too mature to be sharing a camp in the remote African wilderness with a man.

'My sisters!' Her eyes were huge with sleep and shock. 'First my father, and now my sisters. Ryder, you never told me that they were in the harem. You said they were safe. Is there never to be an end to this nightmare?'

'But, Saffron, they are safe. They have not been harmed.'

'How do you know that?' she demanded. 'How can they be safe in the den of the pagan and the barbarian?'

'I spoke to Amber not two weeks ago,' Penrod intervened, to comfort her. 'She and Rebecca are brave and are making the best of the hard blows that Fate has dealt them. It may seem impossible, but they are being treated . . . if not kindly then gently enough. The Dervish see them as valuable chattels, and they will want to preserve their worth.'

'But for how long? We have to do something. Especially for Amber. She is so sweet and sensitive. She is not strong like Rebecca and me. We have to rescue her.'

'That is why I am here,' Penrod told her. 'It is the most

523

incredible good fortune that I stumbled across your path. It must be one chance in a million. But now that we have met we can plan the rescue of your sisters.'

'Is that possible? Abyssinia, where we are now, is primitive and backward, but at least the people are Christians. The Sudan is hell on earth, ruled by demons. No white man or woman can remain there long with any chance of survival.'

'I will be going back,' said Penrod. 'I can stay with you only a few minutes more, and then I am going to do what I can for your sisters. But if I am to get them out of the Sudan, I will need all your help.' Penrod turned back to Ryder. 'Can I count on you?'

'I feel insulted that you need to ask,' said Ryder, stiffly.

It was amazing how quickly the two of them could give and take offence, Saffron thought angrily. In these dreadful circumstances why did they have to bicker and posture? Why were men always so pigheaded and arrogant? 'Captain Ballantyne, we will help you,' she promised, 'in every way within our power.'

Penrod noticed that she used the plural 'we' with the proprietary air of a wife. Penrod wondered if she had good reason to do so. The idea was repugnant: despite appearances Saffron was still a child. And a man like Ryder Courtney would never molest her.

'I can waste no more time,' he said. 'I must return to my keepers, if my delicate position of trust with the Dervish is not to be compromised. We have much to plan. First, we must be able to contact each other and exchange news and plans. Tell me about Ras Hailu.'

'He was my friend and trading partner,' Ryder explained. 'He used to travel to Omdurman in his dhow two or three times a year to trade with the Dervish. Tragically he fell foul of the Mahdi, who accused him of spying for Emperor John. He was executed in Omdurman. I have no other agents in the Sudan.'

'Well, we shall have to set up some new line of communication. Do not to try to contact me directly, for I am carefully watched at all times. You must try to get any message to Nazeera. She is allowed much freedom of movement. I shall try to arrange for a messenger of my own. There are other European captives in Omdurman. One of them is Rudolf Slatin, who was the Egyptian governor of Dongola. He is a resourceful fellow, and I suspect that he has ways of communicating with the outside world. If I am successful in finding a messenger, where will he be able to contact you?'

Quickly Ryder gave Penrod a list of his trading posts closest to the Sudanese border, and the names of his trusted agents there. 'Any message they receive will be passed on to me but, as you can see, I am forced to travel great distances in pursuit of my business affairs. It may take an inordinate length of time to reach me.'

'Nothing happens swiftly in Africa,' Penrod agreed. 'What I will ask from you, when the time comes, is that you make the travel arrangements to get us to the Abyssinian border as swiftly as possible. As soon as we leave Omdurman the entire Dervish army will be alerted, and will pursue us relentlessly.'

'The safety of Saffron's sisters takes priority over everything else,' Ryder assured him.

'Where is the *Intrepid Ibis*?' Penrod asked. 'A steamer would be the fastest and surest method of getting us to the border. I should not like to attempt a flight on camels across the desert. The distances are enormous and the going is killing hard on the women.'

'Unfortunately I was obliged to sell the little steamer. Now that the upper reaches of both Niles have been closed to me by the Dervish, I have been forced to restrict my business activities to Abyssinia and Equatoria. The *Ibis* was of no further use to me.'

'That is a great pity, but I shall devise another route.' Penrod stood up. 'I can spend no more time with you. Before I go, there is one other important matter. The reason I am here is that Abdullahi is planning to attack Abyssinia, and seize all the disputed territories from Gondar to Mount Horea. He is going through all the diplomatic motions of lulling Emperor John with overtures of friendship and peace. But he will attack, probably after the big rains of next year. Osman Atalan will command the Dervish army of about thirty thousand. His first and main objective will be the passes here at Atbara gorge and Minkti. His purpose will be to prevent the Emperor coming down from the plateau with his main forces to intervene. I have been sent here by Atalan, may he rot in hell, to scout the terrain over which he will attack.'

'My God!' Ryder looked aghast. 'The Emperor has no inkling of this.'

'Do you have access to him?' Penrod demanded.

'I do, yes. I know him well. I shall be seeing him immediately on my return to Entoto in three or four months' time.'

'Then give him this warning.'

'I will – depend on it. He will be grateful. I am sure he will offer his assistance in the rescue of Rebecca and Amber,' Ryder assured him. 'But tell me, Ballantyne, why do you offer him this warning? What is it to you if the Dervish invade this country?'

'Need you ask? Your enemy is my enemy. The evil that is abroad can only be appreciated by those who have witnessed the sack of a city by the Dervish. You were at Khartoum?' Ryder nodded. 'Emperor John is a Christian monarch. Abdullahi and his bloodthirsty maniacs must be stopped. Perhaps he will be able to put an end to these horrors.' Penrod turned to Saffron. 'What message can I take back to Omdurman for your sisters?' he asked.

Her eyes glistened with tears in the lamplight as she struggled with her reply. 'Tell them that I love them both with all my heart, and always shall. Tell them to be brave. We will help them. We shall all be together again soon. But whatever happens I still love them.'

'I will give them that message,' Penrod promised. 'I am certain it will be of great comfort to them.' He turned back to Ryder, and held out his hand. 'I think we would be wise to forget our personal differences and work together towards our common goal.'

'I agree with all my heart,' said Ryder, and shook the proffered hand.

Penrod stooped over the lamp and blew out the flame, then disappeared out into the night.

It was almost Christmas before Ryder Courtney returned to Entoto, the capital of Abyssinia and the city where he had his main trading compound.

'This must be the bleakest place in the world,' said Saffron, as they rode in through the city gates at the head of the caravan of mules, 'even worse than Khartoum. Why can't we live in Gondar, Ryder?'

'Because, Miss Saffron Benbrook, in the near future you will be living in the village of Bishop's Sutton in Hampshire with your uncle Thomas and aunt Jane.'

'You are being tiresome again, Ryder,' she warned him. 'I don't want to live in England. I want to stay here with you.'

'I am flattered.' He touched the brim of his hat. 'But, most unfortunately for all concerned, you cannot spend the rest of your life traipsing through the African bush like a gypsy. You have to go back to civilization and learn to be a lady. Besides, people are beginning to talk. You are a child no longer – indeed, you are a big girl now.'

Ah, so you have noticed! Saffron thought complacently. I was beginning to think you, Ryder Courtney, were blind. Then, aloud, she reiterated the promise that was usually enough to satisfy him: 'I will go back to England without any fuss when Rebecca and Amber have been rescued,' she spoke with a straight face and total insincerity, 'and when my uncle Thomas promises to take care of us. He has not replied to your letters yet, and it's over a year since you first wrote,' she reminded him smugly. 'Now, let us speak of more interesting matters. How long will we stay in Entoto, and where will we travel to next?'

'I have business here that will take some time.'

'It's so cold and windy in the mountains after the warmth of the lowlands, and there is no firewood for miles. All the trees have been cut down.'

'You must have been talking to Empress Miriam. She shares your opinion of Entoto. That's why the Emperor is moving the capital to the hot springs at Addis Ababa. She is a nag, just like somebody else I know.'

'I am not a nag, but sometimes I know best,' said Saffron sweetly. 'Even though you treat me like a baby.'

Despite her protests, the Courtney compound at Entoto was really very comfortable and welcoming, and she had managed, with the help of Bacheet, to make it even more so. She had even prevailed on Ryder to convert one of the old disused storerooms into a bedroom and studio for her exclusive use. It had not been easy. Ryder was reluctant to do anything that might give her reason to believe that her stay with him was permanent.

In order to procure a studio Saffron had enlisted the help of Lady Alice Packer, wife of the British ambassador to the court of the Emperor, who had taken her under her wing. Of course, her husband had known David Benbrook when they had both worked under Sir Evelyn Baring in the diplomatic agency in Cairo so she felt some responsibility for his orphaned daughter.

Alice was an amateur artist, and when she recognized Saffron's natural talent in the same field she had assumed the role of teacher. She provided Saffron with paints, brushes and art paper brought in from Cairo in the diplomatic pouch, and taught her how to make her own canvas stretchers and charcoal sticks.

Within the time that they had known each other Saffron had almost outstripped her teacher. Her portfolio contained at least fifty lovingly wrought portraits of Ryder Courtney, most of which had been drawn without the subject's know- ledge, and she had completed numerous African landscapes and animal sketches, which astonished both Alice and Ryder with their maturity and virtuosity. Recently she had com- menced a series of drawings and paintings from her memories of Khartoum and the horrors of the siege. They were beautiful but harrowing. Ryder realized that they were a form of catharsis for her, so he encouraged her to continue with them.

Two days after their return to Entoto, Saffron made her way up to the embassy to take tea with Alice. She showed her tutor all the Khartoum sketches, which they discussed at some length. Alice wept as she looked at them. 'These are magnificent, my dear. I stand in awe of your skill.'

Saffron stopped repacking them and turned to Alice, her eyes full of tears.

'What is it, Saffron?' Alice asked kindly. Although she had been sworn to secrecy by Ryder, Saffron blurted out a full account of the nocturnal meeting with Penrod Ballantyne in the Atbara gorge. Alice promised her husband would inform Sir Evelyn Baring at once of the predicament of her sisters and also of Captain Ballantyne. Saffron was much cheered by this. Then, as she was leaving, she asked innocently, 'If any mail for Mr Courtney has arrived, I would be pleased to deliver it to him, and perhaps save one of your staff the trouble.'

Alice sent down to the chancery and a secretary returned with a stack of envelopes addressed to 'Ryder Courtney Esq,' care of the British ambassador at Entoto, Abyssinia.

Saffron examined them as she walked through the town to the market. She recognized the handwriting on the first envelope. It was from Ryder's nephew, Sean Courtney, at the newly discovered goldfields in the Transvaal Republic of South Africa. Saffron knew that Sean was importuning his uncle to invest several thousand pounds in a new mine. The next was a bill for goods supplied by the Army and Navy stores in London. The third envelope bore the seal of 'The Office of the Government Assayer of the Cape of Good Hope', and the fourth was the one that Saffron had been dreading. On the reverse was the inscription:

> Sender:
> The Reverend Thomas Benbrook
> The Vicarage
> Bishop's Sutton
> Hampshire. England

She placed the other letters in her pocket, but this one she hid down the front of her bodice. Saffron spent less time than usual in the market. She bought a large bunch of wild mountain gladioli from her favourite flower-seller. Then she came across a handsome silver hip-flask, which she decided might do for Ryder's birthday. The price was beyond her meagre resources and she was in too much of a hurry to bargain with the merchant, so she promised to return the following day.

She hurried back to the compound and placed the flowers in the tub beside the kitchen door. Then she retired to the earth closet, which was discreetly tucked away in a corner behind the living quarters. She bolted the door, perched on the high seat and carefully split the seal on the fourth envelope. The single sheet was covered with writing on both sides, and dated seven months earlier. She read it avidly;

Dear Mr Courtney,

My wife and I were saddened to receive your letter and to hear of the tragic murder of my brother David in Khartoum, and of the plight of his daughters. I understand your predicament and agree that it is beyond common decency for poor little Saffron to continue in your care, as you are a bachelor and there is no woman with you to see to her upbringing.

I have addressed enquiries to Sebastian Hardy Esquire, my dear brother's solicitor, as you suggested I might. It pains me to have to inform you that the value of my brother's few remaining assets are far exceeded by his substantial debts. Sarah, his deceased wife, was a lady of profligate disposition. None of my brother's daughters will be due any inheritance from his estate.

My wife and I have discussed the possibility of taking Saffron into our home. However, we have nine children of our own to support on my stipend as a country vicar. Alas, we would not be able to feed and clothe the poor orphan. Fortunately I have been able to make adequate arrangements for her to be taken into a suitable institution where she will receive strict Christian instruction and an education that will be adequate for her later entry into respectable employment as governess to a child of the nobility.

If, in your Christian charity, you would be kind enough to provide her with passage to England and the train fare from the port of her arrival to the Bishop's Sutton railway station, I would meet the poor child there and convey her to the institution. Unfortunately I am not able to contribute to her subsequent upkeep and maintenance.

I wait to hear from you.

Your brother in Christ,

Thomas Benbrook

Slowly, and with relish, Saffron tore the letter into shreds, and dropped each scrap separately into the malodorous pit beneath her. Then she pulled up her skirts and urinated vigorously on the remains of the offending document.

'A fitting end for such a nasty piece of rubbish,' she said to herself. 'So much for an institution, Christian instruction and employment as a governess. I would prefer to walk back to Khartoum on my own bare feet.' She stood up and smoothed down her skirts. 'Now I must hurry to see that Ryder's dinner is ready, and to prepare his whisky peg for him.'

For Saffron, dinner-time was the highlight of her busy day. After she had discussed the roasting of the chicken and yams with the cook, she made certain there was hot water, soap and a clean towel on the washstand in Ryder's bedroom, and a freshly ironed shirt folded on the bed. Next she laid the table, and arranged the flowers and candles. She would not trust one of the servants, even Bacheet, with such an important task. Then she unlocked the strongroom with the key that Ryder had entrusted to her and brought out the bottle of whisky, the crystal glass and the cedarwood cigar box. She set them on the table at the end of the veranda, from where there would be a fine view of the sunset over the mountains.

She hurried to her own room and changed the clothes she had worn all day for a dress of her own design and creation. With the help of two Amharic women from the town, who were expert seamstresses, she had assembled her own abundant and unusual wardrobe. Lady Alice Packer and even Empress Miriam had complimented her on her style.

While she was still combing her hair she heard the clatter of hoofs in the courtyard as Ryder returned from the palace, where he had been in day-long discussions with the Emperor and various royal functionaries. She was waiting for him on the veranda when he emerged from his private quarters in the fresh shirt, his face glowing from the hot water and his wet hair combed back neatly. He is the most handsome man in the world, but his hair needs cutting again. I shall see to it tomorrow, she thought, as she held the whisky bottle over the glass. 'Say when,' she invited.

'"When" is a four-letter word that should be uttered only with great deliberation after long reflection,' he replied. It was their private joke, and she poured him a liberal quantity. He tasted it and sighed. 'Too good for human consumption! Such nectar should be drunk only by angels in their flight!' That completed the ritual. He sank down comfortably on to the leather cushions of his favourite chair. She sat opposite him and they watched the sun set in crimson splendour over the mountains.

'Now tell me what you did today,' Ryder said.

'You first,' she replied.

'I spent the morning in council with the Emperor and two of the generals of his army. I told them what Penrod Ballantyne had reported about the intentions of the Dervish to attack his country. Emperor John was grateful for this warning, and I think he has taken it seriously. I did not tell him of our plans to rescue your sisters. I thought it premature to do so. However, I believe that he will be helpful when we are in a position to act.'

Saffron sighed. 'I do wish Captain Ballantyne would be in touch. It seems ages since he was.'

'He and your sisters have probably been travelling in the entourage of Osman Atalan. Penrod is so closely guarded that he might not have been able to find a reliable messenger. We must be patient.'

'So easy to say, so hard to do,' she said.

To distract her he went on with a recital of his day. 'After I left the Emperor, I spent the rest of the day with his treasurer. He finally agreed to renew my licence to trade throughout the country for another year. The bribe he demanded was extortionate, but in all other respects quite reasonable.' He made her laugh – he always made her laugh. 'By the way, I forgot to mention that we are invited to the royal audience next Friday. Emperor John is to award me the Star of the Order of Solomon and Judea, in recognition of my services to the state. I think that the truth of the matter is that Empress Miriam wants to admire your latest high-fashion creation and persuaded her husband to invite us. Either that or she wants you to paint another portrait of her.'

'How exciting. Will the Star of Solomon be enormous and covered with lots of diamonds?'

'I am sure it will be gigantic, and perhaps not diamonds, but at least good-quality cut glass,' he said, and reached across the table to the small stack of mail that Saffron had brought down from the embassy. First he opened the bill from the Army and Navy Stores. 'Good!' he exclaimed with pleasure. 'They have my pair of number-ten rifles ready to ship out to me. I shall arrange payment tomorrow. They should arrive before our next journey to Equatoria where they will be most useful.' He set aside the bill and opened the letter from his nephew. 'Sean is insistent that this new gold reef they have opened will persist to great depth. I do not have the same hopes for it. I believe that the reef will pinch out before long and leave him much poorer in pocket, if richer in experience. I am afraid I shall have to disabuse him of his hopes that I might provide any capital for his venture.' He picked up the letter with the Cape Colony postage stamp, and examined it. 'I have been waiting for this!'

He opened the envelope, took out the assay report, scanned it anxiously, then smiled comfortably. 'Excellent! Oh, so very good indeed.'

'Can you tell me?' Saffron asked.

'Certainly! Before we left for Gondar I sent a bag of rock samples to the assay office of the Cape Colony. The year before I was caught up in the siege of Khartoum I gathered them from the mountains a hundred miles east of Aksum while I was hunting mountain nyala. This is the report on those samples. Over thirty per cent copper, and just on twelve per cent silver. Even taking into account how remote the area is, and the difficulty of reaching it, it should be a highly profitable deposit. The only trouble is that I will have to go back to the royal treasurer to ask for a mining licence. He had my skin today, so tomorrow he will want my scalp and my teeth.'

'*Sans* teeth and *sans* hair, you might set a new fashion,' Saffron suggested, and he laughed.

As usual they sat late after dinner, talking endlessly. When Ryder climbed into his own bed he was still chuckling at her saucy Parthian shot. He blew out the lamp, and as he composed himself for sleep he realized he had not once thought of Rebecca that day.

When they entered the audience hall at the palace, Alice Packer summoned Saffron with a peremptory wave of her fan.

'Will you forgive me, please, Ryder?'

'Off you go and do your duty.' Ryder watched her cross the room, as did almost everybody else. It was not only the yellow dress that was so striking. Youth has beauty inherent in its very nature. He realized he was staring and looked away quickly, hoping no one had noticed.

The rest of the company was made up of a number of Abyssinian princes and princesses, for the Emperor and the other members of the house of Menelik were prolific breeders. There were also generals and bishops, prosperous merchants and landowners, the entire corps of foreign diplomats, with a few foreign travellers and adventurers. The uniforms and costumes were so exotic and colourful that Saffron's dress seemed restrained and understated by comparison.

Suddenly Ryder became aware that somebody in the throng was watching him. He looked about quickly, then started with surprise. The person who had purchased the *Intrepid Ibis* from him was standing at the far corner of the room, but even at that range her Egyptian eyes above the veil had a hypnotic quality that could not be ignored. As soon as she had his attention she resumed her conversation with the elderly general beside her who was resplendent in an array of medals, jewelled orders and a cloak of leopardskins.

'Peace and the blessing of Allah be upon you, Sitt Bakhita al-Masur,' Ryder greeted her in Arabic, as he came to her side.

'And upon you in equal measure, Effendi.' She made a graceful gesture in reply, touching her lips, then her heart with her fingertips.

'You are a long way from your home,' he remarked. Her eyes slanted upwards at the outer corners, and her dark gaze was direct, unusual in an Egyptian lady even of the highest rank, yet also mysterious. Some men would find her irresistible, but she was not to Ryder's taste.

'I came by the river. In my fine new steamer it was not such a long journey from the first cataract.' Her voice was soft and musical.

'You encountered no let or hindrance along the way, I hope? These are troubled times and the *Ibis* is well known.'

'She is the *Ibis* no longer but the *Durkhan Sama*, the Wisdom of the Skies. Her appearance is much altered. No one would recognize her for what she once was. My boat-builders at Aswan have lavished much attention on her. I paid my dues to the men of God in Omdurman when I passed that pestilential if holy city.'

'Where is she moored now?' Ryder demanded eagerly.

Bakhita looked at him quizzically. 'She is at Roseires.' That was the small port at the uppermost limit of navigation on the Blue Nile. It was still within the Sudan, but less than fifty miles from the Abyssinian border.

Ryder was pleased. 'Is Jock McCrump still the engineer?' he asked.

Bakhita smiled. 'He is captain also. I think it would be difficult to dislodge him from his berth.'

Ryder was even better pleased. Jock would be a useful man

to have aboard if they were to use the steamer in any rescue attempt. 'You seem interested in your old steamer, Effendi. Do I imagine it, or is it indeed so?'

Immediately Ryder was wary. He knew little about this woman, except that she was wealthy and had influence in high places in many countries. He had heard it said that even though she was a Muslim she was favourably inclined towards British interests in the Orient, and opposed to those of France and Germany. It was even rumoured that she was an agent of Sir Evelyn Baring in Cairo. If this was true she would not support the Dervish *jihad* in Omdurman, but it was best not to trust her.

'Indeed, Sitt Bakhita, I did have some idea of chartering the steamer from you for a short period but I am not sure that you would be agreeable to the proposition,' he said.

She dropped her voice when she spoke next: 'General Ras Mengetti speaks only Amharic. Nevertheless we should continue this conversation in private. I know the whereabouts of your compound. May I call upon you there? Say, tomorrow an hour before noon?'

'I will be at your disposal.'

'I will have matters of mutual interest to relate to you,' she promised. Ryder bowed and moved away.

Saffron was still with Alice, but the moment Ryder was free she came across to join him. 'Who was the fat Arab lady?' she asked tartly. 'She was making huge cow eyes at you.'

'She may be useful to us in uniting us with friends and family.'

Saffron considered this, then nodded. 'In that case I forgive her.'

Ryder was uncertain as to how Bakhita had transgressed, but before he made the mistake of pursuing the subject, a flourish of trumpets announced the entrance of the Emperor and his wife.

Much later that evening when they returned to the compound, Saffron brought Ryder his slippers and poured him a nightcap. Then she unpinned the Star of Solomon from his lapel and examined it in the lamplight. 'I am certain they are real diamonds,' she said.

'If you are correct then we are probably millionaires.' He chuckled, and noted that he had picked up the habit from her of using the plural pronoun. It seemed somehow to constitute a formal link between them. He wondered if that was wise, and concluded that perhaps it was not. In future I shall be more circumspect, he promised himself.

The following day Bakhita arrived at the compound in a closed coach drawn by four mules. Ryder recognized the coach and driver and knew that they had probably been put at her disposal by the Emperor. This was further proof, if any were needed, of Bakhita al-Masur's influence and importance. Behind the coach half a dozen armed bodyguards followed closely. They waited in the courtyard while Ryder ushered Bakhita into the main room, where Saffron served coffee and little honey cakes.

When she stood up and excused herself, Bakhita held up her hand. 'Please do not go, Sitt Benbrook. What I have to say concerns you above all others.' Saffron sank back on the sofa, and Bakhita went on, 'I have come to Entoto for the main purpose of meeting you and Mr Courtney. The three of us have affairs of great concern that are all linked in Omdur-man. I have a friend to whom I owe complete loyalty, and close members of your family are held in captivity by the Dervish. I am certain that you are as anxious to procure their release as I am. To this end I wanted to pledge to you all the assistance and support of which I am capable.' Ryder and Saffron stared at her in silent astonishment. 'Yes, I know that your elder sister and your twin are in the harem of the Emir Osman Atalan. My friend is the slave of the same man.'

'May we know the name of your friend?' Ryder asked cautiously.

Bakhita did not answer at once then said, 'My English is not good, but I think we must use your language for very few people in Abyssinia understand it.'

'Your English is very good, Sitt Bakhita,' said Saffron. Her latent antagonism towards the other woman had undergone a sea-change.

'You are kind, but it is not so.' She smiled at Saffron, then turned back to Ryder. 'I could refuse to answer your question, but I want us to be honest with each other. I am sure that my friend is well known to both of you. He is Captain Penrod Ballantyne of the 10th Hussars.'

'He is a valiant officer and a fine gentleman,' Saffron exclaimed. 'We last met him at the Atbara gorge not more than five months ago.'

'Oh, please tell me how he was!' Bakhita exclaimed.

'He was well, although indistinguishable in dress and deportment from his captors,' said Saffron.

'I knew he had been captured by the Dervish, but I heard he had been terribly abused and tortured. Your assurances are of much comfort to me.'

While they discussed Penrod, Ryder was thinking swiftly. From Bacheet he had heard a rumour, which Nazeera had told him, that Penrod had an intimate Egyptian friend. From the depth of her concern for him there was little doubt that Bakhita must be the lady in question. Ryder was shocked. Penrod was a highly decorated officer in a first-rate regiment. A liaison of this nature, if it came to light, might easily cost him his commission and his reputation.

'From all that you have told us, Sitt Bakhita, it is clear that we must pool all our intelligence and resources,' he said. 'Our first concern, which has been troubling me deeply, is how to get messages to and from our friends in Omdurman.'

'I believe I am able to offer a means of communication.' Bakhita stood up and went to the door that led into the courtyard. She clapped her hands, and one of her bodyguards appeared before her. 'I think you know this man,' said Bakhita, as he removed his headcloth and made a deep *salaam* towards Ryder.

'May God always protect you, Effendi.'

'Yakub!' Ryder was truly astonished. 'I heard bad things about you. I heard that you had betrayed your master, Abadan Riji.'

'Effendi, sooner would I betray my father and mother, and may Allah hear my words and strike me down into hell if I lie,' said Yakub. 'The only remaining purpose in my life is to bring my master safely out of the clutches of the Dervish into which my uncle so treacherously led him. I will do anything . . .' Yakub hesitated, then qualified his statement: 'I will do anything except have any truck with the despicable Bacheet to save my master from the Dervish. If there is no other way, I may even abide with, for some brief time, the company of the nefarious Bacheet. However, I shall probably kill him afterwards.'

'On the matter of killing,' Ryder told him grimly, 'Abadan Riji believes that you were as much the traitor as your uncle. He slew your uncle, and he means to do the same to you.'

'Then I must go to him and place my life and loyalty in his hands.'

'While you are about it,' said Ryder, drily, 'you may as well take your master a message and return to us with his reply.'

It took five more days for Ryder and Bakhita to evolve an escape plan for the prisoners in Omdurman that had a reasonable chance of success.

On the following day Yakub left alone for the Sudan.

Osman Atalan was well pleased with the report that Penrod brought him back from the passes of the Abyssinian highlands. He listened with great attention to his suggestions concerning the conduct of the campaign against Emperor John, and they discussed all these in exhaustive

539

detail during the course of the long return journey to Omdurman.

Once they reached that city, Penrod found that the conditions of his imprisonment were much relaxed. He had achieved a position of conditional trust, which had been his objective from the first day of his capture. It was what he had set out to achieve by indulging Osman Atalan, and pretending to submit to his will. However, he was still accompanied at all times by selected aggagiers of Osman's personal bodyguard. During the months after their return to Omdurman Osman spent much time with the Khalifat Abdullahi. Al-Noor told Penrod that he was trying to persuade Abdullahi to allow him to return to his tribal domain in the desert. However, Abdullahi was too foxy and devious to allow a man of such power and influence as Osman Atalan to escape his direct supervision and control. Osman was allowed out of Omdurman only for brief punitive raids and reprisals on those persons and tribes who had incurred Abdullahi's displeasure, or for hunting and hawking excursions into the desert.

When he returned to the city, Osman found himself with much time on his hands. One day he sent for Penrod. 'I have watched the way you wield a blade. It is contrary to usage and custom, and lacks even the semblance of grace.'

Penrod lowered his gaze to hide his anger at the insult, and with an effort refrained from reminding him of their first meeting at El Obeid in which the mighty Khalif Atalan had countered Penrod's feint by raising his targe and blocking his own view of the thrust that followed, a riposte that passed close to his heart.

'However,' said Osman, 'it holds some interest.'

Penrod looked up at him and saw the glimmer of mockery in his eyes. 'Exalted Khalif, from such a master swordsman as you are, this is praise that warms my soul,' he mocked in return.

'It will amuse me to practise at arms against you, and to demonstrate the true and noble usage of the long blade,' said Osman. 'We will begin tomorrow after the morning prayers.'

The next morning as they faced each other with naked

blades, Osman set out the rules of engagement. 'I shall try to kill you. You will try to kill me. If I succeed I will hold your memory in contempt. If you succeed, my aggagiers,' he indicated the fifteen men that formed a circle around him, 'will immediately kill you, but you will be buried with much honour. I shall commission a special prayer to be recited in the mosque in your memory. Am I not a benevolent master?'

'The mighty Atalan is fair and just,' Penrod agreed, and they went to it. Twenty minutes later, when Osman was slow on the recovery, Penrod nicked his forearm in warning.

Osman's gaze was murderous. 'Enough for now. We shall fight again in two days' time.'

After that they fought for an hour every second day, and Osman learnt to recover swiftly and riposte like a hussar. Gradually Penrod found himself more seriously taxed, and was forced to exert all his own skill to restrain his opponent. At the end of Ramadan Osman told him, 'I have a gift for you.'

Her name was Lalla. She was a frightened and abused little thing, a child of war, pestilence and famine. She did not remember her father or mother, and in all her short life nobody had ever shown her kindness.

Penrod was kind to her. He paid one of al-Noor's concubines to wash her as though she were a stray puppy, and to dress her tangled hair. He provided her with fresh clothing to replace her rags. He allowed her to cook his meals, launder his clothes, and sweep the floor of the small cell off the courtyard of the aggagiers, which was his lodging. He let her sleep outside his door. He treated her as though she was human, not an animal.

For the first time in her life Lalla had sufficient food. Hunger had been part of her life from as far back as she could remember. She did not grow fat, but her bones were gradually covered with a little flesh. Sometimes he heard crooning softly over the fire as she cooked his meal. Whenever he returned to the courtyard of the aggagiers she smiled. Once when Osman had succeeded in touching his right shoulder with the long blade, Lalla dressed the wound under his instruction. It was a flesh wound and healed swiftly. Penrod told her she was an angel of mercy, and he bought her a cheap silver bracelet in the souk as a reward. She crept away with it to a corner of the yard and wept with happiness. It was the first gift she had ever received.

That night she crept shyly on to Penrod's *angareb*, and he did not have the heart to send her away. When she whimpered with her nightmares, he stroked her head. She woke and cuddled closer to him. When he made love to her it was without lust or passion, but with pity. The following evening while she was cooking his dinner he spoke to her quietly: 'If I asked you to do something dangerous and difficult for me, would you do it, Lalla?'

'My lord, I would do whatever you ask.'

'If I asked you to put your hand in the fire and bring out a burning brand for me, would you do it?' Without hesitation she reached towards the flames and he had to seize her wrist to prevent her thrusting her hand into them. 'No, not that! I want you to carry a message for me. Do you know the woman Nazeera, whom they call Ammi? She works in the harem as a servant of the white concubines.'

'I know her, my lord.'

'Tell her that Filfil is safe with al-Sakhawi in Abyssinia.' Filfil, or Pepper, was Saffron's Arabic name.

Lalla waited her chance to accost Nazeera discreetly at the well, which was a gathering place for all the women, and delivered the message faithfully. Nazeera hurried back to give the news to Rebecca and Amber.

Within days Nazeera had met Lalla again at the well. She had a message for her to take to Penrod. 'Yakub is here in Omdurman,' Lalla reported faithfully.

Penrod was amazed. 'It cannot be the Yakub I know. That rascal disappeared a long time ago.'

'He wants me to meet him,' Lalla said. 'What will you have me do?'

'Where will you meet?'

'I will be with Nazeera in the souk, at the camel market.'

'Will it be safe for you?' Penrod asked.

Lalla shrugged. 'That is of no account. If you ask it, I will do it.'

When she returned he asked, 'How was this Yakub?'

'He has two eyes, but they do not follow each other. One looks east and the other north.'

'That is the Yakub I know.' How could he ever have doubted him, Penrod asked himself.

'He said to tell you that the peerless Yakub is still your servant. He has languished a year and three months in an Egyptian prison, unjustly accused of trading in slaves. Only when he was released was he able to go to the lady of Aswan. Now she has sent him back to you with tidings that are much to your benefit.'

Penrod knew instantly who was the lady of Aswan, and his heart leapt. He had not thought of Bakhita recently, but she was still there, as constant as she had ever been. With her and Yakub he was no longer alone. 'You have done well, Lalla. No one could have done better,' he said, and her face glowed.

He had now established a line of communication to the outside world, but Lalla was a simple child, incapable of remembering more than a few sentences at a time, and the meetings with Nazeera and Yakub could be risked only at intervals of several days: Abdullahi and Osman had spies everywhere.

Planning the escape was a long-drawn-out and complicated business. Twice Yakub had to leave Omdurman and make the hazardous journey to Abyssinia to consult Ryder Courtney and Bakhita. But, very slowly, the plan took shape.

The attempt would be made on the first Friday of Ramadan, five months hence. Yakub would have camels waiting on the far bank of the Nile, hidden among the ruins of Khartoum. By some ruse or subterfuge, Penrod would find his own way out of the courtyard of the aggagiers. Nazeera would spirit Rebecca and Amber out of the harem to a waiting felucca that she would arrange. Penrod would meet them there, and the felucca would ferry them across the Nile. Then, on

Yakub's camels, they would dash up the south bank of the Blue Nile to where Jock McCrump would have the old *Ibis* hidden in the Lagoon of the Little Fish. He would take them up to Roseires, where horses would be waiting for the final dash to the Abyssinian border.

'Will you take me with you, my lord?' Lalla asked wistfully.

What on earth would I do with her? Penrod wondered. She was not pretty, but had an endearing monkey face, and she looked at him with worshipful adoration. 'I will take you with me wherever I go,' he promised, and thought, Perhaps I can marry her to Yakub. She would make him a perfect little wife.

Only four weeks later, when everything was at last in place, Lalla brought Penrod another message, which struck him like the broadside of heavy cannon.

'Ammi Nazeera says that al-Zahra has seen her first moon and become a woman. She can hide this from the exalted Osman Atalan, but in one month's time her moon will rise again. She will not be able to conceal it longer from him. The mighty Atalan has already ordered Nazeera to watch for and report to him the first show of her woman's blood. He has announced that, as soon as she is marriageable, he will offer al-Zahra as a gift to the Khalifat Abdullahi, who hungers for her.'

Even if he had to risk all of them, Penrod could not possibly allow Amber to go to Abdullahi. It would be worse than feeding her alive to some obscene carnivorous monster. The entire plan had to be brought forward. They had a month's grace in which to change the arrangements. It would be a near-run thing. He sent the willing Lalla almost daily to carry messages to Yakub.

Two weeks before the new date of the escape attempt, the Khalif Osman Atalan announced a feast and entertainment for all his relatives and his most loyal followers. The main compound was decorated with palm fronds and two dozen prime sheep were roasted on spits. The low tables at which the company sat on soft cushions were piled with dishes of fruit and sweetmeats. Penrod found himself placed in a position of preference, close to the Khalif, with al-Noor at one hand and Mooman Digna on the other.

When all had eaten their fill and the mood was as warm as the sunshine, with laughter rippling like the waters of the Nile, Osman rose, made a short speech of welcome and commended them on their loyalty and duty. 'Now let the entertainment begin!' he ordered, and clapped his hands.

A finger drum began to tap a staccato rhythm and then a murmur of surprise went up. Every head craned towards the side gate of the courtyard. Two men led in a creature on a leash. It was impossible at first to guess the nature of the animal. It moved slowly and painfully on all fours, forced by its handlers to make a torturous circuit of the yard. It was only gradually that they realized it was a human female. Her hands and feet had been crudely amputated at wrists and ankles. The stumps had been dipped in hot pitch to staunch the bleeding. She crawled on elbows and knees. The rest of her naked body had been whipped with thorn branches. The thorns had lacerated her skin. The mutilations were so horrible that even the hardened aggagiers were silenced. Slowly she crawled to where Penrod sat. The handlers tightened the leash and forced her to lift her head.

Cold with horror Penrod stared into Lalla's little monkey face. Blood was trickling from her torn scalp into her empty eye-sockets. They had burned out her eyeballs with hot irons. 'Lalla!' he said softly. 'What have they done to you?'

She recognized his voice, and turned towards him. Blood was still oozing down her cheeks. 'My lord,' she whispered, 'I told them nothing.' Then she collapsed with her face in the dust, and though they yanked on the leash they could not rouse her.

'Abadan Riji!' Osman Atalan called. 'My trusted aggagier of the famous sword arm, put this sorry creature out of her agony.' A terrible silence hung over the gathering. Every man looked at Penrod, not understanding but enthralled by the drama of the moment.

'Kill her for me, Abadan Riji,' Osman repeated.

'Lalla!' Penrod's voice trembled with pity.

She heard him and rolled her head towards him, blindly seeking his face. 'My lord,' she whispered, 'for the love I bear you, do this thing. Give me release, for I can go on no longer.'

Penrod hesitated only a moment. Then he rose and drew his sword from its sheath. As he stood over her she spoke again: 'I will always love you.' And with a single blow he struck her head off the maimed body. Then he placed his foot on the blade and, with a sharp tug at the hilt, snapped it in two.

'Tell me, Abadan Riji,' said Osman Atalan, 'are those tears I see in your eyes? Why do you weep like a woman?'

'They are tears indeed, mighty Atalan, and I weep for the manner of your death, which will be terrible.'

'With the help of this creature, Abadan Riji was planning to escape from Omdurman,' Osman explained to his aggagiers. 'Bring in the *shebba*, and place it round his neck.'

The *shebba* was a device designed to restrain and punish recalcitrant slaves, and to prevent them escaping. It was a heavy Y-shaped yoke cut from the fork of an acacia tree. The prisoner was stripped naked, to add to his humiliation, then the crotch of the *shebba* was fitted against his throat. The thick trunk extended in front of him. They lifted it to shoulder height, and bound the fork in place behind his neck with twisted rawhide ropes. Finally Penrod's bare arms were lashed to the long pole in front of him. With both arms pinioned, he was unable to feed himself or lift a bowl of water to his lips. He could not clean himself of his bodily waste. If he allowed the pole to sink from horizontal the fork would crush his windpipe and choke him. To move he had first to raise the whole massive contraption and keep it balanced. He could not lie on his side or back, nor was he able to sit. If he wished to rest or sleep he must do so on his knees, with the end of the pole resting on the earth in front of him. At best he could only totter a few paces before the weight of the unbalanced pole forced him to his knees again.

The feast continued while Penrod knelt in the centre of the courtyard. Afterwards he was driven back to the courtyard of the aggagiers. Mooman Digna whipped him along like a beast of burden. He was unable to eat or drink, and nobody would help him. He could not sleep for the pain of the *shebba* goaded him awake. It was too large and cumbersome to allow him to enter his cell so he knelt in the open courtyard, with an aggagier assigned to guard him day and night. By the third day he had lost all feeling in his arms, and his hands were blue and swollen. Although he staggered around the wall of the courtyard to keep in the shadow, the sun's rays reflected from the limewashed walls and his naked body reddened and blistered. His tongue was like a dry sponge in his parched mouth for the heat in the noonday was intense.

By the morning of the fourth day he was becoming weak and disoriented, hovering on the verge of unconsciousness. Even his eyeballs were drying out, and still no one would help him. As he knelt in a corner of the courtyard he heard the voices of the aggagiers arguing nearby. They were discussing how much longer he would be able to hold out. Then there was silence and he forced open his swollen eyelids. For a moment he thought he was hallucinating.

Amber was coming towards him across the yard. She carried a large pitcher balanced on her head in the manner of an Arab woman. The aggagiers were watching her, but none tried to intervene. She took the pitcher off her head and placed it on the ground. Then she dipped a sponge into it and held it to his lips. He was unable to speak, but he sucked it gratefully. When she had given him as much as he could drink, she replaced the empty pitcher on her head and said softly, 'I will come again tomorrow.'

At the same time the following day Osman Atalan entered the yard and stood in the shade of the cloister with al-Noor and Mooman Digna. Amber came in shortly after his arrival. She saw him at once and stopped, balancing the pitcher with one hand, slim and graceful as a gazelle on the point of flight. She stared at Osman, then she lifted her chin defiantly and came to where Penrod knelt. She dipped the sponge and gave him drink. Osman did not stop her. When she had finished and was ready to leave, she whispered, without moving her lips, 'Yakub will come for you. Be ready.' She walked past Osman on her way to the gate. He watched her go impassively.

Amber came again the next day. Osman was not there and most of the aggagiers seemed to have lost interest. She gave Penrod water, then fed him *asida* and dhurra porridge, spooning it into his mouth as though he were an infant, wiping the spillage off his chin. Then she used another sponge to wash his filth from the back of his legs and his buttocks. 'I wish you did not have to do that,' he said.

She gave him a particular look and replied, 'You still do not understand, do you?' He was too bemused and weak to try to fathom her meaning. She went on, with barely a pause, 'Yakub will come for you tonight.'

Darkness fell and Penrod knelt in his corner of the court-yard. The aggagier Kabel al-Din was his guard that night. He sat nearby, with his back against the wall and his sheathed sword across his lap.

The muscles in Penrod's arms were cramping so violently that he had to bite his lip to stop himself screaming. The blood in his mouth tasted bitter and metallic. Eventually he slipped into a dark, numb sleep. When he woke he heard a woman's soft laughter nearby. It was a vaguely familiar sound. Then the woman whispered salaciously, 'The enormity of your manhood terrifies me, but I am brave enough to endure it.' Incredibly Penrod realized that it was Nazeera. What was she doing here, he wondered. He opened his eyes. She was lying on her back in the moonlight with her skirts drawn up to her armpits. Kabel al-Din was kneeling between her parted thighs, about to mount her, oblivious to everything about him.

Yakub came over the wall as silently as a moth. As Kabel al-Din humped his back over Nazeera, Yakub sank the point of his dagger into the nape of the man's neck. With the expertise of long practice he found the juncture of the third and fourth vertebrae and severed the spinal column. Al-Din stiffened, then collapsed soundlessly on Nazeera. She pushed aside his limp body and rolled out from beneath him. Then she scrambled to her feet, pulling down her skirts as she came to help Yakub, who was stooped over Penrod. With the blood-smeared dagger Yakub cut the thongs that pinioned his arms and Penrod almost screamed as the blood coursed back into his starved arteries and veins. While Nazeera took the weight of the yoke to prevent it crushing Penrod's larynx, Yakub cut the thongs at the back of his neck. Between them they lifted it off.

'Drink.' Nazeera held a small glass flask to his lips. 'It will deaden the pain.' With three gulps Penrod swallowed the contents. The bitter taste of laudanum was unmistakable. They helped him to his feet and half carried him to the wall. Yakub had left a rope in place. While Nazeera propped him up, Yakub settled the loop on the end of the rope under Penrod's armpits. As he straddled the top of the wall and heaved on the rope Nazeera pushed from below and they hoisted Penrod over. He fell in a heap on the far side. Nazeera slipped quietly away in the direction of the harem. Yakub dropped down beside Penrod and hauled him on to his numb feet.

At first their progress towards the riverbank was torturously slow, but then the laudanum took effect and Penrod pushed away Yakub's hands. 'In future, do not stay away so long, tardy Yakub,' he mumbled, and Yakub giggled at the jest. Penrod broke into a shambling run towards the river, where he knew the felucca was waiting to take them across.

As the favourite of Osman Atalan, Rebecca had her own quarters and Amber was allowed to share them with her. The two waited by the small grilled window through which they had a glimpse of the silver moonlight reflected from the wide river. Rebecca had turned the wick of the oil lamp low, so they could just make out each other's faces. Amber was wearing a light woollen robe and sandals, ready to travel, and she was quivering with excitement.

'It is almost time. You must make ready, Becky,' she entreated. 'Nazeera will be back at any moment to fetch us.'

'Listen to me, my darling Amber.' Rebecca placed her hands on her sister's shoulders. 'You must be brave now. I am not coming with you. You are going alone with Penrod Ballantyne.'

Amber went as still as stone, and stared into her sister's eyes, but they were unfathomable in the gloom. When she spoke at last her voice shook. 'I don't understand.'

'I cannot go with you. I must stay here.'

'But why, Becky? Why, oh, why?'

In reply Rebecca took her sister's hands and guided them under her shift. She placed them on her own naked belly. 'Do you feel that?'

'It's just a little fat,' Amber protested. 'That won't stop you. You must come.'

'There is a baby inside me, Amber.'

'I don't believe it. It cannot be. I still love you and need you.'

'It's a baby,' Rebecca assured her. 'It's Osman Atalan's bastard. Do you know what a bastard is, Amber?'

'Yes.' Amber could not bring herself to say more.

'Do you know what will happen if I go home to England with an Arab bastard inside me?'

'Yes.' Amber's voice was almost inaudible. 'But the midwives could take it away, couldn't they?'

'You mean kill my baby?' Rebecca asked. 'Would you kill your own baby, Amber darling?' Amber shook her head. 'Then you cannot ask me to do it.'

'I will stay with you,' said Amber.

'You saw what a sorry condition Penrod is in.' Rebecca knew it was the strongest lever she had to move Amber. 'You have saved his life already. You fed him and gave him water when he was dying. If you desert him now, he will not survive. You must do your duty.'

'But what about you?' Amber was cruelly torn.

'I will be safe, I promise.' Rebecca hugged her hard, and then her tone became firm and brisk. 'Now, you must take this with you. It's Daddy's journal, which I have added to. When you reach England, take it to his lawyer. His name is Sebastian Hardy. I have written his name and address on the first page. He will know what to do with it.' She handed the book to Amber. She had packed it into a bag of woven palm leaves and bound it up carefully. It was heavy and bulky, but Rebecca had plaited a rope handle to make it easier to carry.

'I don't want to leave you,' Amber blurted.

'I know, darling. Duty can be hard. But you must do it.'

'I will love you for ever and always.'

'I know you will, and I will love you just as hard and just as long.' They clung to each other until Nazeera appeared quietly beside them.

'Come, Zahra. It is time to go. Yakub and Abadan Riji are waiting for you by the riverside.'

There was nothing left to say. They embraced for the last time, then Nazeera took Amber's hand and led her away, with the bag that contained her legacy. Only once she was alone did Rebecca allow her grief to burst out. She threw herself on to their *angareb* below the window and wept. Every sob came up painfully from deep inside her.

Then something inside her was awakened by the strength of her sorrow, and for the first time she felt the infant kick in her womb. It startled her into stillness, and filled her with such bitter joy that she clasped her arms round her belly and whispered, 'You are all I have left now.' She rocked herself and the infant to sleep.

The felucca was anchored close to the muddy strip of beach below the old mosque. It was a battered, neglected craft that stank of river mud and old fish. The owner hoped to replace it with a new vessel paid for out of the exorbitant fee he had been promised for a single crossing of the river. Its amount warned him that he was at great risk, and he was edgy and fidgety as he waited.

The laudanum made Penrod Ballantyne feel muzzy-headed and divorced from reality, but at least he was without pain in his limbs. He and Yakub were lying on the floorboards where they would be concealed from casual inspection. In a whisper Yakub was trying to tell him something that he seemed to think was of prime importance. However, Penrod's mind kept floating off on the wings of opium, and Yakub's words made no sense to him.

Then, vaguely, he was aware that somebody was wading out to the vessel. He lifted himself on one elbow and looked groggily over the side. Nazeera was standing on the beach, and the lithe figure of Amber Benbrook, with a large bag on her head, was moving towards the felucca. 'Where is Rebecca?' he asked, and blinked to make certain he was seeing straight.

Amber pulled herself aboard the felucca, then Nazeera turned away from the water and ran off.

'Where is Nazeera going?' he wondered vaguely.

Amber dropped her bag on the deck and stooped over him. 'Penrod! Thank goodness! How are you feeling? Let me see your arms. I have some ointment for your bruises.'

'Wait until we get to the other side,' he demurred. 'Where is Nazeera going? Where is Rebecca?' Neither Amber nor Yakub answered him. Instead Yakub gave a sharp order to the boat-owner and scrambled to help him hoist the lateen sail. It filled to the night breeze and they bore away.

The felucca sailed closer to the wind than her age would suggest, and she kicked up such a bow wave that the spray splattered over them. On the Khartoum side they went aground with such force that the rotten keel was almost torn off her. Amber and Yakub helped Penrod ashore, and Yakub propped his shoulder under his armpit to steady him as they hurried through the deserted streets of the ruined city. They met not a living soul until they reached Ryder Courtney's abandoned compound. There, a Bedouin boy was waiting for them with a string of camels. As soon as he had handed the lead reins to Yakub, he fled into the shadows.

The riding camels were fully saddled and equipped. They mounted at once, but Yakub had to help Penrod into the saddle and he was almost unseated as the animal lurched to its feet. Yakub took him on the lead rein and led the little caravan through the mud of the almost dry canal and into the desert beyond. There he goaded the camels onwards and they paced away, keeping the river in sight on their left-hand side. Within the first mile, Penrod lost his balance and slipped sideways out of the saddle. He hit the ground heavily and lay for a while like a dead man. They dismounted and helped him back into the saddle.

'I will hold him,' Amber told Yakub. She climbed up, sat behind Penrod and placed both arms round his waist to steady him. They went on for hours without a halt, until in the first light of dawn they picked out the shape of the lagoon ahead in the river mist. There was no sign of the steamer out on the open water.

On the edge of the reed bed Yakub reined in his camel and stood upright on his saddle. He sang out over the lagoon in a high wail that would carry for a mile. 'In God's Name, is there no man or jinnee who hears me?'

Almost immediately, from close by in the reeds, a jinnee replied in a broad Scots burr: 'Och, aye, laddie! I hear you.' Jock McCrump had camouflaged his steamer with cut reeds so that it was almost invisible from the bank of the lagoon. As soon as they had turned the camels loose and were safely aboard he reversed the old *Ibis*, now the *Wisdom of the Skies*, out into the open water and turned her bows eastwards for Roseires, almost two hundred miles upstream. Then he came down to the cabin where Penrod was stretched out on the bunk with Amber anointing his blisters and bruises with the lotion that Nazeera had provided. 'And now you'll be expecting me to make you a cuppa tea, I hae nae doot,' said Jock, morosely. It was Darjeeling Orange Pekoe, with condensed milk, and Penrod had never tasted anything so heavenly. He fell asleep immediately after he had downed a third mug, and did not wake again until they were a hundred miles upriver from Khartoum, and beyond the pursuit of even the swiftest camels of Osman Atalan's aggagiers.

When he opened his eyes Amber was still sitting at the end of his bunk, but she was so engrossed in reading her father's bulky journal that for some time she did not realize he was awake. Penrod studied her countenance as the emotions that her father's writing evoked flitted across it. He saw now that she had become far and away the beauty of the trio of Benbrook girls.

Suddenly she looked at him, smiled and closed the journal. 'How are you feeling now? You have slept for ten hours without moving.'

'I'm a great deal better, thanks to you and Yakub.' He paused. 'Rebecca?'

Amber's smile faded, and she looked bereft. 'She will stay in Omdurman. It was her choice.'

'Why?' he asked, and she told him. They were both silent for a while and then Penrod said, 'If I had had my wits about me, I would have gone back to fetch her.'

'She did the right thing,' Amber said softly. 'Rebecca always does the right thing. She made that sacrifice for love of me. I will never forget it.'

Over the rest of the river voyage, as they talked, Penrod discovered that she was no longer a child in either body or mind, but that she had become a courageous, mature young woman, her character tempered in the forge of suffering.

The horses were waiting at Roseires, and they picked up relays of mules as they journeyed through the foothills of the Abyssinian highlands. They reached Entoto after eleven days of hard going, and as they rode into the courtyard of Ryder Courtney's compound Saffron rushed out to greet her twin. Amber tumbled off her mule and they fell into each other's arms, too overcome to speak. Ryder watched them from the veranda with a benign smile.

Once they had recovered their tongues, the twins could barely pause to draw breath. They sat up all night in Saffron's studio, talking. They wandered hand in hand through the souks and lanes of Entoto, talking. They rode out into the mountains and came back with armfuls of flowers, still talking. Then they read their father's journal aloud to each other, and Rebecca's additions to it, and they hugged each other as they wept for their father and elder sister, both of whom they had lost for ever.

Amber studied Saffron's portfolio of Khartoum sketches. She pronounced them wonderfully accurate and evocative, then suggested a few small changes and improvements, which Saffron, anxious to please her, adopted immediately. Saffron designed and made a complete wardrobe of new clothes for Amber, and took her to have tea with Lady Alice Packer and Empress Miriam. The queen thought Amber's new outfit stylish and fetching, and asked Saffron to design her a dress for the next state dinner.

Amber continued David Benbrook's journal from the point where Rebecca had left off. In it she described her escape from Omdurman and the flight up the Blue Nile to the Abyssinian border. In the process she discovered she had a natural talent with the written word.

Only Ryder was not completely enchanted by Amber's arrival in Entoto. He had become accustomed to having Saffron's undivided attention. Now that it had been diverted to her twin, he realized, with something of a shock, how much he missed it.

Penrod recovered swiftly from the injuries he had suffered in Osman Atalan's *shebba*. He exercised his sword arm in practice with Yakub, and his legs in long, solitary walks in the mountains. His first urgent duty was to report his actions and whereabouts to his superiors in Cairo, but the telegraph line ran only as far as Djibouti on the Gulf of Aden. He wrote letters to Sir Evelyn Baring and Viscount Wolseley, and to his elder brother in England. The British ambassador sent these out in the diplomatic pouch, but they all knew how long it would be before he could expect a reply.

Ryder Courtney had a sealed blank envelope for Penrod. When Penrod weighed it in his hand he realized that it contained more than paper. 'Who is it from?' he asked. 'Regrettably I have been sworn to silence,' Ryder replied, 'but I am sure the answer is contained in it. You must ask nothing more from me concerning the matter, for I am unable to discuss it.'

Penrod took it to the bedroom that Ryder had set aside for him and bolted the door. As he slit open the envelope, a weighty object fell out, but he caught it before it struck the tiles. It lay in his palm, shimmering gold and magnificent, its beauty undiminished by the ages. On the obverse side was the crowned portrait of Cleopatra Thea Philopator and on the reverse the head of Marcus Antonius. In the envelope with the coin was a single line of Arabic written on parchment. 'When my lord needs me, he knows where I shall be.' The coin was her signature.

'Bakhita!' He rubbed the portrait of the woman with his thumb. How did she fit into the scheme of things now? Then he remembered Yakub trying to tell him something important while he was drugged with laudanum on the first night of the escape from Omdurman.

The next day he and Yakub rode up into the mountains where they could be alone. Yakub related in detail how, after Penrod had been captured by Osman Atalan, he had set out for Aswan to enlist the aid of the only person who could and would help them. He explained how he had been arrested on the Egyptian border while travelling with a dealer in slaves, and how he had been imprisoned for over a year before he could go on to Aswan.

'As soon as I found Bakhita al-Masur she travelled with me here to Entoto, and arranged your escape with al-Sakhawi.'

Penrod considered ignoring Ryder Courtney's warning and taxing him with Bakhita's role in their rescue, but in the end he shied away from doing so. He and Bakhita had always maintained the greatest secrecy and discretion in their relationship. It even surprised him that Yakub had known of it. By this time I should have learnt not to be surprised by anything that the intrepid Yakub comes up with. He smiled to himself. Then he considered writing to Bakhita, but this would be equally unwise. Even if the letter went through diplomatic channels, there was no telling which of the embassy staff was in the pay of the ubiquitous Evelyn Baring. There was another reason not to contact Bakhita. This was less clear-cut in his mind but it had to do with Amber Benbrook. He did not want to do anything that might later hurt the child.

Child? He questioned his choice of word as he watched her cross the yard in deep conversation with her twin sister. You deceive yourself, Penrod Ballantyne.

It was five months before Penrod received a reply to the letter he had written to his elder brother Sir Peter Ballantyne, at the family estate on the Scottish Borders. In his reply Sir Peter agreed that the Benbrook sisters might make their home at Clercastle until such time as their future had been decided. Penrod would sail back to England with Amber and Saffron and take care of them until they reached Clercastle. Once they arrived Sir Peter's wife, Jane, would take over the responsibility from him.

As soon as Penrod received his brother's letter he went up to the British Embassy and telegraphed to the office of the Peninsular and Orient Steamship line in Djibouti. He booked passage for himself and the twins on board the SS *Singapore*, sailing via Suez and Alexandria for Southampton in six weeks' time. When Amber learnt that she would be sailing home in company with Penrod Ballantyne, then staying at Clercastle with the Ballantyne family she made no objection. On the contrary she seemed well pleased with the arrangement.

It did not go so easily with the other twin. There followed long and difficult discussions with Saffron, who announced with passion that she could see no reason why she should return to England 'where it rains all the time, and I shall probably expire with double pneumonia on the same day I arrive'. It was necessary to appeal to Alice Packer for a ruling.

'My dear Saffron, you are only fourteen.'

'Fifteen in a month's time,' Saffron corrected her grimly.

'Your education has been somewhat neglected,' Alice went on imperturbably. 'I am sure Sir Peter will provide a governess for you and Amber. After all, he has daughters of very much the same age as you two darling girls.'

'I don't need geography and mathematics,' said Saffron, stubbornly. 'I know all about Africa and I can paint.'

'Ah!' said Alice. 'Sir John Millais is a dear friend of mine. How would you like to study art under him? I'm sure I can arrange it.'

Saffron wavered: Millais was a founder of the Pre-Raphaelite Brotherhood, the most celebrated painter of the day. David Benbrook had kept a book of his paintings in his study at Khartoum. Saffron had spent hours dreaming over them. Then Alice played her trump: 'And, of course, as soon as you are sixteen you will always be welcome to return to Entoto as my guest, whenever and as often as you wish.'

As the day of their departure for Djibouti drew nearer, Saffron spent less time with her twin and more in helping Bacheet look after Ryder. He agreed to pose for an hour or two each evening for one last portrait. Since the twins' future had been agreed upon, his mood had been subdued, but it lightened perceptibly during these daily painting sessions. Saffron was an amusing girl and made him laugh.

Two days before Penrod and the twins were due to leave Entoto for Djibouti, Ryder announced his intention of joining their little caravan, as he was expecting a shipment of trade goods to arrive on board the SS *Singapore* from Calcutta. During the journey down to the coast Ryder and Saffron spent much time riding side by side at the rear of the convoy. The closer they came to Djibouti, the more serious their expressions became. The day before they came in sight of the town and harbour a flaming row broke out between them.

Saffron left Ryder and galloped to the head of the column to ride beside Amber.

That night, as was the custom, the four of them ate supper beside the fire. When Ryder addressed a polite remark to her, Saffron pulled a face and deliberately moved her chair so that her back was turned to him. She did not bid him goodnight when she and Amber went to their tent.

The next day as they came in sight of Djibouti harbour the SS *Singapore* was lying in the roads and discharging cargo into the lighters clustered around her. While Ryder and Bacheet set up camp on the outskirts of the town, Penrod and the twins rode down to the shipping office at the wharf to pay for and receive their tickets for the voyage to Southampton. The shipping clerk assured them that the *Singapore* would sail on schedule at noon the following day. Penrod managed to buy a bottle of Glenlivet whisky from the purser. He and Ryder made short work of it that evening, when the twins had retired to their tent not long after nightfall.

Due to the exigencies of the previous evening's consumption of liquor the two men were late in rising. In the roads the *Singapore* was already making steam in preparation for her sailing in three hours' time. Penrod took the luggage down to the wharf and sent it on board, then rode back to the camp and found it in a state of uproar.

'She has gone!' Bacheet lamented, and wrung his plump hands. 'Filfil has gone!'

'What do you mean, Bacheet? Where has she gone?'

'We do not know, Effendi. During the night she took her mule and rode away. Al-Sakhawi has gone after her, but I think Filfil has six hours' start on him. He won't be able to catch her before nightfall.'

'By that time the *Singapore* will have sailed,' Penrod fumed, and went to find Amber.

'After Saffron and I climbed into bed, I went to sleep directly. When I woke it was already light and Saffy had gone, just like that, without even a goodbye.'

Penrod studied her face for some hint of the truth. He was

sure he had heard the twins whispering when he had passed their tent on the way to his own bed. He knew for certain it had been after midnight, because he had wound his pocket watch before he blew out the lamp. 'We will have to go on board. We cannot miss this sailing. There will not be another for months. I will try to persuade the captain to delay until Saffron is on board,' he said, and Amber agreed with an angelic expression.

While Penrod and Amber stood at the starboard rail of the *Singapore*, Penrod was staring anxiously through a pair of borrowed binoculars as the last boat from the shore approached the ship's side.

'Blue bloody blazes!' he muttered furiously. 'She isn't on board.'

As he lowered the binoculars, the ship's third officer hurried down the ladder from the bridge and came to them. 'The captain's compliments, Captain Ballantyne, but he very much regrets that he is not able to delay the sailing until the arrival of Miss Benbrook. If he does he will be unable to make his reservation for the transit of the Suez Canal.' Just then the ship's siren wailed and cut off the rest of his apology. The capstan in the bows began to clatter and the anchor broke free.

'Now, Miss Amber Benbrook,' Penrod said grimly, 'I think it's time you delivered the truth. Just what is your sister playing at?'

'I should think that is perfectly obvious, Captain Ballantyne, except to a blind man or an imbecile.'

'Nevertheless, I would be most obliged if you could explain it to me.'

'My sister is in love with Mr Ryder Courtney. She has not the slightest intention of leaving him. I am afraid we are to be deprived of her company on this voyage. You will have to make do with mine.'

A prospect that I do not find particularly distressing, he thought, but tried to disguise his pleasure.

The tracks of Saffron's mule headed straight back along the main route towards the Abyssinia border. Except where they had been overridden by other travellers they were easy to follow. Saffron had made no attempt to cover them or to throw off any pursuit. Soon Ryder knew that he was overhauling her, but it was the middle of the afternoon before he made out her mule in the distance. He urged his own mount into a gallop. As he came within hail he let out an angry shout. She stopped and turned back towards him. Then he saw that it was not her at all, but one of the camp servants: a dim-witted lad whose sole employment was chopping fire-wood for the camp. Anything more demanding was beyond his limited capabilities.

'What in the name of God are you up to, Solomon? Where do you think you are going on Filfil's mule?'

'Filfil gave me a Maria Theresa to ride back to Entoto and fetch a box she had forgotten,' he announced importantly, proud of the task with which he had been entrusted.

'Where is Filfil now?'

'Why, Effendi, I know not.' Solomon picked his nose with embarrassment at the complexity of the question. 'Is she not still in Djibouti?'

When Ryder came in sight of the harbour again, the *Singapore's* anchorage was empty, and the smoke from her funnels was merely a dark smear on the watery horizon. Ryder stormed into his camp and shouted at Bacheet: 'Where is Filfil?' Bacheet remained silent but rolled his eyes in the direction of her tent.

Ryder strode to the tent and stooped through the opening of the fly. 'There you are, you scamp.'

Saffron was sitting cross-legged on her camp-bed. She was bare-footed and her most extravagant hat was perched on her head. She was looking extremely pleased with herself.

'What have you to say for yourself?' he demanded.

'All I have to say is that you are my dog and I am your

561

flea. You can scratch and scratch as much as you will, but you'll not get rid of me, Ryder Courtney.'

They were half-way back to Entoto before he had recovered from the shock, and had come to realize how happy he was that she had not sailed with the *Singapore*. 'I still don't know what we should do now,' he said. 'I shall probably be arrested for child abduction. I have no idea of the legal age for marriage in Abyssinia.'

'It's fourteen,' said Saffron. 'I asked the Empress before we left Entoto. Anyway, that is merely a guideline. Nobody pays much attention to it. She was thirteen when the Emperor married her.'

'Have you any other gems of information?' he asked tartly.

'I have. The Empress has expressed her willingness to sponsor our union, should you care to marry me. What do you think of that?'

'I had not thought about it at all,' he exclaimed, 'but, by God, now that you raise the subject it is not the worst notion I have ever heard of.' He reached across, lifted her off the back of her mule, seated her on the pommel of his own saddle and kissed her.

She clamped her hat onto her head with one hand and flung her other arm round his neck. Then she kissed him back with a great deal more vigour than finesse. After a while she broke away to breathe. 'Oh, you wonderful man!' she gasped. 'You cannot imagine how long I have wanted to do that. It feels even nicer than I hoped it might. Let's do it again.'

'An excellent idea,' he agreed.

The Empress was as good as her word. She sat in the front pew of the Entoto cathedral with the Emperor at her side, beaming on the ceremony like the rising sun. She was dressed in a Saffron Benbrook creation, which made her look rather like a large sugar-iced chocolate cake.

Lady Packer had prevailed on her husband, Sir Harold White Packer, Knight Commander of Michael and George, Her Britannic Majesty's ambassador, to give Saffron away. He was in full fig, including his bicorne hat with gold lace and white cockerel feathers. The groom was handsome and nervous in his black frock-coat, with the dazzling Star of the Order of Solomon and Judea on his breast. The Bishop of Abyssinia performed the service.

Saffron had designed her own wedding dress. When she came down the aisle on Sir Harold's arm, Ryder was mildly relieved to see that it was in pure virginal white. Saffron's taste usually ran to brighter hues. When they left the church as man and wife, a troop of the Royal Abyssinian Artillery fired a nine-gun salute. In the fever of the moment, one of the ancient cannon had been double charged and it burst in spectacular fashion on the first discharge. Fortunately nobody was injured, and the bishop declared it a propitious omen. The Emperor provided vast quantities of fiery Tej to the populace, and toasts were drunk to bride and groom for as long as the liquor held out and their well-wishers remained upright and conscious.

For the honeymoon Ryder took his bride into the southern Abyssinian highlands on an expedition to capture the rare mountain nyala. They returned some months later without having caught even a glimpse of the elusive beast. Saffron painted a picture to commemorate the expedition: on a mountain peak in the background stood a creature that bore more than a passing resemblance to a unicorn, and in the foreground a man and woman whose identities were in no doubt. The woman wore a huge yellow hat decorated with seashells and roses. They were not looking at the unicorn, but clasped between them was a large and magnificent bird, half ostrich and half peacock. The legend beneath the painting read, 'We went to find the elusive nyala, but found instead the elusive bird of happiness.'

Ryder was so enchanted by it that he had the picture mounted in an ivory frame, and hung it on the wall above their bed.

The voyage up the Red Sea was calm and peaceful. There were only four passenger cabins on board the SS *Singapore*, two of which were unoccupied. Amber and Penrod dined each evening with the captain, and after dinner they strolled around the deck or danced to the music of the violin played by the Italian chef, who thought Amber was the most lovely creature in all creation.

During the day Amber and Penrod worked together in the card room, editing David Benbrook's journal. Amber exercised her new-found writing talent, and Penrod provided military and historical background. Amber suggested he write his own account of the battle of Abu Klea, his subsequent capture by Osman Atalan and their escape from the captivity of the Dervish. They would combine this with the writings of David and Rebecca. The further they advanced into the project, the greater their enthusiasm for it became. By the time the *Singapore* anchored in Alexandria harbour they had made great progress in expanding and correcting the text. It could now be published as an inspiring true adventure, and they had the remainder of the voyage home to complete it.

Penrod went ashore in Alexandria, and hired a horse. He rode the thirty miles to Cairo, and went directly to the British Agency. Sir Evelyn Baring kept him waiting only twenty minutes before he sent his secretary to summon him into his office. He had the thirty-page letter that Penrod had sent from Entoto spread like a fan on the desk in front of him. On it were many cryptic notations written in red ink in the margins. Baring maintained his usual cold, enigmatic manner and expression during the interview, which lasted almost two hours. At the end he rose to dismiss Penrod without making any comment, expressing any opinion, or offering either censure or approval. 'Colonel Samuel Adams at Army headquarters in Giza is anxious to speak to you,' he told Penrod, at the door.

'Colonel?' Penrod asked.

'Promotion,' Baring replied. 'He will explain everything to you.'

Sam Adams limped only slightly and he no longer used a cane as he came round his desk to greet Penrod warmly. He looked fit and suntanned, although there were a few grey hairs in his moustache.

'Congratulations on the colonel's pips, sir.' Penrod saluted.

Adams was without a cap so he could not return the salute, but he seized Penrod's hand and shook it warmly. 'Delighted to have you back, Ballantyne. Much has happened while you have been away. There is a great deal we must talk about. Shall we go for lunch at the club?'

He had reserved a table in the corner of the dining room at the Gheziera Club. He ordered a bottle of Krug, then waited until the glasses were filled and they had placed their order with the waiter, in red fez and white *galabiyya*, before he got down to business. 'After the disaster of Khartoum, and the murder of that idiot Gordon, there were many unpleasant repercussions. The press at home were looking for scapegoats and fastened on Sir Charles Wilson's delay in pressing on to the relief of Gordon after the victory at Abu Klea. Wilson sought to defend himself by placing the blame on his subordinates. Unfortunately you were one of those to suffer, Ballantyne. He has brought charges of subordination and desertion against you. Now that you have come back from limbo, you will almost certainly be court-martialled. Capital offence, if you're found guilty. Firing squad, don't you know?'

Penrod blanched under his suntan and stared at Adams in horror.

He went on hurriedly: 'You have friends here. Everyone knows your worth. Victoria Cross, derring-do, heroic escapes and all that. However, you will have to resign your commission in the Hussars.'

'Resign my commission?' Penrod exclaimed. 'I will let them shoot me first.'

'It might come to that. But hear me out.' Adams reached across the table and laid his hand on Penrod's arm to prevent him leaping to his feet. 'Drink your champagne and listen to me. Damn fine vintage, by the way. Don't waste it.' Penrod subsided, and Adams went on,

'First, I must give you some other background information. Egypt now belongs to us in all but name. Baring calls it the Veiled Protectorate, but it's a bloody colony for all the pretty words. The decision has been taken by London to rebuild the Egyptian army from a disorganized rabble into a first-rate fighting corps. The new sirdar is Horatio Herbert Kitchener. Do you know him?'

'I cannot say that I do,' Penrod said. The sirdar was the commander-in-chief of the Egyptian army.

'Cross between a tiger and a dragon. Absolute bloody fire-eater. He desperately needs first-class officers for the new army, men who know the desert and the lingo. I mentioned your name. He knows of you. He wants you. If you join him he'll quash all Wilson's charges against you. Kitchener is going up the ladder to the top and will take his people with him. You will start at your equivalent rank of captain, but I can almost guarantee you a battalion within a year, your own regiment within five. For you the choice is between ruin and high rank. What do you say?'

Penrod smoothed his whiskers thoughtfully – on board ship Amber had trimmed his sideburns and moustache for him and once again they were luxuriant. He had learnt never to jump at the first offer.

'Camel Corps.' Adams tossed in another plum. 'Plenty of desert fighting.'

'When can I meet the gentleman?'

'Tomorrow. Nine hundred hours sharp at the new army headquarters. If you love life, don't be late.'

Kitchener was a muscular man of middling height and moved like a gladiator. He had a full head of hair and a cast in one eye, not unlike Yakub's. This made Penrod incline towards him. His jaw had been shot half away in a fight with the Dervish at Suakin when he had been governor of that insalubrious and dangerous corner of Africa. The bone was distorted and the keloid scar was pale pink against his darkly tanned skin. His handshake was iron hard and his manner harsh and unyielding.

'You speak Arabic?' he asked, in that language. He spoke it well, but with an accent that would never allow him to pass him as a native.

'Sirdar effendi! May all your days be perfumed with jasmine.' Penrod made the gesture of respect. 'In truth, I speak the language of the One True God and His Prophet.'

Kitchener blinked. It was perfect. 'When can you come on strength?'

'I need to be in England until Christmas. I have been out of contact with civilization for some time. I must settle my personal affairs, and I shall have to resign my commission with my present regiment.'

'You have until the middle of January next year and then I want you here in Cairo. Adams will go over the details with you. You are dismissed.' His uneven gaze dropped back to the papers on the desk in front of him.

As he and Adams went down the steps of the headquarters building to where the grooms were holding their horses, Penrod said, 'He wastes little time.'

'Not a second,' Adams agreed. 'Not a single bloody second.'

Before he rode back to Alexandria to rejoin the *Singapore*, Penrod went to the telegraph office and sent a wire to Sebastian Hardy, David Benbrook's lawyer, at his chambers in Lincolns Inn Fields. It was a lengthy message and cost Penrod two pounds, nine shillings and fourpence.

Hardy came from London by train to meet the ship when she docked at Southampton. In appearance he reminded Penrod and Amber of Charles Dickens's Mr Pickwick. However, behind his *pince-nez* he had a shrewd and calculating eye. He travelled back to London with them.

'The press has got wind of your escape from Omdurman, and your arrival in this country,' he told them. 'They are agog. I have no doubt they will be waiting at Waterloo station to pounce upon you.'

'How can they know what train we will arrive on?' Amber asked.

'I dropped a little hint,' Hardy admitted. 'What I would refer to as pre-baiting the waters. Now, may I read this manuscript?'

Amber looked to Penrod for guidance, and he nodded. 'I think you should trust Mr Hardy. Your father did.'

Hardy skimmed through the thick sheaf of papers so rapidly that Amber doubted he was reading it. She voiced her concern, and Hardy answered, without looking up, 'Trained eye, my dear young lady.'

As the carriage ran in through the suburbs he shuffled the papers together. 'I think we have something here. Will you allow me to keep this for a week? I know a man in Bloomsbury who would like to read it.'

Five journalists were waiting on the platform, including one from *The Times* and another from the *Telegraph*. When they saw the handsome, highly decorated hero of El Obeid and Abu Klea, with the young beauty on his arm, they knew they had a story that would electrify the whole country. They barked hysterically as a pack of mongrels who had chased a squirrel up a tree. Hardy gave them a tantalizing statement about the horrifying ordeal the couple had survived, mentioning Gordon, the Mahdi and Khartoum more than once, all evocative names. Then he sent the press away and led the couple out to a cab he had waiting at the station entrance.

The cabbie whipped up his horse and they clattered through the foggy city to the hotel in Charles Street where Hardy had booked a room for Amber. Once she was installed they went on to the hotel in Dover Street where Penrod would stay.

'Never do for the two of you to frequent the same lodging. From now on you will be under a magnifying lens.'

Four days later Sebastian Hardy summoned them to his office. He was beaming pinkly through his *pince-nez*. 'Macmillan and Company want to publish. You know they did Sir Samuel White Baker's book on the Nile tributaries of Abyssinia? Your book is caviar and champagne to them.'

'What can the Benbrook sisters expect to receive? You know that Miss Amber wishes any proceeds to be shared equally between them, following the example their father set in his will?'

Hardy sobered and looked apologetic. He removed his reading glasses and polished them with the tail of his shirt. 'I pressed them as hard as I could, but they would not budge beyond ten thousand pounds.'

'Ten thousand pounds!' Amber shrieked. 'I did not know there was that much money outside the Bank of England.'

'You will also receive twelve and a half per cent of the profits. I doubt this will amount to much more than seventy-five thousand pounds.'

They gaped at him in silence. Placed in consols, irredeemable government treasury bonds, that sum would bring in almost three and a half thousand pounds per annum in perpetuity. They would never have to worry about money.

In the event, Hardy's estimate erred on the side of caution.

Months before Christmas *Slaves of the Mahdi* was all the rage. Hatchard's in Piccadilly was unable to keep copies on its shelves for more than an hour. Irate customers vied with each other to snatch them and carry them triumphantly to the till.

In the House of Commons the opposition seized on the book as a weapon with which to belabour the government. The whole sorry business of Mr Gladstone abandoning Chinese Gordon to his fate was resuscitated. Saffron Benbrook's harrowing painting depicting the death of the general, to which she had been an eye-witness, formed the book's frontispiece. It was reported in a leading article in *The Times* that women wept and strong men raged as they looked at it. The British people had tried to forget the humiliation and loss of prestige they had suffered at the hands of the Mad Mahdi, but now the half-healed wound was ripped wide open. A popular campaign for the reoccupation of the Sudan swept the country. The book sold and sold.

Amber and Penrod were invited to all the great houses, and were surrounded by admirers wherever they went. London cabbies greeted them by name, and strangers accosted them in Piccadilly and Hyde Park. Hundreds of letters from readers were forwarded to them by the publishers. There was even a short note of congratulation from the sirdar, Kitchener, in Cairo.

'That will do my new career no harm at all,' Penrod told Amber, as they rode together down Rotten Row, acknowledging waves.

The book sold a quarter of a million copies in the first six weeks, and the printing presses roared night and day churning out fresh copies. They were unable to keep up with the demand. Putnam's of 70 Fifth Avenue, New York, brought out an American edition, which piqued the interest of readers who had never heard of the Sudan. *Slaves of the Mahdi* outsold Mr Stanley's account of his search for Dr Livingstone by three to one.

The French, true to the national character, added their own fanciful illustrations to the Paris edition. Rebecca Benbrook was depicted with her bodice torn open by the evil Mahdi as he prepared to ravish her as she courageously sheltered her beautiful, terrified little sister Amber. The indomitable thrust of her bare bosom declared her defiance in the face of a fate worse than death. Copies were smuggled across the Channel and sold at a premium on stalls in the streets of Soho. Even after the payment of income tax at sixpence in the pound, by Christmas the book had earned royalties little short of two hundred thousand pounds. Amber, at the suggestion of Penrod Ballantyne, instructed Mr Hardy to place this in a trust fund for the three sisters.

Amber and Penrod celebrated Christmas at Clercastle. They walked and rode together every day. When the house-party went out to shoot Sir Peter's high-flying pheasant, Amber stood in the line of guns beside Penrod and, thanks to her father's training, acquitted herself so gracefully and skil-fully that the head keeper came to her after the last drive, tugged at the peak of his cap and mumbled, 'It was a joy to watch you shoot, Miss Amber.'

January came too soon. Penrod had to take up his post in Cairo. Amber, chaperoned by Penrod's sister-in-law Jane, went to see him off from Waterloo station on the boat train. With Jane's assistance, Amber had spent the previous week shopping for the correct attire at such a momentous parting. Of course, price was now of little consequence.

She settled on a dove-grey jacket, trimmed with sable fur, worn over ankle-length skirts and a fashionable bustle. Her high-heeled boots buckled up the sides and peeped out from under the sweeping skirts. The artful cut of the material emphasized her tiny waist. Her wide-brimmed hat was crowned with a wave of ostrich feathers. She wore the amber necklace and earrings that he had given her on the road outside Gallabat.

'When will we see each other again?' Amber was trying desperately but unsuccessfully to hold back her tears until after the train had departed.

'That I cannot say.' Penrod had determined never to lie to her, unless it was absolutely necessary. The tears broke over

Amber's lower lids. She tried to sniff them back, and Penrod hurried on: 'Perhaps you and Jane could come out to Cairo to spend your sixteenth birthday at Shepheard's Hotel. Jane has never been there and you might show her the pyramids.'

'Oh, can we do that, Jane? Please?'

'I will speak to my husband,' Jane promised. She was about the same age as Rebecca, and in the few weeks that Amber had lived at Clercastle they had become as close as sisters. 'I can see no possible reason why Peter should object. It will be the height of the grouse-shooting season and he will be much occupied elsewhere. He will hardly miss us.'

Sam Adams came down from Cairo to meet Penrod when his ship docked in Alexandria. Almost his first words were 'We have all read the book. The sirdar is as pleased as a cat with a saucer of cream. London was starting to have second thoughts about rebuilding the army. Gladstone and those other idiots were dithering with the idea of using the money to build a bloody great dam on the Nile instead of giving it to us. Miss Benbrook's book created such a rumpus in the House that they changed their dim minds sharpish. Kitchener has another million pounds, and to the devil with the dam. Now we will certainly have new Maxim guns. As for myself, well, we desperately need a good number two if we're to have any chance of retaining the Nile Cup this year.'

'After my brief meeting with the sirdar, I estimate that he is not likely to set aside much time for polo.'

Adams's wife had found and rented a comfortable house for Penrod on the bank of the river, close to army headquarters and the Gheziera Club. When Penrod climbed the steps to the shady veranda, a figure in a plain white *jibba* and turban rose from his seat beside the front door and made a deep salaam.

'Effendi, the heart of the faithful Yakub has pined for you as the night awaits the dawn.'

The next morning Penrod found out what Kitchener and

Adams had in store for him. He was to recruit and train three companies of camel cavalry to travel far and fast, and fight hard. 'I want men from the desert tribes,' he told Adams. 'They make the best soldiers. Abdullahi has driven many of the Ashraf out of Sudan, emirs of the Jaalin and the Hadendowa. I want to go after them. Hatred makes a man fight harder. I believe I shall be able to turn them against their former masters.'

'Find them,' Adams ordered.

Penrod and Yakub took the steamer to Aswan. Here they waited thirty-six hours for the sailing of another boat that would carry them up beyond the first cataract, as far as Wadi Halfa. Penrod left Yakub at the dock to guard the baggage, and went alone to the gate at the end of the narrow, winding alley. When old Liala heard his voice she flung open the gate and collapsed in a heap of faded robes and veils, wailing pitifully. 'Effendi, why have you come back? You should have spared my mistress. You should never have returned here.'

Penrod lifted her to her feet. 'Take me to her.'

'She will not see you, Effendi.'

'She must tell me that herself. Go to her, Liala. Tell her I am here.' Sobbing pitifully, the old woman left him beside the fountain in the courtyard and tottered into the back quarters. She was gone a long time. Penrod picked tiny green flies from the flowering fuchsias and dropped them into the pool. The perch rose to the surface and gulped them down.

Liala returned at last. She had stopped weeping. 'She will see you.' She led him to the bead screen. 'Go in.'

Bakhita sat on a silk rug on the far side of the well-remembered room. He knew it was her by her perfume. She was heavily veiled. 'My heart fills with joy to see you safe and well, my lord.'

Her soft, sweet voice tugged at his heart. 'Without you, Bakhita, that would not have been possible. Yakub has told me of the part you played in bringing me to safety. I have come to thank you.'

'And the English girl's Arabic name is al-Zahra. I am told that she is young and very beautiful. Is that so, my lord?'

'It is so, Bakhita.' He was not surprised that she knew. Bakhita knew everything.

'Then she is the one we spoke of. The girl of your own people who will be your wife. I am happy for you.'

'We will still be friends, you and I.'

'Friends and more than that,' she said softly. 'Whenever there is something that you should know I will write to you.'

'I will come to see you.'

'Perhaps.'

'May I see your face once more before I go, Bakhita?'

'It would not be wise.'

He went to her and knelt in front of her. 'I want to see your lovely face again, to look into your eyes and to kiss your lips one last time.'

'I beg of you, lord of my heart, spare me this thing.'

He reached out and touched her veil. 'May I lift it?'

She was silent for a while. Then she sighed. 'Perhaps, after all, it would be easier this way,' she said.

He lifted the veil and stared at her. Slowly she watched the horror dawn in his eyes.

'Bakhita, oh, my dear heart, what has happened to you?' His voice trembled with pity.

'It was the smallpox. Allah has punished me for loving you.' The pockmarks were still fresh and livid. Her luminous eyes shone in the ruins of the face that had once been so lovely. 'Remember me as I once was,' she pleaded.

'I will remember only your courage and your kindness, and that you are my friend,' he whispered, and bent forward to kiss her lips.

'It is you who are kind,' she replied. Then she reached up and covered her face with the veil. 'Now you must leave me.'

He stood up. 'I shall return.'

'Perhaps you will, Effendi.'

But they both knew he never would.

The aggagiers found the corpse of Kabel al-Din lying in the courtyard beside the abandoned yoke of the *shebba*. Osman Atalan called all his men to horse and for many days they scoured both banks of the river. Osman was in a murderous mood when at last he returned to Omdurman without having found any trace of the fugitive. This was a bad time for the women to come to him and tell him that al-Zahra was also missing.

'How long has she been gone?' he demanded.

'Eight days, exalted Khalif.'

'The same time as Abadan Riji,' he exclaimed. 'What of the woman al-Jamal?'

'She is still in the *zenana*, mighty Atalan.'

'Bring her to me, and her servant also.'

They dragged in the two women and flung them at his feet.

'Where is your sister?'

'Lord, I do not know,' Rebecca replied.

Osman looked at al-Noor. 'Beat her,' he ordered. 'Beat her until she answers truthfully.'

'Mighty Khalif!' Nazeera cried. 'If you beat her she will lose your child. It may be a son. A son with golden hair like his mother and the lionheart of his sire.' Osman looked startled. He hesitated, staring at Rebecca's belly. Then he snarled at his aggagiers, 'Leave us. Do not return until I call you.'

They hurried out of the room, relieved to be sent away, for when a *khalif* and emir of the Beja is angry all men around him are in jeopardy.

'Disrobe,' he ordered. Rebecca rose to her feet and let her robe drop to her feet. Osman stared at her white, protruding belly. Then he went to her and placed his hand upon it.

Move! Please, my darling, move! Rebecca begged silently, and the foetus kicked.

Osman jerked away his hand and jumped back.

575

'In God's Name, it is alive.' He stared in awe at the bulge. 'Cover yourself!'

While Nazeera helped her to dress, Osman tugged furiously in his beard as he considered his dilemma. Suddenly he let out another angry shout and his aggagiers trooped back into the room. 'This woman.' He pointed at Nazeera. 'Beat her until al-Jamal tells us the whereabouts of her sister.'

Two of them held Nazeera's arms and Mooman Digna grabbed the cloth at the back of her neck and ripped it open to the knees. Al-Noor hefted the kurbash in his right hand. The first blow raised a red stripe across her shoulder-blades.

'Yi! Yi!' screeched Nazeera, and tried to throw herself flat, but the aggagiers held her.

'Yi!' she howled.

'Wait, Lord. I will tell you everything.' Rebecca could bear it no longer.

'Stop!' Osman ordered. 'Tell me.'

'A stranger came and led al-Zahra away,' Rebecca gabbled. 'I think they went north towards Metemma and Egypt, but I cannot be certain of it. Nazeera had nothing to do with this.'

'Why did you not go with them?'

'You are my master, and the father of my son,' Rebecca replied. 'I will leave you only when you kill me or send me away.'

'Beat the old whore again.' Osman waved to assuage his fury without endangering the well-being of the son who might have blue eyes and golden hair.

Rebecca clutched her belly with both hands and cried, 'I can feel the distress of my son within me. If you beat this woman, who is as my own mother, I shall not be able to hold the boy longer in my womb.'

'Hold!' Osman shouted. He was torn. He wanted to see blood. He drew his sword and Nazeera quailed under his gaze. Then he rushed at the stone column in the centre of the room and struck it with such force that sparks showered from the steel.

'Take these two women to the mosque at the oasis of Gedda.' It was a lonely place run by a few old mullahs fifty leagues out in the desert, a religious retreat for the devout, and for students of the Noble Koran. 'If the child that al-Jamal brings forth is a female, kill all three of them. If it is a son, bring them back to me and make certain they remain alive, especially my son.'

Five months later, lying on a rug spread on the floor of her cell at Gedda, while Nazeera attended her and the mullahs waited at the door, Rebecca gave birth to her first child. As soon as she felt the slippery burden she had carried for so long rush out of her, she struggled up on her elbows. Nazeera held the infant in her arms, all shiny with blood and mucus, still bound to Rebecca by the thick cord.

'What is it?' Rebecca gasped. 'Is it a boy? Sweet God, let it be a boy.'

Nazeera cackled like a broody hen and presented the child for her inspection. 'This one is a little stallion.' With her forefinger she tickled the baby's tiny penis. 'See how hard he stands already. You could crack an egg on the end of it. Beware anyone in skirts who stands in this one's way.'

The mullahs of Gedda sent word to Omdurman, and within days twenty aggagiers headed by al-Noor came to escort them back to the Holy City. When they reached the gates of Osman Atalan's palace, he was waiting to meet them. During the past five months his fury had had time to abate. However, he was trying not to appear too benign, and stood with one hand on the hilt of his sword, scowling hideously.

Al-Noor dismounted and took the child from Rebecca's arms. He was wrapped in cotton swaddling clothes and his face was covered to protect him from the sunlight and the dust. 'Mighty Atalan, behold your son!'

Osman glared at al-Noor. 'This I must see for myself.'

He took the bundle and placed it in the crook of his left arm. With his right hand he unwrapped it. He stared at the tiny creature. His head was bald, except for a single copper-tinted quiff. His skin was the colour of goat's milk with a splash of coffee added to it. His eyes were the colour of the waters of the Bahr al-Azrek, the Blue Nile. Osman opened the lower folds of his covering, and his scowl slipped, hovered on the verge of a smile.

The infant felt the cool river breeze fan his genitals, and let fly a yellow stream that splashed down his father's brightly patched *jibba*.

Osman let forth a startled roar of laughter. 'Behold! This is my son. As he pisses on me, so he shall piss on my enemies.' He held the child high, and he said, 'This is my son, Ahmed Habib abd Atalan. Approach and show him respect.' One after another his aggagiers came forward and, with a full salaam, greeted Ahmed, who kicked and gurgled with amusement. Osman had not glanced in the direction of the two waiting women, but now he handed the infant to al-Noor, and said offhandedly, 'Give the child to his mother, and tell her that she will return to her quarters in the harem, and there await my pleasure.'

Over the following eighteen months Rebecca saw Osman only three or four times, and then at a distance as he came and went on affairs of war and state. Whenever he returned he would send al-Noor to fetch Ahmed, and would keep the child away for hours on end, until it was time for him to be fed.

The child flourished. Rebecca fancied that she saw in him a resemblance to her own father, and to Amber, which made her loneliness more acute. She had only Nazeera and the baby: the other women of the harem were silly, scatter-brained creatures. She missed her sisters, and thought of them when she awoke to another empty day, and when she composed herself to sleep with Ahmed at her bosom.

Then, slowly, she became aware that she wanted Osman Atalan to send for her. Her body had recovered from the damage of childbirth, except for the stretchmarks across her belly and the soft sag of her breasts. Sometimes when she awoke in the night and could not sleep again she thought of the men she had known, but her mind returned variably to Osman. She needed somebody to talk to, somebody to be with, somebody to make love to her, and nobody had done that with the same skill as Osman Atalan.

Then the rumour in the harem was that there was to be a great new *jihad*, a war against the Christian infidels of Abyssinia. Osman Atalan would lead the army, and Allah would go with him. Ahmed was now toddling and talking. She hoped that Osman would take them with him. She remembered how it had been at Gallabat when she had conceived. She thought about that a great deal. She had vivid dreams about it, of how he had looked and how he had felt inside her. Her loneliness was an ache deep within her. She devoted herself entirely to the child, but the nights were long.

Then the news ran through the harem. Osman was taking three wives and eight concubines with him to the *jihad*; Rebecca was chosen as one of the eight. Ahmed and Nazeera would go with her, but none of Osman's other children. She understood that he was interested solely in the child, and that she and Nazeera were merely Ahmed's nursemaids. Her empty body ached.

They rode to the Abyssinian border forty thousand strong, a mighty warlike array. Osman left Rebecca and his other women at Gallabat. He rushed into Abyssinia and struck with all his cavalry at the passes.

The Abyssinians were also a warlike nation, and warriors to the blood. Although they had been alerted by Ryder Courtney's warning, even they could not stand before the ferocity of Osman Atalan's attack. He drove hard for the mountain passes at Minkti and Atbara, and seized them against desperate and courageous resistance. He slaughtered all the Abyssinian prisoners that he took, and led his army into the Minkti pass. They toiled up through bitter cold.

Ras Adal, the Abyssinian general, had not expected them to come so high and he made the mistake of allowing them to debouch unopposed on to the plain of Debra Sin before he attacked them.

The battle was fierce and bloody, but at last Ras Adal broke before the savagery of Osman's assault. He and all his army were driven into the river at their backs and most of them drowned. The entire province of Amhara fell to Osman, and he was able to advance unopposed to capture Gondar, the ancient capital of Abyssinia.

Gondar was the city in which Osman intended to set up his own capital, but he had never experienced a winter in the Abyssinian highlands. His Beja were men of the sands and deserts: they shivered, sickened and died. Osman abandoned his conquests, sacked and burned Gondar and led his men back to Gallabat. He arrived on a litter, drawn by his own warhorse, al-Buq. The cold of the mountains had entered his lungs and he was a sick man. They laid him on his *angareb* and waited for him to die.

Osman wheezed for breath. He choked and hawked and spat up slugs of greenish-yellow phlegm, 'Send for al-Jamal,' he ordered.

Rebecca came to his bedside and nursed him. She dosed him with a brew of selected herbs and roots that Nazeera prepared, and sweated him with hot stones. When his crisis came she brought Ahmed to him. 'You cannot die, mighty Atalan. Your son needs his father.'

It took several weeks, but at last Osman was on the road to recovery. During his convalescence he sent for Rebecca on most evenings and resumed the long conversations with her as though they had never ceased. Rebecca was lonely no more.

As he grew stronger, he made love to her again, possessing her masterfully and completely, filling the aching emptiness deep inside her. He declared Ahmed his heir and, in the unpredictable fashion in which he often did things, sent for the mullah and made Rebecca his wife.

It was only when she lay beside him on the first night as his wife that she could bring herself to face the truth squarely. He had made her his slave, in body and in heart. He had snuffed out the last spark of her once indomitable spirit. The suffering he inflicted upon her so casually had become a drug that she could not live without. In a bizarre and unnatural way he had forced her to love him. She knew she could never be without him now.

Emperor John and all his subjects were infuriated by the capture of the province of Amhara and the sack of Gondar. With an army of more than a hundred thousand behind him he came down upon Gallabat to take his revenge. He sent a warning to Osman Atalan that he was coming, so he might not be seen as a sneaking coward. Osman decapitated his messenger and sent the man's head back to him.

Heavily outnumbered, Osman transformed the town into a huge defensive zareba. He placed the women and children in the centre, and stood to meet the Abyssinian fury. It burst upon him. Al-Noor's division of four thousand men was almost wiped out, and al-Noor himself was gravely wounded. The exultant Abyssinians broke into the centre of the *zareba* where the women were, and the rape and slaughter began.

When Osman realized the day was lost, he leapt on to al-Buq, and spurred him forward, going for the head of the serpent. The Emperor had once been a legendary warrior, but he was a young man no longer. In his leopardskins, bronze cuirassier and the gold crown of the Negus on his head, he was tall and regal but his beard was more silver than black. He drew his sword when he saw Osman charging at him through the carnage. The Dervish commander cut down the bodyguards that tried to interpose themselves. He had learnt from Penrod Ballantyne, and he never took his eye from the Emperor's blade. His riposte was like a bolt of silver lightning.

'The Emperor is dead. The Negus has gone!' The cry went up from the Abyssinian host. The moment of complete victory had been transformed into defeat and rout by a single stroke of Osman Atalan's long blade.

Osman rode back to Omdurman with the heads of Emperor John and his generals carried on the lances of his bodyguard. They planted them at the entrance to Khalifat Abdullahi's palace.

Seven months later Rebecca gave birth to her second child, a girl. Osman was not sufficiently interested in a female

581

to bother himself with a name for her. Rebecca named her Kahruba, which in Arabic means Amber. After some months Osman forgave her for bearing a girl, and resumed their nightly conversations and lovemaking. When Kahruba turned into a pretty little thing with smoked-honey hair, he sometimes stroked her head. Once he even took her up on the front of his saddle and ran al-Buq at full gallop. Kahruba squealed with glee, which caused Osman to remark as he handed her back to Rebecca, 'You erred grievously, wife. You should have made her a boy, for she has the heart of one.'

None of his other daughters received any sign of his affection. They were not allowed to speak to him, or to touch him. When Kahruba was six years old, at the feast of Kurban Bairam, she left the women and, with one finger in her mouth, she went to where Osman sat among his aggagiers. He watched her coldly as she approached. Undeterred she scrambled on to his lap.

Osman was flabbergasted. His aggagiers had difficulty in maintaining their sober expressions. Osman scowled at them as though daring any to laugh. Then he deliberately selected a sweetmeat from the bowl in front of him and placed it in the child's mouth. She retaliated by throwing both arms round his neck. However, this was going too far. Osman replaced her on the ground and slapped her little bottom. 'Be off with you, you shameless vixen!' he said.

M r Hiram Steven Maxim sat on a low stool in the brilliant sunshine of the Nile delta. In front of him on a steel tripod was an ungainly-looking weapon with a thick water-jacketed barrel. On his left side stood a five-gallon water can, connected to the weapon by a sturdy rubber hose. At his right hand dozens of wooden crates of ammunition were piled high. His three assistants hovered about him. Despite the heat they wore thick tweed jackets and flat cloth caps. Mr Maxim had stripped down to his shirtsleeves, and his bowler hat was pushed to the back of his head. Since he had come from

America to settle in England, he had adopted British ways and dress.

Now he rolled the unlit cigar from one side of his jaw to the other. 'Major Ballantyne,' he sang out. His accent still proclaimed that he had been born in Sangerville, Maine. 'Would you be good enough to note the time?' At a short distance behind him was a small group of uniformed officers. In the front rank stood the sirdar, General Horatio Herbert Kitchener, a stocky, powerful figure flanked by his staff.

'General, sir?' Penrod glanced at Kitchener for permission to reply.

'Carry on, Ballantyne.' Kitchener nodded.

'Time mark!' Penrod called out. Six hundred yards ahead of the machine-gun, at the foot of a high dun-coloured sand dune, was a line of fifty wooden models of the human form. They were dressed in Dervish *jibbas* and carried wooden spears. Mr Maxim leant forward and took hold of the firing handles. By squeezing the finger-grips he lifted the safety catch off the firing button.

'Commencing firing, now!' He thrust his thumbs down on the trigger button. The gun shuddered and roared. The separate shots were too rapid for the ear to distinguish. It was a prolonged thunder like a high waterfall in spate. The recoil of each shot kicked back the mechanism, and ejected the spent cartridge cases in a blur of glittering bronze. The forward stroke of the action reloaded the chamber, cocked and fired. It was too fast for the eye to follow the sequence.

Mr Maxim traversed the barrel. One after another the wooden figures exploded in a storm of splinters. The sands of the dune behind the targets boiled into sheets of dust. He reached the end of the line and traversed back again. The shattered remains of the targets hung from their frames. The returning torrent of bullets blew them to fragments.

The British officers watched in awed silence. The roar of the gun numbed their eardrums. They could not speak. They did not move. Mr Maxim's assistants had performed this demonstration numerous times and in many countries. They had been drilled to perfection. As one of the ammunition boxes emptied it was dragged away and a full one substituted. A fresh belt of ammunition was hitched to the end of the previous belt as it was sucked into the breech. There was no check, no jamming of the action, no diminution in the rate of fire. The water in the cooling jacket boiled, but the powerful emission of steam was drawn away through the pliable hose into the can of cold water. It was cooled and condensed. There was no steam cloud to betray the position of the gun to the enemy. The cooled water was recycled through the barrel jacket. The clamour of the gun continued without check. The final belt of ammunition was fed through the breech, and only when the last empty cartridge case was flung clear did silence fall.

'Time check,' Mr Maxim shouted.

'Three minutes and ten seconds.'

'Two thousand rounds in three minutes,' Mr Maxim announced proudly. 'Almost seven hundred rounds a minute, without a stoppage.'

'No stoppage,' Colonel Adams repeated. 'This is the end of cavalry as we know it.'

'It changes the face of warfare,' Penrod agreed. 'Just look at the accuracy.' He pointed to the row of targets. Splinters were spread over a wide area. Not even the poles that had supported the targets still stood upright. A thick cloud of dun-coloured dust kicked up by the stream of bullets hung in the air above the dunes.

'Now let the Dervish come!' murmured the sirdar, and his dark moustache seemed to stand erect, like the bristles on the back of an enraged wild boar.

Penrod and Adams rode back to Cairo together. They were both in high spirits, and when a jackal broke from the scrub at the side of the track they drew their sabres and rode it down. Penrod spurted ahead and turned back the drab terrier-like creature. Adams leant low out of the saddle and ran it through between the shoulders, then let its weight swing his blade back until the carcass slipped from the blade, rolled in the dust and at last lay still. 'Beats pig-sticking in the Punjab.'

He laughed. When they reached the gates of the Gheziera Club, he said, 'Do you care for a peg?'

'Not this evening,' replied Penrod. 'I have guests from home to entertain.'

'Ah, yes! So I have heard. What does Miss Amber Benbrook think of your new pips?'

Penrod glanced down at the shiny new major's crowns on his epaulettes.

'If you remember her name, you must have received the invitation to the ball. It is her sixteenth birthday, you know. Will you be attending?'

'The remarkable young lady who wrote *Slaves of the Mahdi?*' Adams exclaimed. 'I would not miss it for the world. My wife would assassinate me if I so much as contemplated the idea.'

Amber's birthday ball was held at Shepheard's Hotel. The band of the new Egyptian army played until dawn. White-robed waiters served silver trays of brimming champagne glasses. Every commissioned officer of the army from the rank of ensign upwards, a hundred and fifteen in all, had accepted the invitation to attend. Their smart new dress uniforms made a handsome foil to the ballgowns of the ladies. Even the sirdar and Sir Evelyn Baring made a brief appearance, and each danced a Vienna waltz with Amber. They both left early, aware that their presence had an inhibiting effect on the festivities.

Ryder and Saffron had made the long circuitous journey down from the highlands of Abyssinia, across the desert by camel, up the Red Sea and through the Suez Canal to Alexandria to be there. Saffron's evening dress caused a mild sensation, even in this glittering company. She was two months pregnant, but of course that was not yet apparent.

At the beginning of the evening, after he had collected Amber and his sister-in-law Jane from the suite they were sharing on the top floor of the hotel, Penrod filled in Amber's dance card. He reserved fifteen of her twenty dances. She was a little peeved that he had been so restrained. At the stroke of midnight the band broke into a rousing rendition of 'For She's a Jolly Good Fellow'. The guests applauded wildly. The champagne flowed like the Nile, and everybody was in jovial, expansive mood.

Penrod climbed the bandstand with Amber on his arm. The band welcomed them with a long drumroll, and Penrod held up his hands for silence. He was only partially successful in achieving it while he proposed the birthday toast. They drank it with gusto, and Ryder Courtney burst into 'When You Were Sweet Sixteen'. The band and the rest of the guests picked up the tune. Amber blushed and clung to Penrod's arm.

At the end of the song he quietened them again. 'I have another announcement to make. Thank you!' The uproar subsided to a buzz of interest. 'My lords, ladies, and fellow officers, who fall into neither of the first two categories!' They hooted, and again he had to bring them to order. 'It gives me ineffable pleasure to inform you that Miss Amber Benbrook has consented to become my wife, and in so doing she has made me the happiest man in creation.'

A little later Colonel Sam Adams was smoking a quiet cigarette on the darkened terrace when he overheard the conversation of two young subalterns who had imbibed copious quantities of champagne.

'They say she has made herself a flash hundred thousand iron men from the book. Happiest man in creation? Ballantyne has that great gong stuck on his chest, pips on his shoulders, his own battalion, and to top it all the lucky blighter has dug himself a gold mine with his pork shovel. Why shouldn't he be happy?'

'Lieutenant Stuttaford.' A cold, familiar voice spoke from the shadows close at hand.

Pale with shock, Stuttaford came unsteadily to attention. 'Colonel Adams, sir!'

'Kindly present yourself at my office at ten o'clock tomorrow morning.'

By noon the next day Lieutenant Stuttaford, still suffering from a vile hangover, found himself packing for immediate departure to the desert outpost at Suakin, one of the most desolate and dreary postings in the Empire.

'The Egyptian army has always been considered a music-hall turn, the Gilbert and Sullivan opera of the Nile. The standing army at home, and those in the Indian Service snigger when they speak our name,' Penrod told the other members of the party. He and Ryder lolled against the transom of the felucca. Jane Ballantyne, Saffron and Amber sat on gaily coloured cushions on the deck. They were sailing upstream in the hired felucca to climb to the summit of the pyramid of Cheops at Giza, and afterwards to picnic in the shadow of the Sphinx.

'How vulgar and silly of them.' Amber came immediately to his defence.

'In all truth they had good reason at one time,' Penrod admitted, 'but that was the old army, in the bad old days. Now the men are paid. The officers do not steal their rations, and turn tail and run at the first shot. The men are not beaten when they fall sick, but are sent to the doctor and the hospital. All of you must come to the review on Monday. You will see some parading and drilling that will astonish you.'

'My father was a colonel in the Black Watch, as you know, Penrod,' said Jane. 'I cannot claim to be a great expert, but I have read something of military affairs. Papa saw to that. As soon as we knew that we were coming to Cairo, Amber and I read every book about Egypt on the shelves of the library at Clercastle, as well as Sir Alfred Milner's excellent *England in Egypt*. Nowhere have I heard it suggested that the Egyptian *fellahin* are good soldierly material.'

'What you say is true. It was always unlikely that the rich and fertile delta, with its enervating climate, would produce warriors. The *fellahin* may be cruel and callous, but they are not fierce and bloodthirsty. On the other hand, they are stoic and strong. They meet pain and hardship with indifference. Theirs is a kind of docile courage that we more warlike peoples can only admire. They are obedient and honest, quick to learn and, above all, strong. What they lack in nerve they make up for in muscle.'

'Pen darling, that is all well and good about the Egyptians but tell us about your Arabs,' Amber interjected.

'Ah, but you know them well, my heart.' Penrod smiled tenderly at her. 'If the Egyptian *fellahin* are mastiffs, then the Arabs are Jack Russell terriers. They are intelligent and quick. They are venal and excitable. They do not lend themselves willingly to discipline. You can never trust them entirely, but their courage is daunting. At Abu Klea they came against the square as if they gloried in death. If they give you their loyalty, and they seldom do, it is a link of steel that binds them to you. War is their way of life. They are warriors, and I respect them. Some I have learnt to love. Yakub is one of those.'

'Nazeera is another,' Amber agreed.

'Oh, I wonder what has become of her, and of our dear sister Rebecca.' Saffron shook her head sorrowfully. 'I dream of her most nights. Is there nobody in Military Intelligence who can discover this for us?'

'Believe me, I have tried diligently to find news of Rebecca. However, the Sudan is closed off from the world, as though in a steel casket. It slumbers in its own nightmare. Would that one day we have the will and the way to end the horror and set her people free. Rebecca is the first of those we would liberate.'

Rebecca sat with the other wives in the cloister of the inner courtyard of the palace of Osman Atalan. It was the cool of the evening and Osman was demonstrating to his followers the courage of his blue-eyed son. For many months Rebecca had known that her son faced this ordeal. She covered her face with her veil so that none of the other women would know of her fear.

Only three months previously Ahmed Habib abd Atalan had been circumcised. Rebecca had wept as she dressed his mutilated penis, but Nazeera had rebuked her: 'Ahmed is a man now. Be proud for him, al-Jamal. Your tears will unman him.'

Now Ahmed stood before his father, trying to be brave. His head was bare and his fists were clenched at his side.

'Open your eyes, my son.' Osman's voice crackled. He tossed his sword into the air and it spun like a cartwheel before the hilt dropped back into his hand. 'Open your eyes. I want Allah and all the world to know that you are a man. I want you to show me, your father, your courage.'

Ahmed opened his eyes. They were no longer milky, but a dark blue like the African sky when stormclouds gather. His lower lip quivered and tiny droplets of perspiration dewed the upper. Osman flourished the long blade and cut at the side of his head with such force that the steel hummed in the air. The stroke could have bisected a grown man at the trunk. It swept past Ahmed's temple. His unruly coppery hair fluttered in the wind of its passage. The watching aggagiers growled with admiration. Ahmed swayed on his feet.

'You are my son,' Osman whispered. 'Hold fast!' He stroked the tip of his son's ear with the flat of the blade. Ahmed shrank away from the cool touch of steel.

'Do not move,' Osman warned him, 'or I will cut it off.'

Ahmed leant forward and vomited on the ground at his feet.

An expression of contempt and shame crossed Osman's face, and was smoothed away immediately. 'Go back to your mother,' he said softly.

Ahmed tried to choke back his sobs. 'I do not feel well,' he murmured hopelessly, and wiped his mouth on the back of his hand.

Osman stepped back and glared at him. 'Go and sit with the women,' he ordered.

Ahmed ran to his mother and buried his face in Rebecca's skirt.

A tense silence held the watchers. Nobody spoke and

nobody moved. They were barely able to draw breath. Osman was turning away when a small, delicate figure rose to her feet from among the ranks of seated women. Rebecca tried to hold her back, but Kahruba pushed away her hand and went to her father. He grounded the point of his blade and watched her stop in front of him. He studied her face, then demanded ominously, 'What disrespect is this? Why do you pester me so?'

'My father, I want to show you and Allah my courage,' said the child. She removed her headcloth and shook out her tawny hair.

'Go back to your mother. This is no childish game.'

'Exalted father, I do not wish to play games.' She looked straight into his eyes.

He raised the sword and stepped towards her, like a leopard stalking a gazelle. She stood her ground. Suddenly he cut, forehanded, at her face. The blade flashed inches from her eyes. She blinked, but stood like a statue.

He cut again, backhanded. A curl dropped from the loose mop of her hair, and floated to the ground at her bare feet. Behind her Rebecca cried out, 'Oh, my darling!'

Kahruba ignored her, and held her father's eyes steadfastly.

'You provoke me,' he said, and slowly traced the outline of her body with the blade. Never further than a finger's breadth from her flesh, the scalpel-sharp edge moved up from the outside of one knee, over her thigh, round the curve of her hip, along her arm and shoulder to the side of her neck. He touched her and she closed her eyes, then opened them as she felt the steel on her cheek. It moved up over the top of her head and down again to her other knee. She did not flinch.

Osman narrowed his eyes and brought the blade back along the same route, but faster, and then again, even faster. The steel dissolved into a silver blur. It danced in front of the child's eyes like a dragonfly. It hummed and whispered in her ears as it passed close to her tender skin. Rebecca was weeping silently, and Nazeera held her hand hard, but she, too, was close to tears. 'Do not make a sound,' she whispered. 'If Kahruba moves, she is dead.'

The dancing blade held Kahruba in a cage of light. Then, abruptly, it stopped, pointing at her right eye from the distance of an inch. The point advanced slowly, until it touched her lower lashes. The child blinked but did not pull away.

'Enough!' said Osman, and stepped back. He threw the sword to al-Noor, who snatched it out of the air. Then Osman stooped and picked up his daughter. He held her close to his chest, and looked around at their taut expressions. 'In this one, at least, my blood has bred true,' he told them. Then he tossed her high in the air, caught her as she fell back and carried her to Rebecca. 'Breed me another like this one,' he ordered, 'but, wife, this time make certain it is a boy.'

Later that evening Rebecca lay sprawled on his *angareb*. She still felt devastated by the events of the day and by the controlled fury of his lovemaking, which had ended only minutes before. She had watched her daughter come close to death under the dancing silver blade, while she herself seemed to have come even closer.

She was stark naked, a vessel overflowing with his fresh seed, aching pleasurably where he had been deep inside her. The lovemaking had rendered her *harom*, unclean in the eyes of God. She should cover herself, or go immediately to bathe and cleanse her body, but she felt languorous and wanton. She opened her eyes and found that he had come back from the bedroom window and was standing over her. He was still half erect, his glans glistening with the juices of her body. As she studied him she felt herself becoming aroused once more. She knew, with sure feminine instinct, that he had just impregnated her again, and that she would be forced to many months of abstinence until she was delivered of the infant. She wanted him, but saw that now his seed was spent his restless mind had moved on to other concerns.

'There is aught that troubles you, my husband.' She sat up and covered herself with the light bedcloth.

'We spoke once of the steamer that runs on land, that travels on ribbons of steel,' he said.

'I recall that, my lord, but it was many years ago.'

591

'I wish to discuss this machine again. What was the name you gave it?'

'Railway engine,' she enunciated slowly and clearly.

He imitated her, but he lisped and garbled the sounds. He saw in her eyes that he had not succeeded. 'It is too difficult, this language of yours.' He shook his head angrily, hating to fail in anything he attempted. 'I shall call it the land steamer.'

'I shall understand what you mean. It is a better name than mine, more powerful and descriptive.' At times he was like a small boy and must be jollied along.

'How many men can travel upon this machine. Ten? Twenty? Surely not fifty?' he asked hopefully.

'If the land over which it passes is levelled it can carry many hundreds of men, perhaps as many as a thousand, perhaps many thousands.'

Osman looked alarmed. 'How far can this thing travel?'

'To the end of its lines.'

'But surely it cannot cross a great river like the Atbara? It must stop there.'

'It can, my lord.'

'I do not believe it. The Atbara is deep and wide. How is that possible?'

'They have men they call engineers who have the skills to build a bridge over it.'

'The Atbara? They cannot build over a river so wide.' He was trying desperately to convince himself. 'Where will they find tree trunks long and strong enough to span the Atbara?'

'They will make the bridge of steel, like the rails it runs upon. Like the blade of your sword,' Rebecca explained. 'But why do you ask these questions, my husband?'

'My spies in the north have sent a message that these God-cursed Englishmen have begun to lay these steel ribbons from Wadi Halfa south across the great bight of the river, towards Metemma and the Atbara.' Then, suddenly, his temper flared. 'They are devils, these infidel tribesmen of yours,' he shouted.

'They are no longer my tribesmen, exalted husband. Now I am of your tribe and no other.'

His anger subsided as suddenly as it had arisen.

'I am leaving at dawn tomorrow to go to the north and see this monstrosity with my own eyes,' he told her.

She dropped her eyes sadly: she would be alone again. Without him she was incomplete.

The year 1895 dawned and events were put in train that would change the history and face of Africa. British South Africa's conquests were consolidated under the new nation of Rhodesia, and almost immediately the predatory men who had brought it into existence attacked the Boer nation of the Transvaal, their neighbours to the south. It was a puny invasion under Dr Starr Jamieson that was immediately dubbed the Jamieson Raid. They had been promised support by their countrymen on the Witwatersrand goldfields, which never materialized, and the tiny band of aggressors capitulated to the Boers without firing a shot. However, the raid presaged the conflict between Boer and Briton that, only a few years later, would cost hundreds of thousands of lives, before the Transvaal and its fabulously rich goldfields came under the sway of Empire.

In England the Liberal Party of Gladstone and Lord Rosebery was ousted by a Conservative and Unionist administration under the Marquess of Salisbury. In opposition they had always been vociferously opposed to Gladstone's Egyptian policies. Now they had a massive majority in the House of Commons, and were in a position to change the direction of affairs in that crucial corner of the African continent.

The nation still smarted from the humiliation of Khartoum and the murder of General Gordon. Books such as *Slaves of the Mahdi* had set the mood for exonerating Gordon of shame. In the new Egypt, which was now virtually a colony of Great Britain, the tool was at hand in the shape of the new Egyptian army, reorganized, trained and equipped as no army in Africa before. The man to lead it was already at its helm in the person of Horatio Herbert Kitchener. Great Britain contemplated the prospect of repossessing the Sudan with increasing pleasure and enthusiasm.

By the beginning of 1896 Britain was ready to act. It needed only a spark to set off the conflagration. On 2 March, at the battle of Adowa, the Abyssinians inflicted a crushing defeat on Italy. Another European power had been thrashed by an African kingdom. This sent a clarion call to all colonial possessions. Almost immediately the gloomy forebodings of rebellion were fulfilled. The Dervish Khalifat Abdullahi threatened Kassala and raided Wadi Halfa. Reports reached Cairo of the gathering of a great Dervish army in Omdurman. Added to this, the French made covert hostile moves towards British possessions in Africa, especially in southern Sudan.

Thus a number of concurrent events had cast Great Britain in the role of far-seeing saviour of the world from anarchy, the avenger of Khartoum and Gordon, the protector of the Egyptian state. The honour and pride of the Empire must be preserved.

The order went out from London to General Kitchener. He was to recapture the Sudan. He was to do it swiftly and, above all, cheaply. The attempts to rescue Gordon and destroy the Mahdi had cost Britain thirteen million pounds: defeat is always more costly than victory. Kitchener was allowed a little over one million pounds to succeed in the job that, thirteen years before, had been botched.

Kitchener summoned his senior officers and told them the momentous news. They were ecstatic. This was the culmination of years of gruelling training and desert skirmishes, and the laurels were at last within their reach. 'There will be more sweat and blisters than glory,' the sirdar cautioned them. Never one to seek popularity, he preferred to be feared rather than liked. 'From the twenty-second to the sixteenth parallel of north latitude we are faced with waterless desert. We will go to capture the Nile, but we cannot use that river as a means of access. The cataracts stand in our way. The only route open to us is the railway we will build to carry us overland into battle. We can use the river only in the final

stage of our advance.' He regarded them with his cold misan-
thropic stare. 'There are no mountains to cross, the desert is
level and good going. It will not be a matter so much of
engineering technique as of hard work. We will not rely on
private contractors. Our own engineers will do the job.'

'What about the Atbara river, sir? At its confluence with
the Nile it is almost a thousand yards wide,' said Colonel Sam
Adams.

'I have already called for tenders to supply the components
for a bridge to be manufactured in sections that can be taken
up on the railway trucks. Another call for tenders will soon
be going out for the supply of steel-hulled river gunboats.
They will be sent up by rail to the clear water above the fifth
cataract. There, they will be reassembled and launched.'

The Egyptian officer corps was immediately plunged into a
hurly-burly of planning and action.

There was only one respect in which the times and
circumstances were not propitious. The delta of Egypt
had been the bread basket of the Mediterranean since the
time of Julius Caesar and Jesus Christ. For the first time in a
hundred years the abundant fertility of its black alluvial soils
had failed. The production of wheat and dhurra had fallen
short of the needs of the civilian population, let alone those
of a great expeditionary army.

'We are short of at least five thousand tons of the flour
needed for the primary stage of the campaign,' the quartermaster general told the sirdar. 'After the first three months,
we will require an additional fifteen hundred tons per month
for the duration of hostilities.'

Kitchener frowned. Bread, the staple of any modern army
– made from wholesome clean grain, and not too much hard
biscuit – ensured the health of the troops. Now they were
telling him that he did not have it.

'Come back tomorrow,' he told his quartermaster.

He went immediately to see Sir Evelyn Baring at the

British Agency – it would have been political suicide for anybody to call it Government House, but that was what it was. Baring had championed Kitchener's appointment to commander-in-chief above the claims of better qualified men. Although they were not friends, they thought alike. Baring listened, then said, 'I think I know the man who can get your bread for you. He provisioned Gordon in Khartoum during the siege. Most fortuitously, he is in Cairo at this very moment.'

Within two hours a mystified Ryder Courtney found himself under Kitchener's reptilian stare.

'Can you do it?' Kitchener asked.

Ryder's business instincts clicked into place. 'Yes, I can. However, I will need four per cent commission for myself, General.'

'That is known as profiteering, Mr Courtney. I can offer you two and a half.'

'That is known as highway robbery, General,' Ryder replied.

Kitchener blinked. He was unaccustomed to being addressed in that fashion.

Ryder went on smoothly, 'However, in the name of patriotism I will accept your offer. On the condition that the army provides a suitable home in Cairo for me and my family, in addition to a stipend of two hundred pounds a month to cover my immediate expenses.'

Ryder rode back to Penrod's riverside home where he and Saffron had been guests since their arrival in Cairo. He was in jubilant mood. Saffron had been agitating: rather than return to Abyssinia, she wanted to remain in this civilized, salubrious city, where she could be close to Amber. When Saffron agitated it was much like living on the slopes of an active volcano. Now her power to persuade was even more formidable than usual as she was pregnant again. Ryder had seen no good commercial sense in setting up business in Egypt, but Herbert Kitchener had just changed that.

Ryder left his horse with the groom in the stables and went down to the lawns above the riverbank. Jane Ballantyne,

Amber and Saffron were taking tea in the summer-house. They were rereading and animatedly discussing the letter from Sebastian Hardy, which had arrived on the mail ship from England and had been delivered to Amber's suite at Shepheard's Hotel that morning.

Mr Hardy took great pleasure in informing Miss Amber Benbrook of the recent resuscitation of public interest in her book *Slaves of the Mahdi*, owing to the prospect of war against the evil Dervish Empire in Omdurman. The amounts paid by Macmillan Publishers in respect of royalties earned over the past three months amounted to £56,483 10s. 6d. In addition, Mr Hardy begged to inform her and the other beneficiaries that the investments he had made on behalf of the Benbrook family trust had been most favourably affected by the same considerations as the book. He had placed large sums in the common stock of the Vickers Company, which had purchased Mr Maxim's patent in his machine-gun. This investment had almost doubled in value. The value of assets of the trust now amounted to a little over three hundred thousand pounds. In addition Macmillan were eager to publish Amber's new manuscript, provisionally entitled *African Dreams and Nightmares*.

Ryder strode down the lawns, but the twins were so excited by Mr Hardy's good tidings that they were oblivious to his presence until his shadow fell over the tea-table. They looked up. 'What is all this laughter and high jinks?' he demanded. 'You know I cannot bear to see anybody having so much fun.'

Saffron jumped to her feet, a little ungainly under her maternal burden, and stood on tiptoe to embrace him. 'You will never guess what,' she whispered in his ear. 'You are married to a rich woman.'

'Indeed, I am married to a rich woman who resides permanently in Cairo, in a house paid for by General Kitchener and the Egyptian army.'

She leant back, holding him at arm's length, and stared at him in astonishment and delight. 'If this is another of your atrocious jokes, Ryder Courtney, I will . . .' She searched for a suitable threat. 'I will throw you into the Nile.'

He grinned complacently. 'Too early for a swim. Besides,

you and I cannot waste precious time. We have to go hunting for our new home.'

He would tell her later that he must leave within days for the United States and Canada to negotiate for the purchase of twenty thousand tons of wheat. It was not the ideal time to break such news to a pregnant wife. *At least she will have enough to keep her fully occupied in my absence.* He had learnt by hard experience that when she was bored Saffron was more difficult to handle than the entire Dervish army.

The ground shook to the thunder of hoofs. Eight horsemen raced each other down the long green field. The spectators shrieked and roared. The atmosphere was feverish and electric. Once again the Nile Cup and the honour of the army polo team were at stake.

The white ball rolled over the uneven turf. Colonel Adams overhauled it swiftly, and leant low out of the saddle, mallet poised. His bay mare was as adept as her rider. She turned in neatly behind the bouncing ball, placing him in the perfect position to make the crossing shot. Mallet and ball met with a crisp thwack, and the ball sailed in a high arc over the heads of the opposing team, dropping directly in the path of Penrod's charging grey gelding. Penrod picked it up on the first bounce after it struck earth. He tapped it ahead, and his nimble pony chased after it, like a whippet behind a rabbit. Tap and tap again – the ball skipped towards the goalposts at the far end of the field. The other riders pursued the grey, their heels hammering into the ribs of their mounts, shouting and pumping the reins for greater speed, but they were unable to catch Penrod. He ran the ball between the posts, and the umpires waved their flags to signal a goal and the end of the match. Once again, the army had retained the Nile Cup against all comers.

Penrod rode back to the pony lines. Under her parasol, Amber was waiting for him. She watched him with pride and devotion. He was marvellously handsome and tanned, although there were crow's feet at the corners of his eyes from squinting into the desert glare. His body was lean and hard, tempered by years of hard riding and still harder fighting. He was no longer a youth, but a man approaching his prime. He swung one booted leg over the pony's withers and dropped to the ground, landing like a cat. The grey trotted on to meet his grooms: he could smell the bucket of water and the bag of dhurra meal they had ready for him.

Amber ran to Penrod, and threw herself against his chest. 'I am so proud of you.'

'Then let's get married,' Penrod said, and kissed her.

She made the kiss endure, but when at last she must relinquish his lips, she laughed at him. 'We are getting married, you silly old thing, or have you forgotten?'

'I mean now. Immediately. At once. Not next year. We've waited far too long.'

She stared at him. 'You jest!' she accused him.

'Never been more serious in my life. In ten days I am away again into the desert. We have a spot of business to take care of in Omdurman. Let us be married before I go.'

They were swept up in the feverish madness of war when custom and convention no longer counted. Amber did not hesitate. 'Yes!' she said, and kissed him again. She had Saffron and Jane to help her with the arrangements. 'Yes! Oh, yes, please!'

Every pew in the cathedral was filled. They held the reception at the Gheziera Club. Sir Evelyn Baring placed the Agency houseboat at their disposal for the honeymoon.

They cruised upriver as far as Giza. In the evening they drank champagne and danced on the deck, while before them rose the silhouette of the pyramids backlit by the sunset. Later, in the great stern cabin on the wide bed with green silk covers, Penrod led her gently along enchanted pathways to a mountain peak of whose existence she had only dreamed. He was a wonderful guide, patient and skilled, and experienced, oh, so very experienced.

Penrod left Amber in the care of Saffron and Jane, and took the steamer south to Aswan and Wadi Halfa to rejoin his regiment.

He found Yakub waiting for him at the river landing, wearing his new khaki uniform with panache. He stamped his feet as he saluted, his grin was infectious, and one eye rolled sideways. Yakub, the outcast, had a home at last. He wore the chevrons of a sergeant on the sleeve of the uniform of the Camel Corps of the Egyptian army. His turban had been replaced with a peaked cap and neck flap. He was still becoming accustomed to breeches and puttees rather than a long *galabiyya* so his stance was slightly bowlegged. 'Effendi, the peerless and faithful Sergeant Yakub looks upon your face with the same awe and devotion that the moon feels towards the sun.'

'My bags are in the cabin, O faithful and peerless one.'

They rode southwards on one of the flat-bed track-laying bogies of the new railway. The smoke from the engine stack blew back over them. The soot darkened Penrod's tanned skin and even Yakub turned a deeper brown while dust and sparks stung their eyes. At last the locomotive reached the railhead, and came to a hissing halt with clouds of steam billowing from her brakes.

The railway line had already been driven sixty-five miles into Dervish territory. Penrod's regiment was waiting for him and his orders were to scout the few small villages along the intended line of rail, then sweep the terrain ahead for the first sign of the Dervish cavalry, which they knew must already be on its way northwards to dispute the right of way.

Penrod found it good to breathe the hot, dry air of the desert again, and to have a camel under him. The excitement of the chase and the battle ahead made his nerves sing like copper telegraph lines in the wind. The sensation of being young, strong and alive was intoxicating.

They reached the village at the wells of Wadi Atira. Penrod opened the ranks of his squadron and they encircled the cluster of mud buildings, which were deserted and falling into ruins. There was one chilling reminder of the Dervish occupation: at the entrance to the village stood a makeshift but obviously effective gallows, made from telegraph poles that the army had abandoned when it withdrew after the fall of Khartoum. The skeletons of the souls who had perished upon it had been cleaned and polished by the abrasive, dust-laden wind. They still wore their chains.

Penrod moved forward past Tanjore where the desolation was similar. The old British fort at Akasha, relic of the Gordon relief expedition, was in ruins. The storerooms had been used by the Dervish as execution chambers: desiccated human carcasses lay in abandoned attitudes on a dusty floor, which was thick with the droppings of lizards and the shed skins of vipers and scorpions.

Penrod converted Akasha into an entrenched camp, a base from which the Camel Corps could sally out. He left two of his squadrons to hold the camp, and with the remainder of his regiment he pressed on into the Desert of the Mother of Stones to search for the Dervish.

While he scoured the land along the Nile, behind him the railhead reached Akasha and his rudimentary camp was transformed into an impregnable fortress and staging station, guarded by artillery and Maxim machine-gun detachments.

As Penrod's camels approached Firket, a few Bedouin galloped towards them, waving their arms and shouting that they were friendly. They reported to Penrod that, only hours before, they had been pursued by a marauding party of Dervish cavalry, and although they had escaped, five of their comrades had been overtaken and massacred. He sent a troop of his camels forward to scout the caravan route that led through a narrow boulder-strewn defile towards Firket five miles ahead. No sooner had they entered the defile than the troop commander found himself confronted by at least two hundred and fifty Dervish horsemen, supported closely by almost two thousand spearmen.

Trapped in the defile, the commander wheeled his men round in an attempt to extricate them and bring them back to the support of Penrod's main force. Before they could complete the manoeuvre the Dervish horses charged. Immediately both sides became entangled in wildest confusion, and covered by a dense fog of brown dust thrown up by the hoofs of the horses and the pads of the camels. In the tumult all words of command were drowned.

From the mouth of the defile Penrod saw that disaster was about to engulf his embattled squadron. 'Forward!' he shouted, and drew his sabre. 'Charge! Go straight at them!' With three troops of camels behind him, he crashed into the struggling mass of men and beasts. With his left hand he fired his Webley, and hacked with his sabre at the *jibba*-clad figures half hidden in the swirling curtains of dust.

For minutes the outcome hung in the balance, then the Dervish broke and scattered back behind the shields of their spearmen. They left eighteen of their dead lying on the sand and retreated towards Firket. Penrod sensed they were trying to lead him into a trap, and let them go.

Instead he turned aside and climbed Firket mountain. From the towering heights he glassed the town below, and saw immediately that his instinct had been true. He had found the main body of the Dervish army. It was massed among the mud-brick buildings, and the cavalry lines extended as far as the banks of the Nile a mile beyond the city.

'At a rough estimate three thousand horse, and only Allah knows how many spears,' he said grimly.

Osman Atalan arrived at Firket two weeks after the skirmish with the Egyptian Camel Corps. He had travelled fast, covering the distance from Omdurman in only fourteen days. He was accompanied by ten of his trusted aggagiers.

Since the first word on the British advance, and the commencement of the work on the railway line from Wadi Halfa, Firket had been under the command of the Emir Hammuda. Osman listened to the report of this indolent and careless man. He was appalled. 'He cares only for what lies between the buttocks of his pretty boys,' he told al-Noor. 'We must go forward ourselves to find the enemy and discover what they are planning.'

They came no closer to the village of Akasha than five miles before they were attacked by elements of the Camel Corps, and driven off with the loss of two good men. They made a wide circle round the village, and the next day captured two Bedouin coming from the direction of the village. Osman's aggagiers stripped and searched them. They found foreign cigarettes and tins of toffees with a picture of the English queen painted on the lids.

The aggagiers held down the Bedouin and sliced off the soles of their feet. Then they forced them to walk over the baking stones. This induced them to talk freely. They described the huge build-up of infidel troops and equipment at Firket.

Osman realized that this was the forward base from which the main infidel attack on Firket would be launched. He circled back through the Mother of Stones towards the Nile, coming in ten miles to the north of Akasha. He was searching for the railway line from Wadi Halfa that the Bedouin had reported. The railway had been in the forefront of his mind since al-Jamal had described it to him.

When he came upon it, it seemed innocuous, twin silver threads lying on the burning sands. He left al-Noor and the rest of his band on the crest of the dunes and rode down alone to inspect it. He dismounted, and warily approached the shining rails. They were fastened by fish-plates to heavy teak sleepers. He kicked the rail: it was solid and immovable. He knelt beside it and tried to lever out one of the iron bolts with the point of his dagger. The blade snapped in two.

He stood up and hurled away the hilt. 'Accursed thing of Shaitan! This is not an honourable way to make war.'

Even in his scorn and anger he became aware of a sound that trembled in the desert air, a distant susurration, like the breath of a sleeping giant. Osman stood upright on al-Buq's saddle, and gazed northwards along the line of rail. He saw a tiny feather of smoke on the horizon. As he watched, it drew closer, so rapidly that he was taken by surprise, the alien shape seeming to swell before his eyes as it rushed towards him. He knew that this was the land steamer of which al-Jamal had told him.

He swung al-Buq's head round and urged him into a gallop. He had a quarter of a mile to cover before he reached the foot of the dune. The machine was coming on apace. He looked ahead to the crest of the dune and saw his aggagiers on the skyline. They had dismounted and were holding their horses, allowing them to rest.

'Get down!' Osman roared as he raced across the open ground. 'Let not the infidel see you!' But his men were four hundred yards away and his voice did not carry to them. They stood and watched the approaching machine with amazement. Suddenly a blast of white steam shot up from the land steamer and it emitted a howl like a maddened jinn. Stupefied, making no effort to conceal themselves, they stood and stared at it. It was a mighty serpent, with a head that hissed, howled and shot out clouds of smoke and steam, and whose body seemed to reach back to the skyline.

'They have seen you!' Osman tried to warn them. 'Beware! Beware!' Now they could see that the rolling trucks were stacked with steel rails and crates. On the last they made out the heads of half a dozen men, who were crouched behind some strange contraption.

'Beware!' Osman was racing up the slip-face of the dune, almost at the top. His voice held a high, despairing note. Suddenly the yellow sands under the feet of the group of aggagiers and the hoofs of their horse exploded into flying clouds of dust. It was as though a *khamsin* wind had torn over them. The terrible sound of the Maxim gun followed close behind the spray of bullets. The troop of men and horse disintegrated, blown away like dead leaves.

The gun traversed back towards Osman, but before the dancing pattern of bullets reached him, al-Buq lunged over the crest. Osman swung down from the saddle. He was still stunned by the enormity and menace of the machine, but he ran to where his men lay. Most of them were dead. Only al-Noor and Mooman Digna were still on their feet. 'See to the others,' Osman ordered. He threw himself flat on the top of the dune and peered down the far side. He watched the long train of wagons wind away along the floor of the valley towards Akasha.

In the few moments that they had been exposed to the fire of the Maxim gun, eight of his men had been killed outright, four were gravely wounded and would die. Four had survived. Five horses were untouched. Osman destroyed the wounded animals, left a waterskin with the wounded men to ease their passing, gathered up his surviving aggagiers and rode back to Firket.

Now that he had had his first glimpse of the juggernaut that was rolling down on them, he realized that his options were limited. There was little he could do to oppose and hold the enemy here at Firket. He determined to assemble and concentrate all his array on the banks of the Atbara river and strike the enemy there in overwhelming force.

He replaced the depraved and ineffectual Emir Hammuda with the Emir Azrak. This man was completely different from Hammuda: he was a fanatical devotee of the Mahdi; he had carried out many daring and brutal raids on the Turk and the infidel; his name was well known in Cairo, and he could expect little mercy if he were captured; he would fight to the death. Osman gave Azrak orders to delay the enemy at Firket for as long as possible, but at the last moment to fall back on the Atbara river with all his army. He left him, and rode back to Omdurman.

No sooner had Osman ridden away than Hammuda refused to accept that he had been replaced and engaged in a bitter dispute with Azrak, which left both men powerless.

While they wrangled the sirdar built up his base at Akasha. Men and equipment, supplies and munitions were brought down the railway line with machine-like efficiency. Then, with nine thousand men under his personal command, General Kitchener fell upon the town of Firket. The Dervish were decimated and the survivors driven out helter-skelter. Hammuda died in the first charge. Azrak escaped with less than a thousand men and röde southwards to the confluence of the Atbara to meet Osman. With his Camel Corps Kitchener followed the fleeing Dervish along the riverbank, and captured hundreds of men and horses and great stores of grain.

Within weeks the entire Dervish province of Dongola had fallen to the sirdar. The juggernaut resumed its deliberate and ponderous advance southwards towards the Atbara river. Month after month and mile after weary mile the railway line unreeled like a silken thread across the desert. On most days the track advanced a mile or so, but on occasions up to three miles.

The workmen encountered unexpected hardships and setbacks. Cholera broke out and hundreds of graves were hastily dug in the empty desert. The first false flood of the inundation brought the 'green tide', all the sewage that had settled on the exposed banks during the Low Nile, downstream. There was no other water to drink. Dysentery racked the army camps. Terrible thunderstorms poured out of a sky that usually never rained. Miles of track were washed away, miles more were swamped under six feet of water.

Zafir, the first of the new stern-wheel gunboats, was brought in sections from Wadi Halfa, and reassembled in a makeshift boatyard at Koshesh on the clear-water section above the cataracts. Her appearance was stately and impressive, and she was launched with General Kitchener and his staff on board. As the boilers built up a full head of steam there was an explosion like a salvo of heavy artillery as they burst. The *Zafir* was out of action until new boilers could be brought out from England and installed.

Yet the remorseless advance continued. The Dervish garrisons at Abu Hamed and Metemma were overrun, and driven back on the Atbara river. Here Kitchener bombarded Osman Atalan's great defensive *zareba*, then smashed it wide open with bullet and bayonet. The Arabs either fled or fought to the death. The black Sudanese troops who would fight as willingly for the infidel as they had for the Dervish were recruited into the sirdar's army.

Victory on the Atbara was decisive. Kitchener's expeditionary force went into summer quarters. He planned and mustered his powers and waited for the river to rise before the final advance on Omdurman.

Penrod, who had received a spear wound through the thigh during the fighting, was granted convalescent leave. He travelled back, by rail and river steamer from Aswan, to Cairo.

When Penrod limped into Cairo, Amber was beside herself with joy to have him at her side, and in her bed. Lady Jane Ballantyne had returned to Clercastle at the insistence of her husband. What had been planned as a three-month sojourn had extended to almost two years. Sir Peter had long ago tired of the bachelor existence.

Ryder Courtney had returned from a highly successful visit to the United States and Canada. The wheat he had purchased was already offloading in Alexandria docks. He had arrived home just in time for the birth of his son. He had learnt that as soon as the Sudanese campaign ended, Sir Evelyn Baring would turn all his energy and the resources of the Khedive to the building of the great irrigation works on the upper Nile, which had been long projected. Almost two hundred thousand acres of rich black soil would be brought under permanent irrigation and would no longer be dependent on the annual inundation from the Nile. Ryder had purchased twenty thousand of these acres in a speculative move. It was a wise decision that, within ten years, would make him a cotton millionaire.

Penrod's wound healed cleanly, and he discovered that he had been gazetted for the Distinguished Service Order for his conduct in the battles of Firket and Atbara. Amber missed her moon, but on Saffron's advice she did not tell Penrod of this momentous occurrence. 'Wait until you are certain,' Saffron told her.

'What if he guesses the truth before I tell him?' Amber was nervous. 'He would take that hard.'

'My darling, Penrod is a man. He would not recognize a pregnancy if he tripped over it.'

With the approaching cool season heralding High Nile, and conditions conducive to resuming campaigning, Penrod kissed Amber farewell and, oblivious of his impending elevation to fatherhood, returned upriver to the great military camp on the Atbara.

When he arrived he found that the encampment now stretched for many miles along the riverbank, and the Nile itself resembled the port of some prosperous European city. It was a forest of masts and funnels. Feluccas and gyassas, barges, steamers and gunboats crowded the anchorage. There were six newly assembled armoured-screw gunboats. They were a hundred and forty feet long and twenty-four wide. They were armed with twelve- and six-pounder quick-firing guns, and with batteries of Maxim machine-guns on their upper decks. They were equipped with modern machinery: ammunition hoists, searchlights and steam winches. Yet they drew only thirty-nine inches of water, and their stern screws could drive them at speeds of up to twelve knots. In addition there were four elderly stern-wheel gunboats, dating from Chinese Gordon's era, which also carried twelve-pounders and Maxim guns.

The sirdar had asked London for first-line British troops to reinforce his already formidable new Egyptian army. His request had been granted and battalions of the Royal Warwickshires, Lincolns, Seaforth Highlanders, Cameron Highlanders, Grenadier Guards, Northumberland Fusiliers, Lancashire Fusiliers, the Rifle Brigade and the 21st Lancers had already joined and were encamped in the great zareba. The array of artillery was formidable and ranged from forty-pounder howitzers to field and horse batteries. The sirdar's large white tent stood on an eminence in the centre of the zareba, with the Egyptian flag waving on a tall staff above it.

Penrod found his camels fat and strong and his men in much the same condition. Life in summer quarters, without the presence of their commander, had been restful. Penrod stirred them into action with a vengeance.

As the first green flood of the rising Nile had poured down through the Shabluka gorge, the grand advance began. Thirty thousand fighting men and their battle train moved southwards to the first staging camp at the entrance to the gorge. Here the mile-wide river was compressed into a mere two hundred yards between the black and precipitous cliffs. They were fifty-six miles from Khartoum and Omdurman. The next staging camp was only seven miles upstream opposite Royan Island above the gorge, but these were seven difficult and dangerous miles.

The gunboats thrashed their way up through the racing, whirling rapids, towing the barges behind them. The ill-fated gunboat *Zafir* now sprang a leak and sank by the bows in the jaws of the gorge. Her officers and men had barely time to escape with their lives.

For the infantry and cavalry the march to Royan Island was doubled in length. To avoid the rocky Shabluka hills they had to circle far out into the desert. Penrod's camels carried water for them in iron tanks.

Once they had reached Royan Island, the road to Omdurman was clear and open before them. The vast array of men, animals, boats and guns moved forward relentlessly, ponderously and menacingly.

At last only the low line of the Kerreri hills concealed the city of Omdurman from the binoculars of the British officers. There was still no sign of the Dervish. Perhaps they had abandoned the city and fled. The sirdar sent his cavalry to find out.

The Khalifat Abdullahi had assembled all his army at Omdurman. They numbered almost a hundred thousand. Abdullahi reviewed them before the city, on the wide plain below the Kerreri hills. The prophecy of one of the saintly mullahs on his deathbed was that a great battle would be fought upon the hills that would define the future of Mahdism and the land of Sudan.

Anyone looking upon the mighty Dervish array could not doubt the outcome of the battle. The galloping regiments were strung out over four miles, wave after wave of horsemen and massed black Sudanese spearmen. At the climax of the review, Abdullahi addressed them passionately. He charged them in the name of Allah and the Mahdi to do their duty. 'Before God, I swear to you that I will be in the forefront of the battle.'

The threat that the emirs and *khalifs* feared above all others was that presented by the gunboats. Their spies had reported the power of these vessels to them. Abdullahi devised a counter to this menace. Among his European captives still in Omdurman was an old German engineer. Abdullahi had him brought before him, and his chains were struck off. This was usually the prelude to execution and the German was prostrated with terror.

'I want you to build me explosive mines to lay in the river,' Abdullahi told him.

The old engineer was delighted to have this reprieve. He flung himself into the project with enthusiasm and energy. He filled two steel boilers each with a thousand pounds of gunpowder. As a detonator he fixed in them a loaded, cocked and charged pistol. To the pistol's triggers he attached a length of stout line. A firm tug on this would fire the pistol, and the discharge would ignite the explosive contents of the boiler.

The first massive mine was loaded on to one of the Dervish steamers, the *Ishmaelia*. With the German engineer and a hundred and fifty men on board it was taken out into mid-channel and lowered over the side. As it touched the bottom of the river the steamer's captain, for reasons he never had an opportunity to explain, decided to yank the trigger cord.

The efficacy of the mine was demonstrated convincingly to Abdullahi, his emirs and commanders who were watching from the shore. The *Ishmaelia*, with her captain, crew and the German engineer, was blown out of the water.

Once Abdullahi had recovered from the mild concussion induced by the explosion, he was delighted with his new weapon. He ordered the captain of one of his other steamers to place the second mine in the channel. This worthy had been as impressed as everybody else with the first demonstration. Wisely he took the precaution of flooding the mine with water before he took it on board. The mine, rendered harmless, was then laid in the channel of the Nile without further mishap. Abdullahi praised him effusively and showered him with rewards.

The Dervish commanders waited for the infidel to come. Each day their spies brought reports of the slow but relentless approach. Better than anyone Osman Atalan understood the strength and determination of these stern new-age crusaders. When the infidel advance reached Merreh, only four miles beyond the Kerreri Hills, he rode out with al-Noor and Mooman Digna and gazed down from the heights upon the host. Through the dust they raised, he saw the marching columns and the lanceheads of the cavalry glittering in the sunlight. He watched the heliographs flashing messages he could not understand. Then he gazed at the flotilla of gunboats, beautiful and deadly, coming up the flow of the Nile. He rode back to his palace in Omdurman and called for his wives. 'I am sending you with all the children to the mosque at the oasis of Gedda. You will wait for me there. When the battle is won, I will come to find you.'

Rebecca and Nazeera packed their possessions on to the camels, gathered up the three children and, under an escort of aggagiers, left the town.

'Why do these infidels wish to hurt us?' Ahmed asked pitifully. 'What shall we do if they kill our exalted and beloved father?' Ahmed lacked the fine looks of his parents. His eyes were blue, but close-set and furtive. His front teeth protruded beyond his upper lip. This gave him the appearance of a large, ginger rodent.

'Do not snivel, my brother. Whatever Allah decrees, we must be brave and take care of our honoured mother,' Kahruba answered.

Rebecca felt her heart squeezed. They were so different: Ahmed plain-featured, timid and afraid; Kahruba beautiful, fearless and wild. She hugged the infant to her breast as she swayed on the camel saddle. Under the cotton sheet she had spread over her to protect her from the sun, her baby daughter lay listlessly against her bosom. The tiny body was hot and sweaty with the fever that consumed her. Omdurman was a plague city.

The little caravan of women and children reached the oasis an hour after dark.

'You will like it here,' Rebecca told Ahmed. 'This is where you were born. The mullahs are learned and wise. They will instruct you in many things.' Ahmed was a born scholar, hungry for knowledge. She did not bother to try to influence Kahruba. She was her own soul, and not amenable to any views that did not coincide with her own.

That night as she lay on the narrow *angareb*, holding her sick baby, Rebecca's mind turned to the twins. This had happened more often recently, ever since she had known that the Egyptian army was moving irresistibly southwards down the river towards them.

It was many years since she had parted from Amber, even longer since Saffron had run off through the dark streets of Khartoum. She still had a vivid picture of them in her mind. Her eyes stung with tears. What did they look like now? Were they married? Did they have children of their own? Were they even alive? Of course they would not recognize her. She knew she had become an Arab wife, drawn and haggard with childbirth, drab and aged with care. She sighed with regret, and the infant whimpered. Rebecca forced herself to remain still, to allow her baby to rest.

She was seized with a strange unfocused terror for what the next few days would bring. She had a premonition of disaster. The existence to which she had become inured, the world to which she now belonged, would be shattered, her husband dead, perhaps her children also. What was there still to hope for? What was there still to be endured?

At last she fell into a dark, numbed sleep. When she awoke the infant in her arms was cold and dead. Despair filled her soul.

The British and Egyptian cavalry moved forward together. The Nile lay on their left hand, and on it they could see the gunboats sailing up the stream in line astern. Before them stood the line of the Kerreri hills. Penrod's camels were on the right flank of the advance. They climbed the first slope, and came out abruptly on the crest. Spread below him, Penrod saw the confluence of the two great Niles, and between them the long-abandoned ruins of Khartoum.

Directly ahead, in Omdurman, rose the brown dome of a large building. It had not been there when Penrod had escaped. He knew, however, that this must be the tomb of the Mahdi in the centre of the city. Nothing else had changed.

The wide plain ahead was speckled with coarse clumps of thornbush, and enclosed on three sides by harsh, stony hills. In the centre of the plain, like another monument, was the conical Surgham Hill. Abutting the hill, a long low uneven ridge hid the fold of ground immediately beyond it. There was no sign of the Dervish. Obedient to his express orders, Penrod halted his troops on the high ground and they watched the squadron of British cavalry ride forward cautiously.

Suddenly there was movement. Hundreds of tiny specks left what appeared to be the walls of a zareba of thorn branches. It was the Dervish vanguard. They moved forward to meet the British cavalry. The front echelon of troopers dismounted and, at long range, opened fire with their carbines on the approaching Dervish. A few fell, and their comrades rode unhurriedly back to the zareba.

Then a remarkable transformation took place. The dark wall of the zareba came to life. It was not made of thornbush but of men, tens of thousands of Dervish warriors. Behind them another vast mass appeared over the low ridge in the centre of the plain. Like an infestation of locusts, they swarmed forward. Around and between their divisions individual horsemen rode back and forth, and squadrons of their wild cavalry swirled. Hundreds of banners waved above their ranks, and myriad spearheads glittered. Even at this distance Penrod could hear the booming of the war drums and the braying of the *ombeyas*.

Through his binoculars he searched the front ranks of this massive concentration of the enemy, and in the centre he picked out the distinctive scarlet and black war banner of Osman Atalan. 'So my enemy has come,' he whispered, reverting instinctively to Arabic.

Beside him, Sergeant Yakub grinned evilly and rolled his one eye. '*Kismet*,' he said. 'This has been written!'

Then their attention was diverted from the awe-inspiring spectacle of the Dervish advance to the river on their left. The flotilla of gunboats, with a crash of cannon, engaged the Dervish forts on both banks, which guarded the river approaches to the city. The Dervish guns responded, and the thunder of artillery echoed from the hills. But the fire from the gunboats was fast and deadly accurate. The embrasures of the forts were smashed to rubble and the guns behind them blown off their mountings. The Maxim guns scoured the rifle trenches on each side of the forts, and slaughtered the Dervish in them.

The British and Egyptian cavalry withdrew slowly ahead of the advancing Dervish army. In the meantime Kitchener's main army came marching up along the riverbank, and laagered around the tiny abandoned fishing village of Eigeiga. In this defensive position they awaited the first assault of the Dervish.

Suddenly the mass of advancing Dervish halted. They fired their rifles into the air, a salute and a challenge, but instead of coming on to the attack they lay down on the earth. By now it was late in the afternoon, and it was soon evident that they would not mount their main attack that day.

The flotilla of gunboats had reduced all the Dervish forts, and shelled the tomb of the Mahdi, destroying the dome. Now they dropped back down the current and anchored opposite the army zareba. Night fell.

At the rear of the Dervish army, Osman Atalan sat with the Khalifat Abdullahi at the small campfire in front of his tent. They were discussing the day's actions and skirmishes, and planning for the morrow. Suddenly, from the centre of the river, a huge cyclopean eye of brilliant light swept over them. Abdullahi sprang to his feet and shouted, 'What is this magic?'

'Exalted Abdullahi, the infidel are watching us.'

'Pull down my tent!' Abdullahi screamed. 'They will see it.' He covered his eyes with both hands, lest the light blind him, and threw himself on to the ground. He feared no man, but this was witchcraft.

Four miles apart the two great armies passed the hours of darkness in fitful slumber and constant vigilance, impatiently awaiting the dawn. At half past four in the morning the bugles of the river camp sounded the reveille. The drums and fifes joined in. The infantrymen and gunners stood to arms and the cavalry mounted up.

Before sunrise the cavalry patrols trotted forward. Because there had been no night attack they suspected that the Dervish had crept away during the hours of darkness, and that the hillside would be deserted. At the head of three troops of his camels, Penrod reached the crest of the slope in front of the zareba and looked down the back slope towards the city and Surgham Hill. Even in the dim light he could see that the dome of the Mahdi's tomb had been shot away by the gunboats. He searched the plain below him, and saw that it was covered with dark patches and streaks. Then the light strengthened with the swiftness of the African dawn.

Far from having absconded, the entire might of the Dervish army lay before him. It began to roll forward on a solid front almost five miles wide. Spear points shimmered above the ranks, and the Dervish cavalry galloped before and about the slowly moving masses of men. Then the war drums began to beat, the ivory *ombeyas* blared, and the Dervish to cheer. The uproar was almost deafening.

As yet the Dervish masses were hidden from the main Egyptian army on the river, and the gunboats anchored behind them. However, the tumult carried to them. The attack developed swiftly. The Dervish legions were well disciplined and moved with purpose and determination. The British and Egyptian cavalry dropped back before them.

The Dervish front ranks, waving hundreds of huge coloured banners and beating the drums, topped the rise. Below them they saw the waiting infidel army. They did not hesitate, but fired their rifles into the air in challenge and rushed down the slope. The sirdar let them come, waiting until they were exposed on the open hillside. The ranges were accurately known to his gunners, and to the captains of the gunboats. However, it was not the British who opened the conflict. The Dervish had brought up a few ancient Krupps field cannon and their shells burst in front of the British zareba.

Immediately the gunboats and field batteries returned fire. The sky above the advancing Dervish masses was pocked with bursting puffs of shrapnel, like cotton pods opening in the sun. The sea of waving banners toppled and fell, like grass blown down by a whirlwind. Then they rose again as the men coming up behind the fallen lifted them high and charged forward.

The cavalry cleared the field to give the guns full play. The Dervish came on, but their ranks thinned steadily and they left the hillside thickly strewn with tiny inert figures. Then the Dervish were in range of the rifles and the Maxims. The slaughter mounted. The rifles grew so hot that they had to be exchanged with those of the reserve companies in the rear. The Maxims boiled away all the water in their reservoirs and were refilled from the water bottles of their crews.

The frontal attack had been planned, by Osman and Abdullahi, to allow their main forces to hook round the flanks and crush in to the sides of the infidel line. The men being massacred by the guns on the open ground were brave, but they were not the élite of the Dervish army. This was coming up behind the ridge.

Penrod had retired on to the flank, and was ready to deal with the survivors of the first charge when they tried to escape, when suddenly he was confronted by thousands of fresh enemy cavalry coming at him from over the crest of the ridge at close range. He must fly with his troops, and try to reach the safety of the lines before they were wiped out. They raced away but the Dervish and their excited clamour were close upon them. One of the gunboats, playing nursemaid, had been watching this dangerous situation develop. It dropped back down the river, and just as it seemed that Penrod's troops must be overtaken by overwhelming numbers of cavalry, it opened up with the deadly Maxims. The range was short and the results stunning. The Dervish cavalry fell in tangled masses, and their rear ranks pulled up and turned back. Penrod led his squadrons into the shelter of the zareba.

Now the sirdar could leave the zareba and begin the final assault towards the city. The Dervish were in full retreat and the way was open. The lines of cavalry, bayonets and guns crossed the ridge and moved down towards the shattered tomb of the Mahdi.

But the Dervish were not beaten. As the British lines neared Surgham Hill and the sandy ridge they found that Osman Atalan and the Khalifat had concealed the flower of their army in this fold of ground. Twenty-five thousand aggagiers and desert warriors burst out from ambush, and poured down on the British.

The fighting was terrible. The gunboats on the river could take no part in it. The British lancers were surprised by the close proximity of Osman's lurking aggagiers and were forced to charge straight at them. Savage, undisciplined infantry could not withstand the charge of British lancers, but these were horsemen. They ran forward to press the muzzles of their rifles against the flanks of the British horses, then fired; they hamstrung others with the long blades, they dragged the riders from their saddles.

The lancers suffered terrible casualties. Al-Noor killed three men. This short but bloody action was only a tiny cameo in the main battle that raged across the plain and around Surgham Hill.

The British and the Egyptians fought superbly. The brigades manoeuvred with parade-ground precision to meet every fresh charge. The officers directed their fire with cool expertise. The Maxims came up to exacerbate the slaughter. But the Dervish courage was inhuman. The fires of fanaticism were unquenchable. They charged and were shot down in tangled heaps, but immediately fresh hordes of *jibba*-bright figures sprang up, seemingly from the ground, and ran upon the guns and bayonets and died. From the gunsmoke that hung over their mangled corpses fresh figures charged forward.

And the Maxims sang the chorus.

By noon it was over. Abdullahi had fled the field, leaving almost half his army dead upon it. The British and the Egyptians had lost forty-eight men, almost half of whom were lancers who had died in the fatal two minutes of that brave but senseless charge.

Penrod was among the first men into the city of Omdurman. There were still small pockets of resistance among the pestilential hovels and stinking slums, but he ignored them and, with a troop of his men, rode to the palace of Osman Atalan. He dismounted in the courtyard. The buildings were deserted. He strode into them with his bared sabre in his hand, calling her name: 'Rebecca! Where are you?' His voice echoed through the empty rooms.

Suddenly he heard a furtive movement behind him, and whirled round just in time to deflect the dagger that had been aimed between his shoulder-blades. He flicked back his blade, catching his assailant as he struck again, slicing open his wrist to the bone. The Arab screamed and the dagger fell from his hand. With the point of the sabre to his throat Penrod pinned him to the wall behind him. He recognized him as one of Osman Atalan's aggagiers. 'Where are they?' Penrod demanded. 'Where are al-Jamal and Nazeera?' Clutching his wrist, the blood from his severed artery pumping sullenly, the Arab spat at him.

'Effendi.' Yakub spoke from behind Penrod's shoulder. 'Leave this one to me. He will speak to me.'

Penrod nodded. 'I will wait with the camels. Do not be long.'

'The remorseless Yakub will waste little time.'

Twice Penrod heard the captured Arab scream, the second time weaker than the first, but at last Yakub came out. 'The oasis of Gedda,' he said, and wiped the blade of his dagger on his camel's neck.

The oasis of Gedda lay in a basin of chalk hills. There was no surface water, only a single deep well with a coping of limestone. It was surrounded by a grove of date palms. The dome of the saint's tomb was separated from the taller dome of the mosque and the flat-roofed quarters of the mullahs.

As Penrod's troop rode in from the desert they saw a group of children playing among the palm trees, small, barefooted boys and girls in long, grubby robes. A copper-haired boy pursued the others, and they squealed with laughter and scattered before him. As soon as they saw the camel troop approaching they froze into silence and stared with huge dark eyes. Then the eldest boy turned and ran back towards the mosque. The others followed him. After they had disappeared the oasis seemed silent and deserted.

Penrod rode forward, and heard a horse whinny. The animal was standing behind the angle of the side wall. It was knee-haltered and had been feeding on a pile of cut fodder. It was a dark-coloured stallion. 'Al-Buq!'

He reined in well short of the front doors of the mosque, jumped down and threw the reins to Yakub. Then he unsheathed his sabre and walked forward slowly. The doors were wide open and the interior of the mosque was impenetrably dark in contrast to the bright sunlight without.

'Osman Atalan!' Penrod shouted, and the echoes from the hills mocked him. The silence persisted.

Then he saw dim movement in the gloom of the building's interior. Osman Atalan stepped out into the sunlight. His fierce and cruel features were inscrutable. He carried the long blade in his right hand, but he had no shield. 'I have come for you,' Penrod said.

'Yes,' Osman answered. Penrod saw the glint of silver threads in his beard. But his gaze was dark and unwavering. 'I expected you. I knew that you would come.'

'Nine years,' said Penrod.

'Too long,' Osman replied, 'but now it is time.' He came down the steps, and Penrod retreated ten paces to give him space to fight. They circled each other, a graceful minuet. Lightly they touched blades and the steel rang like fine crystal.

They circled again, watching each other's eyes, looking for any weakness that might have developed in the years since they had last fought. They found none. Osman moved like a cobra, tensed and poised for the strike. Penrod was his mongoose, quick and fluid.

They crossed and turned, and then as if at a signal, leapt at each other. Their blades slithered together. They broke apart, circled and came together again. The silver blades blurred, glittered and clattered against each other. Penrod drove in hard, forcing Osman on to his back foot, keeping the pressure on him, the blades dancing. Osman stepped back, and then counter-attacked, just as furiously. Penrod gave ground to him, leading him on, making him buy each inch.

Penrod watched him carefully, then cut hard at his head. Osman blocked. Their blades were locked together. Now they both stood solidly and all their weight was on their sword wrists. Tiny beads of sweat popped out on their foreheads. They stared into each other's eyes and pushed. Penrod felt the sponginess in Osman's grip. To test him he broke the lock and jumped back.

As their blades disengaged Osman had a fleeting opening and tried for it, thrusting at Penrod's right elbow to disable his sword arm, but it was one of his old tricks and Penrod was ready for it. It seemed to him that Osman was slow. He hit the long blade and pirouetted clear.

Not slow. He changed his mind as they circled again. Just not as fast as he used to be. But, then, am I?

He feinted at Osman's face, then leant back, not making it obvious that he was inviting the riposte. Osman almost caught him. His counter-stroke came like thunder. Penrod just managed to turn it. Osman was at full extension, and there was the lag again, his old bad habit, slow on the recovery. Penrod hit him.

It was a glancing blow that skidded along Osman's ribcage under his arm. The point sliced down to the bone, but did not find the gap between the ribs. They circled again. Osman was bleeding profusely. The blood loss must weaken him swiftly, and the damaged muscles would soon stiffen. He was running out of time and threw everything into the attack. He came with all his weight and skill. His blade turned to dancing light. It was cut and thrust high in the line of defence, then cross and go back-handed for the thigh, then at the head. He kept it up relentlessly, never breaking, never giving Penrod a chance to come on to his front foot, forcing him on to the defensive.

He cut Penrod high in the left shoulder. It was a light wound, and Osman was losing blood more heavily. Each fresh

621

attack was less fiery, each recovery after the thrust just a little slower. Penrod let him expend himself, holding him off and waiting his moment. He watched Osman's eyes.

During the entire bout Osman had not gone for Penrod's hip. Penrod knew from experience that it was his favourite and most deadly stroke with which he had crippled innumerable enemies. At last Penrod offered it to him, turning his lower body into Osman's natural line.

Osman went for the opening, and once he was committed Penrod turned back so the razor edge slit the cloth of his jodhpurs but did not break the skin. Osman was fully extended and could not recover quickly enough.

Penrod hit him. His thrust split the sternum at the base of Osman's ribs and went on to transfix him cleanly as a fish on a skewer. Penrod felt his steel grate on his opponent's spinal column.

Osman froze, and Penrod stepped in close. He seized his opponent's sword wrist to prevent a last thrust. Their faces were only inches apart. Penrod's eyes were hard and cold. Osman's were dark with bitter rage, but slowly they became opaque as stones. The sword dropped from his hand. His legs buckled, but Penrod held his weight on the sabre. Osman opened his lips to speak, but a snake of dark blood trickled from the corner of his mouth and crawled down his chin.

Penrod relaxed his wrist and let him slide off the blade. He fell at Penrod's feet, and lay still upon his back with his arms spread wide.

As Penrod stepped back a woman screamed. He looked up. He became aware for the first time of the small group of Arab women and children huddled in the doorway of the mosque. He recognized the little ones as those who had run to hide as he rode up. But he knew none of the women.

'Nazeera!' It was Yakub's voice. He saw one of the women react, and then he recognized her. Nazeera held two children against her legs. One was the ugly copper-haired boy, and the other an exquisite little girl, a few years younger than the boy. Both children were weeping and trying to break out of Nazeera's grip, but she held them fast.

Then an Arab woman left the group and came slowly down the steps towards him. She moved like a sleep-walker, and her eyes were fastened on the dead man at his feet. There was something dreadfully familiar about her. Instinctively Penrod backed away, still staring at her in fascination. Then he exclaimed, 'Rebecca!'

'No,' the stranger replied in English. 'Rebecca died long ago.' Her face was a pitiful travesty of that of the lovely young woman he had once known. She knelt beside Osman and picked up his sword. Then she looked up into Penrod's face. Her eyes were old and hopeless. 'Look after my children,' she said. 'You owe me that at least, Penrod Ballantyne.'

Before he understood what she intended and could move to prevent her, she reversed the sword. She placed the pommel on the hard ground and the point under her bottom ribs and fell forward upon it with all her weight. The length of the blade disappeared into her body, and she collapsed on top of Osman Atalan.

The children screamed, broke from Nazeera's grip, rushed down the steps and threw themselves on to the bodies of their parents. They wailed and shrieked. It was a dreadful sound that cut to the core of Penrod's being.

He sheathed his sabre, turned away and walked away towards the palm grove. As he passed Yakub he said, 'Bury Osman Atalan. Do not mutilate his body or take his head. Bury al-Jamal beside him. Nazeera and the children will come with us. They will ride my camel. I will ride al-Buq. When all is ready call me.'

He went into the grove and found a fallen palm trunk on which to sit. He was very tired, and the cut on his shoulder throbbed. He opened his tunic and folded his handkerchief over the wound.

The two children, the boy and the girl, must be Rebecca's, he realized. What will become of them? Then he remembered Amber and Saffron. They have two aunts who will fight over them. He smiled sadly. Of course, they will have Rebecca's share of the trust fund, and they have Nazeera. They will lack for nothing.

Within the hour Yakub came to call him. On the way back to the mosque they stopped beside the newly filled double grave. 'Do you think she loved him, Yakub?'

'She was a Muslim wife,' Yakub replied. 'Of course she loved him. In God's eyes, she had no choice.'

They mounted up. Nazeera had the two children with her on the camel, and Yakub rode beside her. Penrod was on the stallion, and led them back to Omdurman.

Ahmed Habib abd Atalan, the son of Rebecca and Osman Atalan, became uglier as he grew older, but he was very clever. He attended Cairo University where he studied law. He fell in with a group of politically active fellow students, who were violently opposed to the British occupation of their country. He devoted the rest of his life to the same *jihad* against that hated nation and Empire as his father. He was a German supporter during both world wars and spied for Erwin Rommel in the second. He was an active member of the Revolutionary Command Council in the bloodless coup that ousted the Egyptian King Farouk, the British puppet.

Rebecca's daughter Kahruba remained small but she became more beautiful with every year that passed. At an early age she discovered in herself an extraordinary talent for dancing and acting. For twenty years she burned bright as a meteor across the stages of all the great theatres of Europe. With her wild, free spirit, she became a legend in her own lifetime. Her lovers, both men and women, were legion. Finally she married a French industrialist, who manufactured motor-cars, and they lived together in regal state and pomp in their palatial mansion in Deauville.

The Khalifat Abdullahi escaped from Omdurman, but Penrod Ballantyne and his Camel Corps pursued him relentlessly for more than a year. In the end he deigned to run no further. With his wives and devotees around him he sat on a silk carpet in the centre of his camp in the remote wilderness.

When the troops rushed in he offered no further resistance. They shot him dead where he sat.

The tomb of the Mahdi was razed to the ground. His remains were exhumed, and his skull was turned into an inkwell. It was presented to General Kitchener, who was horrified. He had it reburied in a secret grave in the wilderness.

After the battle of Omdurman Kitchener became the darling of the Empire. He was rewarded with a peerage and a huge money grant. When the Boers in South Africa inflicted a series of disastrous defeats on the British army, Kitchener was sent to retrieve the situation. He burnt the farms and herded the women and children into concentration camps. The Boers were crushed.

During the First World War, Kitchener was promoted to field marshal and commander-in-chief to steer the Empire through the most destructive war in all human history. In 1916 while he was on board the cruiser *Hampshire*, *en route* to Russia, the ship struck a German mine off the Orkneys. He drowned at the high noon of his career.

Sir Evelyn Baring became the 1st Earl of Cromer. He returned to England where he spent his days writing and, in the House of Lords, championing free trade.

Nazeera helped to raise all the children of the three Benbrook sisters. This occupied most of her time and energy, but what remained she divided impartially between Bacheet and Yakub.

Bacheet and Yakub pursued their vendetta for the rest of their lives. Bacheet was referred to by his rival as the Despicable Lecher. Yakub was the Jaalin Assassin. In their later years they took to frequenting the same coffee-house where they sat at opposite ends of the room, smoking their water-pipes, never addressing each other but deriving great comfort from their mutual antagonism. When Bacheet died of old age, Yakub never returned to the coffee-house.

Ryder Courtney's cotton acres flourished. He invested his millions in Transvaal gold and Mesopotamian oil. He doubled and redoubled his fortune. In time his mercantile influence encompassed almost all of Africa and the Mediterranean. But to Saffron he remained always a benign and indulgent husband.

General Sir Penrod Ballantyne went to South Africa on Kitchener's staff, and was present when the Boers surrendered at the peace of Vereeniging in the Transvaal. In the First World War he rode with Allenby's cavalry against the Ottoman Turks in Palestine. He fought at Gaza and Megiddo, where he won further honours. He continued to play first-class polo well into his seventies. He and Amber lived in their house on the Nile, and in it raised a large family.

Amber and Saffron outlived both their husbands. They grew ever closer as the years passed. Amber flourished as an author. Her novels faithfully captured the romance and mystery of Africa. She was twice nominated for the Nobel Prize for Literature. Saffron's marvellously colourful paintings were hung in galleries in New York, Paris and London. Her Nile series of paintings was eagerly sought by wealthy collectors on two continents, and commanded enormous prices. Picasso said of her, 'She paints the way a sunbird flies.'

But they are all gone now, for in Africa only the sun triumphs eternally.

GLOSSARY

Arab names will not go into English, exactly, for their consonants are not the same as ours, and their vowels, like ours, vary from district to district. There are scientific systems of transliteration, helpful to people who know enough Arabic not to need helping, but a wash out for the world. I spell my names anyhow, to show what rot the systems are

T. E. Lawrence, *The Seven Pillars of Wisdom*

Abadan Riji – 'One who never turns back'; Penrod Ballantyne's Arabic name

abd – slave

aggagiers – élite warriors of the Beja tribe of desert Arabs

Ammi – aunt

angareb – a native bed with leather thong lacing

Ansars – 'The Helpers', warriors of the Mahdi

ardeb – Oriental measure of volume. Five *ardeb*s equal one cubic metre

asida – porridge of dhurra (*q.v.*) flavoured with chili

Bahr El Abiad – the White Nile

Bahr El Azrek – the Blue Nile

Beia – oath of allegiance required by the Mahdi from his Ansars

Beit el Mal – the treasury of the Mahdi

bombom – bullets or cannon shells

Buq, al- – War Trumpet, Osman Atalan's charger

cantar – Oriental measure of weight: one cantar equals a hundredweight dhurra – *Sorghum vulgare*; staple grain food of men and domestic animals

djinni *see* jinnee

Effendi – lord, a title of respect

falja – a gap between the front top teeth; a mark of distinction, much admired in the Sudan and many Arabic countries

fellah (pl. *fellahin*) – Egyptian peasant

ferenghi – foreigner

Filfil – pepper; Saffron Benbrook's Arabic name

Franks – Europeans

galabiyya – traditional long Arabic robe

Hulu Mayya – Sweet Water, one of Osman Atalan's steeds

Jamal, al- – 'the Beautiful One'; Rebecca Benbrook's Arabic name

jibba – the uniform of the Mahdists; long tunic decorated with multi-coloured patches

jihad – holy war

jinnee (pl. jinn) – a spirit from Muslim mythology, able to assume animal or human form and influence mankind, with supernatural powers

jiz – scarab or dung beetle

Karim, al- – 'Kind and Generous'; variation of Ryder Courtney's Arabic name

khalifa – deputy of the Mahdi

khalifat – the senior and most powerful *khalifa*

khedive – the ruler of Egypt

kittar – bush with wicked hooked thorns

kufi – Muslim traditional skull cap

Kurban Bairam – Islamic festival of sacrifice, commemorating the sacrifice of the ram by Abraham in place of his son Isaac; one of the most important holidays in Islam

kurbash – whip made from hippo hide

Mahdi – 'the Expected One', the successor to the Prophet Muhammad

Mahdist – follower of the Mahdi

Mahdiya – the rule of the Mahdi

mulazemin – the servants and retainers of an eminent Arab

nullah – dry or water-filled streambed

ombeya – war trumpet carved from a single elephant tusk

Sakhawi, al- – 'Generosity'; Ryder Courtney's Arabic name

shufta – bandit

sirdar – the title of the commander-in-chief of the Egyptian Army

sitt – title of respect, equivalent to 'my lady' in English

souk – bazaar

Tej – strong beer made from dhurra

Tirbi Kebir – the great graveyard, large salt pan in the Bight of the Nile

Turk – derogatory term for Egyptian

wadi – gully or dried watercourse

Yom il Guma – Friday, the Muslim Sabbath

Zahra, al- – 'The Flower'; Amber Benbrook's Arabic name

zareba – fortified stockade of stones or thorn bush

zenana – women's quarters in an Arabic household

WILD JUSTICE

This book is for my wife and the jewel of my life

MOKHINISO

with all my love and gratitude for the enchanted years

that I have been married to her

There were only fifteen joining passengers for the British Airways flight at Victoria Airport on the island of Mahé in the oceanic republic of the Seychelles.

Two couples formed a tight group as they waited their turn for departure formalities. They were all young, all deeply tanned and they seemed still carefree and relaxed by their holiday in that island paradise. However, one of them made her three companions seem insignificant by the sheer splendour of her physical presence.

She was a tall girl, with long limbs and her head set on a proud, shapely neck. Her thick, sun-gilded blonde hair was twisted into a braid and coiled high on top of her head, and the sun had touched her with gold and brought out the bloom of youth and health upon her skin.

As she moved with the undulating grace of one of the big predatory cats, bare feet thrust into open sandals, so the big pointed breasts joggled tautly under the thin cotton of her tee-shirt and the tight round buttocks strained the faded denim of her hacked-off shorts.

Across the front of her tee-shirt was blazoned the legend 'I AM A LOVE NUT' and below it was drawn the suggestive outline of a coco-de-mer.

She smiled brilliantly at the dark-skinned Seychellois immigration officer as she slid the green United States passport with its golden eagle across the desk to him, but when she turned to her male companion she spoke in quick fluent German. She retrieved her passport and led the others through into the security area.

Again she smiled at the two members of the Seychelles

1

Police Force who were in charge of the weapons search, and she swung the net carry bag off her shoulder.

'You want to check these?' she asked, and they all laughed. The bag contained two huge coco-de-mer; the grotesque fruit, each twice the size of a human head, were the most popular souvenirs of the Islands. Each of her three companions carried similar trophies in net bags, and the police officer ignored such familiar objects and instead ran his metal detector in a perfunctory manner over the canvas flight bags which made up the rest of their hand luggage. It buzzed harshly on one bag and the boy who carried it shamefacedly produced a small Nikkormat camera. More laughter and then the police officer waved the group through into the final Departure Lounge.

It was already crowded with transit passengers who had boarded at Mauritius, and beyond the lounge windows the huge Boeing 747 Jumbo squatted on the tarmac, lit harshly by floodlights as the refuelling tenders fussed about her.

There were no free seats in the lounge and the group of four formed a standing circle under one of the big revolving punkah fans, for the night was close and humid – and the mass of humanity in the closed room sullied the air with tobacco smoke and the smell of hot bodies.

The blonde girl led the gay chatter and sudden bursts of laughter, standing inches above her two male companions and a full head above the other girl, so that they were a focus of attention for the hundreds of other passengers. Their manner had changed subtly since they entered the lounge; there was a sense of relief as though a serious obstacle had been negotiated, and an almost feverish excitement in the timbre of their laughter. They were never still, shifting restlessly from foot to foot, hands fiddling with hair or clothing.

Although they were clearly a closed group, quarantined by an almost conspiratorial air of camaraderie, one of the

2

transit passengers left his wife sitting and stood up from his seat across the lounge.

'Say, do you speak English?' he asked, as he approached the group.

He was a heavy man in his middle fifties with a thick thatch of steel-grey hair, dark horn-rimmed spectacles, and the easy confident manner of success and wealth.

Reluctantly the group opened for him, and it was the tall blonde girl who answered, as if by right.

'Sure, I'm American also.'

'No kidding?' The man chuckled. 'Well, what do you know.' And he was studying her with open admiration. 'I just wanted to know what those things are.' He pointed to the net bag of nuts that lay at her feet.

'They are coco-de-mer,' the blonde answered.

'Oh yeah, I've heard of them.'

'They call them "love nuts",' the girl went on, stooping to open the heavy bag at her feet. 'And you can see why.' She displayed one of the fruit for him.

The double globes were joined in an exact replica of a pair of human buttocks.

'Back end.' She smiled, and her teeth were so white they appeared as translucent as fine bone china.

'Front end.' She turned the nut, and offered for his inspection the perfect *mons veneris* complete with a feminine gash and a tuft of coarse curls, and now it was clear she was flirting and teasing; she altered her stance, thrusting her hips forward slightly, and the man glanced down involuntarily at her own plump *mons* beneath the tight blue denim, its deep triangle bisected by the fold of material which had rucked up into the cleft.

He flushed slightly and his lips parted with a small involuntary intake of breath.

'The male tree has a stamen as thick and as long as your arm.' She widened her eyes to the size and colour of blue

3

pansies, and across the lounge the man's wife stood up and came towards them, warned by some feminine instinct. She was much younger than her husband and very heavy and awkward with child.

'The Seychellois will tell you that in the full moon the male pulls up its roots and walks around to mate with the females—'

'As long and as thick as your arm—' smiled the pretty little dark-haired girl beside her, ' – wow!' She was also teasing now, and both girls dropped their gaze deliberately down the front of the man's body. He squirmed slightly, and the two young men who flanked him grinned at his discomfort.

His wife reached him and tugged at his arm. There was a red angry rash of prickly heat on her throat and little beads of perspiration across her upper lip, like transparent blisters.

'Harry, I'm not feeling well,' she whined softly.

'I've got to go now,' he mumbled with relief, his poise and confidence shaken, and he took his wife's arm and led her away.

'Did you recognize him?' asked the dark-haired girl in German, still smiling, her voice pitched very low.

'Harold McKevitt,' the blonde replied softly in the same language. 'Neurosurgeon from Forth Worth. He read the closing paper to the convention on Saturday morning.' She explained. 'Big fish – very big fish,' and like a cat she ran the pink tip of her tongue across her lips.

Of the four hundred and one passengers in the final Departure Lounge that Monday evening three hundred and sixty were surgeons, or their wives. The surgeons, including some of the most eminent in the world of medicine, had come from Europe and England and the United States, from Japan and South America and Asia, for the convention that had ended twenty-four hours previously on the island of Mauritius, five hundred miles to the south of Mahé

4

island. This was one of the first flights out since then and it had been fully booked ever since the convention had been convoked.

'British Airways announces the departure of Flight BA 070 for Nairobi and London; will transit passengers please board now through the main gate.' The announcement was in the soft singsong of the Creole accent, and there was a massed movement towards the exit.

'Victoria Control this is Speedbird Zero Seven Zero request push back and start clearance.'

'Zero Seven Zero you are cleared to start and taxi to holding point for runway Zero One.'

'Please copy amendment to our flight plan for Nairobi. Number of Pax aboard should be 401. We have a full house.'

'Roger, Speedbird, your flight plan is amended.'

The gigantic aircraft was still in its nose-high climb configuration and the seat belt and no-smoking lights burned brightly down the length of the first-class cabin. The blonde girl and her companion sat side by side in the roomy seats 1a and 1b directly behind the forward bulkhead that partitioned off the command area and the first-class galley. The seats that the young couple occupied had been reserved many months previously.

The blonde nodded to her companion and he leaned forward to screen her from the passengers across the aisle while she slipped one of the coco-de-mer from its net bag and held it in her lap.

Through its natural division the nut had been carefully sawn into two sections to allow removal of the milk and the

5

white flesh, then the two sections had been glued together again just as neatly. The joint was only apparent after close inspection.

The girl inserted a small metal instrument into the joint and twisted it sharply, and with a soft click the two sections fell apart like an Easter egg.

In the nests formed by the double husk of the shells, padded with strips of plastic foam, were two smooth, grey, egg-like objects – each the size of a baseball.

They were grenades of East German manufacture, with the Warsaw Pact command designation MK IV(C). The outer layer of each grenade was of armoured plastic, of the type used in landmines to prevent discovery by electronic metal detectors. The yellow stripe around each grenade indicated that it was not a fragmentation type, but was designed for high impact concussion.

The blonde girl took a grenade in her left hand, unlatched her lap belt and slipped quietly from her seat. The other passengers paid her only passing interest as she ducked through the curtains into the galley area. However, the purser and the two stewardesses, still strapped into their fold-down seats, looked up sharply as she entered the service area.

'I'm sorry, madam, but I must ask you to return to your seat until the captain extinguishes the seat-belt lights.'

The blonde girl held up her left hand and showed him the shiny grey egg.

'This is a special grenade, designed for killing the occupants of a battle tank,' she said quietly. 'It could blow the fuselage of this aircraft open like a paper bag or kill by concussion any human being within fifty yards.'

She watched their faces, saw the fear bloom like an evil flower.

'It is fused to explode three seconds after it leaves my hand.' She paused again, and her eyes glittered with excitement and her breath was quick and shallow.

'You—' she selected the purser, ' – take me to the flight deck; you others stay where you are. Do nothing, say nothing.'

When she ducked into the tiny cockpit, hardly large enough to contain the members of the flight crew and its massed banks of instruments and electronic equipment, all three men turned to look back at her in mild surprise – and she lifted her hand and showed them what she carried.

They understood instantly.

'I am taking command of this aircraft,' she said, and then, to the flight engineer, 'Switch off all communications equipment.'

The engineer glanced quickly at his captain, and when he nodded curtly, began obediently to shut down his radios – the very high frequency sets, then the high frequency, the ultra high frequency—

'And the satellite relay,' the girl commanded. He glanced up at her, surprised by her knowledge.

'And don't touch the bug.' He blinked at that. Nobody, but nobody outside the company should have known about the special relay which, when activated by the button beside his right knee, would instantly alert Heathrow Control to an emergency and allow them to monitor any conversation on the flight deck. He lifted his hand away.

'Remove the fuse to the bug circuit.' She indicated the correct box above his head, and he glanced at the captain again, but her voice stung like the tail of a scorpion:

'Do what I tell you.'

Carefully he removed the fuse and she relaxed slightly.

'Read your departure clearance,' she instructed.

'We are cleared to radar departure on track for Nairobi and an unrestricted climb to cruise altitude of thirty-nine thousand feet.'

'When is your next "operations normal" due?'

Operations normal was the routine report to Nairobi

7

Control to assure them that the flight was proceeding as planned.

'In eleven minutes and thirty-five seconds.' The engineer was a young, dark-haired, rather handsome man with a deep forehead, pale skin and the quick, efficient manner instilled by his training.

The girl turned to the captain of the Boeing and their gazes locked as they measured each other. The captain's hair was more grey than black and cropped close to his big rounded skull. He was bull-necked, and had the beefy, ruddy face of a farmer or of a butcher – but his eyes were steady and his manner calm and unshakeable. He was a man to watch, the girl recognized instantly.

'I want you to believe that I am committed entirely to this operation,' she said, 'and that I would welcome the opportunity to sacrifice my life to my cause.' Her dark blue eyes held his without fear, and she read the first growth of respect in him. That was good, all part of her careful calculations.

'I believe that,' said the pilot, and nodded once.

'Your duty is to the four hundred and seventeen lives aboard this aircraft,' she went on. He did not have to reply. 'They will be safe, just as long as you follow my commands implicitly. That I promise you.'

'Very well.'

'Here is our new destination.' She handed him a small white typewritten card. 'I want a new course with forecast winds, and a time of arrival. Your turn onto the new heading to commence immediately after your next "operations normal" report in—' She glanced back at the engineer for the time.

'Nine minutes fifty-eight seconds,' he said promptly.

' – and I want your turn to the new heading to be very gentle, very balanced. We don't want any of the passengers to spill their champagne – do we?'

In the few minutes that she had been on the flight deck

she had already established a bizarre rapport with the captain; it was a blend of reluctant respect and overt hostility and of sexual awareness. She had dressed deliberately to reveal her body, and in her excitement her nipples had hardened and darkened, pushing out through the thin cotton shirt with its suggestive legend, and the musky woman's smell of her body again intensified by her excitement filled the confined cockpit.

Nobody spoke again for many minutes, then the flight engineer broke the silence.

'Thirty seconds to "operations normal".'

'All right, switch on the HF and make the report.'

'Nairobi Approach this is Speedbird Zero Seven Zero.'

'Go ahead Speedbird Zero Seven Zero.'

'Operations normal,' said the engineer into his headset.

'Roger, Zero Seven Zero. Report again in forty minutes.'

'Zero Seven Zero.'

The blonde girl sighed with relief. 'All right, shut down the set.' Then to the captain, 'Disengage the flight director and make the turn to the new heading by hand; let's see how gentle you can be.'

The turn was a beautiful exhibition of flying, two minutes to make a change of 76° of heading, the needles of the turn-and-balance indicator never deviating a hair's breadth, and when it was completed, the girl smiled for the first time.

It was a gorgeous sunny flash of very white teeth.

'Good,' she said, smiling directly into the captain's face. 'What is your name?'

'Cyril,' he replied after a moment's hesitation.

'You can call me Ingrid,' she invited.

There was no set routine to the days in this new command of Peter Stride's, except the obligatory hour on the range with pistol and automatic weapons. No member of Thor Command – not even the technicians – were spared daily range practice.

The rest of Peter's day had been filled with unrelenting activity, beginning with a briefing on the new electronic communications equipment that had just been installed in his command aircraft. This had taken half the morning, and he had been only just in time to join his striker force in the main cabin of the Hercules transport for the day's exercise.

Peter jumped with the first stick of ten men. They jumped from five hundred feet, the parachutes seeming to snap open only seconds before they hit the ground. However, the crosswind had been strong enough to spread them out a little even from that height. The first landing had not been tight enough for Peter. They had taken two minutes fifty-eight seconds from jump to penetration of the deserted administration block standing forlornly in one of the military zones of Salisbury Plain.

'If they had been holding hostages in here, we'd have arrived just in time to start mopping up the blood,' Peter told his men grimly. 'We'll do it again!'

This time they had cut one minute fifty seconds off their time, falling in a tightly steered pattern about the building – beating the time of Colin Noble's No 2 striker team by ten seconds.

To celebrate Peter had scorned the military transports and they had run the five miles to the airstrip, each man in full combat kit and carrying the enormous bundle of his used parachute silk.

The Hercules was waiting to fly them back to base, but it was after dark before they landed and taxied into Thor Command's security compound at the end of the main runway.

For Peter the temptation to leave the debriefing to Colin

Noble had been strong indeed. His driver would have picked up Melissa-Jane at East Croydon Station and she would already be waiting alone in the new cottage, only half a mile from the base gates.

He had not seen her for six weeks, not since he had taken command of Thor, for in all that time he had not allowed himself a single day's respite. He felt a tickle of guilt now, that he should be allowing himself this indulgence, and so he lingered a few minutes after the briefing to transfer command to Colin Noble.

'Where are you going for the weekend?' Colin demanded.

'She's taking me to a pop concert tomorrow night – The Living Dead, no less,' Peter chuckled. 'Seems I haven't lived until I hear the Dead.'

'Give M.J. my love, and a kiss,' Colin told him.

Peter placed high value on his new-found privacy. He had lived most of his adult life in officers' quarters and messes, constantly surrounded by other human beings. However, this command had given him the opportunity to escape.

The cottage was only four and a half minutes' drive from the compound but it might have been an island. It had come furnished and at a rental that surprised him pleasantly. Behind a high hedge of dog rose, off a quiet lane, and set in a sprawling rather unkempt garden, it had become home in a few weeks. He had even been able to unpack his books at last. Books accumulated over twenty years, and stored against such an opportunity. It was a comfort to have them piled around his desk in the small front room or stacked on the tables beside his bed, even though there had been little opportunity to read much of them yet. The new job was a tough one.

Melissa-Jane must have heard the crunch of gravel under the Rover's tyres, and she would certainly have been waiting for it. She came running out of the front door into the driveway, directly into the beam of the headlights, and

11

Peter had forgotten how lovely she was. He felt his heart squeezed.

When he stepped out of the car she launched herself at him and clung with both arms around his chest. He held her for a long moment, neither of them able to speak. She was so slim and warm, her body seeming to throb with life and vitality.

At last he lifted her chin and studied her face. The huge violet eyes swam with happy tears, and she sniffed loudly. Already she had that old-fashioned English porcelain beauty; there would never be the acne and the agony of puberty for Melissa-Jane.

Peter kissed her solemnly on the forehead. 'You'll catch your death,' he scolded fondly.

'Oh, Daddy, you are a real fusspot.' She smiled through the tears and on tip-toe she reached up to kiss him full on the mouth.

They ate lasagne and cassata at an Italian restaurant in Croydon, and Melissa-Jane did most of the talking. Peter watched and listened, revelling in her freshness and youth. It was hard to believe she was not yet fourteen, for physically she was almost fully developed, the breasts under the white turtle-neck sweater no longer merely buds; and she conducted herself like a woman ten years older, only the occasional gleeful giggle betraying her or the lapse as she used some ghastly piece of Roedean slang – 'grotty' was one of these.

Back at the cottage she made them Ovaltine and they drank it beside the fire, planning every minute of the weekend ahead of them and skirting carefully around the pitfalls, the unwritten taboos of their relationship which centred mostly on 'Mother'.

When it was time for bed she came and sat in his lap and traced the lines of his face with her fingertip.

'Do you know who you remind me of?'

'Tell me,' he invited.

'Gary Cooper – only much younger, of course,' she added hurriedly.

'Of course,' Peter chuckled. 'But where did you ever hear of Gary Cooper?'

'They had *High Noon* as the Sunday movie on telly last week.'

She kissed him again and her lips tasted of sugar and Ovaltine, and her hair smelled sweet and clean.

'How old are you, anyway, Daddy?'

'I'm thirty-nine.'

'That isn't really so terribly old.' She comforted him uncertainly.

'Sometimes it's as old as the dinosaurs—' and at that moment the bleeper beside his empty cup began its strident, irritating electronic tone, and Peter felt the slide of dread in his stomach.

Not now, he thought. Not on this day when I have been so long without her.

The bleeper was the size of a cigarette pack, the globe of its single eye glared redly, insistent as the audio-signal. Reluctantly Peter picked it up and, with his daughter still in his lap, he switched in the miniature two-way radio and depressed the send button.

'Thor One,' he said.

The reply was tinny and distorted, the set near the limit of its range.

'General Stride, Atlas has ordered condition Alpha.'

Another false alarm, Peter thought bitterly. There had been a dozen Alphas in the last month, but why on this night. Alpha was the first stage of alert with the teams embarked and ready for condition Bravo which was the GO.

'Inform Atlas we are seven minutes from Bravo.'

Four and a half of those would be needed for him to

13

reach the compound, and suddenly the decision to rent the cottage was shown up as dangerous self-indulgence. In four and a half minutes innocent lives can be lost.

'Darling,' he hugged Melissa-Jane swiftly, 'I'm sorry.'

'That's all right.' She was stiff and resentful.

'There will be another time soon, I promise.'

'You always promise,' she whispered, but she saw he was no longer listening. He dislodged her and stood up, the heavy jawline clenched and thick dark brows almost meeting above the narrow, straight, aristocratic nose.

'Lock the door when I'm gone, darling. I'll send the driver for you if it's Bravo. He will drive you back to Cambridge and I will let your mother know to expect you.'

He stepped out into the night, still shrugging into his duffle coat, and she listened to the whirl of the starter, the rush of tyres over gravel and the dwindling note of the engine.

The controller in Nairobi tower allowed the British Airways flight from Seychelles to run fifteen seconds past its reporting time. Then he called once, twice and a third time without reply. He switched frequencies to the channels reserved for information, approach, tower and, finally, emergency, on one at least of which 070 should have been maintaining listening watch. There was still no reply.

Speedbird 070 was forty-five seconds past 'operations normal' before he removed the yellow slip from his approach rack and placed it in the emergency 'lost contact' slot, and immediately search and rescue procedures were in force.

Speedbird 070 was two minutes and thirteen seconds past 'operations normal' when the telex pull sheet landed on the British Airways desk at Heathrow Control, and sixteen seconds later Atlas had been informed and had placed Thor Command on condition Alpha.

The moon was three days short of full, its upper rim only slightly indented by the earth's shadow. However, at this altitude it seemed almost as big as the sun itself and its golden light was certainly more beautiful.

In the tropical summer night great silver cloud ranges towered into the sky, and mushroomed into majestic thunder heads, and the moonlight dressed them in splendour.

The aircraft fled swiftly between the peaks of cloud, like a monstrous black bat on back-swept wings it bored into the west.

Under the port-side wing a sudden dark chasm opened in the clouds like the mouth of hell itself, and deep in its maw there was the faint twinkle of far light, like a dying star.

'That will be Madagascar,' said the captain, his voice over-loud in the quiet cockpit. 'We are on track.' And behind his shoulder the girl stirred and carefully transferred the grenade into her other hand before she spoke for the first time in half an hour.

'Some of our passengers might still be awake and notice that.' She glanced at her wristwatch. 'It's time to wake up the others and let them know the good news.' She turned back to the flight engineer. 'Please switch on all the cabin lights and the seat-belt lights and let me have the microphone.'

Cyril Watkins, the captain, was reminded once again that this was a carefully planned operation. The girl was timing her announcement to the passengers when their resistance would be at its lowest possible ebb; at two o'clock in the morning after having been awoken from the disturbed rest of intercontinental flight their immediate reaction was likely to be glum resignation.

'Cabin and seat-belt lights are on,' the engineer told her, and handed her the microphone.

'Good morning, ladies and gentlemen.' Her voice was warm, clear and bright. 'I regret having to waken you at such an inconvenient hour. However, I have a very important announcement to make and I want all of you to pay the most careful attention.' She paused, and in the cavernous and crowded cabins there was a general stir and heads began to lift, hair tousled and eyes unfocused and blinking away the cobwebs of sleep. 'You will notice that the seat-belt lights are on. Will you all check that the persons beside you are fully awake and that their seat belts are fastened. Cabin staff please make certain that this is done.'

She paused again; the belts would inhibit any sudden movement, any spontaneous action at the first shock. Ingrid noted the passage of sixty seconds on the sweep hand of her wristwatch before going on.

'First let me introduce myself. My name is Ingrid. I am a senior officer of the Action Commando for Human Rights—' Captain Watkins curled his lip cynically at the pompous self-righteous title, but kept silent, staring ahead into the starry, moonlit depths of space ' – and this aircraft is under my command. Under no circumstances whatsoever will any of you leave your seats without the express permission of one of my officers – if this order is disobeyed, it will lead directly to the destruction of this aircraft and all aboard by high explosive.'

She repeated the announcement immediately in fluent German, and then in less proficient but clearly intelligible French before reverting to English once again.

'Officers of the Action Commando will wear red shirts for immediate identification and they will be armed.'

As she spoke her three companions in the front of the first-class cabin were stripping out the false bottoms from their canvas flight bags. The space was only two inches deep by fourteen by eight, but it was sufficient for the broken-down twelve bore pistols, and ten rounds of buckshot cartridges. The barrels of the pistols were fourteen inches long, the bores were smooth and made of armoured plastic. This material would not have withstood the passage of a solid bullet through rifling or any of the newer explosive propellants but it had been designed for use with the lower velocity and pressures of multiple shot and cordite. The breech piece was of plastic as were the double pistol grips, and these clipped swiftly into position. The only metal in the entire weapon was the case-steel firing pin and spring, no bigger than one of the metal studs in the canvas flight bag, so they would not have activated the metal detectors of the security check at Mahé airport. The ten cartridges contained in each bag had plastic cases and bases; again only the percussion caps were of aluminium foil, which would not disturb an electrical field. The cartridges were packed in looped cartridge belts which buckled around the waist.

The weapons were short, black and ugly; they required reloading like a conventional shotgun, the spent shells were not self-ejecting and the recoil was so vicious that it would break the wrists of the user who did not bear down heavily on the pistol grips. However, at ranges up to thirty feet the destructive power was awesome, at twelve feet it would disembowel a man and at six feet it would blow his head off cleanly – yet it did not have the penetrating power to hole the pressure hull of an intercontinental airliner.

It was the perfect weapon for the job in hand, and within a few seconds three of them had been assembled and loaded and the two men had slipped on the bright scarlet shirts that identified them over their tee-shirts and moved to their positions – one in the back of the first-class cabin and one in the back of the tourist cabin, they stood with their grotesque weapons ostentatiously displayed.

The slim, pretty, dark-haired German girl stayed in her seat a little longer, working swiftly and neatly as she opened the remaining coco-de-mer and transferred their contents into two of the netting bags. These grenades differed only from the one carried by Ingrid in that they had double red lines painted around the middle. This signified that they were electronically fused.

Now Ingrid's clear young voice resumed over the cabin address system, and the long rows of passengers – all fully awake now – sat rigid and attentive, their faces reflecting an almost uniform expression of shock and trepidation.

' – The officer of the action commando who is moving down the cabin at this time is placing high explosive grenades—' The dark-haired girl started down the aisle, and every fifteen rows she opened one of the overhead lockers and placed a grenade in it, closed the locker and moved on. The passengers' heads revolved slowly in unison as they watched her with the fascination of total horror. 'A single one of those grenades has the explosive power to destroy this aircraft – they were designed to kill by concussion the crew of a battle tank protected by six inches of armour – the officer is placing fourteen of these devices along the length of this aircraft. They can be detonated simultaneously by an electronic transmitter under my control—' the voice contained a hint of mischief now, a little undercurrent of laughter ' – and if that happened they'd hear the bang at the North Pole!'

The passengers stirred like the leaves of a tree in a vagrant breeze; somewhere a woman began to weep. It was a strangled passionless sound and nobody even looked in her direction.

'But don't worry yourselves. That isn't going to happen. Because everybody is going to do exactly as they are told, and when it's all over you are going to be proud of your part in this operation. We are all partners in a noble and glorious mission, we are all warriors for freedom and for the dignity of man. Today we take a mighty step forward into the new world – a world purged and cleansed of injustice and tyranny and dedicated to the welfare of all its peoples.'

The woman was still weeping, and now a child joined her on a higher, more strident note.

The dark-haired girl returned to her seat and now she retrieved the camera that had activated the metal detector at Mahé airport. She slung it around her neck and crouched again to assemble the two remaining shot pistols; carrying them and the cartridge belts she hurried forward to the flight deck where the big blonde kissed her delightedly and unashamedly on the lips.

'Karen, *Liebling*, you were wonderful.' And then she took the camera from her and slung it around her own neck.

'This—' she explained to the captain ' – is not what it appears to be. It is the remote radio detonator for the grenades in the fuselage.'

He nodded without replying, and with obvious relief Ingrid disarmed the grenade that she had carried for so long by replacing the safety pin. She handed it to the other girl.

'How much longer to the coast?' she asked as she strapped and buckled the cartridge belt around her waist.

'Thirty-two minutes,' said the flight engineer promptly, and Ingrid opened the breech of the pistol, checked the load and then snapped it closed again.

'You and Henri can stand down now,' she told Karen. 'Try and sleep.'

The operation might last many days still, and exhaustion would be the most dangerous enemy they would have to contend with. It was for this reason alone that they had employed such a large force. From now on, except in an emergency, two of them would be on duty and two would be resting.

'You have done a very professional job,' said the pilot, Cyril Watkins, ' – so far.'

'Thank you.' Ingrid laughed, and over the back of his

seat placed a comradely hand on his shoulder. 'We have practised very hard for this day.'

Peter Stride dipped his lights three times as he raced down the long narrow alley that led to the gates of the compound without slowing the Rover, and the sentry swung the gate open just in time for him to roar through.

There were no floodlights, no bustling activity – just the two aircraft standing together in the echoing cavern of the hangar.

The Lockheed Hercules seemed to fill the entire building, that had been built to accommodate the smaller bombers of World War II. The tall vertical fin of its epinage reached to within a few feet of the roof girders.

Beside it the Hawker Siddeley HS 125 executive jet seemed dainty and ineffectual. The differing origins of the machines emphasized that this unit was a co-operative venture between two nations.

This was underscored once more when Colin Noble hurried forward to meet Peter as he cut the Rover's engine and lights.

'A grand night for it, Peter.' There was no mistaking the drawl of mid-Western America, although Colin looked more like a successful used-car salesman than a colonel in the U.S. Marines. In the beginning Peter had believed that this strict apportioning of material and manpower on equal national lines might weaken the effectiveness of Atlas. He no longer had those doubts.

Colin wore the nondescript blue overalls and cloth cap, both embroidered with the legend 'THOR COMMUNI-CATIONS' which deliberately made him look more of a technician than a soldier.

Colin was Peter's second in command. They had known each other only the six weeks since Peter had assumed command of Thor – but after a short period of mutual wariness the two men had formed one of those fast bonds of liking and mutual respect.

Colin was of medium height, but none the less a big man. First glance might have given the impression that he was fat, for his body had a certain toad-like spread to it. There was no fat upon his frame, however, it was all muscle and bone. He had boxed heavyweight for Princeton and the marines, and his nose above the wide laughing mouth had been broken just below the bridge, it was lumped and twisted slightly.

Colin cultivated the boisterous bluff manner of a career athlete, but his eyes were the colour of burned toffee and were brightly intelligent and all-seeing. He was tough and leery as an old alley cat. It was not easy to earn the respect of Peter Stride. Colin had done so in under six weeks.

He stood now between the two aircraft, while his men went about their Alpha preparation with quick understated efficiency.

Both aircraft were painted in commercial airline style, blue and white and gold, with a stylized portrait of the Thunder God on the tail fin and the 'THOR COMMUNICATIONS' title down the fuselage. They could land at any airport in the world without causing undue comment.

'What is the buzz, Colin?' Peter Stride demanded as he slammed the Rover's door and hurried to meet the American. It had taken him some time and conscious effort to adapt his language and mode of address to fit in with his new second-in-command. He had learned very early not to expect that, merely because he was the youngest major-general in the British army, Colonel Colin Noble was going to call him 'Sir' every time he spoke.

'Missing aircraft.' It could have been a train, an embassy,

even an ocean liner, Peter realized. 'British Airways. For Chrissake let's get out of the cold.' The wind was flapping the legs of Colin's overalls and tugging at his sleeves.

'Where?'

'Indian Ocean.'

'Are we set for Bravo?' Peter asked as they climbed into his command plane.

'All set.'

The interior of the Hawker had been restyled to make it a compact headquarters and communications centre.

There was comfortable seating for four officers directly behind the flight deck. Then the two electronic engineers and their equipment occupied a separate rear compartment, beyond which were the small toilet and galley in the extreme rear.

One of the technicians looked through the communicating door as Peter stooped into the cabin. 'Good evening, General Stride – we have a direct link with Atlas established.'

'Put him on the screen,' he ordered as he sank into the padded leather of his chair behind the small working desk.

There was a single fourteen-inch main television screen in the panel directly facing Peter, and above it four smaller six-inch screens for conference communication. The main screen came alive, and the image of the big noble leonine head firmed.

'Good afternoon, Peter.' The smile was warm, charismatic, compelling.

'Good evening, sir.'

And Dr Kingston Parker tilted his head slightly to acknowledge the reference to the time difference between Washington and England.

'Right at this moment we are in the dark completely. All we have is that BA 070 with four hundred and one passengers and sixteen crew on a flight from Mahé to Nairobi has not reported for thirty-two minutes.'

Parker was Chairman of the Intelligence Oversight Board, among other duties, and he reported directly to the President of the United States in that capacity. He was the President's personal and trusted friend. They had been in the same class at Annapolis, both of them had graduated in the top twenty but, unlike the President, Parker had gone directly into government.

Parker was an artist, a talented musician, the author of four scholarly works of philosophy and politics, and a grand master of chess. A man of overwhelming presence, of vast humanity and towering intelligence. Yet also he was a secret man, avoiding the glaring scrutiny of the media, hiding his ambitions, if ambitions he had – although the presidency of the United States would not be an impossible dream to such a man – only taking up with rare skill and strength any burden that was thrust upon him.

Peter Stride had met him personally on half a dozen occasions since being seconded to Thor. He had spent a weekend with Parker at his New York home, and his respect for the man had become boundless. Peter realized that he was the perfect head for such a complex concept as Atlas: it needed the philosopher's tempering influence over trained soldiers, it needed the tact and charisma of the diplomat to deal directly with the heads of two governments, and it needed that steely intellect to make the ultimate decision that could involve hundreds of innocent lives and incur fearsome political consequences.

Now swiftly and incisively he told Peter what little they knew of Flight 070 and what search and rescue routine was already in force, before going on, 'Without being alarmist, this does seem to be the perfect target. The flight carries most of the world's leading surgeons, and the convention was public knowledge eighteen months ago. Doctors have the necessary image to appeal to public sentiment and their nationalities are nicely mixed – American, British, French, Scandinavian, German, Italian – three of those countries

23

have notoriously *soft* records with militant activity. It's a British aircraft, and the final destination would probably have been chosen to further complicate the issue and inhibit any counter-action.'

Parker paused, and a small crease of worry appeared for a moment in the broad smooth forehead.

'I have put Mercury on condition Alpha as well – if this is a strike the final destination could just as easily be eastwards of the aircraft's last reported position.'

Atlas's offensive arm comprised three identical units. Thor would be used only in Europe or Africa. Mercury was based on the American Naval base in Indonesia and covered Asia and Australasia, while Diana was in Washington itself and ready for counteraction in either of the American continents.

'I have Tanner of Mercury on the other relay now. I will be back to you in a few seconds, Peter.'

'Very well, sir.'

The screen went blank, and in the chair beside him Colin Noble lit one of his expensive Dutch cheroots and crossed his ankles on the desk in front of him.

'Seems the great god Thor came down to earth for a little poontang. When he'd finished pleasuring one of the vestal virgins he thought he'd let her know the honour she'd been given. "I'm Thor," he told her. "Tho am I," she agreed, "but it wath loth of fun."'

Peter shook his head sorrowfully. 'That's funny?' he asked.

'Helps to while away the time.' Colin glanced at his wristwatch. 'If this is another false alarm, it's going to make it thirteen straight.' He yawned. There was nothing to do. It had all been done before. Everything was in the ultimate state of readiness. In the huge Hercules transport, every item of a comprehensive arsenal of equipment was ready for instant use. The thirty highly trained soldiers were embarked. The flight crews of both aircraft were at their

24

stations, the communications technicians had set up their links with satellites and through them to the available intelligence computers in Washington and London. It remained only to wait – the greater part of a soldier's life was spent waiting, but Peter had never become hardened to it. It helped now to have the companionship of Colin Noble.

In a life spent in the company of many men it was difficult to form close relationships. Here in the smaller closed ranks of Thor in shared endeavour they had achieved that and become friends, and their conversation was relaxed and desultory, moving casually from subject to subject, but without relaxing the undercurrent of alertness that gripped both men.

At one stage Kingston Parker came on the screen again to tell them that search and rescue aircraft had found no indications at the last reported position of 070, and that a photographic run by the 'Big Bird' reconnaissance satellite had been made over the same area, but that film would not be ready for appraisal for another fourteen hours. Speedbird 070 was now one hour six minutes past 'operations normal' and suddenly Peter remembered Melissa-Jane. He asked communications for a telephone line and dialled the cottage. There was no reply, so the driver would have collected her already. He hung up and rang Cynthia in Cambridge.

'Damn it, Peter. This really is most inconsiderate of you.' Freshly aroused from sleep, her voice was petulant, immediately awakening only antipathies. 'Melissa has been looking forward to this—'

'Yes, I know, and so have I.'

' – and George and I had arranged—' George, her new husband, was a Political History don; despite himself Peter quite liked the man. He had been very good to Melissa-Jane.

'The exigencies of the service.' Peter cut in lightly – and her voice took on a bitter edge.

25

'How often I had to listen to that – I hoped never to hear it again.' They were on the same futile old treadmill, and he had to stop it.

'Look, Cynthia. Melissa is on her way—'

In front of him the big television screen lit and Kingston Parker's eyes were dark with regret, as though he mourned for all mankind.

'I have to go,' Peter told the woman whom once he had loved, and broke the connection, leaning forward attentively towards the image on the screen.

'The South African radar defences have painted an unidentified target approaching their airspace,' Kingston Parker told him. 'Its speed and position correspond with those of 070. They have scrambled a Mirage flight to intercept – but in the meantime I'm assuming that it's a militant strike and we'll go immediately to condition Bravo, if you please, Peter.'

'We are on our way, sir.'

And beside him Colin Noble took his feet off the desk and thumped them together onto the floor. The cheroot was still clamped between his teeth.

The target was live and the pilot of the leading Mirage F.1 interceptor had his flight computer in 'attack' mode and all his weaponry – missiles and cannon – were armed. The computer gave him a time to intercept of thirty-three seconds, and the target's heading was constant at 210° magnetic and its ground speed at 483 knots.

Ahead of him the dawn was rising in wildly theatrical display. Avalanches of silver and pink cloud tumbled down the sky, and the sun, still below the horizon, flung long lances of golden light across the heavens. The pilot leaned forward against his shoulder straps and lifted the Polaroid visor of his helmet with one gloved hand, straining ahead for the first glimpse of the target.

His trained gunfighter's eye picked out the dark speck against the distracting background of cloud and sunlight and he made an almost imperceptible movement of the controls to avoid the direct head-on approach to the target.

The speck swelled in size with disturbing rapidity as they converged at combined speeds of nearly fifteen hundred miles per hour, and at the instant he was certain of his identification the leader took his flight, still in a tight 'finger five', up into a vertical climb from which they rolled out neatly five thousand feet above the target and on the same heading, immediately reducing power to conform in speed to the big aircraft far below.

'Cheetah, this is Diamond leader – we are visual, and target is a Boeing 747 bearing British Airways markings.'

'Diamond Leader, this is Cheetah, conform to target, maintain five thousand feet separation and avoid any threatening attitudes. Report again in sixty seconds.'

Major-General Peter Stride's executive jet was arrowing southwards and leaving its enormous protégé lumbering ponderously along in its wake. Every minute increased the distance between the two aircraft, and by the time they reached their ultimate destination – wherever that might be – there would probably be a thousand miles or more separating them.

However, the big Hercules's slow speed became a virtue when the need arose to take its heavy load of men and equipment into short unsurfaced strips in unlikely corners of the earth – perhaps in the 'hot and high' conditions that a pilot most dreads.

It was the Hawker's job to get Peter Stride to the scene of terrorist activity as swiftly as possible, and the general's job once there to stall and procrastinate and bargain until Colin Noble's assault team caught up with him.

The two men were still in contact, however, and the small central television screen in front of Peter was permanently lit with a view of the interior of the Hercules's main hold. When he lifted his head from his work, Peter Stride could see a picture of his troops, all in the casual Thor overalls, lounging or sprawled in abandoned attitudes of relaxation down the central aisle of the Hercules. They also were veterans at the hard game of waiting, while in the foreground Colin Noble sat at his small work desk, going through the voluminous check list for 'condition Charlie' which was the next state of alert when terrorist activity was confirmed.

Watching Colin Noble at work, Peter Stride found a moment to ponder once again the enormous cost of maintaining Atlas, most of it paid by the United States intelligence budget, and the obstacles and resistance that had been overcome to launch the project in the first place. Only the success of the Israelis at Entebbe and of the Germans at Mogadishu had made it possible, but there was still violent opposition in both countries to maintaining a dual national counteraction force.

With a preliminary click and hum the central screen of Peter's communications console came alive and Dr Parker spoke before his image had properly hardened.

'I'm afraid it's condition Charlie, Peter,' he said softly, and Peter was aware of the rush of his blood through his veins. It was natural for a soldier whose entire life had been spent in training for a special moment in time to welcome the arrival of that moment – yet he found contempt for himself in that emotion; no sane man should anticipate violence and death, and all the misery and suffering which attended them.

' – the South Africans have intercepted and identified 070. It entered their airspace forty-five seconds ago.'

'Radio contact?' Peter asked.

'No.' Parker shook his great head. 'It is declining contact, and we must assume that it is under the control of militants – so now I'm going to be at this desk until this thing is settled.' Kingston Parker never used the emotive word 'terrorist' and he did not like to hear it from his subordinates either.

'Never hate your adversary blindly,' he had told Peter once. 'Understand his motives, recognize and respect his strengths – and you will be better prepared to meet him.'

'What co-operation can we expect?' Peter asked.

'All African States that we have so far been able to contact have offered full co-operation, including overflight, landing and refuelling facilities – and the South Africans are being helpful. I have spoken to their defence minister and he has offered the fullest possible co-operation. They will refuse 070 landing clearance, of course, and I anticipate that it will have to go on to one of the black states farther north, which is probably the militants' intention anyway. I think you know my views about South Africa – but in this instance I must say they are being very good.'

Parker brought into the television shot a black briar pipe with a big round bowl, and began to stuff it with tobacco. His hands were large, like the rest of his body, but the fingers were long and supple as those of a pianist – which of course he was. And Peter remembered the scented smell of the tobacco he smoked. Even though he was a non-smoker, Peter had not found the odour offensive. Both men were silent, deep in thought, Parker frowning slightly as he seemed to concentrate on his pipe. Then he sighed and looked up again.

'All right, Peter. Let's hear what you have.'

Peter shuffled through the notes he had been making. 'I have prepared four tentative scenarios and our responses to each, sir. The most important consideration is whether this is a strike "à l'allemande" or "à l'italienne"—'

Parker nodded, listening; although this was well-travelled ground they must go over it again. A strike in the Italian fashion was the easier to resolve, a straight demand for cash. The German tradition involved release of prisoners, social and political demands that crossed national boundaries. They worked on for another hour before they were interrupted again.

'Good God.' It was a measure of Kingston Parker's astonishment that he used such strong language. 'We have a new development here—'

I t was only when 070 joined the eastern airway and began to initiate a standard approach and let down, without however obtaining air traffic control clearance, that South African Airforce Command suddenly realized what was about to happen.

Immediately emergency silence was imposed on all the aviation frequencies while the approaching flight was bombarded by urgent commands to immediately vacate national airspace. There was no response whatsoever, and one hundred and fifty nautical miles out from Jan Smuts International Airport the Boeing reduced power and commenced a sedate descent to enter controlled airspace.

'British Airways 070 this is Jan Smuts Control, you are expressly refused clearance to join the circuit. Do you read me, 070?'

'British Airways 070 this is Airforce Command. You are warned that you are in violation of national airspace. You are ordered to climb immediately to thirty thousand feet and turn on course for Nairobi.'

The Boeing was a hundred nautical miles out and descending through fifteen thousand feet.

'Diamond Leader, this is Cheetah. Take the target under command and enforce departure clearance.'

The long sleek aircraft in its mottled green and brown battle camouflage dropped like a dart, rapidly overhauling the huge multi-engined giant, diving down just behind the tailplane and then pulling up steeply in front of the gaily painted red, white and blue nose.

Skilfully the Mirage pilot stationed his nimble little machine one hundred feet ahead of the Boeing and rocked his wings in the 'Follow me' command.

The Boeing sailed on serenely as though it had not seen or understood. The Mirage pilot nudged his throttles and the gap between the two aircraft narrowed down to fifty feet. Again he rocked his wings and began a steady rate-one turn onto the northerly heading ordered by Cheetah.

The Boeing held rock steady on its standard approach towards Johannesburg, forcing the Mirage leader to abandon his attempts to lead her away.

He edged back alongside, keeping just above the jet-blast of the Boeing's port engines until he was level with the cockpit and could stare across a gap of merely fifty feet.

'Cheetah, this is Diamond One. I have a good view into target's flight deck. There is a fourth person in the cockpit. It's a woman. She appears to be armed with a machine pistol.'

The faces of the two pilots were white as bone as they turned to watch the interceptor. The woman leaned over the back of the left-hand seat, and lifted the clumsy black weapon in an ironic salute. She smiled and the Mirage pilot was close enough to see how white her teeth were.

' – a young woman, blonde hair, *mooi, baie mooi*—' the Mirage pilot reported. 'Pretty – very pretty.'

'Diamond One, this is Cheetah. Position for head-on attack.'

The Mirage thundered instantly ahead and climbed away swiftly, the other four aircraft of the flight sweeping in to resume their tight 'finger five' formation as they went out in a wide turn ahead of the Boeing.

'Cheetah. We are in position for a head-on attack.'

'Diamond Flight. Simulate. Attack in line astern. Five-second intervals. Minimum separation. Do not, I say again, do not open fire. This is a simulated attack. I say again, this is a simulated attack.'

'Diamond One – understands simulated attack.'

And the Mirage F.1 winged over and dived, its speed rocketing around the mach scale, booming through the sonic barrier in a fearsomely aggressive display.

Cyril Watkins saw him coming from seven miles ahead.

'Jesus,' he shouted. 'This is real,' and he lunged forward to take manual control of the Boeing, to pull her off the automatic approach that the electronic flight director was performing.

'Hold her steady.' Ingrid raised her voice for the first time. 'Hold it.' She swung the gaping double muzzles of the shot pistol onto the flight engineer. 'We don't need a navigator now.'

The captain froze, and the Mirage howled down on them, seemed to grow until it filled the whole view through the windshield ahead. At the last possible instant of time the nose lifted slightly and it flashed only feet overhead, but the supersonic turbulence of its passage struck and tossed even that huge machine like a piece of thistledown.

'Here comes another,' Cyril Watkins shouted.

'I mean it.' Ingrid pressed the muzzles so fiercely into the back of the flight engineer's neck that his forehead struck the edge of his computer console, and there was the quick bright rose of blood on the pale skin.

The jet blasts struck the Boeing one after the other as the Mirages attacked. Ingrid clutched wildly for support with her free hand, but kept the pistol jammed into the navigator's neck. 'I mean it,' she kept shouting. 'I'll kill him,' and they could hear the screams of the passengers even through the bulkhead of the flight deck.

Then the last Mirage was passed and gone and the Boeing's flight director recovered from the battering of close separation and quickly realigned the aircraft on the radio navigational beacons of Jan Smuts Airport.

'They won't buzz us again.' Ingrid stepped back from the flight engineer, allowing him to lift his head and wipe away the trickle of blood on the sleeve of his shirt. 'They can't come again. We are into controlled airspace.' She pointed ahead. 'Look!'

The Boeing was down to five thousand feet, but the horizon was obscured by the haze of smog and summer heat. To the right rose the smooth silhouette of the Kempton Park Power Station cooling towers and, closer at hand, the poisonous yellow tablelands of the mine dumps squatted on the flat and featureless plain of the African highveld. Around them human habitation was so dense that hundreds of windowpanes caught the early morning sun and glittered like beacons.

Closer still was the long, straight, blue streak of the main runway of Jan Smuts Airport.

'Take her straight in on runway 21,' Ingrid ordered.

'We can't—'

'Do it,' snapped the girl. 'Air traffic control will have cleared the circuit. They can't stop us.'

'Yes, they can,' Cyril Watkins answered. 'Just take a look at the runway apron.'

They were close enough now to count five fuel tenders, to see the Shell company insignia on the tanks.

'They are going to block the runway.'

With the tankers were five brilliant red vehicles of the fire service and two big white ambulances. They bumped wildly over the grass verge of the runway and then, one after the other, tenders and fire control vehicles and ambulances parked at intervals of a few hundred yards down the white-painted centre line of the runway.

'We can't land,' said the captain.

'Take her off automatic and fly her in by hand.' The girl's voice was different, hard, cruel.

The Boeing was sinking through a thousand feet, lined up for runway 21 and directly ahead the revolving red beacons on top of the fire vehicles seemed to flash a direct challenge.

'I can't pile into them,' Cyril Watkins decided, and there was no longer hesitation nor doubt in his tone. 'I'm going to overshoot and get out of here.'

'Land on the grass,' the girl shrieked. 'There is open grass on the left of the runway – put her down there.'

But Cyril Watkins had leaned forward in his seat and rammed the bank of throttles forward. The engines howled and the Boeing surged into a nose-high climb.

The young flight engineer had swivelled his stool and was staring ahead through the windscreen. His whole body was rigid, his expression intense and the smear of blood across his forehead was in vivid contrast to the pallor of his skin.

With his right hand he gripped the edge of his desk, and the knuckles of his fist were white and shiny as eggshell.

Without seeming to move the blonde girl had pinned the wrist of that rigid right hand, pressing the muzzles of the pistol into it.

There was a crash of sound, so violent in the confines of the cabin that it seemed to beat in their eardrums. The weapon kicked up as high as the girl's golden head and there was the immediate acrid stench of burned cordite.

The flight engineer stared down incredulously at the desk top. There was a hole blown through the metal as big as a teacup, and the edges were jagged with bright bare metal.

The blast of shot had amputated his hand cleanly at the wrist. The severed member had been thrown forward into the space between the pilots' seats, with the shattered bone protruding from the mangled meat. It twitched like a crushed and maimed insect.

'Land,' said the girl. 'Land or the next shot is through his head.'

'You bloody monster,' shouted Cyril Watkins, staring at the severed hand.

'Land or you will be responsible for this man's life.'

The flight engineer clutched the stump of his arm against his belly and doubled over it silently, his face contorted by the shock.

Cyril Watkins tore his stricken gaze from the severed hand and looked ahead once more. There was wide open grass between the runway markers and the narrow taxiway. The grass had been mown knee-high, and he knew the ground beneath it would be fairly smooth.

Cyril's hand on the throttle bank pulled back smoothly, almost of its own volition, the engine thunder died away and the nose dropped again.

He held his approach aligned with the main runway until he was well in over the threshold lights. He did not want to alert the drivers of the blocking vehicles to his intention while they still had time to counter it.

'You murderous bitch,' he said under his breath. 'You filthy murderous bitch.'

He banked the Boeing steeply, realigned it with the long strip of open grass and cut the throttles completely, bringing her in nose-high and just a fraction above the stall, flaring out deliberately low and banging the Boeing down into the grass for positive touch down.

The huge machine settled to the rough strip, jolting and lurching wildly as Cyril Watkins fought the rudders to keep them lined up, holding his nose wheel off with the control yoke, while his co-pilot threw all her giant engines into reverse thrust and trod firmly down on the main landing gear brakes.

The fire engines and fuel tankers flashed past the starboard wing tip. The startled faces of their crews seemed very close and white – then 070 was past, her speed bleeding off sharply so her nose wheel dropped and she rocked and swayed gradually to a dead stop just short of the brick building which housed the approach and landing beacons, and the main radar installations.

It was 7.25 a.m. local time and Speedbird 070 was down.

'Well, they are down,' intoned Kingston Parker. 'And you can well understand the extreme efforts that were made to prevent them. Their choice of final destination settles one of your queries, Peter.'

'"À l'allemande"—' Peter nodded. 'It's got to be political. I agree, sir.'

'And you and I must now face in dreadful reality what we have discussed only in lofty theory—' Parker held a taper to his pipe and puffed twice before going on. ' – Morally justifiable militancy.'

'Again we have to differ, sir.' Peter cut in swiftly. 'There is no such thing.'

'Is there not?' Parker asked, shaking his head. 'What of the German officers killed in the streets of Paris by the French resistance?'

'That was war,' Peter exclaimed.

'Perhaps the group that seized 070 believes that they are at war—'

'With innocent victims?' Peter shot back.

'The *Haganah* took innocent victims – yet what they were fighting for was right and just.'

'I'm an Englishman, Dr Parker – you cannot expect me to condone the murder of British women and children.' Peter had stiffened in his chair.

'No,' Parker agreed. 'So let us not speak of the MauMau

36

in Kenya, nor of present-day Ireland then – but what of the French Revolution or the spreading of the Catholic faith by the most terrible persecution and tortures yet devised by man – were those not morally justifiable militancy?'

'I would prefer to call it understandable but reprehensible. Terrorism in any form can never be morally justifiable.' Provoked himself, Peter used the word deliberately to provoke and saw the small lift of Parker's thick bushy eyebrows.

'There is terrorism from above – as well as from below.' Parker picked up the word and used it deliberately. 'If you define terrorism as extreme physical or physiological coercion used to induce others to submit to the will of the terrorist – there is the legal terror threat of the gallows, the religious terror threat of hell fire, the paternal terror threat of the cane – are those more morally justifiable than the aspiration of the weak, the poor, the politically oppressed, the powerless victims of an unjust society? Is their scream of protest to be strangled—'

Peter shifted uncomfortably in his chair. 'Protest outside the law—'

'Laws are made by man, almost always by the rich and the powerful – laws are changed by men, usually only after militant action. The women's suffragette movement, the civil rights campaign in this country—' Parker broke off and chuckled. 'I'm sorry, Peter. Sometimes I confuse myself. It's often more difficult to be a liberal than it is to be a tyrant. At least the tyrant seldom has doubts.' Parker lay back in his chair, a dismissive gesture. 'I propose to leave you in peace for an hour or two now. You will want to develop your plans in line with the new developments. But I personally have no doubts now that we are dealing with politically motivated militants, and not merely a gang of old-fashioned kidnappers after a fast buck. Of one other thing I am certain: before we see this one through we will be forced to examine our own consciences very closely.'

'Take the second right,' said Ingrid quietly, and the Boeing swung off the grass onto the taxiway. There seemed to be no damage to her landing gear, but now that she had left her natural element, the aircraft had lost grace and beauty and became lumbering and ungainly.

The girl had never been on the flight deck of a grounded Jumbo before, and the height was impressive. It gave her a feeling of detachment, of being invulnerable.

'Now left again,' she instructed, and the Boeing turned away from the main airport building towards the southern end of the runway. The observation deck of the airport's flat roof was already lined with hundreds of curious spectators, but all activity on the apron was suspended. The waiting machines and tenders were deserted, not a single human figure on the tarmac.

'Park there.' She pointed ahead to an open area four hundred yards from the nearest building, midway between the terminal and the cluster of service hangars and the main fuel depot. 'Stop on the intersection.'

Grimly silent, Cyril Watkins did as he was ordered, and then turned in his seat.

'I must call an ambulance to get him off.'

The co-pilot and a stewardess had the flight engineer stretched out on the galley floor, just beyond the door to the flight deck. They were using linen table napkins to bind up the arm and try and staunch the bleeding. The stench of cordite still lingered and mingled with the taint of fresh blood.

'Nobody leaves this aircraft.' The girl shook her head. 'He knows too much about us already.'

'My God, woman. He needs medical attention.'

'There are three hundred doctors aboard—' she pointed out indifferently. 'The best in the world. Two of them may come forward and attend to him.'

She perched sideways on the flight engineer's blood-splattered desk, and thumbed the internal microphone.

Cyril Watkins noticed even in his outrage that it needed only a single demonstration and Ingrid was able to work the complicated communications equipment. She was bright and very well trained.

'Ladies and gentlemen, we have landed at Johannesburg Airport. We will be here for a long time – perhaps days, even weeks. All our patience will be tried, so I must warn you that any disobedience will be most severely dealt with. Already one attempt at resistance has been made – and in consequence a member of the crew has been shot and gravely wounded. He may die of this wound. We do not want a repetition of this incident. However, I must again warn you that my officers and I will not hesitate to shoot again, or even to detonate the explosives above your heads – if the need arises.'

She paused and watched a moment as two selected doctors came forward and knelt on each side of the flight engineer. He was shaking like a fever victim with shock, his white shirt splashed and daubed with blood. Her expression showed no remorse, no real concern, and her voice was calm and light as she went on.

'Two of my officers will now pass down the aisles and they will collect your passports from you. Please have these documents ready.'

Her eyes flicked sideways, as movement caught her eye. From beyond the service hangars a line of four armoured cars emerged in line ahead. They were the locally manufactured version of the French Panhard with heavily lugged tall tyres, a raked turret and the disproportionately long barrels of the cannons trained forward. The armoured vehicles circled cautiously and parked three hundred yards out, at the four points – wing tips, tail and nose – around the aircraft, with the long cannon trained upon her.

The girl watched them disdainfully until one of the doctors pushed himself in front of her. He was a short, chubby little man, balding – but brave.

'This man must be taken to a hospital immediately.'

'That is out of the question.'

'I insist. His life is in danger.'

'All our lives are in danger, doctor.' She paused and let that make its effect. 'Draw up a list of your requirements. I will see that you get them.'

'They have been down for sixteen hours now and the only contact has been a request for medical supplies and for a power link-up to the electrical mains.' Kingston Parker had removed his jacket and loosened the knot of his tie, but was showing no other ill effects of his vigil.

Peter Stride nodded at the image on the screen. 'What have your medics made of the supplies?' he asked.

'Looks like a gunshot casualty. Whole blood type AB Positive, that's rare but one of the crew is cross-matched AB Positive on his service record. Ten litres of plasmalyte B, a blood-giving set and syringes, morphine and intravenous penicillin, tetanus toxoid – all the equipment needed to treat massive physical trauma.'

'And they are on mains power?' Peter asked.

'Yes, four hundred people would have suffocated by now without the air-conditioning. The airport authority has laid a cable and plugged it into the external socket. All the aircraft's support system – even the galley heating – will be fully functional.'

'So we will be able to throw the switch on them at any time.' Peter made a note on the pad in front of him. 'But no demands yet? No negotiator called for?'

'No, nothing. They seem fully aware of the techniques of bargaining in this type of situation – unlike our friends, the host country. I am afraid we are having a great deal of trouble with the Wyatt Earp mentality—' Parker paused. 'I'm sorry, Wyatt Earp was one of our frontier marshals—'

'I saw the movie, and read the book,' Peter answered tartly.

'Well, the South Africans are itching to storm the aircraft, and both our ambassador and yours are hard pressed to restrain them. They are all set to kick the doors of the saloon open and rush in with six-guns blazing. They must also have seen the movie.'

Peter felt the crawl of horror down his spine. 'That would be a certain disaster,' he said quickly. 'These people are running a tight operation.'

'You don't have to convince me,' Parker agreed. 'What is your flying time to Jan Smuts now?'

'We crossed the Zambesi River seven minutes ago.' Peter glanced sideways through the perspex bubble window, but the ground was obscured by haze and cumulus cloud. 'We have another two hours ten minutes to fly – but my support section is three hours forty behind us.'

'All right, Peter. I will get back onto them. The South African Government has convened a full cabinet meeting, and both our ambassadors are sitting in as observers and advisers. I think I am going to be obliged to tell them about the existence of Atlas.'

He paused a moment. 'Here at last we are seeing Atlas justified, Peter. A single unit, cutting across all national considerations, able to act swiftly and independently. I think you should know that I have already obtained the agreement of the President and of your Prime Minister to condition Delta – at my discretion.'

Condition Delta was the kill decision.

' – but again I emphasize that I will implement Delta only as a last possible resort. I want to hear and consider the demands first, and in that respect we are open to negotiation – fully open—'

Parker went on speaking, and Peter Stride shifted slightly, dropping his chin into the cup of his hand to hide his irritation. They were into an area of dispute now – and once again Peter had to voice disagreement.

'Every time you let a militant walk away from a strike you immediately create the conditions for further strikes, to free the captive.'

'I have the clearance for condition Delta,' Parker reiterated with a trace of acid in his tone now, 'but I am making it clear that it will be used only with the greatest discretion. We are not an assassination unit, General Stride.' Parker nodded to an assistant off-screen. 'I am going through to the South Africans now to explain Atlas.' The image receded into darkness.

Peter Stride leapt up abruptly and tried to pace the narrow aisle between the seats, but there was insufficient headroom for his tall frame and he flung himself angrily into the seat again.

Kingston Parker stood up from his communications desk in the outer office of his suite in the west wing of the Pentagon. The two communications technicians scurried out of his way and his personal secretary opened the door to his inner office.

He moved with peculiar grace for such a large man, and there was no excess weight on his frame, his big heavy bones lean of flesh. His clothes were of fine cloth, well cut – the best that Fifth Avenue could offer – but they were worn almost to the point of shoddiness, the button-down collar slightly frayed, the Italian shoes scuffed at the toes as though material trappings counted not at all with him. Nevertheless he wore them with a certain unconscious panache, and he looked ten years younger than his fifty-three, only a few silver strands in the thick bushy mane of hair.

The inner office was Spartan in its furnishings, all of it U.S. Government issue, utilitarian and impersonal, only the books that filled every shelf and the grand piano were his own. The piano was a Bechstein grand and much too large for the room. Parker ran his right hand lightly across the keyboard as he passed it – but he went on to the desk.

He dropped into the swivel chair and shuffled through the dozen intelligence folders on his desk. Each of them contained the latest computer print-outs that he had requested. There were personal histories, appraisals, and character studies of all the personalities that had so far become involved in the taking of Speedbird 070.

Both the ambassadors – their pink files signified the highest security ratings, and were marked 'Heads of Departments only'. Four other files in lower echelon green were devoted to the South African Government personalities with decision-making capabilities in an emergency. The thickest file was that of the South African Prime Minister – and once again Parker noted wryly that the man had been imprisoned by the pro-British government of General Jan Smuts during World War II as a militant opponent of his country's involvement in that war. He wondered just how much sympathy he would have for other militants now.

There were files for the South African Ministers of Defence and of Justice, and still slimmer green files for the Commissioner of Police and for the Assistant Commissioner who had been given the on-site responsibility of handling the emergency. Of them all only the Prime Minister emerged as a distinct personality – a powerful bulldog figure, not a man easily influenced or dissuaded, and instinctively Kingston Parker recognized that ultimate authority rested here.

There was one other pink file at the bottom of the

considerable stack, so well handled that the cardboard cover was splitting at the hinge. The original print-out in this file had been requisitioned two years previously, with quarterly up-dates since that time.

'STRIDE PETER CHARLES' it was headed – and reclassified 'Head of Atlas only'.

Kingston Parker could probably have recited its contents by heart – but he untied the ribbons now, and opened it in his lap.

Puffing deliberately at his pipe he began to turn slowly through the loose pages.

There were the bare bones of the subject's life. Born 1939, one of twin war-time babies of a military family, his father killed in action three years later when the armoured brigade of guards he commanded was overrun by one of Erwin Rommel's devastating drives across the deserts of North Africa. The elder twin brother had inherited the baronetcy and Peter followed the well-travelled family course, Harrow and Sandhurst, where he must have disconcerted the family by his academic brilliance and his reluctance to participate in team sports – preferring the loner activities of golf and tennis and long-distance running.

Kingston Parker pondered that a moment. They were pointers to the man's character that had disconcerted him as well. Parker had the intellectual's generalized contempt for the military, and he would have preferred a man who conformed more closely to his ideal of the brass-headed soldier.

Yet when the young Stride had entered his father's regiment, it seemed that the exceptional intelligence had been diverted into conventional channels and the preference for independent thought and action held in check, if not put aside completely – until his regiment was sent to Cyprus at the height of the unrest in that country. Within a week of arrival the young Stride had been seconded, with his commanding officer's enthusiastic approval, to central army intelligence. Perhaps the commanding officer had already become aware of the problems involved in harbouring a wonder-boy in the tradition-bound portals of his officers' mess.

For once the military had made a logical, if not an outright brilliant, choice. Stride in the sixteen years since then had not made a single mistake, apart from the marriage which had ended in divorce within two years. Had he remained with his regiment that might have affected his career – but since Cyprus Stride's progress had been as unconventional and meteoric as his brain.

In a dozen different and difficult assignments since then, he had honed his gifts and developed new talents; rising against the trend of reduced British expenditure on defence, he had reached staff rank before thirty years of age.

At NATO Headquarters he had made powerful friends and admirers on both sides of the Atlantic, and at the end of his three-year term in Brussels he had been promoted to major-general and been transferred to head British Intelligence in Ireland, bringing his own particular dedication and flair to the job.

A great deal of the credit for containing the sweep of Irish terrorism through Britain was his, and his in-depth study of the urban guerrilla and the mind of the militant, although classified departmentally, was probably the definitive work on the subject.

The Atlas concept was first proposed in this study, and so it was that Stride had been on the short list to head the project. It seemed certain the appointment would be made – the Americans had been impressed with his study and his friends from NATO had not forgotten him. His appointment was approved in principle. Then at the last moment there had developed sudden and intense opposition to the appointment of a professional soldier to head such a sensitive agency. The opposition had come from both Whitehall and Washington simultaneously, and had prevailed.

Kingston Parker knocked out his pipe, and carried the file across the room and laid it open on the music rack of the piano. He seated himself at the keyboard and, still studying the printout sheets, began to play.

The stream of music, the lovely ethereal strains of Liszt, did not interrupt his thoughts but seemed to buoy them brightly upwards.

Parker had not wanted Stride, had considered from the very first that he was dangerous, sensing in him ambitions and motivations which would be difficult to control. Parker would have preferred his own nominees – Tanner, who now commanded the Mercury arm of Atlas, or Colin Noble – and had expected that Stride would have declined a command so far below his capability.

However, Stride had accepted the lesser appointment and headed Thor. Parker suspected that there was unusual motivation in this, and had made every effort to study the man at first hand. On five separate occasions he had ordered Stride to Washington, and focused upon him the full strength of his charisma and personality. He had even invited him to stay with him in his New York home, spending many hours with him in deep far-ranging discussions – from which he had developed a prudent respect for the man's mind, but had been able to reach no firm conclusions as to his future in Atlas.

Parker turned a page of the character appraisal. When he looked for the weakness in an opponent, Parker had long ago learned to start at the groin. With this man there was no evidence of any unnatural sexual leanings. Certainly he was not homosexual, if anything too much the opposite. There had been at least a dozen significant liaisons with the opposite sex since his divorce. However, all of these had been discreet and dignified. Although three of the ladies had been married, none of them were the wives of his subordinates in the armed services, nor of brother officers or of men who might be able to adversely affect his career.

The women he chose all had certain qualities in common – they all tended to be tall, intelligent and successful. One was a journalist who had her own syndicated column, another was a former fashion model who now designed and marketed her clothes through her own prestigious outlets in London and on the continent. Then there was an actress who was a leading female member of the Royal Shakespeare Company – Parker skimmed the list impatiently, for Parker himself had no sympathy nor patience with a man who succumbed to the dictates of his body.

Parker had trained himself to be totally celibate, channelling all his sexual energies into pursuits of the mind, while this man Stride, on the other hand, was not above conducting two or three of his liaisons concurrently.

Parker moved on to the second area of weakness. Stride's inheritance had been decimated by the punitive British death duties – yet his private income even after savage taxation was still a little over twenty thousand pounds sterling a year, and when this was added to his salary and privileges as a general officer, it enabled him to live in good style. He could even indulge in the mild extravagance of collecting rare books – and, Parker observed acidly, the greater extravagance of collecting rare ladies.

However, there was no trace of any illicit hoard – no Swiss bank accounts, no deposits of gold bullion, no foreign properties, no shares in off-share companies held by nominees – and Parker had searched diligently for them, for they would have indicated payments received, perhaps from foreign governments. A man like Stride had much to sell, at prices he could set himself – but it seemed he had not done so.

Stride did not smoke; Parker removed the old black briar from his own mouth, regarded it affectionately for a moment. It was his one indulgence, a harmless one despite what the surgeon-general of the United States had determined, and he took the stem firmly between his teeth again.

Stride took alcohol in moderation and was considered knowledgeable on the subject of wine. He raced occasionally, more as a social outing than as a serious punter, and the odd fifty pounds he could well afford. There was no evidence of other gambling. However, he did not hunt, nor did he shoot – traditional pursuits of the English gentleman. Perhaps he had moral objections to blood sports, Parker thought, though it seemed unlikely, for Stride was a superlative marksman with rifle, shotgun and pistol. He had represented Britain at the Munich Olympics as a pistol shot, winning a gold in the fifty metre class, and he spent at least an hour every day on the range.

Parker turned to the page of the print-out that gave the man's medical history. He must be superbly fit as well – his body weight at the age of thirty-nine was one pound less than it had been at twenty-one, and he still trained like a front-line soldier. Parker noticed that he had logged sixteen parachute jumps the previous month. Since joining Atlas he had no opportunity or time for golf, though when he was with NATO Stride had played off a handicap of three.

Parker closed the folder and played on softly, but neither the sensual polished feel of cool ivory beneath his fingertips nor the achingly lovely lilt of the music could dispel his sense of disquiet. Exhaustive as the report was, yet it left unanswered questions, like why Stride had downgraded himself to accept the command of Thor – he was not the kind of man who acted ill-advisedly. Yet the most haunting questions that nagged at Parker were just how strong were his qualities of resilience and independent thought, just how strongly was he driven by his ambitions and that penetrating intellect – and just how great a threat such a man would present to the evolution of Atlas into its ultimate role.

'Doctor Parker, sir—' his assistant knocked lightly and entered, ' – there are new developments.'

Parker sighed softly. 'I'm coming,' he said, and let the

last sad and beautiful notes fall from his long, powerful fingers before he stood up.

The Hawker slid almost silently down the sky. The pilot had closed down power at five thousand feet and made his final approach without touching the throttles again. He was ten knots above the stall as he passed over the boundary fence and he touched down twenty feet beyond the chevron markings of the threshold of runway One Fife, instantly applying maximum safe braking. One Fife was the secondary cross-wind runway and the Hawker's roll-out was so short that every part of the approach and landing had been screened by the buildings of the main airport terminal from where Speedbird 070 stood at the southern intersection of the main taxiway.

The pilot swung the Hawker through 360° and back-tracked sedately up runway 15, using just enough power to keep her rolling.

'Well done,' grunted Peter Stride, crouching behind the pilot's seat. He was almost certain that nobody aboard 070 had remarked their arrival.

'They've prepared a slot for us, with hook up to the electrical mains at the north—' Peter broke off as he saw the apron marshal waving them in with the bats, and beyond him a tight group of four men waiting. Three of them wore camouflage battle dress and the other the trim blue uniform, cap and gold insignia of a senior South African police officer.

The uniformed officer was the first to greet Peter as he came down the Hawker's fold-out air-stairs.

'Prinsloo.' He shook hands. 'Lieutenant-General.'

He ranked Peter, but it was a police, not a military appointment. He was a stocky man, with steel-rimmed spectacles, a little paunchy, and not less than fifty-five years of age. He had the rather heavy features, the fleshiness of jowl and lips, that Peter had noticed so often in Belgian and Dutch peasants during his NATO tour in the Netherlands. A man of the earth, dour and conservative.

'Let me introduce Commandant Boonzaier.' This was a military rank, equivalent to that of colonel, and he was a younger man, but with the same thick accent and his features cast in the same mould. A tall man, however, only an inch or so shorter than Peter – but both of the South Africans were suspicious and resentful, and the reason was immediately apparent.

'I have been instructed to take my orders from you, General,' and there was a subtle shift of position, the two officers ranging themselves beside Peter, but facing each other, and he was aware instantly that not all the hostility was directed at him. There had been friction between police and military already – and the basic value of Atlas was underlined yet again.

A single clean-cut line of command and of responsibility was absolutely essential – Peter's mind flicked back to the shoot-out at Larnaca Airport between Egyptian commandos and Cypriot national guardsmen, from which the hijackers of the grounded jet emerged unscathed while the airfield was littered with the burning wreckage of the Egyptian transport aircraft and dozens of dead and dying Cypriots and Egyptians.

The first principle of terrorist strategy was to strike at the point where national responsibilities were blurred. Atlas cut through that.

'Thank you.' Peter accepted command without flaunting it. 'My back-up team will land in just over three hours' time. We will, of course, use force only as a last resort – but if it comes to that, I will use exclusively Atlas personnel in any counter-strike. I would like to make that quite clear immediately.' And he saw the line of the soldier's mouth harden with disappointment.

'My men are the élite—'

'It's a British aircraft, most of the hostages are British or American nationals – it's a political decision, Colonel. But I would value your help in other areas.' Peter turned him aside tactfully.

'Firstly, I want you to suggest a position where I can place my surveillance equipment – and then we will go over the ground together.'

Peter had no difficulty selecting his forward observation post. The service manager's roomy, sparsely furnished office on the third floor of the terminal building overlooked the entire service area and the southern portion of the taxiway where the Boeing stood.

The windows had been left open when the offices were evacuated, so there was no need to change the external appearance of the room.

The overhang of the observation balcony on the floor above shaded the interior, and the office was deep enough to ensure that an observer out there in the bright glare of sunshine would not be able to see into the room, even with a powerful lens. The militants would expect surveillance from the glass control tower high above – any deception, however trivial, was worth while.

The surveillance equipment was lightweight and compact, the television cameras were neither of them bigger than a super 8-mm home movie camera and a man could carry in one hand both of the aluminium extension tripods. However, the cameras could zoom to 800-mm focal length, and they repeated on the screens of the command console in the cabin of the Hawker, while the image was simultaneously stored on videotape.

The audio intensifier was more bulky, but no heavier. It had a four-foot dish antenna, with the sound collector in the centre. The telescopic sight could aim the intensifier at a sound source with the accuracy of a sniper's rifle – could focus on the lips of a human being at eight hundred yards' distance and clearly record normal conversation at that range, passing sound directly to the command console and at the same time storing it on the big magnetic tape spools.

Two of Peter's communications team were posted here, with a plentiful supply of coffee and doughnuts, and Peter, accompanied by the South African colonel and his staff, went up in the elevator to the glass house of the control tower.

From the air traffic control tower there was an unobstructed view across the airfield and over the apron and service areas around the terminal. The observation platform below the tower had been cleared of all but military personnel.

' – I have road blocks at all the main entrances to the airfield. Only passengers with confirmed reservations and current tickets are being allowed through – no thrill seekers – and we are using only the northern section of the terminal for traffic.'

Peter nodded and turned to the senior controller. 'What is the state of your traffic pattern?'

'We have refused clearance to all private flights, incoming and departing. All domestic scheduled flights have been re-routed to Lanseria and Germiston airports, and we are landing and despatching only international scheduled flights – but the backlog has delayed departures by three hours.'

'What separation are you observing from 070?' Peter asked.

'Fortunately the international departures terminal is the farthest from the aircraft, and we are not using the taxiways or the apron of the southern section. As you see, we have cleared the entire area – except for those three S.A. Airways aircraft which are undergoing overhaul and servicing, there are no other aircraft within a thousand yards of 070.'

'I may have to freeze all traffic, if—' Peter paused, 'or should I say, when we have an escalation.'

'Very well, sir.'

'In the meantime, you may continue as you are at present.' Peter lifted his binoculars and once again very carefully examined the huge Boeing.

It stood in stately isolation, silent and seemingly abandoned. The bright, almost gaudy marking gave her a carnival air. Red and blue and crisp sparkling white in the brilliant sunlight of the highveld. She was parked fully broadside to the tower, and all her hatches and doors were still armed and locked.

Peter traversed slowly along the line of perspex windows down the length of the fuselage – but over each of them the sunshades had been firmly closed from the interior, turning them into the multiple eyes of a blinded insect.

Peter lifted his scrutiny slightly onto the windshield and side panels of the flight deck. These again had been screened with blankets, hung over them from inside, completely thwarting any glimpse of the crew or their captors – and certainly preventing a shot into the flight deck, although the range from the nearest corner of the terminal was not more than four hundred yards, and with the new laser sights one of Thor's trained snipers could pick through which eye of the human head he would put a bullet.

Snaking across the open tarmac of the taxiway was the thin black electrical cable that connected the aircraft to the mains supply, a long, vulnerable umbilical cord. Peter studied it thoughtfully, before turning his attention to the four Panhard armoured cars. A little frown of irritation crossed his forehead.

'Colonel, please recall those vehicles.' He tried not to let the irritation come through in his tone. 'With the turrets

53

battened down, your crews will be roasting like Christmas geese.'

'General, I feel it my duty—' Boonzaier began, and Peter lowered the glasses and smiled. It was a charming, friendly grin that took the man by surprise, after the previous stern set of features – and yet the eyes were devoid of humour, cracking blue and hard in the craggy granite of the face.

'I want to defuse the atmosphere as much as possible.' The necessity to explain irked Peter, but he maintained the smile. 'Somebody with four great cannons aimed at him is more likely to make a bad decision, and pull the trigger himself. You may keep them in close support, but get them out of sight into the terminal car park, and let your men rest.'

With little grace the colonel passed the order over the walkie-talkie on his belt, and as the vehicles started up and slowly pulled away behind the line of hangars, Peter went on remorselessly.

'How many men have you got deployed?' He pointed to the line of soldiers along the parapet of the observation balcony, and then to the heads visible as specks between the soaring blue of the African sky and the silhouette of the service hangars.

'Two hundred and thirty.'

'Pull them out,' Peter instructed, 'and let the occupants of the aircraft see them go.'

'All of them?' incredulously.

'All of them,' Peter agreed, and now the smile was wolfish, 'and quickly, please, colonel.'

The man was learning swiftly, and he lifted the miniaturized walkie-talkie to his mouth again. There were a few moments of scurrying and confusion among the troops on the observation deck below before they could be formed up and marched away in file. Their steel helmets, like a bobbing line of button mushrooms, and the muzzles of their slung weapons would show above the parapet, and would be clearly visible to an observer in the Boeing.

'If you treat these people, these animals—' the colonel's voice was choked slightly with frustration, ' – if you treat them soft—'

Peter knew exactly what was coming, ' – and if you keep waving guns in their faces, you will keep them alert and on their toes, Colonel. Let them settle down a little and relax, let them get very confident.' He spoke without lowering the binoculars. With a soldier's eye for ground he was picking the site for his four snipers. There was little chance that he would be able to use them – they would have to take out every single one of the enemy at the same instant – but a remote chance might just offer itself, and he decided to place one gun on the service hangar roof, there was a large ventilator which could be pierced and would command the port side of the aircraft, two guns to cover the flight deck from both sides – he could use the drainage ditch down the edge of the main runway to get a man into the small hut that housed the approach radar and ILS beacons. The hut was in the enemy's rear. They might not expect fire from that quarter – point by point from his mental checklist Peter planned his dispositions, scribbling his decisions into the small leather-covered notebook, poring over the large-scale map of the airport, converting gradients and angles into fields of fire, measuring 'ground to cover' and 'time to target' for an assault force launched from the nearest vantage points, twisting each problem and evaluating it, striving for novel solutions to each, trying to think ahead of an enemy that was still faceless and infinitely menacing.

It took him an hour of hard work before he was satisfied. Now he could pass his decisions to Colin Noble on board the incoming Herc, and within four minutes of the big landing wheels hitting tarmac his highly trained team with their complex talents and skills would be in position.

Peter straightened up from the map and tucked the notebook under the flap of his button-down breast pocket. Once again he scrutinized every inch of the silent, battened-down aircraft through his glasses – but this time he allowed himself the luxury of gut emotion.

He felt the anger and the hatred rise from some hidden depth of his soul and flush his blood and tighten the muscles of his belly and thighs.

Once again he was confronted by the many-headed monster. It crouched out there in ambush, waiting for him as it had so often before.

He remembered suddenly the shards of splintered glass littering the cobbles of a Belfast street and glittering like diamond chips in the arc lamps, the smell of explosives and blood thick in the air.

He remembered the body of a young woman lying in the gutted interior of a fashionable London restaurant. Her lovely young body stripped by the blast of all but a flimsy pearl-coloured pair of French lace panties.

He remembered the smell of a family, father, mother and three small children, burning in the interior of their saloon car, the bodies blackening and twisting in a slow macabre ballet as the flames scorched them. Peter had not been able to eat pork since that day.

He remembered the frightened eyes of a child, through a mask of blood, a dismembered arm lying beside her, the pale fingers still clutching a grubby little rag doll.

The images flashed in disjointed sequences across his memory, feeding his hatred until it pricked and stung behind his eyes and he had to lower the binoculars and wipe his eyes with the back of his hand.

It was the same enemy that he had hunted before, but his instincts warned him that it had grown even stronger and more inhuman since last he had met and fought it. He tried to suppress the hatred now, lest it cloud his judgement, lest it handicap him during the difficult hours and days that

56

he knew lay ahead – but it was too powerful, had been too long nurtured.

He recognized that hatred was the enemy's vice, that from it sprang their twisted philosophy and their monstrous actions, and that to descend to hatred was to descend to their sub-human levels – yet still the hatred persisted.

Peter Stride understood clearly that his hatred was not only for the ghastly death and mutilation that he had witnessed so often. More it was fostered by the threat that he recognized to an entire society and its civilized rule of law. If this evil should be allowed to triumph, then in the future laws would be made by the wild-eyed revolutionary, with a gun in his fist – the world would be run by the destroyers instead of the builders, and Peter Stride hated that possibility more even than the violence and the blood, and those he hated as a soldier hates. For only a soldier truly knows the horror of war.

His soldier's instinct now was to immediately engage the enemy and destroy him – but the scholar and philosopher in him warned that this was not the moment, and with an enormous effort of will he held that fighting man's instinct in check.

Yet still he was deeply aware that it was for this moment, for this confrontation of the forces of evil, that he had jeopardized his whole career.

When command of Atlas had been plucked away and a political appointee named in his place, Peter should have declined the offer of a lesser position in Atlas. There were other avenues open to him, but instead he had elected to stay with the project – and he hoped that nobody had guessed at the resentment he felt. God knows, Kingston Parker had no cause for complaint since then. There was no harder working officer on Atlas, and his loyalty had been tested more than once.

Now all that seemed worth while, and the moment for which he had worked had arrived. The enemy waited for him out there on the burning tarmac under an African sun, not on a soft green island in the rain nor in the grimy streets of a crowded city – but still it was the same old enemy, and Peter knew his time would come.

H is communications technicians had Colin Noble on the main screen as Peter ducked into the Hawker's cabin that was now his command headquarters, and settled into his padded seat. On the top right screen was a panoramic view of the southern terminal area, with the Boeing squatting like a brooding eagle upon its nest in the centre of the shot. On the next screen beside it was a blow-up through the 800-mm zoom lens of the Boeing's flight deck. So crisp was the detail that Peter could read the maker's name on the tab of the blanket that screened the windshield. The third small screen held a full shot of the interior of the air traffic control tower. In the foreground the controllers in shirt sleeves sitting over the radar repeaters, and beyond them through the floor to ceiling windows still another view of the Boeing. All these were being shot through the cameras installed an hour earlier in the terminal building. The remaining small screen was blank, and Colin Noble's homely, humorous face filled the main screen.

'Now if only it had been the cavalry instead of the U.S. Marines,' Peter said, 'you'd have been here yesterday—'

'What's your hurry, pal. Doesn't look like the party has started yet.' Colin grinned at him from the screen and pushed his baseball cap to the back of his head.

'Damned right,' Peter agreed. 'We don't even know who is throwing the party. What's your latest estimate on arrival time?'

'We've picked up a good wind – one hour twenty-two minutes to fly now,' Colin told him.

'Right, let's get down to it,' Peter said, and he began his briefing, going carefully over the field notes he had taken. When he wanted to emphasize a point, Peter called for a change of shot from his cameramen, and they zoomed in or panned to his instruction, picking up the radar shed or the service hangar ventilator where Peter was siting his snipers. The image was repeated not only on the command console but in the cavernous body of the approaching Hercules so that the men who would be called to occupy those positions could study them now and prepare themselves thoroughly for the moment. The same images were hurled across the stratosphere to the circling satellite and from there bounced down to appear, only slightly distorted, on the screens of Atlas Command in the west wing of the Pentagon. Sagging like an old lion in his armchair, Kingston Parker followed every word of the briefing, rousing himself only when a long telex message was passed to him by his assistant, then he nodded a command to have his own televised image superimposed on Peter's command console.

'I'm sorry to interrupt you, Peter, but we've got a useful scrap here. Assuming that the militant group boarded 070 at Mahé, we asked the Seychelles Police to run a check on all joining passengers. There were fifteen of them, ten of whom were Seychelles residents. A local merchant and his wife, and eight unaccompanied children between nine and fourteen years of age. They are the children of expatriate civil servants employed on contract by the Seychelles Government, returning to schools in England for the new term.'

Peter felt the weight of dread bring down upon him like a physical burden. Children, the young lives seemed somehow more important, somehow more vulnerable. But Parker was reading from the telex flimsy in his left hand, the right scratching the back of his neck with the stem of his pipe.

'There is one British businessman, Shell Oil Company, and well-known on the island, and there are four tourists, an American, a Frenchman and two Germans. These last four appeared to be travelling in a group, the immigration and security officers remember them well. Two women and two men, all young. Names Sally-Anne Taylor, twenty-five years, American, Heidi Hottschauser, twenty-four and Gunther Retz, twenty-five, the two Germans and Henri Larousse, twenty-six, the Frenchman. The police have run a back check on the four. They stayed two weeks at the Reef Hotel outside Victoria, the women in one double room and the two men in another. They spent most of the time swimming and sunbathing – until five days ago when a small ocean-going yacht called at Victoria. Thirty-five foot, single-hander around the world, skippered by another American. The four spent time on board her every day of her stay, and the yacht sailed twenty-four hours before the departure of the 070.'

'If the yacht delivered their arms and munitions, then this operation has been planned for a long time,' Peter pondered, 'and damn well planned.'

Peter felt the tingling flush of his blood again, the form of the enemy was taking shape now, the outline of the beast becoming clearer, and always it was uglier and more menacing.

'You have run the names through the computer?' he asked.

'Nothing,' Parker nodded. 'Either there is no intelligence record of them, or the names and passports are false—'

He broke off as there was sudden activity on the screen that monitored the air traffic control tower, and another voice boomed out of the secondary speaker; the volume was set too high, and the technician at the control board adjusted it swiftly. It was a female voice, a fresh, clear young voice speaking English with the lilt and inflexion of the west coast of America in it.

'Jan Smuts tower, this is the officer commanding the task

force of the Action Commando for Human Rights that has control of Speedbird 070. Stand by to copy a message.'

'Contact!' Peter breathed. 'Contact at last.'

On the small screen Colin Noble grinned and rolled his cheroot expertly from one side of his mouth to the other. 'The party has begun,' he announced, but there was the razor edge in his voice not entirely concealed by his jocular tone.

The three-man crew had been moved back from the flight deck, and were held in the first class seats vacated by the group of four.

Ingrid had made the cockpit of the Boeing her headquarters, and she worked swiftly through the pile of passports, filling in the name and nationality of each passenger on the seating plan spread before her.

The door to the galley was open and except for the hum of the air-conditioning, the huge aircraft was peculiarly silent. Conversation in the cabins was prohibited, and the aisles were patrolled by the red-shirted commandos to enforce this edict.

They also ordered the use of the toilets: a passenger must return to his seat before another was allowed to rise. The toilet doors had to remain open during use, so that the commandos could check at a glance.

Despite the silence, there was a crackling atmosphere of tension down the full length of the cabin. Very few of the passengers, mostly the children, were asleep, but the others sat in rigid rows, their faces taut and strained – watching their captors with a mixture of hatred and of fear.

Henri, the Frenchman, slipped into the cockpit.

'They are pulling back the armoured cars,' he said. He was slim, with a very youthful face and dreaming poet's eyes. He had grown a drooping blond gunfighter's moustache, but the effect was incongruous.

Ingrid looked up at him. 'You are so nervous, *chéri*.' She shook her head. 'It will all be all right.'

'I am not nervous,' he answered her stiffly.

She chuckled fondly, and reached up to touch his face. 'I did not mean it as an insult.' She pulled his face down and kissed him, thrusting her tongue deeply into his mouth. 'You have proved your courage – often,' she murmured.

He dropped his pistol onto the desk with a clatter and reached for her. The top three buttons of her red cotton shirt were unfastened, and she let him grope and find her breasts.

They were heavy and pointed and his breathing went ragged as he teased out her nipples. They hardened erect like jelly beans – but when he reached down with his free hand for the zipper of her shorts, she pushed him away roughly.

'Later,' she told him brusquely, 'when this is over. Now get back into the cabin.' And she leaned forward and lifted a corner of the blanket that screened the side window of the cockpit. The sunlight was very bright but her eyes adjusted swiftly and she saw the row of helmeted heads above the parapet of the observation deck. So they were pulling back the troops as well. It was nearly time to begin talking – but she would let them stew in their own juice just a little longer.

She stood up, buttoned her shirt and adjusted the camera on its strap around her neck, paused in the galley to rearrange the shiny mass of golden hair – and then walked slowly back down the full length of the central aisle, pausing to adjust the blanket over a sleeping child, to listen attentively to the complaints of the pregnant wife of the Texan neurosurgeon.

'You and the children will be the first off this plane – I promise you.'

When she reached the prone body of the flight engineer, she knelt beside him.

'How is he?'

'He is sleeping now. I shot him full of morphine,' the fat little doctor muttered, not looking at her, so she could not read the hatred in his expression. The injured arm was elevated to control the bleeding, sticking up stiffly in its cocoon of pressure bandages, oddly foreshortened with the bright ooze of blood through the dressing.

'You are doing good—' She touched his arm. 'Thank you.' And now he glanced at her startled, and she smiled – such a radiant lovely smile, that he began to melt.

'Is that your wife?' Ingrid dropped her voice, so that he alone could hear – and he nodded, glancing at the plump little Jewish woman in the nearest seat. 'I will see she is amongst the first to leave,' she murmured, and his gratitude was pathetic. She stood and went on down the aircraft.

The red-shirted German stood at the head of the tourist cabin, beside the curtained entrance to the second galley. He had the intense drawn face of a religious zealot, dark burning eyes, long black hair falling almost to his shoulders – a white scar twisted the corner of his upper lip into a perpetual smirk.

'Kurt, everything is all right?' she asked in German.

'They are complaining of hunger.'

'We will feed them in another two hours – but not as much as they expect—' and she ran a contemptuous glance down the cabin. 'Fat,' she said quietly, ' – big fat bourgeoisie pigs,' and she stepped through the curtains into the galley and looked at him in invitation. He followed her immediately, drawing the curtains behind them.

'Where is Karen?' Ingrid asked, as he unbuckled his belt. She needed it very badly, the excitement and the blood had inflamed her.

'She is resting – at the back of the cabin.'

Ingrid slipped the button that held the front of her shorts

63

together and drew down the zipper. 'All right Kurt,' she whispered huskily, 'but quickly, very quickly.'

Ingrid sat in the flight engineer's seat; at her shoulder stood the dark-haired girl. She wore the cartridge belt across the shoulder of her bright red shirt, like a bandolier – and she carried the big ugly pistol on her hip.

Ingrid held the microphone to her lips, and combed the fingers of her other hand through the thick golden tangle of her tresses as she spoke.

' – One hundred and ninety-eight British subjects. One hundred and forty-six American nationals—' She was reading the list of her captives. 'There are one hundred and twenty-two women on board, and twenty-six children under the age of sixteen years.' She had been speaking for nearly five minutes and now she broke off and shifted in her seat, turning to smile at Karen over her shoulder. The dark-haired girl smiled in return and reached across to caress the fine mass of golden hair with a narrow bony hand, before letting it drop back to her side.

'We have copied your last transmission.'

'Call me Ingrid.' She spoke into the mike with the smile turning into a wicked grin. There was a moment's silence as the controller in the tower recovered from his shock.

'Roger, Ingrid. Do you have any further messages for us?'

'Affirmative, Tower. As this is a British aircraft and as three hundred and forty-four of my passengers are either British or American, I want a spokesman, representing the embassies of those countries. I want him here in two hours' time to hear my terms for the release of passengers.'

'Stand by, Ingrid. We will be back to you immediately we have been able to contact the ambassadors.'

'Don't horse around, Tower.' Ingrid's voice snapped. 'We both know damned well they are breathing down your neck.

Tell them I want a man here in two hours – otherwise I am going to be forced to put down the first hostage.'

Peter Stride was stripped down to a pair of bathing trunks, and he wore only canvas sneakers on his feet. Ingrid had insisted on a face-to-face meeting, and Peter had welcomed the opportunity to assess at close range.

'We'll be covering you every inch of the way there and back,' Colin Noble told Peter, fussing over him like a coach over his fighter before the gong. 'I'm handling the gunners, personally.'

The snipers were armed with specially hand-built .222 magnums with accurized barrels that threw small light bullets with tremendous velocity and striking power. The ammunition was match-grade, each round lovingly hand finished and polished. The infra-red telescopic sights were readily interchangeable with the laser sights, making the weapon deadly accurate either in daylight or at night. The bullet had a clean, flat trajectory up to seven hundred yards. They were perfectly designed mankillers, precision weapons that reduced the danger to bystanders or hostages. The light bullet would slam a man down with savage force, as though he had been hit by a charging rhinoceros, but it would break up in his body, and not over-penetrate to kill beyond the target.

'You're getting into a lather,' Peter grunted. 'They want to talk, not shoot – not yet, anyway.'

'The female of the species—' Colin warned, ' – that one is real poison.'

'More important than the guns are the cameras, and sound equipment.'

'I went up there and kicked a few arses. You'll get pictures that will win you an Oscar – my personal guarantee.' Colin checked his wristwatch. 'Time to go. Don't keep the lady waiting.' He punched Peter's shoulder lightly. 'Hang loose,' he said, and Peter walked out into the sunshine, lifting both hands above his shoulders, palms open, fingers extended.

The silence was as oppressive as the dry fierce heat, but it was intentional. Peter had frozen all air traffic, and had ordered the shut down of all machinery in the entire terminal area. He did not want any interference with his sound equipment.

There was only the sound of his own footfalls, and he stepped out briskly – but still it was the longest walk of his life, and the closer he got to the aircraft, the higher it towered above him. He knew that he had been required to strip almost naked, not only to ensure that he carried no weapons, but to place him at a disadvantage – to make him feel ill at ease, vulnerable. It was an old trick – the Gestapo always stripped the victim for an interrogation – so he held himself proud and tall, pleased that his body was so lean and hard and muscled like an athlete's. He would have hated to drag a big, pendulous gut and sagging old-man's tits across those four hundred yards.

He was half-way there when the forward door, just behind the cockpit, slid back and a group of figures appeared in the square opening. He narrowed his eyes: there were two uniformed figures, no three – British Airways uniforms, the two pilots and between them the shorter slimmer feminine figure of a stewardess.

They stood shoulder to shoulder, but beyond them he could make out another head, a blonde head – but the angle and the light were against him.

Closer, he saw that the older pilot was on the right, short-cropped grey curls, ruddy round face – that would be Watkins, the commander. He was a good man, Peter had studied his service record. He ignored the co-pilot and stewardess and strained for a glimpse of the figure beyond them, but it was only when he stopped directly below the open hatch that she moved to let him get a clear view of her face.

Peter was startled by the loveliness of that golden head, by the smooth gloss of young sun-polished skin and the thundering innocence of wide-set, steady, green eyes – for a moment he could not believe she was one of them, then she spoke.

'I am Ingrid,' she said. Some of the most poisonous flowers are the loveliest, he thought.

'I am the accredited negotiator for the British and American Governments,' he said, and switched his gaze to the beefy red face of Watkins. 'How many members of your commando are aboard?' he asked.

'No questions!' Ingrid snapped fiercely, and Cyril Watkins extended four fingers of his right hand down his thigh without a change of expression.

It was vital confirmation of what they already suspected, and Peter felt a rush of gratitude towards the pilot.

'Before we discuss your terms,' Peter said, 'and out of common humanity, I would like to arrange for the well-being and comfort of your hostages.'

'They are well cared for.'

'Do you need food or drinking water?'

The girl threw back her head and laughed delightedly. 'So you can dope it with laxative – and have us knee-deep in shit? Stink us out, hey?'

Peter did not pursue it. The doped trays had already been prepared by his doctor.

'You have a gunshot casualty on board?'

'There are no wounded aboard,' the girl denied flatly, cutting her laughter short – but Watkins made the circular affirmative sign of thumb and forefinger, effectively contradicting her, and Peter noticed the spots of dried blood on the sleeves of his white shirt. 'That's enough,' Ingrid warned Peter. 'Ask one more question and we'll break off—'

'All right,' Peter agreed quickly. 'No more questions.'

67

'The objective of this commando is the ultimate downfall of the brutally fascist, inhuman, neo-imperialistic regime that holds this land in abject slavery and misery – denying the great majority of the workers and the proletariat their basic rights as human beings.'

And that, thought Peter bitterly, even though it's couched in the garbled jargon of the lunatic left, is every bit as bad as it can be. Around the world hundreds of millions would have immediate sympathy, making Peter's task just that little bit more difficult. The hijackers had picked a soft target.

The girl was still speaking, with an intense, almost religious fervour, and as he listened Peter faced the growing certainty that the girl was a fanatic, treading the thin line which divided sanity from madness. Her voice became a harsh screech as she mouthed her hatred and condemnation, and when she had finished he knew that she was capable of anything – no cruelty, no baseness was beyond her. He knew that she would not stop even at suicide, the final act of destroying the Boeing, its passengers and herself – he suspected she might even welcome the opportunity of martyrdom, and he felt the chill of it tickle up along his spine.

They were silent now, staring at each other, while the hectic flush of fanaticism receded from the girl's face and she regained her breath, and Peter waited, controlling his own misgivings, waiting for her to calm herself and continue.

'Our first demand—' the girl had steadied and was watching Peter shrewdly now, ' – our first demand is that the statement I have just made be read on every television network in Britain and the United States, and also here upon the South African network.' Peter felt his loathing of that terrible little box rise to the surface of his emotions. That mind-bending electronic substitute for thought, that deadly device for freezing, packaging and distributing opinion. He hated it, almost as much as the violence and sensation it purveyed so effectively. 'It must be read at the next occurrence of 7 p.m. local time in Los Angeles, New York, London and Johannesburg—' Prime time, of course, and the media would gobble it up hungrily, for this was their meat and their drink – the pornographers of violence!

High above him in the open hatch the girl brandished a thick buff envelope. 'This contains a copy of that statement for transmission – it contains also a list of names. One hundred and twenty-nine names, all of them either imprisoned or placed under banning orders by this monstrous police regime. The names on this list are the true leaders of South Africa.' She flung the envelope, and it landed at Peter's feet.

'Our second demand is that every person on that list be placed aboard an aircraft provided by the South African Government. Aboard the same aircraft there will be one million gold Kruger Rand coins also provided by the same government. The aircraft will fly to a country chosen by the freed political leaders. The gold will be used by them to establish a government in exile, until such time as they return to this country as the true leaders of the people.'

Peter stooped and picked up the envelope. He was calculating swiftly. A single Kruger Rand coin was worth $170 at the very least. The ransom demand was, therefore, worth one hundred and seventy million dollars.

There was another calculation. 'One million Krugers will weigh well over forty tons,' he told the girl. 'How are they going to get all that on one aircraft?'

The girl faltered. It was a little comfort to Peter to realize that they hadn't thought out everything perfectly. If they made one small mistake, then they were capable of making others.

'The government will provide sufficient transport for all the gold and all the prisoners,' the girl said sharply. The hesitation had been momentary only.

'Is that all?' Peter asked; the sun was stinging his naked shoulders and a cold drop of sweat tickled down his flank. He had never guessed it could be this bad.

'The aircraft will depart before noon tomorrow, or the execution of hostages will begin then.' Peter felt the crawl of horror. 'Execution.' She was using the jargon of legality, and he realized at that moment that what she promised she would deliver.

'When those aircraft arrive at the destination chosen by the occupants, a pre-arranged code will be flashed to us, and all women and children aboard this aircraft will immediately be released.'

'And the men?' Peter asked.

'On Monday the sixth – three days from now, a resolution is to be tabled before the General Assembly of the United Nations in New York. It will call for immediate total mandatory economic sanctions on South Africa – including withdrawal of all foreign capital, total oil and trade embargoes, severance of all transport and communications links, blockade of all ports and air borders by a U.N. peace-keeping force – pending free elections under universal suffrage supervised by U.N. inspectors—'

Peter's mind was racing to keep ahead of the girl's demands. He knew of the U.N. motion, of course, it had been tabled by Sri Lanka and Tanzania. It would be vetoed in the Security Council. That was a certainty – but the girl's timing brought forward new and frightening considerations. The beast had changed shape again, and what he had heard sickened him. It surely could not be merely coincidence that the resolution was to be tabled within three days of this strike – the implications were too horrible to contemplate. The connivance, if not the direct involvement, of world leaders and governments in the strategy of terror.

The girl spoke again deliberately. 'If any member of the Security Council of the U.N. – America, Britain or France

– uses the veto to block the resolution of this General Assembly, this aircraft and all aboard her will be destroyed by high explosive.'

Peter had lost the power of speech. He stood gaping up at the lovely blonde child, for child she seemed, so young and fresh.

When he found voice again, it croaked hoarsely. 'I don't believe you could have got high explosive aboard this aircraft to carry out that threat,' he challenged her.

The blonde girl said something to somebody who was out of sight, and then a few moments later she tossed a dark round object down to Peter.

'Catch!' she shouted, and he was surprised by the weight of it in his hands. It took only a moment to recognize it.

'Electronically fused!' The girl laughed. 'And we have so many I can afford to give you a sample.'

The pilot, Cyril Watkins, was trying to tell him something, touching his own chest – but Peter was occupied with the explosive in his hands. He knew that a single one of these would be fully capable of destroying the Boeing and all aboard her.

What was Watkins trying to tell him? Touching his neck again. Peter transferred his attention to the girl's neck. She wore a small camera slung around her neck. Something connecting camera and grenade – perhaps? Is that what the pilot was trying to tell him?

But now the girl was speaking again. 'Take that to your masters, and let them tremble. The wrath of the masses is upon them. The revolution is here and now,' she said, and the door of the hatchway was swung closed. He heard the lock fall into place.

Peter turned and began the long walk back, carrying an envelope in one hand, a grenade in the other, and sick loathing in his guts.

Colin Noble's rugged frame almost filled the hatchway of the Hawker, and for once his expression was deadly serious, no trace of laughter in his eyes or at the corners of the wide friendly mouth.

'Doctor Parker is on the screen.' He greeted Peter who was still buttoning his overalls as he hurried to the command plane. 'We copied every word, and he was hooked into the system.'

'Christ, it's bad, Colin,' Peter grunted.

'That was the good news,' Colin told him. 'When you have finished with Parker, I've got the bad news for you.'

'Thanks, pal.' Peter shouldered his way past him into the cabin, and dropped into his leather command chair.

On the screen Kingston Parker was hunched over his desk, poring over the teleprinter sheet on which the entire conversation between Ingrid and Peter had been recorded, the cold empty pipe gripped between his teeth, the broad brow creased with the weight of his responsibility as he studied the demands of the terrorist commando.

The communications director's voice from off-screen alerted Parker.

'General Stride, sir.' And Parker looked up at the camera.

'Peter. This is you and me alone. I have closed the circuit and we will restrict to single tape recording. I want your first reaction, before we relay to Sir William and Constable—' Sir William Davies was the British Ambassador and Kelly Constable was the United States Ambassador to Pretoria.

'I want your first reaction.'

'We are in serious trouble, sir,' Peter said, and the big head nodded.

'What is the militant capability?'

'I am having my explosives team take down the grenade – but I have no doubt that they have the physical capability to destroy 070, and all aboard. I reckon they have an overkill potential of at least ten.'

'And the psychological capability.'

'In my view, she is the child of Bakunin and Jean Paul Sartre—' Again Parker nodded heavily and Peter went on. 'The anarchist conception that destruction is the only truly creative act, that violence is man recreating himself. You know Sartre said that when the revolutionary kills, a tyrant dies and a free man emerges.'

'Will she go all the way?' Parker insisted.

'Yes, sir.' Peter answered without hesitation. 'If she is pressed she'll go all the way – you know the reasoning. If destruction is beautiful, then self-destruction is immortality. In my view, she'll go all the way.'

Parker sighed and knocked the stem of his pipe against his big white teeth.

'Yes, it squares with what we have on her.'

'You have read her?' Peter asked eagerly.

'We got a first-class voice print, and the computer cross-matched with her facial structure print.'

'Who is she?' Peter cut in impatiently; he did not have to be told that the sound intensifier and the zoom video cameras had been feeding her voice and image into the intelligence computer even as she issued her demands.

'Her born name is Hilda Becker. She is a third-generation American of German extraction. Her father is a successful dentist widowed in 1959. The girl is thirty-one years old—' Peter had thought her younger, that fresh young skin had misled him. ' – I.Q. 138. University of Columbia 1965–68, Master's degree in Modern Political History. Member of SDS – that's Students for a Democratic Society—'

'Yes.' Peter was impatient. 'I know.'

' – Activist in Vietnam war protests. Worker for the draft evasion pipeline to Canada. One arrest for possession of marijuana 1967, not convicted. Implicated with Weathermen – and one of the leaders of on-campus rioting in the spring of 1968. Arrested for bombing of Butler University and released. Left America in 1970 for further study at

Dusseldorf. Doctorate in Political Economics 1972. Known association with Gudrun Ensslin and Horst Mahler of the Baader-Meinhof. Went underground in 1976 after suspicion of implication in the abduction and murder of Heinrich Kohler, the West German industrialist—' Her personal history was an almost classical development of the modern revolutionary, Peter reflected bitterly, a perfect picture of the beast. 'Believed to have received advanced training from the PFLP in Syria during 1976 and 1977. No recorded contact since then. She is a habitual user of cannabis-based drugs, reported voracious sexual activity with members of both sexes—' Parker looked up. 'That's all we have,' he said.

'Yes,' Peter repeated softly. 'She'll go all the way.'

'What is your further assessment?'

'I believe that this is an operation organized at high level – possibly governmental—'

'Substantiate!' Parker snapped.

'The co-ordination with U.N.O. proposals sponsored by the unaligned nations points that way.'

'All right, go on.'

'For the first time we have a highly organized and heavily supported strike that is not seeking some obscure, partisan object. We've got demands here about which a hundred million Americans and fifty million Englishmen are going to say in unison, "Hell, these aren't unreasonable."'

'Go on,' said Parker.

'The militants have picked a soft target which is the outcast pariah of Western civilization. That U.N. resolution is going to be passed a hundred to nil, and those millions of Americans and Englishmen are going to have to ask themselves if they are going to sacrifice the lives of four hundred of their most prominent citizens to support a government whose racial policies they abhor.'

'Yes?' Parker was leaning forward to stare into the screen. 'Do you think they'll do a deal?'

'The militants? They might.' Peter paused a moment and then went on. 'You know my views, sir. I oppose absolutely dealing with these people.'

'Even in these circumstances?' Parker demanded.

'Especially now. My views of the host country's policies are in accord with yours, Doctor Parker. This is the test. No matter how much we personally feel the demands are just, yet we must oppose to the death the manner in which they are presented. If these people win their objects, it is a victory for the gun – and we place all mankind in jeopardy.'

'What is your estimate for a successful counterstrike?' Parker demanded suddenly, and even though he had known the question must come, still Peter hesitated a long moment.

'Half an hour ago I would have put the odds at ten to one in our favour that I could pull off condition Delta with only militant casualties.'

'And now?'

'Now I know that these are not fuddle-headed fanatics. They are probably as well trained and equipped as we are, and they have had years to set this operation up.'

'And now?' Parker insisted.

'We have a four to one in our favour of getting them out with a Delta strike, with say less than ten casualties.'

'What is the next best chance?'

'I would say there is no middle ground. If we failed, we would be into a situation with one hundred per cent casualties – we would lose the aircraft and all aboard, including all Thor personnel involved.'

'All right then, Peter.' Parker leaned back in his chair, the gesture of dismissal. 'I am going to speak with the President and the Prime Minister, they are setting up the link now. Then I will brief the ambassadors – and be back to you within the hour.'

His image flickered into darkness, and Peter realized that

all his hatred was suppressed. He felt cold, and functional as the surgeon's blade. Ready to do the job for which he had trained so assiduously, and yet able to assess and evaluate the enemy and the odds against success.

He pressed the call button. Colin had been waiting beyond the soundproof doors of the command cabin, and he came through immediately.

'The explosives boys have taken down the grenade. It's a dandy. The explosive is the new Soviet CJ composition, and the fusing is factory manufacture. Professional stuff – and it will work. Oh, baby, will it ever work.'

Peter hardly needed this confirmation, and Colin went on as he flung himself untidily in the chair opposite Peter.

'We put the list of names and the text of the militant statement on the teleprinter for Washington—' He leaned forward and spoke into the cabin intercom. 'Run that loop – without sound first.' Then he told Peter grimly. 'Here's the bad news I promised.'

The loop of video tape began to run on the central screen. It had clearly been shot from the observation post in the office overlooking the service area.

It was a full shot of the Boeing, the background flattened by the magnification of the lens and swimming and wavering with heat mirage rising from the tarmac of the main runway beyond the aircraft.

In the foreground were Peter's own naked back and shoulders as he strode out towards the aircraft. The lens had again flattened the action so that Peter appeared to be marking time on the same spot without advancing at all.

Suddenly the forward hatch of the Boeing changed shape as the door was slid aside, and the cameraman instantly zoomed in for the closer shot.

The two pilots and the air hostess in the doorway, the camera checked for a few frames and then zoomed closer. The aperture of the lens adjusted swiftly, compensating for the gloom of the interior, and the shot was close and tight on the blonde girl's head for a heartbeat, then the head turned slightly and the lovely line of her lips moved as she spoke – it seemed like three words – before she turned back full face to the camera.

'Okay,' Colin said. 'Run it again – with neutral balance on the sound.'

The entire loop reran, the cabin door opened, there were the three hostages, the fine golden head turned, and then the words 'Let's slide,' from Ingrid, but there was background hiss and clutter.

'"Let's slide"?' Peter asked.

'Run it again with the bass density filter on the sound,' Colin ordered.

The same images on the screen, the golden head turning on the long neck.

'"It's slide."' Peter could not quite catch it.

'Okay,' Colin told the technician. 'Now with full filter and resonance modulation.'

The repetitive images, the girl's head, the full lips parting, speaking to somebody out of sight in the body of the aircraft.

Very clearly, unmistakably, she said, 'It's Stride.' And Peter felt it jolt in his belly like a fist.

'She recognized you,' said Colin. 'No, hell, she was expecting you!'

The two men stared at each other, Peter's handsome craggy features heavy with foreboding. Atlas had one of the highest security classifications. Only twenty men outside the close ranks of Atlas itself were privy to its secrets. One of those was the President of the United States – another was the Prime Minister of Great Britain.

Certainly only four or five men knew who commanded the Thor arm of Atlas – and yet there was no mistaking those words the girl had spoken.

'Run it again,' Peter ordered brusquely.

And they waited tensely for those two words, and when

they came they were in the clear lilt of that fresh young voice.

'It's Stride,' said Ingrid, and the screen went blank.

Peter massaged his closed eyelids with thumb and fore-finger. He realized with mild surprise that he had not slept for nearly forty-eight hours, but it was not physical weariness that assailed him now but the suddenly overwhelming knowledge of treason and betrayal and of undreamed-of evil.

'Somebody has blown Atlas,' said Colin softly. 'This is going to be a living and breathing bastard. They'll be waiting for us at every turn of the track.'

Peter dropped his hand and opened his eyes. 'I must speak to Kingston Parker again,' he said. And when Parker's image reappeared on the main screen he was clearly agitated and angry.

'You have interrupted the President.'

'Doctor Parker—' Peter spoke quickly. ' – Circumstances have altered. In my opinion the chances of a successful Delta strike have dropped. We have no better than an even chance.'

'I see.' Parker checked the anger. 'That's important. I will inform the President.'

The lavatories were all blocked by this time, the bowls almost filled, and the stench permeated all the cabins despite the air-conditioning.

Under the strict rationing of food and water most of the passengers were suffering from the lethargy of hunger, and the children were petulant and weepy.

The terrible strain was beginning to show on the hijack-ers themselves. They were standing a virtual non-stop watch, four hours of broken rest followed by four of ceaseless vigil and activity. The red cotton shirts were rumpled and sweat-stained at the armpits, the sweat of nervous and physical strain, eyes bloodshot and tempers uncertain.

Just before nightfall, the dark-haired girl, Karen, had lost her temper with an elderly passenger who had been slow to respond to her command to return to his seat after using the toilet. She had worked herself up into an hysterical shrieking rage, and repeatedly struck the old man in the face with the short barrel of her shot pistol, laying his cheek open to the bone. Only Ingrid had been able to calm her, leading her away to the curtained tourist galley where she pampered and hugged her.

'It will be all right, *Liebchen*.' She stroked her hair. 'Only a little longer now. You have been so strong. In a few more hours we will all take the pills. Not long now.' And within minutes Karen had controlled the violent trembling of her hands, and although she was pale, she was able to take her position at the rear of the tourist cabin again.

Only Ingrid's strength seemed without limits. During the night she passed slowly down the aisles, pausing to talk quietly with a sleepless passenger, comforting them with the promise of imminent release.

'Tomorrow morning we will have an answer to our demands, and all the women and children will be free – it's going to be all right, you just wait and see.'

A little after midnight the little roly-poly doctor sought her out in the cockpit.

'The navigator is very ill,' he told her. 'Unless we get him to a hospital immediately we will lose him.'

Ingrid went back and knelt beside the flight engineer. His skin was dry and burning hot and his breathing rasped and sawed.

'It's renal failure,' said the doctor, hovering over them. 'Breakdown of the kidneys from delayed shock. We cannot treat him here. He must be taken to hospital.'

Ingrid took the semi-conscious flight engineer's unin-jured hand. 'I'm sorry, but that's impossible.'

She went on holding his hand for another minute.

'Don't you feel anything?' the doctor demanded of her bitterly.

'I feel pity for him – as I do for all mankind,' she answered quietly. 'But he is only one. Out there are millions.'

The towering flat-topped mountain was lit by flood-lights. It was high holiday season and the fairest cape in all the world was showing her beauty to the tens of thousands of tourists and holidaymakers.

On the penthouse deck of the tall building, named for a political mediocrity as are so many buildings and public works in South Africa, the cabinet and its special advisers had been in session for most of the night.

At the head of the long table brooded the heavily built figure of the Prime Minister, bulldog-headed, powerful and unmovable as one of the granite kopjes of the African veld. He dominated the large panelled room, although he had hardly spoken, except to encourage the others with a nod or a few gruff words.

At the far end of the long table sat the two ambassadors, shoulder to shoulder, to emphasize their solidarity. At short intervals the telephones in front of them would ring, and they would listen to the latest reports from their embassies or instructions from the heads of their governments.

On the Prime Minister's right hand sat the handsome moustached Minister of Foreign Affairs, a man with enormous charisma and a reputation for moderation and common sense – but now he was grim and hard faced.

'Your own governments have both pioneered the policy of non-negotiation, of total resistance to the demands of terrorists – why now do you insist that we take the soft line?'

'We do not insist, minister, we have merely pointed out the enormous public interest that this affair is generating in both the United Kingdom and in my own country.' Kelly Constable was a slim, handsome man, intelligent and persuasive, a democratic appointee of the new American administration. 'It is in your government's interest even more than ours to see this through to a satisfactory conclusion. We merely suggest that some accommodation to the demands might bring that about.'

'The Atlas Commander on the spot has assessed the chances of a successful counter-strike as low as fifty-fifty. My government considers that risk unacceptable.' Sir William Davies was a career diplomat approaching retirement age, a grey, severe man with gold-rimmed spectacles, his voice high pitched and querulous.

'My men think we can do better than that ourselves,' said the Minister of Defence, also bespectacled, but he spoke in the thick blunt accent of the Afrikaaner.

'Atlas is probably the best equipped and most highly trained anti-terrorist group in the world,' Kelly Constable said, and the Prime Minister interrupted harshly.

'At this stage, gentlemen, let us confine ourselves to finding a peaceful solution.'

'I agree, Prime Minister.' Sir William nodded briskly.

'However, I think I should point out that most of the demands made by the terrorists are directly in line with the representations made by the government of the United States—'

'Sir, are you expressing sympathy with these demands?' the Prime Minister asked heavily, but without visible emotion.

'I am merely pointing out that the demands will find sympathy in my country, and that my government will find it easier to exercise its veto on the extreme motion of the General Assembly on Monday if some concessions are made in other directions.'

'Is that a threat, sir?' the Prime Minister asked, a small humourless smile hardly softening the question.

'No, Prime Minister, it's common sense. If that U.N. motion was carried and implemented, it would mean the economic ruin of this country. It would be plunged into anarchy and political chaos, a ripe fruit for futher Soviet encroachment. My government does not desire that – however, nor does it wish to endanger the lives of four hundred of its citizens.' Kelly Constable smiled. 'We have to find a way out of our mutual predicament, I'm afraid.'

'My Minister of Defence has suggested a way out.'

'Prime Minister, if your military attack the aircraft without the prior agreement of both the British and American heads of state, then the veto will be withheld in the Security Council and regretfully we will allow the majority proposal to prevail.'

'Even if the attack is successful?'

'Even if the attack is successful. We insist that military decisions are made by Atlas only,' Constable told him solemnly; and then, more cheerfully, 'Let us examine the minimum concessions that your government would be prepared to make. The longer we can keep open the lines of communication with the terrorists, the better our chances of a peaceful solution. Can we offer to fulfil even one small item on the list of demands?'

Ingrid supervised the serving of breakfast personally. Each passenger was allowed one slice of bread and one biscuit with a cup of heavily sweetened coffee. Hunger had lowered the general resistance of the passengers, they were apathetic and listless once they had gobbled their meagre meal.

Ingrid went amongst them again, passing out cigarettes from the duty-free store. Talking gently to the children, stopping to sympathize with a mother – smiling and calm. Already the passengers were calling her 'the nice one'.

When Ingrid reached the first-class galley she called her companions to her one at a time, and they each ate a full breakfast of eggs and buttered toast and kippers. She wanted them as strong and alert as the arduous ordeal would allow. She could not begin to use the stimulants until midday. The use of drugs could only be continued for seventy-two hours with the desired effects. After that the subject would become unpredictable in his actions and decisions. Ratification of the sanctions vote by the Security Council of the United Nations would take place at noon New York time on the following Monday – that was seven p.m. local time on Monday night.

Ingrid had to keep all her officers alert and active until then, she dared not use the stimulants too early and risk physical disintegration before the decisive hour, and yet she realized that lack of sleep and tension were corroding even her physical reserves; she was jumpy and nervous, and when she examined her face in the mirror of the stinking first-class toilets, she saw how inflamed her eyes were, and for the first time noticed the tiny lines of ageing at the corners of her mouth and eyes. This angered her unreasonably. She hated the thought of growing old, and she could smell her own unwashed body even in the overpowering stench from the lavatory.

The German, Kurt, was slumped in the pilot's seat, his pistol in his lap, snoring softly, his red shirt unbuttoned to the waist and his muscular hairy chest rising and falling with each breath. He was unshaven and the lank, black hair fell over his eyes. She could smell his sweat, and somehow that excited her, and she studied him carefully. There was an air of cruelty and brutality about him, the machismo of the revolutionary, which always attracted her strongly – had perhaps been the original reason for her radical leanings so many years ago. Suddenly she wanted him very badly.

However, when she woke him with a hand down the front of his thin linen slacks, he was bleary-eyed and foul-breathed, not even her skilful kneading could arouse him, and in a minute she turned away with an exclamation of disgust.

As a displacement activity, she picked up the microphone, switched on the loudspeakers of the passenger cabins. She knew she was acting irrationally, but she began to speak.

'Now listen to me, everybody, I have something very important to tell you.' Suddenly she was angry with them. They were of the class that had devised and instituted the manifestly unjust and sick society against which she was in total rebellion. They were the fat, complacent bourgeoisie. They were like her father and she hated them as she hated her father. As she began to speak she realized that they would not even understand the language she was using, the language of the new political order, and her anger and frustration against them and their society mounted. She did not realize she was raving, until suddenly she heard as from afar the shriek of outrage in her own voice, like the death wail of a mortally wounded animal – and she stopped abruptly.

She felt giddy and light-headed, so she had to clutch at the desk top for support and her heart banged wildly against her ribs. She was panting as though she had run a long way, and it took nearly a full minute for her to bring herself under control.

When she spoke again, her tone was still ragged and breathless.

'It is now nine o'clock,' she said. 'If we do not hear from the tyrant within three hours I shall be forced to begin executing hostages. Three hours—' She repeated ominously, ' – only three hours.'

Now she prowled the aircraft like a big cat paces along the bars of its cage as feeding time approaches.

'Two hours,' she told them, and the passengers shrank away from her as she passed.

'One hour.' There was a bright sadistic splinter of anticipation in her voice. 'We will choose the first hostages now.'

'But you promised,' pleaded the fat little doctor as Ingrid pulled his wife out of her seat and the Frenchman hustled her forward towards the flight deck.

Ingrid ignored him, and turned to Karen. 'Get children, a boy and a girl—' she instructed, ' – oh yes, and the pregnant one. Let them see her big belly. They won't be able to resist that.'

Karen herded the hostages into the forward galley and forced them at pistol point to sit in a row upon the fold-down air-crew seats.

The door to the flight deck was open and Ingrid's voice carried clearly to the galley, as she explained to the Frenchman Henri, speaking in English.

'It is of the utmost importance that we do not allow a deadline to pass without retaliating strongly. If we miss one deadline, then our credibility is destroyed. It will only be necessary once, we must show the steel at least once. They must learn that every one of our deadlines are irrevocable, not negotiable—'

The girl began to cry. She was thirteen years old, able to understand the danger. The plump doctor's wife put her arm around her shoulders and hugged her gently.

'Speedbird 070—' the radio squawked suddenly, ' – we have a message for Ingrid.'

'Go ahead, Tower, this is Ingrid.' She had jumped up to take the microphone, pushing the door to the flight deck closed.

'The negotiator for the British and American governments has proposals for your consideration. Are you ready to copy?'

'Negative.' Ingrid's voice was flat and emphatic. 'I say

85

again negative. Tell the negotiator I will talk only face to face – and tell him we are only forty minutes to the noon deadline. He had better get out here fast,' she warned. She hooked the microphone and turned to Henri.

'All right. We will take the pills now – it has truly begun at last.'

It was another cloudless day, brilliant sunlight that was flung back in piercing darts of light from the bare metal parts of the aircraft. The heat came up through the soles of his shoes and burned down upon Peter's bare neck.

The forward hatch opened, as it had before, when Peter Stride was half-way across the tarmac.

This time there were no hostages on display, the hatchway was a dark empty square. Suppressing the urge to hurry, Peter carried himself with dignity, head up, jaw clenched firmly.

He was fifty yards from the aircraft when the girl stepped into the opening. She stood with indolent grace, her weight all on one leg, the other cocked slightly, long, bare, brown legs. She carried the big shot pistol on one hip, and the cartridge belt emphasized the narrow waist.

She watched Peter come on, with a half-smile on her lips. Suddenly a medallion of light appeared on her chest, a dazzling speck like a brilliant insect and she glanced down at it contemptuously.

'This is provocation,' she called. Clearly she knew that the bright speck was the beam thrown by the laser sight of one of the marksmen covering her from the airport building. A few ounces more of pressure on the trigger would send a .222 bullet crashing precisely into that spot, tearing her heart and lungs to bloody shreds.

Peter felt a flare of anger at the sniper who had activated his laser sight without the order, but his anger was tempered by reluctant admiration for the girl's courage. She could sneer at that mark of certain death upon her breast.

Peter made a cut out sign with his right hand, and almost immediately the speck of light disappeared as the gunner switched off his laser sight.

'That's better,' the girl said, and she smiled, running her gaze appraisingly down Peter's body.

'You've a good shape, baby,' she said, and Peter's anger flared again under her scrutiny.

'Nice flat belly—' she said, ' – good legs, and you didn't get those muscles sitting at a desk and pushing a pen.' She pursed her lips thoughtfully. 'You know I think you're a cop or a soldier. That's what I think, baby. I think you're a goddamned pig.' Her voice had a new harsh quality, and the skin seemed drier and drawn – older than it had been before.

He was close enough now to see the peculiar diamantine glitter in her eyes, and he recognized the tension that seemed to rack her body, the abrupt restless gestures. She was onto drugs now. He was certain of it. He was dealing with a political fanatic, with a long history of violence and death, whose remaining humane traits would be now entirely suppressed by the high of stimulant drugs. He knew she was more dangerous now than a wounded wild animal, a cornered leopard, a man-eating shark with the taste of blood exciting it to the killing frenzy.

He did not reply, but held her gaze steadily, keeping his hands in view, coming to a halt below the open hatchway.

He waited quietly for her to begin, and the itch of the drug in her blood would not allow her to stand still; she fidgeted with the weapon in her hands, touched the camera still hanging from around her neck. Cyril Watkins had tried to tell him something about that camera – and suddenly Peter realized what it was. The trigger for the fuses? he pondered, as he waited. Almost certainly, he decided, that was why it was with her every moment. She saw the direction of his eyes, and dropped her hand guiltily, confirming his conclusion.

'Are the prisoners ready to leave?' she demanded. 'Is the gold packed? Is the statement ready for transmission?'

'The South African Government has acceded to urgent representations by the governments of Great Britain and the United States of America.'

'Good.' She nodded.

'As an act of common humanity the South Africans have agreed to release all the persons on your list of detainees and banned persons—'

'Yes.'

'They will be flown to any country of their choice.'

'And the gold?'

'The South African Government refuses categorically to finance or to arm an unconstitutional foreign-based opposition. They refuse to provide funds for the persons freed under this agreement.'

'The television transmission?'

'The South African Government considers the statement to be untrue in substance and in fact and to be extremely prejudicial to the maintenance of law and order in this country. It refuses to allow transmission of the statement.'

'They have accepted only one of our demands—' The girl's voice took on an even more strident tone, and her shoulders jerked in an uncontrolled spasm.

'The release of political detainees and banned persons is subject to one further condition—' Peter cut in swiftly.

'And what is that—' The girl demanded, two livid burning spots of colour had appeared in her cheeks.

'In return for the release of political prisoners, they demand the release of all hostages, not only the women and children, all persons aboard the aircraft – and they will guarantee safe passage for you and all members of your party to leave the country with the released detainees.'

The girl flung back her head, the thick golden mane

flying wildly about her head as she screeched with laughter. The laughter was a wild, almost maniacal sound, and though it went on and on, there was no echo of mirth in her eyes. They were fierce as eagles' eyes, as she laughed. The laughter was cut off abruptly, and her voice was suddenly flat and level.

'So they think they can make demands, do they? They think they can draw the teeth from the U.N. proposals, do they? They think that without hostages to account for, the fascist governments of Britain and America can again cast their veto with impunity?'

Peter made no reply.

'Answer me!' she screamed suddenly. 'They do not believe we are serious, do they?'

'I am a messenger only,' he said.

'You're not,' she screamed in accusation. 'You're a trained killer. You're a pig!' She lifted the pistol and aimed with both hands at Peter's face.

'What answer must I take back?' Peter asked, without in any way acknowledging the aim of the weapon.

'An answer—' Her voice dropped again to an almost conversational level. 'Of course, an answer.' She lowered the pistol and consulted the stainless steel Japanese watch on her wrist. 'It's three minutes past noon – three minutes past the deadline, and they are entitled to an answer, of course.'

She looked around her with an almost bewildered expression. The drug was having side effects, Peter guessed. Perhaps she had overdosed herself, perhaps whoever had prescribed it had not taken into account the forty-eight sleepless hours of strain that preceded its use.

'The answer,' he prodded her gently, not wanting to provoke another outburst.

'Yes. Wait,' she said, and disappeared abruptly into the gloom of the interior.

K aren was standing over the four hostages on the fold-down seats. She looked around at Ingrid with smouldering dark eyes. Ingrid nodded once curtly, and Karen turned back to her prisoners.

'Come,' she said softly, 'we are going to let you go now.' Almost gently she lifted the pregnant woman to her feet with a hand on her shoulder.

Ingrid left her and passed swiftly into the rear cabins. She nodded again to Kurt, and with a toss of his head he flicked the lank locks of hair from his eyes and thrust the pistol into his belt.

From the locker above his head he brought down two of the plastic grenades. Holding one in each fist he pulled the pins with his teeth and held the rings hooked over his little fingers.

With his arms spread like a crucifix, he ran lightly down the aisle.

'These grenades are primed. Nobody must move, nobody must leave their seats – no matter whatever happens. Stay where you are.'

The fourth hijacker took up the cry from him, holding primed grenades in both hands above his head.

'Nobody move. No talking. Sit still. Everybody still.' He repeated in German and in French and his eyes had the same hard, glossy glitter of the drug high.

Ingrid turned back towards the flight deck.

'Come, sweetheart.' She placed an arm round the girl's shoulder, shepherding her towards the open hatchway – but the child shrank away from her with dread.

'Don't touch me,' she whispered, and her eyes were huge with terror. The boy was younger, more trusting. He took Ingrid's hand readily.

He had thick curly hair, and honey brown eyes as he looked up at her. 'Is my daddy here?' he asked.

'Yes, darling.' Ingrid squeezed his hand. 'You be a good boy now, and you'll see your daddy very soon.'

She led him to the open hatchway. 'Stand there,' she said.

Peter Stride was uncertain what to expect, as the boy stepped into the open hatchway high above him. Then next to him appeared a plump middle-aged woman in an expensive but rumpled, high-fashion silk dress, probably a Nina Ricci, Peter decided irrelevantly. The woman's elaborate lacquered hairstyle was coming down in wisps around her ears, but she had a kindly humorous face and she placed a protective arm about the boy-child's shoulders.

The next person was a taller and younger woman, with a pale sensitive skin; her nostrils and eyelids were inflamed pink from weeping or from some allergy and there were blotches of angry prickly heat on her throat and upper arms. Under the loose cotton maternity dress her huge belly bulged grotesquely, throwing her off balance; she stood with her thin white legs knock-kneed awkwardly – and blinked in the brilliant sparkling sunshine, her eyes still attuned to the shaded gloom of the cabin.

The fourth and last person was a young girl, and with a sudden blinding stab of agony below the ribs Peter thought it was Melissa-Jane. It took a dozen racing beats of his heart before he realized it was not her – but she had the same sweet Victorian face, the classical English skin of rose petals, the finely bred body of almost woman with delicate breast-buds and long coltish legs below narrow boyish hips.

There was naked terror in her huge eyes, and almost instantly she seemed to realize that Peter was her hope of salvation. The eyes turned on him pleading, hope starting to awaken.

'Please,' she whispered. 'Don't let them hurt us.' So softly

91

that Peter could hardly catch the words. 'Please, sir. Please help us.'

But Ingrid was there, her voice rising stridently.

'You must believe that what we promise, we mean. You and your evil capitalist masters must understand completely that we will not let a single deadline pass without executions. We have to prove that for the revolution we are without mercy. You must be made to understand that our demands must be met in full, that they are not negotiable. We must demonstrate the price for missing a deadline.' She paused. 'The next deadline is midnight tonight. If our demands are not met in full by then – you must know the price you will be made to pay.' She halted again, and then her voice rose into that hysterical shriek. 'This is the price!' and she stepped back out of sight.

Helpless with dread, Peter Stride tried to think of some way to prevent the inevitable.

'Jump!' he shouted, lifting both hands towards the girl. 'Jump, quickly. I will catch you!'

But the child hesitated, the drop was almost thirty feet, and she teetered uncertainly.

Behind her, ten paces back, the dark-haired Karen and the blonde lion-maned girl stood side by side, and in unison they lifted the short, big bored pistols, holding them in the low double-handed grip, positioning themselves at the angle and range which would allow the mass of soft heavy lead beads with which the cartridges were packed to spread sufficiently to sweep the backs of the four hostages.

'Jump!' Peter's voice carried clearly into the cabin, and Ingrid's mouth convulsed in a nervous rictus, an awful parody of a smile.

'Now!' she said, and the two women fired together. The two shots blended in a thunderous burst of sound, a mind-stopping roar, and blue powder smoke burst from the gaping muzzles, flying specks of burning wadding hurled across the cabin, and the impact of lead shot into living flesh sounded like a handful of watermelon pips thrown against a wall.

Ingrid fired the second barrel a moment before Karen, so this time the two shots were distinct stunning blurts of sound, and in the dreadful silence that followed the two men in the passenger cabins were screaming wildly.

'Nobody move! Everybody freeze!'

For Peter Stride those fractional seconds seemed to last for long hours. They seemed to play on endlessly through his brain, like a series of frozen frames in a grotesque movie. Image after image seemed separated from the whole, so that forever afterwards he would be able to recreate each of them entire and undistorted and to experience again undiluted the paralysing nausea of those moments.

The pregnant woman took the full blast of one of the first shots. She burst open like an overripe fruit, her swollen body pulled out of shape by the passage of shot from spine to navel, and she was flung forward so she somersaulted out into space. She hit the tarmac in a loose tangle of pale thin limbs, and was completely still, no flicker of life remaining.

The plump woman clung to the boy beside her, and they teetered in the open doorway – around them swirled pale blue wisps of gunsmoke. Though she kept her balance, the tightly stretched beige silk of her dress was speckled with dozens of tiny wounds, as though she had been stabbed repeatedly with a sharpened knitting needle. The same wounds were torn through the boy's white school shirt, and little scarlet flowers bloomed swiftly around each wound, spreading to stain the cloth. Neither of them made any sound, and their expressions were startled and uncomprehending. The next blasts of sound and shot struck them solidly, and they seemed boneless and without substance as they tumbled forward, still locked together. Their fall seemed to continue for a very long time, and then they sprawled together over the pregnant woman's body.

Peter ran forward to catch the girl-child as she fell, and her weight bore him to his knees on the tarmac. He came to his feet running, carrying her like a sleepy baby, one arm under her knees and the other around her shoulders. Her lovely head bumped against his shoulder, and the fine silken hair blew into his face, half blinding him.

'Don't die,' he found himself grunting the words in time to his pounding feet. 'Please don't die.' But he could feel the warm wet leak of blood down his belly, soaking into his shorts, and dribbling down the front of his thighs.

At the entrance to the terminal buildings Colin Noble ran out a dozen paces and tried to take the child from his arms, but Peter resisted him fiercely.

Peter relinquished the frail, completely relaxed body to the Thor doctor, and he stood by without word or expression of regret as the doctor worked swiftly over her. Peter's face was stony and his wide mouth clamped in a hard line when the doctor looked up at last.

'I'm afraid she's dead, sir.'

Peter nodded curtly and turned away. His heels cracked on the echoing marble of the deserted terminal hall and Colin Noble fell in silently beside him. His face was as bleak and expressionless as Peter's, as they climbed into the cabin of the Hawker command aircraft.

'Sir William, you point at us for holding enemies of the State without trial.' The Foreign Minister leaned forward to point the accuser's finger. 'But you British discarded the citizen's right of Habeas Corpus when you passed the Prevention of Terrorism Act, and in Cyprus and Palestine you were holding prisoners without trial long before that. Now your H block in Ulster – is that any better than what we are forced to do here?'

Sir William, the British Ambassador, gobbled indignantly, while he collected his thoughts.

Kelly Constable intervened smoothly. 'Gentlemen, we are trying to find common ground here – not areas of dispute. There are hundreds of lives at stake—'

A telephone shrilled in the air-conditioned hush of the room and Sir William lifted the receiver to his ear with patent relief, but as he listened, all blood drained from his face, leaving it a jaundiced, putty colour.

'I see,' he said once, and then, 'very well, thank you,' and replaced the receiver. He looked down the length of the long polished imbuia wood table to the imposing figure at the end.

'Prime Minister—' his voice quavered a little ' – I regret to inform you that the terrorists have rejected the compromise proposals offered by your government, and that ten minutes ago they murdered four hostages—'

There was a gasp of disbelief from the attentive circle of listening men.

' – The hostages were two women and two children – a boy and a girl – they were shot in the back and their bodies thrown from the aircraft. The terrorists have set a new deadline – midnight tonight – for the acceptance of their terms. Failing which there will be further shootings.'

The silence lasted for almost a minute as head after head turned slowly, until they were all staring at the big hunched figure at the head of the table.

'I appeal to you in the name of humanity, sir.' It was

Kelly Constable who broke the silence. 'We must save the women and children at least. The world will not allow us to sit by as they are murdered.'

'We will have to attack the aircraft and free the prisoners,' said the Prime Minister heavily.

But the American Ambassador shook his head. 'My government is adamant, sir – as is that of my British colleague—' he glanced at Sir William, who nodded support ' – we cannot and will not risk a massacre. Attack the aircraft and our governments will make no attempt to moderate the terms of the U.N. proposals, nor will we intervene in the Security Council to exercise the veto.'

'Yet, if we agree to the demands of these – these animals—' the last words were said fiercely ' – we place our nation in terrible danger.'

'Prime Minister, we have only hours to find a solution – then the killing will begin again.'

'You yourself have placed the success chances of a Delta strike as low as even,' Kingston Parker pointed out, staring grimly at Peter Stride out of the little square screen. 'Neither the President nor I find those odds acceptable.'

'Doctor Parker, they are murdering women and children out there on the tarmac.' Peter tried to keep his tone neutral, his reasoning balanced.

'Very strong pressure is being brought to bear on the South African Government to accede to the terms for release of the women and children.'

'That will solve nothing.' Peter could not restrain himself. 'It will leave us with exactly the same situation tomorrow night.'

'If we can secure the release of the women and children, the number of lives at risk will be reduced, and in forty hours the situation might have changed – we are buying time, Peter, even if we have to pay for it with a heavy coin.'

'And if the South Africans do not agree? If we come to the midnight deadline without an agreement with the hijackers, what happens then, Doctor Parker?'

'This is a difficult thing to say, Peter, but if that happens—' Parker spread those long graceful hands in a gesture of resignation, ' – we may lose another four lives, but that is better than precipitating the massacre of four hundred. And after that the South Africans will not be able to hold out. They will have to agree to free the women and children – at any cost.'

Peter could not truly believe what he had heard. He knew he was on the very brink of losing his temper completely, and he had to give himself a few seconds to steady himself. He dropped his eyes to his own hands that were interlocked on the desk top in front of him. Under the fingernails of his right hand were black half moons, the dried blood of the child he had carried back from the aircraft. Abruptly he unlocked his fingers and thrust both hands deeply into the pockets of his blue Thor overalls. He took a long deep breath, held it a moment, then let it out slowly.

'If that was difficult to say, Doctor Parker – console yourself that it was a bloody sight harder to listen to.'

'I understand how you feel, Peter.'

'I don't think you do, sir.' Peter shook his head slowly.

'You are a soldier—'

' – and only a soldier knows how to really hate violence,' Peter finished for him.

'Our personal feelings must not be allowed to intrude in this.' Kingston Parker's voice had a sharp edge to it now. 'I must once again forcibly remind you that the decision for condition Delta has been delegated to me by the President and your Prime Minister. No strike will be made without my express orders. Do you understand that, General Stride?'

'I understand, Doctor Parker,' Peter said flatly. 'And we hope to get some really good videotapes of the next murders. I'll let you have copies for your personal collection.'

The other 747 had been grounded for servicing when the emergency began, and it was parked in the assembly area only a thousand yards from where Speedbird 070 stood, but the main service hangars and the corner of the terminal buildings effectively screened it from any observation by the hijackers.

Although it wore the orange and blue of South African Airways with the flying Springbok on the tail, it was an almost identical model to its sister ship. Even the cabin configurations were very close to the plans of Speedbird 070, which had been teleprinted from British Airways Headquarters at Heathrow. It was a fortunate coincidence, and an opportunity that Colin Noble had seized immediately. He had already run seven mock Deltas on the empty hull.

'All right, you guys, let's try and get our arses out of low gear on this run. I want to better fourteen seconds from the "go" to penetration—' His strike team glanced at one another as they squatted in a circle on the tarmac, and there were a few theatrical rollings of eyes. Colin ignored them. 'Let's go for nine seconds, gang,' he said and stood up.

There were sixteen men in the actual assault group – seventeen when Peter Stride joined them. The other members of Thor were technical experts – electronics and communications, four marksmen snipers, a weapons quartermaster, and a bomb disposal and explosives sergeant, doctor, cook, three engineering N.C.O.s under a lieutenant, the pilots and other flight personnel – a big team, but every man was indispensable.

The assault group wore single-piece uniforms of close fitting black nylon, for low night visibility. They wore their gas masks loosely around their necks, ready for instant use. Their boots were black canvas lace-ups, with soft rubber soles for silence. Each man wore his specialized weapons and equipment either in a back pack or on his black webbing belt. No bulky bulletproof flak jackets to impede mobility or to snag on obstacles, no hard helmets to tap against metal and tell tales to a wary adversary.

Nearly all the group were young men, in their early twenties, hand picked from the U.S. Marine corps or from the British 22.SAS regiment that Peter Stride had once commanded. They were superbly fit, and honed to a razor's edge.

Colin Noble watched them carefully as they assembled silently on the marks he had chalked on the tarmac, representing the entrances to the air terminal and the service hangars nearest to 070. He was searching for any sign of slackness, any deviation from the almost impossible standards he had set for Thor. He could find none. 'All right, ten seconds – to flares,' he called. A Delta strike began with the launching of phosphorus flares across the nose of the target aircraft. They would float down on their tiny parachutes, causing a diversion which would hopefully bunch the terrorists in the flight deck of the target aircraft as they tried to figure out the reason for the lights. The brilliance of the flares would also sear the retina of the terrorists' eyes and destroy night vision for many minutes afterwards.

'Flares!' shouted Colin, and the assault group went into action. The two 'stick' men led them, sprinting out directly under the gigantic tail of the deserted aircraft. Each of them carried a gas cylinder strapped across his shoulder, to which the long stainless steel probes were attached by flexible armoured couplings – these were the 'sticks' that gave them their name.

The leader carried compressed air in the tank upon his back at a pressure of 250 atmospheres, and on the tip of his twenty-foot probe was the diamond cutting bit of the air-drill. He dropped on one knee under the belly of the aircraft ten feet behind the landing gear and reached up to press the point of the air-drill against the exact spot, carefully plotted from the manufacturer's drawing, where the pressure hull was thinnest and where direct access to the passenger cabins lay just beyond the skin of alloy metal.

The whine of the cutting drill would be covered by the revving of the jet engines of aircraft parked in the southern terminal. Three seconds to pierce the hull, and the second 'stick' man was ready to insert the tip of his probe into the drill hole.

'Power off,' Colin grunted; at that moment electrical power from the mains to the aircraft would be cut to kill the air-conditioning.

The second man simulated the act of releasing the gas from the bottle on his back through the probe and saturating the air in the aircraft's cabins. The gas was known simply as FACTOR V. It smelled faintly of newly dug truffles, and when breathed as a five per cent concentration in air would partially paralyse a man in under ten seconds – loss of motor control of the muscles, unco-ordinated movement, slurred speech and distorted vision, were initial symptoms.

Breathed for twenty seconds the symptoms were total paralysis, for thirty seconds loss of consciousness; breathed for two minutes, pulmonary failure and death. The antidote was fresh air or, better still, pure oxygen, and recovery was rapid with no long-term after-effects.

The rest of the assault group had followed the 'stick' men and split into four teams. They waited poised, squatting under the wings, gas masks in place, equipment and weapons ready for instant use.

Colin was watching his stopwatch. He could not chance exposing the passengers to more than ten seconds of Factor V. There would be elderly people, infants, asthma sufferers aboard; as the needle reached the ten-second mark, he snapped.

'Power on.' Air-conditioning would immediately begin washing the gas out of the cabins again, and now it was 'Go!'

Two assault teams poured up the aluminium scaling ladders onto the wing roots, and knocked out the emergency window panels. The other two teams went for the main doors, but they could only simulate the use of slap-hammers to tear through the metal and reach the locking device on the interior – nor could they detonate the stun grenades.

'Penetration.' The assault leader standing in for Peter Stride on this exercise signalled entry of the cabins, and Colin clicked his stopwatch.

'Time?' asked a quiet voice at his shoulder, and he turned quickly. So intent on his task, Colin had not heard Peter Stride come up behind him.

'Eleven seconds, sir.' The courteous form of address was proof of Colonel Colin Noble's surprise. 'Not bad – but sure as hell not good either. We'll run it again.'

'Rest them,' Peter ordered. 'I want to talk it out a bit.'

They stood together at the full windows in the south wall of the air traffic control tower, and studied the big red, white and blue aircraft for the hundredth time that day.

The heat of the afternoon had raised thunderheads, great purple and silver mushroom bursts of cloud that reached to the heavens. Trailing grey skirts of torrential rain they marched across the horizon, forming a majestic backdrop that was almost too theatrical to be real, while the lowering sun found the gaps in the cloud and shot long groping fingers of golden light through them, heightening the illusion of theatre.

'Six hours to deadline,' Colin Noble grunted, and groped for one of his scented black cheroots. 'Any news of concessions by the locals?'

'Nothing. I don't think they will buy it.'

'Not until the next batch of executions.' Colin bit the end from the cheroot and spat it angrily into a corner. 'For two years I break my balls training for this, and now they tie our hands behind our backs.'

'If they gave you Delta, when would you make your run?' Peter asked.

'As soon as it was dark,' Colin answered promptly.

'No. They are still revved up high on drugs,' Peter demurred. 'We should give them time to go over the top, and start downing. My guess is they will dope again just before the next deadline. I would hit them just before that—' He paused to calculate. ' – I'd hit them at fifteen minutes before eleven – seventy-five minutes before the deadline.'

'If we had Delta,' Colin grunted.

'If we had Delta,' Peter agreed, and they were silent for a moment. 'Listen, Colin, this has been wearing me down. If they know my name, what else does that gang of freaks know about Thor? Do they know our contingency planning for taking an aircraft?'

'God, I hadn't worked it out that far.'

'I have been looking for a twist, a change from the model, something that will give us the jump even if they know what to expect.'

'We've taken two years to set it up tightly—' Colin looked dubious. 'There is nothing we can change.'

'The flares,' said Peter. 'If we went, we would not signal the Delta with the flares, we would go in cold.'

'The uglies would be scattered all through the cabins, mixed up with passengers and crew—'

'The red shirt Ingrid was wearing. My guess is, all four of them will be uniformed to impress their hostages. We would hose anything and everybody in red. If my guess is wrong, then we would have to do it Israeli style.'

Israeli style was the shouted command to lie down, and to kill anyone who disobeyed or who made an aggressive move.

'The truly important one is the girl. The girl with the camera. Have your boys studied the videotapes of her?'

'They know her face better than they do Fawcett Majors',' Colin grunted, and then, 'the bitch is so goddamned lovely – I had to run the video of the executions three times for them, twice in slow motion, to wipe out a little of the old chivalry bit.' It is difficult to get a man to kill a pretty girl, and a moment of hesitation would be critical with a trained fanatic like Ingrid. 'I also made them take a look at the little girl before they put her in a basket and took her down to the morgue. They're in the right mood.' Colin shrugged. 'But what the hell, Atlas isn't going to call Delta. We're wasting our time.'

'Do you want to play make-believe?' Peter asked, and then without waiting for an answer, 'Let's make believe we have a Delta approval from Atlas. I want you to set up a strike timed to "go" at exactly 10.45 local time tonight. Do it as though it was the real thing – get it right in every detail.'

Colin turned slowly and studied his commander's face, but the eyes were level and without guile and the strong lines of jaw and mouth were unwavering.

'Make-believe?' Colin Noble asked quietly.

'Of course,' Peter Stride's tone was curt and impatient, and Colin shrugged.

'Hell, I only work here,' and he turned away.

Peter lifted the binoculars and slowly traversed the length of the big machine from tail to nose, but there was no sign of life, every port and window still carefully covered

– and reluctantly he let his binoculars sink slightly until he was staring at the pitiful pile of bodies that still lay on the tarmac below the forward hatch.

Except for the electrical mains hook-up, the delivery of medicines and the two occasions when Peter himself had made the long trip out there, nobody else had been allowed to approach the machine. No refuelling, no refuse nor sanitary removals, no catering – not even the removal of the corpses of the murdered hostages. The hijackers had learned the lesson of previous hijacking attempts when vital information had been smuggled off the aircraft in refuse and sewerage at Mogadishu, and at Lod where the storming party had come disguised as caterers.

Peter was still gazing at the bodies, and though he was accustomed to death in its most obscene forms, these bodies offended him more deeply than any in his life before. This was a contemptuous flaunting of all the deepest rooted taboos of society. Peter was grimly content now with the decision of the South African police not to allow any television teams or press photographers through the main gates of the airport.

Peter knew that the world media were howling outrage and threats, protesting in the most extreme terms against the infringement of their God-given rights to bring into the homes of all civilized people images of dreadful death and mutilation, lovingly photographed in gorgeous colour with meticulous professional attention to all the macabre details.

Without this enthusiastic chronicling of their deeds, international terrorism would lose most of its impetus and his job would be a lot easier. For sneaking moments he envied the local police the powers they had to force irresponsibles to act in the best interests of society, then as he carried the thought a step further, he came up hard once again against the question of who was qualified to make such decisions on behalf of society. If the police made that decision and exerted it, was it not just another form of the terrorism it was seeking to suppress? 'Christ,' thought Peter angrily, 'I'm going to drive myself mad.'

He stepped up beside the senior air traffic controller.

'I want to try again,' Peter said, and the man handed him the microphone.

'Speedbird 070 this is the tower. Ingrid, do you read me? Come in, Ingrid.'

He had tried a dozen times to make contact in the last few hours, but the hijackers had maintained an ominous silence.

'Ingrid, come in please.' Peter kept trying, and suddenly there was the clear fresh voice.

'This is Ingrid. What do you want?'

'Ingrid, we request your clearance to have an ambulance remove the bodies,' Peter asked.

'Negative, Tower. I say again, negative. No one is to approach this aircraft.' There was a pause. 'We will wait until we have a round dozen bodies for you to remove—' The girl giggled, still on the drug high, ' – wait until midnight, and we'll make it really worth your while.' And the radio clicked into silence.

'We are going to give you dinner now,' Ingrid shouted cheerfully, and there was a stir of interest down the length of the cabin. 'And it's my birthday today. So you're going to have champagne – isn't that great!'

But the plump little Jewish doctor rose suddenly to his feet. His grey sparse hair stood up in comical wisps, and his face seemed to have collapsed, like melting candle wax, ravaged and destroyed by grief. He no longer seemed to be aware of what had been said or what was happening. 'You had no right to kill her.' His voice sounded like a very old man. 'She was a good person. She never hurt anyone—' He looked about him with a confused, unfocused look, and ran the fingers of one hand through his disordered hair. 'You should not have killed her,' he repeated.

'She was guilty,' Ingrid called back at him. 'Nobody is innocent – you are all the cringing tools of international capitalism—' Her face twisted, in an ugly spasm of hatred. ' – You are guilty, all of you, and you deserve to die—' She stopped short, controlled herself with an obvious effort of will, and then smiled again; going forward to the little doctor, she put an arm around his shoulders. 'Sit down,' she said, almost tenderly, 'I know just how you feel, please believe me, I wish there had been another way.'

He sank down slowly, his eyes vacant with sorrow and his fingers plucking numbly at themselves.

'You just sit there quietly,' Ingrid said gently. 'I'm going to bring you a glass of champagne now.'

'Prime Minister—' Kelly Constable's voice was husky with almost two days and nights of unceasing tension, ' – it's after ten o'clock already. We must have a decision soon, in less than two hours—'

The Prime Minister lifted one hand to silence the rest of it.

'Yes, we all know what will happen then.'

An airforce jet has delivered a copy of the videotape from Johannesburg, a thousand miles away, and the cabinet and the ambassadors had watched the atrocity in detail, recorded by an 800-mm lens. There was not a man at the table who did not have children of his own. The toughest right-wingers amongst them wavered uncertainly, even the puckish little Minister of Police could not meet the ambassador's eyes as he swept the table with a compelling gaze.

'And we all know that no compromise is possible, we must meet the demands in full or not at all.'

'Mr Ambassador—' the Prime Minister broke the silence at last, ' – if we agree to the terms, it will be only as an act of humanity. We will be paying a very high price indeed for the lives of your people – but if we agree to that price, can we be absolutely assured of your support – the support of both Britain and the United States – in the Security Council the day after tomorrow at noon?'

'The President of the United States has empowered me to pledge his support in return for your co-operation,' said Kelly Constable.

'Her Britannic Majesty's Government has asked me to assure you of the same support,' intoned Sir William. 'And our governments will make good the 170 million dollars demanded by the hijackers.'

'Still I cannot make the decision on my own. It is too onerous for one man,' the Prime Minister sighed. 'I am going to ask my ministers, the full cabinet—' he indicated the tense, grim faces around him, ' – to vote. I am going to ask you gentlemen to leave us alone now for a few minutes while we decide.'

And the two ambassadors rose together and bowed slightly to the brooding, troubled figure before leaving the room.

'Where is Colonel Noble?' Kingston Parker asked. 'He is waiting—' Peter indicated with a jerk of his head the sound-proof door of the Hawker's command cabin.

'I want him in on this, please,' Parker said from the screen, and Peter pressed the call button.

Colin Noble came in immediately, stooping slightly under the low roof, a chunky powerful figure with the blue Thor cap pulled low over his eyes.

'Good evening, sir.' He greeted the image on the screen and squeezed into the seat beside Peter.

'I'm glad Colonel Noble is here.' Peter's voice was crisp and businesslike. 'I think he will support my contention that the chances of a successful Delta counterstrike will be greatly enhanced if we can launch our attack not later than ten minutes before eleven o'clock.' He tugged back the cuff of his sleeve, and glanced at his watch. 'That is forty minutes from now. We reckon to catch the militants at the moment when the drug cycle is at its lowest, before they take more pills and begin to arouse themselves to meet their deadline. I believe that if we strike then, we will have an acceptable risk—'

'Thank you, General Stride—' Parker interrupted him smoothly, ' – but I wanted Colonel Noble present so there could be no misunderstanding of my orders. Colonel Noble—' Parker's eyes shifted slightly as he changed the object of his attention. 'Commander of Thor has requested an immediate Delta strike against Speedbird 070. I am now, in your presence, disapproving that request. Negotiations with the South African Government are at a critical state, and under no circumstances must there be either overt or covert hostile moves towards the militants. Do I make myself entirely clear?'

'Yes, sir.' Colin Noble's expression was stony.

'General Stride?'

'I understand, sir.'

'Very well. I want you to stand by, please. I am going to confer with the ambassadors. I will re-establish contact as soon as I have further concrete indications.'

The image receded rapidly, and the screen went dark. Colonel Colin Noble turned slowly and looked at Peter Stride, his expression changed slightly at what he saw, and quickly he pressed the censor button on the command console, stopping all recording tapes, killing the video cameras so there would be no record of his words now.

'Listen, Peter, you're in line for that NATO command, everybody knows that. From there the sky is the limit, pal. Right up there to the joint chiefs – just as far as you want to go.'

Peter said nothing, but glanced once more at the gold Rolex wristwatch. It was seventeen minutes past ten o'clock.

'Think, Peter. For God's sake, man. It's taken you twenty heart-breaking years of hard work to get where you are. They would never forgive you, buddy. You'd better believe it. They'll break you and your career. Don't do it, Peter. Don't do it. You're too good to waste yourself. Just stop and think for one minute.'

'I'm thinking,' said Peter quietly. 'I haven't stopped thinking since—' he checked, ' – always it comes back to this. If I let them die – then I am as guilty as that woman who pulls the trigger.'

'Peter, you don't have to beat your head in. The decision is made by someone else—'

'It would be easier to believe that, wouldn't it,' Peter snapped, 'but it won't save those people out there.'

Colin leaned across and placed a large hairy paw on Peter's upper arm. He squeezed slightly. 'I know, but it eats me to see you have to throw it all away. In my book, you're one of the tops, buddy.' It was the first time he had made any such declaration, and Peter was fleetingly moved by it.

'You can duck this one, Colin. It doesn't have to touch you or your career.'

'I never was very hot at ducking.' Colin dropped his hand away. 'I think I'll go along for the ride—'

'I want you to record a protest – no sense us all getting ourselves fired,' said Peter, as he switched on the recording equipment, both audio and video; now every word would be recorded.

'Colonel Noble,' he said distinctly, 'I am about to lead an immediate Delta assault on Flight 070. Please make the arrangements.'

Colin turned to face the camera. 'General Stride, I must formally protest at any order to initiate condition Delta without express approval from Atlas Command.'

'Colonel Noble, your protest is noted,' Peter told the camera gravely, and Colin Noble hit the censor button once again, cutting tapes and camera.

'Okay, that's enough crap for one day.' He came nimbly to his feet. 'Let's get out there and take the bastards.'

Ingrid sat at the flight engineer's desk, and held the microphone of the on-board loudspeaker system to her lips. There was a greyish tone beneath the sun-gilded skin; she frowned a little at the throbbing pulse of pain behind her eyes and the hand that held the microphone trembled slightly. She knew these were all symptoms of the drug hangover. She regretted now having increased the initial dosage beyond that recommended on the typed label of the tablet phial – but she had needed that extra lift to be able to carry out the first executions. Now she and her officers were paying the price, but in another twenty minutes she would be able to issue another round of tablets. This time she would stay exactly within the recommended dosage, and she anticipated the rush of it through her blood, the heightened vision and energy, the tingling exhilaration of the drug. She even anticipated the thought of what lay ahead; to be able to wield absolute power, the power of death itself, was one of life's most worthwhile experiences. Sartre and Bakunin and Most had discovered one of the great truths of life – that the act of destruction, of total destruction, was a catharsis, a creation, a reawakening of the soul. She looked forward, even through the staleness

110

and ache of the drug let-down, she looked forward to the next executions.

'My friends—' she spoke into the microphone, ' – we have not heard from the tyrant. His lack of concern for your lives is typical of the fascist imperialist. He does not concern himself with the safety of the people, though he sucks and bloats himself on the blood and sweat—'

Outside the aircraft the night was black and close. Thunderheads blotted out half the sky, and every few minutes lightning lit the clouds internally. Twice since sundown abrupt fierce downpours of torrential rain had hammered briefly against the Boeing hull, and now the airport lights glinted on the puddled tarmac.

' – We have to show the face of unrelenting courage and iron purpose to the tyrant. We cannot afford to show even a moment's hesitation. We must now choose four more hostages. It will be done with the utmost impartiality – and I want you all to realize that we are now all part of the revolution together, you can be proud of that—'

Lightning exploded suddenly, much closer, a crackling greenish, iridescent flaming of the heavens that lit the field in merciless light, and then the flail of the thunder beat down upon the aircraft. The girl Karen exclaimed involuntarily and sprang nervously to her feet and crossed quickly to stand beside Ingrid. Her dark eyes were now heavily underscored by the dark kohl of fatigue and drug withdrawal; she trembled violently, and Ingrid caressed her absently the way she might calm a frightened kitten as she went on speaking into the microphone.

' – We must all of us learn to welcome death, to welcome the opportunity to take our place and add our contribution, no matter how humble it might be, to man's great reawakening.'

Lightning burst in fierce splendour once again, but Ingrid went on talking into the microphone, the senseless words somehow hypnotic and lulling so that her captives sat in quietly lethargic rows, not speaking, unmoving, seeming no longer capable of independent thought.

'I have drawn lots to choose the next martyrs of the revolution. I will call out the seat numbers and my officers will come to fetch you. Please co-operate by moving quickly forward to the first-class galley.' There was a pause, and then Ingrid's voice again. 'Seat number 63B. Please stand up.'

The scarred German in the red shirt and with the lank black hair hanging over his eyes had to force the thin, middle-aged man to his feet, twisting his wrist up between his shoulder blades. The man's white shirt was crumpled and he wore elastic braces over his shoulders and old-fashioned narrow trousers.

'You can't let them,' the man pleaded with his fellow passengers, as Henri pushed him up the aisle. 'You can't let them kill me, please.' And they looked down at their laps. Nobody moved, nobody spoke.

'Seat number 43F.' It was a handsome dark-haired woman in her middle thirties, and her face seemed to dissolve slowly as she read the number above her seat, and she covered her mouth with one hand to prevent herself crying out – but from the seat exactly across the aisle from her a sprightly old gentleman with a magnificent mane of silver-grey hair rose swiftly to his feet and adjusted his tie.

'Would you care to change seats with me, madam?' he said softly in a clipped English accent, and strode down the aisle, on long, thin, stork-like legs, contemptuously brushing past the blond moustached Frenchman who came hurrying forward to escort him. Without a glance to either side, and with thin shoulders thrown back, he disappeared through the curtains into the forward galley.

The Boeing had a blind spot that extended back from the side windows of the flight deck at an angle of 20° to the tail, but the hijackers were so well equipped and seemed to have considered every eventuality in such detail that there was no reason to fear that they had worked out some arrangement to keep the blind spot under surveillance.

Peter and Colin discussed the possibility quietly as they stood in the angle of the main service hangar, and both of them carefully studied the soaring shape of the Boeing tailplane and the sagging underbelly of the fuselage for the glint of a mirror or some other device. They were directly behind the aircraft and there was a little over four hundred yards to cover, half of that through knee-high grass and the rest over tarmac.

The field was lit only by the blue periphery lights of the taxiway, and the glow of the airport buildings.

Peter had considered dousing all the airport lights, but discarded the idea as self-defeating. It would certainly alert the hijackers, and would slow the crossing of the assault team.

'I can't see anything,' Colin murmured.

'No,' agreed Peter and they both handed their night glasses to a hovering NCO – they wouldn't need them again. The assault team had stripped all equipment down to absolute essentials.

All that Peter carried was a lightweight eleven-ounce VHF transceiver for communicating with his men in the terminal building – and in a quick-release holster on his right hip a Walther PK 38 automatic pistol.

Each member of the assault team carried the weapon of his own choice. Colin Noble favoured the Browning Hi-power .45 for its massive killing power and large fourteen-round magazine, while Peter liked the pinpoint accuracy and light recoil of the 9-mm parabellum Walther with which he could be certain of a snap head-shot at fifty metres.

One item was standard equipment for all members of the assault team. Every one of their weapons was loaded with Super Velex explosive bullets which trebled the knock-down power at impact, breaking up in the human body and thereby reducing the risk of over-penetration and with it the danger to innocents. Peter never let them forget they would nearly always be working with terrorist and victim closely involved.

Beside Peter, Colin Noble unclipped the thin gold chain from around his neck which held the tiny Star of David, twinkling gold on the black bush of his chest hair. He slipped the ornament into his pocket and buttoned down the flap.

'I say, old chap—' Colin Noble gave an atrocious imitation of a Sandhurst accent ' – shall we toddle along then?'

Peter glanced at the luminous dial of his Rolex. It was sixteen minutes to eleven o'clock. The exact moment at which my career ends, he thought grimly, and raised his right arm with clenched fist, then pumped it up and down twice, the old cavalry signal to advance.

Swiftly the two men raced out ahead, absolutely silent on soft rubber soles, carrying their probes at high port to prevent them clattering against tarmac or against the metal parts of the aircraft, dark hunchbacked figures under the burden of the gas cylinders they carried.

Peter gave them a slow count of five, and while he waited he felt the adrenalin charge his blood, every nerve and muscle of his body coming under tension, and he heard his own words to Kingston Parker echo in his ears like the prophecy of doom.

'There is no middle ground. The alternative is one hundred per cent casualties. We lose the aircraft, the passengers and all the Thor personnel aboard her.'

He thrust the thought aside, and repeated the signal to

advance. In two neat files, bunched up close and well in hand, the assault teams went out, at the run. Three men carrying each of the aluminium alloy scaling ladders, four with the sling-bags of stun grenades, others with the slap hammers to tear out the door locks, and each with his chosen weapon – always a big calibre handgun – for Peter Stride would trust nobody with an automatic weapon in the crowded interior of a hijacked aircraft, and the minimum requirement for every member of the assault teams was marksmanship with a pistol that would enable him to pick a small moving target and hit it repeatedly and quickly without endangering innocents.

They ran in almost total silence; the loudest sound was Peter's breathing in his own ears, and he had time now for a moment's regret. It was a gamble which he could never win, the best that could happen was the utter ruin of his life's work, but he steeled himself brutally and thrust aside the thought. He ran on into the night.

Just ahead of him now, silhouetted by the lights of the terminal building, the dark figures of the 'stick' men were in position under the bulging silver belly; and lightning flared suddenly, so that the tall silver thunderheads rippled with intense white fire, and the field was starkly lit, the double column of black-clad figures standing out clearly against the paler grass. If they were observed, it would come now, and the crash of thunder made Peter's nerves jump, expecting detonation and flame of a dozen percussion grenades.

Then it was dark again, and the sponginess of wet grass beneath his feet gave way to flat hard tarmac. Then suddenly they were under the Boeing fuselage, like chickens under the protective belly of the hen, and the two columns split neatly into four separate groups and still in tight order every man dropped onto his left knee, and at the same moment, with the precision of repeated rehearsals, every member of the team lifted his gas mask to cover his nose and mouth.

Peter swept one quick glance back at them, and then depressed the transmit button on his transceiver. He would not speak a word from now until it was over; there was always a remote possibility that the hijackers were monitoring this frequency.

The click of the button was the signal to the members of his team in the terminal – and almost immediately, there was a rising whistling howl of jet engines running up.

Even though the aircraft were parked up in the northern international departures area, they had been turned so the jet exhausts were pointed at the service area, and there were five intercontinental jet liners co-operating. The combined sound output of twenty big jet engines was deafening even at that range – and Peter gave the open hand signal.

The 'stick' man was waiting poised, and at the signal he reached up and placed the drill bit against the belly of the fuselage. Any sound of the compressed air spinning the drill was effectively drowned, and there was only the slight jerk of the long probe as it went through the pressure hull. Instantly the second 'stick' man placed the tip of his probe into the tiny hole, and glanced at Peter. Again the open hand signal, and the gas was spurting into the hull. Peter was watching the sweep hand of his watch.

Two clicks on the transmit button, and the lights behind the row of shaded portholes blinked out simultaneously as the mains power was cut – and the air-conditioning in the Boeing's cabins with it.

The howl of combined jet engines continued a few seconds longer and Peter signalled the ladder men forward.

Gently the rubber-padded tops of the ladders were hooked onto the leading edges of the wings and into the door sills high above them by black-costumed, grotesquely masked figures working with deceptively casual speed.

Ten seconds from discharge of the Factor V gas into the hull, and Peter clicked thrice. Instantly mains power to the Boeing was resumed and the lights flicked on. Now the air-conditioning was running again, washing the gas swiftly from the cabins and flight deck.

Peter drew one long, slow deep breath and tapped Colin's shoulder. They went up the ladders in a concerted silent rush, Peter and Colin leading the teams to each wing surface.

'Nine minutes to eleven,' said Ingrid to Karen. She lifted her voice slightly above the din of jet engines howling somewhere out there in the night. Her throat was dry and sore from the drug withdrawal and a nerve jumped involuntarily in the corner of her eye. Her headache felt as though a knotted rope was being twisted slowly tighter around her forehead. 'It looks as though Caliph miscalculated. The South Africans aren't going to give in—' She glanced with a small anticipatory twist of her lips back through the open door of the flight deck at the four hostages sitting in a row on the fold-down seats. The silver-haired Englishman was smoking a Virginia cigarette in a long amber and ivory holder, and he returned her gaze with disdain, so that Ingrid felt a prickle of annoyance and raised her voice so he could hear her next words. 'It's going to be necessary to shoot this batch also.'

'Caliph has never been wrong before.' Karen shook her head vehemently. 'There is still an hour to deadline—' and at that instant the lights flickered once and then went out. With all the portholes shaded the darkness was complete, and the hiss of the air-conditioning faded into silence before there was a murmur of surprised comment.

Ingrid groped across the control panel for the switch

which transferred the flight deck onto the power from the aircraft's own batteries, and as the soft ruddy glow of the panel lights came on her expression was tense and worried.

'They've switched off the mains,' she exclaimed. 'The air-conditioning – this could be Delta.'

'No.' Karen's voice was shrill. 'There are no flares.'

'We could be—' Ingrid started but she could hear the drunken slur in her own voice. Her tongue felt too large for her mouth, and Karen's face started to distort before her eyes, the edges blurring out of focus.

'Karen—' she said, and now in her nostrils the unmistakable aroma of truffles and on her tongue the taste of raw mushrooms.

'Christ!' she screamed wildly and lunged for the manual oxygen release. Above each seat the panels dropped open and the emergency oxygen masks dangled down into the cabins on their corrugated hoses.

'Kurt! Henri!' Ingrid shrieked into the cabin intercom. 'Oxygen! Take oxygen! It's Delta. They are going to Delta.'

She grabbed one of the dangling oxygen masks and sucked in deep pumping breaths, cleansing the numbing paralysing gas from her system. In the first-class galley one of the hostages collapsed slowly forward and tumbled onto the deck, another slumped sideways.

Still breathing oxygen, Ingrid unslung the camera from around her neck, and Karen watched her with huge terrified dark eyes. She lifted the oxygen mask from her face to ask:

'You're not going to blow, Ingrid?'

Ingrid ignored her and used the oxygen in her lungs to shout into the microphone.

'Kurt! Henri! They will come as soon as the mains are switched on again. Cover your eyes and ears for the stun grenades and watch the doors and wing windows.' Ingrid slapped the oxygen mask back over her mouth and panted wildly.

'Don't blow us up, Ingrid,' Karen pleaded around her mask. 'Please, if we surrender Caliph will have us free in a month. We don't have to die.'

At that moment the lights of the cabin came on brightly, and there was the hiss of the air-conditioning. Ingrid took one last breath of oxygen and ran back into the first-class cabin, jumping over the unconscious figures of the hostages and of two air hostesses. She grabbed another of the dangling oxygen masks above a passenger seat and looked down the long fuselage.

Kurt and Henri had obeyed her orders. They were breathing oxygen from the roof panels. The German was ready at the port wing panel, and Henri waited at the rear doorway hatch – both of them had the short big-mouthed shot pistols ready, but their faces were covered with the yellow oxygen masks, so Ingrid could not see nor judge their expressions.

Only a small number of the passengers had been quick enough and sensible enough to grab the dangling oxygen masks and remain conscious – but hundreds of others slumped in their seats or had fallen sideways into the aisles.

A thicket of dangling, twisting, swinging oxygen hoses filled the cabin like a forest of lianas, obscuring and confusing the scene, and after the darkness the cabin lights were painfully bright.

Ingrid held the camera in her free hand, for she knew that they must continue breathing oxygen. It would take the air-conditioning many minutes longer to cleanse the air of all trace of Factor V, and she held a mask over her mouth and waited.

Karen was beside her, with her shot pistol dangling from one hand and the other pressing a mask to her mouth.

'Go back and cover the front hatch,' Ingrid snapped at her. 'There will be—'

'Ingrid, we don't have to die,' Karen pleaded, and with a

crash the emergency exit panel over the port wing burst inward, and at the same instant two small dark objects flew threw the dark opening into the cabin.

'Stun grenades!' Ingrid howled. 'Get down!'

Peter Stride was light and jubilant as an eagle in flight. His feet and hands hardly seemed to touch the rungs of the ladder, now in the swift all-engulfing rush of action there were no longer doubts, no more hesitations – he was committed, and it was a tremendous soaring relief.

He went up over the smooth curved leading edge of the wing with a roll of his shoulders and hips, and in the same movement was on his feet, padding silently down the broad glistening metal pathway. The raindrops glittered like diamonds under his feet, and a fresh wind tugged at his hair as he ran.

He reached the main hull, and dropped into position at the side of the panel, his fingertips finding the razor-tight joint while his number-two man knelt swiftly opposite him. The grenade men were ready facing the panel, balanced like acrobats on the curved slippery upper surface of the great wing.

'Under six seconds.' Peter guessed at the time it had taken them to reach this stage from the 'go'. It was as swift and neat as it had never been in training, all of them armed by the knowledge of waiting death and horror.

In unison Peter and his number two hurled their combined strength and weight onto the releases of the emergency escape hatch, and it flew inwards readily, for there was no pressurization to resist, and at exactly the same instant the stun grenades went in cleanly, thrown by the waiting grenade men, and all four members of Peter's team bowed like Mohammedans in prayer to Mecca, covering eyes and ears.

Even outside the cabin, and even with ears and eyes

covered, the thunder of the explosions was appalling, seeming to beat in upon the brain with oppressive physical force, and the glare of burning phosphorus powder painted an X-ray picture of Peter's own fingers on the fleshy red of his closed eyelids. Then the grenade men were shouting into the interior, 'Lie down! Everybody down!' They would keep repeating that order Israeli style as long as it lasted.

Peter was a hundredth of a second slow, numbed by the blast, fumbling slightly at the butt of the Walther, thumbing the hammer as it snapped out of the quick-release holster, and then he went in – feet first through the hatch, like a runner sliding for home base. He was still in the air when he saw the girl in the red shirt running forward brandishing the camera, and screaming something that made no sense, though his brain registered it even in that unholy moment. He fired as his feet touched the deck and his first shot hit the girl in the mouth, punching a dark red hole through the rows of white teeth and snapping her head back so viciously that he heard the small delicate bones of her neck crackle as they broke.

I ngrid used both arms to cover eyes and ears, crouching forward into the appalling blast of sound and light that swept through the crowded cabins like a hurricane wind, and even when it had passed she was reeling wildly clutching for support at a seat back, trying to steady herself and judge the moment when the attackers were into the hull.

Those outside the hull would escape the direct force of the explosives she was about to detonate; there was a high survival chance for them. She wanted to judge the moment when the entire assault team penetrated the hull, she wanted maximum casualties, she wanted to take as many with her as possible, and she lifted the camera above her head with both hands.

'Come on!' she shrieked, but the cabin was thick with swirling clouds of white acrid smoke, and the dangling hoses twisted and writhed like the head of the Medusa. She heard the thunder of a shot pistol and somebody screamed, voices were chanting, 'Lie down! Everybody down!'

It was all smoke and sound and confusion, but she watched the dark opening of the emergency hatchway, waiting for it, finger on the detonator button of the camera. A supple black-clad figure in a grotesque mask torpedoed feet first into the cabin, and at that same instant Karen shrieked beside her.

'No, don't kill us,' and snatched the camera from Ingrid's raised hands, jerking it away by the strap, leaving Ingrid weaponless. Karen ran down the aisle through the smoke, still screaming, 'Don't kill us!' holding the camera like a peace offering. 'Caliph said we would not die.' She ran forward screaming frantically. 'Caliph—' and the black-clad and masked figure twisted lithely in the air, arching his back to land feet first in the centre of the aisle; as his feet touched the deck so the pistol in his right hand jerked up sharply but the shot seemed muted and unwarlike after the concussion of the stun grenades.

Karen was running down the aisle towards him, screaming and brandishing the camera, when the bullet took her in the mouth and wrenched her head backwards at an impossible angle. The next two shots blended into a single blurt of sound, fired so swiftly as to cheat the hearing, and from such close range that even the Velex explosive bullets ripped the back out of Karen's shirt and flooded it with a brighter wetter scarlet as they erupted from between her shoulder blades. The camera went spinning high across the cabin, landing in the lap of an unconscious passenger slumped in one of the central seats between the aisles.

Ingrid reacted with the instinctive speed of a jungle cat, diving forward, flat on the carpet aisle below the line of fire;

shrouded by the sinking white smoke of the grenades she wriggled forward on her belly to reach the camera.

It was twenty feet to where the camera had landed, but Ingrid moved with the speed of a serpent; she knew that the smoke was hiding her, but she knew also that to reach the camera she would have to come to her feet again and reach across two seats and two unconscious bodies.

Peter landed in balance on the carpeted aisle, and he killed the girl swiftly, and danced aside, clearing space for his number two to land.

The next man landed lightly in the space Peter had made for him, and the German in the red shirt jumped out from the angle of the rear galley and hit him in the small of the back with a full charge of buckshot. It almost blew his body into two separate parts, and he seemed to break in the middle like a folding penknife as he collapsed against Peter's legs.

Peter whirled at the shot, turning his back on Ingrid as she crawled forward through the phosphorous smoke.

Kurt was desperately trying to pull down the short, thick barrel of the pistol, for the recoil had thrown it high above his head. His scarlet shirt was open to the navel, shiny hard brown muscle and thick whorls of black body hair, mad glaring eyes through a greasy fringe of black hair, the scarred lip curled in a fixed snarl.

Peter hit him in the chest, taking no chance, and as he reeled backwards still fighting to aim the pistol, Peter hit again, in the head through the temple just in front of the left ear; the eyelids closed tightly over those wild eyes, his features twisted out of shape like a rubber mask and he went down face first into the aisle.

'Two.' Peter found that, as always in these desperate moments, he was functioning very coldly, very efficiently.

His shooting had been as reflexively perfect as if he were walking a combat shoot with jump-up cardboard targets.

He had even counted his shots, there were four left in the Walther.

'And two more of them,' he thought, but the smoke was still so thick that his visibility was down to under fifteen feet, and the swirling forest of dangling oxygen hose still agitated by the grenade blasts cut down his visibility further.

He jumped over the broken body of his number two, the blood squelching under his rubber soles, and suddenly the chunky black figure of Colin Noble loomed across the cabin. He was in the far aisle, having come in over the starboard wing. In the writhing smoke he looked like some demon from the pit, hideous and menacing in his gas mask. He dropped into the marksman's crouch, holding the big Browning in a double-handed grip, and the clangour of the gun beat upon the air like one of the great bronze bells of Notre Dame.

He was shooting at another scarlet-shirted figure, half seen through the smoke and the dangling hoses, a man with a round boyish face and drooping sandy moustache. The big Velex bullets tore the hijacker to pieces with the savagery of a predator's claws. They seemed to pin him like an insect to the central bulkhead, and they smashed chunks of living flesh from his chest and splinters of white bone from his skull.

'Three,' thought Peter. 'One left now – and I must get the camera.'

He had seen the black camera in the hands of the girl he had killed, had seen it fall, and he knew how deadly important it was to secure the detonator before it fell into the hands of the other girl, the blonde one, the dangerous one.

It had been only four seconds since he had penetrated the hull, yet it seemed like a dragging eternity. He could hear the crash of the slap-hammers tearing out the door locks, both fore and aft. Within seconds there would be Thor assault teams pouring into the Boeing through every opening, and he had not yet located the fourth hijacker, the truly dangerous one.

'Get down! Everybody down!' chanted the grenade men, and Peter spun lightly, and ran for the flight deck. He was certain the blonde girl would be there at the control centre.

Then, in front of him lay the girl he had shot down, the long, dark hair spread out around her pale, still terrified face. Her hair was already sodden with dark blood, and the black gap in her white teeth made her look like an old woman. She blocked the aisle with a tangle of slim boneless limbs.

The forward hatch crashed open as the lock gave way, but there were still solid curtains of white smoke ahead of him. Peter gathered himself to jump over the girl's body, and at that instant the other girl, the blonde girl, bounded up from the deck, seeming to appear miraculously from the smoke, like some beautiful but evil apparition.

She dived half across the block of central seating, groping for the camera, and Peter was slightly off balance, blocking himself in the turn to bring his gun hand on to her. He changed hands smoothly, for he was equally accurate with either, but it cost him the tenth part of a second, and the girl had the strap of the camera now and was tugging desperately at it. The camera seemed to be snagged, and Peter swung on her, taking the head shot for she was less than ten paces away, and even in the smoke and confusion he could not miss.

One of the few passengers who had been breathing oxygen from his hanging mask, and was still conscious, ignored the chanted orders 'Get down! Stay down!' and suddenly stumbled to his feet, screaming, 'Don't shoot! Get me out of here! Don't shoot!' in a rising hysterical scream. He was directly between Peter and the red-shirted girl, blocking Peter's field of fire, and Peter wrenched the gun off him at the moment that he fired. The bullet slammed into the roof, and the passenger barged into Peter, still screaming.

'Get me out! I want to get out!'

Peter tried desperately to clear his gun hand, for the girl had broken the strap of the camera and was fumbling with the black box. The passenger had an arm around Peter's gun arm, was shaking him wildly, weeping and screaming.

From across the central block of seats, Colin Noble fired once. He was still in the starboard aisle and the angle was almost impossible, for he had to shoot nine inches past Peter's shoulder, and through the forest of dangling hose.

His first shot missed, but it was close enough to flinch the girl's head violently, the golden hair flickered with the passage of shot, and she stumbled backwards, groping with clumsy fingers for the detonator.

Peter chopped the hysterical passenger in the throat with the stiffened fingers of his right hand and hurled him back into his seat, trying desperately to line up for a shot at the girl – knowing he must get the brain and still her fingers instantly.

Colin fired his second shot, one hundredth of a second before Peter, and the big bullet flung the girl aside, jerking her head out of the track of Peter's shot.

Peter saw the strike of Colin's bullet, it hit her high in the right shoulder, almost in the joint of the scapula and the humerus, shattering the bone with such force that her arm was flung upwards in a parody of a communist salute, twisting unnaturally and whipping above her head; once again the camera was flung aside and the girl's body was thrown violently backwards down the aisle as though she had been hit by a speeding automobile.

Peter picked his shot, waiting for a clean killing hit in the head as the girl tried to drag herself upright – but before he could fire, a mass of black-costumed figures swarmed out of the smoke, and covered the girl, pinning her kicking and screaming on the carpet of the aisle. The Thor team had come in through the forward hatch, just in time to save her life, and Peter clipped the Walther into his holster and stooped to pick up the camera gingerly. Then he pulled off his mask with his other hand.

'That's it. That's all of them,' he shouted. 'We got them all. Cease fire. It's all over.' Then into the microphone of the transceiver, 'Touch down! Touch down!' The code for total success. Three of his men were holding the girl down, and despite the massive spurting wound in her shoulder, she fought like a leopard in a trap.

'Get the emergency chutes down,' Peter ordered, and from each exit the long plastic slides inflated and drooped to the tarmac – already his men were leading the conscious passengers to the exits and helping them into the slide.

From the terminal building a dozen ambulances with sirens howling, gunned out across the tarmac. The back-up members of Thor were running out under the glare of floodlights, cheering thinly. 'Touch down! Touch down!'

Like prehistoric monsters the mechanical stairways lumbered down from the northern apron, to give access to the body of the Boeing.

Peter stepped up to the girl, still holding the camera in his hands, and he stood looking down at her. The icy coldness of battle still gripped him, his mind felt needle sharp and his vision clear, every sense enhanced.

The girl stopped struggling, and looked back at him. The image of a trapped leopard was perfect. Peter had never seen eyes so fierce and merciless, as she glared at him. Then she drew her head back like a cobra about to strike, and spat at him. White frothy spittle splattered down the front of Peter's legs.

Colin Noble was beside Peter now, pulling off his gas mask.

'I'm sorry, Peter. I was going for the heart.'

'You'll never hold me,' shrieked the girl suddenly. 'I'll be free before Thanksgiving!'

And Peter knew she was right. The punishment that a befuddled world society meted out to these people was usually only a few months' imprisonment, and that often suspended. He remembered the feel of the dying child in his arms, the warm trickle of her blood running over his belly and legs.

'My people will come for me,' the girl spat again, this time into the face of one of the men who held her down. 'You will never hold me. My people will force you to free me.'

Again she was right, her capture was a direct invitation for further atrocity, the wheel of vengeance and retribution was set in motion. For the life of this trapped and vicious predator, hundreds more would suffer, and dozens more would die.

The reaction was setting in now, the battle rage abating, and Peter felt the nausea cloying his bowels. It had been in vain, he thought; he had thrown away a lifetime's strivings and endeavour to win only a temporary victory. He had checked the forces of evil, not beaten them – and they would regroup and attack again, stronger and more cunning than ever, and this woman would lead them again.

'We are the revolution.' The girl lifted her uninjured arm in the clenched fist salute. 'We are the power. Nothing, nobody can stop us.'

When this woman had fired a load of buckshot through the swollen body of the pregnant woman it had distorted her shape completely. The image was recaptured entire and whole in Peter's memory, the way she had burst open like the pod of a ripe fruit.

The blonde woman shook the clenched fist into Peter's face.

'This is only the beginning – the new era has begun.'

There was a taunt and a sneering threat in her voice, uttered in complete confidence – and Peter knew it was not misplaced. There was a new force unleashed in the world, something more deadly than he had believed possible, and Peter had no illusions as to the role that blind fortune had played in his small triumph. He had no illusion either that the beast was more than barely wounded; next time it would be more powerful, more cunning, having learned from this inconsequential failure – and with the reaction from battle came a powerful wave of dread and despair that seemed to overwhelm his soul. It had all been in vain.

'You can never win,' taunted the woman, splattered with her own blood, but undaunted and unrepentant, seeming to read his very thoughts.

'And we can never lose,' she shrieked.

'**G**entlemen.' The South African Prime Minister spoke with painful deliberation. 'My cabinet and I are firmly of the opinion that to accede to the terrorists' demands is to take a seat on the back of the tiger, from which we will never be able to dismount.' He stopped, hung his great granite-hewn head for a moment and then looked up at the two ambassadors. 'However, such is the duty we owe to humanity and the dignity of human life, and such is the pressure which two great nations can bring to bear upon one much smaller, that we have decided unanimously to agree in full to all the conditions necessary for the release of the women and children—'

A telephone on the table top in front of the American Ambassador began to shrill irritatingly, and the Prime Minister paused, frowned slightly.

'However, we place complete faith in the undertaking

given by your governments—' He stopped again for the telephone insisted. ' – You had better answer that, sir—' he told Kelly Constable.

'Excuse me, Prime Minister.' The American lifted the receiver, and as he listened an expression of utter disbelief slowly changed his features. 'Hold the line,' he said into the receiver, and then, covering the mouthpiece with his hand, he looked up. 'Prime Minister – it is a very great pleasure to inform you that three minutes ago the Thor assault team broke into Flight 070 and killed three of the terrorists – they wounded and captured a fourth terrorist, but there were no casualties among the passengers. They got them all out, every last one of them. Safe and sound.'

The big man at the head of the table sagged with relief in his seat, and as the storm of jubilation and self-congratulation broke about him, he started to smile. It was a smile that transformed his forbidding features, the smile of an essentially fatherly and kindly man. 'Thank you, sir,' he said, still smiling. 'Thank you very much.'

'You are guilty of blatant dereliction of your duty, General Stride,' Kingston Parker accused grimly.

'My concern was entirely with the lives of hostages and the force of moral law.' Peter answered him quietly; it was less than fifteen minutes since he had penetrated the hull of the Boeing in a blaze of fire and fury. His hands were still shaking slightly and the nausea still lay heavily on his guts.

'You deliberately disobeyed my specific orders.' Parker was an enraged lion, the mane of thick shot-silver hair seemed to bristle, and he glowered from the screen; the vast power of his personality seemed to fill the command cabin of the Hawker. 'I have always had grave reservations as to your suitability for the high command with which you have been entrusted. I have already expressed those reservations in writing to your superiors, and they have been fully justified.'

'I understand by all this that I have been removed from command of Thor,' Peter cut in brusquely, his anger seething to the surface, and Parker checked slightly.

Peter knew that even Kingston Parker could not immediately fire the hero of such a successful counter-strike. It would take time, a matter of days, perhaps, but Peter's fate was sealed. There could be no doubt of that, and Parker went on to confirm this.

'You will continue to exercise command under my direct surveillance. You will make no decision without referring directly back to me, no decision whatsoever. Do you understand that, General Stride?'

Peter did not bother to reply; he felt a wildly reckless mood starting to buoy his sagging spirits, a sense of freedom and choice of action such as he had never known before. For the first time in his career he had deliberately disobeyed a superior officer, and luck or not, the outcome had been a brilliant success.

'Your first duty now will be to withdraw all Thor units, and swiftly and in as good an order as possible. The militant you have taken will be returned to London for questioning and trial—'

'Her crimes were committed here. She should be tried here for murder – I have already had demands from the local—'

'Arrangements are being made with the South African authorities.' Parker's anger had not abated but he had it better under control. 'She will return to Britain aboard your command aircraft, with the Thor doctor in attendance.'

Peter remembered what had happened to the terrorist Leila Khaled, dragged from the El Al airliner where she was being held by Israeli security agents. As a guest of the British police, she had spent six short days in captivity, and then been released in a blaze of publicity and glory, heroine of the communications media, Joan of Arc of terror – released to plan and execute the death and destruction of hundreds more innocents, to lead the attack on the foundations of civilization, to shake the columns that held aloft the rule of law and society.

'I want this woman in London within twenty-four hours. She is to be strictly guarded at all times against retaliation. We cannot afford another bloodbath – like the one you led on 070.'

Peter Stride walked very erect, very tall into the echoing, marble-columned domestic departures hall of the airport, and his men called to him as he came.

'Well done, sir.'

'Great stuff, General.'

'Way to go—'

They were tending the released passengers, re-assembling their scattered gear, dismantling the security and communications equipment and packing it away – within the hour they would be ready to pull out – but now they left their tasks to crowd about him, competing to shake his hand.

The passengers realized that this must be the architect of their salvation and they cheered him as he passed slowly through the hall, and now he was smiling, acknowledging their pitiful gratitude, stopping to talk with an old lady, and submitting to her tearful embrace.

'God bless you, my boy. God bless you.' And her body trembled against him. Gently Peter set her aside and went on, and though he smiled it was with his lips only, for there was steel in his heart.

There were Thor guards on the main administrative offices on the mezzanine floor armed with submachine guns, but they stood aside for him and Peter went through.

Colin Noble was still in his black skin-tight assault suit with the big .45 on his hip, and a cheroot clamped between his teeth.

'Take a look at this lot,' he called to Peter. The desk was covered with explosives and weapons. 'Most of it's iron-curtain stuff – but God alone knows where they got these.' He indicated the double-barrelled shot pistols. 'If they had these custom built, it would have cost them plenty.'

'They have got plenty,' Peter answered drily. 'The ransom for the OPEC ministers was one hundred and fifty million dollars, for the Braun brothers twenty-five million, for Baron Altmann another twenty million – that's the defence budget for a nation.' He picked up one of the shot pistols and opened the breech. It had been unloaded.

'Is this the one she used to gun down the hostages?'

Colin shrugged. 'Probably, it's been fired through both barrels.' Colin was right, there were black specks of burned powder down the short smooth bores.

Peter loaded it with buckshot cartridges from the pile on the desk, and walked on down the long office with the covered typewriters on the deserted desks and the airline travel posters decorating the wall.

Along one wall the three bodies of the hijackers were laid out in a neat row, each encapsulated in its separate translucent plastic envelope.

Two Thor men were assembling the contents of their pockets – personal jewellery, meagre personal effects – and they were packing them into labelled plastic bags.

The body of Peter's Number Two was against the far wall, also in his plastic body-bag, and Peter stooped over him. Through the plastic he could make out the features of the dead man's face. The eyes were wide and the jaw hung open slackly. Death is always so undignified, Peter thought, and straightened up.

Still carrying the shot pistol, Peter went on into the inner office, and Colin Noble followed him.

They had the girl on another stretcher, a plasma drip suspended above her, and the Thor doctor and his two orderlies were working over her quietly, but the young doctor looked up irritably as Peter pushed open the door, then his expression changed as he recognized Peter.

'General, if we are going to save this arm, I have to get her into theatre pretty damned quickly. The joint of the shoulder is shattered—'

The girl rolled the lovely head towards Peter. The thick springing golden hair was matted with drying blood, and there was a smear of it across one cheek.

Now her face was completely drained of all colour, like the head of an angel carved out of white marble. The skin had a waxen, almost translucent, lustre and only the eyes were still fierce, not dulled by the painkilling drugs that they had injected into her.

' – I have asked the South Africans for co-operation—' the doctor went on, ' – they have two top orthopaedic surgeons standing by, and they have offered a helicopter to fly her into the Central Hospital at Edenvale.'

Already she was being treated, even by Thor, as the major celebrity she was. She had taken her first step along the rose-strewn pathway to glory, and Peter could imagine how the media would extol her beauty – they had gone berserk with extravagant praise for the swarthy ferrety-eyed Leila Khaled with her fine dark moustache – they would go over the top for this one.

Peter had never known any emotion so powerful as the emotion that gripped him now.

'Get out,' he said to the doctor.

'Sir?' The man looked startled.

'Get out,' Peter repeated, 'all of you.' And he waited until the opaque glass door closed behind them, before he spoke to the girl in conversational tones.

'You have made me abandon my own principles, and descend to your level.'

The girl watched him uncertainly, her eyes flickered to the shot pistol that Peter held dangling from his right hand.

'You have forced me, a career soldier, to disobey the orders of a superior officer in the face of the enemy.' He paused. 'I used to be a proud man, but when I have done what I must do now I will no longer have much of which to be proud.'

'I demand to see the American Ambassador,' said the girl huskily, still watching the pistol. 'I am an American citizen. I demand the protection—'

Peter interrupted her, again speaking quickly. 'This is not revenge. I am old and wise enough to know that revenge has the most bitter taste of all human excesses.'

'You cannot do it—' The girl's voice rose, the same strident tones, but now shriller still with fear. 'They will destroy you.'

But Peter went on as though she had not spoken. 'It is not revenge,' he repeated. 'You, yourself, gave the reason clearly. If you continue to exist, they will come to get you back. As long as you live, others must die – and they will die stripped of all human dignity. They will die in terror, the same way you murdered—'

'I am a woman. I am wounded. I am a prisoner of war,' screamed the girl, trying to struggle upright.

'Those are the old rules,' Peter told her. 'You tore up the book, and wrote a new one – I am playing to your rules now. I have been reduced to your level.'

'You cannot kill me,' the girl's voice range wildly. 'I still have work—'

'Colin,' Peter said quietly, without looking at the American. 'You'd better get out now.'

Colin Noble hesitated, his right hand on the butt of the Browning, and the girl rolled her head towards him imploringly.

'You can't let him do it.'

'Peter—' Colin said.

'You were right, Colin,' Peter spoke quietly. 'That kid did look a lot like Melissa-Jane.'

Colin Noble dropped his hand from the pistol and turned to the door. Now the girl was shrieking obscenity and threat, her voice incoherent with terror and hatred.

Colin closed the door softly and stood with his back to it. The single crash of shot was shockingly loud, and the stream of filthy abuse was cut off abruptly. The silence was even more appalling than the harrowing sounds which had preceded it. Colin did not move. He waited four, five seconds before the door clicked open and General Peter Stride came out into the main office. He handed the shot pistol to Colin and one barrel was hot in his hand.

Peter's handsome aristocratic features seemed ravaged, as though by a long wasting disease. The face of a man who had leapt into the abyss.

Peter Stride left the glass door open, and walked away without looking back. Despite the terrible expression of despair, he still carried himself like a soldier and his tread was firm.

Colin Noble did not even look through the open door.

'All right,' he called to the doctor. 'She's all yours now.' And he followed Peter Stride down the broad staircase.

There was a long hard gallop over good going and open pasture to the crest of the ridge, with only one gate. Melissa-Jane led on her bay filly, her Christmas gift from Uncle Steven. She was in the midst of the passionate love affair that most pubescent girls have with horses, and she looked truly good astride the glistening thoroughbred. The cold struck high colour into her cheeks and the braid of honey-coloured hair thumped gaily down her back at each stride. She had blossomed even in the few weeks since last Peter had seen her – and he realized with some awe and considerable pride that she was fast becoming a great beauty.

Peter was up on one of Steven's hunters, a big rangy animal with the strength to carry his weight, but the gelding was slogging hard to hold the flying pair that danced ahead of him.

At the hedge, Melissa-Jane scorned the gate, gathered the filly with fine strong hands and took her up and over. Her little round bottom lifted out of the saddle as she leaned into the jump, and clods of black earth flew from the filly's hooves.

As soon as she was over she swivelled in the saddle to watch him, and Peter realized that he was under challenge. The hedge immediately appeared to be head-high and he noticed for the first time how the ground fell away at a steep angle beyond. He had not ridden for almost two years, and it was the first time he had been up on this gelding – but the horse went for the jump gamely, and they brushed the top of the hedge, landed awkwardly, stumbled with Peter up on his neck for an appalling instant of time in which he was convinced he was to take a toss in front of his daughter's critical eye; caught his balance, held the gelding's head up and they came away still together.

'Super-Star!' Melissa-Jane shouted laughing, and by the time he caught her she had dismounted under the yew tree at the crest, and was waiting for him with her breath steaming in the crisp calm air.

'Our land once went right as far as the church—' Peter pointed to the distant grey needle of stone that pricked the belly of the sky, ' – and there almost to the top of the downs.' He turned to point in the opposite direction.

'Yes.' Melissa-Jane slipped her arm through his as they stood close together under the yew. 'The family had to sell it when Grandfather died. You told me. And that's right too. One family shouldn't own so much.'

Peter glanced down at her, startled. 'My God, a communist in the family. An asp in the bosom.'

She squeezed his arm. 'Don't worry, Daddy darling. It's Uncle Steven who is the bloated plutocrat. You're not a capitalist – you aren't even employed any more—' And the instant she had said it, her laughter collapsed around her and she looked stricken. ' – Oh, I didn't mean that. I truly didn't.'

It was almost a month now since Peter's resignation had been accepted by the War Office, but the scandal had not yet run out of steam.

The first heady paeans of praise for the success of Thor's Delta strike had lasted only a few days. The glowing editorials, the full front pages, the lead news item on every television channel, the effusive messages of congratulations from the leaders of the Western governments, the impromptu triumph for Peter Stride and his little band of heroes, had quickly struck an odd note, a sudden souring of the ecstasies.

The racist Government of South Africa had actually agreed to the release of political prisoners *before* the assault, one of the hijackers had been taken alive, and died of gunshot wounds received in the terminal buildings. Then one of the released hostages, a freelance journalist who had been covering the medical convention in Mauritius and was returning aboard the hijacked aircraft, published a sensational eye-witness account of the entire episode, and a dozen other passengers supported his claims that there had been screams from the fourth hijacker, screams for mercy, before she was shot to death after her capture.

A storm of condemnation and vilification from the extreme left of the British Labour Government had swept through the Westminster parliament, and had been echoed by the Democrats in the American Congress. The very existence of the Thor Command had come under scrutiny and been condemned in extravagant terms. The Communist

138

parties of France and Italy had marched, and the detonation of an M.26 hand grenade – one of those stolen by the Baader-Meinhof gang from the American base in Metz – amongst the crowd leaving the Parc des Princes football stadium in Paris had killed one and injured twenty-three. A telephone call to the offices of *France Soir* by a man speaking accented French claimed that this fresh atrocity was revenge for the murder of four hijackers by the Imperialist execution squad.

Pressure for Peter's discharge had come initially from the Pentagon, and there was very little doubt that Dr Kingston Parker was the accuser, though, as head of Atlas, he was never identified, total secrecy still surrounding the project. The media had begun to demand an investigation of all the circumstances surrounding Thor. ' – And if it is ascertained that criminal irregularities did indeed exist in the conduct of the operation, that the person or persons responsible be brought to trial either by a military tribunal or the civil courts.' Fortunately the media had not yet unravelled the full scope of Atlas Command. Only Thor was under scrutiny; they did not yet suspect the existence of either Mercury or Diana.

Within the War Office and the governments of both America and Britain, there had been much sympathy and support for Peter Stride – but he had made it easier for his friends and for himself by tendering his resignation. The resignation had been accepted, but still the left was clamouring for more. They wanted blood, Peter Stride's blood.

Now Melissa-Jane's huge pansy violet eyes flooded with the tears of mortification. 'I didn't mean that. I truly didn't.'

'One thing about being out of a job – I have more time to be with my favourite girl.' He smiled down at her, but she would not be mollified.

'I don't believe the horrible things they are saying. I know you are a man of honour, Daddy.'

'Thank you.' And he felt the ache of it, the guilt and the

sorrow. They were silent a little longer, still standing close together, and Peter spoke first.

'You are going to be a palaeontologist—' he said.

'No. That was last month. I've changed my mind. I'm not interested in old bones any more. Now I'm going to be a doctor, a child specialist.'

'That's good.' Peter nodded gravely. 'But let's go back to old bones for a moment. The age of the great reptiles. The dinosaurs – why did they fade into extinction?'

'They could not adapt to a changing environment.' Melissa-Jane had the answer promptly.

Peter murmured, ' – A concept like honour. Is it outdated in today's world, I wonder?' Then he saw the puzzlement, the hurt in her eyes, and he knew they had wandered onto dangerous ground. His daughter had a burning love for all living things, particularly human beings. Despite her age, she had a developed political and social conscience, distinguished by total belief in shining ideals and the essential beauty and goodness of mankind. There would be time in the years ahead for the agony of disillusion. The term 'man or woman of honour' was Melissa-Jane's ultimate accolade. No matter that it could be applied to any of her current heroes or heroines – the Prince of Wales, or the singer of popular songs with an outrageous name that Peter could never remember, to Virginia Wade, the former Wimbledon champion, or to the Fifth Form science teacher at Roedean who had aroused Melissa-Jane's interest in medicine – Peter knew that he should feel proper gratitude for being included in this exalted company.

'I will try to live up to your opinion of me.' He stooped and kissed her, surprised at the strength of his love for this child-woman. 'And now it's too cold to stand here any longer, and Pat will never forgive us if we are late for lunch.'

They clattered over the stone cobbles of the stable yard, riding knee to knee, and before he dismounted, Peter indulged himself in the pleasure of his favourite view of the house that had always been home, even though it belonged now, together with the title, to Steven, the older brother, older by three hours only, but older none the less.

The house was red brick with a roof that ran at fifty different unlikely angles. It missed being hideous by a subtle margin and achieved a fairytale enchantment. Peter could never grudge it to Steven, who loved the sprawling edifice with something close to passion.

Perhaps the desire to own the house and to restore it to its former magnificence was the goad which had pricked Steven to the superhuman effort that a British resident must make against taxation and socialist restrictions in order to amass anything like a fortune.

Steven had made that effort and now Abbots Yew stood immaculate and well-beloved in glorious gardens, and Sir Steven kept baronial style.

His affairs were so complicated, spread over so many continents that even the British taxman must have been daunted. Peter had once skirted this subject with his twin brother, and Steven had replied quietly.

'When a law is patently unjust, such as our tax law is, it's the duty of an honest man to subvert it.'

Peter's old-fashioned sense of rightness had baulked at such logic, but he let it pass.

It was strange that it had worked this way for the two brothers, for Peter had always been the brilliant one, and the family had always referred to 'Poor Steven'. Nobody was very surprised when Steven left Sandhurst amid dark whispers halfway through his final year – but two years later Steven was already a millionaire while Peter was a lowly second lieutenant in the British Army. Peter grinned without rancour at the memory. He had always been particularly fond of his elder brother – but at that moment his train of thought was interrupted as his eye caught the mirror-like finish of the silver limousine parked at the end of the stable yard. It was one of those long Mercedes-Benz favoured by pop stars, Arab oil men, or heads of state. The chauffeur was uniformed in sober navy blue and was busy burnishing the paintwork to an even higher gloss. Even Steven did not run to that sort of transportation, and Peter felt mildly intrigued. House guests at Abbots Yew were always interesting. Steven Stride did not concern himself with those who did not wield either power, wealth or extraordinary talent. Beyond the Mercedes 600 was parked another smaller model; this one was black and the two men in it had the hard closed faces that marked them as bodyguards.

Melissa-Jane rolled her eyes at the automobile. 'Another bloated plutocrat, I expect,' she muttered. It was the currently favoured term of extreme disapproval, a great advance on 'grotty' which had preceded it, Peter could not help thinking as he helped his daughter unsaddle and then rub down the horses. They went up through the rose garden, arm in arm, and then laughing together into the main drawing-room.

'Peter old boy!' Steven came to meet him, as tall as his brother, and once he had been as lean, but good living had thickened his body while at the same time the strains of being a professional deal maker had greyed his hair at the temples and laced his moustache with silver bristles. His face was not quite a mirror image of Peter's, slightly more fleshy and florid – but the twin resemblance was still strongly marked, and now his face was alive with pleasure.

'Thought you'd broken your bloody neck, what!' Steven carefully cultivated the bluff manner of the country squire to shield his quick and shrewd intelligence.

Now he turned to Melissa-Jane and hugged her with barely a touch of incestuous pleasure. 'How did Florence Nightingale go?'

'She's a darling, Uncle Steven. I will never be able to thank you.'

'Peter, I would like you to meet a very charming lady—'

She had been talking to Patricia Stride, Steven's wife, and now as she turned, the winter sunshine through the bay windows behind lit her with a soft romantic aura.

Peter felt as though the earth had tilted under his feet, and a fist closed around his ribs constricting his breathing and inhibiting the action of his heart.

He recognized her immediately from the photographs in the official file during the long-drawn-out kidnapping and subsequent murder of her husband. At one stage it had seemed that the kidnappers had crossed the Channel with their victim, and Thor had gone to condition Alpha for almost a week. Peter had studied the photographs that had been assembled from a dozen sources, but even the glossy coloured portraits from *Vogue* and *Jours de France* had not been able to capture the magnificence of the woman.

Surprisingly, he saw his own immediate recognition reflected. There was no change in her expression, but it flared briefly like dark-green emerald fire in her eyes. There was no question in Peter's mind but that she had recognized him, and as he stepped towards her he realized she was tall, but the fine proportion of her body had not made that immediately apparent. Her skirt was of a fine wool crêpe which moulded the long, stately legs of a dancer.

'Baroness, may I present my brother. General Stride.'

'How do you do, General.' Her English was almost perfect, a low husky voice, the slight accent very attractive, but she pronounced his rank as three distinct syllables.

'Peter, this is Baroness Altmann.'

Her thick glossy black hair was scraped back severely from the forehead with a perfect arrowhead of widow's peak at the centre, emphasizing the high Slavic cheekbones and the unblemished perfection of her skin – but her jawline was too square and strong for beauty, and the mouth had an arrogant determined line to it. Magnificent, but not beautiful – and Peter found himself violently attracted. The breathless wholesale feeling he had not experienced for twenty years.

She seemed to epitomize everything he admired in a woman.

Her body was in the condition of a trained athlete. Beneath the oyster silk of her blouse her arms were delicately sculpted from toned muscle, the waist narrow, the breasts very small and unfettered, their lovely shape pressing clearly through fine material, her clean lightly tanned skin glowed with health and careful grooming. All this contributed to his attraction.

However, the greater part was in Peter's own mind. He knew she was a woman of extraordinary strength and achievement, that was pure aphrodisiac for him, and she exuded also the challenging air of being unattainable. The regal eyes mocked his evident masculinity with the untouchable aloofness of a queen or a goddess. She seemed to be smiling inwardly, a cool patronizing smile at his admiration, which she realized was no more than her due. Quickly Peter reviewed what he knew of her.

She had begun her association with the Baron as his private secretary, and in five years had become indispensable to him. The Baron had recognized her ability by rapidly elevating her to the boards of directors, first of some of the group's lesser subsidiaries, and finally to that of the central holding company. When the Baron's physical strength had begun to decline in his losing battle with an inexorable cancer, he came to rely more upon her, trust well placed as it soon turned out. For she ran the complex empire of heavy industrial companies, of electronics and armaments corporations, of banking and shipping and property developments, like the son he never had. When he married her he was fifty-eight years of age, almost thirty years her senior, and she had been a perfect wife as she had been a perfect business partner.

She had assembled and personally delivered the massive ransom demanded by his abductors, against the advice of the French police, going alone and unguarded to a meeting with merciless killers, and when they had returned the Baron's fearfully mutilated corpse to her, she had mourned him and buried him and continued to run the empire she had inherited, with vision and strength so far beyond her years.

She was twenty-nine years old. No, that had been two years ago, Peter realized, as he bowed over her hand, not quite touching the smooth cool fingers with his lips. She would be thirty-one years old now. She wore a single ring on her wedding finger, a solitaire diamond, not a particularly large diamond, not more than six carats but of such a perfect whiteness and fire that it seemed to be endowed with its own life. It was the choice of a woman of immense wealth and even greater style.

As Peter straightened, he realized that she was appraising him as carefully as he was her. It seemed that he would be unable to conceal anything from those slanted emerald eyes, but he returned her gaze steadily, knowing without conceit that he could withstand any such scrutiny; still intrigued, however, with the certainty that she had known him.

'Your name has been much in the news recently,' she said, as if in explanation.

There were sixteen for lunch, including Steven and Pat's three children and Melissa-Jane. It was a happy, relaxed meal, but the Baroness was seated at a distance that made it impossible for Peter to speak directly to her, and though he strained to follow her conversation, her voice was low and addressed mostly to Steven and the editor of one of the national daily newspapers who flanked her. Peter found himself fully occupied in fending off the breathless attention of the pretty but feather-brained blonde on his left. She was a starlet who had married well and divorced even better. She had been handpicked by Pat Stride. Peter's sister-in-law was indefatigable in her efforts to find him a suitable replacement for Cynthia. Twelve years of straight failures had not daunted her in the least.

There was still time for Peter to notice that though the Baroness sipped once or twice at her wine, the level in the glass never fell, and she picked only lightly at her plate.

Though Peter watched her covertly, the Baroness never glanced once in his direction. It was only as they went through for coffee that she came directly and unaffectedly to his side.

'Steven tells me there are Roman ruins on the estate,' she said.

'I could show them to you. It is a lovely walk up through the woods.'

'Thank you. I do have some business to discuss with Steven before that; shall we meet at three o'clock?'

She had changed into a loose tweed skirt and jacket that would have looked bulky on a shorter or plumper woman, and high boots in the same lavender tinted brown. Under it she wore a cashmere roll-neck jersey, and a scarf of the same fine wool hung down her back. A wide-brimmed hat with a bright feather in the band was pulled down over her eyes.

She walked in silence, hands thrust deeply into the big pockets of her jacket, making no effort to protect the expensive boots from mud, thorns of damp bracken. She moved with a flowing, long-legged grace, swinging from the hips so that her shoulder and head seemed to float beside Peter, at a not much lower level than his own. Had she not been a world leader in finance and industry, she might have made a great model, he decided. She had a talent for making clothes look important and elegant, while treating them with indifference.

Peter respected her silence, pleased to be able to step out to match her pace, as they went up through the dark dripping woods that smelt of leaf mould and cold rain, the oaks bare and moss-pelted, seeming to beseech a purple-grey sky with arthritic limbs held high.

They came out on the higher open ground without having stopped once, although the path had been steep and the ground soft underfoot.

She was breathing deeply but evenly, and she had coloured just sufficiently to flatter the high Slavic cheeks. She must be in peak physical condition, he thought.

'Here they are.' Peter indicated the barely discernible grass-covered ditch that circled the hilltop. 'They are not very impressive, but I didn't want to warn you in advance.'

She smiled now. 'I have been here before,' she said in that intriguing husky accent.

'Well, we are off to a flying start. We have both deceived each other at our first meeting—' Peter chuckled.

'I came all the way from Paris,' she explained. 'It was most inconvenient really – the business I had to discuss with Sir Steven could have been completed by telephone in five minutes. What I had to discuss with you could only be done face by face—' She corrected herself immediately. 'I am sorry, face to face.' It was a rare slip. Steven had been strangely insistent that Peter spend this particular weekend at Abbots Yew, and was certainly party to this encounter.

'I am flattered by the interest of such a beautiful lady—'

Instantly she frowned, and with a gesture of irritation cut short the compliment as frivolous.

'Very recently you were approached by the Narmco section of Seddler Steel with an offer to head their Sales Division,' she said, and Peter nodded. Since his resignation had been accepted by the War Office, there had been many offers. 'The terms of employment offered were extraordinarily generous.'

'That is true.'

'You prefer the cloistered academic life, perhaps?' she asked, and though Peter's expression did not change, he was taken off balance. It seemed impossible that she could know

147

of the offer of the Chair of Modern Military History that he had been offered by a leading American university, an offer with which he was still toying idly.

'There are some books I want to read and write,' Peter said.

'Books. You have an important collection, and I have read those you have written. You are an interesting contradiction, General Stride. The man of direct action, and at the same time of deep political and social thought.'

'I confuse myself at times,' Peter smiled. 'So what chance do you have to understand me?'

She did not rise to the smile. 'A great deal of your writing coincides with my own conviction. As for your action, if I had been a man and in your position, I might have acted as you did.'

Peter stiffened, resenting any allusion to the taking of Flight 070, and again she seemed to understand instinctively.

'I refer to your entire career, General. From Cyprus to Johannesburg – and including Ireland.' And he relaxed slightly.

'Why did you refuse the Narmco offer?' she asked.

'Because it was presented with the unstated conviction that I could not refuse. Because the terms were so generous that they left a strange unsatisfying odour in my nostrils. Because I believe that I would have been required to perform duties in line with the reputation I seem to have acquired since the taking of Flight 070.'

'What reputation is that?' She leaned slightly towards him, and he smelled her particular aroma. The way perfume reacted upon that petally-smooth skin, heated by the exertion of the climb up the hill. She smelled faintly of crushed lemon blossom and clean healthy mature woman. He felt himself physically aroused by it, and had an almost undesirable impulse to reach out and touch her, to feel the warmth and glossiness of her skin.

'A man who makes accommodations, perhaps,' he answered her.

'What did you think you might have been asked to do?'

This time he shrugged. 'Perhaps carry bribes to my one-time colleagues in NATO Command, to induce them to consider favourably the products of Narmco.'

'Why would you believe that?'

'I was once a decision-making officer in that Command.'

She turned away from him and looked out across the special greens of an English winter landscape, the orderly fields and pastures, the dark wedges and geometrical shapes of the woods and copses.

'Do you know that through Altmann Industries and other companies I control a majority shareholding in Seddler Steel, and naturally in Narmco?'

'No,' Peter admitted. 'But I cannot say I am surprised.'

'Did you know that the offer from Narmco was in reality from me personally?'

This time he said nothing.

'You are quite right, of course, your contacts with the upper echelon of NATO and with the British and American high commands would have been worth every centime of the extravagant salary you were offered. As for bribes—' She smiled then suddenly, and it altered her face entirely, making her seem many years younger, and there was a warmth and a sense of fun that he would not have suspected, ' – this is a capitalist society, General. We prefer to talk about commissions and introducer's fees.'

He found himself smiling back at her, not because of what she had said, but simply because her smile was irresistible.

'However, I give you my solemn word that you would never have been expected to offer or carry – no, since Lockheed were indiscreet, it has changed. Nothing disreputable could ever be traced back to Narmco, and certainly not to the top men there. Certainly not to you.'

'It's all academic now,' Peter pointed out. 'I've refused the offer.'

'I disagree, General Stride.' The brim of the hat covered her eyes as she looked down. 'I hope that when you hear what I had hoped to achieve you may reconsider. I made the error of trying to keep us at arms' length to begin with. I relied on the generosity of the offer to sway you. I do not usually misjudge people so dismally—' and she looked up and smiled again, and this time reached out and touched his arm. Her fingers were like her limbs, long and slim, but they were delicately tapered and the nails were shaped and lacquered to a glossy fleshy pink. She left them on his arm as she went on speaking.

'My husband was an extraordinary man. A man of vast vision and strength and compassion. Because of that they tortured and killed him—' her voice had sunk to a hoarse catchy whisper ' – they killed him in the most vile manner—' She stopped, but made no attempt to turn her head away, she was unashamed of the tears that filled both eyes but did not break over the lower lids. She did not even blink, and it was Peter who looked away first. Only then she moved her hand, slipping it lightly into the crook of Peter's elbow and coming beside him so her hip almost touched his.

'It will rain soon,' she said, her voice level and controlled. 'We should go down.' And as they started, she went on talking.

'The butchers who did that to Aaron went free, while an impotent society looked on. A society which has systematically stripped itself of defence against the next attack. America has virtually disbanded its intelligence system, and so shackled and exposed what is left that it is powerless. Your own country is concerned only with its particular problems, as are we in the rest of Europe – there is no international approach to a problem that is international in

150

scope. Atlas was a fine concept, limited as it was by the fact that it was a force that could only be used in retaliation and then only in special circumstances. However, if they ever suspect that it exists, the denizens of the left will mass to tear it down like a hunting pack of hyena.' She squeezed his arm lightly, and looked sideways at him with a solemn slant of the emerald eyes. 'Yes, General, I do know about Atlas – but do not ask me how.'

Peter said nothing, and they entered the forest, stepping carefully, for the path was slick and steep.

'After the death of my husband, I began to think a great deal about how we could protect the world that we know, while still remaining within the laws which were first designed to do that. With Altmann Industries I had inherited a comprehensive system of international information-gathering; naturally it was attuned almost entirely to commercial and industrial considerations—' She went on talking in that low intense voice that Peter found mesmeric, describing how she had gradually used her massive fortune and influence to reach across borders closed to most to gain the overall view of the new world of violence and intimidation. ' – I was not tied by considerations such as that of Interpol, forbidden by suicidal laws to involve itself in any crime that has political motivation. It was only when I was able to pass on what I had learned that I found myself coming up against the same self-destructive state of mind that masquerades as democracy and individual freedom. Twice I was able to anticipate a terrorist strike and to warn the authorities, but intention is not a crime, I was told, and both the culprits were quietly escorted to the border and turned free to prepare themselves almost openly for the next outrage. The world must wait and cringe for the next stroke, prohibited from making any pre-emptive strike to prevent it, and when it comes they are hampered by confused national responsibilities and by the complicated concept of minimum force—' The Baroness broke off. 'But you know all this! You have written in depth of the same subject.'

'It's interesting to hear it repeated.'

'I will come soon enough to the interesting part – but we are almost back at the house.'

'Come,' Peter told her, and led her past the stables to the swimming pool pavilion. The surface of the heated pool steamed softly, and lush tropical plants were in odd contrast to the wintry scene beyond the glass walls.

They sat side by side on a swing seat, close enough to be able to talk in subdued tones, but the intense mood was broken for the moment. She took off her hat, scarf and jacket, and tossed them onto the cane chair opposite, and she sighed as she settled back against the cushions.

'I understand from Sir Steven that he wants you to go into the bank.' She slanted her eyes at him. 'It must be difficult to be so sought after.'

'I don't think I have Steven's reverence for money.'

'It's a readily acquired taste, General Stride,' she assured him. 'One that can become an addiction.'

At that moment the children of both Stride brothers arrived in a storm of shouted repartee and laughter, which moderated only marginally when they realized that Peter and the Baroness were in the swing seat.

Steven's youngest son, bulging over the top of his costume with puppy-fat and with silver braces on his front teeth, rolled his eyes in their direction and in a stage whisper told Melissa-Jane, *'Je t'aime, ma chérie*, swoon! swoon!' His accent was frighteningly bad and he received a hissed rebuke and a shove in the small of the back that hurled him into the deep end of the pool.

The Baroness smiled. 'Your daughter is very protective—' she turned slightly to examine Peter's face again ' – or is it merely jealousy?' Without waiting for an answer she went straight on to ask another question. Against the background of shouts and splashes, Peter thought he had misheard.

'What did you say?' he asked carefully, certain that his expression had revealed nothing, and she repeated.

'Does the name Caliph mean anything to you?'

He frowned slightly, pretending to consider, while his memory darted back to the terrible micro-seconds of mortal combat, of smoke and flame and gunfire and a dark-haired girl in a scarlet shirt screaming:

'Don't kill us! Caliph said we would not die. Caliph—' And his own bullets stopping the rest of it, smashing into the open mouth. The word had haunted him since then, and he had tried a thousand variations, looking for sense and meaning, considering the possibility that he had misheard. Now he knew he had not.

'Caliph?' he asked, not knowing why he was going to deny it, merely because it seemed vital that he keep something in reserve, that he were not carried headlong on the torrent of this woman's presence and personality. 'It's a Mohammedan title – I think it literally means the heir of Mohammed, the successor to the prophet.'

'Yes.' She nodded impatiently. 'It's the title of a civil and religious leader – but have you heard it used as a code name?'

'No. I am sorry, I have not. What is the significance?'

'I am not sure, even my own sources are obscure and confused.' She sighed, and they watched Melissa-Jane in silence. The child had been waiting for Peter's attention, and when she had it she ran lightly out along the springboard and launched herself, light as a swallow in flight, into a clean one-and-a-half somersault, entering the water with hardly a ripple and surfacing immediately with fine pale hair slick down across her face, immediately looking again for Peter's approval.

'She's a lovely child,' said the Baroness. 'I have no

children. Aaron wanted a son – but there was not one.' And there was real sorrow in the green eyes that she masked quickly. Across the pool Melissa-Jane climbed from the pool and quickly draped a towel around her shoulders, covering her bosom which was now large enough and yet so novel as to provide her with a constant source of embarrassment and shy pride.

'Caliph,' Peter reminded the Baroness quietly, and she turned back to him.

'I first heard the name two years ago, in circumstances I shall never forget—' She hesitated. 'May I take it that you are fully aware of the circumstances surrounding my husband's kidnapping and murder? I do not wish to repeat the whole harrowing story – unless it is necessary.'

'I know it,' Peter assured her.

'You know that I delivered the ransom, personally.'

'Yes.'

'The rendezvous was a deserted airfield near the East German border. They were waiting with a light twin-engined aircraft, a Russian-built reconnaissance machine with its markings sprayed over—' Peter remembered the meticulous planning and the special equipment used in the hijacking of 070. It all tallied. ' – There were four men, masked. They spoke Russian, or rather two of them spoke Russian. The other two never spoke at all. It was bad Russian—' Peter remembered now that the Baroness spoke Russian and five other languages. She had a Middle European background. Peter wished he had studied her intelligence file more thoroughly. Her father has escaped with her from her native Poland when she was a small child. ' – Almost certainly, the aircraft and the Russian were intended to cover their real identity,' she mused. 'I was with them for some little time. I had forty-five million Swiss francs to deliver and even in notes of large denomination it was a bulky and heavy cargo to load aboard the aircraft. After the first few minutes, when they realized that I had no police escort, they relaxed and joked amongst themselves as they worked at loading the money. The word "Caliph" was used in the English version, in a Russian exchange that roughly translates as "He was right again" and the reply "Caliph is always right". Perhaps the use of the English word made me remember it so clearly—' She stopped again, grief naked and bleak in the green eyes.

'You told the police?' Peter asked gently, and she shook her head.

'No. I don't know why not. They had been so ineffectual up to that time. I was very angry and sad and confused. Perhaps even then I had already decided that I would hunt them myself – and this was all I had.'

'That was the only time you heard the name?' he asked, and she did not reply immediately. They watched the children at play – and it seemed fantasy to be discussing the source of evil in such surroundings, against a background of laughter and innocent high spirits.

When the Baroness answered, she seemed to have changed direction completely.

'There had been that hiatus in international terrorism. The Americans seemed to have beaten the hijacking problem with their Cuban agreement and the rigorous airport searches. Your own successful campaign against the Provisional wing of the IRA in this country, the Entebbe raid and the German action at Mogadishu were all hailed as breakthrough victories. Everybody was beginning to congratulate themselves that it was beaten. The Arabs were too busy with the war in the Lebanon and with inter-group rivalries. It had been a passing thing.' She shook her head again. 'But terrorism is a growth industry – the risks are less than those of financing a major movie. There is a proven sixty-seven per cent chance of success, the capital outlay is minimal, with outrageous profits in cash and publicity, with instant results – and potential power not even calculable. Even in the event of total failure, there is still a better than fifty per cent survival rate for the participants.' She smiled again, but now there was no joy and no warmth in it. 'Any businessman will tell you it's better than the commodity markets.'

'The only thing against it is that the business is run by amateurs,' Peter said, 'or by professionals blinded by hatred or crippled by parochial interests and limited goals.'

And now she turned to him, wriggling around in the canvas swing seat, curling those long legs up under her in that double-jointed woman's manner, impossible for a man.

'You are ahead of me, Peter.' She caught herself. 'I am sorry, but General Stride is too much to say, and I have the feeling I have known you so long.' The smile now was fleeting but warm. 'My name is Magda,' she went on simply. 'Will you use it?'

'Thank you, Magda.'

'Yes.' She picked up the thread of conversation again. 'The business is in the hands of amateurs – but it is too good to stay that way.'

'Enter Caliph,' Peter guessed.

'That is the whisper that I have heard; usually there is no name. Just that there was a meeting in Athens, or Amsterdam or East Berlin or Aden – only once have I heard the name Caliph again. But if he exists already he must be one of the richest men in the world, and soon he will be the most powerful.'

'One man?' Peter asked.

'I do not know. Perhaps a group of men – perhaps even a government. Russia, Cuba, an Arab country? Who knows yet?'

'And the goals?'

'Money, firstly. Wealth to tackle the political objectives – and finally power, raw power.' Magda Altmann stopped herself, and made a self-deprecating gesture. 'This is guesswork again, my own guessing – based only on past performance. They have the wealth now, provided by OPEC and – myself

156

amongst others. Now he or they have started on the
political objectives, a soft target first. An African racist
minority government unprotected by powerful allies. It
should have succeeded. They should have won an entire
nation – a mineral-rich nation – for the price of a dozen
lives. Even had they failed to gain the main prize, the
consolation prize was forty tons of pure gold. That's good
business, Peter. It should have succeeded. It *had* succeeded.
The Western nations actually put pressure on the victims,
and forced them to accede to the demands – it was a trial
run, and it worked perfectly, except for one man.'

'I am afraid,' said Peter softly, 'as afraid as I have ever
been in my life.'

'Yes, I am also, Peter. I have been afraid ever since that
terrible phone call on the night they took Aaron, and the
more I learn the more afraid I become.'

'What happens next?'

'I do not know – but the name he has chosen has the
hint of megalomania, perhaps a man with visions of godlike
domination—' She spread her fine narrow hands and the
diamond flashed white fire. ' – We cannot hope to fathom
the mind of a man who could embark on such a course.
Probably he believes that what he is doing is for the
eventual good of mankind. Perhaps he wants to attack the
rich by amassing vast wealth, to destroy the tyrant with
universal tyranny, to free mankind by making it a slave to
terror. Perhaps he seeks to right the wrongs of the world
with evil and injustice.'

She touched his arm again, and this time the strength of
those long fingers startled Peter. 'You have to help me find
him, Peter. I am going to put everything into the hunt,
there will be no reservations, all the wealth and influence
that I control will be at your disposal.'

'You choose me because you believe that I murdered a
wounded woman prisoner?' Peter asked. 'Are those my

credentials?' And she recoiled from him slightly, and stared at him with the slightly Mongolian slant of eyes, then her shoulders slumped slightly.

'All right, that is part of it, but only a small part of it. You know I have read what you have written, you must know that I have studied you very carefully. You are the best man available to me, and finally you have proved that your involvement is complete. I know that you have the strength and skill and ruthlessness to find Caliph and destroy him – before he destroys us and the world we know.'

Peter was looking inwards. He had believed that the beast had a thousand heads, and for each that was struck off a thousand more would grow – but now for the first time he imagined the full shape of the beast, it was still in ambush, not clear yet, but there was only a single head. Perhaps, after all, it was mortal.

'Will you help me, Peter?' she asked.

'You know I will,' he answered quietly. 'I do not have any choice.'

She flew in the brilliance of high sunlight reflected from snowfields of blazing white, jetting through her turns with flowing elegance, carving each turn with a crisp rush of flying snow, swaying across the fall line of the mountain in an intricate ballet of interlinked movement.

She wore a slim-fitting skin suit of pearly grey, trimmed in black at the shoulders and cuffs, she was shod with gleaming black Heierling snowbirds, and her skis were long, narrow, black Rossignol professionals.

Peter followed her, pressing hard not to lose too much ground, but his turns were solid Christies without the stylish fallback unweighting of the jet turn which gave her each time a fractional gain.

> The dun he ran like a stag of ten
> But the mare like a new roused fawn

Kipling might have been describing them, and she was a hundred yards ahead of him as they entered the forest.

The pathway was barred with the shadows of the pines, and sugary ice roared under his skis as he pushed the narrow corners dangerously fast. Always she was farther ahead, flickering like a silver-grey wraith on those long lean legs, her tight round buttocks balancing the narrow waist and swinging rhythmically into the turns, marvellous controlled broadsides where the icy roadway denied purchase, coming out fast and straight, leaning into the rush of the wind, and her faint sweet laughter came back to Peter as he chased. There is an expertise that must be learned in childhood, and he remembered then that she was Polish, would probably have skied before she was weaned, and suppressed the flare of resentment he always felt at being outclassed by another human being, particularly by the woman who was fast becoming his driving obsession.

He came round another steeply banked turn, with the sheer snow wall rising fifteen feet on his right hand and on his left the tops of the nearest pines at his own level, so steep the mountain fell away into the valley.

The ice warning signs flashed past, and there was a wooden bridge, its boards waxen, opalescent with greenish ice. He felt control go as he hit the polished iron-hard surface. The bridge crossed a deep sombre gorge, with a frozen waterfall skewered to the black mountain rock by its own cruel icicles, like crucifixion nails.

To attempt to edge in, or to stem the thundering rush across the treacherous going, would have invited disaster, to lean back defensively would have brought him down instantly and piled him into the sturdy wooden guide rails. At the moment he was lined up for the narrow bridge Peter flung himself forward so that his shins socked into the pads of his boots, and in a swoop of terror and exhilaration he went through, and found that he was laughing aloud though his heart leaped against his ribs and his breathing matched the sound of the wind in his own ears.

She was waiting for him where the path debouched onto the lower slopes. She had pushed her goggles to the top of her head, and stripped off her gloves, both sticks planted in the snow beside her.

'You'll never know how much I needed that.' She had flown into Zurich that morning in her personal Lear jet. Peter had come in on the Swissair flight from Brussels, and they had motored up together. 'You know what I wish, Peter?'

'Tell me,' he invited.

'I wish that I could take a whole month, thirty glorious days, to do what I wish. To be ordinary, to be like other people and not feel a moment's guilt.'

He had seen her on only three occasions in the six weeks since their first meeting at Abbots Yew. Three too brief and, for Peter, unsatisfying meetings.

Once in his new office suite at the Narmco headquarters in Brussels, again at La Pierre Bénite, her country home outside Paris, but then there had been twenty other guests for dinner. The third time had been in the panelled and tastefully decorated cabin of her Lear jet on a flight between Brussels and London.

Though they had made little progress as yet in the hunt for Caliph, Peter was still exploring the avenues that had occurred to him and had cast a dozen lines, baited and hooked.

During their third meeting Peter had discussed with her the need to restructure her personal safety arrangements. He had changed her former bodyguards, replacing them with operatives from a discreet agency in Switzerland which trained its own men. The director of the agency was an old and trusted friend.

They had come to this meeting now so that Peter might report back on his progress to Magda. But for a few hours the snow had seduced them both.

'There is still another two hours before the light goes.' Peter glanced across the valley at the village church. The gold hands of the clock showed a little after two o'clock. 'Do you want to run the Rheinhorn?'

She hesitated only a moment. 'The world will keep turning, I'm sure.' Her teeth were very white, but one of them was slightly crooked, a blemish that was oddly appealing as she smiled up at him. 'Certainly it will wait two hours.'

He had learned that she kept unbelievable hours, beginning her day's work when the rest of the world still slept, and still hard at it when the offices of Altmann Industries in Boulevard Capucine were deserted, except her own office suite on the top floor. Even during the drive up from Zurich she had gone through correspondence and dictated quietly to one of her secretaries. He knew that at the chalet across the valley her two secretaries would be waiting already, with a pile of telex flimsies for her consideration and the line held open for her replies.

'There are better ways to die than working yourself to death.' He was suddenly out of patience with her single-mindedness, and she laughed easily with high colour in her cheeks and the sparkle of the last run in the green eyes.

'Yes, you are right, Peter. I should have you near to keep reminding me of that.'

'That's the first bit of sense I've had from you in six weeks.' He was referring to her opposition to his plans for her security. He had tried to persuade her to change established behaviour patterns, and though the smile was still on her lips, her eyes were deadly serious as she studied his face.

'My husband left me a trust—' she seemed suddenly sad beneath the laughter ' – a duty that I must fulfil. One day I should like to explain that to you – but now we only have two hours.'

It was snowing lightly, and the sun had disappeared behind the mountains of rock and snow and cloud as they walked back through the village. The lights were burning in the richly laden shop windows and they were part of the gaily clad stream returning from the slopes, clumping along the frozen sidewalks in their clumsy ski boots, carrying skis and sticks over one shoulder and chattering with the lingering thrill of the high piste that even the lowering snow-filled dusk could not suppress.

'It feels good to be free of my wolves for a while.' Magda caught his arm as her snowbirds skidded on dirty ridged ice, and after she had regained her balance she left her gloved hand there.

Her wolves were the bodyguards that Peter had provided, the silent vigilant men who followed her either on foot or in a second car. They waited outside her offices while she worked, and others guarded the house while she slept.

That morning, however, she had told Peter, 'Today I have as a companion a gold medal Olympic pistol champion, I don't need my wolves.'

Narmco marketed its own version of the 9-mm parabellum pistol. It was called 'Cobra', and after a single morning in the underground range Peter had taken a liking to the weapon. It was lighter and flatter than the Walther he was accustomed to, easier to carry and conceal, and the single action mechanism saved a flicker of time with the first shot, for there was no need to cock the action. He had had no trouble obtaining a permit to carry one as a trade sample, although it was necessary to check it before every commercial flight, but it carried neatly in a quick-release shoulder holster.

He had felt theatrical and melodramatic at first, but with a little sober thought had convinced himself that to follow on Caliph's tracks unarmed was shortening the odds against himself.

Now it was becoming habit, and he was barely aware of the comforting shape and weight in his armpit, until Magda spoke.

'I am close to dying from thirst,' she went on, and they racked their skis and went into the jovial warmth and clouds of steam that billowed from one of the coffee shops that lined the main street.

They found a seat at a table already crowded with young people, and they ordered glasses of steaming hot *Glühwein*.

Then the four-piece band thumped out a popular dance tune and their table companions swarmed onto the tiny dance floor.

Peter raised a challenging eyebrow at her and she asked with amusement, 'Have you ever danced in ski boots?'

'There has to be a first time for everything.'

She danced like she did everything else, with complete absorption, and her body was strong and hard and slim against his.

It was completely dark as they climbed the narrow track above the village and went in through the electronically controlled gate in the protective wall around the chalet.

It was somehow typical of her that she had avoided the fashionable resorts, and that externally the chalet seemed not much different from fifty others that huddled in the edge of the pine forest.

There was patent relief amongst her entourage at her return, and she seemed almost defiant at their concern as though she had just proved something to herself – but still she did not change from her sports clothes before disappearing into the office suite on the first floor with her two male secretaries. 'I work better with men,' she had explained to Peter once. As Peter dressed in slacks, blazer and silk rollneck after a scalding shower, he could still hear the clatter of the telex machine from the floor below, and it was an hour later when she called him on the house telephone.

The entire top floor was her private domain and she was standing at the windows looking out over the snow-fuzzed lights of the valley as he entered.

She wore green slacks tucked in après-ski boots, and a blouse of the same colour, a perfect match for her eyes. The moment Peter entered, she pressed a concealed switch and the curtains slid silently closed, then she turned to him.

'A drink, Peter?' she asked.

'Not if we are going to talk.'

'We are going to talk,' she said positively, and indicated the soft squashy leather armchair across from the fireplace. She had resisted the traditional Swiss cuckoo-clock and knotty pine decor, and the carpeting was thick Wilton to match the curtains, the furniture low and comfortable but modern, sporty and good fun, the very best made to appear natural and unaffected, blending easily with the modern art on the walls and abstract sculpture in marble and grained wood.

She smiled suddenly at him. 'I had no idea that I had found myself a gifted Sales Director for Narmco – I really am impressed with what you have done in so short a time.'

'I had to establish a plausible cover—' Peter deprecated the compliment. 'And I used to be a soldier – the job interests me.'

'You English!' she told him with mock exasperation. 'Always so modest.' She did not seat herself but moved about the room; although never at rest, neither did she give the feeling of restlessness. 'I am informed that there is to be a definite NATO testing of Kestrel – after almost two years of procrastination.'

Kestrel was Narmco's medium-range ground-to-ground infantry portable missile.

'I am further informed that the decision was made to test after you had met with some of your former colleagues.'

'The whole world runs on the old boy system—' Peter chuckled, ' – you should know that.'

'And you are on old boy terms with the Iranians?' She cocked her head at him.

'That was a small stroke of luck. Five years ago I was on a staff college course with their new military adviser.'

'Luck again.' She smiled. 'Isn't it strange that luck so often favours those who are clever and dedicated and who move faster than the pack?'

'I have had less luck in other directions,' Peter pointed out, and immediately there was no trace of laughter left upon her lips nor in the emerald eyes, but Peter went on. 'So far I have been unsuccessful with the contact we spoke about on our last meeting—'

They had discussed the possibility of access to the Atlas computer link, of requisitioning a printout on 'Caliph' from the Central Intelligence bank, if there was one programmed.

'As I explained, there was the one remote possibility of access, somebody who owed me a favour. He was of no help. He believes that if there is a "Caliph" listing, it's blocked and buzzed.' Which meant that any unauthorized requisition would sound an alarm in intelligence control. 'We'd trigger a Delta condition in Atlas if we put in a printout requisition.'

'You did not give him the name?' Magda asked sharply.

'No. No names, just a general discussion over dinner at Brooks's – but all the implications were there.'

'Do you have any further avenues – ?'

'I think so. One more, but it's a last resort,' Peter said. 'Before we come to that, though, perhaps you can tell me if you have anything further from your sources.'

'My sources—' Magda had never made more explicit descriptions, and Peter had instinctively known not to pry. There was a certain finality to the way she said it. 'My sources have been mostly negative. The seizure of the Netherlands Embassy in Bonn was unconnected with

165

Caliph. It was exactly what it purported to be – South Moluccan extremists. The hijackers of Cathay Airlines and Transit Airlines were both enthusiastic amateurs, as evidence the methods and the outcome—' She smiled drily and drifted back across the room to touch the Hundedwasser collage that hung on the side wall, rearranging the hang of the frame in an essentially feminine gesture. ' – There is only one recent act that has the style of Caliph.'

'Prince Hassied Abdel Hayek?' Peter asked, and she turned to face him, thrusting out one hip with her hand upon it, the nails very red against the light-green cloth and the marquise cut diamond sparkling.

'What did you make of it?' she asked. The Prince had been shot dead, three bullets of .22 calibre in the back of the head while asleep in his rooms on the Cambridge campus. A nineteen-year-old grandson of King Khalid of Saudi Arabia, not one of the particular favourites of the king, a bespectacled scholarly youth who seemed content to remain outside the mainstream of palace power and politics. There had been no attempt at abduction, no sign of a struggle, no evidence of robbery – the young Prince had no close friends nor apparent enemies.

'It does not seem to have reason or motive,' Peter admitted. 'That's why I thought of Caliph.'

'The deviousness of Caliph—' Magda turned away and her haunches rippled under the elastic of her green slacks. There was no ruck line of panties, and her buttocks were perfect spheres, with the shadow of the deep cleft between them showing through the thin material. Peter watched her legs as she paced, realizing for the first time that her feet were long and narrow as her hands, fine and graceful bones in perfect proportion.

'If I told you that Saudi Arabia last week made clear to the other members of OPEC that, far from supporting a rise in the price of crude, she will press for a *five per cent* reduction in the world price at the organization's next meeting—'

Peter straightened up in his chair slowly and Magda went on softly ' – and that she will be supported by Iran in her proposal. If I told you that, what would you think?'

'The King has other, more favoured grandchildren – grandsons and sons as well, brothers, nephews—'

'Seven hundred of them,' Magda agreed, and then went on musing. 'The Shah of Iran has children that he divorced one wife to obtain—'

'The Shah paid his hundred-million-dollar ransom promptly to save his oil minister during the Carlos abduction – what would he do for his own children?' Peter stood up now, unable to stay still with the itch of new ideas.

'And the King of Saudi-Arabia is an Arab. You know how Mohammedans are about sons and grandsons.' Magda came to stand so close to him that he could feel the warmth of her flesh through the narrow space between them, and her perfume subtly underlined the ripe sweet woman's smell of her body, disturbing him, but strangely heightening his awareness. 'Perhaps King Khalid has also been reminded of his own mortality.'

'All right.' Peter hunched his shoulders and frowned in concentration. 'What are we suggesting? That Caliph has struck another easy formula? Two men who control the economic destiny of the Western world? Two men who make decisions at the personal level, who are not answerable to cabinets or causes or governments?'

'Men who are therefore vulnerable to personal terrorism, who have records of appeasement to terrorist pressure.' Magda paused. 'The old truths are still good. "Uneasy lies the head that wears a crown." Both the Shah and the King will be no strangers to the fear of the assassin's blade. They will understand the law of the knife, because they have always lived by it.'

'Hell, you have to admire it.' Peter shook his head. 'There is no need to take and hold hostages. No need for exposure. You kill one obscure member of a large royal family, and you promise that there will be others, each one more important, closer to the head.'

'Both families have a high profile. The Shah loves the bright lights. He's up at Gstaad right this moment. It would need only a sniper up in the treeline to pick one of his children. His sister Shams is in Mauritius now. As for the King's family – any time you want to drop into the Dorchester you'll find one of his sons or grandsons sipping coffee in the public lounge. They are soft targets, and there are plenty of them. You might even have to kill two princelings or three – but secretly the world will feel that they had it coming to them anyway. There will not be oceans wept for men who have themselves held the world to ransom.'

Peter's frown smoothed away, and he grinned wryly. 'Not only do you have to admire it – you've got to have a sneaking sympathy for the object. A dead brake to the crippling inflation of the world, a slowing of disruptive imbalance in trade.'

And Magda's expression was fierce as he had never seen it before. 'That is the trap, Peter. To see the end only, and to harden yourself to the means. That was the trap that Caliph set with the taking of 070. His demands coincided with those of the Western powers, and they placed additional pressure on the victim. Now, if we are correct and Caliph is pressuring the oil dictators for a moderation of their demands, how much more support can he expect from the Western capitalist powers?'

'You are a capitalist,' Peter pointed out. 'If Caliph succeeds you will be one of the first to benefit.'

'I'm a capitalist, yes. But before that I am a human being, and a thinking human being. Do you really believe that if

168

Caliph succeeds now that this will be the last we hear of him?'

'Of course not.' Peter spread his hands in resignation. 'Always his demands will be harsher – with each success he must become bolder.'

'I think we can have that drink now,' Magda said softly, and turned away from him. The black onyx top of the coffee table slid aside at her touch to reveal the array of bottles and glasses beneath.

'Whisky, isn't it?' she asked, and poured a single malt Glenlivet into one of the cut glass tumblers. As she handed it to him their fingers touched and he was surprised at how cool and dry her skin felt.

She poured half a flute glass of white wine and filled it with Perrier water. As she replaced the wine bottle in the ice bucket, Peter saw the label. It was Le Montrachet 1969. Probably the greatest white wine in the world, and Peter had to protest at the way in which she had desecrated it.

'Alexander Dumas said it should be drunk only on bended knee and with head reverently bared—'

' – He forgot the mineral water,' Magda purred with throaty laughter. 'Anyway you can't trust a man who employed other people to write his books for him.' She lifted the adulterated wine to him. 'Long ago I decided to live my life on my own terms. To hell with Messrs Dumas and Caliph.'

'Shall we drink to that?' Peter asked, and they watched each other over the rims. The level of Magda's glass had not lowered and she set the glass aside, moving across to adjust the bowl of hothouse tulips in the chunky free-form crystal bowl.

'If we are right. If this is Caliph at work – then it disturbs the instinctive picture I had formed of him.' Peter broke the silence.

'How?' she asked without looking up from the flowers.

'Caliph – it's an Arabic name. He is attacking the leader of the Arab world.'

'The deviousness of Caliph. Was the name deliberately chosen to confuse the hunters – or perhaps there are other demands apart from the oil price – perhaps pressure is also being put on Khalid for closer support of the Palestinians, or one of the other extremist Arab movements. We do not know what else Caliph wants from Saudi Arabia.'

'But then, the oil price. It is Western orientated. Somehow it has always been accepted that terrorism is a tool of the far left,' Peter pointed out, shaking his head. 'The hijacking of 070 – even the kidnapping of your husband – were both aimed against the capitalist society.'

'He kidnapped Aaron for the money, and killed him to protect his identity. The attack on the South African Government, the attack on the oil cartel, the choice of name, all point to a person with god-like pretensions.' Magda broke the head off one of the tulips with an abrupt, angry gesture, and crushed it in her fist. She let the petals fall into the deep onyx ashtray. 'I feel so helpless, Peter. We seem to be going round in futile circles.' She came back to him as he stood by the curtained windows. 'You said earlier that there was one sure way to flush out Caliph?'

'Yes,' Peter nodded.

'Can you tell me?'

'There was an old trick of the Indian shikari. When he got tired of following the tiger in thick jungle without a sight of the beast, he used to stake out a goat and wait for the tiger to come to it.'

'A goat?'

'My Zodiacal sign is Capricorn – the goat.' Peter smiled slightly.

'I don't understand.'

'If I were to put the word out that I was hunting Caliph—' He smiled again. 'Caliph knows me. The hijacker spoke my

170

name, clearly, unmistakenly. She had been warned. So I believe that Caliph would take me seriously enough to consider it necessary to come after me.'

He saw the lingering colour drain dramatically from her high cheeks, and the sudden shadow in the depths of her eyes.

'Peter—'

'That's the only way I'm going to get close to him.'

'Peter—' She placed her hand on his forearm, but then she could not go on. Instead she stared at him silently and her eyes were green and dark and unfathomable. He saw there was a pulse that throbbed softly in her long graceful neck, just below the ear. Her lips parted, as though she were about to speak. They were delicately sculptured lips, and she touched them with the pink tip of her tongue, leaving them moist and soft and somehow defenceless. She closed them, without speaking, but the pressure of her fingers on his arm increased, and the carriage of her whole body altered. Her back arched slightly so her lower body swayed towards him and her chin lifted slightly.

'I have been so lonely,' she whispered. 'So lonely, for so very long. I only realized how lonely today – while I was with you.'

Peter felt a choking sensation in his throat, and the prickle of blood behind his eyes.

'I don't want to be lonely again, ever.'

She had let her hair come down. It was very thick and long. It fell in a straight rippling curtain shot through with glowing lights, to her waist.

She had parted it in the centre; a thin straight line of white scalp divided the great black wings and they framed her face, making it appear pale and childlike with eyes too large and vulnerable, and as she came towards where Peter lay the glossy sheets of hair slid silently across the brocade of her gown.

The hem of the gown swept the carpet, and her bare toes peeped out from under it with each step. Narrow finely boned feet, and the nails were trimmed and painted with a colourless lacquer. The sleeves of the gown were wide as batwings and lined internally with satin, the collar buttoned up in a high Chinese style.

Beside the bed she stopped and her courage and poise seemed to desert her, her shoulders slumped a little and she clasped the long narrow fingers before her in a defensive gesture.

'Peter, I don't think I am going to be very good at this.' The throaty whisper was barely audible, and her lips trembled with the strength of her appeal. 'And I want so badly to be good.'

Silently he reached out one hand towards her, palm upwards. The bedclothes covered him to the waist, but his chest and arms were bare, lightly tanned and patterned with dark wiry body hair. As he reached for her the muscle bunched and expanded beneath the skin, and she saw that there was no surplus flesh on his waist, nor on his shoulders and upper arms. He looked lean and hard and tempered, yet supple as the lash of a bullwhip, and she did not respond immediately to the invitation, for his masculinity was overpowering.

He folded back the thick down-filled duvet between them, and the sheet was crisp and smoothly ironed in the low rosy light.

'Come,' he ordered gently, but she turned away and with her back to him she undid the buttons of the embroidered gown, beginning at the throat and working downwards.

She slipped the gown from her shoulders, and held it for a moment in the crook of her elbows. The smooth pale flesh

172

gleamed through the fall of dark hair, and she seemed to steel herself like a diver bracing for the plunge into unknown depths.

She let the gown drop with a rustling slide down the full length of her body, and it lay around her ankles in a shallow puddle of peacock colours.

She heard him gasp aloud, and she threw the hair back from her shoulders with a toss of the long, swan-white neck. The hair hung impenetrably to the small of her back; just above the deep cleft of her lower body it ended in a clean line and her buttocks were round and neat and without blemish, but even as he stared the marble smoothness puckered into a fine rash of gooseflesh as though his eyes had physically caressed her, and she had responded with an appealingly natural awareness that proved how her every sense must be aroused and tingling. At the knowledge Peter felt his heart squeezed. He wanted to rush to her and sweep her into his arms, but instinct warned him that she must close the last gap herself, and he lay quietly propped on one elbow, feeling the deep ache of wanting spread through his entire body.

She stooped to pick up the gown, and for a moment the long legs were at an awkward coltish angle to each other and the spheres of her buttocks altered shape. No longer perfectly symmetrical, but parted slightly, and in the creamy niche they formed with her thighs there was an instant's heart-stopping glimpse of a single dense tight curl of hair and the light from beyond tipped the curl with glowing reddish highlights, then she had straightened again, once more lithe and tall, and she dropped the robe across the low couch and in the same movement turned back to face Peter.

He gasped again and his sense of continuity began to break up into a mosaic of distinct, seemingly unconnected images and sensations.

Her breasts were tiny as those of a pubescent child, but

173

the nipples were startlingly prominent, the colour and texture of ripening young berries, dark wine-red, already fully erect and hard as pebbles.

The pale plain of her belly, with the deep pit of the navel at its centre, that ended at last on the plump darkly furred mound pressed into the deep wedge between her thighs, like a small frightened living creature crouching from the stoop of the falcon.

The feel of her face pressed to his chest, and the tickle of her quick breath stirring his body hair, the almost painful grip of slim powerful arms locked with desperate strength around his waist.

The taste of her mouth as her lips parted slowly, softly, to his and the uncertain flutter of her tongue becoming bolder, velvety on top and slick and slippery on the underside.

The sound of her breathing changing to a deep sonorous pulse in his ears, seeming to keep perfect time with his own.

The smell of her breath, heavy with the aromatic musk of her arousal, and blending with the orangy fragrance of her perfume and the ripe woman smell of her body.

And always the feel of her – the warmth and the softness, the hardness of toned muscle and the running ripple of long dark hair about his face and down his body, the crisp electric rasp of tight, tense curls parting to unbearable heat and going on for ever to depths that seemed to reach beyond the frontier of reality and reason.

And then later the stillness of complete peace that reached out from the centre where she lay against his heart and seemed to spread to the farthest corners of his soul.

'I knew that I was lonely,' she whispered. 'But I did not realize just how terribly deeply.' And she held him as though she would never relinquish her grip.

Magda woke him in the cold utter darkness three hours before dawn, and it was still dark when they left the chalet. The headlights of the following Mercedes that carried her wolves swept the interior of their saloon through each bend in the steep twisting road down from the mountains.

On take-off from Zurich Magda was in the Lear jet's left-hand seat, flying as pilot-in-command, and she handled the powerful machine with the sedate lack of ostentation which marks the truly competent aviator. Her personal pilot, a grizzled and taciturn Frenchman, who was flying now as her co-pilot, evidently held her skill in high regard and watched over her with an almost fatherly pride and approval as she cleared Zurich controlled airspace and levelled out at cruise altitude for Paris Orly before she left him to monitor the auto-pilot and came back to the main cabin. Though she sat beside Peter in the black calfskin armchairs, her manner was unchanged from the way it had been during their last flight together in this machine – reserved and polite – so that he found it difficult to believe the wonders they had explored together the previous night.

She worked with the two dark-suited secretaries opposite her, speaking her fluent rippling French with the same enchanting trace of accent that marked her English. In the short time since he had joined Narmco, Peter had been forced to make a crash revision of his own French. Now once again he could manage, if not with éclat, at least with competence, in technical and financial discussion. Once or twice Magda turned to him for comment or opinion, and her gaze was serious and remote, seeming as impersonal and efficient as an electronic computer – and Peter understood that they were to make no show of their new relationship before employees.

Immediately she proved him wrong, for her co-pilot called her over the cabin speaker.

'We will join the Orly circuit in four minutes, Baroness.'

And she turned easily and naturally and kissed Peter's cheek, still speaking French.

'Pardon me, *chéri*. I will make the landing. I need the flying time in my logbook.'

She greased the sleek swift aircraft onto the runway as though she was spreading butter on hot toast. The co-pilot had radioed ahead so that when she parked in the private hangar there were a uniformed immigration *policier* and a *douanier* already waiting.

As they came aboard, they saluted her respectfully and then barely glanced at her red diplomatic passport. They took a little longer with Peter's blue and gold British passport, and Magda murmured to Peter with a trace of a smile.

'I must get you a little red book. It's so much easier.' Then to the officials. 'It is a cold morning, gentlemen, I hope you will take a glass.' And her white-jacketed steward was hovering already. They left the two Frenchmen removing their kepis and pistol belts, settling down comfortably in the leather armchairs to make a leisurely selection of the cigars and cognac that the steward had produced for their approval.

There were three cars waiting for them, parked in the back of the hangar with drivers and guards. Peter's lip curled as he saw the Maserati.

'I told you not to drive that thing,' he said gruffly. 'It's like having your name in neon lights.'

They had argued about this vehicle while Peter was reorganizing her personal security, for the Maserati was an electric silver-grey, one of her favourite colours, a shimmering dart of metal. She swayed against him with that husky little chuckle of hers.

'Oh, that is so very nice to have a man being masterful again. It makes me feel like a woman.'

'I have other ways of making you feel like that.'

'I know,' she agreed, with a wicked flash of green eyes.

'And I like those even better, but not now – please! What in the world would my staff think!' Then seriously, 'You take the Maserati, I ordered it for you, anyway. Somebody may as well enjoy it. And please do not be late this evening. I have especially made it free for us. Try and be at La Pierre Bénite by eight o'clock – will you please?'

By the time Peter had to slow for the traffic along the Pont Neuilly entrance to Paris, he had accustomed himself to the surging power and acceleration of the Maserati, and, as she had suggested, he was enjoying himself. Even in the mad Parisian traffic he used the slick gear box to knife through the merest suspicion of an opening, bulling out of trouble or overtaking with the omnipotent sense of power that control of the magnificent machine bestowed upon its driver.

He knew then why Magda loved it so dearly, and when he parked it at last in the underground garage on the Champs-Elysées side of Concorde he grinned at himself in the mirror.

'Bloody cowboy!' he said, and glanced at his Rolex. He had an hour before his first appointment, and as a sudden thought unclipped the holster of the Cobra and, with the pistol still in it, locked it in the glove compartment of the Maserati. He grinned again as he pondered the inadvisability of marching into French Naval Headquarters armed to the teeth.

The drizzle had cleared, and the chestnut trees in the Elysèe gardens were popping their first green buds as he came out into Concorde. He used one of the call boxes in the Concorde Metro station to make a call to the British Embassy. He spoke to the Military Attaché for two minutes, and when he hung up he knew the ball was probably already in play. If Caliph had penetrated the Atlas Command deeply enough to know him personally as the commander of Thor – then it would not be too long before he knew that the former commander had picked up the spoor. The

Military Attaché at the Paris Embassy had other more clandestine duties than kissing the ladies' hands at diplomatic cocktail parties.

Peter reached the main gates of the Marine Headquarters on the corner of the rue Royale with a few minutes to spare, but already there was a secretary waiting for him below the billowing Tricolour. He smoothed Peter's way past the sentries, and led him to the armaments committee room on the third floor overlooking a misty grey view of the Seine and the gilded arches of the Pont Neuf. Two of Peter's assistants from Narmco were there ahead of him with their briefcases unpacked and the contents spread upon the polished walnut table.

The French Flag captain had been in Brussels, and on one unforgettable evening he had conducted Peter on a magic carpet tour of the brothels of that city. He greeted him now with cries of Gallic pleasure and addressed him as 'tu' and 'toi' – which all boded very well for the meeting ahead.

At noon precisely, the French captain moved that the meeting adjourn across the street to a private room on the first floor of Maxim's, blissful in the certainty that Narmco would pick up the tab, if they were really serious about selling the Kestrel rocket motors to the French Navy.

It required all Peter's tact not to make it obvious that he was taking less than his share of the Clos de Vougeot or of the Rémy Martin, and more than once he found that he had missed part of the discussion which was being conducted at a steadily increasing volume. He found that he was thinking of emerald eyes and small pert bosoms.

From Maxim's back to the Ministry of Marine, and later it required another major act of diplomacy on Peter's part when the captain smoothed his moustache and cocked a knowing eye at Peter. 'There is a charming little club, very close and wonderfully friendly—'

By six o'clock Peter had disentangled himself from the

Frenchman's company, with protestations of friendship and promises to meet again in ten days' time. An hour later Peter left his two sales assistants at the Hôtel Meurice after a quick but thorough summation of the day's achievements. They were, all three, agreed that it was a beginning but a long, long road lay ahead to the ending.

He walked back along Rivoli; despite the frowsiness of a long day of endless talk and the necessity for quick thinking in a language which was still strange on the tongue, despite a slight ache behind the eyes from the wine and cognac and despite the taste of cigar and cigarette smoke he had breathed, he was buoyed by a tingling sense of anticipation, for Magda was waiting, and he stepped out briskly.

As he paused for traffic lights, he caught a glimpse of his own reflection in a shop window. He was smiling without realizing it.

While he waited on the ramp of the parking garage for his turn to pay and enter the traffic stream, with the Maserati engine whispering impatiently, he glanced in the rear view mirror. He had acquired the habit long ago when one of the captured Provo death lists had begun with his name; since then he had learned to look over his shoulder.

He noticed the Citroën two back in the line of vehicles because the windshield was cracked and there was a scrape which had dented the mudguard and exposed a bright strip of bare metal.

He noticed the same black Citroën still two back as he waited for pedestrian lights in the Champs-Elysées, and when he ducked his head slightly to try and get a look at the driver, the headlights switched on as though to frustrate him and at that moment the lights changed and he had to drive on.

Going around the Étoile, the Citroën had fallen back four places in the grey drizzling dusk of early autumn, but he spotted it once again when he was halfway down the Avenue de la Grande Armée, for by now he was actively searching for it. This time it changed lanes and slipped off the main thoroughfare to the left. It was immediately lost in the maze of side streets and Peter should have been able to forget it and concentrate on the pleasure of controlling the Maserati, but there lingered a sense of foreboding and even after he had shot the complicated junction of roads that got him onto the periphery route and eventually out on the road to Versailles and Chartres, he found himself changing lanes and speed while he scanned the road behind in the mirror.

Only when he left Versailles and was on the Rambouillet road did he have a clear view back a mile down the straight avenue of plane trees, and he was certain there was no other vehicle on the road. He relaxed completely and began to prepare himself for the final turn off that would bring him at last to La Pierre Bénite.

The shiny wet black python of road uncoiled ahead of him and then humped abruptly. Peter came over the rise at 150 kilometres an hour and instantly started to dance lightly on brake and clutch, avoiding the temptation of tramping down hard and losing adhesion on the slippery uneven tarmac. Ahead of him there was a gendarme in a shiny white plastic cape, wet with rain, brandishing a torch with a red lens; there were reflective warning triangles bright as rubies, a Peugeot in the ditch beside the road with headlights glaring at the sky, a dark blue police Kombi van half blocking the road, and in the stage lit by the Kombi's headlights two bodies were laid out neatly, and all of it hazed by the soft insistent mantle of falling rain – a typical roadside accident scene.

Peter had the Maserati well in hand, bringing her neatly down through the gears to a crawl, and as he was lowering the side window, the electric motor whining softly and the icy gust of night air into the heated interior, the gendarme gestured with the flashlight for him to pull over into the narrow gap between hedge and the parked Kombi, and at that moment the unexpected movement caught Peter's eye. It was one of the bodies lying in the roadway under the headlights. The movement was the slight arch of the back that a man makes before rising from the prone position.

Peter watched him lift his arm, not more than a few inches, but it was just enough for Peter to realize he had been holding an object concealed down the outside of his thigh, and even in the rain and the night Peter's trained eye recognized the perforated air-cooled sleeve enclosing the short barrel of a fold-down machine pistol.

Instantly his brain was racing so that everything about him seemed to be taking place in dreamy slow motion.

The Maserati! he thought. They're after Magda.

The gendarme was coming round to the driver's side of the Maserati, and he had his right hand under the white plastic cape, at the level of his pistol belt.

Peter went flat on the gas pedal, and the Maserati bellowed like a bull buffalo shot through the heart. The rear wheels broke from the wet surface, and with a light touch Peter encouraged the huge silver machine to swing like a scythe at the gendarme. It should have cut him down, but he was too quick. As he dived for the hedge, Peter saw that he had brought the pistol out from under his cape but was too busy at that moment to use it.

The side of the Maserati touched the hedge with a fluttering rustle of foliage, and Peter lifted his right foot, caught the enraged charge of the machine and swung her the other way. The moment she was lined up he hit the gas again, and the Maserati howled. This time she burned blue rubber smoke off her rear wheels.

There was a driver at the wheel of the blue police Kombi, and he tried to pull across to block the road completely, but he was not fast enough.

The two vehicles touched, with a crackle and scream of metal that jarred Peter's teeth, but what concerned him was that the two bodies in the headlights were no longer flat.

The nearest was on one knee and he was swinging the short stubby machine pistol – it looked like a Stirling or the new Sidewinder, but he was using the fold-down wire butt, wasting vital fractions of a second to get the weapon to his shoulder. He was also blocking the field of fire of the man who crouched behind him with another machine pistol pinned to his hip, pointing with index finger and forearm, ready to trigger with his second finger – 'That's the way it should be done.' Peter recognized professional skill, and his brain was running so swiftly that he had time to applaud it.

The Maserati cannoned off the police Kombi, and Peter lifted his right foot to take traction off the rear wheels, and spun the wheel the hard lock to the right. The Maserati swung her tail with a screech of rubber and went into a left side slide towards the two figures in the road, and Peter ducked down below the level of the door. He had deliberately induced the left-hand slide, so that he had some little protection from the engine compartment and bodywork.

As he ducked he heard the familiar sound, like a giant ripping heavyweight canvas, an automatic weapon throwing bullets at a cyclic rate of almost two thousand rounds a minute, and the bullets tore into the side of the Maserati, beating in the metal with an ear-numbing clangor, while glass exploded in upon Peter like the glittering spray as a storm-driven wave strikes a rock. Glass chips pelted across his back, and stung his cheek and the back of his neck. They sparkled like a diamond tiara in his hair.

Whoever was doing the shooting had certainly emptied the magazine in those few seconds, and now Peter bobbed up in his seat, slitting his eyes against the cloud of glass splinters. He saw a looming nightmare of dark hedges and spun the wheel back to hold the Maserati. She swayed to the limits of her equilibrium and Peter had a glimpse of the two gunmen in the road rolling frantically into the half-filled ditch, but at that moment his offrear wheel hit the lip and he was slammed up short against his safety belt with a force that drove the air from his lungs, and the Maserati reared like a stallion smelling the mare and tail-walked, swinging in short vicious surges back and forth across the road, as he desperately fought for control with gear and brake and wheel. He must have spun full circle, Peter realized, for there was a giddy dazzle of light beams and of running and rolling figures, everything hazy and indistinct in the rain, then the open road ahead again, and he sent the car at it with a great howling lunge, at the same moment glancing up at his mirror.

In the headlights he saw the burned blue clouds of smoke and steam thrown up by his own tyres, and through it the figure of the second gunman obscured from the waist by the ditch. He had the machine pistol at his waist, and the muzzle flash bloomed about him.

Peter heard the first burst hit the Maserati and he could not duck again, for there was a bend ahead in the rain, coming up at dazzling speed and he clenched his jaws waiting for it.

The next burst hit the car, like the sound of hail on a tin roof, and he felt the rude tugging, numbing jerk in his upper body.

'Tagged!' he realized. There was no mistaking it, he had been hit before. The first time when he led a patrol into an EOKA ambush a very long time ago, and at the same moment he was evaluating the hit calmly finding he still had use of both hands and all his senses. Either it was a ricochet, or the bullet had spent most of its force in penetrating the rear windshield and seat back.

The Maserati tracked neatly into the bend, and only then he felt the engine surge and falter. Almost immediately the sharp stink of gasoline filled the cab of the Maserati.

'Fuel line,' he told himself, and there was the warm, uncomfortable spread of his own blood down his back and side, and he placed his wound low in the left shoulder. If it had penetrated it would be a lung hit, and he waited for the coppery salt taste of blood in his throat or the bubbling froth of escaping air in his chest cavity.

The engine beat checked again, surged and checked, as it starved for fuel. That first traversing burst of automatic fire must have ripped through the engine compartment, and Peter thought wryly that in the movies the Maserati would have immediately erupted in spectacular pyrotechnics like a miniature Vesuvius – though in reality it didn't happen like that, still gasoline from the severed lead would be spraying over plugs and points.

One last glance backwards, before the bend hid it and he saw three men running for the police van – three men and the driver, that was lousy odds. They would be after him immediately, and the crippled machine made a final brave leap forward that carried them five hundred yards more, and then it died.

Ahead of him, at the limits of the headlight beam, Peter saw the white gates of La Pierre Bénite. They had set the ambush at the point where they could screen out most extraneous traffic, and gather only the silver Maserati in their net.

He cast his mind back swiftly, recalling the lie of the land beyond the main gates of the estate. He had been here only once before, and it had been dark then also – but he had the soldier's eye for ground, and he remembered thick forest on both sides of the road, down to a low bridge over a narrow fast flowing stream with steep banks, a hard left hander and a climb up to the house. The house was half a mile beyond the gates, a long way to go with a body hit and at least four armed men following, and no guarantee that he would be safe there either.

The Maserati was coasting down the slight incline towards the gates, slowing as it ran out of momentum, and now there was the hot smell of oil and burning rubber. The paintwork of the engine hood began to blister and discolour. Peter switched off the ignition to stop the electric pump spraying more fuel onto the burning engine and he slipped his hand into his jacket. He found the wound where he had expected it – low and left. It was beginning to sting and his hand came away sticky and slick with blood. He wiped it on his thigh.

Behind him was the reflected glow of headlights in the rain, a halo of light growing stronger. At any moment they would come through the bend, and he opened the glove compartment.

The 9-mm Cobra gave some little comfort as he slipped it from its holster and thrust it into the front of his belt. There was no spare magazine and the breech was empty, a safety consideration which he now regretted, for it left him with only nine rounds in the magazine – one more might make a lot of difference.

Pretty little fingers of bright flame were waving at him from under the bonnet of the engine compartment, finding the hinge and joint, probing the ventilation slot on the top surface. Peter released his seat belt, held open the door and steered with his other hand for the verge. Here the road was banked and dropped away steeply.

He flicked the wheel back the opposite way and let the change of direction eject him neatly, throwing him clear, while the Maserati swerved back into the centre of the road and rolled away, slowing gradually.

He landed as though from a parachute drop, feet and knees together cushioning the impact and then rolled into it. Pain flared in his shoulder and he felt something tear. He came up in a crouch and ran doubled over for the edge of the woods, and the burning auto lit the dark trees with flickering orange light.

The fingers of his left hand felt swollen and numb as he pumped a round into the chamber of the Cobra, and at that moment the headlights beyond the bend flared with shocking brilliance and Peter had the illusion of being caught in front stage centre of the Palladium. He went down hard on his belly in the soft rain-sodden earth, but still his wound jarred and he felt the warm trickle of running blood under his shirt as he crawled desperately for the tree line.

The police van roared down the stretch of road. Peter flattened and pressed his face to the earth, and it smelled of leaf mould and fungus. The van roared past where he lay.

Three hundred yards down the road the Maserati had coasted to a halt, two wheels still on the road, the offside wheels over the verge so she stood at an abandoned angle, burning merrily.

The van pulled up at a respectful distance from it, aware of the danger of explosion, and a single figure, the gendarme in his plastic cape, ran forward, took one look into the cab and shouted something. The language sounded like French, but the flames were beginning to drum fiercely and the range too long to hear clearly.

The van locked into a U-turn, bumped over the verge, and then started back slowly. The two erstwhile accident victims, still carrying their machine pistols, running ahead like hounds on leash, one on each side of the road, heads down as they searched for signs in the soft shoulders of the road. The white-caped gendarme rode on the running-board of the van, calling encouragement to the hunters.

Peter was up again, doubled over, heading for the edge of the forest, and he ran into the barbed wire fence at full stretch. It brought him down heavily. He felt the slash of steel through the cloth of his trousers, and as he gathered himself again, he thought bitterly. One hundred and seventy guineas. The suit had been tailored in Savile Row. He crawled between the strands of armed wire, and there was a shout behind him. They had picked up his spoor, and as he dodged across the last few yards of open ground, another sharper, more jubilant shout.

They had spotted him in the towering firelight of the blazing Maserati, and again there was the tearing rip of automatic fire; but it was extreme range for the short barrel and low velocity ammunition. Peter heard passing shot like a whisper of bats' wings in the darkness above him and then he reached the first trees and ducked behind one of them.

He found he was breathing deeply, but with a good easy rhythm. The wound wasn't handicapping him yet, and he was into the cold reasoning rage that combat always instilled in him.

The range to the barbed wire fence was fifty metres, he judged, it was one of his best distances – International pistol standard out-of-hand with a 50-mm X circle – but there were no judges out here and he took a double-handed grip, and let them run into the fence just as he had done.

It brought two of them down, and the cries of angry distress were definitely in French; as they struggled to their feet again they were precisely back-lit by the flames, and the Cobra had a luminous foresight. Peter went for the mid-section of one of the machine gunners.

The 9-mm had a vicious whipcrack report, and punched into flesh and bone with 385 foot-pounds of energy. The strike of the bullet sounded like a watermelon hit with the full swing of a baseball bat. It lifted the man off his feet, and threw him backwards, and Peter swung onto the next target, but they were pros. Even though the fire from the edge of the woods had come as a complete surprise, they reacted instantly, and disappeared flat against the dark earth. They gave him no target, and Peter was too low on ammunition to throw down holding fire.

One of them fired a burst of automatic and it tore bark and wood and leaves along the edge of the trees. Peter fired at the muzzle flash only once as a warning and then ducked away and, keeping his head down to avoid lucky random fire, sprinted back into the woods.

They would be held up for two or three minutes by the fence and by the threat of coming under fire again, and Peter wanted to open some ground between them during that time.

The glow of the burning Maserati kept him well orientated and he moved quickly towards the river; however, before he had covered two yards he was starting to shiver uncontrollably. His two-piece city suit was soaked by the persistent drizzle and by the shower from each bush he brushed against. His shoes were light calf leather with leather soles and he had stepped in puddles of mud, and the knee-high grass was sodden. The cold struck through his clothing; he could feel his wound stiffening agonizingly and the first nauseating grip of shock tightened his belly, but he paused every fifty yards or so and listened for sounds of pursuit. Once he heard the sound of a car engine from the direction of the road, passing traffic probably, and he wondered what they would make of the abandoned police vehicle and the blazing Maserati. Even if it was reported to the real police, it would be all over before a patrol arrived and Peter discounted the chance of assistance from that quarter.

He was beginning now to be puzzled by the total lack of any sign of further pursuit, and he looked for and found a good stance in which to wait for it. There was a fallen oak tree and he wriggled in under the trunk, with a clear avenue of retreat, good cover and a low position from which any pursuer would be silhouetted against the sky glow of the burning Maserati. There were only three pursuers now, and seven cartridges in the Cobra. If it were not for the cold and the demoralizing ache through his upper body, he might have felt more confident, but the nagging terror of the hunted animal was still on him.

He waited five minutes, lying completely still, every sense tuned to its finest, the Cobra held out in extended double grip, ready to roll left or right and take the shot as it came. There was no sound but the drip and plop of the rain-soaked woods.

Another ten minutes passed before it occurred to him suddenly that the pursuers must now realize that the wrong quarry had sprung their trap. They were setting for Magda Altmann, and it must be clear to them that they had a man, and an armed one at that. He pondered their reaction. Almost certainly they would pull out now, or had already done so.

Instead of a lady worth twenty or thirty million dollars in ransom money, they must realize they had one of her employees, probably an armed bodyguard, who was driving the Maserati either as a decoy or merely as delivery driver. Yes, he decided, they would pull out – take their casualty and melt away, and Peter was sure they would leave no clues to their identity. He would have enjoyed the opportunity to question one of them, he thought, and grimaced at a new lance of pain in the shoulder.

He waited another ten minutes, utterly still and alert, controlling the spasms of cold and reaction that shook him, then he rose quietly and moved back towards the river. The Maserati must have burned out completely now for the sky was black again and he had to rely on his own sense of direction to keep orientated. Even though he knew he was alone, he paused every fifty yards to listen and look.

He heard the river at last. It was directly ahead and very close. He moved a little faster and almost walked off the bank in the dark. He squatted to rest for a moment, for the shoulder was very painful now, and the cold was draining his energy.

The prospect of wading the river was particularly uninviting. The rain had fallen without a break for days now, and the water sounded powerful and swift – it would certainly be icy cold, and probably shoulder deep rather than waist deep. The bridge must be only a few hundred yards downstream, and he stood up and moved along the bank.

Cold and pain can sap concentration very swiftly, and Peter had to make a conscious effort to keep himself alert, and he felt for every foothold before transferring his weight forward. He held the Cobra hanging at full stretch of his right arm, but ready for instant use, and he blinked his eyes clear of the fine drizzle of rain and the cold sweat of pain and fear.

Yet it was his sense of smell that alerted him. The rank smell of stale Turkish tobacco smoke on a human body, it was a smell that had always offended him, and now he picked it up instantly, even though it was just one faint whiff.

Peter froze in mid stride while his brain raced to adjust to the unexpected. He had almost convinced himself that he was alone.

Now he remembered the sound of a car engine on the main road, and he realized that men who had set up such an elaborate decoy – the faked motor accident, the police van and uniform – would certainly have taken the trouble to plot and study the ground between the ambush point and the victim's intended destination.

They would know better than Peter himself the layout of woods and river and bridge, and would have realized immediately they had taken their first casualty that futility of blundering pursuit through the dark. It was the smart thing to circle back and wait again, and they would choose the river bank or the bridge itself.

The only thing that troubled Peter was their persistence. They *must* know it was not Magda Altmann, and then even in this tense moment of discovery he remembered the Citroën that had followed him down the Champs-Elysées – nothing was what it appeared to be, and slowly he completed the step in which he had frozen.

He stood utterly still, poised every muscle and every nerve screwed to its finest pitch, but the night was black and the rush of the river covered all sound. Peter waited. The other man will always move if you wait long enough, and he waited with the patience of the stalking leopard, although the cold struck through to his bones and the rain slid down his cheeks and neck.

The man moved at last. The squelch of mud and the unmistakeable brush of undergrowth against cloth, then silence. He was very close, within ten feet, but there was no glimmer of light, and Peter shifted his weight carefully to face the direction of the sound. The old trick was to fire one shot at the sound and use the muzzle flash to light the target for a second shot which followed it in almost the same instant of time – but there were three of them and at ten feet that machine pistol could cut a man in half. Peter waited.

Then from upstream there was the sound of a car engine again, still faint but fast approaching. Immediately somebody whistled faintly, a rising double note in the night up towards the bridge, clearly some prearranged signal. A car door banged shut, much closer than the sound of the approaching engine and a starter whirred, another harsher engine roared into life, headlights flared through the rain, and Peter blinked as the whole scene ahead of him lit up.

A hundred yards ahead the bridge crossed the stream, the surface of the water was shiny and black as new-mined coal as it flowed about the supporting piles.

The blue van had parked on the threshold of the bridge, obviously to wait for Peter, but now it was pulling out, probably alarmed by the approach of the other more powerful engine from the direction of La Pierre Bénite. The driver was heading back towards the main road, the phoney gendarme scrambling alongside with his cape flapping as he tried to scramble through the open offside door – and out of the darkness, close to Peter, a voice cried out with alarm.

'*Attendez!*' The third man had no desire to be left by his companions, and he ran forward, abandoning all attempt at concealment. He had his back to Peter now, waving the machine pistol frantically, clearly outlined by the headlights of the van, and the range was under ten feet. It was a dead shot, and Peter went for it instinctively – and only at the very instant of trigger pressure that would have sent a 95 gram bullet between his shoulder blades was Peter able to check himself.

The man's back was turned and the range would make it murder; Peter's training should have cured him of such nice gentlemanly distinctions. However, what really held his trigger finger was the need to know. Peter had to know who these people were and who had sent them, and what they had been sent to do, who they were after.

Now that the man was being deserted, he had abandoned all stealth and was running as though he were chasing a bus, and Peter saw the chance to take him. Roles had been exchanged completely, and Peter darted forward, transferring the Cobra to his injured left hand.

He caught the man in four paces, keeping low to avoid his peripheral vision, and he whipped his good right arm around the throat, going for the half nelson and the spin that would disorientate the man before he slammed the barrel of the Cobra against the temple.

The man was quick as a cat, something warned him – perhaps the squelch of Peter's sodden shoes, and he ducked his chin onto his chest rolling his shoulders and beginning to turn back into the line of Peter's attack.

Peter missed the throat and caught him high, the crook of his elbow locking about the man's mouth, and the unexpected turn had thrown him slightly off balance. If he had had full use of his left arm, he could still have spun his victim, but in an intuitive flash he realized that he had lost the advantage, already the man was twisting his head out of the armlock, bulking his shoulders, and by the feel of him, Peter knew instantly that he was steel-hard with muscle.

The barrel of the machine pistol was short enough to enable him to press the muzzle into Peter's body just as soon as he completed his turn; it would tear Peter to pieces like a chain saw.

Peter changed his grip slightly, no longer opposing the man's turn, but throwing all his weight and the strength of his right arm into the same direction; they spun together like a pair of waltzing dancers, but Peter knew that the moment they broke apart the man would have the killing advantage again.

The river was his one chance, he realized that instinctively, and before the advantage passed back from him to his adversary, he hurled himself backwards, keeping his grip on the man's head.

They went out into black space, falling together in a short gut-swooping drop with Peter underneath. If there was rock below the steep bank of the river, he realized he would be crushed by the other's weight.

They struck the surface of the fast black water, and freezing cold struck like a club so that Peter almost released the air from his lungs as a reflex.

The shock of cold water seemed to have stunned the man in his grip momentarily, and Peter felt the whoosh of air from his lungs as he let go. Peter changed his grip, wedging his elbow under the chin, but not quite able to get at the throat – immediately the man began the wild panic-stricken struggles of somebody held under icy water with empty lungs.

He had lost the machine pistol, for he was tearing at Peter's arms and face with both hands as the water swirled them both end over end down towards the bridge.

Peter had to keep him from getting air, and as he held his own precious single breath, he tried to get on top and stay there.

Fingers hooked at his closed eyes, and then into his mouth as the man reached back desperately over his own shoulders. Peter opened his mouth slightly and the other man thrust his fingers deeply in, trying to tear at his tongue. Immediately Peter locked his teeth into the fingers with a force that made his jaw ache at the hinges, and his mouth filled with the sickening warm spurt of the other man's blood.

Fighting his own revulsion, he hung on desperately with teeth and arms. He had lost his own weapon, dropping it into the black flood from numbed and crippled fingers, and the man was fighting now with the animal strength of his starved lungs and mutilated fingers; every time he tried to yank his hand out of Peter's mouth the flesh tore audibly in Peter's ears and fresh blood made him gag and choke.

They came out on the surface and through streaming eyes Peter had one glimpse of the bridge looming above him. The blue van had disappeared, but Magda Altmann's Mercedes limousine was parked in the centre of the bridge, and in the wash of its headlights he recognized her two bodyguards. They were leaning far out over the guardrail, and Peter had a moment's dread that one of them might try a shot – then they were flung into the concrete piles of the bridge with such force that they lost the deathlock they had upon each other.

The back eddy beyond the bridge swung them in towards the bank. Gasping and swallowing with cold and exhaustion and pain, Peter fought for footing on gravel and rock. The machine-gunner had found bottom also and was stumbling desperately towards the bank. In the headlights of the limousine Peter saw Magda's two bodyguards racing back across the bridge to head him off.

Peter realized that he would not be able to catch the man before he reached the bank.

'Carl!' he screamed at the bodyguard who was leading. 'Stop him. Don't let him get away.'

The bodyguard vaulted over the guardrail, landing cat-like in complete balance, with the pistol double-handed at the level of his navel.

Below him the machine-gunner dragged himself waist deep towards the bank. It was only then that Peter realized what was going to happen.

'No!' He choked on blood and water. 'Take him alive. Don't kill him, Carl!'

The bodyguard had not heard, or had not understood. The muzzle blast seemed to join him and the wallowing figure in the river below him, a blood-orange rope of flame and thunderous explosion. The bullets smacked into the machine-gunner's chest and belly like an axeman cutting down a tree.

'No!' Peter yelled helplessly. 'Oh Jesus, no! No!'

Peter lunged forward and caught the corpse before it slid below the black water, and he dragged it by one arm to the bank. The bodyguards took it from him and hauled it up, the head lolling like an idiot's, and the blood diluted to pale pink in the reflected headlights.

Peter made three attempts to climb the bank, each time slithering back tiredly into the water, then Carl reached down and gripped his wrist.

Peter knelt on the muddy bank, still choking with the water and blood he had swallowed, and he retched weakly.

'Peter!' Magda's voice rang with concern, and he looked up and wiped his mouth on the back of his forearm. She had slipped out of the back door of the limousine and was running back along the bridge, long-legged in black boots and ski-pants, her face dead white with concern and her eyes frantic with worry.

Peter pushed himself onto his feet and swayed drunkenly. She reached him and caught him, steadying him as he teetered.

'Peter, oh God, darling. What happened—'

'This beauty and some of his friends wanted to take you for a ride – and they got the wrong address.'

They stared down at the corpse. Carl had used a .357 magnum and the damage was massive. Magda turned her head away.

'Nice work,' Peter told the bodyguard bitterly. 'He's not going to answer any questions now, is he?'

'You said to stop him.' Carl growled as he reloaded the pistol.

'I wonder what you would have done if I'd said to really clobber him.' Peter began to turn away with disgust, and pain checked him. He gasped.

'You're hurt.' Magda's concern returned in full strength. 'Take his other arm,' she ordered Carl, and they helped him over the parapet to the limousine.

Peter stripped off the torn and sodden remains of his clothing and Magda wrapped him in the Angora wool travel rug before examining his wound under the interior light of the cab.

The bullet hole was a perfect little blue puncture in the smooth skin, already surrounded by a halo of inflammation, and the bullet was trapped between his ribs and the sheet of flat, hard trapezium muscles. She could see the outline of it quite clearly, the size of a ripe acorn in his flesh, swollen out angry purple.

'Thank God—' she whispered, and unwound the Jean Patou scarf from her long pale throat. She bound the wound carefully. 'We'll take you directly to the hospital at Versailles. Drive fast, Carl.'

She opened the walnut-fronted cocktail cabinet in the bodywork beside her and poured half a tumbler of whisky from the crystal decanter.

It washed the taste of blood from Peter's mouth and then went warmly all the way down his throat to soothe the cramps of cold and shock in his belly.

'What made you come?' he asked, his voice still rough with the fierce spirit, the timely arrival nagged at his sense of rightness.

'The police at Rambouillet had a report of a car smash – they knew the Maserati, and the inspector rang La Pierre Bénite immediately. I guessed something bad—'

At that moment they reached the gates at the main road. The remains of the Maserati lay smouldering on the side of the road; around it like boy scouts around a camp fire were half a dozen gendarmes in their white plastic capes and pillbox kepis. They seemed uncertain of what they should do next.

Carl slowed the limousine and Magda spoke tersely through the window to a sergeant, who treated her with immense respect. '*Oui*, madame la Baronne, *d'accord. Tout à fait vrai*—' She dismissed him with a final nod, and he and his men saluted the departing limousine.

'They will find the body at the bridge—'

'There may be another one on the edge of the forest there—'

'You are very good, aren't you?' She slanted her eyes at him.

'The really good ones don't get hit,' he said, and smiled at her. The whisky had taken some of the sting and stiffness out of the wound and unknotted his guts. It was good to still be alive, he started to appreciate that again.

'You were right about the Maserati then – they were waiting for it.'

'That's why I burned it,' he told her, but she did not answer his smile.

'Oh, Peter. You'll never know how I felt. The police told me that the driver of the Maserati was still in it and had been burned. I thought – I felt as though part of me had been destroyed. It was the most terrifying feeling—' She shivered. 'I nearly did not come, I didn't want to see it. I nearly sent my wolves, but then I had to know – Carl saw you in the river as we turned onto the bridge. He said it was you, I just couldn't believe it—' She stopped herself and shuddered at the memory. 'Tell me what happened, tell me

197

all of it,' she demanded and poured more whisky into his tumbler.

For some reason that he was not sure of himself, Peter did not mention the Citroën that had followed him out of Paris. He told himself that it could not have been relevant. It must have been a coincidence, for if the driver of the Citroën had been one of them he would have been able to telephone ahead and warn the others that Baroness Magda Altmann was not in the Maserati, so that would have meant that they were not after her – but after him, Peter Stride, and that didn't make sense because he had only set himself up as bait that very morning, and they would not have had time yet. He stopped the giddy carousel of thoughts – shock and whisky, he told himself. There would be time later to think it all out more carefully. Now he would simply believe that they were waiting for Magda, and he had run into their net. He told it that way, beginning from the moment that he had seen the police van parked in the road. Magda listened with complete attention, the huge eyes clinging to his face, and she touched him every few moments as if to reassure herself.

When Carl parked under the portico of the emergency entrance of the hospital, the police had radioed ahead and there were an intern and two nurses waiting for Peter with a theatre trolley.

Before she opened the door to let them take Peter, Magda leaned to him and kissed him full on the lips.

'I'm so very glad to have you still,' she whispered, and then with her lips still very close to his ear she went on. 'It was Caliph again, wasn't it?'

He shrugged slightly, grimaced at the stab of pain, and answered, 'I can't think of anyone else offhand that would do such a professional job.'

Magda walked beside the trolley as far as the theatre doors, and she was beside his bed in the curtained cubicle as he struggled up through the deadening, suffocating false death of the anaesthetic.

The French doctor was with her, and he produced the gruesome blood-clotted souvenir with a magician's flourish.

'I did not have to cut,' he told Peter proudly. 'Probe only.' The bullet had mushroomed impressively, had certainly lost much of its velocity in penetrating the bodywork of the Maserati. 'You are a very lucky man,' the doctor went on. 'You are in fine condition, muscles like a racehorse that stopped the bullet going deep. You will be well again very soon.'

'I have promised to look after you, so he is letting you come home now.' Magda hovered over him also. 'Aren't you, doctor?'

'You will have one of the world's most beautiful nurses.' The doctor bowed gallantly towards Magda with a certain wistfulness in his expression.

T he doctor was right, the bullet wound gave him less discomfort than the tears in his thighs from the barbed wire, but Magda Altmann behaved as though he were suffering from an irreversible and terminal disease.

When she did have to go up to her office suite in the Boulevard des Capucines the next day, she telephoned three times for no other reason than to make sure he was still alive and to ask for his size in shoes and clothing. The cavalcade of automobiles carrying her and her entourage were back at La Pierre Bénite while it was still daylight.

'You are keeping civil service hours,' he accused when she came directly to the main guest suite overlooking the terraced lawns and the artificial lake.

'I knew you were missing me,' she explained, and kissed

him before beginning to scold him. 'Roberto tells me you have been wandering around in the rain. The doctor said you were to stay in bed. Tomorrow I will have to stay here to take care of you myself.'

'Is that a threat?' he grinned at her. 'For that sort of punishment I would let Caliph shoot another hole—'

Swiftly she laid her fingers on his lips. 'Peter, *chéri*, don't joke like that.' And the shadow that passed across her eyes was touched with fear, then immediately she was smiling again. 'Look what I have bought you.'

Peter's valise had been in the trunk of the Maserati, and she had replaced it with one in black crocodile from Hermes. To fill it she must have started at the top end of the Faubourg St Honoré and worked her way down to the Place Vendôme.

'I had forgotten how much fun it is to buy presents for one who you—' She did not finish the sentence, but held up a brocade silk dressing-gown. ' – Everybody in St Laurent knew what I was thinking when I chose this.'

She had forgotten nothing. Shaving gear, silk handkerchiefs and underwear, a blue blazer, slacks and shoes from Gucci, even cufflinks in plain gold, each set with a small sapphire.

'You have such blue eyes,' she explained. 'Now I will go and make myself respectable for dinner. I told Roberto we would eat here, for there are no other guests tonight.'

She had changed from the gunmetal business suit and turban into floating cloud-light layers of gossamer silk, and her hair was down to her waist, more lustrous than the cloth.

'I will open the champagne,' she said. 'It needs two hands.'

He wore the brocade gown, with his left arm still in a sling, and they stood and admired each other over the top of the champagne glasses.

'I was right.' She nodded comfortably. 'Blue is your

colour. You must wear it more often.' And he had to smile at the quaint compliment, and touched her glass with his. The crystal pinged musically and they saluted each other before they drank. Immediately she set the glass aside, and her expression became serious.

'I spoke with my friends in the Sûreté. They agree that it was a kidnap attempt against me, and because I asked it, they will not trouble you to make a statement until you feel better. I told them to send a man tomorrow to speak to you. There was no sign of the second man you shot at on the edge of the woods, he must have been able to walk or been carried by his friends.'

'And the other man?' Peter asked. 'The dead one.'

'They know him well. He had a very ugly past. Algeria with the paras. The mutiny.' She spread her hands eloquently. 'My friends were very surprised that he had not killed you when he tried to do so. I did not say too much about your own past. It is better, I think?'

'It's better,' Peter agreed.

'When I am with you like this, I forget that you also are a very dangerous man.' She stopped and examined his face carefully. 'Or is it part of the reason I find you so—' she searched for the word ' – so compelling? You have such a gentle manner, Peter. Your voice is so soft and—' She shrugged. 'But there is something in the way you smile sometimes, and in certain light your eyes are so blue and hard and cruel. Then I remember that you have killed many men. Do you think that is what attracts me?'

'I hope it is not.'

'Some women are excited by blood and violence – the bullfight, the prize ring, there are always as many women as men at these, and I have watched their faces. I have thought about myself, and still I do not know it all. I know only that I am attracted by strong men, powerful men. Aaron was such a man. I have not found many others since then.'

'Cruelty is not strength,' Peter told her.

'No, a truly strong man has that streak of gentleness and compassion. You are so strong, and yet when you make love to me it is with extreme gentleness, though I can always feel the strength and cruelty there, held in bate, like the falcon under the hood.'

She moved away across the room furnished in cream and chocolate and gold, and she tugged the embroidered bell-pull that dangled from the corniced ceiling with its hand-painted panels, pastoral scenes of the type that Marie Antoinette had so admired. Peter knew that much of the furnishing of La Pierre Bénite had been purchased at the auction sales with which the revolutionary committee dispersed the accumulated treasures of the House of Bourbon. With the other treasures there were flowers, wherever Magda Altmann went there were flowers.

She came back to him as Roberto, the Italian butler, supervised the entry of the dinner trolley, and then Roberto filled the wine glasses himself, handling the bottles with white gloves as though they were part of the sacrament, and stationed himself ready to serve the meal, but Magda dismissed him with a curt gesture and he bowed himself out silently.

There was a presentation-wrapped parcel at Peter's place setting, tissue paper and an elaborately tied red ribbon. He looked up at her inquiringly as she served the soup into fragile Limoges bowls.

'Once I began buying presents, I could not stop myself,' she explained. 'Besides, I kept thinking that bullet might have been in my back.' Then she was impatient. 'Are you not going to open it?'

He did so carefully, and then was silent.

'Africa, it is your speciality, is it not?' she asked anxiously. 'Nineteenth-century Africa?'

He nodded, and reverently opened the cover of the volume in its bed of tissue paper. It was fully bound in

202

maroon leather, and the state of preservation was quite extraordinary, only the dedication on the flyleaf in the author's handwriting was faded yellow.

'Where on earth did you find this?' he demanded. 'It was at Sotheby's in 1971. I bid on it then.' He had dropped out of the bidding at five thousand pounds.

'You do not have a first edition of Cornwallis Harris?' she asked again anxiously, and he shook his head, examining one of the perfectly preserved colour plates of African big game.

'No, I do not. But how did you know that?'

'Oh, I know as much about you as you do yourself,' she laughed. 'Do you like it?'

'It is magnificent. I am speechless.' The gift was too extravagant, even for someone of her fortune. It troubled him, and he was reminded of the comedy situation of the husband who brings home flowers unexpectedly and is immediately accused by his wife. 'Why do you have a guilty conscience?'

'Do you truly like it? I know so little about books.'

'It is the one edition I need to complete my major works,' he said. 'And it is probably the finest specimen left outside the British Museum.'

'I'm so glad.' She was genuinely relieved. 'I was truly worried.' And she put down the silver soup ladle and lifted both arms to welcome his embrace.

During the meal she was gay and talkative, and only when Roberto had wheeled away the trolley and they settled side by side on the down-filled couch before the fire did her mood change again.

'Peter, today I have been unable to think of anything but this business – you and me and Caliph. I have been afraid, and I am still afraid. I keep thinking of Aaron, what they did to him – and then I think of you and what nearly happened.'

They were silent, staring into the flames and sipping

coffee from the demi-tasses, then suddenly she had changed direction again. He was growing accustomed to these mercurial switches in thought.

'I have an island – not one island, but nine little islands – and in the centre of them is a lagoon nine kilometres wide. The water is so clear you can see the fish fifty feet down. There is an airstrip on the main atoll. Just under two hours' flying time to Tahiti. Nobody would ever know we were there. We could swim all day, walk in the sand, make love under the stars. You would be king of the islands, and I would be your queen. No more Altmann Industries – I would find somebody as good or better than myself to run it. No more danger. No more fear. No more Caliph – no more—' She stopped abruptly, as though she had been about to commit herself too far, but she went on quickly. 'Let's go there, Peter. Let's forget all this. Let's just run away and be happy together, for ever.'

'It's a pretty thought.' He turned to her, feeling deep and genuine regret.

'It would work for us. We would make it work.'

And he said nothing, just watching her eyes, until she looked away and sighed.

'No.' She mirrored his regret. 'You are right. Neither of us could ever give up living like that. We have to go on – but, Peter, I am so afraid. I am afraid of what I know about you and of what I do not know. I am afraid of what you do not know about me, and what I never can tell you – but we must go on. You are right. We have to find Caliph, and then destroy him. But, oh God, I pray we do not destroy ourselves, what we have found together – I pray we will be able to keep that intact.'

'The best way to conjure up emotional disaster is to talk about it.'

'All right, let's play riddles instead. My turn first. What is the most miserable experience known to the human female?'

204

'I give up.'

'Sleeping alone on a winter's night.'

'Salvation is at hand,' he promised her.

'But what about your poor shoulder?'

'If we combine our vast talents and wisdom, I am sure we will manage something.'

'I think you are right,' she purred and nestled against him like a sleek and silken cat. 'As always.'

There is always a delightfully decadent feeling about buying underwear for a beautiful woman, and Peter was amused by the knowing air of the middle-aged sales lady. She clearly had her own ideas about the relationship, and slyly produced a tray filled with filmy lace and iniquitously expensive wisps of silk.

'Yes,' Melissa-Jane approved rapturously. 'Those are exactly—' She held one of them to her cheek, and the sales lady preened at her own foresight. Peter hated to disillusion her, and he played the role of sugar-daddy a few moments longer as he glanced up at the mirror behind her head.

The tail was still there, a nondescript figure in a grey overcoat, browsing through a display of brassieres across the hall with the avid interest and knowledgeable air of a closet queen.

'I don't really think your mother will approve, darling,' Peter said, and the sales woman looked startled.

'Oh, please, Daddy. I will be fourteen next month.'

They had had a tail on him since he had arrived at Heathrow the previous afternoon, and Peter could not decide who they were. He began to regret he had not yet replaced the Cobra he had lost in the river.

'I think we'd better play it safe—' Peter told his daughter, and both Melissa-Jane and the sales lady looked crestfallen.

'Not bloomers!' Melissa-Jane wailed. 'Not elastic legs.'

'Compromise,' Peter suggested. 'No elastic legs – but no lace, not until you're sixteen. I think painted fingernails is enough for right now.'

'Daddy, you can be so medieval, honestly!'

He glanced at the mirror again, and they were changing the guard across the sales hall. The man in the shabby grey overcoat and checked woollen scarf drifted away and disappeared into one of the lifts. It would take some little time for Peter to spot his replacement – and then he grinned to himself; no it would not. Here he came now. He wore a tweed sports jacket in a frantic hounds tooth pattern, above Royal Stewart tartan trews and a grin like an amiable toad.

'Son of a gun. This is a surprise.' He came up behind Peter and hit him an open-handed blow between the shoulder blades that made Peter wince. At least he knew who they were at last.

'Colin.' He turned and took the massive paw with its covering of wiry black hair across the back. 'Yes, it is a surprise. I've been falling over your gorillas since yesterday.'

'Oafs,' Colin Noble agreed amiably. 'All of them, oafs!' And turned to seize Melissa-Jane. 'You're beautiful,' he told her and kissed her with more than avuncular enthusiasm.

'Uncle Colin. You come straight from heaven.' Melissa-Jane broke from the embrace and displayed the transparent panties. 'What do you think of these?'

'It's you, honey. You've just got to have them.'

'Tell my father, won't you?'

Colin looked around the Dorchester suite and grunted. 'This is really living. You don't get it this good in this man's army.'

'Daddy is truly becoming a bloated plutocrat – just like Uncle Steven,' Melissa-Jane agreed.

'I notice that you and Vanessa and the other comrades all wear lace panties,' Peter counter-attacked his daughter.

'That's different.' Melissa-Jane back-tracked swiftly, and hugged the green Harrod's package defensively. 'You can have a social conscience without dressing like a peasant, you know.'

'Sounds like a good life.' Peter threw his overcoat across the couch and crossed to the liquor cabinet. 'Bourbon?'

'On the rocks,' said Colin.

'Is there a sweet sherry?' Melissa-Jane asked.

'There is Coke,' Peter answered. 'And you can take it through to your own room, young lady.'

'Oh Daddy, I haven't seen Uncle Colin for ages.'

'Scat,' said Peter, and when she had gone, 'sweet sherry, forsooth.'

'It's a crying bastard when they start growing up – and they look like that.' Colin took the glass from Peter and rattled the ice cubes together as he lay back in the armchair. 'Aren't you going to congratulate me?'

'With pleasure.' Peter took his own glass and stood at the windows, against the backdrop of bare branches and grey misty skies over Hyde Park. 'What did you do?'

'Come on, Pete! Thor – they gave me your job, after you walked out.'

'Before they fired me.'

'After you walked out,' Colin repeated firmly. He took a sip of the Bourbon and gargled it loudly. 'There are a lot of things we don't understand – "Ours not to reason why, ours but to do and die." Shakespeare.'

He was still playing the buffoon, but the small eyes were as honey bright and calculating as those of a brand new teddy bear on Christmas morning. Now he waved his glass around the suite.

'This is great. Really it's great. You were wasted in Thor – everybody knew that. You must be pulling down more than all the joint-chiefs put together now.'

'Seven gets you five that you've already seen a Xeroxed copy of my contract of employment with Narmco.'

'Narmco!' Colin whistled. 'Is that who you're working for? No kidding, Pete baby, that's terrific!'

And Peter had to laugh, it was a form of capitulation. He came across and took the seat opposite Colin.

'Who sent you, Colin?'

'That's a lousy question—'

'That's just an opener.'

'Why should somebody have sent me? Couldn't I just want to chew the fat with an old buddy?'

'He sent you because he worked it out that I might bust the jaw of anybody else.'

'Sure now and everybody knows we love each other like brothers.'

'What's the message, Colin?'

'Congratulations, Peter baby, I am here to tell you that you have just won yourself a return ticket to the Big Apple.' He placed one hand across his heart and sang with a surprisingly mellow baritone. 'New York, New York, it's a wonderful town.'

Peter sat staring impassively at Colin, but he was thinking swiftly. He knew he had to go. Somehow he was certain that something was surfacing through muddied waters, the parts were beginning to click together. This was the sort of thing he had hoped for when he put the word on the wind.

'When?'

'There is an airforce jet at Croydon right now.'

'Melissa-Jane?'

'I've got a driver downstairs to take her home.'

'She's going to hate you.'

'Story of my life,' Colin sighed. 'Only the dogs love me.'

They played gin-rummy and drank teeth-blackening airforce coffee, all the way across the Atlantic. Colin Noble did most of the talking, around the stub of his cheroot. It was shop, Thor shop, training and personnel details, small anecdotes about men and things they both knew well – and he made no effort to question Peter about his job and Narmco, other than to remark that he would have Peter back in London for the series of Narmco meetings he had arranged starting on the following Monday. It was a deliberate and not very subtle intimation of just how much Atlas knew about Peter and his new activities.

They landed at Kennedy a little after midnight, and there was an army driver to take them to a local Howard Johnson for six hours' sleep, that kind of deep black coma induced by jet-lag.

Peter still felt prickly-eyed and woollen-headed as he watched with a feeling of disbelief as Colin devoured one of those amazing American breakfasts of waffles and maple syrup, wieners and bacon and eggs, sugar cakes and sticky buns, washed down with countless draughts of fruit juice and coffee. Then Colin lit his first cheroot and announced, 'Hell, now I know I'm home. Only now I realize I've been slowly fading away with malnutrition for two years.'

The same army driver was waiting for them at the front entrance of the motel. The Cadillac was an indication of their status in the military hierarchy. Peter looked out with detachment from the air-conditioned and padded interior onto the brooding ghettoes of Harlem. From the elevated highway along the East River, it reminded Peter of a deserted battle ground – where a few survivors lurked in dark doorways or scuttled along the littered and pitted sidewalks in the cold misty morning. Only the graffiti that adorned the bare brick walls had passion and vitality.

Their drive caught the junction of Fifth and One Hundred and Eleventh Street, and ran south down the park past the Metropolitan Art Museum in the thickening rush-hour traffic, then slipped off and into the cavernous mouth of a parking garage beneath one of the monolithic structures that seemed to reach to the grey cold heavens.

The garage entrance was posted 'Residents Only', but the doorman raised the electronically controlled grid and waved them through. Colin led Peter to the bank of elevators and they rode up with the stomach-dropping swoop while the lights above the elevator door recorded their ascent to the very top of the building.

There they stepped out into a reception area protected by ornamental, but none the less functional screens.

A guard in military police uniform and wearing a side-arm surveyed them through the grille and checked Colin's Atlas pass against his register before allowing them through.

The apartment occupied the entire top level of the building, for there were hanging gardens beyond the sliding glass panels and a view across the sickening canyons of space to the other tall structures farther down Island – the Pan Am building and the twin towers of the World Trade Center.

The decor was Oriental, stark interiors in which were displayed works of art that Peter knew from his previous visit were of incalculable value – antique Japanese brush paintings on silk panels, carvings in jade and ivory, a display of tiny netsuke – and in an atrium through which they passed was a miniature forest of Bonsai trees in their shallow ceramic bowls, the frozen contortions of their trunks and branches a sign of their great age.

Incongruously, the exquisite rooms were filled with the thunder of von Karajan leading the Berlin Philharmonic Orchestra through the glories of the Eroica.

Beyond the atrium was a plain door of white oak, and Colin Noble pressed the buzzer beside the lintel and almost immediately the door slid open.

Colin led into a long carpeted room, the ceiling of which was covered with acoustic tiles. The room contained besides the crowded bookshelves and work table an enormous concert piano, and down the facing wall an array of hi-fi turntables and loudspeakers that would have been more in place in a commercial recording studio.

Kingston Parker stood beside the piano, a heroic figure, tall and heavy in the shoulder, his great shaggy head hanging forward onto his chest, his eyes closed and an expression of almost religious ecstasy glowing upon his face.

The music moved his powerful frame the way the storm wind sways a giant of the forest. Peter and Colin stopped in the doorway, for it seemed an intrusion on such a private, such an intimate moment, but it was only a few seconds before he became aware of them and lifted his head. He seemed to shake off the spell of the music with the shudder that a spaniel uses to shake itself free of water when it reaches dry land, and he lifted the arm of the turntable from the spinning black disc.

The silence seemed to tingle after the great crashing chords of sound.

'General Stride,' Kingston Parker greeted him. 'Or may I still call you Peter?'

'Mr Stride will do very nicely,' said Peter, and Parker made an eloquent little gesture of regret, and without offering to shake hands indicated the comfortable leather couch across the room.

'At least you came,' he said, and as Peter settled into the couch, he nodded.

'I have always had an insatiable curiosity.'

'I was relying on that,' Kingston Parker smiled. 'Have you breakfasted?'

'We've had a snack,' Colin cut in but Peter nodded.

'Coffee then,' said Parker, and spoke quietly into the intercom set, before turning back to them.

'Where to begin?' Parker combed the thick greying hair back with both hands, leaving it even more tousled than it had been.

'Begin at the beginning,' Peter suggested. 'As the King of Hearts said to Alice.'

'At the beginning—' Parker smiled softly. ' – All right, at the beginning I opposed your involvement with Atlas.'

'I know.'

'I did not expect that you would accept the Thor command, it was a step backwards in your career. You surprised me there, and not for the first time.'

A Chinese manservant in a white jacket with brass buttons carried in a tray. They were silent as he offered coffee and cream and coloured crystal sugar and then, when he had gone, Parker went on.

'At that time, my estimate of you, General Stride, was that although you had a record of brilliance and solid achievement, you were an officer of rigidly old-fashioned thought. The Colonel Blimp mentality more suited to trench warfare than to the exigencies of war from the shadows – the kind of wars that we are fighting now, and will be forced to fight in the future.'

He shook the great shaggy head and unconsciously his fingers caressed the smooth cool ivory keyboard, and he settled down on the stool before the piano.

'You see, General Stride, I saw the role of Atlas to be too limited by the original terms of reference placed upon it. I did not believe that Atlas could do what it was designed for if it was only an arm of retaliation. If it had to wait for a hostile act before it could react, if it had to rely entirely on other organizations – with all their internecine rivalries and bickerings – for its vital intelligence. I needed officers who were not only brilliant, but who were capable of unconventional thought and independent action. I did not believe you had those qualities, although I studied you very carefully. I was unable to take you fully into my confidence.'

Parker's slim fingers evoked a fluent passage from the keyboard as though to punctuate his words, and for a moment he seemed completely enraptured by his own music, then he lifted his head again.

'If I had done so, then the conduct of your rescue operation of Flight 070 might have been completely different. I have been forced radically to revise my estimate of you, General Stride – and it was a difficult thing to do. For by demonstrating those qualities which I thought you lacked, you upset my judgement. I admit that personal chagrin swayed my reasoned judgement – and by the time I was thinking straight again you had been provoked into offering your resignation—'

'I know that the resignation was referred to you personally, Doctor Parker – and that you recommended that it be accepted.' Peter's voice was very cold, the tone clipped with controlled anger – and Parker nodded.

'Yes, you are correct. I endorsed your resignation.'

'Then it looks as though we are wasting our time here and now.' Peter's lips were compressed into a thin, unforgiving line, and the skin across his cheeks and over the finely chiselled flare of his nostrils seemed tightly drawn and pale as porcelain.

'Please, General Stride – let me explain first.' Parker reached out one hand to him as though to physically restrain him from rising, and his expression was earnest, compelling. Peter sank back into the couch, his eyes wary and his lips still tight.

'I have to go back a little first, in order to make any sense at all.' Parker stood up from the piano and crossed to the rack of pipes on the work table between the hi-fi equipment. He selected one carefully, a meerschaum mellowed to the colour of precious amber. He blew through the empty pipe and then tramped back across the thick carpet to stand in front of Peter.

'Some months before the hijacking of 070 – six months to be precise, I had begun to receive hints that we were entering a new phase in the application of international terrorism. Only hints at first, but these were confirmed and followed by stronger evidence.' Parker was stuffing the meerschaum from a leather wallet as he spoke, now he zipped this closed and tossed it onto the piano top. 'What we were looking at was a consolidation of the forces of violence under some sort of centralized control – we were not sure what form this control was taking.' He broke off and studied Peter's expression, seemed to misinterpret it for utter disbelief, for he shook his head. 'Yes, I know it sounds far-fetched, but I will show you the files. There was evidence of meetings between known militant leaders and some other shadowy figures, perhaps the representatives of an Eastern government. We were not sure then, nor are we now. And immediately after this a complete change in the conduct and apparent motivation of militant activity. I do not really have to detail this for you. Firstly the systematic accumulation of immense financial reserves by the highly organized and carefully planned abduction of prominent figures, starting with the ministers of OPEC, then leading industrialists and financial figures—' Parker struck a match and puffed on his pipe and perfumed smoke billowed around his head. ' – So that it appeared that the motivation had not really changed and was still entirely self gain or parochial political gain. Then there was the taking of 070. I had not confided in you before and once you were on your way to Johannesburg it was too late. I could do nothing more than try to control your actions by rather heavy-handed commands. I could not explain to you that we suspected that this was the leading wave of the new militancy, and that we must allow it to reveal as much as possible. It was a terrible decision, but I had to gamble a few human lives for vital information – and then you acted as I had believed you were incapable of acting.' Parker removed his pipe from his mouth and he smiled; when he smiled you could believe anything he said and forgive him for it, no matter how outrageous. 'I admit, General Stride, that my first reaction was frustrated rage. I wanted your head, and your guts also. Then suddenly I began using my own head instead. You had just proved you were the man I wanted, my soldier capable of unconventional thought and action. If you were discredited and cast adrift, there was just a chance that this new direction of militancy would recognize the same qualities in you that I had been forced to recognize. If I allowed you to ruin your career, and become an outcast – an embittered man, but one with vital skills and invaluable knowledge, a man who had proved he could be ruthless when it was necessary—' Parker broke off and made that gesture of appeal. ' – I am sorry, General Stride, but I had to recognize the fact that you would be very attractive to—' he made an impatient gesture ' – I do not have a name for them, shall we just call them "the enemy". I had to recognize the fact that you would be of very great interest to the enemy. I endorsed your resignation.' He nodded sombrely. 'Yes, I endorsed your resignation, and without your own knowledge you became an Atlas agent at large. It seemed perfect to me. You did not have to act a role – you believed it yourself. You were the outcast, the wronged and discredited man ripe for subversion.'

'I don't believe it,' Peter said flatly, and Parker went back to the work table, selected an envelope from a Japanese ceramic tray and brought it back to Peter.

It took Peter a few moments to realize that it was a Bank Statement – Crédit Suisse in Geneva – the account was in his name, and there were a string of deposits. No withdrawals or debits. Each deposit was for exactly the same amount, the net salary of a major-general in the British Army.

'You see,' – Parker smiled – 'you are still drawing your Atlas salary. You are still one of us, Peter. And all I can say is that I am very sorry indeed that we had to subject you to the pretence – but it seems it was all worth while.'

Peter looked up at him again, not entirely convinced, but with the hostility less naked in his expression.

'What do you mean by that, Doctor Parker?'

'It seems that you are very much back in play again.'

'I am Sales Director for Northern Armaments Company,' he said flatly.

'Yes, of course, and Narmco is part of the Altmann Industrial Empire – and Baron Altmann and his lovely wife are, or rather were, an extraordinarily interesting couple. For instance, did you know that the Baron was one of the top agents of Mossad in Europe?'

'Impossible,' Peter shook his head irritably. 'He was a Roman Catholic. Israeli intelligence does not make a habit of recruiting Catholics.'

'Yes,' Parker agreed. 'His grandfather converted to Catholicism – and changed the name of the family home to La Pierre Bénite. It was a business decision, that we are certain of, there was not much profit in being Jewish in nineteenth-century France. However, the young Altmann was much influenced by his grandmother and his own mother. He was a Zionist from a very early age, and he unswervingly used his enormous wealth and influence in that cause – right up until the time of his murder. Yet he did it so cunningly, with such subtlety that very few people were aware of his connections with Judaism and Zionism. He never made the mistake of converting back to his ancestral religion, realizing that he could be more effective as a practising Christian.'

Peter was thinking swiftly. If this was true, then it all had changed shape again. It must affect the reasons for the

Baron's death – and it would change the role of Magda Altmann in his life.

'The Baroness?' he asked. 'Was she aware of this?'

'Ah, the Baroness!' Kingston Parker removed his pipe from between his teeth, and smiled with reluctant admiration. 'What a remarkable lady. We are not certain of very much about her – except her beauty and her exceptional talents. We know she was born in Warsaw. Her father was a professor of medicine at the university there, and he escaped to the West when the Baroness was still a child. He was killed a few years later, a traffic accident in Paris. Hit and run driver, while the professor was leaving his faculty in the Sorbonne. A small mystery still hangs around his death. The child seems to have drifted from family to family, friends of her father, distant relatives. She already was showing academic leanings, musical talent, at thirteen a chess player of promise – then for a period there is no record of her. She seems to have disappeared entirely. The only hint is from one of her foster mothers, a very old lady now, with a fading memory. "I think she went home for a while – she told me she was going home."' Parker spread his hands. 'We do not know what that means. Home? Warsaw? Israel? Somewhere in the East?'

'You have researched her very carefully,' Peter said. What he had heard had left him uneasy.

'Of course, we have done so to every contact you have made since leaving Atlas Command. We would have been negligent not to do so – but especially we have been interested in the Baroness. She has been the most fascinating, you understand that, I am sure.'

Peter nodded, and waited. He did not want to ask for more. Somehow it seemed disloyal to Magda, distrustful and petty – but still he waited and Parker went on quietly.

'Then she was back in Paris. Nineteen years of age now – a highly competent private secretary, speaking five languages fluently, beautiful, always dressed in the height of fashion, soon with a string of wealthy, influential and powerful admirers – the last of these was her employer, Baron Aaron Altmann.' Parker was silent then, waiting for the question, forcing Peter to come to meet him.

'Is she Mossad also?'

'We do not know. It is possible – but she has covered herself very carefully. We are rather hoping you will be able to find that out for us.'

'I see.'

'She must have known that her husband was a Zionist. She must have suspected that it had something to do with his abduction and murder. Then there are the missing six years of her life – from thirteen to nineteen, where was she?'

'Is she Jewish?' Peter asked. 'Was her father Jewish?'

'We believe so, although the professor showed no interest in religion and did not fill in the question on his employment application to the Sorbonne. His daughter showed the same lack of religious commitment – we know only that her marriage to the Baron was a Catholic ceremony followed by a civil marriage in Rambouillet.'

'We have drifted a long way from international terrorism,' Peter pointed out.

'I do not think so.' Kingston Parker shook his big shaggy head. 'The Baron was a victim of it, and almost as soon as you – one of the world's leading experts on militancy and urban warfare – as soon as you are associated with her there is an assassination attempt, or an abduction attempt made on the Baroness.'

Peter was not at all surprised that Parker knew of that night on the road to La Pierre Bénite – it was only a few days since Peter's arm had been out of the sling.

'Tell me, Peter. What was your estimate of that affair? I have seen an excerpt of the statement that you made to the French police – but what can you add to that?'

Peter had a vivid cameo memory of the Citroën that had

218

followed him out of Paris, and then almost simultaneously the tearing sound of automatic fire in the night.

'They were after the Baroness,' Peter said firmly.

'And you were driving her car?'

'That's right.'

'You were at the place at the time that the Baroness usually passed?'

'Right.'

'Who suggested that? You?'

'I told her that the car was too conspicuous.'

'So you suggested taking it down to La Pierre Bénite that night.'

'Yes.' Peter lied without knowing why he did so.

'Did anybody else know that the Baroness would not be driving?'

'Nobody.' Except her bodyguards, the two chauffeurs who had met them on their return from Switzerland, Peter thought.

'You are certain?' Parker persisted.

'Yes,' Peter snapped. 'Nobody else.' Except Magda, only Magda. He pushed the thought aside angrily.

'All right, so we must accept that the Baroness was the target – but was it an assassination or an abduction attempt? That could be significant. If it was assassination, it would indicate that it was the elimination of a rival agent, that the Baroness was probably also a Mossad agent, recruited by her husband. On the other hand, an abduction would suggest that the object was monetary gain. Which was it, Peter?'

'They had blocked the road—' he said, but not completely he remembered. 'And the police impersonator signalled me to stop—' or at least to slow down, he thought, slow down sufficiently to make an easy target before they started shooting ' – and they did not open fire until I made it clear that I was not going to stop.' – But they had been ready to begin shooting at the instant Peter made the decision to send the Maserati through the roadblock. The intention of the two machine-gunners had seemed evident. ' – I would say the object was to seize the Baroness alive.'

'All right,' Parker nodded. 'We will have to accept that for the time being.' He glanced at Colin. 'Colonel Noble? You had a question?'

'Thank you, Doctor. We haven't heard from Peter in what terms he was approached by Narmco or the Baroness. Who made the first contact?'

'I was approached by a London firm who specializes in making top executive placements. They came directly from the Narmco Board—' And I turned them down flat, he thought. It was only later at Abbots Yew—

'I see.' Colin frowned with disappointment. 'There was no question of a meeting with the Baroness?'

'Not at that stage.'

'You were offered the sales appointment – no mention of any other duties, security, industrial intelligence—'

'No, not then.'

'Later?'

'Yes. When I met the Baroness, I realized her personal security arrangements were inadequate. I made changes.'

'You never discussed her husband's murder?'

'Yes, we did.'

'And?'

'And nothing.' Peter was finding it difficult to improvise answers, but he used the old rule of telling as much of the truth as possible.

'There was no mention by the Baroness of a hunt for her husband's murderers? You were not asked to use your special talents to lead a vendetta?'

Peter had to make a swift decision. Parker would know of his leak to the British military attaché in Paris – the bait he had so carefully placed to attract Caliph. Of course Parker would know: he was head of Atlas with access to the

Central Intelligence computer. Peter could not afford to deny it.

'Yes, she asked me to relay any information which might point to her husband's murderers. I asked G.2 in Paris for any information he might have. He couldn't help me.'

Parker grunted. 'Yes. I have a note that G.2 filed a routine report – but I suppose her request was natural enough.' He wandered back to his work table to glance at a pad on which was scribbled some sort of personal shorthand.

'We know of eight sexual liaisons that the Baroness formed prior to her marriage, all with politically powerful or wealthy men. Six of them married men—'

Peter found himself trembling with anger so intense that it surprised him. He hated Parker for talking like this of Magda. With a huge effort he kept his expression neutral, the hand in his lap was relaxed and the fingers spread naturally, though he felt a driving desire to bunch it and drive it into Parker's face.

' – all these affairs were conducted with utmost discretion. Then during her marriage there is no evidence of any extra-marital activity. Since the Baron's murder there have been three others, a minister in the French Government, an American businessman – head of the world's second largest oil company—' He dropped the pad back on the desk and swung back to face Peter. 'And recently there has been one other.' He stared at Peter with a bright penetrating gaze. 'The lady certainly believes in mixing business with pleasure. All her partners have been men who are able to deliver very concrete proof of their affections. I think this rule probably applies to her latest choice of sexual partner.'

Colin Noble coughed awkwardly, and shifted in his chair, but Peter did not even glance at him, he went on staring impassively at Kingston Parker. He and Magda had made very little secret of their relationship – still it was bitterly distasteful to have to discuss it with anybody else.

'I think that you are in a position now to gather vital intelligence. I think that you are very near the centre of this nameless and formless influence – I think that you will be able to make some sort of contact with the enemy, even if it is only another military brush with them. The only question is whether or not you find any reason, emotional or otherwise, that might prevent you fulfilling this duty?' Kingston Parker cocked his head on one side, making the statement into a question.

'I have never let my private life interfere with my duty, Doctor,' Peter said quietly.

'No,' Kingston Parker agreed. 'That is true. And I am sure that now you know a little more about Baroness Altmann you will appreciate just how vital is our interest in that lady.'

'Yes, I do.' Peter had his anger under control completely. 'You want me to use a privileged relationship to spy on her. Is that correct?'

'Just as we can be sure she is using the same relationship to her own ends—' Parker broke off as an odd thought seemed to occur. 'I do hope I have not been too blunt, Peter. I haven't destroyed some cherished illusion.' Now Parker's attitude was dismissive. The interview was over.

'At my age, Doctor – a man has no more illusions.' Peter rose to his feet. 'Do I report to you direct?'

'Colonel Noble will make the arrangements for all communications.' Kingston Parker held out his hand. 'I would not have asked this of you if I had a choice.'

Peter did not hesitate, but took the hand. Parker's hand was cool and dry. Although he made no show of it, Peter could sense the physical power in those hard pianist's fingers.

'I understand, sir,' said Peter – and he thought grimly, and even if that is also a lie, I'm going to understand pretty damned soon.

P eter made the excuse of tiredness to avoid the gin-rummy game, and pretended to sleep during most of the long trans-Atlantic flight. With his eyes closed he tried to marshal his thoughts into some sort of pattern, but always they seemed to come around full circle and leave him chasing his tail. He could not even achieve any certainty about his feelings and loyalties to Magda Altmann. They seemed to keep changing shape every time he examined them, and he found himself brooding on irrelevancies. 'Sexual liaisons' – what a ridiculously stilted expression Parker had used, and why had it angered Peter so much? Eight liaisons before marriage, six with married men, two others since marriage – all wealthy or powerful. He found himself trying to flesh out these bare statistics, and with a shock of bitter resentment imagined those faceless, formless figures with the slim smooth body, the tiny, perfectly shaped breasts, and the long smoky fall of shimmering hair. He felt somehow betrayed, and immediately scorned himself for this adolescent reaction.

There were other more dire questions and chances that Kingston Parker had raised, the Mossad connection, the six missing years in Magda's life – and yet he came back again to what had happened between them. Was she capable of such skilful deception, or was it not deception? Was he merely suffering from hurt pride now, or somehow unbeknown to him had she been able to force him into a more vulnerable position? Had she succeeded in making him fall in love with her?

How did he feel about her? At last he had to face that question directly and try to answer it, but when they landed again he still had no answer, except that the prospect of seeing her again pleased him inordinately and the thought that she had deliberately used him to her own ends and was capable of discarding him as she had done those others left him with an aching sense of dismay. He dreaded the answer for which he had to search, and suddenly he remembered her suggestion of an island to which they could escape together. He realized then that she was a victim of the same dread, and with a clairvoyant shudder he wondered if they were somehow preordained to destroy each other.

There were three separate messages from her at the Dorchester. She had left the Rambouillet number, each time. He telephoned immediately he reached the suite.

'Oh, Peter. I was so worried. Where were you?' And it was hard to believe her concern was faked, and it was even harder to discount the pleasure when, the following noon, she met him at Charles de Gaulle Airport herself instead of sending a chauffeur.

'I needed to get out of the office for an hour,' she explained, and then she tucked her hand into the crook of his elbow and pressed herself against him. 'That's a lie, of course. I came because I couldn't wait the extra hour to see you.' Then she chuckled huskily. 'I am behaving shamelessly, I can't imagine what you must think of me!'

They were with a party of eight that evening, dinner at Le Doyen and then the theatre at the Palais de Chaillot. Peter's French was still not up to Molière, so he took his pleasure in surreptitiously watching Magda, and for a few hours he succeeded in suppressing all those ugly questions; only on the midnight drive back to La Pierre Bénite did he begin the next move in the complicated game.

'I couldn't tell you on the telephone—' he said in the intimate darkness and warmth of her limousine. 'I had an approach from Atlas. The head of Atlas summoned me to New York. That's where I was when you called. They are also onto Caliph.'

She sighed then, and her hand stole into his. 'I was waiting for you to tell me, Peter,' she said simply, and she sighed again. 'I knew you'd gone to America, and I had a terrible premonition that you were going to lie to me. I don't know what I would have done then.' And Peter felt a lance of conscience driven up under his ribs, and with it the throb of concern – she had known of his journey to New York, but how? Then he remembered her 'sources'.

'Tell me,' she said, and he told her – everything, except the nagging question marks which Kingston Parker had placed after her name. The missing years, the Mossad connection with the Baron, and those ten nameless men.

'They don't seem to know that Caliph uses that name,' Peter told her. 'But they seem to be pretty certain that you are hunting him, and you've hired me for that purpose.'

They discussed it quietly as the small cavalcade of cars rushed through the night, and later when she came to his suite, they went on talking, holding each other as they whispered in the night, and Peter was surprised that he could act so naturally, that the doubts seemed to evaporate so easily when he was with her.

'Kingston Parker still has me as a member of Atlas,' Peter explained. 'And I did not deny it, nor protest. We want to find Caliph, and if I still have status with Atlas it will be useful, of that I am certain,'

'I agree. Atlas can help us – especially now that they are also aware that Caliph exists.'

They made love in the dawn, very deeply satisfying love that left bodies and minds replete, and then keeping her discretion she slipped away before it was light, but they met again an hour later for breakfast together in the Garden Room.

She poured coffee for him, and indicated the small parcel beside his plate.

'We aren't quite as discreet as we think we are, *chéri*.' She chuckled. 'Somebody seems to know where you are spending your evenings.'

He weighed the parcel in his right palm; it was the size of a roll of 35-mm film, wrapped in brown paper, sealed with red wax.

'Apparently it came special delivery yesterday evening.' She broke one of the crisp croissants into her plate, and smiled at him with that special slant of her green eyes.

The address was typed on a stick-on label, and the stamps were British, franked in south London the previous morning.

Suddenly Peter was assailed with a terrifying sense of foreboding; the presence of some immense overpowering evil seemed to pervade the gaily furnished room.

'What is it, Peter?' Her voice cracked with alarm.

'Nothing,' he said. 'It's nothing.'

'You suddenly went deadly pale, Peter. Are you sure you are all right?'

'Yes. I'm all right.'

He used his table knife to lift the wax seal and then unrolled the brown paper.

It was a small screw-topped bottle of clear glass, and the liquid it contained was clear also. Some sort of preservative, he realized immediately, spirits or formaldehyde.

Hanging suspended in the liquid was a soft white object.

'What is it?' Magda asked.

Peter felt cold tentacles of nausea closing around his stomach.

The object turned slowly, floating free in its bottle, and there was a flash of vivid scarlet.

'Does your mother allow you to wear nail varnish now, Melissa-Jane?' He heard the question echoed in his memory, and saw his daughter flirt her hands, and the scarlet flash of her nails. The same vivid scarlet.

'Oh yes – though not to school, of course. You keep forgetting I'm almost fourteen, Daddy.'

The floating white object was a human finger. It had been severed at the first joint, and the preservative had bleached the exposed flesh a sickly white. The skin had puckered and wrinkled like that of a drowned man. Only the painted fingernail was unaltered, pretty and festively gay.

The nausea caught Peter's throat, choking him and he heaved and retched drily as he stared at the tiny bottle.

T he telephone rang three times before it was answered.

'Cynthia Barrow.' Peter recognized his ex-wife's voice, even though it was ragged with strain and grief.

'Cynthia, it's Peter.'

'Oh, thank God, Peter. I have been trying to find you for two days.'

'What is it?'

'Is Melissa-Jane with you, Peter?'

'No.' He felt as though the earth had lurched under his feet.

'She's gone, Peter. She's been gone for two nights now. I'm going out of my mind.'

'Have you informed the police?'

'Yes, of course.' The edge of hysteria was in her voice.

'Stay where you are,' Peter said. 'I'm coming to England right now, but leave any message for me at the Dorchester.' He hung up quickly, sensing that her grief would overflow at any moment and knowing that he could not handle it now.

Across the ormolu Louis Quatorze desk Magda was pale, tense, and she did not have to ask the question, it was in the eyes that seemed too large for her face.

He did not have to reply to that question. He nodded once, an abrupt jerky motion, and then he dialled again and while he waited he could not take his eyes from the macabre trophy that stood in its bottle in the centre of the desk.

'Colonel Noble.' Peter snapped into the mouthpiece. 'Tell him it's General Stride and it's urgent.'

Colin came on within the minute. 'Peter, is that you?'

'They've taken Melissa-Jane.'

'Who? I don't understand.'

'The enemy. They've taken her.'

'Jesus God! Are you sure?'

'Yes, I'm sure. They sent me her finger in a bottle.'

Colin was silent for a few seconds, and then his voice was subdued. 'That's sick. Christ, that's really sick.'

'Get onto the police. Use all your clout. They must be keeping quiet on it. There has been no publicity. I want to be in on the hunt for these animals. Get Thor involved, find out what you can. I'm on my way now. I'll let you know what flight I am on.'

'I'll keep a listening watch at this number round the clock,' Colin promised. 'And I'll have a driver meet you.' Colin hesitated. 'Peter, I'm sorry. You know that.'

'Yes. I know.'

'We will all be with you, all the way.'

Peter dropped the receiver onto its arm, and across the desk Magda stood up resolutely.

'I'll come with you to London,' she said, and Peter reached out and took her hand.

'No,' he said gently. 'Thank you, but no. There will be nothing for you to do.'

'Peter, I want to be with you through this terrible thing. I feel as though it's all my fault.'

'That's not true.'

'She's such a lovely child.'

'You will be more help to me here,' said Peter firmly. 'Try through all your sources, any little scrap of information.'

'Yes, very well.' She accepted the decision, without further argument. 'Where can I find you if I have anything?'

He gave her Colin Noble's private number at Thor, scribbling it on the pad beside the telephone. 'Either there or at the Dorchester,' he said.

'At least I will come with you as far as Paris,' she said.

T he news had broken by the time Peter landed at Heathrow Airport. It was on the front page of the *Evening Standard* and Peter snatched a copy off the news stand and read it avidly during the drive up to London.

The victim was abducted at the front gate of her home in Leaden Street, Cambridge at eleven o'clock on Thursday. A neighbour saw her speak to the occupants of a maroon Triumph saloon car, and then enter the back door of the vehicle, which drove off immediately.

'I thought there were two people in the car,' Mrs Shirley Callon, 32, the neighbour, told our correspondent, 'and Melissa-Jane did not seem alarmed. She appeared to enter the Triumph quite willingly. I know that her father, who is a senior officer in the army, often sends different cars to fetch her or bring her home. So I thought nothing about it.'

The alarm was not raised for nearly twenty-four hours, as the missing girl's mother also believed that she might be with her ex-husband.

Only when she was unable to contact Major-General Stride, the girl's father, did she inform the police. The Cambridge police found a maroon Triumph abandoned in the car park at Cambridge railway station. The vehicle had been stolen in London the previous day, and immediately a nation-wide alert was put in force for the missing girl.

Chief-Inspector Alan Richards is the police officer in charge of the investigation and any person who may be able to provide information should telephone—

There followed a London number and a detailed description of Melissa-Jane and the clothes she was wearing at the time she disappeared.

Peter crumpled the newspaper and dropped it on the front seat. He sat staring ahead, cupping his anger to him like a flame, husbanding it carefully – because the heat was infinitely more bearable than the icy despair which waited to engulf him.

Inspector Alan Richards was a wiry little man, more like a jockey than a policeman. He had a prematurely wizened face, and he had combed long wisps of hair across his balding pate to disguise it. Yet his eyes were quick and intelligent, and his manner direct and decisive.

He shook hands when Colin Noble introduced them. 'I must make it very clear that this is a police matter, General. However, in these very special circumstances I am prepared to work very closely with the military.'

Swiftly Richards went over the ground he had already covered. He had mounted the investigation from the two offices set aside for him on the third floor of Scotland Yard, with a view over chimney pots of the spires of Westminster Abbey and the Houses of Parliament.

Richards had two young policewomen answering the telephone calls coming in through the number they had advertised in the Press and on television. So far they had accepted over four hundred of these. 'They range from long shots to the completely crazy, but we have to investigate all of them.' For the first time his expression softened. 'It's going to be a long, slow process, General Stride, but we have a few more leads to follow – come through.'

The inner office was furnished in the same nondescript Public Works Department furniture, solid and characterless, but there was a kettle boiling on the gas ring, and Richards poured the tea as he went on.

'Three of my men are taking the kidnap car to pieces. We are sure it is the right car. Your ex-wife has identified a purse found on the floor of the vehicle. It is your daughter's. We have lifted over six hundred fingerprints, and these are

230

being processed. It will take some time until we can isolate each and hope for an identification of any alien prints. However, two of these correspond to prints lifted from your daughter's room – Sugar? Milk?'

Richards brought the cup to Peter as he went on.

' – The neighbour, Mrs Callon, who saw the pick-up, is working on an identikit portrait of the driver, but she did not get a very good view of him. That is a very long shot.'

Richards sipped his tea. 'However, we will show the final picture on television and hope for another lead from it. I am afraid that in cases like this, this is all we can do. Wait for a tip, and wait for the contact from the kidnappers. We do not expect the contact will be made through your ex-wife but of course we have a tap on her telephone and men watching over her.' Richards spread his hands. 'That's it, General Stride. Now it's your turn. What can you tell us? Why should anybody want to snatch your daughter?'

Peter exchanged a glance with Colin Noble, and was silent as he collected his thoughts, but Inspector Richards insisted quietly:

'I understand you are not a very wealthy man, General – but your family? Your brother?'

Peter dismissed the idea with a shake of his head. 'My brother has children of his own. They would be the more logical targets.'

'Vengeance? You were very active against the Provos in Ireland. You commanded the recapture of Flight 070.'

'It's possible.'

'You are no longer connected with the army, I understand.'

Peter was not going to be drawn further in that direction. 'I do not think this type of guesswork will profit us much. We will know the motive as soon as the kidnappers make their demands known.'

'That is true.' Richards rattled his teacup, a little nervous gesture. 'They could not have sent you her—' He broke off

231

as he saw Peter's expression change. ' – I'm sorry, General. It is horrible and terribly distressing, but we have to accept the finger as proof that your daughter is still alive and that the contact, when it comes, will be made to you. It was an expression of their earnest intention, and a threat – but—'

The telephone on his desk rang shrilly and Richards snatched it up.

'Richards!' he snapped, and then listened at length, occasionally grunting encouragement to the caller. When he hung up the receiver he did not speak immediately, but offered Peter a rumpled pack of cigarettes. When Peter refused, the policeman lit one himself and his voice was diffident.

'That was the laboratory. You know your daughter was a white cell donor, don't you?'

Peter nodded. It was part of Melissa-Jane's social commitment. If she had not been tactfully dissuaded, she would have donated her blood and marrow by the bucketful.

'We were able to get a tissue typing from the Cambridge hospital. The amputated finger matches your daughter's tissue type. I'm afraid we must accept that it is hers – I cannot imagine that the kidnappers would have gone to the lengths of finding a substitute of the same type.'

Peter had been secretly cherishing the belief that it was a bluff. That he had been sent the fingertip from a corpse, from a medical sample, from the casualty ward of a city hospital – and now as that hope died he was assailed by the cold spirit-sapping waves of despair. They sat in silence for fully a minute, and now it was Colin Noble who broke it.

'Inspector, you are aware of the nature of the Thor Command?'

'Yes, of course. There was a great deal of publicity at the time of the Johannesburg hijacking. It is an anti-terrorist unit.'

'We are probably the most highly trained specialists in

232

the world at removing hostages safely from the hands of militants—'

'I understand what you are trying to tell me, Colonel,' Richards murmured drily. 'But let us track down our militants first, and then any rescue attempts will be entirely under the control of the Commissioner of Police.'

It was after three o'clock in the morning when Peter Stride checked in with the night receptionist at the Dorchester Hotel in Park Lane.

'We have been holding your suite since midday, General.'

'I'm sorry.' Peter found himself slurring his words, exhaustion and nervous strain, he realized. He had only left Police Headquarters when he could convince himself that everything possible was being done, and that he could place complete trust in Chief-Inspector Richards and his team. He had Richards's solemn undertaking that he would be informed, no matter at what time of day or night, as soon as there was any new development.

Now he signed the register, blinking at the gritty swollen feeling of his eyelids.

'There are these messages for you, General.'

'Thank you again, and goodnight.'

In the elevator he glanced at the mail the clerk had given him.

The first was a telephone slip.

'Baroness Altmann asks you to return her call to either the Paris or Rambouillet number.'

The second was another telephone slip.

'Mrs Cynthia Barrow called. Please call her at Cambridge 699 – 313.'

The third was a sealed envelope, good-quality white paper, undistinguished by crest or monogram.

His name had been printed in capitals, very regular lettering, an old-fashioned copper-plate script. No stamp, so it would have been delivered by hand.

Peter split the flap with his thumb, and withdrew a single sheet of lined writing paper, again good but undistinguished. There would be a stack of these sheets in any stationery department throughout the United Kingdom.

The writing was the same regular, unnatural script, so that Peter realized that the writer had used a stencil to form each letter, one of those clear plastic cut-out stencils obtainable from any toy store or stationery department. A completely effective method of disguising handwriting.

A finger you have already, next you will have the hand, then another hand, then a foot, then another foot – and at last the head.

The next package will arrive on April 20th, and there will be another delivery every seven days.

To prevent this you must deliver a life for a life. The day Dr Kingston Parker dies, your daughter will return to you immediately, alive and suffering no further harm.

Destroy this letter and tell nobody, or the head will be delivered immediately.

The letter was signed with the name which had come to loom so largely in Peter's life:

'CALIPH'

The shock of it seemed to reach to the extremities of his soul. To see the name written. To have complete confirmation of all the evil that they had suspected, to see the mark of the beast deeply printed and unmistakable.

The shock was made greater, almost unbearable, by the contents of the letter. Peter found that such cruelty, such utter ruthlessness, tested his credibility to its limits.

The letter was fluttering in his hands, and he realized with a start of surprise that he was shaking like a man in high fever. The porter carrying his black crocodile valise was staring at him curiously, and it required a huge physical effort to control his hands and fold the sheet of white paper.

He stood rigidly, as though on the parade ground, until the elevator door opened and then he marched stiffly down the passage to his suite. He gave the porter a banknote, without glancing at it, and the moment the latch clicked closed, he unfolded the sheet again, and standing in the centre of the living-room floor scanned the stilted script again, and then again until the words seemed to melt together and lose coherence and meaning.

He realized that for the first time in his life he was in complete panic, that he had lost all resolution and direction.

He took a deep breath and closed his eyes, counting slowly to one hundred, emptying his mind completely, and then giving himself the command:

'Think!'

All right, Caliph knew his movements intimately. Even to when he was expected at the Dorchester. Who knew that? Cynthia, Colin Noble, Magda Altmann and the secretary at Rambouillet who had made the reservation, Colin's secretary at Thor, the Dorchester staff, and anybody else who had made even an idle study of Peter's movements would know he always stayed at the Dorchester. That was a cul-de-sac.

'Think!'

Today was April fourth. There were sixteen days before Caliph sent him Melissa-Jane's severed hand. He felt the panic mounting again, and he forced it back.

'Think!'

Caliph had been watching him, studying him in detail, assessing his value. Peter's value was that he could move unsuspected in high places. He could reach the head of Atlas by simply requesting an audience. More than that, he could probably get access to any head of state if he wanted it badly enough.

For the first time in his life Peter felt the need for liquor. He crossed quickly to the cabinet and fumbled with the key. A stranger's face stared at him out of the gilt-framed mirror above it. The face was pale, haggard, with deep parentheses framing the mouth. There were plum-coloured bruises of fatigue below the eyes, and the gaunt, bony jaw was gun-metal blue with a new beard – and the sapphire blue of the eyes had a wild deranged glitter. He looked away from his own image. It only increased his sense of unreality.

He poured half a tumbler of Scotch whisky, and drank half of it straight off. He coughed at the sting of the liquor and a drop of it broke from the corner of his mouth and trickled down his chin. He wiped it away with his thumb, and turned back to study the sheet of white paper again. It was crumpled already, where he had gripped it too hard. He smoothed it carefully.

'Think!' he told himself. This was how Caliph worked, then. Never exposing himself. Picking his agents with incredible attention to detail. Fanatics, like the girl, Ingrid who had led the taking of Flight 070. Trained assassins, like the man he had killed in the river at La Pierre Bénite. Experts in high places, like General Peter Stride. Studying them, assessing them and their capabilities, and finally finding their price.

Peter had never believed the old law that every man had his price. He had believed himself above that general rule. Now he knew he was not – and the knowledge sickened him.

Caliph had found his price, found it unerringly. Melissa-Jane. Suddenly Peter had a vivid memory of his daughter on horseback, swivelling in the saddle to laugh and call back to him.

'Super-Star!' And the sound of her laughter on the wind.

Peter shivered, and without realizing it he crumpled the sheet of paper to a ball in his fist.

Ahead of him he saw the road that he was destined to follow. With a new flash of insight, he realized that he had already taken his first steps along the road. He had done so when he had put the gun to the blonde killer in the terminal of Johannesburg Airport, when he had made himself judge and executioner.

Caliph had been responsible for that first step on the road to corruption, and now it was Caliph who was driving him farther along it.

With a sudden prophetic glimpse ahead, Peter knew it would not end with the life of Kingston Parker. Once he was committed to Caliph, it would be for ever – or until one of them, Peter Stride, or Caliph, was completely destroyed.

Peter drank the rest of the whisky in the tumbler.

Yes, Melissa-Jane was his price. Caliph had made the correct bid. Nothing else would have driven him to it.

Peter picked the booklet of matches off the liquor cabinet and like a sleepwalker moved through to the bathroom. He twisted the sheet of paper into a taper and lit the end of it, holding it over the toilet bowl. He held it until the flame scorched his fingers painfully, then dropped it into the bowl and flushed the ash away.

He went back into the lounge, and refilled the glass with whisky. He picked the comfortable armchair below the window and sank into it. Only then did he realize how very weary he was. The nerves in his thighs quivered and twitched uncontrollably.

He thought about Kingston Parker. A man like that had an incalculable amount to offer mankind. It will have to look like an assassination attempt aimed at me, Peter thought. One that finds the wrong victim.

'A bomb,' Peter thought. He hated the bomb. Somehow

it seemed to be the symbol of the senseless violence which he hated. He had seen it used in Ireland and in London town, and he hated it. The undirected destruction, mindless, merciless.

'It will have to be a bomb,' he decided, and with surprise he found that his hatred had found a new target. Again for the first time ever, he hated himself for what he was going to do.

Caliph had won. He knew that against an adversary of that calibre there was no chance they would find where Melissa-Jane was hidden. Caliph had won, and Peter Stride sat the rest of the night planning an act which he had dedicated his life, until then, to prevent.

'I cannot understand why we haven't had the demand contact yet.' Inspector Richards ran his hand distractedly across his pate, disturbing the feathery wisps that covered it and leaving them standing out at a startled angle. 'It's five days now. Still no demands.'

'They know where to contact Peter,' Colin Noble agreed. 'The interview he gave covered that.'

Peter Stride had appeared on BBC TV to broadcast an appeal to the kidnappers not to maim his daughter further, and to the general public to offer any information that might lead to her rescue.

On the same programme they had displayed the police identikit portrait of the driver of the maroon Triumph prepared by the one witness.

The response had been overwhelming, jamming the switchboard at Inspector Richards's special headquarters, and a mixed bag had fallen into the net.

A fourteen-year-old runaway had the police barge into the Bournemouth apartment where she was in bed with her thirty-two-year-old lover. She was returned weeping bitterly to the bosom of her family, and had again disappeared within twenty-four hours.

In North Scotland the police sadly bungled a raid on a remote cottage hired by a man with the same lank dark hair and gunfighter's moustache as the identikit portrait. He turned out to be a cottage-industry manufacturer of LSD tablets, and he and his four assistants, one of them a young girl who vaguely fitted the description of Melissa-Jane in that she was female and blonde, had scattered across the Highlands before being overtaken and borne to earth by sweating pounding members of the Scottish Constabulary.

Peter Stride was furious. 'If it had been Melissa-Jane, they would have had fifteen minutes in which to put her down—' He raged at Richards. 'You've got to let Thor go in to the next raid.'

Through the Thor communications net he spoke directly to Kingston Parker on the video screens.

' – We'll put all our influence into it,' Parker agreed, and then with deep compassion in his eyes, 'Peter, I'm living every minute of this with you. I cannot escape the knowledge that I have placed you into this terrible situation. I did not expect the attack would come through your daughter. I think you know that you can call on me for any support you need.'

'Thank you, sir,' said Peter and for a moment felt his resolve weaken. In ten days he would have to execute this man. He steeled himself by thinking of a puckered dead-white finger floating in its tiny bottle.

Kingston Parker's influence worked immediately. Six hours later the order came down from Downing Street via the Commissioner of Police, that the next raid on a suspect hideout would be conducted by Thor Command.

The Royal Air Force placed two helicopters at Thor's disposal for the duration of the operation, and Thor's assault unit went into intensive training for penetration and removal under urban conditions. Peter trained with them, he and Colin swiftly re-establishing the old rapport of concerted action.

When they were not practising and refining the exit and assembly from the hovering helicopters, Peter spent much of his time in the enclosed pistol range, trying to drown his awareness in the crash of gunfire, but the days passed swiftly in a series of false alarms and misleading clues.

Each night when Peter examined his face in the mirror above the liquor cabinet, it was more haggard, the blue eyes muddied by fatigue and terrible gut-eroding terror of what the next day might bring forth.

There were six days left when Peter left the hotel room before breakfast, caught the tube at Green Park and left it again at Finsbury Park. In a garden supplies shop near the station he purchased a twenty-pound plastic bag of ammonium nitrate garden fertilizer. He carried it back to the Dorchester in a locked Samsonite suitcase and stored it in the closet behind his hanging trenchcoat.

That night, when he spoke to Magda Altmann, she pleaded once again to be allowed to come to London.

'Peter, I know I can be of help to you. Even if it's just to stand beside you and hold your hand.'

'No. We've been over that.' He could hear the brutal tone in his own voice, but could not control it. He knew that he was getting very close to the edge. 'Have you heard anything?'

'I'm sorry, Peter. Nothing, absolutely nothing. My sources are doing all that is possible.'

Peter bought the dieseline from a pump at the Lex Garage in Brewer Street. He took five litres in a plastic screw-topped container that had contained a household detergent. The pump attendant was a pimply teenager in dirty overalls. He was completely uninterested in the transaction.

In his bathroom Peter worked on the dieseline and the nitrate from the garden shop. He produced twenty-one pounds of savagely weight-efficient high explosive that was, none the less, docile until activated by a blasting cap – such as he had devised with a flashlight bulb.

It would completely devastate the entire suite, utterly destroying everybody and everything in it. However, the damage should be confined to those three rooms.

It would be a simple matter to lure Kingston Parker to the suite under the pretence of having urgent information about Caliph to deliver, information so critical that it could only be delivered in person and in private.

That night the face in the mirror above the liquor cabinet was that of a man suffering from a devouring terminal disease, and the whisky bottle was empty. Peter broke the seal on a fresh bottle; it would make it easier to sleep, he told himself.

T he wind came off the Irish Sea like the blade of a harvester's scythe, and the low lead-coloured cloud fled up the slopes of the Wicklow hills ahead of it.

There were weak patches in the cloud layer through which a cold and sickly sun beamed swiftly across the green forested slopes. As it passed so the rain followed – icy grey rain slanting in on the wind.

A man came up the deserted street of the village. The tourists had not yet begun the annual invasion, but the 'Bed and Breakfast' signs were already out to welcome them on the fronts of the cottages.

The man passed the pub, in its coat of shocking salmon pink paint – and lifted his head to read the billboard above the empty car park. 'Black is Beautiful – drink Guinness' it proclaimed, and the man did not smile but lowered his head and trudged on over the bridge that divided the village in two.

On the stone balustrades of the bridge a midnight artist

had used an aerosol paint can to spray political slogans in day-glo colours.

'BRITS OUT' on the left-hand balustrade and 'STOP H BLOCK TORTURE' on the other. This time the man grimaced sourly.

Below him the steely grey water boiled about the stone piers before hissing down towards the sea.

The man wore a cyclist's plastic cape and a narrow-brimmed tweed cap pulled down over his eyes. The wind dashed at him, flogging the skirts of the cape against his Wellington boots.

He seemed to cringe to the wind, hunching down against its cold fury, as he trudged on past the few buildings of the village. The street was deserted, though the man knew that he was being watched from curtained windows.

This village on the lower slopes of the Wicklow hills, a mere thirty miles from Dublin, would not have been his choice. Here isolation worked against them, making them conspicuous. He would have preferred the anonymity of the city. However, his preferences had never been asked for.

This was only the third time he had left the house since they had arrived. Each time it had been for some emergency provision, something that a little more forethought might have prevented, which should have been included when the old house was stocked for their stay. That came from having to rely on a drinking man, but here again he had not been consulted.

He was discontented and in a truculent, smouldering mood. It had rained most of the time, and the oil-fired central heating was not working, the only heating was the smoking peat fires in the small fireplaces in each of the two big rooms they were using. The high ceilings and sparse furnishings had made the rooms more difficult to warm – and he had been cold ever since they had arrived. They were using only the two rooms, and had left the rest of the house locked and shuttered. It was a gloomy building, with the smell of damp pervading it. He had only the company of a whining alcoholic, day after cold rainy day. The man was ripe and over-ripe for trouble, for any diversion to break the grinding monotony – but now he was reduced to errand boy and house servant, roles for which he was unsuited by temperament and training, and he scowled darkly as he trudged over the bridge towards the village store, with its row of petrol pumps standing before it like sentries.

The storekeeper saw him coming, and called through into the back of the shop.

'It's himself from down at the Old Manse.'

His wife came through, wiping her hands on her apron, a short plump woman with bright eyes and ready tongue.

'City people have no more sense than they need, out in this weather.'

'Sure and it's not baked beans nor Jameson whiskey he's after buying.'

Speculation about the new occupant of the Old Manse had swiftly become one of the village's main diversions, with regular bulletins broadcast by the girl on the local telephone exchange – two overseas telephone calls, by the postman – no mail deliveries, by the dustman – the disposals into the dustbins were made up mainly of empty Heinz baked beans cans and Jameson whiskey bottles.

'I still think he's from the trouble up north,' said the shopkeeper's wife. 'He's got the look and the sound of an Ulster man.'

'Hush, woman.' Her husband cautioned her. 'You'll bring bad luck upon us. Get yourself back into the kitchen now.'

The man came in out of the rain and swept the tweed cap off his head, beating the water from it against the jamb of the door. He had black straight hair, cut into a ragged fringe above the dark Irish visage and fierce eyes, like those of a falcon when first the leather hood is slipped.

243

'The top of the morning to you, Mr Barry,' the shop-keeper greeted him heartily. 'Like as not it will stop raining, before it clears.'

The man they knew as Barry grunted, and as he slipped the waterproof cape from his shoulders, swept the cluttered interior of the little general dealer's store with a quick, all-embracing glance.

He wore a rough tweed jacket over a cable-stitched jersey and brown corduroys tucked into the top of the Wellington boots.

'You finished writing on your book, have you?' Barry had told the milkman that he was writing a book about Ireland. The Wicklow hills were a stronghold of the literary profession, there were a dozen prominent or eccentric writers living within twenty miles, taking advantage of Ireland's tax concessions to writers and artists.

'Not yet,' Barry grunted, and went across to the shelves nearest the till. He made a selection of half a dozen items and laid them on the worn counter top.

'When it's good and wrote I'm going to ask the library to keep a copy for me,' the shopkeeper promised, as though that was exactly what a writer would want to hear, and began to ring up the purchases on his register.

Barry's upper lip was still unnaturally smoother and paler than the rest of his face. He had shaved away the dark droopy moustache the day before arriving in the village, and at the same time had cut the fringe of his hair that hung almost to his eyes.

The shopkeeper picked up one of the purchases and looked inquiringly at Barry, but when the dark Irish face remained impassive and he volunteered no explanation, the shopkeeper dropped his eyes self-consciously and rang up the package with the other purchases and dropped it into a paper carrier.

'That will be three pounds twenty pence,' he said, and closed the cash drawer with a clang, waiting while Barry slung the cape over his shoulders and adjusted the tweed cap.

'God be with you then, Mr Barry.'

There was no reply and the shopkeeper watched him set off back across the bridge before he called his wife again.

'He's a surly one, all right, he is.'

'He's got him a girlfriend down there.' The shopkeeper was bursting with the importance of his discovery. 'He's up to a nice little bit of hanky-panky.'

'How do you know that?'

'He was after buying women's things – you know.' He hooded a knowing eye.

'No, I don't know,' his wife insisted.

'For the curse – you know. Women's things,' and his wife glowed with the news, and began to untie her apron.

'You're sure now?' she demanded.

'Would I ever be lying to you?'

'I think I'll go across to Mollie for a cuppa tea,' said his wife eagerly; the news would make her the woman of the hour throughout the village.

The man they knew as Barry trudged into the narrow, high-walled lane that led up to the Old Manse. It was only the heavy boots and voluminous cape that gave him a clumsy gait, for he was a lithe, lean man in prime physical condition, and under the brim of his cap the eyes were never still, hunter's eyes probing and darting from side to side.

The wall was twelve feet high, the stonework blotched with silver-grey lichen, and although it was cracked and sagging at places, yet it was still substantial and afforded complete privacy and security to the property beyond.

At the end of the lane there was a pair of rotten and warping double doors, but the lock was a bright new brass Yale and the cracks in the wood and the gaping seams had been covered with fresh white strips of pine so that it was impossible to see into the interior of the garage.

Barry unlocked the brass Yale lock and slipped through, pulling the latch closed behind him.

There was a dark blue Austin saloon car parked facing the doors for immediate departure. It had been stolen in Ulster two weeks before, resprayed and fitted with a roof rack to alter its appearance, and with new licence plates. The engine had been tuned and checked and Barry had paid nearly twice its market value.

Now he slipped behind the wheel and turned the key in the ignition. The engine fired and caught immediately. He grunted with satisfaction; seconds could mean the difference between success and failure, and in his life failure and death were synonymous. He listened to the engine beat for half a minute, checking the oil pressure and fuel gauges before switching off the engine again and going out through the rear door of the garage into the overgrown kitchen yard.

The old house had the sad unloved air of approaching dereliction. The fruit trees in the tiny orchard were sick with fungus diseases and surrounded by weed banks.

The thatch roof was rotten-green with moss, and the windows were blindman's eyes, unseeing and uncaring.

Barry let himself in through the kitchen door and dropped his cape and cap on the scullery floor and set the carrier on the draining board of the sink. Then he reached into the cutlery drawer and brought out a pistol. It was a British officer's service pistol, had in fact been taken during a raid on a British Army arsenal in Ulster three years previously.

Barry checked the handgun with the expertise of a long familiarity and then thrust it into his belt. He had felt naked and vulnerable for the short time that he was without the weapon – but he had reluctantly decided not to risk carrying it in the village.

Now he tapped water into the kettle, and at the sound a voice called through from the dim interior.

'Is that you?'

'None other,' Barry answered drily, and the other man came through and stood in the doorway to the kitchen.

He was a thin, stooped man in his fifties with the swollen inflamed face of the very heavy drinker.

'Did you get it?' His voice was husky and rough with whiskey, and he had a seedy run-down air, a day's stubble of grey hairs that grew at angles on the blotchy skin.

Barry indicated the package on the sink.

'It's all there, doctor.'

'Don't call me that, I'm not a doctor any more,' the man snapped irritably.

'Oh, but you are a damned fine one. Ask the girls who dropped their bundles—'

'Leave me alone, damn you.'

Yes, he had been a damn fine doctor. Long ago, before the whiskey, now however it was the abortions and the gunshot wounds of fugitives, and jobs like this one. He did not like to think about this one. He crossed to the sink and sorted through the packages.

'I asked you for adhesive tape,' he said.

'They had none. I brought the bandage.'

'I cannot—' the man began, but Barry whirled on him savagely, his face darkening with angry blood.

'I've had a gutsful of your whining. You should have brought what you needed, not sent me to get it for you.'

'I did not expect the wound—'

'You didn't expect anything but another dram of Jamesons, man. There is no adhesive tape. Now get on with it and tie the bitch's hand up with the bandage.'

The older man backed away swiftly, picked up the packages and shuffled through into the other room.

Barry made the tea and poured it into the thick china mug, spooned in four spoons of sugar and stirred noisily, staring out of the smeared panes. It was raining again. He thought that the rain and the waiting would drive him mad.

The doctor came back into the kitchen, carrying a

bundle of linen soiled with blood and the yellow ooze of sepsis.

'She is sick,' he said. 'She needs drugs, antibiotics. The finger—'

'Forget it,' said Barry.

From the other room there was a long-drawn-out whimper, followed by the incoherent gabble of a young girl deep in the delirium induced by fever and hypnotic drugs.

'If she is not taken to proper care, I won't be responsible.'

'You'll be responsible,' Barry told him heavily. 'I'll see to that.'

The doctor dropped the bundle of linen into the sink and let the water run over it.

'Can I have a drink now?' he asked.

Barry made a sadistic display of consulting his watch.

'No. Not yet,' he decided.

The doctor poured soapflakes into the sink.

'I don't think I can do the hand,' he whispered, shaking his head. 'The finger was bad enough – but I can't do the hand.'

'You'll do the hand,' said Barry. 'Do you hear me, you whiskey-guzzling old wreck? You'll do the hand, and anything else I tell you to do.'

Sir Steven Stride offered a reward of fifty thousand pounds to anyone giving information that led to the recovery of his niece, and the offer was widely reported on television and in the press with reprints of the identikit portrait. It led to a revival of the flagging public interest in the case.

Inspector Richards had been able to reduce his telephone answering staff to one the last few days, but with the renewed spate of informers and speculators, he had to ask for the other policewoman to return to the third floor, and he had two sergeants processing the material that flowed in.

'I feel like Littlewoods,' he growled to Peter. 'Everybody taking a ticket on the pools, or getting his three-pence worth of advertising.' He picked up another message slip. 'Here is another claim for responsibility – the Democratic People's Party for the Liberation of Hong Kong – Have we ever heard of them before?'

'No, sir.' The senior sergeant looked up from his lists. 'But that makes one hundred and forty-eight confessions or claims for responsibility so far.'

'And 'Enry the Eighth was on again half an hour ago.' One of the girls at the switchboard turned and smiled around her mouthpiece. 'Hasn't missed a day.'

'Enry the Eighth was a sixty-eight-year-old pensioner who lived in a council estate in South London. His hobby was confessing to the latest spectacular crime from rape to bank robbery, and he had called regularly every morning.

'Come and get me,' he challenged each time. 'But I warn you I won't come peaceful like—' When the local constable had made a courtesy call, while on his regular beat, 'Enry the Eighth had his suitcase packed and ready to go. His disappointment was heart-rending when the bobby tactfully explained that they weren't going to arrest him, but when the bobby assured him that they would be keeping him under close surveillance as the Commissioner considered him a very dangerous man, he brightened up considerably and offered the constable a cup of tea.

'The trouble is we dare not dismiss any of it, even the real loonies, it all has to be checked out,' Richards sighed, and motioned Peter to go through to the inner office.

'Still nothing?' Richards asked. It was an unnecessary question. They had a tap on his telephone, at the hotel and at Thor Headquarters, to record any contact from the kidnappers.

'No, nothing,' Peter lied, but the lie had become easy now – just as he had learned to accept whatever else was necessary for Melissa-Jane's release.

'I don't like it, General. I really don't like the fact that there has been no attempt to contact you. I don't want to be despondent, but every day of silence makes it look more like an act of vengeance—' Richards broke off and covered his embarrassment by lighting a cigarette. 'Yesterday the Deputy-Commissioner telephoned me. He wanted my opinion as to how much longer I thought it necessary to maintain this special unit.'

'What did you tell him?' Peter asked.

'I told him that if we did not have some firm evidence within ten days, at least some sort of demand from the kidnappers – then I would have to believe that your daughter was no longer alive.'

'I see.' Peter felt a fatalistic calm. He knew. He was the only one who knew. There were four days to Caliph's deadline, he had worked out his timetable. Tomorrow morning he would request his urgent meeting with Kingston Parker. He expected it would take less than twelve hours to arrange it, he would make it too attractive for Parker to refuse.

Parker would have to come, but against the remote possibility that he did not, Peter had left himself three clear days before the deadline in which to put into action his alternative plan. This would mean going to Kingston Parker. The first plan was the better, the more certain – but if it failed, Peter would accept any risk.

Now he realized that he had been standing in the centre of Richards's office, staring vacantly at the wall above the little inspector's head. He started as he realized that Richards was staring at him with a mingling of pity and concern.

'I am sorry, General. I understand how you feel – but I cannot keep this unit functioning indefinitely. We just do not have enough people—'

'I understand.' Peter nodded jerkily, and wiped his face with an open hand. It was a weary, defeated gesture.

'General, I think you should see your doctor. I really do.' Richards's voice was surprisingly gentle.

'That won't be necessary – I'm just a little tired.'

'A man can take just so much.'

'I think that's what these bastards are relying on,' Peter agreed. 'But I'll be all right.'

From the next door office there was the almost constant tinkle of telephone bells, and the murmur of female voices as the two policewomen answered the incoming stream of calls. It had become a steady background effect, so that when the call for which they had prayed and pleaded and waited finally came, neither of the two men was aware of it, and there was no excitement on the switchboard.

The two girls sat side by side on swivel stools in front of the temporary switchboard. The blonde girl was in her middle twenties, she was pretty and pert, with big round breasts buttoned primly under her blue uniform jacket. The blonde hair was twisted into a bun at the back of her neck to free her ears, but the headset made her appear older and businesslike.

The bell pinged and a panel lit in front of her; she plugged in the switch and spoke into the headset.

'Good morning. This is the Police Special Information Unit—' She had a pleasant middle-class accent, but was unable to keep the trace of boredom out of it. She had been on this job for twelve days now. There was the warning tone of a public telephone and then the click of small change fed into the slot.

'Can you hear me?' The accent was foreign.

'Yes, sir.'

'Listen carefully. Gilly O'Shaughnessy has her—' No, it was an imitation, the foreign accept slipped a little with the pronunciation of the name.

'Gilly O'Shaughnessy,' the police girl repeated.

'That's right. He's holding her at Laragh.'

'Spell that, please.' Again the accent slipped as the man spelled the name.

'And where is that, sir?'

'County Wicklow, Ireland.'

'Thank you, sir. What is your name, please?'

There was the clack of a broken connection and the hum of the dialling tone. The girl shrugged, and scribbled the message on the pad before her, glancing at her wrist-watch simultaneously.

'Seven minutes to tea time,' she said. 'Roll on death, battle with the angels.' She tore the sheet off the pad and passed it over her shoulder to the burly, curly-headed sergeant who sat behind her.

'I'll buy you a sticky bun,' he promised.

'I'm on a diet,' she sighed.

'That's daft, you look a treat—' The sergeant broke off. ' – Gilly O'Shaughnessy. Why do I know that name?'

The older sergeant looked up sharply.

'Gilly O'Shaughnessy?' he demanded. 'Let me see that.' And he snatched the sheet, scanning it swiftly, his lips moving as he read the message. Then he looked up again.

'You know the name because you've seen it on the wanted posters, and heard it on the telly. Gilly O'Shaugh-nessy, strewth man, he's the one who bombed the Red Lion at Leicester, and shot the Chief Constable in Belfast.'

The curly-headed policeman whistled softly. 'This looks like a hot one. A real hot one—' But his colleague was already barging into the inner office without the formality of knocking.

R ichards had the connection to the Dublin police within seven minutes.

'Impress upon them that there must be no attempt—' Peter fretted, while they waited, and Richards cut him short.

'All right, General. Leave this to me. I understand what has to be done—' At that moment the Dublin connection was made, and Richards was transferred quickly to a Deputy-Commissioner. He spoke quietly and earnestly for nearly ten minutes before he replaced the receiver.

'They will use the local constabulary, not to waste time in sending a man down from Dublin. I have their promise that no approach will be made if a suspect is located.'

Peter nodded his thanks. 'Laragh,' he said. 'I have never heard of it. It cannot have a population of more than a few hundred.'

'I've sent for a map,' Richards told him, and when it came they studied it together.

'It's on the slopes of the Wicklow hills – ten miles from the coast—' And that was about all there was to learn from the large-scale map.

'We'll just have to wait for the Dublin police to call back—'

'No,' Peter shook his head. 'I want you to call them again, and ask them to contact the surveyor-general. He must have trig maps of the village, aerial photographs, street layouts. Ask them to get them down with a driver to Enniskerry Airfield—'

'Should we do that now? What if this turns out to be another false alarm.'

'We'll have wasted a gallon of petrol and the driver's time—' Peter was no longer able to sit still, he jumped out of the chair and began to pace restlessly about the office; it was too small for him suddenly, he felt as though he were on the point of suffocation. 'I don't think it is, however. I have the smell of it. The smell of the beast.'

Richards looked startled and Peter deprecated the exaggerated phrase with a dismissive gesture. 'A manner of speech,' he explained, and then stopped as a thought struck him. 'The helicopters will have to refuel, they haven't got the range to make it in one hop, and they are so bloody slow!' He paused and reached a decision, then leaned across Richards's desk to pick up the telephone and dialled Colin Noble's private number at Thor.

'Colin.' He spoke curtly with the tension that gripped him like a mailed fist. 'We've just had a contact. It's still unconfirmed, but it looks the best yet.'

'Where?' Colin broke in eagerly.

'Ireland.'

'That's to hell and gone.'

'Right, what's the flight time for the whirly birds to reach Enniskerry?'

'Stand by.' Peter heard him talking to somebody else – probably one of the R.A.F. pilots. He came back within the minute.

'They will have to refuel en route—'

'Yes?' Peter demanded impatiently.

'Four and a half hours,' Colin told him.

'It's twenty past ten now – almost three o'clock before they reach Enniskerry. With this weather it will be dark before five.' Peter thought furiously; if they sent the Thor team all the way to Ireland on a false trail – and while they were there the correct contact was made in Scotland, or Holland, or—

'It's got the smell. It's got to be right,' he told himself, and took a deep breath. He could not order Colin Noble to go to Bravo. Peter was no longer commander of Thor.

'Colin,' he said. 'I think this is it. I have the deep-down gut feel for it. Will you trust me and go to Bravo now? If we wait even another half hour we'll not get Melissa-Jane out before nightfall – if she is there.'

There was a long silence, broken only by Colin Noble's light quick breath.

'Hell, it can only cost me my job,' he said easily at last. 'Okay, Pete baby, it's Bravo, we'll be airborne in five minutes. We'll pick you up from the helipad in fifteen minutes; be ready.'

The cloud was breaking up, but the wind was still bitter and spiteful, and up on the exposed helipad it cut cruelly through Peter's trench coat, blazer and roll-neck jersey. They looked out across the churned surface of the River Thames, eyes watering in the wind, for the first glimpse of the helicopters.

'What if we have a confirmation before you reach Enniskerry?'

'You can reach us on the R.A.F. frequencies, through Biggin Hill,' Peter told him.

'I hope I don't have bad news for you.' Richards was holding his bowler hat in place with one hand, the skirts of his jacket slapping around his skinny rump and his face blotchy with the cold.

The two ungainly craft came clattering in, low over the rooftops, hanging on the whirling silver coins of their rotors.

At a hundred feet Peter could plainly recognize the broad shape of Colin Noble in the open doorway of the fuselage, just forward of the brilliant R.A.F. roundels, and the down-draught of the rotors boiled the air about them.

'Good hunting.' Richards raised his voice to a shout. 'I wish I was coming with you.'

Peter ran forward lightly, and jumped before the helicopter gear touched the concrete pad. Colin caught him by the upper arm and helped to swing him aboard without removing the cheroot from his wide mouth.

'Welcome aboard, buddy. Now let's get this circus on the road.' And he hitched the big .45 pistol on his hip.

'She's not eating.' The doctor came through from the inner room and scraped the plate into the rubbish bin below the sink. 'I'm worried about her. Very worried.'

Gilly O'Shaughnessy grunted but did not look up from his own plate. He broke a crust off the slice of bread and very carefully wiped up the last of the tomato ketchup. He popped the bread into his mouth and followed it with a gulp of steaming tea, and while he chewed it all together, he leaned back on the kitchen chair and watched the other man.

The doctor was on the verge of cracking up. He would probably not last out the week before his nerve went completely; Gilly O'Shaughnessy had seen better men go to pieces under less strain.

He realized then that his own nerves were wearing away.

It was more than just the rain and the waiting that was working on him. He had been the fox for all of his life, and he had developed the instincts of the hunted animal. He could sense danger, the presence of the pursuers, even when there was no real evidence. It made him restless to stay longer in one place than was necessary, especially when he was on a job. He had been here twelve days, and it was far too long. The more he thought about it the more uneasy he became. Why had they insisted he bring the brat to this isolated, and therefore conspicuous, little dead-end? There was only one road in and out of the village, a single avenue of escape. Why had they insisted that he sit and wait it out in this one place? He would have liked to keep moving. If he had had the running of it, he would have bought a second-hand caravan, and kept rolling from one park to another – his attention wandered for a few moments as he thought how he would have done it – if he had been given the planning of it.

He lit a cigarette and gazed out of the rain-blurred window panes, hardly aware of the muttered complaints and misgivings of his companion. What they should have done was crop the brat's fingers and bottle all of them to send to her father at intervals, and then they should have held a pillow over her face and buried her in the vegetable garden or weighted her and dumped her out beyond the hundred-fathom line of the Irish Sea – that way they would not have had to bother with a doctor, and the nursing—

Everything else had been done with professional skill, starting with the contact they had made with him in the *favela* of Rio de Janeiro, where he was hiding out in a sleazy one-room shack with the half-caste Indian woman, and down to his last fifty quid.

That had given him a real start, he thought he had covered his tracks completely, but they had him made. They had the passport and travel papers in the name of Barry, and they did not look like forgeries. They were good papers, he was sure of it, and he knew a lot about papers.

Everything else had been as well planned, and swiftly delivered. The money – a thousand pounds in Rio, another five thousand the day after they grabbed the brat, and he was confident that the final ten would be there as it was promised. It was better than an English gaol, the 'Silver City' as the Brits called their concentration camp at the Maze. That was what Caliph had promised, if he didn't take the job.

Caliph, now that was a daft name, Gilly O'Shaughnessy decided for the fiftieth time as he dropped the stub of his cigarette into the dregs of his teacup and it was extinguished with a sharp hiss. A real daft name, but somehow it had the ability to put a chill on the blood, and he shivered not only from the cold.

He stood up and crossed to the kitchen window. It had all been done with such speed and purpose and planning – everything so clearly thought out, that when there was a lapse it was more troubling.

Gilly O'Shaughnessy had the feeling that Caliph did nothing without good reason – then why had they been ordered to back themselves into this dangerously exposed bottleneck, without the security of multiple escape routes, and to sit here and wait?

He picked up the cyclist cape and tweed cap. 'Where are you going?' the doctor demanded anxiously. 'I'm going to take a shufti,' Gilly O'Shaughnessy grunted as he pulled the cap down over his eyes.

'You're always prowling around,' the doctor protested. 'You make me nervous.'

The dark Irishman pulled the pistol from under his jacket and checked the load before thrusting it back into his belt. 'You just go on playing nursemaid,' he said brusquely. 'And leave the man's work to me.'

T he small black Austin crawled slowly up the village street, and the rain hammered on the cab and bonnet in tiny white explosions that blurred the outline, giving the machine a softly focused appearance, and the streaming windscreen effectively hid the occupants. It was only when the Austin parked directly in front of Laragh's only grocery store and both front doors opened that the curiosity of watchers from behind the curtained windows all down the street was satisfied.

The two members of the Irish constabulary wore the service blue winter uniform with darker epaulettes. The soft rain speckled the patent leather peaks of their caps as they hurried into the shop.

'Good morning, Maeve, me old love,' the sergeant greeted the plump red-faced lady behind the counter.

'Owen O'Neill, I do declare—' She chuckled as she recognized the sergeant – there had been a time, thirty years before, when the two of them had given the priest some fine pickings at the confessional. 'And what brings you all the way up from the big city?'

That was a generous description of the quaint seaside resort town of Wicklow, fifteen miles down the road.

'The sight of your blooming smile—'

They chatted like old friends for ten minutes, and her husband came through from the little storeroom when he heard the rattle of teacups.

'So what is new in Laragh, then?' the sergeant asked at last. 'Any new faces in the village?'

'No, all the same faces. Nothing changes in Laragh, bless the Lord for that.' The shopkeeper wagged his head. 'No, indeed – only new face is the one down at the Old Manse, he and his lady friend—' he winked knowingly ' – but seeing as how he's a stranger, we aren't after counting him.'

The sergeant ponderously delved for his notebook, opened it and extracted a photograph from it; it was the usual side view and full face of police records. He held the name covered with his thumb as he showed it to them.

'No.' The woman shook her head positively. 'Himself down at the manse is ten years older than that, and he does not have a moustache.'

'This was taken ten years ago,' said the sergeant.

'Oh, well, why didn't you say so.' She nodded. 'Then that's him. That's Mr Barry for certain sure.'

'The Old Manse, you say.' The sergeant seemed to inflate visibly with importance, as he put the photograph back into his notebook. 'I'm going to have to use your telephone now, dear.'

'Where will you be after telephoning?' The shopkeeper asked suspiciously.

'Dublin,' the sergeant told him. 'It's police business.'

'I'll have to charge you for the call,' the shopkeeper warned him quickly.

'There,' said the wife as they watched the sergeant making his request to the girl on the village switchboard. 'I told you he had the look of trouble, didn't I. The first time I laid eyes on him I knew he was from up in the North, and carrying trouble like the black angel.'

Gilly O'Shaughnessy kept close in under the stone wall, keeping out of the slanting rain and out of the line of sight of a casual watcher on the slope beyond the river. He moved carefully and quietly as a tomcat on his midnight business, stopping to examine the earth below the weakened or tumbled places in the wall where a man could have come over, studying the wet drooping weeds for the brush marks where a man might have passed.

At the farthest corner of the garden, he stepped up onto the leaning main stem of an apple tree to see over the wall, wedging himself against the lichen-encrusted stone, so that the silhouette of his head did not show above the wall.

He waited and watched for twenty minutes, with the absolute animal patience of the predator, then he jumped down and went on around the perimeter of the wall, never for a moment relaxing his vigilance, seemingly oblivious to the discomfort of the cold and the insistent rain.

There was nothing, not the least sign of danger, no reason for the nagging disquiet – but still it was there. He reached another vantage point, the iron gate that led into the narrow walled alley, and he leaned against the stone jamb, cupping his hands to protect match and cigarette from the wind, and then shifting slightly so he could see through the crack between wall and gate and cover the walled lane, and the road beyond as far as the bridge.

Once again he assumed the patient watching role, closing his mind against the physical discomfort and letting his eyes and his brain work at their full capacity.

Not for the first time he pondered the unusual system of signals and exchanges of material that Caliph had insisted upon.

The payments had been made by bearer deposit certificates, in Swiss francs, sent through the post to his Rio address and then to his collection address in London.

He had made one delivery to Caliph, the bottle and its contents – and two telephone calls. The delivery had been made within two hours of grabbing the girl, while she was still under the effects of the initial shot of the drug. The doctor – Dr Jameson, as Gilly O'Shaughnessy liked to think of him – had done the job in the back of the second car. It had been waiting in the car park at Cambridge railway station, a little green Ford delivery van with a completely enclosed rear compartment. They had moved the girl from the maroon Triumph to the Ford in the covering dusk of the autumn evening, and they had parked again in the lot of a roadside café on the A10 while Dr Jameson did the job. All the instruments had been ready for him in the van, but he had botched it badly, his hands shaking with nerves and the need for liquor. The brat had bled copiously, and now the hand was infected.

Gilly O'Shaughnessy felt his irritation rising sharply when he thought of the doctor. Everything he touched seemed to turn to disaster.

He had delivered the bottle to a pick-up car that had been exactly where he was told it would be, and it had dipped its headlights in the prearranged signal. Gilly had hardly stopped, but merely drawn up alongside and handed the bottle across, then driven straight into the West, and caught the early morning ferry long before any general alarm was out for the girl.

Then there were the telephone calls. They worried Gilly O'Shaughnessy as much as anything else in this whole bloody business. He had made the first call immediately they reached Laragh. It was an international call, and he had to say one sentence: 'We arrived safely.' And then hang up. A week later a call to the same number, and again only one sentence: 'We are enjoying ourselves.' And then immediately break the connection.

Gilly remembered how each time the girl on the local exchange had called him back to ask if the contact had been satisfactory – and each time she had sounded puzzled and intrigued.

It was not the way Caliph had worked up until then, it was leaving a trail for the hunters to follow and he would have protested – if there had been somebody to protest to, but there was only the international telephone number, no other way of contacting Caliph. He decided as he stood by the gate that he would not make the next telephone call to that number which was due in four days' time.

Then he remembered that was the day the hand was due – and he would probably receive his orders for delivery of the hand when he made the call – but he didn't like it. Not even for the money – and suddenly his mind went back to an incident long ago.

They had wanted to pass false information to the English, details of an intended operation – which would in fact take place at a different place and a different time. They had fed the detailed but duff information to a young unreliable Provo, one who they knew would not hold out under interrogation, and they had put him in a safe house in the Shankhill Road – and that was where the English took him.

Gilly O'Shaughnessy felt a little electric prickle run down his spine like ghost-fire, and that feeling had never let him down before – never. He looked at his cheap Japanese wristwatch; it was almost four o'clock, and evening was lowering on the hills of grey and cold green. When he looked up again, there was movement on the road.

From the top of the hill a vehicle was following the curve of the road, down towards the bridge. It was a small black saloon car, and it went out of sight behind the hedge.

Gilly O'Shaughnessy watched for it to reappear without particular interest, still worrying about those two telephone calls. Trying to find the need for them, why Caliph should want to take that chance.

The small black car turned onto the bridge, and came directly down towards the Manse, but the light was wrong and Gilly could make out only the shape of two heads beyond the rhythmically flogging windscreen wipers.

The car began to slow up, coming down almost to walking speed, and Gilly straightened up instinctively, suddenly completely alert as he peered through the slit. There was the pale blur of faces turned towards him, and the car slowed almost to a halt. The nearest side window was lowered slowly and for the first time he could see clearly into the interior. He saw the peak of the uniform cap, and the silver flash of a cap badge above the straining white face. The ghost-fire flared up Gilly O'Shaughnessy's spine and he felt his breath suddenly scalding his throat.

The small black car disappeared beyond the corner of the stone wall, and he heard it accelerate away swiftly.

Gilly O'Shaughnessy whirled with the cape ballooning around him and he ran back to the house. He felt very cold and sure and calm now that the moment of action had come.

The kitchen was empty and he crossed it in half a dozen strides, and threw open the door to the second room.

The doctor was working over the bed and he looked up angrily.

'I've told you to knock.'

They had argued this out before. The doctor still retained some bizarre vestige of professional ethics in his treatment of his patient. He might surgically mutilate the child for the money he so desperately needed, but he had protested fiercely when Gilly O'Shaughnessy had lingered at the doorway to ogle the maturing body whenever the doctor stripped it for cleansing, treatment or for the performance of its natural functions.

The dark Irishman had half-heartedly attempted to force him to back down, but when he had encountered surprisingly courageous opposition he had abandoned his voyeuristic pleasures and had returned to the inner room only when called to assist.

Now the child lay face down on the soiled sheets. Her blonde hair was matted and snarled into greasy tresses; the doctor's attempts at cleanliness were as bumbling and ineffectual as his surgery.

The infection and the use of drugs had wasted the flesh off the tender young body, each knuckle of her spine stood out clearly and her naked buttocks seemed pathetically vulnerable, shrunken and pale.

Now the doctor pulled the grubby sheet up to her shoulders, and turned to stand protectively over her. It was an absurd gesture, when you looked at the untidy, stained dressing that bound up her left hand – and Gilly O'Shaughnessy snarled at him fiercely.

'We are getting out.'

'You can't move her now,' protested the doctor. 'She's really sick.'

'Suit yourself,' Gilly agreed grimly. 'Then we'll leave her.' He reached under the dripping cape, and brought out the pistol. He thumbed back the hammer and stepped up to the bed. The doctor grabbed at his arm, but Gilly pushed him away easily, sending him reeling back against the wall.

'You are right, she'll be a nuisance,' he said, and placed the muzzle of the pistol against the base of the child's skull.

'No,' shrieked the doctor. 'No, don't do that. We'll take her.'

'We are leaving as soon as it's dark.' Gilly stepped back and uncocked the pistol. 'Be ready by then,' he warned.

The two helicopters flew almost side by side, with the number two only slightly behind and higher than the leader; below them the Irish Sea was a sheet of beaten lead flecked with feathers of white water.

They had refuelled at Caernarvon and had made good time since leaving the Welsh coast, for the wind drove them on, but still the night was overtaking them and Peter Stride fretted, glancing at his wristwatch every few seconds.

It was only ninety miles of open water to cross, but to Peter it seemed like the entire Atlantic. Colin slumped beside him on the bench that ran the length of the hold, with the cold stump of a cheroot in the corner of his mouth in deference to the 'No smoking' light that burned on the bulkhead behind the flight deck. The rest of the Thor team had adopted their usual attitudes of complete relaxation, some of them sprawled on the deck using their equipment as pillows, the others stretched out full length on the benches.

Peter Stride was the only one tensed up, as though his blood fizzed with nervous energy. He stood up once again to peer through the perspex window, checking the amount of daylight and trying to judge the height and position of the sun through the thick cloud cover.

'Take it easy,' Colin counselled him as he dropped back into his seat. 'You will give yourself an ulcer.'

'Colin, we've got to decide. What are our priorities on this strike?' He had to shout above the racket of wind and motor.

'There are no priorities. We have only one object – to get Melissa-Jane out, and out safely.'

'We aren't going to try for prisoners to interrogate?'

'Peter baby, we are going to hit anything and everything that moves in the target area, and we are going to hit them hard.'

Peter nodded with satisfaction. 'They will only be goons anyway, you can be certain that their paymaster will not let them connect to him – but what about Kingston Parker, he would want prisoners?'

'Kingston Parker?' Colin removed the stub of cheroot from his mouth. 'Never heard of him – around here it's Uncle Colin makes the decisions.' And he grinned at Peter, that friendly lopsided grin, and at that moment the flight engineer crossed the cabin and yelled at Colin.

'Irish coast ahead – we'll be landing at Enniskerry in seven minutes, sir.'

Air traffic control at Enniskerry had been apprised of the emergency. They stacked the other traffic in holding pattern above circuit altitude and cleared the two R.A.F. helicopters for immediate landing.

They came clattering out of the low grey cloud and rain, and settled on the hangar apron. Immediately a police car with headlights burning in the gloom, sped out from between the hangars and parked beside the leading machine. Before the rotors had stopped turning, two members of the Irish Constabulary and a representative of the surveyor general's office were scrambling up into the camouflaged fuselage.

'Stride.' Peter introduced himself quickly. He was dressed now in Thor assault gear, the one piece fitted black suit and soft boots, the pistol on its webbing belt strapped down to his right thigh.

'General, we've had a confirmation,' the police inspector

told him while they were still shaking hands. 'Local people have identified O'Shaughnessy from a police photograph. He is staying in the area all right.'

'Have they found where?' Peter demanded.

'They have, sir. It's an old rambling building on the edge of the village—' He motioned the bespectacled surveyor to come forward with the file he was clutching to his chest. There was no chart table in the stripped-out hull of the helicopter, and they spread the survey map and photographs on the deck.

Colin Noble ordered across the team from the second helicopter, and twenty men crowded into a huddle about the maps. 'There, that's the building.' The surveyor placed a circle on the map with a blue pencil.

'Right,' grunted Colin. 'We've got good fixes – we pick up either the river or the road and follow it to the bridge and the church. The target is between them.'

'Haven't we got a blow-up of the building, a plan of the interior?' one of the Thor team asked.

'Sorry, there wasn't time to do a proper search,' the surveyor apologized.

'The local police reported again a few minutes ago, and we got a relay on the radio. They say the house is enclosed by a high stone wall and that there are no signs of activity.'

'They haven't been near it?' Peter demanded. 'They were strictly ordered not to approach the suspects.'

'They drove past once on the public road.' The inspector looked slightly abashed. 'They wanted to make certain that—'

'If it's O'Shaughnessy, he needs only one sniff and he'll be gone—' Peter's expression was stony, but his eyes sparkled blue with anger. ' – Why can't these people do what they are told?' He turned quickly to the helicopter pilot in his yellow life jacket and helmet with its built-in microphone and earphones.

'Can you get us in?'

The pilot did not answer immediately but glanced up at the nearest window; a fresh gout of rain splashed against the pane.

'It will be dark in ten minutes, or even earlier, and the ceiling is down to the deck now, we only got down here using the airport V.O.R. beacons—' He looked dubious. ' – There is nobody aboard who will recognize the target, hell – I don't know – I could get you in at first light tomorrow.'

'It has to be tonight, now. Right now.'

'If you could get the local police to mark the target—' the pilot suggested, ' – with torches or a flare.'

'There is no chance of that – we have to go in cold, and the longer we sit here talking the less our chances. Will you give it your best shot?' Peter was almost pleading, the go decision is one that cannot be forced on a pilot, even air traffic control cannot force a pilot-in-command to operate beyond his personal judgement.

'We will have to try and keep ground contact all the way; it's classic conditions for trouble, rising terrain and deteriorating weather—'

'Try it—' Peter said, ' – please.'

The pilot hesitated five seconds longer.

'Let's go!' he said abruptly, and there was a concerted rush for the hatchway as the second Thor team made for the other machine, and the police and surveyor made certain they were not included on the passenger list.

Turbulence slogged the helicopter like the punches of a heavyweight prize fighter, and she dipped and staggered to them with a nauseatingly giddy action.

The ground flickered past under them, very close, and yet darkly insubstantial in the wild night. The headlights of a solitary vehicle on a lonely country road, the cluttered lights of a village, each a distinct yellow rectangle they were so close, these were the only landmarks with any meaning – the rest was dark patches of woods, the threads of hedges and stone walls drawn lightly across sombre fields, and every few minutes even that was gone as a fresh squall of grey clouds and rain washed away all vision, and the pilot concentrated all his attention on the dull glow of the flight instruments arranged in their distinctive T layout in front of him.

Each time they emerged from cloud, the light seemed to have diminished and the dark menace of earth loomed more threateningly as they were forced lower and lower to keep contact.

Peter was squeezed into the jump seat of the helicopter's flight deck, between the two pilots, and Colin crowded in behind him, all of them peering ahead, all silent and tense as the ungainly machines lumbered low and heavy over the earth, groping for the shoreline.

They hit the coast, the ghostly white line of surf flared with phosphorescence only fifty feet below them, and the pilot swung them to run south with it – and seconds later another brighter field of lights appeared below them.

'Wicklow,' said the pilot, and his co-pilot called the new heading; now they had made a fix they could head for Laragh directly.

They swung onto the new heading, following the road inland.

'Four minutes to target,' the co-pilot shouted at Peter, stabbing ahead with his finger, and Peter did not try to answer in the clatter and roar of the rotors, but he reached down and checked the Walther in its quick-release holster; it came out cleanly in his fist.

Gilly O'Shaughnessy threw his few personal possessions into the blue canvas airways grip, a change of underclothing and his shaving gear. Then he pulled the iron bedstead away from the wall, ripped back the skirting board and cleared out the hiding-place he had made there by removing a single brick.

There were the new papers and passports. Caliph had even provided papers for the brat – Helen Barry – his daughter. Caliph had thought of everything. With the papers was six hundred pounds sterling in travellers' cheques, and a package of spare ammunition for the pistol. He thrust these into the pocket of his jacket, and took one last look around the bare bleak room. He knew that he had left nothing to lead the hunters, because he never carried anything that could be used to identify him. Yet he was obsessed by the need to destroy all sign of his passing. He had long ago ceased to think of himself by the name of Gilly O'Shaughnessy. He had no name, and only one purpose – that purpose was destruction. The magnificent passion to reduce all life to decay and mortification.

He could recite by heart most of Bakunin's *The Revolutionary Catechism*, especially the definition of the true revolutionary:

The lost man, who has no belongings, no outside interest, no personal ties of any sort – not even a name. Possessed of but one thought, interest and passion – the revolution. A man who has broken with Society, broken with its laws and conventions. He must despise the opinions of others, and be prepared for death and torture at any time. Hard towards himself, he must be hard to others, and in his heart there must be no place for love, friendship, gratitude or even honour.

As he stood now in the empty room, he saw himself in a

rare moment of revelation, as the man he had set out to become – the true revolutionary, and his head turned for a moment to indulge in the vanity of regarding his own image in the mirror screwed to the peeling wallpaper above the iron bedstead.

It was the dark cold face of the lost man, and he felt proud to belong to that élite class, the cutting edge of the sword, that was what he was.

He picked up the canvas grip, and strode through into the kitchen.

'Are you ready?' he called.

'Help me.'

He dropped the grip and stepped to the window. The last of the light was fading swiftly, glowing pink and mother-of-pearl within the drooping, pregnant belly of the sky. It seemed so close he could reach out and touch it. Already the trees of the unkempt orchard were melding into the darkness as the night encroached.

'I cannot carry her on my own,' the doctor whined, and he swung away from the window. It was time to go again. In his life there was always the moving onwards, and always the hunters baying hard upon his scent. It was time to run again, run like the fox.

He went through into the second room. The doctor had the child wrapped in a grey woollen blanket, and he had tried to lift her from the bed, but had failed. She was sprawled awkwardly, half onto the floor.

'Help me,' repeated the doctor.

'Get out of the way.' Gilly O'Shaughnessy pushed him roughly aside, and stooped over the girl. For a second their faces were within inches of each other.

Her eyes were opened, half conscious, although the pupils were widely dilated by the drug. The lids were pink-rimmed and there were little butter-yellow lumps of mucus in the corners. Her lips were dried to white scales, and cracked through to the raw flesh at three places.

271

'Please tell my daddy,' she whispered. 'Please tell him I'm here.'

His nostrils flared at the sick sour smell of her body, but he picked her up easily with an arm under her knees and the other under her shoulders, and carried her out across the kitchen, kicking open the door so the lock burst and it slammed back against its hinges.

Quickly he carried her across the yard to the garage, with the doctor staggering along after them carrying a carton of medical supplies and equipment against his chest, cursing miserably at the cold, and sliding and slipping in the treacherous footing.

Gilly O'Shaughnessy waited while the doctor opened the rear door of the car, and then he bundled her in so roughly that the child cried out weakly. He ignored her and went to the double garage doors and dragged them open. It was so dark now that he could not see as far as the bridge.

'Where are we going?' bleated the doctor.

'I haven't decided yet,' Gilly told him brusquely. 'There is a safe house up North, or we might go back across the sea to England—' He thought of the caravan again, that was a good one—

'But why are we leaving now, so suddenly?'

He did not bother to reply but left the garage and ran back into the kitchen. Always he was obsessed by the need to cover his tracks, to leave no sign for the hunters.

Though he had brought little with him, and was taking that now, yet he knew the old house contained signs, even if it was only his fingerprints. There was also the single remaining appetite for destruction to assuage.

He ripped the wooden doors off the kitchen cupboards and smashed them to splinters under his heel, piled them in the centre of the wood floor. He crumpled the newspapers piled on the table and added them to the pile, threw the table and chairs upon it.

He lit a match and held it to the crumpled newsprint. It flared readily, and he straightened and opened the windows and doors. The flames fed on the cold fresh air and climbed greedily, catching on the splintered doors.

Gilly O'Shaughnessy picked up the canvas grip and stepped out into the night, crouching to the wind and the rain – but halfway to the garage he straightened again abruptly and paused to listen.

There was a sound on the wind, from the direction of the coast. It might have been the engine note of a heavy truck coming up the hills, but there was a peculiar thin whistling sound mingled with the engine beat, and the volume of sound escalated too sharply to be that of a lumbering truck. It was coming on too swiftly, the sound seemed to fill the air, to emanate from the very clouds themselves.

Gilly O'Shaughnessy stood with his face lifted to the fine silver drizzle, searching the belly of the clouds, until a throbbing regular glow began to beat like a pulse in the sky, and it was a moment until he recognized it as the beacon light of a low-flying aircraft, and at the same moment he knew that the shrill whistle was the whirling of rotors bringing the hunters.

He cried aloud in the certainty of betrayal and onrushing death. 'Why? God, why?' He called to the god he had so long ago denied, and he began to run.

'It's no good.' The pilot twisted his neck to shout at Peter without taking his eyes from the flight instruments which kept the great ungainly machine level and on course. They had lost contact with the other machine.

'We are socked in, blind.' The cloud frothed over the

canopy like boiling milk over the lip of the pot. 'I'm going to have to climb out, and head back for Enniskerry before we run into my number two.'

The risk of collision with the other helicopter was now real and imminent.

The beacon light throbbed above them, reflected off the impenetrable press of soft cloud – but the other pilot would not see it until too late.

'Hold on. Just another minute,' Peter shouted back at him, his expression tortured in the glow of the instrument panel. The entire operation was disintegrating about him, would soon end in tragedy or in fiasco, but he must go on.

'It's no good—' the pilot began, and then shouted with fright and hurled the helicopter over onto its side, at the same instant altering pitch and altitude so the machine shuddered and lurched as though she had run into a solid obstruction, and then bounded upwards, gaining a hundred feet in a swoop.

The spire of a church had leapt at them out of the cloud, like a predator from ambush, and now it flickered by only feet from where they crouched in the flight deck, but it had disappeared again instantly as they roared past.

'The church!' Peter yelled. 'That's it! Turn back.'

The pilot checked the machine, hovering blindly in the chaos of rain and cloud churned to a fury by the down-draught of their own rotor.

'I can't see a damned thing,' shouted the pilot.

'We've got one hundred and seventy feet on the radio altimeter,' his co-pilot called; that was actual height from the ground and still they could see nothing below them.

'Get us down. For God's sake, get us down,' Peter pleaded.

'I can't take the chance. We don't have any idea of what is under us.' The pilot's face was sickly orange in the instrument glow, his eyes the dark pits of a skull. 'I'm climbing out and heading back—'

Peter reached down and the butt of the Walther jumped into his hand, like a living thing. He realized coldly that he was capable of killing the pilot, to force the co-pilot to land – but at the moment there was a hole in the cloud, just enough to make out the dark loom of the earth below them.

'Visual,' Peter shouted. 'We've visual, get us down!' And the helicopter sank swiftly, breaking out suddenly into the clear.

'The river.' Peter saw the glint of water. 'And the bridge—'

'There's the churchyard—' Colin roared eagerly, ' – and that's the target.'

The thatched roof was a black oblong, and light spilled from the windows of one side of the building, so they could see the high enclosing wall. The pilot spun the helicopter on its axis like a compass needle, and dived towards the building.

Colin Noble scrambled down into the cabin, shouting to his team. 'Delta! We are going to Delta—' And the flight engineer slid the hatch cover open. Immediately a fine swirling mist filled the cabin as the down-draught of the rotors churned the rain filled air.

The Thor team were on their feet, forming up on each side of the open hatch, while Colin towered over the flight engineer as he took lead position – 'point' as he always called it.

The dark earth rushed up to meet them, and Colin spat out the cheroot stub and braced himself in the doorway.

'Hit anything that moves,' he yelled. 'But for Chrissake watch out for the kid. Let's go, gang. Let's go!'

Peter was jammed into the jump seat by the swooping drop of the machine, unable to follow, wasting precious seconds – but he had a clear view ahead through the canopy.

The light in the windows of the building wavered unnaturally, and Peter realized that it was burning. Those were flames, and his concern was heightened by the knowledge, but he did not have a chance to ponder this new development. In the shadows of the walled yard he saw movement, just the dark blur of it in the glow of the flames, and what was left of the daylight – but it was the shape of a man, running, crouched low, disappearing almost immediately into one of the outbuildings that flanked the narrow stone walled lane.

Peter dragged himself out of the seat against the G force, scrambling awkwardly down into the cabin as the helicopter dropped the last few feet, and then hung, swaying slightly, suspended ten feet above the open yard at the rear of the house – and black-clad figures spilled out of her, dropping lightly onto their feet and racing forward as they touched ground, seeming to disappear again miraculously through the doors and windows of the building. Even in the grinding tension of the moment Peter felt the flare of pride in the way it was done, instant and seemingly effortless penetration, the lead man using the sandbags to break in glass and wooden shutters and the man behind him going in with a clean controlled dive.

Peter was the last man left aboard, and something made him check in the open hatchway before jumping. Perhaps it was that glimpse of movement outside the main building that he had been given; he looked back that way, and suddenly lights leapt in solid white lances down the walled lane – the headlights of a motor vehicle, and at the same moment the vehicle launched itself from the dark derelict outbuilding and rocketed away down the lane.

Peter teetered in the open hatch, for he had been in the very act of jumping, but he caught his balance now, grabbing wildly at the nylon line above the door. The vehicle slowed for the turn into the main road at the bridge – and Peter caught the flight engineer and shook his shoulder violently, pointing after the escaping vehicle. His lips were inches from the man's face.

'Don't let it get away!' he screamed, and the flight engineer was quick and alert; he spoke urgently into his microphone, directly to the pilot in the flight deck above them, and obediently the helicopter swung around and the beat of the engines changed as the rotors altered pitch and roared in forward thrust – the machine lunged forward, skimming the garage roof by mere feet and then hammered out into the night in pursuit of the dwindling glow of headlights.

Peter had to hang out of the hatchway to see ahead, and the wind clamoured around his head and tore at his body, but they were swiftly overhauling the vehicle as it raced down the twisting narrow road towards the coast.

It was two hundred yards ahead, and the dark tree tops seemed to rush by at the same level as the hatch in which Peter stood. A hundred yards ahead now, the headlights blazing through the drivel of rain, etching fleeting cameos of hedges and starkly lit stone walls from the night.

They were close enough now for Peter to make out that it was a smallish vehicle with an estate car body, not quite large enough to be a station wagon – the driver was throwing it through the curves and twists of the road with reckless skill, but the helicopter crept up behind him.

'Tell him to switch off the beacon light.' Peter swung inboard to shout in the flight engineer's ear. He did not want to warn the driver that he was being followed, but as the engineer lifted the microphone to his mouth the headlights snapped out into darkness. The driver had become aware, and after the brilliance of the headlights the night seemed totally dark, and the car disappeared into it.

Peter felt the helicopter lurch, as the pilot was taken by surprise, and his own dismay was a lance.

We have lost them, he thought, and he knew that it was suicide to fly on in darkness only a few feet above the treetops, but the pilot of the helicopter steadied the craft and then suddenly the earth below them was lit by a blaze of stark white light that startled Peter until he realized that the pilot had switched on his landing lights. There were two of them, one on each side of the fuselage; they were aimed down and slightly forward.

The escaping car was caught fairly in their brilliance.

The helicopter dropped lower, edging in between the telegraph poles and trees that lined the narrow road.

Now Peter could see that the car was a dark blue Austin, with a carrying rack bolted to the long roof. It was that carrying rack which decided him. Without it no human being could have hoped for purchase on the smooth rounded roof of the lurching, swaying car.

The doctor in the back seat of the Austin had been the one who spotted the helicopter. The engine noise and the drumming of the wind had covered the whistling whine of the rotors, and Gilly O'Shaughnessy had chuckled with grim triumph and self-congratulation. He had deliberately waited for the helicopter to discharge its load of fighting men before he had switched on his headlights and roared out of the garage into the lane.

He knew it would be many minutes before the assault team realized that the burning house was empty and that it would take as long again to regroup and board the helicopter to continue the hunt – and by that time he would be clear; there was a safe house in Dublin – or there had been, four year previously. Perhaps it was blown now; in that case he would have to get rid of the brat and Dr Jameson, a bullet each in the back of the head, and drive the Austin into the Irish Sea.

The wild exhilaration of danger and death was upon him again, the waiting was over at last and he was living again the way he had chosen – the fox running ahead of the hounds, he was alive again, with his right foot thrust flat to the floor boards and the Austin rocketing through the night.

The girl was screaming weakly from the back seat, in pain and panic; the doctor was trying to quieten her, and Gilly laughed aloud. The tyres screeched wildly as he skidded out in the turn, brushing the hedge with the side before he was through.

'They are following,' screamed the doctor, as he straightened the car into the next stretch, then Gilly glanced back over his shoulder. He could see nothing through the rear windows.

'What?'

'The helicopter—'

Gilly lowered his window and, driving with one hand, thrust his head out. The flashing aircraft beacon was close behind and above, and he ducked back in and looked ahead to make sure that the road ran straight, then he switched off the headlights.

In total darkness he did not diminish speed, and now when he laughed it was a wild and reckless sound.

'You're mad,' the doctor shrieked. 'You'll kill us all!'

'Right you are, doctor!' But his night vision was clearing and he caught the Austin before she wandered into the stone wall on the left-hand side, and at the same moment he jerked the pistol from under his cape and laid it on the seat beside him.

'There is not going to be—' he began and then broke off as the blinding light burst over them. The helicopter had switched on its landing lights – the road ahead was brightly lit, and he skidded into the next turn with rubber squealing.

'Stop!' the doctor pleaded, trying to hold the semi-conscious child from being hurled about in the swaying cab. 'Let's give up now, before they kill us.'

'They've got no fighting men on board,' Gilly yelled back at him. 'There's nothing they can do.'

'Give up,' the doctor whined. 'Let's get out of this alive.'

And Gilly O'Shaughnessy threw back his head and roared with laughter.

'I'm keeping three bullets, doctor, one for each of us—'

'They're right on top of us.'

Gilly snatched up the pistol and once again thrust his head and right shoulder out, twisting to look upwards.

The eye-searing lights beamed down upon him, very close above. It was all he could see and he fired at them, the crash of the shots lost in the clattering whistling roar of the rotors and the tearing rush of the wind.

Poised in the hatchway, Peter counted the bright orange spurts of gunfire. There were five of them, but there was no sound of passing shot, no thump of the strike.

'Get lower!' he shouted at the engineer, reinforcing the order with urgent hand signals, and obediently the big machine sank down upon the racing Austin.

Peter gathered himself, judging his moment carefully, and when it came he launched himself clear of the hatchway, and his guts seemed to cram into his throat as he dropped.

He dropped with all four limbs spread and braced to land together, but for a moment he thought he had misjudged it and would fall behind the Austin, into the metalled roadway, to be crushed and shredded by the forward impetus of the low-flying helicopter.

Then the Austin swerved and checked slightly and Peter crashed into its roof with stunning force; he felt the metal buckle and sag under him, and then he was rolling and slipping sideways. His whole left side was numbed by the force of impact, and he clutched wildly with his right hand, his fingernails tearing at the paintwork, but still he slid towards the edge, his legs kicking wildly in dark rushing space.

At the last instant before he was hurled into the roadway, his clawed fingers hooked in the framework of the roof rack, and he hung bat-like from his one arm. It had taken only a small part of a second, and immediately the driver of the Austin realized that there was a man on the roof. He slewed the little car from one side of the road to the other, short wrenching turns that brought her over on two outside wheels before slamming back and twisting the other way. The tyres squealed harsh protest, and Peter was flung brutally back and forth, the muscle and tendons of his right arm popping and creaking with the strain of holding on – but feeling was flooding swiftly back into his numbed left side.

He had to move quickly, he could not survive another of those wrenching swerves, and he gathered himself, judged the Austin's momentum, and used it to roll and grab with his free hand; at the same moment the toes of his soft boots found purchase on one of the struts of the roof carrier, and he pressed himself belly down, clinging with both arms and legs to the wildly swinging machine.

The Austin checked and steadied as a steep turn appeared ahead in the arc lights of the helicopter which still hung over them. The driver shot the car into the corner, and ahead of them was a long extended drop as the road twisted down the hills towards the coast.

Peter half lifted himself and was about to slide forward when the metal six inches in front of his nose exploded outwards, leaving a neatly punched hole through the roof, and tiny fragments of flying metal stung his cheek; at the same moment the concussion of the pistol shot beat in upon his eardrums. The driver of the Austin was firing blindly up through the coachwork, and he had misjudged Peter's position above him by inches. Peter threw himself desperately to one side, for an instant almost losing his grip on the struts of the carrier – and another pistol bullet clanged out through the metal roof, that one would have taken him through the belly, and Peter had a fleeting image of the kind of wound that it would have inflicted, the bullet would have been mushroomed and deformed by the roof and would have broken up inside his body.

Desperately Peter threw himself back the opposite way, trying to outguess the gunman below him, and once again the crash of the shot and the metal roof erupted in a little jagged pockmark, flecking the paintwork away so the rim of the bullet hole shone like polished silver shilling. Again it would have hit him, if he had not moved.

Peter rolled again, tensing his belly muscles in the anticipation of the tearing, paralysing impact, expecting the gun shot – which did not come. Only then he remembered the wasted pistol fire the driver had thrown up at the hovering helicopter. He had emptied his pistol and as the realization dawned on Peter there was another completely compelling sound, very faint in the drumming rush of the wind and the engine roar – but unmistakable. It was the sound of a young girl screaming and it galvanized Peter as nothing else, even the threat of death, could have done.

He came up on toes and fingers, like a cat, and he went forward and to the right, until he was directly above the driver's seat.

The girl screamed again, and he recognized Melissa-Jane's voice. There was no question of it, and he slipped the Walther from its quick-release holster and cocked the hammer with the same movement, one glance ahead and they were rushing down on another turn in the narrow road. The driver would be using both hands to control the swaying and bucking little machine.

'Now!' he told himself, and dropped forward, so that he was peering backwards and upside-down through the windscreen directly into the driver's pale face and at a distance of only eighteen inches.

In the thousandth part of a second Peter recognized the dark, wolfish features and the cold, merciless eyes of the killer. He had hunted this man for many years and studied his photograph endlessly when the hunting of the Provo terrorists had been his life's work.

Gilly O'Shaughnessy was driving with both hands, the pistol still gripped in one of them and the chamber open for reloading. He snarled at Peter like an animal through the bars of its cage, and Peter fired with the muzzle of the Walther touching the glass of the windscreen.

The glass starred into a glittering sheet, white and opaque, and then it collapsed inwards with the force of the wind, filling the interior of the Austin with flying diamond chips of sparkling glass.

Gilly O'Shaughnessy had thrown up both hands to his face, but bright blood burst from between them, spattering his chest and soaking swiftly into the lank black hair.

Still hanging upside down across the Austin's cab, Peter thrust the Walther in through the shattered windscreen until it almost touched the man's body and he fired twice more into his chest, where the explosive Velex bullets would break up against bone, and would not overpenetrate to harm anybody else in the interior. Melissa-Jane's screams still rang clearly in his ears, as he killed Gilly O'Shaughnessy. He did it as coldly as a veterinary surgeon would put down a rabid dog, and with as little pleasure, and the bullets punched Gilly O'Shaughnessy back on the bucket seat, head lolling from side to side, and Peter expected the howl of the engine to cut out now as the dead man's foot slipped from the accelerator.

It did not happen. There was no change in the engine beat, the body had slid forward and jammed, the knee under the dashboard bearing down fully on the pedal, and the little car flew down the slope of the hill, the stone walls on each side blurring past as though down a tunnel in the depths of the earth.

Peter wriggled forward and thrust both arms through the shattered windscreen and caught the untended wheel as it began to spin aimlessly. He checked the Austin and swung her back into the road but she had been driven to her limits, rocking and swaying crazily before she righted herself and flew down the hill.

It was almost impossible to judge the control needed to keep her on the road.

Peter was hanging head down, gripping only with knees and toes, and he had to manipulate the wheel from this inverted position with his upper arms sawing across the teeth of jagged glass still remaining in the frame of the windscreen.

The wind whipped and clawed him, and Gilly O'Shaughnessy's body flopped forward bonelessly onto the wheel, jamming it at a critical moment, so that while Peter used one hand to shove him backwards, the side of the Austin touched the stone wall with a screech of rending metal and a shower of orange sparks. Peter wrenched her back into the road, and she began a series of uncontrolled broadsides, swinging wildly from side to side, touching the wall with another jarring shock, then swinging back sideways to bounce over the verge, then back again.

She was going over, Peter knew it, and he would be crushed under the metal roof and smeared along the abrasive surface of the macadam road. He should jump now, and take his chances – but grimly he stayed with the crazed machine, for Melissa-Jane was in her and he could not leave.

She survived one more skid, and ahead Peter had the glimpse of a barred wooden gate in the wall. Deliberately he turned the front wheels into the direction of the next skid, no longer trying to counteract it, but aggravating it –

steering directly for the gate, and the Austin smashed into it.

A wooden beam cartwheeled over Peter's head, and a scalding cloud of steam from the shattered radiator stung his face and hands, and then the Austin was into the open field, bouncing and thudding over the rocks that studded it, the drag of soft muddy earth slowing her, and the steep slope of the hillside against her – within fifty feet the front end dropped heavily into a drainage ditch, and the little car shuddered to a halt, canted at an abandoned angle.

Peter slipped over the side and landed on his feet. He jerked open the rear door and a man half fell from the cab. He dropped onto his knees in the mud, blubbering incoherently and Peter drove his right knee into his face. Bone and cartilage crunched sharply and there was the crackle of breaking teeth. His voice was cut off abruptly and, as he dropped, Peter chopped him with the stiffened blade of his right hand, a controlled blow – judged finely to immobilize but not to kill, and before the unconscious body dropped, Peter had gone in over it.

He lifted his daughter out of the Austin, and the frail wasted body felt unsubstantial in his arms, and the heat of fever and infection burned against his chest.

He was possessed by an almost uncontrollable desire to crush her body to him with all the strength of his arms, but instead he carried her as though she was made of some precious and fragile substance, stepping carefully over the uneven rocky surface of the field to where the helicopter was settling cumbersomely out of the darkness.

The Thor doctor was still aboard her; he jumped clear before the helicopter touched and ran towards Peter in the brilliant glare of the landing lights.

Peter found he was crooning softly.

'It's all right now, darling. It's all over now. It's all finished, my baby – I'm here, little one—'

285

Then Peter made another discovery. It was not sweat running down his cheeks and dripping from his chin, and he wondered unashamedly when last it was he had wept. He could not remember, and it did not seem important, not now, not with his daughter in his arms.

Cynthia came down to London, and Peter relived some of those horrors from their marriage.

'Everybody around you always has to suffer, Peter. Now it's Melissa-Jane's turn.'

He could not avoid her, nor her martyred expression, for she was always at Melissa-Jane's bedside. While he bore her recriminations and barbed accusations, he wondered that she had ever been gay and young and attractive. She was two years younger than he was but she already had the shapeless body and greying mind that made her seem twenty years older.

Melissa-Jane responded almost miraculously to the antibiotics, and although she was still weak and skinny and pale, the doctor discharged her on the third day, and Peter and Cynthia had their final degrading haggling and bargaining session which Melissa-Jane settled for them.

'Mummy, I'm still so afraid. Can't I go with Daddy – just for a few days?'

Finally Cynthia agreed with sighs and pained airs that left them both feeling a little guilty. On the drive down to Abbots Yew, where Steven had invited them for as long as was necessary for Melissa-Jane's convalescence, she sat very quietly beside Peter, her left hand still in the sling and the finger wearing a small neat white turban. She spoke only after they had passed the Heathrow turn off on the M4.

'All the time I knew you were going to come. I can't remember much else. It was always dark and giddymaking –

things kept changing. I'd look at a face and it would fade away, and then we'd be somewhere else—'

'It was the drug they were giving you,' Peter explained.

'Yes, I know that. I remember the prick of the needle—' Reflexively she rubbed her upper arm, and shivered briefly. 'But even with the drug I always knew you were going to come. I remember lying in the darkness listening for your voice—'

There was the temptation to try to pretend it had never happened, and Melissa-Jane had not spoken about it until now – but Peter knew she must be allowed to talk it out.

'Would you like to tell me about it?' he invited gently, knowing that it was essential to the healing process. He listened quietly as she spilled out drug-haunted memories, disjointed scraps of conversation and impressions. The terror was back in her voice when she spoke of the dark one.

'He looked at me sometimes. I remember him looking at me—' And Peter remembered the cold killer's eyes.

'He is dead now, darling.'

'Yes, I know. They told me.' She was silent for a moment, and then went on. 'He was so different from the one with grey hair. I liked him, the old one. His name was Doctor Jameson.'

'How did you know that?' Peter asked.

'That's what the dark one called him.' She smiled. 'Doctor Jameson, I remember he always smelled like cough mixture and I liked him—'

The one who had done the amputation, and would have taken her hand as well, Peter thought grimly.

'I never saw the other one. I knew he was there, but I never saw him.'

'The other one?' Peter turned to her sharply. 'Which other one, darling?'

'There was another one – and even the dark one was afraid of him. I knew that, they were all afraid of him.'

'You never saw him?'

'No, but they were always talking about him, and arguing about what he would do—'

'Do you remember his name?' Peter asked, and Melissa-Jane frowned in concentration.

'Did he have a name?' Peter prompted.

'Usually they just talked about *him*, but, yes, I remember now. The dark one called him "Casper".'

'Casper?'

'No, not that, not Casper. Oh, I can't remember.' Her voice had risen, a shrill note in terror that ripped at Peter's nerves.

'Don't worry about it.' He tried to soothe her, but she shook her head with frustration.

'Not Casper, a name like that. I knew he was the one who really wanted to hurt me – they were just doing what he told them. He was the one I was truly afraid of.' Her voice ended with a sob, and she was sitting bolt upright in the seat.

'It's over now, darling.' Peter swung into the verge of the road and braked to a halt. He reached for her but she was rigid in his arms and at his touch she began to shake uncontrollably. Peter's alarm flared, and he held her to his chest.

'Caliph!' she whispered. 'That's his name. Caliph.' And she relaxed against him softly, and sighed. The shaking stopped slowly. Peter went on holding her, trying to control the terrible consuming waves of anger that engulfed him, and it was some little time before he realized suddenly that Melissa-Jane had fallen asleep.

It was as though uttering the name had been a catharsis for her terror, and now she was ready to begin the healing inside.

Peter laid her gently back in the seat and covered her with the angora rug before he drove on, but every few seconds he glanced across to make sure she was at peace.

Twice Peter called Magda Altmann from Abbots Yew, both times to her private number, but she was unobtainable and there was no message for him. That was five days he had not been able to reach her, not since the Delta Strike which had freed Melissa-Jane. She seemed to have disappeared completely, and Peter pondered the implications during the quiet days when he was almost always alone with his daughter.

Then Dr Kingston Parker arrived at Abbots Yew, and Sir Steven Stride was delighted to have as his guest such a distinguished statesman.

Kingston Parker's giant personality seemed to fill the beautiful old home. When he put himself out, his graciousness was irresistible. Steven was delighted with him, particularly when he discovered that despite Parker's image as a liberal and his well-known concern with human rights, he was also a champion of the capitalist system, and determined that his country should take more seriously its responsibilities as leader of the Western world. They both deplored the loss of the B1 bomber and the delaying of the neutron bomb programme, and the restructuring of America's intelligence agencies. They spent much of the first afternoon in Steven's redwood-panelled study exploring each other's views, and came out of it fast friends.

When they emerged, Parker completed his conquest of the Stride household by showing he shared with Patricia Stride a scholarly knowledge and love of antique porcelain. His concern and warmth for Melissa-Jane and his relief at her safety were too spontaneous not to be entirely genuine. His conquest of that young lady's affections was complete when he went down with her to the stables to meet Florence Nightingale and prove that he was also a fair judge of horseflesh.

'He's a lovely man. I think he is truly an honourable man,' Melissa-Jane told Peter, when he went up to her bedroom to bid her goodnight – 'And he's so kind and funny—' Then, lest there be any question of disloyalty, 'But you are still my most favourite man in all the world.'

Her cure and convalescence seemed almost complete, and as Peter went down to rejoin the company he marvelled again at the resilience of young flesh and young minds.

As usual at Abbots Yew there was glittering and stimulating company at dinner, with Kingston Parker at its centre, but afterwards he and Peter exchanged a single glance down the length of Pat Stride's silver- and candle-decorated table and they left them to the port and cognac and cigars and slipped out unobtrusively into the walled rose garden.

While they paced side by side on the crunching gravel pathway, Kingston Parker stoked his meerschaum and then began to talk quietly. Once his bodyguard coughed in the shadows where he waited just out of range of their subdued voices, but that was the only intrusion and the spring night was still and balmy. Their conversation seemed utterly incongruous in these surroundings, talk of death and violence, the use and abuse of power, and the manipulations of vast fortunes by a single mysterious figure.

'It's been five days since I arrived in England—' Kingston Parker shrugged. 'One does not rush through the echoing passages of Whitehall. There was much to discuss—' Peter knew that he had met with the Prime Minister on two separate occasions ' – and it wasn't just Atlas business, I'm afraid—' Parker was one of the President's confidants. They would have taken full advantage of his visit to exchange views with the British Government. 'However, we did discuss Atlas in depth and detail. You know very well that Atlas has opponents and critics on both sides of the Atlantic. They tried very hard to squash it, and when they could not they saw to it that its power and duties were severely curtailed—' Parker paused and his pipe gurgled. He flicked out the juices from the mouthpiece onto the gravel path. 'The opponents of Atlas are all highly intelligent concerned and informed men. Their motives and their reasoning in opposing Atlas are laudable. I find myself a little in sympathy despite myself. If you create a strike force such as Atlas, where enormous powers are placed in the hands of a single man or a small élite leadership, you could very well be creating a Frankenstein – a monster more frightening than you are setting out to destroy.'

'That depends on the man who controls it, Dr Parker. I believe that they have the right man.'

'Thank you, Peter.' Parker turned his big shaggy head and smiled. 'Won't you please call me Kingston.'

Peter nodded agreement, while Parker went on. 'Atlas has had some spectacular successes – at Johannesburg and now in Ireland – but that makes it more dangerous. There will be a readier acceptance of the whole concept by the public; if Atlas asks for wider powers, it is more likely they would be granted. And, believe me, if it is to do the job it needs wider powers, Peter. I find myself torn down the centre—'

'And yet,' Peter pointed out, 'we cannot take on the most dangerous animal in the world, man the killer, we cannot do it without arming ourselves in every possible way.'

Kingston Parker sighed. 'And if Atlas achieves those powers, who can say when they will be abused, when will the rule of force supersede the rule of law?'

'The rules have changed. The rule of law is so often powerless in the face of those who have no respect for the law.'

'There is another aspect, Peter. One that I have thought about half my life. What about the rule of unjust law? The laws of oppression and greed. A law that enslaves or deprives a man because of the colour of his face or the god he worships? If a duly constituted parliament makes racial laws – or if the General Assembly of the United Nations declares that Zionism is a form of Imperialism and must be outlawed. – What if a handful of men gain control of the world's resources and legally manipulate them in a manner dictated by personal greed to the detriment of all mankind, such as the Committee of the OPEC, the Shah and the King of Saudi Arabia—' Kingston Parker made a helpless gesture, spreading those long sensitive fingers. 'Must we respect those laws? The rule of law, even unjust law, is it sacrosanct?'

'Balance,' said Peter. 'There has to be a balance between law and force.'

'Yes, but what is the balance, Peter?' He abruptly closed his hands into fists. 'I have asked for greater powers for Atlas, wider scope for its use, and I think these will be granted. When they are, we will have need of good men, Peter.' Kingston Parker reached out and took Peter's shoulder in a surprisingly powerful grip. 'Just men, who can recognize when the rule of law has either failed or is unjust, and who have the courage and the vision to act to restore the balance that you spoke of a moment ago.'

His hand was still on Peter's shoulder and he left it there. It was a natural gesture, without affectation.

'I believe you are one of those men.' He let the hand drop, and his manner changed. 'Tomorrow I have arranged that we meet with Colonel Noble. He has been busy breaking down and examining the entire Irish operation, and I hope he will have come up with something for us to get our teeth into. Then there is much else to discuss. Two o'clock at Thor Command, will it suit you, Peter?'

'Of course.'

'Now let's go in and join the company.'

'Wait.' Peter stopped him. 'I have something I must tell you, Kingston. It's been tearing at my guts, and after you have heard it you may alter your opinion of me – my suitability for my role at Atlas.'

'Yes?' Parker turned back and waited quietly.

'You know that the people who kidnapped my daughter

made no demands for her return, made no attempt to contact me or the police to negotiate.'

'Yes,' Parker answered. 'Of course. It was one of the puzzling things about the whole business.'

'It was untrue. There was a contact and a demand.'

'I don't understand.' Parker frowned and thrust his face closer to Peter's, as though trying to study his expression in the poor light from the windows.

'The kidnappers contacted me. A letter which I destroyed—'

'Why?' Parker shot at him.

'Wait. I'll explain,' Peter replied. 'There was a single condition for my daughter's release, and a deadline of two weeks. If I did not meet the condition by that time, they would have sent me parts of my daughter's body – her hands, her feet, and finally her head.'

'Diabolical,' Parker whispered. 'Inhuman. What was the condition?'

'A life for a life,' said Peter. 'I was to kill you in exchange for Melissa-Jane.'

'Me!' Parker started, throwing back his head with shock. 'They wanted me?'

Peter did not reply, and they stood staring at each other, until Parker raised his hand and combed at his hair, a distracted gesture.

'That changes it all. I will have to think it out carefully – but it makes a whole new scenario.' He shook his head. 'Me. They were going for the head of Atlas. Why? Because I was the champion of Atlas, and they opposed its formation? No! That's not it. There seems only one logical explanation. I told you last time I saw you that I suspected the existence of a central figure – the puppetmaster who was taking control of all known militant organizations and welding them into a single cohesive and formidable entity. Well, Peter, I have been hunting this figure. I have learned much to confirm my suspicions since last we met. I believe

293

this person, or assembly of persons, does in fact exist – part of the new powers I have asked for Atlas were to be used to hunt and destroy this organization before it does grave damage – before it succeeds in so terrifying the nations of the world that it becomes itself a world power—' Parker stopped as though to gather his thoughts, and then went on in quiet, more measured tones. 'I think now that this is absolute proof that it does exist, and that it is aware of my suspicions and intentions to destroy it. When I set you up as Atlas agent at large, I believed you would make contact with the enemy – but, God knows, I did not expect it to come like this.'

He paused again, considering it. 'Incredible!' he marvelled. 'The one person whom I would never have suspected, you Peter. You could have reached me at any time, one of the few people who could. And the leverage! Your daughter – the protracted mutilations – I may have just misjudged the cunning and ruthlessness of the enemy.'

'Have you ever heard the name Caliph?' Peter asked.

'Where did you hear that?' Parker demanded harshly.

'The demand letter was signed Caliph, and Melissa-Jane heard her captors discussing it.'

'Caliph.' Parker nodded. 'Yes, I have heard the name, Peter. Since I last spoke to you. I have heard the name. Indeed I have.' He was silent again, sucking distractedly on his pipe, then he looked up. 'I will tell you how and when tomorrow when we meet at Thor, but now you have given me much to keep me awake tonight.'

He took Peter's arm and led him back towards the house. Warm yellow light and laughter spilled out from the downstairs windows, welcoming and gay, but both of them were withdrawn and silent as they trudged up the smoothly raked path.

At the garden door Kingston Parker paused, holding Peter back from entering.

'Peter, would you have done it?' he asked gruffly.

Peter answered him levelly without attempting to avoid his eyes. 'Yes, Kingston, I would have done it.'

'How?'

'Explosives.'

'Better than poison,' Parker grunted. 'Not as good as the gun.' And then angrily, 'We have to stop him, Peter. It is a duty that supersedes every other consideration.'

'What I have just told you does not alter our relationship?' Peter asked. 'The fact that I would have been your assassin – does not change it?'

'Strangely enough, it merely confirms what I have come to believe of you, Peter. You are a man with the hard ruthless streak we need, if we are to survive.' He smiled bleakly. 'I might wake up sweating in the night – but it doesn't alter what we have to do – you and I.'

Colin Noble with his cheroot, and opposite him Kingston Parker with the amber meerschaum, seemed to be in competition as to who could soonest render the air in the room incapable of supporting human life. It was already thick and blue, and the temporary headquarters of Thor Command lacked air-conditioning – but within minutes Peter had become so immersed in what he was hearing that the discomfort was forgotten.

Colin Noble was going over the details of the Irish operation, and all that had been gleaned from it.

'The house, the Old Manse, was burned to the ground, of course. The Irish constabulary had twenty men sifting through the ashes—' He spread his hands. 'A big nix. Nothing at all.'

'Next the contents of the Austin and its – provenance – how do you like that word, Peter baby? Provenance, that's a classy word.'

Parker smiled indulgently. 'Please go on, Colin.'

'The Austin was stolen in Dublin, and resprayed and fitted with the roof carrier. It contained nothing, no papers, nothing in the glove compartment or boot, it had been stripped and cleaned out by an expert—'

'The men,' Parker prompted him.

'Yes, sir. The men. The dead one first. Name of Gerald O'Shaughnessy, also known as "Gilly", born Belfast 1946—' As he spoke Colin picked up the file that lay on the table in front of him. It was five inches thick. ' – Do we want to read all of it? It's a hell of a story. The guy had a track record—'

'Only as far as it concerns Atlas,' Parker told him.

'There is no evidence as to when or how he became involved with this business—' Colin sketched the facts swiftly and succinctly. ' – So we end with the contents of his pockets. Six hundred pounds sterling, thirty-eight rounds of .38 ammunition, and papers in the name of Edward and Helen Barry – forged, but beautifully forged.' Colin closed the file with a slap. 'Nothing,' he repeated. 'Nothing we can use. Now the other man. Morrison – Claude Bertram Morrison – celebrated abortionist and dedicated alcoholic. Struck off the medical rolls in 1969—' Again he recounted the sordid history swiftly and accurately. ' – His price for the digital surgery was three thousand pounds – half in advance. Hell, that's cheaper than the Blue Cross.' Colin grinned but his eyes were black and bright with anger. 'I am pleased to report that he can expect a sentence of approximately fifteen years. They are going to throw the book at him. There is only one item of any possible interest which he could give us. Gilly O'Shaughnessy was the leader from whom he took his orders, O'Shaughnessy in turn took his orders from somebody called—' He paused dramatically. 'Yes, that's right. The name we have all heard before. Caliph.'

'Just one point here,' Kingston Parker interrupted.

'Caliph likes to use his name. He signs it on his correspondence. Even his lowliest thugs are given the name to use. Why?'

'I think I can answer that.' Peter stirred and raised his head. 'He wants us to know that he exists. We must have a focal point for our fear and hatred. When he was merely a nameless, faceless entity he was not nearly as menacing as he is now.'

'I think you are right.' Parker nodded his head gravely. 'By using the name he is building up a store of credibility which he will draw upon later. In future when Caliph says he will kill or mutilate we know he is in deadly earnest, there will be no compromise. He will do exactly as he promises. The man, or men, are clever psychologists.'

'There is just one aspect of the Irish operation we have not yet considered,' Peter broke in, frowning with concentration. 'That is – who was it that tipped us off, and what was the reason for that telephone call?'

They were all silent, until Parker turned to Colin.

'What do you think of that one?'

'I have discussed it with the police, of course. It was one of the first things that puzzled us. The police believe that Gilly O'Shaughnessy picked his hideout in Ireland because he was familiar with the terrain, and had friends there. It was his old stamping ground when he was with the Provos. He could move and disappear, get things fixed.' Colin paused and saw the sceptical expression on Peter's face. 'Well, look at it this way, Peter baby. He had a woman negotiate the lease on the Old Manse – Kate Barry, she called herself and signed it on the lease – so that was one ally. There must have been others, because he was able to buy a stolen and reworked automobile – he would have had difficulty doing that in Edinburgh or London without the word getting about.'

Peter nodded reluctantly. 'All right, having the Irish connection helped him—'

' – But there was the other side of the coin. O'Shaughnessy had enemies, even in the Provos. He was a ruthless bastard with a bloody record. We can only believe that one of those enemies saw the chance to make a score – the one who sold him the stolen auto, perhaps. We have had the recording of the tip-off call examined by language experts and had a run against the voice prints on the computer. Nothing definite. The voice was disguised, probably through a handkerchief and nose plugs, but the general feeling is that it was an Irishman who made the call. The boffins from the telephone department were able to test the loading of the line and guess it was a call from a foreign country – very likely Ireland, although they cannot be certain of that.'

Peter Stride raised one eyebrow slightly, and Colin chuckled weakly and waved the cheroot at him in a wide gesture of invitation.

'Okay. That's my best shot,' he said. 'Let's hear you do better. If you don't like my theories, you must have one of your own.'

'You are asking me to believe it was all a coincidence; that O'Shaughnessy just happened to run into an old enemy who just happened to tip us off twenty-four hours before the deadline for Melissa-Jane's hand to be amputated. Then it just so happened that we reached Laragh at exactly the same moment as O'Shaughnessy was pulling out and making a run for it. Is that what you want me to believe?'

'Something like that,' Colin admitted.

'Sorry, Colin. I just don't like coincidence.'

'Shoot!' Colin invited. 'Let's hear how it really happened.'

'I don't know,' Peter grinned placatingly. 'It is just that I have this feeling that Caliph doesn't deal in coincidence either. I have this other feeling that somehow Gilly O'Shaughnessy had the death mark on his forehead from the beginning. I have this feeling it was all part of the plan.'

'It must be great fun to have these feelings.' Colin was prickling a little. 'But they sure as hell aren't much help to me.'

'Take it easy.' Peter held up one hand in surrender. 'Let's accept tentatively that it happened your way, then—'

'But?' Colin asked.

'No buts – not until we get some more hard evidence—'

'Okay, buster.' There was no smile on Colin's face now, the wide mouth clamped in a grim line. 'You want hard evidence, try this one for size—'

'Hold it, Colin,' Parker shot in quickly, authoritatively. 'Wait for a moment before we come to that.' And Colin Noble deflated with a visible effort, the cords in his throat smoothing out and the line of mouth relaxed into the old familiar grin as he deferred to Kingston Parker.

'Let's backtrack here a moment,' Parker suggested. 'Peter came up with the name Caliph. In the meantime we had picked up the same name – but from an entirely different source. I promised Peter I would tell him about our source – because I think it gives us a new insight into this entire business.' He paused and tinkered with his pipe, using one of those small tools with folding blades and hooks and spikes with which pipe smokers arm themselves. He scraped the bowl and knocked a nub of half-burned tobacco into the ashtray, before peering into the pipe the way a rifleman checks the bore of his weapon. Peter realized that Parker used his pipe as a prop for his performances, the way a magician distracts his audience with flourishes and mumbo-jumbo. He was not a man to underestimate, Peter thought again for the hundredth time. Kingston Parker looked up at him and smiled, a conspiratorial smile as if to acknowledge that Peter had seen through his little act.

'Our news of Caliph comes from an unlikely direction – or rather, considering the name, a more likely direction. East. Riyadh to be precise. Capital city of Saudi Arabia, seat of King Khalid's oil empire. Our battered and beleaguered

Central Intelligence Agency has received an appeal from the King following the murder of one of his grandsons. You recall the case, I'm sure—' Peter had a strange feeling of *déjà-vu* as he listened to Kingston Parker confirming exactly the circumstances that he and Magda Altmann had discussed and postulated together, was it only three weeks before? ' – You see the King and his family are in a very vulnerable position really. Did you know that there are at least seven hundred Saudi princes who are multi-millionaires, and who are close to the King's affections and power structure? It would be impossible to guard that many potential victims adequately. It's really damned good thinking – you don't have to seize a hostage with all the attendant risks. There is virtually an unlimited supply of them walking around, ripe for plucking, and an inexhaustible supply of assassins to be either pressured or paid to do the job, just as long as you have the information and leverage, or just enough money. Caliph seems to have all that.'

'What demand has been made upon Khalid?' Peter asked.

'We know for certain that he has received a demand, and that he has appealed to the CIA for assistance to protect and guard his family. The demand came from an agency or person calling himself Caliph. We do not know what the demand is – but it may be significant that Khalid and the Shah of Persia have both agreed that they will not support a crude oil price increase at the next pricing session of OPEC, but on the contrary they will push for a five per cent decrease in the price of crude.'

'Caliph's thinking has paid off again,' Peter murmured.

'It looks like it, doesn't it.' Parker nodded, and then chuckled bitterly. 'And once again you get the feeling, as with his demands to the South African Government, that his final objective is desirable – even if the way he goes about procuring it is slightly unconventional, to say the least.'

'To say the very least,' Peter agreed quietly, remembering

the feel of Melissa-Jane's fever-racked body against his chest.

'So there is no doubt now that what we feared, is fact. Caliph exists—' said Parker.

'Not only exists, but flourishes,' Peter agreed.

'Alive and well with a nice house in the suburbs.' Colin lit the stub of his cheroot before going on. 'Hell! He succeeded at Johannesburg. He is succeeding at Riyadh – where does he go from there – why not the Federation of Employers in West Germany? The Trade Union leaders in Great Britain? – Any group powerful enough to affect the fate of nations, and small enough to be terrorized as individuals.'

'It's a way to sway and direct the destiny of the entire world – you just cannot guard all the world's decision-makers from personal attack,' Peter agreed. 'And it's no argument to point out that because his first two targets have been South Africa and the oil monopoly, then the long term results will be to the benefit of mankind. His ultimate target will almost certainly be the democratic process itself. I don't think there can be any doubt that Caliph sees himself as a god. He sees himself as the paternal tyrant. His aim is to cure the ills of the world by radical surgery, and to maintain its health by unrestrained force and fear.'

Peter could remain seated no longer. He pushed back his chair and crossed to the windows, standing there in the soldier's stance, balanced on the balls of his feet with both hands clasped lightly behind his back. There was an uninspiring view of the high barbed-wire fence, part of the airfield and the corrugated sheet wall of the nearest hangar. A Thor sentry paced before the gates with a white M.P. helmet on his head and side arm strapped to his waist. Peter watched him without really seeing him, and behind him the two men at the table exchanged a significant glance. Colin Noble asked a silent question and Parker answered with a curt nod of affirmative.

'All right, Peter,' Colin said. 'A little while back you asked for hard facts. I promised to give you a few.'

Peter turned back from the window and waited.

'Item One. During the time that Gilly O'Shaughnessy held Melissa-Jane in Laragh, two telephone calls were made from the Old Manse. They were both international calls. They both went through the local telephone exchange. The first call was made at seven p.m. local time on the first of this month. That would have been the first day that they could have reached the hideout. We have to guess it was an "All Well" report to the top management. The second call was exactly seven days later again at seven o'clock local time precisely. To the same number. We have to guess that it was another report, "All is still well". Both calls were less than one minute in duration. Just time enough to pass a pre-arranged code message—' Colin broke off and looked again at Kingston Parker.

'Go on,' Parker instructed.

'The calls were to a French number. Rambouillet 47–87–47.'

Peter felt it hit him in the stomach, a physical blow, and he flinched his head, for a moment closing both his eyes tightly. He had called that number so often, the numerals were graven on his memory.

'No.' He shook his head, and opened his eyes. 'I'm not going to believe it.'

'It's true, Peter,' Parker said gently.

Peter walked back to his seat. His legs felt rubbery and shaky under him. He sat down heavily.

The room was completely silent. Neither of the other two looked directly at Peter Stride.

Kingston Parker made a gesture to Colin and obediently he slid the red box file, tied with red tapes, across the cheap vinyl-topped table.

Parker untied the tapes and opened the file. He shuffled the papers, scanning them swiftly. Clearly he was adept at speed reading and was able to assimilate each typed double-spaced page at a glance – but now he was merely waiting for Peter to recover from the shock. He knew the contents of the red file almost by heart.

Peter Stride slumped in the steel-framed chair with its uncushioned wooden seat, staring sightlessly at the bulletin board on the opposite wall on which were posted the Thor rosters.

He found it hard to ride the waves of dismay that flooded over him. He felt chilled and numbed, the depth of this betrayal devastated him, and when he closed his eyes again he had a vivid image of the slim, tender body with the childlike breasts peeping through a silken curtain of dark hair.

He straightened in his seat, and Kingston Parker recognized the moment and looked up at him, half closing the file and turning it towards him.

The cover bore the highest security gradings available to Atlas Command – and below them was typed:

ALTMANN MAGDA IRENE. Born KUTCHINSKY

Peter realized that he had never known her second name was Irene. Magda Irene. Hell, they were really ugly names – made special only by the woman who bore them.

Parker turned the file back to himself and began to speak quietly.

'When last you and I met, I told you of the special interest we had in this lady. That interest has continued, unabated, since then, or rather it has gathered strength with every fresh item of information that has come to us.' He opened the file again and glanced at it as if to refresh his memory. 'Colin has been very successful in enlisting the full co-operation of the intelligence agencies of both our countries, who in turn have been able to secure that of the French and – believe it or not – the Russians. Between the

303

four countries we have been able to at last piece together the woman's history—' He broke off. 'Remarkable woman,' and shook his head in admiration. 'Quite incredible really. I can understand how she is able to weave spells around any man she chooses. I can understand, Peter, your evident distress. I am going to be utterly blunt now – we have no time nor space in which to manoeuvre tactfully around your personal feelings. We know that she has taken you as a lover. You notice that I phrase that carefully. Baroness Altmann takes lovers, not the other way around. She takes lovers deliberately and with careful forethought. I have no doubt that once she has made the decision, she accomplishes the rest of it with superb finesse.'

Peter remembered her coming to him and the exact words she had used. 'I am not very good at this, Peter, and I want so badly to be good for you.'

The words had been chosen with the finesse that Kingston Parker had just spoken of. They were exactly turned to make herself irresistible to Peter – and afterwards she had given the gentle lie to them with the skill and devilish cunning of her hands and mouth and body.

'You see, Peter. She had special and expert training in all the arts of love. There are probably few women in the Western world who know as much about reading a man, and then pleasing him. What she knows she did not learn in Paris or London or New York—' Kingston Parker paused and frowned at Peter. 'This is all theory and hearsay, Peter. You are in a better position to say just how much of it is false?'

The ultimate skill in pleasing a man is to fuel his own belief in himself, Peter thought, as he returned Parker's inquiring gaze with expressionless eyes. He remembered how with Magda Altmann he had felt like a giant, capable of anything. She had made him feel like that with a word, a smile, a gift, a touch – that was the ultimate skill.

He did not answer Parker's question. 'Go on please,

Kingston,' he invited. Externally, he had himself completely under control now. His right hand lay on the table top, with the fingers half open, relaxed.

'I told you that even as a child she showed special talents. In languages, mathematics – her father was an amateur mathematician of some importance – chess and other games of skill. She attracted attention. Especially she attracted attention because her father was a member of the Communist Party—' Parker broke off as Peter lifted his head in sharp inquiry. ' – I'm sorry, Peter. We did not know that when last we met. We have learned it since from the French, they have access to the party records in Paris it seems, and it was confirmed by the Russians themselves. Apparently the child used to accompany her father to meetings of the Party, and soon showed a precocious political awareness and understanding. Her father's friends were mostly party members, and after his death – there still remains a mystery around his death. Neither the French nor the Russians are forthcoming on the subject. – Anyway, after his death, Magda Kutchinsky was cared for by these friends. It seemed she was passed on from family to family—' Kingston Parker slid a postcard-sized photograph from a marbline envelope and passed it across the table to Peter, ' – from this period.'

It showed a rather skinny girl in short skirts and dark stockings, wearing the yoked collar and straw bonnet of the French schoolgirl. Her hair was in two short braids, tied with ribbons, and she held a small fluffy white dog in her arms. The background was a Parisian summer park scene, with a group of men playing *boule* and chestnut trees in full leaf.

The child's face was delicately featured with huge beautiful eyes, somehow wise and compassionate beyond her age, and yet still imbued with the fresh innocence of childhood.

'You can see she already had all the markings of spectacular beauty.' Kingston Parker grunted, and reached across to take back the photograph. For a moment Peter's fingers tightened instinctively; he would have like to have kept it, but he relaxed and let it go. Parker glanced at it again and then slipped it back into the envelope.

'Yes. She attracted much interest, and very soon an uncle from the old country wrote to her. There were photographs of her father and the mother she had never known, anecdotes of her infancy and her father's youth. The child was enchanted. She had never known she had an uncle. Her father had never spoken of his relatives, but now at last the little orphan found she had family. It took only a few more letters, exchanges of delight and affection, and then it was all arranged. The uncle came to fetch her in person – and Magda Kutchinsky went back to Poland.' Parker spread his hands. 'It was easy as that.'

'The missing years,' Peter said, and his voice sounded strange in his own ears. He cleared his throat and shifted uncomfortably under Parker's piercing but understanding gaze.

'No longer missing, Peter. We have been fed a little glimmering of what happened during those years – and we have been able to fill in the rest of it from what we knew already.'

'The Russians?' Peter asked, and when Parker nodded, Peter went on with a bitter tang to his voice. 'They seem to be very forthcoming, don't they? I have never heard of them passing information – at least not valuable information – so readily.'

'They have their reasons in this case,' Parker demurred. 'Very good reasons as it turns out – but one will come to those in due course.'

'Very well.'

'The child returned with her uncle to Poland, Warsaw. And there was an extravagant family reunion. We are not certain if this was her real family, or whether the child was provided with a foster family for the occasion. In any event, the uncle soon announced that if Magda would submit to examination there was an excellent chance that she would be provided with a scholarship to one of the élite colleges of the USSR. We can imagine that she passed her examination with great distinction and her new masters must have congratulated themselves on their discovery.

'The college is on the shores of the Black Sea near Odessa. It does not have a name, nor an old school tie. The students are very specially selected, the screening is rigorous and only the brightest and most talented are enrolled. They are soon taught that they are an élite group, and are streamed in the special direction that their various talents dictate. In Magda's case it was languages and politics, finance and mathematics. She excelled and at the age of seventeen graduated to a higher, more specialized branch of the Odessa college. There she was trained in special memory techniques, the already bright mind was honed down to a razor edge. I understand that one of the less difficult exercises was to be given access to a list of a hundred diverse items for sixty seconds. The list had to be repeated from memory, in the correct order, twenty-four hours later.' Parker shook his head again, expressing his admiration.

'At the same time she was also trained to fit naturally into upper-class international Western society. Dress, food, drink, cosmetics, manners, popular music and literature, cinema, theatre, democratic politics, business procedures, the operation of stocks and commodities markets, the more mundane secretarial skills, modern dancing, the art of love-making and pleasuring men – that and much else, all of it taught by experts – flying, skiing, weapons, the rudiments of electronics and mechanical engineering and every other skill that a top-class agent might have to call upon.

'She was the star of her course and emerged from it much as the woman you know. Poised, skilled, beautiful, motivated – and deadly.

'At the age of nineteen she knew more, was capable of

307

more, than most other human beings, male or female, twice her age. The perfect agent, except for a small flaw in her make-up that only showed up later. She was too intelligent and too personally ambitious.' Kingston Parker smiled for the first time in twenty minutes. ' – Which of course is a pseudonym for greed. Her masters did not recognize it in her, and perhaps at that age it was only latent greed. She had not yet been fully exposed to the attractions of wealth – nor of unlimited power.'

Kingston Parker broke off, leaned across the table towards Peter. He seemed to change direction then, smiling an inward knowledgeable smile, as though pondering a hidden truth.

'Greed for wealth alone belongs essentially to the lower levels of human intelligence. It is only the developed and advanced mind that can truly appreciate the need for power—' He saw the protest in Peter's expression. ' – No, no, I don't mean merely the power to control one's own limited environment, merely the power of life and death over a few thousand lives – not that, but true power. Power to change the destiny of nations, power such as Caesar or Napoleon wielded, such as the President of the United States wields – that is the ultimate greed, Peter. A magnificent and noble greed.'

He was silent a moment, as though glimpsing some vision of splendour. Then he went on:

'I digress. Forgive me,' and turned to Colin Noble. 'Do we have some coffee, Colin? I think we could all do with a cup now.'

Colin went to the machine that blooped and gurgled and winked its red eye in the corner, and while he filled the cups, the charged atmosphere in the room eased a little, and Peter tried to arrange his thoughts in some logical sequence. He looked for the flaws and weak places in the story but could find none – instead he remembered only the feel of her mouth, the touch of her hands on his body. Oh

God, it was a stab of physical pain, a deep ache in the chest and groin, as he remembered how she had coursed him like a running stag, driving and goading him on to unvisited depths of his being. Could such skills be taught, he wondered, and if so, by whom? He had a horrifying thought of a special room set on the heights above the Black Sea, with that slim, vulnerable tender body practising its skills, learning love as though it were cookery or small arms practice – and then he shut his mind firmly against it, and Kingston Parker was speaking again, balancing his coffee cup primly with his pinky finger raised, like an old maid at a tea party.

'So she arrived back in Paris and it fell at her feet. It was a triumphant progress.' Kingston Parker prodded in the file with his free hand, spilling out photographs of Magda – Magda dancing in the ballroom of the Elysée Palace, Magda leaving a Rolls-Royce limousine outside Maxim's in the rue Royale, Magda skiing, riding, beautiful, smiling, poised – and always there were men. Rich, well-fed, sleek men.

'I told you once there were eight sexual liaisons.' Kingston Parker used that irritating expression again. 'We have had reason to revise that figure. The French take a very close interest in that sort of thing, they have added to the list.' He flicked over the photographs. 'Pierre Hammond, Deputy Minister of Defence—' And another. 'Mark Vincent, head of mission at the American Consulate—'

'Yes,' Peter cut in short, but still there was a sickly fascination in seeing the faces of these men. He had imagined them accurately, he realized, without particular relish.

'Her masters were delighted – as you can imagine. With a male agent it is sometimes necessary to wait a decade or more for results while he moles his way into the system. With a young and beautiful woman she has her greatest value when those assets are freshest. Magda Kutchinsky gave them magnificent value. We do not know the exact extent of her contributions – our Russian friends have not bared everything to us, I'm afraid, but I estimate that it was about this time they began to realize her true potential. She had the magical touch, but her beauty and youth could not last for ever—' Kingston Parker made a deprecating gesture with the slim pianist's hands. ' – We do not know if Aaron Altmann was a deliberate choice by her masters. But it seems likely. Think of it – one of the richest and most powerful men in Western Europe, one who controlled most of the steel and heavy engineering producers, the single biggest armaments complex, electronics – all associated and sensitive secondary industries. He was a widower, childless, so under French law his wife could inherit his entire estate. He was known to be fighting a slowly losing battle with cancer, so his life term was limited – and he was also a Zionist and one of the most trusted and influential members of Mossad. It was beautiful. Truly beautiful,' said Kingston Parker. 'Imagine being able to undermine a man of that stature, perhaps being able to double him! Though that seemed an extravagant dream – not even the most beautiful siren of history could expect to turn a man like Aaron Altmann. He is a separate study on his own, another incredible human being with the strength and courage of a lion – until the cancer wore him out. Again I digress, forgive me. Somebody, either the Director of the NKVD in Moscow, or Magda Kutchinsky's control at the Russian Embassy in Paris, who was, incidentally, the Chief NKVD Commissar for Western Europe, such was her value, or Magda Kutchinsky herself, picked Aaron Altmann. Within two years she was indispensable to him. She was cunning enough not to use her sexual talents upon him immediately. Altmann could have any woman who took his fancy, and he usually did. His sexual appetites were legendary, and they probably were the cause of his remaining childless. A youthful indiscretion resulted in a venereal disease with complications. It was later completely cured, but the damage was irreversible, he never produced an heir.'

He was a man who would have toyed with her and cast her aside as soon as he tired of her, if she had been callow enough to make herself immediately available to him.

First, she won his respect and admiration. Perhaps she was the first woman he had ever met whose brain and strength and determination matched his own—

Kingston Parker selected another photograph and passed it across the table. Fascinated, Peter stared at the black and white image of a heavily built man with a bull neck, and a solid thrusting jaw. Like so many men of vast sexual appetite, he was bald except for a Friar Tuck frill around the cannon ball dome of his skull. But there were humorous lines chiselled about his mouth, and his eyes, though fierce, looked as though they too could readily crinkle with laughter lines. Portrait of Power, Peter thought.

'When at last she gave him access to her body, it must have been like some great electrical storm.' Kingston Parker seemed to be deliberately dwelling on her past love affairs, and Peter would have protested had not the information he was receiving been so vital. 'This man and woman must have been able to match each other once again. Two very superior persons, two in a hundred million probably – it is interesting to speculate what might have happened if they had been able to produce a child.' Kingston Parker chuckled. 'It would probably have been a mongolian idiot – life is like that.'

Peter moved irritably, hating this turn in the conversation, and Parker went on smoothly.

'So they married, and NKVD had a mole in the centre of Western industry. Narmco, Altmann's armaments complex, was manufacturing top secret American, British and French missile hardware for NATO. The new Baroness was on the Board, was in fact Deputy Chairman of Narmco. We can be sure that armaments blueprints were passed, not by the sheet but by the truckload. Every night, the leaders and decision-makers of the Western world sat at the new

Baroness's board and swilled her champagne. Every conversation, every nuance and indiscretion was recorded by that specially trained memory, and slowly, inevitably, the Baron's strength was whittled away. He began to rely more and more upon her. We do not know exactly when she began to assist him with his Mossad activities – but when it happened the Russians had succeeded in their design. In effect they had succeeded in turning Baron Aaron Altmann, they had his right hand and his heart – for by this time the dying Baron was completely besotted by the enchantress. They could expect to inherit the greater part of Western European heavy industry. It was all very easy – until the latent defect in the Baroness's character began to surface. We can only imagine the alarm of her Russian masters when they detected the first signs that the Baroness was working for herself alone. She was brighter by far than any of the men who had up until that time controlled her, and she had been given a taste of real power. The taste seemed very much to her liking. We can only imagine the gargantuan battle of wills between the puppetmasters and the beautiful puppet that had suddenly developed a mind and ambitions of her very own – quite simply her ambition now was to be the most wealthy and powerful woman since Catherine of Russia, and the makings were almost within her pretty hands – except—'

Kingston Parker stopped; like a born storyteller, he knew instinctively how to build up the tension in his audience. He rattled his coffee cup.

'This talking is thirsty business.' Colin and Peter had to rouse themselves with a physical effort. They had been mesmerized by the story and the personality of the storyteller. When Parker had his cup refilled, he sipped at it, then went on speaking.

'There was one last lever her Russian masters had over her. They threatened to expose her. It was quite a neat stroke, really. A man like Aaron Altmann would have acted like an enraged bull if he had known how he had been deceived. His reaction was predictable. He would have divorced Magda immediately. Divorce is difficult in France – but not for a man like the Baron. Without his protection Magda was nothing, less than nothing, for her value to the Russians would have come to an end. Without the Altmann Empire her dreams of power would disappear like a puff of smoke. It was a good try – it would have worked against an ordinary person, but of course they were not dealing with an ordinary person—'

Parker paused again; it was clear he was as wrapped up by the story as they were, and he was drawing out the pleasure of the telling of it.

'I have been doing a lot of talking,' he smiled at Peter. 'I'm going to let you have a chance now, Peter. You know her a little, you have learned a lot more about her in the last hour. Can you guess what she did?'

Peter began to shake his head – and then it crashed in upon him with sickening force, and he stared at Parker, the pupils of his eyes dilating with the strength of his revulsion.

'I think you have guessed.' Parker nodded. 'Yes, we can imagine that by this stage she was becoming a little impatient herself. The Baron was taking a rather long time to die.'

'Christ, it's horrible.' Peter grunted, as though in pain.

' – From one point of view, I agree.' Parker nodded. 'But if you look at it like a chess player, and remember she is a player of Grand Master standard, it was a brilliant stroke. She arranged that the Baron be kidnapped. There are witnesses to the fact that she insisted on the Baron accompanying her that day. He was feeling very bad, and he did not want to go sailing, but she insisted that the sun and fresh air would be good for him. He never took his bodyguard when he went sailing. There were just the two of them. A very fast cruiser was waiting offshore—' He spread his hands. ' – You know the details?'

'No,' Peter denied it.

'The cruiser rammed the yacht. Picked the Baron out of the water, but left the Baroness. An hour later there was a radio message to the coastguard; they went out and found her still clinging to the wreckage. The kidnappers were very concerned that she survived.'

'They may have wanted a loving wife to bargain with,' Peter suggested swiftly.

'That is possible, of course, and she certainly played the role of the bereaved wife to perfection. When the ransom demand came it was she who forced the Board of Altmann Industries to ante up the twenty-five million dollars. She personally took the cash to the rendezvous – alone.' Parker paused significantly.

'She didn't need the money.'

'Oh, but she did,' Parker contradicted. 'The Baron was not in his dotage, you know. His hands were still very firmly on the reins – and the purse strings. Magda had as much as any ordinary wife could wish for, furs, jewellery, servants, clothes, cars, boats – pocket money, around two hundred thousand dollars a year, paid to her as a salary from Altmann Industries. Any ordinary wife would have been well content – but she was not an ordinary wife. We must believe she had already planned how to carry forward her dreams of unlimited power – and it needed money, not thousands but millions. Twenty-five million would be a reasonable stop-gap, until she could get her pretty little fingers on the big apple. – She drove with the cash, in thousand-Swiss-franc bills, I understand; she drove alone to some abandoned airfield and had a plane come pick it up and fly it out to Switzerland. Damned neat.'

'But—' Peter searched for some means of denial. ' – But the Baron was mutilated. She couldn't—'

'Death is death, mutilation may have served some obscure purpose. God knows, we're dealing with an Eastern mind, devious, sanguinary – perhaps the mutilation was

314

merely to make any suspicion of the wife completely far-fetched – just as you immediately used it to protect her.'

He was right, of course. The mind that could plan and execute the rest of such a heinous scheme would not baulk at the smaller niceties of execution. He had no more protest to make.

'So let us review what she had achieved by this stage. She was rid of the Baron, and the restrictions he placed upon her. An example of these restrictions, for we will find it significant later: she was very strongly in favour of Narmco banning the sale of all weapons and armaments to the South African Government. The Baron, ever the business-man, looked upon that country as a lucrative market. There was also the South African sympathy for Zionism. He overruled her, and Narmco continued to supply aircraft, missiles and light armaments to that country right up until the official UN resolution to enforce a total arms embargo, with France ratifying it. Remember the Baroness's anti-South African attitude. We come to it again later.

'She was rid of the Baron. She was rid of her Russian control, well able to maintain a small army to protect herself. Even her former Russian masters would hesitate to take revenge on her. She was a French Grande Dame now. She had gained significant working capital – twenty-five million for which she was not accountable to another living human being. She had gained an invincible power base at Altmann Industries. Although she was still under certain checks and safeguards from the Board of Directors, yet she had access to all its information-gathering services, to its vast resources. As the head of such a colossus she had the respect of and sympathy of the French Government, and as a fringe benefit – limited but significant access to their intelligence systems. Then there was the Mossad connec-tion: was she not the heir to Aaron Altmann's position—'

Peter suddenly remembered Magda speaking of her 'sources' – and never identifying them. Was she really able to use the French and Israeli intelligence as her own private agencies? It seemed impossible. But he was learning swiftly that when dealing with Magda Altmann, anything was possible – as Kingston Parker had pointed out, she was not an ordinary person – but Parker was speaking again.

'There was a period then of consolidation, a time when she gathered up the reins that Aaron had dropped. There were changes amongst the top management throughout Altmann Industries as she replaced those who might oppose her with her own minions. A time of planning and organizing, and then the first attempt to govern and prescribe the destiny of nations. She chose the nation which most offended her personal view of the new world she was going to build. We will never know what made her choose the name of Caliph—'

'You have to be wrong.' Peter squeezed his eyelids closed with thumb and forefinger. 'You just don't know her.'

'I don't think anybody knows her, Peter,' Kingston Parker murmured, and fiddled with his pipe. 'I'm sorry, we are going pretty fast here. Do you want to back up and ask any questions?'

'No, it's all right.' Peter opened his eyes again. 'Go on, will you, Kingston?'

'One of the most important lessons that Baroness Altmann had learned was the ease with which force and violence can be used, and their tremendous effect and profitability. Bearing this lesson in mind, the Baroness chose her first act as the new ruler of mankind, and the choice was dictated by her early political convictions, those convictions formed at her father's knee and at the Communist Party meetings that she had attended as a precocious child in Paris. There is a further suggestion that the choice was reinforced by the Altmann banking corporation's interests in South African gold sales, for by this time the Baroness had tempered her socialist and communist leanings with a good healthy dollop of capitalistic self-interest. We can only

316

guess, but if the scheme to bring out forty tons of gold – and a black-based government-in-exile – had succeeded, it would not have taken very long for Caliph to gain control of both government and gold—' Parker shrugged. ' – We just cannot say how ambitious, even grandiose, those plans were. But we can say that Caliph, or the Baroness, recruited her team for the execution of the plan with the skill she brought to anything she handled.' He broke off, and smiled. 'I think all three of us remember the taking of Flight 070 vividly enough not to have to go once more over the details. Let me just remind you that it would have succeeded, in fact it had actually succeeded, when Peter here made his unscheduled move that brought it all down. But it succeeded. That was the important thing. Caliph could afford to congratulate herself. Her information was impeccable. She had chosen the right people for the job. She even knew the name of the officer who would command the anti-terrorist force which would be sent to intervene, and her psychology had been excellent. The execution of the four hostages had so shocked and numbed the opposition that they were powerless – the cup had been dashed from her lips by one man alone. Inevitably her interest in that man was aroused. Possibly with feminine intuition she was able to recognize in him the qualities which could be turned to her own purpose. She had that indomitable streak in her make-up that is able to recognize even in the dust of disaster that material for future victory—' Parker shifted his bulk, and made a small deprecatory gesture. ' – I hope this will not seem immodest if I bring myself into the story as this stage. I had been given the hint that something like Caliph existed. In fact this may not have been her first act after the killing of Aaron Altmann. Two other successful kidnappings have her style – one of them the OPEC ministers in Vienna – but we cannot be sure. I had been warned and I was waiting for Caliph to surface. Dearly I would have loved a chance to interrogate one of the hijackers—'

'They would have had nothing to tell you,' Peter interjected brusquely. 'They were merely pawns, like the doctor we captured in Ireland.'

Parker sighed. 'Perhaps you are right, Peter. But at the time I believed that our only lead to Caliph had been severed. Later when the thing had been done and I had recovered from the shock of it, it suddenly occurred to me that the lead was still there – stronger than ever. You were that lead, Peter. That was why I recommended that your resignation be accepted. If you had not resigned, I would have forced you out anyway, but you played along superbly by resigning—' He smiled again. ' – I have never thanked you for that.'

'Don't mention it,' said Peter grimly. 'I like to be of service.'

'And you were. Almost immediately you were on the loose, the Baroness began making her approach. First she collected every known fact about you. Somehow she even got a computer run on you. That's a fact. An unauthorized run was made on the Central Intelligence computer four days after your resignation. She must have liked what she got, for there was the Narmco offer – through conventional channels. Your refusal must have truly excited her interest, for she used her connections to have herself invited down to Sir Steven's country house.' Parker chuckled. 'My poor Peter, you found yourself without warning in the clutches of one of history's most accomplished enchantresses. I know enough about the lady to guess that her approach to you was very carefully calculated from the complete information that she had on you. She knew exactly what type of woman attracted you. Fortunately, she fitted the general physical description—'

'What is that?' Peter demanded. He was unaware that he had a specific type of physical preference.

'Tall, slim and brunette,' Parker told him promptly.

'Think about it,' he invited. 'All your women have been that.'

He was right, of course, Peter realized. Hell, even at thirty-nine years of age it was still possible to learn something about yourself.

'You're a cold-blooded bastard, Kingston. Did anybody ever tell you that?'

'Frequently.' Kingston smiled. 'But it's not true, and compared to Baroness Altmann I am Father Christmas.' And he became serious again. 'She wanted to find out what we at Atlas know about her activities. She knew by this stage that we had our suspicions, and through you she had an inside ear. Of course, your value would deteriorate swiftly the longer you were out of Thor – but you could still be useful in a dozen other ways. As a bonus you could be expected to do a good job at Narmco. All her expectations were fulfilled, and exceeded. You even thwarted an assassination attempt on her life—'

Peter lifted an eyebrow in inquiry.

' – On the road to Rambouillet that night. Here we are only guessing, but it's a pretty well-informed guess. The Russians had by this time despaired of returning her to the fold. They had also suspicions as to her role as Caliph. They decided on a radical cure for their one-time star agent. They either financed and organized the assassination attempt themselves, or they tipped off Mossad that she had murdered Aaron Altmann. I would be inclined to believe that they hired the killers themselves – because the Mossad usually do their own dirty work. Anyway, with NKVD or Mossad as paymasters, an ambush was set up on the Rambouillet road and you drove into it. I know you don't like coincidence, Peter, but I believe it was merely coincidence that you were driving the Baroness's Maserati that night.'

'All right,' Peter murmured. 'If I swallow the rest of the hog, that little crumb goes down easily enough.'

'That attempt severely alarmed the Baroness. She was not certain who had been the author. I think she believed it was Atlas Command, or at the very least that we had something to do with it. Almost immediately after that you were able to confirm our interest in her, and our knowledge that Caliph existed. I invited you to America, Colin brought you to meet me, and when you returned you either told her about it, or in some way confirmed her suspicions of Atlas Command and Kingston Parker. I am guessing again – but how close am I, Peter? Be honest.'

Peter stared at him, trying to keep his face expressionless while his mind raced. That was exactly how it had happened.

'We were all hunting Caliph. You saw no disloyalty in discussing it with her.' Parker prompted him gently, and Peter nodded once curtly.

'You believed that we had common goals,' Parker went on with deep understanding and compassion. 'You thought we were all hunting Caliph. That is right.'

'She knew I had been to America to see you before I told her. I don't know how – but she knew,' Peter said stiffly. He felt like a traitor.

'I understand,' Parker said simply. He reached across the table and once again placed his hand on Peter's shoulder. He squeezed it while he looked into Peter's eyes, a gesture of affirmation and trust. Then he laid both hands on top of the table.

'She knew who was the hunter then, and she knew enough about me to know I was dangerous. You were probably the only man in the world who could reach me and do the job – but you had to be motivated. She picked the one and only lever that would move you. She picked it unerringly – just as she had done everything else. It would have worked – in one stroke she would have gotten rid of the hunter, and she would have acquired a top-class assassin. When you had done the job, you would have belonged to

Caliph for all time. She would have used you to kill again and again, and each time you killed you would be more deeply enmeshed in her net. You really were a very valuable prize, Peter. Valuable enough for her to find it worthwhile to use her sexual wiles upon you.'

He saw the lumps of clenched muscle at the corner of Peter's jaw, and the fire in his eyes.

'You are also a very attractive man, and who knows but she felt the need to combine business and pleasure? She is a lady with strongly developed sexual appetites.'

Peter felt a violent urge to punch him in the face. He needed some outlet for his rage. He felt belittled, soiled and used.

'She was clever enough to realize that the sex was not enough of a hold to force you to commit murder. So she took your daughter, and immediately had her mutilated – just as at Johannesburg she had executed hostages without hesitation. The world must learn to fear Caliph.'

There was no smile on Parker's face now.

'I truly believe that if you had not been able to deliver my head by the deadline, she would not have hesitated to carry out the next mutilation, and the one after that.'

Again Peter was assailed by a wave of nausea as he remembered that shrivelled white lump of flesh with the scarlet fingernail floating horribly in its tiny bottle.

'We were saved from that by the most incredible piece of luck. The Provo informer,' said Parker. 'And again the understandable eagerness of the Russians to co-operate with us. It is a wonderful opportunity for them to hand us their problem. They have let us have an almost full account of the lady and her history.'

'But what are we going to do about it?' Colin Noble asked. 'Our hands are tied. Do we just have to wait for the next atrocity – do we have to hope we will get another lucky break when Caliph kills the next Arab prince, or machine-guns the Shah's sister?'

'That will happen – unless they push through the OPEC decision,' Parker predicted levelly. 'The lady has converted very easily to the capitalist system now that she owns half of Europe's industry. A reduction in the oil price would benefit her probably more than any other individual on earth – and at the same time it will also benefit the great bulk of humanity. How nicely that squares all her political and personal interests.'

'But if she gets away with it—' Colin insisted, ' – what will be her next act of God?'

'Nobody can predict that,' Parker murmured, and they both turned their heads to look at Peter Stride.

He seemed to have aged twenty years. The lines at the corners of his mouth were cut in deeply like the erosion of weathered granite. Only his eyes were blue and alive and fierce as those of a bird of prey.

'I want you to believe what I am going to say now, Peter. I have not told you all this to put pressure on you,' Parker assured him quietly. 'I have told you only what I believe is necessary for you to know – to protect yourself if you should elect to return to the lion's den. I am not ordering you to do so. The risks involved cannot be overestimated. With a lesser man I would term it suicidal. However, now that you are forewarned, I believe you are the one man who could take Caliph on her own ground. Please do not misunderstand what I mean by that. I am not for a moment suggesting assassination. In fact I expressly forbid you to even think in that direction. I would not allow it, and if you acted independently, I would do my utmost to see that you were brought to justice. No, all I ask is that you keep close to Caliph and try to outguess her. Try to expose her so we can lawfully act to take her out of action. I want you to put out of your mind the emotional issues – those hostages at Johannesburg, your own daughter – try to forget them, Peter. Remember we are neither judge nor executioner—' Parker went on speaking quietly and insistently, and Peter watched his lips with narrowed eyes, hardly listening to the words, trying to think clearly and see his course ahead – but his thoughts were a children's carousel, going around and around with fuss and fury but returning with every revolution to the one central conclusion.

There was only one way to stop Caliph. The thought of attempting to bring someone like Baroness Magda Altmann to justice – in a French court – was laughable. Peter tried to force himself to believe that vengeance had no part in his decisions, but he had lived too long with himself to be able to pull off such a deceit. Yes, vengeance was part of it – and he trembled with the rage of remembrance, but it was not all of it. He had executed the German girl Ingrid, and Gilly O'Shaughnessy – and had not regretted the decision to do so. If it was necessary for them to die – then surely Caliph deserved to die a thousand times more.

And there is only one person who can do it, he realized.

Her voice was quick and light and warm, with just that fascinating trace of accent; he remembered it so well, but had forgotten the effect it could have upon him. His heart pounded as though he had run a long way.

'Oh, Peter. It's so good to hear your voice. I have been so worried. Did you get my cable?'

'No, which cable?'

'When I heard that you had freed Melissa-Jane. I sent you a cable from Rome.'

'I didn't get it – but it doesn't matter.'

'I sent it to you via Narmco – in Brussels.'

'It's probably waiting for me there. I haven't been in touch.'

'How is she, Peter?'

'She is fine now—' He found it strangely difficult to use

her name, or any form of endearment. He hoped that the strain would not sound in his voice. 'But we went through a hell of a time.'

'I know. I understand. I felt so helpless. I tried so hard, that's why I was out of contact, Peter *chéri*, but day after day there was no news.'

'It's all over now,' Peter said gruffly.

'I don't think so,' she said swiftly. 'Where are you calling from?'

'London.'

'When will you come back?'

'I telephoned Brussels an hour ago. Narmco wants me back urgently. I am taking a flight this afternoon.'

'Peter, I have to see you. I've been too long without you – but, oh *mon Dieu*, I have to be in Vienna tonight. – Wait, let me see, if I sent the Lear to fetch you now we could meet, even for an hour. You could take the late flight from Orly to Brussels and I could go on to Vienna with the Lear – please, Peter. I missed you so. We could have an hour together.'

One of the airport sub-managers met Peter as he disembarked from the Lear and led him to one of the VIP lounges above the main concourse.

Magda Altmann came swiftly to meet him as he stepped into the lounge – and he had forgotten how her presence could fill a room with light.

She wore a tailored jacket over a matching skirt, severe gun-metal grey and tremendously effective. She moved like a dancer on long graceful legs which seemed to articulate from the narrow waist – and Peter felt awkward and heavy-footed, for the awareness that he was in the presence of evil sat heavily upon him, weighting him down.

'Oh, Peter. What have they done to you?' she asked with quick concern flaring in those huge compassionate eyes. She reached up to touch his cheek.

The strain and horror of the last days had drawn him out to the edge of physical endurance. His skin had a greyish, sickly tone against which the dark new beard darkening his jaws contrasted strongly. There were more fine silver threads at his temples, gull's wings against the thicker darker waves of his hair, and his eyes were haunted. They had sunk deeply into their sockets.

'Oh, darling, darling,' she whispered, low enough so that the others in the room could not hear her, and she reached up with her mouth for his.

Peter had carefully schooled himself for this meeting. He knew how important it was that he should not in any way betray the knowledge he had. Magda must never guess that he had found her out. That would be deadly dangerous. He must act completely naturally. It was absolutely vital, but there was just that instant's remembrance of his daughter's pale wasted fever-racked features, and then he stooped and took Magda's mouth.

He forced his mouth to soften, as hers was soft and warm and moist, tasting of ripe woman and crushed petals. He made his body welcoming as hers was melting and trusting against his – and he thought he had succeeded completely until she broke from his embrace and leaned back, keeping those slim strong hips still pressed against his. She studied his face again, a swift probing, questioning gaze, and he saw it change deep in her eyes. The flame going out of them leaving only a cold merciless green light, like the beautiful spark in the depths of a great emerald.

She had seen something; no there had been nothing to see. She had sensed something in him, the new awareness. Of course, she would have been searching for it. She needed only the barest confirmation – the quirk of expression on his mouth, the new wariness in his eyes, the slight stiffness and reserve in his body – all of which he thought he had been able to control perfectly.

'Oh, I am glad you are wearing blue now.' She touched the lapel of his casual cashmere jacket. 'It does suit you so well, my dear.'

He had ordered the jacket with her in mind, that was true – but now there was something brittle in her manner. It was as though she had withdrawn her true self, bringing down an invisible barrier between them.

'Come.' She turned away, leading him to the deep leather couch below the picture windows. Some airport official had been able to find flowers, yellow tulips, the first blooms of spring, and there was a bar and coffee machine.

She sat beside him on the couch, but not touching him, and with a nod dismissed her secretary. He moved across the room to join the two bodyguards, her grey wolves, and the three of them remained out of earshot, murmuring quietly amongst themselves.

'Tell me, please, Peter.' She was still watching him, but the cold green light in her eyes had been extinguished – she was friendly and concerned, listening with complete attention as he went step by step over every detail of Melissa-Jane's kidnapping.

It was an old rule of his to tell the complete truth when it would serve – and it served now, for Magda would know every detail. He told her of Caliph's demand for Kingston Parker's life, and his own response.

'I would have done it,' he told her frankly, and she hugged her own arms and shuddered once briefly.

'God, such evil can corrupt even the strongest and the best—' and now there was understanding softening her lips.

Peter went on to tell her of the lucky tip-off and the recovery of Melissa-Jane. He went into details of the manner in which she had been abused, of her terror and the psychological damage she had suffered – and he watched

Magda's eyes carefully. He saw something there, emphasized by the tiny frown that framed them. He knew that he could not expect feelings of guilt. Caliph would be far beyond such mundane emotion – but there was something there, not just stagey compassion.

'I had to stay with her. I think she needed those few days with me,' he explained.

'Yes. I am glad you did that, Peter.' She nodded, and glanced at her wristwatch. 'Oh, we have so little time left,' she lamented. 'Let's have a glass of champagne. We have a little to celebrate. At least Melissa-Jane is alive, and she is young and resilient enough to recover completely.'

Peter eased the cork and when it popped he poured creaming pale yellow Dom Perignon into the flutes, and smiled at her over the glass as they saluted each other.

'It's so good to see you, Peter.' She was truly a superb actress; she said it with such innocent spontaneity that he felt a surge of admiration for her despite himself. He crushed it down and thought that he could kill her now and here. He did not really need a weapon. He could use his hands if he had to, but the Cobra parabellum was in the soft chamois leather holster under his left armpit. He could kill her, and the two bodyguards across the room would gun him down instantly. He might take one of them, but the other one would get him. They were top men. He had picked them himself. They would get him.

'I'm sorry we will not be together for very long,' he countered, still smiling at her.

'Oh, *chéri*. I know, so am I.' She touched his forearm, the first touch since the greeting embrace. 'I wish it were different. There are so many things that we have to do, you and I, and we must forgive each other for them.'

Perhaps the words were meant to have a special significance; there was a momentary flash of the warm green fire in her eyes, and something else – perhaps a deep and unfathomable regret. Then she sipped the wine, and lowered the long curled lashes across her eyes, shielding them from his scrutiny.

'I hope we will never have anything terrible to forgive—'

For the first time he faced the act of killing her. Before it had been something clinical and academic, and he had avoided considering the deed itself. But now he imagined the impact of an explosive Velex bullet into that smooth sweet flesh. His guts lurched, and for the first time he doubted if he were capable of it.

'Oh, Peter, I hope so. More than anything in life, I hope that.' She lifted her lashes for a moment, and her eyes seemed to cling to his for an instant, pleading for something – forgiveness, perhaps. If he did not use the gun, then how would he do it, he wondered. Could he stand the feeling of cartilage and bone snapping and crackling under his fingers, could he hold the blade of knife into her flat hard belly and feel her fight it like a marlin fights the gleaming curved hook of the gaff?

The telephone on the bar buzzed, and the secretary picked it up on the second ring. He murmured into it.

'*Oui, oui. D'accord.*' And hung up. 'Ma Baronne, the aircraft is refuelled and ready to depart.'

'We will leave immediately,' she told him, and then to Peter, 'I am sorry.'

'When will I see you?' he asked.

She shrugged, and a little shadow passed over her eyes. 'It is difficult. I am not sure – I will telephone you. But now I must go, Peter. Adieu, my darling.'

When she had gone, Peter stood at the windows over-looking the airfield. It was a glorious spring afternoon, the early marguerites were blooming wild along the grassy verges of the main runways, like scattered gold sovereigns, and a flock of black birds hopped amongst them, probing and picking for insects, completely undisturbed by the jet shriek of a departing Swissair flight.

Peter ran his mind swiftly over the meeting. Carefully

identifying and isolating the exact moment when she had changed. When she had ceased to be Magda Altmann and become Caliph.

There was no doubt left now. Had there ever been, he wondered, or had it merely been his wish to find doubt?

Now he must harden himself to the act. It would be difficult, much more difficult than he had believed possible. Not once had they been alone, he realized then – always the two grey wolves had hovered around them. It was just another sign of her new wariness. He wondered if they would ever be alone together again – now that she was alerted.

Then abruptly he realized that she had not said 'Au revoir, my darling' but instead she had said 'Adieu, my darling'.

Was there a warning in that? A subtle hint of death – for if Caliph suspected him, he knew what her immediate reaction must be. Was she threatening, or had she merely discarded him, as Kingston Parker had warned that she would?

He could not understand the desolate feeling that swamped him at the thought that he might never see her again – except through the gunsight.

He stood staring out of the window, wondering how his career and his life had begun to disintegrate about him since first he had heard the name Caliph.

A polite voice at his shoulder startled him and he turned to the airport sub-manager. 'They are calling the KLM flight to Brussels now, General Stride.'

Peter roused himself with a sigh and picked up his overcoat and the crocodile skin Hermes briefcase that had been a gift from the woman he must kill.

There was such a volume of correspondence and urgent business piling the long desk in his new office that Peter had an excuse to put aside the detailed planning of the pre-emptive strike against Caliph.

To his mild surprise he found himself enjoying the jostle and haggle, the driving pace and the challenge of the market place. He enjoyed pitting wits and judgement against other sharp and pointed minds, he enjoyed the human interaction – and for the first time understood the fascination which this type of life had exerted over his brother Steven.

Three days after arriving back at his desk, the Iranian Air Force made their first order of the Narmco Kestrel missiles. One hundred and twenty units, over a hundred and fifty million dollars' worth. It was a good feeling, and could grow stronger, could finally become addictive, he realized.

He had always looked upon money as rather a nuisance, those degrading and boring sessions with bank managers and clerks of the income tax department, but now he realized that this was a different kind of money. He had glimpsed the world in which Caliph existed, and realized how once a human being became accustomed to manipulating this kind of money, then dreams of godlike power became believable, capable of being transmuted into reality.

He could understand, but could never forgive, and so at last, seven days after his return to Brussels, he forced himself to face up to what he must do.

Magda Altmann had withdrawn. She had made no further contact since that brief and unsatisfactory hour at Orly Airport.

He must go to her, he realized. He had lost his special inside position which would have made the task easier.

He could still get close enough to kill her, of that he was certain. Just as he had the opportunity to do so at Orly. However, if he did it that way it would be suicidal. If he survived the swift retribution of her guards, there would be the slower but inexorable processes of the law. He knew without bothering to consider it too deeply that he would be unable to use the defence of the Caliph story. No court would believe it. It would sound like the rantings of a maniac without the support of Atlas or the Intelligence systems of America and Britain. That support would not be forthcoming – of that he was certain. If he killed Caliph they would be delighted, but they would let him go to the guillotine without raising a voice in his defence. He could imagine the moral indignation of the civilized world if they believed that an unorthodox organization such as Atlas was employing assassins to murder the prominent citizens of a foreign and friendly nation.

No. He was on his own, completely. Parker had made that quite clear. And Peter realized that he did not want to die. He was not prepared to sacrifice his life to stop Caliph – not unless there was no other way. There had to be another way, of course.

As he planned it he thought of the victim only as Caliph – never as Magda Altmann. That way he was able to bring a cold detachment to the problem. The where, the when, and the how of it.

He had complicated the task by replanning her personal security, and his major concern when he did so had been to make her movements as unpredictable as possible. Her social calendar was as closely guarded as a secret of state, there were never any forward press reports of attendance at public or state events.

If she were invited to dine at the Élysée Palace, the fact was reported the day after, not the day before – but there were some annual events that she would never miss. Together they had discussed these weaknesses in her personal security.

'Oh, Peter – you cannot make a convict of me.' She had laughed in protest when he mentioned them. 'I have so few

331

real pleasures – you would not take them from me, would you?'

The first seasonal showing of Yves St Laurent's collections, that she would never miss – or the Grande Semaine of the spring racing season which culminates with the running of the Grand Prix de Paris at Longchamp. This year she had high hopes of victory with her lovely and courageous bay mare, Ice Leopard. She would be there. It was absolutely certain.

Peter began to draw up the list of possible killing grounds, and then crossed off all but the most likely. The estate at La Pierre Bénite, for instance. It had the advantage of being familiar ground for Peter. With a soldier's eye he had noticed fields of fire across the wide terraced lawns that dropped down to the lake; there were stances for a sniper in the forests along the far edge of the lake, and in the little wooded knoll to the north of the house which commanded the yard and stables. However, the estate was well guarded and even there the victim's movements were unpredictable. It would be possible to lie in ambush for the week when she was in Rome or New York. Then again the escape route was highly risky, through a sparsely populated area with only two access roads – both easily blocked by swift police action. No, La Pierre Bénite was crossed from the list.

In the end Peter was left with the two venues that had first sprung to mind – the members' enclosure at Longchamp or Yves St Laurent's premises, at 46 Avenue Victor Hugo.

Both had the advantages of being public and crowded, circumstances favouring pickpockets and assassins, Peter thought wryly. Both had multiple escape routes, and crowds into which the fugitive could blend. There were good stances for a sniper in the grandstands and buildings overlooking the members' enclosure and the saddling paddock at Longchamp or in the multi-storied buildings opposite No 46 in Avenue Victor Hugo.

It would probably be necessary to rent an office suite in one of the buildings – with the attendant risks, even if he used a false name, which put the probability slightly in favour of the racecourse. However, Peter delayed the final decision until he had a chance to inspect each site critically.

There was one last advantage in doing it this way. It would be a stand-off kill. He would be spared the harrowing moments of a kill at close range, with handgun or knife or garrotte.

There would be the detached view of Caliph through the lens of a telescopic sight. The flattened perspectives and the altered colour balances always made for a feeling of unreality. The intervening distance obviated the need for confrontation. He would never have to watch the green light go out in those magnificent eyes, nor hear the last exhalation of breath through the soft and perfectly sculptured lips that had given him so much joy – quickly he thrust those thoughts aside. They weakened his resolve, even though the rage and the lust for vengeance had not abated.

If he could get one of the Thor .222 sniper rifles it would be the perfect tool for this task. With the extra long, accurized barrels designed for use with match grade ammunition and the new laser sights, the weapon could throw a three-inch group at seven hundred yards.

The sniper had only to depress the button on the top of the stock with the forefinger of his left hand. This activated the laser and the beam swept precisely down the projected flight of the bullet. It would show as a bright white coin the size of a silver dime. The sniper looked for the spot of light through the telescopic lens of the sight, and the moment it was exactly on the target he pressed the trigger. Even an unskilled marksman could hardly miss with this sight, in Peter's hands it would be infallible – and Colin Noble would give him one. Not only would Colin give him one, hell, he would probably have it delivered with the compliments of the American Marine Corps by the senior military attaché of the U.S. Embassy in Paris.

Yet Peter found himself drawing out the moment of action, going over his plans so often and with such a critical eye that he knew he was procrastinating.

The sixteenth day after his return to Brussels was a Friday. Peter spent the morning on the NATO range north of the city at a demonstration of the new electronic shield that Narmco had developed to foil the radar guidance on short-range anti-tank missiles. Then he helicoptered back with the three Iranian officers who had attended the demonstration and they lunched at Épaule de Mouton, a magnificent and leisurely meal. Peter still felt guilty spending three hours at the lunch table, so he worked until eight o'clock that evening, on the missile contracts.

It was long after dark when he left through the rear entrance, taking all his usual precautions against the chance that Caliph had an assassin waiting for him in the dark streets. He never left at the same time nor followed the same route, and this evening he bought the evening papers from a *marchand du tabac* in the Grand'Place and stopped to read them at one of the outdoor cafés overlooking the square.

He began with the English papers, and the headlines filled the page from one side to the other; black and bold, they declared:

DROP IN PRICE OF CRUDE OIL

Peter sipped the whisky thoughtfully as he read the article through, turning to Page Six for the continuation.

Then he crumpled the newsprint in his lap, and stared at the passing jostle of spring tourists and early evening revellers.

Caliph had achieved her first international triumph.

From now on there would be no bounds to her ruthless rampage of power and violence.

Peter knew he could delay no longer. He made the go decision then, and it was irrevocable. He would arrange to visit London on Monday morning, there was excuse enough for that. He would ask Colin to meet him at the airport, and it would be necessary to tell him of his plan. He knew he could expect full support. Then he could move on to Paris for the final reconnaissance and choice of killing ground. There was still two weeks until the showing of the spring collections – two weeks to plan it so carefully that there would be no chance of failure.

He felt suddenly exhausted, as though the effort of decision had required the last of his reserves. So exhausted that the short walk back to the hotel seemed daunting. He ordered another whisky and drank it slowly before he could make the effort.

Narmco maintained two permanent suites at the Hilton for their senior executives and other important visitors. Peter had not yet made the effort of finding private accommodation in the city, and he was living out of the smaller of the two suites. It was merely a place to wash and sleep and leave his clothes, for he could not shake off the feeling of impermanence, of swiftly changing circumstances by which he found himself surrounded.

My books are in storage again, he thought with a little chill of loneliness. His collection of rare and beautiful books had been in storage for the greater part of his life, as he roamed wherever his duty took him, living out of barracks and hotel rooms. His books were his only possessions, and as he thought about them now he was filled with an unaccustomed longing to have a base, a place that was his own – and immediately he thrust it aside, smiling cynically at himself as he strode through the streets of another foreign city, alone again.

It must be old age catching up with me, he decided.

There had never been time for loneliness before – but now, but now? Unaccountably he remembered Magda Altmann coming into his arms and saying quietly:

'Oh, Peter, I have been alone for so long.'

The memory stopped him dead, and he stood in the light of one of the street lamps, a tall figure in a belted trench coat with a gaunt and haunted face.

A blonde girl with lewdly painted lips sauntered towards him down the sidewalk, pausing to murmur a proposition, and it brought Peter back to the present.

'*Merci.*' He shook his head in curt refusal and walked on.

As he passed the bookstall in the lobby of the Hilton, a rack of magazines caught his attention and he stopped at the shelf of women's magazines. There would be announcements of the Paris haute couture showings soon, and he thumbed the pages of *Vogue* looking for mention of Yves St Laurent's show – instead he was shocked by the image of a woman's face that leapt out of the page at him.

The elegant cheekbone structure framing the huge slanted Slavic eyes. The shimmering fall of dark hair, the feline grace of movement frozen by the camera flash.

In the photograph she was in a group of four people. The other woman was the estranged wife of a pop singer, the sulky expression, slightly skew eyes and bee-stung lips a landmark on the Parisian social scene. Her partner was a freckled, boyish-faced American actor in a laid-back velvet suit with gold chains around his throat, more famous for his sexual exploits than his film roles. They were not the type of persons with whom Magda Altmann habitually associated, but the man beside her, on whose arm she leaned lightly, was much more her style. He was fortyish, dark and handsome in a fleshy heavily built way, with dense wavy hair, and he exuded the special aura of power and confidence that befitted the head of the biggest German automobile manufacturing complex.

The caption below the photograph had them attending

the opening of an exclusive new Parisian discotheque –
again this was not Magda Altmann's habitual territory, but
she was smiling brilliantly at the tall handsome German, so
obviously enjoying herself that Peter felt a stinging shaft of
emotion thrust up under his ribs. Hatred or jealousy – he
was not certain – and he slapped the magazine closed and
returned it to its rack.

In the impersonal antiseptically furnished suite he
stripped and showered, and then standing naked in the
small lounge of the suite he poured himself a whisky. It was
his third that evening.

Since the kidnapping he had been drinking more than
ever before in his life, he realized. It could exert an insidious
hold when a man was lonely and in grave doubt. He would
have to begin watching it. He took a sip of the smoky
amber liquid and turned to look at himself in the mirror
across the room.

Since he had been back in Brussels, he had worked out
each day in the gymnasium at the NATO officers' club
where he still had membership, and his body was lean and
hard with a belly like a greyhound's – only the face was
ravaged by strain and worry – and, it seemed, by some deep
unutterable regret.

He turned back towards the bedroom of the suite, and
the telephone rang.

'Stride,' he said into the mouthpiece, standing still naked
with the glass in his right hand.

'Please hold on, General Stride. We have an international call for you.'

The delay seemed interminable with heavy buzzing and
clicking on the line, and the distant voices of other
operators speaking bad French or even worse English.

Then suddenly her voice, but faint and so far away that
it sounded like a whisper in a vast and empty hall.

'Peter, are you there?'

'Magda?' He felt the shock of it, and his voice echoed

back at him from the receiver; there was the click before she spoke again, that switch of carrier wave that told him they were on a radio telephone link.

'I have to see you, Peter. I cannot go on like this. Will you come to me, please, Peter?'

'Where are you?'

'Les Neuf Poissons.' Her voice was so faint, so distorted, that he asked her to repeat it.

'Les Neuf Poissons – The Nine Fishes,' she repeated. 'Will you come, Peter?'

'Are you crying?' he demanded, and the silence echoed and clicked and hummed so he thought they had lost contact, and he felt a flare of alarm so his voice was harsh as he asked again. 'Are you crying?'

'Yes.' It was only a breath, he might have imagined it.

'Why?'

'Because I am sad and frightened, Peter. Because I am alone, Peter. Will you come, please will you come?'

'Yes,' he said. 'How do I get there?'

'Ring Gaston at La Pierre Bénite. He will arrange it. But come quickly, Peter. As quickly as you can.'

'Yes. As soon as I can – but where is it?'

He waited for her reply, but now the distances of the ether echoed with the sound of utter finality.

'Magda? Magda?' He found himself shouting desperately, but the silence taunted him and reluctantly he pressed a finger down on the cradle of the telephone.

'Les Neuf Poissons,' he repeated softly, and lifted the finger. 'Operator,' he said, 'please get me a call to France Rambouillet 47–87–47.' And while he waited he was thinking swiftly.

This was what he had been subconsciously waiting for, he realized. There was a feeling of inevitability to it, the wheel could only turn – it could not roll sideways. This was what had to happen.

Caliph had no alternative. This was the summons to

execution. He was only surprised that it had not come sooner. He would see why Caliph would have avoided the attempt in the cities of Europe or England. One such attempt well planned and executed with great force had failed that night on the road to Rambouillet. It would have been a warning to Caliph not to underestimate the victim's ability to retaliate – for the rest, the problems would have been almost the same as those that Peter had faced when planning the strike against Caliph herself.

The when and the where and the how – and Caliph had the edge here. She could summon him to the selected place – but how incredibly skilfully it had been done. As he waited for the call to Rambouillet, Peter marvelled at the woman afresh. There seemed no bottom to her well of talent and accomplishments – despite himself, knowing full well that he was listening to a carefully rehearsed act, despite the fact that he knew her to be a ruthless and merciless killer, yet his heart had twisted at the tones of despair in her voice, the muffled weeping perfectly done, so he had only just been able to identify it.

'This is the residence of Baroness Altmann.'

'Gaston?'

'Speaking, sir.'

'General Stride.'

'Good evening, General. I was expecting your call. I spoke to the Baroness earlier. She asked me to arrange your passage to Les Neuf Poissons. I have done so.'

'Where is it, Gaston?'

'Les Neuf Poissons – it's the Baroness's holiday island in the Îles sous le Vent – it is necessary to take the UTA flight to Papeete-Faaa on Tahiti where the Baroness's pilot will meet you. It's another hundred miles to Les Neuf Poissons and unfortunately the airstrip is too short to accommodate the Lear jet – one has to use a smaller aircraft.'

'When did the Baroness go to Les Neuf Poissons?'

'She left seven days ago, General,' Gaston answered, and

immediately went on in the smooth, efficient secretarial voice to give Peter the details of the UTA flight. ' – The ticket will be held at the UTA check-in counter for you, General, and I have reserved a non-smoking seat at the window.'

'You think of everything. Thank you, Gaston.'

Peter replaced the receiver, and found that his earlier exhaustion had left him – he felt vital and charged with new energy. The elation of a trained soldier facing the prospect of violent action, he wondered, or was it merely the prospect of an end to the indecision and the fear of unknown things? Soon, for good or for evil, it would be settled and he welcomed that.

He went through into the bathroom and pitched the whisky that remained in his glass into the handbasin.

The UTA DC 10 made its final approach to Tahiti-Faaa from the east, slanting down the sky with the jagged peaks of Moorea under the port wing. Peter remembered the spectacularly riven mountains of Tahiti's tiny satellite island as the backdrop of the musical movie *South Pacific* that had been filmed on location here. The volcanic rock was black and unweathered so that its crests were as sharp as sharks' fangs.

They arrowed down across the narrow channel between the two islands, and the runway seemed to reach out an arm into the sea to welcome the big silver machine.

The air was heavy and warm and redolent with the perfume of frangipani blossoms, and there were luscious brown girls swinging and swaying gracefully in a dance of welcome. The islands reached out with almost overpowering sweetness and friendliness – but as Peter picked his single light bag out of the hold luggage and started for the exit doors, something unusual happened. One of the Polynesian customs officers at the gate exchanged a quick word with his companion and then politely stepped into Peter's path.

'Good afternoon, sir.' The smile was big and friendly, but it did not stretch as far as the eyes. 'Would you be kind enough to step this way.' The two customs men escorted Peter into the tiny screened office.

'Please open your bags, sir.' Swiftly but thoroughly they went through his valise and crocodile-skin briefcase; one of them even used a measuring stick to check both cases for a hidden compartment.

'I must congratulate you on your efficiency,' said Peter, smiling also, but his voice tight and low.

'A random check, sir.' The senior officer answered his smile. 'You were just unlucky to be the ten thousandth visitor. Now, sir, I hope you won't object to a body search?'

'A body search?' Peter snapped, and would have protested further, but instead he shrugged and raised both arms. 'Go ahead.'

He could imagine that Magda Altmann was as much the Grande Dame here as she was in mother France. She owned the entire island group, and it would need only a nod to have an incoming visitor thoroughly searched for weapons of any sort.

He could imagine also that Caliph would be very concerned that the intended victim should be suitably prepared for execution, lest he should inadvertently become the executioner.

The one customs officer checked his arms and flanks from armpit to waist, while the other knelt behind him and checked inside the outside of his legs from crotch to ankle.

Peter had left the Cobra in the safe deposit box in the Hilton in Brussels. He had anticipated something like this, it was the way Caliph would work.

'Satisfied?' he asked.

'Thank you for your co-operation, sir. Have a lovely stay on our island.'

341

Magda's personal pilot was waiting for Peter in the main concourse, and hurried forward to shake his hand.

'I was worried that you were not on the flight.'

'A small delay in customs,' Peter explained.

'We should leave immediately, if we are to avoid a night landing on Les Neuf Poissons – the strip is a little difficult.'

Magda's Gates Lear was parked on the hardstand near the service area, and beside it the Norman Britten Tri-Islander looked small and ungainly, a stork-like ugly aircraft capable of the most amazing performance in short take-off and landing situations.

The body of the machine was already loaded with crates and cartons of supplies, everything from toilet rolls to Veuve Cliquot champagne, all tied down under a wide-meshed nylon net.

Peter took the right-hand seat, and the pilot started up and cleared with control, then to Peter:

'One hour's flying. We will just make it.'

The setting sun was behind them as they came in from the west and Les Neuf Poissons lay like a precious necklace of emeralds upon the blue velvet cushion of the ocean.

There were nine islands in the characteristic circular pattern of volcanic formation, and they enclosed a lagoon of water so limpid that every whorl and twist of the coral outcrops showed through as clearly as if they were in air.

'The islands had a Polynesian name when the Baron purchased them back in 1945,' the pilot explained in the clearly articulated rather pedantic French of the Midi. 'They were given by one of the old kings as a gift to a missionary he favoured and the Baron purchased them from his widow. The Baron could not pronounce the Polynesian name so he changed it—' The pilot chuckled. ' – The Baron was a man who faced the world on his own terms.'

Seven of the islands were merely strips of sand and fringes of palms, but the two to the east were larger with hills of volcanic basalt glittering like the skin of a great reptile in the rays of the lowering sun.

As they turned onto their downwind leg, Peter had a view through the window at his elbow of a central building with its roof of palm thatch elegantly curved like the prow of a ship in the tradition of the islands, and around it half-hidden in luscious green gardens were other smaller bungalows. Then they were over the lagoon and there were a clutter of small vessels around the long jetty which reached out into the protected waters – Hobie-cats with bare masts, a big powered schooner which was probably used to ship the heavy stores such as dieseline down from Papeete, power boats for skiing and diving and fishing. One of them was out in the middle of the lagoon, tearing a snowy ostrich feather of wake from the surface as it ran at speed; a tiny figure towed on skis behind it lifted an arm and waved a greeting. Peter thought it might be her, but at that moment the Tri-Islander banked steeply onto its base leg and he was left with only a view of cumulus cloud bloodied by the setting sun.

The runway was short and narrow, hacked from the palm plantation on the strip of level land between beach and hills. It was surfaced with crushed coral. They made their final approach over a tall palisade of palm trees. Peter saw that the pilot had not exaggerated by calling it a little difficult. There was a spiteful crosswind rolling in and breaking over the hills and it rocked the Tri-Islander's wings sickeningly. The pilot crabbed her in, heading half into the wind, and as he skimmed in over the palm tops, closed the throttles, kicked her straight with the rudders, lowered a wing into the wind to hold her from drifting and dropped her neatly fifty feet over the threshold, perfectly aligned with the short runway so she kissed and sat down solidly; instantly the pilot whipped the wheel to full lock into the crosswind to prevent a ground loop and brought her up short.

'*Parfait!*' Peter grunted with involuntary admiration, and the man looked slightly startled as though the feat deserved no special mention. Baroness Altmann employed only the very best.

There was an electric golf cart driven by a young Polynesian girl waiting at the end of the strip amongst the palm trees. She wore only a pareo wrapped around her body below the armpits, a single length of crimson and gold patterned cloth that fell to mid thigh. Her feet were bare, but around her pretty head she wore a crown of fresh flowers – the maeva of the islands.

She drove the golf cart at a furious pace along narrow winding tracks through the gardens that were a rare collection of exotic plants, skilfully laid out, so that there was an exquisite surprise around each turn of the path.

His bungalow was above the beach with white sand below the verandah and the ocean stretching to the horizon, secluded as though it were the only building on the island. Like a child the island girl took his hand, a gesture of perfect innocence, and led him through the bungalow, showing him the controls for the air-conditioning, lighting and the video screen, explaining it all in lisping French patois, and giggling at his expression of pleasure.

There was a fully stocked bar and kitchenette, the small library contained all the current best-sellers, and the newspapers and magazines were only a few days old. The offerings on the video screen included half a dozen recent successful features and Oscar winners.

'Hell, Robinson Crusoe should have landed here,' Peter chuckled, and the girl giggled and wriggled like a friendly little puppy in sympathy.

She came to fetch him again two hours later, after he had showered and shaved and rested and changed into a light cotton tropical suit with open shirt and sandals.

Again she held his hand and Peter sensed that if a man had taken the gesture as licence the girl would have been hurt and confused. By the hand she led him along a path that was demarcated by cunningly concealed glow lights, and the night was filled with the murmur of the ocean and the gentle rustle and clatter of palm fronds moving in the wind.

Then they came to the long ship-roofed building he had seen from the air. There was soft music and laughter, but when he stepped into the light the laughter stopped and half a dozen figures turned to him expectantly.

Peter was not sure what he had expected, but it was not this gay, social gathering, tanned men and women in expensive and elegant casual wear, holding tall frosted glasses filled with ice and fruit.

'Peter!' Magda Altmann broke from the group, and came to him with that gliding hip-swinging walk.

She wore a soft, shimmering, wheaten-gold dress, held high at the throat with a thin gold chain, but completely nude across the shoulders and down her back to within an inch of the cleft of her buttocks. It was breathtaking for her body was smooth as a rose petal and tanned to the colour of new honey. The dark hair was twisted into a rope as thick as her wrist and piled up onto the top of her head, and she had touched her eyes with shadows so they were slanting and green and mysterious.

'Peter,' she repeated, and kissed him lightly upon the lips, a brush like a moth's wing, and her perfume touched him as softly, the fragrance of Quadrille flowering with the warmth and magic of her body.

He felt his senses tilt. With all he knew of her, yet he was still not hardened to her physical presence.

She was cool and groomed and poised as she had ever been, there was no trace at all of the confusion and fearsome loneliness that he had heard in those muffled choked-down sobs from halfway across the world – not until she stepped back to tilt her head on one side, surveying him swiftly, smiling lightly.

'Oh, *chéri*, you are looking so much better. I was so worried about you when last I saw you.'

Only then he thought he was able to detect the shadows deep in her eyes, and the tightness at the corners of her mouth.

'And you are more beautiful than I remembered.'

It was true, so he could say it without reserve, and she laughed, a single soft purr of pleasure.

'You never said that before,' she reminded him, but still her manner was brittle. Her show of affection and friendliness might have convinced him at another time, but not now. 'And I am grateful.'

Now she took his arm, her fingers in the crook of his elbow, and she led him to the waiting group of guests as though she did not trust herself to be alone with him another moment lest she reveal some forbidden part of herself.

There were three men and their wives: an American Democrat senator of considerable political influence, a man with a magnificent head of silver hair, eyes like dead oysters, and a beautiful wife at least thirty years his junior who looked at Peter the way a lion looks at a gazelle and held his hand seconds longer than was necessary.

There was an Australian, heavy in the shoulder and big in the gut. His skin was tanned leathery and his eyes were framed in a network of wrinkles. They seemed to be staring through dust and sun glare at distant horizons. He owned a quarter of the world's known uranium reserves, and cattle stations whose area was twice the size of the British Isles. His wife was as tanned and her handshake was as firm as his.

The third man was a Spaniard whose family name was synonymous with sherry, an urbane and courtly Don, but with that fierce Moorish rake to his thin features. Peter had read somewhere that the sherry and cognac ageing in this man's cellars was valued at over five hundred million dollars, and that formed only a small part of his family's investments. His wife was a darkly brooding Spanish beauty with an extraordinary streak of chalk white through the peak of her otherwise black hair.

As soon as the group had assimilated Peter, the talk turned back easily to the day's sport. The Australian had boated a huge black marlin that morning, a fish over one thousand pounds in weight and fifteen feet from the point of its bill to the tip of its deep sickle tail, and the company was elated.

Peter took little part in the conversation, but watched Magda Altmann covertly. Yet she was fully aware of his scrutiny; he could see it in the way she held her hand, and the tension in her whole long slim body, but she laughed easily with the others and glanced at Peter only once or twice, each time with a smile, but the shadows were in the green depths of her eyes.

Finally she clapped her hands. 'Come, everybody, we are going to open the feast.' She linked arms with the senator and the Australian and led them down onto the beach. Peter was left to cope with the senator's wife, and pushed her bosom against his upper arm and ran her tongue lightly over her lips as she clung to him.

Two of the Polynesian servants were waiting beside a long mound of white beach sand, and at Magda's signal they attacked it with shovels, swiftly exposing a thick layer of seaweed and banana leaves from which poured columns of thick and fragrant steam. Below that was a rack of banyan wood and palm fronds which suspended the feast over another layer of seaweed and live coals.

There were exclamations of delight as the aroma of chicken and fish and pork mingled with those of breadfruit and plantains and spices.

'Ah, a success,' Magda declared gaily. 'If any air is allowed to enter the bake we lose it all. It burns, poof! And we are left with only charcoal.'

While they feasted and drank the talk and laughter became louder and less restrained, but Peter made the single drink last the evening and waited quietly – not joining the conversation and ignoring the blandishments of the senator's wife.

He was waiting for some indication of when and from what direction it would come. Not here, he knew, not in this company. When it came it would be swift and efficient as everything else that Caliph did. And suddenly he wondered at his own conceit, that had allowed him to walk, entirely unarmed and unsupported, into the arena selected and prepared by his enemy. He knew his best defence was to strike first, perhaps this very night if the opportunity offered. The sooner the safer, he realized, and Magda smiled at him across the table set under the palm trees and laden with enough food to feed fifty. When he smiled back at her, she beckoned with a slight inclination of her head, and then while the men argued and bantered loudly, she murmured an apology to the women and slipped unobtrusively into the shadows.

Peter gave her a count of fifty before he followed her. She was waiting along the beach. He saw the flash of her bare smooth back in the moonlight and he went forward to where she stood staring out across the wind-ruffled waters of the lagoon.

He came up behind her, and she did not turn her head but her voice was a whisper.

'I am so glad you came, Peter.'

'I am so glad you asked me to.'

He touched the back of her neck, just behind her ear. The ear had an almost elfin point to it that he had not noticed before and the unswept hair at her nape was silken under his fingertips. He could just locate the axis, that delicate bone at the base of the skull which the hangman aims to crush with the drop. He could do it with the pressure of thumb and it would be as quick as the knot.

'I am so sorry about the others,' she said. 'But I am getting rid of them – with almost indecent haste, I'm afraid.' She reached up over her shoulder and took his hand from her neck, and he did not resist. Gently she spread the hand, and then pressed the open palm to her cheek. 'They will leave early tomorrow. Pierre is flying them back to Papeete, and then we will have Les Neuf Poissons to ourselves – just you and I—' And then that husky little chuckle.' – And thirty-odd servants.'

He could understand exactly why it would be that way. The only witnesses would be the faithful retainers of the Grande Dame of the islands.

'Now we must go back. Unfortunately my guests are very important, and I cannot ignore them longer – but tomorrow will come. Too slowly for me, Peter – but it will come.'

She turned in the circle of his arms and kissed him with a sudden startling ferocity, so his lips were crushed against his teeth, and then she broke from him and whispered close to his ear.

'Whatever way it goes, Peter, we have had something of value, you and I. Perhaps the most precious thing I have had in my life. They can never take that away from me.'

And then she was out of his arms with that uncanny speed and grace of movement and gliding back along the path towards the lights. He followed her slowly, confused and uncertain as to what she had meant by those last words, concluding finally that the purpose had been exactly that – to confuse and unbalance him, and at that moment he sensed rather than heard movement behind him, and instantly whirled and ducked.

The man was ten paces behind him, had come like a leopard, silently from the cover of a fall of lianas and flowering creepers beside the path; only some animal instinct had warned Peter – and his body flowed into the fighting stance, balanced, strung like a nocked arrow, at once ready both to attack and meet attack.

'Good evening, General Stride.' Peter only just managed to arrest himself, and he straightened slowly but with each hand still extended stiffly at his side like the blade of a meat cleaver, and as lethal.

'Carl!' he said. So the grey wolves had been close, within feet of them, guarding their mistress even in that intimate moment.

'I hope I did not alarm you,' said the bodyguard – and though Peter could not see the man's expression, there was a faint mockery in his voice. If there was confirmation needed, complete and final, this was it. Only Caliph would have need of a guard on a romantic assignment. Peter knew then beyond any doubt that either he or Magda Altmann would be dead by sunset the following evening.

Before going into the bungalow he made a stealthy prowling circuit of the bushes and shrubs that surrounded it. He found nothing suspicious but in the interior the bed had been prepared and his shaving gear cleaned and neatly rearranged. His soiled clothing had been taken for cleaning and the other clothing had been pressed and rearranged more neatly than his own unpacking. He could not therefore be certain that his other possessions had not been searched, but it was safe to presume they had. Caliph would not neglect such an elementary precaution.

The locks on doors and windows were inadequate, had probably not been used in years, for there had been no serpents in this paradise, not until recently. So he placed chairs and other obstacles in such a way that an intruder should stumble over them in the dark, and then he rumpled the bed and arranged the pillows to look like a sleeping figure, but took a single blanket to the long couch in the private lounge. He did not really expect an attempt before the other guests left the island, but if it came he would confuse Caliph's scenario as much as possible.

He slept fitfully, jerking awake when a falling palm frond rattled across the roof, or the moon threw picture shadows on the wall across the room. Just before dawn he fell into a deeper sleep and his dreams were distorted and nonsensical, only the sharp clear image of Melissa-Jane's terror-stricken face and her silent screams of horror remained with him when he woke. The memory roused in him the cold lust for vengeance which had abated a little in the weeks since her rescue, and he felt reaffirmed, possessed of a steely purpose once more, determined to resist the softening, fatal allure of Caliph.

He rose in the slippery pearl light of not yet dawn, and went down to the beach. He swam out a mile beyond the reef, and had a long pull back against a rogue current, but he came ashore feeling good and hard and alert as he had not been in weeks.

All right, he thought grimly. Let it come. I'm as ready as I'll ever be.

There was a farewell breakfast for the departing guests, on the sugary sands of the beach that had been swept smooth by the night tide – pink Laurent Perrier champagne and hothouse strawberries flown in from Auckland, New Zealand.

Magda Altmann wore brief green pants that showed off her long shapely legs to perfection, and a matching 'boob tube' across her small neat breasts – but her belly and shoulders and back were bare. It was the body of a finely trained athlete, but drawn by a great artist.

She seemed unnaturally elated to Peter, her gaiety was slightly forced and the low purring laughter just a little too ready – and with a saw-edge to it. It was almost as though she had made some hard decision, and was steeling herself to carry it through. Peter thought of them as true opponents who had trained carefully for the coming configuration – like prize fighters at the weigh-in.

After the breakfast they rode up in a cavalcade of electric carts to the airfield. The senator, revved-up with pink champagne and sweating lightly in the rising heat, gave Magda an over-affectionate farewell, but she skilfully avoided his hands and shunted him expertly into the Tri-Islander after the other passengers.

Pierre, Magda's pilot, stood on the brakes at the end of the runway while he ran all three engines up to full power. Then he let her go, and the moment she had speed he rotated her into a nose-high obstacle-clearance attitude. The ungainly machine jumped into the sky and went over the palms at the end of the short strip with five hundred feet to spare – and Magda turned to Peter ecstatically.

'I hardly slept last night,' she admitted, as she kissed him.

'Neither did I,' Peter told her – and then he added silently ' – for the same reasons, I'm sure.'

'I've planned a special day for us,' she went on. 'And I don't want to waste another minute of it.'

The head boatman had Magda's big forty-five-foot Chriscraft Fisherman singled up at the end of the jetty. It was a beautiful boat, with long low attacking lines that made it seem to be flying even when on its mooring lines, and loving care had very obviously been lavished upon it. The paintwork was unmarked and the stainless steel fittings were polished to a mirror finish. The boatman beamed happily when Magda commended him with a smile and a word.

'Tanks are full, Baronne. The scuba bottles are charged and the light rods are rigged. The water-skis are in the main racks, and the chef came down himself to check the ice-box.'

However, his wide white smile faded when he learned that Magda was taking the boat out alone.

'Don't you trust me?' she laughed.

'Oh, of course, Baronne—' But he could not hide his

352

chagrin at having to give over his charge – even to such a distinguished captain.

He handled the lines himself, casting her off, and calling anxious last-minute advice to Magda as the gap between jetty and vessel opened.

'Ne t'inquiet pas!' she laughed at him, but he made a dejected figure standing on the end of the jetty as Magda slowly opened up both diesels and the Chris-craft came up on the plane and seemed almost to break free of the surface. Her wake was scored deep and clean and straight through the gin-clear water of the lagoon, a tribute to the design of her hull, and then it curved out gracefully behind them as Magda made the turn between the channel markers and lined her up for the passage through the reef, and out into the open Pacific.

'Where are we going?'

'There is an old Japanese aircraft carrier lying in a hundred feet of water beyond the reef. Yankee aircraft sank her back in 'forty-four – It is a beautiful site for scuba diving. We will go there first—'

How? Peter wondered. Perhaps one of the scuba bottles had been partially filled with carbon monoxide gas. It was simply done, with a hose from the exhaust of the diesel generator: simply pass the exhaust gases through a charcoal filter to remove the taste and smell of unconsumed hydrocarbons and the remaining carbon monoxide gas would be undetectable. Fill the bottle to 30 atmospheres of pressure then top it up with clean air to its operating pressure of 110 atmospheres. It would be swift, but not too swift to alarm the victim, a gentle long sleep. When the victim lost his mouthpiece, the bottles would purge themselves of any trace of the gas. That would be a good way to do it.

'After that we can go ashore on Île des Oiseaux. Since Aaron stopped the islanders stealing the eggs to eat, we've got one of the biggest nesting colonies of terns and noddies and frigate birds in the Southern Pacific—'

Perhaps a speargun. That would be direct and effective. At short range, say two feet, even below the surface, the spear arrow would go right through a human torso – in between the shoulder blades and out through the breast bone.

' – And afterwards we can water-ski—'

With an unsuspecting skier in the water, awaiting the pick-up, what could be more effective than opening up both those tremendously powerful diesels to the gates and running the victim down? If the hull did not crush him, the twin screws turning at 500 revolutions per minute would cut him up as neatly as a loaf of pre-sliced bread.

Peter found himself intrigued with the guessing-game. He found himself regretting the fact that he would never know what she intended, and he looked back from where they stood side by side on the tall flying bridge of the Chriscraft. The main island was lowering itself into the water; already they were out of sight of anybody who did not have a pair of powerful binoculars.

Beside him Magda pulled the retaining ribbon out of her hair, and shook loose a black rippling banner that streamed in the wind behind her.

'Let's do this for ever,' she shouted above the wind and the boom of the engines.

'Sold to the lady with the sexy backside,' Peter shouted back, and he had to remind himself that she was one of the most carefully trained killers he would ever meet. He must not allow himself to be lulled by the laughter and the beauty – and he must not allow her to make the first stroke. His chances of surviving that were remote.

He glanced back again at the land. Any minute now, he thought, and moved as though to glance over the side, getting slightly into her rear, but still in the periphery of her vision; she shifted slightly towards him still smiling.

'At this state of the tide there are always amberjack in the channel. I promised the chef I would bring him a couple of them kicking fresh,' she explained. 'Won't you go down and get two of the light rods ready, *chéri*? The feather lures are in the forward starboard seat locker.'

'Okay,' he nodded.

'I'll throttle back to trolling speed when I make the turn into the channel – put the lines in then.'

'*D'accord.*' And then on an impulse. 'But kiss me first.'

She held up her face to him, and he wondered why he had said that. It was not to take farewell of her. He was sure of that. It was to lull her just that fraction, and yet as their lips met he felt the deep ache of regret that he had controlled for so long and as her mouth spread slowly and moistly open under his, he felt as though his heart might break then. For a moment he felt that he might die himself before he could do it; dark waves of despair poured over him.

He slid his hand over her shoulder to the nape of her neck and her body flattened against his; he caressed her lightly, feeling for the place, and then settling thumb and forefinger – a second, another second passed, and then she pulled him back softly.

'Hey, now!' she whispered huskily. 'You stop that before I pile up on the reef.'

He had not been able to do it with his bare hands. He just could not do it like that – but he had to do it quickly, very quickly. Every minute delayed now led him deeper and deeper into deadly danger.

'Go!' she ordered, and struck him a playful blow on the chest. 'We've got time for that later – all the time in the world. Let's savour it, every moment of it.'

He had not been able to do it, and he turned away. It was only as he went down the steel ladder into the cockpit of the Chris-craft that it suddenly occurred to him that during the lingering seconds of that kiss the fingers of her right hand had cupped lovingly under his chin. She could have crushed his larynx, paralysing him with a thumb

355

driven up into the soft vulnerable arch of his throat at the first offensive pressure of his thumb and forefinger.

As his feet hit the deck of the cockpit another thought came to him. Her other hand had lain against his body, stroking him softly under the ribs. That hand could have struck upwards and inwards to tear through his diaphragm – his instincts must have warned him. She had been poised for the stroke, more so than he was; she had been inside the circle of his arms, inside his defences, waiting for him – and he shivered briefly in the hot morning sun at the realization of how close he had been to death.

The realization turned instantly to something else, that slid down his spine cold as water down a melting icicle. It was fear, not the crippling fear of the craven, but fear that edged him and hardened him. Next time he would not hesitate – he could not hesitate.

He was instinctively carrying out her instructions as his mind raced to catch up with the problem. He lifted the lid of the seat locker. In the custom-fitted interior were arranged trays of fishing gear, swivels of brass and stainless steel in fifty different sizes; sinkers shaped for every type of water and bottom; lures of plastic and feathers, of enamel and bright metal; hooks for gigantic bill fish or for fry – and in a separate compartment in the side tray a bait knife.

The knife was a fifty-dollar Ninja with a lexan composition handle, chequered and moulded for grip. The blade was seven inches of hollow ground steel, three inches broad at the hilt and tapering to a stiletto point. It was a brutal weapon, you could probably chop through an oak log with it, as the makers advertised. Certainly it would enter human flesh and go through bone as though it were Cheddar cheese.

It balanced beautifully in Peter's fist as he made one testing slash and return cut with it. The blade hissed in the air, and when he tested the edge too hurriedly it stung like a razor and left a thin line of bright blood across the ball of his thumb.

He kicked off his canvas sneakers, so the rubber soles did not squeak on the deck. He was dressed now in only a thin cotton singlet and boxer-type swimming trunks, stripped down for action.

He went up the first three rungs of the ladder on bare silent feet, and lifted his eyes above the level of the flying bridge.

Magda Altmann stood at the controls of the Chris-craft, conning the big vessel into the mouth of the channel, staring ahead in complete concentration.

Her hair still flew in the wind, snaking and tangling into thick shimmering tresses. Her naked back was turned to him, the deeply defined depression running down her spine and the crest of smooth hard muscle rising on each side of it.

One leg of her pants had rucked up slightly exposing a half-moon of round white buttock, and her legs were long and supple as a dancer's as she balanced on the balls of her narrow feet, raising herself to see ahead over the bows.

Peter had been gone from the bridge for less than ten seconds, and she was completely unaware, completely unsuspecting.

Peter did not make the same mistake again; he went up the ladder in a single swift bound, and the bellow of the diesels covered any sound he might have made.

With the knife you never take the chance of the point turning against bone, if you have a choice of target.

Peter picked the small of the back, at the level of the kidneys where there was no bone to protect the body cavity.

It is essential to put the blade in with all possible power; this decreases the chance of bone-deflection and it peaks the paralysing effect of impact-shock.

Peter put the full weight of his rush behind the thrust.

The paralysis is total if the blade is twisted a half-turn at the same instant that the blade socks in hilt-deep.

The muscles in Peter's right forearm were bunched in anticipation of the moment in which he would twist the blade viciously in her flesh, quadrupling the size and the trauma of the wound.

The polished stainless steel fascia of the Chris-craft's control panel reflected a distorted image, like those funny mirrors of the fairground. Only at the moment that Peter had committed himself completely, at the moment when he had thrown all his weight into the killing stroke, did he realize with a sickening flash that she was watching him in the polished steel control panel; she had been watching him from the moment he reappeared at the head of the ladder.

The curved surface of the steel distorted her face, so that it appeared to consist only of two enormous eyes; it distracted him in that thousandth part of a second before the point of the blade entered flesh. He did not see her move.

Blinding, numbing agony shot down his right flank and arm, from a point in the hollow where his collar bone joined the upper arm, while at the same instant something hit him on the inside of his forearm just below the elbow. The knife stroke was flung outwards, passing an inch from her hip, and the point of the blade crashed into the control panel in front of her, scoring the metal with a deep bright scratch, but Peter's numbed fingers could not keep hold on the hilt. The weapon spun from his grip, ringing like a crystal wine glass as it struck the steel handrail and rebounded over the side of the bridge into the cockpit behind him. He realized that she had struck backwards at him, not turning to face him but using only the reflection in the control panel to judge her blow with precision into the pressure point of his shoulder.

Now pain had crippled him and the natural reaction was

to clutch at the source of it. Instead with some reflexive instinct of survival he flung up his left hand to protect the side of his neck and the next blow, also thrown backwards, felt as though it had come from a full-blooded swing of a baseball bat. He hardly saw it, it came so fast and hard there was just the flicker of movement across his vision, like the blur of a hummingbird's wing, and then the appalling force of it crushing into the muscle of his forearm.

Had it taken him in the neck where it was aimed, it would have killed him instantly; instead it paralysed his other arm, and she was turning into him now effortlessly, matching his bull strength with a combination of speed and control.

He knew he must try and keep her close, smother her with his weight and size and strength and he hooked at her with the clawed crippled fingers of his knife hand; they caught for a moment and then she jerked free. He had ripped away the flimsy strip of elasticized cloth that covered her breasts, and she spun lightly under and out of the sweep of his other arm as he tried desperately to club her down with his forearm.

He saw that her face was bone-white with the adrenalin overdose coursing her blood. Her lips were drawn back into a fixed snarl of concentration and fury and her teeth seemed as sharp as those of a female leopard in a trap.

It was like fighting a leopard; she attacked him with an unrelenting savagery and total lack of fear, no longer human, dedicated only to his total destruction.

The long hair swirled about him, at one moment flicking like a whiplash into his eyes to blind and unbalance him, and she weaved and dodged and struck like a mongoose at the cobra, every movement flowing into the next, her taunting red-tipped breasts dancing and jerking with each blow she hurled at him.

With a jar of disbelief, Peter realized that she was beating him down. So far he had managed barely to survive each blow that he caught on arm and shoulder; each time her bare feet crashed into his thigh or lower belly, each time her knees drove for his groin and jarred against the bone of his pelvis, he felt a little more of his strength dissipate, felt his reactions becoming more rubbery, just that instant slower. He had countered her attack with luck and instinct, but any instant she must land solidly and drop him, for she was never still, cutting him with hands and feet, keeping him off balance – and he had not hurt her yet, had not touched her with any of his counter-strokes. Still there was no feeling in his hands and fingers. He needed respite, he needed a weapon, and he thought desperately of the knife that had fallen into the cockpit behind him.

He gave ground to her next attack, and the bridge rail caught him in the small of the back; at the same moment another of her strokes – aimed at the soft of his throat – deflected off his arm and crunched into his nose. Instantly his eyes flooded with tears, and he felt the warm salt flood of blood over his upper lip and down the back of his throat; he doubled over swiftly, then in the same movement he threw himself backwards, like a diver making a one-and-a-half from the three-metre board. The rail behind him helped his turn in the air, and he had judged it finely. He landed like a cat on both feet on the deck of the cockpit ten feet below the bridge, flexing at the knees to absorb the shock, and flicking the tears from his eyes, wringing his arms to return blood and feeling.

As he spun into a crouch he saw the knife. It had slid down the cockpit into the stern scuppers. He went for it.

The dive had taken her by surprise, just as she was poised for the final killing stroke to the back of his exposed neck, but she swirled to the head of the ladder and gathered herself while below her Peter launched himself across the cockpit for the big ugly Ninja knife.

She went for him feet first, dropping from ten feet, and the bare soles of her feet hit him together, the impetus of her falling body enhanced by the stabbing kick that she released at the moment that she hit him.

She caught him high in the back, hurling him forward so that the top of his head cracked into the bulkhead and darkness rustled through his head. He felt his senses going, and it required all of his resolve to roll over and pull his knees swiftly to his chest, to guard himself against the next killing stroke. He caught it on his shins, and once again launched himself after the knife. His fingers felt swollen and clumsy on the rough chequered surface of the hilt, and at the moment they touched he unwound his doubled-up body like a steel coil spring, lashing out with both feet together. It was a blind stroke, delivered in complete desperation.

It was the first solid blow he had landed; it caught her at the moment when she had already launched herself into her next onslaught; both his feet slammed into her belly just below the ribs, and had the flesh there been soft or yielding it would have ended it; but she was just able to absorb the force of it with flat hard muscle – though it hurled her backwards across the cockpit with the breath hissing from her lungs and the long slim body doubling over in an agonized convulsion.

Peter realized that this was the only chance that he had had, and the only one he would ever have – yet his body was racked with such pain that he could hardly drag himself up onto his elbow, and his vision swam and blurred with tears and blood and sweat.

He did not know how he had managed it, some supreme exertion of will, but he was on his feet with the knife in his hand, instinctively extending the blade down the back of his right thigh to keep it protected until the moment it had to be used, crouching as he went in, left arm raised as a shield – and knowing that now he had to end it swiftly, he could not go on longer. This was his last effort.

Then she had a weapon also. Moving so swiftly that it had happened before she was halfway across the cockpit, she had knocked the retaining clip off the boat hook that stood in the rack beside the cabin entrance.

It was eight feet of heavy varnished ash, with an ornate but vicious brass head, and she cut at him with it, a low swinging warning blow to hold him off while she forced air back into her empty lungs.

She was recovering swiftly, much more swiftly than Peter himself. He could see the cold killing light rekindle in her eyes. He knew he could not go on much longer, he must risk it all in one last total effort.

He threw the knife, aiming at her head. The Ninja, not designed as a throwing weapon, rolled out of line of flight, hilt foremost – but still it forced her to lift the staff of the boat hook and deflect it. It was the distraction he had wanted.

Peter used the momentum of his throw to go in under the swinging staff, and he hit her with his shoulder while her arms were raised.

Both of them reeled backwards into the cabin bulkhead, and Peter groped desperately for a grip. He found it in the thick lustrous tresses of her hair, and he wove his fingers into it.

She fought like a dying animal with strength and fury and courage that he could never have believed possible, but now at last he could pit his superior weight and strength directly against hers.

He smothered her against his chest, trapping one arm between their bodies, while he was able to pull her head backwards at an impossible angle, exposing the long smooth curve of her throat.

And then he scissored his thighs across her, so that those lethal feet and legs were unable to reach him, and they crashed over onto the deck.

She managed with an incredible effort to swing her weight so that she landed on top of him, her breasts sliding against his chest, lubricated by sweat and blood that dribbled down from his nose, but Peter heaved all his remaining strength into his shoulders and rolled back on top of her.

They were locked breast to chest and groin to groin in some bizarre parody of the act of love, only the stock of the boat hook between them.

Peter twisted down hard on the rope of hair in his left hand, pinning her head to the deck so that her eyes were only six inches from his and blood from his nose and mouth dripped onto her upturned face.

Neither of them had spoken a word, the only sound the hiss and suck of laboured breathing, the explosive grunt of a blow delivered or the involuntary gasp of pain as it landed.

They glared into each other's eyes, and at that moment neither of them was a human being, they were two animals fighting to the death, and Peter shifted quickly so the stock of the boat hook fell across her unprotected throat. She had not been ready for that and she ducked her chin too late.

Peter knew he could not dare to release his grip on her hair, nor the arm around her body, nor the scissors that enfolded her legs. He could feel the steely tension of her whole body, that required all his own strength to hold. If he relaxed his grip in the slightest, she would twist away, and he would not have the strength to go on after that.

With the elbow of the hand that held her hair, he began to bear down on the ash staff of the boat hook, slowly crushing down into her throat.

She knew it was over then, but still she fought on. As she weakened Peter was able to transfer more and more of his weight onto the stock of the boat hook. Slowly blood suffused her face, turning it dark mottled plum, her lips quivered with each painful rasping breath and a little frothy saliva broke from the corners of her mouth and ran back down her cheek.

Watching her die was the most horrible thing Peter had ever had to do. He shifted cautiously, going for the few extra ounces of weight which would force the heavy wooden stock down that last eighth of an inch and crush in her throat, and she recognized the moment in her eyes.

She spoke for the first time. It was a croak slurred through swollen and gaping lips.

'They warned me.' He thought he had misheard her, and he checked the final thrust downwards which would pinch out the last spark of life. 'I couldn't believe it.' The faintest whisper, only just intelligible. 'Not you.'

Then the last resistance went out of her, her body relaxed, the complete acceptance of death at last. The fierce green light went out in her eyes, replaced at the very end with a sadness so heavy that it seemed to acknowledge the ultimate betrayal of all goodness and trust.

Peter could not force himself to make the final thrust downwards that would end it. He rolled off her and flung the heavy wooden stock across the cockpit. It crashed into the bulkhead and he sobbed as he crawled painfully across the deck, turning his back to her completely, knowing that she was still alive and therefore still as dangerous as she had ever been – yet no longer caring. He had gone as far as he could go. It didn't matter any more if she killed him; something in him even welcomed the prospect of release.

He reached the rail and tried to drag himself onto his feet, expecting at any moment the killing blow into the nape of his neck as she attacked him again.

It did not come, and he managed to get onto his knees, but his whole body was trembling violently so that his teeth chattered in his jaws and every strained and bruised tendon and muscle screamed for surcease. Let her kill me, he thought, it doesn't matter. Nothing matters now.

Half supporting himself on the rail, he turned slowly and his vision swam and flickered with patches of darkness and little shooting stars of crimson and white flame.

Through the swirl of senses at the end of their usefulness,

he saw that she was kneeling in the centre of the cockpit, facing him.

Her naked torso was splattered and smeared with his blood and the smooth tanned skin oiled with slippery sweat of near death. Her face was still and swollen and inflamed, wreathed in a great tangle of matted and disordered hair. There was a flaming livid weal across her throat where the stock had crushed her, and as she fought for breath her small pert breasts lifted and dropped to the painful pumping of her chest.

They stared at each other, far beyond speech, driven to the very frontiers of their existence.

She shook her head, as though trying desperately to deny the horror of it all, and at last she tried to speak; no sound came and she licked her lips and lifted one slim hand to her throat as though to ease the pain of it.

She tried again, and this time she managed one word. 'Why?'

He could not reply for fully half a minute, his own throat seemed to have closed, grown together like an old wound. He knew that he had failed in his duty and yet he could not yet hate himself for it. He formed the words in his own mind, as though he were trying to speak a foreign language, and when he spoke his voice was a stranger's broken and coarsened by the knowledge of failure.

'I couldn't do it,' he said.

She shook her head again, and tried to frame the next question. But she could not articulate it, only one word came out, the same word again.

'Why – ?'

And he had no answer for her.

She stared at him, then slowly her eyes filled with tears; they ran down her cheeks and hung from her chin like early morning dew on the leaf of the vine.

Slowly she pitched forward onto the deck, and for many

seconds he did not have the strength to go to her, and then he lurched across the deck and dropped to his knees beside her; he lifted her upper body in his arms suddenly terrified that he had succeeded after all, that she was dead.

His relief soared above the pain of his battered body as he felt her breathing still sawing through her damaged throat, and as her head lolled against his shoulder he realized that fat oily tears still welled out from between her closed eyelids.

He began to rock her like a child in his arms, a completely useless gesture, and only then did her words begin to make any sense to him.

'They warned me,' she had whispered.

'I couldn't believe it,' she had said.

'Not you.'

He knew then that had she not spoken he would have gone through with it. He would have killed her and weighted her body and dropped it beyond the 1,000-fathom line – but the words, although they did not yet make sense, had reached deep into some recess of his mind.

She stirred against his chest. She said something, it sounded like his name. It roused him to reality. The big Chris-craft was still roaring blindly through the channels and reefs of the outer passage.

He laid her back gently on the deck, and scrambled up the ladder to the flying bridge. The whole of that horrific conflict had taken less than a minute, from his knife-stroke to her collapse under him.

The steering of the Chris-craft was locked into the automatic pilot and the vessel had run straight out through the channel into the open sea. It reinforced his knowledge that she had been ready for his attack. She had been acting that total concentration in steering the vessel, luring him into the attack while the Chris-craft was on automatic pilot and she was ready to throw that backward blow at him.

It did not make sense, not yet. All that he knew was that

he had made some terrible miscalculation. He threw out the switch of the automatic steering, and shut down both throttles to the idle position before disengaging the main drive. The diesels burbled softly, and she rounded up gently into the wind and wallowed beam-on to the short steep blue seas of the open ocean.

Peter took one glance back over the stern. The islands were just a low dark smudge on the horizon, and then he was stumbling back to the ladder.

Magda had dragged herself into a half sitting position, but she recoiled swiftly as he came to her and for the first time he saw fear pass like cloud shadow across her eyes.

'It's all right,' he told her, his own voice still ragged. Her fear offended him deeply. He did not want her ever to be afraid of him again.

He took her up in his arms, and her body was stiff with uncertainty, like that of a cat picked up against its will, but too sick to resist.

'It's all right,' he repeated awkwardly, and carried her down into the saloon of the Chris-craft. His own body felt battered as though his very bones were bruised and cracked, but he handled her so tenderly that slowly the resistance went out of her and she melted against him.

He lowered her onto the leather padded bench, but when he tried to straighten up she slid one arm around his neck and restrained him, clinging to him.

'I left the knife there,' she whispered huskily. 'It was a test.'

'Let me get the medicine chest.' He tried to pull away.

'No.' She shook her head and winced at the pain in her throat. 'Don't go away, Peter. Stay with me. I am so afraid. I was going to kill you if you took the knife. I nearly did. Oh, Peter, what is happening to us, are we both going mad?'

She held him desperately and he sank to his knees on the deck and bowed over her.

'Yes,' he answered her, holding her to his chest. 'Yes, we

must be going mad. I don't understand myself or any of it any more.'

'Why did you have to take the knife, Peter? Please – you must tell me. Don't lie, tell me the truth, I have to know why.'

'Because of Melissa-Jane – because of what you had done to her—'

He felt her jerk in his arms as though he had struck her again. She tried to speak but now her voice was only a croak of despair, and Peter went on to explain it to her.

'When I discovered that you were Caliph, I had to kill you.'

She seemed to be gathering herself for some major effort, but then when she spoke it was still in that scratchy broken whisper.

'Why did you stop yourself, Peter?'

'Because—' He knew the reason then. ' – Because suddenly I knew that I loved you. Nothing else counted.'

She gasped and was silent again for nearly a minute.

'Do you still think that I am Caliph?' she asked at last.

'I don't know. I don't know anything any more – except that I love you. That's all that matters.'

'What happened to us, Peter?' She lamented softly. 'Oh God, what has happened to us?'

'Are you Caliph, Magda?'

'But Peter, you tried to kill me. That was the test with the knife. You are Caliph.'

Under Magda's direction Peter took the Chris-craft in through a narrow passage in the coral reef that surrounded Île des Oiseaux, while the seabirds wheeled about them in a raucous cloud, filling the air with their wingbeats.

He anchored in five fathoms in the protected lee, and

then called the main island on the VHF radio, speaking to the head boatman.

'The Baronne has decided to sleep on board overnight,' he explained. 'Don't worry about us.'

When he went down to the saloon again Magda had recovered sufficiently to be sitting up. She had pulled on one of the terry towelling track suits from the clothes locker, and she had wound a clean towel around her throat to protect it and to hide the fierce fresh bruise that was already staining her skin like the squeezed juice of an over-ripe plum.

Peter found the medicine box in a locker above the toilet bowl of the heads, and she protested when he brought two Temprapain capsules for the pain, and four tablets of Brufin for the swelling and bruising of her throat and body.

'Take them,' he commanded and held the glass while she did so.

Then he carefully unwrapped the towel from her throat and lightly rubbed a creamy salve into the bruise with his fingertips.

'That feels better already,' she whispered, but now she had lost her voice almost entirely.

'Let's have a look at your stomach.' He pushed her down gently on her back on the long padded bench and unzipped the top of the towelling suit to the waist. The bruise where he had kicked her had spread from just below her small pale breasts to the tiny sculpted navel in the flat hard plane of her belly; again he massaged the soothing cream into her skin and she sighed and murmured with the comfort of it. When he finished she was able to hobble, still painfully doubled over, to the heads. She locked herself in for fifteen minutes while Peter tended his own injuries, and when she emerged again she had bathed her face and combed out her hair.

He poured two crystal old-fashioned glasses half full of Jack Daniel's Bourbon and he handed one to her as she sank onto the padded bench beside him. 'Drink it. For your throat,' he ordered, and she drank and gasped at the sting of the liquor and set the glass aside.

'And you, Peter?' she husked with sudden concern. 'Are you all right?'

'Just one thing,' he said. 'I'd hate you to get really mad at me.' Then he smiled, and she started to chuckle but choked on the pain and ended up clinging to him.

'When can we talk?' he asked her gently. 'We have to talk this out.'

'Yes, I know, but not yet, Peter. Just hold me for a while.' And he was surprised at the comfort that it afforded him. The warm woman shape pressed to him seemed to ease the pain of body and of mind, and he stroked her hair as she nuzzled softly against his throat.

'You said you loved me,' she murmured at last, making it a question. Seeking reassurance, as lovers always must.

'Yes. I love you. I think I knew it all along, but when I learned that you were Caliph, I had to bury it deep. It was only there at the end I had to admit to myself.'

'I'm glad,' she said simply. 'Because you see I love you also. I thought I would never be able to love. I had despaired of it, Peter. Until you. And then they told me you would kill me. That you were Caliph. I thought then I would die – having found you and then lost you. It was too cruel, Peter. I had to give you the chance to prove it wasn't true!'

'Don't talk,' he commanded. 'Just lie there and listen. There is nothing wrong with my voice, so I will tell it first. The way it was with me, and how I knew you were Caliph.'

And he told it to her, holding her to him and speaking softly, steadily. The only other sounds in the cabin were the slap of the wavelets against the hull and the subdued hum of the air-conditioning unit.

'You know everything up to the day Melissa-Jane was taken, all of it. I told you all of it, without reservation and without lying, not once—' He started, and then he went on to tell her in detail of the hunt for Melissa-Jane.

' – I think something must have snapped in my mind during those days. I was ready to believe anything, to try anything to get her back. I would wake up in the night and go to the toilet and vomit with the thought of her hand in a glass jar.'

He told her how he had planned to kill Kingston Parker to meet Caliph's demands, exactly how he intended doing it, the detailed how and where, and she shuddered against him.

'The power to corrupt even the best,' she whispered.

'Don't talk—' he admonished her, and went on to tell her of the tip-off that had led them at last to the Old Manse in Laragh.

'When I saw my daughter like that, I lost what little was left of my reason. When I held her and felt the fever and heard her scream with lingering terror, I would have killed—' He broke off and they were silent until she protested with a small gasp and he realized that his hand had closed on her upper arm and his fingers were biting into her flesh with the force of his memories.

'I'm sorry.' He relaxed his grip, and lifted the hand to touch her cheek. 'Then they told me about you.'

'Who?' she whispered.

'The Atlas Command.'

'Parker?'

'Yes, and Colin Noble.'

'What did they tell you?'

'They told me how your father brought you to Paris when you were a child. They told me that even then you were bright and pretty and special—' He began to recite it for her. ' – When your father was killed—' and she moved restlessly against his chest as he said it ' – you went to live with foster parents, all of them members of the party, and

371

in the end you were so special that they sent somebody to take you back to Poland. Somebody who posed as your uncle—'

'I believed he was—' She nodded. ' – For ten years I believed it. He used to write to me—' She stopped herself with an effort, was silent a moment and then, ' – he was all I ever had after Papa.'

'You were selected to go to Odessa,' Peter went on, and felt her go very still in his arms, so he repeated it with the harshness unconcealed in his tone, ' – to the special school in Odessa.'

'You know about Odessa?' she whispered. 'Or you think you know – but nobody who has never been there could ever really know.'

'I know they taught you to—' He paused, imagining again a beautiful young girl in a special room overlooking the Black Sea, learning to use her body to trap and beguile a man, any man. ' – They taught you many things.' He could not make the accusation.

'Yes,' she murmured. 'Many, many things.'

'Like how to kill a man with your hands.'

'I think that subconsciously I could not bring myself to kill you, Peter. God knows you should not have survived. I loved you, even though I hated you for betraying me, I could not really do it—'

She sighed again, a broken gusty sound.

' – And when I thought that you were going to kill me – it was almost a relief. I was ready to accept that, against living on without the love that I thought I had found.'

'You talk too much.' He stopped her. 'You'll damage your throat further.' He touched her lips with his fingers, to silence her, and then went on. 'And at Odessa you became one of the chosen, one of the élite.'

'It was like entering the church, a beautiful mystic thing—' she whispered. 'I cannot explain it. I would have done everything or anything for the State, for what I knew was right for "Mother Russia".'

'All of this is true?' He marvelled that she made no effort to deny it.

'All of it,' she nodded painfully. 'I will never lie to you again, Peter. I swear it.'

'Then they sent you back to France – to Paris?' he asked, and she nodded.

'You did your job, even better than they had expected you to do it. You were the best, the very best. No man could resist you.'

She did not answer, but she did not lower her eyes from his. It was not a defiance but merely a total acceptance of what he was saying.

'There were men. Rich and powerful men—' His voice was bitter now. He could not help himself. 'Many, many men. Nobody knows how many, and from each of them you gathered harvest.'

'Poor Peter,' she whispered. 'Have you tortured yourself with that?'

'It helped me to hate you,' he said simply.

'Yes, I understand that. There is nothing that I can give you for your comfort – except this. I never loved a man until I met you.'

She was keeping her word. There were no more lies nor deceptions now. He was certain of it.

'Then they decided that you could be used to take over control of Aaron Altmann and his Empire—'

'No,' she whispered, shaking her head. 'I decided on Aaron. He had been the only one man who I had not been able to—' Her voice pinched out and she took a sip of the bourbon and let it trickle slowly down her throat before she went on. 'He fascinated me. I had never met a man like that before. So strong, such raw power.'

'All right,' Peter agreed. 'You might even have grown tired of the other role by then—'

'It's hard work being a courtesan—' She smiled for the first time since he had begun speaking, but it was a sad self-mocking smile.

'You went about it exactly the right way. First you made yourself indispensable to him. Already he was a sick man, beginning to need a crutch, somebody he could trust entirely. You gave him that—'

She said nothing, but memories passed across her eyes, changing the green shadows like sunlight through a deep still pool.

' – And when he trusted you there was nothing you could not supply to your masters. Your value had increased a hundredfold.'

He went on talking quietly while outside the day died in a fury of crimsons and royal purples, slowly altering the light in the cabin and dimming it down so that her face was all that existed in the soft gloom. A pale intense expression, listening quietly to the accusations, to the recitation of betrayals and deceits. Only occasionally she made a little gesture of denial, a shake of her head or the pressure of fingers on his arms. Sometimes she closed her eyes briefly as though she could not accept some particularly cruel memory, and once or twice an exclamation was wrung from her in that strained and tortured whisper.

'Oh God, Peter! It's true!'

He told her how she had gradually developed the taste for the power she was able to wield as Aaron Altmann's wife, and how that flourished as Aaron's strength declined. How she at last even opposed the Baron on some issues.

'Like that of supplying arms to the South African Government,' Peter said, and she nodded and made one of her rare comments.

'Yes. We argued. That was one of the few times we argued.' And she smiled softly, as though at a private memory that she could not share even with him.

He told her how the taste of power and the trappings of

power gradually eroded her commitment to her earlier political ideals, how her masters slowly realized they were losing their hold over her and of the pressures they attempted to apply to force her back into the fold. 'But you were too powerful now to respond to the usual pressures. You had even succeeded in penetrating Aaron's Mossad connections, and had that protection.'

'This is incredible!' she whispered. 'It's so close, so very close that it is the truth.' He waited for her to elaborate, but instead she motioned him to continue.

'When they threatened to expose you to the Baron as a communist agent, you had no choice but to get rid of him – and you did it in such a way that you not only got rid of the threat to your existence but you also achieved control of Altmann Industries, and to put the cherry on the top of the pie you got yourself twenty-five million in operating capital. You arranged the abduction and killing of Aaron Altmann, you paid yourself the twenty-five million and personally supervised its transfer, probably to a numbered account in Switzerland—'

'Oh God, Peter!' she whispered, and in the dark of the cabin her eyes were fathomless and huge as the empty cavities of a skull.

'Is it true?' Peter asked for confirmation for the first time.

'It's too horrible. Go on please.'

'It worked so well that it opened up a new world of possibilities for you. Just about this time you truly became Caliph. The taking of Flight 070 was possibly not the first stroke after the kidnapping of Aaron Altmann – there may have been others. Vienna and the OPEC ministers, the Red Brigade activities in Rome – but 070 was the first time you used the name Caliph. It worked, except for the dereliction of duty by a subordinate officer.' He indicated himself. 'That was all that stopped it – and that was how I attracted your attention originally.'

Now it was almost totally dark in the cabin and Magda

reached across and switched on the reading light beside them, adjusting the rheostat down to a soft golden glow. In its light she studied his face seriously as he went on.

' – By this time you were aware through your special sources, probably the Mossad connection and almost certainly through the French SID, that somebody was onto Caliph. That somebody turned out to be Kingston Parker and his Atlas organization, and I was the ideal person to firstly confirm that Parker was the hunter – and secondly, to assassinate him. I had the special training and talents for the job, I could get close to him without arousing his suspicions, and I needed only to be sufficiently motivated—'

'No,' she whispered, unable to take her eyes from his face.

'It holds together,' he said. 'All of it.' And she had no reply.

'When I received Melissa-Jane's finger, I was ready for anything—'

'I think I am going to be sick.'

'I'm sorry.' He gave her the glass and she drank the shot of dark liquor it contained, gagging a little on it. Then she sat for a few moments with her eyes closed and her hand on her bruised throat.

'All right?' he asked at last.

'Yes. All right now. Go on.'

'It worked perfectly – except for the tip-off to the hide-out in Ireland. But nobody could have foreseen that, not even Caliph.'

'But there was no proof!' she protested. 'It was all conjecture. No proof that I was Caliph.'

'There was,' he told her quietly. 'O'Shaughnessy, the head of the gang that kidnapped Melissa-Jane, made two telephone calls. They were traced to Rambouillet 47–87–47.'

She stared at him wordlessly.

'He was reporting to his master – to Caliph, you see.'
And he waited for her reply. There was none, so after a
minute of silence he went on to tell her the arrangements
he had made for her execution – the sites he had chosen at
Longchamp race course and in the Avenue Victor Hugo,
and she shuddered as though she had felt the brush of the
black angels' wings across her skin.

'I would have been there,' she admitted. 'You chose the
two best sites. Yves has arranged a private showing for me
on the sixth of next month. I would have gone to it.'

' – Then you saved me the trouble. You invited me here.
I knew that it was an invitation to die, that you knew I had
become aware, that I had learned you were Caliph. I saw it
in your eyes during that meeting at Orly Airport, I saw it
proven by the way you were suddenly avoiding me, the way
you were giving me no opportunity to do the job I had to
do.'

'Go on.'

'You had me searched when I landed at Tahiti-Faaa.'

She nodded.

'You had the grey wolves search my room again last
night, and you set it up for today. I knew I had to strike
first, and I did.'

'Yes,' she murmured. 'You did.' And rubbed her throat
again.

He went to recharge the glasses from the concealed
liquor cabinet behind the bulkhead, and came back to sit
beside her.

She shifted slightly, moving inside the circle of his arm,
and he held her in silence. The telling of it had exhausted
him, and his body ached relentlessly, but he was glad it was
said, somehow it was like lancing a malignant abscess – the
release of poisons was a relief, and now the healing process
could begin.

He could feel his own exhaustion echoed in the slim
body that drooped against him, but he sensed that hers was

deeper, she had taken too much already – and when he lifted her in his arms again she made no protest, and he carried her like a sleeping child through to the master cabin and laid her on the bunk.

He found pillows and a blanket in the locker below. He slid into the bunk with her, under the single blanket, and she fitted neatly into the curve of his body, pressing gently against him, her back against his chest, her hard round buttocks against the front of his thighs, and her head pillowed into the crook of his arm, while with his other arm he cuddled her close and his hand naturally cupped one of her breasts. They fell asleep like that, pressing closely, and when he rolled over she moved without waking, reversing their positions, moulding herself to his back and pressing her face into the nape of his neck, clasping him with one arm and with a leg thrown over his lower body as though to enfold him completely.

Once he woke and she was gone, and the strength of his alarm surprised him, a hundred new doubts and fears assailed him from the darkness, then he heard the liquid purr in the bowl of the heads and he relaxed. When she returned to the bunk, she had stripped off the terry towelling track suit and her naked body felt somehow very vulnerable and precious in his arms.

They woke together with sunlight pouring into the cabin through one porthole like stage lighting.

'My God – it must be noon.' She sat up, and tossed back the long mane of dark hair over her tanned bare shoulders – but when Peter tried to rise, he froze and groaned aloud.

'Qu'a tu, chéri?'

'I must have got caught in a concrete mixer,' he moaned. His bruises had stiffened during the night, torn muscle and strained sinews protested his slightest movement.

'There is only one cure for both of us,' she told him. 'It's in three parts.'

And she helped him off the bunk as though he was an

378

old man. He exaggerated the extent of his injuries a little to make her chuckle. The chuckle was a little hoarse, but her voice was stronger and clearer and she favoured her own bruises only a little as she led him up onto the deck. Her powers of recuperation were those of a young and superbly fit thoroughbred animal.

They swam from the diving platform over the Chris-craft's stern.

'It's working,' Peter admitted as the support of warm salt-water soothed his battered body. They swam side by side, both naked, slowly at first and then faster, changing the sedate breast-stroke for a hard overarm crawl, back as far as the reef, treading water there and gasping at the exertion.

'Better?' she panted with her hair floating around her like the tendrils of some beautiful water plant.

'Much better.'

'Race you back.'

They reached the Chris-craft together and clambered up into the cockpit, cascading water and laughing and panting, but when he reached for her, she allowed only a fleeting caress before pulling away.

'First Phase Two of the cure.'

She worked in the galley with only a floral apron around her waist which covered the dark bruises of her belly.

'I never thought an apron could be provocative before.'

'You are supposed to be doing the coffee,' she admonished him and gave him a lewd little bump and grind with her bare backside.

Her omelettes were thick and golden and fluffy, and they ate them in the early sunlight on the upper deck. The trade wind was sheep-dogging a flock of fluffy silver cloud across the heavens, and in the gaps the sky was a peculiar brilliant blue.

They ate with huge appetites, for the bright new morning seemed to have changed the mood of doom that had overpowered them the previous night. Neither of them wanted to break this mood, and they chattered inconsequential nonsense, and exclaimed at the beauty of the day and threw bread crusts to the seagulls, like two children on a picnic.

At last she came to sit in his lap, and made a show of taking his pulse.

'The patient is much improved,' she announced; 'is now probably strong enough for Phase Three of the cure.'

'Which is?' he asked.

'Peter *chéri*, even if you *are* English, you are not that dense.' And she wriggled her bottom in his lap.

They made love in the warm sunlight, on one of the foam mattresses, with the trade wind teasing their bodies like unseen fingers.

It began in banter and with low gurgles of laughter, little gasps of rediscovery, and murmurs of welcome and encouragement – then suddenly it changed, it became charged with almost unbearable intensity, a storm of emotion that sought to sweep all the ugliness and doubt. They were caught up in the raging torrent that carried them helplessly beyond mere physical response into an unknown dimension from which there seemed no way back, a total affirmation of their bodies and their minds that made all else seem inconsequential.

'I love you,' she cried at the very end, as though to deny all else that she had been forced to do. 'I have loved only you.' It was a cry torn from the very depths of her soul.

It took a long time for them to return from the far place to which they had been driven, to become two separate people again, but when they did somehow they both sensed that they would never again be completely separated; there had been a deeper more significant union than just that of their two bodies, and the knowledge sobered them and yet, at the same time, gave them both new strength and a deep elation that neither had to voice – it was there, and they both simply knew it.

They slid the big inflatable Avon S 650 dinghy over the stern, and went ashore, pulling the rubber craft above the high-water level and mooring it to one of the slanting palm boles.

Then they wandered inland, picking their way hand in hand between the seabird nests that had been crudely scraped in the earth. Half a dozen different species of birds were breeding together in one sprawling colony that covered most of the twenty-acre island. Their eggs varied from cool pale blue as big as that of a goose's, to others the size of a pullet's and speckled and spotted in lovely free-form designs. The chicks were either grotesquely ugly with bare parboiled bodies or were cute as Walt Disney animations. The entire island was pervaded by an endless susurration of thousands of wings and the uproar of squawking, screeching, feuding and mating birds.

Magda knew the zoological names of each species, its range and its habits, and its chances of survival or extinction in the changing eco-systems of the oceans.

Peter listened to her tolerantly, sensing that behind this chatter and studied gaiety she was steeling herself to answer the accusations that he had levelled at her.

At the far end of the island was a single massive takamaka tree, with dense green foliage spreading widely over the fluffy white sand. By now the sun was fiercely bright and the heat and humidity smothered them like a woollen blanket dipped in hot water.

They sought the shade of the takamaka gratefully, and sat close together on the sand staring out across the unruffled waters of the lagoon to the silhouette of the main island, five miles away. At this range and angle there was no sign of the buildings nor of the jetty, and Peter had an illusion of the primeval paradise with the two of them the first man and woman on a fresh and innocent earth.

Magda's next words dispelled that illusion entirely.

'Who ordered you to kill me, Peter? How was the

command given? I must know that before I tell you about myself.'

'Nobody,' he answered.

'Nobody? There was no message like the one you received ordering you to kill Parker?'

'No.'

'Parker himself or Colin Noble? They did not order you to do it – or suggest it?'

'Parker expressly ordered me not to do it. You were not to be touched – until you could be taken in jeopardy.'

'It was your own decision?' she insisted.

'It was my duty.'

'To avenge your daughter?'

He hesitated, would have qualified it, then nodded with total self-honesty. 'Yes, that was the most part of it, Melissa-Jane, but I saw it also as my duty to destroy anything evil enough to envisage the taking of 070, the abduction of Aaron Altmann and the mutilation of my daughter.'

'Caliph knows about us. Understands us better than we understand ourselves. I am not a coward, Peter, but now I am truly afraid.'

'Fear is the tool of his trade,' Peter agreed, and she moved slightly, inviting physical contact. He placed one arm about her bare brown shoulders and she leaned lightly against him.

'All that you told me last night was the truth, only the inferences and conclusions were false. Papa's death, the lonely years with strangers as foster-parents – of that period my clearest memories are of lying awake at night and trying to muffle the sound of my weeping with a false blanket. The return to Poland, yes, that was right, and the Odessa school – all of that. I will tell you about Odessa one day, if you truly want to hear it – ?'

'I don't think I do,' he said.

'Perhaps you are wise; do you want to hear about the return to Paris?'

382

'Only what is necessary.'

'All right, Peter. There were men. That was what I had been selected and trained for. Yes, there were men—' She broke off, and reached up to take his face between her hands, turning it so she could look into his eyes. 'Does that make a difference between us, Peter?'

'I love you,' he replied firmly.

She stared into his eyes for a long time looking for evidence of deceit, and then when she found none, 'Yes. It is so. You really mean that.'

She sighed with relief and laid her head against his shoulder, speaking quietly with just that intriguing touch of accent and the occasional unusual turn of phrase.

'I did not like the men, either, Peter. I think that was why I chose Aaron Altmann. One man, yes I could still respect myself—' She shrugged lightly. 'I chose Aaron, and Moscow agreed. It was, as you said, delicate work. First I had to win his respect. He had never respected a woman before. I proved to him I was as good as any man, at any task he wished to set me. After I had his respect, all else followed—' She paused and chuckled softly. ' – Life plays naughty tricks. I found firstly that I liked him, then I grew to respect him also. He was a great ugly bull of a man, but the power ... A huge raw power, like some cosmic force, became the centre of my existence.' She lifted her head to touch Peter's cheek with her lips in reassurance. 'No. Peter, I never came to love him. I never loved before you. But I stood in vast awe of him, like a member of a primitive tribe worships the lightning and the thunder. It was like that. He dominated my existence – more than a father, more than a teacher, as much as a god – but less, very much less than a lover. He was crude and strong. He did not make love, he could only rut and tup like the bull he was.'

She broke off and looked seriously at him. 'Do you understand that, Peter? Perhaps I explained it badly?'

'No,' he assured her. 'You explained it very well.'

'Physically he did not move me, his smell and the hairiness. He had hair on his shoulders and like a pelt down his back. His belly was bulging and hard as iron—' She shivered briefly. ' – But I had been trained to be able to ignore that. To switch off something in the front of my brain. Yet in all other ways he fascinated me. He goaded me to think forbidden thoughts, to open vaults of my mind that my training had securely locked. All right, he taught me about power and its trappings. You accused me of that, Peter, and I admit it. The flavour of power and money was to my taste. I like it. I like it very much indeed. Aaron introduced me to that. He showed me how to appreciate fine and beautiful things, for he was only physically a bull and he had a wonderful appreciation of the refinements of life – he made me come completely alive. Then he laughed at me. God, I can still hear the bellow of his laughter, and see that great hairy belly shaking with it.'

She paused to remember it, almost reverently, and then she chuckled her own husky little laugh.

'"My fine little communist lady," he mocked me. 'Yes, Peter, it was I who was deceived, he had known from the beginning who I was. He also knew about the school at Odessa. He had accepted me as a challenge, certainly he loved me – or his version of love, but he took me knowingly and corrupted my pure ideological convictions. Only then did I learn that all the information which I had been able to pass to Moscow had been carefully screened by Aaron. He doubled me, as I had been sent to double him. He was Mossad, but of course you know that. He was a Zionist, you know that also. And he made me realize that I was a Jewess, and what it meant to be that. He showed me every fatal flaw in the doctrine of Universal Communism, he convinced me of democracy and the Western Capitalist system and then he recruited me to Mossad—'

She stopped again, and shook her head vehemently.

' – To believe that I could have wished to destroy such a

one. That I could have ordered his abduction and mutilation – Towards the end, when he was getting weak, when the pain was very bad, that was the closest I ever came to loving him, the way a mother loves a child. He became pathetically dependent upon me; he used to say the only thing that could lull the pain was my touch. I used to sit for hours rubbing that hairy belly – feeling that awful thing growing bigger inside him each day, like a cauliflower or a grotesque foetus. He would not let them cut it. He hated them, "butchers" he called them. "Butchers with their knives and rubber tubes – "'

She broke off and Peter realized that her eyes were filled with tears. He hugged her a little more firmly and waited for her to recover.

'It must have been about this time that Caliph made contact with Aaron. Thinking back I can remember the time when he became suddenly terribly agitated. It made little sense to me then, but he held long diatribes about right-wing tyranny being indistinguishable from tyranny of the left. He never mentioned the name Caliph, I do not think Caliph had yet used that name – and I do believe that Aaron would eventually have told me of the contact in detail, if he had lived. It was the way he was, even with me, he could be as wary and subtle as he could be overpowering. He would have told me of Caliph – but Caliph saw to it that he did not.'

She pulled away from Peter's arms so she could again see his face.

'You must understand, *chéri*, that much of this I have learned only recently – in the last few weeks. Much of it I can only piece together like a jig puzzle – pardon, a jig-saw puzzle.' She corrected herself swiftly. 'But this is what must have happened. Caliph contacted Aaron with a proposition. It was a very simple proposition. He was invited to become a partner of Caliph. Aaron was to make a substantial financial contribution to Caliph's war-chest, and to place his privileged knowledge and lines of influence at Caliph's disposal. In return he would have a hand in engineering Caliph's brave new world. It was a miscalculation on Caliph's part, perhaps the only mistake he has made up to now. He had misjudged Aaron Altmann. Aaron turned him down flat – but much more dangerously Caliph had made the mistake of revealing his identity to Aaron. I expect that he had to do that in an effort to convince Aaron. You see, Aaron was not a man who would indulge in a game of code-names and hidden identities. That much Caliph had divined correctly. So he had to confront Aaron face to face, and when he discovered that Aaron would not join in a campaign of murder and extortion – no matter how laudable the ultimate ends – Caliph had no choice. He took Aaron, killed him after torturing him hideously for information that could have been useful, mainly information about his Mossad connection I imagine. Then he persuaded me to pay the ransom. He won two major tricks with a single card. He silenced Aaron, and he gained the twenty-five million for his war-chest.'

'How did you learn this? If only you had explained to me before—' Peter heard the bitterness in his own voice.

'I did not know it when we first met, *chéri*, please believe me. I will tell you how I learned it, but please be patient with me. Let me tell it as it happened.'

'I am sorry,' he said simply.

'The first time I heard the name "Caliph" was the day I delivered the ransom. I told you about that, didn't I?'

'Yes.'

'So we come now to your part. I heard of you for the first time with the Johannesburg hijacking of Flight 070. I thought that you might be the one to help me hunt down Caliph. I found out about you, Peter. I was even able to have a computer printout on you—' She paused, and there was that mischievous flash in her eye again. ' – I will admit to being very impressed with the formidable list of your ladies.'

Peter held up both hands in a gesture of surrender.

'Never again,' he pleaded. 'Not another word – agreed?'

'Agreed.' She laughed, and then, 'I'm hungry, and my throat is sore again with all this talking.'

They crossed the island again, with their bare feet baking on the sun-heated sand, and went back on board the Chriscraft.

The chef had stocked the refrigerator with a cornucopia of food, and Peter opened a bottle of Veuve Cliquot champagne.

'You've got expensive tastes,' he observed. 'I don't know if I can afford to keep you – on my salary.'

'I'm sure we could arrange a raise from your boss,' she assured him with the twinkle in her eyes. In tacit agreement they did not mention Caliph again until they had eaten.

' – There is one other thing you must understand, Peter. I am of Mossad, but I do not control them. They control me. It was the same with Aaron. Both of us were and are very valuable agents, possibly amongst the most valuable of all their networks, but I do not make decisions, nor am I able to have access to all their secrets.

'Mossad's single-minded goal is the safety and security of the state of Israel. It has no other reason for existence. I was certain that Aaron had made a full report to Mossad of Caliph's identity, that he had detailed the proposition that Caliph had proposed – and I suspect that Mossad had ordered Aaron to co-operate with Caliph—'

'Why?' Peter demanded sharply.

'I do not know for certain – but I can think of two reasons. Caliph must have been such a powerful and influential man that his support would have been valuable. Then again I suspect that Caliph had pro-Israeli leanings, or professed to have those leanings. Mossad finds allies where it can, and does not question their morals. I think they ordered Aaron to co-operate with Caliph – but—'

'But?' Peter prompted her.

'But you do not order a man like Aaron to go against his deepest convictions, and under that forbidding exterior Aaron Altmann was a man of great humanity. I think that the reason for his agitation was the conflict of duty and belief that he was forced to endure. His instinct warned him to destroy Caliph, and his duty—'

She shrugged, and picked up her fluted champagne glass, twisting it between those long slim fingers and studying the pinpricks of bubbles as they rose slowly through the pale golden wine. When she spoke again she had changed direction disconcertingly.

'A thousand times I had tried to discover what was so different between you and me than with the other men I have known. Why none of them could move me – and yet with you it was almost instantaneous—' She looked up at him again as though she was still seeking the reason. ' – Of course, I knew so much about you. You had the qualities I admire in another human being, so I was disposed favourably – but there are other qualities you cannot detail on a computer printout nor capture in a photograph. There was something about you that made me—' She made a helpless gesture as she searched for the word. ' – You made me tingle.'

'That's a good word,' Peter smiled.

'And I had never tingled before. So I had to be very sure. It was a new experience to want a man merely because he is gentle and strong and—' she chuckled, ' – just plain sexy. You are sexy, you know that, Peter, but also you are something else—' She broke off. 'No, I am not going to flatter you any more. I do not want you to get swollen ankles—' mixing the French idiom quaintly with the English, and this time not correcting herself. She went straight on. 'Caliph must have realized that I had recruited a dangerous ally. He made the attempt to kill you that night on the Rambouillet road—'

'They were after you,' Peter cut in.

'Who, Peter? Who was after me?'

'The Russians – by that time they knew you were a double agent.'

'Yes, they knew—' She cocked her head and narrowed her eyes. 'I had thought about it, of course, and there had been two previous attempts on me, but I do not think the attempt on the Rambouillet road was Russian.'

'All right, Caliph then, but after you – not me,' Peter suggested.

'Perhaps, but again I do not think so. My instinct tells me they had the right target. They were after you.'

'I would have to agree,' Peter said. 'I think I was followed when I left Paris that evening—' and he told her about the Citroën. ' – I think they knew that I was alone in the Maserati.'

'Then we accept it was Caliph,' she stated flatly.

' – or Mossad,' Peter murmured, and her eyes slowly widened, turning a darker thoughtful green as Peter went on.

'What if Mossad did not want an Atlas man getting close to their star agent, they didn't want you to have an ally in your hunt for Caliph? What if they just didn't want me cluttering up the carefully rehearsed scenario?'

'Peter, it's very deep water—'

' – and there are packs of sharks.'

'Let's leave that night on the Rambouillet road for the moment,' she suggested. 'It merely complicates the story I am trying to tell you.'

'All right,' Peter agreed. 'We can come back to it, if we have to.'

'The next significant move was the abduction of Melissa-Jane,' she said, and Peter's expression changed, becoming flat and stony.

'The choice of the victim was genius-inspired,' she said. 'But it required no special knowledge of you or your domestic arrangements. There was no secret that you had an only child, and it needed but a casual appraisal of your character to understand how powerful a lever she could be—' Magda dipped the tip of her finger into the champagne and then sucked it thoughtfully, pursing her lips and frowning slightly.

'You must understand that by this time I had faced the fact that I was in love with you. The gift was supposed to affirm that—' She flushed slightly under her honey tan, and it was appealing and child-like. He had never seen her blush before and it twisted something in his chest.

'The book,' he remembered. 'The Cornwallis Harris first edition.'

'My first love gift ever. I bought it when I finally admitted it to myself – but I was determined that I would not admit it to you. I am old-fashioned enough to believe the man must speak first.'

'I did.'

'God, I'll never forget it,' she said fervently, and they both thought of the savage confrontation the previous day which had ended incongruously in a declaration of love.

'I try to be unconventional,' he said, and she shook her head smiling.

'You succeed, *mon amour*, oh how you succeed.' Then she sobered again. 'I was in love with you. Your distress was mine. The child was a lovely girl, she had captivated me when we met – and on top of all that I felt deadly responsible for her plight. I had inveigled you into joining my hunt for Caliph, and because of that you had lost your daughter.'

He bowed his head slightly, remembering how he had believed that she had engineered it. She recognized the gesture.

'Yes, Peter. For me it was the cruellest stroke. That you

390

should believe it of me. There was nothing that I would not have done to give her back to you – and yet there seemed nothing that I could do. My contacts with French intelligence had nothing for me. They had no inkling of how or where the child was being held – and my control at Mossad was unaccountably evasive. Somehow I had the feeling that Mossad had the key to the kidnapping. If they were not directly involved they knew more than anybody else. I have already explained that I believed Aaron had given them the identity of Caliph. If that was so, then they must know something that could have helped you to recover your child – but from Paris I was powerless to gather that information. I had to go in person to Israel and confront my control there. It was the one chance that I could get them to co-operate. They might believe my value as an agent was worth enough to give me a lead to Melissa-Jane—'

'You threatened Mossad with resignation?' Peter asked wonderingly. 'You would have done that for me?'

'Oh, Peter, don't you understand? I loved you – and I had never been in love before. I would have done anything for you.'

'You make me feel humble,' he said.

She did not reply, but let the statement stand as though she were savouring it, then she sighed contentedly and went on. 'I left everything in Paris. I have an established routine for disappearing when it is necessary. Pierre took me to Rome in the Lear; from there I telephoned you but I could not tell you what I was going to do. Then I switched identity and took a commercial flight to Tel Aviv. My task in Israel was difficult, much more difficult than I had bargained for. It was five days before my control would see me. He is an old friend. No! perhaps not a friend, but we have known each other a long time. He is the deputy-director of Mossad. That is how highly they value my services, to give me such an important controller, but still it took five days before he would see me, and he was cold.

There was no help they could give me, he said. They knew nothing.' She chuckled. 'You have never seen me when I want something really badly, Peter. Ha! – What a battle. There is much I knew that would embarrass Mossad with her powerful allies of the West – with France and Great Britain and the U.S.A. – I threatened to hold a Press conference in New York. He became less cold, he told me that the security of the State took precedence over all personal feelings, and I said something very rude about the security of the State, and reminded him of some outstanding business which I would happily leave outstanding. He became warmer – but all this was taking time, days, many days, too many days. I was going crazy. I remembered how they had found Aaron's body, and I could not sleep at night for worrying about that lovely child. And you, oh Peter, you will never know how I prayed to a god that I was not too sure of. You will never know how I wanted to be with you to comfort you. I wanted so desperately just to hear your voice – but I could not break my cover from Tel Aviv. I could not even telephone you, nor send you a letter—' She broke off. ' – I hoped you would not believe bad things of me. You would not believe that I did not care. That I was not prepared to help you. I could only hope that I would be able to bring you some information of value to prove it was not true – but I never dreamed that one day you would believe that it was I who had taken your daughter and tortured her.'

'I am sorry,' he said quietly.

'No, do not say you are sorry. We were both Caliph's playthings. There is no blame on you.' She laid her hand upon his arm and smiled at him. 'It was not you alone who believed bad things. For at last I had prevailed on my Mossad control to give me some little scraps of information. At first he denied completely that they had ever heard of Caliph, but I risked lying to him. I told him that Aaron had told me he had reported the Caliph contact. He gave ground. Yes, he admitted. They knew of Caliph, but they did not know who he was. I hammered on, demanding to see my controller each day, driving him as mad as I was – until he threatened to have me deported even. But each time we met I wheedled and bullied a little more from him.

'At last he admitted, "All right, we know Caliph but he is very dangerous, very powerful – and he will become more powerful – God willing, he will become one of the most powerful men in the world, and he is a friend of Israel. Or rather we believe he is a friend of Israel."

'I bullied some more and he told me, "We have put an agent close to Caliph, very close to him, and we cannot jeopardize this agent. He is a valuable agent, very valuable but very vulnerable to Caliph. We cannot take the chance that Caliph could trace information back to him. We have to protect our man."

'Now I threatened, and he told me the agent's code-name to protect both of us should we ever have to make contact. The code-name is "CACTUS FLOWER".'

'That was all?' Peter asked, with evident disappointment.

'No, my control gave me another name. As a sop – and as a warning. The name they gave me was so close to Caliph as to be virtually the same. Again he warned me that he was giving me the name for my own protection.'

'What was it?' Peter demanded eagerly.

'Your name,' she said softly. 'Stride.'

Peter made an irritable gesture of dismissal. 'My name is nonsensical. Why would I kidnap and mutilate my own daughter – and Cactus Flower. He might as well have said, "Kentucky Fried Chicken".'

'Now it's my turn to say I'm sorry.'

Peter caught himself, realizing suddenly that he had been too quick to dismiss these scraps of information. He stood up and paced the deck of the Chris-craft with choppy, agitated steps, frowning heavily. 'Cactus Flower,' he repeated. 'Have you ever heard it before?'

'No,' she shook her head.

'Since then?'

'No,' again.

He searched his memory, trying for a sympathetic echo. There was none.

'All right.' He accepted that as having no immediate value. 'We'll just remember it for now. Let's come to my name – Peter Stride. What did you make of that?'

'It didn't mean anything then, except as a shock. Strangely enough I did not immediately think of you, but I thought of confusion between the kidnapper and the victim.'

'Stride?' he asked. 'Peter Stride? I don't understand.'

'No, well – Melissa-Jane is a Stride also.'

'Yes, of course. They didn't give you the name Peter Stride then?'

'No. Just Stride.'

'I see.' Peter stopped in mid-pace as an idea struck him – and stared out thoughtfully to where the ocean met a blue horizon.

'But they gave me your full name later,' she interrupted his thoughts.

'When?'

'After we received the news that Melissa-Jane had been rescued. Of course, I wanted to return to Paris immediately – to be with you. I was able to get onto a flight from Ben-Gurion Airport six hours after we heard the news. My heart was singing, Peter. Melissa-Jane was safe, and I was in love. I was going to be with you very soon. At the airport, while I was going through the security check before departure, the policewoman took me aside – to the security office. My control was waiting for me there. He had rushed out from Tel Aviv to catch me before I left for home, and he was very worried. They had just received an urgent message from Cactus Flower. General Peter Stride was now definitely Caliph-motivated, and would assassinate me at the first opportunity, he told me. And I laughed at him – but he was deadly serious. "My dear Baroness, Cactus Flower is a first-class man. You must take this warning seriously," he kept repeating.'

Magda shrugged. 'I still did not believe it, Peter. It was impossible. I loved you, and I knew you loved me – although perhaps you had not yet realized that yourself. It was crazy. But on the aircraft I had time to think. My control at Mossad has never been wrong before. Can you imagine my dilemma now – how dearly I wanted to be with you, and yet I was now terrified – not that you would kill me. That did not seem important – but that you would truly turn out to be Caliph. That was what really frightened me. You see, I had never loved a man before. I don't think I could have stood it.'

She was quiet for a while, remembering the pain and confusion, and then she shook her head so that the thick fall of dark shimmering hair rustled around her shoulders.

'Once I reached Paris, my first concern was to learn that you and Melissa-Jane were safe at Abbots Yew, and then I could begin to try and find out how much substance there was in Cactus Flower's warning – but until I could decide on how safe it was I could not take the chance of being alone with you. Every time you attempted to contact me, I had to deny you, and it felt as though some little part of me was dying.'

She reached across and took his hand now, opened the fingers and bowed her head to kiss the palm and then held it to her cheek as she went on.

'A hundred times I convinced myself that it could not be true, and I was on the point of going to you. Oh, Peter – finally I could take it no longer. I decided to meet you at Orly that day and find out one way or the other, end the terrible uncertainty. I had the grey wolves with me, as you remember, and they had been warned to expect trouble – I didn't tell them to watch you,' she explained quickly, as if trying to dispel any memory of disloyalty, 'but if you had tried to get at me they would have—' She broke off, and let his hand fall away from her cheek. 'The moment you walked into the private lounge at Orly, I saw it was true. I could sense it, there was an aura of death around you. It was the most frightening and devastating moment of my life, you looked like a different man – not the Peter Stride I knew – your whole face seemed to be altered and restructured by hatred and anger. I kissed you goodbye, because I knew we could never meet again.' Remembering it her face darkened with sadness, as though a cloud shadow had passed over them. 'I even thought that I had to protect myself by—' She gagged the words. ' – You were part of Caliph, you see, and it would have been the wise thing to do. I admit that I thought of it, Peter. Have you killed, before you could kill me – but it was only a thought and it did not go farther than that. Instead I went on with the business of living, work has always been an opiate for me. If I work hard enough I can forget anything – but this time it didn't turn out that way. I've said it before, but it explains so much that I will say it again. I had never been in love before, Peter, and I could not turn it off. It tormented me, and I cherished doubts – about Cactus Flower's warning and what I had seen so clearly in the lounge at Orly Airport. It couldn't be, it just couldn't be true – I loved you and you loved me, and you just couldn't be plotting to kill me. I almost convinced myself of that.'

She laughed curtly, but it had no humour in the sound, only the bitterness of disillusion.

'I came out here—' she made a gesture that embraced sea and sky and islands ' – to be away from the temptation of going to you. A sanctuary where I could recover from my wounds and begin to get over you. But it didn't work, Peter. It was worse here. I had more time to think, to torture myself with wild speculation and grotesque theories. There was only one way. Finally I recognized that. I would bring you out here and give you the chance to kill me.' She laughed again, and now there was the old husky warmth in it. 'It was the most crazy thing I have ever done in my life – but thank God, I did it.'

'We went right to the very brink,' Peter agreed.

'Peter, why didn't you ask me outright if I was Caliph?' she wanted to know.

'The same reason you didn't ask me outright if I was plotting to kill you.'

'Yes,' she agreed. 'We were just caught up in the web that Caliph had spun for us. I have only one more question, Peter *chéri*. If I was Caliph, do you truly believe that I would have been so stupid as to give my telephone number at Rambouillet to the man who kidnapped Melissa-Jane, and instruct him to ring me for a friendly chat whenever he felt like it?'

Peter looked startled, 'I thought—' he began, then stopped. ' – No, I didn't think. I wasn't thinking clearly at all. Of course, you wouldn't have done that – and yet, even the cleverest criminals make the most elementary mistakes.'

'Not those who have been trained at the Odessa school,' she reminded him, and seemed immediately to regret the words, for she went on quickly. 'So there is my side of the story, Peter. I may have left something out – if you can think of anything, then ask me, darling, and I'll try to fill in any missing pieces.'

And so they started once again at the very beginning, and went over the ground minutely, searching for anything they might have overlooked at the first telling of it, this time exhaustively re-examining each fact from every angle, both of them applying their trained minds to the full without being able to come up with more than they already had.

'One thing we must never let out of sight for a moment is the quality of the opposition.' Peter summed it up as the sun began lowering itself towards the western horizon, its majestic progress flanked by cohorts of cumulo-nimbus cloud rising into towering anvil heads over the scattered islands, like silent nuclear explosions.

'There are layers upon layers, reasons behind reasons, the kidnapping of Melissa-Jane was not merely to force me to assassinate Kingston Parker, but you as well – the proverbial two birds – with a third bird to follow. If I had succeeded I would have been hooked into Caliph for ever.'

'Where do you and I go from here, Peter?' she asked, tacitly transferring ultimate decision-making to him.

'How about home, right now,' he suggested. 'Unless you fancy another night out here.'

P eter found that his possessions had been discreetly moved from the guest bungalow to the owner's magnificent private quarters on the north tip of the island.

His toilet articles had been laid out in the mirrored master bathroom, which flanked that of the mistress. His clothing, all freshly cleaned and pressed, was in the master's dressing-room where there was one hundred and fifty-five feet of louvred hanging space – Peter paced it out and calculated it would take three hundred suits of clothing. There were specially designed swinging shelves for another three hundred shirts and racks for a hundred pairs of shoes although all were empty.

His light cotton suit looked as lonely as a single camel in the midst of the Sahara desert. His shoes had been burnished to a gloss that even his batman had never been able to achieve. Despite himself he searched the dressing-room swiftly for the signs of previous occupancy – and was ridiculously relieved to find none.

'I could learn to rough it like this,' he told his reflection in the mirror as he combed the damp, darkly curling locks off his forehead.

The sitting-room off the suite was on three levels, and had been decorated with cane furniture and luxuriant tropical plants growing in ancient Greek wine amphoras or in rockeries that were incorporated into the flowing design of the room. The creepers and huge glossy leaves of the plants toned in artistically with jungle-patterned curtaining and the dense growth of exotic plants beyond the tall picture windows – yet the room was cool and inviting, although the sound of air-conditioning was covered by the twinkle of a waterfall down the cunningly contrived rock face that comprised one curved wall of the room. Tropical fish floated gracefully in the clear pools into which the waterfall spilled, and the perfume of growing flowers pervaded the room, and their blooms glowed in the subdued lighting.

One of the little golden Polynesian girls brought a tray of four tall frosted glasses for Peter to choose from. They were all filled with fruit and he could smell the sweet warm odour of rum mingled with the fruit. He guessed they would be almost lethal and asked for a whisky, then relented with the girl's eyes flooded with disappointment.

'I make them myself,' she wailed.

'In that case—' He sipped while she waited anxiously.

'*Parfait!*' He exclaimed, and she giggled with gratification, and went off wriggling her bottom under the brief pareo like a happy puppy.

Magda came then in a chiffon dress so gossamer-light that it floated about her like a fine green sea mist, through which her limbs gleamed as the light caught them.

He felt the catch in his breathing as she came towards him, and he wondered if he would ever accustom himself to the impact of her beauty.

She took the glass from his hand and tasted it.

'Good,' she said, and handed it back. But when the girl brought the tray she refused with a smile.

They moved about the room, Magda on his arm as she pointed out the rarer plants and fishes.

'I built this wing after Aaron's death,' she told him, and he realized that she wanted him to know that it contained no memories of another man. It amused him that she should find that important – and then he remembered his own furtive search of the dressing-room for signs of a lover before him, and the amusement turned inward.

One wall of the private dining-room was a single sheet of armoured glass, beyond which the living jewels of coral fish drifted in subtly-lit sea caverns and the fronds of magnificent sea plants waved in gentle unseen currents.

Magda ordered the seating changed so they could be side by side in the low lovers' seat facing the aquarium.

'I do not like you to be far away any more,' she explained, and she picked special titbits from the serving dishes for his plate.

'This is a speciality of Les Neuf Poissons. You will eat it nowhere else in the world.' She selected small deep-sea crustaceans from a steaming creole sauce of spices and coconut cream and at the end of the meal she peeled chilled grapes from Australia with those delicate fingers, using the long shell-pink nails with the precision of a skilled surgeon to remove the pips and then placing them between his lips with thumb and forefinger.

'You spoil me,' he smiled.

'I never had a doll when I was a little girl,' she explained, smiling.

A circular stone staircase led to the beach fifty feet below the dining-room and they left their shoes on the bottom step and walked bare-footed on the smooth, damp sand, compacted as hard as cement by the receding tide. The moon was a few days past full, and its reflection drew a pathway of yellow light to the horizon.

'Caliph must be made to believe that he has succeeded,' Peter said abruptly, and she shivered against him.

'I wish we could forget Caliph for one night.'

'We cannot afford to forget him for a moment.'

'No, you are right. How do we make him believe that?'

'You have to die—' He felt her stiffen.

' – or at least appear to do so. It has to look as though I killed you.'

'Tell me,' she invited quietly.

'You told me that you have special arrangements for when you want to disappear.'

'Yes, I do.'

'How would you disappear from here if you had to do so?'

She thought for only a moment. 'Pierre would fly me to Bora-Bora. I have friends there. Good friends. I would take the island airline to Tahiti-Faaa on another passport – and then a scheduled airline in the same name to California or New Zealand.'

'You have other papers?' he demanded.

'Yes, of course.' She sounded so surprised by the question, that he expected her to ask ' – doesn't everybody?'

'Fine,' he said. 'And we'll arrange a suspicious accident here. A scuba diving accident, shark attack in deep water, no corpse.'

'What is the point of all this, Peter?'

'If you are dead – Caliph is not going to make another attempt to have you killed.'

'Good!' she agreed.

'So you stay officially dead until we flush Caliph out,' Peter told her, and it sounded like an order but she did not demur as he went on. 'And if I carry out Caliph's evident wishes by killing you, it's going to make me a very valuable asset. I will have proved myself, and so he will cherish me. It will give me another chance to get close to him. At least it will give me a chance to check out a few wild hunches.'

'Don't let's make my death too convincing, my love. I

am a great favourite of the police on Tahiti,' she murmured. 'I'd hate to have you end up under the guillotine at Tuarruru.'

Peter woke before her and raised himself on one elbow over her to study her face, delighting to find new planes and angles to her high broad cheekbones, gloating in the velvety texture of her skin, so fine that the pores were indefinable from farther than a few inches. Then he transferred his attention to the curve of her eyelashes that interlocked into a thick dark palisade seeming to seal her eyelids perpetually in sleep – yet they sprang open suddenly, the huge black pools of her pupils shrinking rapidly as she focused, and for the first time he realized that the irises were not pure green but were flecked and shot through with gold and violet.

The surprise of finding him over her changed slowly to pleasure, and she stretched her arms out over her head and arched her back, the way a lazy panther does when it rouses itself. The satin sheet slid down to her waist and she prolonged the stretch a little longer than was necessary, a deliberate display of her body.

'Every other morning of my life that I woke without you there was wasted,' she murmured huskily, and raised her arms still at full stretch to him, folding them gracefully around his neck, still holding her back arched so that the prominent dark-red nipples brushed lightly against the crisp dark mat of curls that covered his own chest.

'Let's pretend this will last for ever,' she whispered, with her lips an inch from his, and her breath was rich as an overblown rose, heavy with the smell of vital woman and rising passion; then her lips spread softly, warmly against his and she sucked his tongue deeply into her mouth, with a low moan of wanting – and the hard slim body began to work against his, the hands breaking from his neck and hunting down his spine, long curved nails pricking and goading him just short of pain. His own arousal was so swift and so brutally hard that she moaned again, and the tension went out of her body, it seemed to soften and spread like a wax figure held too close to the flame, her eyelids trembling closed and her thighs falling apart.

'So strong—' she whispered, deep in her throat and he reared up over her, feeling supreme, invincible.

'Peter, Peter,' she cried. 'Oh yes like that. Please like that.' Both of them striving triumphantly for the moment of glory when each was able to lose self and become for a fleeting instant part of the godhead.

Long afterwards they lay side by side in the enormous bed, both of them stretched out flat upon their backs, not touching except for the fingers of one hand intertwined as their bodies had been.

'I will go away—' she whispered, ' – because I have to, but not now. Not yet.'

He did not reply, the effort was beyond him, and her own voice was languorous with a surfeit of pleasure.

'I will make a bargain with you. Give me three days more. Only three days, to be happy like this. For me it is the first time. I have never known this before, and it may be the last time—'

He tried to rouse himself to deny it, but she squeezed his fingers for silence and went on.

' – It may be the last,' she repeated. 'And I want to have it all. Three days, in which we do not mention Caliph, in which we do not think of the blood and striving and suffering out there. If you give me that I will do everything that you want me to do. Is it a bargain, Peter? Tell me we can have that.'

'Yes. We can have that.'

'Then tell me you love me again, I do not think I can hear you say it too often.'

He said it often during those magic days, and she had spoken the truth, each time he told her she accepted with as much joy as the last time, and always each seemed to be within touching distance of the other.

Even when tearing side by side across the warm flat waters of the lagoon, leaning back with straight arms on the tow lines, skis hissing angrily and carving fiercely sparkling wings of water from the surface as they wove back and forth in a *pas de deux* across the streaming, creaming water, laughing together in the wind and the engine roar of the Chris-craft, Hapiti the Polynesian boatman on the flying bridge looking back with a great white grin of sympathy for their joy.

Finning gently through mysterious blue and dappled depths, the only sound the wheezing suck and blow of their scuba valves and the soft clicking and the eternal echoing susurration that is the pulse beat of the ocean, holding hands as they sank down to the long abandoned hull of the Japanese aircraft carrier, now overgrown with a waving forest of sea growth and populated by a teeming fascinating multitude of beautiful and bizarre creatures.

Flying silently down the sheer steel cliff of the canted flight deck, which seemed to reach down into the very oceanic depths, so that there was the eerie fear of suddenly being deprived of support and falling down to where the surface light blued out in nothingness.

Pausing to peer through their glass face-plates into the still gaping wounds rent into the steel by aerial bombs and high explosive, and then entering through those cruel caverns cautiously as children into a haunted house and emerging victoriously with carrier nets of trophies, coins and cutlery, brass and porcelain.

Strolling on the secluded beaches of the outer islands, still hand in hand, naked in the sunlight.

Fishing the seething tide-race through the main channel at full spring tide, and shouting with excitement as the big golden amberjack came boiling up in the wake, bellies flashing like mirrors, to hit the dancing feather lures, and send the Penn reels screeching a wild protest, and the fibreglass rods nodding and kicking.

Out in the humbling silences of the unrestricted ocean, when even the smudge of the islands disappeared beyond the wave crests for minutes at a time, with only the creak and whisper of the rigging, the trembling pregnancy of the main sail, and the rustle as the twin hulls of the big Hobie cat knifed the tops off the swells.

Strolling the long curving beaches in the moonlight, searching for the heavenly bodies that so seldom show through the turbid skies of Europe – Orion the hunter and the Seven Sisters – exclaiming at the stranger constellations of this hemisphere governed by the great fixed cross in the southern heavens.

Each day beginning and ending in the special wonder and mystery of the circular bed, in loving that welded their bodies and their souls together each time more securely.

Then on the fourth day day Peter woke to find her gone, and for a moment experienced an appalling sensation of total loss.

When she came back to him he did not recognize her for a breath of time.

Then he realized that she had cut away the long dark tresses of her hair, cropped it down short so that it curled close against her skull, like the petals of a dark flower. It had the effect of making her seem even taller. Her neck like the stem of the flower, longer, and the curve of the throat accentuated so that it became delicate and swan-like.

She saw his expression, and explained in a matter-of-fact tone.

'I thought some change was necessary, if I am to leave under a new identity. It will grow again, if you want it that way.'

She seemed to have changed completely herself, the

405

languid amorous mood given way to the brisk business-like efficiency of before. While they ate a last breakfast of sweet yellow papaya and the juice of freshly squeezed limes she explained her intentions, as she went swiftly through the buff envelope that her secretary had silently laid beside her plate.

There was a red Israeli diplomatic passport in the envelope.

'I will be using the name Ruth Levy—' and she picked up the thick booklet of airline tickets, ' – and I have decided to go back to Jerusalem. I have a house there. It's not in my name, and I do not think anybody else outside of Mossad is aware of it. It will be an ideal base, close to my control at Mossad. I will try to give you what support I can, try to get further information to assist you in the hunt—'

She passed him a typed sheet of notepaper.

' – That is a telephone number at Mossad where you can get a message to me. Use the name Ruth Levy.'

He memorized the number while she went on talking, and then shredded the sheet of paper.

'I have modified the arrangements for my departure,' she told him. 'We will take the Chris-craft across to Bora-Bora. It's only a hundred miles. I will radio ahead. My friends will meet me off the beach after dark.'

They crept in through a narrow passage in the coral with all the lights on the Chris-craft doused, Magda's boatman using only what was left of the waning moon and his own intimate knowledge of the islands to take her in.

'I wanted Hapiti to see me go ashore alive,' she whispered quietly, leaning against Peter's chest to draw comfort from their last minutes together. 'I did not exaggerate the danger you might be in if the local people thought what we want Caliph to think. Hapiti will keep his mouth shut—' she assured him,' – and will back up your story of a shark attack, unless you order him to tell the truth.'

'You think of everything.'

'I have only just found you, monsieur,' she chuckled. 'I do not want to lose you yet. I have even decided to speak a word to the Chief of Police on Tahiti, when I pass through. He is an old friend. When you get back to Les Neuf Poissons, have my secretary radio Tahiti—'

She went on quietly, covering every detail of her arrangements, and he could find no omissions. She was interrupted by a soft hail from out of the darkness and Hapiti throttled the diesels back to idle. They drifted down closer to the loom of the island. A canoe bumped against the side, and Magda turned quickly in his arms, reaching up for his mouth with hers.

'Please be careful, Peter,' was all that she said, and then she broke away and stepped down into the canoe as Hapiti handed down her single valise. The canoe pushed away immediately, and was lost in the dark. There was nothing to wave at, and Peter liked it better that way, but still he stared back over the stern into the night as the Chris-craft groped blindly for the channel again.

There was a hollow feeling under his ribs, as though part of himself was missing; he tried to fill it with a memory of Magda that had amused him because it epitomized for him her quick and pragmatic mind.

' – When the news of your death hits the market, the bottom is going to drop out of Altmann stock.' He had realized this halfway through their final discussion that morning. 'I hadn't thought of that.' He was troubled by the complication.

'I had,' she smiled serenely. 'I estimate it will lose a hundred francs a share within the first week after the news breaks.'

'Doesn't that worry you?'

'Not really.' She gave that sudden wicked grin. 'I telexed a buying order to Zurich this morning. I expect to show a profit of not less than a hundred million francs when the stock bounces back.' Again the mischievous flash of green eyes. 'I do have to be recompensed for all this inconvenience, *tu ne penses pas?*'

And although he still smiled at the memory, the hollow place remained there inside him.

P ierre flew the Tahitian police out to Les Neuf Poissons in the Tri-Islander, and there followed two days of questions and statements. Nearly every member of the community wished to make a statement to the police, there had seldom been such entertainment and excitement available on the islands.

Nearly all of the statements were glowing eulogies to 'La Baronne' delivered to the accompaniment of lamentation and weeping. Only Hapiti had first-hand information and he made the most of this position of importance, embroidering and gilding the tale. He was even able to give a positive identification of the shark as a 'Dead White' – The English name startled Peter until he remembered that the movie *Jaws* was in the island's cassette video library and was undoubtedly the source of the big boatman's inspiration. Hapiti went on to describe its fangs as long and sharp as cane knives, and to give a gruesome imitation of the sound they made as they closed on 'La Baronne' – Peter would willingly have gagged him to prevent those flights of imagination, which were not supported by Peter's own statement, but the police sergeant was greatly impressed and encouraged Hapiti to further acts of creation with cries of astonishment.

On the last evening there was a funeral feast on the beach for Magda. It was a moving ritual, and Peter found himself curiously affected when the women of the island, swaying and wailing at the water's edge, cast wreaths of frangipani blooms onto the tide to be carried out beyond the reef.

Peter flew back to Tahiti-Faaa with the police the following morning, and they stayed with him, flanking him discreetly, on the drive to the headquarters of gendarmerie in the town. However, his interview with the Chief of Police was brief and courteous – clearly Magda had been there before him – and if there was no actual exchange of winks and nudges, the commissioner's handshake of farewell was firm and friendly.

'Any friend of La Baronne is a friend here.' And he used the present tense, then sent Peter back to the airport in an official car.

The UTA flight landed in California through that sulphurous eye-stinging layer of yellow air trapped between sea and mountains. Peter did not leave the airport, but after he had shaved and changed his shirt in the men's room he found a copy of the *Wall Street Journal* in the first-class Pan-Am Clipper lounge. It was dated the previous day, and the report of Magda Altmann's death was on Page Three. It was a full column, and Peter was surprised by the depth of the Altmann Industries involvement in the American financial scene. The complex of holdings was listed, followed by a résumé of Baron Aaron Altmann's career and that of his widow. The cause of death as given by the Tahitian police was 'Shark Attack' while scuba diving in the company of a friend – General Peter Stride – Peter was grimly satisfied that his name was mentioned. Caliph would read it, wherever he was, and draw the appropriate conclusion. Peter could expect something to happen now; he was not quite sure what, but he knew that he was being drawn closer to the centre like a fragment of iron to the magnet.

He managed to sleep for an hour, in one of the big armchairs, before the hostess roused him for the Pan-Am Polar flight to London's Heathrow.

He called Pat Stride, his sister-in-law, from Heathrow Airport. She was unaffectedly delighted to hear his voice.

' – Steven is in Spain, but I am expecting him home

tomorrow before lunch, that is if his meetings go the way he wants them. They want to build a thirty-six-hole golf course at San Istaban—' Steven's companies owned a complex of tourist hotels on the Spanish coast ' – and Steven had to go through the motions with the Spanish authorities. But, why don't you come down to Abbots Yew tonight? Alex and Priscilla are here, and there will be an amusing house party for the weekend—' He could hear the sudden calculating tone in Pat's voice as she began instinctively to run through the shortlist of potential mates for Peter.

After he had accepted and hung up, he dialled the Cambridge number and was relieved that Cynthia's husband, George Barrow, answered.

Give me a Bolshevik intellectual over a neurotic ex-wife any day, he thought as he greeted Melissa-Jane's stepfather warmly. Cynthia was at a meeting of the Faculty Wives Association, and Melissa-Jane was auditioning for a part in a production of Gilbert and Sullivan by the local drama society.

'How is she?' Peter wanted to know.

'I think she is well over it now, Peter. The hand is completely healed. She seems to have settled down—' They spoke for a few minutes more, then ran out of conversation. The two women were all they had in common.

'Give Melissa-Jane my very best love,' Peter told him, and picked up a copy of *The Financial Times* from a news-stand on his way to the Avis desk. He hired a compact and while waiting for it to be delivered he searched swiftly through the newspaper for mention of Magda Altmann. It was on an inside page, clearly a follow-up article to a previous report of her death. There had been a severe reaction on the London and European stock exchanges – the hundred-franc drop in Altmann stock that Magda had anticipated had already been exceeded on the Bourse – and again there was a brief mention of his own name in a repetition of the circumstances of her death. He was satisfied with the publicity, and with Magda's judgement in buying back her own stock. Indeed it all seemed to be going a little too smoothly. He became aware of the fateful prickle of apprehension down his spine, his own personal barometer of impending danger.

As always Abbots Yew was like coming home, and Pat met him on the gravel of the front drive, kissed him with sisterly affection and linked her arm through his to lead him into the gracious old house.

'Steven will be delighted,' she promised him. 'I expect he will telephone this evening. He always does when he is away.'

There was a buff cable envelope propped on the bedside table of the guest room overlooking the stables that was always reserved for Peter. The message originated at Ben-Gurion Airport, Tel Aviv, and was a single word – the code he had arranged with Magda to let him know that she arrived safely and without complication. The message gave him a sharp pang of wanting, and he lay in a deep hot bath and thought about her, remembering small details of conversation and shared experience that suddenly were of inflated value.

While he towelled himself he regarded his image in the steamed mirror with a critical eye. He was lean and hard and burned dark as a desert Arab by the Pacific sun. He watched the play of muscle under the tanned skin as he moved, and he knew that he was as fit and as mentally prepared for action as he had ever been, glad that Magda was safely beyond the reach of Caliph's talons so that he could concentrate all his energies on what his instincts told him must be the final stage of the hunt.

He went through to his bedroom with the towel around his waist and stretched out on the bed to wait for the cocktail hour in Pat Stride's rigidly run household.

He wondered what made him so certain that this was

the lead which would carry him to Caliph, it seemed so slim a chance and yet the certainty was like a steel thread, and the steel was in his heart.

That made him pause. Once again he went carefully over the changes which had taken place within him since his first exposure to Caliph's malignant influence; the fatal miasma of corruption that seemed to spread around Caliph like the poisonous mists from some evil swamp seemed to have engulfed Peter entirely.

He thought again of his execution of the blonde girl at Johannesburg what seemed like a thousand years before, but with mild surprise realized was months not years ago.

He thought of how he had been prepared to kill both Kingston Parker and Magda Altmann – and realized that contact with violence was brutalizing, capable of eroding the principles and convictions which he had believed inviolate after almost forty years of having lived with them.

If this was so, then after Caliph – if he succeeded in destroying him – what was there after Caliph? Would he ever be the same man again? Had he advanced too far beyond the frontiers of social behaviour and conscience? Would he ever go back? he wondered. Then he thought about Magda Altmann and realized she was his hope for the future, after Caliph there would be Magda.

These doubts were weakening, he told himself. There must be no distractions now, for once again he was in the arena with the adversary. No distraction, no doubts – only total concentration on the conflict ahead.

He stood up from the bed and began to dress.

S teven was delighted to have Peter at Abbots Yew again, as Pat had predicted.

He also was tanned from the short stay in Spain, but he had again put on weight, only a few pounds, but it would soon be a serious problem, good food and drink were two of the occupational hazards of success: the most evident but not the most dangerous temptations that face a man who has money enough to buy whatever idly engages his fancy.

Peter watched him covertly during the lunch, studying the handsome head which was so very much like his own, the same broad brow and straight aristocratic nose, and yet was so different in small but significant details, and it was not only Steven's thick dark moustache.

All right, it's easy to be wise afterwards, Peter told himself, as he watched his twin brother. Seeing again the little marks, which only now seemed to have meaning. The narrower set of eyes, slightly too close together, so that even when he laughed that deep bluff guffaw of his they seemed still to retain a cold cruel light, the mouth that even in laughter was still too hard, too determined, the mouth of a man who would brook no check to his ambitions, no thwarting of his desires. Or am I imagining it now? Peter wondered. It was so easy to see what you looked for expectantly.

The conversation at lunch dwelt almost exclusively on the prospects for the flat-racing season which had opened at Doncaster the previous weekend, and Peter joined it knowledgeably; but as he chatted he was casting back along the years, to the incidents that might have troubled him more if he had not immediately submerged them under an instinctive and unquestioning loyalty to his twin brother.

There was Sandhurst when Steven had been sent down, and Peter had known unquestioningly that it was unjust. No Stride was capable of what Steven had been accused of, and he had not even had to discuss it with his brother. He had affirmed his loyalty with a handshake and a few embarrassed muttered words.

'Thank you, Peter. I'll never forget that,' Steven had told him fervently, meeting Peter's gaze with steady clear eye.

Since then Steven's rise had been meteoric through the post-war years in which it seemed almost impossible for even the most able man to amass a great fortune, a man had to have special talents and take terrible risks to achieve what Steven had.

Now sitting at his brother's board, eating roast saddle of lamb and the first crisp white asparagus shoots of the season flown in from the Continent, Peter was at last covering forbidden ground, examining loyalties which until then had been unquestioned. Yet they were straws scattered by the winds of time, possibly without significance. Peter transferred his thoughts to the present.

'Stride,' Magda's control at Mossad in Tel-Aviv had said. Just the two names: 'Cactus Flower' and 'Stride'. That was fact and not conjecture.

Down the length of the luncheon table Sir Steven Stride caught his brother's eye.

'Wine with you, my dear fellow.' Steven lifted the glass of claret in the old salute.

'Enchanted, I'm sure.' Peter gave the correct reply, a little ritual between them, a hangover from Sandhurst days, and Peter was surprised at the depth of his regret. Perhaps Caliph has not yet succeeded in corrupting me entirely, Peter thought, as he drank the toast.

After lunch there was another of their brotherly rituals. Steven signalled it with a jerk of the head and Peter nodded agreement. Peter's old army duffle coat was in the cupboard below the back staircase with his Wellingtons, and he and Steven changed into rough clothing sitting side by side on the monk's bench in the rear entrance hall as they had so often before.

Then Steven went through into the gunroom, took down

414

a Purdey Royal shotgun from the rack, and thrust a handful of cartridges in his coat pocket.

'Damned vixen has a litter of cubs somewhere in the bottoms, playing merry hell with the pheasant chicks—' he explained as Peter asked a silent question. 'It goes against the grain a bit to shoot a fox but I must put a stop to her – haven't had a chance at her yet—' and he led the way out of the back door through the orchard towards the stream.

It was almost a formal beating of the bounds, the leisurely circuit of the estate boundaries that the two brothers always made on Peter's first day at Abbots Yew, another old comfortable tradition which allowed them time to have each other's news and reaffirm the bond between them

They sauntered along the riverbank, side by side, moving into single file with Steven leading when the path narrowed and turned away from the stream and went up through the woods.

Steven was elated by the success of his visit to Spain, and he boasted of his achievements in obtaining another parcel of prime seafront property on which to build the new golf course and to extend the hotel by another five hundred rooms.

'Now's the time to buy. Mark my words, Peter – we are on the verge of another explosion.'

'The cut-back in oil price is going to help, I'd expect,' Peter agreed.

'That's not the half of it, old boy.' Steven turned to glance back over his shoulder and he winked knowingly at Peter. 'You can expect another five per cent cut in six months, take my word on it. The Arabs and the Shah have come to their senses.' Steven went on swiftly, picking out those types of industry which would benefit most dramatically from the reduction in crude prices, then selecting the leading companies in those sectors. ' – If you have a few pounds lying idle, that's where to put it.' Steven's whole personality seemed to change when he spoke like this of power and great wealth. Then he came out from behind the façade of the English country squire which he was usually at such pains to cultivate; the glitter in his eyes was now undisguised and his bushy moustache bristled like the whiskers of some big dangerous predator.

He was still talking quickly and persuasively as they left the woods and began to cross the open fields towards the ruins of the Roman camp on the crest of the low hills.

' – These people have still to be told what to do, you know. Those damned shop stewards up in Westminster may have thrown the Empire away, but we still have our responsibilities.' Steven changed the Purdey shotgun from one arm to the other, carrying it in the crook of the arm, the gun broken open and the shining brass caps of the Eley Kynoch cartridges showing in the breeches. ' – Government only by those fit to govern.' Steven enlarged on that for a few minutes.

Then suddenly Steven fell silent, almost as though he had suddenly decided that he had spoken too much, even to somebody as trusted as his own younger twin. Peter was silent also, trudging up the curve of the hill with his boots squelching in the soft damp earth. There was something completely unreal about the moment, walking over well-remembered ground in the beautiful mellow sunlight of an English spring afternoon with a man he had known from the day of his birth – and yet perhaps had never known at all.

It was not the first time he had heard Steven talk like this, and yet perhaps it was the first time he had ever listened. He shivered and Steven glanced at him.

'Cold?'

'Goose walked over my grave,' Peter explained, and Steven nodded as they clambered up the shallow earth bank that marked the perimeter of the Roman camp.

They stood on the lip under the branches of a lovely copper beech, resplendent in its new spring growth of russet.

Steven was breathing hard from the pull up the hill, that extra weight was already beginning to tell. There was a spot of high unhealthy colour in each cheek, and little blisters of sweat speckled his chin.

He closed the breech of the shotgun with a metallic clash, and leaned the weapon against the trunk of the copper beech as he struggled to regain his breath.

Peter moved across casually and propped his shoulder against the copper beech, but his thumbs were hooked into the lapels of the duffle coat, not thrust into pockets, and he was still in balance, weight slightly forward on the balls of his feet. Although he seemed to be entirely relaxed and at rest he was in fact coiled like a spring, poised on the brink of violent action – and the shotgun was within easy reach of his right hand.

He had seen that Steven had loaded with number four shot. At ten paces it would disembowel a man. The safety catch on the top of the pistol grip of the butt engaged automatically when the breech was opened and closed again, but the right thumb would instinctively slip the catch forward as the hand closed on the grip.

Steven took a silver cigarette case from the side pocket of his coat and tapped down a cigarette on the lid.

'Damned shame about Magda Altmann,' he said gruffly, not meeting Peter's eyes.

'Yes,' Peter agreed softly.

'Glad they handled it in a civilized fashion. Could have made it awkward for you, you know.'

'I suppose they could have,' Peter agreed.

'What about your job at Narmco?'

'I don't know yet. I will not know until I get back to Brussels.'

'Well, my offer still stands, old boy. I could do with a bit of help. I really could. Somebody I could trust. You'd be doing me a favour.'

'Damned decent of you, Steven.'

'No, really, I mean it.' Steven lit the cigarette with a gold Dunhill lighter and inhaled with evident pleasure, and after a moment Peter asked him:

'I hope you were not in a heavy position in Altmann stock. I see it has taken an awful tumble.'

'Strange that.' Steven shook his head. 'Pulled out of Altmann's a few weeks ago, actually. Needed the money for San Istaban.'

'Lucky,' Peter murmured, or much more than luck. He wondered why Steven admitted the share transaction so readily. 'Of course,' he realized, 'it would have been very substantial and therefore easily traced.'

He studied his brother now, staring at him with a slight scowl of concentration. Was it possible? he asked himself. Could Steven really have masterminded something so complex, where ideology and self-interest and delusions of omnipotence seemed so inextricably snarled and entwined.

'What is it, old boy?' Steven asked, frowning slightly in sympathy.

'I was just thinking that the whole concept and execution has been incredible, Steven. I would never have suspected you were capable of it.'

'I'm sorry, Peter. I don't understand. What are you talking about?'

'Caliph,' Peter said softly.

It was there! Peter saw it instantly. The instant of utter stillness, like a startled jungle animal – but the flinch of the eyes, followed immediately by the effort of control.

The expression of Steven's face had not altered, the little frown of polite inquiry held perfectly, then turning slowly, deeper into puzzlement.

'I'm afraid you just lost me there, old chap.'

It was superbly done. Despite himself Peter was impressed. There were depths to his brother which he had never suspected – but that was his own omission. No matter

418

which way you looked at it, it took an extraordinary ability to achieve what Steven had achieved in less than twenty years, against the most appalling odds. No matter how he had done it, it was the working of a particular type of genius.

He was capable of running Caliph, Peter accepted the fact at last – and immediately had a focal point for the corroding hatred he had carried within him for so long.

'Your only mistake so far, Steven, was to let Aaron Altmann know your name,' Peter went on quietly. 'I suspect you did not then know that he was a Mossad agent, and that your name would go straight onto the Israeli intelligence computer. Nobody, nothing, can ever wipe it from the memory rolls, Steven. You are known.'

Steven's eyes flickered down to the shotgun; it was instinctive, uncontrollable, the final confirmation if Peter needed one.

'No, Steven. That's not for you.' Peter shook his head. 'That's my work. You're fat and out of condition, and you have never had the training. You must stick to hiring others to do the actual killing. You wouldn't even get a hand on it.'

Steven's eyes darted back to his brother's face. Still the expression of his face had not altered.

'I think you've gone out of your head, old boy.'

Peter ignored it. 'You of all people should know that I am capable of killing anybody. You have conditioned me to that.'

'We are getting into an awful tangle now,' Steven protested. 'What on earth should you want to kill anybody for?'

'Steven, you are insulting both of us. I know. There is no point in going on with the act. We have to work out between us what we are going to do about it.'

He had phrased it carefully, offering the chance of

compromise. He saw the waver of doubt in Steven's eyes, the slight twist of his mouth, as he struggled to reach a decision.

' – But please do not underestimate the danger you are in, Steven.' As he spoke Peter produced an old worn pair of dark leather gloves from his pocket and began to pull them on. There was something infinitely menacing in that simple act, and again Steven's eyes were drawn irresistibly.

'Why are you doing that?' For the first time Steven's voice croaked slightly.

'I haven't yet touched the gun,' Peter explained reasonably. 'It has only your prints upon it.'

'Christ, you'd never get away with it, Peter.'

'Why, Steven? It is always dangerous to carry a loaded shotgun over muddy and uneven ground.'

'You couldn't do it, not in cold blood.' The edge of terror was in Steven's voice.

'Why not? You had no such qualms with Prince Hassied Abdel Hayek.'

'I am your brother – he was only a bloody wog—' Steven choked it off, staring now at Peter with stricken eyes, the expression of his face beginning at last to crack and crumble as he realized that he had made the fateful admission.

Peter reached for the shotgun without taking his eyes from his brother's.

'Wait!' Steven cried. 'Wait, Peter!'

'For what?'

'You've got to let me explain.'

'All right, go ahead.'

'You can't just say go ahead, like that. It's so complicated.'

'All right, Steven. Let's start at the beginning – with Flight 070. Tell me why?'

'We had to do it, Peter. Don't you see? There is over four billions of British investment in that country, another three billions of American money. It's the major world producer of gold and uranium, chrome and a dozen other strategic minerals. My God, Peter. Those ham-handed oafs in control now are on a suicide course. We had to take it away from them, and put in a controllable government. If we don't do that the Reds will have it all within ten years – probably much less.'

'You had an alternative government chosen?'

'Of course,' Steven told him urgently, persuasively, watching the shotgun that Peter still held low across his hips. 'It was planned in every detail. It took two years.'

'All right.' Peter nodded. 'Tell me about the murder of Prince Hassied.'

'It wasn't murder, for God's sake, man, it was absolutely essential. It was a matter of survival. They were destroying Western civilization with their childlike irresponsibility. Drunk with power, they were no longer amenable to reason, like spoiled children in a sweet shop – we had to put a stop to it, or face a breakdown of the capitalist system. They have probably done irreparable damage to the prestige of the dollar, they have taken sterling hostage and hold it in daily jeopardy with the threat of withdrawing those astronomic balances from London. We had to bring them to their senses, and look how small a price. We can reduce the price of crude oil gradually to its 1970 level. We can restore sanity to the currencies of the Western world and secure real growth and prosperity for hundreds of millions of peoples – all at the cost of a single life.'

'And anyway, he was only a bloody wog. Wasn't he?' Peter agreed reasonably.

'Look here, Peter. I said that but I didn't mean it. You are being unreasonable.'

'I will try not to be,' Peter assured him mildly. 'Tell me where it goes from here. Who do you bring under control next – the British Trade Union movement, perhaps?'

And Steven stared at him wordlessly for a moment.

'Damn it, Peter. That was a hell of a guess. But could

you imagine if we had a five-year wage freeze, and no industrial action during that time. It's them or us, Peter. We could get back to being one of the major industrial powers of the Western world. Great Britain! We could be that again.'

'You are very convincing, Steven,' Peter acknowledged. 'There are only a few details that worry me a little.'

'What are they, Peter?'

'Why was it necessary to arrange the murder of Kingston Parker and Magda Altmann—'

Steven stared at him, his jaw unhinging slightly and the hard line of his mouth going slack with astonishment. 'No,' he shook his head. 'That's not so.'

' – and why was it necessary to kill Baron Altmann, and torture him to death?'

'That was not my doing – all right, it was done. And I knew it was done – but I had nothing to do with it, Peter. Not the murder at least. Oh God, all right I knew it had to be done, but—' His voice tailed off, and he stared helplessly at Peter.

'From the beginning again, Steven. Let's hear it all—' Peter spoke almost gently.

'I cannot, Peter. You don't understand what might happen, what will happen if I tell you—'

Peter slid the safety catch off the Purdey shotgun. The click of the mechanism was unnaturally loud in the silence, and Steven Stride started and stepped back a pace, blinking at his brother, fastening all his attention on Peter's eyes.

'God,' he whispered. 'You would do it too.'

'Tell me about Aaron Altmann.'

'Can I have another cigarette?'

Peter nodded and Steven lit it with hands that trembled very slightly.

'You have to understand how it worked, before I can explain.'

'Tell me how it worked,' Peter invited.

'I was recruited—'

'Steven, don't lie to me – you are Caliph.'

'No, God, no, Peter. You have it all wrong,' Steven cried. 'It's a chain. I am only a link in Caliph's chain. I am not Caliph.'

'You are a part of Caliph, then?'

'Only a link in the chain,' Steven repeated vehemently.

'Tell me,' Peter invited with a small movement of the shotgun barrel that drew Steven's eyes immediately.

'There is a man I have known a long time. We have worked together before. A man with greater wealth and influence than I have. It was not an immediate thing. It grew out of many discussions and conversations over a long time, years, in which we both voiced our concern with the way that power had shifted to blocks of persons unfit to wield it—'

'All right,' Peter nodded grimly. 'I understand your political and ideological sentiments. Leave them out of the account.'

'Very well,' Steven agreed. ' – Well, finally this man asked me if I would be prepared to join an association of Western world political and industrial leaders dedicated to restoring power to the hands of those fitted by training and upbringing to govern.'

'Who was this man?'

'Peter, I cannot tell you.'

'You have no choice,' Peter told him, and there was a long moment as they locked eyes and wills; then Steven sighed in capitulation.

'It was—' The name was that of a mining magnate who controlled most of the free world supply of nuclear fuel and gold and precious stones.

'So he is the one who would have been in control of the new South African government with which you intended replacing the present regime in that country, if the taking of 070 had succeeded?' Peter demanded, and Steven nodded wordlessly.

'All right,' Peter nodded. 'Go on.'

'He had been recruited as I was,' Steven explained. 'But I was never to know by whom. In my turn I was to recruit another desirable member – but I would be the only one who knew who that was. It was how the security of the chain was to be maintained. Each link would know only the one above and below him, the man who had recruited him and the one who he recruited in his turn—'

'Caliph?' Peter demanded. 'What about Caliph?'

'Nobody knows who he is.'

'Yet he must know who you are.'

'Yes, of course.'

'Then there must be some way for you to get a message to Caliph,' Peter insisted. 'For instance, when you recruit a new member, you must be able to pass on the information? When he wants something from you, he must be able to contact you.'

'Yes.'

'How?'

'Christ, Peter. It's more than my life is worth.'

'We'll come back to it,' said Peter impatiently. 'Go on, tell me about Aaron Altmann.'

'That was a disaster. I chose Aaron as the man I would recruit. He seemed exactly the kind of man we needed. I had known him for years. I knew he could be very tough when it was necessary. So I approached him. He seemed very eager at first, leading me on. Getting me to explain the way Caliph would work. I was delighted to have recruited such an important man. He intimated that he would contribute twenty-five million dollars to the funds of the association, so I passed a message to Caliph. I told him that I had almost succeeded in recruiting Baron Altmann—'

Steven stopped nervously, and dropped the stub of his

cigarette onto the damp turf, grinding it out under his heel.

'What happened then?' Peter demanded.

'Caliph responded immediately. I was ordered to break off all contact with Aaron Altmann at once. I realized I must have chosen a potentially dangerous person. You tell me now he was Mossad. I did not know that – but Caliph must have known it. I did as I was told and dropped Aaron like a hot chestnut – and four days later he was abducted. I had nothing to do with it, Peter. I swear to you. I liked the man immensely. I admired him—'

'Yet he was abducted and horribly tortured. You must have known that Caliph had done it, and that you were responsible?'

'Yes.' Steven said the word flatly, without evasion. Peter felt a small stir of admiration for that.

'They tortured him to find out if he had passed the information you had given him about Caliph to Mossad,' Peter insisted.

'Yes. I expect so. I do not know.'

'If the picture I have of Aaron Altmann was correct they received no information from him.'

'No. He was like that. They must have lost patience with him in the end – to do what they did to him. It was my first moment of disillusionment with Caliph,' Steven muttered sombrely.

They were both silent now, until Peter burst out angrily. 'My God, Steven, can't you see what a disgusting business you are mixed up in?' And Steven was mute. 'Couldn't you see it?' Peter insisted, the anger raw in his voice. 'Couldn't you realize it from the beginning?'

'Not at the beginning.' Steven shook his head miserably. 'It seemed a brilliant solution for all the diseases of the Western world – and then once I began it was like being on board a speeding express train. It was just impossible to get off again.'

425

'All right. So then you tried to have me assassinated on the Rambouillet road?'

'Good God, no.' Steven was truly appalled. 'You're my brother, good God—'

'Caliph did it to stop me getting close to Aaron's widow who was out to avenge him.'

'I didn't know a thing about it, I swear to you. If Caliph did it, he knew better than to let me in on it.' Steven was pleading now. 'You must believe that.'

Peter felt a softening of his resolve, but forced back the knowledge that this man was his brother, someone who had been very dear over a lifetime.

'What was your next operation for Caliph then?' He asked without allowing the softness to reach his voice.

'There wasn't—'

'Damn you, Steven, don't lie to me.' Peter's voice cracked like a whiplash. 'You knew about Prince Hassied Abdel Hayek!'

'All right. I arranged that. Caliph told me what to do and I did it.'

'Then you kidnapped Melissa-Jane and had her mutilated—'

'Oh God! No!' Steven's voice was a sob.

' – To force me to assassinate Kingston Parker—'

'No, Peter. No!'

' – And then to kill Magda Altmann—'

'Peter, I swear to you. Not Melissa-Jane. I love her like one of my own daughters. You must know that. I had no idea it was Caliph.'

Steven was pleading wildly now.

' – You have to believe me. I would never have allowed that to happen. That is too horrible.'

Peter watched him with a steely merciless glint of blue in his eyes, cold and cutting as the edge of the executioner's blade.

'I will do anything to prove to you I had nothing to do

426

with Melissa-Jane. Anything you say, Peter. I'll take any chance to prove it to you. I swear it to you.'

Steven Stride's dismay and sincerity were beyond question. His face was drained of all colour and his lips were marble white and trembling with the strength of his denial.

Peter handed the shotgun to his brother without a word. Startled, Steven held it for a moment at arm's length.

'You are in bad trouble, Steven,' Peter said quietly. He knew that from now on he needed Steven's unreserved and whole-hearted commitment. He could not be forced to do what he must do at the point of a shotgun.

Steven recognized the gesture, and slowly lowered the gun. With his thumb he pushed across the breech-locking mechanism, and the weapon hinged open. He pulled the cartridges from the double eyes of the breeches and dropped them into the pocket of his shooting jacket.

'Let's get down to the house,' Steven said, his voice still unsteady with the trauma of the last minutes. 'I need a stiff whisky—'

There was a log fire burning in the deep walk-in fireplace of Steven's study. The portals were magnificently carved altar surrounds from a sixteenth-century German church, salvaged from the ruins of World War II Allied bombing and purchased by Steven from a Spanish dealer, after having been smuggled out through Switzerland.

Opposite the fireplace, bow windows with leaded panes and ancient wavy glass looked out over the rose garden. The other two walls housed Steven's collection of rare books, each boxed in its individual leather-bound container and lettered in gold leaf. The shelves reached from floor to the high moulded ceiling. It was a passion that the brothers shared.

Steven stood now in the fireplace with his back to the flames, one hand clasped in the small of his back, hoisting up the skirts of his tweed jacket to warm his backside. In the other hand he held a deep crystal tumbler, still half filled with whisky, hardly diluted by the soda he had dashed into it from the syphon.

Steven still looked shaken and pale, and every few minutes he shivered uncontrollably, although the room was oppressively heated by the blazing fire and all the windows were closed tightly.

Peter sprawled in the brocade-upholstered Louis Quatorze chair across the room, his legs thrust out straight and crossed at the ankles, hands thrust deeply into his pockets, and his chin lowered on his chest in deep thought.

'How much was your contribution to Caliph's war chest?' Peter asked abruptly.

'I was not in the same class as Aaron Altmann,' Steven answered quietly. 'I pledged five millions in sterling over five years.'

'So we must imagine a network extending across all international boundaries. Powerful men in every country, each contributing enormous sums of money – and almost unlimited information and influence—'

Steven nodded and took another swallow of his dark-toned whisky.

' – There is no reason to believe that it was only one man in each country. There may be a dozen in England, another dozen in Western Germany, fifty in the United States—'

'It's possible,' Steven agreed.

'So that Caliph could very easily have arranged the kidnapping of Melissa-Jane through another of his chain in this country.'

'You must believe I had nothing to do with it, Peter.'

Peter dismissed this new protestation impatiently, and went on thinking out aloud.

'It is still possible that Caliph is a committee of the founder members – not one man at all.'

'I don't think so—' Steven hesitated. ' – I had a very strong impression that it all was one man. I do not think a committee would be capable of such swift and determined action.' He shook his head, trying to cast his mind back for the exact words which had formed his impressions. ' – You must remember that I have only discussed Caliph with one other person, the man who recruited me. However, you can be certain that we discussed it in depth and over an extended period. I was not about to put out five million on something that didn't satisfy me entirely. No, it was one man who would make the decision for all of us – but the decisions would be in the interest of all.'

'Yet there was no guarantee that any individual member of the chain would be informed of every decision?'

'No. Of course not. That would have been madness. Security was the key to success.'

'You could trust somebody you had never met, whose identity was hidden from you – you could trust him with vast sums of money, and the destiny of the world as we know it?'

Steven hesitated again as if seeking the right words. 'Caliph has an aura that seems to envelop all of us. The man who recruited me—' Steven seemed reluctant to repeat the name again, proof to Peter of the influence that Caliph exerted ' – is a man whose judgement I respect tremendously. He was convinced, and this helped to convince me.'

'What do you think now?' Peter asked abruptly. 'Are you still convinced?'

Steven drained the whisky glass, and then smoothed his moustache with a little nervous gesture.

'Come on, Steven,' Peter encouraged him.

'I still think Caliph had the right idea—' he said reluctantly. ' – The rules have changed, Peter. We were

429

fighting for survival of the world as we know it. We were merely playing to the new morality—'

He crossed to the silver tray on the corner of his desk and refilled the whisky glass.

' – Up to now we have had one hand tied behind our backs, while the Reds and the extreme left and the members of the Third World have had both hands to fight with and a dagger in each one. All Caliph did was to take off our shackles.'

'What has made you change your mind then?' Peter asked.

'I'm not sure that I have changed my mind.' Steven turned back to face him. 'I still think it was the right idea—'

' – But?' Peter insisted.

Steven shrugged. 'The murder of Aaron Altmann, the mutilation of Melissa-Jane—' He hesitated. ' – Other acts of which I suspect Caliph was the originator. They were not for the common good. They were merely to protect Caliph's personal safety, or to satisfy what I am beginning to believe is vaunted and unbridled lust for power.' Steven shook his head again. 'I believed Caliph to be noble and dedicated – but there is no nobility in some of the things he has done. He has acted like a common criminal. He has acted for personal advantage and glorification. I believe in the concept of Caliph – but I know now we have chosen the wrong man. He has been corrupted by the power that we placed in his hands.'

Peter listened to him carefully, his head cocked to one side, his blue eyes clear and quietly searching.

'All right, Steven. So we discover that Caliph is not a deity – but a man with a man's petty greed and self-interest.'

'Yes, I suppose I do.' Steven's handsome florid face was heavy with regret. 'Caliph is not what I believed he might be.'

'Do you accept now that he is evil – truly evil?'

'Yes, I accept that.' Then, fiercely, 'But God, how I wish Caliph had been what I believed he was at the beginning.'

Peter could understand that and he nodded.

'It was what this crazy world of ours needed—' Steven went on bitterly. ' – We need somebody, a strong man to tell us what to do. I thought it was Caliph. I wanted it so badly to be him.'

'So now, do you accept that Caliph was not that man?'

'Yes,' said Steven simply. 'But if there was a man like that I would follow him again, unquestioningly.'

'You said you would do anything to prove to me that you had nothing to do with Melissa-Jane – will you help me to destroy Caliph?'

'Yes.' Steven did not hesitate.

'There will be great personal risk,' Peter pointed out, and now Steven met his eyes steadily.

'I know that. I know Caliph better than you.'

Peter found that his affection for his brother was now reinforced with admiration. Steven lacked very few of the manly virtues, he thought. He had strength and courage and brains, perhaps his major vice was that he had too much of each.

'What do you want me to do, Peter?'

'I want you to arrange a meeting with Caliph – face to face.'

'Impossible.' Steven dismissed it immediately.

'You said that you had means of getting a message to him?'

'Yes, but Caliph would never agree to a meeting.'

'Steven, what is the single – the only weakness that Caliph has shown so far?'

'He has shown no weakness.'

'Yes, he has,' Peter denied.

'What is it?'

'He is obsessed with protecting his personal identity and safety,' Peter pointed out. 'As soon as that is threatened, he immediately reverts to abduction and torture and murder.'

'That isn't a weakness—' Steven pointed out. 'It's a strength.'

'If you can get a message to him – that his identity is in jeopardy. That somebody, an enemy, has penetrated his security screen and has managed to get close to him,' Peter suggested, and Steven considered it long and carefully.

'He would react very strongly,' Steven agreed. 'But it would not take him very long to find out that I was lying. That would immediately discredit me, and as you said earlier I would be at grave risk for no good reason.'

'It isn't a lie,' Peter told him grimly. 'There is a Mossad agent close to Caliph. Very close to him.'

'How do you know that?' Steven asked sharply.

'I cannot tell you,' Peter said. 'But the information is iron-clad. I even know the agent's code-name. I give you my word that the information is genuine.'

'In that case—' Steven thought it out again ' – Caliph would probably already be suspicious and would be prepared to accept my warning. However, all he would do would be to ask me to give him the name – pass it to him along his usual communications channel. That would be it.'

'You would refuse to pass the information – except face to face. You will protest that the information is much too sensitive. You would protest that your personal safety was at stake. What would be his reaction?'

'I would expect him to put pressure on me to divulge the name—'

'If you resisted?'

'I suppose he would have to agree to a meeting. As you have pointed out, it is his major obsession. But, if he met me face to face, his identity would be revealed anyway.'

'Think, Steven. You know how his mind works.'

It took a few seconds, then Steven's expression changed, consternation twisting his lips as though he was in pain.

'Good God – of course. If I forced him to a face-to-face meeting, I would be highly unlikely to survive it.'

'Exactly,' Peter nodded. 'If we baited it with something absolutely irresistible, Caliph would have to agree to meet you – but he would make arrangements to have you silenced immediately, before you had a chance to pass on his identity to anyone else.'

'Hell, Peter, this is creepy. As you told me earlier today, I am fat and out of condition. I wouldn't be much of a match against Caliph.'

'Caliph would take that into consideration when deciding whether to meet you or not,' Peter agreed.

'It sounds like suicide,' Steven persisted.

'You just signed on to be tough,' Peter reminded him.

'Tough is one thing, stupid is another.'

'You would be in no danger until you delivered the message. Caliph would not dare dispose of you until you delivered your message,' Peter pointed out. 'And I give you my word that I will never call on you to go to an assignation with Caliph.'

'I can't ask for more than that, I suppose.' Steven threw up his hands. 'When do you want me to contact him?'

'How do you do it – the contact?'

'Advert in the Personal column,' Steven told him, and Peter grinned with reluctant admiration. Neat, efficient and entirely untraceable.

'Do it as soon as you can,' Peter instructed.

'Monday morning,' Steven nodded, and went on studying his brother with a peculiarly intent expression.

'What is it, Steven?'

'I was just thinking. If only Caliph had been somebody like you, Peter.'

'Me?' For the first time Peter was truly startled.

'The warrior king – utterly ruthless in the pursuit of the vision of justice and rightness and duty.'

'I am not like that.' Peter denied it.

'Yes, you are,' Steven said positively. 'You are the type of man that I hoped Caliph might be. The type of man we needed.'

P eter had to presume that Caliph was watching him. After his murder of Baroness Altmann, Caliph's interest would be intense. Peter had to act predictably.

He caught the early Monday flight back to Brussels, and before midday was at his desk in Narmco headquarters. Here also he was the centre of much interest and power-play. Altmann Industries had lost its chief executive and there were strong undercurrents and court intrigues already afoot. Despite a number of subtle approaches Peter stayed aloof from the struggle.

On Tuesday evening Peter picked up the newspaper from the news-stand in the Hilton lobby. Steven's contact request was in the small-ads section.

The children of Israel asked counsel of the Lord, saying, shall I go up again to battle? Judges. 20:23.

The quotation that Caliph had chosen seemed to epitomize his view of himself. He saw himself as godlike, set high above his fellow men.

Steven had explained to Peter that Caliph took up to forty-eight hours to answer.

Steven would wait each day after the appearance of the personal announcement at his desk in his office suite in Leadenhall Street, from noon until twenty minutes past the hour. He would have no visitors nor appointments for that time, and he would make certain that his direct unlisted telephone line was unengaged to receive the incoming contact.

There was no contact that Wednesday, but Steven had not expected one. On the Thursday Steven paced restlessly up and down the antique silk Kirman carpet as he waited for the call. He was already wearing the jacket of his suit, and his bowler and rolled umbrella were on the corner of the ornate French ormolu desk that squatted like some benign monster beneath the windows which looked across the street at Lloyds Exchange.

Steven Stride was afraid. He acknowledged the fact with direct self-honesty. Intrigue was part of his existence, had been for nearly all of his life – but always the game had been played to certain rules. He knew he was entering a new jungle, a savage wilderness where those few rules ceased entirely to exist. He was going in over his head; Peter had pointed out to him that this was not his way, and he knew Peter was right. Peter was right, and Steven was afraid as he had never been in his life. Yet he knew that he was going ahead with it. He had heard that it was the mark of true courage – to be able to meet and acknowledge fear, and yet control it sufficiently to be able to go ahead and do what duty dictated must be done.

He did not feel like a brave man.

The telephone rang once, too loud, too shrill – and every nerve in his body jumped taut and he found himself frozen, paralysed with fear in the centre of the beautiful and precious carpet.

The telephone rang again, the insistent double note sounded in his ears like the peal of doom, and he felt his bowels filled with the hot oily slime of fear, hardly to be contained.

The telephone rang the third time, and with an enormous effort he forced himself to make the three paces to his desk.

435

He lifted the telephone receiver, and heard the sharp chimes of the interference from the public telephone system.

'Stride,' he said. His voice was strained, high and almost shrill, and he heard the drop of the coin.

The voice terrified him. It was an electronic drone, inhuman, without gender, without the timbre of living emotion, without neither high nor low notes.

'Aldgate and Leadenhall Street,' said the voice.

Steven repeated the rendezvous and immediately the connection was broken.

Steven dropped the receiver onto its cradle and snatched up his bowler and umbrella as he hurried to the door.

His secretary looked up at him and smiled expectantly. She was a handsome grey-haired woman who had been with Steven for fifteen years.

'Sir?' She still called him that.

'I'm popping out for half an hour, May,' Steven told her. 'Look after the shop, there is a dear.' And he stepped into his private elevator and rode down swiftly to the underground garage where his Rolls was kept, together with the private vehicles of his senior executives.

In the elevator mirror he checked the exact angle of his bowler, a slightly raffish tilt over the right eye, and rearranged the bloom of the crimson carnation in the buttonhole of the dark blue Savile Row suit with its faint and elegant chalk stripe. It was important that he looked and acted entirely naturally during the next few minutes. His staff would remark on any departure from the normal.

In the garage he did not approach the dark-maroon Rolls-Royce which glowed in the subdued lighting like some precious gem. Instead he went towards the wicket gate in the steel roll-up garage door, and the doorman in his little glassed cubicle beside the door looked up from his football pools coupons, recognized the master and leaped to his feet.

'Afternoon, guv.'

'Good day, Harold. I won't be taking the car. Just stepping out for a few minutes.'

He stepped over the threshold of the gate, into the street and turned left, down towards the junction of Leadenhall Street and Aldgate. He walked fast, without seeming to hurry. Caliph spaced his intervals very tight, to make it difficult for the subject to pass a message to a surveillance unit. Steven knew he had only minutes to get from his office to the call box on the corner. Caliph seemed to know exactly how long it would take him.

The telephone in the red-framed and glass call box started to ring when he was still twenty paces away. Steven ran the distance.

'Stride,' he said, his voice slightly puffed with exertion, and immediately the coin dropped and the same electronic droning voice gave him the next contact point. It was the public call box at the High Street entrance to Aldgate tube station. Steven confirmed and the voice troubled him deeply, it sounded like that of a robot from some science fiction movie. It would not have been so bad if he had felt human contact.

The two receiving stations, neither of which was predictable, and the distances between them, had been carefully calculated to make it only just possible to reach them in time, to make it impossible for the call to be traced while the line was still open. Caliph or his agent was clearly moving from one call box to the next in another part of the city. Tracing them even a minute after he had left would be of no possible use in trying to establish identity.

The voice distorter that Caliph was using was a simple device no bigger than a small pocket calculator. Peter had told Steven that it could be purchased from a number of firms specializing in electronic surveillance, security and counter-measure equipment. It cost less than fifty dollars, and so altered the human voice – phasing out all sound outside the middle range – that even the most sophisticated recording device would not be able to lift a useable voice-print to compare with a computer bank memory. It would not even be able to determine whether the speaker was a man, a woman or a child.

Steven had an unusually clear path to the station, and found himself waiting outside the call box in the crowded entrance to the station while a young man in paint-speckled overalls, with long greasy blond hair, finished his conversation. Caliph's system allowed for prior use of the chosen public telephone, and as soon as the scruffy youth finished his leisurely chat, Steven pushed into the booth and made a show of consulting the directory.

The phone rang, and even though he was expecting it, Steven jumped with shock. He was perspiring now, with the walk and the tension, and his voice was ragged as he snatched the receiver.

'Stride,' he gulped.

The coin dropped and Caliph's impersonal tones chilled him again.

'Yes?'

'I have a message.'

'Yes?'

'There is danger for Caliph.'

'Yes?'

'A government intelligence agency has put an agent close to him, close enough to be extremely dangerous.'

'Say the source of your information.'

'My brother. General Peter Stride.' Peter had instructed him to tell the truth, as much as was possible.

'Say the government agency involved.'

'Negative. The information is too sensitive. I must have assurance that Caliph receives it personally.'

'Say the name or position of the enemy agent.'

'Negative. For the same reasons.'

Steven glanced at his gold Cartier tank watch with its black alligator strap. They had been speaking for fifteen seconds – he knew the contact would not last longer than thirty seconds. Caliph would not risk exposure beyond that time. He did not wait for the next question or instruction.

'I will pass the information only to Caliph, and I must be certain it is him, not one of his agents. I request a personal meeting.'

'That is not possible,' droned the inhuman voice.

'Then Caliph will be in great personal danger.' Steven found courage to say it.

'I repeat, say the name and position of enemy agent.'

Twenty-five seconds had passed.

'I say again, negative. You must arrange a face-to-face meeting for transfer of this information.'

A single droplet of sweat broke from the hairline of Steven's temple and ran down his cheek. He felt as though he were suffocating in the claustrophobic little telephone box.

'You will be contacted,' droned the voice and the line clicked dead.

Steven took the white silk handkerchief from his top pocket and dabbed at his face. Then he carefully rearranged the scrap of silk in his pocket, not folded into neat spikes but with a deliberately casual drape.

He squared his shoulders, lifted his chin and left the booth. Now for the first time he felt like a brave man. It was a feeling he relished, and he stepped out boldly swinging the rolled umbrella with a small flourish at each pace.

Peter had been within call of the telephone all that week, during the hours of involvement with the series of Narmco projects which he had put in train before his departure for Tahiti, and which all seemed to be maturing simultaneously. There were meetings that began in the morning and lasted until after dark, there were two separate day journeys, one to Oslo and another to Frankfurt, catching the early businessman's plane and back in the Narmco office before evening. Always he was within reach of a telephone and Steven Stride knew the number; even when he was in the NATO Officers Club gymnasium, sharpening his body to peak physical condition, or practising until after midnight in the underground pistol range until the 9-mm Cobra was an extension of his hands – either hand, left or right, equally capable of grouping the X circle at fifty metres, from any position, standing, kneeling or prone, always he was within reach of the telephone.

Peter felt like a prize fighter in training camp, concentrating all his attention on the preparations for the confrontation he knew lay ahead.

At last the weekend loomed, with the prospect of being boring and frustrating. He refused invitations to visit the country home of one of his Narmco colleagues, another to fly down to Paris for the Saturday racing – and he stayed alone in the Hilton suite, waiting for the call from Steven.

On Sunday morning he had all the papers sent up to his room, English and American and French – German which he could read better than he spoke, and even the Dutch and Italian papers which he could stumble through haltingly, missing every third word or so.

He went through them carefully, trying to find a hint of Caliph's activity. New abductions, hijackings or other acts which might give him a lead to some new Caliph-dominated pressures.

Italy was in a political uproar. The confusion so great that he could only guess at how much of it was from the left and how much from the right. There had been an assassination in Naples of five known members of the Terrorist Red Brigade, all five taken out neatly with a single grenade. The grenade type had been determined as standard NATO issue, and the execution had been in the kitchen of a Red

Brigade safe apartment in a slum area of the city. The police had no leads. It sounded like Caliph. There was no reason to believe that his 'chain' did not include prominent Italian businessmen. A millionaire Italian living in his own country had to be the earth's most endangered species after the blue whale, Peter thought wryly, and they might have called on Caliph to go on the offensive.

Peter finished the continental papers, and turned with relief to the English and American. It was a little before Sunday noon, and he wondered how he could live out the desolate hours until Monday morning. He was certain that there would be no reply to Steven's request for a meeting before then.

He started on the English-language newspapers, spinning them out to cover the blank time ahead.

The British Leyland Motor Company strike was in its fifteenth week – with no prospect of settlement. Now there was a case for Caliph, Peter smiled wryly, remembering his discussion with Steven. Knock a few heads together for their own good.

There was only one other item of interest in his morning's reading. The President of the United States had appointed a special negotiator in another attempt to find a solution to the Israeli occupation of the disputed territories in the Middle East. The man he had chosen was Dr Kingston Parker, who was described as a personal friend of the President and one of the senior members of his inner circle of advisors, a man well thought of by all parties in the dispute, and an ideal choice for the difficult job. Again Peter found himself in agreement. Kingston Parker's energies and resources seemed bottomless.

Peter dropped the last paper and found himself facing a void of boredom that would extend through until the following day. There were three books he should read beside his bed, and the Hermes crocodile case was half-filled with

Narmco material, yet he knew that he would not be able to concentrate – not with the prospect of the confrontation with Caliph over-shadowing all else.

He went through into the mirrored bathroom of the suite, and found the package that he had purchased the previous day in the cosmetic section of Galéries Anspach, one of the city's largest departmental stores.

The wig was of good-quality human hair, not the obviously shiny nylon substitute. It was in his own natural colour, but much longer than Peter wore his hair. He arranged it carefully along his own hairline, and then set to work with a pair of scissors, trimming and tidying it. When he had it as close to his liking as possible, he began to tint the temples with 'Italian Boy' hair silvering.

It took him most of the afternoon, for he was in no hurry, and he was critical of his own work. Every few minutes he consulted the snapshot which Melissa-Jane had taken with her new Polaroid camera, Peter's Christmas present to her, at Abbots Yew on New Year's Day. It was a good likeness of both the Stride brothers, Peter and Steven, standing full face and smiling indulgently at Melissa-Jane's command to do so.

It highlighted the resemblances of the two brothers, and also pointed out their physical differences. The natural hair colouring was identical but Steven's was fashionably longer, curling on his collar at the back, and appreciably greyer at the temples and streaked at the front.

Steven's face was heavier, with the first trace of jowls, and his colour was higher, perhaps the first ruddy warnings of heart malfunction or merely the banner of good living in his cheeks. Yet with the wig on his head, Peter's own face seemed much fuller.

Next Peter shaped the moustache, trimming it down into the infantry officer model that Steven favoured. There had been a good selection of artificial moustaches to choose from in the cosmetic section, amongst a display of artificial eyelashes and eyebrows, but none had been exactly right. Peter had to work on it carefully with the scissors, and then tint it with a little silver.

When he fastened it in place with the special adhesive gum, the result was quite startling. The moustache filled out his face even further, and of course the eyes of the twins were almost exactly the same shape and colour. Their noses were both straight and bony. Peter's mouth was a little more generous, and did not have the same hard relentless line of lip – but the moustache concealed much of that.

Peter stood back and examined himself in the full-length mirror. He and Steven were within a quarter of an inch in height, they had the same breadth of shoulder. Steven was heavier in the gut, and his neck was thickening, giving him a thrusting bull-like set to his head and shoulders. Peter altered his stance slightly. It worked. He doubted that anybody who did not know both of them intimately would be able to detect the substitution. There was no reason to believe that Caliph or any of his closest lieutenants would have seen either Steven or Peter in the flesh.

He spent an hour practising Steven's gait, watching himself in the mirror, trying to capture the buoyant cockiness of Steven's movements, searching for little personal mannerisms, the way Steven stood with both hands clasped under the skirts of his jacket; the way he brushed his moustache with one finger, from the parting under his nose – left and right.

Clothing was not a serious problem. Both brothers had used the same tailor since Sandhurst days, and Steven's dress habits were invariable and inviolable. Peter's knew exactly what he would wear in any given situation.

Peter stripped off wig and moustache and repacked them carefully in their Galéries Anspach plastic packets, then buttoned them into one of the interior divisions of the Hermes case.

Next he removed the Cobra parabellum from another

division. It was still in the chamois leather holster, and he bounced the familiar weight of the weapon in the palm of his hand. Reluctantly he decided he could not take it with him. The meeting would almost certainly be in England. The contact that Steven had had on Thursday had clearly originated in London. He had to believe the next contact would be in that same city. He could not take the chance of walking through British customs with a deadly weapon on his person. If he was stopped, there would be publicity. It would instantly alert Caliph. He would be able to get another weapon from Thor Command once he was in England. Colin Noble would supply him, just as soon as Peter explained the need, he was certain of that.

Peter went down and checked the Cobra pistol into the safe deposit box of the hotel reception office, and returned to his room to face the wearying and indefinite wait. It was one of a soldier's duties to which he had never entirely accustomed himself – he always hated the waiting.

However, he settled down to read Robert Asprey's *War in the Shadows*, that definitive tome on the history and practice of guerrilla warfare down the ages. He managed to lose himself sufficiently to be mildly surprised when he glanced at his watch and saw it was after eight o'clock. He ordered an omelette to be sent up by room service, and ten seconds after he replaced the receiver, the telephone rang. He thought it might be a query from the kitchen about his dinner order.

'Yes, what is it?' he demanded irritably.

'Peter?'

'Steven?'

'He has agreed to a meeting.'

Peter felt his heart lunge wildly.

'When? Where?'

'I don't know. I have to fly to Orly tomorrow. There will be instructions for me at the airport.'

Caliph covering and backtracking. Peter should have

expected it. Desperately he cast his mind back to the layout of Orly Airport. He had to find a private place to meet Steven and make the change-over. He discarded swiftly the idea of meeting in one of the lounges or washrooms. That left one other location.

'What time will you be there?' Peter demanded.

'Cooks have got me onto the early flight. I'll be there at eleven fifteen.'

'I'll be there before you,' Peter told him. He knew the Sabena timetable by heart and all senior Narmco executives had special VIP cards which assured a seat on any flight.

'I will book a room at the Air Hotel on the fourth floor of Orly South terminal in your name,' he told Steven now. 'I'll wait in the lobby. Go directly to the reception desk and ask for your key. I will check behind you to make certain you are not followed. Do not acknowledge me in any way. Have you got that, Steven?'

'Yes.'

'Until tomorrow, then.'

Peter broke the connection, and went through into the bathroom. He studied his own face in the mirror.

'Well, that takes care of getting a weapon from Thor.' Caliph had not set the meeting in England. It was clear now that Paris was only a staging point, and that in his usual careful fashion Caliph would move the subject on from there – perhaps through one or more staging points, to the final rendezvous.

The subject would go in unarmed, and unsupported – and Peter was certain that afterwards Caliph would take his usual pains to ensure that the subject would be unable to carry back a report of the meeting.

I am drawing two cards inside for a straight flush, and Caliph is the dealer from a pack that he has had plenty of time to prepare, Peter thought coldly, but at least the waiting was over. He began to pack his toilet articles into the waterproof Gucci bag.

ir Steven Stride marched into the lobby of Orly South Air Hotel at five minutes past noon, and Peter smiled to himself in self-congratulation. Steven was wearing a blue double-breasted blazer, white shirt and cricket-club tie, above grey woollen slacks and black English handmade shoes – none of your fancy Italian footwear for Steven.

It was Steven's standard informal dress, and Peter had only been wrong about the tie – he had guessed that it would be an I Zingari pattern. Peter himself wore a double-breaster and grey slacks under his trench coat and his shoes were black Barkers.

Steven's eyes flickered around the lobby, passing over Peter sitting in a far corner with a copy of *Le Monde*, then Steven moved authoritively to the reception desk.

'My name is Stride, do you have a reservation for me?' Steven spoke slowly, in rich plummy tones, for very few of these damned people spoke English. The clerk checked swiftly, nodded, murmured a welcome and gave Steven the form and the key.

'Four One Six.' Steven checked the number loudly enough for Peter to hear. Peter had been watching the entrance carefully; fortunately there had been very few guests entering the lobby during the few minutes since Steven's arrival, and none of those could possibly have been Caliph surveillance. Of course, if this was a staging point, as Peter was certain it was, then Caliph would have no reason to put surveillance on Steven – not until he got much closer to the ultimate destination.

Steven moved to the elevator with a porter carrying his single small valise, and Peter drifted across and joined the small cluster of guests waiting at the elevators.

He rode up shoulder to shoulder with Steven in the crowded elevator, neither of them acknowledging the other's existence, and when Steven and the porter left at the fourth stage Peter rode on up three floors, walked the length of the corridor and back, then took the descending elevator to Steven's floor.

Steven had left the door to 416 off the catch, and Peter pushed it open and slipped in without knocking.

'My dear boy.' Steven was in his shirt sleeves. He had switched on the television, but now he turned down the sound volume and hurried to greet him with both affection and vast relief.

'No problems?' Peter asked.

'Like clockwork,' Steven told him. 'Would you like a drink? I got a bottle in the duty-free.'

While he hunted for glasses in the bathroom, Peter checked the room swiftly. A view down towards the square functional buildings of the market that had replaced the picturesque Les Halles in central Paris, matching curtains and covers on the twin beds, television and radio sets, between the beds, modern soulless furniture – it was a room, that was the most and the least that could be said for it.

Steven carried in the glasses and handed one to Peter.

'Cheers!'

Peter tasted his whisky. It was too strong and the Parisian tap water tasted of chlorine. He put it aside.

'How is Caliph going to get instructions to you?'

'Got them already.' Steven went to his blazer, hanging over the back of the chair, and found a long white envelope in the inside pocket. 'This was left at the Air France Information Desk.'

Peter took the envelope and as he split the flap he sank onto one of the armchairs. There were three items in the envelope.

A first-class Air France airline ticket, a voucher for a chauffeur-driven limousine and a hotel reservation voucher.

The air ticket could have been purchased for cash at any Air France outlet or agency, the limousine and hotel bookings could have been made equally anonymously. There was no possibility of a trace back from any of these documents.

Peter opened the Air France ticket and read the destination. Something began to crawl against his skin, like the loathsome touch of body vermin. He closed the ticket and checked the two vouchers; now the sick feeling of betrayal and evil spread through his entire body, numbing his fingertips and coating the back of his tongue with a bitter metallic taste like copper salts.

The air ticket was for this evening's flight from Orly to Ben-Gurion Airport in Israel, the hired-car voucher was good for a single journey from there to Jerusalem, the hotel voucher was for a room in the King David Hotel in that ancient and holy city.

'What is it, Peter?'

'Nothing,' said Peter, only then aware that the sickness must have shown on his face. 'Jerusalem,' he went on. 'Caliph wants you in Jerusalem.'

There was one person in Jerusalem at that moment. Somebody who had been in his thoughts almost unceasingly since last he had embraced her in the darkness of Bora-Bora Island – so very long ago.

Caliph was in Jerusalem, and Magda Altmann was in Jerusalem – and the sickness was heavy in the pit of his stomach.

The deviousness of Caliph.

No, he told himself firmly. I have travelled that road already. It cannot be Magda.

The genius of Caliph, evil and effortless.

It is possible. He had to admit it then. With Caliph, anything is possible. Every time Caliph shook the dice box the numbers changed, different numbers, making different totals – but always completely plausible, always completely believable.

It was one of the basic proven theorems of his trade that

448

a man, any man, was blinded and deafened and rendered senseless by love. Peter was in love, and he knew it.

All right. So now I have to try and free my mind and think it all over again, as though I were not besotted.

'Peter, are you all right?' Steven demanded again, now with real concern. It was impossible to think with Steven hovering over him. He would have to put it aside.

'I am going to Jerusalem in your place,' Peter said.

'Come again, old boy?'

'We are changing places – you and I.'

'You won't get away with it.' Steven shook his head decidedly. 'Caliph will take you on the full toss.'

Peter picked up his Hermes case and went through into the bathroom. He worked quickly with the wig and artificial moustache and then called.

'Steven, come here.'

They stood side by side and stared at themselves in the mirror.

'Good God!' Steven grunted. Peter altered his stance slightly, conforming more closely to his brother.

'That's incredible. Never knew you were such a good-looking blighter,' Steven chuckled, and wagged his head wonderingly. Peter imitated the gesture perfectly.

'Damn it, Peter.' The chuckle dried on Steven's lips. 'That's enough. You're giving me the creeps.'

Peter pulled the wig off his head. 'It will work.'

'Yes,' Steven conceded. 'It will work – but how the hell did you know I would be wearing a blazer and greys?'

'Trick of the trade,' Peter told him. 'Don't worry about it. Let's go through the paperwork now.'

In the bedroom they laid out their personal documents in two piles, and went swiftly through them.

The passport photographs would pass readily enough.

'You have to shave your soup-strainer,' Peter told him, and Steven stroked his moustache with one finger, left and right – lingeringly, regretfully.

'Is that absolutely necessary? I'd feel like I was walking around in public with no trousers on.'

Peter took the slim gold ball-point from his inside pocket and a sheaf of hotel stationery from the drawer. He studied Steven's signature in the passport for a minute, and then dashed it off on the top sheet.

'No.' He shook his head, and tried again. It was like Steven's walk, cocky and confident, the 'T' was crossed with a flourishing sword stroke of the pen.

In sixty seconds he had it perfected.

'With that wig on your head you could walk into my bank any day and sign for the whole damned bundle,' Steven muttered uneasily. 'Then go home and climb into bed with Pat.'

'Now, *there* is an idea.' Peter looked thoughtful.

'Don't joke about it,' Steven pleaded.

'Who's joking?' Peter went through the credit cards, club membership cards, driver's licence and all the other clutter of civilized existence.

Steven's mastery of his brother's signature was not nearly as effective, but after twenty minutes' practice was just adequate for hotel registration purposes.

'Here is the address of a hotel on the left bank. Magnificent restaurant, and the management are very understanding if you should want to invite a young lady up to your room for a drink.'

'Perish the thought.' Steven looked smug at the prospect.

'It should only be for a few days, Steven. Just keep very low. Pay cash for everything. Keep clear of the George V or the Meurice, Le Doyen and Maxim's – all the places where they know you.'

They went carefully over the last details of the exchange of identity, while Steven shaved off the moustache and anointed the bare patch tenderly with Eau de Sauvage.

'You'd better move now,' Peter told him at last. 'Wear

this—' It was Peter's buff trenchcoat that would cover his blazer. ' – And let's change ties.'

Steven was ready, and he stood rather awkwardly by the door, in the tightly fitting trenchcoat.

'Steven, can I ask you a question?' Peter did not know why he had to know now, it had been buried so deeply for so long and yet at this moment it was deadly important to know.

'Of course, old boy.' Steven seemed to welcome the postponement of the moment of parting.

'Sandhurst.' Peter tried to keep the embarrassment out of his voice. 'I never asked you before – but you didn't do it, did you, Steven?'

Steven met his eyes calmly, steadily. 'No, Peter. I did not do it. My word on it.'

Peter took his brother's proffered right hand and squeezed it hard. It was ridiculous to feel so relieved.

'I'm glad, Steven.'

'Take care of yourself, old boy.'

'I will,' Peter nodded. 'But if anything happens,' Peter hesitated, ' – Melissa-Jane—'

'Don't worry. I'll take care of it.'

Why do Englishmen have such difficulty talking to each other, Peter wondered, let alone communicating affection and gratitude?

'Well, I'll be getting along then,' said Steven.

'Take a guard on your middle stump, and don't be caught in the slips,' Peter cautioned him with the old inanity.

'Count on it,' said Steven, and went out into the passage, closing the door behind him firmly, leaving his brother to think about Jerusalem.

Only the name had changed from Lod to Ben-Gurion – otherwise the Arrivals Hall was as Peter remembered it. One of the few airports on the globe which has sufficient luggage trolleys, so that the passengers do not have to fight for possession.

In the Arrivals Hall there was a young Israeli driver with the name:

Sir Steven Stride

printed in white chalk on a schoolboy's black slate.

The driver wore a navy-blue cap with a black patent-leather peak. It was his only item of uniform, otherwise he was dressed in sandals and a white cotton shirt. His English had the usual strong American turn to it, and his attitude was casual and friendly – he might be driving the limousine today, but tomorrow he could be at the controls of a Centurion tank, and he was as good a man as his passenger any day.

'Shalom, Shalom,' he greeted Peter. 'Is that all your luggage?'

'Yes.'

'*Beserder*. Let's go.' He did not offer to push Peter's trolley, but chatted amicably as he led him out to the limousine.

It was a stretched-out 240 D Mercedes Benz – almost brand new, lovingly polished – but somebody had painted a pair of squinting eyes on each side of the chrome three-pointed star on the boot of the vehicle.

They had hardly pulled out through the airport gates when one of the characteristic aromas of Israel filled the cab of the Mercedes – the smell of orange blossom from the citrus orchards that lined each side of the road.

For some reason the smell made Peter feel uneasy, a sensation of having missed something, of having neglected some vital aspect. He tried to think it all out again, from

452

the beginning, but the driver kept up a running commentary as they pulled up the new double highway, over the hills through the pine forests towards Jerusalem, and the voice distracted him.

Peter wished he had kept the list that he had drawn up in the hotel room at Orly instead of destroying it. He tried to reconstruct it in his mind.

There were a dozen items on the plus side. The third was:

Magda told me about Cactus Flower. Would she have done so if she was Caliph?

And then directly opposite, in the 'minus' column:

If Magda is Caliph, then 'Cactus Flower' does not exist. It was an invention for some undisclosed reason.

This was the item that pricked him like a burr in a woollen sock. He kept coming back to it; there was a link missing from the logic of it and he tried to tease it loose. It was there just below the surface of his mind, and he knew instinctively that if he missed it the consequences would be dire.

The driver kept chatting, turning to glance back at him every few minutes with a cheerful demand for recognition.

'That's right, isn't it?'

Peter grunted. The man was irritating him – the missing item was there, just beginning to surface. He could see the shape of it. Why had the smell of orange blossom worried him? The smell of flowers? Cactus flower? There was something there, something missing from the list.

If Magda is not Caliph then— Was that it? He was not certain. ' – Will that be all right, then?' The driver was insisting again.

'I'm sorry – what was that?'

'I said, I had to drop a parcel off at my mother-in-law,' the driver explained again. 'It's from my wife.'

'Can't you do that on your way back?'

'I'm not going back tonight—' The driver grinned

winningly over his shoulder. ' – My mother-in-law lives right on our way. It won't take five minutes. I promised my wife I'd get it to her mother today.'

'Oh, very well then,' Peter snapped. There was something about the man he did not like, and he had lost track of the item that had been worrying him.

He felt as though he was in a chess game with a vastly superior opponent, and he had overlooked a castle on an open file, or a knight in a position to fork simultaneous check on his king and queen.

'We turn off here,' the driver explained, and swung off into a section of new apartment blocks, all of them built of the custard-yellow Jerusalem stone, row upon row of them, Israel's desperate attempt to house its new citizens. At this time of evening the streets were deserted, as families gathered for the evening meal.

The driver jinked through the maze of identical-seeming streets with garrulous confidence and then braked and parked in front of one of the square, boxlike, yellow buildings.

'Two minutes,' he promised, and jumped out of the Mercedes, scampered around to the rear and opened the boot. There was a scratching sound, a small bump and then the lid of the boot slammed and the driver came back into Peter's line of vision – carrying a brown paper parcel.

He grinned at Peter, with the ridiculous cap pushed onto the back of his head, mouthed another assurance through the closed window: 'Two minutes—' and went into the main door of the apartment.

Peter hoped he might be longer. The silence was precious. He closed his eyes, and concentrated.

If Magda is not Caliph then – then— There was the ticking sound of the engine cooling, or was it the dashboard clock? Peter thrust the sound to the back of his mind.

– then – then Cactus Flower exists. Yes, that was it!

Cactus Flower exists, and if he exists he is close enough to Caliph to know of Sir Steven Stride's threat to expose him—

Peter sat upright, rigid in his seat. He had believed that Steven Stride would be perfectly safe – until after the meeting with Caliph. That was the terrible mistake.

– Cactus Flower must stop Steven Stride reaching Caliph! Yes, of course. Christ, how had he not seen it before. Cactus Flower was Mossad, and Peter was sitting in a street of Jerusalem – Mossad's front yard – dressed as Steven Stride.

Christ! He felt the certainty of mortal danger. Cactus Flower probably made the arrangements himself. If Magda Altmann is not Caliph, then I am walking right into Cactus Flower's sucker punch!

The damned clock kept ticking, a sound as nerve-racking as a leaky faucet.

I am in Cactus Flower's city – in Cactus Flower's limo—

The ticking. Oh God! It was not coming from the dashboard. Peter turned his head. It was coming from *behind him*; from the boot which the driver had opened and in which he had moved something. Something that was now ticking away quietly.

Peter wrenched the door handle and hit the door with his shoulder, instinctively grabbing the Hermes case with his other hand.

They would have stripped out the metal partition between the boot and the back seat to allow the blast to cut through. There was probably only the leather upholstery between him and whatever was ticking. That was why he had heard it so clearly.

Time seemed to have slowed, so he was free to think it out as the seconds dropped as lingeringly as spilled honey.

Infernal machine, he thought. Why that ridiculously nineteenth-century term should occur to him now, he could not guess, a relic from the childhood days when he read *Boy's Own Paper*, perhaps.

He was out of the Mercedes now, almost losing his balance as his feet hit the unsurfaced and broken sidewalk.

It is probably plastic explosive with a clockwork timer on the detonator, he thought, as he started to run. What delay would they use? Thirty seconds? No, the driver had to get well away. He had said two minutes, said it twice –

The thoughts raced through his mind, but his legs seemed to be shackled, dragging against an enormous weight. Like trying to run waist deep in the sucking surf of a sandy beach.

– It will be two minutes, and he has been gone that long—

Ten paces ahead of him there was a low wall that had been built as a flower box around the apartment block. It was knee high, a double brick wall with the cavity filled with dry yellow earth and precariously sustaining the life of a few wizened oleander bushes.

Peter dived head first over the wall, breaking his fall with shoulder and forearm, and rolling back hard under the protection of the low wall.

Above his head were the large windows of the ground-floor apartments. Lying on his side, peering up at them, Peter saw the reflection of the parked Mercedes as though in a mirror.

He covered his ears with the palms of both hands. The Mercedes was only fifty feet away. He watched it in the glass, his body braced, his mouth wide open to absorb blast shock in his sinuses.

The Mercedes erupted. It seemed to open quite sedately, like one of those time-elapse movies of a rose blooming. The shining metal spread and distorted like grotesque black petals, and bright white flame shot through it – that was all Peter saw, for the row of apartment windows disappeared, blown away in a million glittering shards by the blast wave, leaving the windows gaping like the toothless mouths of old decrepit men, and at the same moment the blast smashed into Peter.

Even though it was muted by the thick wall of the flower box, it crushed him, seemed to drive in his ribs, and the air whooshed from his lungs. The fearsome din of the explosion clamoured in his head, filling his skull with little bright chips of rainbow light.

He thought he must have lost consciousness for a moment, then there was the patter of falling debris raining down around him and something struck him a painful blow in the small of his back. It spurred him.

He dragged himself to his feet, struggling to refill his empty lungs. He knew he had to get away before the security forces arrived, or he could expect intensive interrogation which would certainly disclose the fact that he was not Sir Steven.

He started to run. The street was still deserted, although he could hear the beginning of the uproar which must follow. The cries of anguish and of fear.

He reached the corner and stopped running. He walked quickly to the next alley behind an apartment block. There were no street lights and he paused in the shadows. By now a dozen figures shouting questions and conjecture were hurrying towards the smoke and dust of the explosion.

Peter recovered his breath and dusted down his blazer and slacks, waiting until the confusion and shouting were at their peak. Then he walked quietly away.

On the main road he joined a short queue at the bus stop. The bus dropped him off in the Jaffa Road.

He found a café opposite the bus stop and went through into the men's room. He was unmarked, but pale and strained; his hands still shook from the shock of the blast as he combed his hair.

He went back into the café, found a corner seat and ordered falafel and pitta bread with coffee.

He sat there for half an hour, considering his next move.

If Magda Altmann is not Caliph— he repeated the conundrum which he had solved just in time to save his life.

Magda Altmann is not Caliph! He knew it then with utter certainty. Cactus Flower had tried to stop Sir Steven Stride reaching Caliph with his denunciation. Therefore Magda had told him the truth. His relief flooded his body with a great warm glow – and his first instinct was to telephone her at the Mossad number she had given him. Then he saw the danger. Cactus Flower was Mossad. He dared not go near her – not yet.

What must he do then? And he knew the answer without having to search for it. He must do what he had come to do. He must find Caliph, and the only fragile thread he had to follow was the trail that Caliph had laid for him.

He left the café and found a taxi at the rank on the corner.

'King David Hotel,' Peter said, and sank back in the seat.

At least I know the danger of Cactus Flower now, he thought grimly. I won't walk into the next one blind.

P eter took one glance around the room that had been reserved for him. It was in the back of the hotel and across the road the tall bell tower of the Y.M.C.A. made a fine stance from which a sniper could command the two windows.

'I ordered a suite,' Peter snapped at the reception clerk who had led him up.

'I'm sorry, Sir Steven.' The man was immediately flustered. 'There must have been a mistake.'

Another glance around the room and Peter had noted half a dozen sites at which Cactus Flower might have laid another explosive charge to back up the one that had failed in the back of the Mercedes. He would prefer to spend a night in a pit full of cobras rather than accept the quarters that Cactus Flower had prepared for him.

Peter stepped back into the passage and fixed the clerk with his most imperious gaze. The man scampered and returned within five minutes – looking mightily relieved.

'We have one of our best suites for you.'

Number 122 commanded a magnificent view across the valley to the Jaffa Gate in the wall of the Old City, and in the centre of this vista towered the Church of the Last Supper.

The gardens of the hotel were lush with lawns and tall graceful palms, children shrieked gleefully around the swimming pool while a cool light breeze broke the heat.

The suite abutted onto the long open terrace, and the moment he was alone, Peter lowered the heavy roller shutters across the terrace door. Cactus Flower could too easily send a man in that way. Then Peter stepped out onto the private balcony.

On the tall stone battlements of the French Consulate adjoining the gardens they were lowering the Tricolour against the flaming backdrop of the sunset. Peter watched it for a moment – then concentrated again on the security of the suite.

There was possible access from the room next door, an easy step across from window to balcony. Peter hesitated – then decided to leave the balcony unshuttered. He could not bring himself to accept the claustrophobic effect of a completely shuttered room.

Instead he drew the curtains and ordered a large whisky and soda from room service. He needed it. It had been a long hard day.

Then he stripped off tie and shirt, wig and moustache and washed away some of the tensions. He was towelling himself when there was a tap on the door.

'Damned quick service,' he muttered, and clapped the wig on his head and stepped into the lounge, just as a key rattled in the lock and the door swung open. Peter lifted the towel and pretended to be still drying his face to cover the lack of moustache on his lip.

'Come in,' he gruffed through the towel, and then froze in the doorway, and a vice seemed to close around his heart and restrict his breathing.

She wore a man's open-neck shirt, with patch pockets on the breasts, and khaki combat breeches hugged her narrow hips. The long legs were thrust into soft-soled canvas boots. Yet she carried herself with the same unforced chic as if she had been dressed in the height of Parisian fashion.

'Sir Steven.' She closed the door swiftly behind her, and Peter saw her palm the slim metal pick with which she had turned the lock. 'I'm Magda Altmann, we have met before. I have come to warn you that you are in very grave danger.'

The abundant short curls formed a dark halo around her head, and her eyes were huge and green with concern.

'You must immediately leave this country. I have my private executive jet aircraft at an airfield near here—'

Peter lowered the towel enough to allow himself to speak.

'Why are you telling me this?' he interrupted her brusquely. 'And why should I believe you?'

He saw the quick roses of anger bloom in her cheeks.

'You are dabbling in things you do not understand.'

'Why should you want to warn me?' Peter insisted.

'Because—' she hesitated and then went on sharply, ' – because you are Peter Stride's brother. For that reason and no other I would not want you killed.'

Peter tossed the towel back into the bathroom and with the same movement pulled off the wig and dropped it onto the chair beside him.

'Peter!' Astonishment riveted her and she stared at him, the colour that anger had painted in her cheeks fled and her eyes turned a deep luminous green. He had forgotten once again how beautiful she was.

460

'Well, don't just stand there,' he said, and she ran to him on those long, graceful legs and flung her arms around his neck.

They strained together silently, neither of them found words necessary for many minutes. Then she broke away.

'Peter, darling – I cannot stay long. I took a terrible chance coming here at all. They are watching the hotel and the girls on the switchboard are Mossad. That is why I could not telephone—'

'Tell me everything you can,' he ordered.

'All right, but hold me, *chéri*. I do not wish to waste a minute of this little time we have together.'

She hid in the bathroom when the waiter brought the whisky, then joined Peter on the couch.

'Cactus Flower reported to control that Steven had requested a meeting with Caliph, and that he intended to denounce him. That was all I knew until yesterday – but I could build on that. First of all I was amazed that Steven was the subject of the first Cactus Flower report and not you, Peter—' She caressed the smooth hard brown muscle of his chest as she spoke. ' – It had never occured to me, even when we discussed the fact that the report mentioned no Christian name.'

'It didn't occur to me either, not until I'd already left Les Neuf Poissons.'

'Then, of course, I guessed that you had taxed Steven with it, and told him the source of your information. It would have been a crazy thing to do – not your usual style, at all. But I thought that being your brother—' She trailed off.

'That is exactly what I did—'

'Peter, we could still talk if we were on the bed,' she murmured. 'I have been without you for so long.'

Her bare skin felt like hot satin, and they lay entwined with the hard smooth plain of her belly pressed to his. Her mouth was against his ear.

' – Steven's request for a meeting went directly to Caliph through a channel other than Cactus Flower. He had no chance to head it off—'

'Who is Cactus Flower, have you found that out?'

'No.' She shook her head. 'I still do not know.' And she raked her long fingernails lightly down across his belly.

'If you do that – I cannot think clearly,' he protested.

'I am sorry.' She brought her hand up to his cheek. 'Anyway, Caliph instructed Cactus Flower to arrange the meeting with Steven. I did not know what arrangements were being made – until I saw Sir Steven's name on the immigration lists this evening. I was not particularly looking for his name, but as soon as I saw it I guessed what was happening. I guessed that Cactus Flower had enticed him here to make his interception easier. It took me three hours to find where Sir Steven would be staying.'

They were both silent now, and she lowered her face and pressed it into the soft of his neck, sighing with happiness.

'Oh God, Peter. How I missed you.'

'Listen, my darling. You must tell me everything else you have.' Peter lifted her chin tenderly so he could see her face and her eyes came back into focus.

'Did you know that there was to be an assassination attempt on Steven?'

'No – but it was the logical step for Mossad to protect Cactus Flower.'

'What else?'

'Nothing.'

'You don't know if actual arrangements have been made for a meeting between Caliph and Steven?'

'No, I don't know,' she admitted.

'You still have no indication at all of Caliph's identity?'

'No, none at all.'

They were silent again, but now she propped herself on one elbow and watched his face as he spoke.

'Cactus Flower would have to make the arrangements for the meeting as Caliph instructed. He would not be able to take the chance of faking it – not with Caliph.'

Magda nodded in silent agreement.

'Therefore we have to believe that at this moment Caliph is close, very close.'

'Yes.' She nodded again, but reluctantly.

'That means that I have to go on impersonating Steven.'

'Peter, no. They will kill you.'

'They have already tried—' Peter told her grimly, and quietly outlined the destruction of the Mercedes. She touched the bruise in the small of his back where he had been struck by flying debris from the explosion.

'They won't let you get close to Caliph.'

'They may have no choice,' Peter told her. 'Caliph is so concerned for his own safety – he is going to insist on the meeting.'

'They will try and kill you again,' she implored him.

'Perhaps, but I'm betting the meeting with Caliph is arranged to take place very soon. They won't have much opportunity to set up another elaborate trap like the Mercedes, and I'll be expecting it – I've got to go ahead with it, Magda.'

'Oh, Peter—' But he touched her lips, silencing the protest, and he was thinking aloud again.

'Let's suppose Mossad knew that I was not Steven Stride, that my real purpose was not to denounce Cactus Flower? What difference would that make to the thinking at Mossad?'

She considered that. 'I'm not certain.'

'If they knew it was Peter Stride impersonating Steven Stride,' he insisted, 'would that make them curious enough to let the meeting go ahead?'

'Peter, are you suggesting I turn in a report to my control at Mossad – ?'

'Would you do that?'

'Sweet merciful God,' she whispered. 'I could be signing your death warrant, Peter my darling.'

' – or you could be saving my life.'

'I don't know.' She sat up erect in the bed and ran the fingers of both hands through the short dark curls, the lamplight glowed on her skin with a pale, smooth opalescence and the small fine breasts changed shape as she moved her arms. 'Oh, Peter, I don't know.'

'It could be our only chance to ever get close to Caliph,' he insisted, and the lovely face was racked with indecision.

'Caliph believes I have killed you, he believes that I have transmitted a warning to him through my brother. He will have his guard as low as ever it will be. We will never have a chance again like this.'

'I am so afraid for you, Peter. I am so afraid for myself without you—' She did not finish it, but pulled up her long naked legs and hugged her knees to her breasts. It was a defensive foetal position.

'Will you do it?' he asked gently.

'You want me to tell my control your real identity, to tell him that I believe your real purpose is not to denounce Cactus Flower – but some other unknown—'

'That is right.'

She turned her head and looked at him.

'I will do it in exchange for your promise,' she decided.

'What is that?'

'If I judge from my control at Mossad that you are still in danger, and that they still intend intercepting you before you reach Caliph – then I want your promise that you will abandon the attempt. That you will immediately go to where the Lear is waiting and that you will allow Pierre to fly you out of here to a safe place.'

'You will be honest with me?' he asked. 'You will judge Mossad's reaction fairly – and even if there is a half-decent chance of me reaching Caliph you will allow me to take that chance?'

She nodded, but he went on grimly, making certain of it.

'Swear it to me!'

'I would not try to prevent you – just as long as there is a chance of success.'

'Swear it to me, Magda.'

'On my love for you, I swear it,' she said quietly, and he relaxed slightly.

'And I in turn swear to you that if there is no chance of meeting Caliph – I will leave on the Lear.'

She turned against his chest, wrapping both her arms around his neck.

'Make love to me, Peter. Now! Quickly! I have to have that at least.'

As she dressed she went over the arrangements for communicating.

'I cannot come through the switchboard here – I explained why,' she told him as she laced the canvas boots. 'You must stay here, in this room where I can reach you. If there is danger I will send someone to you. It will be somebody I trust. He will say simply. "Magda sent me," and you must go with him. He will take you to Pierre and the Lear jet.'

She stood up and belted the khaki breeches around her narrow waist, crossing to the mirror to comb out the dark damp tangle of her curls.

'If you hear nothing from me it will mean that I judge there is still a chance of reaching Caliph—' Then she paused and her expression altered. ' – Are you armed, Peter?' She was watching him in the mirror as she worked with her hair. He shook his head.

'I could get a weapon to you – a knife, a pistol?'

And again he shook his head. 'They will search me before I am allowed near Caliph. If they find a weapon—' He did not have to finish it.

'You are right,' she agreed.

She turned back to him from the mirror, buttoning the shirt over the nipples of her breasts, which were still swollen and dark rosy red from their loving.

'It will all happen very quickly now, Peter. One way or the other it will be over by tomorrow night. I have a feeling here—' She touched herself between the small breasts that pushed out the cotton of her shirt. 'Now kiss me. I have stayed too long already – for the safety of both of us.'

P eter slept very little after Magda left him, even though he was very tired. A dozen times he started awake during the night with every nerve strung tightly, rigid and sweating in his bed.

He was up before first light, and ordered one of those strange Israeli breakfasts of salads and hard-boiled eggs with pale green centres to be sent up to his room.

Then he settled down once more to wait.

He waited the morning out, and when there had been no message from Magda by noon, the certainty increased that Mossad had decided not to prevent the meeting with Caliph. If there had been any doubt in Magda's mind she would have sent for him. He had a light lunch sent up to the room.

The flat bright glare of noon gradually mellowed into warm butter-yellow, the shadows crept out timidly from the foot of the palm trees in the garden as the sun wheeled across a sky of clear high aching blue, and still Peter waited.

When there was an hour left of daylight, the telephone rang again. It startled him, but he reached for it quickly.

'Good evening, Sir Steven. Your driver is here to fetch you,' said the girl at the reception desk.

'Thank you. Please tell him I will be down directly,' said Peter.

He was fully dressed, had been ready all that day to move immediately. He needed only to place the crocodile skin case in the cupboard and lock it, then he left the room and strode down the corridor to the elevators.

He had no way of knowing if he was going to meet Caliph, or if he was about to be spirited out of Israel in Magda's Lear jet.

'Your limousine is waiting outside,' the pretty girl at the desk told him. 'Have a nice evening.'

'I hope so,' Peter agreed. 'Thank you.'

The car was a small Japanese compact, and the driver was a woman, plump and grey-haired with a friendly, ugly face like Golda Meir, Peter thought.

He let himself into the back seat, and waited expectantly for the message, 'Magda sent me.'

Instead, the woman bade him 'Shalom Shalom' politely, started the engine, switched on the headlights and drove serenely out of the hotel grounds.

They swept sedately around the outer walls of the old city in the gathering dusk, and dropped down in the valley of Kidron. Glancing back Peter saw the elegant new buildings of the Jewish quarter rising above the tops of the walls.

When last he had been in Jerusalem that area had been a deserted ruin, deliberately devastated by the Arabs.

The resurrection of that holy quarter of Judaism seemed to epitomize the spirit of these extraordinary people, Peter thought.

It was a good conversational opening, and he remarked on the new development to his driver.

She replied in Hebrew, clearly denying the ability to speak English. Peter tried her in French with the same result.

The lady has been ordered to keep her mouth tight shut, he decided.

The night came down upon them as they skirted the lower slopes of the Mount of Olives, and left the last straggling buildings of the Arab settlements. The lady driver settled down to a comfortable speed, and the road was almost deserted. It dropped gently down through a dark shallow valley, with the crests of a desolate desert landscape humped up on each side of the wide metalled road.

The sky was empty of cloud or haze, and the stars were brighter white and clearer, as the last of the day faded from the western sky behind them.

The road had been well sign-posted, ever since they had left the city. Their direction was eastward towards the Jordan, the Dead Sea and Jericho – and twenty-five minutes after leaving the King David, Peter glimpsed in the headlights the signpost on the right-hand side of the road, declaring in English, Arabic and Hebrew that they were now descending below sea level into the valley of the Dead Sea.

Once again Peter attempted to engage the driver in conversation, but her reply was monosyllabic. Anyway, Peter decided, there was nothing she would be able to tell him. The car was from a hire company. There was a plastic nameplate fastened onto the dashboard giving the company's name, address and hire rates. All she would know was their final destination – and he would know that soon enough himself.

Peter made no further attempt to speak to her, but remained completely alert; without detectable movement he performed the pre-jump paratrooper exercises, pitting muscle against muscle so that his body would not stiffen with long inactivity but would be tuned to explode from stillness into instant violent action.

Ahead of them the warning signals of the crossroads caught the headlights, and the driver slowed and signalled the left turn. As the headlights caught the signpost, Peter saw that they had taken the Jericho road, turning away from the Dead Sea, and heading up the valley of the Jordan towards Galilee in the north.

Now the bull's horns of the new moon rose slowly over the harsh mountain peaks across the valley, and gave enough light to pick out small features in the dry blasted desert around them.

Again the driver slowed, this time for the town of Jericho itself, the oldest site of human communal habitation on this earth – for six thousand years men had lived here and their wastes had raised a mountainous tell hundreds of feet above the desert floor. Archaeologists had already excavated the collapsed walls that Joshua had brought crashing down with a blast of his ram's horns.

'A hell of a trick.' Peter grinned in the darkness. 'Better than the nuke bomb.'

Just before they reached the tell, the driver swung off the main road. She took the narrow secondary road between the clustered buildings – souvenir stalls, Arab cafés, antique dealers – and slowed for the twisting uneven surface.

They ground up onto higher dry hills in low gear, and at the crest the driver turned again onto a dirt track. Now fine talcum dust filled the interior and Peter sneezed once at the tickle of it.

Half a mile along the track a noticeboard stood on trestle legs, blocking the right of way.

'Military Zone,' it proclaimed. 'No access beyond this point.'

The driver had to pull out onto the rocky verge to avoid the notice, and there were no sentries to enforce the printed order.

Quite suddenly Peter became aware of the great black cliff face that rose sheer into the starry night ahead of them – blotting out half the sky.

Something stirred in Peter's memory – the high cliffs above Jericho, looking out across the valley of the Dead Sea; of course, he remembered then – this was the scene of the temptation of Christ. How did Matthew record it? Peter cast for the exact quotation:

Again, the devil taketh him up into an exceeding high mountain, and sheweth him all the kingdoms of the world, and the glory of them –

Had Caliph deliberately chosen this place for its mystical association, was it all part of the quasi-religious image that Caliph had of himself?

He shall give his angels charge concerning thee: and in their hands they shall bear thee up –

Did Caliph truly see himself as the heir to ultimate power over all the kingdoms of the world – that power that the ancient chroniclers had referred to as 'The Sixth Order of Angels'?

Peter felt his spirits quail in the face of such monumental madness, such immense and menacing vision, compared to which he felt insignificant and ineffectual. Fear fell over him like a gladiator's net, enmeshing his resolve, weakening him. He struggled with it silently, fighting himself clear of its mesh before it could render him helpless in Caliph's all-embracing power.

The driver stopped abruptly, turned in the seat and switched on the cab light. She studied him for a moment.

Was there a touch of pity in her old and ugly face, Peter wondered?

'Here,' she said gently.

Peter drew his wallet from the inner pocket of his blazer.

'No,' she shook her head. 'No, you owe nothing.'

'*Toda raba*.' Peter thanked her in his fragmentary Hebrew, and opened the side door.

The desert air was still and cold, and there was the sagey smell of the low thorny scrub.

'Shalom,' said the woman through the open window; then she swung the vehicle in a tight turn. The headlights swept the grove of date palms ahead of them, and then turned back towards the open desert. Slowly the small car pitched and wove along the track in the direction from which they had come.

Peter turned his back on it, allowing his eyes to become accustomed to the muted light of the yellow horned moon and the whiter light of the fat desert stars.

After a few minutes he picked his way carefully into the palm grove. There was the smell of smoke from a dung fire, and the fine blue mist of smoke hung amongst the trees.

Somewhere in the grove he heard a goat bleat plaintively, and then the high thin wail of a child – there must be a Bedouin encampment in the oasis. He moved towards it, and came abruptly into an opening surrounded by the palms. The earth had been churned by the hooves of many beasts, and Peter stumbled slightly in the loose footing and then caught his balance.

In the centre of the opening was the stone parapet which guarded a deep fresh-water well. There was a primitive windlass set above the parapet and another dark object which Peter could not immediately identify, dark and shapeless, crouching upon the parapet.

He went towards it cautiously, and felt his heart tumble within him as it moved.

It was a human figure, in some long voluminous robe

that swept the sandy earth, so that it seemed to float towards him in the gloom.

The figure stopped five paces from him, and he saw that the head was covered by a monk's cowl of the same dark woollen cloth, so that the face was in a forbidding black hole beneath the cowl.

'Who are you?' Peter demanded, and his voice rasped in his own ears. The monk did not reply, but shook one hand free of the wide sleeve and beckoned to him to follow, then turned and glided away into the palm grove.

Peter went after him, and within a hundred yards was stepping out hard to keep the monk in sight. His light city shoes were not made for this heavy going, loose sand with scattered outcrops of shattered rock.

They left the palm grove and directly ahead of them, less than a quarter of a mile away, the cliff fell from the sky like a vast cascade of black stone.

The monk led him along a rough but well-used footpath, and though Peter tried to narrow the distance between them, he found that he would have to break into a trot to do so – for although the monk appeared to be a broad and heavy man beneath the billowing robe, yet he moved lithely and lightly.

They reached the cliff, and the path zig-zagged up it, at such a gradient that they had to lean forward into it. The surface was loose with shale and dry earth – becoming progressively steeper. Then underfoot the path was paved, the worn steps of solid rock.

On one hand the drop away into the valley was deeper always and the sheer cliff on the other seemed to lean out as though to press him over the edge.

Always the monk was ahead of him, tireless and quick, his feet silent on the worn steps, and there was no sound of labouring breath. Peter realized that a man of that stamina and bulk must be immensely powerful. He did not move as you might expect a man of God and prayer to move. There was the awareness and balance of a fighting man about him, the unconscious pride and force of the warrior. With Caliph nothing was ever as it seemed, he thought.

The higher they climbed, so the moonlit panorama below them became more magnificent, a soaring vista of desert and mountain with the great shield of the Dead Sea a brilliant beaten silver beneath the stars.

– All the kingdoms of the world, and the glory of them, Peter thought.

They had not paused to rest once on the climb. How high was it, Peter wondered – a thousand feet, fifteen hundred perhaps? His own breathing was deep and steady, he was not yet fully extended and the light sweat that dewed his forehead cooled in the night air.

Something nudged his memory, and he sniffed at the faintly perfumed aroma on the air. It was not steady, but he had caught it faintly once or twice during the climb.

Peter was plagued by the non-smoker's acute sense of smell; perfumes and odours always had special significance for him – and this smell was important, but he could not quite place it now. It nagged at him, but then it was lost in a host of other more powerful odours – the smell of human beings in community.

The smell of cooking smoke, of food and the underlying sickly taint of rotting garbage and primitive sewage disposal.

Somewhere long ago he had seen photographs of the ancient monastery built into the top of these spectacular cliffs, the caves and subterranean chambers honeycombed the crest of the rock face, and walls of hewn rock had been built above them by men dead these thousand years.

Yet the memory of that faint perfumed aroma lingered with Peter, as they climbed the last hundred feet of that terrifying drop and came out suddenly against the stone tower and thick fortification, into which was set a heavy timber door twelve feet high and studded with iron bolts.

At their approach the door swung open. There was a

narrow stone passageway ahead of them lit by a single storm lantern in a niche at the corner of the passageway.

As Peter stepped through the gate, two other figures closed on each side of him out of the darkness and he moved instinctively to defend himself, but checked the movement and stood quiescent with his hand half raised as they searched him with painstaking expertise for a weapon.

Both these men were dressed in single-piece combat suits, and they wore canvas paratrooper boots. Their heads were covered by coarse woollen scarves wound over mouth and nose so only their eyes showed. Each of them carried the ubiquitous Uzi sub-machine guns, loaded and cocked and slung on shoulder straps.

At last they stood back satisfied, and the monk led Peter on through a maze of narrow passages. Somewhere there was the sound of monks at their devotions, the harsh chanting of the Greek Orthodox service. The sound of it, and the smoky cedarwood aroma of burning incense, became stronger, until the monk led Peter into a cavernous, dimly lit church nave hewn from the living rock of the cliff.

In the gloom the old Greek monks sat like long embalmed mummies in their tall dark wooden pews. Their time-worn faces masked by the great black bushes of their beards. Only their eyes glittered, alive as the jewels and precious metals that gilded the ancient religious icons on the stone walls.

The reek of incense was overpowering, and the hoarse chant of the office missed not a single beat as Peter and the robed monk passed swiftly amongst them.

In the impenetrable shadows at the rear of the church, the monk seemed abruptly to disappear, but when Peter reached the spot he discovered that one of the carved pews had been swung aside to reveal a dark secret opening in the rock.

Peter went into it cautiously. It was totally dark – but his feet found shallow stone steps, and he climbed a twisting stairway through the rock – counting the steps to five hundred, each step approximately six inches high.

Abruptly he stepped out into the cool desert night again. He was in a paved open courtyard, with the brilliant panoply of the stars overhead, the cliff rising straight ahead and a low stone parapet protecting the sheer drop into the valley behind him.

Peter realized that this must be one of the remotest and most easily defensible rendezvous that Caliph could have chosen – and there were more guards here.

Again they came forward, two of them, and searched him once again even more thoroughly than at the monastery gate.

While they worked Peter looked around him swiftly. The level courtyard was perched like an eagle's eyrie on the brink of the precipice, the parapet wall was five feet high. Across the courtyard were the oblong entrances to caves carved into the cliff face. They would probably be the retreats of the monks seeking solitude.

There were other men in the courtyard, wearing the same uniform with heads hidden by the Arab shawl head-gear. Two of them were setting out flashlight beacons in the shape of a pyramid.

Peter realized they were beacons for an aircraft. – Not an aircraft. A helicopter was the only vehicle which would be able to get into this precarious perch on the side of the precipice.

All right then, the beacons would serve to direct a helicopter down into the level paved courtyard.

One of the armed guards ended his body search by checking the buckle of Peter's belt, tugging it experimentally to make certain it was not the handle of a concealed blade.

He stood back and motioned Peter forward. Across the courtyard the big monk waited patiently at the entrance to one of the stone cells that opened onto the courtyard.

Peter stooped through the low entrance. The cell was dimly lit by a stinking kerosene lamp set in a stone niche above the narrow cot. There was a crude wooden table against one wall, a plain crucifix above it and no other ornamentation.

Hewn from the rock wall was a ledge which acted as a shelf for a dozen heavy battered leather-bound books and a few basic eating utensils. It was also a primitive seat.

The monk motioned him towards it, but himself remained standing by the entrance to the cell with his hands thrust into the wide sleeves of his cassock, his face turned away and still masked completely by the deep hood.

There was utter silence from the courtyard beyond the doorway, but it was an electric waiting silence.

Suddenly Peter was aware of the perfumed aroma again, here in the crude stone cell, and then with a small tingling shock he recognized it. The smell came from the monk.

He knew instantly who the big man in the monk's cowl was, and the knowledge confused him utterly, for long stricken moments.

Then like the click of a well-oiled lock slipping home it all came together. He knew – oh God – he knew at last.

The aroma he had recognized was the faint trace of the perfumed smoke of expensive Dutch cheroots, and he stared fixedly at the big hooded monk.

Now there was a sound on the air, a faint flutter like moth's wings against the glass of the lantern, and the monk cocked his head slightly, listening intently.

Peter was balancing distances and times and odds in his head.

The monk, the five armed men in the courtyard, the approaching helicopter –

The monk was the most dangerous factor. Now that Peter knew who he was, he knew also that he was one of the most highly trained fighting men against whom he could ever match himself.

The five men in the yard – Peter blinked with sudden realization. *They would not be there any longer*. It was as simple as that. Caliph would never allow himself to be seen by any but his most trusted lieutenants, and by those about to die. The monk would have sent them away. They would be waiting close by, but it would take them time to get back into action.

There were only the monk and Caliph. For he knew that the dinning of rotor and engine was bringing Caliph in to the rendezvous. The helicopter sounded as though it were already directly overhead. The monk's attention was on it. Peter could see how he held his head under the cowl, he was off-guard for the first time.

Peter heard the sound of the spinning rotors change as the pilot altered pitch for the vertical descent into the tiny courtyard. The cell was lit through the doorway by the reflection of the helicopter's landing lights beating down into the courtyard with a relentless white glare.

Dust began to swirl from the down-draught of the rotors, it smoked in pale wisps into the cell and the monk moved.

He stepped to the doorway, the empty dark hole in the cowl which was his face turned briefly away from Peter as he glanced out through the entrance of the cell.

It was the moment for which Peter had waited, his whole body was charged, like the S in an adder's neck before it strikes. At the instant that the monk turned his head away, Peter launched himself across the cell.

He had ten feet to go, and the thunder of the helicopter's engines covered all sound – yet still some instinct of the fighting man warned the huge monk, and he spun into the arc of Peter's attack. The head under the cowl dropped defensively, so that Peter had to change his stroke. He could no longer go for the kill at the neck, and he chose the right shoulder for a crippling blow. His hand was stiff as a headman's blade and it slogged into the monk's shoulder between the neck and the humerus joint of the upper arm.

Peter heard the collar bone break with a sharp brittle crack, high above even the roar of the helicopter's engines.

With his left hand Peter caught the monk's crippled arm at the elbow and yanked it up savagely, driving the one edge of shattered bone against the other so it grated harshly, twisting it so the bone shards were razor cutting edges in their own living flesh – and the monk screamed, doubling from the waist to try and relieve the intolerable agony in his shoulder.

Shock had paralysed him, the big powerful body went slack in Peter's grasp.

Peter used all his weight and the impetus of his rush to drive the monk's head into the doorjamb of the cell; skull met stone with a solid clunk and the big man dropped face-down to the paved floor.

Peter rolled him swiftly and pulled up the skirts of the cassock. Under it the man wore paratrooper boots and the blue full-length overalls of Thor Command. On his webbing belt was the blue steel and polished walnut butt of the Browning Hi-power .45 pistol in its quick-release holster. Peter sprang it from its steel retaining clamp and cocked the pistol with a sweep of the left hand. It would be loaded with Velex explosives.

The woollen folds of the cowl had fallen back from Colin Noble's head, the wide generous mouth now hanging open slackly, the burned-toffee eyes glazed with concussion, the big crooked prize-fighter's nose – all the well-remembered features, once so dearly cherished in comradeship.

Blood was streaming from Colin's thick curling hairline, running down his forehead and under his ear – but he was still conscious.

Peter put the muzzle of the Browning against the bridge of his nose. The Velex bullet would cut the top off his skull. Peter had lost his wig in those desperate seconds, and he saw recognition spark in Colin's stunned eyes.

'Peter! No!' croaked Colin desperately. ' – I'm Cactus Flower!'

The shock of it hit Peter solidly, and he released the pressure on the Browning's trigger. It held him for only a moment and then he turned and ducked through the low doorway leaving Colin sprawling on the stone floor of the cell.

The helicopter had settled into the courtyard. It was a five-seater Bell Jet Ranger, painted in the blue and gold colours of Thor Command – and on its side was the Thor emblem and the words:

THOR COMMUNICATIONS

There was a pilot still at the controls, and one other man who had already left the cabin of the machine and was coming towards the entrance of the cell.

Even though he was doubled over to avoid the swirling rotor blades, there was no mistaking the tall powerful frame. The high wind of the rotors tumbled the thick greying leonine curls about the noble head, and the landing lights lit him starkly like the central character in some Shakespearian tragedy – a towering presence that transcended his mere physical stature.

Kingston Parker straightened as he came out from under the swinging rotor, and for an earth-stopping instant of time he stared at Peter across the stone-paved courtyard. Without the wig he recognized Peter instantly.

Kingston Parker stood for that instant like an old lion brought to bay.

'Caliph!' Peter called harshly, and the last doubt was gone as Kingston Parker whirled, incredibly swiftly for such a big man. He had almost reached the cabin door of the Jet Ranger before Peter had the Browning up.

The first shot hit Parker in the back, and flung him

forward through the open door, but the gun had thrown high and right. It was not a killing shot, Peter knew it, and now the helicopter was rising swiftly, turning on its own axis, rising out over the edge of the precipice.

Peter ran twenty feet and jumped to the parapet of the hewn stone wall. The Jet Ranger soared above him, its belly white and bloated like that of a man-eating shark, the landing lights blazing down, half dazzling Peter. It swung out over the edge of the cliff.

Peter took the Browning double-handed, shooting directly upwards, judging the exact position of the fuel tank in the rear of the fuselage, where it joined the long stalk-like tail – and he pumped the big heavy explosive shells out of the gun, the recoil pounding down his outflung arms and jolting into his shoulders.

He saw the Velex bullets biting into the thin metal skin of the underbelly, the tiny wink of each bullet as it burst, but still the machine reared away above him – and he had been counting his shots. The Browning was almost empty.

Seven, eight – then suddenly the sky above him filled with flame, and the great whooshing concussion of air jarred the stone under his feet.

The Jet Ranger turned over on her back, a bright bouquet of flame, the engine howling its death cry, and it toppled beyond the edge of the precipice and plunged, burning savagely, into the dark void below where Peter stood.

Peter began to turn back towards the courtyard, and he saw the armed men pouring in through the stone gateway.

They were Thor men, picked fighting men, men he had trained himself. There was one bullet left in the Browning. He knew he was not going to make it – but he made a try for the entrance to the stairway, his only escape route.

He ran along the top of the stone wall like a tightrope artist, and he snapped the single remaining bullet at the running men to distract them.

The crackle of passing shot dinned in his head, and he

flinched and missed his footing. He began to fall, twisting sideways away from the edge of the precipice – but then the bullets thumped into his flesh.

He heard the bullets going into his body with the rubbery socking sound of a heavyweight boxer hitting the heavy punch bag, and then he was flung out over the wall into the bottomless night.

He expected to fall for ever, a thousand feet to the desert floor below, where already the helicopter was shooting a hundred-foot fountain of fire into the air to mark Caliph's funeral pyre.

There was a narrow ledge ten feet below the parapet where a thorny wreath of desert scrub had found a precarious hold. Peter fell into it, and the curved thorns hooked into his clothing and into his flesh.

He hung there over the drop, and his senses began to fade.

His last clear memory was Colin Noble's bull bellow of command to the five Thor guards.

'Cease fire! Don't shoot again!' And then the darkness filled Peter's head.

I n the darkness there were lucid moments, each disconnected from the other by eternities of pain and confused nightmare distortions of the mind.

He remembered being lifted up through the hatchway of an aircraft, lying in one of the light body-fitting Thor stretchers, strapped to it tightly, helpless as a newborn infant.

There was the memory of the inside cabin of Magda Altmann's Lear jet. He recognized the hand-painted decoration of the curved cabin roof. There were plasma bottles suspended above him; the whole blood was the beautiful ruby colour of fine claret in a crystal glass, and when he rolled his eyes downwards he saw the tubes connected to the thick bright needles driven into his arms – but he was terribly tired, an utter weariness that seemed to have bruised and crushed his soul – and he closed his eyes.

When he opened his eyes again, there was the roof of a long brightly lit corridor passing swiftly in front of his eyes. The feeling of motion, and the scratchy squeak of the wheels of a theatre trolley.

Quiet voices were speaking in French, and the bottle of beautiful bright blood was held above him by long slim hands that he knew so well.

He rolled his head slightly and he saw Magda's beloved face swimming on the periphery of his vision.

'I love you,' he said, but there was no sound and he realized that his lips had not moved. He could no longer support the weariness and he let his eyelids droop closed.

'How bad is it?' he heard Magda's voice speaking in that beautiful rippling French, and a man replied.

'One bullet is lying very close to the heart – we must remove it immediately.'

Then the prick of something into his flesh searching for the vein, and the sudden musty taste of Pentothal on his tongue, followed by the abrupt singing plunge back into the darkness.

He came back very slowly out of the darkness, conscious first of the bandages that swathed his chest and restricted his breathing.

The next thing he was aware of was Magda Altmann, and how beautiful she was. It seemed that she must have been there all along while he was in the darkness. He watched the joy bloom in her face as she saw that he was conscious.

'Thank you,' she whispered. 'Thank you for coming back to me, my darling.'

Then there was the room at La Pierre Bénite, with its high gilded ceilings and the view through the tall sash windows across the terraced lawns down to the lake. The trees along the edge of the water were in full leaf, and the very air seemed charged with spring and the promise of new life. Magda had filled the room with banks of flowers, and she was with him during most of each day.

'What happened when you walked back into the board-room at Altmann Industries?' was one of the first questions he asked her.

'Consternation, *chéri*.' She chuckled, that husky little laugh of hers. 'They had already divided the spoils.'

The visitor came when Peter had been at La Pierre Bénite for eight days, and was able to sit in one of the brocaded chairs by the window.

Magda was standing beside Peter's chair, ready to protect him from over-exertion – physically or emotionally.

Colin Noble came into the room like a sheepish St Bernard dog. His right arm was strapped and carried in a sling across his chest. He touched it with his good hand.

'If I'd known it was you – and not Sir Steven – I'd never have turned my back on you,' he told Peter, and grinned placatingly.

Peter had stiffened, his face had transformed into a white rigid mask. Magda laid her hand upon his shoulder.

'Gently, Peter,' she whispered.

'Tell me one thing,' Peter hissed. 'Did you arrange the kidnapping of Melissa-Jane?'

Colin shook his head. 'My word on it. Parker used one of his other agents. I did not know it was going to happen.'

Peter stared at him, hard and unforgiving.

'Only after we had recovered Melissa-Jane, only then I knew that Caliph had planned it. If I had known – I would never have let it happen. Caliph must have known that. That is why he did not make me do it.' Colin was speaking quickly, urgently.

'What was Parker's object?' Peter's voice was still a vicious hiss.

'He had three separate objects. Firstly, to convince you that he was not Caliph. That's why his first order was to have you kill Parker himself. Of course, you never would have got near him. Then you were allowed to recover your daughter. It was Caliph himself who gave us O'Shaughnessy's name and where to find him. Then you were turned onto Magda Altmann—' Colin glanced at her apologetically. ' – Once you had killed her, you would have been bound to Caliph by guilt.'

'When did you learn this?' Peter demanded.

'The day after we found Melissa-Jane. By then there was nothing I could do that would not expose me as Cactus Flower – all I could do was to pass a warning to Magda through Mossad.'

'It's true, Peter,' said Magda quietly.

Slowly the rigidity went out of Peter's shoulders.

'When did Caliph recruit you as his Chief Lieutenant?' he asked, his voice also had altered, softened.

'As soon as I took over Thor Command from you. He was never certain of you, Peter, that was why he opposed your appointment to head of Thor – and why he jumped at the first chance to have you fired. That was why he tried to have you killed on the Rambouillet road. Only after the attempt failed did he realize your potential value to him.'

'Are the other Atlas unit commanders Caliph's lieutenants – Tanner at Mercury Command, Peterson at Diana?'

'All three of us. Yes!' Colin nodded, and there was a long silence.

'What else do you want to know, Peter?' Colin asked softly. 'Are there any other questions?'

'Not now.' Peter shook his head wearily. 'There will be many others later.'

Colin looked up at Magda Altmann inquiringly. 'Is he strong enough yet?' he asked. 'Can I tell him the rest of it?'

She hesitated a moment. 'Yes,' she decided. 'Tell him now.'

'Atlas was to be the secret dagger in the sleeve of Western civilization – a civilization which had emasculated itself and abased itself before its enemies. For once we would be able to meet naked violence and piracy with raw force. Atlas is a chain of powerful men of many nations banded together, and Caliph was to be its executive chief. Atlas is the only agency which transcends all national boundaries, and has as its object the survival of Western society as we know it. Atlas still exists, its structure is complete – only Caliph is dead. He died in a most unfortunate air accident over the Jordan valley – but Atlas still exists. It has to go on, once that part which Caliph has perverted is rooted out. It is our hope for the future in a world gone mad.'

Peter had never heard him speak so articulately, so persuasively.

'You know, of course, Peter, that you were the original choice to command Atlas. However, the wrong man superseded you – although nobody could know he was the wrong man at that time. Kingston Parker seemed to have all the qualities needed for the task – but there were hidden defects which only became apparent much later.' Colin began enumerating them, holding up the fingers of his uninjured arm.

'Firstly, he lacked physical courage. He became obsessed with his own physical safety – grossly abusing his powers to protect himself.

'Secondly, he was a man of unsuspected and overbearing ambition, with an ungoverned lust for raw power. Atlas swiftly became the vehicle to carry him to glory. His first

485.

goal was the Presidency of the United States. He was using Atlas to destroy his political opponents. Had he succeeded in achieving the presidency, no man can tell what his next goal would have been.'

Colin dropped his hand and balled it into a fist.

'The decision to allow you to reach the rendezvous with Kingston Parker on the cliffs above Jericho was made by more than one man – in more than one country.'

Colin grinned again, boyishly, disarmingly.

'I did not even know it was you. I believed it was Steven Stride, right up until the moment I turned my back on you!'

'Tell him,' said Magda quietly, 'Get it over with, Colin. He is still very weak.'

'Yes,' Colin agreed. 'I'll do it now. Yesterday at noon, your appointment to succeed Doctor Kingston Parker as head of Atlas Command was secretly confirmed.'

For Peter it was as though a door had at last opened, a door so long closed and locked, but through it now he could see his destiny stretching out ahead of him; clearly he could see it for the first time.

'You are the man best suited by nature and by training to fill the void which Kingston Parker has left.'

Even through the weakness of his abused body, Peter could feel a deep well of strength and determination within himself which he had never before suspected. It was as though it had been reserved expressly for this time, for this task.

'Will you accept the command of Atlas?' Colin asked. 'What answer must I take back with me?'

Magda's long fingers tightened on his shoulder, and they waited while he made his decision. It came almost immediately. There was no alternative open to him, Peter knew that – it was his destiny.

'Yes,' he said clearly. 'Tell them I accept the responsibility.'

It was a solemn moment, nobody smiled nor spoke for long seconds, and then:

'Caliph is dead,' Magda whispered. 'Long live Caliph.'

Peter Stride raised his head to look at her, but his voice when he replied was so cold that it seemed to frost upon his lips.

'Never,' he said, 'call me that again, ever.'

Magda made a small gesture of acquiescence, of total accord, then she stooped to kiss him on the mouth.